WORDS OF
RADIANCE

BY BRANDON SANDERSON

THE STORMLIGHT ARCHIVE
The Way of Kings
Words of Radiance
Oathbringer

THE MISTBORN SAGA

THE ORIGINAL TRILOGY
Mistborn
The Well of Ascension
The Hero of Ages

THE WAX AND WAYNE SERIES
The Alloy of Law
Shadows of Self
The Bands of Mourning

Elantris
Warbreaker
The Rithmatist
Arcanum Unbounded: The Cosmere Collection

ALCATRAZ VS. THE EVIL LIBRARIANS
Alcatraz vs. the Evil Librarians
The Scrivener's Bones
The Knights of Crystallia
The Shattered Lens
The Dark Talent

THE RECKONERS
Steelheart
Firefight
Calamity

BRANDON SANDERSON

WORDS OF RADIANCE

Book Two of

THE STORMLIGHT ARCHIVE

TOR®
fantasy

A TOM DOHERTY ASSOCIATES BOOK · NEW YORK

WORDS OF RADIANCE

Copyright © 2014 by Dragonsteel Entertainment, LLC

All rights reserved.

Illustrations preceding chapters 22 and 49 by Dan dos Santos

Illustrations preceding chapters 3, 17, 30, 45, 54, 70, 75, and 77 by Ben McSweeney

Maps, rear endpapers, illustrations preceding chapters 5, 11, 14, 35, 60, 65, 80, 83, and the Endnote by Isaac Stewart

Front endpapers by Michael Whelan and Ben McSweeney

Edited by Moshe Feder

Designed by Greg Collins

A Tor Book
Published by Tom Doherty Associates
175 Fifth Avenue
New York, NY 10010

www.tor-forge.com

Tor® is a registered trademark of Macmillan Publishing Group, LLC.

The Library of Congress has cataloged the hardcover edition as follows:

Sanderson, Brandon.
    Words of radiance / Brandon Sanderson.—First edition.
        p. cm.
    "A Tom Doherty Associates book."
    ISBN 978-0-7653-2636-2 (hardcover)
    ISBN 978-1-4299-4962-0 (ebook)
 1. Fantasy fiction.   I. Title.
    PS3619.A533 W67 2014
    813'.6—dc23
                                        2014008908

ISBN 978-1-250-16653-1 (trade paperback)

Our books may be purchased in bulk for promotional, educational, or business use. Please contact your local bookseller or the Macmillan Corporate and Premium Sales Department at 1-800-221-7945, extension 5442, or by email at MacmillanSpecialMarkets@macmillan.com.

First Edition: March 2014
First Trade Paperback Edition: September 2017

Printed in the United States of America

For Oliver Sanderson,
    Who was born during the middle of the writing of this book,
and was walking by the time it was done.

ACKNOWLEDGMENTS

As you might imagine, producing a book in the Stormlight Archive is a major undertaking. It involved almost eighteen months of writing, from outline to final revision, and includes the artwork of four different individuals and the editorial eyes of a whole host of people, not to mention the teams at Tor who do production, publicity, marketing, and everything else a major book needs in order to be successful.

For some two decades now, the Stormlight Archive has been my dream—the story I always wished I could tell. The people you'll read about below quite literally make my dreams a reality, and there aren't words to express my gratitude for their efforts. First in line on this novel needs to be my assistant and primary continuity editor, the incumbent Peter Ahlstrom. He worked very long hours on this book, putting up with my repeated insistence that things which did not fit continuity actually did—eventually persuading me I was wrong far more often than not.

As always, Moshe Feder—the man who discovered me as a writer—did excellent editorial work on the book. Joshua Bilmes, my agent, worked hard on the book in both an agenting and editorial capacity. He's joined by Eddie Schneider, Brady "Words of Bradiance" McReynolds, Krystyna Lopez, Sam Morgan, and Christa Atkinson at the agency. At Tor, Tom Doherty put up with me delivering a book even longer than the last one when I promised to make it shorter. Terry McGarry did the copyediting, Irene Gallo is responsible for the art direction for the cover, Greg Collins for interior design, Brian Lipofsky's team at Westchester Publishing Services for compositing, Meryl Gross and Karl Gold for production, Patty Garcia and her team for publicity. Paul Stevens acted as superman whenever we needed him. A big thanks to all of you.

You may have noticed that this volume, like the one before it, includes amazing art. My vision for the Stormlight Archive has always been of a series that transcended common artistic expectations for a book of its nature. As such, it is an honor to once again have my favorite artist, Michael Whelan, involved in the project. I feel that his cover has captured Kaladin perfectly, and I am extremely grateful for the extra time he spent on the cover—at his own insistence—going through three drafts before he was satisfied. To have endpapers of Shallan as well is more than I had hoped to see for the book, and I'm humbled by how well this whole package came together.

When I pitched the Stormlight Archive, I spoke of having "guest star" artists do pieces for the books here and there. We have our first of those in this novel, for which Dan dos Santos (another of my personal favorite artists, and the man who did the cover for *Warbreaker*) agreed to do some interior illustrations.

Ben McSweeney graciously returned to do more brilliant sketchbook pages for us, and he is a pure delight to work with, quick to recognize what I want, sometimes even when I'm not quite sure *what* I want. I've rarely met a person who mixes talent and professionalism in the way Ben does. You can find more of his art at InkThinker.net.

A long time ago, almost ten years now, I met a man named Isaác Stewart who—in addition to being an aspiring writer—was an excellent artist, particularly when it came to things like maps and symbols. I started collaborating with him on books (starting with *Mistborn*) and he eventually set me up on a blind date with a woman named Emily Bushman—whom I subsequently married. So needless to say, I owe Isaac a few big favors. With each progressive book he works on, that debt on my part grows greater as I see the amazing work he has done. This year, we decided to make his involvement a little more official as I hired him full-time to be an in-house artist and to help me with administrative tasks. So if you see him, welcome him to the team. (And tell him to keep working on his own books, which are quite good.)

Also joining us at Dragonsteel Entertainment is Kara Stewart, Isaac's wife, as our shipping manager. (I actually tried to hire Kara first—and Isaac piped up noting that some of the things I wanted to hire her for, he could do. And it ended up that I got both of them, in a very convenient deal.) She's the one you'll interact with if you order T-shirts, posters, or the like through my website. And she's awesome.

We used a few expert consultants on this book, including Matt Bushman for his songwriting and poetry expertise. Ellen Asher gave some great direction on the scenes with horses, and Karen Ahlstrom was an additional poetry and song consultant. Mi'chelle Walker acted as Alethi handwriting consultant. Finally, Elise Warren gave us some very nice notes relating to the psychology of a key character. Thank you all for lending me your brains.

This book had an extensive beta read done under some strict time constraints, and so a hearty bridgeman salute goes to those who participated. They are: Jason Denzel, Mi'chelle Walker, Josh Walker, Eric Lake, David Behrens, Joel Phillips, Jory Phillips, Kristina Kugler, Lyndsey Luther, Kim Garrett, Layne Garrett, Brian Delambre, Brian T. Hill, Alice Arneson, Bob Kluttz, and Nathan Goodrich.

Proofreaders at Tor include Ed Chapman, Brian Connolly, and Norma

Hoffman. Community proofreaders include Adam Wilson, Aubree and Bao Pham, Blue Cole, Chris King, Chris Kluwe, Emily Grange, Gary Singer, Jakob Remick, Jared Gerlach, Kelly Neumann, Kendra Wilson, Kerry Morgan, Maren Menke, Matt Hatch, Patrick Mohr, Richard Fife, Rob Harper, Steve Godecke, Steve Karam, and Will Raboin.

My writing group managed to get through about half of the book, which is a lot, considering how long the novel is. They are an invaluable resource to me. Members are: Kaylynn ZoBell, Kathleen Dorsey Sanderson, Danielle Olsen, Ben-son-son-Ron, E. J. Patten, Alan Layton, and Karen Ahlstrom.

And finally, thanks to my loving (and rambunctious) family. Joel, Dallin, and little Oliver help keep me humble each day by always making me be the "bad guy" who gets beat up. My forgiving wife, Emily, put up with a lot this past year, as tours grew long, and I'm still not sure what I did to deserve her. Thank you all for making my world one of magic.

CONTENTS

ILLUSTRATIONS

NOTE: *Many illustrations, titles included, contain spoilers for material that comes before them in the book. Look ahead at your own risk.*

BOOK

TWO

WORDS OF RADIANCE

ROSHAR

ENDLESS OCEAN

Rall Elorim

RESHI

QUIL ABR KADR

Kasitor

IRI

RIRA

Kurth

Reshi

Eila

BABATHARNAM

MARABETHI

The Mistee Mountains

Panatham

The Purelake

SHINOVAR

YULAY

Fu Nami

DESH

AZIR

AIMIA

Almian Sea

ALM

UEZIER

Azimir

The Valley

LIAFOR

TASHIKK

EMUL

GREATE

HEX

STEEN

Sesemalex Dar

TUKAR MARAT

Icewater

N

LEEWARD

STORMWARD

S

SOUTHERN DEPTHS

STEAMWATER OCEAN

ISLES

Sea

ARAK

SUMI

Northgrip

HERDAZ

Mourn's
Vault

ARAK

Varikev

Ru Parat

TU
BAYLA

Elanar

JAH KEVED

Valath

Horneater Peaks

Kholinar

Shulin

UNCLAIMED HILLS

BAVLAND

ALETHKAR

Rathalas

Dawn's
Shadow

TU
TRIAX

ALLIA

Silnasen

Vedenar

Dumadari

Karanak

Tarat Sea

Shattered
Plains

FROSTLANDS

New Natanan

Kharbranth

Longbrow's Straits

THAYLENAH

The Shallow Crypts

OCEAN of ORIGINS

FOR HIS ROYAL MAJESTY KING GAVILAR KHOLIN
BY HIS ROYAL HIGH CARTOGRAPHER
ISASIK SHULIN
1167

PROLOGUE

TO QUESTION

SIX YEARS AGO

Jasnah Kholin pretended to enjoy the party, giving no indication that she intended to have one of the guests killed.

She wandered through the crowded feast hall, listening as wine greased tongues and dimmed minds. Her uncle Dalinar was in the full swing of it, rising from the high table to shout for the Parshendi to bring out their drummers. Jasnah's brother, Elhokar, hurried to shush their uncle—though the Alethi politely ignored Dalinar's outburst. All save Elhokar's wife, Aesudan, who snickered primly behind a handkerchief.

Jasnah turned away from the high table and continued through the room. She had an appointment with an assassin, and she was all too glad to be leaving the stuffy room, which stank of too many perfumes mingling. A quartet of women played flutes on a raised platform across from the lively hearth, but the music had long since grown tedious.

Unlike Dalinar, Jasnah drew stares. Like flies to rotten meat those eyes were, constantly following her. Whispers like buzzing wings. If there was one thing the Alethi court enjoyed more than wine, it was gossip. Everyone expected Dalinar to lose himself to wine during a feast—but the king's daughter, admitting to heresy? *That* was unprecedented.

Jasnah had spoken of her feelings for precisely that reason.

She passed the Parshendi delegation, which clustered near the high table, talking in their rhythmic language. Though this celebration honored them and the treaty they'd signed with Jasnah's father, they didn't look festive or even happy. They looked nervous. Of course, they weren't human, and the way they reacted was sometimes odd.

Jasnah wanted to speak with them, but her appointment would not wait. She'd intentionally scheduled the meeting for the middle of the feast, as so many would be distracted and drunken. Jasnah headed toward the doors but then stopped in place.

Her shadow was pointing in the wrong direction.

The stuffy, shuffling, chattering room seemed to grow distant. High-prince Sadeas walked right through the shadow, which quite distinctly pointed *toward* the sphere lamp on the wall nearby. Engaged in conversation with his companion, Sadeas didn't notice. Jasnah stared at that shadow—skin growing clammy, stomach clenched, the way she felt when she was about to vomit. *Not again.* She searched for another light source. A reason. Could she find a reason? No.

The shadow languidly melted back toward her, oozing to her feet and then stretching out the other way. Her tension eased. But had anyone else seen?

Blessedly, as she searched the room, she didn't find any aghast stares. People's attention had been drawn by the Parshendi drummers, who were clattering through the doorway to set up. Jasnah frowned as she noticed a non-Parshendi servant in loose white clothing helping them. A Shin man? That was unusual.

Jasnah composed herself. What did these episodes of hers mean? Superstitious folktales she'd read said that misbehaving shadows meant you were cursed. She usually dismissed such things as nonsense, but *some* superstitions were rooted in fact. Her other experiences proved that. She would need to investigate further.

The calm, scholarly thoughts felt like a lie compared to the truth of her cold, clammy skin and the sweat trickling down the back of her neck. But it was important to be rational at all times, not just when calm. She forced herself out through the doors, leaving the muggy room for the quiet hallway. She'd chosen the back exit, commonly used by servants. It was the most direct route, after all.

Here, master-servants dressed in black and white moved on errands from their brightlords or ladies. She had expected that, but had not anticipated the sight of her *father* standing just ahead, in quiet conference with Brightlord Meridas Amaram. What was the king doing out here?

Gavilar Kholin was shorter than Amaram, yet the latter stooped shallowly in the king's company. That was common around Gavilar, who would speak with such quiet intensity that you wanted to lean in and listen, to catch every word and implication. He was a handsome man, unlike his brother, with a beard that outlined his strong jaw rather than covering it. He had a personal magnetism and intensity that Jasnah felt no biographer had yet managed to convey.

Tearim, captain of the King's Guard, loomed behind them. He wore Gavilar's Shardplate; the king himself had stopped wearing it of late, preferring to entrust it to Tearim, who was known as one of the world's great duelists. Instead, Gavilar wore robes of a majestic, classical style.

Jasnah glanced back at the feast hall. When had her father slipped out? *Sloppy,* she accused herself. *You should have checked to see if he was still there before leaving.*

Ahead, he rested his hand on Amaram's shoulder and raised a finger, speaking harshly but quietly, the words indistinct to Jasnah.

"Father?" she asked.

He glanced at her. "Ah, Jasnah. Retiring so early?"

"It's hardly early," Jasnah said, gliding forward. It seemed obvious to her that Gavilar and Amaram had ducked out to find privacy for their discussion. "This is the tiresome part of the feast, where the conversation grows louder but no smarter, and the company drunken."

"Many people consider that sort of thing enjoyable."

"Many people, unfortunately, are idiots."

Her father smiled. "Is it terribly difficult for you?" he asked softly. "Living with the rest of us, suffering our average wits and simple thoughts? Is it lonely to be so singular in your brilliance, Jasnah?"

She took it as the rebuke it was, and found herself blushing. Even her mother, Navani, could not do that to her.

"Perhaps if you found pleasant associations," Gavilar said, "you would enjoy the feasts." His eyes swung toward Amaram, whom he'd long fancied as a potential match for her.

It would never happen. Amaram met her eyes, then murmured words of parting to her father and hastened away down the corridor.

"What errand did you give him?" Jasnah asked. "What are you about this night, Father?"

"The treaty, of course."

The treaty. Why did he care so much about it? Others had counseled that he either ignore the Parshendi or conquer them. Gavilar insisted upon an accommodation.

"I should return to the celebration," Gavilar said, motioning to Tearim. The two moved along the hallway toward the doors Jasnah had left.

"Father?" Jasnah said. "What is it you aren't telling me?"

He glanced back at her, lingering. Pale green eyes, evidence of his good birth. When had he become so discerning? Storms . . . she felt as if she hardly knew this man any longer. Such a striking transformation in such a short time.

From the way he inspected her, it almost seemed that he didn't trust her. Did he know about her meeting with Liss?

He turned away without saying more and pushed back into the party, his guard following.

What is going on in this palace? Jasnah thought. She took a deep breath. She would have to prod further. Hopefully he hadn't discovered her meetings with assassins—but if he had, she would work with that knowledge. Surely he would see that someone needed to keep watch on the family as he grew increasingly consumed by his fascination with the Parshendi. Jasnah turned and continued on her way, passing a master-servant, who bowed.

After walking a short time in the corridors, Jasnah noticed her shadow behaving oddly again. She sighed in annoyance as it pulled *toward* the three Stormlight lamps on the walls. Fortunately, she'd passed from the populated area, and no servants were here to see.

"All right," she snapped. "That's enough."

She hadn't meant to speak aloud. However, as the words slipped out, several distant shadows—originating in an intersection up ahead—stirred to life. Her breath caught. Those shadows lengthened, deepened. Figures formed from them, growing, standing, rising.

Stormfather. I'm going insane.

One took the shape of a man of midnight blackness, though he had a certain reflective cast, as if he were made of oil. No . . . of some other liquid with a coating of oil floating on the outside, giving him a dark, prismatic quality.

He strode toward her and unsheathed a sword.

Logic, cold and resolute, guided Jasnah. Shouting would not bring help quickly enough, and the inky litheness of this creature bespoke a speed certain to exceed her own.

She stood her ground and met the thing's glare, causing it to hesitate. Behind it, a small clutch of other creatures had materialized from the darkness. She had sensed those eyes upon her during the previous months.

By now, the entire hallway had darkened, as if it had been submerged and was slowly sinking into lightless depths. Heart racing, breath quickening, Jasnah raised her hand to the granite wall beside her, seeking to touch something solid. Her fingers sank into the stone a fraction, as if the wall had become mud.

Oh, storms. She had to do something. What? What could she *possibly* do?

The figure before her glanced at the wall. The wall lamp nearest Jasnah went dark. And then . . .

Then the palace disintegrated.

The entire building shattered into thousands upon thousands of small glass spheres, like beads. Jasnah screamed as she fell backward through a dark sky. She was no longer in the palace; she was somewhere else—another land, another time, another . . . *something*.

She was left with the sight of the dark, lustrous figure hovering in the air above, seeming satisfied as he resheathed his sword.

Jasnah crashed into something—an ocean of the glass beads. Countless others rained around her, clicking like hailstones into the strange sea. She had never seen this place; she could not explain what had happened or what it meant. She thrashed as she sank into what seemed an impossibility. Beads of glass on all sides. She couldn't see anything beyond them, only felt herself descending through this churning, suffocating, clattering mass.

She was going to die. Leaving work unfinished, leaving her family unprotected!

She would never know the answers.

No.

Jasnah flailed in the darkness, beads rolling across her skin, getting into her clothing, working their way into her nose as she tried to swim. It was no use. She had no buoyancy in this mess. She raised a hand before her mouth and tried to make a pocket of air to use for breathing, and managed to gasp in a small breath. But the beads rolled around her hand, forcing between her fingers. She sank, more slowly now, as through a viscous liquid.

Each bead that touched her gave a faint impression of something. A door. A table. A shoe.

The beads found their way into her mouth. They seemed to move on their own. They would choke her, destroy her. No . . . no, it was just because they seemed *attracted* to her. An impression came to her, not as a distinct thought but a feeling. They wanted something from her.

She snatched a bead in her hand; it gave her an impression of a cup. She gave . . . something . . . to it? The other beads near her pulled together, connecting, sticking like rocks sealed by mortar. In a moment she was falling not among individual beads, but through large masses of them stuck together into the shape of . . .

A cup.

Each bead was a pattern, a guide for the others.

She released the one she held, and the beads around her broke apart. She floundered, searching desperately as her air ran out. She needed something she could use, something that would help, some way to survive! Desperate, she swept her arms wide to touch as many beads as she could.

A silver platter.

A coat.

A statue.

A lantern.

And then, something ancient.

Something ponderous and slow of thought, yet somehow *strong*. The palace itself. Frantic, Jasnah seized this sphere and forced her power into

21

it. Her mind blurring, she gave this bead everything she had, and then commanded it to rise.

Beads shifted.

A great crashing sounded as beads met one another, clicking, cracking, rattling. It was almost like the sound of a wave breaking on rocks. Jasnah surged up from the depths, something solid moving beneath her, obeying her command. Beads battered her head, shoulders, arms, until finally she *exploded* from the surface of the sea of glass, hurling a spray of beads into a dark sky.

She knelt on a platform of glass made up of small beads locked together. She held her hand to the side, uplifted, clutching the sphere that was the guide. Others rolled around her, forming into the shape of a hallway with lanterns on the walls, an intersection ahead. It didn't look right, of course—the entire thing was made of beads. But it was a fair approximation.

She wasn't strong enough to form the entire palace. She created only this hallway, without even a roof—but the floor supported her, kept her from sinking. She opened her mouth with a groan, beads falling out to clack against the floor. Then she coughed, drawing in sweet breaths, sweat trickling down the sides of her face and collecting on her chin.

Ahead of her, the dark figure stepped up onto the platform. He again slid his sword from his sheath.

Jasnah held up a second bead, the statue she'd sensed earlier. She gave it power, and other beads collected before her, taking the shape of one of the statues that lined the front of the feast hall—the statue of Talenelat'Elin, Herald of War. A tall, muscular man with a large Shardblade.

It was not alive, but she made it move, lowering its sword of beads. She doubted it could fight. Round beads could not form a sharp sword. Yet the threat made the dark figure hesitate.

Gritting her teeth, Jasnah heaved herself to her feet, beads streaming from her clothing. She would *not* kneel before this thing, whatever it was. She stepped up beside the bead statue, noting for the first time the strange clouds overhead. They seemed to form a narrow ribbon of highway, straight and long, pointing toward the horizon.

She met the oil figure's gaze. It regarded her for a moment, then raised two fingers to its forehead and bowed, as if in respect, a cloak flourishing out behind. Others had gathered beyond it, and they turned to each other, exchanging hushed whispers.

The place of beads faded, and Jasnah found herself back in the hallway of the palace. The real one, with real stone, though it had gone dark—the Stormlight dead in the lamps on the walls. The only illumination came from far down the corridor.

She pressed back against the wall, breathing deeply. *I,* she thought, *need to write this experience down.*

She would do so, then analyze and consider. Later. Now, she wanted to be away from this place. She hurried away, with no concern for her direction, trying to escape those eyes she still felt watching.

It didn't work.

Eventually, she composed herself and wiped the sweat from her face with a kerchief. *Shadesmar,* she thought. *That is what it is called in the nursery tales.* Shadesmar, the mythological kingdom of the spren. Mythology she'd never believed. Surely she could find something if she searched the histories well enough. Nearly everything that happened had happened before. The grand lesson of history, and . . .

Storms! Her appointment.

Cursing to herself, she hurried on her way. That experience continued to distract her, but she needed to make her meeting. So she continued down two floors, getting farther from the sounds of the thrumming Parshendi drums until she could hear only the sharpest cracks of their beats.

That music's complexity had always surprised her, suggesting that the Parshendi were not the uncultured savages many took them for. This far away, the music sounded disturbingly like the beads from the dark place, rattling against one another.

She'd intentionally chosen this out-of-the-way section of the palace for her meeting with Liss. Nobody ever visited this set of guest rooms. A man that Jasnah didn't know lounged here, outside the proper door. That relieved her. The man would be Liss's new servant, and his presence meant Liss hadn't left, despite Jasnah's tardiness. Composing herself, she nodded to the guard—a Veden brute with red speckling his beard—and pushed into the room.

Liss stood from the table inside the small chamber. She wore a maid's dress—low cut, of course—and could have been Alethi. Or Veden. Or Bav. Depending on which part of her accent she chose to emphasize. Long dark hair, worn loose, and a plump, attractive figure made her distinctive in all the right ways.

"You're late, Brightness," Liss said.

Jasnah gave no reply. She was the employer here, and was not required to give excuses. Instead, she laid something on the table beside Liss. A small envelope, sealed with weevilwax.

Jasnah set two fingers on it, considering.

No. This was too brash. She didn't know if her father realized what she was doing, but even if he hadn't, too much was happening in this palace. She did not want to commit to an assassination until she was more certain.

Fortunately, she had prepared a backup plan. She slid a second envelope from the safepouch inside her sleeve and set it on the table in place of the first. She removed her fingers from it, rounding the table and sitting down.

Liss sat back down and made the letter vanish into the bust of her dress. "An odd night, Brightness," the woman said, "to be engaging in treason."

"I am hiring you to watch only."

"Pardon, Brightness. But one does not commonly hire an assassin to watch. Only."

"You have instructions in the envelope," Jasnah said. "Along with initial payment. I chose you because you are expert at extended observations. It is what I want. For now."

Liss smiled, but nodded. "Spying on the wife of the heir to the throne? It will be more expensive this way. You sure you don't simply want her dead?"

Jasnah drummed her fingers on the table, then realized she was doing it to the beat of the drums above. The music was so unexpectedly complex—precisely like the Parshendi themselves.

Too much is *happening,* she thought. *I need to be very careful. Very subtle.*

"I accept the cost," Jasnah replied. "In one week's time, I will arrange for one of my sister-in-law's maids to be released. You will apply for the position, using faked credentials I assume you are capable of producing. You will be hired.

"From there, you watch and report. I will tell you if your other services are needed. You move only if I say. Understood?"

"You're the one payin'," Liss said, a faint Bav dialect showing through.

If it showed, it was only because she wished it. Liss was the most skilled assassin Jasnah knew. People called her the Weeper, as she gouged out the eyes of the targets she killed. Although she hadn't coined the cognomen, it served her purpose well, since she had secrets to hide. For one thing, nobody knew that the Weeper was a woman.

It was said the Weeper gouged the eyes out to proclaim indifference to whether her victims were lighteyed or dark. The truth was that the action hid a second secret—Liss didn't want anyone to know that the way she killed left corpses with burned-out sockets.

"Our meeting is done, then," Liss said, standing.

Jasnah nodded absently, mind again on her bizarre interaction with the spren earlier. That glistening skin, colors dancing across a surface the color of tar . . .

She forced her mind away from that moment. She needed to devote her attention to the task at hand. For now, that was Liss.

Liss hesitated at the door before leaving. "Do you know why I like you, Brightness?"

"I suspect that it has something to do with my pockets and their proverbial depth."

Liss smiled. "There's that, ain't going to deny it, but you're also different from other lighteyes. When others hire me, they turn up their noses at the entire process. They're all too eager to use my services, but sneer and wring their hands, as if they hate being forced to do something utterly distasteful."

"Assassination *is* distasteful, Liss. So is cleaning out chamber pots. I can respect the one employed for such jobs without admiring the job itself."

Liss grinned, then cracked the door.

"That new servant of yours outside," Jasnah said. "Didn't you say you wanted to show him off for me?"

"Talak?" Liss said, glancing at the Veden man. "Oh, you mean that *other* one. No, Brightness, I sold that one to a slaver a few weeks ago." Liss grimaced.

"Really? I thought you said he was the best servant you'd ever had."

"Too good a servant," Liss said. "Let's leave it at that. Storming creepy, that Shin fellow was." Liss shivered visibly, then slipped out the door.

"Remember our first agreement," Jasnah said after her.

"Always there in the back o' my mind, Brightness." Liss closed the door.

Jasnah settled in her seat, lacing her fingers in front of her. Their "first agreement" was that if anyone should come to Liss and offer a contract on a member of Jasnah's family, Liss would let Jasnah match the offer in exchange for the name of the one who made it.

Liss would do it. Probably. So would the dozen other assassins Jasnah dealt with. A repeat customer was always more valuable than a one-off contract, and it was in the best interests of a woman like Liss to have a friend in the government. Jasnah's family was safe from the likes of these. Unless she herself employed the assassins, of course.

Jasnah let out a deep sigh, then rose, trying to shrug off the weight she felt bearing her down.

Wait. Did Liss say her old servant was Shin?

It was probably a coincidence. Shin people weren't plentiful in the East, but you did see them on occasion. Still, Liss mentioning a Shin man and Jasnah seeing one among the Parshendi . . . well, there was no harm in checking, even if it meant returning to the feast. Something *was* off about this night, and not just because of her shadow and the spren.

Jasnah left the small chamber in the bowels of the palace and strode out into the hallway. She turned her steps upward. Above, the drums cut off abruptly, like an instrument's strings suddenly cut. Was the party ending so early? Dalinar hadn't done something to offend the celebrants, had he? That man and his wine . . .

Well, the Parshendi had ignored his offenses in the past, so they probably would again. In truth, Jasnah was happy for her father's sudden focus on a treaty. It meant she would have a chance to study Parshendi traditions and histories at her leisure.

Could it be, she wondered, *that scholars have been searching in the wrong ruins all these years?*

Words echoed in the hallway, coming from up ahead. "I'm worried about Ash."

"You're worried about everything."

Jasnah hesitated in the hallway.

"She's getting worse," the voice continued. "We weren't supposed to get worse. Am I getting worse? I think I feel worse."

"Shut up."

"I don't like this. What we've done was wrong. That creature carries *my lord's* own Blade. We shouldn't have let him keep it. He—"

The two passed through the intersection ahead of Jasnah. They were ambassadors from the West, including the Azish man with the white birthmark on his cheek. Or was it a scar? The shorter of the two men—he could have been Alethi—cut off when he noticed Jasnah. He let out a squeak, then hurried on his way.

The Azish man, the one dressed in black and silver, stopped and looked her up and down. He frowned.

"Is the feast over already?" Jasnah asked down the hallway. Her brother had invited these two to the celebration along with every other ranking foreign dignitary in Kholinar.

"Yes," the man said.

His stare made her uncomfortable. She walked forward anyway. *I should check further into these two,* she thought. She'd investigated their backgrounds, of course, and found nothing of note. Had they been talking about a Shardblade?

"Come on!" the shorter man said, returning and taking the taller man by the arm.

He allowed himself to be pulled away. Jasnah walked to where the corridors crossed, then watched them go.

Where once drums had sounded, screams suddenly rose.

Oh no . . .

Jasnah turned with alarm, then grabbed her skirt and ran as hard as she could.

A dozen different potential disasters raced through her mind. What else could happen on this broken night, when shadows stood up and her father looked upon her with suspicion? Nerves stretched thin, she reached the steps and started climbing.

It took her far too long. She could hear the screams as she climbed and finally emerged into chaos. Dead bodies in one direction, a demolished *wall* in the other. How . . .

The destruction led toward her father's rooms.

The entire *palace* shook, and a crunch echoed from that direction.

No, no, no!

She passed Shardblade cuts on the stone walls as she ran.

Please.

Corpses with burned eyes. Bodies littered the floor like discarded bones at the dinner table.

Not this.

A broken doorway. Her father's quarters. Jasnah stopped in the hallway, gasping.

Control yourself, control . . .

She couldn't. Not now. Frantic, she ran into the quarters, though a Shardbearer would kill her with ease. She wasn't thinking straight. She should get someone who could help. Dalinar? He'd be drunk. Sadeas, then.

The room looked like it had been hit by a highstorm. Furniture in a shambles, splinters everywhere. The balcony doors were broken outward. Someone lurched toward them, a man in her father's Shardplate. Tearim, the bodyguard?

No. The helm was broken. It was not Tearim, but Gavilar. Someone on the balcony screamed.

"Father!" Jasnah shouted.

Gavilar hesitated as he stepped out onto the balcony, looking back at her.

The balcony broke beneath him.

Jasnah screamed, dashing through the room to the broken balcony, falling to her knees at the edge. Wind tugged locks of hair loose from her bun as she watched two men fall.

Her father, and the Shin man in white from the feast.

The Shin man glowed with a white light. He fell *onto* the wall. He hit it, rolling, then came to a stop. He stood up, somehow remaining on the outer palace wall and not falling. It defied reason.

He turned, then stalked toward her father.

Jasnah watched, growing cold, helpless as the assassin stepped down to her father and knelt over him.

Tears fell from her chin, and the wind caught them. What was he doing down there? She couldn't make it out.

When the assassin walked away, he left behind her father's corpse. Impaled on a length of wood. He was dead—indeed, his Shardblade had appeared beside him, as they all did when their Bearers died.

"I worked so hard . . ." Jasnah whispered, numb. "Everything I did to protect this family . . ."

How? Liss. Liss had done this!

No. Jasnah wasn't thinking straight. That Shin man . . . she wouldn't have admitted to owning him in such a case. She'd sold him.

"We are sorry for your loss."

Jasnah spun, blinking bleary eyes. Three Parshendi, including Klade, stood in the doorway in their distinctive clothing. Neatly stitched cloth wraps for both men and women, sashes at the waist, loose shirts with no sleeves. Hanging vests, open at the sides, woven in bright colors. They didn't segregate clothing by gender. She thought they did by caste, however, and—

Stop it, she thought at herself. *Stop thinking like a scholar for one storming day!*

"We take responsibility for his death," said the foremost Parshendi. Gangnah was female, though with the Parshendi, the gender differences seemed minimal. The clothing hid breasts and hips, neither of which were ever very pronounced. Fortunately, the lack of a beard was a clear indication. All the Parshendi men she'd ever seen had beards, which they wore tied with bits of gemstone, and—

STOP IT.

"What did you say?" Jasnah demanded, forcing herself to her feet. "Why would it be your fault, Gangnah?"

"Because we hired the assassin," the Parshendi woman said in her heavily accented singsong voice. "We killed your father, Jasnah Kholin."

"You . . ."

Emotion suddenly ran cold, like a river freezing in the heights. Jasnah looked from Gangnah to Klade, to Varnali. Elders, all three of them. Members of the Parshendi ruling council.

"Why?" Jasnah whispered.

"Because it had to be done," Gangnah said.

"*Why?*" Jasnah demanded, stalking forward. "He fought for you! He kept the predators at bay! My father wanted *peace*, you monsters! Why would you betray us now, of all times?"

Gangnah drew her lips to a line. The song of her voice changed. She seemed almost like a mother, explaining something very difficult to a small child. "Because your father was about to do something very dangerous."

"Send for Brightlord Dalinar!" a voice outside in the hall shouted. "Storms! Did my orders get to Elhokar? The crown prince *must* be taken to safety!" Highprince Sadeas stumbled into the room along with a team of soldiers. His bulbous, ruddy face was wet with sweat, and he wore Gavilar's clothing, the regal robes of office. "What are the savages doing here?

Storms! Protect Princess Jasnah. The one who did this—he was in *their* retinue!"

The soldiers moved to surround the Parshendi. Jasnah ignored them, turning and stepping back to the broken doorway, hand on the wall, looking down at her father splayed on the rocks below, Blade beside him.

"There will be war," she whispered. "And I will not stand in its way."

"This is understood," Gangnah said from behind.

"The assassin," Jasnah said. "He walked on the wall."

Gangnah said nothing.

In the shattering of her world, Jasnah caught hold of this fragment. She had seen something tonight. Something that should not have been possible. Did it relate to the strange spren? Her experience in that place of glass beads and a dark sky?

These questions became her lifeline for stability. Sadeas demanded answers from the Parshendi leaders. He received none. When he stepped up beside her and saw the wreckage below, he went barreling off, shouting for his guards and running down below to reach the fallen king.

Hours later, it was discovered that the assassination—and the surrender of three of the Parshendi leaders—had covered the flight of the larger portion of their number. They escaped the city quickly, and the cavalry Dalinar sent after them were destroyed. A hundred horses, each nearly priceless, lost along with their riders.

The Parshendi leaders said nothing more and gave no clues, even when they were strung up, hanged for their crimes.

Jasnah ignored all that. Instead, she interrogated the surviving guards on what they had seen. She followed leads about the now-famous assassin's nature, prying information from Liss. She got almost nothing. Liss had owned him only a short time, and claimed she hadn't known about his strange powers. Jasnah couldn't find the previous owner.

Next came the books. A dedicated, frenzied effort to distract her from what she had lost.

That night, Jasnah had seen the impossible.

She *would* learn what it meant.

PART

ONE

Alight

SHALLAN · KALADIN · DALINAR

SANTHID

To be perfectly frank, what has happened these last two months is upon my head. The death, destruction, loss, and pain are my burden. I should have seen it coming. And I should have stopped it.

—From the personal journal of Navani Kholin, Jeseses 1174

Shallan pinched the thin charcoal pencil and drew a series of straight lines radiating from a sphere on the horizon. That sphere wasn't *quite* the sun, nor was it one of the moons. Clouds outlined in charcoal seemed to stream toward it. And the sea beneath them . . . A drawing could not convey the bizarre nature of that ocean, made not of water but of small beads of translucent glass.

Shallan shivered, remembering that place. Jasnah knew much more of it than she would speak of to her ward, and Shallan wasn't certain how to ask. How did one demand answers after a betrayal such as Shallan's? Only a few days had passed since that event, and Shallan still didn't know exactly how her relationship with Jasnah would proceed.

The deck rocked as the ship tacked, enormous sails fluttering overhead. Shallan was forced to grab the railing with her clothed safehand to steady herself. Captain Tozbek said that so far, the seas hadn't been bad for this part of Longbrow's Straits. However, she might have to go below if the waves and motion got much worse.

Shallan exhaled and tried to relax as the ship settled. A chill wind blew, and windspren zipped past on invisible air currents. Every time the sea grew rough, Shallan remembered that day, that alien ocean of glass beads . . .

She looked down again at what she'd drawn. She had only glimpsed that place, and her sketch was not perfect. It—

She frowned. On her paper, a pattern had *risen*, like an embossing. What had she done? That pattern was almost as wide as the page, a sequence of complex lines with sharp angles and repeated arrowhead shapes. Was it an effect of drawing that weird place, the place Jasnah said was named Shadesmar? Shallan hesitantly moved her freehand to feel the unnatural ridges on the page.

The pattern *moved*, sliding across the page like an axehound pup under a bedsheet.

Shallan yelped and leapt from her seat, dropping her sketchpad to the deck. The loose pages slumped to the planks, fluttering and then scattering in the wind. Nearby sailors—Thaylen men with long white eyebrows they combed back over their ears—scrambled to help, snatching sheets from the air before they could blow overboard.

"You all right, young miss?" Tozbek asked, looking over from a conversation with one of his mates. The short, portly Tozbek wore a wide sash and a coat of gold and red matched by the cap on his head. He wore his eyebrows up and stiffened into a fanned shape above his eyes.

"I'm well, Captain," Shallan said. "I was merely spooked."

Yalb stepped up to her, proffering the pages. "Your accouterments, my lady."

Shallan raised an eyebrow. "Accout*er*ments?"

"Sure," the young sailor said with a grin. "I'm practicing my fancy words. They help a fellow obtain reasonable feminine companionship. You know—the kind of young lady who doesn't smell too bad an' has at least a few teeth left."

"Lovely," Shallan said, taking the sheets back. "Well, depending on your definition of lovely, at least." She suppressed further quips, suspiciously regarding the stack of pages in her hand. The picture she'd drawn of Shadesmar was on top, no longer bearing the strange embossed ridges.

"What happened?" Yalb said. "Did a cremling crawl out from under you or something?" As usual, he wore an open-fronted vest and a pair of loose trousers.

"It was nothing," Shallan said softly, tucking the pages away into her satchel.

Yalb gave her a little salute—she had no idea why he had taken to doing that—and went back to tying rigging with the other sailors. She soon caught bursts of laughter from the men near him, and when she glanced at him, gloryspren danced around his head—they took the shape of little spheres of light. He was apparently very proud of the jape he'd just made.

She smiled. It was indeed fortunate that Tozbek had been delayed in

Kharbranth. She liked this crew, and was happy that Jasnah had selected them for their voyage. Shallan sat back down on the box that Captain Tozbek had ordered lashed beside the railing so she could enjoy the sea as they sailed. She had to be wary of the spray, which wasn't terribly good for her sketches, but so long as the seas weren't rough, the opportunity to watch the waters was worth the trouble.

The scout atop the rigging let out a shout. Shallan squinted in the direction he pointed. They were within sight of the distant mainland, sailing parallel to it. In fact, they'd docked at port last night to shelter from the highstorm that had blown past. When sailing, you always wanted to be near to port—venturing into open seas when a highstorm could surprise you was suicidal.

The smear of darkness to the north was the Frostlands, a largely uninhabited area along the bottom edge of Roshar. Occasionally, she caught a glimpse of higher cliffs to the south. Thaylenah, the great island kingdom, made another barrier there. The straits passed between the two.

The lookout had spotted something in the waves just north of the ship, a bobbing shape that at first appeared to be a large log. No, it was much larger than that, and wider. Shallan stood, squinting, as it drew closer. It turned out to be a domed brown-green shell, about the size of three rowboats lashed together. As they passed by, the shell came up alongside the ship and somehow managed to keep pace, sticking up out of the water perhaps six or eight feet.

A santhid! Shallan leaned out over the rail, looking down as the sailors jabbered excitedly, several joining her in craning out to see the creature. Santhidyn were so reclusive that some of her books claimed they were extinct and all modern reports of them untrustworthy.

"You *are* good luck, young miss!" Yalb said to her with a laugh as he passed by with rope. "We ain't seen a santhid in years."

"You still aren't seeing one," Shallan said. "Only the top of its shell." To her disappointment, waters hid anything else—save shadows of something in the depths that might have been long arms extending downward. Stories claimed the beasts would sometimes follow ships for days, waiting out in the sea as the vessel went into port, then following them again once the ship left.

"The shell is all you ever see of one," Yalb said. "Passions, this is a good sign!"

Shallan clutched her satchel. She took a Memory of the creature down there beside the ship by closing her eyes, fixing the image of it in her head so she could draw it with precision.

Draw what, though? she thought. *A lump in the water?*

An idea started to form in her head. She spoke it aloud before she could think better. "Bring me that rope," she said, turning to Yalb.

"Brightness?" he asked, stopping in place.

"Tie a loop in one end," she said, hurriedly setting her satchel on her seat. "I need to get a look at the santhid. I've never actually put my head underwater in the ocean. Will the salt make it difficult to see?"

"Underwater?" Yalb said, voice squeaking.

"You're not tying the rope."

"Because I'm not a storming fool! Captain will have my head if . . ."

"Get a friend," Shallan said, ignoring him and taking the rope to tie one end into a small loop. "You're going to lower me down over the side, and I'm going to get a glimpse of what's under the shell. Do you realize that nobody has *ever* produced a drawing of a live santhid? All the ones that have washed up on beaches were badly decomposed. And since sailors consider hunting the things to be bad luck—"

"It is!" Yalb said, voice growing more high pitched. "Ain't nobody going to kill one."

Shallan finished the loop and hurried to the side of the ship, her red hair whipping around her face as she leaned out over the rail. The santhid was still there. How did it keep up? She could see no fins.

She looked back at Yalb, who held the rope, grinning. "Ah, Brightness. Is this payback for what I said about your backside to Beznk? That was just in jest, but you got me good! I . . ." He trailed off as she met his eyes. "Storms. You're serious."

"I'll not have another opportunity like this. Naladan chased these things for most of her life and never got a good look at one."

"This is insanity!"

"No, this is scholarship! I don't know what kind of view I can get through the water, but I have to try."

Yalb sighed. "We have masks. Made from a tortoise shell with glass in hollowed-out holes on the front and bladders along the edges to keep the water out. You can duck your head underwater with one on and see. We use them to check over the hull at dock."

"Wonderful!"

"Of course, I'd have to go to the captain to get permission to take one. . . ."

She folded her arms. "Devious of you. Well, get to it." It was unlikely she'd be able to go through with this without the captain finding out anyway.

Yalb grinned. "What happened to you in Kharbranth? Your first trip with us, you were so timid, you looked like you'd faint at the mere thought of sailing away from your homeland!"

Shallan hesitated, then found herself blushing. "This is somewhat foolhardy, isn't it?"

"Hanging from a moving ship and sticking your head in the water?" Yalb said. "Yeah. Kind of a little."

"Do you think . . . we could stop the ship?"

Yalb laughed, but went jogging off to speak with the captain, taking her query as an indication she was still determined to go through with her plan. And she was.

What did *happen to me?* she wondered.

The answer was simple. She'd lost everything. She'd stolen from Jasnah Kholin, one of the most powerful women in the world—and in so doing had not only lost her chance to study as she'd always dreamed, but had also doomed her brothers and her house. She had failed utterly and miserably.

And she'd pulled through it.

She wasn't unscathed. Her credibility with Jasnah had been severely wounded, and she felt that she had all but abandoned her family. But something about the experience of stealing Jasnah's Soulcaster—which had turned out to be a fake anyway—then nearly being killed by a man she'd thought was in love with her . . .

Well, she now had a better idea of how bad things could get. It was as if . . . once she had feared the darkness, but now she had stepped into it. She had experienced some of the horrors that awaited her there. Terrible as they were, at least she knew.

You always knew, a voice whispered deep inside of her. *You grew up with horrors, Shallan. You just won't let yourself remember them.*

"What is this?" Tozbek asked as he came up, his wife, Ashlv, at his side. The diminutive woman did not speak much; she dressed in a skirt and blouse of bright yellow, a headscarf covering all of her hair except the two white eyebrows, which she had curled down beside her cheeks.

"Young miss," Tozbek said, "you want to go swimming? Can't you wait until we get into port? I know of some nice areas where the water is not nearly so cold."

"I won't be swimming," Shallan said, blushing further. What would she *wear* to go swimming with men about? Did people really do that? "I need to get a closer look at our companion." She gestured toward the sea creature.

"Young miss, you know I can't allow something so dangerous. Even if we stopped the ship, what if the beast harmed you?"

"They're said to be harmless."

"They are so rare, can we really know for certain? Besides, there are other animals in these seas that could harm you. Redwaters hunt this area for certain, and we might be in shallow enough water for khornaks to be a worry." Tozbek shook his head. "I'm sorry, I just cannot allow it."

Shallan bit her lip, and found her heart beating traitorously. She wanted to push harder, but that decisive look in his eyes made her wilt. "Very well."

Tozbek smiled broadly. "I'll take you to see some shells in the port at Amydlatn when we stop there, young miss. They have quite a collection!"

She didn't know where that was, but from the jumble of consonants squished together, she assumed it would be on the Thaylen side. Most cities were, this far south. Though Thaylenah was nearly as frigid as the Frostlands, people seemed to enjoy living there.

Of course, Thaylens were all a little off. How else to describe Yalb and the others wearing no shirts despite the chill in the air?

They weren't the ones contemplating a dip in the ocean, Shallan reminded herself. She looked over the side of the ship again, watching waves break against the shell of the gentle santhid. What was it? A great-shelled beast, like the fearsome chasmfiends of the Shattered Plains? Was it more like a fish under there, or more like a tortoise? The santhidyn were so rare—and the occasions when scholars had seen them in person so infrequent—that the theories all contradicted one another.

She sighed and opened her satchel, then set to organizing her papers, most of which were practice sketches of the sailors in various poses as they worked to maneuver the massive sails overhead, tacking against the wind. Her father would never have allowed her to spend a day sitting and watching a bunch of shirtless darkeyes. How much her life had changed in such a short time.

She was working on a sketch of the santhid's shell when Jasnah stepped up onto the deck.

Like Shallan, Jasnah wore the havah, a Vorin dress of distinctive design. The hemline was down at her feet and the neckline almost at her chin. Some of the Thaylens—when they thought she wasn't listening—referred to the clothing as prudish. Shallan disagreed; the havah wasn't prudish, but elegant. Indeed, the silk hugged the body, particularly through the bust—and the way the sailors gawked at Jasnah indicated they didn't find the garment unflattering.

Jasnah *was* pretty. Lush of figure, tan of skin. Immaculate eyebrows, lips painted a deep red, hair up in a fine braid. Though Jasnah was twice Shallan's age, her mature beauty was something to be admired, even envied. Why did the woman have to be so perfect?

Jasnah ignored the eyes of the sailors. It wasn't that she didn't notice men. Jasnah noticed everything and everyone. She simply didn't seem to care, one way or another, how men perceived her.

No, that's not true, Shallan thought as Jasnah walked over. *She wouldn't take the time to do her hair, or put on makeup, if she didn't care how she was perceived.* In that, Jasnah was an enigma. On one hand, she seemed to be a

scholar concerned only with her research. On the other hand, she cultivated the poise and dignity of a king's daughter—and, at times, used it like
a bludgeon.

"And here you are," Jasnah said, walking to Shallan. A spray of water
from the side of the ship chose that moment to fly up and sprinkle her. She
frowned at the drops of water beading on her silk clothing, then looked
back to Shallan and raised her eyebrow. "The ship, you may have noticed,
has two very fine cabins that I hired out for us at no small expense."

"Yes, but they're inside."

"As rooms usually are."

"I've spent most of my life inside."

"So you will spend much more of it, if you wish to be a scholar."

Shallan bit her lip, waiting for the order to go below. Curiously, it did
not come. Jasnah gestured for Captain Tozbek to approach, and he did so,
groveling his way over with cap in hand.

"Yes, Brightness?" he asked.

"I should like another of these . . . seats," Jasnah said, regarding Shallan's box.

Tozbek quickly had one of his men lash a second box in place. As she
waited for the seat to be ready, Jasnah waved for Shallan to hand over her
sketches. Jasnah inspected the drawing of the santhid, then looked over
the side of the ship. "No wonder the sailors were making such a fuss."

"Luck, Brightness!" one of the sailors said. "It is a good omen for your
trip, don't you think?"

"I shall take any fortune provided me, Nanhel Eltorv," she said. "Thank
you for the seat."

The sailor bowed awkwardly before retreating.

"You think they're superstitious fools," Shallan said softly, watching the
sailor leave.

"From what I have observed," Jasnah said, "these sailors are men who
have found a purpose in life and now take simple pleasure in it." Jasnah
looked at the next drawing. "Many people make far less out of life. Captain Tozbek runs a good crew. You were wise in bringing him to my attention."

Shallan smiled. "You didn't answer my question."

"You didn't ask a question," Jasnah said. "These sketches are character-
istically skillful, Shallan, but weren't you supposed to be reading?"

"I . . . had trouble concentrating."

"So you came up on deck," Jasnah said, "to sketch pictures of young
men working without their shirts on. You expected this to *help* your concentration?"

Shallan blushed, as Jasnah stopped at one sheet of paper in the stack.

Shallan sat patiently—she'd been well trained in that by her father—until Jasnah turned it toward her. The picture of Shadesmar, of course.

"You have respected my command not to peer into this realm again?" Jasnah asked.

"Yes, Brightness. That picture was drawn from a memory of my first . . . lapse."

Jasnah lowered the page. Shallan thought she saw a hint of something in the woman's expression. Was Jasnah wondering if she could trust Shallan's word?

"I assume this is what is bothering you?" Jasnah asked.

"Yes, Brightness."

"I suppose I should explain it to you, then."

"Really? You would do this?"

"You needn't sound so surprised."

"It seems like powerful information," Shallan said. "The way you forbade me . . . I assumed that knowledge of this place was secret, or at least not to be trusted to one of my age."

Jasnah sniffed. "I've found that refusing to explain secrets to young people makes them *more* prone to get themselves into trouble, not less. Your experimentation proves that you've already stumbled face-first into all of this—as I once did myself, I'll have you know. I know through painful experience how dangerous Shadesmar can be. If I leave you in ignorance, I'll be to blame if you get yourself killed there."

"So you'd have explained about it if I'd asked earlier in our trip?"

"Probably not," Jasnah admitted. "I had to see how willing you were to obey me. This time."

Shallan wilted, and suppressed the urge to point out that back when she'd been a studious and obedient ward, Jasnah hadn't divulged nearly as many secrets as she did now. "So what is it? That . . . place."

"It's not truly a location," Jasnah said. "Not as we usually think of them. Shadesmar is here, all around us, right now. All things exist there in some form, as all things exist here."

Shallan frowned. "I don't—"

Jasnah held up a finger to quiet her. "All things have three components: the soul, the body, and the mind. That place you saw, Shadesmar, is what we call the Cognitive Realm—the place of the mind.

"All around us you see the physical world. You can touch it, see it, hear it. This is how your physical body experiences the world. Well, Shadesmar is the way that your cognitive self—your unconscious self—experiences the world. Through your hidden senses touching that realm, you make intuitive leaps in logic and you form hopes. It is likely through those extra senses that you, Shallan, create art."

Water splashed on the bow of the ship as it crossed a swell. Shallan wiped a drop of salty water from her cheek, trying to think through what Jasnah had just said. "That made almost *no* sense whatsoever to me, Brightness."

"I should hope that it didn't," Jasnah said. "I've spent six years researching Shadesmar, and I still barely know what to make of it. I shall have to accompany you there several times before you can understand, even a little, the true significance of the place."

Jasnah grimaced at the thought. Shallan was always surprised to see visible emotion from her. Emotion was something relatable, something human—and Shallan's mental image of Jasnah Kholin was of someone almost divine. It was, upon reflection, an odd way to regard a determined atheist.

"Listen to me," Jasnah said. "My own words betray my ignorance. I told you that Shadesmar wasn't a place, and yet I call it one in my next breath. I speak of visiting it, though it is all around us. We simply don't have the proper terminology to discuss it. Let me try another tactic."

Jasnah stood up, and Shallan hastened to follow. They walked along the ship's rail, feeling the deck sway beneath their feet. Sailors made way for Jasnah with quick bows. They regarded her with as much reverence as they would a king. How did she do it? How could she control her surroundings without seeming to do anything at all?

"Look down into the waters," Jasnah said as they reached the bow. "What do you see?"

Shallan stopped beside the rail and stared down at the blue waters, foaming as they were broken by the ship's prow. Here at the bow, she could see a *deepness* to the swells. An unfathomable expanse that extended not just outward, but downward.

"I see eternity," Shallan said.

"Spoken like an artist," Jasnah said. "This ship sails across depths we cannot know. Beneath these waves is a bustling, frantic, unseen world."

Jasnah leaned forward, gripping the rail with one hand unclothed and the other veiled within the safehand sleeve. She looked outward. Not at the depths, and not at the land distantly peeking over both the northern and southern horizons. She looked toward the east. Toward the storms.

"There is an entire world, Shallan," Jasnah said, "of which our minds skim but the surface. A world of deep, profound thought. A world *created* by deep, profound thoughts. When you see Shadesmar, you enter those depths. It is an alien place to us in some ways, but at the same time we formed it. With some help."

"We did what?"

"What are spren?" Jasnah asked.

The question caught Shallan off guard, but by now she was accustomed to challenging questions from Jasnah. She took time to think and consider her answer.

"Nobody knows what spren are," Shallan said, "though many philosophers have different opinions on—"

"No," Jasnah said. "What *are* they?"

"I . . ." Shallan looked up at a pair of windspren spinning through the air above. They looked like tiny ribbons of light, glowing softly, dancing around one another. "They're living ideas."

Jasnah spun on her.

"What?" Shallan said, jumping. "Am I wrong?"

"No," Jasnah said. "You're right." The woman narrowed her eyes. "By my best guess, spren are elements of the Cognitive Realm that have *leaked* into the physical world. They're concepts that have gained a fragment of sentience, perhaps because of human intervention.

"Think of a man who gets angry often. Think of how his friends and family might start referring to that anger as a beast, as a thing that possesses him, as something *external* to him. Humans personify. We speak of the wind as if it has a will of its own.

"Spren are those ideas—the ideas of collective human experience—somehow come alive. Shadesmar is where that first happens, and it is *their* place. Though we created it, they shaped it. They live there; they rule there, within their own cities."

"*Cities?*"

"Yes," Jasnah said, looking back out over the ocean. She seemed troubled. "Spren are wild in their variety. Some are as clever as humans and create cities. Others are like fish and simply swim in the currents."

Shallan nodded. Though in truth she was having trouble grasping any of this, she didn't want Jasnah to stop talking. This was the sort of knowledge that Shallan *needed*, the kind of thing she *craved*. "Does this have to do with what you discovered? About the parshmen, the Voidbringers?"

"I haven't been able to determine that yet. The spren are not always forthcoming. In some cases, they do not know. In others, they do not trust me because of our ancient betrayal."

Shallan frowned, looking to her teacher. "Betrayal?"

"They tell me of it," Jasnah said, "but they won't say what it was. We broke an oath, and in so doing offended them greatly. I think some of them may have died, though how a concept can die, I do not know." Jasnah turned to Shallan with a solemn expression. "I realize this is overwhelming. You will have to learn this, all of it, if you are to help me. Are you still willing?"

"Do I have a choice?"

A smile tugged at the edges of Jasnah's lips. "I doubt it. You Soulcast on your own, without the aid of a fabrial. You are like me."

Shallan stared out over the waters. Like Jasnah. What did it mean? Why—

She froze, blinking. For a moment, she thought she'd seen the same pattern as before, the one that had made ridges on her sheet of paper. This time it had been in the water, impossibly formed on the surface of a wave.

"Brightness . . ." she said, resting her fingers on Jasnah's arm. "I thought I saw something in the water, just now. A pattern of sharp lines, like a maze."

"Show me where."

"It was on one of the waves, and we've passed it now. But I think I saw it earlier, on one of my pages. Does it mean something?"

"Most certainly. I must admit, Shallan, I find the coincidence of our meeting to be startling. Suspiciously so."

"Brightness?"

"They were involved," Jasnah said. "They brought you to me. And they are still watching you, it appears. So no, Shallan, you no longer have a choice. The old ways are returning, and I don't see it as a hopeful sign. It's an act of self-preservation. The spren sense impending danger, and so they return to us. Our attention now must turn to the Shattered Plains and the relics of Urithiru. It will be a long, long time before you return to your homeland."

Shallan nodded mutely.

"This worries you," Jasnah said.

"Yes, Brightness. My family . . ."

Shallan felt like a traitor in abandoning her brothers, who had been depending on her for wealth. She'd written to them and explained, without many specifics, that she'd had to return the stolen Soulcaster—and was now required to help Jasnah with her work.

Balat's reply had been positive, after a fashion. He said he was glad at least one of them had escaped the fate that was coming to the house. He thought that the rest of them—her three brothers and Balat's betrothed—were doomed.

They might be right. Not only would Father's debts crush them, but there was the matter of her father's broken Soulcaster. The group that had given it to him wanted it back.

Unfortunately, Shallan was *convinced* that Jasnah's quest was of the utmost importance. The Voidbringers would soon return—indeed, they were not some distant threat from stories. They lived among men, and had for centuries. The gentle, quiet parshmen who worked as perfect servants and slaves were really destroyers.

Stopping the catastrophe of the return of the Voidbringers was a greater duty than even protecting her brothers. It was still painful to admit that.

Jasnah studied her. "With regard to your family, Shallan. I have taken some action."

"Action?" Shallan said, taking the taller woman's arm. "You've helped my brothers?"

"After a fashion," Jasnah said. "Wealth would not truly solve this problem, I suspect, though I have arranged for a small gift to be sent. From what you've said, your family's problems really stem from two issues. First, the Ghostbloods desire their Soulcaster—which you have broken—to be returned. Second, your house is without allies and deeply in debt."

Jasnah proffered a sheet of paper. "This," she continued, "is from a conversation I had with my mother via spanreed this morning."

Shallan traced it with her eyes, noting Jasnah's explanation of the broken Soulcaster and her request for help.

This happens more often than you'd think, Navani had replied. *The failing likely has to do with the alignment of the gem housings. Bring me the device, and we shall see.*

"My mother," Jasnah said, "is a renowned artifabrian. I suspect she can make yours function again. We can send it to your brothers, who can return it to its owners."

"You'd let me do that?" Shallan asked. During their days sailing, Shallan had cautiously pried for more information about the sect, hoping to understand her father and his motives. Jasnah claimed to know very little of them beyond the fact that they wanted her research, and were willing to kill for it.

"I don't particularly want them having access to such a valuable device," Jasnah said. "But I don't have time to protect your family right now directly. This is a workable solution, assuming your brothers can stall a while longer. Have them tell the truth, if they must—that you, knowing I was a scholar, came to me and asked me to fix the Soulcaster. Perhaps that will sate them for now."

"Thank you, Brightness." Storms. If she'd just gone to Jasnah in the first place, after being accepted as her ward, how much easier would it have been? Shallan looked down at the paper, noticing that the conversation continued.

As for the other matter, Navani wrote, *I'm very fond of this suggestion. I believe I can persuade the boy to at least consider it, as his most recent affair ended quite abruptly—as is common with him—earlier in the week.*

"What is this second part?" Shallan asked, looking up from the paper.

"Sating the Ghostbloods alone will not save your house," Jasnah said. "Your debts are too great, particularly considering your father's actions in alienating so many. I have therefore arranged a powerful alliance for your house."

"Alliance? How?"

Jasnah took a deep breath. She seemed reluctant to explain. "I have taken the initial steps in arranging for you to be betrothed to one of my cousins, son of my uncle Dalinar Kholin. The boy's name is Adolin. He is handsome and well-acquainted with amiable discourse."

"Betrothed?" Shallan said. "You've promised him my hand?"

"I have started the process," Jasnah said, speaking with uncharacteristic anxiety. "Though at times he lacks foresight, Adolin has a good heart—as good as that of his father, who may be the best man I have ever known. He is considered Alethkar's most eligible son, and my mother has long wanted him wed."

"Betrothed," Shallan repeated.

"Yes. Is that distressing?"

"It's wonderful!" Shallan exclaimed, grabbing Jasnah's arm more tightly. "So easy. If I'm married to someone so powerful . . . Storms! Nobody would dare touch us in Jah Keved. It would solve many of our problems. Brightness Jasnah, you're a genius!"

Jasnah relaxed visibly. "Yes, well, it did seem a workable solution. I had wondered, however, if you'd be offended."

"Why on the winds would I be offended?"

"Because of the restriction of freedom implicit in a marriage," Jasnah said. "And if not that, because the offer was made without consulting you. I had to see if the possibility was even open first. It has proceeded further than I'd expected, as my mother has seized on the idea. Navani has . . . a tendency toward the overwhelming."

Shallan had trouble imagining anyone overwhelming Jasnah. "Stormfather! You're worried I'd be offended? Brightness, I spent my entire life locked in my father's manor—I grew up assuming he'd pick my husband."

"But you're free of your father now."

"Yes, and I was so *perfectly* wise in my own pursuit of relationships," Shallan said. "The first man I chose was not only an ardent, but secretly an assassin."

"It doesn't bother you at all?" Jasnah said. "The idea of being beholden to another, particularly a man?"

"It's not like I'm being sold into slavery," Shallan said with a laugh.

"No. I suppose not." Jasnah shook herself, her poise returning. "Well, I will let Navani know you are amenable to the engagement, and we should have a causal in place within the day."

A causal—a conditional betrothal, in Vorin terminology. She would be, for all intents and purposes, engaged, but would have no legal footing until an official betrothal was signed and verified by the ardents.

"The boy's father has said he will not force Adolin into anything," Jasnah explained, "though the boy is recently single, as he has managed to offend yet another young lady. Regardless, Dalinar would rather you two meet before anything more binding is agreed upon. There have been . . . shifts in the political climate of the Shattered Plains. A great loss to my uncle's army. Another reason for us to hasten to the Plains."

"Adolin Kholin," Shallan said, listening with half an ear. "A duelist. A fantastic one. And even a Shardbearer."

"Ah, so you *were* paying attention to your readings about my father and family."

"I was—but I knew about your family before that. The Alethi are the center of society! Even girls from rural houses know the names of the Alethi princes." And she'd be lying if she denied youthful daydreams of meeting one. "But Brightness, are you certain this match will be wise? I mean, I'm hardly the most important of individuals."

"Well, yes. The daughter of another highprince might have been preferable for Adolin. However, it seems that he has managed to offend each and every one of the eligible women of that rank. The boy is, shall we say, somewhat overeager about relationships. Nothing you can't work through, I'm sure."

"Stormfather," Shallan said, feeling her legs go weak. "He's heir to a princedom! He's in line to the throne of Alethkar itself!"

"Third in line," Jasnah said, "behind my brother's infant son and Dalinar, my uncle."

"Brightness, I have to ask. Why Adolin? Why not the younger son? I—I have nothing to offer Adolin, or the house."

"On the contrary," Jasnah said, "if you are what I think you are, then you will be able to offer him something nobody else can. Something more important than riches."

"What is it you think that I am?" Shallan whispered, meeting the older woman's eyes, finally asking the question that she hadn't dared.

"Right now, you are but a promise," Jasnah said. "A chrysalis with the potential for grandeur inside. When once humans and spren bonded, the results were women who danced in the skies and men who could destroy the stones with a touch."

"The Lost Radiants. Traitors to mankind." She couldn't absorb it all. The betrothal, Shadesmar and the spren, and this, her mysterious destiny. She'd known. But speaking it . . .

She sank down, heedless of getting her dress wet on the deck, and sat with her back against the bulwark. Jasnah allowed her to compose herself before, amazingly, sitting down herself. She did so with far more poise, tucking her dress underneath her legs as she sat sideways. They both drew looks from the sailors.

"They're going to chew me to pieces," Shallan said. "The Alethi court. It's the most ferocious in the world."

Jasnah snorted. "It's more bluster than storm, Shallan. I will train you."

"I'll never be like you, Brightness. You have power, authority, wealth. Just look how the sailors respond to you."

"Am I specifically using said power, authority, or wealth right now?"

"You paid for this trip."

"Did you not pay for several trips on this ship?" Jasnah asked. "They did not treat you the same as they do me?"

"No. Oh, they are fond of me. But I don't have your *weight*, Jasnah."

"I will assume that did not have implications toward my girth," Jasnah said with a hint of a smile. "I understand your argument, Shallan. It is, however, dead wrong."

Shallan turned to her. Jasnah sat upon the deck of the ship as if it were a throne, back straight, head up, commanding. Shallan sat with her legs against her chest, arms around them below the knees. Even the ways they *sat* were different. She was nothing like this woman.

"There is a secret you must learn, child," Jasnah said. "A secret that is even more important than those relating to Shadesmar and spren. Power is an illusion of perception."

Shallan frowned.

"Don't mistake me," Jasnah continued. "Some kinds of power are real—power to command armies, power to Soulcast. These come into play far less often than you would think. On an individual basis, in most interactions, this thing we call power—authority—exists only as it is perceived.

"You say I have wealth. This is true, but you have also seen that I do not often use it. You say I have authority as the sister of a king. I do. And yet, the men of this ship would treat me exactly the same way if I were a beggar who had *convinced* them I was the sister to a king. In that case, my authority is not a real thing. It is mere vapors—an illusion. I can create that illusion for them, as can you."

"I'm not convinced, Brightness."

"I know. If you were, you would be doing it already." Jasnah stood up, brushing off her skirt. "You will tell me if you see that pattern—the one that appeared on the waves—again?"

"Yes, Brightness," Shallan said, distracted.

"Then take the rest of the day for your art. I need to consider how to best teach you of Shadesmar." The older woman retreated, nodding at the bows of sailors as she passed and went back down belowdecks.

Shallan rose, then turned and grabbed the railing, one hand to either side of the bowsprit. The ocean spread before her, rippling waves, a scent of cold freshness. Rhythmic crashing as the sloop pushed through the waves.

Jasnah's words fought in her mind, like skyeels with only one rat between them. Spren with cities? Shadesmar, a realm that was here, but unseen? Shallan, suddenly *betrothed* to the single most important bachelor in the world?

She left the bow, walking along the side of the ship, freehand trailing on the railing. How did the sailors regard her? They smiled, they waved. They liked her. Yalb, who hung lazily from the rigging nearby, called to her, telling her that in the next port, there was a statue she had to go visit. "It's this *giant* foot, young miss. Just a foot! Never finished the blustering statue . . ."

She smiled to him and continued. Did she want them to look at her as they looked at Jasnah? Always afraid, always worried that they might do something wrong? Was that power?

When I first sailed from Vedenar, she thought, reaching the place where her box had been tied, *the captain kept urging me to go home. He saw my mission as a fool's errand.*

Tozbek had always acted as if he were doing her a favor in conveying her after Jasnah. Should she have had to spend that entire time feeling as if she'd imposed upon him and his crew by hiring them? Yes, he had offered a discount to her because of her father's business with him in the past—but she'd still been employing him.

The way he'd treated her was probably a thing of Thaylen merchants. If a captain could make you feel like you were imposing on him, you'd pay better. She liked the man, but their relationship left something to be desired. Jasnah would never have stood for being treated in such a way.

That santhid still swam alongside. It was like a tiny, mobile island, its back overgrown with seaweed, small crystals jutting up from the shell.

Shallan turned and walked toward the stern, where Captain Tozbek spoke with one of his mates, pointing at a map covered with glyphs. He nodded to her as she approached. "Just a warning, young miss," he said. "The ports will soon grow less accommodating. We'll be leaving Longbrow's Straits, curving around the eastern edge of the continent, toward New Natanan. There's nothing of worth between here and the Shallow Crypts—and even that's not much of a sight. I wouldn't send my own brother ashore there without guards, and he's killed seventeen men with his bare hands, he has."

"I understand, Captain," Shallan said. "And thank you. I've revised my earlier decision. I need you to halt the ship and let me inspect the specimen swimming beside us."

He sighed, reaching up and running his fingers along one of his stiff, spiked eyebrows—much as other men might play with their mustaches.

"Brightness, that's *not* advisable. Stormfather! If I dropped you in the ocean . . ."

"Then I would be wet," Shallan said. "It is a state I've experienced one or two times in my life."

"No, I simply cannot allow it. Like I said, we'll take you to see some shells in—"

"Cannot allow it?" Shallan interrupted. She regarded him with what she hoped was a look of puzzlement, hoping he didn't see how tightly she squeezed her hands closed at her sides. Storms, but she hated confrontation. "I wasn't aware I had made a request you had the power to allow or disallow, Captain. Stop the ship. Lower me down. That is your order." She tried to say it as forcefully as Jasnah would. The woman could make it seem easier to resist a full highstorm than to disagree with her.

Tozbek worked his mouth for a moment, no sound coming out, as if his body were trying to continue his earlier objection but his mind had been delayed. "It is my ship . . ." he finally said.

"Nothing will be done to your ship," Shallan said. "Let's be quick about it, Captain. I do not wish to overly delay our arrival in port tonight."

She left him, walking back to her box, heart thumping, hands trembling. She sat down, partially to calm herself.

Tozbek, sounding profoundly annoyed, began calling orders. The sails were lowered, the ship slowed. Shallan breathed out, feeling a fool.

And yet, what Jasnah said worked. The way Shallan acted *created* something in the eyes of Tozbek. An illusion? Like the spren themselves, perhaps? Fragments of human expectation, given life?

The santhid slowed with them. Shallan rose, nervous, as sailors approached with rope. They reluctantly tied a loop at the bottom she could put her foot in, then explained that she should hold tightly to the rope as she was lowered. They tied a second, smaller rope securely around her waist—the means by which to haul her, wet and humiliated, back onto the deck. An inevitability, in their eyes.

She took off her shoes, then climbed up over the railing as instructed. Had it been this windy before? She had a moment of vertigo, standing there with socked toes gripping a tiny rim, dress fluttering in the coursing winds. A windspren zipped up to her, then formed into the shape of a face with clouds behind it. Storms, the thing had better not interfere. Was it human imagination that had given windspren their mischievous spark?

She stepped unsteadily into the rope loop as the sailors lowered it down beside her feet, then Yalb handed her the mask he'd told her of.

Jasnah appeared from belowdecks, looking about in confusion. She saw Shallan standing off the side of the ship, and then cocked an eyebrow.

Shallan shrugged, then gestured to the men to lower her.

She refused to let herself feel silly as she inched toward the waters and the reclusive animal bobbing in the waves. The men stopped her a foot or two above the water, and she put on the mask, held by straps, covering most of her face including the nose.

"Lower!" she shouted up at them.

She thought she could *feel* their reluctance in the lethargic way the rope descended. Her foot hit the water, and a biting cold shot up her leg. Stormfather! But she didn't have them stop. She let them lower her farther until her legs were submerged in the frigid water. Her skirt ballooned out in a most annoying way, and she actually had to step on the end of it—inside the loop—to prevent it from rising up about her waist and floating on the water's surface as she submerged.

She wrestled with the fabric for a moment, glad the men above couldn't see her blushing. Once it got wetter, though, it was easier to manage. She finally was able to squat, still holding tightly to the rope, and go down into the water up to her waist.

Then she ducked her head under the water.

Light streamed down from the surface in shimmering, radiant columns. There was *life* here, furious, amazing life. Tiny fish zipped this way and that, picking at the underside of the shell that shaded a majestic creature. Gnarled like an ancient tree, with rippled and folded skin, the true form of the santhid was a beast with long, drooping blue tendrils, like those of a jellyfish, only far thicker. Those disappeared down into the depths, trailing behind the beast at a slant.

The beast itself was a knotted grey-blue mass underneath the shell. Its ancient-looking folds surrounded one large eye on her side—presumably, its twin would be on the other side. It seemed ponderous, yet majestic, with mighty fins moving like oarsmen. A group of strange spren shaped like arrows moved through the water here around the beast.

Schools of fish darted about. Though the depths seemed empty, the area just around the santhid teemed with life, as did the area under the ship. Tiny fish picked at the bottom of the vessel. They'd move between the santhid and the ship, sometimes alone, sometimes in waves. Was this why the creature swam up beside a vessel? Something to do with the fish, and their relationship to it?

She looked upon the creature, and its eye—as big as her head—rolled toward her, focusing, *seeing* her. In that moment, Shallan couldn't feel the cold. She couldn't feel embarrassed. She was looking into a world that, so far as she knew, no scholar had ever visited.

She blinked her eyes, taking a Memory of the creature, collecting it for later sketching.

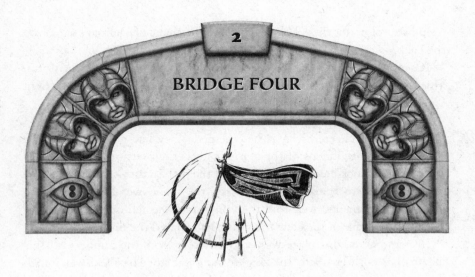

2

BRIDGE FOUR

Our first clue was the Parshendi. Even weeks before they abandoned their pursuit of the gemhearts, their pattern of fighting changed. They lingered on the plateaus after battles, as if waiting for something.

—From the personal journal of Navani Kholin, Jeseses 1174

Breath.

A man's breath was his life. Exhaled, bit by bit, back into the world. Kaladin breathed deeply, eyes closed, and for a time that was all he could hear. His own life. In, out, to the beating of the thunder in his chest.

Breath. His own little storm.

Outside, the rain had stopped. Kaladin remained sitting in the darkness. When kings and wealthy lighteyes died, their bodies weren't burned like those of common men. Instead, they were Soulcast into statues of stone or metal, forever frozen.

The darkeyes' bodies were burned. They became smoke, to rise toward the heavens and whatever waited there, like a burned prayer.

Breath. The breath of a lighteyes was no different from that of a darkeyes. No more sweet, no more free. The breath of kings and slaves mingled, to be breathed by men again, over and over.

Kaladin stood up and opened his eyes. He'd spent the highstorm in the darkness of this small room alongside Bridge Four's new barrack. Alone. He walked to the door, but stopped. He rested his fingers on a cloak he knew hung from a hook there. In the darkness, he could not make out its deep blue color, nor the Kholin glyph—in the shape of Dalinar's sigil—on the back.

It seemed that every change in his life had been marked by a storm. This was a big one. He shoved open the door and stepped out into the light as a free man.

He left the cloak, for now.

Bridge Four cheered him as he emerged. They had gone out to bathe and shave in the riddens of the storm, as was their custom. The line was almost done, Rock having shaved each of the men in turn. The large Horneater hummed to himself as he worked the razor over Drehy's balding head. The air smelled wet from the rain, and a washed-out firepit nearby was the only trace of the stew the group had shared the night before.

In many ways, this place wasn't so different from the lumberyards his men had recently escaped. The long, rectangular stone barracks were much the same—Soulcast rather than having been built by hand, they looked like enormous stone logs. These, however, each had a couple of smaller rooms on the sides for sergeants, with their own doors that opened to the outside. They'd been painted with the symbols of the platoons using them before; Kaladin's men would have to paint over those.

"Moash," Kaladin called. "Skar, Teft."

The three jogged toward him, splashing through puddles left by the storm. They wore the clothing of bridgemen: simple trousers cut off at the knees, and leather vests over bare chests. Skar was up and mobile despite the wound to his foot, and he tried rather obviously not to limp. For now, Kaladin didn't order him to bed rest. The wound wasn't too bad, and he needed the man.

"I want to look at what we've got," Kaladin said, leading them away from the barrack. It would house fifty men along with a half-dozen sergeants. More barracks flanked it on either side. Kaladin had been given an entire block of them—twenty buildings—to house his new battalion of former bridgemen.

Twenty buildings. That Dalinar should so easily be able to find a block of twenty buildings for the bridgemen bespoke a terrible truth—the cost of Sadeas's betrayal. Thousands of men dead. Indeed, female scribes worked near some of the barracks, supervising parshmen who carried out heaps of clothing and other personal effects. The possessions of the deceased.

Not a few of those scribes looked on with red eyes and frazzled composures. Sadeas had just created thousands of new widows in Dalinar's camp, and likely as many orphans. If Kaladin had needed another reason to hate that man, he found it here, manifest in the suffering of those whose husbands had trusted him on the battlefield.

In Kaladin's eyes, there was no sin greater than the betrayal of one's allies in battle. Except, perhaps, for the betrayal of one's own men—of murdering them after they risked their lives to protect you. Kaladin felt an immediate flare of anger at thoughts of Amaram and what he'd done. His slave brand seemed to burn again on his forehead.

Amaram and Sadeas. Two men in Kaladin's life who would, at some point, need to pay for the things they'd done. Preferably, that payment would come with severe interest.

Kaladin continued to walk with Teft, Moash, and Skar. These barracks, which were slowly being emptied of personal effects, were also crowded with bridgemen. They looked much like the men of Bridge Four—same vests and knee-trousers. And yet, in some other ways, they couldn't have looked *less* like the men of Bridge Four. Shaggy-haired with beards that hadn't been trimmed in months, they bore hollow eyes that didn't seem to blink often enough. Slumped backs. Expressionless faces.

Each man among them seemed to sit alone, even when surrounded by his fellows.

"I remember that feeling," Skar said softly. The short, wiry man had sharp features and silvering hair at the temples, despite being in his early thirties. "I don't want to, but I do."

"We're supposed to turn *those* into an army?" Moash asked.

"Kaladin did it to Bridge Four, didn't he?" Teft asked, wagging a finger at Moash. "He'll do it again."

"Transforming a few dozen men is different from doing the same for hundreds," Moash said, kicking aside a fallen branch from the highstorm. Tall and solid, Moash had a scar on his chin but no slave brand on his forehead. He walked straight-backed with his chin up. Save for those dark brown eyes of his, he could have passed for an officer.

Kaladin led the three past barrack after barrack, doing a quick count. Nearly a thousand men, and though he'd told them yesterday that they were now free—and could return to their old lives if they wished—few seemed to want to do anything but sit. Though there had originally been forty bridge crews, many had been slaughtered during the latest assault and others had already been short-manned.

"We'll combine them into twenty crews," Kaladin said, "of about fifty each." Above, Syl fluttered down as a ribbon of light and zipped around him. The men gave no sign of seeing her; she would be invisible to them. "We can't teach each of these thousand personally, not at first. We'll want to train the more eager ones among them, then send them back to lead and train their own teams."

"I suppose," Teft said, scratching his chin. The oldest of the bridgemen, he was one of the few who retained a beard. Most of the others had shaved theirs off as a mark of pride, something to separate the men of Bridge Four from common slaves. Teft kept his neat for the same reason. It was light brown where it hadn't gone grey, and he wore it short and square, almost like an ardent's.

Moash grimaced, looking at the bridgemen. "You assume some of them will be 'more eager,' Kaladin. They all look the same level of despondent to me."

"Some will still have fight in them," Kaladin said, continuing on back toward Bridge Four. "The ones who joined us at the fire last night, for a start. Teft, I'll need you to choose others. Organize and combine crews, then pick forty men—two from each team—to be trained first. You'll be in command of that training. Those forty will be the seed we use to help the rest."

"I suppose I can do that."

"Good. I'll give you a few men to help."

"A few?" Teft asked. "I could use more than a few. . . ."

"You'll have to make do with a few," Kaladin said, stopping on the path and turning westward, toward the king's complex beyond the camp wall. It rose on a hillside overlooking the rest of the warcamps. "Most of us are going to be needed to keep Dalinar Kholin alive."

Moash and the others stopped beside him. Kaladin squinted at the palace. It certainly didn't look grand enough to house a king—out here, everything was just stone and more stone.

"You are willing to trust Dalinar?" Moash asked.

"He gave up his Shardblade for us," Kaladin said.

"He owed it to us," Skar said with a grunt. "We saved his storming life."

"It could have just been posturing," Moash said, folding his arms. "Political games, him and Sadeas trying to manipulate each other."

Syl alighted on Kaladin's shoulder, taking the form of a young woman with a flowing, filmy dress, all blue-white. She held her hands clasped together as she looked up at the king's complex, where Dalinar Kholin had gone to plan.

He'd told Kaladin that he was going to do something that would anger a lot of people. *I'm going to take away their games. . . .*

"We need to keep that man alive," Kaladin said, looking back to the others. "I don't know if I trust him, but he's the only person on these Plains who has shown even a *hint* of compassion for bridgemen. If he dies, do you want to guess how long it will take his successor to sell us back to Sadeas?"

Skar snorted in derision. "I'd like to see them try with a Knight Radiant at our head."

"I'm *not* a Radiant."

"Fine, whatever," Skar said. "Whatever you *are*, it will be tough for them to take us from you."

"You think I can fight them all, Skar?" Kaladin said, meeting the older man's eyes. "Dozens of Shardbearers? Tens of thousands of troops? You think one man could do that?"

"Not one man," Skar said, stubborn. "You."

"I'm not a god, Skar," Kaladin said. "I can't hold back the weight of ten armies." He turned to the other two. "We decided to stay here on the Shattered Plains. Why?"

"What good would it do to run?" Teft asked, shrugging. "Even as free men, we'd just end up conscripted into one army or another out there in the hills. Either that, or we'd end up starving."

Moash nodded. "This is as good a place as any, so long as we're free."

"Dalinar Kholin is our best hope for a *real* life," Kaladin said. "Bodyguards, not conscripted labor. Free men, despite the brands on our foreheads. Nobody else will give us that. If we want freedom, we need to keep Dalinar Kholin alive."

"And the Assassin in White?" Skar asked softly.

They'd heard of what the man was doing around the world, slaughtering kings and highprinces in all nations. The news was the buzz of the warcamps, ever since reports had started trickling in through spanreed. The emperor of Azir, dead. Jah Keved in turmoil. A half-dozen other nations left without a ruler.

"He already killed our king," Kaladin said. "Old Gavilar was the assassin's first murder. We'll just have to hope he's done here. Either way, we protect Dalinar. At all costs."

They nodded one by one, though those nods were grudging. He didn't blame them. Trusting lighteyes hadn't gotten them far—even Moash, who had once spoken well of Dalinar, now seemed to have lost his fondness for the man. Or any lighteyes.

In truth, Kaladin was a little surprised at himself and the trust he felt. But, storm it, Syl liked Dalinar. That carried weight.

"We're weak right now," Kaladin said, lowering his voice. "But if we play along with this for a time, protecting Kholin, we'll be paid handsomely. I'll be able to train you—really train you—as soldiers and officers. Beyond that, we'll be able to teach these others.

"We could never make it on our own out there as two dozen former bridgemen. But what if we were instead a highly skilled mercenary force of a thousand soldiers, equipped with the finest gear in the warcamps? If worst comes to worst, and we have to abandon the camps, I'd like to do so as a cohesive unit, hardened and impossible to ignore. Give me a year with this thousand, and I can have it done."

"Now *that* plan I like," Moash said. "Do I get to learn to use a sword?"

"We're still darkeyes, Moash."

"Not you," Skar said from his other side. "I saw your eyes during the—"

"Stop!" Kaladin said. He took a deep breath. "Just stop. No more talk of that."

Skar fell silent.

"I *am* going to name you officers," Kaladin said to them. "You three, along with Sigzil and Rock. You'll be lieutenants."

"Darkeyed lieutenants?" Skar said. The rank was commonly used for the equivalent of sergeants in companies made up only of lighteyes.

"Dalinar made me a captain," Kaladin said. "The highest rank he said he dared commission a darkeyes. Well, I need to come up with a full command structure for a thousand men, and we're going to need something between sergeant and captain. That means appointing you five as lieutenants. I think Dalinar will let me get away with it. We'll make master sergeants if we need another rank.

"Rock is going to be quartermaster and in charge of food for the thousand. I'll appoint Lopen his second. Teft, you'll be in charge of training. Sigzil will be our clerk. He's the only one who can read glyphs. Moash and Skar . . ."

He glanced toward the two men. One short, the other tall, they walked the same way, with a smooth gait, dangerous, spears always on their shoulders. They were never without. Of all the men he'd trained in Bridge Four, only these two had instinctively *understood*. They were killers.

Like Kaladin himself.

"We three," Kaladin told them, "are each going to focus on watching Dalinar Kholin. Whenever possible, I want one of us three personally guarding him. Often one of the other two will watch his sons, but make no mistake, the Blackthorn is the man we're going to keep alive. At all costs. He is our only guarantee of freedom for Bridge Four."

The others nodded.

"Good," Kaladin said. "Let's go get the rest of the men. It's time for the world to see you as I do."

⋄⋄

By common agreement, Hobber sat down to get his tattoo first. The gap-toothed man was one of the very first who had believed in Kaladin. Kaladin remembered that day; exhausted after a bridge run, wanting to simply lie down and stare. Instead, he'd chosen to save Hobber rather than letting him die. Kaladin had saved himself that day too.

The rest of Bridge Four stood around Hobber in the tent, watching in silence as the tattooist worked carefully on his forehead, covering up the scar of his slave's brand with the glyphs Kaladin had provided. Hobber winced now and then at the pain of the tattoo, but he kept a grin on his face.

Kaladin had heard that you could cover a scar with a tattoo, and it ended up working quite well. Once the tattoo ink was injected, the glyphs drew the eye, and you could barely tell that the skin beneath was scarred.

Once the process was finished, the tattooist provided a mirror for Hobber to look into. The bridgeman touched his forehead hesitantly. The skin was red from the needles, but the dark tattoo perfectly covered the slave brand.

"What does it say?" Hobber asked softly, tears in his eyes.

"Freedom," Sigzil said before Kaladin could reply. "The glyph means freedom."

"The smaller ones above," Kaladin said, "say the date you were freed and the one who freed you. Even if you lose your writ of freedom, anyone who tries to imprison you for being a runaway can easily find proof that you are not. They can go to Dalinar Kholin's scribes, who keep a copy of your writ."

Hobber nodded. "That's good, but it's not enough. Add 'Bridge Four' to it. Freedom, Bridge Four."

"To imply you were freed from Bridge Four?"

"No, sir. I wasn't freed *from* Bridge Four. I was freed *by* it. I wouldn't trade my time there for anything."

It was crazy talk. Bridge Four had been death—scores of men had been slaughtered running that cursed bridge. Even after Kaladin had determined to save the men, he'd lost far too many. Hobber would have been a fool not to take any opportunity to escape.

And yet, he sat stubbornly until Kaladin drew out the proper glyphs for the tattooist—a calm, sturdy darkeyed woman who looked like she could have lifted a bridge all on her own. She settled down on her stool and began adding the two glyphs to Hobber's forehead, tucked right below the freedom glyph. She spent the process explaining—again—how the tattoo would be sore for days and how Hobber would need to care for it.

He accepted the new tattoos with a grin on his face. Pure foolishness, but the others nodded in agreement, clasping Hobber on the arm. Once Hobber was done, Skar sat quickly, eager, demanding the same full set of tattoos.

Kaladin stepped back, folding his arms and shaking his head. Outside the tent, a bustling marketplace sold and bought. The "warcamp" was really a city, built up inside the craterlike rim of some enormous rock formation. The prolonged war on the Shattered Plains had attracted merchants of all varieties, along with tradesmen, artists, and even families with children.

Moash stood nearby, face troubled, watching the tattooist. He wasn't the only one in the bridge crew who didn't have a slave brand. Teft didn't either. They had been made bridgemen without technically being made slaves first. It happened frequently in Sadeas's camp, where running bridges was a punishment that one could earn for all manner of infractions.

"If you don't have a slave's brand," Kaladin said loudly to the men, "you don't need to get the tattoo. You're still one of us."

"No," Rock said. "I will get this thing." He insisted on sitting down after Skar and getting the tattoo right on his forehead, though he had no slave brand. Indeed, every one of the men without a slave brand—Beld and Teft included—sat down and got the tattoo on their foreheads.

Only Moash abstained, and had the tattoo placed on his upper arm. Good. Unlike most of them, he wouldn't have to go about with a proclamation of former slavery in plain view.

Moash stood up from the seat, and another took his place. A man with red and black skin in a marbled pattern, like stone. Bridge Four had a lot of variety, but Shen was in a class all his own. A parshman.

"I can't tattoo him," the artist said. "He's property."

Kaladin opened his mouth to object, but the other bridgemen jumped in first.

"He's been freed, like us," Teft said.

"One of the team," Hobber said. "Give him the tattoo, or you won't see a sphere from any of us." He blushed after he said it, glancing at Kaladin—who would be paying for all this, using spheres granted by Dalinar Kholin.

Other bridgemen spoke out, and the tattoo artist finally sighed and gave in. She pulled over her stool and began working on Shen's forehead.

"You won't even be able to see it," she grumbled, though Sigzil's skin was nearly as dark as Shen's, and the tattoo showed up fine on him.

Eventually, Shen looked in the mirror, then stood up. He glanced at Kaladin, and nodded. Shen didn't say much, and Kaladin didn't know what to make of the man. It was actually easy to forget about him, usually trailing along silently at the back of the group of bridgemen. Invisible. Parshmen were often that way.

Shen finished, only Kaladin himself remained. He sat down next and closed his eyes. The pain of the needles was a lot sharper than he'd anticipated.

After a short time, the tattooist started cursing under her breath.

Kaladin opened his eyes as she wiped a rag on his forehead. "What is it?" he asked.

"The ink won't take!" she said. "I've never seen anything like it. When I wipe your forehead, the ink all just comes right off! The tattoo won't stay."

Kaladin sighed, realizing he had a little Stormlight raging in his veins. He hadn't even noticed drawing it in, but he seemed to be getting better and better at holding it. He frequently took in a little these days while walking about. Holding Stormlight was like filling a wineskin—if you filled it to bursting and unstopped it, it would squirt out quickly, then slow to a trickle. Same with the Light.

He banished it, hoping the tattoo artist didn't notice when he breathed out a small cloud of glowing smoke. "Try again," he said as she got out new ink.

This time, the tattoo took. Kaladin sat through the process, teeth clenched against the pain, then looked up as she held the mirror for him. The face that looked back at Kaladin seemed alien. Clean-shaven, hair pulled back from his face for the tattooing, the slave brands covered up and, for the moment, forgotten.

Can I be this man again? he thought, reaching up, touching his cheek. *This man died, didn't he?*

Syl landed on his shoulder, joining him in looking into the mirror. "Life before death, Kaladin," she whispered.

He unconsciously sucked in Stormlight. Just a little, a fraction of a sphere's worth. It flowed through his veins like a wave of pressure, like winds trapped in a small enclosure.

The tattoo on his forehead melted. His body shoved out the ink, which started to drip down his face. The tattooist cursed again and grabbed her rag.

Kaladin was left with the image of those glyphs melting away. Freedom dissolved, and underneath, the violent scars of his captivity. Dominated by a branded glyph.

Shash. Dangerous.

The woman wiped his face. "I don't know why this is happening! I thought it would stay that time. I—"

"It's all right," Kaladin said, taking the rag as he stood, finishing the cleanup. He turned to face the rest of them, bridgemen now soldiers. "The scars haven't finished with me yet, it appears. I'll try again another time."

They nodded. He'd have to explain to them later what was happening; they knew of his abilities.

"Let's go," Kaladin said to them, tossing a small bag of spheres to the tattooist, then taking his spear from beside the tent entrance. The others joined him, spears to shoulders. They didn't need to be armed while in camp, but he wanted them to get used to the idea that they were free to carry weapons now.

The market outside was crowded and vibrant. The tents, of course, would have been taken down and stowed during last night's highstorm, but they'd already sprung up again. Perhaps because he was thinking about Shen, he noticed the parshmen. He picked out dozens of them with a cursory glance, helping set up a few last tents, carrying purchases for lighteyes, helping shopowners stack their wares.

What do they think of this war on the Shattered Plains? Kaladin wondered. *A war to defeat, and perhaps subjugate, the only free parshmen in the world?*

Would that he could get an answer out of Shen regarding questions like that. It seemed all he ever got from the parshman were shrugs.

Kaladin led his men through the market, which seemed far friendlier than the one in Sadeas's camp. Though people stared at the bridgemen, nobody sneered, and the haggling at nearby stands—while energetic— didn't progress to shouting. There even seemed to be fewer urchins and beggars.

You just want to believe that, Kaladin thought. *You want to believe Dalinar is the man everyone says he is. The honorable lighteyes of the stories. But everyone said the same things about Amaram.*

As they walked, they did pass some soldiers. Too few. Men who had been on duty back in the camp when the others had gone on the disastrous assault where Sadeas had betrayed Dalinar. As they passed one group patrolling the market, Kaladin caught two men at their front raising their hands before themselves, crossed at the wrist.

How had they learned Bridge Four's old salute, and so quickly? These men didn't do it as a full salute, just a small gesture, but they nodded their heads to Kaladin and his men as they passed. Suddenly, the more calm nature of the market took on another cast to Kaladin. Perhaps this wasn't simply the order and organization of Dalinar's army.

There was an air of quiet dread over this warcamp. Thousands had been lost to Sadeas's betrayal. Everyone here had probably known a man who had died out on those plateaus. And everyone probably wondered if the conflict between the two highprinces would escalate.

"It's nice to be seen as a hero, isn't it?" Sigzil asked, walking beside Kaladin and watching another group of soldiers pass by.

"How long will the goodwill last, do you think?" Moash asked. "How long before they resent us?"

"Ha!" Rock, towering behind him, clapped Moash on the shoulder. "No complaining today! You do this thing too much. Do not make me kick you. I do not like kicking. It hurts my toes."

"Kick me?" Moash snorted. "You won't even carry a spear, Rock."

"Spears are not for kicking complainers. But big Unkalaki feet like mine—it is what they were made for! Ha! This thing is obvious, yes?"

Kaladin led the men out of the market and to a large rectangular building near the barracks. This one was constructed of worked stone, rather than Soulcast rock, allowing far more finesse in design. Such buildings were becoming more common in the warcamps, as more masons arrived.

Soulcasting was quicker, but also more expensive and less flexible. He didn't know much about it, only that Soulcasters were limited in what they could do. That was why the barracks were all essentially identical.

Kaladin led his men inside the towering building to the counter, where a grizzled man with a belly that stretched to next week supervised a few parshmen stacking bolts of blue cloth. Rind, the Kholin head quartermaster, to whom Kaladin had sent instructions the night before. Rind was lighteyed, but what was known as a "tenner," a lowly rank barely above darkeyes.

"Ah!" Rind said, speaking with a high-pitched voice that did not match his girth. "You're here, finally! I've got them all out for you, Captain. Everything I have left."

"Left?" Moash asked.

"Uniforms of the Cobalt Guard! I've commissioned some new ones, but this is what stock remained." Rind grew more subdued. "Didn't expect to need so many so soon, you see." He looked Moash up and down, then handed him a uniform and pointed to a stall for changing.

Moash took it. "We going to wear our leather jerkins over these?"

"Ha!" Rind said. "The ones tied with so much bone you looked like some Western skullbearer on feast day? I've heard of that. But no, Brightlord Dalinar says you're each to be outfitted with breastplates, steel caps, new spears. Chain mail for the battlefield, if you need it."

"For now," Kaladin said, "uniforms will do."

"I think I'll look silly in this," Moash grumbled, but walked over to change. Rind distributed the uniforms to the men. He gave Shen a strange look, but delivered the parshman a uniform without complaint.

The bridgemen gathered in an eager bunch, jabbering with excitement as they unfolded their uniforms. It had been a long time since any of them had worn anything other than bridgeman leathers or slave wraps. They stopped talking when Moash stepped out.

These were newer uniforms, of a more modern style than Kaladin had worn in his previous military service. Stiff blue trousers and black boots polished to a shine. A buttoned white shirt, only the edges of its collar and cuffs extending beyond the jacket, which came down to the waist and buttoned closed beneath the belt.

"Now, *there's* a soldier!" the quartermaster said with a laugh. "Still think you look silly?" He gestured for Moash to inspect his reflection in the mirror on the wall.

Moash fixed his cuffs and actually blushed. Kaladin had rarely seen the man so out of sorts. "No," Moash said. "I don't."

The others moved eagerly and began changing. Some went to the stalls at the side, but most didn't care. They were bridgemen and slaves; they'd spent most of their recent lives being paraded about in loincloths or little more.

Teft had his on before anyone else, and knew to do up the buttons in the right places. "Been a long time," he whispered, buckling his belt. "Don't know that I deserve to wear something like this again."

"This is what you are, Teft," Kaladin said. "Don't let the slave rule you."

Teft grunted, affixing his combat knife in its place on his belt. "And you, son? When are *you* going to admit what you are?"

"I have."

"To us. Not to everyone else."

"Don't start this again."

"I'll storming start whatever I want," Teft snapped. He leaned in, speaking softly. "At least until you give me a real answer. You're a Surgebinder. You're not a Radiant yet, but you're going to be one when this is all blown through. The others are right to push you. Why don't you go have a hike up to that Dalinar fellow, suck in some Stormlight, and make him recognize you as a lighteyes?"

Kaladin glanced at the men in a muddled jumble as they tried to get the uniforms on, an exasperated Rind explaining to them how to do up the coats.

"Everything I've ever had, Teft," Kaladin whispered, "the lighteyes have taken from me. My family, my brother, my friends. More. More than you can imagine. They see what I have, and they take it." He held up his hand, and could faintly make out a few glowing wisps trailing from his skin, since he knew what to look for. "They'll take it. If they can find out what I do, they'll *take* it."

"Now, how in Kelek's breath would they do that?"

"I don't know," Kaladin said. "I don't *know*, Teft, but I can't help feeling panic when I think about it. I can't let them have this, can't let them take it—or you men—from me. We remain quiet about what I can do. No more talk of it."

Teft grumbled as the other men finally got themselves sorted out, though Lopen—one armed, with his empty sleeve turned inside out and pushed in so it didn't hang down—prodded at the patch on his shoulder. "What's this?"

"It's the insignia of the Cobalt Guard," Kaladin said. "Dalinar Kholin's personal bodyguard."

"They're dead, gancho," Lopen said. "We aren't them."

"Yeah," Skar agreed. To Rind's horror, he got out his knife and cut the patch free. "We're Bridge Four."

"Bridge Four was your prison," Kaladin protested.

"Doesn't matter," Skar said. "We're Bridge Four." The others agreed, cutting off the patches, tossing them to the ground.

Teft nodded and did likewise. "We'll protect the Blackthorn, but we're not just going to replace what he had before. We're our own crew."

Kaladin rubbed his forehead, but this was what he had accomplished in bringing them together, galvanizing them into a cohesive unit. "I'll draw up a glyphpair insignia for you to use," he told Rind. "You'll have to commission new patches."

The portly man sighed as he gathered up the discarded patches. "I suppose. I've got your uniform over there, Captain. A darkeyed captain! Who would have thought it possible? You'll be the only one in the army. The only one ever, so far as I know!"

He didn't seem to find it offensive. Kaladin had little experience with low-dahn lighteyes like Rind, though they were very common in the warcamps. In his hometown, there had only been the citylord's family—of upper-middle dahn—and the darkeyes. It hadn't been until he'd reached Amaram's army that he'd realized there was an entire spectrum of lighteyes, many of whom worked common jobs and scrambled for money just like ordinary people.

Kaladin walked over to the last bundle on the counter. His uniform was different. It included a blue waistcoat and a double-breasted blue longcoat, the lining white, the buttons of silver. The longcoat was meant to hang open, despite the rows of buttons down each side.

He'd seen such uniforms frequently. On lighteyes.

"Bridge Four," he said, cutting the Cobalt Guard insignia from the shoulder and tossing it to the counter with the others.

3

PATTERN

*Soldiers reported being watched from afar by an unnerving number
of Parshendi scouts. Then we noticed a new pattern of their penetrating close to the camps in the night and then quickly retreating.
I can only surmise that our enemies were even then preparing their
stratagem to end this war.*

—From the personal journal of Navani Kholin, Jeseses 1174

R esearch into times before the Hierocracy is frustratingly difficult, the book
read. *During the reign of the Hierocracy, the Vorin Church had near-
absolute control over eastern Roshar. The fabrications they promoted—
and then perpetuated as absolute truth—became ingrained in the consciousness of
society. More disturbingly, modified copies of ancient texts were made, aligning
history to match Hierocratic dogma.*

In her cabin, Shallan read by the glow of a goblet of spheres, wearing
her nightgown. Her cramped chamber lacked a true porthole and had just
a thin slit of a window running across the top of the outside wall. The only
sound she could hear was the water lapping against the hull. Tonight, the
ship did not have a port in which to shelter.

The church of this era was suspicious of the Knights Radiant, the book read.
*Yet it relied upon the authority granted Vorinism by the Heralds. This created a
dichotomy in which the Recreance, and the betrayal of the knights, was overemphasized. At the same time, the ancient knights—the ones who had lived alongside the Heralds in the shadowdays—were celebrated.*

*This makes it particularly difficult to study the Radiants and the place named
Shadesmar. What is fact? What records did the church, in its misguided attempt*

to cleanse the past of perceived contradictions, rewrite to suit its preferred narrative? Few documents from the period survive that did not pass through Vorin hands to be copied from the original parchment into modern codices.

Shallan glanced up over the top of her book. The volume was one of Jasnah's earliest published works as a full scholar. Jasnah had not assigned Shallan to read it. Indeed, she'd been hesitant when Shallan had asked for a copy, and had needed to dig it out of one of the numerous trunks full of books she kept in the ship's hold.

Why had she been so reluctant, when this volume dealt with the very things that Shallan was studying? Shouldn't Jasnah have given her this right off? It—

The pattern returned.

Shallan's breath caught in her throat as she saw it on the cabin wall beside the bunk, just to her left. She carefully moved her eyes back to the page in front of her. The pattern was the same one that she'd seen before, the shape that had appeared on her sketchpad.

Ever since then, she'd been seeing it from the corner of her eye, appearing in the grain of wood, the cloth on the back of a sailor's shirt, the shimmering of the water. Each time, when she looked right at it, the pattern vanished. Jasnah would say nothing more, other than to indicate it was likely harmless.

Shallan turned the page and steadied her breathing. She had experienced something like this before with the strange symbol-headed creatures who had appeared unbidden in her drawings. She allowed her eyes to slip up off the page and look at the wall—not right at the pattern, but to the side of it, as if she hadn't noticed it.

Yes, it was there. Raised, like an embossing, it had a complex pattern with a haunting symmetry. Its tiny lines twisted and turned through its mass, somehow lifting the surface of the wood, like iron scrollwork under a taut tablecloth.

It was one of those *things*. The symbolheads. This pattern was similar to their strange heads. She looked back at the page, but did not read. The ship swayed, and the glowing white spheres in her goblet clinked as they shifted. She took a deep breath.

Then looked directly at the pattern.

Immediately, it began to fade, the ridges sinking. Before it did, she got a clear look at it, and she took a Memory.

"Not this time," she muttered as it vanished. "This time I have you." She threw away her book, scrambling to get out her charcoal pencil and a sheet of sketching paper. She huddled down beside her light, red hair tumbling around her shoulders.

She worked furiously, possessed by a frantic *need* to have this drawing done. Her fingers moved on their own, her unclothed safehand holding the sketchpad toward the goblet, which sprinkled the paper with shards of light.

She tossed aside the pencil. She needed something crisper, capable of sharper lines. Ink. Pencil was wonderful for drawing the soft shades of life, but this thing she drew was not life. It was something else, something unreal. She dug a pen and inkwell from her supplies, then went back to her drawing, replicating the tiny, intricate lines.

She did not think as she drew. The art consumed her, and creationspren popped into existence all around. Dozens of tiny shapes soon crowded the small table beside her cot and the floor of the cabin near where she knelt. The spren shifted and spun, each no larger than the bowl of a spoon, becoming shapes they'd recently encountered. She mostly ignored them, though she'd never seen so many at once.

Faster and faster they shifted forms as she drew, intent. The pattern seemed impossible to capture. Its complex repetitions twisted down into infinity. No, a pen could never capture this thing perfectly, but she was close. She drew it spiraling out of a center point, then re-created each branch off the center, which had its own swirl of tiny lines. It was like a maze created to drive its captive insane.

When she finished the last line, she found herself breathing hard, as if she'd run a great distance. She blinked, again noticing the creationspren around her—there were *hundreds*. They lingered before fading away one by one. Shallan set the pen down beside her vial of ink, which she'd stuck to the tabletop with wax to keep it from sliding as the ship swayed. She picked up the page, waiting for the last lines of ink to dry, and felt as if she'd accomplished something significant—though she knew not what.

As the last line dried, the pattern *rose* before her. She heard a distinct sigh from the paper, as if in relief.

She jumped, dropping the paper and scrambling onto her bed. Unlike the other times, the embossing didn't vanish, though it *left* the paper—budding from her matching drawing—and moved onto the floor.

She could describe it in no other way. The pattern somehow moved from paper to floor. It came to the leg of her cot and wrapped around it, climbing upward and onto the blanket. It didn't look like something moving beneath the blanket; that was simply a crude approximation. The lines were too precise for that, and there was no stretching. Something beneath the blanket would have been just an indistinct lump, but this was exact.

It drew closer. It didn't look dangerous, but she still found herself trembling. This pattern was different from the symbolheads in her drawings, but it was also somehow the *same*. A flattened-out version, without torso or limbs. It was an abstraction of one of them, just as a circle with a few lines in it could represent a human's face on the page.

Those things had terrified her, haunted her dreams, made her worry she was going insane. So as this one approached, she scuttled from her bed and went as far from it in the small cabin as she could. Then, heart thumping in her chest, she pulled open the door to go for Jasnah.

She found Jasnah herself just outside, reaching toward the doorknob, her left hand cupped before her. A small figure made of inky blackness—shaped like a man in a smart, fashionable suit with a long coat—stood in her palm. He melted away into shadow as he saw Shallan. Jasnah looked to Shallan, then glanced toward the floor of the cabin, where the pattern was crossing the wood.

"Put on some clothing, child," Jasnah said. "We have matters to discuss."

⁙

"I had originally hoped that we would have the same type of spren," Jasnah said, sitting on a stool in Shallan's cabin. The pattern remained on the floor between her and Shallan, who lay prone on the cot, properly clothed with a robe over the nightgown and a thin white glove on her left hand. "But of course, that would be too easy. I have suspected since Kharbranth that we would be of different orders."

"Orders, Brightness?" Shallan asked, timidly using a pencil to prod at the pattern on the floor. It shied away, like an animal that had been poked. Shallan was fascinated by how it raised the surface of the floor, though a part of her did not want to have anything to do with it and its unnatural, eye-twisting geometries.

"Yes," Jasnah said. The inklike spren that had accompanied her before had not reappeared. "Each order reportedly had access to two of the Surges, with overlap between them. We call the powers Surgebinding. Soulcasting was one, and is what we share, though our orders are different."

Shallan nodded. Surgebinding. Soulcasting. These were talents of the Lost Radiants, the abilities—supposedly just legend—that had been their blessing or their curse, depending upon which reports you read. Or so she'd learned from the books Jasnah had given her to read during their trip.

"I'm not one of the Radiants," Shallan said.

"Of course you aren't," Jasnah said, "and neither am I. The orders of knights were a construct, just as all society is a construct, used by men to define and explain. Not every man who wields a spear is a soldier, and not every woman who makes bread is a baker. And yet weapons, or baking, become the hallmarks of certain professions."

"So you're saying that what we can do . . ."

"Was once the definition of what initiated one into the Knights Radiant," Jasnah said.

"But we're women!"

"Yes," Jasnah said lightly. "Spren don't suffer from human society's prejudices. Refreshing, wouldn't you say?"

Shallan looked up from poking at the pattern spren. "There were women among the Knights Radiant?"

"A statistically appropriate number," Jasnah said. "But don't fear that you will soon find yourself swinging a sword, child. The archetype of Radiants on the battlefield is an exaggeration. From what I've read—though records are, unfortunately, untrustworthy—for every Radiant dedicated to battle, there were another three who spent their time on diplomacy, scholarship, or other ways to aid society."

"Oh." Why was Shallan disappointed by that?

Fool. A memory rose unbidden. A silvery sword. A pattern of light. Truths she could not face. She banished them, squeezing her eyes shut.

Ten heartbeats.

"I have been looking into the spren you told me about," Jasnah said. "The creatures with the symbol heads."

Shallan took a deep breath and opened her eyes. "This is one of them," she said, pointing her pencil at the pattern, which had approached her trunk and was moving up onto it and off it—like a child jumping on a sofa. Instead of threatening, it seemed innocent, even playful—and hardly intelligent at all. She had been frightened of this thing?

"Yes, I suspect that it is," Jasnah said. "Most spren manifest differently here than they do in Shadesmar. What you drew before was their form there."

"This one is not very impressive."

"Yes. I will admit that I'm disappointed. I feel that we're missing something important about this, Shallan, and I find it annoying. The Cryptics have a fearful reputation, and yet this one—the first specimen I've ever seen—seems . . ."

It climbed up the wall, then slipped down, then climbed back up, then slipped down again.

"Imbecilic?" Shallan asked.

"Perhaps it simply needs more time," Jasnah said. "When I first bonded with Ivory—" She stopped abruptly.

"What?" Shallan said.

"I'm sorry. He does not like me to speak of him. It makes him anxious. The knights' breaking of their oaths was very painful to the spren. Many spren died; I'm certain of it. Though Ivory won't speak of it, I gather that what he's done is regarded as a betrayal by the others of his kind."

"But—"

"No more of that," Jasnah said. "I'm sorry." **69**

"Fine. You mentioned the Cryptics?"

"Yes," Jasnah said, reaching into the sleeve that hid her safehand and slipping out a folded piece of paper—one of Shallan's drawings of the symbolheads. "That is their own name for themselves, though we would probably name them liespren. They don't like the term. Regardless, the Cryptics rule one of the greater cities in Shadesmar. Think of them as the lighteyes of the Cognitive Realm."

"So this thing," Shallan said, nodding to the pattern, which was spinning in circles in the center of the cabin, "is like . . . a prince, on their side?"

"Something like that. There is a complex sort of conflict between them and the honorspren. Spren politics are not something I've been able to devote much time to. This spren will be your companion—and will grant you the ability to Soulcast, among other things."

"Other things?"

"We will have to see," Jasnah said. "It comes down to the nature of spren. What has your research revealed?"

With Jasnah, everything seemed to be a test of scholarship. Shallan smothered a sigh. This was why she had come with Jasnah, rather than returning to her home. Still, she did wish that sometimes Jasnah would just *tell* her answers rather than making her work so hard to find them. "Alai says that the spren are fragments of the powers of creation. A lot of the scholars I read agreed with that."

"It is one opinion. What does it mean?"

Shallan tried not to let herself be distracted by the spren on the floor. "There are ten fundamental Surges—forces—by which the world works. Gravitation, pressure, transformation. That sort of thing. You told me spren are fragments of the Cognitive Realm that have somehow gained sentience because of human attention. Well, it stands to reason that they were something before. Like . . . like a painting was a canvas before being given life."

"Life?" Jasnah said, raising her eyebrow.

"Of course," Shallan said. Paintings lived. Not lived like a person or a spren, but . . . well, it was obvious to her, at least. "So, before the spren were alive, they were something. Power. Energy. Zen-daughter-Vath sketched tiny spren she found sometimes around heavy objects. Gravitationspren— fragments of the *power* or *force* that causes us to fall. It stands to reason that every spren was a power before it was a spren. Really, you can divide spren into two general groups. Those that respond to emotions and those that respond to forces like fire or wind pressure."

"So you believe Namar's theory on spren categorization?"

"Yes."

"Good," Jasnah said. "As do I. I suspect, personally, that these groupings of spren—emotion spren versus nature spren—are where the ideas of mankind's primeval 'gods' came from. Honor, who became Vorinism's Almighty, was created by men who wanted a representation of ideal human emotions as they saw in emotion spren. Cultivation, the god worshipped in the West, is a female deity that is an embodiment of nature and nature spren. The various Voidspren, with their unseen lord—whose name changes depending on which culture we're speaking of—evoke an enemy or antagonist. The Stormfather, of course, is a strange offshoot of this, his theoretical nature changing depending on which era of Vorinism is doing the talking. . . ."

She trailed off. Shallan blushed, realizing she'd looked away and had begun tracing a glyphward on her blanket against the evil in Jasnah's words.

"That was a tangent," Jasnah said. "I apologize."

"You're so sure he isn't real," Shallan said. "The Almighty."

"I have no more proof of him than I do of the Thaylen Passions, Nu Ralik of the Purelake, or any other religion."

"And the Heralds? You don't think they existed?"

"I don't know," Jasnah said. "There are many things in this world that I don't understand. For example, there is *some* slight proof that both the Stormfather and the Almighty are real creatures—simply powerful spren, such as the Nightwatcher."

"Then he *would* be real."

"I never claimed he was not," Jasnah said. "I merely claimed that I do not accept him as God, nor do I feel any inclination to worship him. But this is, again, a tangent." Jasnah stood. "You are relieved of other duties of study. For the next few days, you have only one focus for your scholarship." She pointed toward the floor.

"The pattern?" Shallan asked.

"You are the only person in centuries to have the chance to interact with a Cryptic," Jasnah said. "Study it and record your experiences—in detail. This will likely be your first writing of significance, and could be of utmost importance to our future."

Shallan regarded the pattern, which had moved over and bumped into her foot—she could feel it only faintly—and was now bumping into it time and time again.

"Great," Shallan said.

4

TAKER OF SECRETS

The next clue came on the walls. I did not ignore this sign, but neither did I grasp its full implications.

—From the journal of Navani Kholin, Jeseses 1174

I'm running through water," Dalinar said, coming to himself. He *was* moving, charging forward.

The vision coalesced around him. Warm water splashed his legs. On either side of him, a dozen men with hammers and spears ran through the shallow water. They lifted their legs high with each step, feet back, thighs lifting parallel to the water's surface, like they were marching in a parade— only no parade had ever been such a mad scramble. Obviously, running that way helped them move through the liquid. He tried to imitate the odd gait.

"I'm in the Purelake, I think," he said, under his breath. "Warm water that only comes up to the knees, no signs of land anywhere. It's dusk, though, so I can't see much.

"People run with me. I don't know if we're running toward something or away from it. Nothing over my shoulder that I can see. These people are obviously soldiers, though the uniforms are antiquated. Leather skirts, bronze helms and breastplates. Bare legs and arms." He looked down at himself. "I'm wearing the same."

Some highlords in Alethkar and Jah Keved still used uniforms like this, so he couldn't place the exact era. The modern uses were all calculated revivals by traditionalist commanders who hoped a classical look would inspire their men. In those cases, however, modern steel equipment would be used alongside the antique uniforms—and he didn't see any of that here.

Dalinar didn't ask questions. He'd found that playing along with these visions taught him more than it did to stop and demand answers.

Running through this water was tough. Though he'd started near the front of the group, he was now lagging behind. The group ran toward some kind of large rock mound ahead, shadowed in the dusk. Maybe this *wasn't* the Purelake. It didn't have rock formations like—

That wasn't a rock mound. It was a *fortress*. Dalinar halted, looking up at the peaked, castle-like structure that rose straight from the still lake waters. He'd never seen its like before. Jet-black stone. Obsidian? Perhaps this place had been Soulcast.

"There's a fortress ahead," he said, continuing forward. "It must not still exist—if it did, it would be famous. It looks like it's created entirely from obsidian. Finlike sides rising toward peaked tips above, towers like arrowheads . . . Stormfather. It's majestic.

"We're approaching another group of soldiers who stand in the water, holding spears wardingly in all directions. There are perhaps a dozen of them; I'm in the company of another dozen. And . . . yes, there's someone in the middle of them. Shardbearer. Glowing armor."

Not just a Shardbearer. Radiant. A knight in resplendent Shardplate that glowed with a deep red at the joints and in certain markings. Armor did that in the shadowdays. This vision was taking place before the Recreance.

Like all Shardplate, the armor was distinctive. With that skirt of chain links, those smooth joints, the vambraces that extended back just so . . . Storms, that looked like Adolin's armor, though this armor pulled in more at the waist. Female? Dalinar couldn't tell for certain, as the faceplate was down.

"Form up!" the knight ordered as Dalinar's group arrived, and he nodded to himself. Yes, female.

Dalinar and the other soldiers formed a ring around the knight, weapons outward. Not far off, another group of soldiers with a knight at their center marched through the water.

"Why did you call us back?" asked one of Dalinar's companions.

"Caeb thinks he saw something," the knight said. "Be alert. Let's move carefully."

The group started away from the fortress in another direction from the one they'd come. Dalinar held his spear outward, sweating at his temples. To his own eyes, he didn't look any different from his normal self. The others, however, would see him as one of their own.

He still didn't know terribly much about these visions. The Almighty sent them to him, somehow. But the Almighty was dead, by his own admission. So how did that work?

"We're looking for something," Dalinar said, under his breath. "Teams of knights and soldiers have been sent into the night to find something that was spotted."

"You all right, new kid?" asked one of the soldiers to his side.

"Fine," Dalinar said. "Just worried. I mean, I don't even really know what we're looking for."

"A spren that doesn't act like it should," the man said. "Keep your eyes open. Once Sja-anat touches a spren, it acts strange. Call attention to anything you see."

Dalinar nodded, then under his breath repeated the words, hoping that Navani could hear him. He and the soldiers continued their sweep, the knight at their center speaking with . . . nobody? She sounded like she was having a conversation, but Dalinar couldn't see or hear anyone else with her.

He turned his attention to the surroundings. He'd always wanted to see the center of the Purelake, but he'd never had a chance to do much besides visit the border. He'd been unable to find time for a detour in that direction during his last visit to Azir. The Azish had always acted surprised that he would want to go to such a place, as they claimed there was "nothing there."

Dalinar wore some kind of tight shoes on his feet, perhaps to keep him from cutting them on anything hidden by the water. The footing was uneven in places, with holes and ridges he felt rather than saw. He found himself watching little fish dart this way and that, shadows in the water, and next to them a face.

A face.

Dalinar shouted, jumping back, pointing his spear downward. "That was a face! In the water!"

"Riverspren?" the knight asked, stepping up beside him.

"It looked like a shadow," Dalinar said. "Red eyes."

"It's here, then," the knight said. "Sja-anat's spy. Caeb, run to the checkpoint. The rest of you, keep watching. It won't be able to go far without a carrier." She yanked something off her belt, a small pouch.

"There!" Dalinar said, spotting a small red dot in the water. It flowed away from him, swimming like a fish. He charged after, running as he'd learned earlier. What good would it do to chase a spren, though? You couldn't catch them. Not with any method he knew.

The others charged behind. Fish scattered away, frightened by Dalinar's splashing. "I'm chasing a spren," Dalinar said under his breath. "It's what we've been hunting. It looks a little like a face—a shadowy one, with red eyes. It swims through the water like a fish. Wait! There's another one.

Joining it. Larger, like a full figure, easily six feet. A swimming person, but like a shadow. It—"

"Storms!" the knight shouted suddenly. "It brought an escort!"

The larger spren twisted, then dove downward in the water, vanishing into the rocky ground. Dalinar stopped, uncertain if he should keep chasing the smaller one or remain here.

The others turned and started to run the other way.

Uh-oh . . .

Dalinar scrambled back as the rocky lake bottom began to shake. He stumbled, splashing down into the water. It was so clear he could see the floor *cracking* under him, as if something large were pounding against it from beneath.

"Come on!" one of the soldiers cried, grabbing him by the arm. Dalinar was pulled to his feet as the cracks below widened. The once-still surface of the lake churned and thrashed.

The ground *jolted*, almost tumbling Dalinar off his feet again. Ahead of him, several of the soldiers did fall.

The knight stood firm, an enormous Shardblade forming in her hands.

Dalinar glanced over his shoulder in time to see rock emerging from the water. A long arm! Slender, perhaps fifteen feet long, it *burst* from the water, then slammed back down as if to get a firm purchase on the lakebed. Another arm rose nearby, elbow toward the sky, then they both heaved as if attached to a body doing a push-up.

A giant body ripped itself out of the rocky floor. It was like someone had been buried in sand and was now emerging. Water streamed from the creature's ridged and pocked back, which was overgrown with bits of shalebark and submarine fungus. The spren had somehow animated the stone itself.

As it stood and twisted about, Dalinar could make out glowing red eyes—like molten rock—set deep in an evil stone face. The body was skeletal, with thin bony limbs and spiky fingers that ended in rocky claws. The chest was a rib cage of stone.

"Thunderclast!" soldiers yelled. "Hammers! Ready hammers!"

The knight stood before the rising creature, which stood thirty feet tall, dripping water. A calm, white light began to rise from her. It reminded Dalinar of the light of spheres. Stormlight. She raised her Shardblade and charged, stepping through the water with uncanny ease, as if it had no purchase on her. Perhaps it was the strength of Shardplate.

"They were created to watch," a voice said from beside him.

Dalinar looked to the soldier who had helped him rise earlier, a long-faced Selay man with a balding scalp and a wide nose. Dalinar reached down to help the man to his feet.

This wasn't how the man had spoken before, but Dalinar recognized the voice. It was the same one that came at the end of most of the visions. The Almighty.

"The Knights Radiant," the Almighty said, standing up beside Dalinar, watching the knight attack the nightmare beast. "They were a solution, a way to offset the destruction of the Desolations. Ten orders of knights, founded with the purpose of helping men fight, then rebuild."

Dalinar repeated it, word for word, focused on catching every one and not on thinking about what they meant.

The Almighty turned to him. "I was surprised when these orders arrived. I did not teach my Heralds this. It was the spren—wishing to imitate what I had given men—who made it possible. You will need to refound them. This is *your* task. Unite them. Create a fortress that can weather the storm. Vex Odium, convince him that he can lose, and appoint a champion. He will take that chance instead of risking defeat again, as he has suffered so often. This is the best advice I can give you."

Dalinar finished repeating the words. Beyond him, the fight began in earnest, water splashing, rock grinding. Soldiers approached bearing hammers, and unexpectedly, these men now also glowed with Stormlight, though far more faintly.

"You were surprised by the coming of the knights," Dalinar said to the Almighty. "And this force, this enemy, managed to kill you. You were never God. God knows everything. God cannot be killed. So who *were* you?"

The Almighty did not answer. He couldn't. Dalinar had realized that these visions were some kind of predetermined experience, like a play. The people in them could react to Dalinar, like actors who could improvise to an extent. The Almighty himself never did this.

"I will do what I can," Dalinar said. "I will refound them. I will prepare. You have told me many things, but there is one I have figured out on my own. If you could be killed, then the other like you—your enemy—probably can be as well."

The darkness came upon Dalinar. The yelling and splashing faded. Had this vision occurred during a Desolation, or between? These visions never told him *enough*. As the darkness evaporated he found himself lying in a small stone chamber within his complex in the warcamps.

Navani knelt beside him, clipboard held before her, pen moving as she scribbled. Storms, she was beautiful. Mature, lips painted red, hair wound about her head in a complex braid that sparkled with rubies. Bloodred dress. She looked at him, noting that he was blinking back awake, and smiled.

"It was—" he began.

"Hush," she said, still writing. "That last part sounded important." She wrote for a moment, then finally removed pen from pad, the latter held through the cloth of her sleeve. "I think I got it all. It's hard when you change languages."

"I changed languages?" he asked.

"At the end. Before, you were speaking Selay. An ancient form of it, certainly, but we have records of that. I hope my translators can make sense of my transcription; my command of that language is rusty. You do need to speak more slowly when you do this, dearest."

"That can be hard, in the moment," Dalinar said, rising. Compared to what he'd felt in the vision, the air here was cold. Rain pelted the room's closed shutters, though he knew from experience that an end to his vision meant that the storm had nearly spent itself.

Feeling drained, he walked to a seat beside the wall and settled down. Only he and Navani were in the room; he preferred it that way. Renarin and Adolin waited out the storm nearby, in another room of Dalinar's quarters and under the watchful eyes of Captain Kaladin and his bridgeman bodyguards.

Perhaps he should invite more scholars in to observe his visions; they could all write down his words, then consult to produce the most accurate version. But storms, he had enough trouble with one person watching him in such a state, raving and thrashing on the ground. He believed in the visions, even depended upon them, but that didn't mean it wasn't embarrassing.

Navani sat down beside him, and wrapped her arms around him. "Was it bad?"

"This one? No. Not bad. Some running, then some fighting. I didn't participate. The vision ended before I needed to help."

"Then why that expression?"

"I have to refound the Knights Radiant."

"Refound the . . . But how? What does that even mean?"

"I don't know. I don't *know* anything; I only have hints and shadowy threats. Something dangerous is coming, that much is certain. I have to stop it."

She rested her head on his shoulder. He stared at the hearth, which crackled softly, giving the small room a warm glow. This was one of the few hearths that hadn't been converted to the new fabrial heating devices.

He preferred the real fire, though he wouldn't say it to Navani. She worked so hard to bring new fabrials to them all.

"Why you?" Navani asked. "Why do you have to do this?"

"Why is one man born a king, and another a beggar?" Dalinar asked. "It is the way of the world."

"It is that easy for you?"

"Not easy," Dalinar said, "but there is no point in demanding answers."

"Particularly if the Almighty is dead. . . ."

Perhaps he should not have shared that fact with her. Speaking of just that one idea could brand him a heretic, drive his own ardents from him, give Sadeas a weapon against the Throne.

If the Almighty was dead, what did Dalinar worship? What did he believe?

"We should record your memories of the vision," Navani said with a sigh, pulling back from him. "While they are fresh."

He nodded. It was important to have a description to match the transcriptions. He began to recount what he'd seen, speaking slowly enough that she could write it all down. He described the lake, the clothing of the men, the strange fortress in the distance. She claimed there were stories of large structures on the Purelake told by some who lived there. Scholars had considered them mythological.

Dalinar stood up and paced as he moved on to the description of the unholy thing that had risen from the lake. "It left behind a hole in the lakebed," Dalinar explained. "Imagine if you were to outline a body on the floor, then watch that body *rip* itself free from the ground.

"Imagine the tactical advantage such a thing would have. Spren move quickly and easily. One could slip in behind battle lines, then stand up and start attacking the support staff. That beast's stone body must have been difficult to break. Storms . . . Shardblades. Makes me wonder if *these* are the things the weapons were truly designed to fight."

Navani smiled as she wrote.

"What?" Dalinar asked, stopping in his pacing.

"You are such a soldier."

"Yes. And?"

"And it's endearing," she said, finishing her writing. "What happened next?"

"The Almighty spoke to me." He gave her the monologue as best he could remember while he paced in a slow, restful walk. *I need to sleep more,* he thought. He wasn't the youth he'd been twenty years ago, capable of staying up all night with Gavilar, listening with a cup of wine as his brother made plans, then charging to battle the next day full of vigor and hungering for a contest.

Once he was done with his narrative, Navani rose, tucking her writing implements away. She'd take what he'd said and have her scholars—well, his scholars, which she'd appropriated—work at matching his Alethi words up with the transcriptions she'd recorded. Though, of course, she'd first remove the lines where he mentioned sensitive issues, such as the Almighty's death.

She'd also search for historical references to match his descriptions.

Navani liked things neat and quantified. She'd prepared a timeline of all of his visions, trying to piece them into a single narrative.

"You're still going to publish the proclamation this week?" she asked.

Dalinar nodded. He'd released it to the highprinces a week ago, in private. He'd intended to release it the same day to the camps, but Navani had convinced him that this was the wiser course. News was seeping out, but this would let the highprinces prepare.

"The proclamation will go to the public within a few days," he said. "Before the highprinces can put further pressure on Elhokar to retract it."

Navani pursed her lips.

"It must be done," Dalinar said.

"You're supposed to unite them."

"The highprinces are spoiled children," Dalinar said. "Changing them will require extreme measures."

"If you break the kingdom apart, we'll never unify it."

"We'll make certain that it doesn't break."

Navani looked him up and down, then smiled. "I *am* fond of this more confident you, I must admit. Now, if I could just borrow a little of that confidence in regards to *us* . . ."

"I am quite confident about us," he said, pulling her close.

"Is that so? Because this traveling between the king's palace and your complex wastes a lot of my time each day. If I were to move my things here—say, into your quarters—think how much more *convenient* everything would be."

"No."

"You're confident they won't let us marry, Dalinar. So what else are we to do? Is it the morality of the thing? You yourself said that the Almighty was dead."

"Something is either right or it's wrong," Dalinar said, feeling stubborn. "The Almighty doesn't come into it."

"God," Navani said flatly, "doesn't come into whether his commands are right or wrong."

"Er. Yes."

"Careful," Navani said. "You're sounding like Jasnah. Anyway, if God is dead—"

"*God* isn't dead. If the Almighty died, then he was never God, that's all."

She sighed, still close to him. She went up on her toes and kissed him—and not demurely, either. Navani considered demureness for the coy and frivolous. So, a passionate kiss, pressing against his mouth, pushing his head backward, hungering for more. When she pulled away, Dalinar found himself breathless.

She smiled at him, then turned and picked up her things—he hadn't noticed her dropping them during the kiss—and then walked to the door. "I am not a patient woman, you realize. I am as spoiled as those highprinces, accustomed to getting what I want."

He snorted. Neither was true. She *could* be patient. When it suited her. What she meant was that it didn't suit her at the moment.

She opened the door, and Captain Kaladin himself peered in, inspecting the room. The bridgeman certainly was earnest. "Watch her as she travels home for the day, soldier," Dalinar said to him.

Kaladin saluted. Navani pushed by him and left without a goodbye, closing the door and leaving Dalinar alone again.

Dalinar sighed deeply, then walked to the chair and settled down by the hearth to think.

He started awake some time later, the fire having burned out. Storms. Was he falling asleep in the middle of the day, now? If only he didn't spend so much time at night tossing and turning, head full of worries and burdens that should never have been his. What had happened to the simple days? His hand on a sword, secure in the knowledge that Gavilar would handle the difficult parts?

Dalinar stretched, rising. He needed to go over preparations for releasing the king's proclamation, and then see to the new guards—

He stopped. The wall of his room bore a series of stark white scratches forming glyphs. They hadn't been there before.

Sixty-two days, the glyphs read. *Death follows.*

⁘

A short time later, Dalinar stood, straight-backed, hands clasped behind him as he listened to Navani confer with Rushu, one of the Kholin scholars. Adolin stood nearby, inspecting a chunk of white rock that had been found on the floor. It had apparently been pried from the row of ornamental stones rimming the room's window, then used to write the glyphs.

Straight back, head up, Dalinar told himself, *even though you want to just slump in that chair.* A leader did not slump. A leader was in control. Even when he least felt like he controlled anything.

Especially then.

"Ah," said Rushu—a young female ardent with long eyelashes and buttonlike lips. "Look at the sloppy lines! The improper symmetry. Whoever did this is *not* practiced with drawing glyphs. They almost spelled death wrong—it looks more like 'broken.' And the meaning is vague. Death follows? Or is it 'follow death'? Or Sixty-Two Days of Death and Following? Glyphs are imprecise."

"Just make the copy, Rushu," Navani said. "And don't speak of this to anyone."

"Not even you?" Rushu asked, sounding distracted as she wrote.

Navani sighed, walking over to Dalinar and Adolin. "She *is* good at what she does," Navani said softly, "but she's a little oblivious sometimes. Anyway, she knows handwriting better than anyone. It's one of her many areas of interest."

Dalinar nodded, bottling his fears.

"Why would anyone do this?" Adolin asked, dropping the rock. "Is it some kind of obscure threat?"

"No," Dalinar said.

Navani met Dalinar's eyes. "Rushu," she said. "Leave us for a moment."

The woman didn't respond at first, but scuttled out at further prompting. As she opened the door, she revealed members of Bridge Four outside, led by Captain Kaladin, his expression dark. He'd escorted Navani away, then come back to find this—and then had immediately sent men to check on and retrieve Navani.

He obviously considered this lapse his fault, thinking that someone had sneaked into Dalinar's room while he was sleeping. Dalinar waved the captain in.

Kaladin hurried over, and hopefully didn't see how Adolin's jaw tightened as he regarded the man. Dalinar had been fighting the Parshendi Shardbearer when Kaladin and Adolin had clashed on the battlefield, but he'd heard talk of their run-in. His son certainly did not like hearing that this darkeyed bridgeman had been put in charge of the Cobalt Guard.

"Sir," Captain Kaladin said, stepping up. "I'm embarrassed. One week on the job, and I've failed you."

"You did as commanded, Captain," Dalinar said.

"I was *commanded* to keep you safe, sir," Kaladin said, anger bleeding into his voice. "I should have posted guards at individual doors inside your quarters, not just outside of the room complex."

"We'll be more observant in the future, Captain," Dalinar said. "Your predecessor always posted the same guard as you did, and it was sufficient before."

"Times were different before, sir," Kaladin said, scanning the room and narrowing his eyes. He focused on the window, too small to let someone slip in. "I still wish I knew how they got in. The guards heard nothing."

Dalinar inspected the young soldier, scarred and dark of expression. *Why,* Dalinar thought, *do I trust this man so much?* He couldn't put his finger on it, but over the years, he'd learned to trust his instincts as a soldier and a general. Something within him urged him to trust Kaladin, and he accepted those instincts.

"This is a small matter," Dalinar said.

Kaladin looked at him sharply.

"Don't worry yourself overly much about how the person got in to scribble on my wall," Dalinar said. "Just be more watchful in the future. Dismissed." He nodded to Kaladin, who retreated reluctantly, pulling the door closed.

Adolin walked over. The mop-haired youth was as tall as Dalinar was. That was hard to remember, sometimes. It didn't seem so long ago that Adolin had been an eager little boy with a wooden sword.

"You said you awoke to this here," Navani said. "You said you didn't see anyone enter or hear anyone make the drawing."

Dalinar nodded.

"Then why," she said, "do I get the sudden and distinct impression that you *know* why it is here?"

"I don't know for certain who made it, but I know what it means."

"What, then?" Navani demanded.

"It means we have very little time left," Dalinar said. "Send out the proclamation, then go to the highprinces and arrange a meeting. They'll want to speak with me."

The Everstorm comes. . . .

Sixty-two days. Not enough time.

It was, apparently, all he had.

Freedom   Bridge 4   Kholin   Tanat

I had to spend hours watching
bridgemen to sketch their stupid
forehead glyphs so you could have
them, my friend. I'm pretty sure
this is how they were designed.
                —Nazh

Traditional   Stylized
Year 1173   Year 1173

sas   nahn

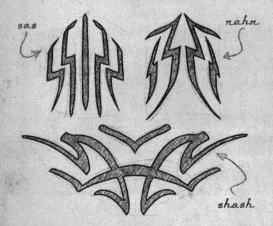

shash

Kaladin's forehead brands   Bridge 4 Uniform Insignia

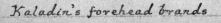

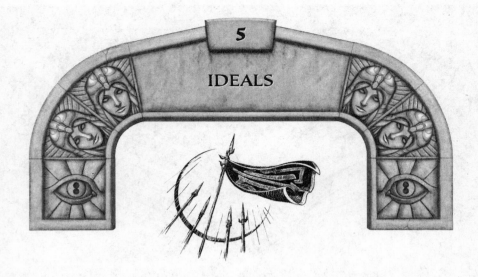

5

IDEALS

The sign on the wall proposed a greater danger, even, than its deadline. To foresee the future is of the Voidbringers.

—From the journal of Navani Kholin, Jeseses 1174

Ovictory and, at long last, vengeance." The crier carried a writ with the king's words on it—bound between two cloth-covered boards—though she obviously had the words memorized. Not surprising. Kaladin alone had made her repeat the proclamation three times.

"Again," he said, sitting on his stone beside Bridge Four's firepit. Many members of the crew had lowered their breakfast bowls, going silent. Nearby, Sigzil repeated the words to himself, memorizing them.

The crier sighed. She was a plump, lighteyed young woman with strands of red hair mixed in her black, bespeaking Veden or Horneater heritage. There would be dozens of women like her moving through the warcamp to read, and sometimes explain, Dalinar's words.

She opened the ledger again. *In any other battalion,* Kaladin thought idly, *its leader would be of a high enough social class to outrank her.*

"Under the authority of the king," she said, "Dalinar Kholin, Highprince of War, hereby orders changes to the manner of collection and distribution of gemhearts on the Shattered Plains. Henceforth, each gemheart will be collected in turn by two highprinces working in tandem. The spoils become the property of the king, who will determine—based on the effectiveness of the parties involved and their alacrity to obey—their share.

"A prescribed rotation will detail which highprinces and armies are responsible for hunting gemhearts, and in what order. The pairings will not always be the same, and will be judged based on strategic compatibility. It is expected that by the Codes we all hold dear, the men and women of these armies will welcome this renewed focus on victory and, at long last, vengeance."

The crier snapped the book closed, looking up at Kaladin and cocking a long black eyebrow he was pretty sure had been painted on with makeup.

"Thank you," he said. She nodded to him, then moved off toward the next battalion square.

Kaladin climbed to his feet. "Well, there's the storm we've been expecting."

The men nodded. Conversation at Bridge Four had been subdued, following the strange break-in at Dalinar's quarters yesterday. Kaladin felt a fool. Dalinar, however, seemed to be ignoring the break-in entirely. He knew far more than he was telling Kaladin. *How am I supposed to do my job if I don't have the information I need?*

Not two weeks on the job, and already the politics and machinations of the lighteyes were tripping him up.

"The highprinces are going to *hate* this proclamation," Leyten said from beside the firepit, where he was working on Beld's breastplate straps, which had come from the quartermaster with the buckles twisted about. "They base pretty much everything on getting those gemhearts. We're going to have discontent aplenty on today's winds."

"Ha!" Rock said, ladling up curry for Lopen, who had come back for seconds. "Discontent? Today, this will mean *riots*. Did you not hear that mention of the Codes? This thing, it is an insult against the others, whom we know do not follow their oaths." He was smiling, and seemed to consider the anger—even rioting—of the highprinces to be amusing.

"Moash, Drehy, Mart, and Eth with me," Kaladin said. "We've got to go relieve Skar and his team. Teft, how goes your assignment?"

"Slowly," Teft said. "Those lads in the other bridge crews . . . they have a long way to go. We need something more, Kal. Some way to inspire them."

"I'll work on it," Kaladin said. "For now, we should try food. Rock, we've only got five officers at the moment, so you can have that last room on the outside for storage. Kholin gave us requisition rights from the camp quartermaster. Pack it full."

"Full?" Rock asked, an enormous grin splitting his face. "How full?"

"*Very*," Kaladin said. "We've been eating broth and stew with Soulcast grain for months. For the next month, Bridge Four eats like kings."

"No shells, now," Mart said, pointing at Rock as he gathered his spear and did up his uniform jacket. "Just because you can fix anything you want, it doesn't mean we're going to eat something stupid."

"Airsick lowlanders," Rock said. "Don't you want to be strong?"

"I want to keep my teeth, thank you," Mart said. "Crazy Horneater."

"I will fix two things," Rock said, hand to his chest, as if making a salute. "One for the brave and one for the silly. You may choose between these things."

"You'll make feasts, Rock," Kaladin said. "I need you to train cooks for the other barracks. Even if Dalinar has extra cooks to spare now with fewer regular troops to feed, I want the bridgemen to be self-sufficient. Lopen, I'm assigning Dabbid and Shen to help you assist Rock from here on out. We need to turn those thousand men into soldiers. It starts the same way it did with all of you—by filling their stomachs."

"It will be done," Rock said, laughing, slapping Shen on the shoulder as the parshman stepped up for seconds. He'd only just started doing things like that, and seemed to hide in the back less than he once had. "I will not even put any dung in it!"

The others chuckled. Putting dung in food was what had gotten Rock turned into a bridgeman in the first place. As Kaladin started out toward the king's palace—Dalinar had an important meeting with the king today—Sigzil joined him.

"A moment of your time, sir," Sigzil said quietly.

"If you wish."

"You promised me that I could have a chance to measure your . . . particular abilities."

"Promised?" Kaladin asked. "I don't remember a promise."

"You grunted."

"I . . . grunted?"

"When I talked about taking some measurements. You seemed to think it was a good idea, and you told Skar we could help you figure out your powers."

"I suppose I did."

"We need to know exactly what you can do, sir—the extent of the abilities, the length of time the Stormlight remains in you. Do you agree that having a clear understanding of your limits would be valuable?"

"Yes," Kaladin said reluctantly.

"Excellent. Then . . ."

"Give me a couple of days," Kaladin said. "Go prepare a place where we can't be seen. Then . . . yes, all right. I'll let you measure me."

"Excellent," Sigzil said. "I've been devising some experiments." He stopped on the path, allowing Kaladin and the others to draw away from him.

Kaladin rested his spear on his shoulder and relaxed his hand. He frequently found his grip on the weapon too strong, his knuckles white. It was like part of him still didn't believe he could carry it in public now, and feared it would be taken from him again.

Syl floated down from her daily sprint around the camp on the morning winds. She alighted on his shoulder and sat, seeming lost in thought.

Dalinar's warcamp was an organized place. Soldiers never lounged lazily here. They were always doing something. Working on their weapons, fetching food, carrying cargo, patrolling. Men patrolled a lot in this camp. Even with the reduced army numbers, Kaladin passed three patrols as his men marched toward the gates. That was three more than he'd ever seen in Sadeas's camp.

He was reminded again of the emptiness. The dead didn't need to become Voidbringers to haunt this camp; the empty barracks did that. He passed one woman, seated on the ground beside one of those hollow barracks, staring up at the sky and clutching a bundle of masculine clothing. Two small children stood on the path beside her. Too silent. Children that small shouldn't be quiet.

The barracks formed blocks in an enormous ring, and in the center of them was a more populated part of camp—the bustling section that contained Dalinar's living complex, along with the quarters of the various highlords and generals. Dalinar's complex was a moundlike stone bunker with fluttering banners and scuttling clerks carrying armfuls of ledgers. Nearby, several officers had set up recruitment tents, and a long line of would-be soldiers had formed. Some were sellswords who had made their way to the Shattered Plains seeking work. Others were bakers or the like, who had heeded the cry for more soldiers following the disaster.

"Why didn't you laugh?" Syl said, inspecting the line as Kaladin hiked around it, on toward the gates out of the warcamp.

"I'm sorry," he replied. "Did you do something funny that I didn't see?"

"I mean earlier," she said. "Rock and the others laughed. You didn't. When you laughed during the weeks things were hard, I knew that you were forcing yourself to. I thought, maybe, once things got better . . ."

"I've got an entire battalion of bridgemen to keep track of now," Kaladin said, eyes forward. "And a highprince to keep alive. I'm in the middle of a camp full of widows. I guess I don't feel like laughing."

"But things are *better*," she said. "For you and your men. Think of what you did, what you accomplished."

A day spent on a plateau, slaughtering. A perfect melding of himself, his weapon, and the storms themselves. And he'd killed with it. Killed to protect a lighteyes.

He's different, Kaladin thought.

They always said that.

"I guess I'm just waiting," Kaladin said.

"For what?"

"The thunder," Kaladin said softly. "It always follows after the lightning. Sometimes you have to wait, but eventually it comes."

"I . . ." Syl zipped up in front of him, standing in the air, moving backward as he walked. She didn't fly—she didn't have wings—and didn't bob in the air. She just stood there, on nothing, and moved in unison with him. She seemed to take no notice of normal physical laws.

She cocked her head at him. "I don't understand what you mean. Drat! I thought I was figuring this all out. Storms? Lightning?"

"You know how, when you encouraged me to fight to save Dalinar, it still hurt you when I killed?"

"Yes."

"It's like that," Kaladin said softly. He looked to the side. He was again gripping his spear too tightly.

Syl watched him, hands on hips, waiting for him to say more.

"Something bad is going to happen," Kaladin said. "Things can't just continue to be good for me. That's not how life is. It might have to do with those glyphs on Dalinar's wall yesterday. They seemed like a countdown."

She nodded.

"Have you ever seen anything like that before?"

"I remember . . . something," she whispered. "Something bad. Seeing what is to come—it isn't of Honor, Kaladin. It's something else. Something dangerous."

Wonderful.

When he said nothing more, Syl sighed and zipped into the air, becoming a ribbon of light. She followed him up there, moving between gusts of wind.

She said that she's honorspren, Kaladin thought. *So why does she still keep up the act of playing with winds?*

He'd have to ask her, assuming she'd answer him. Assuming she even knew the answer.

⟡

Torol Sadeas laced his fingers before himself, elbows on the fine stonework tabletop, as he stared at the Shardblade he'd thrust down through the center of the table. It reflected his face.

Damnation. When had he gotten old? He imagined himself as a young man, in his twenties. Now he was fifty. Storming *fifty*. He set his jaw, looking at that Blade.

Oathbringer. It was Dalinar's Shardblade—curved, like a back arching, with a hooklike tip on the end matched by a sequence of jutting serrations by the crossguard. Like waves in motion, peeking up from the ocean below.

How often had he lusted for this weapon? Now it was his, but he found the possession hollow. Dalinar Kholin—driven mad by grief, broken to the point that battle frightened him—still clung to life. Sadeas's old friend was like a favored axehound he'd been forced to put down, only to find it whimpering at the window, the poison having not quite done its work.

Worse, he couldn't shake the feeling that Dalinar had gotten the *better* of him somehow.

The door to his sitting room opened, and Ialai slipped in. With a slender neck and a large mouth, his wife had never been described as a beauty—particularly as the years stretched long. He didn't care. Ialai was the most dangerous woman he knew. That was more attractive than any simple pretty face.

"You've destroyed my table, I see," she said, eyeing the Shardblade slammed down through the center. She flopped down onto the small couch beside him, draped one arm across his back, and put her feet up on the table.

While with others, she was the perfect Alethi woman. In private, she preferred to lounge. "Dalinar is recruiting heavily," she said. "I've taken the opportunity to place a few more of my associates among the staff of his warcamp."

"Soldiers?"

"What do you take me for? That would be far too obvious; he will have new soldiers under careful watch. However, much of his support staff has holes as men join the call to take up spears and reinforce his army."

Sadeas nodded, still staring at that Blade. His wife ran the most impressive network of spies in the warcamps. Most impressive indeed, since very, very few knew of it. She scratched at his back, sending shivers up the skin.

"He released his proclamation," Ialai noted.

"Yes. Reactions?"

"As anticipated. The others hate it."

Sadeas nodded. "Dalinar should be dead, but since he is not, at least we can depend upon him to hang himself in time." Sadeas narrowed his eyes. "By destroying him, I sought to prevent the collapse of the kingdom. Now I'm wondering if that collapse wouldn't be better for us all."

"What?"

"I'm not meant for this, love," Sadeas whispered. "This stupid game on the plateaus. It sated me at first, but I'm growing to loathe it. I want *war*, Ialai. Not hours of marching on the off chance that we'll find some little skirmish!"

"Those little skirmishes bring us wealth."

Which was why he'd suffered them so long. He rose. "I will need to meet with some of the others. Aladar. Ruthar. We need to fan the flames among the other highprinces, raise their indignation at what Dalinar attempts."

"And our end goal?"

"I will have it back, Ialai," he said, resting his fingers on Oathbringer's hilt. "The conquest."

It was the only thing that made him feel alive any longer. That glorious, wonderful Thrill of being on the battlefield and striving, man against man. Of risking everything for the prize. Domination. Victory.

It was the only time he felt like a youth again.

It was a brutal truth. The best truths, however, were simple.

He grabbed Oathbringer by the hilt and yanked it up out of the table. "Dalinar wants to play politician now, which is unsurprising. He has always secretly wanted to be his brother. Fortunately for us, Dalinar is no good at this sort of thing. His proclamation will alienate the others. He will push the highprinces, and they'll take up arms against him, fracturing the kingdom. And then, with blood at my feet and Dalinar's own sword in my hand, I will forge a new Alethkar from flame and tears."

"What if, instead, he succeeds?"

"That, my dear, is when your assassins will be of use." He dismissed the Shardblade; it turned to mist and vanished. "I will conquer this kingdom anew, and then Jah Keved will follow. After all, the purpose of this life is to train soldiers. In a way, I'm only doing what God himself wants."

⁘

The walk between the barracks and the king's palace—which the king had started calling the Pinnacle—took an hour or so, which gave Kaladin plenty of time to think. Unfortunately, on his way, he passed a group of Dalinar's surgeons in a field with servants, gathering knobweed sap for an antiseptic.

Seeing them made Kaladin think not only of his own efforts gathering the sap, but of his father. Lirin.

If he were here, Kaladin thought as he passed them, *he'd ask why I wasn't out there, with the surgeons. He'd demand to know why, if Dalinar had taken me in, I hadn't requested to join his medical corps.*

In fact, Kaladin could probably have gotten Dalinar to employ all of Bridge Four as surgeons' assistants. Kaladin could have trained them in medicine almost as easily as he had the spear. Dalinar would have done it. An army could never have too many good surgeons.

He hadn't even considered it. The choice for him had been simpler—

either become Dalinar's bodyguards or leave the warcamps. Kaladin had chosen to put his men in the path of the storm again. Why?

Eventually, they reached the king's palace, which was built up the side of a large stone hill, with tunnels dug down into the rock. The king's own quarters sat at the very top. That meant lots of climbing for Kaladin and his men.

They hiked up the switchbacks, Kaladin still lost in thought about his father and his duty.

"That's a tad unfair, you know," Moash said as they reached the top.

Kaladin looked to the others, realizing that they were puffing from the long climb. Kaladin, however, had drawn in Stormlight without noticing. He wasn't even winded.

He smiled pointedly for Syl's benefit, and regarded the cavernous hallways of the Pinnacle. A few men stood guard at the entrance gates, wearing the blue and gold of the King's Guard, a separate and distinct unit from Dalinar's own guard.

"Soldier," Kaladin said with a nod to one of them, a lighteyes of low rank. Militarily, Kaladin outranked a man like this—but not socially. Again, he wasn't certain how all of this was supposed to work.

The man looked him up and down. "I heard you held a bridge, practically by yourself, against hundreds of Parshendi. How'd you do that?" He did not address Kaladin with "sir," as would have been appropriate for any other captain.

"You want to find out?" Moash snapped from behind. "We can show you. Personally."

"Hush," Kaladin said, glaring at Moash. He turned back to the soldier. "I got lucky. That's it." He stared the man in the eyes.

"I suppose that makes sense," the soldier said.

Kaladin waited.

"Sir," the soldier finally added.

Kaladin waved his men forward, and they passed the lighteyed guards. The interior of the palace was lit by spheres grouped in lamps on the walls—sapphires and diamonds blended to give a blue-white cast. The spheres were a small but striking reminder of how things had changed. Nobody would have let bridgemen near such casual use of spheres.

The Pinnacle was still unfamiliar to Kaladin—so far, his time spent guarding Dalinar had mostly been in the warcamp. However, he'd made certain to look over maps of the place, so he knew the way to the top.

"Why did you cut me off like that?" Moash demanded, catching up to Kaladin.

"You were in the wrong," Kaladin said. "You're a soldier now, Moash. You're going to have to learn to act like one. And that means not provoking fights."

"I'm not going to scrape and bow before lighteyes, Kal. Not anymore."

"I don't expect you to scrape, but I *do* expect you to watch your tongue. Bridge Four is better than petty gibes and threats."

Moash fell back, but Kaladin could tell he was still smoldering.

"That's odd," Syl said, landing on Kaladin's shoulder again. "He looks so angry."

"When I took over the bridgemen," Kaladin said softly, "they were caged animals who had been beaten into submission. I brought back their fight, but they were still caged. Now the doors are off those cages. It will take time for Moash and the others to adjust."

They would. During the final weeks as bridgemen, they'd learned to act with the precision and discipline of soldiers. They stood at attention while their abusers marched across bridges, never uttering a word of derision. Their discipline itself had become their weapon.

They'd learn to be real soldiers. No, they *were* real soldiers. Now they had to learn how to act without Sadeas's oppression to push against.

Moash moved up beside him. "I'm sorry," he said softly. "You're right."

Kaladin smiled, this time genuinely.

"I'm not going to pretend I don't hate them," Moash said. "But I'll be civil. We have a duty. We'll do it well. Better than anyone expects. We're Bridge Four."

"Good man," Kaladin said. Moash was going to be particularly tricky to deal with, as more and more, Kaladin found himself confiding in the man. Most of the others idolized Kaladin. Not Moash, who was as close to a real friend as Kaladin had known since being branded.

The hallway grew surprisingly decorative as they approached the king's conference chamber. There was even a series of reliefs being carved on the walls—the Heralds, embellished with gemstones on the rock to glow at appropriate locations.

More and more like a city, Kaladin thought to himself. *This might actually be a true palace soon.*

He met Skar and his team at the door into the king's conference chambers. "Report?" Kaladin asked softly.

"Quiet morning," Skar said. "And I'm fine with that."

"You're relieved for the day, then," Kaladin said. "I'll stay here for the meeting, then let Moash take the afternoon shift. I'll come back for the evening shift. You and your squad get some sleep; you'll be back on duty tonight, stretching to tomorrow morning."

"Got it, sir," Skar said, saluting. He collected his men and moved off.

The chamber beyond the doors was decorated with a thick rug and large unshuttered windows on the leeward side. Kaladin had never been in this

room, and the palace maps—for the protection of the king—only included the basic hallways and routes through the servants' quarters. This room had one other door, probably out onto the balcony, but no exits other than the one Kaladin stepped through.

Two other guards in blue and gold stood on either side of the door. The king himself paced back and forth beside the room's desk. His nose was larger than the paintings of him showed.

Dalinar spoke with Highlady Navani, an elegant woman with grey in her hair. The scandalous relationship between the king's uncle and mother would have been the talk of the warcamp, if Sadeas's betrayal hadn't overshadowed it.

"Moash," Kaladin said, pointing. "See where that door goes. Mart and Eth, stand watch just outside in the hall. Nobody other than a highprince comes in until you've checked with us in here."

Moash gave the king a salute instead of a bow, and checked on the door. It indeed led to the balcony that Kaladin had spotted from below. It ran all around this upmost room.

Dalinar studied Kaladin and Moash as they worked. Kaladin saluted, and met the man's eyes. He wasn't going to fail again, as he'd done the day before.

"I don't recognize these guards, Uncle," the king said with annoyance.

"They're new," Dalinar said. "There is no other way onto that balcony, soldier. It's a hundred feet in the air."

"Good to know," Kaladin said. "Drehy, join Moash out there on the balcony, close the door, and keep watch."

Drehy nodded, jumping into motion.

"I just said there's no way to reach that balcony from the outside," Dalinar said.

"Then that's the way I'd try to get in," Kaladin said, "if I wanted to, sir."

Dalinar smiled in amusement.

The king, however, was nodding. "Good . . . good."

"Are there any other ways into this room, Your Majesty?" Kaladin asked. "Secret entrances, passages?"

"If there were," the king said, "I wouldn't want people knowing about them."

"My men can't keep this room safe if we don't know what to guard. If there are passages nobody is supposed to know about, those are immediately suspect. If you share them with me, I'll use only my officers in guarding them."

The king stared at Kaladin for a moment, then turned to Dalinar. "I *like* this one. Why haven't you put him in charge of your guard before?"

"I haven't had the opportunity," Dalinar said, studying Kaladin with eyes that had a *depth* behind them. A weight. He stepped over and rested a hand on Kaladin's shoulder, pulling him aside.

"Wait," the king said from behind, "is that a *captain's* insignia? On a darkeyes? When did that start happening?"

Dalinar didn't answer, instead walking Kaladin to the side of the room. "The king," he said softly, "is very worried about assassins. You should know this."

"A healthy paranoia makes the job easier for his bodyguards, sir," Kaladin said.

"I didn't say it was healthy," Dalinar said. "You call me 'sir.' The common address is 'Brightlord.'"

"I will use that term if you command, sir," Kaladin said, meeting the man's eyes. "But 'sir' is an appropriate address, even for a lighteyes, if he's your direct superior."

"I'm a highprince."

"Speaking frankly," Kaladin said—he wouldn't ask for permission. This man had put him in the role, so Kaladin would assume it came with certain privileges, unless told otherwise. "Every man I've ever called 'Brightlord' has betrayed me. A few men I've called 'sir' still have my trust to this day. I use one more reverently than the other. Sir."

"You're an odd one, son."

"The normal ones are dead in the chasms, sir," Kaladin said softly. "Sadeas saw to that."

"Well, have your men on the balcony guard from farther to the side, where they can't hear through the window."

"I'll wait with the men in the hall, then," Kaladin said, noticing that the two men of the King's Guard had already moved through the doors.

"I didn't order that," Dalinar said. "Guard the doors, but on the inside. I want you to hear what we're planning. Just don't repeat it outside this room."

"Yes, sir."

"Four more people are coming to the meeting," Dalinar said. "My sons, General Khal, and Brightness Teshav, Khal's wife. They may enter. Anyone else should be kept back until the meeting is over."

Dalinar went back to a conversation with the king's mother. Kaladin got Moash and Drehy positioned, then explained the door protocol to Mart and Eth. He'd have to do some training later. Lighteyes never truly meant "Don't let anyone else in" when they said "Don't let anyone else in." What they meant was "If you let anyone else in, I'd better agree that it was important enough, or you're in trouble."

Then, Kaladin took his post inside the closed door, standing against a wall with carved paneling made of a rare type of wood he didn't recognize. *It's probably worth more than I've earned in my entire lifetime,* he thought idly. *One wooden panel.*

The highprince's sons arrived, Adolin and Renarin Kholin. Kaladin had seen the former on the battlefield, though he looked different without his Shardplate. Less imposing. More like a spoiled rich boy. Oh, he wore a uniform like everyone else, but the buttons were engraved, and the boots . . . those were expensive hogshide ones without a scuff on them. Brand new, likely bought at ridiculous expense.

He did save that woman in the market, though, Kaladin thought, remembering the encounter from weeks ago. *Don't forget about that.*

Kaladin wasn't sure what to make of Renarin. The youth—he might have been older than Kaladin, but sure didn't look it—wore spectacles and walked after his brother like a shadow. Those slender limbs and delicate fingers had never known battle or real work.

Syl bobbed around the room, poking into nooks, crannies, and vases. She stopped at a paperweight on the women's writing desk beside the king's chair, poking at the block of crystal with a strange kind of crab-thing trapped inside. Were those wings?

"Shouldn't that one wait outside?" Adolin asked, nodding toward Kaladin.

"What we're doing is going to put me in direct danger," Dalinar said, hands clasped behind his back. "I want him to know the details. That might be important to his job." Dalinar didn't look toward Adolin or Kaladin.

Adolin walked up, taking Dalinar by the arm and speaking in a hushed tone that was not so soft that Kaladin couldn't hear. "We barely know him."

"We have to trust some people, Adolin," his father said in a normal voice. "If there's one person in this army I can guarantee isn't working for Sadeas, it's that soldier." He turned and glanced at Kaladin, once again studying him with those unfathomable eyes.

He didn't see me with the Stormlight, Kaladin told himself forcefully. *He was practically unconscious. He doesn't know.*

Does he?

Adolin threw up his hands but walked to the other side of the room, muttering something to his brother. Kaladin remained in position, standing comfortably at parade rest. *Yes, definitely spoiled.*

The general who arrived soon after was a limber, bald man with a straight back and pale yellow eyes. His wife, Teshav, had a pinched face and hair streaked blond. She took up position by the writing desk, which Navani had made no move to occupy.

"Reports," Dalinar said from the window as the door clicked shut behind the two newcomers.

"I suspect you know what you'll hear, Brightlord," said Teshav. "They're irate. They sincerely hoped you would reconsider the command—and sending it out to the public has provoked them. Highprince Hatham was the only one to make a public announcement. He plans to—and I quote—'see that the king is dissuaded from this reckless and ill-advised course.'"

The king sighed, settling into his seat. Renarin sat down immediately, as did the general. Adolin found his seat more reluctantly.

Dalinar remained standing, looking out the window.

"Uncle?" the king asked. "Did you hear that reaction? It's a good thing you didn't go so far as you had considered: to proclaim that they *must* follow the Codes or face seizure of assets. We'd be in the middle of a rebellion."

"That will come," Dalinar said. "I still wonder if I should have announced it all at once. When you've got an arrow stuck in you, it's sometimes best to just yank it out in one pull."

Actually, when you had an arrow in you, the best thing to do was leave it there until you could find a surgeon. Often it would plug the blood flow and keep you alive. It was probably best not to speak up and undermine the highprince's metaphor, however.

"Storms, what a ghastly image," the king said, wiping his face with a handkerchief. "Do you have to say such things, Uncle? I *already* fear we'll be dead before the week is out."

"Your father and I survived worse than this," Dalinar said.

"You had allies, then! Three highprinces for you, only six against, and you never fought them all at the same time."

"If the highprinces unite against us," General Khal said, "we will not be able to stand firm. We'll have no choice but to rescind this proclamation, which will weaken the Throne considerably."

The king leaned back, hand to his forehead. "Jezerezeh, this is going to be a disaster. . . ."

Kaladin raised an eyebrow.

"You disagree?" Syl asked, moving over toward him as a cluster of fluttering leaves. It was disconcerting to hear her voice coming from such shapes. The others in the room, of course, couldn't see or hear her.

"No," Kaladin whispered. "This proclamation sounds like a real tempest. I just expected the king to be less . . . well, whiny."

"We need to secure allies," Adolin said. "Form a coalition. Sadeas will gather one, and so we counter him with our own."

"Dividing the kingdom into two?" Teshav said, shaking her head. "I don't see how a civil war would serve the Throne. Particularly one we're unlikely to win."

"This could be the end of Alethkar as a kingdom," the general agreed.

"Alethkar ended as a kingdom centuries ago," Dalinar said softly, staring out that window. "This thing we have created is not Alethkar. Alethkar was justice. We are children wearing our father's cloak."

"But Uncle," the king said, "at least the kingdom is *something*. More than it has been in centuries! If we fail here, and fracture to ten warring princedoms, it will negate everything my father worked for!"

"This isn't what your father worked for, son," Dalinar said. "This game on the Shattered Plains, this nauseating political farce. This isn't what Gavilar envisioned. The Everstorm comes. . . ."

"What?" the king asked.

Dalinar turned from the window finally, walking to the others, and rested his hand on Navani's shoulder. "We're going to find a way to do this, or we're going to destroy the kingdom in the process. I won't suffer this charade any longer."

Kaladin, arms folded, tapped one finger against his elbow. "Dalinar acts like he's the king," he mouthed, whispering so softly only Syl could hear. "And everyone else does as well." Troubling. It was like what Amaram had done. Seizing the power he saw before him, even if it wasn't his.

Navani looked up at Dalinar, raising her hand to rest on his. She was in on whatever he was planning, judging by that expression.

The king wasn't. He sighed lightly. "You've *obviously* got a plan, Uncle. Well? Out with it. This drama is tiring."

"What I really want to do," Dalinar said frankly, "is beat the lot of them senseless. That's what I'd do to new recruits who weren't willing to obey orders."

"I think you'll have a hard time *spanking* obedience into the highprinces, Uncle," the king said dryly. For some reason, he absently rubbed at his chest.

"You need to disarm them," Kaladin found himself saying.

All eyes in the room turned toward him. Brightness Teshav gave him a frown, as if speaking were not Kaladin's right. It probably wasn't.

Dalinar, however, nodded toward him. "Soldier? You have a suggestion?"

"Your pardon, sir," Kaladin said. "And your pardon, Your Majesty. But if a squad is giving you trouble, the first thing you do is separate its members. Split them up, stick them in better squads. I don't think you can do that here."

"I don't know how we'd break apart the highprinces," Dalinar said. "I doubt I could stop them from associating with one another. Perhaps if this war were won, I could assign different highprinces different duties, send them off, then work on them individually. But for the time being, we are trapped here."

"Well, the second thing you do to troublemakers," Kaladin said, "is you disarm them. They're easier to control if you make them turn in their spears. It's embarrassing, makes them feel like recruits again. So . . . can you take their troops away from them, maybe?"

"We can't, I'm afraid," Dalinar said. "The soldiers swore allegiance to their lighteyes, not to the Crown specifically—it's only the highprinces who have sworn to the Crown. However, you are thinking along the right lines."

He squeezed Navani's shoulder. "For the last two weeks," he said, "I've been trying to decide how to approach this problem. My gut tells me that I need to treat the highprinces—the entire lighteyed population of Alethkar—like new recruits, in need of discipline."

"He came to me, and we talked," Navani said. "We can't *actually* bust the highprinces down to a manageable rank, as much as Dalinar would like to do just that. Instead, we need to lead them to believe that we're *going* to take it all from them, if they don't shape up."

"This proclamation will make them mad," Dalinar said. "I *want* them mad. I want them to think about the war, their place here, and I want to remind them of Gavilar's assassination. If I can push them to act more like soldiers, even if it starts with them taking up arms against me, then I might be able to persuade them. I can reason with soldiers. Regardless, a big part of this will involve the threat that I'm going to take away their authority and power if they don't use it correctly. And that begins, as Captain Kaladin suggested, with disarming them."

"Disarm the *highprinces*?" the king asked. "What foolishness is this?"

"It's not foolishness," Dalinar said, smiling. "We can't take their armies from them, but we *can* do something else. Adolin, I intend to take the lock off your scabbard."

Adolin frowned, considering that for a moment. Then a wide grin split his face. "You mean, letting me duel again? For real?"

"Yes," Dalinar said. He turned to the king. "For the longest time, I've forbidden him from important bouts, as the Codes prohibit duels of honor between officers at war. More and more, however, I've come to realize that the others don't see themselves as being at war. They're playing a game. It's time to allow Adolin to duel the camp's other Shardbearers in official bouts."

"So he can humiliate them?" the king asked.

"It wouldn't be about humiliation; it would be about depriving them of their Shards." Dalinar stepped into the middle of the group of chairs. "The highprinces would have a hard time fighting against us if we controlled all of the Shardblades and Shardplate in the army. Adolin, I want you to challenge the Shardbearers of other highprinces in duels of honor, the prizes being the Shards themselves."

"They won't agree to it," General Khal said. "They'll refuse the bouts."

"We'll have to make sure they agree," Dalinar said. "Find a way to force them, or shame them, into the fights. I've considered that this would probably be easier if we could ever track down where Wit ran off to."

"What happens if the lad loses?" General Khal asked. "This plan seems too unpredictable."

"We'll see," Dalinar said. "This is only one part of what we will do, the smaller part—but also the most visible part. Adolin, everyone tells me how good you are at dueling, and you have pestered me incessantly to relax my prohibition. There are thirty Shardbearers in the army, not counting our own. Can you defeat that many men?"

"Can I?" Adolin said, grinning. "I'll do it without breaking a sweat, so long as I can start with Sadeas himself."

So he's spoiled and *cocky,* Kaladin thought.

"No," Dalinar said. "Sadeas won't accept a personal challenge, though eventually bringing him down is our goal. We start with some of the lesser Shardbearers and work up to him."

The others in the room seemed troubled. That included Brightness Navani, who drew her lips to a line and glanced at Adolin. She might be in on Dalinar's plan, but she didn't love the idea of her nephew dueling.

She didn't say so. "As Dalinar indicated," Navani said, "this won't be our entire plan. Hopefully, Adolin's duels won't need to go far. They are meant mostly to inspire worry and fear, to apply pressure to some factions who are working against us. The greater part of what we must do will entail a complex and determined political effort to connect with those who can be swayed to our side."

"Navani and I will work to persuade the highprinces of the advantages of a truly unified Alethkar," Dalinar said, nodding. "Though the Stormfather knows, I'm less certain of my political acumen than Adolin is of his dueling. It is what must be. If Adolin is to be the stick, I must be the feather."

"There will be assassins, Uncle," Elhokar said, sounding tired. "I don't think Khal is right; I don't think Alethkar will shatter immediately. The highprinces have come to like the idea of being one kingdom. But they also like their sport, their fun, their gemhearts. So they will send assassins. Quietly, at first, and probably not directly at you or me. Our families. Sadeas and the others will try to hurt us, make us back down. Are you willing to risk your sons on this? How about my mother?"

"Yes, you are right," Dalinar said. "I hadn't . . . but yes. That is how they think." He sounded regretful to Kaladin.

"And you're still willing to go through with this plan?" the king asked.

"I have no choice," Dalinar said, turning away, walking back toward the window. Looking out westward, in toward the continent.

"Then at least tell me this," Elhokar said. "What is your endgame, Uncle? What is it you want out of all of this? In a year, if we survive this fiasco, what do you want us to be?"

Dalinar put his hands on the thick stone windowsill. He stared out, as if at something he could see and the rest of them could not. "I'll have us be what we were before, son. A kingdom that can stand through storms, a kingdom that is a light and not a darkness. I will have a truly unified Alethkar, with highprinces who are loyal and just. I'll have more than that." He tapped the windowsill. "I'm going to refound the Knights Radiant."

Kaladin nearly dropped his spear in shock. Fortunately, nobody was watching him—they were leaping to their feet, staring at Dalinar.

"The Radiants?" Brightness Teshav demanded. "Are you mad? You're going to try to rebuild a sect of traitors who gave us over to the Voidbringers?"

"The rest of this sounds good, Father," Adolin said, stepping forward. "I know you think about the Radiants a lot, but you see them . . . differently than everyone else. It won't go well if you announce that you want to emulate them."

The king just groaned, burying his face in his hands.

"People are wrong about them," Dalinar said. "And even if they are not, the original Radiants—the ones instituted by the Heralds—are something even the Vorin church admits were once moral and just. We'll need to remind people that the Knights Radiant, as an order, stood for something grand. If they hadn't, then they wouldn't have been able to 'fall' as the stories claim they did."

"But *why*?" Elhokar asked. "What is the point?"

"It is what I must do." Dalinar hesitated. "I'm not completely certain why, yet. Only that I've been instructed to do it. As a protection, and a preparation, for what is coming. A storm of some sort. Perhaps it is as simple as the other highprinces turning against us. I doubt that, but perhaps."

"Father," Adolin said, hand on Dalinar's arm. "This is all well and good, and maybe you can change people's perception of the Radiants, but . . . Ishar's soul, Father! They could do things we cannot. Simply naming someone a Radiant won't give them fanciful powers, like in the stories."

"The Radiants were about more than what they could do," Dalinar said. "They were about an ideal. The kind of ideal we're lacking, these days. We may not be able to reach for the ancient Surgebindings—the powers they had—but we can seek to emulate the Radiants in other ways. I am set on this. Do not try to dissuade me."

The others did not seem convinced.

Kaladin narrowed his eyes. So did Dalinar know about Kaladin's powers, or didn't he? The meeting moved on to more mundane topics, such as how to maneuver Shardbearers into facing Adolin and how to step up patrols of the surrounding area. Dalinar considered making the warcamps safe to be a prerequisite for what he was attempting.

When the meeting finally ended, most people inside departing to carry out orders, Kaladin was still considering what Dalinar had said about the Radiants. The man hadn't realized it, but he'd been very accurate. The Knights Radiant did have ideals—and they'd called them that very thing. The Five Ideals, the Immortal Words.

Life before death, Kaladin thought, playing with a sphere he'd pulled from his pocket, *strength before weakness, journey before destination.* Those Words made up the First Ideal in its entirety. He had only an inkling of what it meant, but his ignorance hadn't stopped him from figuring out the Second Ideal of the Windrunners, the oath to protect those who could not protect themselves.

Syl wouldn't tell him the other three. She said he would know them when he needed to. Or he wouldn't, and would not progress.

Did he want to progress? To become what? A member of the Knights Radiant? Kaladin hadn't asked for someone else's ideals to rule his life. He'd just wanted to survive. Now, somehow, he was headed straight down a path that no man had trod in centuries. Potentially becoming something that people across Roshar would hate or revere. So much attention . . .

"Soldier?" Dalinar asked, stopping by the door.

"Sir." Kaladin stood up straight again and saluted. It felt *good* to do that, to stand at attention, to find a place. He wasn't certain if it was the good feeling of remembering a life he'd once loved, or if it was the pathetic feeling of an axehound finding its leash again.

"My nephew was right," Dalinar said, watching the king retreat down the hallway. "The others might try to hurt my family. It's how they think. I'm going to need guard details on Navani and my sons at all times. Your best men."

"I've got about two dozen of those, sir," Kaladin said. "That's not enough for full guard details running all day protecting all four of you. I should have more men trained before too long, but putting a spear in the hands of a bridgeman does not make him a soldier, let alone a good body-guard."

Dalinar nodded, looking troubled. He rubbed his chin.

"Sir?"

"Your force isn't the only one stretched thin in this warcamp, soldier," Dalinar said. "I lost a lot of men to Sadeas's betrayal. Very good men. Now I have a deadline. Just over sixty days . . ."

Kaladin felt a chill. The highprince was taking the number found scrawled on his wall very seriously.

"Captain," Dalinar said softly, "I need every able-bodied man I can get. I need to be training them, rebuilding my army, preparing for the storm. I need them assaulting plateaus, clashing with the Parshendi, to get battle experience."

What did this have to do with him? "You promised that my men wouldn't be required to fight on plateau runs."

"I'll keep that promise," Dalinar said. "But there are two hundred and fifty soldiers in the King's Guard. They include some of my last remaining battle-ready officers, and I will need to put them in charge of new recruits."

"I'm not just going to have to watch over your family, am I?" Kaladin asked, feeling a new weight settling in his shoulders. "You're implying you want to turn over guarding the *king* to me as well."

"Yes," Dalinar said. "Slowly, but yes. I need those soldiers. Beyond that, maintaining two separate guard forces seems like a mistake to me. I feel that your men, considering your background, are the least likely to include spies for my enemies. You should know that a while back, there may have been an attempt on the king's life. I still haven't figured out who was behind it, but I worry that some of his guards may have been involved."

Kaladin took a deep breath. "What happened?"

"Elhokar and I hunted a chasmfiend," Dalinar said. "During that hunt, at a time of stress, the king's Plate came close to failing. We found that many of the gemstones powering it had likely been replaced with ones that were flawed, making them crack under stress."

"I don't know much of Plate, sir," Kaladin said. "Could they have just broken on their own, without sabotage?"

"Possible, but unlikely. I want your men to take shifts guarding the palace and the king, alternating with some of the King's Guard, to get you familiar with him and the palace. It might also help your men learn from the more experienced guards. At the same time, I'm going to start siphoning off the officers from his guard to train soldiers in my army.

"Over the next few weeks, we'll merge your group and the King's Guard into one. You'll be in charge. Once you've trained bridgemen from those other crews well enough, we'll replace soldiers in the guard with your men, and move the soldiers to my army." He looked Kaladin in the eyes. "Can you do this, soldier?"

"Yes, sir," Kaladin said, though part of him was panicking. "I can."

"Good."

"Sir, a suggestion. You've said you're going to expand patrols outside the warcamps, trying to police the hills around the Shattered Plains?"

"Yes. The number of bandits out there is embarrassing. This is Alethi land now. It needs to follow Alethi laws."

"I have a thousand men I need to train," Kaladin said. "If I could patrol them out there, it might help them feel like soldiers. I could use a large enough force that it sends a message to the bandits, maybe making them withdraw—but my men won't need to see much combat."

"Good. General Khal had been in command of patrol duty, but he's now my most senior commander, and will be needed for other things. Train your men. Our goal will eventually be to have your thousand doing real roadway patrols between here, Alethkar, and the ports to the south and east. I'll want scouting teams, watching for signs of bandit camps and searching out caravans that have been attacked. I need numbers on how much activity is out there, and just how dangerous it is."

"I'll see to it personally, sir."

Storms. How was he going to do all of this?

"Good," Dalinar said.

Dalinar walked from the chamber, clasping his hands behind him, as if lost in thought. Moash, Eth, and Mart fell in after him, as ordered by Kaladin. He'd have two men with Dalinar at all times, three if he could manage it. He'd once hoped to expand that to four or five, but storms, with so many to watch over now, that was going to be impossible.

Who is this man? Kaladin thought, watching Dalinar's retreating form. He ran a good camp. You could judge a man—and Kaladin did—by the men who followed him.

But a tyrant could have a good camp with disciplined soldiers. This man, Dalinar Kholin, had helped unite Alethkar—and had done so by wading through blood. Now . . . now he spoke like a king, even when the king himself was in the room.

He wants to rebuild the Knights Radiant, Kaladin thought. That wasn't something Dalinar Kholin could accomplish through simple force of will.

Unless he had help.

*We had never considered that there might be Parshendi spies hiding
among our slaves. This is something else I should have seen.*

—From the journal of Navani Kholin, Jesesan 1174

Shallan sat again on her box on the ship's deck, though she now wore
a hat on her head, a coat over her dress, and a glove on her freehand—
her safehand was, of course, pinned inside its sleeve.

The chill out here on the open ocean was something unreal. The captain
said that far to the south, the ocean itself actually froze. That sounded incredible; she'd like to see it. She'd occasionally seen snow and ice in Jah
Keved, during the odd winter. But an entire ocean of it? Amazing.

She wrote with gloved fingers as she observed the spren she'd named
Pattern. At the moment, he had lifted himself up off the surface of the
deck, forming a ball of swirling blackness—infinite lines that twisted in ways
she could never have captured on the flat page. Instead, she wrote descriptions supplemented with sketches.

"Food . . ." Pattern said. The sound had a buzzing quality and he vibrated
when he spoke.

"Yes," Shallan said. "We eat it." She selected a small limafruit from the
bowl beside her and placed it in her mouth, then chewed and swallowed.

"Eat," Pattern said. "You . . . make it . . . into you."

"Yes! Exactly."

He dropped down, the darkness vanishing as he entered the wooden
deck of the ship. Once again, he became part of the material—making the
wood ripple as if it were water. He slid across the floor, then moved up the

box beside her to the bowl of small green fruits. Here, he moved *across* them, each fruit's rind puckering and rising with the shape of his pattern.

"Terrible!" he said, the sound vibrating up from the bowl.

"Terrible?"

"Destruction!"

"What? No, it's how we survive. Everything needs to eat."

"Terrible destruction to eat!" He sounded aghast. He retreated from the bowl to the deck.

Pattern connects increasingly complex thoughts, Shallan wrote. *Abstractions come easily to him. Early, he asked me the questions "Why? Why you? Why be?" I interpreted this as asking me my purpose. When I replied, "To find truth," he easily seemed to grasp my meaning. And yet, some simple realities—such as why people would need to eat—completely escape him. It—*

She stopped writing as the paper puckered and rose, Pattern appearing on the sheet itself, his tiny ridges lifting the letters she had just penned.

"Why this?" he asked.

"To remember."

"Remember," he said, trying the word.

"It means . . ." Stormfather. How did she explain memory? "It means to be able to know what you did in the past. In other moments, ones that happened days ago."

"Remember," he said. "I . . . cannot . . . remember . . ."

"What is the first thing you do remember?" Shallan asked. "Where were you first?"

"First," Pattern said. "With you."

"On the ship?" Shallan said, writing.

"No. Green. Food. Food not eaten."

"Plants?" Shallan asked.

"Yes. Many plants." He vibrated, and she thought she could hear in that vibration the blowing of wind through branches. Shallan breathed in. She could almost *see* it. The deck in front of her changing to a dirt path, her box becoming a stone bench. Faintly. Not really there, but *almost*. Her father's gardens. Pattern on the ground, drawn in the dust . . .

"Remember," Pattern said, voice like a whisper.

No, Shallan thought, horrified. *NO!*

The image vanished. It hadn't really been there in the first place, had it? She raised her safehand to her breast, breathing in and out in sharp gasps. No.

"Hey, young miss!" Yalb said from behind. "Tell the new kid here what happened in Kharbranth!"

Shallan turned, heart still racing, to see Yalb walking over with the "new kid," a six-foot-tall hulk of a man who was at least five years Yalb's senior. They'd picked him up at Amydlatn, the last port. Tozbek wanted to be sure they wouldn't be undermanned during the last leg to New Natanan.

Yalb squatted down beside her stool. In the face of the chill, he'd acquiesced to wearing a shirt with ragged sleeves and a kind of headband that wrapped over his ears.

"Brightness?" Yalb asked. "You all right? You look like you swallowed a turtle. And not just the head, neither."

"I'm well," Shallan said. "What . . . what was it you wanted of me, again?"

"In Kharbranth," Yalb said, thumbing over his shoulder. "Did we or did we not meet the king?"

"We?" Shallan asked. "I met him."

"And I was your retinue."

"You were waiting outside."

"Doesn't matter none," Yalb said. "I was your footman for that meeting, eh?"

Footman? He'd led her up to the palace as a favor. "I . . . guess," she said. "You did have a nice bow, as I recall."

"See," Yalb said, standing and confronting the much larger man. "I mentioned the bow, didn't I?"

The "new kid" rumbled his agreement.

"So get to washing those dishes," Yalb said. He got a scowl in response. "Now, don't give me that," Yalb said. "I *told* you, galley duty is something the captain watches closely. If you want to fit in around here, you do it well, and do some extra. It will put you ahead with the captain *and* the rest of the men. I'm giving you quite the opportunity here, and I'll have you appreciate it."

That seemed to placate the larger man, who turned around and went tromping toward the lower decks.

"Passions!" Yalb said. "That fellow is as dun as two spheres made of mud. I worry about him. Somebody's going to take advantage of him, Brightness."

"Yalb, have you been boasting again?" Shallan said.

"'Tain't boasting if some of it's true."

"Actually, that's *exactly* what boasting entails."

"Hey," Yalb said, turning toward her. "What were you doing before? You know, with the colors?"

"Colors?" Shallan said, suddenly cold.

"Yeah, the deck turned green, eh?" Yalb said. "I swear I saw it. Has to do with that strange spren, does it?"

"I . . . I'm trying to determine exactly what kind of spren it is," Shallan said, keeping her voice even. "It's a scholarly matter."

"I thought so," Yalb said, though she'd given him nothing in the way of an answer. He raised an affable hand to her, then jogged off.

She worried about letting them see Pattern. She'd tried staying in her cabin to keep him a secret from the men, but being cooped up had been too difficult for her, and he didn't respond to her suggestions that he stay out of their sight. So, during the last four days, she'd been forced to let them see what she was doing as she studied him.

They were understandably discomforted by him, but didn't say much. Today, they were getting the ship ready to sail all night. Thoughts of the open sea at night unsettled her, but that was the cost of sailing this far from civilization. Two days back, they'd even been forced to weather a storm in a cove along the coast. Jasnah and Shallan had gone ashore to stay in a fortress maintained for the purpose—paying a steep cost to get in—while the sailors had stayed on board.

That cove, though not a true port, had at least had a stormwall to help shelter the ship. Next highstorm, they wouldn't even have that. They'd find a cove and try to ride out the winds, though Tozbek said he'd send Shallan and Jasnah ashore to seek shelter in a cavern.

She turned back to Pattern, who had shifted into his hovering form. He looked something like the pattern of splintered light thrown on the wall by a crystal chandelier—except he was made of something black instead of light, and he was three-dimensional. So . . . Maybe not much like that at all.

"Lies," Pattern said. "Lies from the Yalb."

"Yes," Shallan said with a sigh. "Yalb is far too skilled at persuasion for his own good, sometimes."

Pattern hummed softly. He seemed pleased.

"You like lies?" Shallan asked.

"Good lies," Pattern said. "That lie. Good lie."

"What makes a lie good?" Shallan asked, taking careful notes, recording Pattern's exact words.

"True lies."

"Pattern, those two are opposites."

"Hmmmm . . . Light makes shadow. Truth makes lies. Hmmmm."

Liespren, Jasnah called them, Shallan wrote. *A moniker they don't like, apparently. When I Soulcast for the first time, a voice demanded a truth from me. I still don't know what that means, and Jasnah has not been forthcoming. She doesn't seem to know what to make of my experience either. I do not think that voice belonged to Pattern, but I cannot say, as he seems to have forgotten much about himself.*

She returned to making a few sketches of Pattern both in his floating and flattened forms. Drawing let her mind relax. By the time she was done, there were several half-remembered passages from her research that she wanted to quote in her notes.

She made her way down the steps belowdecks, Pattern following. He drew looks from the sailors. Sailors were a superstitious lot, and some took him as a bad sign.

In her quarters, Pattern moved up the wall beside her, watching without eyes as she searched for a passage she remembered, which mentioned spren that spoke. Not just windspren and riverspren, which would mimic people and make playful comments. Those were a step up from ordinary spren, but there was yet another level of spren, one rarely seen. Spren like Pattern, who had real conversations with people.

The Nightwatcher is obviously one of these, Alai wrote, Shallan copying the passage. *The records of conversations with her—and she is definitely female, despite what rural Alethi folktales would have one believe—are numerous and credible. Shubalai herself, intent on providing a firsthand scholarly report, visited the Nightwatcher and recorded her story word for word. . . .*

Shallan went to another reference, and before long got completely lost in her studies. A few hours later, she closed a book and set it on the table beside her bed. Her spheres were getting dim; they'd go out soon, and would need to be reinfused with Stormlight. Shallan released a contented sigh and leaned back against her bed, her notes from a dozen different sources laid out on the floor of her small chamber.

She felt . . . satisfied. Her brothers loved the plan of fixing the Soulcaster and returning it, and seemed energized by her suggestion that all was not lost. They thought they could last longer, now that a plan was in place.

Shallan's life was coming together. How long had it been since she'd just been able to sit and read? Without worried concern for her house, without dreading the need to find a way to steal from Jasnah? Even before the terrible sequence of events that had led to her father's death, she had always been anxious. That had been her life. She'd seen becoming a true scholar as something unreachable. Stormfather! She'd seen the *next town over* as being unreachable.

She stood up, gathering her sketchbook and flipping through her pictures of the santhid, including several drawn from the memory of her dip in the ocean. She smiled at that, recalling how she'd climbed back up on deck, dripping wet and grinning. The sailors had all obviously thought her mad.

Now she was sailing toward a city on the edge of the world, betrothed to a powerful Alethi prince, and was free to just learn. She was seeing incredible new sights, sketching them during the days, then reading through piles of books in the nights.

She had stumbled into the perfect life, and it was everything she'd wished for.

Shallan fished in the pocket inside her safehand sleeve, digging out some more spheres to replace those dimming in the goblet. The ones her hand emerged with, however, were completely dun. Not a glimmer of Light in them.

She frowned. These had been restored during the previous highstorm, held in a basket tied to the ship's mast. The ones in her goblet were two storms old now, which was why they were running out. How had the ones in her pocket gone dun faster? It defied reason.

"Mmmmm . . ." Pattern said from the wall near her head. "Lies."

Shallan replaced the spheres in her pocket, then opened the door into the ship's narrow companionway and moved to Jasnah's cabin. It was the cabin that Tozbek and his wife usually shared, but they had vacated it for the third—and smallest—of the cabins to give Jasnah the better quarters. People did things like that for her, even when she didn't ask.

Jasnah would have some spheres for Shallan to use. Indeed, Jasnah's door was cracked open, swaying slightly as the ship creaked and rocked along its evening path. Jasnah sat at the desk inside, and Shallan peeked in, suddenly uncertain if she wanted to bother the woman.

She could see Jasnah's face, hand against her temple, staring at the pages spread before her. Jasnah's eyes were haunted, her expression haggard.

This was *not* the Jasnah that Shallan was accustomed to seeing. The confidence had been overwhelmed by exhaustion, the poise replaced by worry. Jasnah started to write something, but stopped after just a few words. She set down the pen, closing her eyes and massaging her temples. A few dizzy-looking spren, like jets of dust rising into the air, appeared around Jasnah's head. Exhaustionspren.

Shallan pulled back, suddenly feeling as if she'd intruded upon an intimate moment. Jasnah with her defenses down. Shallan began to creep away, but a voice from the floor suddenly said, "Truth!"

Startled, Jasnah looked up, eyes finding Shallan—who, of course, blushed furiously.

Jasnah turned her eyes down toward Pattern on the floor, then reset her mask, sitting up with proper posture. "Yes, child?"

"I . . . I needed spheres . . ." Shallan said. "Those in my pouch went dun."

"Have you been Soulcasting?" Jasnah asked sharply.

"What? No, Brightness. I promised I would not."

"Then it is the second ability," Jasnah said. "Come in and close that door. I should speak to Captain Tozbek; it won't latch properly."

Shallan stepped in, pushing the door closed, though the latch didn't catch. She stepped forward, hands clasped, feeling embarrassed.

"What did you do?" Jasnah asked. "It involved light, I assume?"

"I seemed to make plants appear," Shallan said. "Well, really just the color. One of the sailors saw the deck turn green, but it vanished when I stopped thinking about the plants."

"Yes . . ." Jasnah said. She flipped through one of her books, stopping at an illustration. Shallan had seen it before; it was as ancient as Vorinism. Ten spheres connected by lines forming a shape like an hourglass on its side. Two of the spheres at the center looked almost like pupils. The Double Eye of the Almighty.

"Ten Essences," Jasnah said softly. She ran her fingers along the page. "Ten Surges. Ten orders. But what does it mean that the spren have finally decided to return the oaths to us? And how much time remains to me? Not long. Not long . . ."

"Brightness?" Shallan asked.

"Before your arrival, I could assume I was an anomaly," Jasnah said. "I could hope that Surgebindings were not returning in large numbers. I no longer have that hope. The Cryptics sent you to me, of that I have no doubt, because they knew you would need training. That gives me hope that I was at least one of the first."

"I don't understand."

Jasnah looked up toward Shallan, meeting her eyes with an intense gaze. The woman's eyes were reddened with fatigue. How late was she working? Every night when Shallan turned in, there was still light coming from under Jasnah's door.

"To be honest," Jasnah said, "I don't understand either."

"Are you all right?" Shallan asked. "Before I entered, you seemed . . . distressed."

Jasnah hesitated just briefly. "I have merely been spending too long at my studies." She turned to one of her trunks, digging out a dark cloth pouch filled with spheres. "Take these. I would suggest that you keep spheres with you at all times, so that your Surgebinding has the opportunity to manifest."

"Can you teach me?" Shallan asked, taking the pouch.

"I don't know," Jasnah said. "I will try. On this diagram, one of the Surges is known as Illumination, the mastery of light. For now, I would prefer you expend your efforts on learning this Surge, as opposed to Soulcasting. That is a dangerous art, more so now than it once was."

Shallan nodded, rising. She hesitated before leaving, however. "Are you sure you are well?"

"Of course." She said it too quickly. The woman was poised, in control, but also obviously exhausted. The mask was cracked, and Shallan could see the truth.

She's trying to placate me, Shallan realized. *Pat me on the head and send me back to bed, like a child awakened by a nightmare.*

"You're worried," Shallan said, meeting Jasnah's eyes.

The woman turned away. She pushed a book over something wiggling on her table—a small purple spren. Fearspren. Only one, true, but still.

"No . . ." Shallan whispered. "You're not worried. You're *terrified*." Stormfather!

"It is all right, Shallan," Jasnah said. "I just need some sleep. Go back to your studies."

Shallan sat down on the stool beside Jasnah's desk. The older woman looked back at her, and Shallan could see the mask cracking further. Annoyance as Jasnah drew her lips to a line. Tension in the way she held her pen, in a fist.

"You told me I could be part of this," Shallan said. "Jasnah, if you're worried about something . . ."

"My worry is what it has always been," Jasnah said, leaning back in her chair. "That I will be too late. That I'm incapable of doing anything meaningful to stop what is coming—that I'm trying to stop a highstorm by blowing against it *really hard*."

"The Voidbringers," Shallan said. "The parshmen."

"In the past," Jasnah said, "the Desolation—the coming of the Voidbringers—was supposedly always marked by a return of the Heralds to prepare mankind. They would train the Knights Radiant, who would experience a rush of new members."

"But we captured the Voidbringers," Shallan said. "And enslaved them." That was what Jasnah postulated, and Shallan agreed, having seen the research. "So you think a kind of revolution is coming. That the parshmen will turn against us as they did in the past."

"Yes," Jasnah said, rifling through her notes. "And soon. Your proving to be a Surgebinder does not comfort me, as it smacks too much of what happened before. But back then, new knights had teachers to train them, generations of tradition. We have nothing."

"The Voidbringers are captive," Shallan said, glancing toward Pattern. He rested on the floor, almost invisible, saying nothing. "The parshmen can barely communicate. How could they possibly stage a revolution?"

Jasnah found the sheet of paper she'd been seeking and handed it to Shallan. Written in Jasnah's own hand, it was an account by a captain's wife of a plateau assault on the Shattered Plains.

"Parshendi," Jasnah said, "can sing in time with one another no matter how far they are separated. They have some ability to communicate that we do not understand. I can only assume that their cousins the parshmen have the same. They may not need to *hear* a call to action in order to revolt."

Shallan read the report, nodding slowly. "We need to warn others, Jasnah."

"You don't think I've tried?" Jasnah asked. "I've written to scholars and kings all around the world. Most dismiss me as paranoid. The evidence you readily accept, others call flimsy.

"The ardents were my best hope, but their eyes are clouded by the interference of the Hierocracy. Besides, my personal beliefs make ardents skeptical of anything I say. My mother wants to see my research, which is something. My brother and uncle might believe, and that is why we are going to them." She hesitated. "There is another reason we seek the Shattered Plains. A way to find evidence that might convince everyone."

"Urithiru," Shallan said. "The city you seek?"

Jasnah gave her another curt glance. The ancient city was something Shallan had first learned about by secretly reading Jasnah's notes.

"You still blush too easily when confronted," Jasnah noted.

"I'm sorry."

"And apologize too easily as well."

"I'm . . . uh, indignant?"

Jasnah smiled, picking up the representation of the Double Eye. She stared at it. "There is a secret hidden somewhere on the Shattered Plains. A secret about Urithiru."

"You told me the city wasn't there!"

"It isn't. But the path to it may be." Her lips tightened. "According to legend, only a Knight Radiant could open the way."

"Fortunately, we know two of those."

"Again, you are not a Radiant, and neither am I. Being able to replicate some of the things they could do may not matter. We don't have their traditions or knowledge."

"We're talking about the potential end of civilization itself, aren't we?" Shallan asked softly.

Jasnah hesitated.

"The Desolations," Shallan said. "I know very little, but the legends . . ."

"In the aftermath of each one, mankind was broken. Great cities in ashes, industry smashed. Each time, knowledge and growth were reduced to an almost prehistoric state—it took *centuries* of rebuilding to restore civilization to what it had been before." She hesitated. "I keep hoping that I'm wrong."

"Urithiru," Shallan said. She tried to refrain from just asking questions, trying instead to reason her way to the answer. "You said the city was a kind of base or home to the Knights Radiant. I hadn't heard of it before speaking with you, and so can guess that it's not commonly referred to in the literature. Perhaps, then, it is one of the things that the Hierocracy suppressed knowledge of?"

"Very good," Jasnah said. "Although I think that it had begun to fade into legend even before then, the Hierocracy did not help."

"So if it existed before the Hierocracy, and if the pathway to it was locked at the fall of the Radiants . . . then it might contain records that have not been touched by modern scholars. Unaltered, unchanged lore about the Voidbringers and Surgebinding." Shallan shivered. "*That's* why we're really going to the Shattered Plains."

Jasnah smiled through her fatigue. "Very good indeed. My time in the Palanaeum was very useful, but also in some ways disappointing. While I confirmed my suspicions about the parshmen, I also found that many of the great library's records bore the same signs of tampering as others I'd read. This 'cleansing' of history, removing direct references to Urithiru or the Radiants because they were embarrassments to Vorinism—it's infuriating. And people ask me why I am hostile to the church! I need primary sources. And then, there are stories—ones I dare to believe—claiming that Urithiru was holy and protected from the Voidbringers. Maybe that was wishful fancy, but I am not too much a scholar to hope that something like that might be true."

"And the parshmen?"

"We will try to persuade the Alethi to rid themselves of those."

"Not an easy task."

"A nearly impossible one," Jasnah said, standing. She began to pack her books away for the night, putting them in her waterproofed trunk. "Parshmen are such perfect slaves. Docile, obedient. Our society has become far too reliant upon them. The parshmen wouldn't need to turn violent to throw us into chaos—though I'm certain that is what's coming—they could simply walk away. It would cause an economic crisis."

She closed the trunk after removing one volume, then turned back to Shallan. "Convincing everyone of what I say is beyond us without more evidence. Even if my brother listens, he doesn't have the authority to force the highprinces to get rid of their parshmen. And, in all honesty, I fear my brother won't be brave enough to risk the collapse expelling the parshmen might cause."

"But if they turn on us, the collapse will come anyway."

"Yes," Jasnah said. "You know this, and I know it. My mother might believe it. But the risk of being wrong is so immense that . . . well, we will need evidence—overwhelming and irrefutable evidence. So we find the city. At all costs, we *find* that city."

Shallan nodded.

"I did not want to lay all of this upon your shoulders, child," Jasnah said, sitting back down. "However, I will admit that it is a relief to speak of these things to someone who doesn't challenge me on every other point."

"We'll do it, Jasnah," Shallan said. "We'll travel to the Shattered Plains and we'll find Urithiru. We'll get the evidence and convince everyone to listen."

"Ah, the optimism of youth," Jasnah said. "That is nice to hear on occasion too." She handed the book to Shallan. "Among the Knights Radiant, there was an order known as the Lightweavers. I know precious little about them, but of all the sources I've read, this one has the most information."

Shallan took the volume eagerly. *Words of Radiance*, the title read.

"Go," Jasnah said. "Read."

Shallan glanced at her.

"I will sleep," Jasnah promised, a smile creeping to her lips. "And stop trying to mother me. I don't even let Navani do that."

Shallan sighed, nodding, and left Jasnah's quarters. Pattern tagged along behind; he'd spent the entire conversation silent. As she entered her cabin, she found herself much heavier of heart than when she'd left it. She couldn't banish the image of terror in Jasnah's eyes. Jasnah Kholin shouldn't fear anything, should she?

Shallan crawled onto her cot with the book she'd been given and the pouch of spheres. Part of her was eager to begin, but she was exhausted, her eyelids drooping. It really had gotten late. If she started the book now . . .

Perhaps better to get a good night's sleep, then dig refreshed into a new day's studies. She set the book on the small table beside her bed, curled up, and let the rocking of the boat coax her to sleep.

She awoke to screams, shouts, and smoke.

7

OPEN FLAME

I was unprepared for the grief my loss brought—like an unexpected rain—breaking from a clear sky and crashing down upon me. Gavilar's death years ago was overwhelming, but this . . . this nearly crushed me.

—From the journal of Navani Kholin, Jesesach 1174

Still half asleep, Shallan panicked. She scrambled off her cot, accidentally slapping the goblet of mostly drained spheres. Though she used wax to keep it in place, the swat knocked it free and sent spheres tumbling across her cabin.

The scent of smoke was powerful. She ran to her door, disheveled, heart thumping. At least she'd fallen asleep in her clothing. She threw open the door.

Three men crowded in the passageway outside, holding aloft torches, their backs to her.

Torches, sparking with flamespren dancing about the fires. Who brought open flame onto a ship? Shallan stopped in numb confusion.

The shouts came from the deck above, and it seemed that the ship wasn't on fire. But who were these men? They carried axes, and were focused on Jasnah's cabin, which was open.

Figures moved inside. In a frozen moment of horror, one threw something to the floor before the others, who stepped aside to make way.

A body in a thin nightgown, eyes staring sightlessly, blood blossoming from the breast. Jasnah.

"Be sure," one of the men said.

The other one knelt and rammed a long, thin knife right into Jasnah's chest. Shallan heard it hit the wood of the floor beneath the body.

Shallan screamed.

One of the men spun toward her. "Hey!" It was the blunt-faced, tall fellow that Yalb had called the "new kid." She didn't recognize the other men.

Somehow fighting through the terror and disbelief, Shallan slammed her door and threw the bolt with trembling fingers.

Stormfather! Stormfather! She backed away from the door as something heavy hit the other side. They wouldn't need the axes. A few determined smashes of shoulder to door would bring it down.

Shallan stumbled back against her cot, nearly slipping on the spheres rolling to and fro with the ship's motion. The narrow window near the ceiling—far too small to fit through—revealed only the dark of night outside. Shouts continued above, feet thumping on wood.

Shallan trembled, still numb. Jasnah. . . .

"Sword," a voice said. Pattern, hanging on the wall beside her. "Mmmm . . . The sword . . ."

"No!" Shallan screamed, hands to the sides of her head, fingers in her hair. Stormfather! She was trembling.

Nightmare. It was a nightmare! It couldn't be—

"Mmmm . . . Fight . . ."

"*No!*" Shallan found herself hyperventilating as the men outside continued to ram their shoulders against her door. She was not ready for this. She was not prepared.

"Mmmm . . ." Pattern said, sounding dissatisfied. "Lies."

"I don't know how to use the lies!" Shallan said. "I haven't practiced."

"Yes. Yes . . . remember . . . the time before . . ."

The door crunched. Dared she remember? *Could* she remember? A child, playing with a shimmering pattern of light . . .

"What do I do?" she asked.

"You need the Light," Pattern said.

It sparked something deep within her memory, something prickled with barbs she dared not touch. She needed Stormlight to fuel the Surgebinding.

Shallan fell to her knees beside her cot and, without knowing exactly what she was doing, breathed in sharply. Stormlight left the spheres around her, pouring into her body, becoming a storm that raged in her veins. The cabin went dark, black as a cavern deep beneath the earth.

Then Light began to rise from her skin like vapors off boiling water. It lit the cabin with swimming shadows.

"Now what?" she demanded.

"Shape the lie."

What did that mean? The door crunched again, cracking, a large split opening down the center.

Panicked, Shallan let out a breath. Stormlight streamed from her in a cloud; she almost felt as if she could touch it. She could *feel* its potential.

"How!" she demanded.

"Make the truth."

"That makes no sense!"

Shallan screamed as the door broke open. New light entered the cabin, torchlight—red and yellow, hostile.

The cloud of Light *leaped* from Shallan, more Stormlight streaming from her body to join it. It formed a vague upright shape. An illuminated blur. It washed past the men through the doorway, waving appendages that could have been arms. Shallan herself, kneeling by the bed, fell into shadow.

The men's eyes were drawn to the glowing shape. Then, blessedly, they turned and gave chase.

Shallan huddled against the wall, shaking. The cabin was utterly dark. Above, men screamed.

"Shallan . . ." Pattern buzzed somewhere in the darkness.

"Go and look," she said. "Tell me what is happening up on deck."

She didn't know if he obeyed, as he made no sound when he moved. After a few deep breaths, Shallan stood up. Her legs shook, but she stood.

She collected herself somewhat. This was terrible, this was awful, but nothing, *nothing*, could compare to what she'd had to do the night her father died. She had survived that. She could survive this.

These men, they would be of the same group Kabsal had been from—the assassins Jasnah feared. They had finally gotten her.

Oh, Jasnah . . .

Jasnah was dead.

Grieve later. What was Shallan going to do about armed men taking over the ship? How would she find a way out?

She felt her way out into the passageway. There was a little light here, from torches above on the deck. The yells she heard there grew more panicked.

"Killing," a voice suddenly said.

She jumped, though of course it was only Pattern.

"What?" Shallan hissed.

"Dark men killing," Pattern said. "Sailors tied in ropes. One dead, bleeding red. I . . . I do not understand. . . ."

Oh, Stormfather . . . Above, the shouting heightened, but there was no scramble of boots on the deck, no clanging of weapons. The sailors had been captured. At least one had been killed.

In the darkness, Shallan saw shaking, wiggling forms creep up from the wood around her. Fearspren.

"What of the men who chased after my image?" she asked.

"Looking in water," Pattern said.

So they thought she'd jumped overboard. Heart thumping, Shallan felt her way to Jasnah's cabin, expecting at any moment to trip over the woman's corpse on the floor. She didn't. Had the men dragged it above?

Shallan entered Jasnah's cabin and closed the door. It wouldn't latch shut, so she pulled a box over to block it.

She had to do something. She felt her way to one of Jasnah's trunks, which had been thrown open by the men, its contents—clothing—scattered about. In the bottom, Shallan found the hidden drawer and pulled it open. Light suddenly bathed the cabin. The spheres were so bright they blinded Shallan for a moment, and she had to look away.

Pattern vibrated on the floor beside her, form shaking in worry. Shallan looked about. The small cabin was a shambles, clothing on the floor, papers strewn everywhere. The trunk with Jasnah's books was gone. Too fresh to have soaked in, blood was pooled on the bed. Shallan quickly looked away.

A shout suddenly sounded above, followed by a thump. The screaming grew louder. She heard Tozbek bellow for the men to spare his wife.

Almighty above . . . the assassins were executing the sailors one at a time. Shallan had to do something. Anything.

Shallan looked back at the spheres in their false bottom, lined with black cloth. "Pattern," she said, "we're going to Soulcast the bottom of the ship and sink it."

"What!" His vibrating increased, a buzz of sound. "Humans . . . Humans . . . Eat water?"

"We drink it," Shallan said, "but we cannot breathe it."

"Mmmm . . . Confused . . ." Pattern said.

"The captain and the others are captured and being executed. The best chance I can give them is chaos." Shallan placed her hands on the spheres and drew in the Light with a sharp breath. She felt *afire* with it inside of her, as if she were going to burst. The Light was a living thing, trying to press out through the pores of her skin.

"Show me!" she shouted, far more loudly than she'd intended. That Stormlight urged her to action. "I've Soulcast before. I must do it again!" Stormlight puffed from her mouth as she spoke, like breath on a cold day.

"Mmmmm . . ." Pattern said anxiously. "I will intercede. See."

"See what?"

"*See!*"

Shadesmar. The last time she'd gone to that place, she'd nearly gotten herself killed. Only, it wasn't a place. Or was it? Did it matter?

She reached back through recent memory to the time when she'd last Soulcast and accidentally turned a goblet into blood. "I need a truth."

"You have given enough," Pattern said. "Now. See."

The ship vanished.

Everything . . . popped. The walls, the furniture, it all shattered into little globes of black glass. Shallan prepared herself to fall into the ocean of those glass beads, but instead she dropped onto solid ground.

She stood in a place with a black sky and a tiny, distant sun. The ground beneath her reflected light. Obsidian? Each way she turned, the ground was made of that same blackness. Nearby, the spheres—like those that would hold Stormlight, but dark and small—bounced to a rest on the ground.

Trees, like growing crystal, clustered here and there. The limbs were spiky and glassy, without leaves. Nearby, little lights hung in the air, flames without their candles. *People,* she realized. *Those are each a person's mind, reflected here in the Cognitive Realm.* Smaller ones were scattered about her feet, dozens upon dozens, but so small she almost couldn't make them out. *The minds of fish?*

She turned around and came face-to-face with a creature that had a symbol for a head. Startled, she screamed and jumped back. These things . . . they had haunted her . . . they . . .

It was Pattern. He stood tall and willowy, but slightly indistinct, translucent. The complex pattern of his head, with its sharp lines and impossible geometries, seemed to have no eyes. He stood with hands behind his back, wearing a robe that seemed too stiff to be cloth.

"Go," he said. "Choose."

"Choose what?" she said, Stormlight escaping her lips.

"Your ship."

He did not have eyes, but she thought she could follow his gaze toward one of the little spheres on the glassy ground. She snatched it, and suddenly was given the impression of a ship.

The *Wind's Pleasure.* A ship that had been cared for, loved. It had carried its passengers well for years and years, owned by Tozbek and his father before him. An old ship, but not ancient, still reliable. A proud ship. It manifested here as a sphere.

It could actually think. The ship could think. Or . . . well, it reflected the thoughts of the people who served on it, knew it, thought about it.

"I need you to change," Shallan whispered to it, cradling the bead in her hands. It was too heavy for its size, as if the entire weight of the ship had been compressed to this singular bead.

"No," the reply came, though it was Pattern who spoke. "No, I cannot. I must serve. I am happy."

Shallan looked to him.

"I will intercede," Pattern repeated. ". . . Translate. You are not ready."

Shallan looked back to the bead in her hands. "I have Stormlight. Lots of it. I will give it to you."

"No!" the reply seemed angry. "I serve."

It really wanted to stay a ship. She could feel it, the pride it took, the reinforcement of years of service.

"They are dying," she whispered.

"No!"

"You can feel them dying. Their blood on your deck. One by one, the people you serve will be cut down."

She could feel it herself, could see it in the ship. They were being executed. Nearby, one of the floating candle flames vanished. Three of the eight captives dead, though she did not know which ones.

"There is only one chance to save them," Shallan said. "And that is to change."

"Change," Pattern whispered for the ship.

"If you change, they might escape the evil men who kill," Shallan whispered. "It is uncertain, but they will have a chance to swim. To do something. You can do them a last service, *Wind's Pleasure*. Change for them."

Silence.

"I . . ."

Another light vanished.

"I will change."

It happened in a hectic second; the Stormlight *ripped* from Shallan. She heard distant cracks from the physical world as she withdrew so much Light from the nearby gemstones that they shattered.

Shadesmar vanished.

She was back in Jasnah's cabin.

The floor, walls, and ceiling melted into water.

Shallan was plunged into the icy black depths. She thrashed in the water, dress hampering her movements. All around her, objects sank, the common artifacts of human life.

Frantic, she searched for the surface. Originally, she'd had some vague idea of swimming out and helping untie the sailors, if they were bound. Now, however, she found herself desperately even trying to find the way up.

As if the darkness itself had come alive, something wrapped around her.

It pulled her farther into the deep.

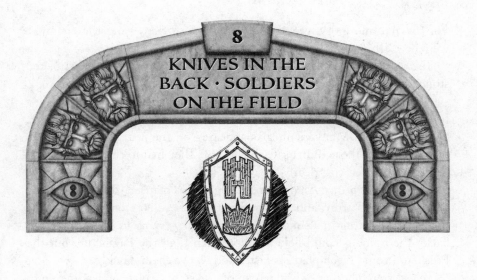

I seek not to use my grief as an excuse, but it is an explanation.
People act strangely soon after encountering an unexpected loss.
Though Jasnah had been away for some time, her loss was unex-
pected. I, like many, assumed her to be immortal.

—From the journal of Navani Kholin, Jesesach 1174

T he familiar scraping of wood as a bridge slid into place. The stomping of feet in unison, first a flat sound on stone, then the ringing
thump of boots on wood. The distant calls of scouts, shouting back
the all-clear.

The sounds of a plateau run were familiar to Dalinar. Once, he had craved
these sounds. He'd been impatient between runs, longing for the chance to
strike down Parshendi with his Blade, to win wealth and recognition.

That Dalinar had been seeking to cover up his shame—the shame of
lying slumped in a drunken stupor while his brother fought an assassin.

The setting of a plateau run was uniform: bare, jagged rocks, mostly the
same dull color as the stone surface they sat on, broken only by the occasional cluster of closed rockbuds. Even those, as their name implied, could
be mistaken for more rocks. There was nothing but more of the same from
here where you stood, all the way out to the far horizon; and everything
you'd brought with you, everything human, was dwarfed by the vastness
of these endless, fractured plains and deadly chasms.

Over the years, this activity had become rote. Marching beneath that
white sun like molten steel. Crossing gap after gap. Eventually, plateau runs
had become less something to anticipate and more a dogged obligation.

For Gavilar and glory, yes, but mainly because they—and the enemy—were here. This was what you did.

The scents of a plateau run were the scents of a great stillness: baked stone, dried crem, long-traveled winds.

Most recently, Dalinar was coming to detest plateau runs. They were a frivolity, a waste of life. They weren't about fulfilling the Vengeance Pact, but about greed. Many gemhearts appeared on the near plateaus, convenient to reach. Those didn't sate the Alethi. They had to reach farther, toward assaults that cost dearly.

Ahead, Highprince Aladar's men fought on a plateau. They had arrived before Dalinar's army, and the conflict told a familiar story. Men against Parshendi, fighting in a sinuous line, each army trying to shove the other back. The humans could field far more men than the Parshendi, but the Parshendi could reach plateaus faster and secure them quickly.

The scattered bodies of bridgemen on the staging plateau, leading up to the chasm, attested to the danger of charging an entrenched foe. Dalinar did not miss the dark expressions on his bodyguards' faces as they surveyed the dead. Aladar, like most of the other highprinces, used Sadeas's philosophy on bridge runs. Quick, brutal assaults that treated manpower as an expendable resource. It hadn't always been this way. In the past, bridges had been carried by armored troops, but success bred imitation.

The warcamps needed a constant influx of cheap slaves to feed the monster. That meant a growing plague of slavers and bandits roaming the Unclaimed Hills, trading in flesh. *Another thing I'll have to change,* Dalinar thought.

Aladar himself didn't fight, but had instead set up a command center on an adjacent plateau. Dalinar pointed toward the flapping banner, and one of his large mechanical bridges rolled into place. Pulled by chulls and full of gears, levers, and cams, the bridges protected the men who worked them. They were also very slow. Dalinar waited with self-disciplined patience as the workers ratcheted the bridge down, spanning the chasm between this plateau and the one where Aladar's banner flew.

Once the bridge was in position and locked, his bodyguard—led by one of Captain Kaladin's darkeyed officers—trotted onto it, spears to shoulders. Dalinar had promised Kaladin his men would not have to fight except to defend him. Once they were across, Dalinar kicked Gallant into motion to cross to Aladar's command plateau. Dalinar felt too light on the stallion's back—the lack of Shardplate. In the many years since he'd obtained his suit, he'd never gone out onto a battlefield without it.

Today, however, he didn't ride to battle—not truly. Behind him, Adolin's own personal banner flew, and he led the bulk of Dalinar's armies to assault the plateau where Aladar's men already fought. Dalinar didn't send any orders regarding how the assault should go. His son had been trained well, and he was ready to take battlefield command—with General Khal at his side, of course, for advice.

Yes, from now on, Adolin would lead the battles.

Dalinar would change the world.

He rode toward Aladar's command tent. This was the first plateau run following his proclamation requiring the armies to work together. The fact that Aladar had come as commanded, and Roion had not—even though the target plateau was closest to Roion's warcamp—was a victory unto itself. A small encouragement, but Dalinar would take what he could get.

He found Highprince Aladar watching from a small pavilion set up on a secure, raised part of this plateau overlooking the battlefield. A perfect location for a command post. Aladar was a Shardbearer, though he commonly lent his Plate and Blade to one of his officers during battles, preferring to lead tactically from behind the battle lines. A practiced Shardbearer could mentally command a Blade to not dissolve when he let go of it, though—in an emergency—Aladar could summon it to himself, making it vanish from the hands of his officer in an eyeblink, then appear in his own hands ten heartbeats later. Lending a Blade required a great deal of trust on both sides.

Dalinar dismounted. His horse, Gallant, glared at the groom who tried to take him, and Dalinar patted the horse on the neck. "He'll be fine on his own, son," he said to the groom. Most common grooms didn't know what to do with one of the Ryshadium anyway.

Trailed by his bridgeman guards, Dalinar joined Aladar, who stood at the edge of the plateau, overseeing the battlefield ahead and just below. Slender and completely bald, the man had skin a darker tan than most Alethi. He stood with hands behind his back, and wore a sharp traditional uniform with a skirtlike takama, though he wore a modern jacket above it, cut to match the takama.

It was a style Dalinar had never seen before. Aladar also wore a thin mustache and a tuft of hair beneath his lip, again an unconventional choice. Aladar was powerful enough, and renowned enough, to make his own fashion—and he did so, often setting trends.

"Dalinar," Aladar said, nodding to him. "I thought you weren't going to fight on plateau runs any longer."

"I'm not," Dalinar said, nodding toward Adolin's banner. There, soldiers streamed across Dalinar's bridges to join the battle. The plateau was small enough that many of Aladar's men had to withdraw to make way, something they were obviously all too eager to do.

"You almost lost this day," Dalinar noted. "It is well that you had support." Below, Dalinar's troops restored order to the battlefield and pushed against the Parshendi.

"Perhaps," Aladar said. "Yet in the past, I was victorious in one out of three assaults. Having support will mean I win a few more, certainly, but will also cost half my earnings. Assuming the king even assigns me any. I'm not convinced that I'll be better off in the long run."

"But this way, you lose fewer men," Dalinar said. "And the total winnings for the entire army will rise. The honor of the—"

"Don't talk to me about honor, Dalinar. I can't pay my soldiers with honor, and I can't use it to keep the other highprinces from snapping at my neck. Your plan favors the weakest among us and undercuts the successful."

"Fine," Dalinar snapped, "honor has no value to you. You will *still* obey, Aladar, because your king demands it. That is the only reason you need. You will do as told."

"Or?" Aladar said.

"Ask Yenev."

Aladar started as if slapped. Ten years back, Highprince Yenev had refused to accept the unification of Alethkar. At Gavilar's order, Sadeas had dueled the man. And killed him.

"Threats?" Aladar asked.

"Yes." Dalinar turned to look the shorter man in the eyes. "I'm done cajoling, Aladar. I'm done asking. When you disobey Elhokar, you mock my brother and what he stood for. I *will* have a unified kingdom."

"Amusing," Aladar said. "Good of you to mention Gavilar, as he didn't bring the kingdom together with honor. He did it with knives in the back and soldiers on the field, cutting the heads off any who resisted. Are we back to that again, then? Such things don't sound much like the fine words of your precious book."

Dalinar ground his teeth, turning away to watch the battlefield. His first instinct was to tell Aladar he was an officer under Dalinar's command, and take the man to task for his tone. Treat him like a recruit in need of correction.

But what if Aladar just ignored him? Would he *force* the man to obey? Dalinar didn't have the troops for it.

He found himself annoyed—more at himself than at Aladar. He'd come on this plateau run not to fight, but to talk. To persuade. Navani was right. Dalinar needed more than brusque words and military commands to save this kingdom. He needed loyalty, not fear.

But storms take him, *how?* What persuading he'd done in life, he'd accomplished with a sword in hand and a fist to the face. Gavilar had always been the one with the right words, the one who could make people listen.

Dalinar had no business trying to be a politician.

Half the lads on that battlefield probably didn't think they had any business being soldiers, at first, a part of him whispered. *You don't have the luxury of being bad at this. Don't complain. Change.*

"The Parshendi are pushing too hard," Aladar said to his generals. "They want to shove us off the plateau. Tell the men to give a little and let the Parshendi lose their advantage of footing; that will let us surround them."

The generals nodded, one calling out orders.

Dalinar narrowed his eyes at the battlefield, reading it. "No," he said softly.

The general stopped giving orders. Aladar glanced at Dalinar.

"The Parshendi are preparing to pull back," Dalinar said.

"They certainly don't act like it."

"They want some room to breathe," Dalinar said, reading the swirl of combat below. "They nearly have the gemheart harvested. They will continue to push hard, but will break into a quick retreat around the chrysalis to buy time for the final harvesting. That's what you'll need to stop."

The Parshendi surged forward.

"I took point on this run," Aladar said. "By your own rules, I get final say over our tactics."

"I observe only," Dalinar said. "I'm not even commanding my own army today. You may choose your tactics, and I will not interfere."

Aladar considered, then cursed softly. "Assume Dalinar is correct. Prepare the men for a withdrawal by the Parshendi. Send a strike team forward to secure the chrysalis, which should be almost opened up."

The generals set up the new details, and messengers raced off with the tactical orders. Aladar and Dalinar watched, side by side, as the Parshendi shoved forward. That singing of theirs hovered over the battlefield.

Then they pulled back, careful as always to respectfully step over the bodies of the dead. Ready for this, the human troops rushed after. Led by Adolin in gleaming Plate, a strike force of fresh troops broke through the Parshendi line and reached the chrysalis. Other human troops poured through the gap they opened, shoving the Parshendi to the flanks, turning the Parshendi withdrawal into a tactical disaster.

In minutes, the Parshendi had abandoned the plateau, jumping away and fleeing.

"Damnation," Aladar said softly. "I *hate* that you're so good at this."

Dalinar narrowed his eyes, noticing that some of the fleeing Parshendi stopped on a plateau a short distance from the battlefield. They lingered there, though much of their force continued on away.

Dalinar waved for one of Aladar's servants to hand him a spyglass, then he raised it, focusing on that group. A figure stood at the edge of the plateau out there, a figure in glistening armor.

The Parshendi Shardbearer, he thought. *The one from the battle at the Tower. He almost killed me.*

Dalinar didn't remember much from that encounter. He'd been beaten near senseless toward the end of it. This Shardbearer hadn't participated in today's battle. Why? Surely with a Shardbearer, they could have opened the chrysalis sooner.

Dalinar felt a disturbing pit inside of him. This one fact, the watching Shardbearer, changed his understanding of the battle entirely. He thought he'd been able to read what was going on. Now it occurred to him that the enemy's tactics were more opaque than he'd assumed.

"Are some of them still out there?" Aladar asked. "Watching?"

Dalinar nodded, lowering his spyglass.

"Have they done that before in any battle you've fought?"

Dalinar shook his head.

Aladar mulled for a moment, then gave orders for his men on the plateau to remain alert, with scouts posted to watch for a surprise return of the Parshendi.

"Thank you," Aladar added, grudgingly, turning to Dalinar. "Your advice proved helpful."

"You trusted me when it came to tactics," Dalinar said, turning to him. "Why not try trusting me in what is best for this kingdom?"

Aladar studied him. Behind, soldiers cheered their victory and Adolin ripped the gemheart free from the chrysalis. Others fanned out to watch for a return attack, but none came.

"I wish I could, Dalinar," Aladar finally said. "But this isn't about you. It's about the other highprinces. Maybe I could trust you, but I'll never trust them. You're asking me to risk too much of myself. The others would do to me what Sadeas did to you on the Tower."

"What if I can bring the others around? What if I can prove to you that they're worthy of trust? What if I can change the direction of this kingdom, and this war? Will you follow me then?"

"No," Aladar said. "I'm sorry." He turned away, calling for his horse.

The trip back was miserable. They'd won the day, but Aladar kept his distance. How could Dalinar do so many things so right, yet still be unable to persuade men like Aladar? And what did it mean that the Parshendi were changing tactics on the battlefield, not committing their Shardbearer? Were they too afraid to lose their Shards?

When, at long last, Dalinar returned to his bunker in the warcamps—after seeing to his men and sending a report to the king—he found an unexpected letter waiting for him.

He sent for Navani to read him the words. Dalinar stood waiting in his private study, staring at the wall that had borne the strange glyphs. Those had been sanded away, the scratches hidden, but the pale patch of stone whispered.

Sixty-two days.

Sixty-two days to come up with an answer. Well, sixty now. Not much time to save a kingdom, to prepare for the worst. The ardents would condemn the prophecy as a prank at best, or blasphemous at worst. To foretell the future was forbidden. It was of the Voidbringers. Even games of chance were suspect, for they incited men to look for the secrets of what was to come.

He believed anyway. For he suspected his own hand had written those words.

Navani arrived and looked over the letter, then started reading aloud. It turned out to be from an old friend who was going to arrive soon on the Shattered Plains—and who might provide a solution to Dalinar's problems.

9

WALKING THE GRAVE

I wish to think that had I not been under sorrow's thumb, I would have seen earlier the approaching dangers. Yet in all honesty, I'm not certain anything could have been done.

—From the journal of Navani Kholin, Jesesach 1174

Kaladin led the way down into the chasms, as was his right.

They used a rope ladder, as they had in Sadeas's army. Those ladders had been unsavory things, the ropes frayed and stained with moss, the planks battered by far too many highstorms. Kaladin had never lost a man because of those storming ladders, but he'd always worried.

This one was brand new. He knew that for a fact, as Rind the quartermaster had scratched his head at the request, and then had one built to Kaladin's specifications. It was sturdy and well made, like Dalinar's army itself.

Kaladin reached the bottom with a final hop. Syl floated down and landed on his shoulder as he held up a sphere to survey the chasm bottom. The single sapphire broam was worth more by itself than the entirety of his wages as a bridgeman.

In Sadeas's army, the chasms had been a frequent destination for bridgemen. Kaladin still didn't know if the purpose had been to scavenge every possible resource from the Shattered Plains, or if it had really been about finding something menial—and will-breaking—for bridgemen to do between runs.

The chasm bottom here, however, was untouched. There were no paths cut through the snarl of stormleavings on the ground, and there were no scratched messages or instructions in the lichen on the walls. Like the other chasms, this one opened up like a vase, wider at the bottom than at the cracked top—a result of waters rushing through during highstorms. The floor was relatively flat, smoothed by the hardened sediment of settling crem.

As he moved forward, Kaladin had to pick his way over all kinds of debris. Broken sticks and logs from trees blown in from across the Plains. Cracked rockbud shells. Countless tangles of dried vines, twisted through one another like discarded yarn.

And bodies, of course.

A lot of corpses ended up in the chasms. Whenever men lost their battle to seize a plateau, they had to retreat and leave their dead behind. Storms! Sadeas often left the corpses behind even if he won—and bridgemen he'd leave wounded, abandoned, even if they could have been saved.

After a highstorm, the dead ended up here, in the chasms. And since storms blew westward, toward the warcamps, the bodies washed in this direction. Kaladin found it hard to move without stepping on bones entwined in the accumulated foliage on the chasm floor.

He picked his way through as respectfully as he could as Rock reached the bottom behind him, uttering a quiet phrase in his native tongue. Kaladin couldn't tell if it was a curse or a prayer. Syl moved from Kaladin's shoulder, zipping into the air, then streaking in an arc to the ground. There, she formed into what he thought of as her true shape, that of a young woman with a simple dress that frayed to mist just below the knees. She perched on a branch and stared at a femur poking up through the moss.

She didn't like violence. He wasn't certain if, even now, she understood death. She spoke of it like a child trying to grasp something beyond her.

"What a mess," Teft said as he reached the bottom. "Bah! This place hasn't seen any kind of care at all."

"It is a grave," Rock said. "We walk in a grave."

"All of the chasms are graves," Teft said, his voice echoing in the dank confines. "This one's just a messy grave."

"Hard to find death that isn't messy, Teft," Kaladin said.

Teft grunted, then started to greet the new recruits as they reached the bottom. Moash and Skar were watching over Dalinar and his sons as they attended some lighteyed feast—something that Kaladin was glad to be able to avoid. Instead, he'd come with Teft down here.

They were joined by the forty bridgemen—two from each reorganized crew—that Teft was training with the hope that they'd make good sergeants for their own crews.

"Take a good look, lads," Teft said to them. "This is where we come from. This is why some call us the order of bone. We're not going to make you go through everything we did, and be glad! We could have been swept away by a highstorm at any moment. Now, with Dalinar Kholin's storm-wardens to guide us, we won't have nearly as much risk—and we'll be staying close to the exit just in case . . ."

Kaladin folded his arms, watching Teft instruct as Rock handed practice spears to the men. Teft himself carried no spear, and though he was shorter than the bridgemen who gathered around him—wearing simple soldiers' uniforms—they seemed thoroughly intimidated.

What else did you expect? Kaladin thought. *They're bridgemen. A stiff breeze could quell them.*

Still, Teft looked completely in control. Comfortably so. This was right. Something about it was just . . . right.

A swarm of small glowing orbs materialized around Kaladin's head, spren the shape of golden spheres that darted this way and that. He started, looking at them. Gloryspren. Storms. He felt as if he hadn't seen the like in years.

Syl zipped up into the air and joined them, giggling and spinning around Kaladin's head. "Feeling proud of yourself?"

"Teft," Kaladin said. "He's a leader."

"Of course he is. You gave him a rank, didn't you?"

"No," Kaladin said. "I didn't give it to him. He claimed it. Come on. Let's walk."

She nodded, alighting in the air and settling down, her legs crossed at the knees as if she were primly seating herself in an invisible chair. She continued to hover there, moving exactly in step with him.

"Giving up all pretense of obeying natural laws again, I see," he said.

"*Natural* laws?" Syl said, finding the concept amusing. "Laws are of men, Kaladin. Nature doesn't have them!"

"If I toss something upward, it comes back down."

"Except when it doesn't."

"It's a law."

"No," Syl said, looking upward. "It's more like . . . more like an agreement among friends."

He looked at her, raising an eyebrow.

"We have to be consistent," she said, leaning in conspiratorially. "Or we'll break your brains."

He snorted, walking around a clump of bones and sticks pierced by a spear. Cankered with rust, it looked like a monument.

"Oh, come on," Syl said, tossing her hair. "That was worth *at least* a chuckle."

Kaladin kept walking.

"A snort is *not* a chuckle," Syl said. "I know this because I am intelligent and articulate. You should compliment me now."

"Dalinar Kholin wants to refound the Knights Radiant."

"Yes," Syl said loftily, hanging in the corner of his vision. "A brilliant idea. I wish I'd thought of it." She grinned triumphantly, then scowled.

"What?" he said, turning back to her.

"Has it ever struck you as unfair," she said, "that spren cannot attract spren? I should *really* have had some gloryspren of my own there."

"I have to protect Dalinar," Kaladin said, ignoring her complaint. "Not just him, but his family, maybe the king himself. Even though I failed to keep someone from sneaking into Dalinar's rooms." He still couldn't figure out how someone had managed to get in. Unless it hadn't been a person. "Could a spren have made those glyphs on the wall?" Syl had carried a leaf once. She had *some* physical form, just not much.

"I don't know," she said, glancing to the side. "I've seen . . ."

"What?"

"Spren like red lightning," Syl said softly. "Dangerous spren. Spren I haven't seen before. I catch them in the distance, on occasion. Stormspren? Something dangerous *is* coming. About that, the glyphs are right."

He chewed on that for a while, then finally stopped and looked at her. "Syl, are there others like me?"

Her face grew solemn. "Oh."

"Oh?"

"Oh, *that* question."

"You've been expecting it, then?"

"Yeah. Sort of."

"So you've had plenty of time to think about a good answer," Kaladin said, folding his arms and leaning back against a somewhat dry portion of the wall. "That makes me wonder if you've come up with a solid explanation or a solid lie."

"Lie?" Syl said, aghast. "Kaladin! What do you think I am? A Cryptic?"

"And what is a Cryptic?"

Syl, still perched as if on a seat, sat up straight and cocked her head. "I actually . . . I actually have no idea. Huh."

"Syl . . ."

"I'm *serious*, Kaladin! I don't know. I don't remember." She grabbed her hair, one clump of white translucence in each hand, and pulled sideways.

He frowned, then pointed. "That . . ."

"I saw a woman do it in the market," Syl said, yanking her hair to the sides again. "It means I'm frustrated. I think it's supposed to hurt. So . . . ow? Anyway, it's not that I don't want to tell you what I know. I do! I just . . . I don't *know* what I know."

"That doesn't make sense."

"Well, imagine how frustrating it *feels*!"

Kaladin sighed, then continued along the chasm, passing pools of stagnant water clotted with debris. A scattering of enterprising rockbuds grew stunted along one chasm wall. They must not get much light down here.

He breathed in deeply the scents of overloaded life. Moss and mold. Most of the bodies here were mere bone, though he did steer clear of one patch of ground crawling with the red dots of rotspren. Just beside it, a group of frillblooms wafted their delicate fanlike fronds in the air, and those danced with green specks of lifespren. Life and death shook hands here in the chasms.

He explored several of the chasm's branching paths. It felt odd to not know this area; he'd learned the chasms closest to Sadeas's camp better than the camp itself. As he walked, the chasm grew deeper and the area opened up. He made a few marks on the wall.

Along one fork he found a round open area with little debris. He noted it, then walked back, marking the wall again before taking another branch. Eventually, they entered another place where the chasm opened up, widening into a roomy space.

"Coming here was dangerous," Syl said.

"Into the chasms?" Kaladin asked. "There aren't going to be any chasmfiends this close to the warcamps."

"No. I meant for me, coming into this realm before I found you. It was dangerous."

"Where were you before?"

"Another place. With lots of spren. I can't remember well . . . it had lights in the air. Living lights."

"Like lifespren."

"Yes. And no. Coming here risked death. Without you, without a mind born of this realm, I couldn't think. Alone, I was just another windspren."

"But you're not windspren," Kaladin said, kneeling beside a large pool of water. "You're honorspren."

"Yes," Syl said.

Kaladin closed his hand around his sphere, bringing near-darkness to the cavernous space. It was day above, but that crack of sky was distant, unreachable.

Mounds of flood-borne refuse fell into shadows that seemed almost to give them flesh again. Heaps of bones took on the semblance of limp arms, of corpses piled high. In a moment, Kaladin remembered it. Charging with a yell toward lines of Parshendi archers. His friends dying on barren plateaus, thrashing in their own blood.

The thunder of hooves on stone. The incongruous chanting of alien tongues. The cries of men both lighteyed and dark. A world that cared nothing for bridgemen. They were refuse. Sacrifices to be cast into the chasms and carried away by the cleansing floods.

This was their true home, these rents in the earth, these places lower than any other. As his eyes adjusted to the dimness, the memories of death receded, though he would never be free of them. He would forever bear those scars upon his memory like the many upon his flesh. Like the ones on his forehead.

The pool in front of him glowed a deep violet. He'd noticed it earlier, but in the light of his sphere it had been harder to see. Now, in the dimness, the pool could reveal its eerie radiance.

Syl landed on the side of the pool, looking like a woman standing on an ocean's shore. Kaladin frowned, leaning down to inspect her more closely. She seemed . . . different. Had her face changed shape?

"There *are* others like you," Syl whispered. "I do not know them, but I know that other spren are trying, in their own way, to reclaim what was lost."

She looked to him, and her face now had its familiar form. The fleeting change had been so subtle, Kaladin wasn't sure if he'd imagined it.

"I am the only honorspren who has come," Syl said. "I . . ." She seemed to be stretching to remember. "I was forbidden. I came anyway. To find you."

"You knew me?"

"No. But I knew I'd find you." She smiled. "I spent the time with my cousins, searching."

"The windspren."

"Without the bond, I am basically one of them," she said. "Though they don't have the capacity to do what we do. And what we do is important. So important that I left everything, defying the Stormfather, to come. You saw him. In the storm."

The hair stood up on Kaladin's arms. He had indeed seen a being in the storm. A face as vast as the sky itself. Whatever the thing was—spren, Herald, or god—it had not tempered its storms for Kaladin during that day he'd spent strung up.

"We are needed, Kaladin," Syl said softly. She waved for him, and he lowered his hand to the shore of the tiny violet ocean glowing softly in the chasm. She stepped onto his hand, and he stood up, lifting her.

She walked up his fingers and he could actually feel a little weight, which was unusual. He turned his hand as she stepped up until she was perched on one finger, her hands clasped behind her back, meeting his eyes as he held that finger up before his face.

"You," Syl said. "You're going to need to become what Dalinar Kholin is looking for. Don't let him search in vain."

"They'll take it from me, Syl," Kaladin whispered. "They'll find a way to take *you* from me."

"That's foolishness. You know that it is."

"I know it is, but I *feel* it isn't. They broke me, Syl. I'm not what you think I am. I'm no Radiant."

"That's not what I saw," Syl said. "On the battlefield after Sadeas's betrayal, when men were trapped, abandoned. That day I saw a hero."

He looked into her eyes. She had pupils, though they were created only from the differing shades of white and blue, like the rest of her. She glowed more softly than the weakest of spheres, but it was enough to light his finger. She smiled, seeming utterly confident in him.

At least one of them was.

"I'll try," Kaladin whispered. A promise.

"Kaladin?" The voice was Rock's, with his distinctive Horneater accent. He pronounced the name "kal-ah-*deen*," instead of the normal "*kal*-a-din."

Syl zipped off Kaladin's finger, becoming a ribbon of light and flitting over to Rock. He showed respect to her in his Horneater way, touching his shoulders in turn with one hand, and then raising the hand to his forehead. She giggled; her profound solemnity had become girlish joy in moments. Syl might only be a cousin to windspren, but she obviously shared their impish nature.

"Hey," Kaladin said, nodding to Rock, and fishing in the pool. He came out with an amethyst broam and held it up. Somewhere up there on the Plains, a lighteyes had died with this in his pocket. "Riches, if we still were bridgemen."

"We are still bridgemen," Rock said, coming over. He plucked the sphere from Kaladin's fingers. "And this is still riches. Ha! Spices they have for us to requisition are *tuma'alki*! I have promised I will not fix dung for the men, but it is hard, with soldiers being accustomed to food that is not much better." He held up the sphere. "I will use *him* to buy better, eh?"

"Sure," Kaladin said. Syl landed on Rock's shoulder and became a young woman, then sat down.

Rock eyed her and tried to bow to his own shoulder.

"Stop tormenting him, Syl," Kaladin said.

"It's so fun!"

"You are to be praised for your aid of us, *mafah'liki*," Rock said to her. "I will endure whatever you wish of me. And now that I am free, I can create a shrine fitting to you."

"A *shrine*?" Syl said, eyes widening. "Ooooh."

"Syl!" Kaladin said. "Stop it. Rock, I saw a good place for the men to practice. It's back a couple of branches. I marked it on the walls."

"Yes, we saw this thing," Rock said. "Teft has led the men there. It is strange. This place is frightening; it is a place that nobody comes, and yet the new recruits . . ."

"They're opening up," Kaladin guessed.

"Yes. How did you know this thing would happen?"

"They were there," Kaladin said, "in Sadeas's warcamp, when we were assigned to exclusive duty in the chasms. They saw what we did, and have heard stories of our training here. By bringing them down here, we're inviting them in, like an initiation."

Teft had been having problems getting the former bridgemen to show interest in his training. The old soldier was always sputtering at them in annoyance. They'd insisted on remaining with Kaladin rather than going free, so why wouldn't they learn?

They had needed to be invited. Not just with words.

"Yes, well," Rock said. "Sigzil sent me. He wishes to know if you are ready to practice your abilities."

Kaladin took a deep breath, glancing at Syl, then nodded. "Yes. Bring him. We can do it here."

"Ha! Finally. I will fetch him."

RED CARPET
ONCE WHITE

SIX YEARS AGO

The world ended, and Shallan was to blame.

"Pretend it never happened," her father whispered. He wiped something wet from her cheek. His thumb came back red. "I'll protect you."

Was the room shaking? No, that was Shallan. Trembling. She felt so small. Eleven had seemed old to her, once. But she was a child, still a child. So small.

She looked up at her father with a shudder. She couldn't blink; her eyes were frozen open.

Father started to whisper, blinking tears. "Now go to sleep in chasms deep, with darkness all around you . . ."

A familiar lullaby, one he always used to sing to her. In the room behind him, dark corpses stretched out on the floor. A red carpet once white.

"Though rock and dread may be your bed, so sleep my baby dear."

Father gathered her into his arms, and she felt her skin squirming. No. No, this affection wasn't right. A monster should not be held in love. A monster who killed, who murdered. *No.*

She could not move.

"Now comes the storm, but you'll be warm, the wind will rock your basket . . ."

Father carried Shallan over the body of a woman in blue and gold. Little blood there. It was the man who bled. Mother lay facedown, so Shallan couldn't see the eyes. The horrible eyes.

Almost, Shallan could imagine that the lullaby was the end to a nightmare. That it was night, that she had awakened screaming, and her father was singing her to sleep . . .

"The crystals fine will glow sublime, so sleep my baby dear."

They passed Father's strongbox set into the wall. It glowed brightly, light streaming from the cracks around the closed door. A monster was inside.

"And with a song, it won't be long, you'll sleep my baby dear."

With Shallan in his arms, Father left the room and closed the door on the corpses.

Shallan made
landfall here.
— Nazh

11

AN ILLUSION
OF PERCEPTION

*But, understandably, we were focused on Sadeas. His betrayal was
still fresh, and I saw its signs each day as I passed empty barracks
and grieving widows. We knew that Sadeas would not simply rest
upon his slaughters in pride. More was coming.*

—From the journal of Navani Kholin, Jesesach 1174

Shallan awoke mostly dry, lying on an uneven rock that rose from the ocean. Waves lapped at her toes, though she could barely feel them through the numbness. She groaned, lifting her cheek from the wet granite. There was land nearby, and the surf sounded against it with a low roar. In the other direction stretched only the endless blue sea.

She was cold and her head throbbed as if she'd banged it repeatedly against a wall, but she was alive. Somehow. She raised her hand—rubbing at the itchy dried salt on her forehead—and hacked out a ragged cough. Her hair stuck to the sides of her face, and her dress was stained from the water and the seaweed on the rock.

How . . . ?

Then she saw it, a large brown shell in the water, almost invisible as it moved toward the horizon. The santhid.

She stumbled to her feet, clinging to the pointy tip of her rock perch. Woozy, she watched the creature until it was gone.

Something hummed beside her. Pattern formed his usual shape on the surface of the churning sea, translucent as if he were a small wave himself.

"Did . . ." She coughed, clearing her voice, then groaned and sat down on the rock. "Did anyone else make it?"

"Make?" Pattern asked.

"Other people. The sailors. Did they escape?"

"Uncertain," Pattern said, in his humming voice. "Ship . . . Gone. Splashing. Nothing seen."

"The santhid. It rescued me." How had it known what to do? Were they intelligent? Could she have somehow communicated with it? Had she missed an opportunity to—

She almost started laughing as she realized the direction her thoughts were going. She'd nearly drowned, Jasnah was dead, the crew of the *Wind's Pleasure* likely murdered or swallowed by the sea! Instead of mourning them or marveling at her survival, Shallan was engaging in scholarly speculation?

That's what you do, a deeply buried part of herself accused her. *You distract yourself. You refuse to think about things that bother you.*

But that was how she survived.

Shallan wrapped her arms around herself for warmth on her stone perch and stared out over the ocean. She *had* to face the truth. Jasnah was dead.

Jasnah was dead.

Shallan felt like weeping. A woman so brilliant, so amazing, was just . . . gone. Jasnah had been trying to save everyone, protect the world itself. And they'd killed her for it. The suddenness of what had happened left Shallan stunned, and so she sat there, shivering and cold and just staring out at the ocean. Her mind felt as numb as her feet.

Shelter. She'd need shelter . . . something. Thoughts of the sailors, of Jasnah's research, those were of less immediate concern. Shallan was stranded on a stretch of coast that was almost completely uninhabited, in lands that froze at night. As she'd been sitting, the tide had slowly withdrawn, and the gap between herself and the shore was not nearly as wide as it had been. That was fortunate, as she couldn't really swim.

She forced herself to move, though lifting her limbs was like trying to budge fallen tree trunks. She gritted her teeth and slipped into the water. She could still feel its biting cold. Not completely numb, then.

"Shallan?" Pattern asked.

"We can't sit out here forever," Shallan said, clinging to the rock and getting all the way down into the water. Her feet brushed rock beneath, and so she dared let go, half swimming in a splashing mess as she made her way toward the land.

She probably swallowed half the water in the bay as she fought through the frigid waves until she finally was able to walk. Dress and hair streaming, she coughed and stumbled up onto the sandy shore, then fell to her knees. The ground here was strewn with seaweed of a dozen different varieties that writhed beneath her feet, pulling away, slimy and slippery. Cremlings and larger crabs scuttled in every direction, some nearby making clicking sounds at her, as if to ward her off.

She dully thought it a testament to her exhaustion that she hadn't even considered—before leaving the rock—the sea predators she'd read about: a dozen different kinds of large crustaceans that were happy to have a leg to snip free and chew on. Fearspren suddenly began to wiggle out of the sand, purple and sluglike.

That was silly. Now she was frightened? *After* her swim? The spren soon vanished.

Shallan glanced back at her rock perch. The santhid probably hadn't been able to deposit her any closer, as the water grew too shallow. Stormfather. She was lucky to be alive.

Despite her mounting anxiety, Shallan knelt down and traced a glyphward into the sand in prayer. She didn't have a means of burning it. For now, she had to assume the Almighty would accept this. She bowed her head and sat reverently for ten heartbeats.

Then she stood and, hope against hope, began to search for other survivors. This stretch of coast was pocketed with numerous beaches and inlets. She put off seeking shelter, instead walking for a long time down the shoreline. The beach was composed of sand that was coarser than she'd expected. It certainly didn't match the idyllic stories she'd read, and it ground unpleasantly against her toes as she walked. Alongside her, it rose in a moving shape as Pattern kept pace with her, humming anxiously.

Shallan passed branches, even bits of wood that *might* have belonged to ships. She saw no people and found no footprints. As the day grew long, she gave up, sitting down on a weathered stone. She hadn't noticed that her feet were sliced and reddened from walking on the rocks. Her hair was a complete mess. Her safepouch had a few spheres in it, but none were infused. They'd be of no use unless she found civilization.

Firewood, she thought. She'd gather that and build a fire. In the night, that might signal other survivors.

Or it might signal pirates, bandits, or the shipboard assassins, if they had survived.

Shallan grimaced. What was she going to do?

Build a small fire to keep warm, she decided. *Shield it, then watch the night for other fires. If you see one, try to inspect it without getting too close.*

A fine plan, except for the fact that she'd lived her entire life in a stately manor, with servants to light fires for her. She'd never started one in a hearth, let alone in the wilderness.

Storms . . . she'd be lucky not to die of exposure out here. Or starvation. What would she do when a highstorm came? When was the next one? Tomorrow night? Or was it the night after.

"Come!" Pattern said.

He vibrated in the sand. Grains jumped and shook as he spoke, rising and falling around him. *I recognize that . . .* Shallan thought, frowning at him. *Sand on a plate. Kabsal . . .*

"Come!" Pattern repeated, more urgent.

"What?" Shallan said, standing up. Storms, but she was tired. She could barely move. "Did you find someone?"

"Yes!"

That got her attention immediately. She didn't ask further questions, but instead followed Pattern, who moved excitedly down the coast. Would he know the difference between someone dangerous and someone friendly? For the moment, cold and exhausted, she almost didn't care.

He stopped beside something halfway submerged in the water and seaweed at the edge of the ocean. Shallan frowned.

A trunk. Not a person, but a large wooden trunk. Shallan's breath caught in her throat, and she dropped to her knees, working the clasps and pulling open the lid.

Inside, like a glowing treasure, were Jasnah's books and notes, carefully packed away, protected in their waterproof enclosure.

Jasnah might not have survived, but her life's work had.

* *

Shallan knelt down by her improvised firepit. A grouping of rocks, filled with sticks she'd gathered from this little stand of trees. Night was almost upon her.

With it came the shocking cold, as bad as the worst winter back home. Here in the Frostlands, this would be common. Her clothing, which in this humidity hadn't completely dried despite the hours walking, felt like ice.

She did not know how to build a fire, but perhaps she could make one in another way. She fought through her weariness—storms, but she was exhausted—and took out a glowing sphere, one of many she'd found in Jasnah's trunk.

"All right," she whispered. "Let's do this." Shadesmar.

"Mmm . . ." Pattern said. She was learning to interpret his humming. This seemed anxious. "Dangerous."

"Why?"

"What is land here is sea there."

Shallan nodded dully. *Wait. Think.*

That was growing hard, but she forced herself to go over Pattern's words again. When they'd sailed the ocean, and she'd visited Shadesmar, she'd found obsidian ground beneath her. But in Kharbranth, she'd dropped into that ocean of spheres.

"So what do we do?" Shallan asked.

"Go slowly."

Shallan took a deep, cold breath, then nodded. She tried as she had before. Slowly, carefully. It was like . . . like opening her eyes in the morning.

Awareness of another place consumed her. The nearby trees *popped* like bubbles, beads forming in their place and dropping toward a shifting sea of them below. Shallan felt herself falling.

She gasped, then blinked back that awareness, closing her metaphoric eyes. That place vanished, and in a moment, she was back in the stand of trees.

Pattern hummed nervously.

Shallan set her jaw and tried again. More slowly this time, slipping into that place with its strange sky and not-sun. For a moment, she hovered between the worlds, Shadesmar overlaying the world around her like a shadowy afterimage. Holding between the two was difficult.

Use the Light, Pattern said. *Bring them.*

Shallan hesitantly drew the Light into herself. The spheres in the ocean below moved like a school of fish, surging toward her, clinking together. In her exhaustion, Shallan could barely maintain her double state, and she grew woozy, looking down.

She held on, somehow.

Pattern stood beside her, in his form with the stiff clothing and a head made of impossible lines, arms clasped behind his back, and hovering as if in the air. He was tall and imposing on this side, and she absently noticed that he cast a shadow the wrong way, *toward* the distant, cold-seeming sun instead of away from it.

"Good," he said, his voice a deeper hum here. "Good." He cocked his head, and though he had no eyes, turned around as if regarding the place. "I am from here, yet I remember so little . . ."

Shallan had a sense that her time was limited. Kneeling, she reached down and felt at the sticks she'd piled to form the place for her fire. She could feel the sticks—but as she looked into this strange realm, her fingers also found one of the glass beads that had surged up beneath her.

As she touched it, she noticed something sweeping through the air above her. She cringed, looking up to find large, birdlike creatures circling around her in Shadesmar. They were a dark grey and seemed to have no specific shape, their forms blurry.

"What . . ."

"Spren," Pattern said. "Drawn by you. Your . . . tiredness?"

"Exhaustionspren?" she asked, shocked by their size here.

"Yes."

She shivered, then looked down at the sphere beneath her hand. She was dangerously close to falling into Shadesmar completely, and could barely see the impressions of the physical realm around her. Only those beads. She felt as if she would tumble into their sea at any moment.

"Please," Shallan said to the sphere. "I need you to become fire."

Pattern buzzed, speaking with a new voice, interpreting the sphere's words. "I am a stick," he said. He sounded satisfied.

"You could be fire," Shallan said.

"I am a stick."

The stick was not particularly eloquent. She supposed that she shouldn't be surprised.

"Why don't you become fire instead?"

"I am a stick."

"How do I make it change?" Shallan asked of Pattern.

"Mm . . . I do not know. You must persuade it. Offer it truths, I think?" He sounded agitated. "This place is dangerous for you. For us. Please. Speed."

She looked back at the stick.

"You want to burn."

"I am a stick."

"Think how much fun it would be?"

"I am a stick."

"Stormlight," Shallan said. "You could have it! All that I'm holding."

A pause. Finally, "I am a stick."

"Sticks need Stormlight. For . . . things . . ." Shallan blinked away tears of fatigue.

"I am—"

"—a stick," Shallan said. She gripped the sphere, feeling both it and the stick in the physical realm, trying to think through another argument. For a moment, she hadn't felt quite so tired, but it was returning—crashing back upon her. Why . . .

Her Stormlight was running out.

It was gone in a moment, drained from her, and she exhaled, slipping into Shadesmar with a sigh, feeling overwhelmed and exhausted.

She fell into the sea of spheres. That awful blackness, millions of moving bits, consuming her.

She threw herself from Shadesmar.

The spheres expanded outward, growing into sticks and rocks and trees, restoring the world as she knew it. She collapsed into her small stand of trees, heart pounding.

All grew normal around her. No more distant sun, no more sea of spheres. Just frigid cold, a night sky, and biting wind that blew between the trees. The single sphere she'd drained slipped from her fingers, clicking against the stone ground. She leaned back against Jasnah's trunk. Her arms still ached from dragging that up the beach to the trees.

She huddled there, frightened. "Do you know how to make fire?" she asked Pattern. Her teeth chattered. Stormfather. She didn't feel cold anymore, but her teeth were chattering, and her breath was visible as vapor in the starlight.

She found herself growing drowsy. Maybe she should just sleep, then try to deal with it all in the morning.

"Change?" Pattern asked. "Offer the change."

"I tried."

"I know." His vibrations sounded depressed.

Shallan stared at that pile of sticks, feeling utterly useless. What was it Jasnah had said? Control is the basis of all true power? Authority and strength are matters of perception? Well, this was a direct refutation of *that*. Shallan could imagine herself as grand, could act like a queen, but that didn't change a thing out here in the wilderness.

Well, Shallan thought, *I'm not going to sit here and freeze to death. I'll at least freeze to death trying to find help.*

She didn't move, though. Moving was hard. At least here, huddled by the trunk, she didn't have to feel the wind so much. Just lying here until morning . . .

She curled into a ball.

No. This didn't seem right. She coughed, then somehow got to her feet. She stumbled away from her not-fire, dug a sphere from her safepouch, then started walking.

Pattern moved at her feet. Those were bloodier now. She left a red trail on the rock. She couldn't feel the cuts.

She walked and walked.

And walked.

And . . .

Light.

She didn't move any more quickly. She couldn't. But she did keep going, shambling directly toward that pinprick in the darkness. A numb part of her worried that the light was really Nomon, the second moon. That she'd march toward it and fall off the edge of Roshar itself.

So she surprised herself by stumbling right into the middle of a small group of people sitting around a campfire. She blinked, looking from one face to another; then—ignoring the sounds they made, for words were meaningless to her in this state—she walked to the campfire and lay down, curled up, and fell asleep.

⁛

"Brightness?"

Shallan grumbled, rolling over. Her face hurt. No, her *feet* hurt. Her face was nothing compared to that pain.

If she slept a little longer, maybe it would fade. At least for that time. . . .

"B-Brightness?" the voice asked again. "Are you feeling well, yes?"

That was a Thaylen accent. Dredged from deep within her, a light surfaced, bringing memories. The ship. Thaylens. The sailors?

Shallan forced her eyes open. The air smelled faintly of smoke from the still-smoldering fire. The sky was a deep violet, brightening as the sun broke the horizon. She'd slept on hard rock, and her body ached.

She didn't recognize the speaker, a portly Thaylen man with a white beard wearing a knit cap and an old suit and vest, patched in a few inconspicuous places. He wore his white Thaylen eyebrows tucked up over his ears. Not a sailor. A merchant.

Shallan stifled a groan, sitting up. Then, in a moment of panic, she checked her safehand. One of her fingers had slipped out of the sleeve, and she pulled it back in. The Thaylen's eyes flicked toward it, but he said nothing.

"You are well, then?" the man asked. He spoke in Alethi. "We were going to pack to go, you see. Your arrival last night was . . . unexpected. We did not wish to disturb you, but thought perhaps you would want to wake before we depart."

Shallan ran her freehand through her hair, a mess of red locks stuck with twigs. Two other men—tall, hulking, and of Vorin descent—packed up blankets and bedrolls. She'd have killed for one of those during the night. She remembered tossing uncomfortably.

Stilling the needs of nature, she turned and was surprised to see three large chull wagons with cages on the back. Inside were a handful of dirty, shirtless men. It took just a moment for it all to click.

Slavers.

She shoved down an initial burst of panic. Slaving was a perfectly legal profession. Most of the time. Only this was the Frostlands, far from the rule of any group or nation. Who was to say what was legal here and what was not?

Be calm, she told herself forcefully. *They wouldn't have awakened you politely if they were planning something like that.*

Selling a Vorin woman of high dahn—which the dress marked her as being—would be a risky gambit for a slaver. Most owners in civilized lands would require documentation of the slave's past, and it was rare indeed that a lighteyes was made a slave, aside from ardents. Usually someone of higher breeding would simply be executed instead. Slavery was a mercy for the lower classes.

"Brightness?" the slaver asked nervously.

She was thinking like a scholar again, to distract herself. She'd need to get past that.

"What is your name?" Shallan asked. She hadn't intended to make her voice quite so emotionless, but the shock of what she'd seen left her in turmoil.

The man stepped back at her tone. "I am Tvlakv, humble merchant."

"Slaver," Shallan said, standing up and pushing her hair back from her face.

"As I said. A merchant."

His two guards watched her as they loaded equipment onto the lead wagon. She did not miss the cudgels they carried prominently at their waists. She'd had a sphere in her hand as she walked last night, hadn't she?

Memories of that made her feet flare up again. She had to grit her teeth against the agony as painspren, like orange hands made of sinew, clawed out of the ground nearby. She'd need to clean her wounds, but bloodied and bruised as they were, she wasn't going to be walking anywhere anytime soon. Those wagons had seats. . . .

They likely stole the sphere from me, she thought. She felt around in her safepouch. The other spheres were still there, but the sleeve was unbuttoned. Had she done that? Had they peeked? She couldn't suppress a blush at the thought.

The two guards regarded her hungrily. Tvlakv acted humble, but his leering eyes were also very eager. These men were one step from robbing her.

But if she left them, she'd probably die out here, alone. Stormfather! What could she do? She felt like sitting down and sobbing. After everything that had happened, now this?

Control is the basis of all power.

How would Jasnah respond to this situation?

The answer was simple. She would be Jasnah.

"I will allow you to assist me," Shallan said. She somehow kept her voice even, despite the anxious terror she felt inside.

". . . Brightness?" Tvlakv asked.

"As you can see," Shallan said, "I am the victim of a shipwreck. My servants are lost to me. You and your men will do. I have a trunk. We will need to go fetch it."

She felt like one of the ten fools. Surely he would see through the flimsy act. Pretending you had authority was not the same as having it, no matter what Jasnah said.

"It would . . . of course be our privilege to help," Tvlakv said. "Brightness . . . ?"

"Davar," Shallan said, though she took care to soften her voice. Jasnah wasn't condescending. Where other lighteyes, like Shallan's father, went about with conceited egotism, Jasnah had simply expected people to do as she wished. And they had.

She could make this work. She had to.

"Tradesman Tvlakv," Shallan said. "I will need to go to the Shattered Plains. Do you know the way?"

"The Shattered Plains?" the man asked, glancing at his guards, one of whom had approached. "We were there a few months ago, but are now heading to catch a barge over to Thaylenah. We have completed our trading in this area, with no need to return northward."

"Ah, but you do have a need to return," Shallan said, walking toward one of the wagons. Each step was agony. "To take me." She glanced around, and gratefully noticed Pattern on the side of a wagon, watching. She walked to the front of that wagon, then held out her hand to the other guard, who stood nearby.

He looked at the hand mutely, scratching his head. Then he looked at the wagon and climbed onto it, reaching down to help her up.

Tvlakv walked over to her. "It will be an expensive trip for us to return without wares! I have only these slaves I purchased at the Shallow Crypts. Not enough to justify the trip back, not yet."

"Expensive?" Shallan asked, seating herself, trying to project amusement. "I assure you, tradesman Tvlakv, the expense is minuscule to me. You will be greatly compensated. Now, let us be moving. There are important people waiting for me at the Shattered Plains."

"But Brightness," Tvlakv said. "You've obviously had a difficult time of events recently, yes, that I can see. Let me take you to the Shallow Crypts. It is much closer. You can find rest there and send word to those waiting for you."

"Did I ask to be taken to the Shallow Crypts?"

"But . . ." He trailed off as she focused her gaze on him.

She softened her expression. "I know what I am doing, and thank you for the advice. Now let us be moving."

The three men exchanged befuddled looks, and the slaver took his knit cap off, wringing it in his hands. Nearby, a pair of parshmen with marbled skin walked into camp. Shallan nearly jumped as they trudged by, carrying dried rockbud shells they'd apparently been gathering for fires. Tvlakv gave them no heed.

Parshmen. Voidbringers. Her skin crawled, but she couldn't worry about them right now. She looked back at the slaver, expecting him to ignore her orders. However, he nodded. And then, he and his men simply . . . did as she said. They hitched up the chulls, the slaver got directions to her trunk, and they started moving without further objection.

They might just be going along for now, Shallan told herself, *because they want to know what's in my trunk. More to rob.* But when they reached it, they heaved it onto the wagon, lashed it in place, and then turned around and headed to the north.

Toward the Shattered Plains.

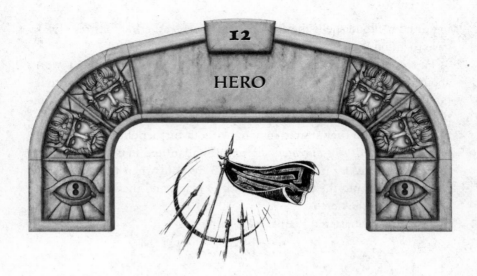

12

HERO

Unfortunately, we fixated upon Sadeas's plotting so much that we did not take note of the changed pattern of our enemies, the murderers of my husband, the true danger. I would like to know what wind brought about their sudden, inexplicable transformation.

—From the journal of Navani Kholin, Jesesach 1174

Kaladin pressed the stone against the wall of the chasm, and it stuck there. "All right," he said, stepping back.

Rock jumped up and grabbed it, then dangled from the wall, bending legs below. His deep, bellowing laugh echoed in the chasm. "This time, he holds me!"

Sigzil made a notation on his ledger. "Good. Keep hanging on, Rock."

"For how long?" Rock asked.

"Until you fall."

"Until I . . ." The large Horneater frowned, hanging from the stone with both hands. "I do not like this experiment any longer."

"Oh, don't whine," Kaladin said, folding his arms and leaning on the wall beside Rock. Spheres lit the chasm floor around them, with its vines, debris, and blooming plants. "You're not dropping far."

"It is not the drop," Rock complained. "It is my arms. I am big man, you see."

"So it's a good thing you have big arms to hold you."

"It does not work that way, I think," Rock said, grunting. "And the handhold is not good. And I—"

The stone popped free and Rock fell downward. Kaladin grabbed his arm, steadying him as he caught himself.

"Twenty seconds," Sigzil said. "Not very long."

"I warned you," Kaladin said, picking up the fallen stone. "It lasts longer if I use more Stormlight."

"I think we need a baseline," Sigzil said. He fished in his pocket and pulled out a glowing diamond chip, the smallest denomination of sphere. "Take all of the Stormlight from this, put it into the stone, then we'll hang Rock from that and see how long he takes to fall."

Rock groaned. "My poor arms . . ."

"Hey, mancha," Lopen called from farther down the chasm, "at least you've got two of them, eh?" The Herdazian was watching to make sure none of the new recruits somehow wandered over and saw what Kaladin was doing. It shouldn't happen—they were practicing several chasms over—but Kaladin wanted someone on guard.

Eventually they'll all know anyway, Kaladin thought, taking the chip from Sigzil. *Isn't that what you just promised Syl? That you'd let yourself become a Radiant?*

Kaladin drew in the chip's Stormlight with a sharp intake of breath, then infused the Light into the stone. He was getting better at that, drawing the Stormlight into his hand, then using it like luminescent paint to coat the bottom of the rock. The Stormlight soaked into the stone, and when he pressed it against the wall, it stayed there.

Smoky tendrils of luminescence rose from the stone. "We probably don't need to make Rock hang from it," Kaladin said. "If you need a baseline, why not just use how long the stone remains there on its own?"

"Well, that's less fun," Sigzil said. "But very well." He continued to write numbers on his ledger. That would have made most of the other bridgemen uncomfortable. A man writing was seen as unmasculine, even blasphemous—though Sigzil was only writing glyphs.

Today, fortunately, Kaladin had with him Sigzil, Rock, and Lopen—all foreigners from places with different rules. Herdaz was Vorin, technically, but they had their own brand of it and Lopen didn't seem to mind a man writing.

"So," Rock said as they waited, "Stormblessed leader, you said there was something else you could do, did you not?"

"Fly!" Lopen said from down the passage.

"I can't fly," Kaladin said dryly.

"Walk on walls!"

"I tried that," Kaladin said. "I nearly broke my head from the fall."

"Ah, gancho," Lopen said. "No flying *or* walking on walls? I need to impress the women. I do not think sticking rocks to walls will be enough."

"I think anyone would find that impressive," Sigzil said. "It defies the laws of nature."

"You do not know many Herdazian women, do you?" Lopen asked, sighing. "Really, I think we should try again on the flying. It would be the best."

"There *is* something more," Kaladin said. "Not flying, but still useful. I'm not certain I can replicate it. I've never done it consciously."

"The shield," Rock said, standing by the wall, staring up at the rock. "On the battlefield, when the Parshendi shot at us. The arrows hit your shield. *All* the arrows."

"Yes," Kaladin said.

"We should test that," Sigzil said. "We'll need a bow."

"Spren," Rock said, pointing. "They pull the stone against the wall."

"What?" Sigzil said, scrambling over, squinting at the rock Kaladin had pressed against the wall. "I don't see them."

"Ah," Rock said. "Then they do not wish to be seen." He bowed his head toward them. "Apologies, *mafah'liki*."

Sigzil frowned, looking closer, holding up a sphere to light the area. Kaladin walked over and joined them. He could make out the tiny purple spren if he looked closely. "They're there, Sig," Kaladin said.

"Then why can't I see them?"

"It has to do with my abilities," Kaladin said, glancing at Syl, who sat on a cleft in the rock nearby, one leg draping over and swinging.

"But Rock—"

"I am *alaii'iku*," Rock said, raising a hand to his breast.

"Which means?" Sigzil asked impatiently.

"That I can see these spren, and you cannot." Rock rested a hand on the smaller man's shoulder. "It is all right, friend. I do not blame you for being blind. Most lowlanders are. It is the air, you see. Makes your brains stop working right."

Sigzil frowned, but wrote down some notes while absently doing something with his fingers. Keeping track of the seconds? The rock finally popped off the wall, trailing a few final wisps of Stormlight as it hit the ground. "Well over a minute," Sigzil said. "I counted eighty-seven seconds." He looked to the rest of them.

"We were supposed to be counting?" Kaladin asked, glancing at Rock, who shrugged.

Sigzil sighed.

"Ninety-one seconds," Lopen called. "You're welcome."

Sigzil sat down on a rock, ignoring a few finger bones peeking out of the moss beside him, and made some notations on his ledger. He scowled.

"Ha!" Rock said, squatting down beside him. "You look like you have eaten bad eggs. What is problem?"

"I don't know what I'm doing, Rock," Sigzil said. "My master taught me to ask questions and find precise answers. But how can I be precise? I would need a clock for the timing, but they are too expensive. Even if we had one, I don't know how to measure Stormlight!"

"With chips," Kaladin said. "The gemstones are precisely weighed before being encased in glass."

"And can they all hold the same amount?" Sigzil asked. "We know that uncut gems hold less than cut ones. So is one that was cut better going to hold more? Plus, Stormlight fades from a sphere over time. How many days has it been since that chip was infused, and how much Light has it lost since then? Do they all lose the same amount at the same rate? We know too little. I think perhaps I am wasting your time, sir."

"It's not a waste," Lopen said, joining them. The one-armed Herdazian yawned, sitting down on the rock by Sigzil, forcing the other man over a little. "We just need to be testing other things, eh?"

"Like what?" Kaladin said.

"Well, gancho," Lopen said. "Can you stick me to the wall?"

"I . . . I don't know," Kaladin said.

"Seems like it would be good to know, eh?" Lopen stood up. "Shall we try?"

Kaladin glanced at Sigzil, who shrugged.

Kaladin drew in more Stormlight. The raging tempest filled him, as if it were battering against his skin, a captive trying to find a way out. He drew the Stormlight into his hand and pressed it against the wall, painting the stones with luminescence.

Taking a deep breath, he picked up Lopen—the slender man was startlingly easy to lift, particularly with a measure of Stormlight still inside Kaladin's veins. He pressed Lopen against the wall.

When Kaladin dubiously stepped back, the Herdazian remained there, stuck to the stone by his uniform, which bunched up under his armpits.

Lopen grinned. "It worked!"

"This thing could be useful," Rock said, rubbing at his strangely cut Horneater beard. "Yes, *this* is what we need to test. You are a soldier, Kaladin. Can you use this in combat?"

Kaladin nodded slowly, a dozen possibilities popping into his head. What if his enemies ran across a pool of Light he had put on the floor? Could he stop a wagon from rolling? Stick his spear to an enemy shield, then yank it from their hands?

"How does it feel, Lopen?" Rock asked. "Does this thing hurt?"

"Nah," Lopen said, wiggling. "I'm worried my coat will rip, or the buttons will snap. Oh. Oh. Question for you! What did the one-armed Herdazian do to the man who stuck him to the wall?"

Kaladin frowned. "I . . . I don't know."

"Nothing," Lopen said. "The Herdazian was 'armless." The slender man burst into laughter.

Sigzil groaned, though Rock laughed. Syl had cocked her head, zipping over to Kaladin. "Was that a joke?" she asked softly.

"Yes," Kaladin said. "A distinctly bad one."

"Ah, don't say that!" Lopen said, still chuckling. "It's the best one I know—and trust me, I'm an expert on one-armed Herdazian jokes. 'Lopen,' my mother always says, 'you must learn these to laugh before others do. Then you steal the laughter from them, and have it all for yourself.' She is a very wise woman. I once brought her the head of a chull."

Kaladin blinked. "You . . . What?"

"Chull head," Lopen said. "Very good to eat."

"You are a strange man, Lopen," Kaladin said.

"No," Rock said. "They really are good. The head, he is best part of chull."

"I will trust you two on that," Kaladin said. "Marginally." He reached up, taking Lopen by the arm as the Stormlight holding him in place began to fade. Rock grabbed the man's waist, and they helped him down.

"All right," Kaladin said, instinctively checking the sky for the time, though he couldn't see the sun through the narrow chasm opening above. "Let's experiment."

⁂

Tempest stoked within him, Kaladin dashed across the chasm floor. His movement startled a group of frillblooms, which pulled in frantically, like hands closing. Vines trembled on the walls and began to curl upward.

Kaladin's feet splashed in stagnant water. He leaped over a mound of debris, trailing Stormlight. He was filled with it, *pounding* with it. That made it easier to use; it *wanted* to flow. He pushed it into his spear.

Ahead, Lopen, Rock, and Sigzil waited with practice spears. Though Lopen wasn't very good—the missing arm was a huge disadvantage—Rock made up for it. The large Horneater would not fight Parshendi and would not kill, but had agreed to spar today, in the name of "experimentation."

He fought very well, and Sigzil was acceptable with the spear. Together on the battlefield, the three bridgemen might once have given Kaladin trouble.

Times changed.

Kaladin tossed his spear sideways at Rock, surprising the Horneater, who had raised his weapon to block. The Stormlight made Kaladin's spear stick to Rock's, forming a cross. Rock cursed, trying to turn his spear around to strike, but in doing so smacked himself on the side with Kaladin's spear.

As Lopen's spear struck, Kaladin pushed it down easily with one hand, filling the tip with Stormlight. The weapon hit the pile of refuse and stuck to the wood and bones.

Sigzil's weapon came in, missing Kaladin's chest by a wide margin as he stepped aside. Kaladin nudged and infused the weapon with the flat of his hand, shoving it into Lopen's, which he'd just pulled out of the refuse, plastered with moss and bone. The two spears stuck together.

Kaladin slipped between Rock and Sigzil, leaving the three of them in a jumbled mess, off balance and trying to disentangle their weapons. Kaladin smiled grimly, jogging down to the other end of the chasm. He picked up a spear, then turned, dancing from one foot to the other. The Stormlight encouraged him to move. Standing still was practically impossible while holding so much.

Come on, come on, he thought. The three others finally got their weapons apart as the Stormlight ran out. They formed up to face him again.

Kaladin dashed forward. In the dim light of the chasm, the glow of the smoke rising from him was strong enough to cast shadows that leaped and spun. He crashed through pools, the water cold on his unshod feet. He'd removed his boots; he wanted to feel the stone underneath him.

This time, the three bridgemen set the butts of their spears on the ground as if against a charge. Kaladin smiled, then grabbed the top of his spear—like theirs, it was a practice one, without a real spearhead—and infused it with Stormlight.

He slapped it against Rock's, intending to yank it out of the Horneater's hands. Rock had other plans, and *hauled* his spear back with a strength that took Kaladin by surprise. He nearly lost his grip.

Lopen and Sigzil quickly moved to come at him from either side. *Nice,* Kaladin thought, proud. He'd taught them formations like that, showing them how to work together on the battlefield.

As they drew close, Kaladin let go of his spear and stuck out his leg. The Stormlight flowed out of his bare foot as easily as it did his hands, and he was able to swipe a large glowing arc on the ground. Sigzil stepped in it and tripped, his foot sticking to the Light. He tried to stab as he fell, but there was no force behind the blow.

Kaladin slammed his weight against Lopen, whose strike was off-center. He shoved Lopen against the wall, then pulled back, leaving the Herdazian stuck to the stone, which Kaladin had infused in the heartbeat they'd been pressed together.

"Ah, not again," Lopen said with a groan.

Sigzil had fallen face-first in the water. Kaladin barely had time to smile before he noticed Rock swinging a log at his head.

An entire log. How had Rock *lifted* that thing? Kaladin threw himself out of the way, rolling on the ground and scraping his hand as the log crashed against the floor of the chasm.

Kaladin growled, Stormlight passing between his teeth and rising into the air in front of him. He jumped onto Rock's log as the Horneater tried to lift it again.

Kaladin's landing slammed the wood back against the ground. He leaped toward Rock, and part of him wondered just what he was thinking, getting into a hand-to-hand fight with someone twice his weight. He slammed into the Horneater, hurling them both to the ground. They rolled in the moss, Rock twisting to pin Kaladin's arms. The Horneater obviously had training as a wrestler.

Kaladin poured Stormlight into the ground. It wouldn't affect or hamper him, he'd found. So, as they rolled, first Rock's arm stuck to the ground, then his side.

The Horneater kept fighting to get Kaladin into a hold. He almost had it, till Kaladin pushed with his legs, rolling both of them so Rock's other elbow touched the ground, where it stuck.

Kaladin tore away, gasping and puffing, losing most of his remaining Stormlight as he coughed. He leaned up against the wall, mopping sweat from his face.

"Ha!" Rock said, stuck to the ground, splayed with arms to the sides. "I almost had you. Slippery as a fifth son, you are!"

"Storms, Rock," Kaladin said. "What I wouldn't do to get you on the battlefield. You are wasted as a cook."

"You don't like the food?" Rock asked, laughing. "I will have to try something with more grease. This thing will fit you! Grabbing you was like trying to keep my hands on a live lakefish! One that has been covered in butter! Ha!"

Kaladin stepped up to him, squatting down. "You're a warrior, Rock. I saw it in Teft, and you can say whatever you want, but I see it in you."

"I am wrong son to be soldier," Rock said stubbornly. "It is a thing of the *tuanalikina*, the fourth son or below. Third son cannot be wasted in battle."

"Didn't stop you from throwing a tree at my head."

"Was small tree," Rock said. "And very hard head."

Kaladin smiled, then reached down, touching the Stormlight infused into the stone beneath Rock. He hadn't ever tried to take it back after using it in this way. Could he? He closed his eyes and breathed in, trying . . . yes.

Some of the tempest within him stoked again. When he opened his eyes, Rock was free. Kaladin hadn't been able to take it all back, but some. The rest was evaporating into the air.

He took Rock by the hand, helping the larger man to his feet. Rock dusted himself off.

"That was *embarrassing*," Sigzil said as Kaladin walked over to free him too. "It's like we're children. The Prime's own eyes have not seen such a shameful show."

"I have a very unfair advantage," Kaladin said, helping Sigzil to his feet. "Years of training as a soldier, a larger build than you. Oh, and the ability to emit Stormlight from my fingers." He patted Sigzil on the shoulder. "You did well. This is just a test, like you wanted."

A more useful type of test, Kaladin thought.

"Sure," Lopen said from behind them. "Just go ahead and leave the Herdazian stuck to the wall. The view here is wonderful. Oh, and is that slime running down my cheek? A fresh new look for the Lopen, who cannot brush it away, because—have I mentioned?—his hand is stuck to *the wall*."

Kaladin smiled, walking over. "You were the one who asked me to stick you to a wall in the first place, Lopen."

"My other hand?" Lopen said. "The one that was cut off long ago, eaten by a fearsome beast? It is making a rude gesture toward you right now. I thought you would wish to know, so that you can prepare to be insulted." He said it with the same lightheartedness with which he seemed to approach everything. He had even joined the bridge crew with a certain crazy eagerness.

Kaladin let him down.

"This thing," Rock said, "it worked well."

"Yes," Kaladin said. Though honestly, he probably could have dispatched the three men more easily just by using a spear and the extra speed and strength the Stormlight lent. He didn't know yet whether that was because he was unfamiliar with these new powers, but he did think that forcing himself to use them had put him in some awkward positions.

Familiarity, he thought. *I need to know these abilities as well as I know my spear.*

That meant practice. Lots of practice. Unfortunately, the best way to practice was to find someone who matched or bested you in skill, strength, and capacity. Considering what he could now do, that was going to be a tall order.

The three others walked over to dig waterskins from their packs, and Kaladin noticed a figure standing in the shadows a little ways down the chasm. Kaladin stood up, alarmed until Teft emerged into the light of their spheres.

"I thought you were going to be on watch," Teft growled at Lopen.

"Too busy being stuck to walls," Lopen said, raising his waterskin. "I thought you had a bunch of greenvines to train?"

"Drehy has them in hand," Teft said, picking his way around some debris, joining Kaladin beside the chasm wall. "I don't know if the lads told you, Kaladin, but bringing that lot down here broke them out of their shells somehow."

Kaladin nodded.

"How did you get to know people so well?" Teft asked.

"It involves a lot of cutting them apart," Kaladin said, looking down at his hand, which he'd scraped while fighting Rock. The scrape was gone, Stormlight having healed the tears in his skin.

Teft grunted, glancing back at Rock and the other two, who had broken out rations. "You ought to put Rock in charge of the new recruits."

"He won't fight."

"He just sparred with you," Teft said. "So maybe he will with them. People like him more than me. I'm just going to screw this up."

"You'll do a fine job, Teft, I won't have you saying otherwise. We have resources now. No more scrimping for every last sphere. You'll train those lads, and you'll do it *right*."

Teft sighed, but said no more.

"You saw what I did."

"Aye," Teft said. "We'll need to bring down the entire group of twenty if we want to give you a proper challenge."

"That or find another person like myself," Kaladin said. "Someone to spar with."

"Aye," Teft said again, nodding, as if he hadn't considered that.

"There were ten orders of knights, right?" Kaladin asked. "Do you know much of the others?" Teft had been the first one to figure out what Kaladin could do. He'd known before Kaladin himself had.

"Not much," Teft said with a grimace. "I know the orders didn't always get along, despite what the official stories say. We'll need to see if we can find someone who knows more than I do. I . . . I kept away. And the people I knew who could tell us, they aren't around any longer."

If Teft had been in a dour mood before, this drove him down even further. He looked at the ground. He spoke of his past infrequently, but Kaladin was more and more certain that whoever these people had been, they were dead because of something Teft himself had done.

"What would you think if you heard that somebody wanted to refound the Knights Radiant?" Kaladin said softly to Teft.

Teft looked up sharply. "You—"

"Not me," Kaladin said, speaking carefully. Dalinar Kholin had let him listen in on the conference, and while Kaladin trusted Teft, there were certain expectations of silence that an officer was required to uphold.

Dalinar is a lighteyes, part of him whispered. *He wouldn't think twice if he were revealing a secret you'd shared with him.*

"Not me," Kaladin repeated. "What if a king somewhere decided he wanted to gather a group of people and name them Knights Radiant?"

"I'd call him an idiot," Teft said. "Now, the Radiants weren't what people say. They weren't traitors. They just *weren't.* But everyone is sure they betrayed us, and you're not going to change minds quickly. Not unless you can Surgebind to quiet them." Teft looked Kaladin up and down. "Are you going to do it, lad?"

"They'd hate me, wouldn't they?" Kaladin said. He couldn't help noticing Syl, who walked through the air until she was close, studying him. "For what the old Radiants did." He held up a hand to stop Teft's objection. "What people *think* they did."

"Aye," Teft said.

Syl folded her arms, giving Kaladin a look. *You promised,* that look said.

"We'll have to be careful about how we do it, then," Kaladin said. "Go gather the new recruits. They've had enough practice down here for one day."

Teft nodded, then jogged off to do as ordered. Kaladin gathered his spear and the spheres he'd set out to light the sparring, then waved to the other three. They packed up their things and began the hike back out.

"So you're going to do it," Syl said, landing on his shoulder.

"I want to practice more first," Kaladin said. *And get used to the idea.*

"It will be fine, Kaladin."

"No. It will be hard. People will hate me, and even if they don't, I'll be set apart from them. Separated. I've accepted that as my lot, though. I'll deal with it." Even in Bridge Four, Moash was the only one who didn't treat Kaladin like some mythological savior Herald. Him and maybe Rock.

Still, the other bridgemen hadn't reacted with the fear he'd once worried about. They might idolize him, but they did not isolate him. It was good enough.

They reached the rope ladder before Teft and the greenvines, but there was no reason to wait. Kaladin climbed up out of the muggy chasm onto the plateau just east of the warcamps. It felt so strange to be able to carry his spear and money out of the chasm. Indeed, the soldiers guarding the approach to Dalinar's warcamp didn't pester him—instead, they saluted and stood up straight. It was as crisp a salute as he'd ever gotten, as crisp as the ones given to a general.

"They seem proud of you," Syl said. "They don't even know you, but they're proud of you."

"They're darkeyes," Kaladin said, saluting back. "Probably men who were fighting on the Tower when Sadeas betrayed them."

"Stormblessed," one of them called. "Have you heard the news?"

Curse the one who told them that nickname, Kaladin thought as Rock and the other two caught up to him.

"No," Kaladin called. "What news?"

"A hero has come to the Shattered Plains!" the soldier yelled back. "He's going to meet with Brightlord Kholin, perhaps support him! It's a good sign. Might help calm things down around here."

"What's this?" Rock called back. "Who?"

The soldier said a name.

Kaladin's heart became ice.

He nearly lost his spear from numb fingers. And then, he took off running. He didn't heed Rock's cry behind him, didn't stop to let the others catch up with him. He dashed through the camp, running toward Dalinar's command complex at its center.

He didn't want to believe when he saw the banner hanging in the air above a group of soldiers, probably matched by a much larger group outside the warcamp. Kaladin passed them, drawing cries and stares, questions if something was wrong.

He finally stumbled to a stop outside the short set of steps into Dalinar's bunkered complex of stone buildings. There, standing in front, the Blackthorn clasped hands with a tall man.

Square-faced and dignified, the newcomer wore a pristine uniform. He laughed, then embraced Dalinar. "Old friend," he said. "It's been too long."

"Too long by far," Dalinar agreed. "I'm glad you finally made your way here, after years of promises. I heard you've even found yourself a Shardblade!"

"Yes," the newcomer said, pulling back and holding his hand to the side. "Taken from an assassin who dared try to kill me on the field of battle."

The Blade appeared. Kaladin stared at the silvery weapon. Etched along its length, the Blade was shaped to look like flames in motion, and to Kaladin it seemed that the weapon was stained red. Names flooded his mind: Dallet, Coreb, Reesh . . . a squad before time, from another life. Men Kaladin had loved.

He looked up and forced himself to see the face of the newcomer. A man Kaladin hated, *hated* beyond any other. A man he had once worshipped.

Highlord Amaram. The man who had stolen Kaladin's Shardblade, branded his forehead, and sold him into slavery.

THE END OF

Part One

INTERLUDES

ESHONAI • YM • RYSN

The Rhythm of Resolve thrummed softly in the back of Eshonai's mind as she reached the plateau at the center of the Shattered Plains. The central plateau. Narak. Exile.

Home.

She ripped the helm of the Shardplate from her head, taking a deep breath of cool air. Plate ventilated wonderfully, but even it grew stuffy after extended exertions. Other soldiers landed behind her—she had taken some fifteen hundred this run. Fortunately, this time they'd arrived well before the humans, and had harvested the gemheart with minimal fighting. Devi carried it; he had earned the privilege by being the one to spot the chrysalis from afar.

Almost she wished it had not been so easy a run. Almost.

Where are you, Blackthorn? she thought, looking westward. *Why have you not come to face me again?*

She thought she'd seen him on that run a week or so back, when they'd been forced off the plateau by his son. Eshonai had not participated in that fight; her wounded leg ached, and the jumping from plateau to plateau had stressed it, even in Shardplate. Perhaps she should not be going on these runs in the first place.

She'd wanted to be there in case her strike force grew surrounded, and needed a Shardbearer—even a wounded one—to break them free. Her leg still hurt, but Plate cushioned it enough. Soon she would have to return to the fighting. Perhaps if she participated directly, the Blackthorn would appear again.

She *needed* to speak with him. She felt an urgency to do so blowing upon the winds themselves.

Her soldiers raised hands in farewell as they went their separate ways.

Many softly sang or hummed a song to the Rhythm of Mourning. These days, few sang to Excitement, or even to Resolve. Step by step, storm by storm, depression claimed her people—the listeners, as they called their race. "Parshendi" was a human term.

Eshonai strode toward the ruins that dominated Narak. After so many years, there wasn't much left. Ruins of ruins, one might call them. The works of men and listeners alike did not last long before the might of the highstorms.

That stone spire ahead, that had probably once been a tower. Over the centuries, it had grown a thick coating of crem from the raging storms. The soft crem had seeped into cracks and filled windows, then slowly hardened. The tower now looked like an enormous stalagmite, rounded point toward the sky, side knobbed with rock that looked as if it had been melted.

The spire must have had a strong core to survive the winds so long. Other examples of ancient engineering had not fared so well. Eshonai passed lumps and mounds, remnants of fallen buildings that had slowly been consumed by the Shattered Plains. The storms were unpredictable. Sometimes huge sections of rock would break free from formations, leaving gouges and jagged edges. Other times, spires would stand for centuries, growing—not shrinking—as the winds both weathered and augmented them.

Eshonai had discovered similar ruins in her explorations, such as the one she'd been on when her people had first encountered humans. Only seven years ago, but also an eternity. She had loved those days, exploring a wide world that felt infinite. And now . . .

Now she spent her life trapped on this one plateau. The wilderness called to her, sang that she should gather up what things she could carry and strike out. Unfortunately, that was no longer her destiny.

She passed into the shadow of a big lump of rock that she always imagined might have been a city gate. From what little they'd learned from their spies over the years, she knew that the Alethi did not understand. They marched over the uneven surface of the plateaus and saw only natural rock, never knowing that they traversed the bones of a city long dead.

Eshonai shivered, and attuned the Rhythm of the Lost. It was a soft beat, yet still violent, with sharp, separated notes. She did not attune it for long. Remembering the fallen was important, but working to protect the living was more so.

She attuned Resolve again and entered Narak. Here, the listeners had built the best home they could during the years of war. Rocky shelves had become barracks, carapace from greatshells forming the walls and roofs. Mounds that had once been buildings now grew rockbuds for food on their leeward sides. Much of the Shattered Plains had once been populated, but the largest city had been here at the center. So now the ruins of her people made their home in the ruins of a dead city.

They had named it Narak—exile—for it was where they had come to be separated from their gods.

Listeners, both malen and femalen, raised hands to her as she passed. So few remained. The humans were relentless in their pursuit of vengeance.

She didn't blame them.

She turned toward the Hall of Art. It was nearby, and she hadn't put in an appearance there for days. Inside, soldiers did a laughable job of painting.

Eshonai strode among them, still wearing her Shardplate, helm under her arm. The long building had no roof—allowing in plenty of light to paint by—and the walls were thick with long-hardened crem. Holding thick-bristled brushes, the soldiers tried their best to depict the arrangement of rockbud flowers on a pedestal at the center. Eshonai did a round of the artists, looking at their work. Paper was precious and canvas nonexistent, so they painted on shell.

The paintings were awful. Splotches of garish color, off-center petals . . . Eshonai paused beside Varanis, one of her lieutenants. He held the brush delicately between armored fingers, a hulking form before an easel. Plates of chitin armor grew from his arms, shoulders, chest, even head. They were matched by her own, under her Plate.

"You are getting better," Eshonai said to him, speaking to the Rhythm of Praise.

He looked to her, and hummed softly to Skepticism.

Eshonai chuckled, resting a hand on his shoulder. "It actually looks like flowers, Varanis. I mean it."

"It looks like muddy water on a brown plateau," he said. "Maybe with some brown leaves floating in it. Why do colors turn brown when they mix? Three beautiful colors put together, and they become the *least* beautiful color. It makes no sense, General."

General. At times, she felt as awkward in the position as these men did trying to paint pictures. She wore warform, as she needed the armor for battle, but she preferred workform. More limber, more rugged. It wasn't that she disliked leading these men, but doing the same thing every day— drills, plateau runs—numbed her mind. She wanted to be seeing new things, going new places. Instead, she joined her people in a long funeral vigil as, one by one, they died.

No. We will find a way out of it.

The art was part of that, she hoped. By her order, each man or woman took a turn in the Hall of Art at their appointed time. And they tried; they tried *hard*. So far, it had been about as successful as trying to leap a chasm with the other side out of sight. "No spren?" she asked.

"Not a one." He said it to the Rhythm of Mourning. She heard that rhythm far too often these days.

"Keep trying," she said. "We will not lose this battle for lack of effort."

"But General," Varanis said, "what is the *point*? Having artists won't save us from the swords of humans."

Nearby, other soldiers turned to hear her answer.

"Artists won't help," she said to the Rhythm of Peace. "But my sister is confident that she is close to discovering new forms. If we can discover how to create artists, then it might teach her more about the process of change—and that might help her with her research. Help her discover forms stronger, even, than warform. Artists won't get us out of this, but some other form might."

Varanis nodded. He was a good soldier. Not all of them were—warform did not intrinsically make one more disciplined. Unfortunately, it did hamper one's artistic skill.

Eshonai had tried painting. She couldn't think the right way, couldn't grasp the abstraction needed to create art. Warform was a good form, versatile. It didn't impede thought, like mateform did. As with workform, you were yourself when you were warform. But each had its quirks. A worker had difficulty committing violence—there was a block in the mind somewhere. That was one of the reasons she liked the form. It forced her to think differently to get around problems.

Neither form could create art. Not well, at least. Mateform was better, but came with a whole host of other problems. Keeping those types focused on anything productive was almost impossible. There were two other forms, though the first—dullform—was one they rarely used. It was a relic of the past, before they'd rediscovered something better.

That left only nimbleform, a general form that was lithe and careful. They used it for nurturing young and doing the kind of work that required more dexterity than brawn. Few could be spared for that form, though it was more skilled at art.

The old songs spoke of hundreds of forms. Now they knew of only five. Well, six if one counted slaveform, the form with no spren, no soul, and no song. The form the humans were accustomed to, the ones they called parshmen. It wasn't really a form at all, however, but a lack of any form.

Eshonai left the Hall of Art, helm under her arm, leg aching. She passed through the watering square, where nimbles had crafted a large pool from sculpted crem. It caught rain during the riddens of a storm, thick with nourishment. Here, workers carried buckets to fetch water. Their forms were strong, almost like that of warform, though with thinner fingers and no armor. Many nodded to her, though as a general she had no authority over them. She was their last Shardbearer.

A group of three mateforms—two female, one male—played in the water, splashing at one another. Barely clothed, they dripped with what others would be *drinking*.

"You three," Eshonai snapped at them. "Shouldn't you be doing something?"

Plump and vapid, they grinned at Eshonai. "Come in!" one called. "It's fun!"

"Out," Eshonai said, pointing.

The three muttered to the Rhythm of Irritation as they climbed from the water. Nearby, several workers shook their heads as they passed, one singing to Praise in appreciation of Eshonai. Workers did not like confrontation.

It was an excuse. Just as those who took on mateform used their form as an excuse for their inane activities. When a worker, Eshonai had trained herself to confront when necessary. She'd even been a mate once, and had proven to herself firsthand that one could indeed be productive as a mate, despite . . . distractions.

Of course, the rest of her experiences as a mate had been an utter disaster.

She spoke to Reprimand to the mateforms, her words so passionate that she actually attracted angerspren. She saw them coming from a ways off, drawn by her emotion, moving with an incredible speed—like lightning dancing toward her across the distant stone. The lightning pooled at her feet, turning the stones red.

That put the fear of the gods into the mateforms, and they ran off to report to the Hall of Art. Hopefully, they wouldn't end up in an alcove along the way, mating. Her stomach churned at the thought. She had never been able to fathom people who wanted to *remain* in mateform. Most couples, in order to have a child, would enter the form and sequester themselves away for a year—then would be out of the form as soon after the child's birth as possible. After all, who would want to go out in public like that?

The humans did it. That had baffled her during those early days, when she'd spent time learning their language, trading with them. Not only did humans not change forms, they were *always* ready to mate, always distracted by sexual urges.

What she wouldn't have given to be able to go among them unnoticed, to adopt their monochrome skin for a year and walk their highways, see their grand cities. Instead, she and the others had ordered the murder of the Alethi king in a desperate gambit to stop the listener gods from returning.

Well, that had worked—the Alethi king hadn't been able to put his plan into action. But now, her people were slowly being destroyed as a result.

She finally reached the rock formation she called home: a small, collapsed dome. It reminded her of the ones on the edge of the Shattered Plains, actually—the enormous ones that the humans called warcamps. Her people had lived in those, before abandoning them for the security of the Shattered Plains, with its chasms the humans couldn't jump.

Her home was much, much smaller, of course. During the early days of living here, Venli had crafted a roof of greatshell carapace and built walls to divide the space into chambers. She'd covered it all over with crem, which had hardened with time, creating something that actually felt like a home instead of a shanty.

Eshonai set her helm on a table just inside, but left the rest of her armor on. Shardplate just felt right to her. She liked the sensation of strength. It let her know that something was still reliable in the world. And with the power of Shardplate, she could mostly ignore the wound to her leg.

She ducked through a few rooms, nodding to the people she passed. Venli's associates were scholars, though no one knew the proper form for true scholarship. Nimbleform was their makeshift substitute for now. Eshonai found her sister beside the window of the farthest chamber. Demid, Venli's once-mate, sat next to her. Venli had held nimbleform for three years, as long as they'd known of the form, though in Eshonai's mind's eye she still saw her sister as a worker, with thicker arms and a stouter torso.

That was the past. Now, Venli was a slender woman with a thin face, her marblings delicate swirling patterns of red and white. Nimbleform grew long hairstrands, with no carapace helm to block them. Venli's, a deep red, flowed down to her waist, where they were tied in three places. She wore a robe, drawn tight at the waist and showing a hint of breasts at the chest. This was not mateform, so they were small.

Venli and her once-mate were close, though their time as mates had produced no children. If they'd gone to the battlefield, they'd have been a warpair. Instead, they were a researchpair, or something. The things they spent their days doing were very un-listener. That was the point. Eshonai's people could not afford to be what they had been in the past. The days of lounging isolated on these plateaus—singing songs to one another, only occasionally fighting—were over.

"So?" Venli asked to Curiosity.

"We won," Eshonai said, leaning back against the wall and folding her arms with a clink of Shardplate. "The gemheart is ours. We will continue to eat."

"That is well," Venli said. "And your human?"

"Dalinar Kholin. He did not come to this battle."

"He will not face you again," Venli said. "You nearly killed him last time." She said it to the Rhythm of Amusement as she rose, picking up a piece of paper—they made it from dried rockbud pulp following a harvest—which she handed to her once-mate. Looking it over, he nodded and began making notes on his own sheet.

That paper required precious time and resources to make, but Venli insisted the reward would be worth the effort. She'd better be right.

Venli regarded Eshonai. She had keen eyes—glassy and dark, like those of all listeners. Venli's always seemed to have an extra depth of secret knowledge to them. In the right light, they had a violet cast.

"What would you do, Sister?" Venli asked. "If you and this Kholin were actually able to stop trying to kill each other long enough to have a conversation?"

"I'd sue for peace."

"We murdered his brother," Venli said. "We slaughtered King Gavilar on a night when he'd invited us into his home. That is not something the Alethi will forget, or forgive."

Eshonai unfolded her arms and flexed a gauntleted hand. That night. A desperate plan, made between herself and five others. She had been part of it despite her youth, because of her knowledge of the humans. All had voted the same.

Kill the man. Kill him, and risk destruction. For if he had lived to do what he told them that night, all would have been lost. The others who had made that decision with her were dead now.

"I have discovered the secret of stormform," Venli said.

"*What?*" Eshonai stood up straight. "You were to be working on a form to help! A form for diplomats, or for scholars."

"Those will not save us," Venli said to Amusement. "If we wish to deal with the humans, we will need the ancient powers."

"Venli," Eshonai said, grabbing her sister by the arm. "Our gods!"

Venli didn't flinch. "The humans have Surgebinders."

"Perhaps not. It could have been an Honorblade."

"You fought him. Was it an Honorblade that struck you, wounded your leg, sent you limping?"

"I . . ." Her leg ached.

"We don't know which of the songs are true," Venli said. Though she said it to Resolve, she sounded tired, and she drew exhaustionspren. They came with a sound like wind, blowing in through the windows and doors like jets of translucent vapor before becoming stronger, more visible, and spinning around her head like swirls of steam.

My poor sister. She works herself as hard as the soldiers do.

"If the Surgebinders have returned," Venli continued, "we must strive for something meaningful, something that can ensure our freedom. The forms of *power*, Eshonai . . ." She glanced at Eshonai's hand, still on her arm. "At least sit and listen. And stop looming like a mountain."

Eshonai removed her fingers, but did not sit. Her Shardplate's weight would break a chair. Instead, she leaned forward, inspecting the table full of papers.

Venli had invented the script herself. They'd learned that concept from the humans—memorizing songs was good, but not perfect, even when you had the rhythms to guide you. Information stored on pages was more practical, especially for research.

Eshonai had taught herself the script, but reading was still difficult for her. She did not have much time to practice.

"So . . . stormform?" Eshonai said.

"Enough people of that form," Venli said, "could control a highstorm, or even summon one."

"I remember the song that speaks of this form," Eshonai said. "It was a thing of the gods."

"Most of the forms are related to them in some way," Venli said. "Can we really trust the accuracy of words first sung so long ago? When those songs were memorized, our people were mostly dullform."

It was a form of low intelligence, low capacity. They used it now to spy on the humans. Once, it and mateform had been the only forms her people had known.

Demid shuffled some of the pages, moving a stack. "Venli is right, Eshonai. This is a risk we must take."

"We *could* negotiate with the Alethi," Eshonai said.

"To what end?" Venli said, again to Skepticism, her exhaustionspren finally fading, the spren spinning away to search out more fresh sources of emotion. "Eshonai, you keep saying you want to negotiate. I think it is because you are fascinated by humans. You think they'll let you go freely among them? A person they see as having the form of a rebellious slave?"

"Centuries ago," Demid said, "we escaped both our gods and the humans. Our ancestors left behind civilization, power, and might in order to secure freedom. I would not give that up, Eshonai. Stormform. With it, we can destroy the Alethi army."

"With them gone," Venli said, "you can return to exploration. No responsibility—you could travel, make your maps, discover places no person has ever seen."

"What I want for myself is meaningless," Eshonai said to Reprimand, "so long as we are all in danger of destruction." She scanned the specks on the page, scribbles of songs. Songs without music, written out as they were. Their souls stripped away.

Could the listeners' salvation really be in something so terrible? Venli and her team had spent five years recording all of the songs, learning the nuances from the elderly, capturing them in these pages. Through collaboration, research, and deep thought, they had discovered nimbleform.

"It is the only way," Venli said to Peace. "We will bring this to the Five, Eshonai. I would have you on our side."

"I . . . I will consider."

Ym carefully trimmed the wood from the side of the small block. He held it up to the spherelight beside his bench, pinching his spectacles by the rim and holding them closer to his eyes.

Such delightful inventions, spectacles. To live was to be a fragment of the cosmere that was experiencing itself. How could he properly experience if he couldn't see? The Azish man who had first created these devices was long deceased, and Ym had submitted a proposal that he be considered one of the Honored Dead.

Ym lowered the piece of wood and continued to carve it, carefully whittling off the front to form a curve. Some of his colleagues bought their lasts—the wooden forms around which a cobbler built his shoes—from carpenters, but Ym had been taught to make his own. That was the old way, the way it had been done for centuries. If something had been done one way for such a long time, he figured there was probably a good reason.

Behind him stood the shadowed cubbies of a cobbler's shop, the toes of dozens of shoes peeking out like the noses of eels in their holes. These were test shoes, used to judge size, choose materials, and decide styles so he could construct the perfect shoe to fit the foot and character of the individual. A fitting could take quite a while, assuming you did it properly.

Something moved in the dimness to his right. Ym glanced in that direction, but didn't change his posture. The spren had been coming more often lately—specks of light, like those from a piece of crystal suspended in a sunbeam. He did not know its type, as he had never seen one like it before.

It moved across the surface of the workbench, slinking closer. When it stopped, light crept upward from it, like small plants growing or climbing from their burrows. When it moved again, those withdrew.

Ym returned to his sculpting. "It will be for making a shoe."

The evening shop was quiet save for the scraping of his knife on wood.

"Sh-shoe . . . ?" a voice asked. Like that of a young woman, soft, with a kind of chiming musicality to it.

"Yes, my friend," he said. "A shoe for young children. I find myself in need of those more and more these days."

"Shoe," the spren said. "For ch-children. Little people."

Ym brushed wooden scraps off the bench for later sweeping, then set the last on the bench near the spren. It shied away, like a reflection off a mirror—translucent, really just a shimmer of light.

He withdrew his hand and waited. The spren inched forward—tentative, like a cremling creeping out of its crack after a storm. It stopped, and light grew upward from it in the shape of tiny sprouts. Such an odd sight.

"You are an interesting experience, my friend," Ym said as the shimmer of light moved onto the last itself. "One in which I am honored to participate."

"I . . ." the spren said. "I . . ." The spren's form shook suddenly, then grew more intense, like light being focused. *"He comes."*

Ym stood up, suddenly anxious. Something moved on the street outside. Was it that one? That watcher, in the military coat?

But no, it was just a child, peering in through the open door. Ym smiled, opening his drawer of spheres and letting more light into the room. The child shied back, just as the spren had.

The spren had vanished somewhere. It did that when others drew near.

"No need to fear," Ym said, settling back down on his stool. "Come in. Let me get a look at you."

The dirty young urchin peered back in. He wore only a ragged pair of trousers, no shirt, though that was common here in Iri, where both days and nights were usually warm.

The poor child's feet were dirty and scraped.

"Now," Ym said, "that won't do. Come, young one, settle down. Let's get something on those feet." He moved out one of his smaller stools.

"They say you don't charge nothin'," the boy said, not moving.

"They are quite wrong," Ym said. "But I think you will find my cost bearable."

"Don't have no spheres."

"No spheres are needed. Your payment will be your story. Your experiences. I would hear them."

"They said you was strange," the boy said, finally walking into the shop.

"They were right," Ym said, patting the stool.

The urchin stepped timidly up to the stool, walking with a limp he tried to hide. He was Iriali, though the grime darkened his skin and hair, both of which were golden. The skin less so—you needed the light to see it right—but the hair certainly. It was the mark of their people.

Ym motioned for the child to raise his good foot, then got out a washcloth, wetted it, and cleaned away the grime. He wasn't about to do a fitting on feet so dirty. Noticeably, the boy tucked back the foot he'd limped on, as if trying to hide that it had a rag wrapped around it.

"So," Ym said, "your story?"

"You're old," the boy said. "Older than anyone I know. Grandpa old. You must know everythin' already. Why do you want to hear from me?"

"It is one of my quirks," Ym said. "Come now. Let's hear it."

The boy huffed, but talked. Briefly. That wasn't uncommon. He wanted to hold his story to himself. Slowly, with careful questions, Ym pried the story free. The boy was the son of a whore, and had been kicked out as soon as he could fend for himself. That had been three years ago, the boy thought. He was probably eight now.

As he listened, Ym cleaned the first foot, then clipped and filed the nails. Once done, he motioned for the other foot.

The boy reluctantly lifted it up. Ym undid the rag, and found a nasty cut on the bottom of that foot. It was already infected, crawling with rotspren, tiny motes of red.

Ym hesitated.

"Needed to get some shoes," the urchin said, looking the other way. "Can't keep on without 'em."

The rip in the skin was jagged. *Done climbing over a fence, perhaps?* Ym thought.

The boy looked at him, feigning nonchalance. A wound like this would slow an urchin down terribly, which on the streets could easily mean death. Ym knew that all too well.

He looked up at the boy, noting the shadow of worry in those little eyes. The infection had spread up the leg.

"My friend," Ym whispered, "I believe I am going to need your help."

"What?" the urchin said.

"Nothing," Ym replied, reaching into the drawer of his table. The light spilling out was just from five diamond chips. Every urchin who had come to him had seen those. So far, Ym had been robbed of them only twice.

He dug more deeply, unfolding a hidden compartment in the drawer and taking a more powerful sphere—a broam—from there, covering its light quickly in his hand while reaching for some antiseptic with the other hand.

The medicine wasn't going to be enough, not with the boy unable to stay off his feet. Lying in bed for weeks to heal, constantly applying expensive medication? Impossible for an urchin fighting for food each day.

Ym brought his hands back, sphere tucked inside of one. Poor child. It must hurt something fierce. The boy probably ought to have been laid out in bed, feverish, but every urchin knew to chew ridgebark to stay alert and awake longer than they should.

Nearby, the sparkling light spren peeked out from underneath a stack of leather squares. Ym applied the medication, then set it aside and lifted the boy's foot, humming softly.

The glow in Ym's other hand vanished.

The rotspren fled from the wound.

When Ym removed his hand, the cut had scabbed over, the color returning to normal, the signs of infection gone. So far, Ym had used this ability only a handful of times, and had always disguised it as medicine. It was unlike anything he had ever heard of. Perhaps that was why he had been given it—so the cosmere could experience it.

"Hey," the boy said, "that feels *a lot* better."

"I'm glad," Ym said, returning the sphere and the medicine to his drawer. The spren had retreated. "Let us see if I have something that fits you."

He began fitting shoes. Normally, after fitting, he'd send the patron away and craft a perfect set of shoes just for them. For this child, unfortunately, he'd have to use shoes he'd already made. He'd had too many urchins never return for their pair of shoes, leaving him to fret and wonder. Had something happened to them? Had they simply forgotten? Or had their natural suspicion gotten the better of them?

Fortunately, he had several good, sturdy pairs that might fit this boy. *I need more treated hogshide,* he thought, making a note. Children would not properly care for shoes. He needed leather that would age well even if unattended.

"You're really gonna give me a pair of shoes," the urchin said. "For *nothin'*?"

"Nothing but your story," Ym said, slipping another testing shoe onto the boy's foot. He'd given up on trying to train urchins to wear socks.

"Why?"

"Because," Ym said, "you and I are One."

"One what?"

"One being," Ym said. He set aside that shoe and got out another. "Long ago, there was only One. One knew everything, but had experienced nothing. And so, One became many—us, people. The One, who is both male and female, did so to experience all things."

"One. You mean God?"

"If you wish to say it that way," Ym said. "But it is not completely true. I accept no god. You should accept no god. We are Iriali, and part of the Long Trail, of which this is the Fourth Land."

"You sound like a priest."

"Accept no priests either," Ym said. "Those are from other lands, come to preach to us. Iriali need no preaching, only experience. As each experience is different, it brings completeness. Eventually, all will be gathered back in—when the Seventh Land is attained—and we will once again become One."

"So you an' me . . ." the urchin said. "Are the same?"

"Yes. Two minds of a single being experiencing different lives."

"That's stupid."

"It is simply a matter of perspective," Ym said, dusting the boy's feet with powder and slipping back on a pair of the test shoes. "Please walk on those for a moment."

The boy gave him a strange look, but obeyed, trying a few steps. He didn't limp any longer.

"Perspective," Ym said, holding up his hand and wiggling his fingers. "From very close up, the fingers on a hand might seem individual and alone. Indeed, the thumb might think it has very little in common with the pinky. But with proper perspective, it is realized that the fingers are part of something much larger. That, indeed, they are One."

The urchin frowned. Some of that had probably been beyond him. *I need to speak more simply, and—*

"Why do you get to be the finger with the expensive ring," the boy said, pacing back the other direction, "while I gotta be the pinky with the broken fingernail?"

Ym smiled. "I know it sounds unfair, but there can *be* no unfairness, as we are all the same in the end. Besides, I didn't always have this shop."

"You didn't?"

"No. I think you'd be surprised at where I came from. Please sit back down."

The boy settled down. "That medicine works real well. Real, real well."

Ym slipped off the shoes, using the powder—which had rubbed off in places—to judge how the shoe fit. He fished out a pair of premade shoes, then worked at them for a moment, flexing them in his hands. He'd want a cushion on the bottom for the wounded foot, but something that would tear off after a few weeks, once the wound was healed. . . .

"The things you're talking about," the boy said. "They sound dumb to me. I mean, if we're all the same person, shouldn't everyone know this already?"

"As One, we knew truth," Ym said, "but as many, we need ignorance.

We exist in variety to experience all kinds of thought. That means some of us must know and others must not—just like some must be rich, and others must be poor." He worked the shoe a moment longer. "More people *did* know this, once. It's not talked about as much as it should be. Here, let's see if these fit right."

He handed the boy the shoes, who put them on and tied the laces.

"Your life might be unpleasant—" Ym began.

"Unpleasant?"

"All right. Downright awful. But it will get better, young one. I promise it."

"I thought," the boy said, stamping his good foot to test the shoes, "that you were gonna tell me that life is awful, but it all don't matter in the end, 'cuz we're going the same place."

"That's true," Ym said, "but isn't very comforting right now, is it?"

"Nope."

Ym turned back to his worktable. "Try not to walk on that wounded foot too much, if you can help it."

The urchin strode to the door with a sudden urgency, as if eager to get away before Ym changed his mind and took back the shoes. He did stop at the doorway, though.

"If we're all just the same person trying out different lives," the boy said, "you don't need to give away shoes. 'Cuz it don't matter."

"You wouldn't hit yourself in the face, would you? If I make your life better, I make my own better."

"That's crazy talk," the boy said. "*I* think you're just a nice person." He ducked out, not speaking another word.

Ym smiled, shaking his head. Eventually, he went back to work on his last. The spren peeked out again.

"Thank you," Ym said. "For your help." He didn't know why he could do what he did, but he knew the spren was involved.

"He's *still here*," the spren whispered.

Ym looked up toward the doorway out onto the night street. The urchin was there?

Something rustled behind Ym.

He jumped, spinning. The workroom was a place of dark corners and cubbies. Had he perhaps heard a rat?

Why was the door into the back room—where Ym slept—open? He usually left that closed.

A shadow moved in the blackness back there.

"If you've come for the spheres," Ym said, trembling, "I have only the five chips here."

More rustling. The shadow separated itself from the darkness, resolving into a man with dark, Makabaki skin—all save for a pale crescent on his cheek. He wore black and silver, a uniform, but not one from any military that Ym recognized. Thick gloves, with stiff cuffs at the back.

"I had to look very hard," the man said, "to discover your indiscretion."

"I . . ." Ym stammered. "Just . . . five chips . . ."

"You have lived a clean life, since your youth as a carouser," the man said, his voice even. "A young man of means who drank and partied away what his parents left him. That is not illegal. Murder, however, is."

Ym sank down onto his stool. "I didn't know. I didn't *know* it would kill her."

"Poison delivered," the man said, stepping into the room, "in the form of a bottle of wine."

"They told me the vintage itself was the sign!" Ym said. "That she'd know the message was from them, and that it meant she would need to pay! I was desperate for money. To eat, you see. Those on the streets are not kind . . ."

"You were an accomplice to murder," the man said, pulling his gloves on more tightly, first one hand, then the other. He spoke with such a stark lack of emotion, he could have been conversing about the weather.

"I didn't know . . ." Ym pled.

"You are guilty nonetheless." The man reached his hand to the side, and a weapon formed from mist there, then fell into his hand.

A *Shardblade*? What kind of constable of the law was this? Ym stared at that wondrous, silvery Blade.

Then he ran.

It appeared that he still had useful instincts from his time on the streets. He managed to fling a stack of leather toward the man and duck the Blade as it swung for him. Ym scrambled out onto the dark street and charged away, shouting. Perhaps someone would hear. Perhaps someone would help.

Nobody heard.

Nobody helped.

Ym was an old man now. By the time he reached the first cross street, he was gasping for air. He stopped beside the old barber shop, dark inside, door locked. The little spren moved along beside him, a shimmering light that sprayed outward in a circle. Beautiful.

"I guess," Ym said, panting, "it is . . . my time. May One . . . find this memory . . . pleasing."

Footsteps slapped on the street behind, getting closer.

"No," the spren whispered. "Light!"

Ym dug in his pocket and pulled out a sphere. Could he use it, some-how, to—

The constable's shoulder slammed Ym against the wall of the barber shop. Ym groaned, dropping the sphere.

The man in silver spun him around. He looked like a shade in the night, a silhouette against the black sky.

"It was *forty* years ago," Ym whispered.

"Justice does not expire."

The man shoved the Shardblade through Ym's chest.

Experience ended.

RYSN

Rysn liked to pretend that her pot of Shin grass was not stupid, but merely contemplative. She sat near the prow of her catamaran, holding the pot in her lap. The otherwise still surface of the Reshi Sea rippled from the paddling of the guide behind her. The warm, damp air made beads of sweat form on Rysn's brow and neck.

It was probably going to rain again. Precipitation here on the sea was the worst kind—not mighty or impressive like a highstorm, not even insistent like an ordinary shower. Here, it was just a misting haze, more than a fog but less than a drizzle. Enough to ruin hair, makeup, clothing—indeed, every element of a careful young woman's efforts to present a suitable face for trading.

Rysn shifted the pot in her lap. She'd named the grass Tyvnk. Sullen. Her babsk had laughed at the name. He understood. In naming the grass, she acknowledged that he was right and she had been wrong; his trade with the Shin people last year had been exceptionally profitable.

Rysn chose not to be sullen at being proven so clearly wrong. She'd let her plant be sullen instead.

They'd traversed these waters for two days now, and then only after waiting at port for weeks until the right time between highstorms for a trip onto the nearly enclosed sea. Today, the waters were shockingly still. Almost as serene as those of the Purelake.

Vstim himself rode two boats over in their irregular flotilla. Paddled by new parshmen, the sixteen sleek catamarans were laden with goods that had been purchased with the profits of their last expedition. Vstim was still resting in the back of his boat. He looked like little more than another bundle of cloth, almost indistinguishable from the sacks of goods.

He would be fine. People got sick. It happened, but he would become well again.

And the blood you saw on his handkerchief?

She suppressed the thought and pointedly turned around in her seat, shifting Tyvnk to the crook of her left arm. She kept the pot *very* clean. That soil stuff the grass needed in order to live was even worse than crem, and it had a proclivity for ruining clothing.

Gu, the flotilla's guide, rode in her own boat, just behind her. He looked a lot like a Purelaker with those long limbs, the leathery skin, and dark hair. Every Purelaker she'd met, however, had cared deeply about those gods of theirs. She doubted Gu had ever cared about *anything*.

That included getting them to their destination in a timely manner.

"You said we were near," she said to him.

"Oh, we are," he said, lifting his oar and then slipping it back down into the water. "Soon, now." He spoke Thaylen rather well, which was why he'd been hired. It *certainly* wasn't for his punctuality.

"Define 'soon,'" Rysn said.

"Define . . ."

"What do you mean by 'soon'?"

"Soon. Today, maybe."

Maybe. Delightful.

Gu continued to paddle, only doing so on one side of the boat, yet somehow keeping them from going in circles. At the rear of Rysn's boat, Kylrm—head of their guards—played with her parasol, opening it and closing it again. He seemed to consider it a wondrous invention, though they'd been popular in Thaylenah for *ages* now.

Shows how rarely Vstim's workers get back to civilization. Another cheerful thought. Well, she'd apprenticed under Vstim wanting to travel to exotic places, and exotic this was. True, she'd expected cosmopolitan and exotic to go hand in hand. If she'd had half a wit—which she wasn't sure she did, these days—she'd have realized that the *really* successful traders weren't the ones who went where everyone else wanted to go.

"Hard," Gu said, still paddling with his lethargic pace. "Patterns are off, these days. The gods do not walk where they always should. We shall find her. Yes, we shall."

Rysn stifled a sigh and turned forward. With Vstim incapacitated again, she was in charge of leading the flotilla. She wished she knew where she was leading it—or even knew how to find their destination.

That was the trouble with islands that moved.

The boats glided past a shoal of branches breaking the sea's surface. Encouraged by the wind, gentle waves lapped against the stiff branches, which reached out of the waters like the fingers of drowning men. The sea was deeper than the Purelake, with its bafflingly shallow waters. Those trees would be dozens of feet tall at the very least, with bark of stone. Gu called them *i-nah*, which apparently meant bad. They could slice up a boat's hull.

Sometimes they'd pass branches hiding just beneath the glassy surface, almost invisible. She didn't know how Gu knew to steer clear of them. In this, as in so much else, they just had to trust him. What would they do if he led them into an ambush out here on these silent waters? Suddenly, she felt very glad that Vstim had ordered their guards to monitor his fabrial that showed if people were drawing near. It—

Land.

Rysn stood up in the catamaran, making it rock precariously. There *was* something ahead, a distant dark line.

"Ah," Gu said. "See? Soon."

Rysn remained standing, waving for her parasol when a sprinkle of rain started to fall. The parasol barely helped, though it was waxed to double as an umbrella. In her excitement, she hardly gave it—or her increasingly frizzy hair—a thought. *Finally.*

The island was much bigger than she'd expected. She'd imagined it to be like a very large boat, not this towering rock formation jutting from the waters like a boulder in a field. It was different from other islands she'd seen; there didn't seem to be any beach, and it wasn't flat and low, but mountainous. Shouldn't the sides and top have eroded over time?

"It's so green," Rysn said as they drew closer.

"The Tai-na is a good place to grow," Gu said. "Good place to live. Except when it's at war."

"When two islands get too close," Rysn said. She'd read of this in preparation, though there were not many scholars who cared enough about the Reshi to write of them. Dozens, perhaps hundreds, of these moving islands floated in the sea. The people on them lived simple lives, interpreting the movements of the islands as divine will.

"Not always," Gu said, chuckling. "Sometimes close Tai-na is good. Sometimes bad."

"What determines?" Rysn asked.

"Why, the Tai-na itself."

"The island decides," Rysn said flatly, humoring him. Primitives. What *was* her babsk expecting to gain by trading here? "How can an island—"

Then the island ahead of them moved.

Not in the drifting way she'd imagined. The island's very shape changed, stones twisting and undulating, a huge section of rock rising in a motion that seemed lethargic until one appreciated the grand scale.

Rysn sat down with a plop, her eyes wide. The rock—the *leg*—lifted, streaming water like rainfall. It lurched forward, then crashed back down into the sea with incredible force.

The Tai-na, the gods of the Reshi Isles, were greatshells.

This was the largest beast she'd ever seen, or ever heard of. Big enough to make mythological monsters like the chasmfiends of distant Natanatan seem like pebbles in comparison!

"Why didn't anyone tell me?" she demanded, looking back at the boat's other two occupants. Surely Kylrm at least should have said something.

"Is better to see," Gu said, paddling with his usual relaxed posture. She did not much care for his smirk.

"And take away that moment of discovery?" Kylrm said. "I remember when I first saw one move. It's worth not spoiling. We never tell the new guards when they first come."

Rysn contained her annoyance and looked back at the "island." Curse those inaccurate accounts from her readings. Too much hearsay, not enough experience. She found it hard to believe that no one had ever recorded the truth. Likely, she simply had the wrong sources.

A falling haze of rain shrouded the enormous beast in mist and enigma. What did a thing so big eat? Did it notice the people living upon its back; did it care? Kelek . . . What was *mating* like for these monsters?

It had to be ancient. The boat drew into its shadow, and she could see the greenery growing across its stony skin. Shalebark mounds made vast fields of vibrant colors. Moss coated nearly everything. Vines and rockbuds wound around trunks of small trees that had gained a foothold in cracks between plates of the animal's shell.

Gu led the convoy around the hind leg—giving it a very wide berth, to her relief—and came up along the creature's flank. Here, the shell dipped down into the water, forming a platform. She heard the people before she saw them, their laughter rising amid splashes. The rain stopped, so Rysn lowered her parasol and shook it over the water. She finally spotted the people, a group of youths both male and female climbing up onto a ridge of shell and leaping from it into the sea.

That was not so surprising. The water of the Reshi Sea, like that of the Purelake, was remarkably warm. She had once ventured into the water near her homeland. It was a frigid experience, and not one to be engaged in while of sound mind. Frequently, alcohol and bravado were involved in any ocean dip.

Out here, though, she expected that swimmers were commonplace. She had not expected them to be unclothed.

Rysn blushed furiously as a group of people ran past on the docklike shell outcropping, as bare as the day they were born. Young men and women alike, uncaring of who saw. She was no Alethi prude, but . . . Kelek! Shouldn't they wear *something*?

Shamespren fell around her, shaped like white and red flower petals that drifted on a wind. Behind her, Gu chuckled.

Kylrm joined him. "That's another thing we don't warn the newcomers about."

Primitives, Rysn thought. She shouldn't blush so. She was an adult. Well, almost.

The flotilla continued toward a section of shell that formed a kind of dock—a low plate that hung mostly above water. They settled in to wait, though for what, she didn't know.

After a few moments, the plate lurched—water streaming off it—as the beast took another lethargic step. Waves lapped against the boats from the splashdown ahead. Once things were settled, Gu guided the boat to the dock. "Up you go," he said.

"Shall we tie the boats to anything?" Rysn said.

"No. Not safe, with movement. We will pull back."

"And at night? How do you dock the boats?"

"When we sleep, we move boats away, tie together. Sleep out there. Find island again in the morning."

"Oh," Rysn said, taking a calming breath and checking to make sure her pot of grass was carefully stored in the bottom of the catamaran.

She stood up. This was not going to be kind to her shoes, which had been *quite* expensive. She had a feeling the Reshi wouldn't care. She could probably meet their king barefooted. Passions! From what she'd seen, she could probably meet him bare-*chested*.

She climbed up carefully, and was pleased to find that despite being an inch or so underwater, the shell was not slippery. Kylrm climbed up with her and she handed him the folded-up parasol, stepping back and waiting as Gu maneuvered his boat away. Another oarsman brought up his boat instead, a longer catamaran with parshmen to help row.

Her babsk huddled inside, wrapped in his blanket despite the heat, head propped up against the back of the boat. His pale skin had a waxy cast.

"Babsk . . ." Rysn said, heart wrenching. "We should have turned around."

"Nonsense," he said, his voice frail. He smiled anyway. "I've suffered worse. The trade must happen. We've leveraged too much."

"I will go to the island's king and traders," Rysn said. "And ask for them to come here to negotiate with you on the docks."

Vstim coughed into his hand. "No. These people aren't like the Shin. My weakness will ruin the deal. Boldness. You must be bold with the Reshi."

"Bold?" Rysn said, glancing at the boat guide, who lounged with fingers in the water. "Babsk . . . the Reshi are a relaxed people. I do not think much matters to them."

"You will be surprised, then," Vstim said. He followed her gaze toward the nearby swimmers, who giggled and laughed as they leaped into the waters. "Life can be simple here, yes. It attracts such people like war attracts painspren."

Attracts . . . One of the women scampered past, and Rysn noticed with shock that she had *Thaylen* eyebrows. Her skin had been tanned in the sun, so the difference in tones hadn't been immediately obvious. Picking through those swimming, Rysn saw others. Two that were probably Herdazians, even . . . an *Alethi*? Impossible.

"People seek out this place," Vstim said. "They like the life of the Reshi. Here, they can simply go with the island. Fight when it fights another island. Relax otherwise. There will be people like this in any culture, for every society is made of individuals. You must learn this. Do not let your assumptions about a culture block your ability to perceive the individual, or you will fail."

She nodded. He seemed so frail, but his words were firm. She tried not to think about the swimming people. The fact that at least one of them was of her own kind made her even *more* embarrassed.

"If you cannot trade with them . . ." Rysn said.

"You must do it."

Rysn felt cold, despite the heat. This was what she'd joined with Vstim to do, wasn't it? How many times had she wished he would let her lead? Why feel so timid now?

She glanced toward her own boat, moving off, carrying her pot of grass. She looked back at her babsk. "Tell me what to do."

"They know much of foreigners," Vstim said. "More than we know of them. This is because so many of us come to live among them. Many of the Reshi are as carefree as you say, but there are also many who are not. Those prefer to fight. And a trade . . . it is like a fight to them."

"To me too," Rysn said.

"I know these people," Vstim said. "We must have Passion that Talik is not here. He is their best, and often goes to trade with other islands. Whichever you do meet for trade, he or she will judge you as they would judge a rival in battle. And to them, battle is about posturing.

"I once had the misfortune to be on an isle during war." He paused, coughing, but spurned the drink Kylrm tried to give him. "As the two islands raged, the people climbed down into boats to exchange insults and boasts. They would each start with their weakest, who would yell out boasts, then progress in a kind of verbal duel up to their greatest. After that, arrows

184

and spears, struggling on ships and in the water. Fortunately, there was more yelling than actual cutting."

Rysn swallowed, nodding.

"You are not ready for this, child," Vstim said.

"I know."

"Good. Finally you realize it. Go now. They will not suffer us long on their island unless we agree to join them permanently."

"Which would require . . . ?" Rysn said.

"Well, for one, it requires giving all you own to their king."

"Lovely," Rysn said, rising. "I wonder how he'd look wearing my shoes." She took a deep breath. "You still haven't told me what we're trading for."

"They know," her babsk said, then coughed. "Your conversation will not be a negotiation. The terms were set years ago."

She turned to him, frowning. "What?"

"This is not about what you can get," Vstim said, "but about whether or not they think you are worthy of it. Convince them." He hesitated. "Passions guide you, child. Do well."

It seemed a plea. If their flotilla was turned away . . . The cost of this trade was not in the goods—woods, cloth, simple supplies purchased cheaply—but in the outfitting of a convoy. It was in traveling so far, paying guides, wasting time waiting for a break between storms, then more time searching for the right island. If she was turned away, they could still sell what they had—but at a stiff devastating loss, considering the high overhead of the trip.

Two of the guards, Kylrm and Nlent, joined her as she left Vstim and walked along the docklike protrusion of shell. Now that they were so close, it was difficult to see a creature and not an island. Just ahead of her, the patina of lichen made the shell nearly indistinguishable from rock. Trees clustered here, their roots draping into the water, their branches reaching high and creating a forest.

She hesitantly stepped onto the only path leading up from the waters. Here, the "ground" formed steps that seemed far too square and regular to be natural.

"They cut into its shell?" Rysn said, climbing.

Kylrm grunted. "Chulls can't feel their shells. This monster probably can't either."

As they walked, he kept his hand on his gtet, a type of traditional Thaylen sword. The thing had a large triangular wedge of a blade with a grip directly at the base; you'd hold the grip like a fist, and the long blade would extend out down past the knuckles, with parts of the hilt resting around the wrist for support. Right now, he wore it in a sheath at his side, along with a bow on his back.

Why was he was so anxious? The Reshi were not supposed to be dangerous. Perhaps when you were a paid guard, it was better to assume *everyone* was dangerous.

The pathway wound upward through thick jungle. The trees here were limber and hale, their branches almost constantly moving. And when the beast stepped, everything shook.

Vines trembled and twisted on the pathway or drooped from branches, and these pulled out of the way at her approach, but crept back quickly after her passing. Soon, she couldn't see the sea, or even smell its brine. The jungle enveloped everything. Its thick green and brown were broken occasionally by pink and yellow mounds of shalebark that seemed to have been growing for generations.

She'd found the humidity oppressive before, but here it was overwhelming. She felt as if she were swimming, and even her thin linen skirt, blouse, and vest seemed as thick as old Thaylen highland winter gear.

After an interminable climb, she heard voices. To her right, the forest opened up to a view of the ocean beyond. Rysn caught her breath. Endless blue waters, clouds dropping a haze of rain in patches that seemed so distinct. And in the distance . . .

"Another one?" she asked, pointing toward a shadow on the horizon.

"Yeah," Kylrm said. "Hopefully going the other way. I'd rather not be here when they decide to war." His grip tightened on the handle of his sword.

The voices came from farther up the way, so Rysn resigned herself to more climbing. Her legs ached from the effort.

Though the jungle remained impenetrable to her left, it remained open to her right, where the massive flank of the greatshell formed ridges and shelves. She caught sight of some people sitting around tents, leaning back and staring out over the sea. They hardly gave her and the two guards more than a glance. Up farther, she found more Reshi.

These were jumping.

Men and women alike—and in various states of undress—were taking turns leaping off the shell's outcroppings with whoops and shouts, plummeting toward the waters far below. Rysn grew nauseated just watching them. How high up *were* they?

"They do it to shock you. They always jump from greater heights when a foreigner is here."

Rysn nodded, then—with a sudden start—realized that the comment hadn't come from one of her guards. She turned and discovered that to her left, the forest had moved back around a large outcrop of shell like a rock mound.

There, hanging upside down and tied by his feet to a point at the top of the shell, was a lanky man with pale white skin verging on blue. He wore only a loincloth, and his skin was covered with hundreds upon hundreds of small, intricate tattoos.

Rysn took a step toward him, but Kylrm grabbed her shoulder and pulled her back. "Aimian," he hissed. "Keep your distance."

The blue fingernails and deep blue eyes should have been a clue. Rysn stepped back, though she couldn't see his Voidbringer shadow.

"Keep your distance indeed," the man said. "Always a wise idea." His accent was unlike any she'd heard, though he spoke Thaylen well. He hung there with a pleasant smile on his face, as if completely indifferent to the fact that he was upside down.

"Are you . . . well?" Rysn asked the man.

"Hmmm?" he said. "Oh, between blackouts, yes. Quite well. I think I'm growing numb to the pain of my ankles, which is just delightful."

Rysn brought her hands up to her chest, not daring to get any closer. Aimian. Very bad luck. She wasn't particularly superstitious—she was even skeptical of the Passions sometimes—but . . . well, this was an *Aimian*.

"What fell curses did you bring on this people, beast?" Kylrm demanded.

"Improper puns," the man said lazily. "And a stench from something I ate that did *not* sit well with me. Are you off to speak with the king, then?"

"I . . ." Rysn said. Behind her, another Reshi whooped and leaped from the shelf. "Yes."

"Well," the creature said, "don't ask about the soul of their god. They don't like to speak of that, it turns out. Must be spectacular, to let the beasts grow this large. Beyond even the spren who inhabit the bodies of ordinary greatshells. Hmmm . . ." He seemed very pleased by something.

"Do not feel for him, trademaster," Kylrm said softly to her, steering her away from the dangling prisoner. "He could escape if he wished."

Nlent, the other guard, nodded. "They can take off their limbs. Take off their skin too. No real body to them. Just something evil, taking human form." The squat guard wore a charm on his wrist, a charm of courage, which he took off and held tightly in one hand. The charm hadn't any properties itself, of course. It was a reminder. Courage. Passion. Want what you need, embrace it, *desire* it and bring it to you.

Well, what *she* needed was her babsk to be here with her. She turned her steps upward again, the confrontation with the Aimian leaving her unnerved. More people ran and leaped from the shelves to her right. Crazy.

Trademaster, she thought. *Kylrm called me "trademaster."* She wasn't, not yet. She was property owned by Vstim; for now just an apprentice who provided occasional slave labor.

She didn't deserve the title, but hearing it strengthened her. She led the way up the steps, which twisted farther around the beast's shell. They passed a place where the ground split, the shell showing skin far beneath. The rift was like a chasm; she couldn't have leaped from one side to the other without falling in.

Reshi she passed on the path refused to respond to her questions. Fortunately, Kylrm knew the way, and when the path split, he pointed to the right fork. At times, the path leveled out for significant distances, but then there were always more steps.

Her legs burning, her clothing damp with sweat, they reached the top of this flight and—at long last—found no more steps. Here, the jungle fell away completely, though rockbuds clutched the shell in the open field— beyond which was only the empty sky.

The head, Rysn thought. *We've climbed all the way to the beast's head.*

Soldiers lined the path, armed with spears bearing colorful tassels. Their breastplates and armguards were of carapace carved wickedly with points, and though they wore only wraps for clothing, they stood as stiff-backed as any Alethi soldier, with stern expressions to match. So her babsk was right. Not every Reshi was the "lounge and swim" type.

Boldness, she thought to herself, remembering Vstim's words. She could not show these people a timid face. The king stood at the end of the pathway of guards and rockbuds, a diminutive figure on the edge of a carapace shelf, looking toward the sun.

Rysn strode forward, passing through a double row of spears. She would have expected the same kind of clothing on the king, but instead the man wore full, voluminous robes of vibrant green and yellow. They looked terribly hot.

As she drew nearer, Rysn got a sense for just how high she had climbed. The waters below shimmered in the sunlight, so far down that Rysn wouldn't have heard a rock hit if she'd dropped one. Far enough that looking over the side made her stomach twist upon itself and her legs tremble.

Getting close to the king would require stepping out onto that shelf where he stood. It would place her within a breath of plummeting down hundreds and hundreds of feet.

Steady, Rysn told herself. She *would* show her babsk that she was capable. She was not the ignorant girl who had misjudged the Shin or who had offended the Iriali. She had learned.

Still, perhaps she should have asked Nlent to lend her his charm of courage.

She stepped out onto the shelf. The king seemed young, at least from behind. Built like a youth, or . . .

No, Rysn thought with a start as the king turned. It was a woman, old enough that her hair was greying, but not so old that she was bent with age.

Someone stepped out onto the shelf behind Rysn. Younger, he wore the standard wrap and tassels. His hair was in two braids that fell over tan, bare shoulders. When he spoke, there wasn't even a *hint* of an accent to his voice. "The king wishes to know why his old trading partner, Vstim, has not come in person, and has instead sent a child in his place."

"And are you the king?" Rysn asked the newcomer.

The man laughed. "You stand beside him, yet ask that of me?"

Rysn looked toward the robed figure. The robes were tied with the front open enough to show that the "king" definitely had breasts.

"We are led by a king," the newcomer said. "Gender is irrelevant."

It seemed to Rysn that gender was part of the definition, but it wasn't worth arguing over. "My master is indisposed," she said, addressing the newcomer—he'd be the island's trademaster. "I am authorized to speak for him, and to accomplish the trade."

The newcomer snorted, sitting down on the edge of the shelf, legs hanging out over the edge. Rysn's stomach did a somersault. "He should have known better. The trade is off, then."

"You are Talik, I assume?" Rysn said, folding her arms. The man was no longer facing her. It seemed an intentional slight.

"Yes."

"My master warned me about you."

"Then he isn't a complete fool," Talik said. "Just mostly."

His pronunciation was astonishing. She found herself checking him for Thaylen eyebrows, but he was obviously Reshi.

Rysn clenched her teeth, then forced herself to sit down beside him on the edge. She tried to do it as nonchalantly as he had, but she just couldn't. Instead, she settled down—not easy in a fashionable skirt—and scooted out beside him.

Oh, Passions! I'm going to fall off of this and die. Don't look down! Do not look down!

She couldn't help it. She glanced downward, and felt immediately woozy. She could see the side of the head down there, the massive line of a jaw. Nearby, standing on a ridge above the eye to Rysn's right, people pushed large bundles of fruit off the side. Tied with vine rope, the bundles swung down beside the maw below.

Mandibles moved slowly, pulling the fruit in, jerking the ropes. The Reshi pulled those back up to affix more fruit, all under the eyes of the king, who was supervising the feeding from the very tip of the nose to Rysn's left.

"A treat," Talik said, noticing where she watched. "An offering. These small bundles of fruit, of course, do not sustain our god."

"What does?"

He smiled. "Why are you still here, young one? Did I not dismiss you?"

"The trade does not have to be off," Rysn said. "My master told me the terms were already set. We have brought everything you require in payment." *Though for what, I don't know.* "Turning me aside would be pointless."

The king, she noticed, had stepped closer to listen.

"It would serve the same purpose as everything in life," Talik said. "To please Relu-na."

That would be the name of their god, the greatshell. "And your island would approve of such waste? Inviting traders all this way, only to send them off empty-handed?"

"Relu-na approves of boldness," Talik said. "And, more importantly, *respect*. If we do not respect the one with whom we trade, then we should not do it."

What ridiculous logic. If a merchant followed that line of reasoning, he'd never be able to trade. Except . . . in her months with Vstim, it seemed that he'd often sought out people who liked trading with him. People he respected. Those kinds of people certainly would be less likely to cheat you.

Perhaps it wasn't bad logic . . . simply incomplete.

Think like the other trader, she recalled. One of Vstim's lessons—which were so different from the ones she'd learned at home. *What do they want? Why do they want it? Why are you the best one to provide it?*

"It must be hard to live out here, in the waters," Rysn said. "Your god is impressive, but you cannot make everything you need for yourselves."

"Our ancestors did it just fine."

"Without medicines," Rysn said, "that could have saved lives. Without cloth from fibers that grow only on the mainland. Your ancestors survived without these things because they had to. You do not."

The trademaster hunched forward.

Don't do that! You'll fall!

"We are not idiots," Talik said.

Rysn frowned. Why—

"I'm so tired of explaining this," the man continued. "We live simply. That does not make us stupid. For years the outsiders came, trying to exploit us because of our ignorance. We are tired of it, woman. Everything you say is true. Not true—*obvious*. Yet you say it as if we'd never stopped to consider. 'Oh! Medicine! Of course we need medicine! Thank you for pointing that out. I was just going to sit here and *die*.'"

Rysn blushed. "I didn't—"

"Yes, you *did* mean that," Talik said. "The condescension dripped from your lips, young lady. We're tired of being taken advantage of. We're tired of foreigners who try to trade us trash for riches. We don't have knowledge of the current economic situation on the mainland, so we can't know for certain if we are being cheated or not. Therefore, we trade *only* with people we know and trust. That is that."

Current economic situation on the mainland . . . ? Rysn thought. "You've trained in Thaylenah," she guessed.

"Of course I have," Talik said. "You have to know a predator's tricks before you can catch him." He settled back, which let her relax a little. "My parents sent me to train as a child. I had one of your babsks. I made trademaster on my own before returning here."

"Your parents being the king and queen?" Rysn guessed again.

He eyed her. "The king and king's consort."

"You could just call her a queen."

"This trade is not happening," Talik said, standing. "Go and tell your master we are sorry for his illness and hope that he recovers. If he does, he may return next year during the trading season and we will meet with him."

"You imply you respect him," Rysn said, scrambling to her feet—and away from that drop. "So just trade with him!"

"He is sickly," Talik said, not looking at her. "It would not do him justice. We'd be taking advantage of him."

Taking advantage of . . . Passions, these people were *strange*. It seemed even odder to hear such things coming from the mouth of a man who spoke such perfect Thaylen.

"You'd trade with me if you respected me," Rysn said. "If you thought I was worthy of it."

"That will take years," Talik said, joining his mother at the front of the shelf. "Go away, and—"

He cut off as the king spoke to him softly in Reshi.

Talik drew his lips into a line.

"What?" Rysn asked, stepping forward.

Talik turned toward her. "You have apparently impressed the king. You argue fiercely. Though you dismiss us as primitives, you're not as bad as some." He ground his teeth for a moment. "The king will hear your argument for a trade."

Rysn blinked, looked from one to the other. Hadn't she just made her argument for a trade, with the king listening?

The woman regarded Rysn with dark eyes and a calm expression. *I've won the first fight,* Rysn realized, *like the warriors on the battlefield. I've dueled and been judged worthy to spar with the one of greater authority.*

The king spoke, and Talik interpreted. "The king says that you are talented, but that the trade cannot—of course—continue. You should return with your babsk when he comes again. In a decade or so, perhaps we will trade with you."

Rysn searched for an argument. "And is that how Vstim gained respect, Your Majesty?" She would *not* fail in this. She couldn't! "Over years, with his own babsk?"

"Yes," Talik said.

"You didn't interpret that," Rysn said.

"I . . ." Talik sighed, then interpreted her question.

The king smiled with apparent fondness. She spoke a few words in their language, and Talik turned to his mother, looking shocked. "I . . . Wow."

"What?" Rysn demanded.

"Your babsk slew a coracot with some of our hunters," Talik said. "On his own? A foreigner? I had not heard of such a thing."

Vstim. Slaying something? With *hunters*? Impossible.

Though he obviously hadn't always been the wizened old ledgerworm that he was now, she'd imagined he'd been a wizened *young* ledgerworm in the past.

The king spoke again.

"I doubt you'll be slaying any beasts, child," Talik interpreted. "Go. Your babsk will recover from this. He is wise."

No. He is dying, Rysn thought. It came to her mind unbidden, but the truth of it terrified her. More than the height, more than anything else she'd known. Vstim was dying. This might be his final trade.

And she was ruining it.

"My babsk trusts me," Rysn said, stepping closer to the king, moving along the greatshell's nose. "And you said you trust him. Can you not trust his judgment that I am worthy?"

"One cannot substitute for personal experience," Talik translated.

The beast stepped, ground trembling, and Rysn clenched her teeth, imagining them all toppling off. Fortunately, up this high, the motion was more like a gentle sway. Trees rustled, and her stomach lurched, but it wasn't any more dangerous than a ship surging on a wave.

Rysn stepped closer to where the king stood beside the beast's nose. "You are king—you know the importance of trusting those beneath you. You cannot be everywhere, know everything. At times, you must accept the judgment of those you know. My babsk is such a man."

"You make a valid point," Talik translated, sounding surprised. "But what you do not realize is that I have already paid your babsk this respect. That is why I agreed to speak with you myself. I would not have done this for another."

"But—"

"Return below," the king said through Talik, her voice growing harder. She seemed to think this was the end. "Tell your babsk that you proceeded far enough to speak with me personally. Doubtless, this is more than he expected. You may leave the island, and return when he is well."

"I . . ." Rysn felt as if a fist were crushing her throat, making it hard for her to speak. She couldn't fail him, not now.

"Give him my best wishes for his recovery," the king said, turning away.

Talik smiled in what seemed to be satisfaction. Rysn glanced at her two guards, who bore grim expressions.

Rysn stepped away. She felt numb. Turned away, like a child demanding sweets. She felt a furious blush consume her as she walked past the men and women preparing more bundles of fruit.

Rysn stopped. She looked to her left, out at the endless expanse of blue. She turned back toward the king. "I believe," Rysn said loudly, "that I need to speak with someone with more authority."

Talik turned toward her. "You have spoken to the king. There *is* nobody with more authority."

"I beg your pardon," Rysn said. "But I do think there is."

One of the ropes shook from having its fruit gift consumed. *This is stupid, this is stupid, this is—*

Don't think.

Rysn scrambled to the rope, causing her guards to cry out. She grabbed the length of rope and let herself over the side, climbing down beside the greatshell's head. The *god's* head.

Passions! This was hard in a skirt. The rope bit into the skin of her arms, and it vibrated as the creature below crunched on the fruit upon its end.

Talik's head appeared above. "What in Kelek's name are you doing, idiot woman?" he screamed. She found it amusing that he'd learned their curses while studying with them.

Rysn clung to the rope, heart rushing in a mad panic. What *was* she doing? "Relu-na," she yelled back at Talik, "approves of boldness!"

"There is a difference between boldness and stupidity!"

Rysn continued to climb down. It was more of a slide. *Oh, Craving, Passion of need . . .*

"Pull her back up!" Talik ordered. "You soldiers, help." He gave further orders in Reshi.

Rysn looked up as workers grabbed the rope to haul her back upward. A new face appeared above, however, looking down. The king. She raised a hand, halting them as she studied Rysn.

Rysn continued on down. She didn't go terribly far, maybe fifty feet or so. Not even down to the creature's eye. She stopped herself, with effort, her fingers burning. "O great Relu-na," Rysn said loudly, "your people refuse to trade with me, and so I come to you to beg. Your people need what I have brought, but I need a trade even more. I cannot afford to return."

The creature, of course, did not reply. Rysn hung in place beside its shell, which was crusted with lichen and small rockbuds.

"Please," Rysn said. "Please."

What am I expecting to happen? Rysn wondered. She didn't expect the thing to make any sort of reply. But maybe she could persuade those above that she was bold enough to be worthy. It couldn't hurt, at least.

The rope quivered in her hands, and she made the mistake of glancing down.

Actually, what she was doing could hurt. Very much.

"The king," Talik said above, "has commanded that you return."

"Will our negotiation continue?" Rysn asked, glancing up. The king actually looked concerned.

"That's not important," Talik said. "You have been issued a command."

Rysn gritted her teeth, clinging to the rope, looking at the plates of chitin before her. "And what do *you* think?" she asked softly.

Down below, the thing bit down, and the rope suddenly became very tight, slapping Rysn against the side of the enormous head. Above, workers shouted. The king yelled at them in a sudden, sharp voice.

Oh no . . .

The rope pulled even tighter.

Then snapped.

The shouts grew frantic above, though Rysn barely noticed them as panic struck. She did not fall gracefully, but as a flurry of screaming cloth and legs, her skirt flapping, her stomach lurching. What had she done? She—

She saw an eye. The god's eye. Only a glimpse as she passed; it was as large as a house, glassy and black, and it reflected her falling form.

She seemed to hang before it for a fraction of a second, and her scream died in her throat.

It was gone in a moment. Then rushing wind, another scream, and a crash into water hard as stone.

Blackness.

⁎

Rysn found herself floating when she awoke. She didn't open her eyes, but she could sense that she was floating. Drifting, bobbing up and down . . .

"She is an idiot." She knew that voice. Talik, the one she'd been trading with.

"Then she fits well with me," Vstim said. He coughed. "I have to say, old friend, you were supposed to help train her, *not* drop her off a cliff."

Floating . . . Drifting . . .

Wait.

Rysn forced her eyes open. She was in a bed inside a hut. It was hot. Her vision swam, and she drifted . . . drifted because her mind was cloudy. What had they given her? She tried to sit up. Her legs wouldn't move. Her *legs wouldn't move.*

She gasped, then began breathing quickly.

Vstim's face appeared above her, followed by a concerned Reshi woman with ribbons in her hair. Not the queen . . . king . . . whatever. This woman spoke quickly in the barking language of the Reshi.

"Calm now," Vstim said to Rysn, kneeling beside her. "Calm . . . They'll get you something to drink, child."

"I lived," Rysn said. Her voice rasped as she spoke.

"Barely," Vstim said, though with fondness. "The spren cushioned your fall. From that height . . . Child, what were you thinking, climbing over the side like that?"

"I needed to do something," Rysn said. "To prove courage. I thought . . . I needed to be bold . . ."

"Oh, child. This is my fault."

"You were his babsk," Rysn said. "Talik, their trader. You set this up with him, so I could have a chance to trade on my own, but in a controlled setting. The trade was never in danger, and you are not as sick as you appear." The words boiled out, tumbling over one another like a hundred men trying to leave through the same doorway at once.

"When did you figure that out?" Vstim asked, then coughed.

"I . . ." She didn't know. It just all kind of fell together for her. "Right now."

"Well, you must know that I feel a true fool," Vstim said. "I thought this would be a perfect chance for you. A practice with real stakes. And then . . . Then you went and fell off the island's head!"

Rysn squeezed her eyes shut as the Reshi woman arrived with a cup of something. "Will I walk again?" Rysn asked softly.

"Here, drink this," Vstim said.

"Will I walk again?" She didn't take the cup, and kept her eyes closed.

"I don't know," Vstim said. "But you *will* trade again. Passions! Daring to go above the king's authority? Being saved by the island's soul itself?" He chuckled. It sounded forced. "The other islands will be clamoring to trade with us."

"Then I accomplished *something*," she said, feeling a complete and utter idiot.

"Oh, you accomplished something indeed," Vstim said.

She felt a prickling pressure on her arm and opened her eyes with a snap. Something crawled there, about as big as the palm of her hand—a creature that looked like a cremling, but with wings that folded along the back.

"What is it?" Rysn demanded.

"Why we came here," Vstim said. "The thing we trade for, a treasure that very few know still exists. They were supposed to have died with Aimia, you see. I came here with all of these goods in tow because Talik sent to me to say they had the corpse of one to trade. Kings pay fortunes for them."

He leaned down. "I have never seen one alive before. I was given the corpse I wanted in trade. This one has been given to you."

"By the Reshi?" Rysn asked, mind still clouded. She didn't know what to make of any of this.

"The Reshi could not command one of the larkin," Vstim said, standing. "This was given you by the island itself. Now drink your medicine and sleep. You shattered both of your legs. We will be staying on this island for a long while as you recover, and as I seek forgiveness for being a foolish, foolish man."

She accepted the drink. As she drank, the small creature flew up toward the rafters of the hut and perched there, looking down at her with eyes of solid silver.

So what kind of spren *is* it?" Thude asked to the slow Rhythm of Curiosity. He held up the gemstone, peering in at the smoky creature moving about inside.

"Stormspren, my sister says," Eshonai replied as she leaned against the wall, arms folded.

The strands of Thude's beard were tied with bits of raw gemstone that shook and twinkled as he rubbed his chin. He held the large cut gemstone up to Bila, who took it and tapped it with her finger.

They were a warpair of Eshonai's own personal division. They dressed in simple garments that were tailored around the chitinous armor plates on their arms, legs, and chests. Thude also wore a long coat, but he wouldn't take that to battle.

Eshonai, by contrast, wore her uniform—tight red cloth that stretched over her natural armor—and a cap on her skullplate. She never spoke of how that uniform imprisoned her, felt like manacles that tied her in place.

"A stormspren," Bila said to the Rhythm of Skepticism as she turned the stone over in her fingers. "Will it help me kill humans? Otherwise, I don't see why I should care."

"This could change the world, Bila," Eshonai said. "If Venli is right, and she can bond with this spren and come out with anything other than dullform . . . well, at the very least we will have an entirely new form to choose. At the greatest we will have power to control the storms and tap their energy."

"So she will try this personally?" Thude asked to the Rhythm of Winds, the rhythm that they used to judge when a highstorm was near.

"If the Five give her permission." They were to discuss it, and make their decision, today.

"That's great," Bila said, "but will it help me *kill humans?*"

Eshonai attuned Mourning. "If stormform is truly one of the ancient powers, Bila, then yes. It will help you kill humans. Many of them."

"Good enough for me, then," Bila said. "Why are you so worried?"

"The ancient powers are said to have come from our gods."

"Who cares? If the gods would help us kill those armies out there, then I'd swear to them right now."

"Don't say that, Bila," Eshonai said to Reprimand. "*Never* say anything like that."

The woman quieted, tossing the stone onto the table. She hummed softly to Skepticism. That walked the line of insubordination. Eshonai met Bila's eyes and found herself softly humming to Resolve.

Thude glanced from Bila to Eshonai. "Food?" he asked.

"Is that your answer to every disagreement?" Eshonai asked, breaking her song.

"It's hard to argue with your mouth full," Thude said.

"I'm sure I've seen you do just that," Bila said. "Many times."

"The arguments end happy, though," Thude said. "Because everyone is full. So . . . food?"

"Fine," Bila said, glancing at Eshonai.

The two withdrew. Eshonai sat down at the table, feeling drained. When had she started worrying if her friends were insubordinate? It was this horrid uniform.

She picked up the gemstone, staring into its depths. It was a large one, about a third the size of her fist, though gemstones didn't have to be large to trap a spren inside.

She hated trapping them. The right way was to go into the highstorm with the proper attitude, singing the proper song to attract the proper spren. You bonded it in the fury of the raging storm and were reborn with a new body. People had been doing this from the arrival of the first winds.

The listeners had learned that capturing spren was possible from the humans, then had figured out the process on their own. A captive spren made the transformation much more reliable. Before, there had always been an element of chance. You could go into the storm wanting to become a soldier, and come out a mate instead.

This is progress, Eshonai thought, staring at the little smoky spren inside the stone. *Progress is learning to control your world. Put up walls to stop the storms, choose when to become a mate.* Progress was taking nature and putting a box around it.

Eshonai pocketed the gemstone, and checked the time. Her meeting with the rest of the Five wasn't scheduled until the third movement of the Rhythm of Peace, and she had a good half a movement until then.

It was time to speak with her mother.

Eshonai stepped out into Narak and walked along the path, nodding to those who saluted. She passed mostly soldiers. So much of their population wore warform these days. Their small population. Once, there had been hundreds of thousands of listeners scattered across these plains. Now a fraction remained.

Even then, the listeners had been a united people. Oh, there had been divisions, conflicts, even wars among their factions. But they had been a single people—those who had rejected their gods and sought freedom in obscurity.

Bila no longer cared about their origins. There would be others like her, people who ignored the danger of the gods and focused only on the fight with the humans.

Eshonai passed dwellings—ramshackle things constructed of hardened crem over frames of shell, huddled in the leeward shadow of lumps of stone. Most of those were empty now. They'd lost thousands to war over the years.

We do *have to do something,* she thought, attuning the Rhythm of Peace in the back of her mind. She sought comfort in its calm, soothing beats, soft and blended. Like a caress.

Then she saw the dullforms.

They looked much like what the humans called "parshmen," though they were a little taller and not nearly as stupid. Still, dullform was a limiting form, without the capacities and advantages of newer forms. There shouldn't have been any here. Had these people bonded the wrong spren by mistake? It happened sometimes.

Eshonai strode up to the group of three, two femalen and one malen. They were hauling rockbuds harvested on one of the nearby plateaus, plants which had been encouraged to grow quickly by use of Stormlight-infused gems.

"What is this?" Eshonai asked. "Did you choose this form in error? Or are you new spies?"

They looked at her with insipid eyes. Eshonai attuned Anxiety. She had once tried dullform—she had wanted to know what their spies would suffer. Trying to force concepts through her brain had been like trying to think rationally while in a dream.

"Did someone ask you to adopt this form?" Eshonai said, speaking slowly and clearly.

"Nobody asked it," the malen said to no rhythm at all. His voice sounded dead. "We did it."

"Why?" Eshonai said. "*Why* would you do this?"

"Humans won't kill us when they come," the malen said, hefting his rockbud and continuing on his way. The others joined him without a word.

Eshonai gaped, the Rhythm of Anxiety strong in her mind. A few fear-spren, like long purple worms, dove in and out of the rock nearby, collecting toward her until they crawled up out of the ground around her.

Forms could not be commanded; every person was free to choose for themselves. Transformations could be cajoled and requested, but they could not be forced. Their gods had not allowed this freedom, so the listeners *would* have it, no matter what. These people could choose dullform if they wished. Eshonai could do nothing about it. Not directly.

She hastened her pace. Her leg still ached from her wound, but was healing quickly. One of the benefits of warform. She could almost ignore the damage at this point.

A city full of empty buildings, and Eshonai's mother chose a shack on the very edge of the city, almost fully exposed to the storms. Mother worked her shalebark rows outside, humming softly to herself to the Rhythm of Peace. She wore workform; she'd always preferred it. Even after nimble-form had been discovered, Mother had not changed. She had said she didn't want to encourage people to see one form as more valuable than another, that such stratification could destroy them.

Wise words. The type Eshonai hadn't heard out of her mother in years.

"Child!" Mother said as Eshonai approached. Solid despite her years, Mother had a neat round face and wore her hairstrands in a braid, tied with a ribbon. Eshonai had brought her that ribbon from a meeting with the Alethi years ago. "Child, have you seen your sister? It is her day of first transformation! We need to prepare her."

"It is attended to, Mother," Eshonai said to the Rhythm of Peace, kneeling down beside the woman. "How goes the pruning?"

"I should be finishing soon," Mother said. "I need to leave before the people who own this house return."

"You own it, Mother."

"No, no. It belongs to two others. They were in the house last night, and told me I needed to leave. I'll just finish with this shalebark before I go." She got out her file, smoothing one side of a ridge, then painting it with sap to encourage growth in that direction.

Eshonai sat back, attuning Mourning, and Peace left her. Perhaps she should have chosen the Rhythm of the Lost instead. It changed in her head.

She forced it back. No. No, her mother was *not* dead.

She wasn't fully alive, either.

"Here, take this," Mother said to Peace, handing Eshonai a file. At least Mother recognized her today. "Work on that outcropping there. I don't want it to keep growing downward. We need to send it up, up toward the light."

"The storms are too strong on this side of the city."

"Storms? Nonsense. No storms here." Mother paused. "I wonder *where* we'll be taking your sister. She'll need a storm for her transformation."

"Don't worry about that, Mother," Eshonai said, forcing herself to speak to Peace. "I will care for it."

"You are so good, Venli," Mother said. "So helpful. Staying home, not running off, like your sister. That girl . . . She's never where she should be."

"She is now," Eshonai whispered. "She's trying to be."

Mother hummed to herself, continuing working. Once, this woman had one of the best memories in the city. She still did, in a way.

"Mother," Eshonai said, "I need help. I think something terrible is going to happen. I can't decide if it is *less* terrible than what is already happening."

Mother filed at a section of shalebark, then blew off the dust.

"Our people are crumbling," Eshonai said. "We're being weathered away. We moved to Narak and chose a war of attrition. That has meant six years with steady losses. People are giving up."

"That's not good," Mother said.

"But the alternative? Dabbling in things we shouldn't, things that might bring the eyes of the Unmade upon us."

"You're not working," Mother said, pointing. "Don't be like your sister."

Eshonai placed her hands in her lap. This wasn't helping. Seeing Mother like this . . .

"Mother," Eshonai said to Supplication, "why did we leave the dark home?"

"Ah, now that's an old song, Eshonai," Mother said. "A dark song, not for a child like you. Why, it's not even your day of first transformation."

"I'm old enough, Mother. Please?"

Mother blew on her shalebark. Had she forgotten, finally, this last part of what she had been? Eshonai's heart sank.

"Long are the days since we knew the dark home," Mother sang softly to one of the Rhythms of Remembrance. "The Last Legion, that was our name then. Warriors who had been set to fight in the farthest plains, this place that had once been a nation and was now rubble. Dead was the freedom of most people. The forms, unknown, were forced upon us. Forms of power, yes, but also forms of obedience. The gods commanded, and we did obey, always. Always."

"Except for that day," Eshonai said along with her mother, in rhythm.

"The day of the storm when the Last Legion fled," Mother continued in song. "Difficult was the path chosen. Warriors, touched by the gods, our only choice to seek dullness of mind. A crippling that brought freedom."

Mother's calm, sonorous song danced with the wind. As frail as she seemed other times, when she sang the old songs, she seemed herself again. A parent who had at times conflicted with Eshonai, but a parent whom Eshonai had always respected.

"Daring was the challenge made," Mother sang, "when the Last Legion abandoned thought and power in exchange for freedom. They risked forgetting all. And so songs they composed, a hundred stories to tell, to remember. I tell them to you, and you will tell them to your children, until the forms are again discovered."

From there, Mother launched into one of the early songs, about how the people would make their home in the ruins of an abandoned kingdom. How they would spread out, act as simple tribes and refugees. It was their plan to remain hidden, or at least ignored.

The songs left out so much. The Last Legion hadn't known how to transform into anything other than dullform and mateform, at least not without the help of the gods. How had they known the other forms were possible? Had these facts originally been recorded in the songs, and then lost over the years as words changed here and there?

Eshonai listened, and though her mother's voice did help her attune Peace again, she found herself deeply troubled anyway. She had come here for answers. Once, that would have worked.

No longer.

Eshonai stood to leave her mother singing.

"I found some of your things," Mother said, breaking the song, "when cleaning today. You should take them. They clutter the home, and I will be moving out soon."

Eshonai hummed Mourning to herself, but went to see just what her mother had "discovered." Another pile of rocks, in which she saw child's playthings? Strips of cloth she imagined were clothing?

Eshonai found a small sack in front of the building. She opened it to find paper.

Paper made from local plants, not human paper. Rough paper, with varied color, made after the old listener way. Textured and full, not neat and sterile. The ink on it was beginning to fade, but Eshonai recognized the drawings.

My maps, she thought. *From those early days.*

Without meaning to, she attuned Remembrance. Days spent hiking across the wilderness of what the humans called Natanatan, passing through forests and jungles, drawing her own maps and expanding the world. She'd started alone, but her discoveries had excited an entire people. Soon, though still in her teenage years, she'd been leading entire expeditions to find new rivers, new ruins, new spren, new plants.

And humans. In a way, this was all her fault.

Her mother started singing again.

Looking through her old maps, Eshonai found a powerful longing within her. Once, she'd seen the world as something fresh and exciting. New, like a blossoming forest after a storm. She was dying slowly, as surely as her people were.

She packed up the maps and left her mother's house, walking toward the center of town. Her mother's song, still beautiful, echoed behind her. Eshonai attuned Peace. That let her know that she was nearly late for the meeting with the rest of the Five.

She did not hasten her pace. She let the steady, sweeping beats of the Rhythm of Peace carry her forward. Unless you concentrated on attuning a certain rhythm, your body would naturally choose the one that fit your mood. Therefore, it was always a conscious decision to listen to a rhythm that did not match how you felt. She did this now with Peace.

The listeners had made a decision centuries ago, a decision that set them back to primitive levels. Choosing to murder Gavilar Kholin had been an act to affirm that decision of their ancestors. Eshonai had not then been one of their leaders, but they had listened to her counsel and given her the right to vote among them.

The choice, horrible though it seemed, had been one of courage. They'd hoped that a long war would bore the Alethi.

Eshonai and the others had underestimated Alethi greed. The gemhearts had changed everything.

In the center of town, near the pool, was a tall tower that remained proudly erect in defiance of centuries' worth of storms. Once, there had been steps within, but crem leaking in windows had filled the building up with rock. So workers had carved steps running around its outside.

Eshonai started up the steps, holding to the chain for safety. It was a long but familiar climb. Though her leg ached, warform had great endurance— though it required more food than any other form to keep it strong. She made it to the top with ease.

She found the other members of the Five waiting for her, one member wearing each known form. Eshonai for warform, Davim for workform, Abronai for mateform, Chivi for nimbleform, and the quiet Zuln for dullform. Venli waited as well, with her once-mate, though he was flushed from the difficult climb. Nimbleform, though good for many delicate activities, did not have great endurance.

Eshonai stepped up onto the flat top of the once-tower, wind blowing against her from the east. There were no chairs up here, and the Five sat on the bare rock itself.

Davim hummed to Annoyance. With the rhythms in one's head, it was difficult to be late by accident. They rightly suspected that Eshonai had dallied.

She sat on the rock and took the spren-filled gemstone from her pocket, setting it on the ground in front of her. The violet stone glowed with Stormlight.

"I am worried about this test," Eshonai said. "I do not think we should allow it to proceed."

"What?" Venli said to Anxiety. "Sister, don't be ridiculous. Our people need this."

Davim leaned forward, arms on his knees. He was broad faced, his workform skin marbled mostly of black with tiny swirls of red here and there. "If this works, it will be an amazing advance. The first of the forms of ancient power, rediscovered."

"Those forms are tied to the gods," Eshonai said. "What if, in choosing this form, we invite them to return?"

Venli hummed Irritation. "In the old day, *all* forms came from the gods. We have found that nimbleform does not harm us. Why would storm-form?"

"It is different," Eshonai said. "Sing the song; hum it to yourself. 'Its coming brings the gods their night.' The ancient powers are dangerous."

"Men have them," Abronai said. He wore mateform, lush and plump, though he controlled its passions. Eshonai had never envied him the position; she knew, from private conversations, that he would have preferred to have another form. Unfortunately, others who held mateform either did so transiently—or did not possess the proper solemnity to join the Five.

"You yourself brought us the report, Eshonai," Abronai continued. "You saw a warrior among the Alethi using ancient powers, and many others confirmed it to us. Surgebindings have returned to men. The spren again betray us."

"If Surgebindings are back," Davim said to Consideration, "then it might indicate that the gods are returning anyway. If so, we'd best be prepared to deal with them. Forms of power will help with that."

"We don't know they will come," Eshonai said to Resolve. "We don't know *any* of this. Who knows if men even have Surgebindings—it might be one of the Honorblades. We left one in Alethkar that night."

Chivi hummed to Skepticism. Her nimbleform face had elongated features, her hairstrands tied back in a long tail. "We are fading as a people.

I passed some today who had taken dullform, and not to remember our past. They did so because they worried that men would kill them otherwise! They prepare themselves to become slaves!"

"I saw them too," Davim said to Resolve. "We must do something, Eshonai. Your soldiers are losing this war, beat by beat."

"The next storm," Venli said. She used the Rhythm of Pleading. "I can test this at the next storm."

Eshonai closed her eyes. Pleading. It was a rhythm not often attuned. It was hard to deny her sister in this.

"We must be unified in this decision," Davim said. "I will accept nothing else. Eshonai, do you insist on objecting? Will we need to spend hours here making this decision?"

She took a deep breath, coming to a decision that had been working its way through the back of her mind. The decision of an explorer. She glanced at the sack of maps she'd set on the floor beside her.

"I will agree to this test," Eshonai said.

Nearby, Venli hummed to Appreciation.

"However," Eshonai continued to Resolve, "I must be the one who tries the new form first."

All humming stopped. The others of the Five gaped at her.

"What?" Venli said. "Sister, no! It is my right."

"You are too valuable," Eshonai said. "You know too much about the forms, and much of your research is held only in your head. I am simply a soldier. I can be spared if this goes wrong."

"You are a Shardbearer," Davim said. "Our last."

"Thude has trained with my Blade and Plate," Eshonai said. "I will leave both with him, just in case."

The others of the Five hummed to Consideration.

"This is a good suggestion," Abronai said. "Eshonai has both strength and experience."

"It was *my* discovery!" Venli said to Irritation.

"And you are appreciated for it," Davim said. "But Eshonai is right; you and your scholars are too important to our future."

"More than that," Abronai added. "You are too close to the project, Venli. The way you speak makes that clear. If Eshonai enters the storms and discovers that something is off about this form, she can halt the experiment and return to us."

"This is a good compromise," Chivi said, nodding. "Are we in agreement?"

"I believe so," Abronai said, turning toward Zuln.

The representative of the dullforms rarely spoke. She wore the smock of a parshman, and had indicated that she considered it her duty to represent them—those with no songs—along with any dullforms among them.

Hers was as noble a sacrifice as Abronai holding to mateform. More so. Dullform was a difficult form to suffer, one that only a few ever experienced for longer than a stormpause or so.

"I agree to this," Zuln said.

The others hummed to Appreciation. Only Venli did not join in the song. If this stormform turned out to be real, would they add another person to the Five? At first, the Five had all been dullforms, then all workers. It was only at the discovery of nimbleform that it had been decided that they would have one of each form.

A question for later. The others of the Five stood up, then began to make their way down the long flight of steps spiraling around the tower. Wind blew from the east, and Eshonai turned toward it, looking out over the broken Plains—toward the Origin of Storms.

During a coming highstorm, she would step into the winds and become something new. Something powerful. Something that would change the destiny of the listeners, and perhaps the humans, forever.

"I nearly had cause to hate you, Sister," Venli said to Reprimand, idling beside where Eshonai sat.

"I did not forbid this test," Eshonai said.

"Instead you take its glory."

"If there is glory to be had," Eshonai said to Reprimand, "it will be yours for discovering the form. That should not be a consideration. Only our future should matter."

Venli hummed to Irritation. "They called you wise, experienced. It makes one wonder if they've forgotten who you were—that you went off recklessly into the wilds, *ignoring* your people, while I stayed home and memorized songs. When did everyone start believing you were the responsible one?"

It's this cursed uniform, Eshonai thought, rising. "Why didn't you tell us what you were researching? You let me believe your studies were to find artform or mediationform. Instead, you were looking for one of the forms of ancient power."

"Does that matter?"

"Yes. It makes all the difference, Venli. I love you, but your ambition frightens me."

"You don't trust me," Venli said to Betrayal.

Betrayal. That was a song rarely sung. It stung enough to make Eshonai wince.

"We'll see what this form does," Eshonai said, picking up her maps and the gemstone with the trapped spren. "Then we will talk further. I just want to be careful."

"You want to do it yourself," Venli said to Irritation. "You always want to be first. But enough. It is done. Come with me; I will need to train you in the proper mindset to help the form work. Then we will pick a high-storm for the transformation."

Eshonai nodded. She would go through this training. In the meantime, she would consider. Perhaps there was another way. If she could get the Alethi to listen to her, find Dalinar Kholin, sue for peace . . .

Perhaps then, this would not be needed.

PART
TWO

Winds' Approach

SHALLAN • KALADIN • ADOLIN • SADEAS

13

THE DAY'S MASTERPIECE

Warform is worn for battle and reign,
Claimed by the gods, given to kill.
Unknown, unseen, but vital to gain.
It comes to those with the will.

—From the Listener Song of Listing, 15th stanza

The wagon rattled and shook its way across the stone ground, Shallan perched on the hard seat next to Bluth, one of the slab-faced mercenaries Tvlakv employed. He guided the chull pulling the wagon, and didn't speak much, though when he thought she wasn't looking, he would inspect her with eyes like beads of dark glass.

It was chilly. She wished the weather would turn, and spring—or even summer—would come for a time. That wasn't likely in a place notorious for its permanent chill. Having improvised a blanket from the lining of Jasnah's trunk, Shallan draped it over her knees and down to her feet, as much to obscure how tattered her skirt had become as against the cold.

She tried to distract herself by studying the surroundings; the flora out here in the southern Frostlands was completely unfamiliar to her. If there was grass, it grew in patches along the leeward sides of rocks, with short spiky blades rather than long, waving ones. The rockbuds never grew larger than a fist, and they didn't open all the way, even when she'd tried pouring water on one. Their vines were lazy and slow, as if numbed by the cold. There were also spindly little shrubs that grew in cracks and along hillsides. Their brittle branches scraped the sides of the wagon, their tiny green leaves the size of raindrops folding and pulling into the stalks.

The shrubs grew prolifically, spreading wherever they could find purchase. As the wagon rolled past a particularly tall clump, Shallan reached out and snapped off a branch. It was tubular, with an open center, and felt rough like sand.

"These are too fragile for highstorms," Shallan said, holding it up. "How does this plant survive?"

Bluth grunted.

"It is common, Bluth," Shallan said, "to engage one's traveling companion in mutually diverting dialogue."

"I'd do that," he said darkly, "if I knew what in Damnation half those words meant."

Shallan started. She honestly hadn't expected a response. "Then we are even," she said, "as you use plenty of words *I* don't know. Admittedly, I think most of them are curses. . . ."

She'd meant it lightheartedly, but his expression only darkened further. "You think I'm as dumb as that stick."

Stop insulting my stick. The words came to her mind, and almost to her lips, unbidden. She should have been better at holding her tongue, considering her upbringing. But freedom—without the fear that her father was looming behind every closed door—had severely diminished her self-control.

She suppressed the taunt this time. "Stupidity is a function of one's surroundings," she said instead.

"You're saying I'm dumb because I was raised that way?"

"No. I'm saying that everyone is stupid in some situations. After my ship was lost, I found myself ashore but unable to make a fire to warm myself. Would you say that I'm stupid?"

He shot her a glance, but did not speak. Perhaps to a darkeyes, that question sounded like a trap.

"Well I am," Shallan said. "In many areas, I'm stupid. Perhaps when it comes to large words, you're stupid. That's why we need both scholars and caravan workers, guardsman Bluth. Our stupidities complement one another."

"I can see why we need fellows who know how to light fires," Bluth said. "But I don't see why we need people to use fancy words."

"Shhhh," Shallan said. "Don't say that so loudly. If the lighteyes hear, they might stop wasting their time making up new words, and instead start interfering with the business of honest men."

He glanced at her again. Not even a glimmer of humor in the eyes beneath that thick brow. Shallan sighed, but turned her attention back to the

plants. How *did* they survive highstorms? She should get out her sketchpad and—

No.

She blanked her mind and let it go. A short time later, Tvlakv called the
midday halt. Shallan's wagon slowed, and one of the others pulled up beside it.

Tag drove this one, with the two parshmen sitting in the cage behind,
working quietly at weaving hats from reeds they'd gathered in the morning. People often ordered parshmen to do such menial work—something
to make sure all of their time was spent earning money for those who
owned them. Tvlakv would sell the hats for a few chips at his destination.

They kept working as the wagon stopped. They would have to be told to
do something else, and had to be trained specifically for each job they did.
But once they were trained, they would work without complaint.

Shallan had difficulty not seeing their quiet obedience as something
pernicious. She shook her head, then held out her hand to Bluth, who
helped her from the wagon without further prodding. On the ground, she
rested her hand on the side of the vehicle and breathed in sharply through
her teeth. *Stormfather*, what had she done to her feet? Painspren wiggled
out of the wall beside her, little orange bits of sinew—like hands with the
flesh removed.

"Brightness?" Tvlakv said, waddling her direction. "I'm afraid we haven't
much to offer you in the way of meals. We are poor for merchants, you see,
and cannot afford delicacies."

"Whatever you have will suffice," Shallan said, trying to keep the pain
from showing in her face, though the spren had already given her away.
"Please have one of your men get down my trunk."

Tvlakv did so without complaint, though he watched hungrily as Bluth
lowered it to the ground. It seemed a particularly bad idea to let him see
what was inside; the less information he had, the better off she would be.

"These cages," Shallan said, looking over the back of her wagon, "from
those clasps at top, it looks like the wooden sides can be affixed over the bars."

"Yes, Brightness," Tvlakv said. "For highstorms, you see."

"You only have enough slaves to fill one of the three wagons," Shallan
said. "And the parshmen ride in another. This one is empty, and will make
an excellent traveling wagon for me. Put the sides on."

"Brightness?" he said with surprise. "You want to be put into the *cage*?"

"Why not?" Shallan asked, meeting his eyes. "Certainly I'm safe in your
custody, tradesman Tvlakv."

"Er . . . yes . . ."

"You and your men must be well acquainted with rough travel," Shallan
said calmly, "but I am not. Sitting day in and out in the sun on a hard

bench will not suit me. A proper carriage, however, would be a welcome amelioration of this wilderness journey."

"Carriage?" Tvlakv said. "It's a slave wagon!"

"Mere words, tradesman Tvlakv," Shallan said. "If you please?"

He sighed, but gave the order, and the men pulled the sides out from beneath the wagon and hooked them up on the outside. They left off the back one, where the cage door was. The result did not look especially comfortable, but it *would* offer some privacy. Shallan had Bluth haul her chest up and inside, to Tvlakv's dismay. Then, she climbed in and pulled the cage door shut. She held her hand out through the bars toward Tvlakv.

"Brightness?"

"The key," she said.

"Oh." He pulled it out of a pocket, regarding it for a moment—too long a moment—before handing it to her.

"Thank you," she replied. "You may send Bluth with my meal when it is ready, but I shall require a bucket of clean water immediately. You have been most accommodating. I will not forget your service."

"Er . . . Thank you." It almost sounded like a question, and as he walked away, he seemed confused. Good.

She waited for Bluth to bring the water, then crawled—to stay off her feet—through the enclosed wagon. It stank of dirt and sweat, and she grew nauseated thinking of the slaves who had been held here. She would ask Bluth to have the parshmen scrub it later.

She stopped before Jasnah's trunk, then knelt and gingerly raised the lid. Light spilled out from the infused spheres inside. Pattern waited there as well—she had instructed him not to be seen—his shape raising the cover of a book.

Shallan had survived, so far. She certainly wasn't safe, but at least she wasn't going to freeze or starve immediately. That meant she finally had to face greater questions and problems. She rested her hand on the books, ignoring her throbbing feet for the moment. "These have to reach the Shattered Plains."

Pattern vibrated with a confused sound—a questioning pitch that implied curiosity.

"Someone needs to continue Jasnah's work," Shallan said. "Urithiru must be found, and the Alethi must be convinced that the return of the Voidbringers is imminent." She shivered, thinking of the marbled parshmen working just one wagon over.

"You . . . mmm . . . continue?" Pattern asked.

"Yes." She'd made that decision the moment she'd insisted that Tvlakv head for the Shattered Plains. "That night before the sinking, when I saw Jasnah with her guard down . . . I know what I must do."

Pattern hummed, again sounding confused.

"It's hard to explain," Shallan said. "It's a human thing."

"Excellent," Pattern said, eager.

She raised an eyebrow toward him. He'd quickly come a long way from spending hours spinning in the center of a room or climbing up and down walls.

Shallan took out some spheres for better light, then removed one of the cloths Jasnah had wrapped around her books. It was immaculately clean. Shallan dipped the cloth into the bucket of water and began to wash her feet.

"Before I saw Jasnah's expression that night," she explained, "before I talked to her through her fatigue and got a sense of just how worried she was, I had fallen into a trap. The trap of a scholar. Despite my initial horror at what Jasnah had described about the parshmen, I had come to see it all as an intellectual puzzle. Jasnah was so outwardly dispassionate that I assumed she did the same."

Shallan winced as she dug a bit of rock from a crack in her foot. *More* painspren wiggled out of the floor of the wagon. She wouldn't be walking great distances anytime soon, but at least she didn't see any rotspren yet. She had better find some antiseptic.

"Our danger isn't just theoretical, Pattern. It is real and it is terrible."

"Yes," Pattern said, voice sounding grave.

She looked up from her feet. He had moved up onto the inside of the chest's lid, lit by the varied light of the differently colored spheres. "You know something about the danger? The parshmen, the Voidbringers?" Perhaps she was reading too much into his tones. He wasn't human, and often spoke with strange inflections.

"My return . . ." Pattern said. "Because of this."

"What? Why haven't you said something!"

"Say . . . speaking . . . Thinking . . . All hard. Getting better."

"You came to me because of the Voidbringers," Shallan said, moving closer to the trunk, bloodied rag forgotten in her hand.

"Yes. Patterns . . . we . . . us . . . Worry. One was sent. Me."

"Why to me?"

"Because of lies."

She shook her head. "I don't understand."

He buzzed in dissatisfaction. "You. Your family."

"You watched me with my family? That long ago?"

"Shallan. Remember . . ."

Again those memories. This time, not a garden seat, but a sterile white room. Her father's lullaby. Blood on the floor.

No.

She turned away and began cleaning her feet again.

"I know . . . little of humans," Pattern said. "They break. Their minds break. You did not break. Only cracked."

She continued her washing.

"It is the lies that save you," Pattern said. "The lies that drew me."

She dipped her rag in the bucket. "Do you have a name? I've called you Pattern, but it's more of a description."

"Name is numbers," Pattern said. "Many numbers. Hard to say. Pattern . . . Pattern is fine."

"As long as you don't start calling me Erratic as a contrast," Shallan said.

"Mmmmmm . . ."

"What does that mean?" she asked.

"I am thinking," Pattern said. "Considering the lie."

"The joke?"

"Yes."

"Please don't think too hard," Shallan said. "It wasn't a particularly good joke. If you want to ponder a real one, consider that stopping the return of the Voidbringers might depend on *me*, of all people."

"Mmmmm . . ."

She finished with her feet as best she could, then wrapped them with several other cloths from the trunk. She had no slippers or shoes. Perhaps she could buy an extra pair of boots from one of the slavers? The mere thought made her stomach churn, but she didn't have a choice.

Next, she sorted through the contents of the trunk. This was only one of Jasnah's trunks, but Shallan recognized it as the one the woman kept in her own cabin—the one the assassins had taken. It contained Jasnah's notes: books and books full of them. The trunk contained few primary sources, but that didn't matter, as Jasnah had meticulously transcribed all relevant passages.

As Shallan set aside the last book, she noticed something on the bottom of the trunk. A loose piece of paper? She picked it up, curious—then nearly dropped it in surprise.

It was a picture of Jasnah, drawn by Shallan herself. Shallan had given it to the woman after being accepted as her ward. She'd assumed Jasnah had thrown it away—the woman had little fondness for visual arts, which she considered a frivolity.

Instead, she'd kept it here with her most precious things. No. Shallan didn't want to think about that, didn't want to face it.

"Mmm . . ." Pattern said. "You cannot keep all lies. Only the most important."

Shallan reached up and found tears in her eyes. For Jasnah. She'd been avoiding the grief, had stuffed it into a little box and set it away.

As soon as she let that grief come, another piled on top of it. A grief that seemed frivolous in comparison to Jasnah's death, but one that threatened to tow Shallan down as much, or even more.

"My sketchpads . . ." she whispered. "All gone."

"Yes," Pattern said, sounding sorrowful.

"Every drawing I've ever kept. My brothers, my father, Mother . . ." All sunk into the depths, along with her sketches of creatures and her musings on their connections, biology, and nature. Gone. Every bit of it gone.

The world didn't depend upon Shallan's silly pictures of skyeels. She felt as if everything was broken anyway.

"You will draw more," Pattern whispered.

"I don't want to." Shallan blinked free more tears.

"I will not stop vibrating. The wind will not stop blowing. You will not stop drawing."

Shallan brushed her fingers across the picture of Jasnah. The woman's eyes were alight, almost alive again—it was the first picture Shallan had drawn of Jasnah, done on the day they'd met. "The broken Soulcaster was with my things. It's now on the bottom of the ocean, lost. I won't be able to repair it and send it to my brothers."

Pattern buzzed in what sounded like a morose tone to her.

"Who are they?" Shallan asked. "The ones who did this, who killed her and took my art from me. Why would they do such horrible things?"

"I do not know."

"But you are certain that Jasnah was right?" Shallan said. "The Void-bringers are going to return?"

"Yes. Spren . . . spren of *him*. They come."

"These people," Shallan said, "they killed Jasnah. They were probably of the same group as Kabsal, and . . . and as my father. Why would they kill the person closest to understanding how, and why, the Voidbringers are coming back?"

"I . . ." He faltered.

"I shouldn't have asked," Shallan said. "I already know the answer, and it is a very human one. These people seek to control the knowledge so that they can profit from it. Profit from the apocalypse itself. We're going to see that doesn't happen."

She lowered the sketch of Jasnah, setting it between the pages of a book to keep it safe.

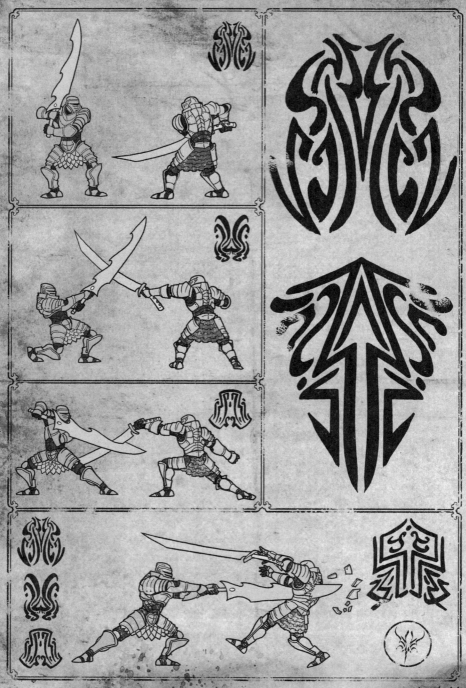

Excerpt from a longer scroll. The bottom half was eaten by an axehound as I fled the place where I'd stolen this.

IRONSTANCE

Mateform meek, for love to share,
Given to life, it brings us joy.
To find this form, one must care.
True empathy one must employ.

—From the Listener Song of Listing, 5th stanza

I t's been a while," Adolin said, kneeling and holding his Shardblade before him, point sunken a few inches into the stone ground. He was alone. Just him and the sword in one of the new preparation rooms, built alongside the dueling arena.

"I remember when I won you," Adolin whispered, looking at his reflection in the blade. "Nobody took me seriously then, either. The fop with the nice clothing. Tinalar thought to duel me just to embarrass my father. Instead I got his Blade." If he'd lost, he would have had to give Tinalar his Plate, which he'd inherited from his mother's side of the family.

Adolin had never named his Shardblade. Some did, some didn't. He'd never thought it appropriate—not because he didn't think the Blade deserved a name, but because he figured he didn't know the right one. This weapon had belonged to one of the Knights Radiant, long ago. That man had named the weapon, undoubtedly. To call it something else seemed presumptuous. Adolin had felt that way even before he'd started thinking of the Radiants in a good light, as his father did.

This Blade would continue after Adolin died. He didn't own it. He was borrowing it for a time.

Its surface was austerely smooth, long, sinuous like an eel, with ridges at the back like growing crystals. Shaped like a larger version of a standard longsword, it bore some resemblance to the enormous, two-handed broadswords he'd seen Horneaters wield.

"A real duel," Adolin whispered to the Blade. "For real stakes. Finally. No more tiptoeing around it, no more limiting myself."

The Shardblade didn't respond, but Adolin imagined that it listened to him. You couldn't use a weapon like this, a weapon that seemed like an extension of the soul itself, and not feel at times that it was alive.

"I speak so confidently to everyone else," Adolin said, "since I know they rely on me. But if I lose today, that's it. No more duels, and a severe knot in Father's grand plan."

He could hear people outside. Stomping feet, a buzz of chatter. Scraping on the stone. They'd come. Come to see Adolin win or be humiliated.

"This might be our last fight together," Adolin said softly. "I appreciate what you've done for me. I know you'd do it for anyone who held you, but I still appreciate it. I . . . I want you to know: I believe in Father. I believe he's right, that the things he sees are real. That the world needs a united Alethkar. Fights like this one are my way to make it happen."

Adolin and his father weren't politicians. They were soldiers—Dalinar by choice, Adolin more by circumstance. They wouldn't be able to just talk their way into a unified kingdom. They'd have to fight their way into one.

Adolin stood up, patting his pocket, then dismissing his Blade to mist and crossing the small chamber. The stone walls of the narrow hallway he entered were etched with reliefs depicting the ten basic stances of swordsmanship. Those had been carved elsewhere, then placed here when this room was built—a recent addition, to replace the tents that dueling preparation had once happened in.

Windstance, Stonestance, Flamestance . . . There was a relief, with depicted stance, for each of the Ten Essences. Adolin counted them off to himself as he passed. This small tunnel had been cut into the stone of the arena itself, and ended in a small room cut into the rock. The bright sunlight of the dueling grounds glared around the edges of the final pair of doors between him and his opponent.

With a proper preparation room for meditation, then this staging room to put on armor or retreat between bouts, the dueling arena at the warcamps was transforming into one as proper as those back in Alethkar. A welcome addition.

Adolin stepped into the staging room, where his brother and aunt were waiting. Stormfather, his hands were sweating. He hadn't felt this nervous when riding into battle, when his life was actually in danger.

Aunt Navani had just finished a glyphward. She stepped away from the pedestal, setting aside her brushpen, and held up the ward for him to see. It was painted in bright red on a white cloth.

"Victory?" Adolin guessed.

Navani lowered it, raising an eyebrow at him.

"What?" Adolin said as his armorers entered, carrying the pieces of his Shardplate.

"It says 'safety and glory,'" Navani said. "It wouldn't kill you to learn some glyphs, Adolin."

He shrugged. "Never seemed that important."

"Yes, well," Navani said, reverently folding the prayer and setting it in the brazier to burn. "Hopefully, you will eventually have a wife to do this for you. Both the reading of glyphs and the making of them."

Adolin bowed his head, as was proper while the prayer burned. Pailiah knew, this wasn't the time to offend the Almighty. Once it was done, however, he glanced at Navani. "And what of the news of the ship?"

They had expected word from Jasnah when she reached the Shallow Crypts, but none had been forthcoming. Navani had checked in with the harbormaster's office in that distant city. They said the *Wind's Pleasure* had not yet arrived. That put it a week overdue.

Navani waved a dismissive hand. "Jasnah was on that ship."

"I know, Aunt," Adolin said, shuffling uncomfortably. What had happened? Had the ship been caught in a highstorm? What of this woman Adolin might be marrying, if Jasnah had her way?

"If the ship is delayed, it's because Jasnah is up to something," Navani said. "Watch. We'll get a communication from her in a few weeks, demanding some task or piece of information. I'll have to pry from her why she vanished. Battah send that girl some sense to go with her intelligence."

Adolin didn't press the issue. Navani knew Jasnah better than anyone else. But . . . he was certainly concerned for Jasnah, and felt a sudden worry that he might not get to meet the girl, Shallan, when expected. Of course, the causal betrothal wasn't likely to work out—but a piece of him wished that it would. Letting someone else choose for him had a strange appeal, considering how loudly Danlan had cursed at him when he'd broken off that particular relationship.

Danlan was still one of his father's scribes, so he saw her on occasion. More glares. But storm it, that one was *not* his fault. The things she'd said to her friends . . .

An armorer set out his boots, and Adolin stepped into them, feeling them click into place. The armorers quickly affixed the greaves, then moved upward, covering him in too-light metal. Soon, all that remained were the gauntlets and the helm. He knelt down, placing his hands into the gauntlets at his side, fingers in their positions. In the strange manner of Shardplate, the armor constricted on its own, like a skyeel curling around its rat, pulling to comfortable tightness around his wrists.

He turned and reached for his helm from the last armorer. It was Renarin.

"You ate chicken?" Renarin asked as Adolin took the helm.

"For breakfast."

"And you talked to the sword?"

"Had an entire conversation."

"Mother's chain in your pocket?"

"Checked three times."

Navani folded her arms. "You still hold to those foolish superstitions?"

Both brothers looked at her sharply.

"They're not superstitions," Adolin said at the same time Renarin said, "It's just good luck, Aunt."

She rolled her eyes.

"I haven't done a formal duel in a long time," Adolin said, pulling on the helm, faceplate open. "I don't want anything to go wrong."

"Foolishness," Navani repeated. "Trust in the Almighty and the Heralds, not whether or not you had the right *meal* before you duel. Storms. Next thing I know, you'll be believing in the Passions."

Adolin shared a look with Renarin. His little traditions probably didn't help him win, but, well, why risk it? Every duelist had his own quirks. His hadn't let him down yet.

"Our guards aren't happy about this," Renarin said softly. "They keep talking about how hard it's going to be to protect you when someone else is swinging a Shardblade at you."

Adolin slammed down his faceplate. It misted at the sides, locking into place, becoming translucent and giving him a full view of the room. Adolin grinned, knowing full well Renarin couldn't see the expression. "I'm so sad to be denying them the chance to babysit me."

"Why do you enjoy tormenting them?"

"I don't like minders."

"You've had guards before."

"On the battlefield," Adolin said. It felt different to be followed about everywhere he went.

"There's more. Don't lie to me, Brother. I know you too well."

Adolin inspected his brother, whose eyes were so earnest behind his spectacles. The boy was too solemn all the time.

"I don't like their captain," Adolin admitted.

"Why? He saved Father's life."

"He just bothers me." Adolin shrugged. "There's something about him that is off, Renarin. That makes me suspicious."

"I think you don't like that he ordered you around, on the battlefield."

"I barely even remember that," Adolin said lightly, stepping toward the door out.

"Well, all right then. Off with you. And Brother?"

"Yes?"

"Try not to lose."

Adolin pushed open the doors and stepped out onto the sand. He'd been in this arena before, using the argument that though the Alethi Codes of War proscribed duels between officers, he still needed to maintain his skills.

To placate his father, Adolin had stayed away from important bouts—bouts for championships or for Shards. He hadn't dared risk his Blade and Plate. Now everything was different.

The air was still chill with winter, but the sun was bright overhead. His breath sounded against the plate of his helm, and his feet crunched in sand. He checked to see that his father was watching. He was. As was the king.

Sadeas hadn't come. Just as well. That might have distracted Adolin with memories of one of the last times that Sadeas and Dalinar had been amiable, sitting together up on those stone steps, watching Adolin duel. Had Sadeas been planning a betrayal even then, while laughing with his father and chatting like an old friend?

Focus. His foe today wasn't Sadeas, though someday . . . Someday soon he'd get that man in the arena. It was the goal of everything he was doing here.

For now, he'd have to settle for Salinor, one of Thanadal's Shardbearers. The man had only the Blade, though he'd been able to borrow a set of the King's Plate for a bout with a full Shardbearer.

Salinor stood on the other side of the arena, wearing the unornamented slate-grey Plate and waiting for the highjudge—Brightlady Istow—to signal the start of the bout. This fight was, in a way, an insult to Adolin. In order to get Salinor to agree to the duel, Adolin had been forced to bet *both* his Plate and his Blade against just Salinor's Blade. As if Adolin weren't worthy, and had to offer more potential spoils to justify bothering Salinor.

As expected, the arena was overflowing with lighteyes. Even if it was speculated that Adolin had lost his former edge, bouts for Shards were very, very rare. This would be the first in over a year's time.

"Summon Blades!" Istow ordered.

Adolin thrust his hand to the side. The Blade fell into his waiting hand ten heartbeats later—a moment before his opponent's appeared. Adolin's heart was beating more quickly than Salinor's. Perhaps that meant his opponent wasn't frightened, and underestimated him.

Adolin fell into Windstance, elbows bent, turned to the side, sword's tip pointing up and backward. His opponent fell into Flamestance, sword held one-handed, other hand touching the blade, standing with a square posture of the feet. The stances were more a philosophy than a predefined set of moves. Windstance: flowing, sweeping, majestic. Flamestance: quick and flexible, better for shorter Shardblades.

Windstance was familiar to Adolin. It had served him well throughout his career.

But it didn't feel right today.

We're at war, Adolin thought as Salinor edged forward, looking to test him. *And every lighteyes in this army is a raw recruit.*

It wasn't time for a show.

It was time for a beating.

As Salinor drew close for a cautious strike to feel out his opponent, Adolin twisted and fell into Ironstance, with his sword held two-handed up beside his head. He slapped away Salinor's first strike, then stepped in and slammed his Blade down into the man's helm. Once, twice, three times. Salinor tried to parry, but he was obviously surprised by Adolin's attack, and two of the blows landed.

Cracks crawled across Salinor's helm. Adolin heard grunts accompanying curses as Salinor tried to bring his weapon back to strike. This wasn't the way it was supposed to go. Where were the test blows, the art, the dance?

Adolin growled, feeling the old Thrill of battle as he shoved aside Salinor's attack—careless of the hit it scored on his side—then brought his Blade in two-handed and *crashed* it into his opponent's breastplate, like he was chopping wood. Salinor grunted again and Adolin raised his foot and *kicked* the man backward, throwing him to the ground.

Salinor dropped his Blade—a weakness of Flamestance's one-handed posture—and it vanished to mist. Adolin stepped over the man and dismissed his own Blade, then kicked down with a booted heel into Salinor's helm. The piece of Plate exploded into molten bits, exposing a dazed, panicked face.

Adolin slammed the heel of his foot against the breastplate next. Though Salinor tried to grab his foot, Adolin kicked relentlessly until the breastplate, too, shattered.

"Stop! *Stop!*"

Adolin halted, lowering his foot beside Salinor's head, looking up at the highjudge. The woman stood in her box, face red, voice furious.

"Adolin Kholin!" she shouted. "This is a duel, not a *wrestling match!*"

"Did I break any rules?" he shouted back.

Silence. It struck him, through the rush in his ears, that the entire crowd had gone quiet. He could hear their breathing.

"Did I break any *rules*?" Adolin demanded again.

"This is not how a duel—"

"So I win," Adolin said.

The woman sputtered. "This duel was to three broken pieces of Plate. You broke only two."

Adolin looked down at the dazed Salinor. Then he reached down, ripped off the man's pauldron, and smashed it between two fists. "Done."

Stunned silence.

Adolin knelt beside his opponent. "Your Blade."

Salinor tried to stand, but with the breastplate missing, doing so was more difficult. His armor wouldn't work properly, and he'd need to roll onto his side and work his way to his feet. Doable, but he obviously didn't have the experience with Plate to perform the maneuver. Adolin slammed him back down to the sand by his shoulder.

"You've lost," Adolin growled.

"You cheated!" Salinor sputtered.

"How?"

"I don't know how! It just— It's not supposed to . . ."

He trailed off as Adolin carefully placed a gauntleted hand against his neck. Salinor's eyes widened. "You wouldn't."

Fearspren crawled out of the sand around him.

"My prize," Adolin said, suddenly feeling drained. The Thrill faded from him. Storms, he'd never before felt like this in a duel.

Salinor's Blade appeared in his hand.

"Judgment," the highjudge said, sounding reluctant, "goes to Adolin Kholin, the victor. Salinor Eved forfeits his Shard."

Salinor let the Blade slip from his fingers. Adolin took it and knelt beside Salinor, holding the weapon with pommel toward the man. "Break the bond."

Salinor hesitated, then touched the ruby at the weapon's pommel. The gemstone flashed with light. The bond had been broken.

Adolin stood, ripping the ruby free, then crushing it in a gauntleted hand. That wouldn't be needed, but it was a nice symbol. Sound finally rose in the crowd, frantic chattering. They'd come for a spectacle and had instead been given brutality. Well, that was how things often went in war. Good for them to see it, he supposed, though as he ducked back into the waiting room he was uncertain of himself. What he'd done was reckless. Dismissing his Blade? Putting himself in a position where the enemy could have gotten at his feet?

Adolin entered the staging room, where Renarin looked at him wide-eyed.

"That," his younger brother said, "was *incredible*. It has to be the shortest Shard bout on record! You were amazing, Adolin!"

"I . . . Thanks." He handed Salinor's Shardblade toward Renarin. "A present."

"Adolin, are you sure? I mean, I'm not exactly the best with the Plate I already have."

"Might as well have the full set," Adolin said. "Take it."

Renarin seemed hesitant.

"Take it," Adolin said again.

Reluctantly, Renarin did so. He grimaced as he took it. Adolin shook his head, sitting down on one of the reinforced benches intended to hold a Shardbearer. Navani stepped into the room, having come down from the seats above.

"What you did," she noted, "would not have worked on a more skillful opponent."

"I know," Adolin said.

"It was wise, then," Navani said. "You mask your true skill. People can assume this was won by trickery, pit-fighting instead of proper dueling. They might continue to underestimate you. I can work with this to get you more duels."

Adolin nodded, pretending that was why he'd done it.

Workform worn for strength and care.
Whispering spren breathe at your ear.
Seek first this form, its mysteries to bear.
Found here is freedom from fear.

—From the Listener Song of Listing, 19th stanza

Tradesman Tvlakv," Shallan said, "I believe that you are wearing a different pair of shoes today than you were on the first day of our trip."

Tvlakv stopped on his way to the evening fire, but adapted smoothly to her challenge. He turned toward her with a smile, shaking his head. "I fear you must be mistaken, Brightness! Just after leaving on this trip, I lost one of my clothing trunks to a storm. I have but this one pair of shoes to my name."

It was a flat-out lie. However, after six days of traveling together, she had discovered that Tvlakv didn't much mind being caught in a lie.

Shallan perched on her wagon's front seat in the dim light, feet bandaged, staring Tvlakv down. She'd spent most of the day milking knobweed stems for their sap, then rubbing it on her feet to keep away the rotspren. She felt extremely satisfied to have noticed the plants—it showed that though she lacked much practical knowledge, some of her studies could be useful in the wild.

Did she confront him about his lie? What would it accomplish? He didn't seem to get embarrassed by such things. He watched her in the darkness, eyes beady, shadowed.

"Well," Shallan said to him, "that is unfortunate. Perhaps in our travels we will meet another merchant group with whom I can trade for proper footwear."

"I will be certain to look for such an opportunity, Brightness." Tvlakv gave her a bow and a fake smile, then continued toward the evening cook fire, which was burning fitfully—they were out of wood, and the parshmen had gone out into the evening to search for more.

"Lies," Pattern said softly, his shape nearly invisible on the seat beside her.

"He knows if I can't walk, I'm more dependent upon him."

Tvlakv settled down beside the struggling fire. Nearby, the chulls—unhooked from their wagons—lumbered around, crunching tiny rockbuds beneath their gargantuan feet. They never strayed far.

Tvlakv started whispering quietly with Tag, the mercenary. He kept a smile on his face, but she didn't trust those dark eyes of his, glittering in the firelight.

"Go see what he's saying," Shallan told Pattern.

"See . . . ?"

"Listen to his words, then come back and repeat them to me. Don't get too close to the light."

Pattern moved down the side of the wagon. Shallan leaned back against the hard seat, then took a small mirror she'd found in Jasnah's trunk out of her safepouch along with a single sapphire sphere for light. Just a mark, nothing too bright, and it was failing at that. *When is that next highstorm due? Tomorrow?*

It was nearing the start of a new year—and that meant the Weeping was coming, though not for a number of weeks. It was a Light Year, wasn't it? Well, she could endure highstorms out here. She'd already been forced to suffer that indignity once, locked within her wagon.

In the mirror, she could see that she looked awful. Red eyes with bags under them, her hair a frazzled mess, her dress frayed and soiled. She looked like a beggar who had found a once-nice dress in a trash heap.

It didn't bother her overly much. Was she worried about looking pretty for slavers? Hardly. However, Jasnah hadn't cared what people thought of her, yet had always kept her appearance immaculate. Not that Jasnah had acted alluringly—never for a moment. In fact, she'd disparaged such behavior in no uncertain terms. *Using a fetching face to make men buy you something is no different from a man using muscle to force someone to do the same,* she'd said. *Both methods are base, and both will fail a person as they age.*

No, Jasnah had not approved of seduction as a tool. However, people responded differently to those who looked in control of themselves.

But what can I do? Shallan thought. *I have no makeup; I don't even have shoes to wear.*

". . . she could be someone important," Tvlakv's voice said abruptly nearby. Shallan jumped, then looked to the side, where Pattern now rested on the seat beside her. The voice came from there.

"She is trouble," Tag's voice said. Pattern's vibrations produced a perfect imitation. "I still think we should just leave her and go."

"It is fortunate for us," Tvlakv's voice said, "that the decision is not yours. You worry about making dinner. I shall worry about our little light-eyed companion. Someone is missing her, someone rich. If we can sell her back to them, Tag, it could be what finally digs us out."

Pattern imitated the sounds of a crackling fire for a short time, then fell silent.

The precise reproduction of the conversation was marvelous. *This*, Shallan thought, *could be very useful*.

Unfortunately, something needed to be done about Tvlakv. She couldn't have him regarding her as something to be sold back to those missing her—that was discomfortingly close to viewing her as a slave. If she let him continue in such a mindset, she'd spend the entire trip worrying about him and his thugs.

So what would Jasnah do, in this situation?

Gritting her teeth, Shallan slipped down off the wagon, stepping gingerly on her wounded feet. She could walk, barely. She waited for the pain-spren to retreat, then—covering up her agony—she approached the meager fire and sat down. "Tag, you are excused."

He looked to Tvlakv, who nodded. Tag retreated to check on the parshmen. Bluth had gone to scout the area, as he often did at night, checking for signs of others passing this way.

"It is time to discuss your payment," Shallan said.

"Service to one so illustrious is payment in itself, of course."

"Of course," she said, meeting his eyes. *Don't back down. You can do this.* "But a merchant must make a living. I am not blind, Tvlakv. Your men do not agree with your decision to help me. They think it a waste."

Tvlakv glanced at Tag, looking unsettled. Hopefully, he wondered what else she had guessed.

"Upon arriving at the Shattered Plains," Shallan said, "I will acquire a grand fortune. I do not have it yet."

"That is . . . unfortunate."

"Not in the slightest," Shallan said. "It is an opportunity, tradesman Tvlakv. The fortune I will acquire is the result of a betrothal. If I arrive safely, those who rescued me—saved me from pirates, sacrificed greatly to see me brought to my new family—will undoubtedly be well rewarded."

"I am but a humble servant," Tvlakv said with a broad, false smile. "Rewards are the farthest thing from my mind."

He thinks I'm lying about the fortune. Shallan ground her teeth in frustration, anger beginning to burn inside of her. This was just what Kabsal had done! Treating her like a plaything, a means to an end, not a real person.

She leaned closer to Tvlakv into the firelight. "Do not toy with me, slaver."

"I wouldn't dare—"

"You have no idea the storm you have wandered into," Shallan hissed, holding his eyes. "You have no idea what stakes have been wagered upon my arrival. Take your petty schemes and stuff them in a crevice. Do as I say, and I will see your debts canceled. You will be a free man again."

"What? How . . . how did you—"

Shallan stood up, cutting him off. She felt somehow stronger than she had before. More determined. Her insecurities fluttered in the pit of her stomach, but she paid them no heed.

Tvlakv didn't know she was timid. He didn't know she had been raised in rural isolation. To him, she was a woman of the court, accomplished at argument and accustomed to being obeyed.

Standing before him, feeling radiant in the glow of the flames—towering above him and his grubby machinations—she *saw*. Expectation wasn't just about what people expected of you.

It was about what you expected of yourself.

Tvlakv leaned away from her like a man before a raging bonfire. He shrank back, eyes wide, raising an arm. Shallan realized that she *was* glowing faintly with the light of spheres. Her dress no longer bore the tears and smudges it had before. It was majestic.

Instinctively, she let the glow from her skin fade, hoping Tvlakv would think it a trick of the firelight. She spun and left him shaking beside the fire as she walked back to the wagon. Darkness was fully upon them, the first moon having yet to rise. As she walked, her feet didn't hurt nearly as much as they had. Was the knobweed sap doing that much good?

She reached the wagon and began climbing back into the seat, but Bluth chose that moment to crash into camp.

"Put out the fire!" he cried.

Tvlakv looked at him dumbfounded.

Bluth dashed ahead, passing Shallan and reaching the fire, where he grabbed the pot of steaming broth. He turned it over onto the flames, splashing out ashes and steam with a hiss, scattering flamespren, which faded away.

Tvlakv jumped up, looking down as filthy broth—faintly lit by the dying embers—ran past his feet. Shallan, gritting her teeth against the pain, got off the wagon and approached. Tag ran up from the other direction.

". . . seem to be several dozen of them," Bluth was saying in a low voice. "They are well armed, but have no horses or chulls, so they are not rich."

"What is this?" Shallan demanded.

"Bandits," Bluth said. "Or mercenaries. Or whatever you want to call them."

"Nobody polices this area, Brightness," Tvlakv said. He glanced at her, then looked away quickly, obviously still shaken. "It is truly a wilderness, you see. The presence of the Alethi on the Shattered Plains means many like to come and go. Trading caravans like ours, craftsmen seeking work, lowborn lighteyed sellswords with an eye toward enlisting. Those two conditions—no laws, but plenty of travelers—attract a certain kind of ruffian."

"Dangerous," Tag agreed. "These types take what they want. Leave only corpses."

"Did they see our fire?" Tvlakv asked, wringing his cap in his hands.

"Don't know," Bluth said, glancing over his shoulder. Shallan could barely make out his expression in the darkness. "Didn't want to get close. I snuck up to get a count, then ran back here fast."

"How can you be sure they're bandits?" Shallan asked. "They might just be soldiers on their way to the Shattered Plains, as Tvlakv said."

"They fly no banners, display no sigils," Bluth said. "But they have good equipment and keep a tight guard. They're deserters. I'd bet the chulls on it."

"Bah," Tvlakv said. "You'd bet my chulls on a hand with the tower, Bluth. But Brightness, for all his terrible gambling sense, I believe the fool is right. We must harness the chulls and depart immediately. The night's darkness is our ally, and we must make the most of it."

She nodded. The men moved quickly, even the portly Tvlakv, breaking down camp and hooking up the chulls. The slaves grumbled at not getting their food for the night. Shallan stopped beside their cage, feeling ashamed. Her family had owned slaves—and not just parshmen and ardents. Ordinary slaves. In most cases, they were nothing worse than darkeyes without the right of travel.

These poor souls, however, were sickly and half-starved.

You're only one step from being in one of those pens yourself, Shallan, she thought with a shiver as Tvlakv passed, hissing curses at the captives. *No. He wouldn't dare put you in there. He'd just kill you.*

Bluth had to be reminded again to give her a hand up into the wagon. Tag ushered the parshmen into their wagon, cursing at them for moving so slowly, then climbed into his seat and took up the tail position.

The first moon began to rise, making it lighter than Shallan would have liked. It seemed to her that each crunching footstep of the chulls was as loud as a highstorm's thunder. They brushed the plants she'd named crustspines, with their branches like tubes of sandstone. Those cracked and shook.

Progress was not quick—chulls never were. As they moved, she picked out lights on a hillside, frighteningly close. Campfires not a ten-minute walk away. A shifting of winds brought the sound of distant voices, of metal on metal, perhaps men sparring.

Tvlakv turned the wagons eastward. Shallan frowned in the night. "Why this way?" she whispered.

"Remember that gully we saw?" Bluth whispered. "Putting it between us and them, in case they hear and come looking."

Shallan nodded. "What can we do if they catch us?"

"It won't be good."

"Couldn't we bribe our way past them?"

"Deserters ain't like common bandits," Bluth said. "These men, they've given up everything. Oaths. Families. When you desert, it breaks you. It leaves you willing to do anything, because you've already given away everything you could have cared about losing."

"Wow," Shallan said, looking over her shoulder.

"I . . . Yeah, you spend your whole life with a decision like that, you do. You wish any honor were left for you, but know you've already given it away."

He fell silent, and Shallan was too nervous to prod him further. She continued watching those lights on the hillside as the wagons—blessedly—rolled farther and farther into the night, eventually escaping into the darkness.

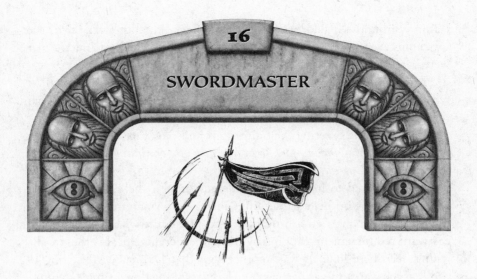

Nimbleform has a delicate touch.
Gave the gods this form to many,
Tho' once defied, by the gods they were crushed.
This form craves precision and plenty.

—From the Listener Song of Listing, 27th stanza

Y ou know," Moash said from Kaladin's side, "I always thought this place would be . . ."

"Bigger?" Drehy offered in his lightly accented voice.

"*Better*," Moash said, looking around the practice grounds. "It looks just like where darkeyed soldiers practice."

These sparring grounds were reserved for Dalinar's lighteyes. In the center, the large open courtyard was filled with a thick layer of sand. A raised wooden walkway ran around the perimeter, stretching between the sand and the narrow surrounding building, which was just one room deep. That narrow building wrapped around the courtyard except at the front, which had a wall with an archway for the entrance, and had a wide roof that extended, giving shade to the wooden walkway. Lighteyed officers stood chatting in the shade or watching men sparring in the sunlight of the yard, and ardents moved this way and that, delivering weapons or drinks.

It was a common layout for training grounds. Kaladin had been in several buildings like this. Mostly back when he'd first been training in Amaram's army.

Kaladin set his jaw, resting his fingers on the archway leading into the training grounds. It had been seven days since Amaram's arrival in the warcamps. Seven days of dealing with the fact that Amaram and Dalinar were friends.

He'd decided to be storming happy about Amaram's arrival. After all, it meant that Kaladin would be able to find a chance to finally stick a spear in that man.

No, he thought, entering the training grounds, *not a spear. A knife. I want to be up close to him, face-to-face, so I can watch him panic as he dies. I want to feel that knife going in.*

Kaladin waved to his men and entered through the archway, forcing himself to focus on his surroundings instead of Amaram. That archway was good stone, quarried nearby, built into a structure with the traditional eastward reinforcement. Judging by the modest crem deposits, these walls hadn't been here long. It was another sign that Dalinar was starting to think of the warcamps as permanent—he was taking down simple, temporary buildings and replacing them with sturdy structures.

"I don't know what you expected," Drehy said to Moash as he inspected the grounds. "How would you make *sparring grounds* different for the lighteyes? Use diamond dust instead of sand?"

"Ouch," Kaladin said.

"I don't know how," Moash said. "It's just that they make such a big deal of it. No darkeyes on the 'special' sparring grounds. I don't see what makes them special."

"That's because you don't think like lighteyes," Kaladin said. "This place is special for one simple reason."

"Why's that?" Moash asked.

"Because *we're* not here," Kaladin said, leading the way in. "Not normally, at least."

He had with him Drehy and Moash, along with five other men, a mix of Bridge Four members and a few survivors of the old Cobalt Guard. Dalinar had assigned those to Kaladin, and to Kaladin's surprise and pleasure, they had accepted him as their leader without a word of complaint. To a man, he'd been impressed with them. The old Guard had deserved its reputation.

A few, all darkeyed, had started eating with Bridge Four. They'd asked for Bridge Four patches, and Kaladin had gotten them some—but ordered them to put their Cobalt Guard patches on the other shoulder, and continue to wear them as a mark of pride.

Spear in hand, Kaladin led his team toward a group of ardents who bustled in their direction. The ardents wore Vorin religious garb—loose trousers and tunics, tied at the waist with simple ropes. Pauper's clothing. They were slaves, and then they also weren't. Kaladin had never given much thought to them. His mother would probably lament how little Kaladin cared for religious observance. The way Kaladin figured it, the Almighty didn't show much concern for him, so why care back?

"This is the *lighteyes'* training ground," said the lead ardent sternly. She was a willowy woman, though you weren't supposed to think of ardents as male or female. She had her head shaven, like all ardents. Her male companions wore square beards with clean upper lips.

"Captain Kaladin, Bridge Four," Kaladin said, scanning the practice grounds and shouldering his spear. It would be very easy for an accident to happen here, during sparring. He'd have to watch for that. "Here to guard the Kholin boys while they practice today."

"Captain?" one of the ardents scoffed. "You—"

Another ardent silenced him by whispering something. News about Kaladin had traveled quickly through camp, but ardents could be an isolated lot, sometimes.

"Drehy," Kaladin said, pointing. "See those rockbuds growing up on the top of the wall there?"

"Yup."

"They're cultivated. That means there's a way up."

"Of course there is," the lead ardent said. "The stairwell is at the northwestern corner. I have the key."

"Good, you can let him in," Kaladin said. "Drehy, keep an eye on things from up there."

"On it," Drehy said, trotting in the direction of the stairwell.

"And what kinds of danger do you expect them to be in here?" the ardent said, folding her arms.

"I see lots of weapons," Kaladin said, "lots of people moving in and out, and . . . are those Shardblades I see? I wonder what could *possibly* go wrong." He gave her a pointed look. The woman sighed, then handed her key to an assistant, who jogged off after Drehy.

Kaladin pointed to positions for his other men to watch from. They moved off, leaving only him and Moash. The lean man had turned immediately at the mention of Shardblades, and now watched them hungrily. A pair of lighteyed men bearing them had moved out into the center of the sands. One Blade was long and thin, with a large crossguard, while the other was wide and enormous, with wicked spikes—slightly flamelike—jutting out of both sides along the lower third. Both weapons had protective strips on the edges, like a partial sheath.

"Huh," Moash said, "I don't recognize either of those men. I thought I knew all the Shardbearers in camp."

"They aren't Shardbearers," the ardent said. "They're using the King's Blades."

"Elhokar lets people use his Shardblade?" Kaladin asked.

"It is a grand tradition," the ardent said, seeming annoyed that she had to explain. "The highprinces used to do it in their own princedoms, before the reunification, and now it is the king's obligation and honor. Men may use the King's Blade and Plate to practice. The lighteyes of our armies must be trained with Shards, for the good of all. Blade and Plate are difficult to master, and if a Shardbearer falls in battle, it is important that others be capable of their immediate use."

That made sense, Kaladin supposed, though he found it hard to imagine any lighteyes letting someone else touch his Blade. "The king has two Shardblades?"

"One is that of his father, kept for the tradition of training Shardbearers." The ardent glanced at the sparring men. "Alethkar has always had the finest Shardbearers in the world. This tradition is part of it. The king has hinted that someday, he might bestow his father's Blade upon a worthy warrior."

Kaladin nodded in appreciation. "Not bad," he said. "I'll bet that a lot of men come to practice with them, each hoping to prove he's the most skilled and most deserving. A good way for Elhokar to trick a bunch of men into training."

The ardent huffed and walked away. Kaladin watched the Shardblades flash in the air. The men using them barely knew what they were doing. The real Shardbearers he'd seen, the real Shardbearers he'd *fought*, hadn't lurched about swinging the oversized swords like polearms. Even Adolin's duel the other day had—

"Storms, Kaladin," Moash said, watching the ardent stalk away. "And you were telling *me* to be respectful?"

"Hmm?"

"You didn't use an honorific for the king," Moash said. "Then you implied that the lighteyes coming to practice were lazy and needed to be tricked into it. I thought we were supposed to avoid antagonizing the lighteyes?"

Kaladin looked away from the Shardbearers. Distracted, he'd spoken thoughtlessly. "You're right," he said. "Thanks for the reminder."

Moash nodded.

"I want you by the gate," Kaladin said, pointing. A group of parshmen came in, bearing boxes, probably foodstuffs. Those wouldn't be dangerous. Would they? "Pay particularly close attention to servants, sword runners, or anyone else seemingly innocuous who approaches Highprince Dalinar's sons. A knife to the side from someone like that would be one of the best ways to pull off an assassination."

"Fine. But tell me something, Kal. Who is this Amaram fellow?"

Kaladin turned sharply toward Moash.

"I see how you look at him," Moash said. "I see how your face gets when the other bridgemen mention him. What did he do to you?"

"I was in his army," Kaladin said. "The last place I fought, before . . ."

Moash gestured to Kaladin's forehead. "That's his work, then?"

"Yeah."

"So he's not the hero people say he is," Moash said. He seemed pleased by that fact.

"His soul is as dark as any I've ever known."

Moash took Kaladin by the arm. "We *are* going to get back at them somehow. Sadeas, Amaram. The ones who have done these things to us?" Angerspren boiled up around him, like pools of blood in the sand.

Kaladin met Moash's eyes, then nodded.

"Good enough for me," Moash said, shouldering his spear and jogging off toward the position Kaladin had indicated, the spren vanishing.

"He's another who needs to learn to smile more," Syl whispered. Kaladin hadn't noticed her flitting nearby, and now she settled down on his shoulder.

Kaladin turned to walk around the perimeter of the practice grounds, noting each entrance. Perhaps he was being overly cautious. He just liked doing jobs well, and it had been a lifetime since he'd had a job other than saving Bridge Four.

Sometimes, though, it seemed like his job was impossible to do well. During the highstorm last week, someone had *again* sneaked into Dalinar's rooms, scrawling a second number on the wall. Counting it down, it pointed at the same date a little over a month away.

The highprince didn't seem worried, and wanted the event kept quiet. Storms . . . was he writing the glyphs himself while he had fits? Or was it some kind of spren? Kaladin was *sure* nobody could have gotten past him this time to get in.

"Do you want to talk about the thing that is bothering you?" Syl asked from her perch.

"I'm worried about what's happening during the highstorms with Dalinar," Kaladin said. "Those numbers . . . something is wrong. You still seeing those spren about?"

"Red lightning?" she asked. "I think so. They're hard to spot. You haven't seen them?"

Kaladin shook his head, hefting his spear and walking over onto the walkway around the sands. Here, he peeked into a storage room. Wooden practice swords, some the size of Shardblades, and sparring leathers lined the wall.

"Is that all that's bothering you?" Syl asked.

"What else would be?"

"Amaram and Dalinar."

"It's not a big deal. Dalinar Kholin is friends with one of the worst murderers I've ever met. So? Dalinar is lighteyed. He's probably friends with a lot of murderers."

"Kaladin . . ." Syl said.

"Amaram's worse than Sadeas, you know," Kaladin said, walking around the storage room, checking for doorways. "Everyone knows that Sadeas is a rat. He's straight with you. 'You're a bridgeman,' he told me, 'and I'm going to use you up until you die.' Amaram, though . . . He promised to be more, a brightlord like those in the stories. He told me he'd protect Tien. He feigned honor. That's worse than any depth Sadeas could ever reach."

"Dalinar's not like Amaram," Syl said. "You know he's not."

"People say the same things about him that they did of Amaram. That they *still do* of Amaram." Kaladin stepped back out into the sunlight and continued his circuit of the grounds, passing dueling lighteyes who kicked up sand as they grunted, sweated, and clacked wooden swords against one another.

Each pair was attended by a half-dozen darkeyed servants carrying towels and canteens—and many had a parshman or two bring them chairs to sit on when they rested. Stormfather. Even in something routine like this, the lighteyes had to be pampered.

Syl zipped out into the air in front of Kaladin, coming down like a storm. *Literally* like a storm. She stopped in the air right in front of him, a cloud boiling from beneath her feet, flashing with lightning. "You can honestly say," she demanded, "that you think Dalinar Kholin is only *pretending* to be honorable?"

"I—"

"Don't you lie to me, Kaladin," she said, stepping forward, pointing. Diminutive though she was, in that moment, she seemed as vast as a highstorm. "No lies. Ever."

He took a deep breath. "No," he finally said. "No, Dalinar gave up his Blade for us. He's a good man. I accept that. Amaram has him fooled. He had me fooled too, so I suppose I can't blame Kholin too much."

Syl nodded curtly, the cloud dissipating. "You should talk to him about Amaram," she said, walking in the air beside Kaladin's head as he continued scouting the structure. Her steps were small, and she should have fallen behind, but she didn't.

"And what should I say?" Kaladin asked. "Should I go to him and accuse a lighteyes of the third dahn of murdering his own troops? Of stealing my Shardblade? I'll sound like either a fool or a madman."

"But—"

"He won't listen, Syl," Kaladin said. "Dalinar Kholin might be a good man, but he won't let me speak ill of a powerful lighteyes. It's the way of the world. And that *is* truth."

He continued his inspection, wanting to know what was in the rooms where people could watch people spar. Some were for storage, others for bathing and resting. Several of those were locked, with lighteyes inside recovering from their daily sparring. Lighteyes liked baths.

The back side of the structure, opposite the entrance gate, held the living quarters for the ardents. Kaladin had never seen so many shaved heads and robed bodies scurrying about. Back in Hearthstone, the citylord had kept only a few wizened old ardents for tutoring his son. Those had also come down to the town periodically to burn prayers and elevate darkeyes' Callings.

These ardents didn't seem to be the same type. They had the physiques of warriors, and would often step in to practice with lighteyes who needed a sparring partner. Some of the ardents had dark eyes, but still used the sword—they weren't considered lighteyed or darkeyed. They were just ardents.

And what do I do if one of them *decides to try killing the princelings?* Storms, but he hated some aspects of bodyguard duty. If nothing happened, then you were never sure if it was because nothing was wrong, or because you had deterred potential assassins.

Adolin and his brother finally arrived, both fully armored in their Shardplate, helms under their arms. They were accompanied by Skar and a handful of former members of the Cobalt Guard. Those saluted Kaladin as he walked up and gestured that they were dismissed, the shift officially changed. Skar would be off to join Teft and the group protecting Dalinar and Navani.

"The area is as secure as I can make it without disrupting training, Brightlord," Kaladin said, walking up to Adolin. "My men and I will keep an eye out while you spar, but don't hesitate to give a holler if something seems amiss."

Adolin grunted, surveying the place, barely paying Kaladin any heed. He was a tall man, his few black Alethi hairs overwhelmed by quite a bit of golden blond. His father didn't have that. Adolin's mother had been from Rira, perhaps?

Kaladin turned to walk toward the northern side of the courtyard, where he'd have a different view from Moash.

"Bridgeman," Adolin called. "You've decided to start using proper titles for people? Didn't you call my father 'sir'?"

"He's in my chain of command," Kaladin said, turning back. The simple answer seemed the best.

"And I'm not?" Adolin asked, frowning.

"No."

"And if I give you an order?"

"I'll comply with any reasonable requests, Brightlord. But if you wish for someone to fetch you tea between bouts, you'll have to send someone else. There should be plenty here willing to lick your heels."

Adolin stepped up to him. Though the deep blue Shardplate added only a few inches to his height, he seemed to tower because of it. Perhaps that line about licking heels had been brash.

Adolin represented something, though. The privilege of the lighteyes. He wasn't like Amaram or Sadeas, who brought out Kaladin's hatred. Men like Adolin just annoyed him, reminding him that in this world, some sipped wine and wore fancy clothing while others were made slaves almost on a whim.

"I owe you my life," Adolin growled, as if it hurt to say the words. "That's the only reason I haven't yet thrown you through a window." He reached up with a gauntleted finger and tapped at Kaladin's chest. "But my patience with you won't extend as far as my father's, little bridgeman. There's something off about you, something I can't put my finger on. I'm watching you. Remember your place."

Great. "I'll keep you alive, Brightlord," Kaladin said, pushing aside the finger. "*That's* my place."

"I can keep myself alive," Adolin said, turning away and tromping across the sand with a clink of Plate. "Your job is to watch over my brother."

Kaladin was more than happy to let him leave. "Spoiled child," he muttered. Kaladin supposed that Adolin was a few years older than him. Just recently, Kaladin had realized that he'd passed his twentieth birthday while a bridgeman, and never known it. Adolin was in his early twenties. But being a child had little to do with age.

Renarin still stood awkwardly near the front gate, wearing Dalinar's former Shardplate, carrying his newly won Shardblade. Adolin's quick duel from yesterday was the talk of the warcamps, and it would take Renarin five days to fully bond his Blade before he could dismiss it.

The young man's Shardplate was the color of dark steel, unpainted. That was how Dalinar had preferred it. By giving his Plate away, Dalinar suggested that he felt he needed to win his next victories as a politician. It was a laudable move; you couldn't always have men following you because they feared you could beat them up—or even because you were the best soldier among them. You needed more, far more, to be a true leader.

Yet Kaladin did wish Dalinar had kept the Plate. Anything that helped the man stay alive would have been a boon for Bridge Four.

Kaladin leaned back against a column, folding his arms, spear in the crook of his arm, watching the area for trouble and inspecting everyone that got too close to the princelings. Adolin walked over and grabbed his brother by the shoulder, towing him across the courtyard. Various people sparring in the square stopped and bowed—if not in uniform—or saluted the princelings as they passed. A group of grey-clothed ardents had gathered at the back of the courtyard, and the woman from earlier stepped forward to chat with the brothers. Adolin and Renarin both bowed formally to her.

It had been three weeks now since Renarin had been given his Plate. Why had Adolin waited so long to bring him here for training? Had he been waiting until the duel, so he could win the lad a Blade too?

Syl landed on Kaladin's shoulder. "Adolin and Renarin are both bowing to her."

"Yeah," Kaladin said.

"But isn't the ardent a slave? One their father owns?"

Kaladin nodded.

"Humans don't make sense."

"If you're only now learning that," Kaladin said, "then you haven't been paying attention."

Syl tossed her hair, which moved realistically. The gesture itself was very human. Perhaps she'd been paying attention after all. "I don't like them," she said airily. "Either one. Adolin or Renarin."

"You don't like anyone who carries Shards."

"Exactly."

"You called the Blades abominations before," Kaladin said. "But the Radiants carried them. So were the Radiants wrong to do so?"

"Of course not," she said, sounding like he was saying something completely stupid. "The Shards weren't abominations back then."

"What changed?"

"The knights," Syl said, growing quiet. "The knights changed."

"So it's not that the weapons are abominations specifically," Kaladin said. "It's that the wrong people are carrying them."

"There are no right people anymore," Syl whispered. "Maybe there never were. . . ."

"And where did they come from in the first place?" Kaladin asked. "Shardblades. Shardplate. Even modern fabrials are nowhere near as good. So where did the ancients get weapons so amazing?"

Syl fell silent. She had a frustrating habit of doing that when his questions got too specific.

"Well?" he prompted.

"I wish I could tell you."

"Then do."

"I wish it worked that way. It doesn't."

Kaladin sighed, turning his attention back to Adolin and Renarin, where it was supposed to be. The senior ardent had led them to the very back of the courtyard, where another group of people sat on the ground. They were ardents too, but something was different about them. Teachers of some sort?

As Adolin spoke to them, Kaladin did another quick scan around the courtyard, then frowned.

"Kaladin?" Syl asked.

"Man in the shadows over there," Kaladin said, gesturing with his spear toward a place under the eaves. A man stood there, leaning cross-armed against a waist-high wooden railing. "He's watching the princelings."

"Um, so is everyone else."

"He's different," Kaladin said. "Come on."

Kaladin wandered over casually, unthreatening. The man was probably just a servant. Long-haired, with a short but scruffy black beard, he wore loose tan clothing tied with ropes. He looked out of place in the sparring yard, and that itself was probably enough to indicate he wasn't an assassin. The best assassins never stood out.

Still, the man had a robust build and a scar on his cheek. So he'd seen fighting. Best to check on him. The man watched Renarin and Adolin intently and, from this angle, Kaladin couldn't see if his eyes were light or dark.

As Kaladin got close, his foot audibly scraped the sand. The man spun immediately, and Kaladin leveled his spear by instinct. He could see the man's eyes now—they were brown—but Kaladin had trouble placing his age. Those eyes seemed old somehow, but the man's skin didn't seem wrinkled enough to match them. He could have been thirty-five. Or he could have been seventy.

Too young, Kaladin thought, though he couldn't say why.

Kaladin lowered his spear. "Sorry, I'm a little jumpy. First few weeks on the job." He tried to say it disarmingly.

It didn't work. The man looked him up and down, still showing the chained menace of a warrior deciding whether or not to strike. Finally, he turned away from Kaladin and relaxed, watching Adolin and Renarin.

"Who are you?" Kaladin asked, stepping up beside the man. "I'm new, as I said. I'm trying to learn everyone's names."

"You're the bridgeman. The one who saved the highprince."

"I am," Kaladin said.

"You don't need to keep prying," the man said. "I'm not going to hurt your Damnation prince." He had a low, grinding voice. Scratchy. Strange accent too.

"He's not my prince," Kaladin said. "Just my responsibility." He looked the man over again, noticing something. The light clothing, tied with ropes, was very similar to what some of the ardents were wearing. The full head of hair had thrown Kaladin off.

"You're a soldier," Kaladin guessed. "Ex-soldier, I mean."

"Yeah," the man said. "They call me Zahel."

Kaladin nodded, the irregularities clicking into place. Occasionally, a soldier retired to the ardentia, if he had no other life to return to. Kaladin would have expected them to require the man to at least shave his head.

I wonder if Hav is in one of these monasteries somewhere, Kaladin thought idly. *What would he think of me now?* He'd probably be proud. He always had seen guard duty as the most respectable of a soldier's assignments.

"What are they doing?" Kaladin asked Zahel, nodding toward Renarin and Adolin—who, despite the encumbrance of their Shardplate, had seated themselves on the ground before the elder ardents.

Zahel grunted. "The younger Kholin has to be chosen by a master. For training."

"Can't they just pick whichever one they want?"

"Doesn't work that way. It's kind of an awkward situation, though. Prince Renarin, he's never practiced much with a sword." Zahel paused. "Being chosen by a master is a step that most lighteyed boys of suitable rank take by the time they're ten."

Kaladin frowned. "Why didn't he ever train?"

"Health problems of some sort."

"And they'd really turn him down?" Kaladin asked. "The highprince's own son?"

"They could, but they probably won't. Not brave enough." The man narrowed his eyes as Adolin stood up and gestured. "Damnation. I knew it was suspicious that he waited for this until I got back."

"Swordmaster Zahel!" Adolin called. "You aren't sitting with the others!"

Zahel sighed, then gave Kaladin a resigned glance. "I'm probably not brave enough either. I'll try not to hurt him too much." He walked around the railing and jogged over. Adolin clasped Zahel's hand eagerly, then pointed to Renarin. Zahel looked distinctly out of place among the other ardents with their bald heads, neatly trimmed beards, and cleaner clothing.

"Huh," Kaladin said. "Did he seem odd to you?"

"You all seem odd to me," Syl said lightly. "Everyone but Rock, who is a complete gentleman."

"He thinks you're a god. You shouldn't encourage him."

"Why not? I *am* a god."

He turned his head, looking at her flatly as she sat on his shoulder. "Syl . . ."

"What? I am!" She grinned and held up her fingers, as if pinching something very small. "A little piece of one. Very, very little. You have permission to bow to me now."

"Kind of hard to do when you're sitting on my shoulder," he mumbled. He noticed Lopen and Shen arriving at the gate, likely bearing the daily reports from Teft. "Come on. Let's see if Teft has anything he needs from me, then we'll do a circuit and check on Drehy and Moash."

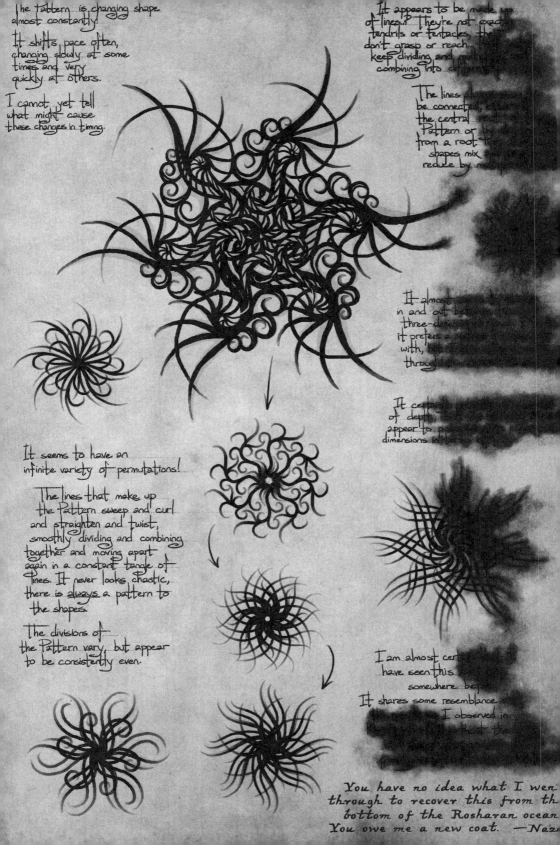

The pattern is changing shape almost constantly.

It shifts pace often, changing slowly at some times and very quickly at others.

I cannot yet tell what might cause these changes in timing.

It appears to be made up of lines... They're not exactly tendrils or tentacles, they don't grasp or reach... they keep dividing and ~~combining into different~~

The lines always ~~seem to~~ be connected, ~~either to~~ the central ~~root~~ Pattern or ~~branching~~ from a root. The shapes mix ~~and~~ reduce by ~~number~~

It ~~moves~~ almost ~~fades~~ in and out ~~of~~ three-~~dimensions~~ it prefers ~~to stay~~ with, ~~but moves~~ through

It ~~certainly~~ ~~has a sense~~ of depth, ~~it~~ ~~doesn't~~ appear to ~~possess~~ dimensions ~~in the~~

It seems to have an infinite variety of permutations!

The lines that make up the Pattern sweep and curl and straighten and twist, smoothly dividing and combining together and moving apart again in a constant tangle of lines. It never looks chaotic, there is always a pattern to the shapes.

The divisions of the Pattern vary, but appear to be consistently even.

I am almost cert~~ain I~~ have seen this ~~pattern~~ somewhere bef~~ore.~~

It shares some resemblance ~~to patterns~~ I observed in

You have no idea what I went through to recover this from the bottom of the Rosharan ocean. You owe me a new coat. —Naz

17

A PATTERN

Dullform dread, with the mind most lost.
The lowest, and one not bright.
To find this form, one need banish the cost.
It finds you and brings you to blight.

—From the Listener Song of Listing, final stanza

Riding on her wagon, Shallan covered her anxiety with scholarship. There was no way to tell if the deserters had spotted the trails of crushed rockbuds made by the caravan. They might be following. They might not be.

No use dwelling on it, she told herself. And so she found a distraction. "The leaves can start their own shoots," she said, holding up one of the small, round leaves on the tip of her finger. She turned it toward the sunlight.

Bluth sat beside her, hulking like a boulder. Today, he wore a hat that was entirely too stylish for him—dusty white, with a brim that folded upward at the sides. He would occasionally flick his guiding reed—it was at least as long as Shallan was tall—on the shell of the chull ahead.

Shallan had made a small list of the beats he used in the back of her book. Bluth hit twice, paused, and hit again. That made the animal slow as the wagon in front of them—driven by Tvlakv—began moving up a hillside covered in tiny rockbuds.

"You see?" Shallan said, showing him the leaf. "That's why the plant's limbs are so fragile. When the storm comes, it will shatter these branches and break off the leaves. They will blow away and start new shoots, building their own shell. They grow so quickly. Faster than I'd have expected out here, in these infertile lands."

Bluth grunted.

Shallan sighed, lowering her finger and putting the tiny plant back in the cup she'd been using to nurture it. She glanced over her shoulder.

No sign of pursuit. She really should just stop worrying.

She turned back to her new sketchbook—one of Jasnah's notebooks that didn't have many pages filled—then began a quick sketch of the small leaf. She didn't have very good materials, only a single charcoal pencil, some pens, and a little ink, but Pattern had been right. She could not stop.

She had begun with a replacement sketch of the santhid as she remembered it from her dip in the sea. The picture wasn't equal to the one she'd crafted right after the event, but having it again—in any form—had started healing the wounds inside.

She finished the leaf, then turned the page and began a sketch of Bluth. She didn't particularly want to restart her collection of people with him, but her options were limited. Unfortunately, that hat really did look silly—it was far too small for his head. The image of him huddled forward like a crab, back to the sky and hat on his head . . . well, at least it would be an interesting composition.

"Where did you get the hat?" she asked as she sketched.

"Traded for it," Bluth mumbled, not looking at her.

"Did it cost much?"

He shrugged. Shallan had lost her own hats in the sinking, but had persuaded Tvlakv to give her one of the ones woven by the parshmen. It wasn't particularly attractive, but it kept the sun off her face.

Despite the bumping wagon, Shallan eventually managed to finish her sketch of Bluth. She inspected it, dissatisfied. It *was* a poor way to start her collection, particularly as she felt she'd caricatured him somewhat. She pursed her lips. What would Bluth look like if he weren't always scowling at her? If his clothing were neater, if he carried a proper weapon instead of that old cudgel?

She flipped the page and started again. A different composition— idealized, perhaps, but somehow also *right*. He could actually look dashing, once you dressed him up properly. A uniform. A spear, planted to his side. Eyes toward the horizon. By the time she'd finished, she was feeling much better about the day. She smiled at the product, then held it up to Bluth as Tvlakv called the midday halt.

Bluth glanced at the picture, but said nothing. He gave the chull a few whacks to stop it alongside the one pulling Tvlakv's wagon. Tag rolled up his wagon—he carried the slaves, this time.

"Knobweed!" Shallan said, lowering her sketch and pointing at a patch of thin reeds growing behind a nearby rock.

Bluth groaned. "More of that plant?"

"Yes. Would you kindly fetch them for me?"

"Can't the parshmen do it? I'm supposed to feed the chulls. . . ."

"Which would you rather make wait, guardsman Bluth? The chulls, or the lighteyed woman?"

Bluth scratched his head underneath the hat, then sullenly climbed down from the wagon and walked toward the reeds. Nearby, Tvlakv stood on his wagon, watching the horizon to the south.

A thin trail of smoke rose in that direction.

Shallan felt an immediate chill. She scrambled from the wagon and hurried to Tvlakv. "Storms!" Shallan said. "Is it the deserters? They *are* following us?"

"Yes. They have stopped to cook for midday, it seems," Tvlakv said from his perch atop his wagon. "They do not care about us seeing their fire." He forced out a laugh. "That is a good sign. They probably know we are only three wagons, and are barely worth chasing. So long as we keep moving and don't stop often, they will give up the chase. Yes. I'm certain."

He hopped down from his wagon, then hurriedly began to water the slaves. He didn't bother to make the parshmen do it—he did the work himself. That, more than anything, testified to his nervousness. He wanted to be moving again quickly.

That left the parshmen to continue weaving in their cage behind Tvlakv's wagon. Anxious, Shallan stood there watching. The deserters had spotted the wagons' trail of broken rockbuds.

She found herself sweating, but what could she do? She couldn't hurry the caravan. She had to simply hope, as Tvlakv said, that they could stay ahead of pursuit.

That didn't seem likely. The chull wagons couldn't be faster than marching men.

Distract yourself, Shallan thought as she started to panic. *Find something to take your mind off the pursuit.*

What about Tvlakv's parshmen? Shallan eyed them. Perhaps a drawing of the two of them in their cage?

No. She was too nervous for drawing, but perhaps she could find something out. She walked to the parshmen. Her feet complained, but the pain was manageable. In fact, in contrast to how she'd covered it up on previous days, now she exaggerated her winces. Better to make Tvlakv think she was less well than she was.

She stopped at the cage's bars. The back was unlocked—parshmen never ran. Buying these two must have been quite an investment for Tvlakv.

Parshmen weren't cheap, and many monarchs and powerful lighteyes hoarded them.

One of the two glanced at Shallan, then turned back to his work. Her work? It was difficult to tell the males from the females without undressing them. Both of these two had red on white marbled skin. They had squat bodies, perhaps five feet tall, and were bald.

It was so difficult to see these two humble workers as a threat. "What are your names?" Shallan asked.

One looked up. The other kept working.

"Your name," Shallan prodded.

"One," the parshman said. He pointed at his companion. "Two." He put his head down and kept working.

"Are you happy with your life?" Shallan asked. "Would you rather be free, given the chance?"

The parshman looked up at her and frowned. He scrunched up his brow, mouthing a few of the words, then shook his head. He didn't understand.

"Freedom?" Shallan prodded.

He hunched down to work.

He actually looks uncomfortable, Shallan thought. *Embarrassed for not understanding.* His posture seemed to say, "Please stop asking me questions." Shallan tucked her sketchbook under her arm and took a Memory of the two of them working there.

These are evil monsters, she told herself forcefully, *creatures of legend who will soon be bent on destroying everyone and everything around them.* Standing here, looking in at them, she found it difficult to believe, even though she had accepted the evidence.

Storms. Jasnah was right. Persuading the lighteyes to rid themselves of their parshmen was going to be nearly impossible. She would need very, very solid proof. Troubled, she walked back to her seat and climbed up, making sure to wince. Bluth had left her a bundle of knobweed, and was now caring for the chulls. Tvlakv was digging out some food for a quick lunch, which they'd probably eat while moving.

She quieted her nerves and forced herself to do some sketches of nearby plants. She soon moved on to a sketch of the horizon and the rock formations nearby. The air didn't feel as cold as it had during her first days with the slavers, though her breath still steamed before her in the mornings.

As Tvlakv passed by, he gave her an uncomfortable glance. He had treated her differently since their confrontation at the fire last night.

Shallan continued sketching. It was certainly a lot flatter out here than back home. And there were far fewer plants, though they were more robust. And . . .

. . . And was that *another* column of smoke up ahead? She stood up and raised a hand to shade her eyes. Yes. More smoke. She looked southward, toward the pursuing mercenaries.

Nearby, Tag stopped, noticing what she had. He hustled over to Tvlakv, and the two started arguing softly.

"Tradesman Tvlakv"—Shallan refused to call him "Trademaster," as would be his proper title as a full merchant—"I would hear your discussion."

"Of course, Brightness, of course." He waddled over, wringing his hands. "You have seen the smoke ahead. We have entered a corridor running between the Shattered Plains and the Shallow Crypts and its sister villages. There is more traffic here than in other parts of the Frostlands, you see. So it is not unexpected that we should encounter others . . ."

"Those ahead?"

"Another caravan, if we are lucky."

And if we're unlucky . . . She didn't need to ask. It would mean more deserters or bandits.

"We can avoid them," Tvlakv said. "Only a large group would dare make smoke for midday meals, as it is an invitation—or a warning. The small caravans, like ourselves, do not risk it."

"If it's a large caravan," Tag said, rubbing his brow with a thick finger, "they'll have guards. Good protection." He looked southward.

"Yes," Tvlakv said. "But we could also be placing ourselves between two enemies. Danger on all sides . . ."

"Those behind *will* catch us, Tvlakv," Shallan said.

"I—"

"A man hunting game will return with a mink if there are no telm to be found," she said. "Those deserters have to kill to survive out here. Didn't you say there was probably going to be a highstorm tonight?"

"Yes," Tvlakv said, reluctant. "Two hours after sunset, if the list I bought is correct."

"I don't know how bandits normally weather the storms," Shallan said, "but they've obviously committed to chasing us down. I'd bet they plan to use the wagons as shelter after killing us. They're not going to let us go."

"Perhaps," Tvlakv said. "Yes, perhaps. But Brightness, if we see that second column of smoke ahead, so might the deserters. . . ."

"Yeah," Tag said, nodding, as if he'd only just realized it. "We cut east. The killers might go after the group ahead."

"We let them attack someone else instead of us?" Shallan said, folding her arms.

"What else would you expect us to do, Brightness?" Tvlakv said, exasperated. "We are small cremlings, you see. Our only choice is to keep away from larger creatures and hope for them to hunt one another."

Shallan narrowed her eyes, inspecting that small column of smoke ahead. Was it her eyes, or was it growing thicker? She looked backward. Actually, the columns looked to be about the same size.

They won't hunt prey their own size, Shallan thought. *They left the army, ran away. They're cowards.*

Nearby, she could see Bluth looking backward as well, watching that smoke with an expression she couldn't read. Disgust? Longing? Fear? No spren to give her a clue.

Cowards, she thought again, *or just men disillusioned? Rocks who started rolling down a hillside, only to start going so quickly they don't know how to stop?*

It didn't matter. Those rocks would crush Shallan and the others, if given the chance. Cutting eastward wouldn't work. The deserters would take the easy kill—slow-moving wagons—instead of the potentially harder kill straight ahead.

"We make for the second column of smoke," Shallan said, sitting down.

Tvlakv looked at her. "You don't get to—" He broke off as she met his eyes.

"You . . ." Tvlakv said, licking his lips. "You won't get . . . to the Shattered Plains as quickly, Brightness, if we get tied up with a larger caravan, you see. It could be bad."

"I will deal with that if the problem arises, tradesman Tvlakv."

"Those ahead will keep moving," Tvlakv warned. "We may arrive at that camp and find them gone."

"In which case," Shallan said, "they will either be moving toward the Shattered Plains or coming this way, along the corridor toward the port cities. We will intersect them eventually one way or another."

Tvlakv sighed, then nodded, calling to Tag to hurry.

Shallan sat down, feeling a thrill. Bluth returned and took his seat, then shoved a few wizened roots in her direction. Lunch, apparently. Shortly, the wagons began rolling northward, Shallan's wagon falling into place third in line this time.

Shallan settled into her seat for the trip—they were hours away from that second group, even if they did manage to catch up to it. To keep from worrying, she finished her sketches of the landscape. She then turned to idle sketches, simply letting her pencil go where it willed.

She drew skyeels dancing in the air. She drew the docks of Kharbranth. She did a sketch of Yalb, though the face felt off to her, and she didn't quite capture the mischievous spark in his eyes. Perhaps the errors related to how sad she became, thinking of what had probably happened to him.

She flipped the page and started a random sketch, whatever came into her mind. Her pencil moved into a depiction of an elegant woman in a stately gown. Loose but sleek below the waist, tight across the chest and stomach. Long, open sleeves, one hiding the safehand, the other cut at the elbow exposing the forearm and draping down below.

A bold, poised woman. In control. Still drawing unconsciously, Shallan added her own face to the elegant woman's head.

She hesitated, pencil hovering above the image. That wasn't her. Was it? Could it be?

She stared at that image as the wagon bumped over rocks and plants. She flipped to the next page and started another drawing. A ball gown, a woman at court, surrounded by the elite of Alethkar as she imagined them. Tall, strong. The woman belonged among them.

Shallan added her face to the figure.

She flipped the page and did another one. And then another.

The last one was a sketch of her standing at the edge of the Shattered Plains as she imagined them. Looking eastward, toward the secrets that Jasnah had sought.

Shallan flipped the page and drew again. A picture of Jasnah on the ship, seated at her desk, papers and books sprawled around her. It wasn't the setting that mattered, but the face. That worried, terrified face. Exhausted, pushed to her limits.

Shallan got this one right. The first drawing since the disaster that captured perfectly what she'd seen. Jasnah's burden.

"Stop the wagon," Shallan said, not looking up.

Bluth glanced at her. She resisted the urge to say it again. He didn't, unfortunately, obey immediately.

"Why?" he demanded.

Shallan looked up. The smoke column was still distant, but she'd been right, it was growing thicker. The group ahead had stopped and built a sizable fire for the midday meal. Judging by that smoke, they were a much larger group than the one behind.

"I'm going to get into the back," Shallan said. "I need to look something up. You can continue when I'm settled, but please stop and call to me once we're near to the group ahead."

He sighed, but stopped the chull with a few whacks on the shell. Shallan climbed down, then took the knobweed and notebook, moved to the back of the wagon. Once she was in, Bluth started up again immediately, shouting back to Tvlakv, who had demanded to know the meaning of the delay.

With the walls up her wagon was shaded and private, particularly with it being last in line so nobody could look in the back door at her. Unfortunately, riding in the back wasn't as comfortable as riding in the front. Those tiny rockbuds caused a surprising amount of jarring and jolting.

Jasnah's trunk was tied in place near the front wall. She opened the lid—letting the spheres inside provide dusky illumination—then settled back on her improvised cushion, a pile of the cloths Jasnah had used to wrap her books. The blanket she used at night—as Tvlakv had been unable to produce one for her—was the velvet lining she had ripped out of the trunk.

Settling back, she unwrapped her feet to apply the new knobweed. They were scabbed over and much improved from their condition just a day before. "Pattern?"

He vibrated from somewhere nearby. She'd asked him to remain in the back so as to not alarm Tvlakv and the guards.

"My feet are healing," she said. "Did you do this?"

"Mmmm . . . I know almost nothing of why people break. I know less of why they . . . unbreak."

"Your kind don't get wounded?" she asked, snapping off a knobweed stem and squeezing the drops onto her left foot.

"We break. We just do it . . . differently than men do. And we do not unbreak without aid. I do not know why you unbreak. Why?"

"It is a natural function of our bodies," she said. "Living things repair themselves automatically." She held one of her spheres close, searching for signs of little red rotspren. Where she found a few of them along one cut, she was quick to apply sap and chase them off.

"I would like to know why things work," Pattern said.

"So would many of us," Shallan said, bent over. She grimaced as the wagon hit a particularly large rock. "I made myself glow last night, by the fire with Tvlakv."

"Yes."

"Do you know why?"

"Lies."

"My dress changed," Shallan said. "I swear the scuffs and rips were gone last night. They've returned now, though."

"Mmm. Yes."

"I have to be able to control this thing we can do. Jasnah called it Lightweaving. She implied it was far safer to practice than Soulcasting."

"The book?"

Shallan frowned, sitting back against the bars on the side of the wagon. Beside her, a long line of scratches on the floor looked like they'd been made by fingernails. As if one of the slaves had tried, in a fit of madness, to claw his way to freedom.

The book Jasnah had given her, *Words of Radiance*, had been swallowed by the ocean. It seemed a greater loss than the other one Jasnah had given her, the *Book of Endless Pages*, which had strangely been blank. She didn't understand the full significance of that yet.

"I never got a chance to actually read that book," Shallan said. "We'll need to see if we can find another copy once we reach the Shattered Plains." Their destination being a warcamp, though, she doubted that many books would be for sale.

Shallan held one of her spheres up before herself. It was growing dim, and needed to be reinfused. What would happen if the highstorm came, and they hadn't caught up to the group ahead? Would the deserters push through the storm itself to reach them? And, potentially, the safety of their wagons?

Storms, what a mess. She needed an edge. "The Knights Radiant formed a bond with spren," Shallan said, more to herself than to Pattern. "It was a symbiotic relationship, like a little cremling who lives in the shalebark. The cremling cleans off the lichen, getting food, but also keeping the shalebark clean."

Pattern buzzed in confusion. "Am I . . . the shalebark or the cremling?"

"Either," Shallan said, turning the diamond sphere in her fingers—the tiny gemstone trapped inside glowed with a vigilant light, suspended in glass. "The Surges—the forces that run the world—are more pliable to spren. Or . . . well . . . since spren are *pieces* of those Surges, maybe it's that the spren are better at influencing one another. Our bond gives me the ability to manipulate one of the Surges. In this case, light, the power of Illumination."

"Lies," Pattern whispered. "And truths."

Shallan gripped the sphere in her fist, the light shining through her skin making her hand glow red. She willed the Light to enter her, but nothing happened. "So, how do I make it work?"

"Perhaps eat it?" Pattern said, moving over onto the wall beside her head.

"Eat it?" Shallan asked, skeptical. "I didn't need to eat it before to get the Stormlight."

"Might work, though. Try?"

"I doubt I could swallow an entire sphere," Shallan said. "Even if I wanted to, which I distinctly do *not*."

"Mmmm," Pattern said, his vibrations making the wood shake. "This . . . is not one of the things humans like to eat, then?"

"Storms, no. Haven't you been paying attention?"

"I have," he said with an annoyed zip of a vibration. "But it is difficult to tell! You consume some things, and turn them into other things . . . Very curious things that you hide. They have value? But you leave them. Why?"

"We are done with that conversation," Shallan said, opening her fist and holding up the sphere again. Though, admittedly, something about what he said felt *right*. She hadn't eaten any spheres before, but she had somehow . . .

consumed the Light. Like drinking it.

She'd breathed it in, right? She stared at the sphere for a moment, then sucked in a sharp breath.

It worked. The Light left the sphere, quick as a heartbeat, a bright line streaming into her chest. From there it spread, filling her. The unusual sensation made her feel anxious, alert, ready. Eager to be about . . . something. Her muscles tensed.

"It worked," she said, though when she spoke, Stormlight—glowing faintly—puffed out in front of her. It rose from her skin, too. She had to practice before it all left. Lightweaving . . . She needed to create something. She decided to go with what she'd done before, improving the look of her dress.

Again, nothing happened. She didn't know what to do, what muscles to use, or even if muscles mattered. Frustrated, she sat there trying to find a way to make the Stormlight work, feeling inept as it escaped through her skin.

It took several minutes for it to dissipate completely. "Well, that was distinctly unimpressive," she said, moving to get more stalks of knobweed. "Maybe I should practice Soulcasting instead."

Pattern buzzed. "Dangerous."

"So Jasnah told me," Shallan said. "But I don't have her to teach me anymore, and so far as I know, she's the only one who could have done so. It's either practice on my own or never learn to use the ability." She squeezed out another few drops of knobweed sap, moved to massage it into a cut on her foot, then stopped. The wound was noticeably smaller than it had been just moments ago.

"The Stormlight is healing me," Shallan said.

"It makes you unbreak?"

"Yes. Stormfather! I'm doing things almost by accident."

"Can something be 'almost' an accident?" Pattern asked, genuinely curious. "This phrase, I do not know what it means."

"I . . . Well, it's mostly a figure of speech." Then, before he could ask further, she continued, "And by that I mean something we say to convey an idea or a feeling, but not a literal fact."

Pattern buzzed.

"What does *that* mean?" Shallan asked, massaging the knobweed in anyway. "When you buzz like that. What are you feeling?"

"Hmmm . . . Excited. Yes. It has been so long since anyone has learned of you and your kind."

Shallan squeezed some more sap onto her toes. "You came to learn? Wait . . . you're a *scholar*?"

"Of course. Hmmm. Why else would I come? I will learn so much before—"

He stopped abruptly.

"Pattern?" she asked. "Before what?"

"A figure of speech." He said it perfectly flatly, absent of tone. He was growing better and better at speaking like a person, and at times he sounded just like one. But now all of the color had gone from his voice.

"You're lying," she accused him, glancing at his pattern on the wall. He had shrunk, growing as small as a fist, half his usual size.

"Yes," he said reluctantly.

"You're a terrible liar," Shallan said, surprised at the realization.

"Yes."

"But you love lies!"

"So fascinating," he said. "You are all so *fascinating*."

"Tell me what you were going to say," Shallan ordered. "Before you stopped yourself. I'll know if you lie."

"Hmmmm. You sound like her. More and more like her."

"Tell me."

He buzzed with an annoyed sound, quick and high pitched. "I will learn what I can of you before you kill me."

"You think . . . You think I'm going to *kill* you?"

"It happened to the others," Pattern said, his voice softer now. "It will happen to me. It is . . . a pattern."

"This has to do with the Knights Radiant," Shallan said, raising her hands to start braiding her hair. That would be better than leaving it wild—though without a comb and brush, even braiding it was hard. *Storms,* she thought, *I need a bath. And soap. And a dozen other things.*

"Yes," Pattern said. "The knights killed their spren."

"How? Why?"

"Their oaths," Pattern said. "It is all I know. My kind, those who were unbonded, we retreated, and many kept our minds. Even still, it is hard to think apart from my kind, unless . . ."

"Unless?"

"Unless we have a person."

"So that's what you get out of it," Shallan said, untangling her hair with her fingers. "Symbiosis. I get access to Surgebinding, you get thought."

"Sapience," Pattern said. "Thought. Life. These are of humans. We are ideas. Ideas that wish to live."

Shallan continued working on her hair. "I'm not going to kill you," she said firmly. "I *won't* do it."

"I don't suppose the others intended to either," he said. "But it is no matter."

"It is an *important* matter," Shallan said. "I won't do it. I'm not one of the Knights Radiant. Jasnah made that clear. A man who can use a sword isn't necessarily a soldier. Just because I can do what I do doesn't make me one of them."

"You spoke oaths."

Shallan froze.

Life before death . . . The words drifted toward her from the shadows of her past. A past she would not think of.

"You live lies," Pattern said. "It gives you strength. But the truth . . . Without speaking truths you will not be able to grow, Shallan. I know this somehow."

She finished with her hair and moved to rewrap her feet. Pattern had moved to the other side of the rattling wagon chamber, settling onto the wall, only faintly visible in the dim light. She had a handful of infused spheres left. Not much Stormlight, considering how quickly that other had left her. Should she use what she had to further heal her feet? Could she even do that intentionally, or would the ability elude her, as Light-weaving had?

She tucked the spheres into her safepouch. She would save them, just in case. For now, these spheres and their Light might be the only weapon available to her.

Bandages redone, she stood up in the rattling wagon and found that her foot pain was nearly gone. She could walk almost normally, though she still wouldn't want to go far without shoes. Pleased, she knocked on the wood nearest to Bluth. "Stop the wagon!"

This time, she didn't have to repeat herself. She rounded the wagon and, taking her seat beside Bluth, immediately noticed the smoke column ahead. It had grown darker, larger, roiling violently.

"That's no cook fire," Shallan said.

"Aye," Bluth said, expression dark. "Something big is burning. Probably wagons." He glanced at her. "Whoever is up there, it doesn't look like things went well for them."

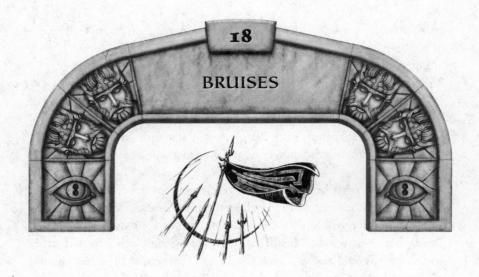

Scholarform shown for patience and thought.
Beware its ambitions innate.
Though study and diligence bring the reward,
Loss of innocence may be one's fate.

—From the Listener Song of Listing, 69th stanza

New guys are coming along, gancho," Lopen said, taking a bite of the paper-wrapped something he was eating. "Wearing their uniforms, talking like real men. Funny. It only took them a few days. Took us weeks."

"It took the rest of the men weeks, but not you," Kaladin said, shading his eyes from the sun and leaning on his spear. He was still on the lighteyes' practice grounds, watching over Adolin and Renarin—the latter of whom was receiving his first instructions from Zahel the swordmaster. "You had a good attitude from the first day we found you, Lopen."

"Well, life was pretty good, you know?"

"Pretty good? You'd just been assigned to carry siege bridges until you died on the plateaus."

"Eh," Lopen said, taking a bite of his food. It looked like a thick piece of flatbread wrapped around something goopy. He licked his lips, then handed it to Kaladin to free his single hand so he could dig in his pocket for a moment. "You have bad days. You have good days. Evens out eventually."

"You're a strange man, Lopen," Kaladin said, inspecting the "food" Lopen had been eating. "What *is* this?"

"Chouta."

"Chowder?"

"Cha-ou-ta. Herdazian food, gon. Good stuff. You can have a bite, if you want."

It seemed to be chunks of undefinable meat slathered in some dark liquid, all wrapped in overly thick bread. "Disgusting," Kaladin said, handing it back as Lopen gave him the thing he'd dug out of his pocket, a shell with glyphs written on both sides.

"Your loss," Lopen said, taking another bite.

"You shouldn't be walking around eating like that," Kaladin noted. "It's rude."

"Nah, it's *convenient*. See, it's wrapped up good. You can walk about, get stuff done, eat at the same time . . ."

"Slovenly," Kaladin said, inspecting the shell. It listed Sigzil's tallies of how many troops they had, how much food Rock thought they'd need, and Teft's assessments of how many of the former bridgemen were fit for training.

That last number was pretty high. If bridgemen lived, they got strong carrying bridges. As Kaladin had proven firsthand, that translated to their making fine soldiers, assuming they could be motivated.

On the reverse side of the shell, Sigzil had outlined a path for Kaladin to take on patrol outside the warcamps. He'd soon have enough of the greenvines ready to begin patrolling the region outside of the warcamps, as he'd told Dalinar he would do. Teft thought it would be good for Kaladin to go himself, as it would let the new men spend time with Kaladin.

"Highstorm tonight," Lopen noted. "Sig says it will come two hours after sunset. He thought you'd want to make preparations."

Kaladin nodded. Another chance for those mysterious numbers to appear—both times before, they'd come during storms. He'd make extra certain Dalinar and his family were being watched.

"Thanks for the report," Kaladin said, tucking the shell into his pocket. "Send back and tell Sigzil his proposed route takes me too far from the warcamps. Have him draw up another one. Also, tell Teft I need a few more men to come here today and relieve Moash and Drehy. They've both been pulling too many hours lately. I'll guard Dalinar tonight myself—suggest to the highprince it would be convenient if his entire family would be together for the highstorm."

"If the winds will, gon," Lopen said, finishing his last bite of chouta. He whistled then, looking in at the practice grounds. "That *is* something, isn't it?"

Kaladin followed Lopen's gaze. Adolin, having left his brother with Zahel, was now executing a training sequence with his Shardblade. Gracefully, he spun and twisted on the sands, sweeping his sword in broad, flowing patterns.

On a practiced Shardbearer, Plate never looked clumsy. Imposing, re-splendent, it fit to the form of the wearer. Adolin's reflected sunlight like a mirror as he made sweeps of the sword, moving from one posture to the next. Kaladin knew it was just a warm-up sequence, more impressive than functional. You'd never do something like this on the battlefield, though many of the individual postures and cuts represented practical movements.

Even knowing that, Kaladin had to shake off a feeling of awe. Shard-bearers in Plate looked inhuman when they fought, more like Heralds than men.

He caught Syl sitting on the edge of the roof overhang near Adolin, watching the young man. She was too distant for Kaladin to make out her expression.

Adolin finished his warm-up in a move where he fell to one knee and slammed his Shardblade into the ground. It sank up to mid-blade, then vanished when he released it.

"I've seen him summon that weapon before," Kaladin said.

"Yeah, gancho, on the battlefield, when we saved his sorry ass from Sadeas."

"No, before that," Kaladin said, remembering an incident with a whore in Sadeas's camp. "He saved someone who was being bullied."

"Huh," Lopen said. "He can't be too bad then, you know?"

"I suppose. Anyway, off with you. Make sure to send that replacement team."

Lopen saluted, collecting Shen, who had been poking at practice swords along the side of the courtyard. Together, they jogged off on the errand.

Kaladin did his rounds, checking on Moash and the others before walking over to where Renarin sat—still armored—on the ground before his new master.

Zahel, the ardent with the ancient eyes, sat in a solemn posture that belied his ragged beard. "You will need to relearn how to fight, wearing that Plate. It changes the way a man steps, grips, moves."

"I . . ." Renarin looked down. It was very odd to see a man wearing spectacles in the magnificent armor. "I will not need to relearn how to fight, master. I never learned in the first place."

Zahel grunted. "That's good. It means I don't have to break down any old, bad habits."

"Yes, master."

"We'll start you off easily, then," Zahel said. "There are some steps at the corner over there. Climb up onto the roof of the dueling grounds. Then jump off."

Renarin looked up sharply. ". . . Jump?"

"I'm old, son," Zahel said. "Repeating myself makes me eat the wrong flower."

Kaladin frowned, and Renarin cocked his head, then looked at Kaladin questioningly. Kaladin shrugged.

"Eat . . . what . . . ?" Renarin asked.

"It means I get angry," Zahel snapped. "You people don't have proper idioms for anything. Go!"

Renarin sprang to his feet, kicking up sand, and hustled away.

"Your helmet, son!" Zahel called.

Renarin stopped, then scrambled back and snatched his helmet off the ground, nearly slipping onto his face as he did so. He spun, off balance, and ran awkwardly toward the stairs. He nearly plowed into a pillar on the way.

Kaladin snorted softly.

"Oh," Zahel said, "and you assume *you'd* do better your first time wearing Shardplate, bodyguard?"

"I doubt I'd forget my helmet," Kaladin said, shouldering his spear and stretching. "If Dalinar Kholin intends to force the other highprinces into line, I think he's going to need better Shardbearers than this. He should have picked someone else for that Plate."

"Like you?"

"Storms no," Kaladin said, perhaps too vehemently. "I'm a soldier, Zahel. I want nothing to do with Shards. The boy is likable enough, but I wouldn't trust men to his command—let alone armor that could keep a much better soldier alive on the field—and that's it."

"He'll surprise you," Zahel replied. "I gave him the whole 'I'm your master and you do what I say' talk, and he actually listened."

"Every soldier hears that on their first day," Kaladin said. "Sometimes they listen. That the boy did is hardly noteworthy."

"If you knew how many spoiled ten-year-old lighteyed brats came through here," Zahel said, "you'd think it worth noting. I thought a nineteen-year-old like him would be insufferable. And don't call him a boy, boy. He's probably close to your own age, and is the son of the most powerful human on this—"

He cut off as scraping from atop the building announced Renarin Kholin charging and throwing himself off into the air, boots grinding against the stone coping of the roof. He sailed a good ten or twelve feet out over the courtyard—practiced Shardbearers could do far better—before floundering like a dying skyeel and crashing down into the sand.

Zahel looked toward Kaladin, raising an eyebrow.

"What?" Kaladin asked.

"Enthusiasm, obedience, no fear of looking foolish," Zahel said. "I can teach him how to fight, but those qualities are innate. This lad is going to do just fine."

"Assuming he doesn't fall on anyone," Kaladin said.

Renarin climbed to his feet. He looked down, as if surprised that he hadn't broken anything.

"Go up and do it again!" Zahel called to Renarin. "This time, fall head-first!"

Renarin nodded, then turned and trotted off toward the stairwell.

"You want him to be confident in how the Plate protects him," Kaladin said.

"Part of using Plate is knowing its limits," Zahel said, turning back to Kaladin. "Plus, I just want him moving in it. Either way he's listening, and that's good. Teaching him is going to be a real pleasure. You, on the other hand, are another story."

Kaladin raised his hand. "Thanks, but no."

"You'd turn down an offer to train with a full weapons master?" Zahel asked. "I can count on one hand the number of darkeyes I've seen given that chance."

"Yes, well, I've already done the 'new recruit' thing. Yelled at by sergeants, worked to the bone, marched for hours on end. Really, I'm fine."

"This isn't the same at all," Zahel said, waving down one of the ardents walking past. The man was carrying a Shardblade with metal guards over the sharp edges, one of the ones the king provided for training use.

Zahel took the Shardblade from the ardent, holding it up.

Kaladin nodded his chin at it. "What's that on the Blade?"

"Nobody's sure," Zahel said, swiping with the Blade. "Fit it to the edges of a Blade, and it will adapt to the shape of the weapon and make it safely blunt. Off the weapons, they break surprisingly easily. Useless in a fight on their own. Perfect for training, though."

Kaladin grunted. Something created long ago, for use in training? Zahel inspected the Shardblade for a moment, then pointed it directly toward Kaladin.

Even with it blunted—even knowing the man wasn't going to really attack him—Kaladin felt an immediate moment of panic. A Shardblade. This one had a slender, sleek form with a large crossguard. The flat sides of the blade were etched with the ten fundamental glyphs. It was a handspan wide and easily six feet long, yet Zahel held it with one hand and didn't seem off balance.

"Niter," Zahel said.

"What?" Kaladin asked, frowning.

"He was head of the Cobalt Guard before you," Zahel said. "He was a good man, and a friend. He died keeping the men of the Kholin house alive. Now you've got the same Damnation job, and you're going to have a tough time doing it half as well as he did."

"I don't see what that has to do with you waving a Shardblade at me."

"Anyone who sends assassins after Dalinar or his sons is going to be powerful," Zahel said. "They'll have access to Shardbearers. That's what you're up against, son. You're going to need far more training than a battle-field gives a spearman. Have you ever fought a man holding one of these?"

"Once or twice," Kaladin said, relaxing against the nearby pillar.

"Don't lie to me."

"I'm not lying," Kaladin said, meeting Zahel's eyes. "Ask Adolin what I pulled his father out of a few weeks back."

Zahel lowered the sword. Behind him, Renarin dove face-first off the roof and crashed into the ground. He groaned inside his helm, rolling over. His helm leaked Light but he seemed otherwise unharmed.

"Well done, Prince Renarin," Zahel called without looking. "Now do a few more jumps and see if you can land on your feet."

Renarin rose and clinked off.

"All right then," Zahel said, sweeping the Shardblade in the air. "Let's see what you can do, kid. Convince me to leave you alone."

Kaladin didn't respond other than to heft his spear and settle into a de-fensive posture, one foot behind, one out front. He held his weapon with the butt forward instead of the point. Nearby, Adolin sparred with another one of the masters, who had the second King's Blade and a suit of Plate.

How would this work? If Zahel scored a hit on Kaladin's spear, would they pretend it had cut through?

The ardent approached in a rush, raising the Blade in a two-handed grip. The familiar calmness and focus of battle enveloped Kaladin. He did not draw in Stormlight. He needed to be certain not to come to rely on it too much.

Watch that Shardblade, Kaladin thought, stepping forward, trying to get inside the weapon's reach. In fighting a Shardbearer, everything became about that Blade. The Blade that nothing could stop, the Blade that didn't just kill the body—but severed the soul itself. The Blade—

Zahel dropped the Blade.

It hit the ground as Zahel got inside Kaladin's reach. Kaladin had been too focused on the weapon, and though he tried to get his spear in position to strike, Zahel twisted and buried his fist into Kaladin's stomach. The next punch—to the face—slammed Kaladin to the floor of the practice grounds.

Kaladin immediately rolled, ignoring the painspren wiggling in the sand. He found his feet as his vision swam. He grinned. "Nice move, that."

Zahel was already turning back to Kaladin, Blade recovered. Kaladin scuttled backward on the sand, spear still forward, staying away. Zahel knew his way around a Blade. He didn't fight like Adolin; fewer sweeping blows, more overhand chops. Quick and furious. He backed Kaladin around the side of the practice ground.

He'll get tired keeping this up, Kaladin's instincts said. *Keep him moving.*

After an almost complete circuit of the grounds, Zahel slowed his offense and instead rounded on Kaladin, watching for an opening. "You'd be in trouble if I had Plate," Zahel said. "I'd be faster, wouldn't tire."

"You don't have Plate."

"And if someone comes for the king wearing it?"

"I'll use a different tactic."

Zahel grunted as Renarin crashed to the ground nearby. The prince almost kept his footing, but stumbled and fell to the side, skidding in the sand.

"Well, if this were a real assassination attempt," Zahel said, "I'd be using different tactics too."

He dashed toward Renarin.

Kaladin cursed, taking off after Zahel.

Immediately, the man reversed, skidding to a stop in the sand and spinning to swing at Kaladin with a powerful two-handed blow. The strike connected with Kaladin's spear, sending a sharp *crack* echoing across the practice grounds. If the Blade hadn't been guarded, it would have split the spear in two and perhaps grazed Kaladin's chest.

A watching ardent tossed Kaladin half a spear. They'd been waiting for his spear to be "cut," and wanted to replicate a real fight as much as possible. Nearby, Moash had arrived, looking concerned, but several ardents intercepted him and explained.

Kaladin looked back to Zahel.

"In a real fight," the man said, "I might have chased down the prince by now."

"In a real fight," Kaladin said, "I might have stabbed you with half a spear when you thought me disarmed."

"I wouldn't have made that mistake."

"Then we'll have to assume I wouldn't have made the mistake of letting you get to Renarin."

Zahel grinned. It looked a dangerous expression on him. He stepped forward, and Kaladin understood. There would be no backing away and leading him off this time. Kaladin wouldn't have that option if he were protecting a member of Dalinar's family. Instead, he had to try his best to pretend to kill this man.

That meant an attack.

A prolonged, close-quarters fight would favor Zahel, as Kaladin couldn't parry a Shardblade. Kaladin's best bet was to strike fast and hope to score an early hit. Kaladin barreled forward, then threw himself to his knees, skidding on the sands underneath Zahel's strike. That would get him close, and—

Zahel kicked Kaladin in the face.

Vision swimming, Kaladin rammed his fake spear into Zahel's leg. The man's Shardblade came down a second later, stopping where Kaladin's shoulder met his neck.

"You're dead, son," Zahel said.

"You've got a spear through the leg," Kaladin said, puffing. "You aren't chasing down Renarin like that. I win."

"You're still dead," Zahel said with a grunt.

"My job is to stop you from killing Renarin. With what I just did, he escapes. Doesn't matter if the bodyguard is dead."

"And what if the assassin had a friend?" another voice asked from behind.

Kaladin twisted to see Adolin, in full Plate and standing with his Shardblade point stuck into the ground before him. He'd removed his helm, and held it in one hand, the other hand resting on the Blade's crossguard.

"If there were two of them, bridgeboy?" Adolin asked with a smirk. "Could you fight two Shardbearers at once? If I wanted to kill Father or the king, I'd never send just one."

Kaladin stood, rolling his shoulder in its socket. He met Adolin's gaze. So condescending. So sure of himself. Arrogant bastard.

"All right," Zahel said. "I'm sure he sees the point, Adolin. No need—"

Kaladin charged the princeling, and he thought he heard Adolin chuckling as he put on his helm.

Something boiled inside of Kaladin.

The nameless Shardbearer who had killed so many of his friends.

Sadeas, sitting regally in red armor.

Amaram, hands on a sword stained with blood.

Kaladin screamed as Adolin's unguarded Shardblade came for him in one of the careful, sweeping strokes from Adolin's practice session. Kaladin pulled himself up short, raising his half-spear and letting the Blade pass right before him. Then he *slapped* the back edge of the Shardblade with his spear, knocking Adolin's grip to the side and fouling up the follow-through.

Kaladin barreled forward and threw his shoulder against the prince. It was like slamming into a wall. Kaladin's shoulder flared with pain, but the momentum—along with the surprise of his cudgel blow—knocked Adolin off balance. Kaladin forced both of them backward, the Shardbearer toppling to the ground with a crash and a surprised grunt.

Renarin made a twin crash, falling to the ground nearby. Kaladin raised his half-spear like a dagger to plunge it toward Adolin's faceplate. Unfortunately, Adolin had dismissed his Blade as they fell. The princeling got a gauntleted hand up underneath Kaladin.

Kaladin slammed his weapon downward.

Adolin heaved upward with one hand.

Kaladin's blow didn't connect; instead he found himself airborne, thrown with all the Plate-augmented strength of a Shardbearer. He floundered in the air before slamming down eight feet away, the sand grinding into his side, the shoulder he'd hit against Adolin flaring in pain again. Kaladin gasped.

"Idiot!" Zahel yelled.

Kaladin groaned, rolling over. His vision swam.

"You could have killed the boy!" He was talking to Adolin somewhere far away.

"He attacked me!" Adolin's voice was muffled by the helm.

"You challenged him, fool child." Zahel's voice was closer.

"Then he asked for it," Adolin said.

Pain. Someone at Kaladin's side. Zahel?

"You're wearing *Plate*, Adolin." Yes, that was Zahel kneeling above Kaladin, whose vision refused to focus. "You don't throw an unarmored sparring partner like he's a bundle of sticks. Your father taught you better than that!"

Kaladin sucked in sharply and forced his eyes open. Stormlight from the pouch at his belt filled him. *Not too much. Don't let them see. Don't let them take it away from you!*

Pain vanished. His shoulder reknit—he didn't know if he'd broken it or just dislocated it. Zahel cried out in surprise as Kaladin pitched himself up to his feet and dashed back toward Adolin.

The prince stumbled away, hand out to his side, obviously summoning his Blade. Kaladin kicked his fallen half-spear up in a spray of sand, then grabbed it in midair as he got near.

In that moment, the strength drained from him. The tempest inside of him fled without warning, and he stumbled, gasping at the returning pain of his shoulder.

Adolin caught him by the arm with a gauntleted fist. The prince's Shardblade formed in his other hand, but in that moment, a second Blade stopped at Kaladin's neck.

"You're dead," Zahel said from behind, holding the Blade against Kaladin's skin. "Again."

Kaladin sank down in the middle of the practice grounds, dropping his half-spear. He felt completely drained. What had happened?

"Go give your brother some help with his jumping," Zahel ordered Adolin. Why did he get to order around princes?

Adolin left and Zahel knelt beside Kaladin. "You don't flinch when someone swings a Blade at you. You actually *have* fought Shardbearers before, haven't you?"

"Yeah."

"You're lucky to be alive, then," Zahel said, probing at Kaladin's shoulder. "You've got tenacity. A stupid amount of it. You have good form, and you think well in a fight. But you hardly know what you're doing against Shardbearers."

"I . . ." What should he say? Zahel was right. It was arrogant to say otherwise. Two fights—three, if he counted today—did not make one an expert. He winced as Zahel prodded a sore tendon. More painspren on the ground. He was giving them a workout today.

"Nothing broken here," Zahel said with a grunt. "How are your ribs?"

"They're fine," Kaladin said, lying back in the sand, staring up at the sky.

"Well, I won't force you to learn," Zahel said, standing up. "I don't think I *could* force you, actually."

Kaladin squeezed his eyes shut. He felt humiliated, but why should he? He'd lost sparring matches before. It happened all the time.

"You remind me a lot of him," Zahel said. "Adolin wouldn't let me teach him either. Not at first."

Kaladin opened his eyes. "I'm nothing like him."

Zahel barked a laugh at that, then stood and walked away, chuckling, as if he'd heard the finest joke in all the world. Kaladin continued to lie on the sand, staring upward at the deep blue sky, listening to the sounds of men sparring. Eventually, Syl flitted over and landed on his chest.

"What happened?" Kaladin asked. "The Stormlight drained from me. I *felt* it go."

"Who were you protecting?" Syl asked.

"I . . . I was practicing how to fight, like when I practiced with Skar and Rock down in the chasms."

"Is that *really* what you were doing?" Syl asked.

He didn't know. He lay there, staring at the sky, until he finally caught his breath and forced himself to his feet with a groan. He dusted himself off, then went to check on Moash and the other guards. As he went, he drew in a little Stormlight, and it worked, slowly healing his shoulder and soothing away his bruises.

The physical ones, at least.

19

SAFE THINGS

FIVE AND A HALF YEARS AGO

The silk of Shallan's new dress was softer than any she had owned before. It touched her skin like a comforting breeze. The left cuff clipped closed over the hand; she was old enough now to cover her safehand. She had once dreamed of wearing a woman's dress. Her mother and she . . .

Her mother . . .

Shallan's mind went still. Like a candle suddenly snuffed, she stopped thinking. She leaned back in her chair, legs tucked up underneath her, hands in her lap. The dreary stone dining chamber bustled with activity as Davar Manor prepared for guests. Shallan did not know which guests, only that her father wanted the place immaculate.

Not that she could do anything to help.

Two maids bustled past. "She saw," one whispered softly to the other, a new woman. "Poor thing was in the room when it happened. Hasn't spoken a word in five months. The master killed his own wife and her lover, but don't let it . . ."

They continued talking, but Shallan didn't hear.

She kept her hands in her lap. Her dress's vibrant blue was the only real color in the room. She sat on the dais, beside the high table. A half-dozen maids in brown, wearing gloves on their safehands, scrubbed the floor and polished the furniture. Parshmen carted in a few more tables. A maid threw open the windows, letting in damp fresh air from the recent highstorm.

Shallan caught mention of her name again. The maids apparently thought that because she didn't speak, she didn't hear either. At times, she wondered if she was invisible. Perhaps she wasn't real. That would be nice. . . .

The door to the hall slammed open, and Nan Helaran entered. Tall, muscular, square-chinned. Her oldest brother was a man. The rest of them . . . they were children. Even Tet Balat, who had reached the age of adulthood. Helaran scanned the chamber, perhaps looking for their father. Then he approached Shallan, a small bundle under his arm. The maids made way with alacrity.

"Hello, Shallan," Helaran said, squatting down beside her chair. "Here to supervise?"

It was a place to be. Father did not like her being where she could not be watched. He worried.

"I brought you something," Helaran said, unwrapping his bundle. "I ordered it for you in Northgrip, and the merchant only just passed by." He took out a leather satchel.

Shallan took it hesitantly. Helaran's grin was so wide, it practically glowed. It was hard to frown in a room where he was smiling. When he was around, she could almost pretend . . . Almost pretend . . .

Her mind went blank.

"Shallan?" he asked, nudging her.

She undid the satchel. Inside was a sheaf of drawing paper, the thick kind—the expensive kind—and a set of charcoal pencils. She raised her covered safehand to her lips.

"I've missed your drawings," Helaran said. "I think you could be very good, Shallan. You should practice more."

She ran the fingers of her right hand across the paper, then picked up a pencil. She started to sketch. It had been too long.

"I need you to come back, Shallan," Helaran said softly.

She hunched over, pencil scratching on paper.

"Shallan?"

No words. Just drawing.

"I'm going to be away a lot in the next few years," Helaran said. "I need you to watch the others for me. I'm worried about Balat. I gave him a new axehound pup, and he . . . wasn't kind to it. You need to be strong, Shallan. For them."

The maids had grown quiet since Helaran's arrival. Lethargic vines curled down outside the window nearby. Shallan's pencil continued to move. As if she weren't doing the drawing; as if it were coming up out of the page, the charcoal seeping out of the texture. Like blood.

Helaran sighed, standing. Then he saw what she was drawing. Bodies, facedown, on the floor with—

He grabbed the paper and crumpled it. Shallan started, pulling back, fingers shaking as she clutched the pencil.

"Draw plants," Helaran said, "and animals. Safe things, Shallan. Don't dwell on what happened."

Tears trickled down her cheeks.

"We can't have vengeance yet," Helaran said softly. "Balat can't lead the house, and I must be away. Soon, though."

The door slammed open. Father was a big man, bearded in careless defiance of fashion. His Veden clothing eschewed the modern designs. Instead, Father wore a skirtlike garment of silk called an ulatu and a tight shirt with a robe over the top. No mink pelts, as his grandfathers might have worn, but otherwise very, very traditional.

He towered taller than Helaran, taller than anyone else on the estate. More parshmen entered after him, carrying bundles of food for the kitchens. All three had marbled skin, two red on black and one red on white. Father liked parshmen. They did not talk back.

"I got word that you told the stable to prepare one of my carriages, Helaran!" Father bellowed. "I'll not have you gallivanting off again!"

"There are more important things in this world," Helaran said. "More important even than you and your crimes."

"Do not speak that way to me," Father said, stalking forward, finger pointed at Helaran. "I am your father." Maids scurried to the side of the room, trying to stay out of the way. Shallan pulled the satchel up against her chest, trying to hide in her chair.

"You are a murderer," Helaran said calmly.

Father stopped in place, face gone red beneath his beard. He then continued forward. "How *dare* you! You think I can't have you imprisoned? Because you're my heir, you think I—"

Something formed in Helaran's hand, a line of mist that coalesced into silvery steel. A Blade some six feet long, curved and thick, with the side that wasn't sharp rising into a shape like burning flames or perhaps ripples of water. It had a gemstone set at the pommel, and as light reflected off the metal, the ridges seemed to move.

Helaran was a Shardbearer. Stormfather! How? When?

Father cut off, pulling up short. Helaran hopped down from the low dais, then leveled the Shardblade at his father. The point touched Father's chest.

Father raised his hands to the sides, palms forward.

"You are a vile corruption upon this house," Helaran said. "I should shove this through your chest. To do so would be a mercy."

"Helaran . . ." The passion seemed to have bled from Father, like the color from his face, which had gone stark white. "You don't know what you think you know. Your mother—"

"I will *not* listen to your lies," Helaran said, rotating his wrist, twisting the sword in his hand, point still against Father's chest. "So easy."

"No," Shallan whispered.

Helaran cocked his head, then turned, not moving the sword.

"No," Shallan said, "please."

"You speak now?" Helaran said. "To defend *him*?" He laughed. A wild bark of a noise. He whipped the sword away from Father's chest.

Father sat down in a dining chair, face still pale. "How? A *Shardblade*. Where?" He glanced suddenly upward. "But no. It's different. Your new friends? They trust you with this wealth?"

"We have an important work to do," Helaran said, turning and striding to Shallan. He laid a hand fondly on her shoulder. He continued more softly. "I will tell you of it someday, Sister. It is good to hear your voice again before I leave."

"Don't go," she whispered. The words felt like gauze in her mouth. It had been months since she'd last spoken.

"I must. Please do some drawings for me while I'm gone. Of fanciful things. Of brighter days. Can you do that?"

She nodded.

"Farewell, Father," Helaran said, turning and striding from the room. "Try not to ruin too much while I'm gone. I *will* come back periodically to check." His voice echoed in the hallway outside as he left.

Brightlord Davar stood, roaring. The few maids left in the room fled out the side door into the gardens. Shallan shrank back, horrified, as her father picked up his chair and slammed it into the wall. He kicked over a small dining table, then took the chairs one at a time and smashed them into the floor with repeated, brutal blows.

Breathing deeply, he turned his eyes on her.

Shallan whimpered at the rage, the lack of humanity, in his eyes. As they focused on her, the life returned to them. Father dropped a broken chair and turned his back toward her, as if ashamed, before fleeing the room.

Artform applied for beauty and hue.
One yearns for the songs it creates.
Most misunderstood by the artist it's true,
Come the spren to foundation's fates.

—From the Listener Song of Listing, 90th stanza

T he sun was a smoldering ember on the horizon, sinking toward
oblivion, as Shallan and her little caravan neared the source of the
smoke in front of them. Though the column had dwindled, she
could now make out that it had three different sources, rising into the air
and twisting into one.

She climbed to her feet on the rocking wagon as they rolled up one last
hill, then stopped on the side, mere feet away from letting her see what
was out there. Of course; cresting the hill would be a very bad idea if bandits waited below.

Bluth climbed down from his wagon and jogged forward. He wasn't
terribly nimble, but he was the best scout they had. He crouched and removed his too-fine hat, then made his way up the hillside to peek over. A
moment later, he stood up straight, no longer attempting stealth.

Shallan hopped down from her seat and hurried over, skirts catching on
the twisted branches of crustspines here and there. She reached the top of
the hill just before Tvlakv did.

Three caravan wagons smoldered quietly below, and the signs of a battle
littered the ground. Fallen arrows, a group of corpses in a pile. Shallan's
heart leaped as she saw the living among the dead. A scattering of tired

figures combed through the rubble or moved bodies. They weren't dressed like bandits, but like honest caravan workers. Five more wagons were clustered on the far side of the camp. Some were scorched, but they all looked functional and still laden with goods.

Armed men and women tended their wounds. Guards. A group of frightened parshmen cared for the chulls. These people had been attacked, but they had survived. "Kelek's breath . . ." Tvlakv said. He turned and shooed Bluth and Shallan backward. "Back, before they see."

"What?" Bluth said, though he obeyed. "But it's another caravan, as we'd hoped."

"Yes, and they needn't know we are here. They might want to speak to us, and that could slow us. Look!" He pointed backward.

In the waning light, Shallan could make out a shadow cresting a hill not far behind them. The deserters. She waved for Tvlakv to surrender his spyglass, and he did so reluctantly. The lens was cracked, but Shallan still got a good look at the force. The thirty or so men *were* soldiers, as Bluth had reported. They flew no banner, and did not march in formation or wear one uniform, but they looked well equipped.

"We need to go down and ask the other caravan for help," Shallan said.

"No!" Tvlakv said, snatching the spyglass back. "We need to flee! The bandits will see this richer but weakened group and will fall upon them instead of us!"

"And you think they won't chase us after that?" Shallan said. "With our tracks so easily visible? You think they won't run us down in the following days?"

"There should be a highstorm tonight," Tvlakv said. "It might cover our tracks, blowing away the shells of the plants we crush."

"Unlikely," Shallan said. "If we stand with this new caravan, we can add our little strength to theirs. We can hold. It—"

Bluth held up a hand suddenly, turning. "A noise." He spun around, reaching for his cudgel.

A figure stood up nearby, hidden by shadows. Apparently, the caravan below had a scout of its own. "You led them right toward us, did you?" asked a woman's voice. "What are they? More bandits?"

Tvlakv held up his sphere, which revealed the scout to be a lighteyed woman of medium height and wiry build. She wore trousers and a long coat that almost looked like a dress, buckled at the waist. She wore a tan glove over her safehand, and spoke Alethi without an accent.

"I . . ." Tvlakv said. "I am just a humble merchant, and—"

"The ones chasing us are certainly bandits," Shallan cut in. "They have chased us all day."

The woman cursed, raising a spyglass of her own. "Good equipment," she mumbled. "Deserters, I'd guess. As if this weren't bad enough. Yix!"

A second figure stood up nearby, wearing tan clothing the color of stone. Shallan jumped. How had she missed spotting him? He was so close! He had a sword at his waist. A lighteyes? No, a foreigner, judging by that golden hair. She never was sure what eye color meant for their social standing. There weren't people with light eyes in the Makabaki region, though they had kings, and practically everyone in Iri had light yellow eyes.

He jogged over, hand on his weapon, watching Bluth and Tag with overt hostility. The woman said something to him in a tongue Shallan didn't know, and he nodded, then jogged off toward the caravan below. The woman followed.

"Wait," Shallan called to her.

"I don't have time to talk," the woman snapped. "We've got two bandit groups to fight."

"Two?" Shallan said. "You didn't defeat the one that attacked you earlier?"

"We fought them off, but they'll be back soon." The woman hesitated on the side of the hill. "The fire was an accident, I think. They were using flaming brands to scare us. They pulled back to let us fight the fires, as they didn't want to lose any more goods."

Two forces, then. Bandits ahead and behind. Shallan found herself sweating in the cold air as the sun finally vanished beneath the western horizon.

The woman was looking northward, toward where her group of bandits must have retreated. "Yeah, they'll be back," the woman said. "They'll want to be done with us before the storm comes tonight."

"I offer you my protection," Shallan found herself saying.

"Your protection?" the woman said, turning back to Shallan, sounding baffled.

"You may accept me and mine into your camp," Shallan said. "I will see to your safety tonight. I will need your service after that to convey me to the Shattered Plains."

The woman laughed. "You are gutsy, whoever you are. You can join our camp, but you'll die there with the rest of us!"

Cries rose from the caravan. A second later, a flight of arrows fell through the night from that direction, pelting wagons and caravan workers.

Screams.

Bandits followed, emerging from the blackness. They weren't nearly as well equipped as the deserters, but they didn't need to be. The caravan had fewer than a dozen guards left. The woman cursed and started running down the hillside.

Shallan shivered, eyes wide at the sudden slaughter below. Then she turned and walked to Tvlakv's wagons. This sudden chill was familiar to her. The coldness of clarity. She knew what she had to do. She didn't know if it would work, but she saw the solution—like lines in a drawing, coming together to transform random scribbles into a full picture.

"Tvlakv," she said, "take Tag below and try to help those people fight."

"What!" he said. "No. No, I will not throw my life away for your foolishness."

She met his eyes in the near darkness, and he stopped. She knew that she was glowing softly; she could feel the storm within. "Do it." She left him and walked to her wagon. "Bluth, turn this wagon around."

He stood with a sphere beside the wagon, looking down at something in his hand. A sheet of paper? Surely *Bluth* of all people didn't know glyphs.

"Bluth!" Shallan snapped, climbing into the wagon. "We need to be moving. *Now!*"

He shook himself, then tucked the paper away and scrambled into the seat beside her. He whipped at the chull, turning it. "What are we doing?" he asked.

"Heading south."

"Into the bandits?"

"Yes."

For once, he did as she told him without complaint, whipping the chull faster—as if he were eager to just get this all over with. The wagon rattled and shook as they went down one hillside, then climbed another.

They reached the top and looked down at the force climbing toward them. The men carried torches and sphere lanterns, so she could see their faces. Dark expressions on grim men with weapons drawn. Their breastplates or leather jerkins might once have held symbols of allegiance, but she could see where those had been cut or scratched away.

The deserters looked at her with obvious shock. They had not expected their prey to come to them. Her arrival stunned them for a moment. An important moment.

There will be an officer, Shallan thought, standing up on her seat. *They are soldiers, or once were. They'll have a command structure.*

She took a deep breath. Bluth raised his sphere, looking at her, and grunted as if surprised.

"Bless the Stormfather that you're here!" Shallan cried to the men. "I need your help desperately."

The group of deserters just stared at her.

"Bandits," Shallan said. "They're attacking our friends in the caravan just two hills over. It's a slaughter! I said I'd seen soldiers back here, moving toward the Shattered Plains. Nobody believed me. Please. You must help."

Again, they just stared at her. *A little like the mink wandering into the whitespine's den and asking when dinner is . . .* she thought. Finally, the men shuffled uneasily and turned toward a man near the center. Tall, bearded, he had arms that looked too long for his body.

"Bandits, you say," the man replied, voice empty of emotion.

Shallan leaped down from the wagon and walked toward the man, leaving Bluth sitting as a silent lump. Deserters stepped away from her, wearing ripped and dirty clothing, with grizzled, unkempt hair and faces that hadn't seen a razor—or a washcloth—in ages. And yet, by torchlight, their weapons gleamed without a spot of rust and their breastplates were polished to the point where they reflected her features.

The woman she glimpsed in one breastplate looked too tall, too stately, to be Shallan herself. Instead of tangled hair, she had flowing red locks. Instead of refugee rags, she wore a gown woven with golden embroidery. She had not been wearing a necklace before, and when she raised her hand toward the leader of the band, her chipped fingernails appeared perfectly manicured.

"Brightness," the man said as she stepped up to him, "we aren't what you think we are."

"No," Shallan replied. "You aren't what *you* think yourselves to be."

Those around her in the firelight regarded her with eager stares, and she felt the hair rising in a shiver across her body. Into the predator's den indeed. Yet the tempest within her spurred her to action, and urged her to greater confidence.

The leader opened his mouth as if to give some order. Shallan cut him off. "What is your name?"

"I'm called Vathah," the man said, turning toward his allies. It was a Vorin name, like Shallan's own. "And I'll decide what to do with you later. Gaz, take this one and—"

"What would you do, Vathah," Shallan said in a loud voice, "to erase the past?"

He looked back toward her, face lit on one side by primal torchlight.

"Would you protect instead of kill, if you had the choice?" Shallan asked. "Would you rescue instead of rob if you could do it over again? Good people are dying as we speak here. You can stop it."

Those dark eyes of his seemed dead. "We can't change the past."

"I can change your future."

"We are wanted men."

"Yes, I came here wanting men. Hoping to find *men*. You are offered the chance to be soldiers again. Come with me. I will see to it you have new lives. Those lives start by saving instead of killing."

Vathah snorted in derision. His face looked unfinished in the night, rough, like a sketch. "Brightlords have failed us in the past."

"Listen," Shallan said. "Listen to the screams."

The piteous sounds reached them from behind her. Shouts for help. Workers, both men and women, from the caravan. Dying. Haunting sounds. Shallan was surprised, despite having pointed them out, how well the sounds carried. How much they sounded like pleas for help.

"Give yourself another chance," Shallan said softly. "If you return with me, I will see that your crimes are erased. I promise it to you, by all that I have, by the Almighty himself. You *can* start over. Start over as heroes."

Vathah held her eyes. This man was stone. She could see, with a sinking feeling, that he wasn't swayed. The tempest inside of her began to fade away, and her fears boiled higher. What was she *doing*? This was crazy!

Vathah looked away from her again, and she knew she'd lost him. He barked the order to take her captive.

Nobody moved. Shallan had focused only on him, not the other two dozen or so men, who had drawn in close, torches raised high. They looked at her with open faces, and she saw very little of the lust she'd noticed before. Instead, they bore wide eyes, longing, reacting to the distant yells. Men fingered their uniforms, where the insignias had been. Others looked down at spears and axes, weapons of their service perhaps not so long ago.

"You fools are *considering* this?" Vathah said.

One man, a short fellow with a scarred face and an eye patch, nodded his head. "I wouldn't mind starting over," he muttered. "Storms, but it would be nice."

"I saved a woman's life once," another said, a tall, balding man who was easily into his forties. "I felt a hero for weeks. Toasts in the tavern. Warmth. Damnation! We're dying out here."

"We left to get away from their oppression!" Vathah bellowed.

"And what have we done with our freedom, Vathah?" a man asked from the back of the group.

In the silence that followed, Shallan could hear only the screams for help.

"Storm it, I'm going," said the short man with the eye patch, jogging up the hill. Others broke off and followed him. Shallan turned—hands clasped in front of her—as nearly the *entire group* took off in a charge. Bluth stood up on his wagon, his shocked face showing in the torchlight that passed. Then he actually *whooped*, jumping down from the wagon and raising his cudgel high as he joined the deserters charging toward the battle.

Shallan was left with Vathah and two other men. Those seemed dumbfounded by what had just happened. Vathah folded his arms, letting out an audible sigh. "Idiots, every one."

"They are not idiots for wanting to be better than they are," Shallan said.

He snorted, looking her over. She had an immediate flash of fear.

Moments ago, this man was ready to rob her and probably worse. He didn't make any moves toward her, though his face looked even more threatening now that most of the torches had gone.

"Who are you?" he asked.

"Shallan Davar."

"Well, Brightness Shallan," he said, "I hope for your sake you can keep your word. Come on, boys. Let's see if we can keep those fools alive." He left with the others who had remained behind, marching up over the hill toward the fighting.

Shallan stood alone in the night, exhaling softly. No Light came out; she'd used it all. Her feet were no longer so much as sore, but she felt *exhausted*, drained like a punctured wineskin. She walked to the wagon and slumped against it, then finally settled down on the ground. Head back, she looked up at the sky. A few exhaustionspren rose around her, little swirls of dust spinning into the air.

Salas, the first moon, made a violet disc in the center of a cluster of bright white stars. The screams and yells of fighting continued. Would the deserters be enough? She didn't know how many bandits there were.

She'd be useless there, only getting in the way. She squeezed her eyes shut, then climbed up into the seat and took out her sketchbook. To the sounds of the fighting and dying, she sketched the glyphs for a prayer of hope.

"They listened," Pattern said, buzzing from beside her. "You changed them."

"I can't believe it worked," Shallan said.

"Ah . . . You are good with lies."

"No, I mean, that was a figure of speech. It seems impossible that they'd actually listen to me. Hardened criminals."

"You are lies and truth," Pattern said softly. "They transform."

"What does that mean?" It was hard to sketch with only the light of Salas to see by, but she did her best.

"You spoke of one Surge, earlier," Pattern said. "Lightweaving, the power of light. But you have something else. The power of transformation."

"Soulcasting?" Shallan said. "I didn't Soulcast anyone."

"Mmmm. And yet, you transformed them. And yet. Mmmm."

Shallan finished her prayer, then held it up, noticing that a previous page had been ripped out of the notebook. Who had done that?

She couldn't burn the prayer, but she didn't think the Almighty would mind. She pressed it close to her breast and closed her eyes, waiting until the shouts from below quieted.

Mediationform made for peace, it's said.
Form of teaching and consolation.
When used by the gods, it became instead
Form of lies and desolation.

—From the Listener Song of Listing, 33rd stanza

hallan closed Bluth's eyes, not looking at the ripped-out hole in his torso, the bloody entrails. Around her, workers salvaged what they could from the camp. People groaned, though some of those groans cut off as Vathah executed the bandits one by one.

Shallan didn't stop him. He did the duty grimly, and as he walked past he didn't look at her. *He's thinking these bandits could have easily been him and his men,* Shallan thought, looking back down at Bluth, his dead face lit by fires. *What separates the heroes from the villains? One speech in the night?*

Bluth wasn't the only casualty of the assault; Vathah had lost seven soldiers. They had killed over twice that many bandits. Exhausted, Shallan rose, but hesitated as she saw something poking out of Bluth's jacket. She leaned down and pushed the jacket open.

There, stuffed in his pocket, was her picture of him. The one that depicted him not as he was, but as she imagined he might once have been. A soldier in an army, in a crisp uniform. Eyes forward, rather than looking down all the time. A hero.

When had he taken it from her sketchbook? She slipped it free and folded it, flattening the wrinkles.

"I was wrong," she whispered. "You were a fine way to restart my collection, Bluth. Fight well for the Almighty in your sleep, bold one."

She rose and looked over the camp. Several of the caravan's parshmen pulled corpses to the fires for burning. Shallan's intervention had rescued the merchants, but not without heavy losses. She hadn't counted, but the toll looked high. Dozens dead, including most of the caravan's guards—among them the Iriali man from earlier in the night.

In her fatigue, Shallan wanted to crawl into her wagon and curl up for sleep. Instead, she went looking for the caravan leaders.

The haggard, bloodstained scout from before stood beside a travel table, where she was talking to an older, bearded man in a felt cap. His eyes were blue, and he moved his fingers through his beard as he looked over a list the woman had brought him.

Both looked up as Shallan approached. The woman rested a hand on her sword; the man continued to stroke his beard. Nearby, caravan workers sorted through the contents of a wagon that had toppled over, spilling bales of cloth.

"And here is our savior," the older man said. "Brightness, the winds themselves cannot speak of your majesty or the wonder of your timely arrival."

Shallan didn't feel majestic. She felt tired, sore, and grungy. Her bare feet—hidden by the bottom of her skirts—had started to ache again, and her ability to Lightweave was expended. Her dress looked almost as bad as a pauper's, and her hair—though braided—was an absolute mess.

"You are the caravan owner?" Shallan asked.

"Macob is my name," he said. She couldn't place his accent. Not Thaylen or Alethi. "You have met my associate Tyn." He nodded toward the woman. "She is head of our guards. Both her soldiers and my goods have . . . dwindled from tonight's encounters."

Tyn folded her arms. She still wore her tan coat, and in the light of Macob's spheres, Shallan could see that it was of fine leather. What to make of a woman who dressed like a soldier and wore a sword at her waist?

"I've been telling Macob of your offer," Tyn said. "Earlier, on the hill."

Macob chuckled, an incongruous sound considering their surroundings. "Offer, she calls it. My associate is under the impression that it was really a threat! These mercenaries obviously work for you. We are wondering what your intention is for this caravan."

"The mercenaries didn't work for me before," Shallan said, "but they do now. It took a little persuasion."

Tyn raised an eyebrow. "That must have been some mighty fine persuasion, Brightness. . ."

"Shallan Davar. All I ask of you is what I said to Tyn before. Accompany me to the Shattered Plains."

"Surely your soldiers can do that," Macob said. "You don't need our assistance."

I want you here to remind the "soldiers" what they've done, Shallan thought. Her instincts said that the more reminders of civilization the deserters had, the better off she would be.

"They are soldiers," Shallan said. "They have no idea how to properly convey a lighteyed woman in comfort. You, however, have nice wagons and goods aplenty. If you can't tell from my humble aspect, I am in dreadful need of a little luxury. I'd rather not arrive at the Shattered Plains looking like a vagabond."

"We *could* use her soldiers," Tyn said. "My own force is reduced to a handful." She inspected Shallan again, this time with curiosity. It wasn't an unfriendly look.

"Then we shall make an accord," Macob said, smiling broadly and reaching across the table toward Shallan. "In my gratitude for my life, I shall see you cared for with new apparel and fine foodstuffs for the duration of our travels together. You and your men will ensure our safety the rest of the way, and then we will part, nothing more owed to one another."

"Agreed," Shallan said, taking his hand. "I shall allow you to join me, your caravan unto mine."

He hesitated. "Your caravan."

"Yes."

"And your authority, then, I assume?"

"You expected otherwise?"

He sighed, but shook on the deal. "No, I suppose not. I suppose not." He released her hand, then waved toward a pair of people off at the side of the wagons. Tvlakv and Tag. "And what of those?"

"They are mine," Shallan said. "I will deal with them."

"Just keep them at the *back* of the caravan, if you will," Macob said, wrinkling his nose. "Grimy business. I'd rather not our caravan stink of those wares. Either way, you'd best be about gathering your people. There will be a highstorm soon. With our lost wagons, we have no extra shelter."

Shallan left them and made her way across the valley, trying to ignore the mingled stench of blood and char. A shape split from the darkness, moving in beside her. Vathah didn't look any less intimidating in the better light here.

"Well?" Shallan asked him.

"Some of my men are dead," he said, his voice a monotone.

"They died doing a very good work," Shallan said, "and the families of these who lived will bless them for their sacrifice."

Vathah took her arm, pulling her to a stop. His grip was firm, even painful. "You don't look like you did before," he said. She hadn't realized how much he towered over her. "Did my eyes mistake me? I saw a queen in the darkness. Now I see a child."

"Perhaps you saw what your conscience needed you to see," Shallan said, tugging—unsuccessfully—on her arm. She blushed.

Vathah leaned in. His breath wasn't particularly sweet. "My men have done worse things than this," he whispered, waving his other hand at the burning dead. "Out in the wilderness, we took. We killed. You think one night absolves us? You think one night will stop the nightmares?"

Shallan felt a hollowness in her stomach.

"If we go with you to the Shattered Plains, we're dead men," Vathah said. "We'll be hanged the moment we return."

"My word—"

"Your word means nothing, woman!" he shouted, grip tensing.

"You should let her go," Pattern said calmly from behind him.

Vathah spun, looking about, but they weren't near anyone in particular. Shallan spotted Pattern on the back of Vathah's uniform as he turned.

"Who said that?" Vathah demanded.

"I heard nothing," Shallan said, somehow managing to sound calm.

"You should let her go," Pattern repeated.

Vathah looked around again, then back at Shallan, who met his gaze with a level stare. She even forced out a smile.

He let go of her and wiped his hand on his trousers, then retreated. Pattern slipped down his back and leg onto the ground, then skimmed toward Shallan.

"That one will be trouble," Shallan said, rubbing the place where he'd gripped her.

"Is this a figure of speech?" Pattern asked.

"No. I mean what I said."

"Curious," Pattern said, watching Vathah retreat, "because I think he already *is* trouble."

"True." She continued her way toward Tvlakv, who sat on the seat of his wagon with hands clasped before him. He smiled toward Shallan as she arrived, though the expression seemed particularly thin on him today.

"So," he asked conversationally, "were you in on it from the start?"

"In on what?" Shallan asked wearily, shooing Tag away so she could talk to Tvlakv in private.

"Bluth's plan."

"Please, do tell."

"Obviously," Tvlakv said, "he was in league with the deserters. That first night, when he came running back to the camp, he'd met with them and promised to let them take us if he could share in the wealth. That was why they did not immediately kill you two when you went to speak with them."

"Oh?" Shallan asked. "And if that were the case, why did Bluth come back and warn us that night? Why did he flee with us, instead of just letting his 'friends' kill us right then?"

"Perhaps he only met with a few of them," Tvlakv said. "Yes, *they* lit fires on that hillside in the night to make us think there were more, and then his friends went to gather a larger crowd . . . And . . ." He deflated. "Storms. That doesn't make any sense. But how, why? We should be dead."

"The Almighty preserved us," Shallan said.

"Your Almighty is a farce."

"You should hope he is," Shallan said, walking to the back of Tag's wagon nearby. "For if he is not, then Damnation itself awaits men like you." She inspected the cage. Five slaves in grimy clothing huddled inside, each one looking alone, though they were crammed in close.

"These are mine now," Shallan told Tvlakv.

"What!" he stood up on his seat. "You—"

"I saved your life, you oily little man," Shallan said. "You will give me these slaves in payment. Dues in recompense for my soldiers protecting you and your worthless life."

"This is robbery."

"This is justice. If it bothers you, submit a grievance with the king in the Shattered Plains, once we arrive."

"I'm not going to the Shattered Plains," Tvlakv spat. "You have someone else to convey you now, *Brightness*. I'm heading south, as I originally intended."

"Then you'll do so without these," Shallan said, using her key—the one he had given her to get into her wagon—to open the cage. "You will give me their writs of slavery. And the Stormfather help you if not everything is in order, Tvlakv. I'm very good at spotting a forgery."

She hadn't ever even seen a writ of slavery, and wouldn't know how to tell if one was faked. She didn't care. She was tired, frustrated, and eager to be done with this night.

One by one, five hesitant slaves stepped from the wagon, shaggy bearded and shirtless. Her trip with Tvlakv had not been pleasant, but it had been luxurious compared to what these men had been through. Several glanced at the darkness nearby, as if eager.

"You may run if you wish," Shallan said, softening her tone. "I will not hunt you. I need servants, however, and I will pay you well. Six firemarks a week if you agree to put five of them toward paying down your slave debt. One if you don't."

One of the men cocked his head. "So . . . we take away the same amount either way? What kind of sense does that make?"

"The best kind," Shallan said, turning to Tvlakv, who sat stewing on the side of his seat. "You have three wagons but only two drivers. Will you sell me the third wagon?" She wouldn't need the chull—Macob would have an extra she could use, since several of his wagons had burned.

"Sell the wagon? Bah! Why not just steal it from me?"

"Stop being a child, Tvlakv. Do you want my money or not?"

"Five sapphire broams," he snapped. "And it's a steal at that price; don't you argue otherwise."

She didn't know if it was or not, but she could afford it, with the spheres she had, even if most of them were dun.

"You can't have my parshmen," Tvlakv snapped.

"You can keep them," Shallan said. She would need to talk to the caravan master about shoes and clothing for her servants.

As she walked off to see if she could use an extra chull of Macob's, she passed a group of the caravan workers waiting to the side of one of the bonfires. The deserters threw the last body—one of their own—into the flames, then stepped back, wiping brows.

One of the darkeyed caravan women stepped up, holding out a sheet of paper to a former deserter. He took it, scratching at his beard. He was the shorter, one-eyed man who'd spoken during her speech. He held up the sheet to the others. It was a prayer made from familiar runes, but not one of mourning, as Shallan would have expected to see. It was a prayer of thanks.

The former deserters gathered in front of the flames and looked at the prayer. Then they turned and looked outward, seeing—as if for the first time—the two dozen people standing there and watching. Silent in the night. Some had tears on their cheeks; some held the hands of children. Shallan had not noticed the children before, but was not surprised to see them. Caravan workers would spend their lives traveling, and their families would travel with them.

Shallan stopped just beyond the caravaneers, mostly hidden in the darkness. The deserters didn't seem to know how to react, surrounded by that constellation of thankful eyes and tearful appreciation. Finally, they burned the prayer. Shallan bowed her head as they did, as did most of those watching.

She left them standing taller, watching the ashes of that prayer rise toward the Almighty.

A page from a folio of fashion pages out of
Liafor. The model, it should be noted, is Alethi,
as this folio was intended for sale in the Alethi
and Veden markets.

22

LIGHTS IN THE STORM

Stormform is said to cause
A tempest of winds and showers,
Beware its powers, beware its powers.
Though its coming brings the gods their night,
It obliges a bloodred spren.
Beware its end, beware its end.

—From the Listener Song of Winds, 4th stanza

Kaladin watched the window shutters. Motion came in bursts.

First stillness. Yes, he could hear a distant howling, the wind passing through some hollow, but nothing nearby.

A tremble. Then wood rattling wickedly in its frame. Violent shaking, with water seeping in at the joints. Something was out there, in the dark chaos of the highstorm. It thrashed and pounded at the window, wanting in.

Light flashed out there, glistening through the drops of water. Another flash.

Then the light stayed. Steady, like glowing spheres, just outside. Faintly red. For some reason he couldn't explain, Kaladin had the impression of eyes.

Transfixed, he raised his hand toward the latch, to open it and see.

"Someone really needs to fix that loose shutter," King Elhokar said, annoyed.

The light faded. The rattling stopped. Kaladin blinked, lowering his hand.

"Someone remind me to ask Nakal to see to it," Elhokar said, pacing behind his couch. "The shutter shouldn't leak. This is my palace, not a village tavern!"

"We'll make sure it's seen to," Adolin said. He sat in a chair beside the hearth, flipping through a book filled with sketches. His brother sat in a chair next to him, hands clasped in his lap. He was probably sore from his training, but he didn't show it. Instead, he had gotten a small box out of his pocket and was repeatedly opening it, turning it in his hand, rubbing one side, then shutting it with a click. He did it over and over and over.

He stared at nothing as he did it. He seemed to do that a lot.

Elhokar continued pacing. Idrin—head of the King's Guard—stood near the king, straight-backed, green eyes forward. He was dark-skinned for an Alethi, perhaps with some Azish blood in him, and wore a full beard.

Men from Bridge Four had been taking shifts with his men, as Dalinar suggested, and so far Kaladin had been impressed by the man and the team he had run. However, when the horns for a plateau run sounded, Idrin would turn toward them and his expression would grow longing. He wanted to be out there fighting. Sadeas's betrayal had made a lot of the soldiers in camp similarly eager—as if they wanted the chance to prove how strong Dalinar's army was.

More rumbling came from the storm outside. It was odd not to be cold during a highstorm—the barrack always felt chilly. This room was well heated, though not by a fire. Instead, the hearth held a ruby the size of Kaladin's fist, one that could have paid to feed everyone in his hometown for weeks.

Kaladin left the window and sauntered toward the fireplace under the pretext of inspecting the gemstone. He really wanted a glimpse of whatever it was Adolin was looking through. Many men refused to even look at books, considering it unmasculine. Adolin didn't seem to be bothered by that. Curious.

As he approached the hearth, Kaladin passed the door to a side room where Dalinar and Navani had retired at the advent of the storm. Kaladin had wanted to post a guard inside. They'd refused.

Well, this is the only way into that room, he thought. *There's not even a window.* This time, if words appeared on the wall, he would know for certain nobody was sneaking in.

Kaladin stooped down, inspecting the ruby in the hearth, which was held in place by a wire enclosure. Its strong heat made his face prickle with sweat; storms, that ruby was so large that the Light infusing it should have blinded him. Instead, he could stare into its depths and see the Light moving inside.

People thought that the illumination from gemstones was steady and calm, but that was just in contrast to flickering candlelight. If you looked deeply into a stone, you could see the Light shifting with the chaotic pattern of a blowing storm. It was not calm inside. Not by a wind or a whisper.

"Never seen a heating fabrial before, I assume?" Renarin asked.

Kaladin glanced at the bespectacled prince. He wore an Alethi highlord's uniform, like that of Adolin. In fact, Kaladin had never seen them wearing anything else—other than Shardplate, of course.

"No, I haven't," Kaladin said.

"New technology," Renarin said, still playing with his little metal box. "My aunt built that one herself. Every time I turn around, it seems the world has changed somehow."

Kaladin grunted. *I know how that feels.* Part of him yearned to suck in the Light of that gemstone. A foolish move. There'd be enough in there to make him glow like a bonfire. He lowered his hands and strolled past Adolin's chair.

The sketches in Adolin's book were of men in fine clothing. The drawings were quite good, their faces done in as much detail as their garments.

"Fashion?" Kaladin asked. He hadn't intended to speak, but it came out anyway. "You're spending the highstorm looking for new clothing?"

Adolin snapped the book closed.

"But you only wear uniforms," Kaladin said, confused.

"Do you *need* to be here, bridgeboy?" Adolin demanded. "Surely nobody is going to come for us during a highstorm, of all things."

"The fact that you assume that," Kaladin said, "is why I need to be here. What better time would there be for an assassination attempt? The winds would cover shouts, and help would be slow in coming when everyone has taken cover to wait out the storm. Seems to me this is one of the times when His Majesty most needs guards."

The king stopped pacing and pointed. "That makes sense. Why hasn't anyone else ever explained that to me?" He looked at Idrin, who remained stoic.

Adolin sighed. "You could at least leave Renarin and me out of it," he said softly to Kaladin.

"It's easier to protect you when you're all together, Brightlord," Kaladin said, walking away. "Plus, you can defend each other."

Dalinar had been intending to stay with Navani during the storm anyway. Kaladin approached the window again, listening to the storm pass outside. Had he really seen the things he thought he had during his time out in the storm? A face as vast as the sky? The Stormfather himself?

I am a god, Syl had said. *A little piece of one.*

Eventually, the storm passed, and Kaladin opened the window to a black sky, a few phantom clouds shining with Nomon's light. The storm had started a few hours into the night, but nobody could sleep during a storm. He hated when a highstorm came so late; he often felt exhausted the next day.

The side room door opened and Dalinar stepped out, trailed by Navani. The statuesque woman carried a large notebook. Kaladin had heard, of course, about the highprince's fits during storms. His men were divided on the topic. Some thought Dalinar was frightened of highstorms, and his terror sent him into convulsions. Others whispered that with age, the Blackthorn was losing his mind.

Kaladin badly wanted to know which it was. His fate, and that of his men, was tied to this man's health.

"Numbers, sir?" Kaladin asked, peeking into the room, looking at the walls.

"No," Dalinar said.

"Sometimes they come just after the storm," Kaladin said. "I have men in the hall outside. I would prefer if everyone remained here for a short time."

Dalinar nodded. "As you wish, soldier."

Kaladin walked to the exit. Beyond, some men of Bridge Four and of the King's Guard stood on watch. Kaladin nodded to Leyten, then pointed for them to watch out on the balcony. Kaladin *would* catch the phantom scratching those numbers. If, indeed, such a person existed.

Behind, Renarin and Adolin approached their father. "Anything new?" Renarin asked softly.

"No," Dalinar said. "The vision was a repeat. But they're not coming in the same order as last time, and some are new, so perhaps there is something to learn we have not yet discovered . . ." Noticing Kaladin, he trailed off, then changed the topic. "Well, as long as we're waiting here, perhaps I can get an update. Adolin, when can we expect more duels?"

"I'm trying," Adolin said with a grimace. "I thought beating Salinor would drive others to want to try me, but they're stalling instead."

"Problematic," Navani said. "Weren't you always saying that everyone wanted to duel you?"

"They did!" Adolin said. "When I couldn't duel, at least. Now, every time I make an offer, people start shuffling their feet and looking away."

"Have you tried anyone in Sadeas's camp?" the king asked eagerly.

"No," Adolin said. "But he's only got one Shardbearer other than himself. Amaram."

Kaladin felt a shiver.

"Well, you won't be dueling *him*," Dalinar said, chuckling. He sat down on the couch, Brightness Navani settling in beside him, hand fondly on his knee. "We might have him on our side. I've been speaking to Highlord Amaram . . ."

"You think you can get him to secede?" the king asked.

"Is that possible?" Kaladin asked, surprised.

The lighteyes turned to him. Navani blinked, as if noticing him for the first time.

"Yes, it is possible," Dalinar said. "Most of the territory that Amaram oversees would remain with Sadeas, but he could bring his personal land to my princedom—along with his Shards. Usually it requires a land trade with a princedom bordering the one a highlord wishes to join."

"It hasn't happened in over a decade," Adolin said, shaking his head.

"I'm working on him," Dalinar said. "But Amaram . . . he wants to bring Sadeas and me together instead. He thinks we can get along again."

Adolin snorted. "*That* possibility blew away the day Sadeas betrayed us."

"Probably long before that day," Dalinar said, "even if I didn't see it. Is there anyone else you could challenge, Adolin?"

"I'm going to try Talanor," Adolin said, "and then Kalishor."

"Neither full Shardbearers," Navani said with a frown. "The first has only the Blade, the second only the Plate."

"All of the full Shardbearers have refused me," Adolin said with a shrug. "Those two are eager, thirsty for notoriety. One of them might agree where others haven't."

Kaladin folded his arms, leaning back against the wall. "And if you defeat them, won't it scare off others from fighting you?"

"*When* I beat them," Adolin said, glancing at Kaladin's relaxed posture and frowning, "Father will maneuver others into agreeing to duels."

"But it will have to stop sometime, right?" Kaladin asked. "Eventually the other highprinces will realize what's happening. They'll refuse to be goaded into further duels. It might be happening already. That's why they don't accept."

"Someone will," Adolin said, standing. "And once I start winning, others will begin to see me as a real challenge. They'll want to test themselves."

That seemed optimistic to Kaladin.

"Captain Kaladin is right," Dalinar said.

Adolin turned toward his father.

"There's no need to fight every Shardbearer in camp," Dalinar said softly. "We need to narrow our attack, choose duels for you that point us toward the ultimate goal."

"Which is?" Adolin asked.

"Undermining Sadeas." Dalinar almost sounded regretful. "Killing him in a duel, if we have to. Everyone in camp knows the sides in this power struggle. This won't work if we punish everyone equally. We need to show those in the middle, those deciding whom to follow, the advantages of trust. Cooperation on plateau runs. Help from one another's Shardbearers. We show them what it's like to be part of a *real* kingdom."

The others grew quiet. The king turned away with a shake of his head. He didn't believe, at least not fully, in what Dalinar wished to achieve.

Kaladin found himself annoyed. Why should he be? Dalinar had agreed with him. He stewed for a moment, and realized that he was probably still upset because someone had mentioned Amaram.

Even hearing the man's name put Kaladin out of sorts. He kept thinking something should happen, something should change, now that such a murderer was in camp. Yet everything just kept on going. It was frustrating. Made him want to lash out.

He needed to do something about it.

"I assume we've waited long enough?" Adolin said to his father. "I can go?"

Dalinar sighed, nodding. Adolin pulled open the door and strode away; Renarin followed at a slower pace, hauling that Shardblade he was still bonding, sheathed in its protective strips. As they passed the group of guards Kaladin had put outside, Skar and three others broke off to follow them.

Kaladin walked to the door, doing a quick count of who was left. Four men total. "Moash," Kaladin said, noticing the man yawning. "How long have you been on duty today?"

Moash shrugged. "One shift guarding Brightness Navani. One shift with the King's Guard."

I'm working them too hard, Kaladin thought. *Stormfather. I don't have enough men. Even with the leftover Cobalt Guard that Dalinar is sending to me.* "Head back and get some sleep," Kaladin said. "You too, Bisig. I saw you on shift this morning."

"And you?" Moash asked Kaladin.

"I'm fine." He had Stormlight to keep him alert. True, using Stormlight that way could be dangerous—it provoked him to act, to be more impulsive. He wasn't sure he liked what it did to him when he used it outside of battle.

Moash raised an eyebrow. "You've *got* to be at least as tired as I am, Kal."

"I'll go back in a bit," Kaladin said. "You need some time off, Moash. You'll get sloppy if you don't take it."

"I have to pull two shifts," Moash said, shrugging. "At least, if you want me to train with the King's Guard as well as doing my regular guard duty."

Kaladin drew his lips to a line. That *was* important. Moash needed to think like a bodyguard, and there was no better way than serving on an already-established crew.

"My shift here with the King's Guard is almost over," Moash noted. "I'll head back after."

"Fine," Kaladin said. "Keep Leyten with you. Natam, you and Mart guard Brightness Navani. I'll see Dalinar back to camp and post guards at his door."

"Then you'll get some sleep?" Moash asked. The others glanced at Kaladin. They were worried as well.

"Yes, fine." Kaladin turned back to the room, where Dalinar was helping Navani to her feet. He'd walk her to her door, as he did most evenings.

Kaladin debated for a moment, then stepped up to the highprince. "Sir, there's something I need to talk to you about."

"Can it wait until I'm done here?" Dalinar said.

"Yes, sir," Kaladin said. "I'll wait at the palace's front doors, then will be your guard on the way back to camp."

Dalinar led Navani away, joined by two bridgeman guards. Kaladin made his own way down the corridor, thinking. Servants had already come by to open the corridor windows, and Syl floated in through one as a spinning swirl of mist. Giggling, she spun around him a few times before going out another window. She always got more sprenlike during a highstorm.

The air smelled wet and fresh. The whole world felt clean after a highstorm, scrubbed by nature's abrasive.

He reached the front of the palace, where a pair of the King's Guard stood on watch. Kaladin nodded to them and got crisp salutes in return, then he fetched a sphere lantern from the guard post and filled it with his own spheres.

From the front of the palace, Kaladin could look out over all ten warcamps. As always after a storm, the Light of refreshed spheres sparkled everywhere, their gemstones ablaze with captured fragments of the tempest that had passed.

Standing there, Kaladin confronted what he needed to say to Dalinar. He rehearsed it silently more than once, but still wasn't ready when the highprince emerged at last from the palace doors. Natam saluted from behind them, handing Dalinar off to Kaladin, then jogged back to join Mart outside Brightness Navani's door.

The highprince started down the switchbacks of the side route down from the Pinnacle to the stables below. Kaladin fell in beside him. Dalinar appeared deeply distracted by something.

He hasn't ever announced anything about his fits during highstorms, Kaladin thought. *Shouldn't he say something?*

They'd talked about visions, earlier. What was it Dalinar saw, or thought he saw?

"So, soldier," Dalinar said as they walked. "What is it you wanted to discuss?"

Kaladin took a deep breath. "A year ago, I was a soldier in Amaram's army."

"So that's where you learned," Dalinar said. "I should have guessed. Amaram is the only general in Sadeas's princedom with any real leadership ability."

"Sir," Kaladin said, stopping on the steps. "He betrayed me and my men."

Dalinar stopped and turned to look at him. "A poor battle decision, then? Nobody is perfect, soldier. If he sent your men into a bad situation, I doubt he intended to do so."

Just push through it, Kaladin told himself, noticing Syl sitting on a shale-bark ridge just to the right. She nodded at him. *He has to know.* It was just . . .

He'd never spoken of this, not in full. Not even to Rock, Teft, and the others.

"It wasn't that, sir," Kaladin said, meeting Dalinar's eyes by spherelight. "I know where Amaram got his Shardblade. I was there. I killed the Shardbearer carrying it."

"That can't be the case," Dalinar said slowly. "If you had, you'd hold the Plate and Blade."

"Amaram took it for himself, then slaughtered everyone who knew the truth," Kaladin said. "Everyone but a lone soldier who, in his guilt, Amaram branded a slave and sold rather than murdering."

Dalinar stood in silence. From this angle, the hillside behind him was completely dark, lit only by stars. A few spheres glowed in Dalinar's pocket, shining through the fabric of his uniform.

"Amaram is one of the best men I know," Dalinar said. "His honor is spotless. I've never even known him to take undue advantage of an opponent in a duel, despite cases when it would have been acceptable."

Kaladin didn't respond. He'd believed that too, at one point.

"Do you have any proof?" Dalinar asked. "You understand that I can't take one man's word on something of this nature."

"One darkeyed man's word, you mean," Kaladin said, gritting his teeth.

"It's not the color of your eyes that is the problem," Dalinar said, "but the severity of your accusation. The words you speak are dangerous. Do you have any *proof,* soldier?"

"There were others there when he took the Shards. Men of his personal guard did the actual killing at his command. And there was a stormwarden there. Middle-aged, with a peaked face. He wore a beard like an ardent." He paused. "They were all complicit in the act, but maybe . . ."

Dalinar sighed softly in the night. "Have you spoken this accusation to anyone else?"

"No," Kaladin said.

"Continue to hold your tongue. I'll talk to Amaram. Thank you for telling me of this."

"Sir," Kaladin said, taking a step closer to Dalinar. "If you really believe in justice, you—"

"That's enough for the moment, son," Dalinar cut in, voice calm but cool. "You've had your say, unless you can offer me anything else by way of evidence."

Kaladin forced down his immediate burst of anger. It was difficult.

"I appreciated your input when we were talking about my son's duels earlier," Dalinar said. "This is the second time you've added something important to one of our conferences, I believe."

"Thank you, sir."

"But soldier," Dalinar said, "you're walking quite a line between helpfulness and insubordination in the way you treat me and mine. You have a chip on your shoulder the size of a boulder. I ignore it, because I know what was done to you, and I can see the soldier beneath. That's the man I hired for this job."

Kaladin ground his teeth, and nodded. "Yes, sir."

"Good. Now run along."

"Sir, but I must escort—"

"I think I'll return to the palace," Dalinar said. "I don't think I'll get much sleep tonight, so I might want to pester the dowager with my thoughts. Her guards can watch over me. I'll take one with me when I return to my camp."

Kaladin let out a long breath. Then saluted. *Fine,* he thought, continuing down the dark, damp path. When he reached the bottom, Dalinar was still standing up above, now just a shadow. He seemed lost in thought.

Kaladin turned and walked back toward Dalinar's warcamp. Syl flitted up and landed on his shoulder. "See," she said. "He listened."

"No he didn't, Syl."

"What? He replied and said—"

"I told him something he didn't want to hear," Kaladin said. "Even if he does look into it, he'll find plenty of reasons to dismiss what I said. In the end, it will be my word against Amaram's. Stormfather! I shouldn't have said anything."

"You'd let it go, then?"

"Storms, no," Kaladin said. "I'd find my own justice."

"Oh . . ." Syl settled on his shoulder.

They walked for a long while, eventually approaching the warcamp.

"You're not a Skybreaker, Kaladin," Syl finally said. "You're not supposed to be like this."

"A what?" he asked, stepping over scuttling cremlings in the dark. They came out in force after a storm, when plants unfolded to lap up the water. "That was one of the orders, wasn't it?" He did know some little of them. Everyone did, from the legends.

"Yes," Syl said, voice soft. "I'm worried about you, Kaladin. I thought things would be better, once you were free from the bridges."

"Things *are* better," he said. "None of my men have been killed since we were freed."

"But you . . ." She didn't seem to know what else to say. "I thought you might be like the person you were before. I can remember a man on a field of battle . . . A man who fought . . ."

"That man is dead, Syl," Kaladin said, waving to the guards as he entered the warcamp. Once again, light and motion surrounded him, people running quick errands, parshmen repairing buildings damaged by the storm. "During my time as a bridgeman, all I had to worry about was my men. Now things are different. I have to become someone. I just don't know who yet."

When he reached Bridge Four's barrack, Rock was dishing out the evening stew. Far later than usual, but some of the men were on odd shifts. The men weren't limited to stew any longer, but they still insisted on it for the evening meal. Kaladin took a bowl gratefully, nodding to Bisig, who was relaxing with several of the others and chatting about how they actually *missed* carrying their bridge. Kaladin had instilled in them a respect for it, much as a soldier respected his spear.

Stew. Bridges. They spoke so fondly of things that had once been emblems of their captivity. Kaladin took a bite, then stopped, noticing a new man leaning against a rock beside the fire.

"Do I know you?" he asked, pointing at the bald, muscular man. He had tan skin, like an Alethi, but he didn't seem to have the right face shape. Herdazian?

"Oh, don't mind Punio," Lopen called from nearby. "He's my cousin."

"You had a cousin on the bridge crews?" Kaladin asked.

"Nah," Lopen said. "He just heard my mother say we needed more guards, so he came to help. I got him a uniform and things."

The newcomer, Punio, smiled and raised his spoon. "Bridge Four," he said with a thick Herdazian accent.

"Are you a soldier?" Kaladin asked him.

"Yes," the man said. "Brightlord Roion army. Not worry. I swore to Kholin instead, now. For my cousin." He smiled affably.

"You can't just leave your army, Punio," Kaladin said, rubbing his forehead. "It's called desertion."

"Not for us," Lopen called. "We're Herdazian—nobody can tell us apart anyway."

"Yes," Punio said. "I leave for the homeland once a year. When I come back, nobody remembers me." He shrugged. "This time, I come here."

Kaladin sighed, but the man looked like he knew his way around a spear, and Kaladin *did* need more men. "Fine. Just pretend you were one of the bridgemen from the start, all right?"

"Bridge Four!" the man said enthusiastically.

Kaladin passed him and found his customary place by the fire to relax and think. He didn't get that chance, however, as someone stepped up and squatted down before him. A man with marbled skin and a Bridge Four uniform.

"Shen?" Kaladin asked.

"Sir."

Shen continued to stare at him.

"Is there something you wanted?" Kaladin asked.

"Am I really Bridge Four?" Shen asked.

"Of course you are."

"Where is my spear?"

Kaladin looked Shen in the eyes. "What do you think?"

"I think that I am not Bridge Four," Shen said, taking time to think with each word. "I am Bridge Four's slave."

It was like a punch to Kaladin's gut. He'd hardly heard a dozen words out of the man during their time together, and now this?

The words smarted either way. Here was a man who, unlike the others, wasn't welcome to leave and make his way in the world. Dalinar had freed the rest of Bridge Four—but a parshman . . . he'd be a slave no matter where he went or what he did.

What could Kaladin say? Storms.

"I appreciate your help when we were scavenging. I know it was difficult for you to see what we did down there sometimes."

Shen waited, still squatting, listening. He regarded Kaladin with those impenetrable, solid black parshman eyes of his.

"I *can't* start arming parshmen, Shen," Kaladin said. "The lighteyes barely accept us as it is. If I gave *you* a spear, think of the storm it would cause."

Shen nodded, face displaying no hint of his emotions. He stood up straight. "A slave I am, then."

He withdrew.

Kaladin knocked his head back against the stone behind him, staring up at the sky. Storming man. He had a good life, for a parshman. Certainly more freedom than any other of his kind.

And were you satisfied with that? a voice inside him asked. *Were you happy to be a well-treated slave? Or did you try to run, fight your way to freedom?*

What a mess. He mulled over those thoughts, digging into his stew. He got two bites down before Natam—one of the men who'd been guarding at the palace—came stumbling into their camp, sweating, frantic, and red-cheeked from running.

"The king!" Natam said, puffing. "An assassin."

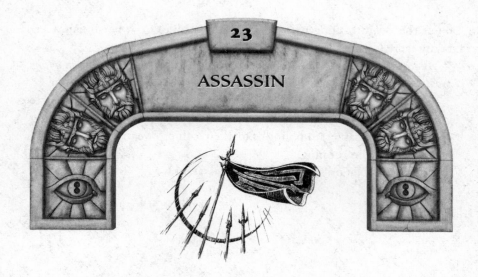

Nightform predicting what will be,
The form of shadows, mind to foresee.
As the gods did leave, the nightform whispered.
A new storm will come, someday to break.
A new storm a new world to make.
A new storm a new path to take, the nightform listens.

—From the Listener Song of Secrets, 17th stanza

The king was fine.

One hand on the doorframe, Kaladin stood gasping from his run back to the palace. Inside, Elhokar, Dalinar, Navani, and both of Dalinar's sons spoke together. Nobody was dead. Nobody was dead.

Stormfather, he thought, stepping into the room. *For a moment, I felt like I did on the plateaus, watching my men charge the Parshendi.* He hardly knew these people, but they were his duty. He hadn't thought that his protectiveness could apply to lighteyes.

"Well, at least *he* ran here," the king said, waving off the attentions of a woman who was trying to bandage a gash on his forehead. "You see, Idrin. This is what a *good* bodyguard looks like. I bet he wouldn't have let this happen."

The captain of the King's Guard stood near the door, red-faced. He looked away, then stalked out into the hallway. Kaladin raised a hand to his head, bewildered. Comments like that one from the king were *not* going to help his men get along with Dalinar's soldiers.

Inside the room, a mess of guards, servants, and members of Bridge

Four stood around, looking confused or embarrassed. Natam was there—he'd been on duty with the King's Guard—as was Moash.

"Moash," Kaladin called. "You're supposed to be back in the camp asleep."

"So are you," Moash said.

Kaladin grunted, trotting over, speaking more softly. "Were you here when it happened?"

"I'd just left," Moash said. "Finishing my shift with the King's Guard. I heard yelling, and came back as quickly as I could." He nodded toward the open balcony door. "Come have a look."

They walked out onto the balcony, which was a circular stone pathway that ran around the peak rooms of the palace—a terrace cut into the stone itself. From such a height, the balcony offered an unparalleled view overlooking the warcamps and the Plains beyond. Some members of the King's Guard stood here, inspecting the balcony railing with sphere lamps. A section of the ironwork structure had twisted outward and hung precariously over the drop.

"From what we've figured," Moash said, pointing, "the king came out here to think, as he likes to do."

Kaladin nodded, walking with Moash. The stone floor beneath was still wet from highstorm rain. They reached the place where the railing was ripped, several guards making way for them. Kaladin looked down over the side. The drop was a good hundred feet onto the rocks below. Syl drifted through the air down there, making lazy glowing circles.

"Damnation, Kaladin!" Moash said, taking his arm. "Are you trying to make me panic?"

I wonder if I could survive that fall.... He'd dropped half that once before, filled with Stormlight, and had landed without trouble. He stepped back for Moash's sake, though even before gaining his special abilities, heights had fascinated him. It felt liberating to be up so high. Just you and the air itself.

He knelt down, looking at the places where the footings of the iron railing had been mortared into holes in the stone. "The railing pulled free of its mountings?" he asked, poking his finger into a hole, then pulling it out with mortar dust on his fingers.

"Yeah," Moash said, several of the men of the king's guard nodding.

"Could just be a flaw in the design," Kaladin said.

"Captain," said one of the guardsmen. "I was here when it happened, watching him on the balcony. It fell right out. Barely a sound. I was standing here, looking out at the Plains and thinking to myself, and next I knew His Majesty was hanging right there, holding on for his life and cursing like a caravan worker." The guard blushed. "Sir."

Kaladin stood, inspecting the metalwork. So the king had leaned against this section of the railing, and it had bent forward—the mountings at the bottom giving way. It had almost come free completely, but fortunately one bar had held tight. The king had grabbed hold and clung to it long enough to be rescued.

This should never have been possible. The thing looked as if it had been constructed of wood and rope first, then Soulcast into iron. Shaking another section, he found it incredibly secure. Even a few footings giving out shouldn't have let the whole thing fall off—the metal pieces would have had to come apart.

He moved to the right, inspecting some of those that had ripped free of one another. The two pieces of metal had been sheared at a joint. Smoothly, cleanly.

The doorway into the king's chamber darkened as Dalinar Kholin stepped out onto the balcony. "In," he said to Moash and the other guards. "Close the door. I'd like to speak to Captain Kaladin."

They obeyed, though Moash went reluctantly. Dalinar walked up to Kaladin as the windows closed, giving them privacy. Despite his age, the highprince's figure was an intimidating one, wide shouldered, built like a brick wall.

"Sir," Kaladin said. "I should have—"

"This wasn't your fault," Dalinar said. "The king wasn't under your care. Even if he was, I wouldn't reprimand you—just as I won't reprimand Idrin. I wouldn't expect bodyguards to inspect architecture."

"Yes, sir," Kaladin said.

Dalinar knelt down to inspect the mountings. "You like to take responsibility for things, don't you? A commendable attribute in an officer." Dalinar rose and looked at the place where the rail had been cut. "What is your assessment?"

"Someone definitely chipped at the mortar," Kaladin said, "and sabotaged the railing."

Dalinar nodded. "I agree. This was a deliberate attempt on the king's life."

"However . . . sir . . ."

"Yes?"

"Whoever tried this is an idiot."

Dalinar looked to him, raising an eyebrow in the lantern light.

"How could they know where the king would lean?" Kaladin said. "Or even that he would? This trap could easily have caught someone else, and then the would-be assassins would have exposed themselves for nothing. In fact, that *is* what happened. The king survived, and now we're aware of them."

"We've been expecting assassins," Dalinar said. "And not just because of the incident with the king's armor. Half the powerful men in this camp are probably contemplating some kind of assassination attempt, so an attempt on Elhokar's life doesn't tell us as much as you'd think. As to how they knew to catch him here, he has a favorite spot for standing, leaning against the rail and looking out over the Shattered Plains. Anyone who watches his patterns would have known where to apply their sabotage."

"But sir," Kaladin said, "it's just so *convoluted*. If they have access to the king's private chambers, then why not hide an assassin inside? Or use poison?"

"Poison is as unlikely to work as this was," Dalinar said, waving toward the railing. "The king's food and drink is tasted. As for a hidden assassin, one might run into guards." He stood up. "But I agree that such methods would probably have had a greater chance at success. The fact that they didn't try it that way tells us something. Assuming these are the same people who planted those flawed gemstones in the king's armor, they prefer nonconfrontational methods. It's not that they're idiots, they're . . ."

"They're cowards," Kaladin realized. "They want to make the assassination look like an accident. They're timid. They may have waited this long so that suspicion would die down."

"Yes," Dalinar said, rising, looking troubled.

"This time, though, they made a big mistake."

"How?"

Kaladin walked to the cut section he had inspected earlier and knelt down to rub the smooth section. "What cuts iron so cleanly?"

Dalinar leaned down, inspecting the cut, then took out a sphere for more light. He grunted. "It's supposed to look like the joint came apart, I'd guess."

"And does it?" Kaladin asked.

"No. That was a Shardblade."

"Narrows down our suspects a tad, I'd think."

Dalinar nodded. "Don't tell anyone else. We'll hide that we noticed the Shardblade cut, maybe gain an edge. It's too late to pretend that we think this was an accident, but we don't have to reveal everything."

"Yes, sir."

"The king is insisting that I put you in charge of guarding him," Dalinar said. "We might have to move up our timetable for that."

"I'm not ready," Kaladin said. "My men are stretched thin with the duties they already have."

"I know," Dalinar said softly. He seemed hesitant. "This was done by someone on the inside, you realize."

Kaladin felt cold.

"The king's own chambers? That means a servant. Or one of his guards.

Men in the King's Guard might have had access to his armor, too." Dalinar looked at Kaladin, face lit by the sphere in his hand. A strong face, with a nose that had once been broken. Blunt. *Real.* "I don't know whom I can trust these days. Can I trust you, Kaladin Stormblessed?"

"Yes. I swear it."

Dalinar nodded. "I'm going to relieve Idrin of this post and assign him to a command in my army. It will sate the king, but I'll make certain Idrin knows he isn't being punished. I suspect he'll enjoy the new command more anyway."

"Yes, sir."

"I'll ask him for his best men," Dalinar said, "and those will be under your command for now. Use them as little as possible. I eventually want the king being guarded only by men from the bridge crews—men you trust, men who have no part in warcamp politics. Choose carefully. I don't want to replace potential traitors with former thieves who can be easily bought."

"Yes, sir," Kaladin said, feeling a large weight settle on his shoulders.

Dalinar stood up. "I don't know what else to do. A man needs to be able to trust his own guards." He walked back toward the door into the room. The tone of his voice sounded deeply troubled.

"Sir?" Kaladin asked. "This wasn't the assassination attempt you were expecting, was it?"

"No," Dalinar said, hand on the doorknob. "I agree with your assessment. This wasn't the work of someone who knows what they're doing. Considering how contrived it was, I'm actually surprised at how close it came to working." He leveled his gaze at Kaladin. "If Sadeas decides to strike—or, worse, the assassin who claimed my brother's life—it will not go so well for us. The storm is yet to come."

He pulled open the door, letting out the complaints of the king, which had been muffled behind it. Elhokar was ranting that nobody took his safety seriously, that nobody listened, that they should be looking for the things he saw over his shoulder in the mirror, whatever that meant. The tirade sounded like the whining of a spoiled child.

Kaladin looked at the twisted rail, imagining the king dangling from it. He had good reason to be out of sorts. But then, wasn't a king supposed to be better than that? Didn't his Calling demand that he be able to keep his composure under pressure? Kaladin found it difficult to imagine Dalinar reacting with such ranting, regardless of the situation.

Your job isn't to judge, he told himself, waving to Syl and walking away from the balcony. *Your job is to protect these people.*

Somehow.

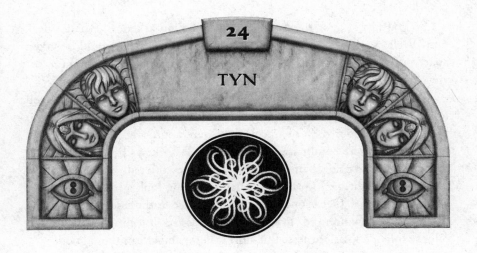

Decayform destroys the souls of dreams.
A form of gods to avoid, it seems.
Seek not its touch, nor beckon its screams, deny it.
Watch where you walk, your toes to tread,
O'er hill or rocky riverbed
Hold dear the fears that fill your head, defy it.

—From the Listener Song of Secrets, 27th stanza

Well, you see," Gaz said as he sanded the wood on Shallan's wagon. She sat nearby, listening as she worked. "Most of us, we joined the fight at the Shattered Plains for revenge, you know? Those marbles killed the king. It was gonna be this grand thing and such. A fight for vengeance, a way to show the world that the Alethi don't stand for betrayal."

"Yeah," Red agreed. The lanky, bearded soldier pulled free a bar from her wagon. With this one removed, it left only three at each corner to hold up the roof. He dropped the bar with satisfaction, then dusted off his work gloves. This would help transform the vehicle from a rolling cage into a conveyance more suitable for a lighteyed lady.

"I remember it," Red continued, sitting down on the wagon's bed, legs dangling. "The call to arms came to us from Highprince Vamah himself, and it moved through Farcoast like a bad stench. Every second man of age joined the cause. People wondered if you were a coward if you went to the pub for a drink but didn't wear a recruit's patch. I joined up with five of my buddies. They're all dead now, rotting in those storm-cursed chasms."

"So you just . . . got tired of fighting?" Shallan asked. She had a desk now. Well, a table—a small piece of travel furniture that could be taken apart easily. They'd moved it out of the wagon, and she was using it to review some of Jasnah's notes.

The caravan was making camp as the day waned; they'd traveled well today, but Shallan wasn't pushing them hard, after what they'd all been through. After four days of travel, they were approaching the section of the corridor where bandit strikes were much less likely. They were getting close to the Shattered Plains, and the safety they offered.

"Tired of fighting?" Gaz said, chuckling as he took a hinge and began nailing it in place. Occasionally, he would glance to the side, a kind of nervous tic. "Damnation, no. It wasn't us, it was the storming lighteyes! No offense intended, Brightness. But storm them, and storm them good!"

"They stopped fighting to win," Red softly added. "And they started fighting for spheres."

"Every day," Gaz said. "Every storming day, we'd get up and fight on those plateaus. And we wouldn't make any progress. Who cared if we made progress? It was the gemhearts the highprinces were after. And there we were, locked into virtual slavery by our military oaths. No right of travel as good citizens should have, since we'd enlisted. We were dying, bleeding, and suffering so they could get rich! That was all. So we left. A bunch of us who drank together, though we served different highprinces. We left them and their war behind."

"Now, Gaz," Red said. "That isn't everything. Be honest with the lady. Didn't you owe some spheres to the debtmongers too? What was that you told us about being one step from being turned into a bridgeman—"

"Here now," Gaz said. "That's my old life. Ain't nothing in that old life that matters anymore." He finished with the hammer. "Besides. Brightness Shallan said our debts would be taken care of."

"Everything will be forgiven," Shallan said.

"See?"

"Except your breath," she added.

Gaz looked up, a blush rising on his scarred face, but Red just laughed. After a moment, Gaz gave in to chuckling. There was something desperately affable about these soldiers. They had seized the chance to live a normal life again and were determined to hold to it. There hadn't been a single problem with discipline in the days they'd been together, and they were quick, even eager, to be of service to her.

Evidence of that came as Gaz folded the side of her wagon back up—then opened a latch and lowered a small window to let the light in. He gestured with a smile at his new window. "Maybe not nice enough to befit a lighteyed lady, but at least you'll be able to see out now."

"Not bad," Red said, clapping slowly. "Why didn't you tell us you'd trained as a carpenter?"

"I haven't trained as one," Gaz said, expression turning oddly solemn. "I spent some time around a lumberyard, that's all. You pick up a few things."

"It's very nice, Gaz," Shallan said. "I appreciate it deeply."

"It's nothing. You should probably have one on the other side too. I'll see if I can scrounge another hinge off the merchants."

"Already kissing the feet of our new master, Gaz?" Vathah stepped up to the group. Shallan hadn't noticed him approaching.

The leader of the former deserters held a small bowl of steaming curry from the dinner cauldron. Shallan could smell the pungent peppers. While it would have made a nice change from the stew she'd eaten with the slavers, the caravan had proper women's food, which she was obliged to eat. Maybe she could sneak a bite of the curry when nobody was looking.

"You didn't ever offer to make things like this for me, Gaz," Vathah said, dipping his bread and tearing off a chunk with his teeth. He spoke while chewing. "You seem happy to have been made a servant to the lighteyes again. It's a wonder your shirt isn't torn up from all the crawling and scraping you've been doing."

Gaz blushed again.

"So far as I know, Vathah," Shallan said, "you didn't have a wagon. So what is it you'd have wanted Gaz to make a window in? Your head, perhaps? I'm certain we can arrange that."

Vathah smiled as he ate, though it wasn't a particularly pleasant smile. "Did he tell you about the money he owes?"

"We will handle that problem when the time comes."

"This lot is going to be more trouble than you think, little lighteyes," Vathah said, shaking his head as he dipped his bread again. "Going right back to where they were before."

"This time they'll be heroes for rescuing me."

He snorted. "This lot will *never* be heroes. They're crem, Brightness. Pure and simple."

Nearby Gaz looked down and Red turned away, but neither disagreed with the assessment.

"You're trying very hard to beat them down, Vathah," Shallan said, standing. "Are you *that* afraid of being wrong? One would assume you'd be accustomed to it by now."

He grunted. "Be careful, girl. You wouldn't want to accidentally insult a man."

"The last thing I'd want to do is accidentally insult you, Vathah," Shallan said. "To think that I couldn't manage it on purpose if I wanted!"

He looked at her, then flushed and took a moment, trying to come up with a response.

Shallan cut in before he could do so. "I'm not surprised you're at a loss for words, as it's *also* an experience I'm sure you're accustomed to. You must feel it every time someone asks you a challenging question—such as the color of your shirt."

"Cute," he said. "But words aren't going to change these men or the troubles they are in."

"On the contrary," Shallan said, meeting his eyes, "in my experience, words are where most change begins. I have promised them a second chance. I *will* keep my promise."

Vathah grunted, but wandered away without further comment. Shallan sighed, sitting down and returning to her work. "That one always walks around acting like a chasmfiend ate his mother," she said with a grimace. "Or perhaps the chasmfiend *was* his mother."

Red laughed. "If you don't mind me saying, Brightness. You have quite the clever tongue on you!"

"I've never actually had someone's tongue *on* me," Shallan said, turning a page and not looking up, "clever or not. I'd hazard to consider it an unpleasant experience."

"It ain't so bad," Gaz said.

They both looked at him.

He shrugged. "Just saying. It ain't . . ."

Red laughed, slapping Gaz on the shoulder. "I'm going to get some food. I'll help you hunt down that hinge afterward."

Gaz nodded, though he glanced to the side again—that same nervous tic—and didn't join Red as the taller man walked toward the dinner cauldron. Instead, he settled down to begin sanding the floor of her wagon where the wood had begun to splinter.

She set aside the notebook in front of her, in which she had been attempting to devise ways to help her brothers. Those included everything from trying to buy one of the Soulcasters owned by the Alethi king to trying to track down the Ghostbloods and somehow deflect their attention. She couldn't do anything, however, until she reached the Shattered Plains—and then, most of her plans would require her to have powerful allies.

Shallan needed to make the betrothal to Adolin Kholin go forward. Not just for her family, but for the good of the world. Shallan would need the allies and resources that would give her. But what if she couldn't maintain the betrothal? What if she couldn't bring Brightness Navani to her side? She might need to proceed in finding Urithiru and preparing for the Voidbringers on her own. That terrified her, but she wanted to be ready.

She dug out a different book—one of the few from Jasnah's stash that didn't describe the Voidbringers or legendary Urithiru. Instead, it listed the current Alethi highprinces and discussed their political maneuvers and goals.

Shallan had to be ready. She had to know the political landscape of the Alethi court. She couldn't afford ignorance. She had to know who among these people might be potential allies, if all else failed her.

What of this Sadeas? she thought, flipping to a page in the notebook. It listed him as conniving and dangerous, but noted that both he and his wife were sharp of wit. A man of intelligence might listen to Shallan's arguments and understand them.

Aladar was listed as another highprince that Jasnah respected. Powerful, known for his brilliant political maneuvers. He was also fond of games of chance. Perhaps he would risk an expedition to find Urithiru, if Shallan highlighted the potential riches to be found.

Hatham was listed as a man of delicate politics and careful planning. Another potential ally. Jasnah didn't think much of Thanadal, Bethab, or Sebarial. The first she called oily, the second a dullard, and the third outrageously rude.

She studied them and their motivations for some time. Eventually, Gaz stood up and dusted sawdust from his trousers. He nodded in respect to her and moved to get himself some food.

"A moment, Master Gaz," she said.

"I'm no master," he said, walking up to her. "Sixth nahn only, Brightness. Never could buy myself anything better."

"How bad, exactly, are these debts of yours?" she asked, digging some spheres out of her safepouch to put in the goblet on her desk.

"Well, one of the fellows I owed was executed," Gaz said, rubbing his chin. "But there is more." He hesitated. "Eighty ruby broams, Brightness. Though they might not take them anymore. It's my head they may want, these days."

"Quite a debt for a man such as yourself. Are you a gambler, then?"

"Ain't no difference," he said. "Sure."

"And that's a lie," Shallan said, cocking her head. "I would know the truth from you, Gaz."

"Just turn me over to them," he said, turning and walking toward the soup. "Ain't no matter. I'd rather that than be out here, wondering when they'll find me, anyways."

Shallan watched him go, then shook her head, turning back to her studies. *She says that Urithiru is not on the Shattered Plains,* Shallan thought, turning a few pages. *But how is she certain? The Plains were never fully explored, because of the chasms. Who knows what is out there?*

Fortunately, Jasnah was very complete in her notes. It appeared that most of the old records spoke of Urithiru as being in the mountains. The Shattered Plains filled a basin.

Nohadon could walk there, Shallan thought, flipping to a quote from *The Way of Kings.* Jasnah questioned the validity of that statement, though Jasnah questioned pretty much everything. After an hour of study as the sun sank down through the sky, Shallan found herself rubbing her temples.

"Are you well?" Pattern's voice asked softly. He liked to come out when it was darker, and she did not forbid him. She searched and found him on the table, a complex formation of ridges in the wood.

"Historians," Shallan said, "are a bunch of liars."

"Mmmmm," Pattern said, sounding satisfied.

"That wasn't a compliment."

"Oh."

Shallan slammed her current book closed. "These women were supposed to be scholars! Instead of recording facts, they wrote opinions and presented them as truth. They seem to take great pains to contradict one another, and they dance around topics of import like spren around a fire—never providing heat themselves, just making a show of it."

Pattern hummed. "Truth is individual."

"What? No it's not. Truth is . . . it's *Truth.* Reality."

"Your truth is what you see," Pattern said, sounding confused. "What else could it be? That is the truth that you spoke to me, the truth that brings power."

She looked at him, his ridges casting shadows in the light of her spheres. She'd renewed those in the highstorm last night, while she was cooped up in her box of a wagon. Pattern had started buzzing in the middle of the storm—a strange, angry sound. After that, he'd ranted in a language she didn't understand, panicking Gaz and the other soldiers she'd invited into the shelter. Luckily, they took it for granted that terrible things happened during highstorms, and none had spoken of it since.

Fool, she told herself, flipping to an empty page in the notes. *Start acting like a scholar. Jasnah would be disappointed.* She wrote down what Pattern had said just now.

"Pattern," she said, tapping her pencil—one she'd gotten from the merchants, along with paper. "This table has four legs. Would you not say that is a truth, independent of my perspective?"

Pattern buzzed uncertainly. "What is a leg? Only as it is defined by you. Without a perspective, there is no such thing as a leg, or a table. There is only wood."

"You've told me the table perceives itself this way."

"Because people have considered it, long enough, as being a table," Pattern said. "It becomes truth to the table because of the truth the people create for it."

Interesting, Shallan thought, scribbling away at her notebook. She wasn't so interested in the nature of truth at the moment, but in how Pattern perceived it. *Is this because he's from the Cognitive Realm? The books say that the Spiritual Realm is a place of pure truth, while the Cognitive is more fluid.*

"Spren," Shallan said. "If people weren't here, would spren have thought?"

"Not here, in this realm," Pattern said. "I do not know about the other realm."

"You don't sound concerned," Shallan said. "Your entire existence might be dependent on people."

"It is," Pattern said, again unconcerned. "But children are dependent upon parents." He hesitated. "Besides, there are others who think."

"Voidbringers," Shallan said, cold.

"Yes. I do not think that my kind would live in a world with only them. They have their own spren."

Shallan sat up sharply. "Their *own* spren?"

Pattern shrank on her table, scrunching up, his ridges growing less distinct as they mashed together.

"Well?" Shallan asked.

"We do not speak of this."

"You might want to start," Shallan said. "It's important."

Pattern buzzed. She thought he was going to insist on the point, but after a moment, he continued in a very small voice. "Spren are . . . power . . . shattered power. Power given thought by the perceptions of men. Honor, Cultivation, and . . . and another. Fragments broken off."

"Another?" Shallan prodded.

Pattern's buzz became a whine, going so high pitched she almost couldn't hear it. "Odium." He spoke the word as if needing to force it out.

Shallan wrote furiously. Odium. Hatred. A type of spren? Perhaps a large unique one, like Cusicesh from Iri or the Nightwatcher. Hatred-spren. She'd never heard of such a thing.

As she wrote, one of her slaves approached in the darkening night. The timid man wore a simple tunic and trousers, one of the sets given to Shallan by the merchants. The gift was welcome, as the last of Shallan's spheres were in the goblet before her, and wouldn't be enough to buy a meal at some of the finer restaurants in Kharbranth.

"Brightness?" the man asked.

"Yes, Suna?"

"I . . . um . . ." He pointed. "The other lady, she asked me to tell you . . ."

He was pointing toward the tent used by Tyn, the tall woman who was leader of the few remaining caravan guards.

"She wants me to visit her?" Shallan asked.

"Yes," Suna said, looking down. "For food, I guess?"

"Thank you, Suna," Shallan said, freeing him to go back toward the fire where he and the other slaves were helping with the cooking while parshmen gathered wood.

Shallan's slaves were a quiet group. They had tattoos on their foreheads, rather than brands. It was the kinder way to do it, and usually marked a person who had entered servitude willingly, as opposed to being forced into it as a punishment for a violent or terrible crime. They were men with debts or the children of slaves who still bore the debt of their parents.

These were accustomed to labor, and seemed frightened by the idea of what she was paying them. Pittance though it was, it would see most of them freed in under two years. They were obviously uncomfortable with that idea.

Shallan shook her head, packing away her things. As she walked toward Tyn's tent, Shallan paused at the fire and asked Red to lift her table back into the wagon and secure it there.

She did worry about her things, but she no longer kept any spheres in there, and had left it open so Red and Gaz could glimpse inside and see only books. Hopefully there would be no incentive for people to go rooting through them.

You dance around the truth too, she thought to herself as she walked away from the fire. *Just like those historians you were ranting about.* She pretended these men were heroes, but had no illusions about how quickly they could change coats in the wrong circumstances.

Tyn's tent was large and well lit. The woman didn't travel like a simple guard. In many ways, she was the most intriguing person here. One of the few lighteyes aside from the merchants themselves. A woman who wore a sword.

Shallan peeked in through the open flaps and found several parshmen setting up a meal on a low travel table, meant for people to eat at while sitting on the floor. The parshmen hurried out, and Shallan watched them suspiciously.

Tyn herself stood by a window cut into the cloth. She wore her long, tan coat, buckled at the waist and almost closed. It had a dresslike feel to it, though it was far stiffer than any dress Shallan had worn, matched by the stiff trousers the woman wore underneath.

"I asked your men," Tyn said without turning, "and they said you hadn't dined yet. I had the parshmen bring enough for two."

"Thank you," Shallan said, entering and trying to keep the hesitation from her voice. Among these people, she wasn't a timid girl but a powerful woman. Theoretically.

"I've ordered my people to keep the perimeter clear," Tyn said. "We can speak freely."

"That is well," Shallan said.

"It means," Tyn said, turning around, "that you can tell me who you really are."

Stormfather! What did *that* mean? "I'm Shallan Davar, as I have said."

"Yes," Tyn said, walking over and sitting down at the table. "Please," she said, gesturing.

Shallan seated herself carefully, using a ladylike posture, with legs bent to the side.

Tyn sat cross-legged after flipping her coat out behind her. She dug into her meal, dipping flatbread in a curry that seemed too dark—and smelled too peppery—to be feminine.

"Men's food?" Shallan asked.

"I've always hated those definitions," Tyn said. "I was raised in Tu Bayla by parents who worked as interpreters. I didn't realize certain foods were supposed to be for women or men until I visited my parents' homeland for the first time. Still seems stupid to me. I'll eat what I want, thank you very much."

Shallan's own meal was more proper, smelling sweet rather than savory. She ate, only now realizing how hungry she was.

"I have a spanreed," Tyn said.

Shallan looked up, tip of her bread in her dipping bowl.

"It's connected to one over in Tashikk," Tyn continued, "at one of their new information houses. You hire an intermediary there, and they can perform services for you. Research, make inquiries—even relay messages for you via spanreed to any major city in the world. Quite spectacular."

"That sounds useful," Shallan said carefully.

"Indeed. You can find out all kinds of things. For example, I had my contact find what they could on House Davar. It's apparently a small, out-of-the-way house with large debts and an erratic house leader who may or may not still be alive. He has a daughter, Shallan, whom nobody seems to have met."

"I am that daughter," Shallan said. "So I'd say that 'nobody' is a stretch."

"And why," Tyn said, "would an unknown scion of a minor Veden family be traveling the Frostlands with a group of slavers? All the while claiming she's expected at the Shattered Plains, and that her rescue will be celebrated? That she has powerful connections, enough to pay the salaries of a full mercenary troop?"

"Truth is sometimes more surprising than a lie."

Tyn smiled, then leaned forward. "It's all right; you don't need to keep up the front with me. You're actually doing a good job here. I've discarded my annoyance with you and have decided to be impressed instead. You're new to this, but talented."

"This?" Shallan asked.

"The art of the con, of course," Tyn said. "The grand act of pretending to be someone you aren't, then running off with the goods. I like what you pulled with those deserters. It was a big gamble, and it paid off.

"But now you're in a predicament. You're pretending to be someone several steps above your station, and are promising a grand payoff. I've run that scam before, and the trickiest part is the end. If you don't handle this well, these 'heroes' you've recruited will have no qualms stringing you up by the neck. I've noticed that you're dragging your feet moving us toward the Plains. You're uncertain, aren't you? In over your head?"

"Most definitely," Shallan said softly.

"Well," Tyn said, digging into her food, "I'm here to help."

"At what cost?" This woman certainly did like to talk. Shallan was inclined to let her continue.

"I want in on whatever you're planning," Tyn said, stabbing her bread down into the bowl like a sword into a greatshell. "You came all the way here to the Frostlands for *something*. Your plot is likely no small con, but I can't help but assume you don't have the experience to pull it off."

Shallan tapped her finger against the table. Who would she be for this woman? Who did she *need* to be?

She seems like a master con artist, Shallan thought, sweating. *I can't fool someone like this.*

Except that she already had. Accidentally.

"How did you end up here?" Shallan asked. "Leading guards on a caravan? Is that part of a con?"

Tyn laughed. "This? No, it wouldn't be worth the trouble. I may have exaggerated my experience in talking to the caravan leaders, but I needed to get to the Shattered Plains and didn't have the resources to do it on my own. Not safely."

"How does a woman like you end up without resources, though?" Shallan asked, frowning. "I'd think you would never be without."

"I'm not," Tyn said, gesturing. "As you can plainly see. You're going to have to get used to rebuilding, if you want to join the profession. It comes, it goes. I got stuck down south without any spheres, and am finding my way to more civilized countries."

"To the Shattered Plains," Shallan said. "You have a job there of some sort as well? A . . . con you're intending to pull?"

Tyn smiled. "This isn't about me, kid. It's about you, and what I can do for you. I know people in the warcamps. It's practically the new capital of Alethkar; everything interesting in the country is happening there. Money is flowing like rivers after a storm, but everyone considers it a frontier, and so laws are lax. A woman can get ahead if she knows the right people."

Tyn leaned forward, and her expression darkened. "But if she doesn't, she can make enemies really quickly. Trust me, you want to know who I know, and you want to work with them. Without their approval, nothing big happens at the Shattered Plains. So I ask you again. What are you hoping to accomplish there?"

"I . . . know something about Dalinar Kholin."

"Old Blackthorn himself?" Tyn said, surprised. "He's been living a boring life lately, all superior, like he's some hero from the legends."

"Yes, well, what I know is going to be very important to him. Very."

"Well, what is this secret?"

Shallan didn't answer.

"Not willing to divulge the goods yet," Tyn said. "Well, that's understandable. Blackmail is a tricky one. You'll be glad you brought me on. You *are* bringing me on, aren't you?"

"Yes," Shallan said. "I do believe I could learn some things from you."

Smokeform for hiding and slipping between men.
A form of power, like human Surges.
Bring it 'round again.
Though crafted of gods,
It was by Unmade hand.
Leaves its force to be but one of foe or friend.

—From the Listener Song of Histories, 127th stanza

K aladin figured that it took a lot to put him in a situation he'd never before seen. He'd been a slave and a surgeon, served on a battle-field and in a lighteyes' dining room. He'd seen a lot for his twenty years. Too much, it felt at times. He had many memories he'd rather be without.

Regardless, he had not expected this day to present him with something so utterly and disconcertingly unfamiliar. "Sir?" he asked, taking a step backward. "You want me to do *what?*"

"Get on that horse," Dalinar Kholin said, pointing toward an animal grazing nearby. The beast would stand perfectly still, waiting for grass to creep up out of its holes. Then it would pounce, taking a quick bite, which would cause the grass to shoot back down into its burrows. It got a mouthful each time, often pulling the grass out by its roots.

It was one of many such animals dawdling and prancing through the area. It never ceased to stun Kaladin just how rich people like Dalinar were; each horse was worth spheres in profusion. And Dalinar wanted him to climb on one of them.

"Soldier," Dalinar said, "you need to know how to ride. The time might come when you need to guard my sons on the battlefield. Besides, how long did it take you to reach the palace the other night, when coming to hear about the king's accident?"

"Almost three-quarters of an hour," Kaladin admitted. It had been four days since that night, and Kaladin had frequently found himself on edge since then.

"I have stables near the barracks," Dalinar said. "You could have made that trip in a fraction of the time if you could ride. Perhaps you won't spend much of your time in the saddle, but this is going to be an important skill for you and your men to know."

Kaladin looked back at the other members of Bridge Four. Shrugs all around—a few timid ones—except for Moash, who nodded eagerly. "I suppose," Kaladin said, looking back at Dalinar. "If you think it's important, sir, we'll give it a try."

"Good man," Dalinar said. "I'll send over Jenet, the stablemaster."

"We'll await him with eagerness, sir," Kaladin said, trying to sound like he meant it.

Two of Kaladin's men escorted Dalinar as he walked toward the stables, a set of large, sturdy stone buildings. From what Kaladin saw, when the horses weren't inside, they were allowed to roam freely inside this open area west of the warcamp. A low stone wall enclosed it, but surely the horses could jump that at will.

They didn't. The brutes wandered about, stalking grass or lying down, snorting and whinnying. The entire place smelled strange to Kaladin. Not of dung, just . . . of horse. Kaladin eyed one eating nearby, just inside the wall. He didn't trust it; there was something too *smart* about horses. Proper beasts of burden like chulls were slow and docile. He'd ride a chull. A creature like this, though . . . who knew what it was thinking?

Moash stepped up beside him, watching Dalinar go. "You like him, don't you?" he asked softly.

"He's a good commander," Kaladin said, as he instinctively sought out Adolin and Renarin, who were riding their horses nearby. Apparently, the things needed to be exercised periodically to keep them functioning properly. Devilish creatures.

"Don't get too close to him, Kal," Moash said, still watching Dalinar. "And don't trust him too far. He's lighteyed, remember."

"I'm not likely to forget," Kaladin said dryly. "Besides, you're the one who looked like you'd faint from joy the moment he offered to let us ride these monsters."

"Have you ever faced a lighteyes riding one of these things?" Moash asked. "On the battlefield, I mean?"

Kaladin remembered thundering hooves, a man in silvery armor. Dead friends. "Yes."

"Then you know the advantage it offers," Moash said. "I'll take Dalinar's offer gladly."

The stablemaster turned out to be a she. Kaladin raised an eyebrow as the pretty, young lighteyed woman walked up to them, a pair of grooms in tow. She wore a traditional Vorin gown, though it wasn't silk but something coarser, and was slit up the front and back, ankle to thigh. Underneath, she wore a feminine pair of trousers.

The woman wore her dark hair in a tail, no ornaments, and had a tautness to her face that he didn't expect in a lighteyed woman. "The highprince says I'm to let you ruffians touch my horses," Jenet said, folding her arms. "I'm not pleased about it."

"Fortunately," Kaladin said, "neither are we."

She looked him up and down. "You're that one, aren't you? The one everyone is talking about?"

"Maybe."

She sniffed. "You need a haircut. All right, listen up, soldier boys! We're going to do this properly. I won't have you hurting my horses, all right? You listen, and you listen well."

What proceeded was one of the dullest, most protracted lectures of Kaladin's life. The woman went on and on about posture—straight-backed, but not too tense. About getting the horses to move—nudges with the heels, nothing too sharp. About how to ride, how to respect the animal, how to hold the reins properly and how to balance. All before being allowed to even *touch* one of the creatures.

Eventually, the boredom was interrupted by the arrival of a man on horseback. Unfortunately, it was Adolin Kholin, riding that white monster of a horse of his. It was several hands taller than the one Jenet was showing them. Adolin's almost looked a completely different species, with those massive hooves, glistening white coat, and unfathomable eyes.

Adolin looked the bridgemen over with a smirk, then caught the stablemaster's eye and smiled in a less condescending way. "Jenet," he said. "Looking fetching today, as always. Is that a new riding dress?"

The woman bent down without looking—she was now talking about how to guide the horses—and selected a stone from the ground. Then she turned and threw it at Adolin.

The princeling flinched, raising an arm protectively over his face, though Jenet's aim was off.

"Oh, come on now," Adolin said. "You're not still sore that—"

Another rock. This one clipped him on the arm.

"Right, then," Adolin said, jogging his horse away, hunched down to present a smaller target for rocks.

Eventually, after demonstrating saddling and bridling on her horse, Jenet finished the lecture and deemed them worthy of touching some horses. A flock of her grooms, both male and female, scurried out onto the field to select proper mounts for the six bridgemen.

"Lots of women on your staff," Kaladin noted to Jenet as the grooms worked.

"Horseback riding isn't mentioned in *Arts and Majesty*," she replied. "Horses weren't terribly well known back then. Radiants had Ryshadium, but even kings had little access to ordinary horses." She wore her safehand in a sleeve, unlike most of the darkeyed groom women, who wore gloves.

"Which matters because . . . ?" Kaladin said.

Frowning, she looked at him, baffled. *"Arts and Majesty* . . ." she prompted. "Foundation of masculine and feminine arts . . . Of course. I keep looking at those captain's knots on your shoulder, but—"

"But I'm just an ignorant darkeyes?"

"Sure, if that's how you want to put it. Whatever. Look, I'm not going to give you a lecture on the arts—I'm tired of talking to you people already. Let's just say that anyone who wants can be a groom, all right?"

She lacked a polished refinement that Kaladin had come to expect in lighteyed women, and he found it refreshing. Better a woman who was *overtly* condescending than the alternative. The grooms walked the horses out of their enclosure and to a riding ground, shaped like a ring. A group of parshmen with eyes downcast brought the saddles, saddle pads, and bridles—equipment that, following Jenet's lecture, Kaladin could name.

Kaladin selected a beast that didn't look too evil, a shorter horse with a shaggy mane and a brown coat. He saddled it with help from a groom. Nearby, Moash finished and threw himself up into his saddle. Once the groom let go, Moash's horse wandered off without him asking it to do so.

"Hey!" Moash said. "Stop. Whoa. How do I get it to stop walking?"

"You dropped the reins," Jenet called after him. "Storming fool! Were you even listening?"

"Reins," Moash said, scrambling for them. "Can't I just slap it over the head with a reed, like you do a chull?"

Jenet rubbed her forehead.

Kaladin looked into the eye of his own chosen beast. "Look," he said softly, "you don't want to do this. I don't want to do this. Let's just be pleasant to one another and get it over with as quickly as possible."

The horse snorted softly. Kaladin took a deep breath, then grabbed the saddle as instructed, lifting one foot into the stirrup. He rocked a few times, then threw himself up into the saddle. He grabbed the saddle horn in a death grip and held on tight, ready to be thrown about as the beast went charging away.

His horse bent her head and began licking some rocks.

"Hey, now," Kaladin said, raising the reins. "Come on. Let's move."

The horse ignored him.

Kaladin tried cuing it in the flanks as he'd been told. The horse didn't budge.

"You're supposed to be some kind of wagon with legs," Kaladin said to the thing. "You're worth more than a village. Prove it to me. Get going! Forward! Onward!"

The horse licked the rocks.

What is *the thing doing?* Kaladin thought, leaning to the side. With surprise, he noticed grass poking out of its holes. *Licking fools the grass into thinking rain has come.* Often after a storm, plants would unfold to glut themselves on the water even if insects decided to chew them. *Clever beast. Lazy. But clever.*

"You need to show her you're in charge," Jenet said, wandering past. "Tighten the reins, sit up straight, pull her head up, and don't let her eat. She'll walk all over you if you aren't firm."

Kaladin tried to obey, and did manage—finally—to pull the horse away from her meal. The horse did smell odd, but it wasn't a bad smell really. He got her walking, and once that happened, steering wasn't *that* difficult. It felt strange to have some other thing in control of where he was going, however. Yes, he had the reins, but at any time this horse could just up and take off running and he'd be unable to do anything about it. Half of Jenet's training had been about not spooking the horses—about remaining still if one started to gallop, and about never surprising one from behind.

It looked higher from atop the horse than he'd assumed it would. That was a long fall to the ground. He guided the horse about, and after a short time, he managed to pull up beside Natam on purpose. The long-faced bridgeman held his reins as if they were precious gemstones, afraid to yank them or direct his horse.

"Can't believe people ride these things on storming purpose," Natam said. He had a rural Alethi accent, his words bluntly clipped, like he was biting them off before he'd quite finished them. "I mean, we ain't moving any faster than walking, right?"

Again, Kaladin remembered the image of that charging mounted Shardbearer from long ago. Yes, Kaladin could see the reason for horses. Sitting up higher made it easier to strike with power, and the size of the horse—its bulk and momentum—frightened soldiers on foot and sent them scattering.

"I think most go faster than these," Kaladin said. "I'd bet they gave us the old horses to practice on."

"Yeah, I suppose," Natam said. "It's warm. Didn't expect that. I've ridden chulls before. This thing shouldn't be so . . . warm. Hard to feel like this thing is worth as much as it is. It's like I'm riding about on a pile of emerald broams." He hesitated, glancing backward. "Only, emeralds' backsides ain't nearly so busy . . ."

"Natam," Kaladin asked. "Do you remember much about the day when someone tried to kill the king?"

"Oh, sure," Natam said. "I was with the guys who ran out there and found him flapping in the wind, like the Stormfather's own ears."

Kaladin smiled. Once, this man would barely say two sentences together, instead always staring at the ground, somber. Used up by his time as a bridgeman. These last few weeks had been good for Natam. Good for them all.

"Before the storm that night," Kaladin said. "Was anyone out on the balcony? Any servants you didn't recognize? Any soldiers who weren't from the King's Guard?"

"No servants that I recall," Natam said, squinting. The once-farmer got a pensive look on his face. "I guarded the king all day, sir, with the King's Guard. Ain't nothing standing out to me. I— Whoa!" His horse had suddenly picked up speed, outpacing Kaladin's.

"Think about it!" Kaladin called to him. "See what you can remember!"

Natam nodded, still holding his reins like they were glass, refusing to pull them tight or steer the horse. Kaladin shook his head.

A small horse galloped past him. In the air. Made of light. Syl giggled, changing shape and spinning around as a ribbon of light before settling on the neck of Kaladin's horse, just in front of him.

She lounged back, grinning, then frowned at his expression. "You're not enjoying yourself," Syl said.

"You're starting to sound a lot like my mother."

"Captivating?" Syl said. "Amazing, witty, meaningful?"

"Repetitive."

"Captivating?" Syl said. "Amazing, witty, meaningful?"

"Very funny."

"Says the man not laughing," she replied, folding her arms. "All right, so what is drearifying you today?"

"Drearifying?" Kaladin frowned. "Is that a word?"

"You don't know?"

He shook his head.

"Yes," Syl said solemnly. "Yes, it absolutely is."

"Something's off," he said. "About the conversation I just had with

Natam." He tugged on the reins, stopping the horse from trying to bend down and nibble at grass again. The thing was *very* focused.

"What did you talk about?"

"The assassination attempt," Kaladin said, narrowing his eyes. "And if he'd seen anyone before the . . ." He paused. "Before the storm."

He looked down and met Syl's eyes.

"The storm itself would have blown down the railing," Kaladin said.

"Bending it!" Syl said, standing up and grinning. "Ooohhh . . ."

"It was cut clean through, the mortar on the bottom chipped away," Kaladin continued. "I'll bet the force of the winds was easily equal to the weight the king put on it."

"So the sabotage must have happened *after* the storm," Syl said.

A much narrower time frame. Kaladin turned his horse toward where Natam was riding. Unfortunately, catching up wasn't easy. Natam was moving at a trot, much to his obvious dismay, and Kaladin couldn't get his mount to go faster.

"Having trouble, bridgeboy?" Adolin asked, trotting up.

Kaladin glanced at the princeling. Stormfather, but it was difficult not to feel tiny when riding beside that monster of Adolin's. Kaladin tried to kick his horse faster. She kept clopping along at her one speed, walking around the circle here that was a kind of running track for horses.

"Spray might have been fast during her youth," Adolin said, nodding at Kaladin's mount, "but that was fifteen years ago. I'm surprised she's still around, honestly, but she seems perfectly suited for training children. And bridgemen."

Kaladin ignored him, eyes forward, still trying to get the horse to pick up her pace and catch Natam.

"Now, if you want something with more spunk," Adolin said, pointing toward the side, "Dreamstorm over there might be more to your liking."

He indicated a larger, leaner animal in its own enclosure, saddled and roped to a pole firmly mortared into a hole in the ground. The long rope let it run in short bursts, though only around in a circle. It tossed its head, snorting.

Adolin heeled his own animal forward and past Natam.

Dreamstorm, eh? Kaladin thought, inspecting the creature. It certainly did seem to have more spunk than Spray. It also looked like it wanted to take a bite out of anyone who drew too close.

Kaladin turned Spray in that direction. Once near, he slowed—Spray was all too happy to do *that*—and climbed off. Doing so proved more difficult than he'd expected, but he managed to avoid tripping onto his face.

Once down, he put his hands on his hips and inspected the running horse inside its fence.

"Weren't you just complaining," Syl said, walking up onto Spray's head, "that you'd rather walk than let a horse carry you about?"

"Yeah," Kaladin said. He hadn't realized it, but he had been holding some Stormlight. Just a tad. It escaped when he spoke, invisible unless he looked closely and detected a slight warping of the air.

"So what are you doing thinking about riding *that*?"

"This horse," he said, nodding to Spray, "is only for walking. I can walk just fine on my own. That other one, that's an animal for war." Moash was right. Horses were an advantage on the battlefield, so Kaladin should be at least familiar with them.

The same argument Zahel made to me about learning to fight against a Shardblade, Kaladin thought with discomfort. *And I turned him down.*

"What do you think you're doing?" Jenet asked, riding up to him.

"I'm going to get on *that*," Kaladin said, pointing at Dreamstorm.

Jenet snorted. "She'll throw you in a heartbeat and you'll break your crown, bridgeman. She's not good with riders."

"She has a saddle on."

"So she can get used to wearing one."

The horse finished a round of cantering and slowed.

"I don't like that look in your eyes," Jenet told him, turning her own animal to the side. It stomped impatiently, as if eager to be running.

"I'm going to give it a try," Kaladin said, walking forward.

"You won't even be able to get on," Jenet said. She watched him carefully, as if curious what he'd do—though it seemed to him she might be more worried for the horse's safety than his.

Syl alighted on Kaladin's shoulder as he walked.

"This is going to be like back at the lighteyed practice grounds, isn't it?" Kaladin asked. "I'm going to end up on my back, staring at the sky, feeling like a fool."

"Probably," Syl said lightly. "So why are you doing this? Because of Adolin?"

"Nah," Kaladin said. "The princeling can storm away."

"Then why?"

"Because I'm scared of these things."

Syl looked at him, seeming baffled, but it made perfect sense to Kaladin. Ahead, Dreamstorm—huffing out huge breaths from her run—looked at him. She met his eyes.

"Storms!" Adolin's voice called from behind. "Bridgeboy, don't actually *do* it! Are you mad?"

Kaladin stepped up to the horse. She danced a few steps back, but let him touch the saddle. So he breathed in a little more Stormlight and threw himself at the saddle.

"Damnation! What—" Adolin shouted.

That was all Kaladin heard. His Stormlight-aided leap let him get higher than an ordinary man could probably have managed, but his aim was off. He got hold of the pommel and threw one leg over, but the horse started thrashing.

The beast was incredibly strong, a distinct and powerful contrast to Spray. Kaladin was quite nearly hurled from the seat on the first buck.

With a wild swipe of the hand, Kaladin poured Stormlight onto the saddle and stuck himself in place. That only meant that instead of being tossed from horseback like a limp cloth, he got whipped back and forth like a limp cloth. He somehow managed to get hold of the horse's mane and, with teeth gritted, did his best to keep from being bounced senseless.

The stable grounds were a blur. The only sounds he could hear were his beating heart and the smashing hooves. The Voidbringer beast moved like a storm itself, but Kaladin was stuck to the saddle as surely as if he'd been nailed there. After what seemed an eternity, the horse—blowing out big, frothy breaths—stilled.

Kaladin's swimming vision cleared to show a group of bridgemen— keeping their distance—cheering him on. Adolin and Jenet, both mounted, stared at him with what seemed to be a mixture of horror and awe. Kaladin grinned.

Then, in one last, powerful motion, Dreamstorm bucked him free.

He hadn't realized that the Stormlight in the saddle was exhausted. In a fitting fulfillment of his earlier prediction, Kaladin found himself dazed, lying on his back staring at the sky, having trouble remembering the last few seconds of his life. A number of painspren wiggled out of the ground beside him, little orange hands that grabbed this way and that.

An equine head with unfathomably dark eyes leaned down over Kaladin. The horse snorted at him. The smell was moist and grassy.

"You monster," Kaladin said. "You waited until I was relaxed, *then* threw me."

The horse snorted again, and Kaladin found himself laughing. Storms, but that had felt good! He couldn't explain why, but the act of clinging for dear life to the thrashing animal had been truly exhilarating.

As Kaladin stood and dusted himself off, Dalinar himself broke through the crowd, brow furrowed. Kaladin hadn't realized the highprince had still been nearby. He looked from Dreamstorm to Kaladin, then raised an eyebrow.

"You don't chase down assassins on a placid mount, sir," Kaladin said, saluting.

"Yes," Dalinar said, "but it is customary to start training men by using weapons *without* edges, soldier. Are you all right?"

"Fine, sir," Kaladin said.

"Well, it seems your men are taking to the training," Dalinar said. "I'm going to put in a requisition release. You and five others you select are to come here and practice every day for the next few weeks."

"Yes, sir." He'd find the time. Somehow.

"Good," Dalinar said. "I received your proposal for initial patrols outside of the warcamps, and thought it looked good. Why don't you start in two weeks, and bring some horses with you to practice out in the field."

Jenet made a strangled sound. "Outside the city, Brightlord? But . . . bandits . . ."

"The horses are here to be used, Jenet," Dalinar said. "Captain, you'll be sure to bring enough troops to protect the horses, won't you?"

"Yes, sir," Kaladin said.

"Good. But *do* leave that one behind," Dalinar said, waving toward Dreamstorm.

"Er, yes, sir."

Dalinar nodded, moving off and raising his hand toward someone Kaladin couldn't see. Kaladin rubbed his elbow, which he'd smacked. The remaining Stormlight in his body had healed his head first, then run out before getting to his arm.

Bridge Four moved to their horses as Jenet called out for them to remount and start a second phase of training. Kaladin found himself standing near Adolin, who remained mounted.

"Thanks," Adolin said, grudgingly.

"For?" Kaladin asked, walking past him toward Spray, who continued to chew at grass, uncaring of the fuss.

"Not telling Father I put you up to that."

"I'm not an idiot, Adolin," Kaladin said, swinging into his saddle. "I could see what I was getting myself into." He turned his horse away from her meal with some difficulty, and got some more pointers from a groom.

Eventually, Kaladin trotted over toward Natam again. The gait was bouncy, but he mostly got the hang of moving with the horse—they called it posting—to keep from slapping around too much.

Natam watched him as he moved up. "That's unfair, sir."

"What I did with Dreamstorm?"

"No. The way you just ride like that. Seems so natural for you."

Didn't feel that way. "I want to talk some more about that night."

"Sir?" the long-faced man asked. "I haven't thought of anything yet. Been a little distracted."

"I have another question," Kaladin said, bringing their horses up beside one another. "I asked you about your shift during the day, but what about right after I left? Did anyone other than the king go out onto the balcony?"

"Just guards, sir," Natam said.

"Tell me which ones," Kaladin said. "Maybe they saw something."

Natam shrugged. "I mainly watched the door. The king remained in the sitting room for a time. I guess Moash went out."

"Moash," Kaladin said, frowning. "Wasn't his shift supposed to be done soon?"

"Yeah," Natam said. "He stayed around a little extra time; said he wanted to see the king settled. While waiting, Moash went out to watch the balcony. You usually want one of us out there."

"Thanks," Kaladin said. "I'll ask him."

Kaladin found Moash diligently listening to Jenet explain something. Moash seemed to have picked up riding quickly—he seemed to pick up everything quickly. Certainly, he'd been the best student among the bridgemen when it came to fighting.

Kaladin watched him for a few moments, frowning. Then it struck him. *What are you thinking? That Moash might have had something to do with the assassination attempt? Don't be stupid.* That was ridiculous. Besides, the man didn't have a Shardblade.

Kaladin turned his horse away. As he did, however, he saw the person Dalinar had gone to meet. Brightlord Amaram. The two were too far away for Kaladin to hear them, but he could see the amusement on Dalinar's face. Adolin and Renarin rode up to them, smiling broadly as Amaram waved to them.

The anger that surged within Kaladin—sudden, passionate, almost *chokingly* strong—made him clench his fists. His breath hissed out. That surprised him. He'd thought the hatred buried deeper than that.

He turned his horse pointedly the other direction, suddenly looking forward to the chance to go on patrol with the new recruits.

Getting away from the warcamps sounded very good to him.

26

THE FEATHER

They blame our people
For the loss of that land.
The city that once covered it
Did range the eastern strand.
The power made known in the tomes of our clan
Our gods were not who shattered these plains.

—From the Listener Song of Wars, 55th stanza

Adolin crashed into the Parshendi line, ignoring weapons, throwing his shoulder against the enemy at the front. The Parshendi man grunted, his song faltering, as Adolin spun about himself and swept with his Shardblade. Tugs on the weapon marked when it passed through flesh.

Adolin came out of his spin, ignoring the glow of Stormlight coming from a crack at his shoulder. Around him, bodies dropped, eyes burning in their skulls. Adolin's breath, hot and humid, filled his helm as he puffed in and out.

There, he thought, raising his Blade and charging, his men filling in around him. Not those bridgemen, for once, but real soldiers. He'd left the bridgemen back on the assault plateau. He didn't want men around him who didn't want to fight Parshendi.

Adolin and his soldiers pushed through the Parshendi, joining up with a frantic set of soldiers in green uniforms with gold accents, led by a Shardbearer in matching colors. The man fought with a large Shardbearer's hammer—he had no Blade of his own.

Adolin pushed through to him. "Jakamav?" he asked. "You all right?"

"All right?" Jakamav asked, voice muffled by his helm. He slammed the faceplate up, revealing a grin. "I'm wonderful." He laughed, pale green eyes alight with the Thrill of the fight. Adolin recognized that feeling well.

"You were almost surrounded!" Adolin said, turning to face a group of Parshendi running up in pairs. Adolin respected them for coming at Shardbearers, rather than fleeing. It meant almost certain death, but if you won, you could turn the tide of a battle.

Jakamav laughed, sounding as pleased now as when enjoying a winehouse singer, and that laughter was infectious. Adolin found himself grinning as he engaged the Parshendi, sweeping them down with blow after blow. He never enjoyed simple warfare as much as a good duel, but for the moment, despite its crassness, he found challenge and joy in the fight.

Moments later, the dead lying at his feet, he spun about and searched for another challenge. This plateau was shaped very strangely; it had been a tall hill before the Plains were shattered, but half of it had ended up on the adjacent plateau. He couldn't imagine what kind of force would have split the hill down the center, as opposed to cracking it at the base.

Well, it wasn't an ordinary-shaped hill, so maybe that had something to do with the split. It was shaped more like a wide, flat pyramid with only three steps. A large base, a second plateau atop it that was perhaps a hundred feet across, then a third, smaller peak atop the other two, placed right in the center. Almost like a cake with three tiers that had been cut with a large knife right down the center.

Adolin and Jakamav fought on the second tier of the battlefield. Technically, Adolin wasn't required to be on this run. It wasn't his army's turn in the rotation. However, the time had come to implement another part of Dalinar's plan. Adolin had arrived with only a small strike force, but it was a good thing he had. Jakamav had been surrounded up here, on the second tier, and the regular army hadn't been able to break through.

Now, the Parshendi had been pushed back to the sides of this tier. They still held the top tier completely; it was where the chrysalis had appeared. That put them in a bad position. Yes, they had the high ground, but they also had to hold the slopes between tiers to secure their withdrawal. They'd obviously hoped to get the harvesting done before the humans arrived.

Adolin kicked a Parshendi soldier over the edge, toppling him down thirty feet or so onto those fighting on the bottom tier, then looked to his right. The slope upward was there, but the Parshendi had the approach clogged. He'd really like to reach the top. . . .

He looked at the sheer cliff face between his tier and the one above. "Jakamav," he called, pointing.

Jakamav followed Adolin's gesture, looking upward. Then stepped back from the fighting.

"That's crazy!" Jakamav said as Adolin jogged up.

"Sure is."

"Let's be at it, then!" He handed his hammer to Adolin, who slipped it into the sheath on his friend's back. Then the two of them ran to the rock wall and started to climb.

Adolin's Plated fingers ground against rock as he pulled himself straight up. Soldiers below cheered them on. There were handholds aplenty, though he would never have wanted to do this without Plate to propel his climb and protect him if he fell.

It was still crazy; they'd end up surrounded. However, two Shardbearers could do amazing things when supporting one another. Besides, if they got overwhelmed, they could always jump off the cliff, assuming their Plate was healthy enough to survive the fall.

It was the sort of risky move that Adolin would never dare when his father was on the battlefield.

He paused halfway up the cliff. Parshendi gathered on the edge of the tier above, preparing for them.

"You have a plan for getting a foothold up there?" Jakamav asked, clinging to the rocks beside Adolin.

Adolin nodded. "Just be ready to support me."

"Sure." Jakamav scanned the heights, face hidden behind his helm. "What are you doing here, by the way?"

"I figured no army would turn away some Shardbearers who wanted to help."

"Shardbearers? Plural?"

"Renarin is down below."

"Hopefully not fighting."

"He's surrounded by a large squad of soldiers with careful instructions *not* to let him get into the fighting. Father wanted him to see a few of these, though."

"I know what Dalinar is doing," Jakamav said. "He's trying to show a spirit of cooperation, trying to get the highprinces to stop being rivals. So he sends his Shardbearers to help, even when the run isn't his."

"Are you complaining?"

"Nope. Let's see you make an opening up there. I'll need a moment to get the hammer out."

Adolin grinned inside his helmet, then continued climbing. Jakamav was a landlord and Shardbearer under Highprince Roion, and a fairly good friend. It was important that lighteyes like Jakamav saw Dalinar and Adolin actively working toward a better Alethkar. Perhaps a few episodes like this would show the value of a trustworthy alliance, instead of the back-stabbing, temporary coalition Sadeas represented.

Adolin climbed farther, Jakamav close behind, until he was a dozen feet from the top. The Parshendi clustered there, hammers and maces at the ready—weapons for fighting a man in Shardplate. A few farther down launched arrows, which bounced ineffectively off the Plate.

All right, Adolin thought, holding his hand to the side—clinging to the rocks with the other—and summoned his Blade. He slammed it directly into the rock wall with the flat of the blade facing upward. He climbed up beside the sword.

Then he stepped onto the flat of the blade.

Shardblades couldn't break—they could barely bend—so it held him. He suddenly had leverage and good footing, and so when he crouched down and leaped, the Plate hurled him upward. As he passed the edge of the top tier, he grabbed the rock there—just beneath the feet of the Parshendi—and pulled on it to throw himself into the waiting foe.

They broke off their singing as he smashed into them with the force of a boulder. He got his feet underneath him, mentally sending a summons to his Blade, then slammed his shoulder into one group. He began to lay about himself with punches, smashing the chest of one Parshendi, then the head of another. The soldiers' carapace armor cracked with sickening sounds, and the punches flung them backward, knocking some off the cliff.

Adolin took a few hits on his forearms before his Blade finally re-formed in his hands. He swung about, so focused on holding his ground that he didn't notice Jakamav until the Shardbearer in green fell in beside him, crushing Parshendi with his hammer.

"Thanks for tossing a platoon's worth of Parshendi down on my head," Jakamav called as he swung. "That was a wonderful surprise."

Adolin grinned, pointing. "Chrysalis."

The top tier wasn't well populated—though more Parshendi were flooding up the incline. He and Jakamav had a direct path to the chrysalis, a hulking, oblong boulder of brown and faint green. It was matted to the rocks with the same stuff that made up its shell.

Adolin leaped over the twitching form of a Parshendi with dead legs and charged the chrysalis, Jakamav following at a clanking jog. Getting to a gemheart was tough—the chrysalises had skin like rock—but with a Shardblade, it could be easy. They just had to kill the thing, then cut a hole so they could rip out the heart and—

The chrysalis was already open.

"No!" Adolin said, scrambling up to it, grabbing the sides of the hole and peering into the slushy violet interior. Chunks of carapace floated within the goop, and a conspicuous gap lay where the gemheart normally connected to veins and sinew.

Adolin spun, searching across the top of the plateau. Jakamav clanked up and cursed. "How did they get it out so quickly?"

There. Nearby, Parshendi soldiers scattered, yelling in their impenetrable, rhythmic language. Standing behind them was a tall figure in silvery Shardplate, a red cloak billowing out behind. The armor had peaked joints, ridges rising like the points on a crab's shell. The figure was easily seven feet tall, the armor making him look massive, perhaps because it covered a Parshendi who had that carapace armor growing from his skin.

"It's him!" Adolin said, running forward. This was the one his father had fought on the Tower, the only Shardbearer they'd seen among the Parshendi for weeks, maybe months.

Perhaps the last one they had.

The Shardbearer turned toward Adolin, gripping a large uncut gemstone in his hand. It dripped ichor and plasma.

"Fight me!" Adolin said.

A group of Parshendi soldiers charged past the Shardbearer, running toward the long drop-off at the back of the formation, where the hill had been split down the center. The Shardbearer handed his gemheart to one of these charging men, then turned and watched them jump.

They soared across the gap to land on the top of the other half of the hill, the one on the adjacent plateau. It still amazed Adolin that these Parshendi soldiers could leap chasms. He felt a fool as he realized that these heights were not a trap for them as they would be for humans. To them, a mountain split in half was just another chasm to leap.

More and more of the Parshendi made the leap, flowing away from the humans below and jumping to safety. Adolin did spot one who stumbled as he leapt. The poor fellow screamed as he plummeted into the chasm. This was dangerous for them, but it was obviously less so than trying to fight off the humans.

The Shardbearer remained. Adolin ignored the fleeing Parshendi— ignored Jakamav, who called for him to fall back—and ran up to that Shardbearer, swinging his Blade full force. The Parshendi raised his own Blade, slapping aside Adolin's blow.

"You are the son, Adolin Kholin," the Parshendi said. "Your father? Where is?"

Adolin froze in place. The words were in Alethi—heavily accented, yes, but understandable.

The Shardbearer slammed up his faceplate. And, to Adolin's shock, there was no beard on that face. Didn't that make this a woman? Telling the difference with Parshendi was difficult for him. The vocal timbre was rough and low-pitched, though he supposed it could be feminine.

"I must need speak to Dalinar," the woman said, stepping forward. "I met him one time, much long ago."

"You refused our every messenger," Adolin said, backing away, sword out. "Now you wish to speak with us?"

"That was long ago. Time does change."

Stormfather. Something inside of Adolin urged him to go in swinging, to batter this Shardbearer down and get some answers, win some Shards. Fight! He was here to *fight*!

His father's voice, in the back of his mind, held him at bay. Dalinar would want this chance. It could change the course of the entire war.

"He will want to contact you," Adolin said, taking a deep breath, shoving down the Thrill of battle. "How?"

"Will send messenger," the Shardbearer said. "Do not kill one who comes." She raised her Shardblade toward him in salute, then let it drop and dematerialize. She turned to charge toward the chasm and hurled herself across in a prodigious leap.

⁘

Adolin pulled off his helm as he strode across the plateau. Surgeons saw to the wounded while the hale sat around in groups, drinking water and grousing about their failure.

A rare mood hovered over the armies of Roion and Ruthar this day. Usually when the Alethi lost a plateau run it was because the Parshendi pushed them back in a wild scrambling retreat across bridges. It wasn't often that a run ended with the Alethi controlling the plateau, but with no gemheart to show for it.

He released one gauntlet, the straps undoing themselves automatically at his will, then hooked it at his waist. He used a sweaty hand to push back sweatier hair. Now where had Renarin gotten to?

There, on the staging plateau, sitting on a rock surrounded by guards. Adolin tromped across one of the bridges, raising a hand to Jakamav, who was removing his Plate nearby. He'd want to ride back in comfort.

Adolin jogged up to his brother, who sat on a boulder with his helm off, staring at the ground in front of him.

"Hey," Adolin said. "Ready to head back?"

Renarin nodded.

"What happened?" Adolin asked.

Renarin continued staring at the ground. Finally, one of the bridgeman guards—a compact man with silvering hair—nodded his head to the side. Adolin walked with him a short distance away.

"A group of shellheads tried to seize one of the bridges, Brightlord," the bridgeman said softly. "Brightlord Renarin insisted on going to help. Sir, we tried hard to dissuade him. Then, when he got near and summoned his Blade, he just kind of . . . stood there. We got him away, sir, but he's been sitting on that rock ever since."

One of Renarin's fits. "Thank you, soldier," Adolin said. He walked back over and laid his ungauntleted hand on Renarin's shoulder. "It's all right, Renarin. It happens."

Renarin shrugged again. Well, if he was in one of his moods, there was nothing to do but let him stew. The younger man would talk about it when he was ready.

Adolin organized his two hundred troops, then paid his respects to the highprinces. Neither seemed very grateful. In fact, Ruthar seemed convinced that Adolin and Jakamav's stunt had driven the Parshendi off with the gemheart. As if they wouldn't have withdrawn the moment they had it anyway. Idiot.

Adolin smiled affably, regardless. Hopefully Father was right, and the extended hand of fellowship would help. Personally, Adolin just wanted a chance at each of them in the dueling ring, where he could teach them a little respect.

On his way back to his army, he searched out Jakamav, who sat under a small pavilion, having a cup of wine as he watched the rest of his army trudge back across the bridges. There were a lot of slumped shoulders and long faces.

Jakamav gestured for his steward to get Adolin a cup of sparkling yellow wine. Adolin took it in his unarmored hand, though he didn't drink.

"That was quite nearly awesome," Jakamav said, staring out at the battle plateau. From this lower vantage, it looked truly imposing, with those three tiers.

Almost looks man-made, Adolin thought idly, considering the shape. "Nearly," Adolin agreed. "Can you imagine what an assault would look like if we had twenty or thirty Shardbearers on the battlefield at once? What chance would the Parshendi have?"

Jakamav grunted. "Your father and the king are seriously committed to this course, aren't they?"

"As am I."

"I can see what you and your father are doing here, Adolin. But if you keep dueling, you're going to lose your Shards. Even you can't *always* win. Eventually you'll hit an off day. Then it will all be gone."

"I might lose at some point," Adolin agreed. "Of course by then I'll have won half the Shards in the kingdom, so I should be able to arrange a replacement."

Jakamav sipped his wine, smiling. "You are a cocky bastard, I'll give you that."

Adolin smiled, then settled down in a squat beside Jakamav's chair—he couldn't sit in one himself, not in Shardplate—so he could meet his friend's eyes. "The truth is, Jakamav, I'm not really worried about losing my Shards—I'm more worried about finding duels in the *first* place. I can't seem to get any Shardbearers to agree to a bout, at least not for Shards."

"There have been certain . . . inducements going around," Jakamav admitted. "Promises made to Shardbearers if they refused you."

"Sadeas."

Jakamav inspected his wine. "Try Eranniv. He's been boasting that he's better than the standings give him credit for. Knowing him, he'll see everyone else refusing, and see it as an opportunity for him to do something spectacular. He's pretty good, though."

"So am I," Adolin said. "Thanks, Jak. I owe you."

"What's this I hear about you being betrothed?"

Storms. How had that gotten out? "It's just a causal," Adolin said. "And it might not even get that far. The woman's ship seems to have been severely delayed."

Two weeks now, with no word. Even Aunt Navani was getting worried. Jasnah should have sent word.

"I never thought you were the type to let yourself be nailed into an arranged marriage, Adolin," Jakamav said. "There are lots of winds to ride out there, you know?"

"Like I said," Adolin replied, "it's far from official."

He still didn't know how he felt about all this. Part of him had wanted to push back simply because he resisted being subject to Jasnah's manipulation. But then, his recent track record wasn't anything to boast of. After what had happened with Danlan . . . It wasn't his fault, was it, that he was a friendly man? Why did every woman have to be so jealous?

The idea of letting someone else just take care of it all for him was more tempting than he'd ever publicly admit.

"I can tell you the details," Adolin said. "Maybe at the winehouse later tonight? Bring Inkima? You can tell me how stupid I'm being, give me some perspective."

Jakamav stared at his wine.

"What?" Adolin asked.

"Being seen with you isn't good for one's reputation these days, Adolin," Jakamav said. "Your father and the king aren't particularly popular."

"It will all blow over."

"I'm sure it will," Jakamav said. "So let's . . . wait until then, shall we?"

Adolin blinked, the words hitting him harder than any blow on the battlefield. "Sure," Adolin forced himself to say.

"Good man." Jakamav actually had the audacity to smile at him and lift his cup of wine.

Adolin set aside his own cup untouched and stalked off.

Sureblood was ready and waiting for him when he reached his men. Adolin moved to swing into the saddle, stewing, but the white Ryshadium nudged him with a butt of the head. Adolin sighed, scratching at the horse's ears. "Sorry," he said. "Haven't been paying much attention to you lately, have I?"

He gave the horse a good scratch, and felt somewhat better after climbing into the saddle. Adolin patted Sureblood's neck, and the horse pranced a bit as they started moving. He often did that when Adolin was feeling annoyed, as if trying to improve his master's mood.

His four guards for the day followed behind him. They'd obligingly brought their old bridge from Sadeas's army to get Adolin's team where they needed to go. They seemed to find it very amusing that Adolin had his soldiers take shifts carrying the thing.

Storming Jakamav. *This has been coming,* Adolin admitted to himself. *The more you defend Father, the more they'll pull away.* They were like children. Father really *was* right.

Did Adolin have *any* true friends? Anyone who would actually stand by him when things were difficult? He knew practically everyone of note in the warcamps. Everyone knew him.

How many of them actually cared?

"I didn't have a fit," Renarin said softly.

Adolin shook out of his brooding. They rode side by side, though Adolin's mount was several hands taller. With Adolin astride a Ryshadium, Renarin looked like a child on a pony by comparison, even in his Plate.

Clouds had rolled across the sun, giving some relief from the glare, though the air had turned cold lately and it looked like winter was here for a season. The empty plateaus stretched ahead, barren and broken.

"I just stood there," Renarin said. "I wasn't frozen because of my . . . ailment. I'm just a coward."

"You're no coward," Adolin said. "I've seen you act as brave as any man. Remember the chasmfiend hunt?"

Renarin shrugged.

"You don't know how to fight, Renarin," Adolin said. "It's a good thing you froze. You're too new at this to go into battle right now."

"I shouldn't be. You started training when you were six."

"That's different."

"You're different, you mean," Renarin said, eyes forward. He wasn't wearing his spectacles. Why was that? Didn't he need them?

Trying to act like he doesn't, Adolin thought. Renarin so desperately wanted to be useful on a battlefield. He'd resisted all suggestions that he should become an ardent and pursue scholarship, as might have better suited him.

"You just need more training," Adolin said. "Zahel will whip you into shape. Just give it time. You'll see."

"I need to be ready," Renarin said. "Something is coming."

The way he said it gave Adolin a shiver. "You're talking about the numbers on the walls."

Renarin nodded. They'd found another scratched set of them, after the recent highstorm, outside Father's room. *Forty-nine days. A new storm comes.*

According to the guards, nobody had gone in or out—different men from last time, which made it unlikely it had been one of them. Storms. That had been scratched on the wall while Adolin had been sleeping just one room away. Who, or what, had done it?

"Need to be ready," Renarin said. "For the coming storm. So little time . . ."

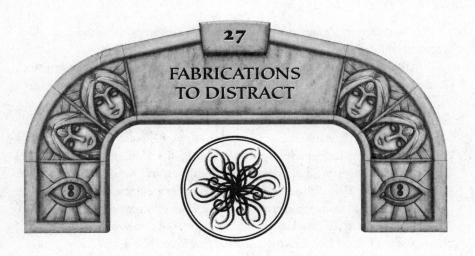

FIVE YEARS AGO

S hallan longed to stay outside. Here in the gardens, people didn't scream at each other. Here there was peace.

Unfortunately, it was a fake peace—a peace of carefully planted shalebark and cultivated vines. A fabrication, designed to amuse and distract. More and more she longed to escape and visit places where the plants weren't carefully trimmed into shapes, where people didn't step lightly, as if afraid of causing a rockslide. A place away from the shouting.

A cool mountain breeze came down from the heights and swept through the gardens, making vines shy backward. She sat away from the flowerbeds, and the sneezing they would bring her, instead studying a section of sturdy shalebark. The cremling she sketched turned at the wind, its enormous feelers twitching, before leaning back down to chew on the shalebark. There were so *many* kinds of cremlings. Had anyone tried to count them all?

By luck, her father had owned a drawing book—one of the works of Dandos the Oilsworn—and she used that for instruction, letting it rest open beside her.

A yell sounded from inside the nearby manor house. Shallan's hand stiffened, making an errant streak across her sketch. She took a deep breath and tried to return to her drawing, but another series of shouts put her on edge. She set her pencil down.

She was nearly out of sheets from the latest stack her brother had brought her. He returned unpredictably but never for long, and when he came, he and Father avoided one another.

Nobody in the manor knew where Helaran went when he left.

She lost track of time, staring at a blank sheet of paper. That happened to her sometimes. When she raised her eyes, the sky was darkening. Almost time for Father's feast. He had those regularly now.

Shallan packed up her things in the satchel, then took off her sun hat and walked toward the manor house. Tall and imposing, the building was an exemplar of the Veden ideal. Solitary, strong, towering. A work of square blocks and small windows, dappled by dark lichen. Some books called manors like this the soul of Jah Keved—isolated estates, each brightlord ruling independently. It seemed to her that those writers romanticized rural life. Had they ever actually visited one of the manors, experienced the true dullness of country life in person, or did they merely fantasize about it from the comfort of their cosmopolitan cities?

Inside the house, Shallan turned up the stairs toward her quarters. Father would want her looking nice for the feast. There would be a new dress for her to wear as she sat quietly, not interrupting the discussion. Father had never said so, but she suspected he thought it a pity she had begun speaking again.

Perhaps he did not wish her to be able to speak of things she'd seen. She stopped in the hallway, her mind going blank.

"Shallan?"

She shook herself to find Van Jushu, her fourth brother, on the steps behind her. How long had she been standing and staring at the wall? The feast would start soon!

Jushu's jacket was undone and hung askew, his hair mussed, his cheeks flushed with wine. No cufflinks or belt; they had been fine pieces, each with a glowing gemstone. He'd have gambled those away.

"What was Father yelling about earlier?" she asked. "Were you here?"

"No," Jushu said, running his hand through his hair. "But I heard. Balat has been starting fires again. Nearly burned down the storming servants' building." Jushu pushed past her, then stumbled, grabbing the bannister to keep from falling.

Father was not going to like Jushu coming to the feast like this. More yelling.

"Storms-cursed idiot," Jushu said as Shallan helped him right himself. "Balat is going straight crazy. I'm the only one left in this family with any sense. You were staring at the wall again, weren't you?"

She didn't reply.

"He'll have a new dress for you," Jushu said as she helped him toward his room. "And nothing for me but curses. Bastard. He loved Helaran, and none of us are him, so we don't matter. Helaran is never here! He betrayed Father, almost killed him. And still, he's the only one who matters. . . ."

They passed Father's chambers. The heavy stumpweight door was open a crack as a maid tidied the room, allowing Shallan to see the far wall.

And the glowing strongbox.

It was hidden behind a painting of a storm at sea that did nothing to dim the powerful white glow. Right through the canvas, she saw the outline of the strongbox blazing like a fire. She stumbled, pulling to a stop.

"What are you staring at?" Jushu demanded, holding to the bannister.

"The light."

"What light?"

"Behind the painting."

He squinted, lurching forward. "What in the Halls are you talking about, girl? It really did ruin your mind, didn't it? Watching him kill Mother?" Jushu pulled away from her, cursing softly to himself. "I'm the only one in this family who hasn't gone crazy. The only storming one . . ."

Shallan stared into that light. There hid a monster.

There hid Mother's soul.

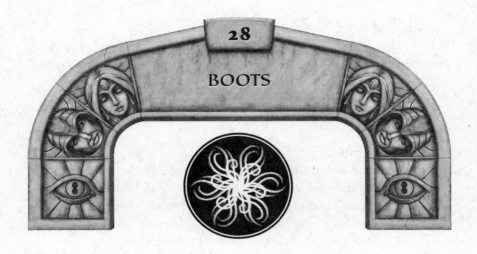

The betrayal of spren has brought us here.
They gave their Surges to human heirs,
But not to those who know them most dear, before us.
'Tis no surprise we turned away
Unto the gods we spent our days
And to become their molding clay, they changed us.

—From the Listener Song of Secrets, 40th stanza

Th'information'll cost ya twelve broams," Shallan said. "Ruby, you see. I'll check each one."

Tyn laughed, tossing her head back, jet-black hair falling free around her shoulders. She sat in the driver's seat of the wagon. Where Bluth used to sit.

"You call *that* a Bav accent?" Tyn demanded.

"I've only heard them three or four times."

"You sounded like you have rocks in your mouth!"

"That's how they sound!"

"Nah, it's more like they have pebbles in their mouths. But they talk really slow, with overemphasized sounds. Like this. 'Oi looked over the paintings that ya gave me, and they're roit nice. Roit nice indeed. Ain't never had a cloth for my backside that was so pleasant.'"

"You're exaggerating that!" Shallan said, though she couldn't help laughing.

"A tad," Tyn said, leaning back and sweeping her long, chull-guiding reed in front of her like a Shardblade.

"I don't see why knowing a Bav accent would be useful," Shallan said. "They're not a very important people."

"Kid, that's *why* they're important."

"They're important because they're unimportant," Shallan said. "All right, I know I'm bad at logic sometimes, but something about that statement seems off."

Tyn smiled. She was so relaxed, so . . . free. Not at all what Shallan had expected after their first encounter.

But then the woman had been playing a part. Leader of the guard. This woman Shallan was talking to now, this seemed real.

"Look," Tyn said, "if you're going to fool people, you'll need to learn how to act beneath them as well as above them. You're getting the whole 'important lighteyes' thing down. I assume you've had good examples."

"You could say that," Shallan replied, thinking of Jasnah.

"Thing is, in a lot of situations, being an important lighteyes is useless."

"Being unimportant is important. Being important is useless. Got it."

Tyn eyed her, chewing on some jerky. Her sword belt hung from a peg on the side of the seat, swaying to the rhythm of the chull's gait. "You know, kid, you get kind of mouthy when you let your mask down."

Shallan blushed.

"I like it. I prefer people who can laugh at life."

"I can guess what you're trying to teach me," Shallan said. "You're saying that a person with a Bav accent, someone who looks lowly and simple, can go places a lighteyes never could."

"And can hear or do things a lighteyes never could. Accent is important. Elocute with distinction, and it often won't matter how little money you have. Wipe your nose on your arm and speak like a Bav, and sometimes people won't even glance to see if you're wearing a sword."

"But my eyes are light blue," Shallan said. "I'll never pass for lowly, no matter what my voice sounds like!"

Tyn fished in her trouser pocket. She had slung her coat over another peg, and so wore only the pale tan trousers—tight, with high boots—and a buttoned shirt. Almost a worker's shirt, though of nicer material.

"Here," Tyn said, tossing something to her.

Shallan barely caught it. She blushed at her clumsiness, then held it up toward the sun: a small vial with some dark liquid inside.

"Eyedrops," Tyn said. "They'll darken your eyes for a few hours."

"*Really?*"

"Not hard to find, if you have the right connections. Useful stuff."

Shallan lowered the vial, suddenly feeling a chill. "Is there—"

"The reverse?" Tyn cut in. "Something to turn a darkeyes into a lighteyes? Not that I know of. Unless you believe the stories about Shardblades."

"Makes sense," Shallan said, relaxing. "You can darken glass by painting it, but I don't think you can lighten it without melting down the whole thing."

"Anyway," Tyn said, "you'll need a good backwater accent or two. Herdazian, Bavlander, something like that."

"I probably *have* a rural Veden accent," Shallan admitted.

"That won't work out here. Jah Keved is a cultured country, and your internal accents are too similar to one another for outsiders to recognize. Alethi won't hear rural from you, like a fellow Veden would. They'll just hear exotic."

"You've been to a lot of places, haven't you?" Shallan asked.

"I go wherever the winds take me. It's a good life, so long as you're not attached to stuff."

"Stuff?" Shallan asked. "But you're—pardon—you're a *thief*. That's all about getting more stuff!"

"I take what I can get, but that just proves how transient *stuff* is. You'll take some things, but then you'll lose them. Just like the job I pulled down south. My team never returned from their mission; I'm half convinced they ran off without seeing me paid." She shrugged. "It happens. No need to get worked up."

"What kind of job was it?" Shallan asked, blinking pointedly to take a Memory of Tyn lounging there, sweeping her reed as if conducting musicians, not a care in the world. They'd nearly died a couple of weeks back, but Tyn took it in stride.

"It was a big job," Tyn said. "Important, for the kinds of people who make things change in the world. I still haven't heard back from the ones who hired us. Maybe my men didn't run off; maybe they just failed. I don't know for certain." Here, Shallan caught tension in Tyn's face. A tightening of the skin around the eyes, a distance to her gaze. She was worried about what her employers might do to her. Then it was gone, smoothed away. "Have a look," Tyn said, nodding up ahead.

Shallan followed the gesture and noticed moving figures a few hills over. The landscape had slowly changed as they approached the Plains. The hills grew steeper, but the air a little warmer, and plant life was more prevalent. Stands of trees clustered in some of the valleys, where waters would flow after highstorms. The trees were squat, different from the flowing majesty of the ones she'd known in Jah Keved, but it was still nice to see something other than scrub.

The grass here was fuller. It pulled smartly away from the wagons, sinking into its burrows. The rockbuds here grew large, and shalebark cropped up in patches, often with lifespren bouncing about like tiny green motes. During their days traveling they'd passed other caravans, more plentiful now that they were closer to the Shattered Plains. So Shallan wasn't surprised to see someone up ahead. The figures, however, rode *horses*. Who could afford animals like that? And why didn't they have an escort? There seemed to be only four of them.

The caravan rolled to a stop as Macob yelled an order from the first wagon. Shallan had learned, through awful experience, just how dangerous *any* encounter out here could be. None were taken lightly by caravan masters. She was the authority here, but she allowed those with more experience to call stops and choose their path.

"Come on," Tyn said, stopping the chull with a whack of the stick, then hopping down from the wagon and grabbing her coat and sword off their pegs.

Shallan scrambled down, putting on her Jasnah face. She let herself be herself with Tyn. With the others, she needed to be a leader. Stiff, stern, but hopefully inspiring. To that end, she was pleased with the blue dress that Macob had given her. Embroidered with silver, made of the finest silk, it was a wonderful upgrade from her tattered one.

They walked past where Vathah and his men marched just behind the lead wagon. The leader of the deserters shot Tyn a glare. His dislike of the woman was only more reason to respect her, despite her criminal proclivities.

"Brightness Davar and I will handle this," Tyn said to Macob as they passed.

"Brightness?" Macob said, standing and looking toward Shallan. "What if they are bandits?"

"There are only four of them, Master Macob," Shallan said lightly. "The day I can't handle four bandits on my own is a day I deserve to be robbed."

They passed the wagon, Tyn tying on her belt.

"What if they *are* bandits?" Shallan hissed once they were out of earshot.

"I thought you said you could handle four."

"I was just going along with your attitude!"

"That's dangerous, kid," Tyn said with a grin. "Look, bandits wouldn't let us see them, and they *certainly* wouldn't just sit there."

The group of four men waited on the top of the hill. As Shallan drew closer, she could see that they were wearing crisp blue uniforms that looked quite genuine. At the bottom of the ravine between hills, Shallan stubbed her toe on a rockbud. She grimaced—Macob had given her lighteyed shoes to match her dress. They were luxurious, and probably worth a fortune, but they were little more than slippers.

"We'll wait here," Shallan said. "They can come to us."

"Sounds good to me," Tyn said. Indeed, up above, the men started moving down the hillside when they noticed Shallan and Tyn were waiting for them. Two more came and followed after them on foot, men not in uniforms, but workers' clothing. Grooms?

"Who are you going to be?" Tyn asked softly.

". . . Myself?" Shallan replied.

"What's the fun in that?" Tyn said. "How's your Horneater?"

"Horneater! I—"

"Too late," Tyn said as the men rode up.

Shallan found horses intimidating. The large brutish things weren't docile like chulls. Horses were always stomping about, snorting.

The lead rider reined in his horse with some obvious annoyance. He didn't seem in complete control of the beast. "Brightness," he said, nodding to her as he saw her eyes. Shockingly, he was darkeyed, a tall man with black Alethi hair he wore down to his shoulders. He looked over Tyn, noting the sword and the soldier's uniform, but let slip no reaction. A hard man, this one.

"Her Highness," Tyn announced in a loud voice, gesturing toward Shallan, "Princess Unulukuak'kina'autu'atai! You are in the presence of royalty, darkeyes!"

"A Horneater?" the man said, leaning down, inspecting Shallan's red hair. "Wearing a Vorin dress. Rock would have a fit."

Tyn looked to Shallan and raised an eyebrow.

I'm going to strangle you, woman, Shallan thought, then took a deep breath. "This thing," Shallan said, gesturing at her dress. "He is not what you have a princess wear? He is good for me. You will be respect!" Fortunately, her red face would fit for a Horneater. They were a passionate people.

Tyn nodded to her, looking appreciative.

"I'm sorry," the man said, though he didn't seem very apologetic. What was a darkeyes doing riding an animal of such value? One of the man's companions was inspecting the caravan through a spyglass. He was dark-eyed too, but looked more comfortable on his mount.

"Seven wagons, Kal," the man said. "Well guarded."

The man, Kal, nodded. "I've been sent out to look for signs of bandits," he said to Tyn. "Has all been well with your caravan?"

"We ran into some bandits three weeks ago," Tyn said, thumbing over her shoulder. "Why do you care?"

"We represent the king," the man said. "And are from the personal guard of Dalinar Kholin."

Oh, *storms.* Well, that was going to be inconvenient.

"Brightlord Kholin," Kal continued, "is investigating the possibility of a wider range of control around the Shattered Plains. If you really were attacked, I would like to know the details."

"*If* we were attacked?" Shallan asked. "You doubt our word?"

"No—"

"I am offend!" Shallan declared, folding her arms.

"You'd better watch yourself," Tyn told the men. "Her Highness does not like to be offended."

"How surprising," Kal said. "Where did the attack take place? You fought it off? How many bandits were there?"

Tyn filled him in on the details, which gave Shallan a chance to think. Dalinar Kholin was her future father-in-law, if the causal matured into a marriage. Hopefully, she wouldn't run into these particular soldiers again.

I really am going to strangle you, Tyn. . . .

Their leader listened to the details of the attack with a stoic air. He didn't seem like a very pleasant man.

"I am sorry to hear of your losses," Kal said. "But you're only a day and a half by caravan from the Shattered Plains now. You should be safe the rest of the way."

"I am curiosity," Shallan said. "These animals, they are horses? Yet you are darkeyed. This . . . Kholin trusts you well."

"I do my duty," Kal said, studying her. "Where are the rest of your people? That caravan looks as if it's all Vorin. Also, you look a little spindly for a Horneater."

"Did you just insult the princess's weight?" Tyn asked, aghast.

Storms! She was good. She actually managed to produce angerspren with the remark.

Well, nothing to do but soldier on.

"I am offend!" Shallan yelled.

"You have offended Her Highness again!"

"*Very* offend!"

"You'd better apologize."

"No apologize!" Shallan declared. "Boots!"

Kal leaned back, looking between the two of them, trying to parse what had just been said. "Boots?" he asked.

"Yes," Shallan said. "I am liking your boots. You will apology with boots."

"You . . . want my boots?"

"Did you not hear Her Highness?" Tyn asked, arms folded. "Are soldiers of this Dalinar Kholin's army so disrespectful?"

"I'm not disrespectful," Kal said. "But I'm not giving her my boots."

"You insult!" Shallan declared, stepping forward, pointing at him. Stormfather, those horses were enormous! "I will tell all who are to listen! When arriving, I will say, 'Kholin is stealer of boots and taker of women's virtue!'"

Kal sputtered. "Virtue!"

"Yes," Shallan said; then she glanced over to Tyn. "Virtue? No, wrong word. Virture . . . No . . . Vesture. Vesture! Taker of woman's vesture! That is word I wanted."

The soldier glanced to his companions, looking confused. *Drat,* Shallan thought. *Good puns are lost on men with poor vocabulary.*

"Is no matter," Shallan said, throwing up her hand. "All will know what you have done in wronging me. You have laid me bare, here in this wilderness. Stripping me! Is an insult to my house and my clan. All will know that Kholin—"

"Oh, stop, stop," Kal said, reaching down and awkwardly pulling his boot from his foot while on horseback. His sock had a hole in the heel. "Storming woman," he muttered. He tossed the first boot down to her, then removed the other.

"Your apology is accepted," Tyn said, fetching the boots.

"By Damnation, it had better be," Kal said. "I'll pass along your story. Maybe we can get this storming place patrolled. Come on, men." He turned and left them without another word, perhaps fearing another Horneater diatribe.

Once they were out of earshot, Shallan looked at the boots, then started laughing uncontrollably. Joyspren rose around her, like blue leaves that started at her feet then moved up in a swirl before flaring out above her as if in a blast of wind. Shallan watched them with a big smile. Those were very rare.

"Ah," Tyn said with a smile. "No use denying. That was fun."

"I'm *still* going to strangle you," Shallan said. "He knew we were playing with him. That has to be the worst Horneater impression a woman has ever done."

"It was actually pretty good," Tyn said. "You overdid the words, but the accent itself was spot on. That wasn't the point, though." She handed back the boots.

"What *was* the point?" Shallan asked as they hiked back toward the caravan. "Making a fool out of me?"

"Partially," Tyn said.

"That was sarcasm."

"If you're going to learn to do this," Tyn said, "you have to be comfortable in situations like that. You can't be embarrassed when you pose as someone else. The more outrageous the attempt, the straighter you have to play it. The only way to get better is to practice—and in front of people who very well might catch you."

"I suppose," Shallan said.

"Those boots are too big for you," Tyn noted. "Though I *did* love the look on his face when you asked for them. 'No apologize. Boots!'"

"I *really* need some boots," Shallan said. "I'm tired of walking around on rock barefoot or in slippers. A little padding, and these will fit." She held them up. They *were* rather large. "Er, maybe." She looked backward. "I hope he'll be all right without them. What if he has to fight bandits on his way back?"

Tyn rolled her eyes. "We're going to have to talk about that kindheartedness of yours sometime, kid."

"It's not a bad thing to be nice."

"You're training to be a con artist," Tyn said. "For now, let's get back to the caravan. I want to talk you through the finer points of a Horneater accent. With that red hair of yours, you'll probably find more chances to use it than you would others."

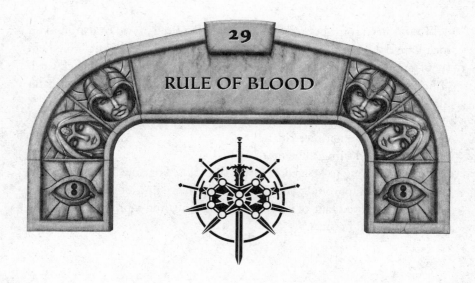

Artform for colors beyond our ken;
For its grand songs we yearn.
We must attract creationspren;
These songs suffice 'til we learn.

—From the Listener Song of Revision, 279th stanza

Torol Sadeas closed his eyes and rested Oathbringer on his shoulder, breathing in the sweet, moldy scent of Parshendi blood. The Thrill of battle surged within him, a blessed and beautiful strength.

His own blood pumped so loudly in his ears he almost couldn't hear the battlefield shouts and groans of pain. For a moment, he reveled only in the delicious glow of the Thrill, the heady euphoria at having spent an hour engaged in the only thing that brought true joy anymore: contending for his life, and taking those of enemies lesser than himself.

It faded. As always, the Thrill was fleeting once battle itself ended. It had grown less and less sweet during these raids on the Parshendi, likely because he knew deep inside that this contest was pointless. It did not stretch him, did not carry him further toward his ultimate goals of conquest. Slaughtering crem-covered savages in a Heralds-forsaken land had truly lost its savor.

He sighed, lowering his Blade, opening his eyes. Amaram approached across the battlefield, stepping over corpses of men and Parshendi. His Shardplate was bloodied purple up to the elbows, and he carried a glimmering gemheart in one gauntleted hand. He kicked aside a Parshendi corpse and joined Sadeas, his own honor guard fanning out to join those of his highprince. Sadeas spared a moment of annoyance for how efficiently they moved, particularly when compared to his own men.

Amaram pulled off his helm and hefted the gemheart, tossing it up and catching it. "Your maneuver here today failed, you realize?"

"Failed?" Sadeas said, lifting his faceplate. Nearby, his soldiers slaughtered a pocket of fifty Parshendi who hadn't managed to get off the plateau when the rest retreated. "I think this went quite nicely."

Amaram pointed. A stain had appeared on the plateaus to the west, toward the warcamps. The banners indicated that Hatham and Roion, the two highprinces who were *supposed* to have gone on this plateau run, had arrived together—they used bridges like Dalinar's, slow plodding things it had been easy to outrun. One of the advantages of the bridge crews Sadeas preferred was that they needed very little training to function. If Dalinar had thought to slow him down with his stunt of trading Oathbringer for Sadeas's bridgemen, he had been proven a fool.

"We needed to get out here," Amaram said, "seize the gemheart, and return before the others arrived. Then you could have claimed that you didn't realize you weren't in the rotation today. The arrival of both other armies removes that shred of deniability."

"You mistake me," Sadeas said. "You assume I still care about deniability." The last Parshendi died with enraged screams; Sadeas felt proud of that. Others said Parshendi warriors on the field never surrendered, but he'd seen them try it once, long ago, in the first year of the war. They'd laid down their weapons. He'd slaughtered them all personally, with Shardhammer and Plate, beneath the eyes of their retreating companions watching from a nearby plateau.

Never again had any Parshendi denied him or his men their right to finish a battle the proper way. Sadeas waved for the vanguard to gather and escort him back to the warcamps while the rest of the army licked its wounds. Amaram joined him, crossing a bridge and passing idling bridgemen who lay on the ground and slept while better men died.

"I am duty-bound to join you on the battlefield, Your Highness," Amaram said as they walked, "but I want you to know that I do not approve of our actions here. We should be seeking to bridge our differences with the king and Dalinar, not trying to agitate them further."

Sadeas snorted. "Don't give me that noble talk. It works fine for others, but I know you for the ruthless bastard you really are."

Amaram set his jaw, eyes forward. When they reached their horses, he reached out, hand on Sadeas's arm. "Torol," he said softly, "there is so much more to the world than your squabbles. You're right about me, of course. Take that admission with the understanding that to you, above all others, I can speak the truth. Alethkar needs to be strong for what is coming."

Sadeas climbed the mounting block the groom had set out. Getting onto a horse in Shardplate could be dangerous to the animal if not done correctly. Besides, he'd once had a stirrup snap on him when he stepped into it to haul himself into the saddle. He'd ended up on his backside.

"Alethkar does need to be strong," Sadeas said, holding out a gauntleted hand. "So I'll make it so by force of fist and the rule of blood."

Amaram reluctantly placed the gemheart there, and Sadeas gripped it, holding his reins in the other hand.

"Do you ever worry?" Amaram asked. "About what you do? About what *we* must do?" He nodded toward a group of surgeons, carrying wounded men across the bridges.

"Worry?" Sadeas said. "Why should I? It gives the wretches a chance to die in battle for something worthwhile."

"You say things like that a lot these days, I've noticed," Amaram said. "You weren't like that before."

"I've learned to accept the world as it is, Amaram," Sadeas said, turning his horse. "That's something very few people are willing to do. They stumble along, hoping, dreaming, pretending. That doesn't change a single storming thing in life. You have to stare the world in the eyes, in all its grimy brutality. You have to acknowledge its depravities. Live with them. It's the only way to accomplish anything meaningful."

With a squeeze of the knees, Sadeas started his horse forward, leaving Amaram behind for the moment.

The man would remain loyal. Sadeas and Amaram had an understanding. Even Amaram now being a Shardbearer would not change that.

As Sadeas and his vanguard approached Hatham's army, he noticed a group of Parshendi on a nearby plateau, watching. Those scouts of theirs were getting bold. He sent a team of archers to go chase them off, then rode toward a figure in resplendent Shardplate at the front of Hatham's army: the highprince himself, seated upon a Ryshadium. Damnation. Those animals were far superior to any other horseflesh. How to get one?

"Sadeas?" Hatham called out to him. "What have you *done* here?"

After a quick moment of decision, Sadeas lifted his arm back and hurled the gemheart across the plateau separating them. It hit the rock near Hatham and bounced along in a roll, glowing faintly.

"I was bored," Sadeas shouted back. "I thought I'd save you some trouble."

Then, ignoring further questions, Sadeas continued on his way. Adolin Kholin had a duel today, and he'd decided not to miss it, just in case the youth embarrassed himself again.

A few hours later, Sadeas settled down into his place in the dueling arena, tugging at the stock on his neck. Insufferable things—fashionable, but insufferable. He would never tell a soul, not even Ialai, that he secretly wished he could just go about in a simple uniform like Dalinar.

He couldn't ever do that, of course. Not just because he wouldn't be seen bowing to the Codes and the king's authority, but because a military uniform was actually the *wrong* uniform for these days. The battles they fought for Alethkar at the moment weren't battles with sword and shield.

It was important to dress the part when you had a role to play. Dalinar's military outfits proved he was lost, that he didn't understand the game he was playing.

Sadeas leaned back to wait as whispers filled the arena like water in a bowl. A large attendance today. Adolin's stunt in his previous duel had drawn attention, and anything novel was of interest to the court. Sadeas's seat had a space cleared around it to give him extra room and privacy, though it was really just a simple chair built onto the stone bleachers of this pit of an arena.

He hated how his body felt outside of Shardplate, and he hated more how he looked. Once, he'd turned heads as he walked. His power had filled a room; everyone had looked to him, and many had *lusted* when seeing him. Lusted for his power, for who he was.

He was losing that. Oh, he was still powerful—perhaps more so. But the look in their eyes was different. And every way of responding to his loss of youthfulness made him look petulant.

He was dying, step by step. Like every man, true, but he *felt* that death looming. Decades away, hopefully, but it cast a long, long shadow. The only path to immortality was through conquest.

Rustling cloth announced Ialai slipping into the seat beside his. Sadeas reached out absently, resting his hand on the small of her back and scratching at that place she liked. Her name was symmetrical. A tiny bit of blasphemy from her parents—some people dared imply such holiness of their children. Sadeas liked those types. Indeed, the name was what had first intrigued him about her.

"Mmmm," his wife said with a sigh. "Very nice. The duel hasn't started yet, I see."

"Mere moments away, I believe."

"Good. I can't stand waiting. I hear you gave away the gemheart you captured today."

"Threw it at Hatham's feet and rode away, as if I didn't have a care."

"Clever. I should have seen that as an option. You'll undermine Dalinar's claim that we only resist him because of our greed."

Below, Adolin finally stepped out onto the field, wearing his blue Shardplate. Some of the lighteyes clapped politely. Across the way, Eranniv left his own preparatory room, his polished Plate its natural color except across the breastplate, which he'd painted a deep black.

Sadeas narrowed his eyes, still scratching Ialai's back. "This duel should not even be happening," he said. "Everyone was supposed to be too afraid, or too dismissive, to accept his challenges."

"Idiots," Ialai said softly. "They know, Torol, what they're supposed to do—I've dropped the right hints and promises. And yet every one of them secretly wants to be the man who brings down Adolin. Duelists are not a particularly dependable lot. They are brash, hotheaded, and care too much about showing off and gaining renown."

"His father's plan cannot be allowed to work," Sadeas said.

"It won't."

Sadeas glanced at where Dalinar had set up. Sadeas's own position was not too far away—within shouting distance. Dalinar didn't look at him.

"I built this kingdom," Sadeas said softly. "I know how fragile it is, Ialai. It should not be so difficult to knock the thing down." That would be the only way to properly build it anew. Like reforging a weapon. You melted down the remnants of the old before you created the replacement.

The duel began down below, Adolin striding across the sands toward Eranniv, who wielded old Gavilar's Blade, with its wicked design. Adolin engaged too quickly. Was the boy that eager?

In the crowd, lighteyes grew quiet and darkeyes shouted, eager for another display like last time. However, this didn't devolve into a wrestling match. The two exchanged testing blows and Adolin backed away, having taken a hit on his shoulder.

Sloppy, Sadeas thought.

"I finally discovered the nature of that disturbance at the king's chambers two weeks ago," Ialai noted.

Sadeas smiled, eyes still on the bout. "Of course you did."

"Assassination attempt," she said. "Someone sabotaged the king's balcony in a crude attempt at dropping him a hundred feet to the rocks. From what I hear, it nearly worked."

"Not so crude then, if it almost killed him."

"Pardon, Torol, but *almost* is a big distinction in assassinations."

True.

Sadeas searched within himself, seeking some sign of emotion at hearing that Elhokar had almost died. He found none beside a faint sense of pity. He was fond of the boy, but to rebuild Alethkar, all vestiges of former rule would need to be removed. Elhokar would need to die. Preferably in a quiet manner, after Dalinar had been dealt with. Sadeas expected he'd have to cut the boy's throat himself, out of respect for old Gavilar.

"Who commissioned the assassins, do you suppose?" Sadeas asked, speaking softly enough that—with the buffer his guards kept around their seats—he didn't have to worry about being overheard.

"Hard to tell," Ialai replied, scooting to the side and twisting to get him to scratch a different part of her back. "It wouldn't be Ruthar or Aladar."

Both were solidly in Sadeas's palm. Aladar with some resignation, Ruthar eagerly. Roion was too much a coward, others too careful. Who else could have done it?

"Thanadal," Sadeas guessed.

"He's the most likely. But I will see what I can discover."

"It might be the same ones as with the king's armor," Sadeas said. "Perhaps we could find out more if I exercise my authority."

Sadeas was Highprince of Information—one of the old designations, from previous centuries, which split duties in the kingdom among highprinces. It technically gave Sadeas authority over investigations and policing.

"Perhaps," Ialai said hesitantly.

"But?"

She shook her head, watching another exchange of the duelists down below. This bout of fighting left Adolin with Stormlight streaming from one gauntlet, to the booing of some of the darkeyes. Why were those people even allowed in? There were lighteyes who were unable to attend because Elhokar reserved seating for their inferiors.

"Dalinar," Ialai said, "has responded to our ploy of making you Highprince of Information. He used it as precedent for making himself Highprince of War. And so now, every step you take invoking your rights as Highprince of Information cements *his* authority over this conflict."

Sadeas nodded. "You have a plan, then?"

"Not quite yet," Ialai said. "But I'm forming one. You've noticed how he started up patrols outside of the camps? And in the Outer Market. Should that be your duty?"

"No, that's the job of a Highprince of Commerce, which the king hasn't appointed. However, I *should* have authority over policing all ten camps, and appointing judges and magistrates. He should have involved me the moment an attempt was made on the king's life. But he didn't." Sadeas chewed on the thought for a moment, removing his hand from Ialai's back, letting her sit up straight.

"There is a weakness here we can exploit," Sadeas said. "Dalinar has always had a problem giving up authority. He never *really* trusts anyone to do their job. He didn't come to me when he should have. This weakens his claims that all parts of the kingdom should work together. It's a chink in his armor. Can you ram a dagger in it?"

Ialai nodded. She'd use her informants to start questions in court: Why, if Dalinar was trying to forge a better Alethkar, was he unwilling to give up any power? Why hadn't he involved Sadeas in the king's protection? Why wouldn't he open his doors to Sadeas's judges?

What authority did the Throne have, really, if it made assignments like the one to Sadeas, only to pretend they hadn't been given?

"You should renounce your appointment as Highprince of Information in protest," Ialai said.

"No. Not yet. We wait until the rumors have nipped at old Dalinar, made him decide he needs to let me do my job. Then, the moment before he tries to involve me, I renounce."

It would widen the cracks that way, both in Dalinar, and in the kingdom itself.

Adolin's bout continued below. He certainly didn't look like his heart was in it. He kept leaving himself open, taking hits. This was the youth who had bragged about his skill so often? He was good, of course, but not nearly *that* good. Not as good as Sadeas had himself seen when the boy had been on the battlefield fighting the . . .

He was faking.

Sadeas found himself grinning. "Now that's almost *clever*," he said softly.

"What?" Ialai asked.

"Adolin is fighting beneath his capacity," Sadeas explained as the youth got a hit—barely—on Eranniv's helm. "He's reluctant to display his real skill, as he fears it will scare others away from dueling him. If he looks *barely* capable enough to win this fight, others might decide to pounce."

Ialai narrowed her eyes, watching the fight. "Are you sure? Couldn't he just be having an off day?"

"I'm sure," Sadeas said. Now that he knew what to watch for, he could easily read it in Adolin's specific moves, the way he teased Eranniv to attack him, then barely fended off the blows. Adolin Kholin was cleverer than Sadeas had given him credit for.

Better at dueling as well. It took skill to win a bout—but it took *true mastery* to win while making it look the whole time that you were behind. As the fight progressed, the crowd got into it, and Adolin made it a close contest. Sadeas doubted many others would see what he did.

When Adolin, moving lethargically and leaking Light from a dozen hits—all carefully allowed on different sections of Plate, so none shattered and exposed him to real danger—managed to bring down Eranniv with a "lucky" blow at the end, the crowd roared in appreciation. Even the lighteyes seemed drawn in.

Eranniv stormed off, shouting about Adolin's luck, but Sadeas found himself quite impressed. *There might be a future for this boy,* he thought. *More so than his father, at least.*

"Another Shard won," Ialai said with dissatisfaction as Adolin raised a hand and walked off the field. "I'll redouble my efforts to make certain this doesn't happen again."

Sadeas tapped his finger against the side of his seat. "What was it you said about duelists? That they're brash? Hotheaded?"

"Yes. And?"

"Adolin is both of those things and more," Sadeas said softly, considering. "He can be goaded, pushed around, brought to anger. He has passion like his father, but he controls it less securely."

Can I get him right up to the cliff's edge, Sadeas thought, *then shove him off?*

"Stop discouraging people from fighting him," Sadeas said. "Don't encourage them *to* fight him, either. Step back. I want to see how this develops."

"That sounds dangerous," Ialai said. "That boy is a weapon, Torol."

"True," Sadeas said, standing, "but you are rarely cut by a weapon if you are the one holding its hilt." He helped his wife to her feet. "I also want you to tell Ruthar's wife that he can ride with me next time I decide to strike out on my own for a gemheart. Ruthar is eager. He can be of use to us."

She nodded, walking toward the exit. Sadeas followed, but hesitated, casting a glance toward Dalinar. How would this be if the man weren't trapped in the past? If he'd been willing to see the real world, rather than imagining it?

You'd probably have ended up killing him then too, Sadeas admitted to himself. *Don't try to pretend otherwise.*

Best to be honest, at the very least, with oneself.

the left shows distinct grains of crem buildup,
esulting in large spikes that rim the edge
the predominant direction of the winds.

Many of these species are new to me.
The plant life here isn't nearly as lush
as it was on Father's estates, or even
Kharbranth, but there is a frantic
determination to the way it grows.

'Tis said it was warm in the land far away
When Voidbringers entered our songs.
We brought them home to stay
And then those homes became their own,
It happened gradually.
And years ahead 'twil still be said 'tis how it has to be.

—From the Listener Song of Histories, 12th stanza

Shallan gasped at the sudden flare of color.

It disrupted the landscape like breaking lightning in an otherwise clear sky. Shallan set down her spheres—Tyn was having her practice palming them—and stood up in the wagon, steadying herself with her freehand on the back of her seat. Yes, it was unmistakable. Brilliant red and yellow on an otherwise dull canvas of brown and green.

"Tyn," Shallan said. "What's that?"

The other woman lounged with feet out, a wide-brimmed white hat tipped over her eyes despite the fact that she was supposed to be driving. Shallan wore Bluth's hat, which she'd recovered from his things, to keep the sun off.

Tyn turned to the side, lifting her hat. "Huh?"

"Right there!" Shallan said. "The color."

Tyn squinted. "I don't see anything."

How could she miss that color, so vibrant when compared to the rolling hills full of rockbuds, reeds, and patches of grass? Shallan took the woman's spyglass and raised it to look more closely. "Plants," Shallan said. "There's a rock overhang there, sheltering them from the east."

"Oh, is that all?" Tyn settled back, closing her eyes. "Thought it might be a caravan tent or something."

"Tyn, it's *plants.*"

"So?"

"Divergent flora in an otherwise uniform ecosystem!" Shallan exclaimed. "We're going! I'll go tell Macob to steer the caravan that way."

"Kid, you're kind of strange," Tyn said as Shallan yelled at the other wagons to stop.

Macob was reluctant to agree to the detour, but fortunately he accepted her authority. The caravan was about a day out from the Shattered Plains. They'd been taking it easy. Shallan struggled to contain her excitement. So much out here in the Frostlands was uniformly dull; something new to draw was exciting beyond normal reason.

They approached the ridge, which had caused a high shelf of rock at exactly the right angle to form a windbreak. Larger versions of these formations were called laits. Sheltered valleys where a town could flourish. Well, this wasn't nearly so large, but life had still found it. A grove of short, bone-white trees grew here. They had vivid red leaves. Vines of numerous varieties draped the rock wall itself, and the ground teemed with rockbuds, a variety that remained open even when there wasn't rain, blossoms drooping with heavy petals from the inside, along with tonguelike tendrils that moved like worms, seeking water.

A small pond reflected the blue sky, feeding the rockbuds and trees. The leafy shade in turn gave shelter to a bright green moss. The beauty was like veins of ruby and emerald in a drab stone.

Shallan hopped down the moment the wagons pulled up. She frightened something in the underbrush, and a few very small, feral axehounds burst away. She wasn't sure of the breed—she honestly wasn't even sure they were axehounds, they moved so quickly.

Well, she thought, walking into the tiny lait, *that probably means I don't have to worry about anything larger.* A predator like a whitespine would have frightened away smaller life.

Shallan walked forward with a smile. It was almost like a garden, though the plants were obviously wild rather than cultivated. They moved quickly to retract blooms, feelers, and leaves, opening a patch around her. She stifled a sneeze and pushed through to find a dark green pond.

Here, she set down a blanket on a boulder, then settled herself to sketch. Others from the caravan went scouting through the lait or around the top of the rock wall.

Shallan breathed in the wonderful humidity as the plants relaxed.

Rockbud petals stretching out, timid leaves unfolding. Color swelled around her like nature blushing. Stormfather! She hadn't realized how much she'd missed the variety of beautiful plants. She opened her sketchbook and drew out a quick prayer in the name of Shalash, Herald of Beauty, Shallan's namesake.

The plants retracted again as someone moved through them. Gaz stumbled past a group of rockbuds, cursing as he tried not to step on their vines. He came up to her, then hesitated, looking down at the pool. "Storms!" he said. "Are those fish?"

"Eels," Shallan guessed as something rippled the green surface of the pool. "Bright orange ones, it appears. We had some like them back in my father's ornamental garden."

Gaz leaned down, trying to get a good look, until one of the eels broke the surface with a flipping tail, spraying him with water. Shallan laughed, taking a Memory of the one-eyed man peering into those verdant depths, lips pursed, wiping his forehead.

"What do you want, Gaz?"

"Well," he said, shuffling. "I was wondering . . ." He glanced at the sketchpad.

Shallan flipped to a new page in the pad. "Of course. Like the one I did for Glurv, I assume?"

Gaz coughed into his hand. "Yeah. That one looked right nice."

Shallan smiled, then started sketching.

"Do you need me to pose or something?" Gaz asked.

"Sure," she said, mostly to keep him busy while she drew. She tidied up his uniform, smoothing out his paunch, taking liberties with his chin. Most of the difference, however, had to do with the expression. Looking up, into the distance. With the right expression, that eye patch became noble, that scarred face became wise, that uniform became a mark of pride. She filled it in with some light background details reminiscent of that night beside the fires, when the people of the caravan had thanked Gaz and the others for their rescue.

She removed the sheet from the pad, then turned it toward him. Gaz took it reverently, running his hand through his hair. "Storms," he whispered. "Is that really what I looked like?"

"Yes," Shallan said. She could faintly feel Pattern as he vibrated softly nearby. A lie . . . but also a truth. That was certainly how the people Gaz saved had viewed him.

"Thank you, Brightness," Gaz said. "I . . . Thank you." Ash's eyes! He actually seemed to be tearing up.

"Keep it safe," Shallan said, "and don't fold it until tonight. I'll lacquer it so it won't smudge."

He nodded and walked, frightening the plants again as he retreated. He was the sixth of the men to ask her for a likeness. She encouraged the requests. Anything to remind them of what they could, and should, be.

And you, Shallan? she thought. *Everyone seems to want you to be something. Jasnah, Tyn, your father . . . What do you want to be?*

She flipped back through her sketchbook, finding the pages where she'd drawn herself in a half-dozen different situations. A scholar, a woman of the court, an artist. Which did she want to be?

Could she be them all?

Pattern hummed. Shallan glanced to the side, noticing Vathah lurking in the trees nearby. The tall mercenary leader hadn't said anything of the sketches, but she saw his sneers.

"Stop frightening my plants, Vathah," Shallan said.

"Macob says we'll stop for the night," Vathah replied, then moved away.

"Trouble . . ." Pattern buzzed. "Yes, trouble."

"I know," Shallan said, waiting as the foliage returned, then sketching it. Unfortunately, though she'd been able to get charcoal and lacquer from the merchants, she didn't have any colored chalks, or she might have tried something more ambitious. Still, this would be a nice series of studies. Quite a change from the rest in this sketchbook.

She pointedly did not think about what she had lost.

She drew and drew, enjoying the simple peace of the small thicket. Lifespren joined her, the little green motes bobbing between leaves and blossoms. Pattern moved out onto the water and, amusingly, began quietly counting the leaves on a nearby tree. Shallan got a good half-dozen drawings of the pond and trees, hoping she'd be able to identify those from a book later on. She made sure to do some close-up views showing the leaves in detail, then moved on to drawing whatever struck her.

It was so *nice* to not be moving on a wagon while sketching. The environment here was just perfect—sufficient light for drawing, still and serene, surrounded by life . . .

She paused, noticing what she'd drawn: a rocky shore near the ocean, with distinctive cliffs rising behind. The perspective was distant; on the rocky shore, several shadowy figures helped one another out of the water. She *swore* one of them was Yalb.

A hopeful fancy. She wished so much for them to be alive. She would probably never know.

She turned the page and drew what came to her. A sketch of a woman kneeling over a body, raising a hammer and chisel, as if to slam it down into the person's face. The one beneath her was stiff, wooden . . . maybe even stone?

Shallan shook her head as she lowered her pencil and studied this drawing. Why had she drawn it? The first one made sense—she was worried about Yalb and the other sailors. But what did it say about her subconscious that she'd drawn this strange depiction?

She looked up, realizing that shadows had grown long, the sun easing down to rest on the horizon. Shallan smiled at it, then jumped as she saw someone standing not ten paces away.

"Tyn!" Shallan said, raising her safehand to her breast. "Stormfather! You gave me a fright."

The woman picked her way through the foliage, which shied away from her. "Those drawings are nice, but I think you should spend more time practicing to forge signatures. You're a natural at that, and it's a kind of work you could do without having to worry about getting into trouble."

"I do practice it," Shallan said. "But I need to practice my art too."

"You get really into those drawings, don't you?"

"I don't get into them," Shallan said, "I put others into them."

Tyn grinned, reaching Shallan's stone. "Always fast with a quip. I like that. I need to introduce you to some friends of mine once we reach the Shattered Plains. They'll spoil you right quick."

"That doesn't sound very pleasant."

"Nonsense," Tyn said, hopping up onto a dry part of the next rock over. "You'd still be yourself. Your jokes would merely be dirtier."

"Lovely," Shallan said, blushing.

She thought the blush might make Tyn laugh, but instead the woman became thoughtful. "We *are* going to have to figure out a way to give you a taste of realism, Shallan."

"Oh? Does it come in the form of a tonic these days?"

"No," Tyn said, "it comes in the form of a punch to the face. It leaves nice girls crying, assuming they're lucky enough to survive."

"I think you'll find," Shallan said, "that my life hasn't been one of nonstop blossoms and cake."

"I'm sure you think that," Tyn said. "Everyone does. Shallan, I like you, I really do. I think you've got heaps of potential. But what you're training for . . . it will require you to do very difficult things. Things that wrench the soul, rip it apart. You're going to be in situations that you've never been in before."

"You barely know me," Shallan said. "How can you be so certain I've never done things like this?"

"Because you aren't broken," Tyn said, expression distant.

"Perhaps I'm faking."

"Kid," Tyn said, "you draw pictures of criminals to turn them into heroes. You dance around in flower patches with a sketchpad, and you blush at the mere *hint* of something racy. However bad you think you've had it, brace yourself. It's going to get worse. And I honestly don't know that you'll be able to handle it."

"Why are you telling me this?" Shallan asked.

"Because in a little over a day's time, we're going to reach the Shattered Plains. This is the last chance for you to back out."

"I . . ."

What *was* she going to do about Tyn when she arrived? Admit that she had only gone along with Tyn's assumptions in order to learn from her? *She knows people,* Shallan thought. *People in the warcamps who might be very useful to know.*

Should Shallan continue with the subterfuge? She wanted to, though part of her knew it was because she liked Tyn, and didn't want to give the woman a reason to stop teaching her. "I am committed," Shallan found herself saying. "I want to go through with my plan."

A lie.

Tyn sighed, then nodded. "All right. Are you ready to tell me what this grand scam is?"

"Dalinar Kholin," Shallan said. "His son is betrothed to a woman from Jah Keved."

Tyn raised an eyebrow. "Now that's curious. And the woman isn't going to arrive?"

"Not when he expects," Shallan said.

"And you look like her?"

"You could say that."

Tyn smiled. "Nice. You had me thinking it would be blackmail, which is very tough. This, though, this is a scam you might actually be able to do. I'm impressed. It's bold, but attainable."

"Thank you."

"So what's your plan?" Tyn said.

"Well, I'll go introduce myself to Kholin, indicate I'm the woman his son is to marry, and let him set me up in his household."

"No good."

"No?"

Tyn shook her head sharply. "It puts you too much in Kholin's debt. It will make you seem needy, and that will undermine your ability to be respected. What you're doing here is called a pretty face con, an attempt to relieve a rich man of his spheres. That kind of job is all about presentation and image. You want to set up in an inn somewhere in a different warcamp and act like you're completely self-sufficient. Maintain an air of mystery. Don't be too easy for the son to capture. Which one is it, by the way? The older one or the younger one?"

"Adolin," Shallan said.

"Hmmm . . . Not sure if that's better or worse than Renarin. Adolin Kholin is a flirt by reputation, so I can see why his father wants him married off. It will be tough to keep his attention, though."

"Really?" Shallan asked, feeling a spike of real concern.

"Yeah. He's been almost engaged a dozen times. I think he *has* been engaged before, actually. It's good you met me. I'll have to work on this one awhile to determine the right approach, but you are certainly *not* going to accept Kholin hospitality. Adolin will never express interest if you're not in some way unobtainable."

"Hard to be unobtainable when we're already in a causal."

"Still important," Tyn said, raising a finger. "You're the one who wants to do a love scam. They're tricky, but relatively safe. We'll figure this out."

Shallan nodded, though inside, her worries had spiked. What *would* happen with the betrothal? Jasnah wasn't around to push for it any longer. The woman had wanted Shallan tied to her family, presumably because of the Surgebinding potential. Shallan doubted the rest of the Kholin house would be so determined to have a nobody Veden girl marry into the family.

As Tyn rose, Shallan stuffed away her anxiety. If the betrothal ended, so be it. She had far more important concerns in Urithiru and the Voidbringers. She *would* have to figure out a way to deal with Tyn, though—a way that didn't involve actually scamming the Kholin family. Just one more thing to juggle.

Oddly, she found herself excited by the prospect as she decided to do one more drawing before finding some food.

Smokeform for hiding and slipping 'tween men.
A form of power—like Surges of spren.
Do we dare to wear this form again? It spies.
Crafted of gods, this form we fear.
By Unmade touch its curse to bear,
Formed from shadow—and death is near. It lies.

—From the Listener Song of Secrets, 51st stanza

Kaladin led his troop of sore, tired men up to Bridge Four's barrack, and—as he'd secretly requested—the men got a round of cheers and welcoming calls. It was early evening, and the familiar scent of stew was one of the most inviting things Kaladin could imagine.

He stepped aside and let the forty men tromp past him. They weren't members of Bridge Four, but for tonight, they'd be considered such. They held their heads higher, smiles breaking out as men passed them bowls of stew. Rock asked one how the patrolling had gone, and though Kaladin couldn't hear the soldier's reply, he could definitely hear the bellowing laughter it prompted from Rock.

Kaladin smiled, leaning back against the barrack wall, folding his arms. Then he found himself checking the sky. The sun hadn't quite set, but in the darkening sky, stars had begun to appear around Taln's Scar. The Tear hung just above the horizon, a star much brighter than the others, named for the single tear that Reya was said to have shed. Some of the stars moved—starspren, nothing to be surprised by—but something felt odd about the evening. He breathed in deeply. Was the air stale?

"Sir?"

Kaladin turned. One of the bridgemen, an earnest man with short dark hair and strong features, had not joined the others at the stew cauldron. Kaladin searched for his name . . .

"Pitt, isn't it?" Kaladin said.

"Yes, sir," the man replied. "Bridge Seventeen."

"What did you need?"

"I just . . ." The man glanced at the inviting fire, with members of Bridge Four laughing and chatting with the patrol group. Nearby, someone had hung a few distinctive suits of armor on the barrack walls. They were carapace helms and breastplates, attached to the leathers of common bridgemen. Those had now been replaced with fine steel caps and breastplates. Kaladin wondered who had hung the old suits up. He hadn't even known that some of the men had fetched them; they were the extra suits that Leyten had crafted for the men and stashed down in the chasms before being freed.

"Sir," Pitt said, "I just want to say that I'm sorry."

"For?"

"Back when we were bridgemen." Pitt raised a hand to his head. "Storms, that seems like a different life. I couldn't think rightly during those times. It's all hazy. But I remember being *glad* when your crew was sent out instead of mine. I remember hoping you'd fail, since you dared to walk with your chin up . . . I—"

"It's all right, Pitt," Kaladin said. "It wasn't your fault. You can blame Sadeas."

"I suppose." Pitt got a distant look on his face. "He broke us right good, didn't he, sir?"

"Yes."

"Turns out, though, men can be reforged. I wouldn't have thought that." Pitt looked over his shoulder. "I'm going to have to go do this for the other lads of Bridge Seventeen, aren't I?"

"With Teft's help, yes, but that's the hope," Kaladin said. "Do you think you can do it?"

"I'll just have to pretend to be you, sir," Pitt said. He smiled, then moved on, taking a bowl of stew and joining the others.

These forty would be ready soon, ready to become sergeants to their own teams of bridgemen. The transformation had happened more quickly than Kaladin had hoped. *Teft, you marvelous man,* he thought. *You did it.*

Where was Teft, anyway? He'd gone on the patrol with them, and now he'd vanished. Kaladin glanced over his shoulder but didn't see him; perhaps he'd gone to check on some of the other bridge crews. He did catch Rock shooing away a lanky man in an ardent's robe.

"What was that?" Kaladin asked, catching the Horneater as he passed.

"That one," Rock said. "Keeps loitering here with sketchbook. Wants to draw bridgemen. Ha! Because we are famous, you see."

Kaladin frowned. Strange actions for an ardent—but, then, all ardents were strange, to an extent. He let Rock return to his stew and stepped away from the fire, enjoying the peace.

Everything was so quiet out there, in the camp. Like it was holding its breath.

"The patrol seems to have worked out," Sigzil said, strolling up to Kaladin. "Those men are changed."

"Funny what a couple of days spent marching as a unit can do to soldiers," Kaladin said. "Have you seen Teft?"

"No, sir," Sigzil said. He nodded toward the fire. "You'll want to get some stew. We won't have much time for chatting tonight."

"Highstorm," Kaladin realized. It seemed like too soon since the last one, but they weren't always regular—not in the way he thought of it. The stormwardens had to do complex mathematics to predict them; Kaladin's father had made a hobby of it.

Perhaps that was what he was noticing. Was he suddenly predicting highstorms because the night seemed too . . . something?

You're imagining things, Kaladin thought. Shrugging off his fatigue from the extended ride and march, he went over to get some stew. He'd have to eat quickly—he'd want to go join the men guarding Dalinar and the king during the storm.

The men from the patrol cheered him as he filled his bowl.

⁘

Shallan sat on the rattling wagon and moved her hand over the sphere on the seat beside her, palming it and dropping another.

Tyn raised an eyebrow. "I heard the replacement hit."

"Drynets!" Shallan said. "I thought I had it."

"Drynets?"

"It's a curse," Shallan said, blushing. "I heard it from the sailors."

"Shallan, do you have any idea at *all* what that means?"

"Like . . . for fishing?" Shallan said. "The nets are dry, maybe? They haven't been catching any fish, so it's bad?"

Tyn grinned. "Dear, I'm going to do my *very* best to corrupt you. Until then, I think you should avoid using sailor curses. Please."

"All right." Shallan passed her hand over the sphere again, swapping the spheres. "No clink! Did you hear that? Or, um, did you *not* hear that? It didn't make a noise!"

"Nice," Tyn said, getting out a pinch of some kind of mossy substance. She began rubbing it between her fingers, and Shallan thought she saw *smoke* rising from the moss. "You *are* getting better. I also feel like we should figure out some way to use that drawing talent of yours."

Shallan already had an inkling of how it would come in handy. More of the former deserters had asked her for pictures.

"You've been working on your accents?" Tyn asked, eyes glazing as she rubbed the moss.

"I have indeed, my good woman," Shallan said with a Thaylen accent.

"Good. We'll get around to costuming once we have more resources. I, for one, am going to be very amused to watch your face when you have to go out in public with that hand of yours uncovered."

Shallan immediately pulled her safehand up to her breast. "What!"

"I warned you about difficult things," Tyn said, smiling in a devious way. "West of Marat, almost all women go out with both hands uncovered. If you're going to go to those places and not stand out, you'll have to be able to do as they do."

"It's immodest!" Shallan said, blushing furiously.

"It's just a hand, Shallan," Tyn said. "Storms, you Vorins are so prim. That hand looks *exactly* like your other hand."

"A lot of women have breasts that aren't much more pronounced than male ones," Shallan snapped. "That doesn't make it right for them to go out wearing no shirt, like a man would!"

"Actually, in parts of the Reshi Isles and Iri, it's not uncommon for women to walk about topless. It gets hot up there. Nobody minds. I rather like it, myself."

Shallan raised both hands to her face—one clothed, one not—hiding her blush. "You're doing this just to provoke me."

"Yeah," Tyn said, chuckling. "I am. This is the girl that scammed an entire troop of deserters and took over our caravan?"

"I didn't have to go naked to do *that*."

"Good thing you didn't," Tyn said. "You still think you're experienced and worldly? You blush at the mere mention of exposing your safehand. Can't you see how it's going to be hard for you to run any kind of productive scam?"

Shallan took a deep breath. "I guess."

"Showing your hand off isn't going to be the toughest thing you need to do," Tyn said, looking distant. "Not the toughest by a breeze or a stormwind. I . . ."

"What?" Shallan asked.

Tyn shook her head. "We'll talk about it later. Can you see those warcamps yet?"

Shallan stood up on her seat, shading her eyes against the setting sun in the west. To the north, she saw a haze. Hundreds of fires—no, thousands—seeping darkness into the sky. Her breath caught in her throat. "We're there."

"Call camp for the night," Tyn said, not moving from her relaxed position.

"It looks like it's only a few hours away," Shallan said. "We could push on—"

"And arrive after nightfall, then be forced to camp anyway," Tyn said. "Better to arrive fresh in the morning. Trust me."

Shallan settled down, calling for one of the caravan workers, a youth who walked barefoot—his calluses must be frightening—alongside the caravan. Only those senior among them rode.

"Ask Trademaster Macob what he thinks of stopping here for the night," Shallan said to the young man.

He nodded, then jogged up the line, passing lumbering chulls.

"You don't trust my assessment?" Tyn asked, sounding amused.

"Trademaster Macob doesn't like being told what to do," Shallan said. "If stopping is a good move, perhaps he'll suggest it. It seems like a better way to lead."

Tyn closed her eyes, face toward the sky. She still held one hand up, absently rubbing moss between her fingers. "I might have some information for you tonight."

"About?"

"Your homeland." Tyn cracked an eye. Though her posture was lazy, that eye was curious.

"That's nice," Shallan said, noncommittal. She tried not to say much about her home or her life there—she also hadn't told Tyn about her trip, or about the sinking of the ship. The less Shallan said about her background, the less likely that Tyn would realize the truth about her new student.

It's her own fault for jumping to conclusions about me, Shallan thought. *Besides, she's the one teaching me about pretending. I shouldn't feel bad about lying to her. She lies to everyone.*

Thinking that made her wince. Tyn was right; Shallan *was* naive. She couldn't help feeling guilty about lying, even to a professed con woman!

"I'd have expected more from you," Tyn said, closing her eye. "Considering."

That provoked Shallan, and she found herself wiggling on her seat. "Considering what?" she finally asked.

"So you *don't* know," Tyn said. "I thought as much."

"There are many things I don't know, Tyn," Shallan said, exasperated.

"I don't know how to build a wagon, I don't know how to speak Iriali, and I *certainly* don't know how to prevent you from being annoying. Not that I haven't tried to figure out all three."

Tyn smiled, eyes closed. "Your Veden king is dead."

"Hanavanar? Dead?" She'd never met the highprince, let alone the king. The monarchy was a far-off thing. She found that it didn't particularly matter to her. "His son will inherit, then?"

"He would. If he weren't dead too. Along with six of Jah Keved's highprinces."

Shallan gasped.

"They say it was the Assassin in White," Tyn said softly, eyes still closed. "The Shin man who killed the Alethi king six years back."

Shallan pushed through her confusion. Her brothers. Were they all right? "Six highprinces. Which ones?" If she knew that, it might tell her how her own princedom was faring.

"I don't know for certain," Tyn said. "Jal Mala and Evinor for sure, and probably Abrial. Some died in the attack, others before that, though the information is vague. Getting any kind of reliable information out of Vedenar these days is tough."

"Valam. He still lives?" Her own highprince.

"He was fighting for the succession, reports say. I have my informants sending me word tonight via spanreed. Might have something for you then."

Shallan settled back. The king, dead? A succession war? Stormfather! How could she find out about her family and their estate? They were nowhere near the capital, but if the entire country was consumed by war, it could reach even to the backwater areas. There was no easy way to reach her brothers. She'd lost her own spanreed in the sinking of the *Wind's Pleasure*.

"Any information would be appreciated," Shallan said. "Any at all."

"We'll see. I'll let you come by for the report."

Shallan settled back to digest this information. *She suspected I didn't know, but didn't tell me until now.* Shallan liked Tyn, but had to remember that the woman made a profession of hiding information. What else did Tyn know that she wasn't sharing?

Ahead, the caravan youth walked back down the line of moving wagons. As he reached Shallan, he turned and walked beside her vehicle. "Macob says you are wise to ask, and says we should probably camp here. The warcamps each have secure borders, and aren't likely to let us in during the night. Beyond that, he is uncertain if we could reach the camps before tonight's storm."

To the side, eyes still closed, Tyn grinned.

"We camp, then," Shallan said.

32

THE ONE
WHO HATES

The spren betrayed us, it's often felt.
Our minds are too close to their realm
That gives us our forms, but more is then
Demanded by the smartest spren,
We can't provide what the humans lend,
Though broth are we, their meat is men.

—From the Listener Song of Spren, 9th stanza

In his dream, Kaladin was the storm.

He claimed the land, surging across it, a cleansing fury. All washed before him, broke before him. In his darkness, the land was reborn.

He soared, alive with lightning, his flashes of inspiration. The wind's howling was his voice, the thunder his heartbeat. He overwhelmed, overcame, overshadowed, and—

And he had done this before.

An awareness came to Kaladin, like water seeping under a door. Yes. He'd dreamed this dream before.

With effort, he turned around. A face as large as eternity stretched behind him, the force behind the tempest, the Stormfather himself.

SON OF HONOR, said a voice like roaring wind.

"This is real!" Kaladin yelled into the storm. He was wind itself. Spren. He found voice somehow. "You are real!"

SHE TRUSTS YOU.

"Syl?" Kaladin called. "Yes, she does."

SHE SHOULD NOT.

"Are you the one who forbade her to come to me? Are you the one who keeps the spren back?"

You will kill her. The voice, so deep, so *powerful*, sounded regretful. Mournful. You will murder my child and leave her corpse to wicked men.

"I will *not*!" Kaladin shouted.

You begin it already.

The storm continued. Kaladin saw the world from above. Ships in sheltered harbors rocking on violent swells. Armies huddled in valleys, preparing for war in a place of many hills and mountains. A vast lake going dry ahead of his arrival, the water retreating into holes in the rock beneath.

"How can I prevent it?" Kaladin demanded. "How can I protect her?"

You are human. You will be a traitor.

"No I won't!"

You will change. Men change. All men.

The continent was so vast. So many people speaking languages he could not comprehend, everyone hiding in their rooms, their caverns, their valleys.

Ah, the Stormfather said. So it will end.

"What?" Kaladin shouted into the winds. "What changed? I feel—"

He comes for you, little traitor. I am sorry.

Something rose before Kaladin. A second storm, one of red lightning, so enormous as to make the continent—the *world itself*—into nothing by comparison. Everything fell into its shadow.

I am sorry, the Stormfather said. He comes.

Kaladin awoke, heart thundering in his chest.

He almost fell from his chair. Where was he? The Pinnacle, the king's conference chamber. Kaladin had sat down for a moment and . . .

He blushed. He'd dozed off.

Adolin stood nearby, talking to Renarin. "I'm not sure if anything will come from the meeting, but I'm glad Father agreed to it. I'd almost given up hope of it happening, with how long the Parshendi messenger took to arrive."

"You're sure the one you met out there was a woman?" Renarin asked. He seemed more at ease since he had finished bonding his Blade a couple weeks back, and no longer needed to carry it around. "A woman Shardbearer?"

"The Parshendi are pretty odd," Adolin said with a shrug. He glanced toward Kaladin, and his lips rose in a smirk. "Sleeping on the job, bridgeboy?"

The leaking shutter shook nearby, water dribbling in under the wood. Navani and Dalinar would be in the room next door.

The king wasn't there.

"His Majesty!" Kaladin cried, scrambling to his feet.

"In the privy, bridgeboy," Adolin said, nodding to another door. "You can sleep during a highstorm. That's impressive. Almost as impressive as how much you drool when you're dozing."

No time for gibes. That dream . . . Kaladin turned toward the balcony door, breathing quickly.

He comes. . . .

Kaladin pulled open the balcony door. Adolin shouted and Renarin called out, but Kaladin ignored them, facing the tempest.

The wind still howled and rain pelted the stone balcony with a sound like sticks breaking. There was no lightning, however, and the wind—while violent—was not nearly strong enough to fling boulders or topple walls. The bulk of the highstorm had passed.

Darkness. Wind from the depths of nothingness, battering him. He felt as if he were standing above the void itself, Damnation, known as Braize in the old songs. Home to demons and monsters. He stepped out hesitantly, light from the still-open door spilling onto the wet balcony. He found the railing—a part that was still secure—and clenched it in cold fingers. Rain bit him on the cheek, seeping through his uniform, burrowing through the cloth and seeking warm skin.

"Are you *mad*?" Adolin demanded from the doorway. Kaladin could barely hear his voice over the wind and distant rumbles of thunder.

⁘

Pattern hummed softly as rain fell on the wagon.

Shallan's slaves huddled together and whimpered. She wished she could quiet the blasted spren, but Pattern wasn't responding to her promptings. At least the highstorm was nearly over. She wanted to get away and read what Tyn's correspondents had to say about Shallan's homeland.

Pattern's hums sounded almost like a whimper. Shallan frowned and leaned down close to him. Were those words?

"Bad . . . bad . . . so bad . . ."

⁘

Syl shot out of the highstorm's dense darkness, a sudden flash of light in the black. She spun about Kaladin before coming to rest on the iron railing before him. Her dress seemed longer and more flowing than usual. The rain passed through her without disturbing her shape.

Syl looked into the sky, then turned her head sharply over her shoulder. "Kaladin. Something is wrong."

"I know."

Syl spun about, twisting this way, then that. Her small eyes opened wide. "He's coming."

"Who? The storm?"

"The one who hates," she whispered. "The darkness inside. Kaladin, he's watching. Something's going to happen. Something bad."

Kaladin hesitated only a moment, then scrambled back into the room, pushing past Adolin and entering the light. "Get the king. We're leaving. *Now.*"

"What?" Adolin demanded.

Kaladin threw open the door into the small room where Dalinar and Navani waited. The highprince sat on a sofa, expression distant, Navani holding his hand. That wasn't what Kaladin had expected. The highprince didn't seem frightened or mad, just thoughtful. He was speaking softly.

Kaladin froze. *He sees things during the storms.*

"What are you doing?" Navani demanded. "How *dare* you?"

"Can you wake him?" Kaladin asked, stepping into the room. "We need to leave this room, leave this palace."

"Nonsense." It was the king's voice. Elhokar stepped into the room behind him. "What are you babbling about?"

"You're not safe here, Your Majesty," Kaladin said. "We need to get you out of the palace and take you to the warcamp." Storms. Would that be safe? Should he go somewhere nobody would expect?

Thunder rumbled outside, but the sound of rainfall slackened. The storm was dying.

"This is ridiculous," Adolin said from behind the king, throwing his hands into the air. "This is the safest place in the warcamps. You want us to leave? Drag the king out into the storm?"

"We need to wake the highprince," Kaladin said, reaching for Dalinar.

Dalinar caught his arm as he did so. "The highprince is awake," Dalinar said, his gaze clearing, returning from the distant place where it had been. "What is going on here?"

"The bridgeboy wants us to evacuate the palace," Adolin said.

"Soldier?" Dalinar asked.

"It's not safe here, sir."

"What makes you say that?"

"Instinct, sir."

The room grew still. Outside, the rainfall slackened to a gentle patter. The riddens had arrived.

"We go, then," Dalinar said, rising.

"What?" the king demanded.

"You put this man in charge of your guard, Elhokar," Dalinar said. "If he thinks our position is not safe, we should do as he says."

There was an implied *for now* after that sentence, but Kaladin didn't care. He shoved past the king and Adolin, rushing back through the main chamber to the doorway out. His heart hammered inside of him, his muscles tense. Syl, visible only to his eyes, flitted through the room, frantic.

Kaladin threw open the doors. Six men stood on watch in the hallway beyond, mostly bridgemen with one member of the King's Guard, a man named Ralinor. "We're leaving," Kaladin said, pointing. "Beld and Hobber, you're an advance squad. Scout the way out of the building—the back way, down through the kitchens—and give a shout if you see anything unusual. Moash, you and Ralinor are the rear guard—watch this room until I've got the king and the highprince out of sight, then follow. Mart and Eth, you stay at the king's side, no matter what."

The guards scrambled into action without question. As the scouts ran ahead, Kaladin moved back to the king and grabbed him by the arm, then hauled him toward the door. Elhokar allowed it, a stunned expression on his face.

The other lighteyes followed. The bridgeman brothers Mart and Eth fell in, flanking the king, Moash holding the doorway. He gripped his spear nervously, pointing it in one direction, then another.

Kaladin rushed the king and his family down the corridor along the chosen path. Instead of heading left and down the incline toward the palace's formal entrance, they would head right, farther into its bowels. Down to the right, through the kitchens, then out into the night.

The hallways were silent. Everyone was sheltering in their rooms during the highstorm.

Dalinar joined Kaladin at the front of the group. "I will be curious to hear exactly what prompted this, soldier," he said. "Once we are safely evacuated."

My spren is having a fit, Kaladin thought, watching her zip back and forth in the corridor. *That's what prompted it.* How was he going to explain that? That he'd listened to a *windspren*?

Deeper they went. Storms, these empty corridors were disturbing. Much of the palace was really just a burrow cut through the rock of the peak, with windows carved out of the sides.

Kaladin froze in place.

The lights ahead were out, the corridor dimming into the distance until it was dark as a mine.

"Wait," Adolin said, stopping in place. "Why is it dark? What happened to the spheres?"

They've been drained of Light.

Damnation. And what was that on the wall of the hallway up ahead? A large patch of blackness. Kaladin frantically fished a sphere from his pocket and raised it. It was a hole! A doorway had been cut into this corridor from the outside, sliced directly through the rock. A cold breeze blew inward.

Kaladin's light also illuminated something on the floor just ahead. A body lying where corridors crossed. It wore a blue uniform. Beld, one of the men Kaladin had sent on ahead.

The huddle of people stared at the body in horror. The corridor's eerie silence, the lack of lights, had stilled even the king's protests.

"He's here," Syl whispered.

A solemn figure stepped out of the side corridor, holding a long, silvery Blade that cut a trail in the stone floor. The figure had flowing white clothing: filmy trousers and an overshirt that rippled with each step. Bald head, pale skin. Shin.

Kaladin recognized the figure. Every person in Alethkar had heard of this man. The Assassin in White. Kaladin had seen him once in a dream, like the one earlier, though he hadn't recognized him at that point.

Stormlight streamed from the assassin's body.

He was a Surgebinder.

"Adolin, with me!" Dalinar shouted. "Renarin, protect the king! Take him back the way we came!" With that, Dalinar—the Blackthorn—seized a spear from one of Kaladin's men and charged the assassin.

He's going to get himself killed, Kaladin thought, running after him. "Go with Prince Renarin!" he yelled at his men. "Do as he tells you! Protect the king!"

The men—including Moash and Ralinor, who had caught up to them—began a frantic retreat, towing away Navani and the king.

"Father!" Renarin cried. Moash grabbed him by the shoulder and hauled him back. "I can fight!"

"Go!" Dalinar bellowed. "Protect the king!"

As Kaladin charged with Dalinar and Adolin, the last thing he heard of the group was King Elhokar's whimpering voice. "He's come for me. I always knew he would. Like he came for Father . . ."

Kaladin drew in as much Stormlight as he dared. The Assassin in White stood calmly in the corridor, streaming with his own Light. How could he be a Surgebinder? What spren had chosen this man?

Adolin's Shardblade formed in his hands.

"Trident," Dalinar said softly, slowing as the three of them approached the assassin. "I'm the middle. You familiar with that, Kaladin?"

"Yes, sir." It was a simple, small-squad battlefield formation.

"Let me handle this, Father," Adolin said. "He has a Shardblade, and I don't like the look of that glow—"

"No," Dalinar said, "we hit him together." His eyes narrowed as he regarded the assassin, still standing calmly above the body of poor Beld. "I'm not asleep at the table this time, you bastard. You're not taking another one from me!"

The three charged together. Dalinar, as the middle tine of the trident, would try to hold the assassin's attention while Kaladin and Adolin attacked from either side. He'd wisely taken the spear for reach, rather than using his side sword. They charged in a rush to confuse and overwhelm.

The assassin waited until they were close, then jumped, trailing Light. He twisted in the air as Dalinar bellowed and thrust with his spear.

The assassin did not come down. Instead, he landed on the *ceiling* of the corridor some twelve feet above.

"It's true," Adolin said, sounding haunted. He bent back, raising his Shardblade to attack at the awkward angle. The assassin, however, *ran down the wall* in a rustle of white cloth, battering aside Adolin's Shardblade with his own, then slammed his hand into Adolin's chest.

Adolin flipped upward as if he'd been tossed. His body streamed Stormlight and he crashed into the ceiling above. He groaned, rolling over, but remained on the ceiling.

Stormfather! Kaladin thought, pulse pounding, tempest within raging. He thrust his spear alongside that of the Blackthorn in an attempt to hit the assassin.

The man didn't dodge.

Both spears struck flesh, Dalinar's in the shoulder, Kaladin's in the side. The assassin spun, sweeping his Shardblade through the spears and cutting them in half, as if he didn't even care about the wounds. He lunged forward, slapping Dalinar across the face, sending him sprawling to the ground, then swept his Blade toward Kaladin.

Kaladin barely ducked the blow, then scrambled backward, the top of his spear clattering to the ground beside Dalinar, who rolled with a groan, holding a hand to his cheek where the assassin had struck him. Blood seeped from torn skin. The blow of a Surgebinder bearing Stormlight could not just be shaken off.

The assassin stood poised and confident in the center of the corridor. Stormlight swirled in the slashes in his now-reddened clothing, healing his flesh.

Kaladin backed away, holding a spear missing its head. The things this man did . . . He couldn't be a *Windrunner*, could he?

Impossible.

"Father!" Adolin shouted from above. The youth had climbed to his feet, but the Stormlight streaming from him had nearly run out. He tried to attack the assassin, but slipped from the ceiling and crashed to the ground, landing on his shoulder. His Shardblade vanished as it fell from his fingers.

The assassin stepped over Adolin, who stirred but did not rise. "I am sorry," the assassin said, Stormlight streaming from his mouth. "I don't want to do this."

"I won't give you the chance," Kaladin growled, dashing forward. Syl spun around him, and he felt the wind stirring. He felt the tempest raging, urging him onward. He came at the assassin with the remnant of his spear wielded like a quarterstaff, and *felt* the wind guiding him.

Strikes made with precision, a moment of oneness with the weapon. He forgot his worries, forgot his failures, forgot even his rage. Just Kaladin and a spear.

As the world was meant to be.

The assassin took a blow to the shoulder, then the side. He couldn't ignore them all—his Stormlight would run out as it healed him. The assassin cursed, letting out another mouthful of Light, and backed away, his Shin eyes—slightly too large, colored like pale sapphires—widening at the continued flurry of strikes.

Kaladin sucked in the rest of his Stormlight. So little. He hadn't picked up new spheres before coming to guard duty. Stupid. Sloppy.

The assassin turned his shoulder, lifting his Shardblade, preparing to thrust. *There,* Kaladin thought. He could *feel* what would happen. He would twist around the strike, bringing up the butt of his spear. It would hit the assassin on the side of the head, a powerful blow that even Stormlight would not easily compensate for. He'd be left dazed. An opening.

I have him.

Somehow, the assassin twisted out of the way.

He moved too quickly, faster than Kaladin anticipated. As quickly . . . as Kaladin himself. Kaladin's blow found only open air, and he narrowly avoided being run through by the Shardblade.

Kaladin's next moves came by instinct. Years of training gave his muscles minds of their own. If he'd been fighting an ordinary foe, the way he automatically shifted his weapon to block the next swing would have been perfect. But the assassin had a Shardblade. Kaladin's instincts—instilled so diligently—betrayed him.

The silvery weapon sheared through the remnant of Kaladin's spear, then through Kaladin's right arm, just below the elbow. A shock of incredible pain washed through Kaladin, and he gasped, falling to his knees.

Then . . . nothing. He couldn't feel the arm. It turned grey and dull, lifeless, the palm opening, fingers spreading as half of his spear shaft dropped from his fingers and thumped to the ground.

The assassin kicked Kaladin out of the way, slamming him against the wall. Kaladin groaned, slumping there.

The man in the white clothing turned up the corridor in the direction the king had gone. He again stepped over Adolin.

"Kaladin!" Syl said, her form a ribbon of light.

"I can't beat him," Kaladin whispered, tears in his eyes. Tears of pain. Tears of frustration. "He's one of us. A Radiant."

"No!" Syl said forcefully. "No. He's something far more terrible. No spren guides him, Kaladin. Please. Get up."

Dalinar had regained his feet in the corridor between the assassin and the path to the king. The Blackthorn's cheek was a bloody mess, but his eyes were lucid. "I won't let you have him!" Dalinar bellowed. "Not Elhokar. You took my brother! You won't take the only thing I have left of him!"

The assassin stopped in the corridor just in front of Dalinar. "But I'm not here for him, Highprince," he whispered, Stormlight puffing from his lips. "I'm here for you." The assassin lunged forward, slapping away Dalinar's strike, and kicked the Blackthorn in the leg.

Dalinar went down on one knee, his grunt echoing in the hallway as he dropped his spear. A frigid wind blew into the corridor through the opening in the wall just beside him.

Kaladin growled, forcing himself to stand and charge down the corridor, one hand useless and dead. He'd never wield a spear again. He couldn't think about that. He *had* to reach Dalinar.

Too slow.

I'm going to fail.

The assassin swung his terrible Blade down in a final overhead sweep. Dalinar did not dodge.

Instead, he caught the Blade.

Dalinar brought the heels of his palms together as the Blade fell, and he *caught* it just before it hit.

The assassin grunted in surprise.

At that moment, Kaladin plowed into him, using his weight and momentum to throw the assassin against the wall. Except there wasn't a wall here. They hit the place where the assassin had cut his entrance into the corridor.

Both tumbled out into the open air.

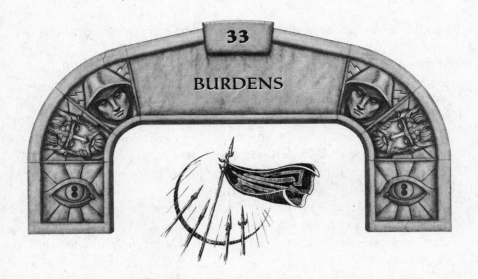

33

BURDENS

Kaladin fell with the rain.

He clung to the assassin's bone-white clothing with his one working hand. The assassin's dropped Shardblade exploded into mist beside them, and together they plummeted toward the ground a hundred feet below.

The tempest within Kaladin was almost still. Too little Stormlight!

The assassin suddenly started glowing more powerfully.

He has spheres.

Kaladin breathed in sharply, and Light streamed from spheres in pouches at the assassin's waist. As the Light streamed into Kaladin, the assassin kicked at him. One handhold was not enough, and Kaladin was thrown free.

Then he hit.

He hit hard. No preparation, no getting his feet beneath him. He smacked against cold, wet stone, and his vision flashed like lightning.

It cleared a moment later, and he found himself lying on the rocks at the base of the rise that led to the king's palace, a gentle rain sprinkling him. He looked up at the distant light of the hole in the wall above. He'd survived.

One question answered, he thought, struggling to his knees on the wet rock. The Stormlight was already working on his skin, which was shredded along his right side. He'd broken something in his shoulder; he could feel its healing as a burning pain that slowly retreated.

But his right forearm and hand, faintly lit by the Stormlight rising from the rest of him, were still a dull grey. Like a dead candle in a row, this part of him did not glow. He couldn't feel it; he couldn't even move the fingers. They drooped, limp, as he cradled the hand.

Nearby, the Assassin in White stood up straight in the rain. He'd somehow gotten his feet beneath him and landed, in control, with poise. This man had a level of experience with his powers that made Kaladin look like a new recruit.

The assassin turned on Kaladin, then stopped short. He spoke softly in a language Kaladin didn't understand, the words breathy and sibilant, bearing lots of "sh" sounds.

Got to move, Kaladin thought. *Before he summons that Blade again.* Unfortunately, he failed to shove down the horror at having lost the hand. No more spear fighting. No more surgery. Both men he had learned to be were now lost to him.

Except . . . he could *almost* feel . . .

"Did I Lash you?" the assassin asked in accented Alethi. His eyes had darkened, losing their sapphire blue quality. "To the ground? But why did you not die falling? No. I must have Lashed you upward. Impossible." He stepped back.

A moment of surprise. A moment to live. Perhaps . . . Kaladin felt the Light working, the tempest within straining and pushing. He gritted his teeth and *heaved* somehow.

The color returned to his hand, and feeling—cold pain—suddenly flooded his arm, hand, fingers. Light began to stream from his hand.

"No . . ." the assassin said. "No!"

Whatever Kaladin had done to his hand had consumed much of his Light and his overall glow faded, leaving him barely alight. Still on his knees, gritting his teeth, Kaladin grabbed the knife from his belt, but found his grip weak. He almost fumbled the weapon as he got it free.

He swapped the knife to his off hand. It would have to do.

He threw himself to his feet and charged the assassin. *Have to hit him quickly to have a chance.*

The assassin jumped backward, soaring a good ten feet, his white clothing rippling in the night air. He landed with a lithe grace, Shardblade appearing in his hand. "What are you?" he demanded.

"Same thing you are," Kaladin said. He felt a wave of nausea, but forced himself to appear firm. "Windrunner."

"You can't be."

Kaladin held up the knife, the few wisps of remaining Light steaming from his skin. Rain sprinkled him.

The assassin scrambled backward, eyes as wide as if Kaladin had turned into a chasmfiend. "They told me I was a liar!" the assassin screamed. "They told me I was wrong! Szeth-son-son-Vallano . . . Truthless. They named me *Truthless!*"

Kaladin stepped forward as threateningly as he could manage, hoping his Stormlight would last long enough to be imposing. He breathed out, letting it puff before him, faintly luminescent in the darkness.

The assassin scrambled back through a puddle. "Are they back?" he demanded. "Are they *all* back?"

"Yes," Kaladin said. It seemed like the right answer. The answer that would keep him alive, at least.

The assassin stared at him a moment longer, then turned and fled. Kaladin watched the glowing form run, then lurch into the sky. He zipped eastward as a streak of light.

"Storms," Kaladin said, then breathed out the last of his Light and collapsed in a heap.

⁂

When he regained consciousness, Syl stood beside him on the rocky ground, hands on her hips. "Sleeping when you're supposed to be on guard duty?"

Kaladin groaned and sat up. He felt horribly weak, but he was alive. Good enough. He held up his hand, but couldn't see much in the darkness now that his Stormlight had faded.

He could move his fingers. His entire hand and forearm ached, but it was the most wonderful ache he'd ever felt.

"I healed," he whispered, then coughed. "I healed from a *Shardblade* wound. Why didn't you tell me I could do that?"

"Because I didn't know you could do it until you did it, silly." She said it as if it were the most obvious fact in the world. Her voice grew softer. "There are dead. Up above."

Kaladin nodded. Could he walk? He managed to get to his feet, and slowly made his way around the base of the Pinnacle, toward the steps on the other side. Syl flitted around him anxiously. His strength began to return a little as he found the steps and began to climb. He had to stop several times to catch his breath, and at one point he ripped off the sleeve of his coat to hide that it had been cut through with a Shardblade.

He reached the top. Part of him feared that he'd find everyone dead. The hallways were silent. No shouts, no guards. Nothing. He continued on, feeling alone, until he saw light ahead.

"Stop!" called a trembling voice. Mart, of Bridge Four. "You in the dark! Identify yourself!"

Kaladin continued forward into the light, too exhausted to reply. Mart and Moash stood guard at the door to the king's chambers, along with some of the men from the King's Guard. They let out whoops of surprise as they recognized Kaladin. They ushered him into the warmth and light of Elhokar's quarters.

Here, he found Dalinar and Adolin—alive—sitting on the couches. Eth tended their wounds; Kaladin had trained a number of the men in Bridge Four in basic field medicine. Renarin slumped in a chair near the corner, his Shardblade discarded at his feet like a piece of refuse. The king paced at the back of the room, speaking softly with his mother.

Dalinar stood up, shaking off Eth's attention, as Kaladin entered. "By the Almighty's tenth name," Dalinar said, voice hushed. "You're *alive*?"

Kaladin nodded, then slumped down in one of the plush royal chairs, uncaring if he got water or blood on it. He let out a soft groan—half relief at seeing them all well, half exhaustion.

"How?" Adolin demanded. "You fell. I was barely awake, but I *know* I saw you fall."

I am a Surgebinder, Kaladin thought as Dalinar looked over at him. *I used Stormlight.* He wanted to say the words, but they wouldn't come out. Not in front of Elhokar and Adolin.

Storms. I'm a coward.

"I had a good grip on him," Kaladin said. "I don't know. We tumbled in the air, and when we hit, I wasn't dead."

The king nodded. "Didn't you say he stuck *you* to the ceiling?" he said to Adolin. "They probably floated all the way down."

"Yeah," Adolin said. "I suppose."

"After you landed," the king said, hopefully, "did you kill him?"

"No," Kaladin said, "He ran off, though. I think he was surprised we fought back as capably as we did."

"Capably?" Adolin asked. "We were like three children attacking a chasmfiend with sticks. Stormfather! I've never been routed so soundly in my life."

"At least we were alerted," the king said, sounding shaken. "This bridge-man . . . he makes a good bodyguard. You will be commended, young man."

Dalinar stood and crossed the room. Eth had cleaned up his face and plugged his bleeding nose. His skin was split along the left cheekbone, his nose broken, though surely not for the first time in Dalinar's long military career. Both were wounds that looked worse than they really were.

"How did you know?" Dalinar asked.

Kaladin met his eyes. Behind him, Adolin glanced over, narrowing his eyes. He looked down at Kaladin's arm and frowned.

That one saw something, Kaladin thought. As if he didn't have enough trouble with Adolin as it was.

"I saw a light moving in the air outside," Kaladin said. "I moved by instinct."

Nearby, Syl zipped into the room and looked pointedly at him, frowning. But it wasn't a lie. He *had* seen a light in the night. Hers.

"All those years ago," Dalinar said, "I dismissed the stories the witnesses told of my brother's assassination. Men walking on walls, others falling up instead of down . . . Almighty above. What *is* he?"

"Death," Kaladin whispered.

Dalinar nodded.

"Why has he come back now?" Navani asked, moving up to Dalinar's side. "After all these years?"

"He wants to claim me," Elhokar said. His back was to them, and Kaladin could make out a cup in his hand. He downed the contents, then immediately refilled it from a jug. Deep violet wine. Elhokar's hand was trembling as he poured.

Kaladin met Dalinar's eyes. The highprince had heard. This Szeth had not come for the king, but Dalinar.

Dalinar didn't say anything to correct the king, so Kaladin didn't either.

"What do we do if he comes back?" Adolin asked.

"I don't know," Dalinar said, sitting back down on the couch beside his son. "I don't know . . ."

Tend his wounds. It was the voice of Kaladin's father, whispering inside him. The surgeon. *Stitch that cheek. Reset the nose.*

He had a more important duty. Kaladin forced himself to his feet, though he felt like he was carrying lead weights, and took a spear from one of the men at the door. "Why are the hallways silent?" he asked Moash. "Do you know where the servants are?"

"The highprince," Moash said, nodding to Dalinar. "Brightlord Dalinar sent a couple of the men to the servants' quarters to move everyone out. He thought that if the assassin came back, he might start killing indiscriminately. Figured the more people who left the palace, the fewer casualties there would be."

Kaladin nodded, taking a sphere lamp and moving out into the hallway. "Hold here. I need to do something."

Adolin slumped in his seat as the bridgeboy left. Kaladin gave no explanation, of course, and didn't ask the king for permission to withdraw. Storming man seemed to consider himself above lighteyes. No, the storming man seemed to consider himself above the *king*.

He did fight alongside you, part of him said. How many men, lighteyed or dark, would stand so firm against a Shardbearer?

Troubled, Adolin stared up at the ceiling. He couldn't have seen what he thought he had. He'd been dazed from his fall from the ceiling. Surely the assassin hadn't *actually* cut Kaladin through the arm with his Shardblade. The arm seemed perfectly fine now, after all.

But why was the sleeve missing?

He fell with the assassin, Adolin thought. *He fought, and looked like he was wounded, but it turns out he wasn't.* Could this all be part of some ruse?

Stop it, Adolin thought at himself. *You'll get as paranoid as Elhokar.* He glanced at the king, who was staring—face pale—at his empty wine cup. Had he really gone through everything in the pitcher? Elhokar walked toward his bedroom, where there would be more waiting for him, and pulled open the door.

Navani gasped, causing the king to freeze in place. He turned toward the door. The back side of the wood had been scratched with a knife, jagged lines forming a series of glyphs.

Adolin stood up. Several of those were numbers, weren't they?

"Thirty-eight days," Renarin read. "The end of all nations."

⁂

Kaladin moved tiredly through the palace hallways, retracing the route he'd led them along only a short time before. Down toward the kitchens, into the hallway with the hole cut out into the air. Past the place where Dalinar's blood spotted the floor, to the intersection.

Where Beld's corpse lay. Kaladin knelt down, rolling the body over. The eyes were burned out. Above those dead eyes remained the tattoos of freedom that Kaladin had designed.

Kaladin closed his own eyes. *I've failed you,* he thought. The balding, square-faced man had survived Bridge Four and the rescue of Dalinar's armies. He'd survived Damnation itself, only to fall here, to an assassin with powers he should not have.

Kaladin groaned.

"He died protecting." Syl's voice.

"I should be able to keep them alive," Kaladin said. "Why didn't I just let them go free? Why did I bring them to this duty, and more death?"

"Someone has to fight. Someone has to protect."

"They've done enough! They've bled their share. I should banish them all. Dalinar can find different bodyguards."

"They made the choice," Syl said. "You can't take that from them."

Kaladin knelt, struggling with his grief.

You have to learn when to care, son. His father's voice. *And when to let go. You'll grow calluses.*

He never had. Storm him, he never had. It was why he'd never made a good surgeon. He couldn't lose patients.

And now, now he killed? Now he was a soldier? How did that make any sense? He hated how good he was at killing.

He took a deep breath, regaining control, with effort. "He can do things I can't," he finally said, opening his eyes and looking toward Syl, who stood in the air near him. "The assassin. Is it because I have more Words to speak?"

"There are more," Syl said. "You're not ready for them yet, I don't think. Regardless, I think you could already do what he does. With practice."

"But how is he Surgebinding? You said that the assassin had no spren."

"No honorspren would give that creature the means to slaughter as he does."

"Perspectives can be different among humans," Kaladin said, trying to keep the emotion from his voice as he turned Beld facedown so he wouldn't have to see those shriveled, burned-out eyes. "What if the honorspren thought this assassin was doing the right thing? You gave me the means to slaughter Parshendi."

"To protect."

"In their eyes, the Parshendi are protecting their kind," Kaladin said. "To them, I'm the aggressor."

Syl sat down, wrapping her arms around her knees. "I don't know. Maybe. But no other honorspren are doing what I do. I am the only one who disobeyed. But his Shardblade . . ."

"What of it?" Kaladin asked.

"It was different. Very different."

"It looked ordinary to me. Well, as ordinary as a Shardblade can."

"It was *different*," she repeated. "I feel I should know why. Something about the amount of Light he was consuming . . ."

Kaladin rose, then walked down the side corridor, holding up his lamp. It bore sapphires, turning the walls blue. The assassin had cut that hole with his Blade, entered the corridor, and killed Beld. But Kaladin had sent *two* men on ahead.

Yes, another body. Hobber, one of the first men Kaladin had saved in Bridge Four. Storms take that assassin! Kaladin remembered saving this man after he had been left by everyone else to die on the plateau.

Kaladin knelt beside the corpse, rolled it over.

And found it weeping.

"I . . . I'm . . . sorry," Hobber said, overcome with emotion and barely able to speak. "I'm sorry, Kaladin."

"Hobber!" Kaladin said. "You're alive!" Then he noticed that the legs of Hobber's uniform had been sliced through at midthigh. Beneath the fabric, Hobber's legs were darkened and grey, dead, as Kaladin's arm had been.

"I didn't even see him," Hobber said. "He cut me down, then stabbed Beld straight through. I listened to you fighting. I thought you'd all died."

"It's all right," Kaladin said. "You're all right."

"I can't feel my legs," Hobber said. "They're gone. I'm no soldier anymore, sir. I'm useless now. I—"

"No," Kaladin said firmly. "You're still Bridge Four. You're *always* Bridge Four." He forced himself to smile. "We'll just have Rock teach you how to cook. How are you with stew?"

"Awful, sir," Hobber said. "I can burn broth."

"Then you'll fit right in with most military cooks. Come on, let's get you back to the others." Kaladin strained, getting his arms under Hobber, trying to lift him.

His body would have none of it. He let out an involuntary groan, putting Hobber back down.

"It's all right, sir," Hobber said.

"No," Kaladin said, sucking in the Light of one of the spheres in the lamp. "It's not." He heaved again, lifting Hobber, then carried him back toward the others.

Our gods were born splinters of a soul,
Of one who seeks to take control,
Destroys all lands that he beholds, with spite.
They are his spren, his gift, his price.
But the nightforms speak of future life,
A challenged champion. A strife even he must requite.

—From the Listener Song of Secrets, final stanza

*H*ighprince Valam might be dead, Brightness Tyn, the spanreed wrote. *Our informants are uncertain. He was never in the best of health, and now there are rumors that his illness finally overcame him. His forces are gearing up to seize Vedenar, however, so if he's dead, his bastard son is likely pretending he is not.*

Shallan sat back, though the reed continued writing. It moved seemingly of its own volition, paired to an identical reed used by Tyn's associate somewhere in Tashikk. They'd set up regular camp following the highstorm, Shallan joining Tyn in her magnificent tent. The air still smelled of rain, and the floor of the tent let some water leak through, wetting Tyn's rug. Shallan wished she'd worn her oversized boots instead of slippers.

What would it mean for her family if the highprince *was* dead? He had been one of her father's main problems in the latter days of his life, and her house had gone into debt securing allies to win the highprince's ear or perhaps—instead—to try to unseat him. A succession war could pressure the people who held her family's debts, and that might make them come to her brothers demanding payments. Or, instead, the chaos could cause the creditors to forget about Shallan's brothers and their insignificant house. And what of the Ghostbloods? Would the succession war make them more or less likely to come, demanding their Soulcaster?

Stormfather! She needed more information.

The reed continued to move, listing the names of those who were making a play for the throne of Jah Keved. "Do you know any of these people personally?" Tyn asked, arms crossed contemplatively as she stood beside the writing table. "What's happening might offer us some opportunities."

"I wasn't important enough for those types," Shallan said with a grimace. It was true.

"We might want to make our way to Jah Keved, regardless," Tyn said. "You know the culture, the people. That'll be useful."

"It's a war zone!"

"War means desperation, and desperation is our mother's milk, kid. Once we follow your lead at the Shattered Plains—maybe pick up another member or two for our team—we probably will want to go visit your homeland."

Shallan felt an immediate stab of guilt. From what Tyn said, the stories she told, it had become clear that she often chose to have someone like Shallan under her wing. An acolyte, someone to nurture. Shallan suspected that was at least partly because Tyn liked having someone around to impress.

Her life must be so lonely, Shallan thought. *Always moving, always taking whatever she can get, but never giving. Except once in a while, to a young thief she can foster . . .*

A strange shadow moved across the wall of the tent. Pattern, though Shallan only noticed him because she knew what to look for. He could be practically invisible when he wanted to be, though unlike some spren he could not vanish completely.

The spanreed continued to write, giving Tyn a longer rundown of conditions in various countries. After that, it produced a curious statement.

I have checked with informants at the Shattered Plains, the pen wrote. *The ones you asked after are, indeed, wanted men. Most are former members of the army of Highprince Sadeas. He is not forgiving of deserters.*

"What's this?" Shallan asked, rising from her stool and going to look more closely at what the pen wrote.

"I implied earlier we'd have to discuss this," Tyn said, changing the paper for the spanreed. "As I keep explaining, the life we lead requires doing some harsh things."

The leader, whom you call Vathah, is worth a bounty of four emerald broams, the pen wrote. *The rest, two broams each.*

"Bounty?" Shallan demanded. "I gave promises to these men!"

"Hush!" Tyn said. "We're not alone in this camp, fool child. If you want us dead, all you need to do is let them overhear this conversation."

"We're *not* turning them in for money," Shallan said more softly. "Tyn, I gave my word."

"Your word?" Tyn said, laughing. "Kid, what do you think we are? Your *word*?"

Shallan blushed. On the table, the spanreed continued to write, oblivious to the fact they weren't paying attention. It was saying something about a job Tyn had done before.

"Tyn," Shallan said, "Vathah and his men can be useful."

Tyn shook her head, walking over to the side of the tent, pouring herself a cup of wine. "You should be proud of what you did here. You have barely any experience, yet you took over three *separate* groups, convincing them to put you—practically sphereless and completely without authority—in charge. Brilliant!

"But here's the thing. The lies we tell, the dreams we create, they're not real. We can't let them be real. This might be the hardest lesson you have to learn." She turned to Shallan, her expression having gone hard, all sense of relaxed playfulness gone. "When a good con woman dies, it's usually because she starts believing her own lies. She finds something good and wants it to continue. She keeps it going, thinking she can juggle it. One day more, she tells herself. One day more, and then . . ."

Tyn dropped the cup. It hit the ground, the wine splashing bloodred across the tent floor and Tyn's rug.

Red carpet . . . once it was white . . .

"Your rug," Shallan said, feeling numb.

"You think I can afford to haul a *rug* with me when I leave the Shattered Plains?" Tyn asked softly, stepping across the spilled wine, taking Shallan by the arm. "You think we can take *any* of this? It's meaningless. You've lied to these men. You've built yourself up, and tomorrow—when we enter that warcamp—the truth will hit you like a slap in the face.

"You think you can *actually* get clemency for these men? From a man like Highprince Sadeas? Don't be an idiot. Even if you get the con going with Dalinar, you want to spend what little credibility we can fake in order to free murderers from Dalinar's political enemy? How long did you think you could keep this lie going?"

Shallan sat back down on the stool, agitated—both at Tyn and at herself. She shouldn't be surprised that Tyn wanted to betray Vathah and his men—she knew what Tyn was, and had eagerly let the woman teach her. In truth, Vathah and his men probably *did* deserve their punishments.

That didn't mean Shallan was going to betray them. She had told them they could change. She had given her word.

Lies . . .

Just because you learned how to lie didn't mean you had to let the lie rule you. But how could she protect Vathah without alienating Tyn? Did she even have that option?

What would Tyn do when Shallan proved to *actually* be the woman betrothed to Dalinar Kholin's son?

How long did you think you could keep this lie going . . .

"Here now," Tyn said, smiling broadly. "*That's* some good news."

Shallan shook herself from her ruminations, glancing at what the span-reed had been writing.

In regards to your mission in Amydlatn, it read, *our benefactors have written to say that they are pleased. They* do *want to know if you recovered the information, but I think this is secondary to them. They let slip that they've found the information they need elsewhere, something about a city they've been researching.*

For your part, there is no news of the target surviving. It seems that your worry about the mission's failure is unfounded. Whatever happened aboard the ship, it worked to our favor. The Wind's Pleasure *is reported lost with all hands. Jasnah Kholin is dead.*

Jasnah Kholin is dead.

Shallan gaped, jaw dropping. *That . . . it isn't . . .*

"Maybe those idiots *did* manage to complete the job," Tyn said, satisfied. "It looks like I'll be paid after all."

"Your mission in Amydlatn," Shallan whispered. "It was to assassinate Jasnah Kholin."

"Run the operation, at least," Tyn said, distracted. "Would have gone myself, but can't stand ships. Those churning seas turn my stomach inside out. . . ."

Shallan couldn't speak. Tyn was an assassin. Tyn had been behind the hit on Jasnah Kholin.

The spanreed was still writing.

. . . some interesting news. You asked after House Davar in Jah Keved. It looks like Jasnah, before leaving Kharbranth, took a new ward . . .

Shallan reached for the spanreed.

Tyn caught her hand, the woman's eyes widening as the reed wrote a few last sentences.

. . . a girl named Shallan. Red hair. Pale skin. Nobody knows much about her. Didn't seem important news to our informants until I pried.

Shallan looked up just as Tyn did, meeting the woman's eyes.

"Ah, *Damnation*," Tyn said.

Shallan tried to pull free. Instead, she found herself being hauled off the chair.

She couldn't follow Tyn's quick motions as the woman slammed her to the ground, face-first. The woman's boot followed to Shallan's back, knocking the air from her and throwing a shock through her body. Shallan's vision fuzzed as she gasped for air.

"Damnation, *Damnation*!" Tyn said. "You're Kholin's ward? Where's Jasnah? Did she live?"

"Help!" Shallan croaked, barely able to speak as she tried to crawl toward the tent wall.

Tyn knelt on Shallan's back, pressing the air from her lungs again. "I had my men clear the area around this tent. I was worried about you alerting the deserters that we would turn them in. Stormfather!" She knelt down, head closer to Shallan's ear. As Shallan struggled, Tyn grabbed her on the shoulder and squeezed hard. "*Did. Jasnah. Live?*"

"No," Shallan whispered, tears of pain coming to her eyes.

"The ship, you may have noticed," Jasnah's voice said from behind them, "has two very fine cabins which I hired out for us at no small expense."

Tyn cursed, leaping up and spinning to see who had spoken. It was, of course, Pattern. Shallan didn't give him a glance, but scrambled toward the tent wall. Vathah and the others were out there, somewhere. If she could just—

Tyn caught her leg, yanking her backward.

I can't escape, a primal part of her thought. Panic surged within Shallan, bringing with it memories of days spent completely impotent. Her father's increasingly destructive violence. A family falling apart.

Powerless.

Can't run, can't run, can't run . . .

Fight.

Shallan pulled her leg free of Tyn and spun, launching herself at the woman. She would not be powerless again. She would *not*!

Tyn gasped as Shallan attacked with everything she had. A clawing, angry, frantic mess. It wasn't effective. Shallan knew next to nothing about how to fight, and in moments she found herself croaking in pain a second time, Tyn's fist buried in her stomach.

Shallan sank to her knees, tears on her cheeks. She tried, ineffectively, to inhale. Tyn cracked her on the side of the head, making her vision go all white.

"Where did *that* come from?" Tyn said.

Shallan blinked, looking up, vision swimming. She was on the ground again. Her fingernails had left a set of bloody rips across Tyn's cheek. Tyn reached up, hand coming away red. Her expression darkened, and she reached to the table, where her sword rested in its sheath.

"What a mess," Tyn growled. "Storm it! I'm going to have to invite that Vathah here, then find a way to blame this on him." Tyn pulled the sword from its sheath.

Shallan struggled to her knees, then tried to climb to her feet, but her legs were unsteady and the room lurched around her, as if she were still on the ship.

"Pattern?" she croaked. "Pattern?"

She heard something outside. Shouts?

"I'm sorry," Tyn said, voice cold. "I'm going to have to tie this up tight. In a way, I'm proud of you. You fooled me. You'd have been good at this."

Calm, Shallan told herself. *Be calm!*

Ten heartbeats.

But for her, it didn't have to be ten, did it?

No. It must be. Time, I need time!

She had spheres in her sleeve. As Tyn approached, Shallan breathed in sharply. Stormlight became a raging tempest inside of her and she raised her hand, thrusting out a pulse of Light. She couldn't form it into anything— she still didn't know how—but it seemed for a moment to show a rippling image of Shallan, standing proudly like a woman of the court.

Tyn stopped short at the sight of the projection of light and color, then waved her sword out in front of her. The Light rippled, dissipating into smoky trails.

"So I'm going mad," Tyn said. "Hearing voices. Seeing things. I guess part of me doesn't want to do this." She advanced, raising her blade. "I'm sorry that you have to learn the lesson this way. Sometimes, we must do things we don't like, kid. Difficult things."

Shallan growled, thrusting her hands forward. Mist twisted and writhed in her hands as a brilliantly silver Blade formed there, spearing Tyn through the chest. The woman barely had time to gasp in surprise as her eyes burned in her skull.

Tyn's corpse slid back off the weapon, collapsing in a heap.

"Difficult things," Shallan growled. "Yes. I believe I *told* you. I've learned that lesson already. Thank you." She crawled to her feet, wobbling.

The tent flap ripped open and Shallan turned, holding up the Shard-blade point-first toward the opening. Vathah, Gaz, and a few other soldiers stopped there in a jumble, weapons bloodied. They looked from Shallan to the corpse on the floor with its burned-out eyes, then back to Shallan.

She felt numb. She wanted to dismiss the Blade, hide it. It was *terrible.*

She did not. She crushed those emotions and hid them deep within. At the moment, she needed something strong to hold to, and the weapon served that purpose. Even if she hated it.

"Tyn's soldiers?" Was that *her* voice, completely cold, purged of emotion?

"Stormfather!" Vathah said, stepping into the tent, hand to his chest as he stared at the Shardblade. "That night, when you pled with us, you could have killed us every one, and the bandits too. You could have done it on your own—"

"Tyn's men!" Shallan shouted.

"Dead, Brightness," Red said. "We heard . . . heard a voice. Telling us to come get you, and they wouldn't let us pass. Then we heard you screaming, and—"

"Was it the voice of the Almighty?" Vathah asked in a whisper.

"It was my spren," Shallan said. "That is all you need know. Search this tent. This woman was hired to assassinate me." It was true, after a fashion. "There might be records of who hired her. Bring me anything you find with writing on it."

As they swarmed in and set to work, Shallan sat down on the stool beside the table. The spanreed still waited there, hovering, paused at the bottom of the page. It needed a new sheet.

Shallan dismissed the Shardblade. "Do not speak of what you saw here to the others," she told Vathah and his men. Though they promised quickly, she doubted that would hold for long. Shardblades were near-mythical objects, and a *woman* holding one? Rumors would spread. Just what she needed.

You're alive because of that cursed thing, she thought to herself. *Again. Stop complaining.*

She took the spanreed up and changed the paper, then set it with its point at the corner. After a moment, Tyn's distant accomplice started writing again.

Your benefactors on the Amydlatn job wish to meet with you, the pen wrote. *It seems that the Ghostbloods have something else for you to do. Would you like me to arrange a meeting with them in the warcamps?*

The pen stopped in place, waiting for a response. What had the spanreed said above? That these people—Tyn's benefactors, the Ghostbloods—had found the information they sought . . . information about a city.

Urithiru. The people who had killed Jasnah, the people who threatened her family, were searching for the city too. Shallan stared at the paper and its words for an extended moment as Vathah and his men began pulling clothing out of Tyn's trunk, knocking on its sides to find anything hidden.

Would you like me to arrange a meeting with them . . .

Shallan took the spanreed, switched the fabrial's setting, then wrote a single word.

Yes.

THE END OF

Part Two

INTERLUDES

ESHONAI • ZAHEL • TALN

THE RIDER OF STORMS

In the city of Narak, people closed up windows tightly as night approached and the storm loomed. They stuffed rags under doors, shoved bracing boards into position, pounded large, square blocks of wood into windows.

Eshonai did not join in the preparations, but stood outside Thude's dwelling, listening to his report—he'd just returned from meeting with the Alethi, arranging a parley to discuss peace. She had wanted to send someone earlier, but the Five had deliberated and complained until Eshonai wanted to throttle the lot of them. At least they'd finally agreed to let her send a messenger.

"Seven days," Thude said. "The meeting will happen on a neutral plateau."

"Did you see him?" Eshonai asked, eager. "The Blackthorn?"

Thude shook his head.

"What of the other one?" Eshonai asked. "The Surgebinder?"

"No sign of him either." Thude looked troubled. He looked eastward. "You'd better go. I can give you more details after the storm is done."

Eshonai nodded, resting her hand on her friend's shoulder. "Thank you."

"Good luck," Thude said to Resolve.

"To all of us," she replied as he shut the door, leaving her alone in a dark, seemingly empty city. Eshonai checked the stormshield on her back, then took the sphere with Venli's captive spren from her pocket and attuned the Rhythm of Resolve.

The time had come. She ran toward the storm.

Resolve was a stately beat with a steady, rising sense of import and power. She left Narak, and reaching the first chasm, she jumped. Only warform had the strength for such leaps; for the workers to reach outer plateaus and grow food, they used rope bridges that were pulled back and stowed before each storm.

She landed in full stride, her footsteps falling to the beat of Resolve. The stormwall appeared in the distance, barely visible in the darkness. Winds rose, pushing against her, as if to hold her back. Above, windspren zipped and danced in the air. They were heralds of what was to come.

Eshonai jumped two more chasms, then slowed, striding up to the top of a low hill. The stormwall now dominated the night sky, advancing at a terrible pace. The enormous sheet of darkness mingled debris with rain, a banner of water, rock, dust, and fallen plants. Eshonai unhooked the large shield on her back.

For the listeners, there was a certain romanticism to going out in the storm. Yes, the storms were terrible—but every listener would have to spend a number of nights out in them, alone. The songs said that someone seeking a new form would be protected. She wasn't certain if this was fancy or fact, but the songs didn't prevent most listeners from hiding in a cleft of rock to avoid the stormwall, then coming out once it had passed.

Eshonai preferred a shield. It felt more like facing the Rider straight on. This one, the soul of the storm, was the one the humans called Stormfather—and he was not one of her people's gods. In fact, the songs named him a traitor—a spren who had chosen to protect humans instead of the listeners.

Still, her people respected him. He would kill any who did not respect him.

She placed the base of the shield against a ridge of rock on the ground, then turned her shoulder against it, lowered her head, and braced herself with one foot back. Her other hand held the stone with the spren in it. She'd have preferred to wear her Plate, but for some reason having it on interfered with the transformation process.

She felt and heard the storm approach. The ground shook, the air roared. Bits of leaves swept across her in a chill gust, like scouts before an oncoming army that charged behind, the howling wind its battle cry.

She squeezed her eyes shut.

It slammed against her.

Despite her posture and her braced muscles, something *cracked* against the shield and flipped it away. The wind caught it and ripped it from her fingers. She stumbled backward, then threw herself to the ground, shoulder to the wind, head ducked.

Thunder beat against her as the raging wind tried to pull her off the plateau and toss her into the air. She kept her eyes closed, as all was black within the storm save for the flashes of lightning. It did not seem to her she was being protected. Her shoulder against the wind, huddling down behind a hillock, it seemed that the wind was doing its best to destroy her. Rocks crunched against the dark plateau nearby, shaking the ground. All she could hear was the roar of wind in her ears, punctuated occasionally by thunder. A terrible song without rhythm.

She kept Resolve attuned inside of her. She could feel that, at least, even if she couldn't hear.

Rain that fell like arrowheads beat into her body, bouncing off her skullplate and her armor. She set her jaw against the deep, bone-chilling cold and stayed in place. She had done this many times before, either when transforming or when on the occasional surprise raid against the Alethi. She could survive. She *would* survive.

She focused on the rhythm in her head, clinging to some rocks as the wind tried to push her back off the plateau. Demid, Venli's once-mate, had started a movement where people who wanted to transform waited inside buildings until the storm had been going for a while. They only stepped out once the initial burst of fury was past. That was risky, as you never knew when the point of transformation would come.

Eshonai had never tried it. The storms were violent, they were dangerous, but they were also things of discovery. Within them, the familiar became something grand, majestic, and terrible. She did not look forward to entering them, but when she had to, she always found the experience thrilling.

She lifted her head, eyes closed, and put her face to the winds—feeling them blast her, shake her. She felt the rain on her skin. The Rider of Storms was a traitor, yes—but you could not have a traitor who had not originally been a friend. These storms belonged to her people. The listeners were *of* the storms.

The rhythms changed in her mind. In a moment, they all aligned and became the same. No matter which one she attuned, she heard the same rhythm—single, steady beats. Like that of a heart. The moment had arrived.

The storm vanished. Wind, rain, sound . . . gone. Eshonai stood up, dripping wet, her muscles cold, her skin numb. She shook her head, spraying water, and looked up into the sky.

The face was there. Infinite, expansive. The humans spoke of their Stormfather, yet they never knew him as a listener did. As wide as the sky itself, with eyes full of countless stars. The gemstone in Eshonai's hand burst alight.

Power, energy. She imagined it coursing through her, energizing her, *enlivening* her. Eshonai threw the gemstone against the ground, smashing it and releasing the spren. She worked hard to get the proper *feel* down, as Venli had trained her.

Is this really what you want? The voice reverberated through her like crashing thunder.

The Rider had *spoken* to her! That happened in songs, but not . . . never . . . She attuned Appreciation, but of course it was the same rhythm now. *Beat. Beat. Beat.*

The spren escaped from its prison and spun around her, giving off a strange red light. Splinters of lightning sprang from it. Angerspren?

This was wrong.

I suppose this must be, the Rider of Storms said. It was going to happen.

"No," Eshonai said, stepping back from that spren. In a moment of panic, she cast from her mind the preparations that Venli had given her. "No!"

The spren became a streak of red light and hit her in the chest. Tendrils of red spread outward.

I cannot stop this, the Rider of Storms said. I would shelter you, little one, if I were given that power. I am sorry.

Eshonai gasped, the rhythms fleeing her mind, and fell to her knees. She felt it wash through her, the transformation.

I am sorry.

The rains came again, and her body began to change.

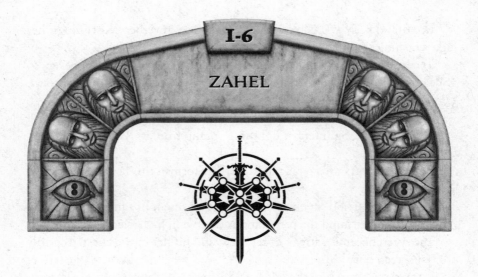

ZAHEL

Someone was near.

Zahel awoke, snapping his eyes open, knowing instantly that someone was approaching his room.

Blast! It was the middle of the night. If this was another lighteyed brat he'd turned away, come to beg . . . He grumbled to himself, climbing off his cot. *I am far, far too old for this.*

He pulled open his door, revealing the courtyard of the practice grounds at night. The air was wet. Oh, right. One of those storms had come, Invested to the hilt and looking for a place to stick it all. Cursed things.

A young man, hand poised to knock, jumped back in surprise from the opening door. Kaladin. The bridgeman-turned-bodyguard. The one with that spren Zahel could sense always spinning about.

"You look like death itself," Zahel snapped at the boy. Kaladin's clothing was bloodied, his uniform ripped up on one side. The right sleeve was missing. "What happened?"

"Attempt on the king's life," the boy said softly. "Not two hours ago."

"Huh."

"Is your offer to learn how to fight a Shardblade still good?"

"No." Zahel slammed the door. He turned to walk back toward his cot.

The boy pushed the door open, of course. Blasted monks. Saw themselves as property and couldn't own anything, so they figured they didn't need locks on the doors.

"Please," the boy said. "I—"

"Kid," Zahel said, turning back toward him. "Two people live in this room."

The boy frowned, looking at the single cot.

"The first," Zahel said, "is a grouchy swordsman who has a soft spot for kids who are in over their heads. He comes out by day. The other is a very, *very* grouchy swordsman who finds everything and everyone utterly contemptible. He comes out when some fool wakes him at a horrid hour of the night. I suggest you ask the first man and *not* the second. All right?"

"All right," the boy said. "I'll be back."

"Good," Zahel said, settling down on the bed. "And don't be green from the ground."

The boy paused by the door. "Don't be . . . Huh?"

Stupid language, Zahel thought, climbing into his cot. *No proper metaphors at all.* "Just leave your attitude and come to learn. I hate beating up people younger than me. It makes me feel like a bully."

The kid grunted, sliding the door shut. Zahel pulled up his blanket—damn monks only got one—and turned over on his cot. He expected a voice to speak in his mind as he drifted off. Of course, there wasn't one.

Hadn't been one in years.

TALN

O f fires that burned and yet they were gone. Of heat he could feel when others felt not. Of screams his own that nobody heard. Of torture sublime, for life it meant.

"He just stares like that, Your Majesty."

Words.

"He doesn't seem to see anything. Sometimes he mumbles. Sometimes he shouts. But always, he just *stares*."

The Gift and words. Not his. Never his. Now his.

"Storms, it's haunting, isn't it? I had to ride all this way with that, Your Majesty. Listening to him ranting in the back of the wagon half the time. Then feeling him stare at the back of my head the rest."

"And Wit? You mentioned him."

"Started on the trip with me, Your Majesty. But on the second day, he declared that he needed a rock."

"A . . . rock."

"Yes, Your Majesty. He hopped out of the wagon and found one, then, er, he hit himself on the head with it, Your Majesty. Did it three or four times. Came right back to the wagon with an odd grin, and said . . . um . . ."

"Yes?"

"Well, he said that he'd needed, uh, I had this remembered for you. He said, 'I needed an objective frame of reference by which to judge the experience of your company. Somewhere between four and five blows, I place it.' I don't rightly understand what he meant, sir. I think he was mocking me."

"Safe bet."

Why didn't they scream? That *heat*! Of death. Of death and the dead and the dead and their talking and not screaming of death except of the death that did not come.

"After that, Your Majesty, Wit just kind of, well, ran off. Into the hills. Like some storming Horneater."

"Don't try to understand Wit, Bordin. You'll only cause yourself pain."

"Yes, Brightlord."

"I *like* this Wit."

"We're quite aware, Elhokar."

"Honestly, Your Majesty, I preferred the madman for company."

"Well of course you did. If people *liked* to be around Wit, he wouldn't be much of a Wit, would he?"

They were on fire. The walls were on fire. The floor was on fire. Burning and the inside of a cannot where to be and then at all. Where?

A trip. Water? Wheels?

Fire. Yes, fire.

"Can you hear me, madman?"

"Elhokar, look at him. I doubt he understands."

"I am Talenel'Elin, Herald of War." Voice. He spoke it. He didn't think it. The words came, like they always came.

"What was that? Speak louder, man."

"The time of the Return, the Desolation, is near at hand. We must prepare. You will have forgotten much, following the destruction of the times past."

"I can make out some of it, Elhokar. It's Alethi. Northern accent. Not what I'd have expected from one with such dark skin."

"Where did you get the Shardblade, madman? Tell me. Most Blades are accounted for through the generations, their lineage and history recorded. This one is completely unknown. From whom did you take it?"

"Kalak will teach you to cast bronze, if you have forgotten this. We will Soulcast blocks of metal directly for you. I wish we could teach you steel, but casting is so much easier than forging, and you must have something we can produce quickly. Your stone tools will not serve against what is to come."

"He said something about bronze. And stone?"

"Vedel can train your surgeons, and Jezrien . . . he will teach you leadership. So much is lost between Returns . . ."

"The Shardblade! Where did you get it?"

"How did you separate it from him, Bordin?"

"We didn't, Brightlord. He just dropped it."

"And it didn't vanish away? Not bonded, then. He couldn't have had it for long. Were his eyes this color when you found him?"

"Yes, sir. A darkeyed man with a Shardblade. Odd sight, that."

"I will train your soldiers. We should have time. Ishar keeps talking about a way to keep information from being lost following Desolations.

And you have discovered something unexpected. We will use that. Surge-binders to act as guardians . . . Knights . . ."

"He's said this all before, Your Majesty. When he mumbles, uh, he just keeps at it. Over and over. I don't think he even knows what he's saying. Eerie, how his expression doesn't change as he talks."

"That *is* an Alethi accent."

"He looks like he's been living in the wild for some time, with that long hair and those broken nails. Perhaps a villager lost their mad father."

"And the Blade, Elhokar?"

"Surely you don't think it's *his*, Uncle."

"The coming days will be difficult, but with training, humanity *will* survive. You must bring me to your leaders. The other Heralds should join us soon."

"I am willing to consider anything, these days. Your Majesty, I suggest you send him to the ardents. Perhaps they can help his mind to recover."

"What will you do with the Shardblade?"

"I'm certain we can find a good use for it. In fact, something occurs to me right now. I might have need of you, Bordin."

"Whatever you need, Brightlord."

"I think . . . I think I am late . . . this time . . ."

How long had it been?

How long had it been?

How long had it been?

How long had it been?

How long had it been?

How long had it been?

How long had it been?

Too long.

A FORM OF POWER

They were waiting for Eshonai when she returned.

A gathering of thousands crowded the edge of the plateau just outside of Narak. Workers, nimbles, soldiers, and even some mates who had been drawn away from their hedonism by the prospect of something novel. A new form, a form of *power*?

Eshonai strode toward them, marveling at the energy. Tiny, almost invisible lines of red lightning flared from her hand if she made a fist quickly. Her marbled skin tone—mostly black, with a slight grain of red streaks—had not changed, but she'd lost the bulky armor of warform. Instead, small ridges peeked out through the skin of her arms, which was stretched tightly in places. She'd tested the new armor against stones and found it very durable.

She had hairstrands again. How long had it been since she'd felt those? More wondrous, she felt *focused*. No more worries about the fate of her people. She knew what to do.

Venli pushed to the front of the crowd as Eshonai reached the edge of the chasm. They looked across the void at one another, and Eshonai could see the question on her sister's lips. *It worked?*

Eshonai leapt the chasm. She didn't require the running start that warform used; she crouched down, then threw herself up and into the air. The wind seemed to writhe around her. She shot over the chasm and landed among her people, red lines of power running up her legs as she crouched, absorbing the impact of the landing.

People backed away. So clear. Everything was *so clear*.

"I have returned from the storms," she said to Praise, which could also be used for true satisfaction. "I bring with me the future of two peoples. Our time of loss is at an end."

"Eshonai?" It was Thude, wearing his long coat. "Eshonai, your *eyes*."

"Yes?"

"They're red."

"They are a representation of what I've become."

"But, in the songs—"

"Sister!" Eshonai called to Resolve. "Come look upon what you have wrought!"

Venli approached, timid at first. "Stormform," she whispered to Awe. "It works, then? You can move in the storms without danger?"

"More than that," Eshonai said. "The winds obey me. And Venli, I can feel something . . . something *building*. A storm."

"You feel a storm right now? In the rhythms?"

"Beyond the rhythms," Eshonai said. How could she explain it? How could she describe taste to one with no mouth, sight to one who had never seen? "I feel a tempest brewing just beyond our experience. A powerful, angry tempest. A highstorm. With enough of us bearing this form together, we could bring it. We could *bend* the storms to our will, and could bring them down upon our enemies."

Humming to the Rhythm of Awe spread through those who watched. As they were listeners, they could feel the rhythm, hear it. All were in tune, all were in rhythm with one another. Perfection.

Eshonai held out her arms to the sides and spoke in a loud voice. "Cast aside despair and sing to the Rhythm of Joy! I have looked into the depths of the Storm Rider's eyes, and I have seen his betrayal. I know his mind, and have seen his intent to help the humans against us. But my sister has discovered salvation! With this form we can stand on our own, independent, and we can sweep our enemies from this land like leaves before the tempest!"

The humming to Awe grew louder, and some began to sing. Eshonai gloried in it.

She pointedly ignored the voice deep within her that was screaming in horror.

THREE

Deadly

SHALLAN • KALADIN • ADOLIN • NAVANI

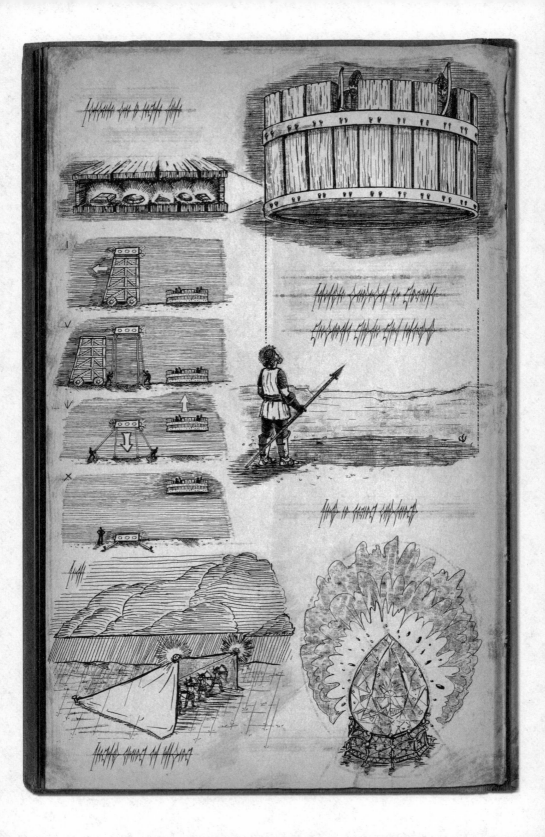

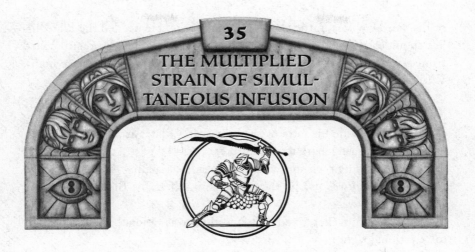

They also, when they had settled their rulings in the nature of each bond's placement, called the name of it the Nahel bond, with regard to its effect upon the souls of those caught in its grip; in this description, each was related to the bonds that drive Roshar itself, ten Surges, named in turn and two for each order; in this light, it can be seen that each order would by necessity share one Surge with each of its neighbors.

—From *Words of Radiance*, chapter 8, page 6

Adolin threw his Shardblade.

Wielding the weapons was about more than just practicing stances and growing accustomed to the too-light swordplay. A master of the Blade learned to do more with the bond. He learned to command it to remain in place after being dropped, and learned to summon it back from the hands of those who might have picked it up. He learned that man and sword were, in some ways, one. The weapon became a piece of your soul.

Adolin had learned to control his Blade in this way. Usually. Today, the weapon disintegrated almost immediately after leaving his fingers.

The long, silvery Blade transmuted to white vapor—holding its shape for just a brief moment, like a smoke ring—before exploding in a puff of writhing white streams. Adolin growled in frustration, pacing back and forth on the plateau, hand held out to the side as he resummoned the weapon. Ten heartbeats. At times, it felt like an eternity.

He wore his Plate without the helm, which sat atop a nearby rock, and so his hair blew free in the early morning breeze. He needed the Plate; his left shoulder and side were a mass of purple bruises. His head still ached from slamming into the ground during the assassin's attack last night. Without the Plate, he wouldn't be nearly so nimble today.

Besides, he *needed* its strength. He kept looking over his shoulder, expecting the assassin to be there. He'd stayed up all night last night, sitting on the floor outside his father's room, wearing Plate, arms crossed on his knees, chewing ridgebark to stay awake.

He'd been caught without his Plate once. Not again.

And what will you do? he thought to himself as his Blade reappeared. *Wear it all the time?*

The part of him that asked such questions was rational. He didn't want to be rational right now.

He shook the condensation from his Blade, then twisted and hurled it, transmitting the mental commands that would tell it to hold together. Once again, the weapon shattered to mist moments after it left his fingers. It didn't even cross half the distance to the rock formation he was aiming for.

What was wrong with him? He'd mastered Blade commands years ago. True, he hadn't often practiced *throwing* his sword—such things were forbidden in duels, and he hadn't ever thought he'd need to use the maneuver. That was before he'd been trapped on the *ceiling* of a hallway, unable to properly engage an assassin.

Adolin walked to the edge of the plateau, staring out over the uneven expanse of the Shattered Plains. A huddle of three guards watched him nearby. Laughable. What would three *bridgemen* do if the Assassin in White returned?

Kaladin was worth something in the attack, Adolin thought. *More than you were.* That man had been suspiciously effective.

Renarin said that Adolin was unfair toward the bridgeman captain, but there *was* something strange about that man. More than his attitude—the way he always acted like by talking to you, he was doing you a favor. The way he seemed so decidedly gloomy at everything, angry at the world itself. He was unlikable, plain and simple, but Adolin had known plenty of unlikable people.

Kaladin was also strange. In ways Adolin couldn't explain.

Well, for all that, Kaladin's men were just doing their duty. No use in snapping at them, so he gave them a smile.

Adolin's Shardblade dropped into his fingers again, too light for its size. He had always felt a certain strength when holding it. Never before had Adolin felt powerless when bearing his Shards. Even surrounded by the Parshendi, even certain he was going to die, he'd still felt *power.*

Where was that feeling now?

He spun and threw the weapon, focusing as Zahel had taught him years before, sending a direct *instruction* to the Blade—picturing what he needed it to do. It held together, spinning end over end, flashing in the air. It sank up to its hilt into the stone of the rock formation. Adolin let out the breath he had been holding. Finally. He released the Blade, and it burst into mist, which streamed like a tiny river from the hole left behind.

"Come," he said to his bodyguards, snatching his helm from the rock and walking toward the nearby warcamp. As one might expect, the crater edge that formed the warcamp wall was most weathered here, in the east. The camp had spilled out like the contents of a broken turtle egg, and—over the years—had even started to creep down onto the near plateaus.

Emerging from that creep of civilization was a distinctly odd procession. The congregation of robed ardents chanted in unison, surrounding parshmen who carried large poles upright like lances. Silk cloth shimmered between these poles, a good forty feet wide, rippling in the breeze and cutting off the view of something in the center.

Soulcasters? They didn't normally come out during the day. "Wait here," he told his bodyguards, then jogged over toward the ardents.

The three bridgemen obeyed. If Kaladin had been with them, he would have insisted on following. Maybe the way the fellow acted was a result of his strange position. Why had father put a darkeyed soldier *outside* the command structure? Adolin was all for treating men with respect and honor regardless of eye shade, but the Almighty had put some men in command and others beneath them. It was simply the natural order of things.

The parshmen carrying the poles watched him come, then looked down at the ground. Nearby ardents let Adolin pass, though they looked uncomfortable. Adolin was allowed to see Soulcasters, but having him visit them was irregular.

Inside the temporary silk room, Adolin found Kadash—one of the foremost of Dalinar's ardents. The tall man had once been a soldier, as the scars on his head testified. He spoke with ardents in bloodred robes.

Soulcasters. It was the word for both the people who performed the art and the fabrials they used. Kadash was not one himself; he wore the standard grey robes instead of red, his head shaven, face accented by a square beard. He noticed Adolin, hesitated briefly, then bowed his head in respect. Like all of the ardents, Kadash was technically a slave.

That included the five Soulcasters. Each stood with right hand to breast, displaying a sparkling fabrial across the back of the palm. One of the ardents glanced at Adolin. Stormfather—that gaze wasn't completely human, not any longer. Prolonged use of the Soulcaster had transformed the eyes so that they sparkled like gemstones themselves. The woman's skin had hardened to something like stone, smooth, with fine cracks. It was as if the person were a living statue.

Kadash hustled over toward Adolin. "Brightlord," he said. "I had not realized you were coming to supervise."

"I'm not here to supervise," Adolin said, glancing with discomfort at the Soulcasters. "I'm just surprised. Don't you usually do this at night?"

"We can't afford to any longer, bright one," Kadash said. "There are too many demands upon the Soulcasters. Buildings, food, removal of waste . . . To fit it all in, we are going to need to start training multiple ardents on each fabrial, then working them in shifts. Your father approved this earlier in the week."

This drew glances from several of the red-robed ardents. What did they think about others training on their fabrials? Their almost-alien expressions were unreadable.

"I see," Adolin said. *Storms, we rely on these things a lot.* Everyone talked about Shardblades and Shardplate, and their advantages in war. But in truth, it was these strange fabrials—and the grain they created—that had allowed this war to proceed as it had.

"May we proceed, bright one?" Kadash asked.

Adolin nodded, and Kadash walked back to the five and gave a few brief commands. He spoke quickly, nervous. It was odd to see that in Kadash, who was normally so placid and unflappable. Soulcasters had that effect on everyone.

The five started softly chanting, a harmony to the singing of the ardents outside. The five stepped forward and raised their hands in a line, and Adolin found his face breaking out in a sweat, blown cold by the wind that managed to sneak past the silken walls.

At first there was nothing. And then *stone.*

Adolin thought he caught a brief glimpse of mist coalescing—like the moment a Shardblade appeared—as a massive wall sprang into existence. Wind blew inward, as if sucked by that materializing rock, making the cloth flap violently, snapping and writhing in the air. Why should the wind pull inward? Shouldn't it have been blown outward by rock displacing it?

The large barrier abutted the cloth on either side, causing the silk screens to bulge outward, and rose high into the air.

"We'll need taller poles," Kadash muttered to himself.

The stone wall had the same utilitarian look as the barracks, but this was a new shape. Flat on the side facing the warcamps, it was sloped on the other side, like a wedge. Adolin recognized it as something his father had been deliberating building for months now.

"A windbreak!" Adolin said. "That's wonderful, Kadash."

"Yes, well, your father seemed to like the proposal. A few dozen of these out here, and the construction yards will be able to expand onto the entire plateau without fear of highstorms."

That wasn't *completely* true. You always had to worry about highstorms, since they could hurl boulders and blow hard enough to rip buildings from their foundations. But a good solid windbreak would be a blessing of the Almighty out here in the stormlands.

The Soulcasters retreated, not speaking with the other ardents. The parshmen scrambled to keep up, those on one side of the barrier running along behind it with their silk and opening the back of the room to let the new windbreak slip out of the enclosure. They passed by Adolin and Kadash, leaving them exposed on the plateau and standing in the shade of the large new stone structure.

The silk wall went back up, blocking sight of the Soulcasters. Just before it did, Adolin noticed one of the Soulcasters' hands. The fabrial's glow was gone. Likely one or more of the gemstones in it had shattered.

"I still find it incredible," Kadash said, looking up at the stone barrier. "Even after all these years. If we needed proof of the Almighty's hand in our lives, this is certainly it." A few gloryspren appeared around him, spinning and golden.

"The Radiants could Soulcast," Adolin said, "couldn't they?"

"It is written that they could," Kadash said carefully. The Recreance— the term for the Radiants' betrayal of mankind—was often seen as a failure of Vorinism as a religion. The way the Church sought to seize power in the centuries that followed was even more embarrassing.

"What else could the Radiants do?" Adolin asked. "They had strange powers, right?"

"I have not read on it extensively, bright one," Kadash said. "Perhaps I should have spent more time learning about them, if only to remember the evils of pride. I will be certain to do this, bright one, in order to remain faithful and remember the proper place of all ardents."

"Kadash," Adolin said, watching the shimmering silken procession retreat, "I need information right now, not humility. The Assassin in White has returned."

Kadash gasped. "The disturbance at the palace last night? The rumors are *true*?"

"Yes."

There was no use hiding it. His father and the king had told the highprinces, and were planning on how to release the information to everyone else.

Adolin met the ardent's eyes. "That assassin walked on the walls, as if the pull of the earth were nothing to him. He fell a hundred feet without injury. He was like a Voidbringer, death given form. So I ask you again. What could the Radiants do? Were abilities like these ascribed to them?"

"Those and more, bright one," Kadash whispered, face drained of color. "I spoke with some of the soldiers who survived that first terrible night when the old king was killed. I thought the things they claimed to have seen the result of trauma—"

"I need to know," Adolin said. "Look into it. Read. Tell me what this creature might be capable of doing. We have to know how to fight him. He *will* return."

"Yes," Kadash said, visibly shaken. "But . . . Adolin? If what you say is true . . . Storms! It could mean the Radiants are not dead."

"I know."

"Almighty preserve us," Kadash whispered.

◆◆

Navani Kholin loved warcamps. In ordinary cities, everything was so *messy*. Shops where they hardly belonged, streets that refused to run in straight lines.

Military men and women, however, valued order and rationality—at least, the better ones did. Their camps reflected that. Barracks in neat rows, shops confined to marketplaces, as opposed to popping up on every corner. From her vantage atop her observation tower, she could see much of Dalinar's camp. So *neat*, so *intentional*.

This was the mark of humankind: to take the wild, unorganized world and make something logical of it. You could get so much more done when everything was in its place, when you could easily find what or whom you needed. Creativity required such things.

Careful planning was, indeed, the water that nourished innovation.

She took in a deep breath and turned back toward the engineering grounds, which dominated the eastern section of Dalinar's warcamp. "All right, everyone!" she called. "Let's give it a try!" This test had been planned long before the assassin's attack, and she'd decided to proceed. What else was she going to do? Sit around and worry?

The grounds below became a buzz of activity. Her elevated observation platform was perhaps twenty-five feet high, and gave her a good view of the engineering grounds. She was flanked by a dozen different ardents and scholars—and even Matain and a few other stormwardens. She still wasn't sure what she thought of those fellows—they spent too much time talking about numerology and reading the winds. They called it a science in an attempt to dodge Vorin prohibitions of predicting the future.

They *had* offered some useful wisdom from time to time. She'd invited them for that reason—and because she wanted to keep an eye on them.

The object of her attention, and the subject of today's test, was a large circular platform at the center of the engineering yards. The wooden structure looked like the top of a siege tower that had been cut off and laid on the ground. Crenellations ringed it, and they'd set up dummies at those, the kinds that the soldiers used for archery practice. Next to that grounded platform was a tall wooden tower with a latticework of scaffolding up the sides. Workers scuttled over it, checking that everything was operational.

"You really should read this, Navani," Rushu said, looking over a report. The young woman was an ardent, and had no right whatsoever to have such lush eyelashes or delicate features. Rushu had joined the ardentia to escape the advances of men. A silly choice, judging by the way male ardents always wanted to work with her. Fortunately, she was also brilliant. And Navani could always find a use for someone brilliant.

"I'll read it later," Navani said in a gently chiding voice. "We have work to do now, Rushu."

". . . changed even when he was in the other room," Rushu mumbled, flipping to another page. "Repeatable and measurable. Only flamespren so far, but so many potential other applications . . ."

"Rushu," Navani said, a little more firmly this time. "The test?"

"Oh! Sorry, Brightness." The woman tucked the folded pages into a pocket of her robes. Then she ran her hand across her shaved head, frowning. "Navani, have you ever wondered why the Almighty gave beards to men, but not women? For that matter, why do we consider it feminine for a woman to have long hair? Should not more hair be a *masculine* trait? Many of them have quite a lot of it, you see."

"Focus, child," Navani said. "I want you watching when the test happens." She turned to the others. "That goes for all of you. If this thing crashes to the ground again, I don't want to lose another week attempting to figure out what went wrong!"

The others nodded, and Navani found herself growing excited, some of the tension from the night's attack finally bleeding away. She went over the protocols for the test in her head. People moved out of danger . . . Ardents on various platforms nearby, watching intently with quills and paper to record . . . Stones infused . . .

Everything had been done and checked three times over. She stepped up to the front of her platform—holding the railing tightly with freehand and gloved safehand—and blessed the Almighty for the distracting power of a good fabrial project. She'd used this one at first to divert herself from worrying about Jasnah, though she'd eventually realized that Jasnah would be fine. True, reports now said the ship had been lost with all hands, but this wasn't the first time that supposed disaster had struck Navani's daughter. Jasnah played with danger as a child played with a captive cremling, and she always came through.

The assassin's return, though . . . Oh, *Stormfather*. If he took Dalinar as he had Gavilar . . .

"Give the signal," she said to the ardents. "We've checked everything more times than is useful."

The ardents nodded and wrote, via spanreed, to the workers below. Navani noticed with annoyance that a figure in blue Shardplate had wandered onto the engineering grounds, helm under arm, exposing a messy mop of blond hair speckled black. The guards were supposed to have kept people out, but such prohibitions would not apply to the highprince's heir. Well, Adolin would know to keep his distance. She hoped.

She turned back to the wooden tower. Ardents at the top had activated the fabrials there, and now climbed down the ladders at the sides, unhooking latches as they went. Once they were down, workers carefully pulled the sides away on their rollers. Those were the only things that had been holding the top of the tower in place. Without them, it should fall.

The top of the platform, however, remained in place—hanging impossibly in the air. Navani's breath caught. The only thing connecting it to the ground was a set of two pulleys and ropes, but those offered no support. That square, thick section of wood now hung in the air completely unsupported.

The ardents around her murmured in excitement. Now for the real test. Navani waved, and the men below worked the cranks on the pulleys, pulling down the floating section of wood. The archer parapet nearby shook, wobbled, then began to rise into the air in a motion exactly opposite to the square's.

"It's working!" Rushu exclaimed.

"I don't like that wobble," said Falilar. The ancient engineer scratched at his ardent's beard. "That ascent should be smoother."

"It's not falling," Navani said. "I'll settle for that."

"Winds willing, I'd have been up there," Rushu said, raising a spyglass. "I can't see even a sparkle from the gemstones. What if they're cracking?"

"Then we'll find out eventually," Navani said, though in truth she wouldn't have minded being on top of the rising parapet herself. Dalinar would have had a heart attack if he'd learned of her doing such a thing. The man was a dear, but he was a touch overprotective. In the way a highstorm was a touch windy.

The parapet wobbled its way upward. It acted as if it were being hoisted, though it had no support at all. Finally, it peaked. The square of wood that had been hanging in the air before was now down against the ground and tied in place. The round parapet hung in the air instead, slightly off-kilter.

It did not fall.

Adolin clomped up the steps to her viewing platform, rattling and shaking the entire thing with that Shardplate of his. By the time he reached her, the other scholars were chattering among themselves and furiously making notes. Logicspren, in the shape of tiny stormclouds, rose around them.

It had worked. *Finally*.

"Hey," Adolin said. "Is that platform *flying*?"

"And you only just now noticed this, dear?" Navani asked.

He scratched his head. "I've been distracted, Aunt. Huh. That . . . That's really odd." He seemed troubled.

"What?" Navani asked him.

"It's, it's like . . ."

Him. The assassin, who had—according to both Adolin and Dalinar—somehow manipulated gravityspren.

Navani looked to the scholars. "Why don't you all go down and have them lower the platform? You can inspect the gemstones and see if any broke."

The others heard it as a dismissal and went down the steps in an excited bunch, though Rushu—dear Rushu—remained. "Oh!" the woman said. "It would be better to watch from up here, in case—"

"I will speak with my nephew. Alone, please." Sometimes, working with scholars, you had to be a touch blunt.

Rushu finally blushed, then bobbed a bow and hastened away. Adolin stepped up to the railing. It was difficult to not feel dwarfed by a man wearing Plate, and when he reached out to hold the railing, she thought she could hear the wood groan from the strength of that grip. He could have snapped that rail without a second thought.

I will figure out how to make more of that, she thought. While she was no warrior, there might be things she could do to protect her family. The more she understood the secrets of technology and the power of spren locked within gemstones, the closer she grew to finding what she sought.

Adolin was staring at her hand. Oh, so he'd finally noticed that, had he?

"Aunt?" he said, voice strained. "A *glove*?"

"Far more practical," she said, holding up her safehand and wiggling the fingers. "Oh, don't look like that. Darkeyed women do it all the time."

"You're not darkeyed."

"I'm the dowager queen," Navani said. "Nobody cares what in Damnation I do. I could prance around completely nude, and they'd all just shake their heads and talk about how eccentric I am."

Adolin sighed, but let the matter drop, instead nodding toward the platform. "How did you do it?"

"Conjoined fabrials," Navani said. "The trick was finding a way to overcome the structural weaknesses of the gemstones, which succumb easily to the multiplied strain of simultaneous infusion drain and physical stress. We . . ."

She trailed off as she caught Adolin's eyes glazing over. He was a bright young man when it came to most social interactions, but he didn't have a single scholarly breath in him. Navani smiled, switching to layman's terms.

"If you split a fabrial gemstone in a certain way," Navani said, "you can link the two pieces together so they mimic each other's motions. Like a spanreed?"

"Ah, right," Adolin said.

"Well," Navani said, "we can also make two halves that move *opposite* one another. We filled the floor of that parapet with such gemstones and put their other halves in the wooden square. Once we engage them all—so they are mimicking one another in reverse—we can pull one platform down and make the other go up."

"Huh," Adolin said. "Can you make this work on a battlefield?"

That was, of course, the exact thing Dalinar had asked when she'd shown him the concepts. "Proximity is a problem right now," she said. "The farther the pairs grow from one another, the weaker their interaction, and that causes them to crack more easily. You don't see it with something light like a spanreed, but when working with heavy weights . . . Well, we can probably get them working on the Shattered Plains. That's our goal right now. You could roll one of these out there, then engage it and write back to us via reed. We pull the platform here down, and your archers get raised up fifty feet to gain a perfect archery position."

This, finally, seemed to get Adolin excited. "The enemy wouldn't be able to topple it or climb it! Stormfather. The tactical advantage!"

"Exactly."

"You don't sound enthusiastic."

"I am, dear," Navani said. "But this isn't the most ambitious idea we've had for this technique. Not by a faint breeze or a stormwind."

He frowned at her.

"It's all very technical and theoretical right now," Navani said, smiling. "But just wait. When you see the things the ardents are imagining—"

"Not you?" Adolin asked.

"I'm their patron, dear," Navani said, patting him on the arm. "I don't have time to make all of the diagrams and figures, even were I up to the task." She looked down at the gathered ardents and women scientists who were inspecting the floor of the parapet platform. "They suffer me."

"Surely it's more than that."

Perhaps in another life it could have been. She was sure some of them saw her as a colleague. Many, however, just saw her as the woman who sponsored them so she'd have new fabrials to show off at parties. Perhaps she was just that. A lighteyed lady of rank had to have some hobbies, didn't she?

"I assume you're here to escort me to the meeting?" The highprinces, abuzz about the assassin's attack, had demanded that Elhokar meet with them today.

Adolin nodded, twitching and glancing over his shoulder as he heard a noise, instinctively stepping protectively to put himself between Navani and whatever it was. The noise, however, was just some workers taking the side off one of Dalinar's massive rolling bridges. Those were the main purpose of these grounds; she'd merely appropriated the area for her test.

She held her arm out to him. "You're as bad as your father."

"Perhaps I am," he said, taking her arm. That Plated hand of his might have made some women uncomfortable, but she'd been around Plate far, far more often than most.

They started down the wide steps together. "Aunt," he said. "Have you been, uh, doing anything to encourage my father's advances? Between you two, I mean." For a boy who spent half his life flirting with anything in a dress, he certainly did blush a lot when he said that.

"Encourage him?" Navani said. "I did more than that, child. I practically had to *seduce* the man. Your father is certainly stubborn."

"I hadn't noticed," Adolin said dryly. "You realize how much more difficult you've made his position? He's trying to force the other highprinces to follow the Codes using the social constraints of honor, yet he's pointedly ignoring something similar."

"A bothersome tradition."

"You seem content to ignore only the ones you find bothersome, while expecting us to follow all the others."

"Of course," Navani said, smiling. "You haven't figured that out before now?"

Adolin's expression grew grim.

"Don't sulk," Navani said. "You're free from the causal for now, as Jasnah has apparently decided to gallivant off someplace. I won't have the chance to marry you off quite yet, at least not until she reappears." Knowing her, that could be tomorrow—or it could be months from now.

"I'm not sulking," Adolin said.

"Of course you aren't," she said, patting his armored arm as they reached the bottom of the steps. "Let's get to the palace. I don't know if your father will be able to delay the meeting for us if we're tardy."

And when they were spoken of by the common folk, the Releasers claimed to be misjudged because of the dreadful nature of their power; and when they dealt with others, always were they firm in their claim that other epithets, notably "Dustbringers," often heard in the common speech, were unacceptable substitutions, in particular for their similarity to the word "Voidbringers." They did also exercise anger in great prejudice regarding it, though to many who speak, there was little difference between these two assemblies.

—From *Words of Radiance,* chapter 17, page 11

Shallan awoke as a new woman.

She wasn't yet completely certain who that woman was, but she knew who that woman was not. She was not the same frightened girl who had suffered the storms of a broken home. She was not the same naive woman who had tried to steal from Jasnah Kholin. She was not the same woman who had been deceived by Kabsal and then Tyn.

That did not mean she was not still frightened or naive. She was both. But she was also tired. Tired of being shoved around, tired of being misled, tired of being dismissed. During the trip with Tvlakv, she'd pretended she could lead and take charge. She no longer felt the need to pretend.

She knelt beside one of Tyn's trunks. She'd resisted letting the men break it open—she wanted a few trunks for keeping clothing—but her search of the tent hadn't found the proper key.

"Pattern," she said. "Can you look inside of this? Squeeze in through the keyhole?"

"Mmm . . ." Pattern moved onto the side of the trunk, then shrank down to be the size of her thumbnail. He moved in easily. She heard his voice from inside. "Dark."

"Drat," she said, fishing out a sphere and holding it up to the keyhole. "Does that help?"

"I see a pattern," he said.

"A pattern? What kind of—"

Click.

Shallan started, then reached to lift the lid of the trunk. Pattern buzzed happily inside.

"You unlocked it."

"A pattern," he said happily.

"You can move things?"

"Push a little here and there," he said. "Very little strength on this side. Mmm . . ."

The trunk was filled with clothing and had a pouch of spheres in a black cloth bag. Both would be very useful. Shallan searched through and found a dress with fine embroidery and a modern cut. Tyn needed it, of course, for times when she pretended to be of a higher status. Shallan put it on, found it loose through the bust but otherwise acceptable, then did her face and hair at the mirror using the dead woman's makeup and brushes.

When she left the tent that morning, she felt—for the first time in what seemed ages—like a true lighteyed woman. That was well, for today she would finally reach the Shattered Plains. And, hopefully, destiny.

She strode out into the morning light. Her men worked alongside the caravan's parshmen to break down camp. With Tyn's guards dead, the only armed force in the camp belonged to Shallan.

Vathah fell into step beside her. "We burned the bodies last night as you instructed, Brightness. And another guard patrol stopped by this morning while you were getting ready. They obviously wanted us to know that they intend to keep the peace. If someone camps in this spot and finds the bones of Tyn and her soldiers in the ashes, it could lead to questions. I don't know that the caravan workers will keep your secret if asked."

"Thank you," Shallan said. "Have one of the men gather the bones into a sack. I'll deal with them."

Had she really just said that?

Vathah nodded curtly, as if this were the expected answer. "Some of the men are uncomfortable, now that we're so close to the warcamps."

"Do you still think I'm incapable of keeping my promises to them?"

He actually smiled. "No. I think I've been right convinced, Brightness."

"Well then?"

"I'll reassure them," he said.

"Excellent." They parted ways as Shallan sought out Macob. When she found him, the bearded, aging caravan trademaster bowed to her with far more respect than he'd ever shown her before. He'd already heard about the Shardblade.

"I will need one of your men to run down to the warcamps and find me a palanquin," Shallan said. "Sending one of my soldiers is currently impossible." She wouldn't risk them being recognized and imprisoned.

"Certainly," Macob said, voice stiff. "The price will be . . ."

She gave him a pointed stare.

". . . paid out of my own purse, as thanks to you for a safe arrival." He put an odd emphasis on the word *safe*, as if it were of questionable merit in the sentence.

"And the price for your discretion?" Shallan asked.

"My discretion can always be assured, Brightness," the man said. "And my lips are not the ones that should trouble you."

True enough.

He climbed up into his wagon. "One of my men will run on ahead, and we will send a palanquin back for you. With that, I bid you farewell. I hope it is not insulting for me to say, Brightness, that I hope we never meet again."

"Then our views in that regard are in agreement."

He nodded to her and tapped his chull. The wagon rolled away.

"I listened to them last night," Pattern said with a buzzing, excited voice from the back of her dress. "Is nonexistence really such a fascinating concept to humans?"

"They spoke of death, did they?" Shallan asked.

"They kept wondering if you would 'come for them.' I realize that nonexistence is not something to look forward to, but they talked on, and on, and *on* about it. Fascinating indeed."

"Well, keep your ears open, Pattern. I suspect this day is going to only get *more* interesting." She walked back toward the tent.

"But, I don't have ears," he said. "Ah yes. A metaphor? Such delicious lies. I will remember that idiom."

⁘

The Alethi warcamps were so much *more* than Shallan had expected them to be. Ten compact cities in a row, each casting up smoke from thousands of fires. Lines of caravans streamed in and out, passing the crater rims that made up their walls. Each camp flew hundreds of banners proclaiming the presence of high-ranked lighteyes.

As the palanquin carried her down a slope, she was truly *stunned* at the magnitude of the population. Stormfather! She'd once considered the regional fair on her father's lands to be a huge gathering. How many mouths were there to feed down below? How much water did they require from each highstorm?

Her palanquin lurched. She'd left the wagon behind; the chulls belonged to Macob. She'd try to sell the wagon, if it remained when she sent her men for it later. For now, she rode the palanquin, which was carried by parshmen under the watchful eyes of a lighteyed man who owned them and rented out the vehicle. He strolled along ahead. The irony of being carried on the backs of Voidbringers as she entered the warcamps was not lost on her.

Behind the vehicle marched Vathah and her eighteen guards, then her five slaves, who carried her trunks. She'd dressed them in shoes and clothing from the merchants, but you couldn't cover up months of slavery with a new outfit—and the soldiers weren't much better. Their uniforms had only been washed when a highstorm hit, and that was more of a *douse* than a *wash*. The occasional whiff she got of them was why she had them marching *behind* her palanquin.

She hoped she wasn't as bad. She had Tyn's perfume, but the Alethi elite preferred frequent bathing and a clean scent—part of the wisdom of the Heralds. *Wash with the coming highstorm, both servant and brightlord, to ward away rotspren and purify the body.*

She'd done what she could with some pails of water, but did not have the luxury of stopping to prepare more properly. She needed the protection of a highprince, and quickly. Now that she had arrived, the immensity of her tasks struck her afresh: Discover what Jasnah had been looking for on the Shattered Plains. Use the information there to persuade the Alethi leadership to take measures against the parshmen. Investigate the people Tyn had been meeting with and . . . do what? Scam them somehow? Find out what they knew about Urithiru, deflect their attention away from her brothers, and perhaps find a way to repay them for what they'd done to Jasnah?

So *much* to do. She would need resources. Dalinar Kholin was her best hope for that.

"But will he take me in?" she whispered.

"Mmmm?" Pattern said from the seat nearby.

"I will need him as a patron. If Tyn's sources know that Jasnah is dead, then Dalinar probably knows as well. How will he react to my unexpected arrival? Will he take her books, pat me on the head, and send me back to Jah Keved? The Kholin house has no need of a bond to a minor Veden like me. And I . . . I'm just rambling out loud, aren't I?"

"Mmmm," Pattern said. He sounded drowsy, though she didn't know if spren could get tired.

Her anxiety grew as her procession approached the warcamps. Tyn had been adamant that Shallan *not* ask for Dalinar's protection, as that would make her beholden to him. Shallan had killed the woman, but she still respected Tyn's opinion. Was there merit to what she'd said about Dalinar?

A knock came at her palanquin window. "We're going to have the parshmen put you down for a bit," Vathah said. "Need to ask around and see where the highprince is."

"Fine."

She waited impatiently. They must have sent the palanquin owner on the errand—Vathah was as nervous as she was at the idea of sending one of his men into the warcamps alone. She eventually heard a muffled conversation outside, and Vathah returned, his boots scraping rock. She drew back the curtain, looking up at him.

"Dalinar Kholin is with the king," Vathah said. "The whole lot of the highprinces are there." He looked disturbed as he turned toward the warcamps. "Something's on the winds, Brightness." He squinted. "Too many patrols. Lots of soldiers out. The palanquin owner won't say, but from the sound of it, something happened recently. Something deadly."

"Take me to the king, then," Shallan said.

Vathah raised an eyebrow at her. The king of Alethkar was arguably the most powerful man in the world. "You aren't going to kill him, are you?" Vathah asked softly, leaning down.

"*What?*"

"I figure it's one reason a woman would have . . . you know." He didn't meet her eyes. "Get close, summon the thing, have it through a man's chest before anyone knows what happened."

"I'm not going to kill your king," she said, amused.

"Wouldn't care if you did," Vathah said softly. "Almost hope you would. He's a child wearing his father's clothes, that one is. Everything's gotten worse for Alethkar since he took the throne. But my men, we'd have a hard time getting away if you did something like that. Hard time indeed."

"I will keep my promise."

He nodded, and she let the drapes fall back down over the palanquin window. Stormfather. Give a woman a Shardblade, get her close . . . Had anyone ever tried that? They must have, though thinking about it made her sick.

The palanquin turned northward. Passing the warcamps took a long time; they were enormous. Eventually, she peeked out and saw a tall hill to the left with a building sculpted from—and onto—the stone of the top. A palace?

What if she did convince Brightlord Dalinar to take her in and trust her with Jasnah's research? What would she be in Dalinar's household? A lesser scribe, to be tucked aside and ignored? That was how she'd spent most of her life. She found herself suddenly, passionately determined *not* to let it happen again. She needed the freedom and the funding to investigate Urithiru and Jasnah's murder. Shallan would accept nothing else. She *could* accept nothing else.

So make it happen, she thought.

Would that it were so easy as wishing. As the palanquin turned up the switchbacks leading to the palace, her new satchel—from Tyn's things— shook and hit her foot. She picked it up and flipped through the pages inside, finding the crinkled sketch of Bluth as she'd imagined him. A hero instead of a slaver.

"Mmmmm . . ." Pattern said from the seat beside her.

"This picture is a lie," Shallan said.

"Yes."

"And yet it isn't. This is what he became, at the end. To a small degree."

"Yes."

"So what is the lie, and what is the truth?"

Pattern hummed softly to himself, like a contented axehound before the hearth. Shallan fingered the picture, smoothing it. Then she pulled out a sketchpad and a pencil, and started drawing. It was a difficult task in the lurching palanquin; this would not be her finest drawing. Still, her fingers moved across the sketch with an intensity she hadn't felt in weeks.

Broad lines at first, to fix the image in her head. She wasn't copying a Memory this time. She was searching for something nebulous: a lie that could be real if she could just imagine it correctly.

She scratched frantically at the paper, hunkering down, and soon stopped feeling the rhythm of the porters' steps. She saw only the drawing, knew only the emotions she bled onto that page. Jasnah's determination. Tyn's confidence. A sense of *rightness* that she could not describe, but which she drew from her brother Helaran, the best person she'd ever known.

It all *poured* from her into the pencil and onto the page. Streaks and lines that became shadows and patterns that became figures and faces. A quick sketch, hurried, yet one alive. It depicted Shallan as a confident young woman standing before Dalinar Kholin, as she imagined him. She'd put him in Shardplate as he, and those around him, studied Shallan with penetrating consternation. She stood strong, hand raised toward them as she spoke with confidence and power. No trembling here. No fear of confrontation.

This is what I would have been, Shallan thought, *if I had not been raised in a household of fear. So this is what I will be today.*

It wasn't a lie. It was a different truth.

A knock came at the palanquin's door. It had stopped moving; she'd barely noticed. With a nod to herself, she folded the sketch and slipped it into the pocket of her safehand sleeve. Then she stepped out of the vehicle and onto cold rock. She felt invigorated, and realized she had sucked in a tiny amount of Stormlight without meaning to.

The palace was both finer and more mundane than she might have expected. Certainly, this was a warcamp, and so the king's seat wouldn't match the majesty of the royal dwellings of Kharbranth. At the same time, it was amazing that such a structure could have been crafted here, away from the culture and resources of Alethkar proper. The towering stone fortress of sculpted rock, several stories high, perched at the pinnacle of the hill.

"Vathah, Gaz," she said. "Attend me. The rest of you, take up position here. I will send word."

They saluted her; she wasn't certain if that was appropriate or not. She strode forward, and noticed with amusement that she'd chosen one of the tallest of the deserters and one of the shortest to accompany her, and so when they flanked her, it created an even slope of height: Vathah, herself, Gaz. Had she really just chosen her guards based on aesthetic appeal?

The front gates of the palace complex faced west, and here Shallan found a large group of guards standing before open doors that led to a deep tunnel of a corridor into the hill itself. Sixteen guards at the door? She had read that King Elhokar was paranoid, but this seemed excessive.

"You'll need to announce me, Vathah," she said softly as they walked up. "As?"

"Brightness Shallan Davar, ward of Jasnah Kholin and causal betrothed of Adolin Kholin. Wait to say it until I indicate."

The grizzled man nodded, hand on his axe. Shallan didn't share his discomfort. If anything, she was *excited*. She strode by the guards with head held high, acting as if she belonged.

They let her pass.

Shallan almost stumbled. Over a dozen guards at the door, and they didn't challenge her. Several raised hands as if to do so—she saw this from the corner of her eye—but they backed down into silence. Vathah snorted softly from beside her as they entered the tunnel-like corridor beyond the gates.

The acoustics caught echoing whispers as the guards at the door conversed. Finally, one of them did call out after her. ". . . Brightness?"

She stopped, turning toward them and raising an eyebrow.

"I'm sorry, Brightness," the guard called. "But you are . . . ?"

She nodded to Vathah.

"You don't recognize Brightness Davar?" he barked. "The causal *betrothed* of Brightlord Adolin Kholin?"

The guards hushed, and Shallan turned around to continue on her way. The conversation behind started up again almost immediately, loud enough this time that she could catch a few words. ". . . never can keep track of that man's women . . ."

They reached an intersection. Shallan looked one way, then the other. "Upward, I'd guess," she said.

"Kings do like to be at the top of everything," Vathah said. "Attitude might get you past the outer door, Brightness, but it's not going to get you in to see Kholin."

"Are you *really* his betrothed?" Gaz asked nervously, scratching at his eye patch.

"Last I checked," Shallan said, leading the way. "Which, granted, was before my ship sank." She wasn't worried about getting in to see Kholin. She'd at least get an audience.

They continued upward, asking servants for directions. Those scuttled about in clusters, jumping when spoken to. Shallan recognized that kind of timidity. Was the king as terrible a master as her father had been?

As they went higher, the structure seemed less like a fortress and more like a palace. There were reliefs on the walls, mosaics on the floor, carved shutters, an increasing number of windows. By the time they approached the king's conference chamber near the top, wood trim framed the stone walls, with silver and gold leaf worked into the carvings. Lamps held massive sapphires, beyond the size of ordinary denominations, radiating bright blue light. At least she wouldn't lack for Stormlight, should she need it.

The passage into the king's conference room was *clogged* with men. Soldiers in a dozen different uniforms.

"Damnation," Gaz said. "Those are Sadeas's colors there."

"And Thanadal, and Aladar, and Ruthar . . ." Vathah said. "He's meeting with all the highprinces, as I said."

Shallan could pick out factions easily, dredging from her studies of Jasnah's book the names—and heraldry—of all ten highprinces. Sadeas's soldiers chatted with those of Highprince Ruthar and Highprince Aladar. Dalinar's stood alone, and Shallan could sense hostility between them and the others in the hallway.

Dalinar's guards had very few lighteyes among them. That was odd. And did that one man at the door look familiar? The tall darkeyed man with the blue coat that went down to his knees. The man with the shoulder-length hair, curling slightly . . . He was speaking in a low voice with another soldier, who was one of the men from the gates below.

"Looks like they beat us up here," Vathah said softly.

The man turned and looked her right in the eyes, then glanced down toward her feet.

Oh no.

The man—an officer, by the uniform—strode directly toward her. He ignored the hostile stares of the other highprinces' soldiers as he walked right up to Shallan. "Prince Adolin," he said flatly, "is engaged to a Horneater?"

She'd almost forgotten the encounter two days outside of the warcamps. *I'm going to strangle that—* She cut off, feeling a stab of depression. She *had* ended up killing Tyn.

"Obviously not," Shallan said, raising her chin and not using the Horneater accent. "I was traveling alone through the wilderness. Revealing my true identity did not seem prudent."

The man grunted. "Where are my boots?"

"Is this how you address a lighteyed lady of rank?"

"It's how I address a thief," the man said. "I'd just gotten those boots."

"I'll have a dozen new pairs sent to you," Shallan said. "After I have spoken with Highprince Dalinar."

"You think I'm going to let you see him?"

"You think you get to choose?"

"I'm captain of his guard, woman."

Blast, she thought. That was going to be inconvenient. At least she wasn't trembling from the confrontation. She really *was* past that. Finally.

"Well tell me, *Captain,*" she said. "What is your name?"

"Kaladin." Odd. That sounded like a lighteyes's name.

"Excellent. Now I have a name to use when I tell the highprince about you. He's not going to like his son's betrothed being treated this way."

Kaladin waved to several of his soldiers. The men in blue surrounded her and Vathah and . . .

Where had Gaz gotten off to?

She turned and found him backing down the corridor. Kaladin spotted him, and started visibly.

"Gaz?" Kaladin demanded. "What is this?"

"Uh . . ." The one-eyed man stammered. "Lordsh . . . Um, Kaladin. You're, ah, an officer? So things have been going well for you . . ."

"You know this man?" Shallan asked Kaladin.

"He tried to get me killed," Kaladin said, voice even. "On multiple occasions. He's one of the most hateful little rats I've ever known."

Great.

"You're not Adolin's betrothed," Kaladin said, meeting her gaze as several of his men gleefully seized Gaz, who had backed into other guards coming up from below. "Adolin's betrothed has drowned. *You* are an op-

426

portunist with a very bad sense of timing. I doubt that Dalinar Kholin will be pleased to find a swindler trying to capitalize on the death of his niece."

She finally started to feel nervous. Vathah glanced at her, obviously worried that this Kaladin's guesses were correct. Shallan steadied herself and reached into her safepouch, pulling out a piece of paper she'd found in Jasnah's notes. "Is Highlady Navani in that room?"

Kaladin didn't reply.

"Show her this, please," Shallan said.

Kaladin hesitated, then took the sheet. He looked it over, but obviously couldn't tell that he was holding it upside down. It was one of the written communications between Jasnah and her mother, arranging for the causal. Communicated via spanreed, there would be two copies—the one that had been written on Jasnah's side, and the one on Brightness Navani's side.

"We'll see," Kaladin said.

"We'll . . ." Shallan found herself sputtering. If she couldn't get in to see Dalinar, then . . . Then . . . Storm this man! She took his arm in her free-hand as he turned to give orders to his men. "Is this really all because I lied to you?" she demanded more softly.

He looked back at her. "It's about doing my job."

"Your job is to be offensive and asinine?"

"No, I'm offensive and asinine on my own time too. My *job* is to keep people like you away from Dalinar Kholin."

"I guarantee he will want to see me."

"Well, forgive me for not trusting the word of a Horneater princess. Would you like some shells to chew on while my men tow you away to the dungeons?"

All right, that's enough.

"The dungeons sound wonderful!" she said. "At least there, I'd be away from *you*, idiot man!"

"Only for a short time. I'd be by to interrogate you."

"What? I couldn't pick a more pleasant option? Like being executed?"

"You're assuming I could find a hangman willing to put up with your blathering long enough to fit the rope."

"Well, if you want to kill me, you could always let your breath do the job."

He reddened, and several guards nearby started snickering. They tried to stifle their reaction as Captain Kaladin looked at them.

"I should envy you," he said, turning back to her. "My *breath* needs to be up close to kill, while that face of yours can kill any man from a distance."

"Any man?" she asked. "Why, it's not working on you. I guess that's proof that you're not much of a man."

"I misspoke. I didn't mean *any* man, just males of your own species—but don't worry, I'll take care not to let our chulls get close."

"Oh? Your parents are in the area, then?"

His eyes widened, and for the first time she seemed to have really gotten under his skin. "My parents have nothing to do with this."

"Yes, that makes sense. I'd *expect* that they want nothing to do with you."

"At least my ancestors had the sense not to breed with a sponge!" he snapped, probably a reference to her red hair.

"At least I *know* my parentage!" she snapped back.

They glared at each other. Part of Shallan felt satisfaction at being able to make him lose his temper, though from the heat she felt in her face, she'd let go of hers as well. Jasnah would have been disappointed. How often had she tried to get Shallan to control her tongue? True wit was controlled wit. It shouldn't be allowed to run free, any more than an arrow should be loosed in a random direction.

For the first time, Shallan realized that the large hallway had grown silent. A great number of the soldiers and attendants were staring at her and the officer.

"Bah!" Kaladin shook her arm free of his—she hadn't let go after getting his attention earlier. "I revise my opinion of you. You're obviously a highborn lighteyes. Only they are capable of being *this* infuriating." He stalked away from her toward the doors to the king's chamber.

Nearby, Vathah relaxed visibly. "Getting into a shouting match with the head of Highprince Dalinar's guard?" he whispered to her. "Was that wise?"

"We created an incident," she said, calming herself. "Now Dalinar Kholin will hear of this one way or another. That guardsman won't be able to keep my arrival secret from him."

Vathah hesitated. "So it was part of the *plan*."

"Hardly," Shallan said. "I'm not nearly that clever. But it should work anyway." She looked to Gaz, who was released by Kaladin's guards so he could join the two of them, though all were still under careful watch.

"Even for a deserter," Vathah said under his breath, "you're a coward, Gaz."

Gaz just stared at the ground.

"How do you know him?" Shallan asked.

"He was a slave," Gaz said, "at the lumberyards where I used to work. Storming man. He's dangerous, Brightness. Violent, a troublemaker. I don't know how he got to such a high position in such a short time."

Kaladin hadn't entered the conference chamber. However, the doors cracked a moment later. The meeting appeared to be over, or at least on break. Several aides rushed in to see if their highprinces needed anything, and chatter started up among the guards. Captain Kaladin shot her a glance, then reluctantly entered, carrying her sheet of paper.

Shallan forced herself to stand with hands clasped before her—one sleeved, the other not—to keep herself from looking nervous. Eventually, Kaladin stepped back out, a look of annoyed resignation on his face. He pointed at her, then thumbed over his shoulder, indicating she could enter. His guards let her pass, though they restrained Vathah when he tried to follow her.

She waved him back, took a deep breath, then strode through the moving crowd of soldiers and aides, entering the king's conference chamber.

37

A MATTER OF PERSPECTIVE

Now, as each order was thus matched to the nature and temperament of the Herald it named patron, there was none more archetypal of this than the Stonewards, who followed after Talenelat'Elin, Stonesinew, Herald of War: they thought it a point of virtue to exemplify resolve, strength, and dependability. Alas, they took less care for imprudent practice of their stubbornness, even in the face of proven error.

—From *Words of Radiance,* chapter 13, page 1

The meeting finally reached a break. They weren't done—Stormfather, it didn't seem like they'd *ever* be done—but the arguing was over for the moment. Adolin stood, wounds along his leg and side protesting, and left his father and aunt to speak in hushed tones as the large chamber filled with a buzz of conversation.

How did Father stand it? A full two hours had passed, according to Navani's fabrial clock on the wall. Two hours of highprinces and their wives complaining about the Assassin in White. Nobody could agree on what should be done.

They all ignored the truth stabbing them in the face. Nothing *could* be done. Nothing other than Adolin staying alert and practicing, training to face the monster when he returned.

And you think you can beat him? When he can walk on walls and make the very spren of nature obey him?

It was a discomforting question. At his father's suggestion, Adolin had reluctantly changed out of his Plate and into something more appropriate. *We need to project confidence at this meeting*, Dalinar had said, *not fear*.

General Khal wore the armor instead, hiding in a room to the side with a strike force. Father seemed to think it unlikely the assassin would strike during the meeting. If the assassin wanted to kill the highprinces, he could take them much more easily alone, in the night. Attacking them all together, in the company of their guards and dozens of Shardbearers, seemed like it would be an imprudent decision. Indeed, there were Shards aplenty at this meeting. Three of the highprinces wore their Plate, and the others had Shardbearers in attendance. Abrobadar, Jakamav, Resi, Relis . . . Adolin had rarely seen so many collected together at once.

Would any of it matter? Accounts had been flooding in from around the world for weeks. Kings slaughtered. Ruling bodies decapitated all across Roshar. In Jah Keved, the assassin had reportedly killed dozens of soldiers bearing half-shard shields that could block his Blade, as well as *three* Shardbearers, including the king. It was a crisis that spanned the entire world, and one man was behind it. Assuming he was even a man.

Adolin found himself a cup of sweet wine at the edge of the room, poured by an eager servant in blue and gold. Orange wine, basically just juice. Adolin downed an entire cup anyway, then went looking for Relis. He needed to be doing *something* other than sitting and listening to people complain.

Fortunately, he'd concocted something while sitting there.

Relis, Ruthar's son and star Shardbearer, was a man with a face like a shovel—flat and wide, with a nose that seemed like it had been smashed. He wore a frilly outfit of green and yellow. It wasn't even interesting. He had the choice to wear anything, and he chose this?

He was a full Shardbearer, one of the few in the camps. He was also the current dueling champion—which, along with his parentage, made him of particular interest to Adolin. He stood speaking with his cousin Elit and a group of three of Sadeas's attendants: women in the traditional Vorin havah. One of those women, Melali, gave Adolin a pointed glare. She was as pretty as she'd ever been, her hair up in complex braids and stuck with hairspikes. What had he done to annoy her, again? It had been forever since they'd courted.

"Relis," Adolin said, raising his cup, "I just wanted you to know that I found it very brave of you to offer to fight the assassin yourself, when you spoke earlier. It is inspiring that you'd be willing to die for the Crown."

Relis scowled at Adolin. How *did* someone get a face so flat? Had he been dropped as a child? "You're assuming I'd lose."

"Well, of course you would," Adolin said, chuckling. "I mean, let's be honest, Relis. You've been sitting on your title for almost half a year. You haven't won a duel of any importance since you defeated Epinar."

"This from a man who spent years refusing almost all challenges," Melali said, looking Adolin up and down. "I'm surprised your daddy let you free to come talk. Isn't he afraid you might hurt yourself?"

"Nice to see you too, Melali," Adolin said. "How's your sister?"

"Off limits."

Oh, right. That was what he'd done. Honest mistake. "Relis," Adolin said. "You claim you'd face this assassin, yet you're frightened of dueling *me*?"

Relis spread his hands, one holding a shimmering goblet of red wine. "It's protocol, Adolin! I'll duel you once you fight up through the brackets for a year or two. I can't just take on any old challenger, particularly not in a bout with our Shards on the line!"

"Any old challenger?" Adolin said. "Relis, I'm one of the best there is."

"Are you?" Relis asked, smiling. "After that display with Eranniv?"

"Yes, Adolin," said Elit, Relis's short, balding cousin. "You've only had a handful of duels of any consequence in recent memory—in one of those you basically cheated, and in the second you won by sheer luck!"

Relis nodded. "If I bend the rules and accept your challenge, then it will break the stormwall. I'll have dozens of inferior swordsmen nipping at me."

"No you won't," Adolin said. "Because you won't be a Shardbearer any longer. You'll have lost to me."

"So confident," Relis said, chuckling, turning to Elit and the women. "Listen to him. He ignores the rankings for months, then leaps back in and assumes he can beat me."

"I'll wager both my Plate and Blade," Adolin said. "And my brother's Plate and Blade, along with the Shard I won from Eranniv. Five Shards to your two."

Elit started. The man was a Shardbearer with only the Plate—given to him by his cousin. He turned to Relis, looking hungry.

Relis paused. Then he closed his mouth and cocked his head lazily to the side as he met Adolin's eyes. "You're a fool, Kholin."

"I'm offering it here, before witnesses," Adolin said. "You win this bout, you take every Shard my family owns. What's stronger? Your fear or your greed?"

"My *pride*," Relis said. "No contest, Adolin."

Adolin ground his teeth. He'd hoped the duel with Eranniv would make others underestimate him, make them more likely to duel him. It wasn't working. Relis barked out a laugh. He held out his arm to Melali, and tugged her away, his attendants following.

Elit hesitated.

Well, it's better than nothing, Adolin thought, a plan forming. "What about you?" Adolin asked the cousin.

Elit looked him up and down. Adolin didn't know the man well. He was said to be a passable duelist, though he was often in his cousin's shadow.

But that *hunger*—Elit wanted to be a full Shardbearer.

"Elit?" Relis said.

"Same offer?" Elit said, meeting Adolin's gaze. "Your five to my one?"

What a terrible deal.

"Same offer," Adolin said.

"I'm in," Elit said.

Behind him, Ruthar's son groaned. He grabbed Elit by the shoulder, towing him to the side with a growl.

"You told me to fight up through the brackets," Adolin said to Relis. "I'm doing that."

"*Not* my cousin."

"Too late," Adolin said. "You heard it. The ladies heard it. When do we fight, Elit?"

"Seven days," Elit said. "On Chachel."

Seven days—a long wait, considering a challenge like this. So, he wanted time to train, did he? "How about tomorrow instead?"

Relis snarled at Adolin, a very un-Alethi display, and shoved his cousin farther away. "I can't see why you're so eager, Adolin. Shouldn't you focus on protecting that father of yours? It's always sad when a soldier lives long enough to see his wits go. Has he started wetting himself in public yet?"

Steady, Adolin told himself. Relis was trying to goad him, maybe get Adolin to take a hasty swing. That would let him petition to the king for redress and a voiding of all contracts with his house—including the dueling agreement with Elit. But the insult went too far. His companions gasped slightly, pulling away at the very un-Alethi bluntness.

Adolin didn't give in to the desperate goading. He had what he wanted. He wasn't certain what he could do about the assassin—but this, this was a way to help. Elit wasn't ranked highly, but he served Ruthar, who was—more and more—acting as Sadeas's right-hand man. Beating him would take Adolin one step closer to the real goal. A duel with Sadeas himself.

He turned to leave, and stopped short. Someone stood behind him—a stout man with a bulbous face and black curly hair. His complexion was ruddy, the nose too red, fine veins visible in his cheeks. The man had the arms of a soldier, despite his frivolous outfit—which was, Adolin admitted grudgingly, quite fashionable. Dark slacks that were trimmed with forest green silk, a short open coat over a stiff matching shirt. Scarf at the neck.

Torol Sadeas, highprince, Shardbearer, and the very man Adolin had been thinking of—the single person he hated most in the world.

"Another duel, young Adolin," Sadeas said, taking a sip of wine. "You really are determined to embarrass yourself out there. I still find it strange your father abandoned his prohibition of you dueling—indeed, I thought it a matter of honor to him."

Adolin pushed past Sadeas, not trusting himself to speak so much as a single word to this eel of a man. Sight of the man brought memories of stark panic as he watched Sadeas retreat from the field of battle to leave Adolin and his father alone and surrounded.

Havar, Perethom, and Ilamar—good soldiers, good friends—had died that day. They and six thousand more.

Sadeas grabbed Adolin's shoulder as he passed. "Think what you will, son," the man whispered, "but what I did was intended as a kindness to your father. A tip of the sword to an old ally."

"*Let. Go.*"

"If you lose your mind as you age, pray to the Almighty there are people like myself willing to give you a good death. People who care enough not to snicker, but instead hold the sword for you as you fall on it."

"I'll have your throat in my hands, Sadeas," Adolin hissed. "I'll squeeze and squeeze, then I'll sink my dagger into your gut and *twist*. A quick death is too good for you."

"Tsk," Sadeas said, smiling. "Careful. It's a full room. What if someone heard you threatening a highprince?"

The Alethi way. You could abandon an ally on the battlefield, and everyone could know it—but an offense in person, well, that just wouldn't do. *Society* would *frown* on that. Nalan's hand! His father was right about them all.

Adolin turned in a quick motion, reversing out of Sadeas's grip. His next moves were by instinct, his fingers balling, stepping in preparation to plant a fist in that smiling, self-satisfied face.

A hand fell on Adolin's shoulder, causing him to hesitate.

"I don't think that would be wise, Brightlord Adolin," said a soft but stern voice. It reminded Adolin of his father, though the timbre was off. He glanced at Amaram, who had stepped up beside him.

Tall, with a face like chipped stone, Brightlord Meridas Amaram was one of the only lighteyed men in the room who wore a proper uniform. As much as Adolin wished he himself could wear something more fashionable, he had come to realize the importance of the uniform as a symbol.

Adolin took a deep breath, lowering his fist. Amaram nodded to Sadeas, then turned Adolin by his shoulder and walked him away from the highprince.

"You mustn't let him provoke you, Your Highness," Amaram said softly. "He'll use you to embarrass your father, if he can."

They moved through the room full of chattering attendants. Drinks and finger food had been distributed. It had turned from a short break during the meeting into a full-blown party. Not surprising. With all the important lighteyes here, people would want to mingle and connive.

"Why do you remain with him, Amaram?" Adolin asked.

"He is my liege lord."

"You're of a rank that you could choose a new liege. Stormfather! You're a Shardbearer now. Nobody would even question you. Come to our camp. Join with Father."

"In doing that, I would create a divide," Amaram said softly. "So long as I remain with Sadeas, I can help bridge gaps. He trusts me. So does your father. My friendship with both is a step toward keeping this kingdom together."

"Sadeas will betray you."

"No. Highprince Sadeas and I have an understanding."

"We thought *we* had one. Then he set us up."

Amaram's expression grew distant. Even the way he walked was so full of decorum, straight back, nodding with respect to many they passed. The perfect lighteyed general—brilliantly capable, yet not lofty. A sword for his highprince to employ. He'd spent the majority of the war diligently training new troops and sending the best of them to Sadeas while guarding sections of Alethkar. Amaram was half the reason that Sadeas had been so effective out here on the Shattered Plains.

"Your father is a man who cannot bend," Amaram said. "I wouldn't have it any other way, Adolin—but it does mean that the man he has become is not someone who can work with Highprince Sadeas."

"And you're different?"

"Yes."

Adolin snorted. Amaram was one of the finest the kingdom had, a man with a sterling reputation. "I doubt that."

"Sadeas and I agree that the means we choose to reach an honorable goal are allowed to be distasteful. Your father and I agree on what that goal should be—a better Alethkar, a place without all of this squabbling. It is a matter of perspective. . . ."

He continued talking, but Adolin found his mind drifting. He'd heard enough of this speech from his father. If Amaram started quoting *The Way of Kings* at him, he'd probably scream. At least—

Who was *that*?

Gorgeous red hair. There wasn't a *single* lock of black in it. A slender build, so different from the curvaceous Alethi. A silken blue dress, simple yet elegant. Pale skin—it almost had a Shin look to it—matched by light blue eyes. A slight dusting of freckles under the eyes, giving her an exotic cast.

The young woman seemed to glide through the room. Adolin twisted about, watching her pass. She was so *different*.

"Ash's eyes!" Amaram said, chuckling. "You're still doing that, are you?"

Adolin pried his eyes away from the girl. "Doing what?"

"Letting your eyes be drawn by every flitting little thing that swishes by. You need to settle down, son. Pick one. Your mother would be mortified to find you still unwed."

"Jasnah's unwed too. She's a decade older than me." Assuming she was still alive, as Aunt Navani was convinced.

"Your cousin is hardly a role model in that regard." His tone implied more. *Or any regard.*

"*Look* at her, Amaram," Adolin said, craning to the side and watching the young woman approach his father. "That hair. Have you ever seen anything such a deep shade of red?"

"Veden, I'd warrant," Amaram said. "Horneater blood. There are family lines that pride themselves on it."

Veden. It couldn't be . . . Could it?

"Excuse me," Adolin said, breaking away from Amaram and shoving—politely—his way over to where the young woman was speaking to his father and his aunt.

"Brightlady Jasnah did go down with the ship, I'm afraid," the woman was saying. "I'm sorry for your loss . . ."

Now, as the Windrunners were thus engaged, arose the event which has hitherto been referenced: namely, that discovery of some wicked thing of eminence, though whether it be some rogueries among the Radiants' adherents or of some external origin, Avena would not suggest.

—From *Words of Radiance*, chapter 38, page 6

". . . sorry for your loss," Shallan said. "I have brought with me what things of Jasnah's I was able to recover. My men have them outside."

She found it surprisingly difficult to say the words with an even tone. She'd grieved for Jasnah during her weeks traveling, yet speaking of the death—remembering that terrible night—returned the emotions like surging waves, threatening to overwhelm again.

The image she'd drawn of herself came to her rescue. She could be that woman today—and that woman, while not emotionless, could push through the loss. She focused her attention on the moment, and the task at hand—specifically the two people in front of her. Dalinar and Navani Kholin.

The highprince was exactly what she'd expected him to be: a man with blunted features, short black hair silvering at the sides. His stiff uniform made him seem the only one in the room who knew anything about combat. She wondered if those bruises on his face were the result of the campaign against the Parshendi. Navani looked like a version of Jasnah twenty years older, still pretty, though with a motherly air. Shallan could never imagine Jasnah being motherly.

Navani had been smiling as Shallan approached, but now that levity was gone. *She still had hope for her daughter,* Shallan thought as the woman sat down in a nearby seat. *I just crushed it.*

"I thank you for bringing us this news," Brightlord Dalinar said. "It is . . . good to have confirmation."

It felt terrible. Not just to be reminded of the death, but to weigh others down with it as well. "I have information for you," Shallan said, trying to be delicate. "About the things Jasnah was working on."

"More about those parshmen?" Navani snapped. "Storms, that woman was too fascinated by them. Ever since she got it into her head that she was to blame for Gavilar's death."

What was this? That wasn't a side of all this that Shallan had ever heard.

"Her research can wait," Navani said, eyes fierce. "I want to know exactly what happened when you think you saw her die. Precisely as you remember it, girl. No details passed over."

"Perhaps after the meeting . . ." Dalinar said, resting a hand on Navani's shoulder. The touch was surprisingly tender. Was this not his brother's wife? That look in his eyes; was that familial affection for his sister, or was it something more?

"No, Dalinar," Navani said. "Now. I would hear it now."

Shallan took a deep breath, preparing to begin, steeling herself against the emotions—and finding herself surprisingly in control. As she gathered her thoughts, she noticed a blond-haired young man watching her. That would likely be Adolin. He was handsome, as rumors indicated, and wore a blue uniform like his father. And yet Adolin's was somehow more . . . stylish? Was that the right word? She liked how his somewhat unruly hair contrasted with the crisp uniform. It made him seem more real, less picturesque.

She turned back to Navani. "I woke in the middle of the night to shouting and the smell of smoke. I opened my door to unfamiliar men crowded around the doorway to Jasnah's cabin, across the companionway from my own. They had her body on the floor, and . . . Brightness, I watched them stab her through the heart. I'm sorry."

Navani tensed, head flinching, as if she'd been slapped.

Shallan continued. She tried to give Navani as much truth as she could, but obviously the things Shallan had done—weaving light, Soulcasting the ship—weren't wise to share, at least for now. Instead, she indicated that she'd barricaded herself in her cabin, a lie she'd already prepared.

"I heard the men yelling up above as they were being executed, one by one," Shallan said. "I realized that the only hope I could give them was a crisis for the brigands, so I used the torch I'd taken and set the ship on fire."

"On *fire?*" Navani asked, horrified. "With my daughter unconscious?"

"Navani—" Dalinar said, squeezing her shoulder.

"You doomed her," Navani said, locking eyes with Shallan. "Jasnah wouldn't have been able to swim, like the others. She—"

"Navani," Dalinar repeated, more firmly. "This child's choice was a good one. You can hardly expect her to have taken on a band of men single-handed. And what she saw . . . Jasnah was not unconscious, Navani. It was too late to do anything for her at that point."

The woman took a deep breath, obviously struggling to keep her emotions in check. "I . . . apologize," she said to Shallan. "I am not myself at the moment, and I stray toward the irrational. Thank . . . thank you for bringing word to us." She stood. "Excuse me."

Dalinar nodded, letting her make a reasonably graceful exit. Shallan stepped back, hands clasped before herself, feeling impotent and strangely ashamed as she watched Navani leave. She hadn't expected that to go particularly well. And it hadn't.

She took the moment to check on Pattern, who was on her skirt, practically invisible. Even if he was noticed, he'd be thought an odd part of the fabric design—assuming, that was, he did as she'd ordered and didn't move or speak.

"I assume your trip here was an ordeal," Dalinar said, turning to Shallan. "Shipwrecked in the Frostlands?"

"Yes. Fortunately, I met with a caravan and traveled with them this way. We did encounter bandits, I regret to say, but were rescued by the timely arrival of some soldiers."

"Soldiers?" Dalinar said, surprised. "From what banner?"

"They did not say," Shallan replied. "I take it they were formerly of the Shattered Plains."

"Deserters?"

"I have not asked for specifics, Brightlord," Shallan said. "But I *did* promise them clemency for previous crimes, in recognition of their act of nobility. They saved dozens of lives. Everyone in the caravan I joined can vouch for the bravery of these men. I suspect they sought atonement and a chance to start over."

"I will see that the king seals pardons for them," Dalinar said. "Prepare a list for me. Hanging soldiers always feels like a waste."

Shallan relaxed. One item dealt with.

"There is another matter of some delicacy we must discuss, Brightlord," Shallan said. They both turned toward Adolin, loitering nearby. He smiled.

And he *did* have a very nice smile.

When Jasnah had first explained the causal to her, Shallan's interest had been completely abstract. Marriage into a powerful Alethi house? Allies for her brothers? Legitimacy, and a way to continue working with Jasnah for the salvation of the world? These had seemed like wonderful things.

Looking at Adolin's grin, however, she didn't consider *any* of those advantages. Her pains of speaking of Jasnah didn't fade completely, but she found it much easier to ignore them when looking at him. She found herself blushing.

This, she thought, *could be dangerous.*

Adolin stepped up to join them, the hum of conversation all around giving them some privacy within the crowd. He had found a cup of orange wine for her somewhere, which he held out. "Shallan Davar?" he asked.

"Um . . ." Was she? Oh, right. She took the wine. "Yes?"

"Adolin Kholin," he said. "I am sorry to hear of your hardships. We will need to speak to the king of his sister. I can spare you that task, if I might go in your place."

"Thank you," Shallan said. "But I would prefer to see him myself."

"Of course," Adolin said. "As for our . . . involvement. It *did* make a lot more sense when you were Jasnah's ward, didn't it?"

"Probably."

"Though, now that you're here, perhaps we should go for a walk and just see how things feel."

"I like to walk," Shallan said. *Stupid! Quick, say something witty.* "Um. Your hair is nice."

A part of her—the part trained by Tyn—groaned.

"My hair?" Adolin said, touching it.

"Yes," Shallan said, trying to get her sluggish brain working again. "Blond hair isn't often seen in Jah Keved."

"Some people see it as a mark of my bloodline being impure."

"Funny. They say the same about me because of my hair." She smiled at him. That seemed the right move, since he smiled back. Her verbal recovery hadn't been the deftest of her career, but she couldn't be doing too poorly, so long as he was smiling.

Dalinar cleared his throat. Shallan blinked. She'd completely forgotten that the highprince was there.

"Adolin," he said, "fetch me some wine."

"Father?" Adolin turned to him. "Oh. All right, then." He walked off. Ash's *eyes,* that man was handsome. She turned to Dalinar who, well, wasn't. Oh, he was distinguished, but his nose had been broken at some point, and his face was a tad unfortunate. The bruises didn't help either.

In fact, he was downright intimidating.

"I would know more of you," he said softly, "the precise status of your family, and why you are so eager to be involved with my son."

"My family is destitute," Shallan said. Frankness seemed the right approach with this man. "My father is dead, though the people to whom we owe money do not yet know it. I had not considered a union with Adolin until Jasnah suggested it, but I would seize it eagerly, if allowed. Marriage into your house would provide my family with a great deal of protection."

She still didn't know what to do about the Soulcaster her brothers owed. One step at a time.

Dalinar grunted. He wouldn't have expected her to be so direct. "So you have nothing to offer," he said.

"From what Jasnah said to me of your opinions," Shallan said, "I did not assume that my monetary or political offerings would be your first consideration. If such a union was your goal, you'd have had Prince Adolin married off years ago." She winced at her forwardness. "With all due respect, Brightlord."

"No offense taken," Dalinar said. "I like it when people are direct. Just because I want to let my son have a say in the matter doesn't mean I don't want him to marry well. A woman from a minor foreign house who professes her family is destitute and who brings nothing to the union?"

"I did not say I could offer nothing," Shallan replied. "Brightlord, how many wards has Jasnah Kholin taken in the last ten years?"

"None that I know of," he admitted.

"Do you know how many she has turned away?"

"I've an inkling."

"Yet she took me. Might that not constitute an endorsement of what I can offer?"

Dalinar nodded slowly. "We will maintain the causal for now," he said. "The reason I agreed to it in the first place still stands—I want Adolin to be seen as unavailable to those who would manipulate him for political gain. If you can somehow persuade me, Brightness Navani, and of course the lad himself, we can progress the causal to a full betrothal. In the meantime, I'll give you a position among my lesser clerks. You can prove yourself there."

The offer, though generous, felt like ropes tightening about her. The stipend of a lesser clerk would be enough to live on, but nothing to brag about. And she had no doubt that Dalinar would be watching her. Those eyes of his were scarily discerning. She wouldn't be able to move without her actions being reported to him.

His charity would be her prison.

"That is generous of you, Brightlord," she found herself saying, "but I actually have—"

"Dalinar!" one of the others in the room called. "Are we going to start this meeting again sometime today, or am I going to have to order in a proper dinner!"

Dalinar turned toward a plump, bearded man in traditional clothing—an open-fronted robe over a loose shirt and warrior's skirt, called a takama. *Highprince Sebarial,* Shallan thought. Jasnah's notes dismissed him as obnoxious and useless. She'd had kinder words even for Highprince Sadeas, whom she had noted was not to be trusted.

"Fine, fine, Sebarial," Dalinar said, breaking away from Shallan and walking to a group of seats in the center of the room. He settled down in one beside the desk there. A proud man with a prominent nose settled down next to him. That would be the king, Elhokar. He was younger than Shallan had pictured. Why had Sebarial called on Dalinar to reconvene the meeting, and not the king?

The next few moments were a test of Shallan's preparation as highborn men and women settled themselves in the lavish chairs. Beside each one was a small table and behind that, a master-servant for important needs. A number of parshmen kept the tables filled with wine, nuts, and fresh and dried fruit. Shallan shivered each time one of those passed her.

She counted the highprinces off in her head. Sadeas was easy to pick out, red-faced from visible veins under the skin, like her father had displayed after drinking. Others nodded to him and let him seat himself first. He seemed to command as much respect as Dalinar. His wife, Ialai, was a slender-necked woman with thick lips, large bust, and a wide mouth. Jasnah had noted that she was as shrewd as her husband.

Two highprinces sat to either side of the couple. One was Aladar, a renowned duelist. The short man was listed in Jasnah's notes as a powerful highprince, fond of taking risks, known to gamble in the type of games of random chance that the devotaries forbade. He and Sadeas seemed to be on very friendly terms. Weren't they enemies? She'd read that they often squabbled over lands. Well, that was obviously a broken stone, for they seemed united as they regarded Dalinar.

Joining them were Highprince Ruthar and his wife. Jasnah considered them to be little more than thieves, but warned that the pair were dangerous and opportunistic.

The room seemed oriented so that all eyes were on those two factions. The king and Dalinar against Sadeas, Ruthar, and Aladar. Obviously, the political alignments had changed since Jasnah made her notes.

The room hushed, and nobody seemed to care that Shallan was watching. Adolin took a seat behind his father, next to a younger man in spectacles and an empty seat probably vacated by Navani. Shallan carefully rounded the room—the peripheries were clogged with guards, attendants, and even some men in Shardplate—getting out of Dalinar's direct line of sight, just in case he noticed her and decided to eject her.

Brightlady Jayla Ruthar spoke first, leaning forward over clasped hands. "Your Majesty," she said, "I fear that our conversation this day has run in circles, and that nothing is being accomplished. Your safety is, of course, our greatest concern."

Across the circle of highprinces, Sebarial snorted loudly as he chewed on slices of melon. Everyone else seemed to pointedly ignore the obnoxious, bearded man.

"Yes," Aladar said. "The Assassin in White. We *must* do something. I will not wait in my palace to be assassinated."

"He is murdering princes and kings all across the world!" Roion added. The man looked like a turtle to Shallan, with those hunched shoulders and that balding head. What had Jasnah said about him . . . ?

That he's a coward, Shallan thought. *He always chooses the safe option.*

"We must present a unified Alethkar," Hatham said—she recognized him immediately, with that long neck and refined way of speaking. "We must not allow ourselves to be attacked one at a time, and we must not squabble."

"That's precisely why you should follow my commands," the king said, frowning at the highprinces.

"No," Ruthar said, "it is why we must abandon these ludicrous restrictions you have placed upon us, Your Majesty! This is not a time to look foolish before the world."

"Listen to Ruthar," Sebarial said dryly, leaning back in his chair. "He's an expert at looking like a fool."

The arguing continued, and Shallan got a better feel for the room. There were actually three factions. Dalinar and the king, the team with Sadeas, and what she dubbed the peacemakers. Led by Hatham—who seemed, when he spoke, the most natural politician in the room—this third group sought to mediate.

So that's what it's really about, she thought, listening as Ruthar argued with the king and Adolin Kholin. *They're each trying to persuade these neutral highprinces to join their faction.*

Dalinar said little. The same for Sadeas, who seemed content to let Highprince Ruthar and his wife speak for him. The two watched each other, Dalinar with a neutral expression, Sadeas with a faint smile. It seemed innocent enough until you saw their eyes. Locked on to one another, rarely blinking.

There was a storm in this room. A silent one.

Everyone seemed to fall into one of the three factions except for Sebarial, who kept rolling his eyes, occasionally throwing out commentary that bordered on the obscene. He obviously made the other Alethi, with their haughty airs, uncomfortable.

Shallan slowly picked apart the conversation's subtext. This talk of prohibitions and rules placed by the king . . . it wasn't the rules *themselves* that seemed to matter, but the authority behind them. How much would the highprinces submit to the king, and how much autonomy could they demand? It was fascinating.

Right up to the moment when one of them mentioned her.

"Wait," said Vamah—one of the neutral highprinces. "Who is that girl over there? Does someone have a Veden in their retinue?"

"She was speaking with Dalinar," Roion said. "Is there news of Jah Keved that you're keeping from us, Dalinar?"

"You, girl," said Ialai Sadeas. "What can you tell us of your homeland's succession war? Do you have information on this assassin? Why would someone in the employ of the Parshendi seek to undermine *your* throne?"

All eyes in the room turned toward Shallan. She felt a moment of sheer panic. The most important people in the world, interrogating her, their eyes drilling into her—

And then she remembered the drawing. *That* was who she was.

"Alas," Shallan said, "I will be of little use to you, Brightlords and Brightladies. I was away from my homeland when that tragic assassination occurred, and I have no insight into its cause."

"Then what are you doing here?" Hatham asked, polite, but insistent.

"She's watching the zoo, obviously," Sebarial said. "The lot of you making fools of yourselves is the best free entertainment to be found in this frozen wasteland."

It probably *was* wise to ignore that one. "I am the ward of Jasnah Kholin," Shallan said, meeting Hatham's eyes. "My purpose here is of a personal nature."

"Ah," Aladar said. "The phantom betrothal I've heard rumors of."

"That's right," Ruthar said. He had a decidedly oily look about him, with dark slicked hair, burly arms, and a beard around the mouth. Most disturbing, however, was that smile of his—a smile that seemed far too predatory. "Child, what would it take for you to visit my warcamp and speak to my scribes? I need to know what is happening in Jah Keved."

"I will do better than that," Roion said. "Where are you staying, girl? I offer an invitation to visit my palace. I too would hear of your homeland."

But . . . she'd just said she didn't know anything . . .

Shallan dredged up Jasnah's training. They didn't care about Jah Keved. They wanted to get information about her betrothal—they suspected that there was more to the story.

The two who had just invited her were among those Jasnah rated the least politically savvy. The others—like Aladar and Hatham—would wait until a private time to make the invitation, so they didn't reveal their interest in public.

"Your concern is unwarranted, Roion," Dalinar said. "She is, of course, staying in my warcamp and has a position among my clerks."

"Actually," Shallan said, "I didn't get a chance to respond to your offer, Brightlord Kholin. I would love the opportunity to be in your service, but alas, I have already taken a position in another warcamp."

Stunned silence.

She knew what she *wanted* to say next. A huge gamble, one of which Jasnah would never have approved. She found herself speaking anyway, trusting her instincts. It worked in art, after all.

"Brightlord Sebarial," Shallan said, looking toward the bearded man that Jasnah so thoroughly detested, "was the first to offer me a position and invite me to stay with him."

The man almost choked on his wine. He looked up over the cup toward her, narrowing his eyes.

She shrugged with what she hoped was an innocent gesture, and smiled. *Please . . .*

"Uh, that's right," Sebarial said, leaning back. "She's a distant family relation. Couldn't possibly live with myself if I didn't give her a place to stay."

"His offer was quite generous," Shallan said. "Three full broams a week support."

Sebarial's eyes bugged out.

"I wasn't aware of this," Dalinar said, looking from Sebarial to her.

"I'm sorry, Brightlord," Shallan said. "I should have told you. I didn't find it appropriate to be staying in the house of someone who was courting me. Surely you understand."

He frowned. "What I'm having trouble understanding is why anyone would want to be closer to Sebarial than they need to be."

"Oh, Uncle Sebarial is quite tolerable, once you get used to him," Shallan said. "Like a very annoying noise that you eventually learn to ignore."

Most seemed horrified at her comment, though Aladar smiled. Sebarial—as she'd hoped—laughed out loud.

"I guess that is settled," Ruthar said, dissatisfied. "I do hope you'll at least be willing to come brief me."

"Give it up, Ruthar," Sebarial said. "She's too young for you. Though with you involved, I'm sure it *would* be brief."

Ruthar sputtered. "I wasn't implying . . . You moldy old . . . Bah!"

Shallan was glad that attention then turned from her back to the topics at hand, because that last comment had her blushing. Sebarial *was* inappropriate. Still, he seemed to be making an effort to leave himself out of these political discussions, and that seemed like the place where Shallan wanted to be. The position with the most freedom. She *would* still work with Dalinar and Navani on Jasnah's notes, but she didn't want to be beholden to them.

Who is to say being beholden to this man is any different? Shallan thought, rounding the room to approach where Sebarial sat, without wife or family members to attend him. He was unmarried.

"Almost threw you out on your ear, girl," Sebarial said quietly, sipping his wine and not looking at her. "Stupid move, putting yourself in my hands. Everyone knows I like to set things on fire and watch them burn."

"And yet you *didn't* throw me out," she said. "So it wasn't a stupid move. Merely a risk that paid rewards."

"Still might drop you. I'm certainly not paying that three broams. That's almost as much as my mistress costs, and at least I get something from that arrangement."

"You'll pay," Shallan said. "It's a matter of public record now. But don't worry. I will earn my keep."

"You have information about Kholin?" Sebarial asked, studying his wine.

So he *did* care.

"Information, yes," Shallan said. "Less about Kholin, and more about the world itself. Trust me, Sebarial. You've just entered into a very profitable arrangement."

She'd have to figure out why that was.

The others continued arguing about the Assassin in White, and she gathered that he had attacked here but had been fought off. As Aladar steered the conversation to a complaint that his gemstones were being taken by the Crown—Shallan didn't know the reason they'd been seized—Dalinar Kholin slowly stood up. He moved like a rolling boulder. Inevitable, implacable.

Aladar trailed off.

"I passed a curious pile of stones along my path," Dalinar said. "Of a type I found remarkable. The fractured shale had been weathered by highstorms, blown up against stone of a more durable nature. This pile of thin wafers lay as if stacked by some mortal hand."

The others looked at Dalinar as if he were mad. Something about the words tugged at Shallan's memory. They were a quotation from something she'd once read.

Dalinar turned, walking toward the open windows on the leeward side of the room. "But no man had stacked these stones. Precarious though they looked, they were actually quite solid, a formation from once-buried strata now exposed to open air. I wondered how it was possible they remained in such a neat stack, with the fury of the tempests blowing against them.

"I soon ascertained their true nature. I found that force from one direction pushed them back against one another and the rock behind. No amount of pressure I could produce in that manner caused them to shift. And yet, when I removed one stone from the bottom—pulling it out instead of pushing it in—the entire formation collapsed in a miniature avalanche."

The room's occupants stared at him until Sebarial finally spoke for all of them. "Dalinar," the plump man said, "what in *Damnation's* eleventh name are you on about?"

"Our methods aren't working," Dalinar said, looking back at the lot of them. "Years at war, and we find ourselves in the same position as before. We can no more fight this assassin now than on the night he killed my brother. The king of Jah Keved put three Shardbearers and half an army up against the creature, then died with a Blade through the chest, his Shards left to be scavenged by opportunists.

"If we cannot defeat the assassin, then we must remove his reason for attacking. If we can capture or eliminate his employers, then perhaps we can invalidate whatever contract binds him. Last we knew, he was employed by the Parshendi."

"Great," Ruthar said dryly. "All we have to do is win the war, which we've only been trying to do for five years."

"We *haven't* been trying," Dalinar said. "Not hard enough. I intend to make peace with the Parshendi. If they will not have it on our terms, then I will set out into the Shattered Plains with my army and any who will join me. No more games on plateaus, fighting over gemhearts. I will strike toward the Parshendi camp, find it, and defeat them once and for all."

The king sighed softly, leaning back behind his desk. Shallan guessed he'd been expecting this.

"Out onto the Shattered Plains," Sadeas said. "That sounds like a marvelous thing for you to try."

"Dalinar," Hatham said, speaking with obvious care, "I don't see that our situation has changed. The Shattered Plains are still largely unexplored, and the Parshendi camp could be literally *anywhere* out there, hidden among miles and miles of terrain that our army cannot traverse without great difficulty. We agreed that attacking their camp was imprudent, so long as they were willing to come to us."

"Their willingness to come to us, Hatham," Dalinar said, "has proved to be a problem, because it puts the battle on their terms. No, our situation hasn't changed. Merely our resolve. This war has persisted far too long already. I will finish it, one way or another."

"Sounds wonderful," Sadeas repeated. "Will you be off tomorrow or wait until the next day?"

Dalinar gave him a disdainful look.

"Just trying to estimate when there will be an open warcamp," Sadeas said innocently. "I've almost outgrown mine, and wouldn't mind spilling into a second once the Parshendi slaughter you and yours. To think, after all the trouble you got yourself into by getting surrounded out there, that you're going to go do it again."

Adolin stood up behind his father, face red, angerspren bubbling at his feet like pools of blood. His brother coaxed him back down into his seat. There was something here, obviously, that Shallan was missing.

I wandered into the middle of all this without nearly enough context, she thought. *Storms, I'm lucky I haven't been chewed up already.* Suddenly, she wasn't quite so proud of her accomplishments this day.

"Before the highstorm last night," Dalinar said, "we had a messenger from the Parshendi—the first willing to speak with us in ages. He said that his leaders wished to discuss the possibility of peace."

The highprinces looked stunned. *Peace?* Shallan thought, heart leaping. That would certainly make it easier to get out and search for Urithiru.

"That very night," Dalinar said softly, "the assassin struck. Again. Last time he came was just after we had signed a peace treaty with the Parshendi. Now, he comes again the day of another peace offer."

"Those bastards," Aladar said softly. "Is this some kind of twisted ritual of theirs?"

"It might be a coincidence," Dalinar said. "The assassin has been striking all over the world. Surely the Parshendi haven't contacted all of these people. However, the events make me wary. Almost, I wonder if the Parshendi are being framed—if someone is using this assassin to make certain that Alethkar never knows peace. But then, the Parshendi *did* claim to have hired him to kill my brother. . . ."

"Maybe they're desperate," Roion said, hunkering down in his chair. "One faction among them sues for peace while the other does whatever it can to destroy us."

"Either way, I intend to plan for the worst," Dalinar said, looking to Sadeas. "I *will* be making my way to the center of the Shattered Plains—either to defeat the Parshendi for good, or to accept their surrender and disarmament—but such an expedition will take time to arrange. I'll need to train my men for an extended operation and send scouts to map farther into the middle of the Plains. Beyond that, I need to choose some new Shardbearers."

". . . new Shardbearers?" Roion asked, turtle-like head rising in curiosity.

"I will soon come into the possession of more Shards," Dalinar said.

"And are we allowed to know the source of this amazing trove?" Aladar asked.

"Why, Adolin is going to win them from all of you," Dalinar said.

Some of the others chuckled, as if it were a joke. Dalinar did not seem to intend it as one. He sat back down, and the others took this as marking an end to the meeting—once again, it seemed that Dalinar, and not the king, truly led.

The entire balance of power has shifted here, Shallan thought. *As has the nature of the war.* Jasnah's notes about the court were *definitely* outdated.

"Well, I suppose you're going to accompany me back to my camp now," Sebarial said to her, rising. "Which means this meeting wasn't just the usual waste of time listening to blowhards make veiled threats to one another—it actually cost me money as well."

"It could be worse," Shallan said, helping the older man rise, as he seemed somewhat unsteady on his feet. That passed once he was standing, and he pulled his arm free.

"Worse? How?"

"I could be boring as well as expensive."

He looked at her, then laughed. "I suppose that's true. Well, come on then."

"Just a moment," Shallan said, "you go on ahead, and I'll catch up at your carriage."

She walked off, seeking the king, to whom she personally delivered news of Jasnah's death. He took it well, with regal dignity. Dalinar had probably already informed him.

That task done, she sought out the king's scribes. A short time later, she left the conference chamber and found Vathah and Gaz waiting nervously outside. She handed a sheet of paper to Vathah.

"What's this?" he asked, twisting it about.

"Writ of pardon," she said. "Sealed by the king. It's for you and your men. We'll soon receive specific ones with their names on them, but meanwhile this will keep you from being arrested."

"You actually did it?" Vathah asked, looking it over, though he obviously couldn't make sense of the writing. "Storms, you actually kept your word?"

"Of course I did," Shallan said. "Note that it only covers *past* crimes, so tell the men to be on their best behavior. Now, let's be going. I have arranged a place for us to stay."

FOUR YEARS AGO

Father held feasts because he wanted to pretend that everything was all right. He invited local brightlords from nearby hamlets, he fed them and gave them wine, he displayed his daughter.

Then, the next day after everyone was gone, he sat at his table and listened to his scribes tell him how impoverished he had grown. Shallan saw him afterward sometimes, holding his forehead, staring straight ahead at nothing.

For tonight, however, they feasted and pretended.

"You've met my daughter, of course," Father said, gesturing to Shallan as his guests were seated. "The jewel of House Davar, our pride above all others."

The visitors—lighteyes from two valleys over—nodded politely as Father's parshmen brought wine. Both the drink and the slaves were a way to display riches Father didn't actually possess. Shallan had begun helping with the accounts, her duty as daughter. She knew the truth of their finances.

The evening's chill was offset by the crackling hearth; this room might have felt homey somewhere else. Not here.

The servants poured her wine. Yellow, mildly intoxicating. Father drank violet, prepared in its strength. He settled himself down at the high table, which ran the width of the room—the same room where Helaran had threatened to kill him a year and a half ago. They'd received a brief letter from Helaran six months back, along with a book by the famous Jasnah Kholin for Shallan to read.

Shallan had read his note to her father in a trembling whisper. It hadn't said much. Mostly veiled threats. That night, Father had beaten one of the maids near to death. Isan still walked with a limp. The servants no longer gossiped about Father having killed his wife.

Nobody does anything at all to resist him, Shallan thought, glancing toward her father. *We're all too scared.*

Shallan's three other brothers sat in a huddled knot at their own table. They avoided looking at their father or interacting with the guests. Several small sphere goblets glowed on the tables, but the room as a whole could have used more light. Neither spheres nor hearthlight were enough to drive out the gloom. She thought that her father liked it that way.

The visiting lighteyes—Brightlord Tavinar—was a slender, well-dressed man with a deep red silk coat. He and his wife sat close together at the high table, their teenaged daughter between them. Shallan had not caught her name.

As the evening progressed, Father tried to speak to them a few times, but they gave only terse responses. For all that it was supposed to be a feast, nobody seemed to be enjoying themselves. The visitors looked as if they wished they'd never accepted the invitation, but Father was more politically important than they, and good relations with him would be valuable.

Shallan picked at her own food, listening to her father boast about his new axehound breeding stud. He spoke of their prosperity. Lies.

She did not want to contradict him. He had been good to her. He was always good to her. Yet, shouldn't someone do something?

Helaran might have. He'd left them.

It's growing worse and worse. Someone needs to do something, say something, to change Father. He shouldn't be doing the things that he did, growing drunk, beating the darkeyes . . .

The first course passed. Then Shallan noticed something. Balat—whom Father had started calling Nan Balat, as if he were the oldest—kept glancing at the guests. That was surprising. He usually ignored them.

Tavinar's daughter caught his eye, smiled, then looked back at her food. Shallan blinked. Balat . . . and a girl? How odd to consider.

Father didn't seem to notice. He eventually stood and raised his cup to the room. "Tonight, we celebrate. Good neighbors, strong wine."

Tavinar and his wife hesitantly raised their cups. Shallan had only just begun to study propriety—it was hard to do, as her tutors kept leaving—but she knew that a good Vorin brightlord was not supposed to celebrate drunkenness. Not that they *wouldn't* get drunk, but it was the Vorin way not to talk about it. Such niceties were not her father's strong point.

"It is an important night," Father said after taking a sip of his wine. "I have just received word from Brightlord Gevelmar, whom I believe you know, Tavinar. I have been without a wife for too long. Brightlord Gevelmar is sending his youngest daughter along with writs of marriage. My ardents will perform the service at the end of the month, and I will have a wife."

Shallan felt cold. She pulled her shawl closer. The aforementioned ardents sat at their own table, dining silently. The three men were greying in equal measure, and had served long enough to know Shallan's grandfather as a youth. They treated her with kindness, however, and studying with them brought her pleasure when all other things seemed to be collapsing.

"Why does nobody speak?" Father demanded, turning around the room. "I have just become betrothed! You look like a bunch of storming Alethi. We're Veden! Make some noise, you idiots."

The visitors clapped politely, though they looked even more uncomfortable than they had before. Balat and the twins shared looks, and then lightly thumped the table.

"To the void with all of you." Father slumped back into his chair as his parshmen approached the low table, each bearing a box. "Gifts for my children to mark the occasion," Father said with a wave of the hand. "Don't know why I bother. Bah!" He drank the rest of his wine.

The boys got daggers, very fine pieces engraved like Shardblades. Shallan's gift was a necklace of fat silvery links. She held it silently. Father didn't like her speaking much at feasts, though he always placed her table close to the high table.

He never shouted at her. Not directly. Sometimes, she wished he would. Maybe then Jushu wouldn't resent her so. It—

The door to the feast hall slammed open. The poor light revealed a tall man in dark clothing standing at the threshold.

"What is this!" Father demanded, rising, slamming his hands on the table. "Who interrupts my feast?"

The man strode in. His face was so long and slender, it looked as if it had been pinched. He wore ruffles at the cuffs of his soft maroon coat, and the way he pursed his lips made him look as if he'd just found a latrine that had overflowed in the rain.

One of his eyes was intense blue. The other dark brown. Both lighteyed and dark. Shallan felt a chill.

A Davar house servant dashed up to the high table, then whispered to Father. Shallan did not catch what was said, but whatever it was, it drained the thunder right out of Father's expression. He remained standing, but his jaw dropped.

A handful of servants in maroon livery filed in around the newcomer. He stepped forward with a precise air, as if choosing his steps with some care to avoid stepping in anything. "I have been sent by His Highness, Highprince Valam, ruler of these lands. It has come to his attention that dark rumors persist in these lands. Rumors regarding the death of a light-eyed woman." He met Father's eyes.

"My wife was killed by her lover," Father said. "Who then killed himself."

"Others tell a different story, Brightlord Lin Davar," the newcomer said. "Such rumors are . . . troublesome. They provoke dissatisfaction with His Highness. If a brightlord under his rule *were* to have murdered a light-eyed woman of rank, it is not something he can ignore."

Father did not respond with the outrage Shallan would have predicted. Instead he waved his hands toward Shallan and the visitors. "Away," he said. "Give me space. You there, messenger, let us speak alone. No need to drag mud into the hallway."

The Tavinars rose, looking all too eager to be going. The girl did glance back at Balat as they left, whispering softly.

Father looked toward Shallan, and she realized she'd frozen in place again at the mention of her mother, sitting at her table just before the high table.

"Child," Father said softly, "go sit with your brothers."

She withdrew, passing the messenger as he stepped up to the high table. Those eyes . . . It was Redin, the highprince's bastard son. His father used him as an executioner and assassin, it was said.

Since her brothers hadn't been explicitly banished from the room, they took chairs around the hearth, far enough away to give father privacy. They left a spot for Shallan, and she settled down, the fine silk of her dress rumpling. The voluminous way it enveloped her made her feel as if she weren't really there and only the dress mattered.

The highprince's bastard settled down at the table with Father. At least someone was confronting him. But what if the highprince's bastard decided Father was guilty? What then? Inquest? She didn't want Father to fall; she wanted to stop the darkness that was slowly strangling them all. It seemed like their light had gone out when Mother died.

When Mother . . .

"Shallan?" Balat asked. "Are you well?"

She shook herself. "Can I see the daggers? They looked quite fine from my table."

Wikim just stared at the fire, but Balat tossed his to her. She caught it clumsily, then pulled it from its sheath, admiring the way the metal folds reflected the hearthlight.

The boys watched the flamespren dance on the fire. The three brothers never talked anymore.

Balat glanced over his shoulder, toward the high table. "I wish I could hear what was being said," he whispered. "Maybe they'll drag him away. That would be fitting, for what he's done."

"He didn't kill Mother," Shallan said softly.

"Oh?" Balat snorted. "Then what did happen?"

"I . . ."

She didn't know. She couldn't think. Not of that time, that day. Had Father actually done it? She felt cold again, despite the fire's warmth.

The silence returned.

Someone . . . someone needed to *do* something.

"They're talking about plants," Shallan said.

Balat and Jushu looked at her. Wikim continued staring at the fire.

"Plants," Balat said flatly.

"Yes. I can hear them faintly."

"I can't hear a thing."

Shallan shrugged from within her too-enveloping dress. "My ears are better than yours. Yes, plants. Father is complaining that the trees in his gardens never listen when he tells them to obey. 'They have been dropping their leaves because of a sickness,' he says, 'and they refuse to grow new ones.'

"'Have you tried beating them for their disobedience?' the messenger asks.

"'All the time,' Father replies. 'I even break off their limbs, yet they still do not obey! It is untidy. At the very least, they should clean up after themselves.'

"'A problem,' the messenger says, 'as trees without foliage are hardly worth keeping. Fortunately, I have the solution. My cousin once had trees that acted this way, and he found that all he needed to do was sing to them and their leaves popped right back out.'

"'Ah, of course,' Father says. 'I will try that immediately.'

"'I hope that it works for you.'

"'Well, if it does, I will certainly be relieved.'"

Her brothers stared at her, baffled.

Finally, Jushu cocked his head. He was the youngest of the brothers, just above Shallan herself. "Re . . . leaf . . . ed . . ."

Balat burst into laughter—loud enough that their father glared at them. "Oh, that is *awful*," Balat said. "That is purely awful, Shallan. You should be ashamed."

She huddled down in her dress, grinning. Even Wikim, the older twin, cracked a smile. She hadn't seen him smile in . . . how long?

Balat wiped his eyes. "I actually thought, for a moment, you could really hear them. You little Voidbringer." He let out a deep breath. "Storms, but that felt good."

"We should laugh more," Shallan said.

"This hasn't been a place for laughter," Jushu said, sipping his wine.

"Because of Father?" Shallan asked. "There's one of him and four of us. We just need to be more optimistic."

"Being optimistic does not change facts," Balat said. "I wish Helaran hadn't left." He thumped his fist down on the side of his chair.

"Do not begrudge him his travels, Tet Balat," Shallan said softly. "There are so many places to see, places we will probably never visit. Let one of us go to them. Think of the stories he will bring back to us. The colors."

Balat looked across the drab blackrock room, with its muted hearths glowing red-orange. "Colors. I wouldn't mind a little more color around here."

Jushu smiled. "Anything would be a nice change from Father's face."

"Now, don't be down on Father's face," Shallan said. "It's quite adept at doing its duty."

"Which is?"

"Reminding us all that there are worse things than his odor. It's really quite a noble Calling."

"Shallan!" Wikim said. He looked dramatically unlike Jushu. Spindly and sunken-eyed, Wikim had hair cut so short he almost looked like an ardent. "Don't say such things where Father could hear."

"He's engrossed in conversation," Shallan said. "But you are right. I probably shouldn't mock our family. House Davar is distinctive and enduring."

Jushu raised his cup. Wikim nodded sharply. ·

"Of course," she added, "the same could be said for a wart."

Jushu just about spat out his wine. Balat let out another roaring laugh.

"Stop that racket!" Father shouted at them.

"It's a feast!" Balat called back. "Did you not ask us to be more Veden?"

Father glared at him, then returned to his conversation with the messenger. The two huddled together at the high table, Father's posture supplicating, the highprince's bastard sitting back with an arched eyebrow and a still face.

"Storms, Shallan," Balat said. "When did you become so clever?"

Clever? She didn't feel clever. Suddenly, the forwardness of what she'd said caused her to shrink back into her chair. These things, they'd simply slid out of her mouth. "Those are just things . . . just things I read in a book."

"Well, you should read more of those books, small one," Balat said. "It seems brighter in here for it."

Father slammed his hand down on the table, shaking cups, rattling plates. Shallan glanced at him, worried as he pointed his finger at the messenger and said something. It was too soft and far away for Shallan to make it out, but she knew that look in her father's eyes. She had seen it many times before he took his cane—or even once the fireplace poker—to one of the servants.

The messenger stood up in a smooth motion. His refinement seemed a shield that rebuffed Father's temper.

Shallan envied him.

"It appears I will get nowhere with this conversation," the messenger said loudly. He looked at Father, but his tone seemed to imply that his words were for them all. "I came prepared for that inevitability. The high-prince has given me authority, and I would very much like to know the *truth* of what happened in this household. Any lighteyes of birth who can provide witness will be welcomed."

"They need the testimony of a lighteyes," Jushu said softly to his siblings. "Father is important enough that they can't just remove him."

"There was one," the messenger said loudly, "who was willing to speak to us of the truth. He has since made himself unavailable. Do any of you have his courage? Will you come with me and testify to the highprince of the crimes committed on these lands?"

He looked toward the four of them. Shallan huddled in her chair, trying to look small. Wikim didn't look away from the flames. Jushu looked like he might stand, but then turned to his wine, cursing, his face growing red.

Balat. Balat grabbed the sides of his chair as if to stand, but then glanced at Father. That intensity in Father's eyes remained. When his rage was red-hot, he yelled, he threw things at the servants.

It was now, when his rage became cold, that he grew truly dangerous. This was when Father got quiet. This was when the yelling stopped.

Father's yelling, at least.

"He'll kill me," Balat whispered. "If I say a word, he'll kill me." His earlier bravado melted away. He seemed not a man any longer, but a youth—a terrified teenager.

"You could do it, Shallan," Wikim hissed at her. "Father won't dare hurt you. Besides, you actually *saw* what happened."

"I didn't," she whispered.

"You were there!"

"I don't know what happened. I don't remember it."

It didn't happen. It didn't.

A log shifted in the hearth. Balat stared at the floor, and did not stand. None of them would. A whirling group of translucent flower petals stirred among them, fading into view. Shamespren.

"I see," the messenger said. "If any of you . . . *remember* the truth at some point in the future, you will find willing ears in Vedenar."

"You will not tear this house apart, bastard," Father said, standing. "We stand by one another."

"Save for those who can no longer stand, I assume."

456   "Leave this house!"

The messenger gave Father a look of disgust, a demeaning sneer. It said, *I am a bastard, but even I am not as low as you*. He then left, sweeping from the room and gathering his men outside, his terse orders indicating that he wished to be back on the road despite the late hour, on another errand beyond Father's estates.

Once he was gone, Father placed both of his hands on the table and breathed out deeply. "Go," he said to the four of them, lowering his head.

They hesitated.

"Go!" Father roared.

They fled the room, Shallan scrambling after her brothers. She was left with the sight of her father sinking down into his seat, holding his head. The gift he'd given her, the fine necklace, sat forgotten in the opened box on the table just before him.

40

PALONA

*That they responded immediately and with great consternation is
undeniable, as these were primary among those who would for-
swear and abandon their oaths. The term Recreance was not then
applied, but has since become a popular title by which this event is
named.*

—From *Words of Radiance,* chapter 38, page 6

Sebarial shared his carriage with Shallan as they left the king's palace
and rode toward his warcamp. Pattern kept vibrating softly on the
folds of her skirt, and she had to shush him.

The highprince sat across from her, head tilted back against the cushioned wall, snoring softly as the carriage rattled. The ground here had
been scraped clean of rockbuds and set with a line of flagstones down the
center, to divide left from right.

Her soldiers were safe, and would catch up later. She had a base of operations and an income. In the tension of the meeting, and then Navani's
withdrawal, the Kholin house hadn't yet demanded that Shallan turn over
Jasnah's things. She still needed to approach Navani about helping with
the research, but so far, the day had actually worked out quite well.

Now Shallan just needed to save the world.

Sebarial snorted and shook awake from his short nap. He settled into
his seat, wiping his cheek. "You've changed."

"Excuse me?"

"You look younger. In there, I would have guessed you were twenty,
maybe twenty-five. But now I see that you can't be older than *fourteen.*"

"I am seventeen," Shallan said dryly.

"Same difference." Sebarial grunted. "I could have sworn your dress was more vibrant before, your features sharper, prettier . . . Must have been the light."

"Do you always make a habit of insulting the looks of young ladies?" Shallan asked. "Or is it only after you drool in front of them?"

He grinned. "You weren't trained in the court, obviously. I like that. But be careful—insult the wrong people in this place, and retribution can be swift."

Through the carriage window Shallan saw that they were finally approaching a warcamp flying Sebarial's banner. It bore the glyphs *sebes* and *laial* stylized into a skyeel, deep gold on a black field.

The soldiers at the gates saluted, and Sebarial gave orders for one to conduct Shallan's men to his manor when they arrived. The carriage continued, and Sebarial settled back to watch her, as if anticipating something.

She couldn't fathom what. Perhaps she was reading him wrong. She turned her attention out the window, and soon decided that this place was a warcamp in name only. The streets were straighter than you might have in a city that had grown naturally, but Shallan saw far more civilians than she did soldiers.

They passed taverns, open markets, shops, and tall buildings that surely could hold a dozen different families. People crowded many of the streets. The place wasn't as varied and vibrant as Kharbranth had been, but the buildings were of solid wood and stone, constructed up against one another to share support.

"Rounded roofs," Shallan said.

"My engineers say they repel the winds better," Sebarial said proudly. "Also, buildings with rounded corners and sides."

"So many people!"

"Almost all permanent residents. I have the most complete force of tailors, artisans, and cooks in the camps. Already, I've set up twelve manufactories—textiles, shoes, ceramics, several mills. I control the glassblowers as well."

Shallan turned back toward him. That pride in his voice didn't *at all* match what Jasnah had written of the man. Of course, most of her notes and knowledge of the highprinces came from infrequent visits to the Shattered Plains, and none had been recent.

"From what I've heard," Shallan said, "your forces are among the least successful in the war against the Parshendi."

Sebarial got a twinkle in his eyes. "The others hunt quick income from gemhearts, but what will they spend their money on? My textile mills will soon produce uniforms at a much cheaper price than they can be shipped in for, and my farmers will provide food far more varied than what is supplied through Soulcasting. I'm growing both lavis and tallew, not to mention my hog farms."

"You sly eel," Shallan said. "While the others fight a war, you've been building an economy."

"I've had to be careful," he confided, leaning in. "I didn't want them to notice what I was doing at first."

"Clever," Shallan said. "But why are you telling me?"

"You'll see it anyway, if you're to act as one of my clerks. Besides, the secrecy doesn't matter anymore. The manufactories are now producing, and my armies barely go on a single plateau run a month. I have to pay Dalinar's fines for avoiding them and forcing him to send someone else, but it's worth the cost. Anyway, the smarter highprinces have figured out what I'm up to. The others just think I'm a lazy fool."

"And so you're not a lazy fool?"

"Of course I am!" he exclaimed. "Fighting is too much work. Besides, soldiers die, and that makes me pay out to their families. It's just useless all around." He looked out the window. "I saw the secret three years back. Everyone was moving here, but nobody thought of the place as permanent—despite the value of those gemhearts, which ensured that Alethkar would always have a presence here. . . ." He smiled.

The carriage eventually pulled up to a modest manor-style home amid the taller tenement buildings. The manor had grounds filled with ornamental shalebark, a flagstone drive, and even some trees. The stately home, while not enormous, had a refined classical design, with pillars along the front. It used the row of taller stone buildings behind it as a perfect windbreak.

"We probably have a room for you," Sebarial said. "Maybe in the cellars. Never do seem to have enough space for all of the stuff I'm expected to have. Three full sets of dining furniture. Bah! As if I'm ever going to have anyone over."

"You really don't think highly of the others, do you?" Shallan asked.

"I hate them," Sebarial said. "But I try to hate everyone. That way, I don't risk leaving out anyone who is particularly deserving. Anyway, here we are. Don't expect me to help you out of the carriage."

She didn't need his help, as a footman quickly arrived and assisted her as she stepped out onto the stone steps built in beside the driveway. Another footman went to Sebarial, who cursed at him, but accepted the aid.

A short woman in a fine dress stood on the manor's steps, hands on her hips. She had curly dark hair. From northern Alethkar, then?

"Ah," Sebarial said as he and Shallan walked up toward the woman. "The bane of my existence. Please try to hold your laughter until we separate. My frail, aging ego can no longer handle the mockery."

Shallan gave him a confused look.

Then the woman spoke. "*Please* tell me you didn't kidnap her, Turi."

No, not Alethi at all, Shallan thought, trying to judge the woman's accent. *Herdazian.* The fingernails, with a rocklike cast to them, proved that. She was darkeyed, but her fine dress indicated she was not a servant.

Of course. The mistress.

"She insisted on coming with me, Palona," Sebarial said, climbing the steps. "I couldn't dissuade her. We'll have to give her a room or something."

"And who *is* she?"

"Some foreigner," Sebarial said. "When she said she wanted to come with me, it seemed to annoy old Dalinar, so I allowed it." He hesitated. "What was your name?" he asked, turning to Shallan.

"Shallan Davar," Shallan said, bowing to Palona. She might be darkeyed, but she was apparently head of this household.

The Herdazian woman cocked an eyebrow. "Well, she is polite, which means she probably won't fit in here. I honestly can't believe you brought home a random girl because you thought it would annoy one of the other highprinces."

"Bah!" Sebarial said. "Woman, you make me the most henpecked man in all of Alethkar—"

"We aren't *in* Alethkar."

"—and I'm not even storming married!"

"I'm not marrying you, so stop asking," Palona said, folding her arms, looking Shallan up and down speculatively. "She's far too young for you."

Sebarial grinned. "I used that line already. On Ruthar. It was delightful—he sputtered so much, you could have mistaken him for a storm."

Palona smiled, then waved him inside. "There's mulled wine in your study."

He sauntered toward the door. "Food?"

"You ran the cook off. Remember?"

"Oh, right. Well, you could have made the food."

"As could you."

"Bah. You're useless, woman! All you do is spend my money. Why do I put up with you, again?"

"Because you love me."

"Can't be that," Sebarial said, pausing beside the front doors. "I'm not capable of love. Too much a curmudgeon. Well, do something with the girl." He walked inside.

Palona beckoned Shallan up to join her. "What *really* happened, child?"

"He didn't say anything untrue," Shallan said, realizing that she was blushing. "But he did leave out a few facts. I have come for the purpose of an arranged marriage to Adolin Kholin. I thought staying in the Kholin household might leave me too restricted, so I sought other options."

"Huh. That actually makes it sound like Turi—"

"Don't call me that!" a voice called from inside.

"—that the idiot did something politically savvy."

"Well," Shallan said, "I *did* kind of bully him into taking me in. And I implied publicly that he was going to give me a very generous stipend."

"Too large a one!" the voice said from inside.

"Is he . . . standing in there listening?" Shallan asked.

"He's good at skulking," Palona said. "Well, come along. Let's get you settled. Make sure you tell *me* how much he's promised—even by implication—for your stipend. I'll make sure it happens."

Several footmen unloaded Shallan's trunks from the coach. Her soldiers hadn't arrived yet. Hopefully, they hadn't run into trouble. She followed Palona into the building, which proved to have as classic a decor as the exterior implied. Lots of marble and crystal. Statues trimmed in gold. A sweeping, broad staircase leading to a second-floor balcony overlooking the entrance hall. Shallan didn't notice the highprince around, skulking or otherwise.

Palona led Shallan to a very nice set of rooms in the eastern wing. They were all white, and richly furnished, the hard stone walls and floors softened with silk hangings and thick rugs. She hardly deserved such rich decor.

I suppose I shouldn't feel that way, Shallan thought as Palona checked the closet for towels and linen. *I'm betrothed to a prince.*

Still, so much finery reminded her of her father. The lace, jewelry, and silk he'd given her in attempts to make her forget about . . . other times . . .

Shallan blinked, turning to Palona, who was speaking about something.

"Excuse me?" Shallan asked.

"Servants," Palona said. "You have your own lady's maid?"

"I don't," Shallan said. "I've got eighteen soldiers, though, and five slaves."

"And they'll be helping you change clothes?"

Shallan blushed. "I mean that I'd like them to be housed, if you can manage it."

"I can," Palona said lightly. "I can probably even find something productive for them to do. You'll want them paid out of your stipend, I assume—your maid as well, which I'll get for you. Food is served at second bell, noon, and tenth bell. If you want something at other times, ask at the kitchens. Cook might swear at you, assuming I can get him to come back this time. We've a storm cistern, so there's usually running water. If you want it warm for a bath, the boys will need an hour or so to heat it."

"Running water?" Shallan said, eager. She'd seen this for the first time in Kharbranth.

"As I said, storm cistern." Palona pointed upward. "Each highstorm fills it, and the shape of the cistern sifts out the crem. Don't use the system until midday after a highstorm, or the water will be brown. And you look entirely too eager about this."

"Sorry," Shallan said. "We didn't have this sort of thing in Jah Keved."

"Welcome to civilization. I trust you left your club and loincloth at the door. Let me set to finding you a maid." The short woman started to leave.

"Palona?" Shallan asked.

"Yes, child?"

"Thank you."

Palona smiled. "Winds know, you're not the first stray he's brought home. Some of us even end up staying." She left.

Shallan sat down on the plush, white bed, and sank almost down to her neck. What had they made the thing out of? Air and wishes? It felt luxurious.

In her sitting room—her *sitting room*—thumps announced the footmen arriving with her trunks. They left a moment later, closing the door. For the first time in quite a long while, Shallan found herself not fighting for her survival or worrying about being murdered by one of her traveling companions.

So she fell asleep.

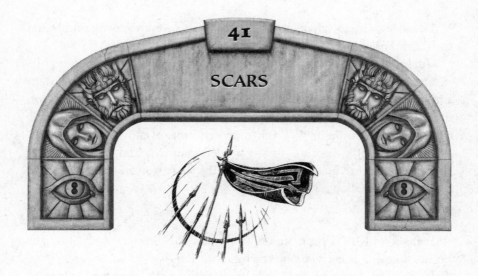

This act of great villainy went beyond the impudence which had
hitherto been ascribed to the orders; as the fighting was particu-
larly intense at this time, many attributed this act to a sense of
inherent betrayal; and after they withdrew, about two thousand
made assault upon them, destroying much of the membership; but
this was only nine of the ten, as one said they would not abandon
their arms and flee, but instead entertained great subterfuge at the
expense of the other nine.

—From *Words of Radiance,* chapter 38, page 20

K aladin rested his fingers on the chasm wall as Bridge Seventeen
formed up behind him.

He remembered being frightened of these chasms when he first descended into them. He had feared that heavy rains would cause a flash flood while his men were scavenging. He was a little surprised Gaz hadn't found a way to "accidentally" get Bridge Four assigned to chasm duty on the day of a highstorm.

Bridge Four had embraced its punishment, claiming these pits. Kaladin was startled to realize that coming down here felt more like coming home than returning to Hearthstone and his parents would have. The chasms were *his.*

"The lads are ready, sir," Teft said, stepping up beside him.

"Where were you the other night?" Kaladin asked, looking up toward the crack of open sky above.

"I was off duty, sir," Teft said. "Went to see what I could find in the market. Do I need to report every little thing I do?"

"You went to the market," Kaladin said, "in a highstorm?"

"Time may have gotten away from me for a breath or two . . ." Teft said, looking away.

Kaladin wanted to press further, but Teft was entitled to his privacy. *They're not bridgemen anymore. They don't have to spend all of their time together. They'll start having lives again.*

He wanted to encourage that. Still, it was disturbing. If he didn't know where they all were, how could he make sure they were all safe?

He turned around to regard Bridge Seventeen—a motley crew. Some had been slaves, purchased for the bridges. Others had been criminals, though the crimes punishable by bridge duty in Sadeas's army could be practically anything. Falling into debt, insulting an officer, fighting.

"You," Kaladin said to the men, "are Bridge Seventeen, under the command of Sergeant Pitt. You are not soldiers. You may wear the uniforms, but they don't fit you yet. You're playing dress-up. We're going to change that."

The men shuffled and looked about. Though Teft had been working with them and the other crews for weeks now, these didn't yet *see* themselves as soldiers. As long as that was true, they'd hold those spears at awkward angles, look around lazily when being addressed, and shuffle in line.

"The chasms are mine," Kaladin said. "I give you leave to practice here. Sergeant Pitt!"

"Yes, sir!" Pitt said, standing at attention.

"This is a sloppy mess of stormleavings you've got to work with, but I've seen worse."

"I find that hard to believe, sir!"

"Believe it," Kaladin said, looking over the men. "I was in Bridge Four. Lieutenant Teft, they're yours. Make them sweat."

"Aye, sir," Teft said. He began to call out orders as Kaladin picked up his spear and made his way farther down the chasms. It would be slow going, getting all twenty crews into shape, but at least Teft had successfully trained the sergeants. Heralds send that the same training worked on the common men.

Kaladin wished he could explain, even to himself, why he felt so anxious about getting these men ready. He felt he was racing toward something. Though what, he didn't know. That writing on the wall . . . Storms, it had him on edge. Thirty-seven days.

He passed Syl sitting on the frond of a frillbloom growing from the wall. It pulled closed at Kaladin's approach. She didn't notice, but remained sitting in the air.

"What is it that you want, Kaladin?" she asked.

"To keep my men alive," he said immediately.

"No," Syl said, "that was what you *wanted*."

"You're saying I don't want them to be safe?"

She slid down onto his shoulder, moving like a stiff breeze had blown her. She crossed her legs, sitting ladylike, skirt rippling as he walked.

"In Bridge Four, you dedicated everything you had to saving them," Syl said. "Well, they're saved. You can't go about protecting every one like a . . . um . . . Like a . . ."

"Father kurl watches over his eggs?"

"Exactly!" She paused. "What's a kurl?"

"A crustacean," Kaladin said, "about the size of a small axehound. Looks kind of like a cross between a crab and a tortoise."

"Ooooo . . ." Syl said. "I wanna see one!"

"They don't live out here."

Kaladin walked with his eyes forward, so she poked him in the neck until he looked at her. Then she rolled her eyes exaggeratedly. "So you admit that your men are relatively safe," she said. "That means you haven't really answered my question. What do you want?"

He passed piles of bones and wood, overgrown with moss. On one pile, rotspren and lifespren spun about one another, little motes of red and green glowing around the vines that sprouted incongruously from the mass of death.

"I want to beat that assassin," Kaladin said, surprised by how vehemently he felt it.

"Why?"

"Because it's my job to protect Dalinar."

Syl shook her head. "That's not it."

"What? You think you've gotten that good at reading human intentions?"

"Not all humans. Just you."

Kaladin grunted, stepping carefully around the edge of a dark pool. He'd rather not spend the rest of the day with soaked boots. These new ones didn't hold out the water as well as they should.

"Maybe," he said, "I want to beat that assassin because this is all his fault. If he hadn't killed Gavilar, Tien wouldn't have been drafted, and I wouldn't have followed him. Tien wouldn't have died."

"And you don't think Roshone would have found another way of getting back at your father?"

Roshone was the citylord of Kaladin's hometown back in Alethkar.

Sending Tien into the army had been an act of petty vengeance on his part, a way to get back at Kaladin's father for not being a good enough surgeon to save Roshone's son.

"He probably would have done something else," Kaladin admitted. "Still, that assassin deserves to die."

He heard the others before he reached them, their voices echoing down the cavernous chasm bottom.

"What I'm trying to explain," one said, "is that nobody seems to be asking the right questions." Sigzil's voice, with his elevated Azish accent. "We call the Parshendi savages, and everyone says they hadn't ever met people until that day they encountered the Alethi expedition. If those things are true, then what storm brought them a *Shin* assassin? A Shin assassin who can Surgebind, no less."

Kaladin stepped into the light of their spheres sprinkled about on the floor of the chasm, which had been cleared of debris since the last time Kaladin had been here. Sigzil, Rock, and Lopen sat on boulders, waiting for him.

"Are you implying that the Assassin in White never really worked for the Parshendi?" Kaladin asked. "Or are you implying that the Parshendi lied about being as isolated as they claimed?"

"I'm not implying anything," Sigzil said, turning toward Kaladin. "My master trained me to ask questions, so I'm asking them. Something doesn't make sense about this whole matter. The Shin are extremely xenophobic. They rarely leave their lands, and you never find them working as mercenaries. Now this one goes about assassinating kings? With a Shardblade? Is he still working for the Parshendi? If so, why did they wait so long to unleash him against us again?"

"Does it matter who he's working for?" Kaladin asked, sucking in Stormlight.

"Of course it does," Sigzil said.

"Why?"

"Because it's a *question*," he said, as if offended. "Besides, discovering his true employer might give us a clue to their goal, and knowing that might help us defeat him."

Kaladin smiled, then tried to run up the wall.

After falling to the ground, ending up flat on his back, he sighed.

Rock's head leaned in over him. "Is fun to watch," he said. "But this thing, you are certain she can work?"

"The assassin walked on the ceiling," Kaladin said.

"Are you sure he wasn't just doing what we did?" Sigzil asked skeptically. "Using the Stormlight to stick one object to another? He could have sprayed the ceiling with Stormlight, then jumped up into it to stick there."

"No," Kaladin said, Stormlight escaping his lips. "He jumped up and landed on the ceiling. Then he ran down the wall and sent *Adolin* to the ceiling somehow. The prince didn't stick there, he *fell* that way." Kaladin watched his Stormlight rise and evaporate. "At the end of it all, the assassin . . . he flew away."

"Ha!" Lopen said from his rock perch. "I knew it. When we have this figured out, the king of all Herdaz, he will say to me, 'Lopen, you are glowing, and this is impressive. But you can also fly. For this, you may marry my daughter.'"

"The king of Herdaz doesn't have a daughter," Sigzil said.

"He doesn't? I have been lied to all this time!"

"You don't know your royal family?" Kaladin asked, sitting up.

"Gon, I haven't been to Herdaz since I was a baby. There are as many Herdazians in Alethkar and Jah Keved these days as there are in our homeland. Flick my sparks, I'm practically an Alethi! Only not so tall and not so grouchy."

Rock gave Kaladin a hand and pulled him to his feet. Syl had taken a perch on the wall.

"Do you know how this works?" Kaladin asked her.

She shook her head.

"But the assassin *is* a Windrunner," Kaladin said.

"I think?" Syl said. "Something like you? Maybe?" She shrugged.

Sigzil followed the direction that Kaladin was looking. "I wish I could see it," he mumbled. "It would be a— Gah!" He jumped backward, pointing. "It looks like a little person!"

Kaladin raised an eyebrow toward Syl.

"I like him," she said. "Also, Sigzil, I'm a 'she' and not an 'it,' thank you very much."

"Spren have genders?" Sigzil asked, amazed.

"Of course," she said. "Though, technically, it probably has something to do with the way people view us. Personification of the forces of nature or some similar gobbletyblarthy."

"Doesn't that bother you?" Kaladin asked. "That you might be a creation of human perception?"

"You're a creation of your parents. Who cares how we were born? I can think. That's good enough." She grinned in a mischievous way, then zipped down as a ribbon of light toward Sigzil, who had settled down on a rock with a stunned expression. She stopped right in front of him, returned to the form of a young woman, then leaned in and made her face look exactly like his.

"Gah!" Sigzil cried again, scrambling away, making her giggle and change her face back.

Sigzil looked toward Kaladin. "She talks . . . She talks like a real person." He raised a hand to his head. "The stories say the Nightwatcher might be capable of that. . . . Powerful spren. Vast spren."

"Is he calling me vast?" Syl said, cocking her head to the side. "Not sure what I think of that."

"Sigzil," Kaladin said, "could the Windrunners fly?"

The man gingerly sat back down, still staring at Syl. "Stories and lore aren't my specialty," he said. "I tell of different places, to make the world smaller and to help men understand each other. I've heard legends speak of people dancing on the clouds, but who is to say what is fancy and what is truth, from stories so old?"

"We've got to figure this out," Kaladin said. "The assassin will return."

"So," Rock said, "jump at wall some more. I will not laugh much." He settled down on a boulder and plucked a small crab off the ground beside him. He inspected it, then popped it into his mouth and began chewing.

"Ew," Sigzil said.

"Tastes good," Rock said, speaking with his mouth full. "But better with salt and oil."

Kaladin regarded the wall, then closed his eyes and drew in more Stormlight. He felt it inside of him, beating against the walls of his veins and arteries, trying to escape. Daring him forward. To jump, to move, to *do*.

"So," Sigzil said to the others, "are we assuming that the Assassin in White was the one who sabotaged the king's railing?"

"Bah," Rock said. "Why would he do this thing? He could kill more easily."

"Yeah," Lopen agreed. "Maybe the railing was done by one of the other highprinces."

Kaladin opened his eyes and looked at his arm, palm against the slick wall of the chasm, elbow straight. Stormlight rose from his skin. Curling wisps of Light that vaporized in the air.

Rock nodded. "All highprinces want the king dead, though they will not speak of this. One of them sent saboteur."

"So how did this saboteur get to the balcony?" Sigzil asked. "It must have taken some time to cut through the railing. It was metal. Unless . . . How smooth was that cut, Kaladin?"

Kaladin narrowed his eyes, watching that Stormlight rise. It was raw power. No. "Power" was the wrong term. It was a force, like the Surges that ruled the universe. They made fire burn, made rocks fall, made light glow. These wisps, they were the Surges reduced to some primal form.

He could use it. Use it to . . .

"Kal?" Sigzil's voice asked, though it seemed distant. Like an unimportant buzzing. "How smooth was the cut to the railing? Could it have been a Shardblade?"

The voice faded. For a moment, Kaladin thought he saw shadows of a world that was not, shadows of another place. And in that place, a distant sky with a sun enclosed, almost as if by a corridor of clouds.

There.

He made the direction of the wall become down.

Suddenly, his arm was all that was supporting him. He fell forward into the wall, grunting. His awareness of his surroundings returned in a crash—only, his perspective was bizarre. He scrambled to his feet, and found himself standing *on* the wall.

He backed up a few paces—walking up the side of the chasm. To him, that wall was the floor, and the other three bridgemen stood on the actual floor, which looked like the wall. . . .

This, Kaladin thought, *is going to get confusing.*

"Wow," Lopen said, standing up excitedly. "Yeah, this is *really* going to be fun. Run up the wall, gancho!"

Kaladin hesitated, then turned and started running. It was like he was in a cave, the two walls of the chasm the top and bottom. Those slowly squeezed together as he moved toward the sky.

Feeling the rush of the Stormlight within him, Kaladin grinned. Syl streaked along beside him, laughing. The closer they got to the top, the narrower the chasm became. Kaladin slowed, then stopped.

Syl streaked out in front of him, zipping out of the chasm as if leaping from the mouth of the cave. She turned about, a ribbon of light.

"Come on!" she called to him. "Out onto the plateau! Into the sunlight!"

"There are scouts out there," he said, "watching for gemhearts."

"Come out anyway. Stop hiding, Kaladin. *Be.*"

Lopen and Rock whooped below in excitement. Kaladin stared outward at the blue sky. "I have to know," he whispered.

"Know?"

"You ask me why I protect Dalinar. I have to know if he really is what he seems, Syl. I *have* to know if one of them lives up to his reputation. That will tell me—"

"Tell you?" she asked, becoming the image of a full-size young woman standing on the wall before him. She was nearly as tall as he was, her dress fading to mist. "Tell you what?"

"If honor is dead," Kaladin whispered.

"He is," Syl said. "But he lives on in men. And in me."

Kaladin frowned.

"Dalinar Kholin is a good man," Syl said.

"He is friends with Amaram. He could be the same, inside."

"You don't believe that."

"I have to *know*, Syl," he said, stepping forward. He tried to take her arm as he would a human's, but she was too insubstantial. His hand passed through. "I can't just believe it. I need to know it. You asked what I want. Well, that's it. I want to know if I can trust Dalinar. And if I can . . ."

He nodded toward the light of the day outside the chasm.

"If I can, I'll tell him what I can do. I will believe that at least one lighteyes won't try to take everything from me. Like Roshone did. Like Amaram did. Like Sadeas did."

"And that is what it will take?" she asked.

"I warned you that I was broken, Syl."

"No. You've been reforged. It can happen to men."

"To other men, yes," Kaladin said, raising his hand, feeling the scars on his forehead. Why had the Stormlight never healed those? "I'm not certain about myself yet. But I will protect Dalinar Kholin with everything I have. I will learn who he is, who he *really* is. Then, maybe . . . we'll give him his Knights Radiant."

"And Amaram? What of him?"

Pain. Tien. "Him I'm going to kill."

"Kaladin," she said, hands clasped before her, "don't let this destroy you."

"It can't," he said, Stormlight running out. His uniform coat began to fall backward, toward the ground, as did his hair. "Amaram already took care of that."

The ground below fully reasserted itself, and Kaladin fell backward away from her. He sucked in Stormlight, twisting in the air as his veins flared back to life. He landed feet-first in a rush of power and Light.

The other three remained silent for a few moments as he stood up straight.

"That," Rock said, "was very fast way to get down. Ha! But it did not include falling on face, which would be fun. So you get only soft clap." He proceeded to clap. It was indeed soft. Lopen, however, cheered and Sigzil nodded with a wide grin.

Kaladin snorted, grabbing a waterskin. "The king's railing *was* cut with a Shardblade, Sigzil." He took a drink. "And no, it wasn't the Assassin in White. That attempt on Elhokar's life was too crude."

Sigzil nodded.

"What's more," Kaladin said, "the railing must have been cut *after* the highstorm that night. Otherwise, the wind would have blown the railing out of shape. So our saboteur, a Shardbearer, somehow got out onto the balcony after the storm."

Lopen shook his head, catching the waterskin as Kaladin threw it back.

"We're supposed to believe that one of the camp's Shardbearers snuck through the palace and got onto that balcony, gon? And nobody noticed him?"

"Could someone else do this thing?" Rock said, gesturing to the wall. "Walk up it?"

"I doubt it," Kaladin said.

"A rope," Sigzil said.

They looked to him.

"If I wanted to sneak a Shardbearer in, I'd bribe some servant to let down a rope." Sigzil shrugged. "One could be smuggled out onto the railing easily, perhaps wrapped around the servant's body under their clothing. The saboteur and maybe some friends could climb up the rope, cut the railing and dig at the mortar, then climb back down. The accomplice then cuts the rope and goes back inside."

Kaladin nodded slowly.

"So," Rock said, "we find out who went on balcony after storm, and we find accomplice. Easy! Ha. Maybe you are not airsick, Sigzil. No. Probably just a little."

Kaladin felt unsettled. Moash had been out on that balcony between the storm and the king's near fall.

"I'll ask around," Sigzil said, rising.

"No," Kaladin said quickly. "I'll do it. Don't speak a word of this to anyone else. I want to see what I can find."

"All right," Sigzil said. He nodded toward the wall. "Can you do that again?"

"More tests?" Kaladin asked with a sigh.

"We have time," Sigzil said. "Besides, I believe Rock wants to see if you fall on your face."

"Ha!"

"All right," Kaladin said. "But I'm going to have to drain some of those spheres we're using for light." He glanced toward them sitting in little piles on the too-clean ground. "By the way, why did you clear away the rubble in this area?"

"Clear it away?" Sigzil asked.

"Yeah," Kaladin said. "There was no need to go moving remains around, even if they are just skeletons. It . . ."

He trailed off as Sigzil picked up a sphere and held it up toward the wall, exposing something Kaladin had missed before. Deep gouges where the moss had been scraped off, the rock scored.

Chasmfiend. One of the massive greatshells had passed through the area, and its bulk had scraped everything away.

"I didn't think they came this close to the warcamps," Kaladin said. "Maybe we shouldn't train the lads down here for a while, just in case."

The others nodded.

"Is gone now," Rock said. "Otherwise, we'd have been eaten. Is obvious. So, back to training."

Kaladin nodded, though those gouges haunted him as he practiced.

⁂

A few hours later, they led a tired group of former bridgemen back into their barrack block. Exhausted as they looked, the men of Bridge Seventeen seemed *more* lively than they'd been before going down into the chasm. They perked up even more when they reached their barrack and found one of Rock's apprentice chefs fixing them a big pot of stew.

It was dark by the time Kaladin and Teft got back to Bridge Four's own barrack. Another of Rock's apprentices was fixing the stew here, Rock himself—having gotten back a little earlier than Kaladin—tasting and giving criticism. Shen moved behind Rock, stacking bowls.

Something was wrong.

Kaladin stopped just outside the light of the firepit, and Teft froze beside him. "Something is off," Teft said.

"Yeah," Kaladin agreed, scanning the men. They were clumped together on one side of the fire, some seated, others standing in a group. Their laughter forced, their postures nervous. When you trained men for war, they started to use combat stances whenever they were uncomfortable. Something on the other side of that fire was a threat.

Kaladin stepped into the light and found a man sitting there in a nice uniform, hands down at his side, head bowed. Renarin Kholin. Oddly, he was rocking back and forth with a small motion, staring at the ground.

Kaladin relaxed. "Brightlord," Kaladin said, stepping over to him. "Is there something you need?"

Renarin scrambled to his feet and saluted. "I would like to serve under your command, sir."

Inside, Kaladin groaned. "Let's talk away from the fire, Brightlord." He took the spindly prince by the arm, leading him away from the ears of the others.

"Sir," Renarin said, speaking softly, "I want—"

"You shouldn't call me sir," Kaladin whispered. "You're lighteyed. Storms, you're the son of the most powerful man in eastern Roshar."

"I want to be in Bridge Four," Renarin said.

Kaladin rubbed his forehead. During his time as a slave, dealing with much larger problems, he had forgotten about the headaches of dealing with highborn lighteyes. Once, he might have assumed he'd heard the most outlandish of their ridiculous demands. Not so, it seemed.

"You can't be in Bridge Four. We're bodyguards for your own family. What are you going to do? Guard yourself?"

"I won't be a liability, sir. I'll work hard."

"I don't doubt you would, Renarin. Look, *why* do you want to be in Bridge Four?"

"My father and my brother," Renarin said softly, face shadowed, "they're warriors. Soldiers. I'm not, if you haven't noticed."

"Yes. Something about . . ."

"Physical ailments," Renarin said. "I've a blood weakness."

"That's a folk description of many different conditions," Kaladin said. "What do you really have?"

"I'm epileptic," Renarin said. "It means—"

"Yes, yes. Is it idiopathic or symptomatic?"

Renarin stood absolutely still in the darkness. "Uh . . ."

"Was it caused by a specific brain injury," Kaladin asked, "or is it something that just started happening for no reason?"

"I've had it since I was a kid."

"How bad are the seizures?"

"They're fine," Renarin said quickly. "It's not as bad as everyone says. It's not like I fall to the ground or froth like everyone thinks. My arm will jerk a few times, or I'll twitch uncontrollably for a few moments."

"You retain consciousness?"

"Yeah."

"Myoclonic, probably," Kaladin said. "You've been given bitterleaf to chew?"

"I . . . Yes. I don't know if it helps. The jerking isn't the whole problem. A lot of times, when it's happening, I get really weak. Particularly along one side of my body."

"Huh," Kaladin said. "I suppose that could fit with the seizures. Have you ever had any persistent relaxation of the muscles, an inability to smile on one side of your face, for example?"

"No. How do you know these things? Aren't you a soldier?"

"I know some field medicine."

"Field medicine . . . for epilepsy?"

Kaladin coughed into his hand. "Well, I can see why they didn't want you going into battle. I've seen men with wounds that caused similar symptoms, and the surgeons always dismissed those men from duty. It's no shame to not be fit enough for battle, Brightlord. Not every man is needed for fighting."

"Sure," Renarin said bitterly. "Everyone tells me that. Then they all go back to fighting. The ardents, they claim every Calling is important, but then what do they teach about the afterlife? That it's a big war to reclaim the Tranquiline Halls. That the best soldiers in this life are glorified in the next."

"If the afterlife really is a big war," Kaladin said, "then I hope I end up in Damnation. At least there I might be able to get a wink or two of sleep. Regardless, you're no soldier."

"I want to be."

"Brightlord—"

"You don't have to set me to doing anything important," Renarin said. "I came to you, instead of one of the other battalions, because most of your men spend their time patrolling. If I'm patrolling, I won't be in much danger, and my fits won't hurt anyone. But at least I can see, I can *feel* what it's like."

"I—"

He rushed on. Kaladin had never heard so many words from the normally quiet young man.

"I will obey your commands," Renarin said. "Treat me like a new recruit. When I'm here, I'm not a prince's son, I'm not a lighteyes. I'm just another soldier. Please. I want to be part of it. When Adolin was young, my father made him serve in a spearman squad for two months."

"He did?" Kaladin asked, genuinely surprised.

"Father said every officer should serve in the shoes of his men," Renarin said. "I have Shards now. I'm going to be in war, but I've never felt what it's like to really be a soldier. I think this is the closest I'll be able to get. *Please.*"

Kaladin folded his arms, looking the youth over. Renarin looked anxious. *Very* anxious. He'd formed his hands to fists, though Kaladin could see no sign of the box Renarin often fiddled with when nervous. He'd begun breathing deeply, but had set his jaw, and kept his eyes forward.

Coming to see Kaladin, to ask this of him, *terrified* the young man for some reason. He'd done it anyway. Could one ask anything more of a recruit?

Am I really considering this? It seemed ludicrous. And yet, one of Kaladin's jobs was to protect Renarin. If he could pound some solid self-defense skills into him, that would go a long way toward helping him survive assassination attempts.

"I should probably point out," Renarin said, "how much easier it will be to guard me if I'm spending time training with your men. Your resources are thin, sir. Having one fewer person to protect must be appealing. The only times I'll leave are the days when I practice with my Shards under Swordmaster Zahel."

Kaladin sighed. "You really want to be a soldier?"

"Yes, sir!"

"Go take those dirty stew bowls and wash them," Kaladin said, pointing. "Then help Rock clean his cauldron and put away the cooking implements."

"Yes, sir!" Renarin said with an enthusiasm Kaladin had never heard from anyone assigned washing duty. Renarin jogged over and began happily snatching up bowls.

Kaladin folded his arms and leaned against the barrack. The men didn't know how to react to Renarin. They'd hand over bowls of half-finished stew to please him, and conversation hushed when he was too near. But they'd been nervous around Shen too, before eventually coming to accept him. Could they ever do the same for a lighteyes?

Moash had refused to hand his bowl to Renarin, washing it himself, as was their common practice. Once done, he strolled over to Kaladin. "You're really going to let him join?"

"I'll speak to his father tomorrow," Kaladin said. "Get the highprince's read on it."

"I don't like it. Bridge Four, our nightly conversations . . . these things are supposed to be safe from *them*, you know?"

"Yeah," Kaladin said. "But he's a good kid. I think if any lighteyes could fit in here, he could."

Moash turned, raising an eyebrow toward him.

"You disagree, I presume?" Kaladin asked.

"He doesn't act right, Kal. The way he talks, the way he looks at people. He's strange. That's not important, though—he's lighteyed, and that should be enough. It means we can't trust him."

"We don't need to," Kaladin said. "We're just going to keep an eye on him, maybe try to train him to defend himself."

Moash grunted, nodding. He seemed to accept those as good reasons for letting Renarin stay.

I've got Moash here, Kaladin thought. *Nobody else is close enough to hear. I should ask . . .*

But how did he form the words? *Moash, were you involved in a plot to kill the king?*

"Have you thought about what we're going to do?" Moash asked. "Regarding Amaram, I mean."

"Amaram is my problem."

"You're Bridge Four," Moash said, taking Kaladin by the arm. "Your problem *is* our problem. He's the one who made you a slave."

"He did more than that," Kaladin growled softly, ignoring Syl's gesturing that he should remain quiet. "He killed my friends, Moash. Right before my eyes. He's a murderer."

"Then something has to be done."

"It does," Kaladin asked. "But what? You think I should go to the authorities?"

Moash laughed. "What are *they* going to do? You have to get the man into a duel, Kaladin. Bring him down, man against man. Until you do it, something's going to feel wrong to you, deep down in your gut."

"You sound like you know what this feels like."

"Yeah." Moash gave a little half smile. "I have some Voidbringers in my past too. Maybe that's why I understand you. Maybe that's why you understand me."

"Then what—"

"I don't really want to talk about it," Moash said.

"We're Bridge Four," Kaladin said, "like you said. Your problems are mine." *What did the king do to your family, Moash?*

"Suppose that's true," Moash said, turning away. "I just . . . Not tonight. Tonight, I just want to relax."

"Moash!" Teft called from nearer the fire. "You coming?"

"I am," Moash called back. "What about you, Lopen? You ready?"

Lopen grinned, standing up and stretching beside the fire. "I am the Lopen, which means I am ready for anything at any time. You should know this by now."

Nearby, Drehy snorted and flipped a chunk of stewed longroot at Lopen. It splatted against the Herdazian's face.

Lopen kept right on talking. "As you can see, I was perfectly ready for that, as shown by the poise I display as I make this decidedly rude gesture."

Teft chuckled as he, Peet, and Sigzil walked over to join Lopen. Moash moved to go with them, then hesitated. "You coming, Kal?"

"Where?" Kaladin asked.

"Out," Moash said, shrugging. "Visit a few taverns, play some rings, get something to drink."

Out. The bridgemen had rarely done such things in Sadeas's army, at least not as a group, with friends. At first, they had been too beaten down to care for anything other than sticking their noses in drink. Later, lack of funds and the general prejudice against them among the troops had worked to keep the bridgemen to themselves.

That wasn't the case any longer. Kaladin found himself stammering. "I . . . probably ought to stay . . . uh, to go look in at the fires of the other crews . . ."

"Come on, Kal," Moash said. "You can't *always* work."

"I'll go with you another time."

"Fine." Moash jogged over to join the others.

Syl left the fire, where she'd been dancing with a flamespren, and zipped over to Kaladin. She hung in the air, watching the group walk off into the evening.

"Why didn't you go?" she asked him.

"I can't live that life anymore, Syl," Kaladin said. "I wouldn't know what to do with myself."

"But—"

Kaladin walked away and got himself a bowl of stew.

But as for Ishi'Elin, his was the part most important at their incep-
tion; he readily understood the implications of Surges being
granted to men, and caused organization to be thrust upon them;
as having too great power, he let it be known that he would destroy
each and every one, unless they agreed to be bound by precepts and
laws.

—From *Words of Radiance*, chapter 2, page 4

Shallan awoke to humming. She opened her eyes, finding herself
snuggled into the luxurious bed in Sebarial's manor. She'd fallen
asleep in her clothing.

The humming was Pattern on the comforter beside her. He looked almost like lace embroidery. The window shades had been drawn—she
didn't remember doing that—and it was dark outside. The evening of the
day she'd arrived at the Plains.

"Did someone come in?" she asked Pattern, sitting up, pushing stray
locks of red hair from her eyes.

"Mmm. Someones. Gone now."

Shallan rose and wandered into her sitting room. Ash's eyes, she almost
didn't want to walk on the pristine white carpeting. What if she left tracks
and ruined it?

Pattern's "someones" had left food on the table. Suddenly ravenous,
Shallan sat down on the sofa, lifting the lid off the tray to find flatbread
that had been baked with sweet paste in the center, along with dipping
sauces.

"Remind me," she said, "to thank Palona in the morning. That woman is divine."

"Mmm. No. I think she is . . . Ah . . . Exaggeration?"

"You catch on quickly," Shallan said as Pattern became a three-dimensional mass of twisting lines, a ball hanging in the air above the seat beside her.

"No," he said. "I am too slow. You prefer some food and not others. Why?"

"The taste," Shallan said.

"I should understand this word," Pattern said. "But I do not, not really."

Storms. How did you describe taste? "It's like color . . . you see with your mouth." She grimaced. "And that was an awful metaphor. Sorry. I have trouble being insightful on an empty stomach."

"You say you are 'on' the stomach," Pattern said. "But I know you do not mean this. Context allows me to infer what you truly mean. In a way, the very phrase is a lie."

"It's not a lie," Shallan said, "if everyone understands and knows what it means."

"Mm. Those are some of the best lies."

"Pattern," Shallan said, breaking off a piece of flatbread, "sometimes you're about as intelligible as a Bavlander trying to quote ancient Vorin poetry."

A note beside the food said that Vathah and her soldiers had arrived, and had been quartered in a tenement nearby. Her slaves had been incorporated into the manor's staff for the time being.

Chewing on the bread—it was delightful—Shallan went over to her trunks with the intent of unpacking. When she opened the first, however, she was confronted by a blinking red light. Tyn's spanreed.

Shallan stared at it. That would be the person who relayed Tyn's information. Shallan assumed it was a woman, though since the information relay station was in Tashikk, they might not even be Vorin. It could be a man.

She knew so little. She was going to have to be very careful . . . storms, she might get herself killed even if she *was* careful. Shallan was tired, however, of being pushed around.

These people knew something about Urithiru. It was, dangerous or not, Shallan's best lead. She took out the spanreed, prepared its board with paper, and placed the reed. Once she turned the dial to indicate she had set up, the pen remained hanging there, immobile, but did not immediately start writing. The person trying to contact her had stepped away—the pen could have been in there blinking for hours. She'd have to wait until the person on the other side returned.

"Inconvenient," she said, then smiled at herself. Was she really complaining about waiting a few minutes for instantaneous communication across half the world?

I will need to find a way to contact my brothers, she thought. That would be distressingly slow, without a spanreed. Could she arrange a message through one of these relay stations in Tashikk using a different intermediary, perhaps?

She settled back down on the couch—pen and writing board near the tray of food—and looked through the stack of previous communications that Tyn had exchanged with this distant person. There weren't many. Tyn had probably destroyed them periodically. The ones remaining involved questions regarding Jasnah, House Davar, and the Ghostbloods.

One oddity stood out to Shallan. The way Tyn spoke of this group wasn't like that of a thief and one-off employers. Tyn spoke of "getting in good" and "moving up" within the Ghostbloods.

"Pattern," Pattern said.

"What?" Shallan asked, looking toward him.

"Pattern," he replied. "In the words. Mmm."

"Of this sheet?" Shallan asked, holding up the page.

"There and others," Pattern said. "See the first words?"

Shallan frowned, inspecting the sheets. In each one, the first words came from the remote writer. A simple sentence asking after Tyn's health or status. Tyn replied simply each time.

"I don't understand," Shallan said.

"They form groups of five," Pattern said. "Quintets, the letters. Mmm. Each message follows a pattern—first three words start with one each of three of the quintet of letters. Tyn's reply, the two that match."

Shallan looked it over, though she couldn't see what Pattern meant. He explained it again, and she *thought* she grasped it, but the pattern was complex.

"A code," Shallan said. It made sense; you'd want a way to authenticate that the right person was on the other end of the spanreed. She blushed as she realized she had almost ruined this opportunity. If Pattern hadn't seen this, or if the spanreed had started writing immediately, Shallan would have exposed herself.

She couldn't do this. She couldn't infiltrate a group skilled and powerful enough to bring down Jasnah herself. She just *couldn't*.

And yet she had to.

She got out her sketchbook and started to draw, letting her fingers move on their own. She needed to be older, but not too much older. She'd be darkeyed. People would remark upon a lighteyes they didn't know moving through camp. A darkeyes would be more invisible. To the right people, though, she could imply that she was using the eyedrops.

Dark hair. Long, like her real hair, but not red. Same height, same build, but a much different face. Worn features, like Tyn's. A scar across the chin, a more angular face. Not as pretty, but not ugly either. More . . . straightforward.

She sucked in Stormlight from the lamp beside her, and that *energy* made her draw more quickly. It wasn't excitement. It was a need to go forward.

She finished with a flourish, and found a face staring back at her from the page, almost alive. Shallan breathed out Light and felt it envelop her, twist about her. Her vision clouded for a moment, and she saw only the glow of that fading Stormlight.

Then it was gone. She didn't feel any different. She prodded at her face. It felt the same. Had she—

The lock of hair hanging down over her shoulder was black. Shallan stared at it, then rose from her seat, eager and timid at the same time. She crossed to the washroom and stepped up to the mirror there, looking at a face transformed, one with tan skin and dark eyes. The face from her drawing, given color and life.

"It works . . ." she whispered. This was more than changing scuffs in her dress or making herself look older, as she'd done before. This was a complete transformation. "What can we do with this?"

"Whatever we imagine," Pattern said from the wall nearby. "Or whatever you can imagine. I am not good with what is *not*. But I like it. I like the . . . taste . . . of it." He seemed very pleased with himself at that comment.

Something was off. Shallan frowned, holding up her sketch, realizing she'd left a spot unfinished on the side of the nose. The Lightweaving there didn't cover up her nose completely, and had a kind of fuzzy gap in the side. It was small; someone else would probably just see it as a strange scar. To her, it seemed glaring, and offended her artistic sense.

She prodded at the rest of the nose. She'd made it slightly larger than her real one, and could reach *through* the image to touch her nose. The image had no substance to it. In fact, if she moved her finger quickly through the tip of the false nose, it fuzzed to Stormlight, like smoke that had been blown away by a gust.

She removed her fingers, and the image snapped back into place, though it still had that gap on the side. Sloppy drawing on her part.

"How long will the image last?" she asked.

"It feeds on Light," Pattern said.

Shallan dug the spheres from her safepouch. They were all dun—she'd likely used those up in the conversation with the highprinces. She took one from the lamp on the wall, replacing it with a dun sphere of the same denomination, and carried it in her fist.

Shallan went back into the sitting room. She'd need a different outfit, of course. A darkeyed woman wouldn't—

The spanreed was writing.

Shallan hastened over to the sofa, breath catching as she saw the words appear. *I think some information I have today will work.* A simple introduction, but it followed the right pattern for the code.

"Mmm," Pattern said.

She needed the first two words of her reply to start with the proper letters. *But you said that last time,* she wrote, hopefully completing the code.

Don't worry, the messenger wrote. *You'll like this, though the timing might be tight. They want to meet.*

Good, Shallan wrote back, relaxing—and blessing the time Tyn had spent forcing her to practice forgery techniques. She'd taken to it quickly, as it was a kind of drawing, but Tyn's suggestions now let her imitate the woman's own sloppier writing with demonstrable skill.

They want to meet tonight, Tyn, the reed wrote.

Tonight? What time was it? A clock on the wall read half past first night bell. It was just first moon, right after dark. She picked up the spanreed and started to write, "I don't know if I'm ready," but stopped herself. That wasn't how Tyn would say it.

I'm not ready, she wrote instead.

They were insistent, the messenger returned. *It is why I tried to contact you earlier. Apparently, Jasnah's ward arrived today. What happened?*

It is none of your concern, Shallan wrote back, matching the tone Tyn had used previously in these conversations. The person on the other end was a servant, not a colleague.

Of course, the reed wrote. *But they want to meet you tonight. If you refuse, it might mean a severing of ties.*

Stormfather! Tonight? Shallan ran her fingers through her hair, staring at the page. Could she do it tonight?

Would waiting really change anything?

Heart thumping, she wrote, *I thought I had Jasnah's ward captive, but the girl betrayed me. I'm not well. But I will send my apprentice.*

Another one, Tyn? the reed wrote. *After what happened with Si? Anyway, I doubt they'll like meeting with an apprentice.*

They don't have a choice, Shallan wrote.

Perhaps she could have created a Lightweaving around herself that made her look like Tyn, but she doubted she was ready for something like that. Pretending to be someone she'd invented would be tough enough— but imitating a specific person? She'd be discovered for sure.

I'll see, the messenger wrote.

Shallan waited. In distant Tashikk, the messenger would be getting out another spanreed and acting as intermediary to the Ghostbloods. Shallan spent the time checking on the sphere she'd carried in from the washroom.

Its light had faded a small amount. Keeping this Lightweaving going would require her to keep a stock of infused spheres on her person.

The spanreed started writing again. *They'll do it. Can you get to Sebarial's warcamp quickly?*

I think I can, Shallan wrote. *Why there?*

It's one of the few with gates open all night, the messenger wrote. *There is a tenement where your employers will meet your apprentice. I'll draw you a map. Have your apprentice arrive at Salas's moonheight. Good luck.*

A sketch followed, indicating the location. Salas's moonheight? She'd have twenty-five minutes, and she didn't know the camp at all. Shallan leaped to her feet, then froze. She couldn't go like this, dressed as a light-eyed woman. She hurried to Tyn's trunk and dug through clothing.

A few minutes later she stood in front of the mirror, wearing loose brown trousers, a white buttoned shirt, and a thin glove on her safehand. She felt naked with her hand exposed like that. The trousers weren't so bad—darkeyed women wore them when working the plantation back home, though she'd never seen a lighteyed lady in them. But that glove . . .

She shivered, noticing that her false face blushed when she did. The nose moved when she wrinkled her own as well. That was a good thing, though she'd been hoping to be able to hide her embarrassment.

She pulled on one of Tyn's white coats. The stiff thing went all the way down to the top of her boots, and she tied it at the waist with a thick black hogshide belt so that it was mostly closed in front, as Tyn had worn it. She finished by replacing the spheres in the pouch in her pocket with infused ones from the lamps in the room.

That flaw in her nose still bothered her. *Something to shade the face,* she thought, hurrying back to her trunk. There, she dug out Bluth's white hat, the one with the sides that folded upward at a slant. Hopefully it would look better on her than it had on Bluth.

She put it on, and when she returned to the mirror, she was pleased with how it shaded her face. It did look kind of silly. But then, she felt that *everything* about this outfit looked silly. A gloved hand? Trousers? The coat had seemed imposing on Tyn—it indicated experience and a sense of personal style. When Shallan wore it, she looked like she was pretending. She saw through the illusion to the frightened girl from rural Jah Keved.

Authority is not a real thing. Jasnah's words. *It is mere vapors—an illusion. I can create that illusion . . . as can you.*

Shallan stood up taller, straightened the hat, then went to the bedroom and tucked a few things in her pockets, including the map of where to go. She walked to the window and pulled it open. Fortunately, she was on the ground floor.

"Here we go," she whispered to Pattern.

Out she went, into the night.

And thus were the disturbances in the Revv toparchy quieted, when, upon their ceasing to prosecute their civil dissensions, Nalan'Elin betook himself to finally accept the Skybreakers who had named him their master, when initially he had spurned their advances and, in his own interests, refused to countenance that which he deemed a pursuit of vanity and annoyance; this was the last of the Heralds to admit to such patronage.

—From *Words of Radiance*, chapter 5, page 17

The warcamp was still busy, despite the hour. She wasn't surprised; her time in Kharbranth had taught her that not everyone treated the arrival of night as a reason to stop working. Here, there were nearly as many people about in the streets as when she'd first ridden through.

And almost nobody paid attention to her.

For once, she didn't feel conspicuous. Even in Kharbranth, people had glanced at her—noticed her, considered her. Some had thought of robbing her, others of how to use her. A young lighteyes without proper escort was distinctive, and possibly an opportunity. However, while wearing straight dark hair and dark brown eyes, she might as well have been invisible. It was *wonderful*.

Shallan smiled, stuffing her hands in the pockets of her coat—she still felt embarrassed by that gloved safehand, though nobody even *looked* at it.

She reached an intersection. In one direction, the warcamp glittered with torches and oil lanterns. A market, busy enough that nobody trusted spheres in their lamps. Shallan walked toward it; she'd be safer on the more traveled streets. Her fingers crinkled on the paper in her pocket, and she drew it out as she stopped to wait for a group of chattering people to move from in front of her.

The map looked easy enough to parse. She just needed to get her bearings. She waited, then finally realized that the group in front of her *wasn't* going to move. She was expecting them to defer to her as they would a lighteyes. Shaking her head at her foolishness, she went around them.

It continued like that; she was forced to squeeze through tight places between bodies, and was jostled as she walked. This market flowed like two rivers passing one another, with shops on either side and vendors peddling food in the center. It was even covered in some places by awnings that stretched across to the buildings on the other side.

Perhaps only ten paces across, it was a claustrophobic, bustling, jabbering mess. And Shallan loved it. She found herself wanting to stop and sketch half the people she passed. They all seemed so full of life, whether haggling or simply walking with a friend and chewing on a snack. Why hadn't she gone out more in Kharbranth?

She stopped, grinning at a man performing a show with puppets and a box. Farther down the way, a Herdazian used a sparkflicker and some kind of oil to make bursts of flame in the air. If she could just stop off a little time and do a sketch of him . . .

No. She had business to be about. Part of her didn't want to go forward with it, obviously, and her mind was trying to distract her. She was becoming increasingly aware of this defense of hers. She used it, she *needed* it, but she couldn't let it control her life.

She did stop at the cart of a woman selling glazed fruit, however. They looked juicy and red, and had been stabbed through with a little stick before being dipped in a glassy melted sugar. Shallan pulled a sphere from her pocket and held it out.

The woman froze, staring at the sphere. Others stopped nearby. What was the problem? It was just an emerald mark. It wasn't like she'd gotten out the broam.

She looked at the glyphs listing prices. A stick of candied fruit was a single clearchip. Denominations of spheres wasn't something she'd often had to think about, but if she remembered . . .

Her mark was worth two hundred and fifty times the cost of the treat. Even in her family's strained state, this wouldn't have been considered much money to them. But that was on the level of houses and estates, not the level of street vendors and working darkeyes.

"Uh, I don't think I can change that," the woman said. "Er . . . citizen." A title given to a wealthy darkeyes of the first or second nahn.

Shallan blushed. How many times was she going to prove just how naive she was? "It's for one of the treats, and for some help. I'm new to the area. I could use some directions."

"Expensive way to get directions, miss," the woman said, but pocketed the sphere with deft fingers nonetheless.

"I need to find Nar Street."

"Ah. You're going the wrong storming way, miss. Back up the market flow, turn right. You'll need to go, uh, six blocks, I think? It's easy to find; the highprince made everyone lay out their buildings in squares, like in a proper city. Look for the taverns, and you'll be there. But miss, I don't think that's the sort of place one like you should be visiting, if you don't mind me saying."

Even as a darkeyes, people thought her incapable of taking care of herself. "Thank you," Shallan said, plucking out one of the sticks of candied fruit. She hastened away, crossing the flow to join those walking in the opposite direction through the market.

"Pattern?" she whispered.

"Mmm." He was clinging to the outside of her coat, near the knees.

"Trail behind and watch to see if anyone follows me," Shallan said. "Do you think you can do that?"

"They will make a pattern if they come," he said, dropping to the ground. For a brief moment in the air, between coat and stone, he was a dark mass of twisting lines. Then he vanished like a drop of water hitting a lake.

Shallan hurried along with the flow, safehand securely gripping the sphere pouch in her coat pocket, freehand carrying the stick of fruit. She remembered all too well how Jasnah's deliberate flashing of too much money in Kharbranth had lured thieves like vines to stormwater.

Shallan followed the directions, her sense of liberation replaced by anxiety. The corner she took out of the market led her to a roadway that was much less crowded. Was the fruit vendor trying to direct Shallan into a trap where she could be robbed easily? Head down, she hurried along the road. She couldn't Soulcast to protect herself, not as Jasnah had. Storms! Shallan hadn't even been able to make sticks catch fire. She doubted she'd be able to transform living bodies.

She had Lightweaving, but she was already using that. Could she Lightweave a second image at the same time? How *was* her disguise doing, anyway? It would be draining the Light from her spheres. She almost pulled them out to see how much was gone, then stopped herself. Fool. She was worried about being robbed, and so she considered revealing a handful of money?

She stopped after two blocks. Some people did walk this street, a handful of men in workers' clothing heading home for the night. The buildings here certainly weren't as nice as the ones she'd left behind.

"Nobody follows," Pattern said from her feet.

Shallan jumped nearly to the rooftops. She raised her freehand to her breast, breathing in and out deeply. She really thought she could infiltrate a group of assassins? Her own *spren* often made her jump.

Tyn said that nothing would teach me, Shallan thought, *but personal experience. I'm just going to have to muddle through these first few times and hope I get used to this before I get myself killed.*

"Let's keep moving," Shallan said. "We're running out of time." She started forward, digging into the fruit. It really was good, though her nerves prevented her from fully enjoying it.

The street with the taverns was actually five blocks away, not six. Shallan's increasingly wrinkled paper showed the meeting place as a tenement building across from a tavern with blue light shining through the windows.

Shallan tossed aside her fruit stick as she stepped up to the tenement building. It couldn't be old—nothing in these warcamps could be more than five or six years old—but it *looked* ancient. The stones weathered, the window shutters hanging askew in places. She was surprised a highstorm hadn't blown the thing over.

Fully aware that she could be striding into the whitespine's den for dinner, she walked up and knocked. The door was opened by a darkeyed man the size of a boulder who had a beard trimmed like a Horneater's. His hair *did* seem to have some red in it.

She resisted the urge to shuffle from one foot to the next as he looked her up and down. Finally, he opened the door all the way, motioning her in with thick fingers. She didn't miss the large axe that leaned against the wall just next to him, illuminated by the single feeble Stormlight lamp—it looked like it only had a chip in it—on the wall.

Taking a deep breath, Shallan entered.

The place smelled moldy. She heard water dripping from somewhere farther inside, stormwater infallibly making its way from a leaking roof down, down, down to the ground floor. The guard did not speak as he led her along the hall. The floor was *wood*. There was something about walking on wood that made her feel as if she were going to fall through. It seemed to groan with every step. Good stone never did anything like that.

The guard nodded toward an opening in the wall, and Shallan stared into the blackness there. Steps. Down.

Storms, what am I doing?

Not being timid. That was what she was doing. Shallan glanced at the brutish guard and raised an eyebrow, forcing her voice to sound calm. "You really went all-out on the decor. How long did you have to look to find a den in the Shattered Plains that had a creepy staircase in it?"

The guard actually smiled. It didn't make him look any less intimidating.

"The stairs aren't going to collapse under me, are they?" Shallan asked.

"Is fine," the guard said. His voice was surprisingly high pitched. "He did not collapse for me, and I had two breakfasts today." He patted his stomach. "Go. They wait for you."

She got out a sphere for light and started down the stairwell. The stone walls here had been cut. Who would go to the trouble to burrow out a basement for a rotting tenement building? The answer came as she noticed several extended crem dribbles on the wall. A little like wax melting down the side of a candle, these had hardened to stone long ago.

This hole was here before the Alethi came, she thought. When settling this warcamp, Sebarial had built this building above an already-existent basement. The warcamp craters must have once held people. There was no other explanation. Who had they been? The Natan people of long ago?

The steps led down into a small, empty room. How odd to find a basement in such a ramshackle building; normally, you found them only in wealthy homes, as the precautions one needed to take to prevent flooding were extensive. Shallan folded her arms, confused, until one corner of the floor opened, bathing the room in light. Shallan stepped back, breath catching. A part of the rock floor was false, hiding a trapdoor.

The basement had a basement. She stepped up to the edge of the hole and saw a ladder heading down toward red carpet and light that seemed almost blinding following the dimness she'd been in. This place must flood something fierce after a storm.

She swung onto the ladder and made her way down, glad for the trousers. The trapdoor closed above—it appeared to have some sort of pulley mechanism.

She hopped off onto the carpet and turned, finding a room that was incongruously palatial. A long dining table ran down the center, and it sparkled with glass goblets that had gemstones set in their sides; their glow sprayed the room with light. Cozy shelves lined the walls, each laden with books and ornaments. Many were in small glass cases. Trophies of some sort?

Of the half-dozen or so people in the room, one drew her attention most. Straight-backed, with jet-black hair, he wore white clothing and stood in front of the room's crackling hearth. He reminded her of someone, a man from her childhood. The messenger with the smiling eyes, the enigma who knew so much. *Two blind men waited at the end of an era, contemplating beauty. . . .*

The man turned around, revealing light violet eyes and a face scarred by old wounds, including a cut that ran down his cheek and deformed his upper lip. Though he looked refined—holding a goblet of wine in his left hand and dressed in the finest of suits—his face and hands told another story. Of battles, of killing, and of strife.

This was not the messenger from Shallan's past. The man raised his right hand, in which he held some kind of long reed. He placed this to his lips. He held it like a weapon, pointed right at Shallan.

She froze in place, unable to move, staring down that weapon across the room. Finally, she glanced over her shoulder. A target hung on the wall in the form of a tapestry with various creatures on it. Shallan yelped and jumped to the side just before the man blew on his weapon, shooting a small dart through the air. It passed within inches of her before embedding itself in one of the figures on the wall hanging.

Shallan raised her safehand to her breast and took a deep breath. *Steady,* she thought at herself. *Steady.*

"Tyn," the man said, lowering the blowgun, "is unwell?" The quiet way he spoke made Shallan shiver. She could not place his accent.

"Yes," Shallan said, finding her voice.

The man set his goblet on the mantel beside him, then slipped another dart from his shirt pocket. He tucked this carefully into the end of the blowgun. "She does not seem the type to let something so trivial keep her from an important meeting."

He looked up at Shallan, blowgun loaded. Those violet eyes seemed like glass, his scarred face expressionless. The room seemed to hold its breath.

He'd seen through her lie. Shallan felt a cold sweat.

"You are right," Shallan said. "Tyn is well. However, the plan did not go as she promised. Jasnah Kholin is dead, but the implementation of the assassination was sloppy. Tyn felt it prudent to work through an intermediary for now."

The man narrowed his eyes, then finally raised his reed and blew sharply. Shallan jumped, but the dart did not strike her, instead flying to hit the wall hanging.

"She reveals herself as a coward," he said. "You came here willingly, knowing that I might just kill you for her mistakes?"

"Every woman starts somewhere, Brightlord," Shallan said, voice trembling rebelliously. "I can't claw my way upward without taking a few chances. If you don't kill me, then I have had a chance to meet people that Tyn probably would never have introduced me to."

"Bold," the man said. He gestured with two fingers, and one of the people sitting beside the hearth—a spindly lighteyed man with teeth so large, he might have had some rat in his heritage somewhere—scrambled forward and plunked something down on the long table near Shallan.

A sack of spheres. Inside it must be broams; the sack, though dark brown, glowed brightly.

"Tell me where she is, and you may have that money," said the scarred man, loading another dart. "You have ambition. I like that. I will not only pay you for her location, but will attempt to find you a position in my organization."

"Pardon, Brightlord," Shallan said. "But you know I won't sell her out to you." Surely he could see her fear, sweat dampening the lining of her hat, trickling down her temples. Indeed, fearspren wiggled up through the ground beside her, though his view of them might be blocked by the table. "If I were willing to betray Tyn for a price, then of what worth would I ever be to you? You'd know that I'd do the same to you, if offered a big enough bounty."

"Honor?" the man asked, expression still blank, dart pinched between two fingers. "From a thief?"

"Pardon again, Brightlord," Shallan said. "But I am no mere thief."

"And if I were to torture you? I could get the information that way, I assure you."

"I don't doubt that you could, Brightlord," Shallan said. "But do you really think Tyn would send me with knowledge of her location? What would be the point of torturing me?"

"Well," the man said, looking down and tucking the dart into place, "for one thing, it would be fun."

Breathe, Shallan told herself. *Slowly. Normally.* It was hard to manage. "I don't think you'll do that, Brightlord."

He raised the reed and blew with a swift motion. The dart *thumped* as it stuck into the wall. "And why not?"

"Because you don't seem the type to throw away something useful." She nodded toward the relics in glass boxes.

"You presume to be of use to me?"

Shallan raised her head, meeting his gaze. "Yes."

He held her eyes. The hearth crackled.

"Very well," he finally said, turning toward his fireplace and picking up his cup again. He continued to hold the reed in one hand, but drank with the other, his back to her.

Shallan felt like a puppet whose strings had been cut. She exhaled in relief, legs wobbling, and sat down on one of the chairs beside the dining table. Fingers trembling, she got out a handkerchief and wiped her brow and temples, pushing back the hat.

When she stopped to put the handkerchief away, she realized that someone had taken the seat beside her. Shallan hadn't even seen him move, and his presence gave her a start. The short, tan-skinned person had some kind of carapace mask tied to his face, pulled tight. In fact, it looked like . . . like the skin had started to grow around the edges of the mask somehow.

The arrangement of red-orange carapace pieces was like a mosaic, giving a hint of eyebrows, of anger and rage. Behind that mask, a pair of dark eyes regarded her, unblinking, and an impassive mouth and chin were also left exposed. The man . . . no, the *woman*—Shallan noticed the hint of breasts and shape of the torso. The exposed safehand had thrown her.

Shallan stifled a blush. The woman wore dark brown clothing, simple, tied at the waist with an intricate belt, studded with more carapace. Four other people wearing more traditional Alethi clothing chatted softly beside the fire. The tall man who had questioned her did not speak again.

"Um, Brightlord?" Shallan said, looking toward him.

"I am considering," the man said. "I had been expecting to kill you and hunt down Tyn. You can tell her she would have been fine coming to me—I am not angry that she did not retrieve the information from Jasnah. I hired the hunter I felt best for the task, and I understood the risks. Kholin is dead, and Tyn was to achieve that at all other costs. I may not have commended her on the job, but I was satisfied.

"Deciding not to come explain in person, however—that cowardice turns my stomach. She hides, like prey." He took a sip of his wine. "You are not a coward. She sent someone she knew I would not kill. She always has been clever."

Great. What did that mean for Shallan? She hesitantly rose from her seat, wanting to be away from the strange little woman with the unblinking eyes. Instead, Shallan took the chance to inspect the room in greater detail. Where was the smoke from the fire going? Had they cut a flue all the way down here?

The right wall had the greater number of trophies, including several enormous gemhearts. Those were, together, likely worth more than her father's estates. Fortunately, they weren't infused. Even uncut as they were, they'd probably glow enough to blind. There were also shells that Shallan vaguely recognized. That tusk was probably from a whitespine. And that eye socket, that looked frighteningly close to the structure of a santhid's skull.

Other curiosities baffled her. A vial of pale sand. A couple of thick hairpins. A lock of golden hair. The branch of a tree with writing on it she couldn't read. A silver knife. An odd flower preserved in some kind of solution. There were no plaques to explain these mementos. That chunk of pale pink crystal looked like it might be some kind of gemstone, but why was it so delicate? Bits of it had flaked off in its case, as if simply setting it down had almost crushed it.

She stepped, hesitantly, closer to the back of the room. Smoke from the fire rose, then curled and twisted around something hanging at the top of the hearth. A gemstone? . . . No, a fabrial. It gathered the smoke as a spool gathered thread. She'd never seen anything like it.

"Do you know the man named Amaram?" asked the scarred man in white.

"No, Brightlord."

"I am called Mraize," the man said. "You may use that title for me. And you are?"

"I'm called Veil," Shallan said, using a name she'd been toying with.

"Very well. Amaram is a Shardbearer in the court of Highprince Sadeas. He is also my current prey."

Hearing it spoken like that sent a shiver through Shallan. "And what do you wish of me, Mraize?" She tried, but didn't get the pronunciation of the title quite right. It wasn't a Vorin term.

"He owns a manor near Sadeas's palace," Mraize said. "Inside, Amaram hides secrets. I would know which ones. Tell your mistress to investigate and return to me with information next week on Chachel. She will know what I seek. If she does this, my disappointment with her will fade."

Sneaking into the manor of a Shardbearer? Storms! Shallan had no idea how she'd accomplish such a thing. She should leave this place, abandon her disguise, and count herself lucky for having escaped alive.

Mraize set down his empty cup of wine, and she saw that his right hand was scarred, the fingers crooked, as if they had been broken and badly reset. There, glistening and golden on Mraize's middle finger, was a signet ring bearing the same symbol that Jasnah had drawn. The symbol Shallan's steward had carried, the symbol that Kabsal had tattooed on his body.

There was no backing out. Shallan would do whatever she had to in order to find out what these people knew. About her family, about Jasnah, and about the end of the world itself.

"The task will be done," Shallan said to Mraize.

"No question of payment?" Mraize asked, amused, removing a dart from his pocket. "Your mistress always asked."

"Brightlord," Shallan said, "one does not haggle at the finest winehouses. Your payment will be accepted."

For the first time since she'd entered, she saw Mraize smile, though he didn't look toward her. "Do not harm Amaram, little knife," he warned. "His life belongs to another. Do not alert anyone or bring suspicion. Tyn is to investigate and return. Nothing more."

He turned around and blew a dart into the wall. Shallan glanced at the other four people by the fire and took Memories of them with a quick blink each. Then—sensing she had been dismissed—she walked to the ladder.

She felt Mraize's eyes on her back as he raised his blowgun one last time. The trapdoor opened above. Shallan felt the gaze follow her as she climbed up the ladder.

A dart passed just beneath her, between the rungs, and stabbed the wall. Breathing quickly, Shallan left the hidden chamber, entering the dusty upper basement again. The trapdoor closed, shutting her away into the darkness.

Her poise broke, and she scrambled up the steps and out of the building. She stopped outside, breathing deeply. The street outside had grown *more* busy, not less, with those taverns drawing a crowd. Shallan hurried on her way.

She realized now that she hadn't had much of a plan in coming to meet with the Ghostbloods. What was she going to do? Get information from them somehow? That would require earning their trust. Mraize didn't seem the type to trust anyone. How would she find out what he knew about Urithiru? How to call his people off her brothers? How would she—

"Following," Pattern said.

Shallan pulled up short. "What?"

"People follow," Pattern said, voice pleasant, as if he had no idea how tense this entire experience had been for Shallan. "You asked me to watch. I watched."

Of *course* Mraize would send someone to tail her. Her cold sweat returning, Shallan forced herself to move, not looking over her shoulder. "How many?" she asked Pattern, who had climbed up onto the side of her coat.

"One," Pattern said. "The person with the mask, though she now wears a black cloak. Should we go speak with her? You are friends now, right?"

"No. I wouldn't say that."

"Mmm . . ." Pattern said. She suspected he was trying to figure out the nature of human interactions. Good luck.

What to do? Shallan doubted she could lose her tail. The woman would have practice with this sort of thing, while Shallan . . . well, she had a lot of practice reading books and sketching pictures.

Lightweaving, she thought. *Can I do something with that?* Her disguise was still working—the dark hair trailing down her shoulder proved that. Could she change to a different image overlaying herself?

She drew in Stormlight, and that made her increase her pace. Up ahead, an alley turned between two groups of tenements. Ignoring memories of a similar alleyway in Kharbranth, Shallan turned in to this one with a quick step, then immediately breathed out Stormlight, trying to shape it. Perhaps into the image of a large man, to cover over her coat, and . . .

And the Stormlight just puffed in front of her, doing nothing. She panicked, but forced herself to keep moving down the alleyway.

It didn't work. Why didn't it work? She'd been able to make it work in her rooms!

The only thing she could think that was different was her sketch. In her rooms, she'd drawn a detailed picture. She didn't have that now.

She reached into her pocket, taking out the sheet of paper with the map sketched on it. The back was blank. She fished in the other pocket for the pencil she'd instinctively put there and tried to draw while walking. Impossible. Salas had almost set, and it was too dark. Besides, she couldn't do good detail while moving and with nothing firm to back the paper. If she stopped and sketched, would that arouse suspicion? Storms, she was so nervous, she had trouble keeping the pencil straight.

She needed a place where she could hide, crouch down, and do a solid sketch. Like one of those doorway nooks she'd passed in the alleyway.

She started to draw a wall.

That she *could* do while walking. She turned down a side street, the light from an open tavern spilling across her. She ignored the ruckus of laughter and shouts, though a few of those seemed to be directed at her, and drew a simple stone wall on her sheet.

She had no idea if this would work, but she might as well try. She turned in to another alleyway—almost stumbling over the snoring form of a drunk who was missing his shoes—then took off at a run. A short distance in, she ducked into a doorway recess a couple of feet deep. Breathing out her remaining Stormlight, she imagined the wall she'd drawn covering over the doorway.

Everything went black.

The alley had been dark anyway, but now she couldn't see *anything*. No phantom light of the moon, no glow from the torchlit tavern at the end of the alley. Did that mean her image was working? She pushed back against the door behind her, pulling off her hat, trying to make sure none of her poked through the illusory wall. She heard a faint scrape outside, boots on stone, and a sound like clothing brushing against the wall across from her. Then nothing.

Shallan remained there, frozen, straining her ears but hearing only the thud of her heart. Finally, she whispered, "Pattern. Are you here?"

"Yes," he said.

"Go and see if the woman is outside somewhere near."

He made no sound as he left and then returned. "She is gone."

Shallan let out the breath she'd been holding. Then, bracing herself, she stepped through the wall. A glow, like that of Stormlight, filled her vision. Then she was out, standing in the alleyway. The illusion behind her swirled briefly like disturbed smoke, then quickly re-formed.

The imitation was actually pretty good. Examined closely, the joints between her stones didn't align perfectly with the real ones, but that was hard to see at night. Only a few moments later, though, the illusion shattered back to swirling Stormlight and evaporated. She had no Light left to sustain it.

"Your disguise is gone," Pattern noted.

Red hair. Shallan gasped, then immediately shoved her safehand into her pocket. The darkeyed con woman that Tyn had trained could go about half-clothed, but not Shallan herself. It just wasn't right.

It was also stupid, and she knew that, but she couldn't change her feelings. She hesitated briefly, then took off the coat. With that and the hat removed, and with her hair and face changed, she was a different person. She left out the opposite end of the alley from where she assumed the masked woman had gone.

Shallan hesitated, getting her bearings. Where was the mansion? She tried retracing her route mentally, but had trouble fixing her position. She needed something she could see. She took out her wrinkled paper and drew a quick map of the path she'd taken so far.

"I can lead you back to the mansion," Pattern said.

"I can manage." Shallan held up the map and nodded.

"Mmm. It is a pattern. You can see this one?"

"Yes."

"But not the pattern of letters with the spanreed?"

How could she explain? "Those were words," Shallan said. "The warcamp is a place, something I can draw." The picture of the path back was clear to her.

"Ah . . ." Pattern said.

She returned to the mansion without incident, but she couldn't be certain she'd cleanly slipped the tail, nor whether someone from Sebarial's staff had seen her crossing the grounds and climbing into the window. That was the problem with sneaking about. If nothing seemed to have gone wrong, you rarely knew if it was because you were safe, or if someone had spotted you and just hadn't done anything. Yet.

After pulling her shutters closed and snapping the drapes into place, Shallan threw herself back onto the plush bed, breathing deeply and trembling.

That was, she thought, *the most ridiculous thing I've ever done.*

And yet she found herself excited, flushed with the thrill of it. Storms! She'd *enjoyed* that. The tension, the sweat, the talking her way out of being killed, even the chase at the end. What was wrong with her? When she'd tried to steal from Jasnah, every part of the experience had made her sick.

I'm not that girl anymore, Shallan thought, smiling and staring at the ceiling. *I haven't been for weeks now.*

She *would* find a way to investigate this Brightlord Amaram, and she would earn the trust of Mraize so she could find out what he knew. *I still need an alliance with the Kholin family,* she thought. *And the path to that is Prince Adolin.* She'd have to find a way to interact with him again as soon as possible, but somehow that didn't make her look desperate.

The part involving him seemed likely to be the most pleasant of her tasks. Still smiling, she threw herself off the bed and went to see if any food remained on that tray she'd been left.

But as for the Bondsmiths, they had members only three, which number was not uncommon for them; nor did they seek to increase this by great bounds, for during the times of Madasa, only one of their order was in continual accompaniment of Urithiru and its thrones. Their spren was understood to be specific, and to persuade them to grow to the magnitude of the other orders was seen as seditious.

—From *Words of Radiance*, chapter 16, page 14

K aladin never felt more uncomfortably conspicuous than when visiting Dalinar's lighteyed training grounds, where all of the other soldiers were highborn.

Dalinar mandated that his soldiers wear uniforms during duty hours, and these men obeyed. In his own blue uniform, Kaladin shouldn't have felt set off from them, but he did. Theirs were more lavish, with bright buttons up the sides of the fine coats and gemstones set into the buttons. Others ornamented their uniforms with embroidery. Colorful scarves were growing popular.

The lighteyed looked over Kaladin and his men as they entered. As much as the regular soldiers treated his men like heroes—as much as even these officers respected Dalinar and his decisions—their postures were hostile toward him and his.

You are not wanted here, those stares said. *Everyone has a place. You're out of yours. Like a chull in a dining hall.*

"May I be relieved from duty for today's training, sir?" Renarin asked Kaladin. The youth wore a Bridge Four uniform.

Kaladin nodded. His departure made the other bridgemen relax. Kaladin pointed toward three watch positions, and three of his men ran off to stand guard. Moash, Teft, and Yake stayed with him.

Kaladin marched them up to Zahel, who stood at the back of the sand-covered courtyard. Though the other ardents all busied themselves carrying water, towels, or sparring weapons to dueling lighteyes, Zahel had drawn a circle in the sand and was throwing little colored rocks into it.

"I'm taking you up on your offer," Kaladin said, stepping up to him. "I brought three of my men to learn with me."

"Didn't offer to train four of you," Zahel said.

"I know."

Zahel grunted. "Do forty laps around the outside of this building at a jog, then report back. You have until I get tired of my game to return."

Kaladin gestured sharply, and all four of them took off at a run.

"Wait," Zahel called.

Kaladin stopped, boots crunching sand.

"I was just testing how willing you were to obey me," Zahel said, throwing a rock into his circle. He grunted, as if pleased with himself. Finally, he turned to look at them. "I suppose I don't need to toughen you up. But boy, you've got red on your ears like I've never seen."

"I— Red on my ears?" Kaladin asked.

"Damnation language. I mean that you feel you've got something to prove, that you are spoiling for a fight. It means you're angry at everything and everyone."

"Can you blame us?" Moash asked.

"I suppose I can't. But if I'm going to train you lads, I can't have your red ears getting in the way. You're going to listen, and you're going to do what I say."

"Yes, Master Zahel," Kaladin said.

"Don't call me master," Zahel said. He thumbed over his shoulder toward Renarin, who was putting on his Shardplate with the assistance of some ardents. "I'm his master. For you lads, I'm just an interested party who wants to help you keep my friends alive. Wait here until I get back."

He turned to walk toward Renarin. As Yake picked up one of the colored stones Zahel had been throwing, the man said, without looking, "And don't touch my rocks!"

Yake jumped and dropped the stone.

Kaladin settled back, leaning against one of the pillars that held up the roof overhang, watching Zahel give instruction to Renarin. Syl zipped down and began inspecting the little rocks with a curious expression, trying to figure out what was special about them.

A short time later, Zahel walked past with Renarin, explaining the lad's training for today. Apparently, he wanted Renarin to eat lunch. Kaladin smiled as some ardents hurriedly carried out a table, dining ware, and a heavy stool that could support a Shardbearer. They even had a tablecloth. Zahel left the bemused Renarin, who sat in his hulking Shardplate with his faceplate up, regarding a full lunch. He awkwardly picked up a fork.

"You're teaching him to be delicate with his newfound strength," Kaladin said to Zahel as the man passed back the other way.

"Shardplate is powerful stuff," Zahel said, not looking at Kaladin. "Controlling it is about more than punching through walls and jumping off buildings."

"So when do we—"

"Keep waiting." Zahel wandered off.

Kaladin glanced at Teft, who shrugged. "I like him."

Yake chuckled. "That's because he's almost as grouchy as you are, Teft."

"I ain't grouchy," Teft snapped. "I just have a low threshold for stupidity."

They waited until Zahel jogged back toward them. The men grew immediately alert, eyes widening. Zahel carried a Shardblade.

They'd been hoping for it. Kaladin had told them they might be able to hold one as part of this training. Their eyes followed that Blade as they'd follow a gorgeous woman taking off her glove.

Zahel stepped up, then slammed the Blade into the sandy ground in front of them. He took his hand off the hilt and waved. "All right. Try it out."

They stared at it. "Kelek's breath," Teft finally said. "You are serious, aren't you?"

Nearby, Syl had turned from the rocks and stared at the Blade.

"The morning after talking to your captain in the middle of the Damnation night," Zahel said, "I went to Brightlord Dalinar and the king and asked permission to train you in sword stances. You don't have to carry swords around or anything, but if you're going to fight an assassin with a Shardblade, you need to know the stances and how to respond to them."

He looked down, resting his hand on the Shardblade. "Brightlord Dalinar suggested letting you handle one of the king's Shardblades. Smart man."

Zahel removed his hand and gestured. Teft reached out to touch the Shardblade, but Moash seized the thing first, taking it by the hilt and yanking it—too hard—out of the ground. He stumbled backward, and Teft backed away.

"Be careful, now!" Teft barked. "You'll cut off your own storming arm if you act like a fool."

"I'm no fool," Moash said, holding the sword up, pointing it outward. A single gloryspren faded into existence near his head. "It's heavier than I expected."

"Really?" Yake said. "Everyone says they're light!"

"Those are people used to a regular sword," Zahel said. "If you've trained all of your life with a longsword, then pick up something that looks like it has two or three times as much steel to it, you expect it to weigh more. Not less."

Moash grunted, delicately swiping with the weapon. "From the way the stories are told, I thought it wouldn't have any weight at all. Like it would be as light as a breeze." He hesitantly stuck it into the ground. "It has more resistance when it cuts than I thought too."

"Guess it's about expectations again," Teft said, scratching at his beard and waving Yake to have the weapon next. The stout man pulled it free more carefully than Moash had.

"Stormfather, but it feels strange to hold this," Yake said.

"It's just a tool," Zahel said. "A valuable one, but still just a tool. Remember that."

"It's more than a tool," Yake said, swiping it. "I'm sorry, but it just *is*. I might believe that about a regular sword, but this . . . this is art."

Zahel shook his head in annoyance.

"What?" Kaladin asked as Yake reluctantly handed the Shardblade over to Teft.

"Men prohibited from using the sword because they're too lowborn," Zahel said. "Even after all these years, it strikes me as silly. There's nothing holy about swords. They're better in some situations, worse in others."

"You're an ardent," Kaladin said. "Aren't you supposed to uphold Vorin arts and traditions?"

"Well," Zahel said, "if you haven't noticed, I'm not a very good ardent. I just happen to be an excellent swordsman." He nodded toward the sword. "You going to take a turn?"

Syl looked at Kaladin sharply.

"I'll pass unless you demand it," Kaladin said to Zahel.

"Not curious at all how it feels?"

"Those things have killed too many of my friends. I'd rather not have to touch it, if it's all the same to you."

"Suit yourself," Zahel said. "Brightlord Dalinar's suggestion was to get you used to these weapons. To take away some of the awe. Half the time a man dies by one of those, it's because he's too busy staring to dodge."

"Yeah," Kaladin said softly. "I've seen that. Swing it at me. I need practice facing one down."

"Sure. Let me get the sword's guard."

"No," Kaladin said. "No guard, Zahel. I need to be afraid."

Zahel studied Kaladin for a moment, then nodded, walking over to take the sword from Moash—who had begun a second turn swinging it.

Syl zipped past, twisting around the heads of the men, who couldn't see her. "Thank you," she said, settling onto Kaladin's shoulder.

Zahel walked back and fell into a stance. Kaladin recognized it as one of the lighteyed dueling stances, but he didn't know which one. Zahel stepped forward and swung.

Panic.

Kaladin couldn't keep it from rising. In an instant, he saw Dallet die— the Shardblade shearing through his head. He saw faces with burned-out eyes reflecting on the Blade's too-silvery surface.

The Blade passed a few inches in front of him. Zahel stepped into the swing and brought the Blade around again in a flowing maneuver. This time it would hit, so Kaladin had to step back.

Storms, those monsters were beautiful.

Zahel swung again, and Kaladin had to jump to the side to dodge. *A bit overzealous there, Zahel,* he thought. He dodged again, then reacted to a shadow he'd seen from the corner of his eye. He spun, and came face-to-face with Adolin Kholin.

They stared one another in the eyes. Kaladin waited for a wisecrack. Adolin's eyes flicked toward Zahel and the Shardblade, then turned back to Kaladin. Finally, the prince gave a shallow nod. He turned about and walked toward Renarin.

The implication was simple. The Assassin in White had bested both of them. There was nothing to mock in preparing to fight him again.

Doesn't mean he's not a spoiled blusterer, Kaladin thought, turning back to Zahel. The man had waved over a fellow ardent, and was delivering the Shardblade to him.

"I have to go train Prince Renarin," Zahel said. "Can't leave him alone all day for you fools. Ivis here will go through some sparring moves with you and let you each face down a Shardblade, as Kaladin has done. Get comfortable with the sight, so you don't freeze when one comes for you."

Kaladin and the others nodded. Only after Zahel had trotted away did Kaladin notice that the new ardent, Ivis, was a woman. Though she was an ardent, she kept her hand gloved, so there was some acknowledgment of her gender, even if the flowing ardent clothing and shaved head masked some of the other obvious signs.

A woman with a sword. An odd sight. Of course, was it any odder than darkeyed men holding a Shardblade?

Ivis gave them lengths of wood that, weight and balance wise, were decent approximations of a Shardblade. Like a child's scribble with chalk could be a decent approximation of a person. Then she put them through several routines, demonstrating the ten Shardblade sword stances.

Kaladin had been looking to kill lighteyes from the moment he'd first touched a spear, and during the later years—before being enslaved—he'd gotten pretty good at it. But those lighteyes he'd hunted on the battlefield hadn't been terribly skilled. The majority of men who were truly good with a sword had made their way to the Shattered Plains. So the stances were new to him.

He started to see and understand. Knowing the stances would let him anticipate a swordsman's next move. He didn't have to be wielding a sword himself—he still thought it an inflexible weapon—to make use of that.

An hour or so later, Kaladin set down his practice sword and stepped over to the water barrel. No ardents or parshmen ran drinks to him or his men. He was just fine with that; he wasn't some pampered rich boy. He leaned against the barrel, taking a ladle of water, feeling the good exhaustion deep in his muscles that told him he'd been doing something worthwhile.

He scanned the grounds for Adolin and Renarin. He wasn't on duty watching either of them—Adolin would have come with Mart and Eth, and Renarin was under the watch of the three that Kaladin had assigned earlier. Still, he couldn't help looking to see how they were. An accident here could be—

A woman was on the practice grounds. Not an ardent, but a true lighteyed woman, the one with the vibrant red hair. She had just wandered in, and was scanning the grounds.

He didn't bear a grudge about the incident with his boots. It simply typified how, to a lighteyes, men like Kaladin were playthings. You toyed with darkeyes, took what you needed from them, and gave no thought to having left them far worse for the interaction.

It was how Roshone had been. It was how Sadeas was. It was how this woman was. She wasn't evil, really. She just didn't care.

She's probably a good match for the princeling, he thought as Yake and Teft jogged over for some water. Moash stayed with his practice, intent on his sword forms.

"Not bad," Yake said, following Kaladin's gaze.

"Not bad at what?" Kaladin asked, trying to figure out what the woman was doing.

"Not bad *looking,* Captain," Yake said with a laugh. "Storms! Sometimes, it seems the only thing you think about is who has to be on duty next."

Nearby, Syl nodded emphatically.

"She's lighteyed," Kaladin said.

"So?" Yake said, slapping him on the shoulder. "A lighteyed lady can't be attractive?"

"No." It was as simple as that.

"You are a strange one, sir," Yake said.

Eventually, Ivis called for Yake and Teft to stop idling and return to practice. She didn't call for Kaladin. He seemed to intimidate many of the ardents.

Yake jogged back, but Teft lingered for a moment, then nodded toward the girl, Shallan. "You think we have to worry about her? Foreign woman about whom we know very little, sent in to suddenly be Adolin's betrothed. Sure would make a good assassin."

"Damnation," Kaladin said. "I should have seen that. Good eye, Teft."

Teft shrugged modestly, then jogged back to his training.

He'd assumed the woman was an opportunist, but could she actually be an assassin? Kaladin picked up his practice sword and wandered toward her, passing Renarin, who was training in some of the same stances that Kaladin's men were practicing.

As Kaladin walked toward Shallan, Adolin clanked up beside him in Shardplate.

"What is she doing here?" Kaladin asked.

"Come to watch me while I spar, presumably," Adolin said. "I usually have to kick them out."

"Them?"

"You know. Girls who want to gawk at me while I fight. I wouldn't mind, but if we allowed it, they'd clog the entire grounds every time I came. Nobody would be able to get any sparring done."

Kaladin raised an eyebrow at him.

"What?" Adolin asked. "You don't get women coming to watch while you spar, bridgeboy? Little darkeyed ladies, missing seven teeth and afraid of bathing . . ."

Kaladin looked away from Adolin, drawing his lips to a line. *Next time,* he thought, *I let the assassin have this one.*

Adolin chuckled for a moment, though his laughter trailed off awkwardly. "Anyway," he continued, "she probably has a better reason to be here than others, considering our relationship. We'll still have to kick her out. Can't set a bad precedent."

"You really let this happen?" Kaladin asked. "A betrothal to a woman you'd never met?"

Adolin shrugged armored shoulders. "Things always go so well at first, and then . . . they fall apart on me. I can never figure out where I go wrong. I thought, maybe if there were something more formal in place . . ."

He scowled, as if remembering who he was talking to, and tromped forward at a faster pace to get away from Kaladin. Adolin reached Shallan, who—humming to herself—passed him right by without looking. Adolin raised a hand, mouth opened to speak, as he turned and watched her walk farther across the courtyard. Her eyes were on Nall, head ardent of the practice grounds. Shallan bowed to her in reverence.

Adolin scowled, turning to jog after Shallan, passing Kaladin, who smirked at him.

"Come to watch you, I see," Kaladin said. "Completely fascinated by you, obviously."

"Shut up," Adolin growled.

Kaladin strolled after Adolin, reaching Shallan and Nall in the middle of a conversation.

". . . visual records of these suits are *pathetic*, Sister Nall," Shallan was saying, handing Nall a bound leather portfolio. "We need new sketches. Though much of my time will be spent clerking for Brightlord Sebarial, I would like a few projects of my own during my time at the Shattered Plains. With your blessing, I wish to proceed."

"Your talent is admirable," Nall said, flipping through pages. "Art is your Calling?"

"Natural History, Sister Nall, though sketching is a priority for me in that line of study as well."

"As well it should be." The ardent turned another page. "You have my blessing, dear child. Tell me, which devotary do you call your own?"

"That is . . . a subject of some consternation on my part," Shallan said, taking the portfolio back. "Oh! Adolin. I didn't notice you there. My, but you *do* loom when you wear that armor, don't you?"

"You're letting her stay?" Adolin asked Nall.

"She wishes to update the royal record of Shardplate and Shardblades in the warcamps with new sketches," Nall said. "This seems wise. The king's current accounting of the Shards includes many rough sketches, but few detailed drawings."

"So you're going to need me to pose for you?" Adolin asked, turning to Shallan.

"Actually, the sketches of your Plate are quite complete," Shallan said, "thanks to your mother. I'll focus first on the King's Plate and Blades, which nobody has thought to sketch in any detail."

"Just stay out of the way of the men sparring, child," Nall said as someone called for her. She walked off.

"Look," Adolin said, turning to Shallan. "I can see what you're up to."

"Five foot six inches," Shallan said. "I suspect that's all I will ever be up to, unfortunately."

"Five foot . . ." Adolin said, frowning.

"Yes," Shallan said, scanning the practice grounds. "I thought it was a good height, then I came here. You Alethi really are freakishly tall, aren't you? I'd guess everyone here is a good two inches taller than the Veden average."

"No, that's not . . ." Adolin frowned. "You're here because you want to watch me spar. Admit it. The sketching is a ruse."

"Hmmm. Someone has a high opinion of himself. Comes with being royalty, I suppose. Like funny hats and a fondness for beheadings. Ah, and it's our captain of the guard. Your boots are on the way to your barracks via courier."

Kaladin started as he realized she was talking to him. "Is that so?"

"I had the soles replaced," Shallan said. "They were terribly uncomfortable."

"I liked how they fit!"

"Then you must have stones for feet." She glanced down, then cocked an eyebrow.

"Wait," Adolin said, frowning more deeply. "You wore the bridgeboy's *boots*? How did that happen?"

"Awkwardly," Shallan replied. "And with three pairs of socks." She patted Adolin's armored arm. "If you really want me to sketch you, Adolin, I will. No need to act jealous, though I do still want that walk you promised me. Oh! I *need* to get that. Excuse me."

She strode toward where Renarin was taking hits on his armor from Zahel, presumably to get him used to taking a beating while wearing Plate. Shallan's green gown and red hair were vibrant slashes of color on the grounds. Kaladin inspected her, wondering just how far she could be trusted. Probably not far.

"Insufferable woman," Adolin growled. He glanced at Kaladin. "Stop leering at her backside, bridgeboy."

"I'm *not* leering. And what do you care? You just said she was insufferable."

"Yeah," Adolin said, looking back toward her with a wide grin. "She all but ignored me, didn't she?"

"I suppose."

"Insufferable," Adolin said, though he seemed to mean something completely different. His smile widened and he strode after her, moving with the grace of Shardplate that was so discordant with its apparent bulk.

Kaladin shook his head. Lighteyes and their games. How had he found himself in such a position that he had to spend so much time around them? He walked back to the barrel and got another drink. Soon after, a practice sword crunching to the sand announced Moash joining him.

Moash nodded gratefully as Kaladin handed over the ladle. Teft and Yake were having a turn facing down the Shardblade.

"She let you go?" Kaladin asked, nodding toward their trainer.

Moash shrugged, gulping water. "I didn't flinch."

Kaladin nodded appreciatively.

"What we're doing here is good," Moash said. "*Important*. After the way you trained us in those chasms, I thought I didn't have anything left to learn. Shows how much I knew."

Kaladin nodded, folding his arms. Adolin displayed several dueling stances for Renarin, Zahel nodding approvingly. Shallan had settled down to sketch them. Was this all an excuse to get her close, so she could wait for the right time to slide a knife into Adolin's gut?

A paranoid way to think, perhaps, but that *was* his job. So he kept an eye on Adolin as the man turned and began sparring with Zahel, to give Renarin some perspective on how to use the stances.

Adolin *was* a good swordsman. Kaladin would give him that much. So was Zahel, for that matter.

"It was the king," Moash said. "He had my family executed."

It took Kaladin a moment to realize what Moash was talking about. The person that Moash wanted to kill, the person he had a grudge against. It *was* the king.

Kaladin felt a shock spike through him, as if he'd been punched. He turned on Moash.

"We're Bridge Four," Moash continued, staring off to the side at nothing in particular. He took another drink. "We stick together. You should know about . . . why I am the way I am. My grandparents were the only family I ever knew. Parents died when I was a child. Ana and Da, they raised me. The king . . . he killed them."

"How did it happen?" Kaladin asked softly, checking to make sure none of the ardents were close enough to hear.

"I was away," Moash said, "working a caravan that ran out here, to this wasteland. Ana and Da, they were second nahn. Important for darkeyes, you know? Ran their own shop. Silversmiths. I never picked up on the trade. Liked to be out walking. Going somewhere.

"Well, a lighteyed man owned two or three silversmith shops in Kholinar, one of which was across from my grandparents. He never did like the competition. This was a year or so before the old king died, and Elhokar was left in charge of the kingdom while Gavilar was out at the Plains. Anyway, Elhokar was good friends with the lighteyes who was in competition with my grandparents.

"So, he did his friend a favor. Elhokar had Ana and Da dragged in on some charge or another. They were important enough to demand a right to trial, an inquest before magistrates. I think it surprised Elhokar that he couldn't completely ignore the law. He pled lack of time and sent Ana and Da to the dungeons to wait until an inquest could be arranged." Moash dipped the ladle back into the barrel. "They died there a few months later, still waiting for Elhokar to approve their paperwork."

"That's not exactly the same as killing them."

Moash met Kaladin's eyes. "You doubt that sending a seventy-five-year-old couple to the palace *dungeons* is a death sentence?"

"I guess . . . well, I guess you're right."

Moash nodded sharply, tossing the ladle into the barrel. "Elhokar knew they'd die in there. That way, the hearing would never go before the magistrates, exposing his corruption. That bastard killed them—murdered them to keep his secret. I came home from my trip with the caravan to an empty house, and the neighbors told me my family was already two months dead."

"So now you're trying to assassinate King Elhokar," Kaladin said softly, feeling a chill to be speaking it. Nobody was close enough to hear, not over the sounds of weapons and shouting common to sparring grounds. Still, the words seemed to hang in front of him, as loud as a trumpeter's call.

Moash froze, looking him in the eye.

"That night on the balcony," Kaladin said, "did you make it look like a Shardblade cut the railing?"

Moash took him by the arm in a tight grip, looking about. "We shouldn't talk about this here."

"Stormfather, Moash!" Kaladin said, the depth of it sinking in. "We've been hired to *protect* the man!"

"Our *job*," Moash said, "is to keep Dalinar alive. I can agree with that. He doesn't seem too bad, for a lighteyes. Storms, this kingdom would be a lot better off if he were king instead. Don't tell me you think differently."

"But killing the king—"

"Not here," Moash hissed through clenched teeth.

"I can't just let it go. Nalan's hand! I'm going to have to tell—"

"You'd do that?" Moash demanded. "You'd turn on a member of Bridge Four?"

They locked gazes.

Kaladin turned away. "Damnation. No, I won't. At least, not if you'll agree to stop. You may have a grudge with the king, but you can't just try to . . . you know . . ."

"And what else am I supposed to do?" Moash asked softly. By now, he'd pulled right up to Kaladin. "What kind of justice can a man like me get on a *king*, Kaladin? Tell me."

This can't be happening.

"I'll stop for now," Moash said. "If you'll agree to meet with someone."

"Who?" Kaladin asked, looking back to him.

"This plan wasn't my idea. Some others are involved. All I had to do was throw them a rope. I want you to listen to them."

"Moash . . ."

"Listen to what they have to say," Moash said, grip tightening on Kaladin's arm. "Just *listen*, Kal. That's all. If you don't agree with what they tell you, I'll back out. Please."

"You promise not to do anything else against the king until we've had this meeting?"

"On my grandparents' honor."

Kaladin sighed, but nodded. "All right."

Moash relaxed visibly. He nodded, scooping up his mock sword, then ran back to do some more practice with the Shardblade. Kaladin sighed, turning to grab his sword, and came face-to-face with Syl hovering behind him. Her tiny eyes had gone wide, hands as fists to her sides.

"What did you just do?" she demanded. "I only heard the last part."

"Moash *was* involved," Kaladin whispered. "I need to follow this through, Syl. If someone is trying to kill the king, it's my job to investigate them."

"Oh." She frowned. "I felt something. Something else." She shook her head. "Kaladin, this is dangerous. We should go to Dalinar."

"I promised Moash," he said, kneeling and untying his boots and removing his socks. "I can't go to Dalinar until I know more."

Syl followed him as a ribbon of light as he took the fake Shardblade and walked out into the sands of the dueling grounds. The sand was cold under his bare feet. He wanted to feel it.

He fell into Windstance and practiced a few of the swings that Ivis had taught them. Nearby, a group of lighteyed men nudged one another, nodding toward him. One said something soft, making the others laugh, though several others continued frowning. The image of a darkeyed man with even a practice Shardblade was not something they found amusing.

This is my right, Kaladin thought, swinging, ignoring them. *I defeated a Shardbearer. I belong here.*

Why weren't darkeyes encouraged to practice like this? The darkeyed men in history who had won Shardblades were praised in song and story. Evod Markmaker, Lanacin, Raninor of the Fields . . . These men were revered. But modern darkeyes, well, they were told not to think beyond their station. Or else.

But what was the purpose of the Vorin church? Of ardents and Callings and the arts? Improve yourself. Be better. Why *shouldn't* men like him be expected to dream big dreams? None of it seemed to fit. Society and religion, they just flat-out contradicted each other.

Soldiers are glorified in the Tranquiline Halls. But without farmers, soldiers can't eat—so being a farmer is probably all right too.

Better yourself with a Calling in life. But don't get *too* ambitious or we'll lock you away.

Don't get revenge upon the king for ordering the death of your grandparents. But do get revenge on the Parshendi for ordering the death of someone you never met.

Kaladin stopped swinging, sweating but feeling unfulfilled. When he fought or trained, it wasn't supposed to be like this. It was supposed to be Kaladin and the weapon, as one, not all of these problems bouncing around in his head.

"Syl," he said, trying a thrust with the sword, "you're honorspren. Does that mean you can tell me the right thing to do?"

"Definitely," she said, hanging nearby in the form of a young woman, legs swinging off an invisible ledge. She wasn't zipping around him in a ribbon, as she often did when he sparred.

"Is it wrong for Moash to try to kill the king?"

"Of course."

"Why?"

"Because killing is wrong."

"And the Parshendi I killed?"

"We've talked about this. It had to be done."

"And what if one of them was a Surgebinder," Kaladin said. "With his own honorspren?"

"Parshendi can't become Surgebin—"

"Just pretend," Kaladin said, grunting as he tried another thrust. He wasn't getting it right. "I'd guess all the Parshendi want to do at this point is survive. Storms, the ones involved in Gavilar's death, they might not even still be alive. Their leaders were executed back in Alethkar, after all. So you tell me, if a common Parshendi who is protecting his people comes up against me, what would his honorspren say? That he's doing the right thing?"

"I . . ." Syl hunched down. She hated questions like this. "It doesn't matter. You said you won't kill the Parshendi anymore."

"And Amaram? Can I kill him?"

"Is that justice?" Syl asked.

"One form."

"There's a difference."

"What?" Kaladin demanded, thrusting. Storm it! Why couldn't he make the stupid weapon go where it should?

"Because of what it does to you," Syl said softly. "Thinking about him changes you. Twists you. You're supposed to *protect*, Kaladin. Not kill."

"You have to kill to protect," he snapped. "Storms. You're starting to sound as bad as my father."

He tried a few more stances, until finally Ivis came over and gave him some corrections. She laughed at his frustration as he held the sword wrong again. "You expected to pick this up in one day?"

He kind of had. He knew the spear; he'd trained long and hard. He thought that maybe, this would all just *click*.

It didn't. He kept on anyway, going through the motions, kicking up cold sand, mixing among the lighteyes sparring and practicing their own forms. Eventually, Zahel wandered by.

"Keep at it," the man said without even inspecting Kaladin's forms.

"I was under the impression you'd be training me personally," Kaladin called after him.

"Too much work," Zahel called back, digging a canteen of something from a bundle of cloth beside one of the pillars. Another ardent had piled his colored rocks there, which made Zahel scowl.

Kaladin jogged up to him. "I saw Dalinar Kholin, while unarmed and unarmored, catch a Shardblade in midair with the flats of his palms."

Zahel grunted. "Old Dalinar pulled off a lastclap, eh? Good for him."

"Can you teach me?"

"It's a stupid maneuver," Zahel said. "When it works, it's only because most Shardbearers learn to swing their weapons without as much force as they would a regular blade. And it *doesn't* usually work; it usually fails, and you're dead when it does. Better to focus your time practicing things that will actively help you."

Kaladin nodded.

"Not going to push me on it?" Zahel asked.

"Your argument is good," Kaladin said. "Solid soldier's logic. Makes sense."

"Huh. Might be hope for you after all." Zahel took a swig from his canteen. "Now go get back to practicing."

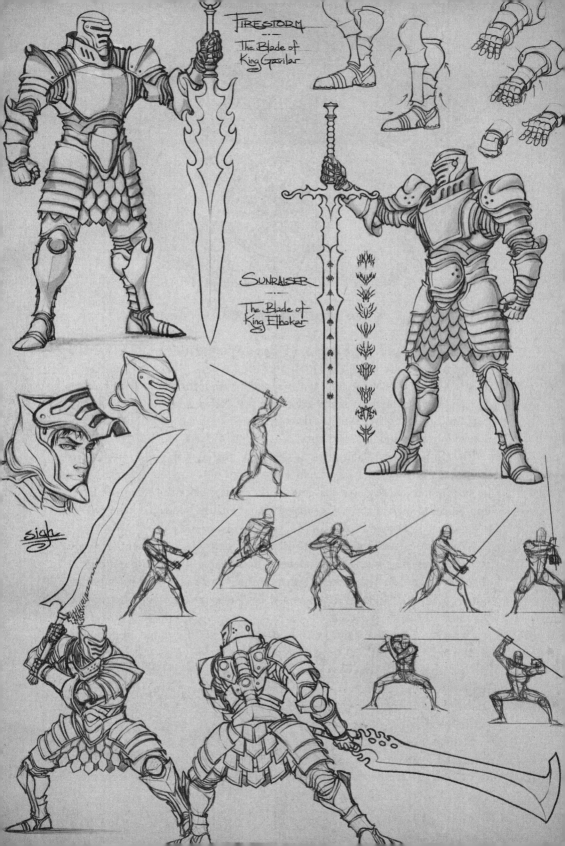

FIRESTORM
The Blade of King Gavilar

SUNRAISER
The Blade of King Elhokar

sigh

THREE AND A HALF YEARS AGO

Shallan poked at the cage, and the colorful creature inside shifted on its perch, cocking its head at her.

It was the most bizarre thing she'd ever seen. It stood on two feet like a person, though its feet were clawed. It was only about as tall as two fists atop one another, but the way it turned its head as it looked at her showed unmistakable personality.

The thing only had a little bit of shell—on the nose and mouth—but the strangest part was its hair. It had *bright green* hair that covered its entire body. The hair lay flat, as if manicured. As she watched, the creature turned and began to pick at the hair—a large flap of it lifted up, and she could see it grew out of a central spine.

"What does the young lady think of my chicken?" the merchant said proudly, standing with hands clasped behind his back, ample stomach thrust forward like the prow of a ship. Behind, people moved through the fair in a throng. There were so many. Five hundred, perhaps even *more,* people in the same place.

"Chicken," Shallan said, poking at the cage with a timid finger. "I've eaten chicken before."

"Not this breed!" the Thaylen man said with a laugh. "Chickens for eating are stupid—this one is smart, almost as smart as a man! It can speak. Listen. Jeksonofnone! Say your name!"

"Jeksonofnone," the creature said.

Shallan jumped back. The word was mangled by the creature's inhuman voice, but it was recognizable. "A Voidbringer!" she hissed, safehand to her chest. "An animal that speaks! You'll bring the eyes of the Unmade upon us."

The merchant laughed. "These things live all over Shinovar, young lady. If their speech drew the Unmade, the entire country would be cursed!"

"Shallan!" Father stood with his bodyguards where he had been speaking to another merchant across the way. She hurried toward him, looking over her shoulder at the strange animal. Deviant though the thing was, if it could talk, she felt sorry for its being trapped in that cage.

The Middlefest Fair was a highlight of the year. Set during the midpeace—a period opposite the Weeping when there were no storms—it drew people from hamlets and villages all around. Many of the people here were from lands her father oversaw, including lesser lighteyes from families who had ruled the same villages for centuries.

The darkeyes came too, of course, including merchants—citizens of the first and second nahns. Her father didn't speak of it often, but she knew he found their wealth and station inappropriate. The Almighty had chosen the lighteyes to rule, not these merchants.

"Come along," Father said to her.

Shallan followed him and his bodyguards through the busy fair, which was laid out on her father's estates about a half day's travel from the mansion. The basin was fairly well sheltered, the slopes nearby covered in jella trees. Their strong branches grew spindly leaves—long spikes of pink, yellow, and orange, and so the trees looked like explosions of color. Shallan had read in one of her father's books that the trees drew in crem, then used it to make their wood hard, like rock.

In the basin itself, most of the trees had been broken down, though some were instead used to hold up canopies dozens of yards wide, tied in place high above. They passed a merchant cursing as a windspren darted through his enclosure, making objects stick together. Shallan smiled, pulling her satchel out from under her arm. There wasn't time to sketch, however, as her father barreled on toward the dueling grounds where—if this was like previous years—she would spend most of the fair.

"Shallan," he said, causing her to scurry to catch up. At fourteen, she felt horribly gangly and far too boyish in figure. As womanhood had begun to come upon her, she had learned that she should be embarrassed by her red hair and freckled skin, as they were a mark of an impure heritage. They were traditional Veden colorings, but that was because—in their past—their lines had mixed with the Horneaters up in the peaks.

Some people were proud of the coloring. Not her father, so neither was Shallan.

"You are coming to an age where you must act more like a lady," Father said. The darkeyes gave them plenty of room, bowing as her father passed. Two of Father's ardents trailed after them, hands behind their backs, contemplative. "You will need to stop gawking so often. It will not be long before we will want to find a husband for you."

"Yes, Father," she said.

"I may need to stop bringing you to events like these," he said. "All you do is run around and act like a child. You need a new tutor, at the very least."

He'd scared off the last tutor. The woman had been an expert in languages, and Shallan had been picking up Azish quite well—but she'd left soon after one of Father's . . . episodes. Shallan's stepmother had appeared the next day with bruises on her face. Brightness Hasheh, the tutor, had packed her things and fled without giving notice.

Shallan nodded to her father's words, but secretly hoped that she'd be able to sneak away and find her brothers. Today she had work to do. She and her father approached the "dueling arena," which was a grandiose term for a section of roped-off ground where parshmen had dumped half a beach's worth of sand. Canopied tables had been erected for the lighteyes to sit at, dine, and converse.

Shallan's stepmother, Malise, was a young woman less than ten years older than Shallan herself. Short of stature with buttonlike features, she sat straight-backed, her black hair brightened by a few streaks of blond. Father settled in beside her in their box; he was one of four men of his rank, fourth dahn, who would be attending the fair. The duelists would be the lesser lighteyes from the surrounding region. Many of them would be landless, and duels would be one of their only ways to gain notoriety.

Shallan sat in the seat reserved for her, and a servant handed her chilled water in a glass. She had barely taken a single sip before someone approached the box.

Brightlord Revilar might have been handsome, if his nose hadn't been removed in a youthful duel. He wore a wooden replacement, painted black—a strange mixture of covering up the blemish and drawing attention to it at the same time. Silver-haired, well-dressed in a suit of a modern design, he had the distracted look of someone who had left his hearth burning untended back at home. His lands bordered Father's; they were two of the ten men of similar rank who served under the highprince.

Revilar approached with not one, but two master-servants at his side. Their black-and-white uniforms were a distinction that ordinary servants were denied, and Father eyed them hungrily. He'd tried to hire master-servants. Each had cited his "reputation" and had refused.

"Brightlord Davar," Revilar said. He did not wait for permission before climbing up the steps into the box. Father and he were the same rank, but everyone knew the allegations against Father—and that the highprince saw them as credible.

"Revilar," Father said, eyes forward.

"May I sit?" He took a seat beside Father—the one that Helaran, as heir, would have used if he'd been there. Revilar's two servants took up places behind him. They somehow managed to convey a sense of disapproval of Father without saying anything.

"Is your son going to duel today?" Father asked.

"Actually, yes."

"Hopefully he can keep all of his parts. We wouldn't want your experience to become a tradition."

"Now, now, Lin," Revilar said. "That is no way to speak to a business associate."

"Business associate? We have dealings of which I am not aware?"

One of Revilar's servants, the woman, set a small sheaf of pages on the table before Father. Shallan's stepmother took them hesitantly, then began to read them out loud. The terms were for an exchange of goods, Father trading some of his breachtree cotton and raw shum to Revilar in exchange for a small payment. Revilar would then take the goods to market for sale.

Father stopped the reading three-quarters of the way through. "Are you delusional? One clearmark a bag? A tenth of what that shum is worth! Considering patrols of roadways and maintenance fees paid back to the villages where the materials are harvested, I would *lose* spheres on this deal."

"Oh, it is not so bad," Revilar said. "I think you will find the arrangement quite agreeable."

"You're insane."

"I'm popular."

Father frowned, growing red-faced. Shallan could remember a time when she'd rarely, if ever, seen him angry. Those days were long, long dead. "Popular?" Father demanded. "What does—"

"You may or may not know," Revilar said, "that the highprince himself recently visited my estates. It seems he likes what I have been doing for this princedom's textiles. That, added to my son's dueling prowess, has drawn attention to my house. I have been invited to visit the highprince in Vedenar one week out of ten, starting next month."

At times, Father was not the cleverest of men, but he did have a mind for politics. So Shallan thought, at least, though she did so want to believe the best about him. Either way, he saw this implication immediately.

"You rat," Father whispered.

"You have very few options open to you, Lin," Revilar said, leaning toward him. "Your house is on the decline, your reputation in shambles. You need allies. *I* need to look the part of a financial genius to the highprince. We can assist one another."

Father bowed his head. Outside the box, the first duelists were announced, an inconsequential bout.

"Everywhere I step, I find only corners," Father whispered. "Slowly, they trap me."

Revilar pushed the papers toward Shallan's stepmother once more. "Would you start again? I suspect your husband was not listening carefully the last time." He glanced at Shallan. "And does the child need to be here?"

Shallan left without a word. It was what she'd wanted anyway, though she did feel bad leaving Father. He didn't often speak with her, let alone ask for her opinion, but he did seem to be stronger when she was near.

He was so disconcerted that he didn't even send one of the guards with her. She slipped out of the box, satchel under her arm, and passed through the Davar servants who were preparing her father's meal.

Freedom.

Freedom was as valuable as an emerald broam to Shallan, and as rare as a larkin. She hurried away, lest her father realize he had given no orders for her to be accompanied. One of the guards at the perimeter—Jix—stepped toward her anyway, but then looked back at the box. He went that way instead, perhaps intending to ask if he should follow.

Best to not be easily found when he returned. Shallan took a step toward the fair, with its exotic merchants and wonderful sights. There would be guessing games and perhaps a Worldsinger telling tales of distant kingdoms. Over the polite clapping of the lighteyes watching the duel behind her, she could hear drums from the common darkeyes along with singing and merriment.

Work first. Darkness lay over her house like a storm's shadow. She would find the sun. She *would*.

That meant turning back to the dueling grounds, for now. She rounded the back of the boxes, weaving between parshmen who bowed and darkeyes who gave her nods or bows, depending on their rank. She eventually found a box where several lesser lighteyed families shared space in the shade.

Eylita, daughter of Brightlord Tavinar, sat on the end, just within the sunlight shining through the side of the box. She stared at the duelists with a vapid expression, head slightly cocked, a whimsical smile on her face. Her long hair was a pure black.

Shallan stepped up beside the box and hissed at her. The older girl turned, frowning, then raised hands to her lips. She glanced at her parents, then leaned down. "Shallan!"

"I told you to expect me," Shallan whispered back. "Did you think about what I wrote you?"

Eylita reached into the pocket of her dress, then slipped out a small note. She grinned mischievously and nodded.

Shallan took the note. "You'll be able to get away?"

"I'll need to take my handmaid, but otherwise I can go where I want."

What would that be like?

Shallan ducked away quickly. Technically, she outranked Eylita's parents, but age was a funny thing among the lighteyes. Sometimes, the higher-ranked child didn't seem nearly as important when speaking to adults of a lower dahn. Besides, Brightlord and Brightness Tavinar had been there on *that* day, when the bastard had come. They were not fond of Father, or his children.

Shallan backed away from the boxes, then turned toward the fair itself. Here, she paused nervously. The Middlefest Fair was an intimidating collage of people and places. Nearby, a group of tenners drank at long tables and placed bets on the matches. The lowest rank of lighteyes, they were barely above darkeyes. They not only had to work for their living, they weren't even merchants or master craftsmen. They were just . . . people. Helaran had said there were many of them in the cities. As many as there were darkeyes. That seemed very odd to her.

Odd and fascinating at the same time. She itched to find a corner to watch where she would not be noticed, her sketchpad out and her imagination boiling. Instead, she forced herself to move around the edge of the fair. The tent that her brothers had spoken of would be on the outer perimeter, wouldn't it?

Darkeyed fairgoers gave her a wide berth, and she found herself afraid. Her father spoke of how a young lighteyed girl could be a target for the brutish people of the lower classes. Surely nobody would harm her here in the open, with so many people about. Still, she clutched her satchel to her chest and found herself trembling as she walked.

What would it be like, to be brave like Helaran? As her mother had been.

Her mother . . .

"Brightness?"

Shallan shook herself. How long had she been standing there, on the path? The sun had moved. She turned sheepishly to find Jix the guard standing behind her. Though he had a gut and rarely kept his hair combed, Jix was strong—she had once seen him pull a cart out of the way when the chull's hitch broke. He'd been one of her father's guards for as long as she could remember.

"Ah," she said, trying to cover her nervousness, "you're here to accompany me?"

"Well, I was *gonna* bring you back. . . ."

"Did my father order you to?"

Jix chewed on the yamma root, called cussweed by some, in his cheek. "He was busy."

"Then you will accompany me?" She shook from the nervousness of saying it.

"I suppose."

She breathed out a sigh of relief and turned around on the pathway, stone where rockbuds and shalebark had been scraped away. She turned one way, then the other. "Um . . . We need to find the gambling pavilion."

"That's not a place for a lady." Jix eyed her. "Particularly not one of your age, Brightness."

"Well, I suppose you can go tell my father what I'm doing." She shuffled from one foot to the other.

"And in the meantime," Jix said, "you'll try to find it on your own, won't you? Go in by yourself if you find it?"

She shrugged, blushing. That was exactly what she'd do.

"Which means I'd have left you wandering around in a place like that without protection." He groaned softly. "Why do you defy him like this, Brightness? You're just going to make him angry."

"I think . . . I think he will anger no matter what I or anyone does," she said. "The sun will shine. The highstorms will blow. And Father will yell. That's just how life is." She bit her lip. "The gambling pavilion? I promise that I will be brief."

"This way," Jix said. He didn't walk particularly quickly as he led her, and he frequently glared at darkeyed fairgoers who passed. Jix was lighteyed, but only of the eighth dahn.

"Pavilion" turned out to be too grand a term for the patched and ripped tarp strung up at the edge of the fairgrounds. She'd have found it on her own soon enough. The thick canvas, with sides that hung down a few feet, made it surprisingly dark inside.

Men crowded together in there. The few women that Shallan saw had the fingers cut out of the gloves on their safehands. Scandalous. She found herself blushing as she stopped at the perimeter, looking in at the dark, shifting forms. Men shouted inside with raw voices, any sense of Vorin decorum left out in the sunlight. This was, indeed, not a place for someone like her. She had trouble believing it was a place for *anyone*.

"How about I go in for you," Jix said. "Is it a bet you're wanting to—"

Shallan pushed forward. Ignoring her own panic, her discomfort, she moved into the darkness. Because if she did not, then it meant that none of them were resisting, that nothing would change.

Jix stayed at her side, shoving her some space. She had trouble breathing inside; the air was dank with sweat and curses. Men turned and glanced at her. Bows—even nods—were slow in coming, if they were offered at all. The implication was clear. If she wouldn't obey social conventions by staying out, they didn't have to obey them by showing her deference.

"Is there something specific you're searching for?" Jix asked. "Cards? Guessing games?"

"Axehound fights."

Jix groaned. "You're gonna end up stabbed, and I'm gonna end up on a roasting spit. This is crazy. . . ."

She turned, noting a group of men cheering. That sounded promising. She ignored the increasing trembling in her hands, and also tried to ignore a group of drunk men sitting in a ring on the ground, staring at what appeared to be vomit.

The cheering men sat on crude benches with others crowded around. A glimpse between bodies showed two small axehounds. There were no spren. When people crowded about like this, spren were rare, even though the emotions seemed to be very high.

One set of benches was not crowded. Balat sat here, coat unbuttoned, leaning on a post in front of him with arms crossed. His disheveled hair and stooped posture gave him an uncaring look, but his eyes . . . his eyes lusted. He watched the poor animals killing one another, fixated on them with the intensity of a woman reading a powerful novel.

Shallan stepped up to him, Jix remaining a little ways behind. Now that he'd seen Balat, the guard relaxed.

"Balat?" Shallan asked timidly. "Balat!"

He glanced at her, then nearly toppled off his bench. He scrambled up to his feet. "What in the . . . Shallan! Get out of here. What are you doing?" He reached for her.

She cringed down despite herself. He sounded like Father. As he took her by the shoulder, she held up the note from Eylita. The lavender paper, dusted with perfume, seemed to glow.

Balat hesitated. To the side, one axehound bit deeply into the leg of the other. Blood sprayed the ground, deep violet.

"What is it?" Balat asked. "That is the glyphpair of House Tavinar."

"It's from Eylita."

"Eylita? The daughter? Why . . . what . . ."

Shallan broke the seal, opening the letter to read for him. "She wishes to walk with you along the fairgrounds stream. She says she'll be waiting there, with her handmaid, if you want to come."

Balat ran a hand through his curling hair. "Eylita? She's here. Of course she's here. Everyone is here. You talked to her? Why— But—"

"I know how you've looked at her," Shallan said. "The few times you've been near."

"So you talked to her?" Balat demanded. "Without my permission? You said I'd be interested in something like"—he took the letter—"like this?"

Shallan nodded, wrapping her arms around herself.

Balat looked back toward the fighting axehounds. He bet because it was expected of him, but he didn't come here for the money—unlike Jushu would.

Balat ran his hand through his hair again, then looked back at the letter. He wasn't a cruel man. She knew it was a strange thing to think, considering what he sometimes did. Shallan knew the kindness he showed, the strength that hid within him. He hadn't acquired this fascination with death until Mother had left them. He could come back, stop being like that. He *could*.

"I need . . ." Balat looked out of the tent. "I need to go! She'll be waiting for me. I shouldn't make her wait." He buttoned up his coat.

Shallan nodded eagerly, following him from the pavilion. Jix trailed along behind, though a couple of men called out to him. He must be known in the pavilion.

Balat stepped out into the sunlight. He seemed a changed man, just like that.

"Balat?" Shallan asked. "I didn't see Jushu in there with you."

"He didn't come to the pavilion."

"What? I thought—"

"I don't know where he went," Balat said. "He met some people right after we arrived." He looked toward the distant stream that ran down from the heights and through a channel around the fairgrounds. "What do I say to her?"

"How should I know?"

"You're a woman too."

"I'm fourteen!" She wouldn't spend time courting, anyway. Father would choose her a husband. His only daughter was too precious to be wasted on something fickle, like her own powers of decision.

"I guess . . . I guess I'll just talk to her," Balat said. He jogged off without another word.

Shallan watched him go, then sat down on a rock and trembled, arms around herself. That place . . . the tent . . . it had been *horrible*.

She sat there for an extended time, feeling ashamed of her weakness, but also proud. She'd done it. It was small, but she'd done something.

Eventually, she rose and nodded to Jix, letting him lead the way back toward their box. Father should be finished with his meeting by now.

It turned out that he had finished that meeting only to start another. A man she did not know sat next to Father with a cup of chilled water in one hand. Tall, slender, and blue-eyed, he had deep black hair without a hint of impurity and wore clothing the same shade. He glanced at Shallan as she stepped up into the box.

The man started, dropping his cup to the table. He caught it with a swift lunge, keeping it from tipping over, then turned to stare at her with a slack jaw.

It was gone in a second, replaced with an expression of practiced indifference.

"Clumsy fool!" Father said.

The newcomer turned away from Shallan, speaking softly to Father. Shallan's stepmother stood to the side, with the cooks. Shallan slipped over to her. "Who is that?"

"Nobody of consequence," Malise said. "He claims to have brought word from your brother, but is of low enough dahn that he can't even produce a writ of lineage."

"My brother? Helaran?"

Malise nodded.

Shallan turned back to the newcomer. She caught, with a subtle movement, the man slipping something from his coat pocket and moving it up toward the drinks. A shock coursed through Shallan. She raised a hand. Poison—

The newcomer covertly dumped the pouch's contents into his *own* drink, then raised it to his lips, gulping down the powder. What had it been?

Shallan lowered her hand. The newcomer stood up a moment later. He didn't bow to Father as he left. He gave Shallan a smile, then was down the steps and out of the box.

Word from Helaran. What had it been? Shallan timidly moved to the table. "Father?"

Father's eyes were on the duel in the center of the ring. Two men with swords, no shields, harking back to classical ideals. Their sweeping methods of fighting were said to be an imitation of fighting with a Shardblade.

"Word from Nan Helaran?" Shallan prodded.

"You will not speak his name," Father said.

"I—"

"You will *not* speak of that one," Father said, looking to her, thunder in his expression. "Today I declare him disinherited. Tet Balat is officially now Nan Balat, Wikim becomes Tet, Jushu becomes Asha. I have only three sons."

She knew better than to push him when he was like this. But how would she discover what the messenger had said? She sank into her chair, shaken again.

"Your brothers avoid me," Father said, watching the duel. "Not one chooses to dine with their father as would be proper."

Shallan folded her hands in her lap.

"Jushu is probably drinking somewhere," Father said. "The Stormfather only knows where Balat has run off to. Wikim refuses to leave the carriage."

He downed the wine in his cup. "Will you speak with him? This has not been a good day. If I went to him, I . . . worry what I would do."

Shallan rose, then rested a hand on her father's shoulder. He slumped, leaning forward, one hand around the empty wine flagon. He raised his other hand and patted hers on his shoulder, his eyes distant. He *did* try. They all did.

Shallan sought out their carriage, which stood parked with a number of others near the western slope of the fairgrounds. Jella trees here rose high, their hardened trunks colored the light brown of crem. The needles sprouted like a thousand tongues of fire from each limb, though the nearest ones pulled in as she approached.

She was surprised to see a mink slinking in the shadows; she'd expected all those in the area to have been trapped by now. The coachmen played cards in a ring nearby; some of them had to stay and watch the carriages, though Shallan had heard Ren speaking of some kind of rotation so that they all got a chance at the fair. In fact, Ren wasn't there at the moment, though the other coachmen bowed as she passed.

Wikim sat in their carriage. The slender, pale youth was only fifteen months older than Shallan. He shared some resemblance to his twin, but few people mistook them for one another. Jushu looked older, and Wikim was so thin he looked sickly.

Shallan climbed in to sit across from Wikim, setting her satchel on the seat beside her.

"Did Father send you," Wikim asked, "or did you come on one of your new little missions of mercy?"

"Both?"

Wikim turned away from her, looking out the window toward the trees, away from the fair. "You can't fix us, Shallan. Jushu will destroy himself. It's only a matter of time. Balat is becoming Father, step by step. Malise spends one night in two weeping. Father will kill her one of these days, like he did Mother."

"And you?" Shallan asked. It was the wrong thing to say, and she knew it the moment it came out of her mouth.

"Me? I won't be around to see any of it. I'll be dead by then."

Shallan wrapped her arms around herself, pulling her legs up beneath her on the seat. Brightness Hasheh would have chided her for the unladylike posture.

What did she do? What did she say? *He's right,* she thought. *I can't fix this. Helaran could have. I can't.*

They were all slowly unraveling.

"So what was it?" Wikim said. "Out of curiosity, what did you come up with to 'save' me? I'm guessing you used the girl on Balat."

She nodded.

"You were obvious about that," Wikim said. "With the letters you sent her. Jushu? What of him?"

"I have a list of the day's duels," Shallan whispered. "He so wishes he could duel. If I show him the fights, maybe he'll want to come watch them."

"You'll have to find him first," Wikim said with a snort. "And what about me? You have to know that neither swords nor pretty faces will work for me."

Feeling a fool, Shallan dug in her satchel and came out with several sheets of paper.

"Drawings?"

"Math problems."

Wikim frowned and took them from her, absently scratching the side of his face as he looked them over. "I'm no ardent. I'll not be boxed up and forced to spend my days convincing people to listen to the Almighty—who suspiciously has nothing to say for himself."

"That doesn't mean you can't study," Shallan said. "I gathered those from Father's books, equations for determining highstorm timing. I translated and simplified the writing to glyphs, so you could read them. I figured you could try to guess when the next ones would come. . . ."

He shuffled through the papers. "You copied and translated it all, even the drawings. Storms, Shallan. How long did this take you?"

She shrugged. It had taken weeks, but she had nothing but time. Days sitting in the gardens, evenings sitting in her room, the occasional visit to the ardents for some peaceful tutoring about the Almighty. It was good to have things to do.

"This is stupid," Wikim said, lowering the papers. "What do you think you'll accomplish? I can't believe you wasted so much time on this."

Shallan bowed her head and then, blinking tears, scrambled out of the carriage. It felt horrible—not just Wikim's words, but the way her emotions betrayed her. She couldn't hold them in.

She hastened away from the carriages, hoping the coachmen wouldn't see her wiping her eyes with her safehand. She sat down on a stone and tried to compose herself, but failed, tears flowing freely. She turned her head aside as a few parshmen trotted past, running their master's axehounds. There would be several hunts as part of the festivities.

"*Axehound*," a voice said from behind her.

Shallan jumped, safehand to breast, and spun.

He rested up on a tree limb, wearing his black outfit. He moved as she saw him, and the spiky leaves around him retreated in a wave of vanishing red and orange. It was the messenger who had spoken to Father earlier.

"I have wondered," the messenger said, "if any of you find the term odd. You know what an *axe* is. But what is a *hound*?"

"Why does that matter?" Shallan asked.

"Because it is a word," the messenger replied. "A simple word with a world embedded inside, like a bud waiting to open." He studied her. "I did not expect to find you here."

"I . . ." Her instincts told her to back away from this strange man. And yet, he had news of Helaran—news her father would never share. "Where did you expect to find me? At the dueling grounds?"

The man swung around the branch and dropped to the ground.

Shallan stepped backward.

"No need for that," the man said, settling onto a rock. "You needn't fear me. I'm terribly ineffective at hurting people. I blame my upbringing."

"You have news of my brother Helaran."

The messenger nodded. "He is a very determined young man."

"Where is he?"

"Doing things he finds very important. I would fault him for it, as I find nothing more frightening than a man trying to do what he has decided is important. Very little in the world has ever gone astray—at least on a grand scale—because a person decided to be frivolous."

"He *is* well, though?" she asked.

"Well enough. The message for your father was that he has eyes nearby, and is watching."

No wonder it had put Father in a bad mood. "Where is he?" Shallan said, timidly stepping forward. "Did he tell you to speak to me?"

"I'm sorry, young one," the man said, expression softening. "He gave me only that brief message for your father, and that only because I mentioned I would be traveling this direction."

"Oh! I assumed he'd sent you here. I mean, that coming to us was your primary purpose."

"Turns out that it was. Tell me, young one. Do spren speak to you?"

The lights going out, life drained from them.

Twisted symbols the eye should not see.

Her mother's soul in a box.

"I . . ." she said. "No. Why would a spren speak to me?"

"No voices?" the man said, leaning forward. "Do spheres go dark when you are near?"

"I'm sorry," Shallan said, "but I should be getting back to my father. He will be missing me."

"Your father is slowly destroying your family," the messenger said. "Your brother was right on that count. He was wrong about everything else."

"Such as?"

"Look." The man nodded back toward the carriages. She was at the right angle to see into the window of her father's carriage. She squinted.

Inside, Wikim leaned forward, using a pencil taken from her satchel—which she'd left behind. He scribbled at the mathematical problems she'd left.

He was smiling.

Warmth. That warmth she felt, a deep glow, was like the joy she had known before. Long ago. Before everything had gone wrong. Before Mother.

The messenger whispered. "Two blind men waited at the end of an era, contemplating beauty. They sat atop the world's highest cliff, overlooking the land and seeing nothing."

"Huh?" She looked to him.

"'Can beauty be taken from a man?' the first asked the second.

"'It was taken from me,' the second replied. 'For I cannot remember it.' This man was blinded in a childhood accident. 'I pray to the God Beyond each night to restore my sight, so that I may find beauty again.'

"'Is beauty something one must see, then?' the first asked.

"'Of course. That is its nature. How can you appreciate a work of art without seeing it?'

"'I can hear a work of music,' the first said.

"'Very well, you can hear some kinds of beauty—but you cannot know full beauty without sight. You can know only a small portion of beauty.'

"'A sculpture,' the first said. 'Can I not feel its curves and slopes, the touch of the chisel that transformed common rock into uncommon wonder?'

"'I suppose,' said the second, 'that you can know the beauty of a sculpture.'

"'And what of the beauty of food? Is it not a work of art when a chef crafts a masterpiece to delight the tastes?'

"'I suppose,' said the second, 'that you can know the beauty of a chef's art.'

"'And what of the beauty of a woman,' the first said. 'Can I not know her beauty in the softness of her caress, the kindness of her voice, the keenness of her mind as she reads philosophy to me? Can I not know this beauty? Can I not know most kinds of beauty, even without my eyes?'

"'Very well,' said the second. 'But what if your ears were removed, your hearing taken away? Your tongue taken out, your mouth forced shut, your sense of smell destroyed? What if your skin were burned so that you could no longer feel? What if all that remained to you was pain? You could not know beauty then. It *can* be taken from a man.'"

The messenger stopped, cocking his head at Shallan.

"What?" she asked.

"What think you? Can beauty be taken from a man? If he could not touch, taste, smell, hear, see . . . what if all he knew was pain? Has that man had beauty taken from him?"

"I . . ." What did this have to do with anything? "Does the pain change day by day?"

"Let us say it does," the messenger said.

"Then beauty, to that person, would be the times when the pain lessens. Why are you telling me this story?"

The messenger smiled. "To be human is to seek beauty, Shallan. Do not despair, do not end the hunt because thorns grow in your way. Tell me, what is the most beautiful thing you can imagine?"

"Father is probably wondering where I am. . . ."

"Indulge me," the messenger said. "I will tell you where your brother is."

"A wonderful painting, then. That is the most beautiful thing."

"Lies," the messenger said. "Tell me the truth. What is it, child? Beauty, to you."

"I . . ." What was it? "Mother still lives," she found herself whispering, meeting his eyes.

"And?"

"And we are in the gardens," Shallan continued. "She is speaking to my father, and he is laughing. Laughing and holding her. We are all there, including Helaran. He never left. The people my mother knew . . . Dreder . . . never came to our home. Mother loves me. She teaches me philosophy, and she shows me how to draw."

"Good," the messenger said. "But you can do better than that. What is that place? What does it *feel* like?"

"It's spring," Shallan shot back, growing annoyed. "And the mossvines bloom a vigorous red. They smell sweet, and the air is moist from the morning's highstorm. Mother whispers, but there is music to her tone, and Father's laugh doesn't echo—it rises high into the air, bathing us all.

"Helaran is teaching Jushu swords, and they spar nearby. Wikim laughs as Helaran is struck on the side of the leg. He is studying to be an ardent, as Mother wanted. I am sketching them all, charcoal scratching paper. I feel warm, despite the slight chill to the air. I have a steaming cup of cider beside me, and I taste the sweetness in my mouth from the sip I just took. It is beautiful because it *could* have been. It *should* have been. I . . ."

She blinked tears. She saw it. Stormfather, but she *saw* it. She heard her mother's voice, saw Jushu giving up spheres to Balat as he lost the duel, but laughing as he paid, uncaring of the loss. She could feel the air, smell the scents, hear the sounds of songlings in the brush. Almost, it became real.

Wisps of Light rose before her. The messenger had gotten out a handful of spheres and held them toward her while staring into her eyes. The steamy Stormlight rose between them. Shallan lifted her fingers, the image of her ideal life wrapped around her like a comforter.

No.

She drew back. The misty light faded.

"I see," the messenger said softly. "You do not yet understand the nature of lies. I had that trouble myself, long ago. The Shards here are very strict. You will have to see the truth, child, before you can expand upon it. Just as a man should know the law before he breaks it."

Shadows from her past shifted in the depths, surfacing just briefly toward the light. "Could you help?"

"No. Not now. You aren't ready, for one, and I have work to be about. Another day. Keep cutting at those thorns, strong one, and make a path for the light. The things you fight aren't completely natural." He stood up, then bowed to her.

"My brother," she said.

"He is in Alethkar."

Alethkar? "Why?"

"Because that is where he feels he is needed, of course. If I see him again, I will give him word of you." The messenger walked away on light feet, his steps smooth, almost like moves in a dance.

Shallan watched him go, the deep things within her settling again, returning to the forgotten parts of her mind. She realized she had not even asked the man his name.

When Simol was informed of the arrival of the Edgedancers, a concealed consternation and terror, as is common in such cases, fell upon him; although they were not the most demanding of orders, their graceful, limber movements hid a deadliness that was, by this time, quite renowned; also, they were the most articulate and refined of the Radiants.

—From *Words of Radiance*, chapter 20, page 12

Kaladin reached the end of the line of bridgemen. They stood at attention, spears to shoulders, eyes forward. The transformation was marvelous. He nodded under the darkening sky.

"Impressive," he said to Pitt, the sergeant of Bridge Seventeen. "I've rarely seen such a fine platoon of spearmen."

It was the kind of lie that commanders learned to give. Kaladin didn't mention how some of the bridgemen shuffled while they stood, or how their maneuvers in formation were sloppy. They were trying. He could sense it in their earnest expressions, and in the way they had begun taking pride in their uniforms, their identity. They were ready to patrol, at least close to the warcamps. He made a mental note to have Teft start taking them out in a rotation with the other two crews that were ready.

Kaladin was proud of them, and he let them know it as the hour stretched long and night arrived. He then dismissed them to their evening meal, which smelled quite different from Rock's Horneater stew. Bridge Seventeen considered their nightly bean curry to be part of their identity. Individuality through meal choice; Kaladin found that amusing as he moved off into the night, shouldering his spear. He had three more crews to look in on.

The next, Bridge Eighteen, was one of those having problems. Their sergeant, though earnest, didn't have the presence necessary for a good officer. Or, well, none of the bridgemen had *that*. He was just particularly weak. Prone to begging instead of ordering, awkward in social situations.

It couldn't all be blamed on Vet, however. He'd also been given a particularly discordant group of men. Kaladin found the soldiers of Eighteen sitting in isolated bunches, eating their evening meal. No laughter, no camaraderie. They weren't as solitary as they'd been as bridgemen. Instead, they'd splintered into little cliques who didn't mingle.

Sergeant Vet called them to order and they rose sluggishly, not bothering to stand in a straight line or salute. Kaladin saw the truth in their eyes. What could he do to them? Surely nothing as bad as their lives had been as bridgemen. So why make an effort?

Kaladin spoke to them of motivation and unity for a time. *I'll need to do another training session in the chasms with this lot,* he thought. And if that didn't work either . . . well, he'd probably have to break them up, stick them in other platoons that were working.

He eventually left Eighteen, shaking his head. They didn't seem to want to be soldiers. Why had they taken Dalinar's offer then, instead of leaving?

Because they don't want to make choices anymore, he thought. *Choices can be hard.*

He knew how that felt. Storms, but he did. He remembered sitting and staring at a blank wall, too morose to even get up and go kill himself.

He shivered. Those were not days he wanted to remember.

As he made his way toward Bridge Nineteen, Syl floated past on a current of wind in the form of a small patch of mist. She melded into a ribbon of light and zipped around him in circles before coming to rest on his shoulder.

"Everyone else is eating their dinners," Syl said.

"Good," Kaladin said.

"That wasn't a status report, Kaladin," she said. "It was a point of contention."

"Contention?" He stopped in the darkness near the barrack of Bridge Nineteen, whose men were doing well, eating around their fire as a group.

"You're working," Syl said. "Still."

"I need to get these men ready." He turned his head to look at her. "You know something is coming. Those countdowns on the walls . . . Have you seen more of those red spren?"

"Yes," she admitted. "I think so, at least. In the corners of my eyes, watching me. Very infrequently, but there."

"Something is coming," Kaladin said. "That countdown points right toward the Weeping. Whatever happens then, I'll have the bridgemen ready to weather it."

"Well, you won't if you drop dead from exhaustion first!" Syl hesitated. "People really can do that, right? I heard Teft saying he felt like he was going to do so."

"Teft likes to exaggerate," Kaladin said. "It's one mark of a good sergeant."

Syl frowned. "And that last part . . . was a joke?"

"Yes."

"Ah." She looked into his eyes. "Rest anyway, Kaladin. Please."

Kaladin looked toward Bridge Four's barrack. It was a distance away, down the rows, but he thought he could hear Rock's laughter echoing through the night.

Finally, he sighed, acknowledging his exhaustion. He could check on the last two platoons tomorrow. Spear in hand, he turned and hiked back. The advent of darkness meant it would be about two hours before men started turning in for the night. Kaladin arrived to the familiar scent of Rock's stew, though Hobber—sitting on a tall stump the men had fashioned for him, a blanket across his grey, useless legs—was doing the serving. Rock stood nearby, arms folded, looking proud.

Renarin was there, taking and washing the dishes of those who'd finished. He did that every night, kneeling quietly beside the washbasin in his bridgeman uniform. The lad certainly was earnest. He didn't display any of the spoiled temperament of his brother. Though he had insisted on joining them, he often sat at the edges of the group, near the back of the bridgemen at night. Such an odd young man.

Kaladin passed Hobber and gripped the man's shoulder. He nodded, meeting Hobber's eyes, raising a fist. *Fight on.* Kaladin reached for some stew, then froze.

Sitting nearby on a log were not one, but *three* beefy, thick-armed Herdazians. All wore Bridge Four uniforms, and Kaladin only recognized Punio out of the three.

Kaladin found Lopen nearby, staring at his hand—which he held before himself in a fist for some reason. Kaladin had long since given up on understanding Lopen.

"Three?" Kaladin demanded.

"Cousins!" Lopen replied, looking up.

"You have too many of those," Kaladin said.

"That's impossible! Rod, Huio, say hello!"

"Bridge Four," the two men said, raising their bowls.

Kaladin shook his head, accepting his own stew and then walking past the cauldron into the darker area beside the barrack. He peeked into the storage room, and found Shen stacking sacks of tallew grain there, lit only by a single diamond chip.

"Shen?" Kaladin said.

The parshman continued stacking bags.

"Fall in and attention!" Kaladin barked.

Shen froze, then stood up, back straight, at attention.

"At ease, soldier," Kaladin said softly, stepping up to him. "I spoke to Dalinar Kholin earlier today and asked if I could arm you. He asked if I trusted you. I told him the truth." Kaladin held out his spear to the parshman. "I do."

Shen looked from the spear to Kaladin, dark eyes hesitant.

"Bridge Four doesn't have slaves," Kaladin said. "I'm sorry for being frightened before." He urged the man to take the spear, and Shen finally did so. "Leyten and Natam practice in the mornings with a few men. They're willing to help you learn so that you don't have to train with the greenvines."

Shen held the spear with what seemed to be reverence. Kaladin turned to leave the storage room.

"Sir," Shen said.

Kaladin paused.

"You are," Shen said, speaking in his slow way, "a good man."

"I've spent my life being judged for my eyes, Shen. I won't do something similar to you because of your skin."

"Sir, I—" The parshman seemed troubled by something.

"Kaladin!" Moash's voice came from outside.

"Was there something you wanted to say?" Kaladin asked Shen.

"Later," the parshman said. "Later."

Kaladin nodded, then stepped out to see what the disturbance was. He found Moash looking for him near the cauldron.

"Kaladin!" Moash said, spotting him. "Come on. We're going out, and you're coming with us. Even Rock is coming tonight."

"Ha! Stew is in good hands," Rock said. "I will go do this thing. Will be good to get away from stink of little bridgemen."

"Hey!" Drehy said.

"Ah. And stink of big bridgemen too."

"Come on," Moash said, waving to Kaladin. "You promised."

He'd done no such thing. He just wanted to settle down by the fire, eat his stew, and watch the flamespren. Everyone was looking at him, though. Even the ones who weren't going with Moash tonight.

"I . . ." Kaladin said. "Fine. Let's go."

They cheered and clapped. Storming fools. They cheered to see their commander go out drinking? Kaladin slurped down a few bites of stew, then handed the rest to Hobber. With reluctance, he then walked over to join Moash, as did Lopen, Peet, and Sigzil.

"You know," Kaladin growled under his breath to Syl, "if this had been one of my old spearman crews, I'd assume they wanted me out of the camp so they could get away with something while I'm gone."

"I doubt it's that," Syl said, frowning.

"No," Kaladin said. "These men just want to see me as human." He *did* need to go, for that reason. He was already too separate from the men. He didn't want them thinking of him as they would a lighteyes.

"Ha!" Rock said, jogging up to join them. "These men, they claim they can drink more than Horneater. Airsick lowlanders. Is not possible."

"A drinking contest?" Kaladin said, groaning inwardly. What was he getting into?

"None of us are on duty until the late morning," Sigzil said with a shrug. Teft was watching the Kholins overnight, along with Leyten's team.

"Tonight," Lopen said, finger to the air, "I will be victorious. It is said you should never bet against the one-armed Herdazian in a drinking contest!"

"It is?" Moash asked.

"It *will be* said," Lopen continued, "you should never bet against the one-armed Herdazian in a drinking contest!"

"You weigh about as much as a starved axehound, Lopen," Moash said skeptically.

"Ah, but I have *focus*."

They continued, turning down a pathway that led toward the market. The warcamp was laid out with blocks of barracks forming a large circle around the lighteyed buildings closer to the center. On the way out toward the market, which was in the outer ring of camp followers beyond the soldiers, they passed plenty of other barracks manned by ordinary soldiers—and the men there were busy in tasks that Kaladin had rarely seen in Sadeas's army. Sharpening spears, oiling breastplates, before their dinner call came.

Kaladin's men weren't the only ones going out for the night, though. Other groups of soldiers had already eaten, and these strolled toward the market, laughing. They were recovering, slowly, from the slaughter that had left Dalinar's army crippled.

The market was aglow with life, torches and oil lanterns shining from most buildings. Kaladin wasn't surprised. An ordinary army would have had camp followers aplenty, and that was for a moving army. Here, merchants showed off wares. Criers sold news they claimed had come via spanreed, reporting events in the world. What was that about a war in Jah

Keved? And a new emperor in Azir? Kaladin had only a vague idea of where that was.

Sigzil jogged over to get an earful of news, paying the crier a sphere while Lopen and Rock argued which tavern was the best to visit for the night. Kaladin watched the flow of life. Soldiers passing on the night watch. A group of chatting darkeyed women moving from spice merchant to spice merchant. A lighteyed courier posting projected highstorm dates and times on a board, her husband yawning nearby and looking bored—as if he'd been forced to come along to keep her company. The Weeping was coming up soon, the time of constant rain with no highstorms—the only break was Lightday, right in the middle. It was an off year in the thousand-day cycle of two years, which meant the Weeping would be a calm one this time.

"Enough arguing," Moash said to Rock, Lopen, and Peet. "We're going to the Ornery Chull."

"Aw!" Rock said. "But they do not have Horneater lagers!"

"That's because Horneater lagers melt your teeth," Moash said. "Anyway, it's my pick tonight." Peet nodded eagerly. That tavern had been his choice as well.

Sigzil got back from hearing the news, and he'd apparently stopped somewhere else as well, as he carried something steaming and wrapped in paper.

"Not you too," Kaladin said, groaning.

"It's good," Sigzil said defensively, then took a bite of the chouta.

"You don't even know what it is."

"Of course I do." Sigzil hesitated. "Hey, Lopen. What's *in* this stuff?"

"Flangria," Lopen said happily as Rock ran off to the street vendor to get himself some chouta too.

"Which is?" Kaladin asked.

"Meat."

"What kind of meat?"

"The meaty kind."

"Soulcast," Kaladin said, looking at Sigzil.

"You ate Soulcast food every night as a bridgeman," Sigzil said, shrugging and taking a bite.

"Because I had no choice. Look. He's *frying* that bread."

"You fry the flangria too," Lopen said. "Make little balls of it, mixed with ground lavis. Batter it up and fry it, then stuff it in fried bread and pour on gravy." He made a satisfied sound, licking his lips.

"It's cheaper than *water*," Peet noted as Rock jogged back.

"That's probably because even the grain is Soulcast," Kaladin said. "It will all taste like mold. Rock, I'm disappointed in you."

The Horneater looked sheepish, but took a bite. His chouta crunched.

"Shells?" Kaladin asked.

"Cremling claws." Rock grinned. "Deep-fried."

Kaladin sighed, but they finally struck out again through the crowd, eventually reaching a wooden building built on the leeward side of a larger stone structure. Everything here was, of course, arranged so that as many doorways as possible could point away from the Origin, streets designed so that they could run east to west and provide a way for winds to blow.

Warm, orange light spilled from the tavern. Firelight. No tavern would use spheres for light. Even with locks on the lanterns, the rich glow of spheres might be just a little too tempting for the intoxicated patrons. Shouldering their way inside, the bridgemen were confronted by a low roar of chatter, yelling, and singing.

"We'll never find seats," Kaladin said over the din. Even with the reduced population of Dalinar's warcamp, this place was packed.

"Of course we will find seat," Rock said, grinning. "We have secret weapon." He pointed to where Peet, oval-faced and quiet, was working his way through the room toward the front bar. A pretty darkeyed woman stood polishing a glass there, and she smiled brightly when she saw Peet.

"So," Sigzil said to Kaladin, "have you given thought to where you're going to house the married men of Bridge Four?"

Married men? Looking at Peet's expression as he leaned across the bar, chatting with the woman, it seemed that might not be far off. Kaladin *hadn't* given any thought to it. He should have. He knew that Rock was married—the Horneater had already sent letters to his family, though the Peaks were so far away, news had not yet returned. Teft had been married, but his wife was dead, as was much of his family.

Some of the others might have families. When they'd been bridgemen, they hadn't spoken much of their pasts, but Kaladin had teased out hints here and there. They would slowly reclaim normal lives, and families would be part of that, particularly here with the stable warcamp.

"Storms!" Kaladin said, raising a hand to his head. "I'll have to ask for more space."

"There are many barracks partitioned to allow families," Sigzil noted. "And some of the married soldiers rent places in the market. Men could move to one of those choices."

"This thing would break up Bridge Four!" Rock said. "It cannot be allowed."

Well, married men tended to make better soldiers. He'd have to find a way to make it work. There *were* a lot of empty barracks around in Dalinar's camp now. Maybe he should ask for a few more.

Kaladin nodded toward the woman at the bar. "She doesn't own the place, I assume."

"No, Ka is just barmaid," Rock said. "Peet is quite taken with her."

"We'll need to see if she can read," Kaladin said, stepping aside as a semi-drunk patron pushed out into the night. "Storms, but it would be good to have someone around to do that." In a normal army, Kaladin would be lighteyed, and his wife or sister would act as the battalion's scribe and clerk.

Peet waved them over, and Ka led them through to a table set off to the side. Kaladin settled himself with his back to the wall, near enough to a window that he could look out if he wanted, but where he wouldn't be silhouetted. He spared some pity for Rock's chair as the Horneater settled down. Rock was the only one in the crew who had a few inches' height on Kaladin, and he was practically twice as broad.

"Horneater lager?" Rock asked hopefully, looking at Ka.

"It melts our cups," she said. "Ale?"

"Ale," Rock said with a sigh. "This thing should be a drink for women, not for large Horneater men. At least he is not wine."

Kaladin told her to bring whatever, barely paying attention. This place was not *inviting*, really. It was loud, obnoxious, smoky, and smelly. It was also alive. Laughing. Boasts and calls, mugs clanking. This . . . this was what some people lived for. A day of honest labor, followed by an evening at the tavern with friends.

That was not so bad a life.

"It's loud tonight," Sigzil noticed.

"Is always loud," Rock replied. "But tonight, maybe more."

"The army won a plateau run along with Bethab's army," Peet said.

Good for them. Dalinar hadn't gone, but Adolin had, along with three men from Bridge Four. They hadn't been required to go into battle, though—and any plateau run that didn't endanger Kaladin's men was a good one.

"So many people is nice," Rock said. "Makes tavern warmer. Is too cold outside."

"Too cold?" Moash said. "You're from the storming Horneater Peaks!"

"And?" Rock asked, frowning.

"And those are *mountains*. It's got to be colder up there than anything down here."

Rock actually sputtered, an amusing mixture of indignation and incredulity, bringing a red cast to his light Horneater skin. "Too much air! Hard for you to think. Cold? Horneater Peaks is warm! Wonderfully warm."

"Really?" Kaladin asked, skeptical. This could be one of Rock's jokes. Sometimes, those didn't make much sense to anyone but Rock himself.

"It's true," Sigzil said. "The peaks have hot springs to warm them."

"Ah, but these are not springs," Rock said, wagging a finger at Sigzil. "This is lowlander word. The Horneater oceans are waters of life."

"Oceans?" Peet asked, frowning.

"Very small oceans," Rock said. "One for every peak."

"The top of each mountain forms a kind of crater," Sigzil explained, "which is filled with a large lake of warm water. The heat is enough to create a pocket of livable land, despite the altitude. Walk too far from one of the Horneater towns, though, and you'll end up in freezing temperatures and ice fields left by the highstorms."

"You are telling story wrong," Rock said.

"These are facts, not a story."

"Everything is story," Rock said. "Listen. Long ago, the Unkalaki—my people, ones you call Horneaters—did not live in peaks. They lived down where air was thick and thinking was difficult. But we were hated."

"Who would hate Horneaters?" Peet said.

"Everyone," Rock replied as Ka brought the drinks. More special attention. Most everyone else was having to go to the bar to pick up drinks. Rock smiled at her and grabbed his large mug. "Is first drink. Lopen, you are trying to beat me?"

"I'm at it, mancha," Lopen said, raising his own mug, which was not quite so large.

The large Horneater took a pull on his drink, which left froth on his lip. "Everyone wanted to kill Horneaters," he said, thumping his fist on the table. "They were frightened of us. Stories say we were too good at fighting. So we were hunted and nearly destroyed."

"If you were so good at fighting," Moash said, pointing, "then how come you were nearly destroyed?"

"There are few of us," Rock said, hand proudly to his chest. "And very many of you. You are all over down here in lowlands. Man cannot step without finding toes of Alethi beneath his boot. So the Unkalaki, we were nearly destroyed. But our *tana'kai*—is like a king, but more—went to the gods to plead for help."

"Gods," Kaladin said. "You mean spren." He sought out Syl, who had chosen a perch on a rafter up above, watching a couple of little insects climb on a post.

"These are gods," Rock said, following Kaladin's gaze. "Yes. Some gods, though, they are more powerful than others. The *tana'kai*, he sought the strongest among them. He went first to gods of the trees. 'Can you hide us?' he asked. But gods of the trees could not. 'Men hunt us too,' they said.

'If you hide here, they will find you, and will use you for wood just like they use us.'"

"Use Horneaters," Sigzil said blandly, "as wood."

"Hush," Rock replied. "Next, *tana'kai*, he visited gods of the waters. 'Can we live in your depths?' he pled. 'Give to us power to breathe as fish, and we will serve you beneath oceans.' Alas, waters could not help. 'Men dig into our hearts with hooks, and bring forth those we protect. If you were to live here, you would become their meals.' So we could not live there.

"Last, *tana'kai*—desperate—visited most powerful of gods, gods of the mountains. 'My people are dying,' he pled. 'Please. Let us live on your slopes and worship you, and let your snows and ice provide our protection.'

"Gods of the mountains thought long. 'You cannot live upon our slopes,' they said, 'for is no life here. This is place of spirits, not of men. But if you can find way to make him a place of men *and* of spirits, we will protect you.' And so, *tana'kai* returned to gods of the waters and said, 'Give to us your water, that we may drink and live upon mountains.' And he was promised. *Tana'kai* went to gods of the trees and said, 'Give to us your fruit in bounty, that we may eat and live upon the mountains.' And he was promised. Then, *tana'kai* returned to mountains, and said, 'Give to us your heat, this thing that is in your heart, that we may live upon your peaks.'

"And this thing, he pleased gods of mountains, who saw that Unkalaki would work hard. They would not be burden upon the gods, but would solve problems on their own. And so, gods of mountains withdrew their peaks into themselves, and made open place for waters of life. The oceans were created of gods of the waters. Grass and fruit to give life were had of promise of gods of trees. And heat from heart of the mountains gave a place that we may live."

He sat back, taking a deep drink of his mug, then slammed it down on the table, grinning.

"So the gods," Moash said, nursing his own drink, "were pleased that you solved problems on your own . . . by going to other gods and begging them for help instead?"

"Hush," Rock said. "Is good story. And is truth."

"But you did call the lakes up there water," Sigzil said. "So they're hot springs. Just like I said."

"Is different," Rock replied, raising his hand and waving toward Ka, then smiling very deeply and wagging his mug in a supplicating way.

"How?"

"Is not just water," Rock said. "Is water of life. It is connection to gods. If Unkalaki swim in it, sometimes they see place of gods."

Kaladin leaned forward at that. His mind had been drifting toward how to help Bridge Eighteen with their discipline problems. This struck him. "Place of the gods?"

"Yes," Rock said. "Is where they live. The waters of life, they let you see place. In it, you commune with gods, if you are lucky."

"Is that why you can see spren?" Kaladin asked. "Because you swam in these waters, and they did something to you?"

"Is not part of story," Rock said as his second mug of ale arrived. He grinned at Ka. "You are very wonderful woman. If you come to the Peaks, I will make you family."

"Just pay your tab, Rock," Ka said, rolling her eyes. As she moved off to collect some empty mugs, Peet jumped up to help her, surprising her by gathering some from another table.

"You can see the spren," Kaladin pressed, "because of what happened to you in these waters."

"Is not part of story," Rock said, eyeing him. "It is . . . involved. I will say no more of this thing."

"I'd like to visit," Lopen said. "Go for a dip myself."

"Ha! Is death to one not of our people," Rock said. "I could not let you swim. Even if you beat me at drinking tonight." He raised an eyebrow at Lopen's drink.

"Swimming in the emerald pools is death to outsiders," Sigzil said, "because you execute outsiders who touch them."

"No, this is not true. Listen to story. Stop being boring."

"They're just hot springs," Sigzil grumbled, but returned to his drink.

Rock rolled his eyes. "On top, is water. Beneath, is not. Is something else. Water of life. The place of the gods. This thing is true. I have met a god myself."

"A god like Syl?" Kaladin asked. "Or maybe a riverspren?" Those were somewhat rare, but supposedly able to speak at times in simple ways, like windspren.

"No," Rock said. He leaned in, as if saying something conspiratorial. "I saw Lunu'anaki."

"Uh, great," Moash said. "Wonderful."

"Lunu'anaki," Rock said, "is god of travel and mischief. Very powerful god. He came from depths of peak ocean, from realm of gods."

"What did he look like?" Lopen asked, eyes wide.

"Like person," Rock said. "Maybe Alethi, though skin was lighter. Very angular face. Handsome, perhaps. With white hair."

Sigzil looked up sharply. "White hair?"

"Yes," Rock said. "Not grey, like old man, but white—yet he is young man. He spoke with me on shore. Ha! Made mockery of my beard. Asked what year it was, by Horneater calendar. Thought my name was funny. Very powerful god."

"Were you scared?" Lopen asked.

"No, of course not. Lunu'anaki cannot hurt man. Is forbidden by other gods. Everyone knows this." Rock downed the rest of his second mug and raised it to the air, grinning and wagging it toward Ka *again* as she passed.

Lopen hurriedly drank the rest of his first mug. Sigzil looked troubled, and had only touched half of his drink. He stared at it, though when Moash asked him what was wrong, Sigzil made an excuse about being tired.

Kaladin finally took a sip of his own drink. Lavis ale, sudsy, faintly sweet. It reminded him of home, though he'd only started drinking it once in the army.

The others moved on to a conversation about plateau runs. Sadeas had apparently been disobeying orders to go on plateau runs in teams. He'd gone on one a bit back on his own, seizing the gemheart before anyone got there, then tossing it away as if it was unimportant. Just a few days back, though, Sadeas and Highprince Ruthar had gone on another run together—one they weren't supposed to go on. They claimed to have failed to get the gemheart, but it was open knowledge they'd won and hidden the winnings.

These overt slaps in Dalinar's face were the buzz of the warcamps. More so because Sadeas seemed outraged that he wasn't being allowed to put investigators into Dalinar's warcamp to search for "important facts" he said related to the safety of the king. It was all a game to him.

Someone needs to put Sadeas down, Kaladin thought, sipping his drink, swishing the cool liquid in his mouth. *He's as bad as Amaram—tried to get me and mine killed repeatedly. Don't I have reason, even right, to return the favor?*

Kaladin was learning how to do what the assassin did—how to run up walls, maybe reach windows that were thought inaccessible. He could visit Sadeas's camp in the night. Glowing, violent . . .

Kaladin could *bring* justice to this world.

His gut told him that there was something wrong with that reasoning, but he had trouble producing it logically. He drank a little more, and looked around the room, noticing again how relaxed everyone seemed. This was their life. Work, then play. That was enough for them.

Not for him. He needed something more. He got out a glowing sphere—just a diamond chip—and began to idly roll it on the table.

After about an hour of conversation, Kaladin taking part only sporadically, Moash nudged him in the side. "You ready?" he whispered.

"Ready?" Kaladin frowned.

"Yeah. Meeting is in the back room. I saw them come in a bit ago. They'll be waiting."

"Who . . ." He trailed off, realizing what Moash intended. Kaladin had said he'd meet with Moash's friends, the men who had tried to kill the king. Kaladin's skin went cold, the air suddenly seeming chill. "That's why you wanted me to come tonight?"

"Yeah," Moash said. "I thought you'd figured it out. Come on."

Kaladin looked down into his mug of yellow-brown liquid. Finally, he downed the rest and stood up. He needed to know who these men were. His duty demanded it.

Moash excused them, saying he'd noticed an old friend he wanted to introduce to Kaladin. Rock, looking not the least bit drunk, laughed and waved them on. He was on his . . . sixth drink? Seventh? Lopen was already tipsy after his third. Sigzil had only barely finished his second, and didn't seem inclined to continue.

So much for the contest, Kaladin thought, letting Moash lead him. The place was still busy, though not quite as packed as it had been earlier. Tucked away in the back of the tavern was a hallway with private dining rooms, the type used by wealthy merchants who didn't want to be subjected to the crudeness of the common room. A swarthy man lounged outside of one. He might have been part Azish, or maybe just a very tan Alethi. He carried very long knives at his belt, but didn't say anything as Moash pushed open the door.

"Kaladin . . ." Syl's voice. Where was she? Vanished, apparently, from even his eyes. Had she done that before? "Be careful."

He stepped into the room with Moash. Three men and a woman drank wine at a table inside. Another guard stood at the back, wrapped in a cloak, a sword at his waist and his head down, as if he were barely paying attention.

Two of the seated people, including the woman, were lighteyes. Kaladin should have expected this, considering the fact that a Shardblade was involved, but it still gave him pause.

The lighteyed man stood up immediately. He was perhaps a little older than Adolin, and he had jet-black Alethi hair, styled crisply. He wore an open jacket and an expensive-looking black shirt underneath, embroidered with white vines running between the buttons, and a stock at his throat.

"So this is the famous Kaladin!" the man exclaimed, stepping forward and reaching out to clasp Kaladin's hand. "Storms, but it is a pleasure to meet you. Embarrassing Sadeas while saving the Blackthorn himself? Good show, man. Good *show*."

"And you are?" Kaladin asked.

"A patriot," the man said. "Call me Graves."

"And are you the Shardbearer?"

"Straight to the point, are you?" Graves said, gesturing for Kaladin to sit at the table.

Moash took a seat immediately, nodding to the other man at the table—he was darkeyed, with short hair and sunken eyes. *Mercenary,* Kaladin guessed, noting the heavy leathers he was wearing and the axe beside his seat. Graves continued to gesture, but Kaladin delayed, inspecting the young woman at the table. She sat primly and sipped her cup of wine held in two hands, one covered in her buttoned sleeve. Pretty, with pursed red lips, she wore her hair up and stuck through with sundry metal decorations.

"I recognize you," Kaladin said. "One of Dalinar's clerks."

She watched him, careful, though she tried to appear relaxed.

"Danlan is a member of the highprince's retinue," Graves said. "Please, Kaladin. Sit. Have some wine."

Kaladin sat down, but did not pour a drink. "You are trying to kill the king."

"He *is* direct, isn't he?" Graves asked Moash.

"Effective, too," Moash said. "It's why we like him."

Graves turned to Kaladin. "We are patriots, as I said before. Patriots of Alethkar. The Alethkar that *could* be."

"Patriots who wish to murder the kingdom's ruler?"

Graves leaned forward, clasping his hands on the table. A bit of the humor left him, which was fine. He'd been trying too hard anyway. "Very well, we shall be on with it. Elhokar is a supremely *bad* king. Surely you've noticed this."

"It's not my place to pass judgment on a king."

"Oh please," Graves said. "You're telling me you haven't seen the way he acts? Spoiled, petulant, paranoid. He squabbles instead of consulting, he makes childish demands instead of leading. He is blowing this kingdom to the ground."

"Have you any idea the kinds of policies he put into place before Dalinar got him under control?" Danlan asked. "I spent the last three years in Kholinar helping the clerks there sort through the mess he made of the royal codes. There was a time when he'd sign practically *anything* into law if he was cajoled the right way."

"He is incompetent," said the darkeyed mercenary, whose name Kaladin didn't know. "He gets good men killed. Lets that bastard Sadeas get away with high treason."

"So you try to assassinate him?" Kaladin demanded.

Graves met Kaladin's eyes. "Yes."

"If a king is destroying his country," the mercenary said, "is it not the right—the duty—of the people to see him removed?"

"If he *were* removed," Moash said, "what would happen? Ask yourself that, Kaladin."

"Dalinar would probably take the throne," Kaladin said. Elhokar had a son back in Kholinar, a child, barely a few years old. Even if Dalinar only proclaimed himself regent in the name of the rightful heir, he would rule.

"The kingdom would be far better off with him at the head," Graves said.

"He practically rules the place anyway," Kaladin said.

"No," Danlan said. "Dalinar holds himself back. He knows he should take the throne, but hesitates out of love for his dead brother. The other highprinces interpret this as weakness."

"We need the Blackthorn," Graves said, pounding the table. "This kingdom is going to fall otherwise. The death of Elhokar would spur Dalinar to action. We would get back the man we had twenty years ago, the man who unified the highprinces in the first place."

"Even if that man didn't fully return," the mercenary added, "we certainly couldn't be worse off than we are now."

"So yes," Graves said to Kaladin. "We're assassins. Murderers, or would-be ones. We don't want a coup, and we don't want to kill innocent guards. We just want the king removed. Quietly. Preferably in an accident."

Danlan grimaced, then took a drink of wine. "Unfortunately, we have not been particularly effective so far."

"And that's why I wanted to meet with you," Graves said.

"You expect me to *help* you?" Kaladin asked.

Graves raised his hands. "Think about what we've said. That is all I ask. Think about the king's actions, watch him. Ask yourself, 'How much longer will the kingdom last with this man at its head?'"

"The Blackthorn must take the throne," Danlan said softly. "It *will* happen eventually. We want to help him along, for his own good. Spare him the difficult decision."

"I could turn you in," Kaladin said, meeting Graves's eyes. To the side, the cloaked man—who had been leaning against the wall and listening—shuffled, standing up straighter. "Inviting me here was a risk."

"Moash says you were trained as a surgeon," Graves said, not looking at all concerned.

"Yes."

"And what do you do if the hand is festering, threatening the entire body? Do you wait and hope it gets better, or do you act?"

Kaladin didn't reply.

"You control the King's Guard now, Kaladin," Graves said. "We will need an opening, a time when no guards will be hurt, to strike. We didn't want the actual blood of the king on our hands, wanted to make this seem an accident, but I have realized this is cowardly. I will do the deed myself. All I want is an opening, and Alethkar's suffering will be over."

"It will be better for the king this way," Danlan said. "He is dying a slow death on that throne, like a drowning man far from land. Best to be done with it quickly."

Kaladin stood up. Moash rose hesitantly.

Graves looked at Kaladin.

"I will consider," Kaladin said.

"Good, good," Graves said. "You can get back to us through Moash. Be the surgeon this kingdom needs."

"Come on," Kaladin said to Moash. "The others will be wondering where we got to."

He walked out, Moash following after making a few hasty farewells. Kaladin, honestly, expected one of them to try to stop him. Didn't they worry that he'd turn them in, as he'd threatened?

They let him go. Back out into the clattering, chattering common room.

Storms, he thought. *I wish their arguments hadn't been so good.* "How did you meet them?" Kaladin asked as Moash jogged up to join him.

"Rill, that's the fellow who was sitting at the table, he was a mercenary on some of the caravans I worked before ending up in the bridge crews. He came to me once we were free of slavery." Moash took Kaladin by the arm, halting him before they got back to their table. "They're right. You know they are, Kal. I can see it in you."

"They're traitors," Kaladin said. "I want nothing to do with them."

"You said you'd consider!"

"I said that," Kaladin said softly, "so that they'd let me leave. We have a *duty*, Moash."

"Is it greater than the duty to the country itself?"

"You don't care about the country," Kaladin snapped. "You just want to pursue your grudge."

"All right, fine. But Kaladin, did you notice? Graves treats all men the same, regardless of eye color. He doesn't care that we're darkeyed. He married a darkeyed woman."

"Really?" Kaladin had heard of wealthy darkeyes marrying lowborn lighteyes, but never anyone as high-dahn as a Shardbearer.

"Yeah," Moash said. "One of his sons is even a one-eye. Graves doesn't give a storm about what other people think of him. He does what is right. And in this case, it's—" Moash glanced around. They were now surrounded by people. "It's what he said. Someone has to do it."

"Don't speak of this to me again," Kaladin said, pulling his arm free and walking back toward the table. "And don't meet with them anymore."

He sat back down, Moash slinking into his place, annoyed. Kaladin tried to get himself to rejoin the conversation with Rock and Lopen, but he just couldn't.

All around him, people laughed or shouted.

Be the surgeon this kingdom needs. . . .

Storms, what a mess.

47

FEMININE WILES

Yet, were the orders not disheartened by so great a defeat, for the Lightweavers provided spiritual sustenance; they were enticed by those glorious creations to venture on a second assault.

—From *Words of Radiance,* chapter 21, page 10

I t doesn't make sense," Shallan said. "Pattern, these maps are baffling."

The spren hovered nearby in his three-dimensional form full of twisting lines and angles. Sketching him had proven difficult, as whenever she looked closely at a section of his form, she found that it had so much detail as to defy proper depiction.

"Mmm?" Pattern asked in his humming voice.

Shallan climbed off her bed and tossed the book onto her white-painted writing desk. She knelt beside Jasnah's trunk, digging through it before coming out with a map of Roshar. It was ancient, and not terribly accurate; Alethkar was depicted as far too large and the world as a whole was misshapen, with trade routes emphasized. It clearly predated modern methods of survey and cartography. Still, it was important, for it showed the Silver Kingdoms as they had supposedly existed during the time of the Knights Radiant.

"Urithiru," Shallan said, pointing toward a shining city depicted on the map as the center of everything. It wasn't in Alethkar, or Alethela as it had been known at the time. The map put it in the middle of the mountains near what might have been modern Jah Keved. However, Jasnah's annotations said other maps from the time placed it elsewhere. "How could they not *know* where their capital was, the center of the orders of knights? Why does every map argue with its fellows?"

"Mmmmmm . . ." Pattern said, thoughtful. "Perhaps many had heard of it, but never visited."

"Cartographers as well?" Shallan asked. "And the kings who commissioned these maps? Surely *some* of them had been to the place. Why on Roshar would it be so difficult to pinpoint?"

"They wished to keep its location secret, perhaps?"

Shallan stuck the map to the wall using some weevilwax from Jasnah's supplies. She backed away, folding her arms. She hadn't dressed for the day yet, and wore her dressing gown, hands uncovered.

"If that's the case," Shallan said, "they did too good a job of it." She dug out a few other maps from the time, created by other kingdoms. In each, Shallan noted, the country of origin was presented far larger than it should have been. She stuck these to the wall too.

"Each shows Urithiru in a different location," Shallan said. "Notably close to their own lands, yet not *in* their lands."

"Different languages on each," Pattern said. "Mmm . . . There are patterns here." He started to try sounding them out.

Shallan smiled. Jasnah had told her that several of them were thought to have been written in the Dawnchant, a dead language. Scholars had been trying for years to—

"Behardan King . . . something I do not understand . . . order, perhaps . . ." Pattern said. "Map? Yes, that would likely be map. So the next is perhaps to draw . . . draw . . . something I do not understand . . ."

"You're *reading* it?"

"It is a pattern."

"You're *reading the Dawnchant*."

"Not well."

"You're reading the *Dawnchant*!" Shallan exclaimed. She scrambled up to the map beside which Pattern hovered, then rested her fingers on the script at the bottom. "Behardan, you said? Maybe Bajerden . . . Nohadon himself."

"Bajerden? Nohadon? Must people have so many names?"

"One is honorific," Shallan said. "His original name wasn't considered symmetrical enough. Well, I guess it wasn't really symmetrical at all, so the ardents gave him a new one centuries ago."

"But . . . the new one isn't symmetrical either."

"The *h* sound can be for any letter," Shallan said absently. "We write it as the symmetrical letter, to make the word balance, but add a diacritical mark to indicate it sounds like an *h* so the word is easier to say."

"That— One can't just *pretend* that a word is symmetrical when it isn't!"

Shallan ignored his sputtering, instead staring at the alien script of what was supposedly the Dawnchant. *If we do find Jasnah's city,* Shallan thought, *and if it does have records, they might be in this language.* "We need to see how much of the Dawnchant you can translate."

"I did not read it," Pattern said, annoyed. "I postulated a few words. The name I could translate because of the sounds of the cities above."

"But those aren't written in the Dawnchant!"

"The scripts are derived from one another," Pattern said. "Obviously."

"So obvious that no human scholar has ever figured it out."

"You are not as good with patterns," he said, sounding smug. "You are abstract. You think in lies and tell them to yourselves. That is fascinating, but it is not good for patterns."

You are abstract . . . Shallan rounded the bed and slipped a book from the pile there, one written by the scholar Ali-daughter-Hasweth of Shinovar. The Shin scholars were among the most interesting to read, as their perspectives on the rest of Roshar could be so frank, so different.

She found the passage she wanted. Jasnah had highlighted it in her notes, so Shallan had sent out for the full book. Sebarial's stipend to her—which he *was* paying—came in very handy. Vathah and Gaz, by her request, had spent the last few days visiting book merchants asking after *Words of Radiance*, the book Jasnah had given her just before dying. So far no luck, though one merchant had claimed he might be able to order it in from Kholinar.

"Urithiru was the connection to all nations," she read from the Shin writer's work. "And, at times, our only path to the outside world, with its stones unhallowed." She looked up at Pattern. "What does that mean to you?"

"It means what it says," Pattern replied, still hovering beside the maps. "That Urithiru was well connected. Roads, perhaps?"

"I've always read the phrase metaphorically. Connected in purpose, in thought, and scholarship."

"Ah. Lies."

"What if it's not a metaphor? What if it's like what you say?" She rose and crossed the room toward the maps, resting her fingers on Urithiru at the center. "Connected . . . but not by roads. Some of these maps don't have any roads leading to Urithiru at all. They all place it in the mountains, or at least the hills. . . ."

"Mmm."

"How do you reach a city if not by roads?" Shallan asked. "Nohadon could walk there, or so he claimed. But others do not speak of riding, or walking, to Urithiru." True, there were few accounts of people visiting the city. It was a legend. Most modern scholars considered it a myth.

She needed more information. She scrambled over to Jasnah's trunk, digging out one of her notebooks. "She said that Urithiru wasn't on the

Shattered Plains," Shallan said, "but what if the *pathway* to it is here? Not an ordinary pathway, though. Urithiru was the city of Surgebinders. Of ancient wonders, like Shardblades."

"Mm . . ." Pattern said softly. "Shardblades are no wonder . . ."

Shallan found the reference she was searching for. It wasn't the quote she found curious, but Jasnah's annotation of it. *Another folktale, this one recorded in* Among the Darkeyed, *by Calinam. Page 102. Stories of instantaneous travel and the Oathgates pervade these tales.*

Instantaneous travel. Oathgates.

"That's what she was coming here for," Shallan whispered. "She thought she could find a passageway here, on the Plains. But they're barren stormlands, just stone, crem, and greatshells." She looked up at Pattern. "We *really* need to get out there, onto the Shattered Plains."

Her announcement was accompanied by an ominous chime from the clock. Ominous in that it meant the hour was far later than she'd assumed. Storms! She needed to meet Adolin by noon. She had to leave in a half hour if she was going to meet him on time.

Shallan yelped and ran for the washroom. She turned the spigot for water to fill the tub. After a moment of it spitting out dirty cremwater, clean, warm water began to flow, and she put in the stopper. She put her hand underneath it, marveling yet again. Flowing warm water. Sebarial said that artifabrians had visited recently, arranging to set up a fabrial that would keep the water in the cistern above perpetually warm, like the ones in Kharbranth.

"I," she said, shucking off her dressing gown, "am going to allow myself to grow very, very accustomed to this."

She climbed into the tub as Pattern moved along the wall above her. She had decided not to be bashful around him. True, he had a male voice, but he wasn't *really* a man. Besides, there were spren everywhere. The tub probably had one in it, as did the walls. She'd seen for herself that everything had a soul, or a spren, or whatever. Did she care if the walls watched her? No. So why should she care about Pattern?

She did have to repeat this line of reasoning every time he saw her undress. It would help if he weren't so blasted *curious* about everything.

"The anatomical differences between genders are so slight," Pattern said, humming to himself. "Yet so profound. And you augment them. Long hair. Blush on the cheeks. I went and watched Sebarial bathe last night and—"

"Please tell me you didn't," Shallan said, blushing as she grabbed some pasty soap from the jar beside the iron tub.

"But . . . I just told you that I did. . . . Anyway, I wasn't seen. I would not need to do this if you'd be more accommodating."

"I am *not* doing nude sketches for you."

She had made the mistake of mentioning that many of the great artists had trained themselves this way. After much pleading back home, she'd gotten several of the maids to pose for her, so long as she promised to destroy the sketches. Which she had. She'd never sketched men that way. Storms, that would be embarrassing!

She didn't let herself linger in the bath. A quarter hour later—by the clock—she stood dressed and combing her damp hair before the mirror.

How would she ever go back to Jah Keved and a placid, rural life again? The answer was simple. She probably would never return. Once, that thought would have horrified her. Now it thrilled her—though she was determined to bring her brothers to the Shattered Plains. They would be far safer here than at her father's estates, and what would they be leaving behind? Barely anything at all. She'd begun to think it was a far better solution than anything else, and let them dodge the issue of the missing Soulcaster, to an extent.

She'd gone to one of the information stations connected to Tashikk— there was one in every warcamp—and paid to have a letter, along with a spanreed, sent by messenger from Valath to her brothers. It would take weeks to arrive, unfortunately. If it even did. The merchant she'd talked to at the information station had warned her that moving through Jah Keved was difficult these days, with the succession war. To be careful, she'd sent a second letter from Northgrip, which was as far from the battlefields as one could get. Hopefully at least one of the two would arrive safely.

When she established contact again, she'd make a single argument to her brothers. Abandon the Davar estates. Take the money Jasnah had sent and flee to the Shattered Plains. For now, she'd done what she could.

She rushed through the room, hopping on one foot as she pulled on a slipper, and passed the maps. *I'll deal with you later.*

It was time to go woo her betrothed. Somehow. The novels she'd read made it seem easy. A batting of eyelashes, blushes at appropriate times. Well, she had that last one down in good measure. Except maybe the appropriate part. She buttoned up the sleeve over her safehand, then paused at the door as she looked back and saw her sketchbook and pencil lying on the table.

She didn't want to leave without those ever again. She tucked both in her satchel and rushed out. On the way through the white-marbled house, she passed Palona and Sebarial in a room with enormous glass windows, facing leeward over the gardens. Palona lay facedown, getting a massage— completely bare-backed—while Sebarial reclined and ate sweets. A young woman stood at a lectern in the corner, reciting poetry to them.

Shallan had a difficult time judging those two. Sebarial. Was he a clever civil planner or an indolent glutton? Both? Palona certainly did like the luxuries of wealth, but she didn't seem the least bit arrogant. Shallan had spent the last three days poring over Sebarial's house ledgers, and had found them an absolute *mess*. He seemed so smart in some areas. How could he have let his ledgers get so overgrown?

Shallan wasn't especially good with numbers, not compared to her art, but she did enjoy math on occasion and was determined to tackle those ledgers.

Gaz and Vathah waited for her outside the doors. They followed her toward Sebarial's coach, which waited for her to use, along with one of her slaves to act as footman. En said he'd done the job before, and he smiled at her as she stepped up. That was good to see. She couldn't remember any of the five smiling on their trip out, even when she'd released them from the cage.

"You are being treated well, En?" she asked as he opened the coach door for her.

"Yes, mistress."

"You'd tell me if you weren't?"

"Er, yes, mistress."

"And you, Vathah?" she asked, turning to him. "How are you finding your accommodations?"

He grunted.

"I assume that means they're accommodating?" she asked.

Gaz chuckled. The short man had an ear for wordplay.

"You've kept your bargain," Vathah said. "I'll give you that. The men are happy."

"And you?"

"Bored. All we do every day is sit around, collect what you pay us, and go drinking."

"Most men would consider that an ideal profession." She smiled at En, then climbed into the coach.

Vathah shut the door for her, then looked in the window. "Most men are idiots."

"Nonsense," Shallan said, smiling. "By the law of averages, only half of them are."

He grunted. She was learning to interpret those, which was essential to speaking Vathahese. This one roughly meant, "I'm not going to acknowledge that joke because it would spoil my reputation as a complete and utter dunnard."

"I suppose," he said, "we have to ride up top."

"Thank you for offering," Shallan said, then pulled down the window shade. Outside, Gaz chuckled again. The two climbed into the guard positions on the top back of the carriage, and En joined the coachman up front. It was a true proper coach, pulled by horses and everything. Shallan had originally felt bad about asking to use it, but Palona had laughed. "Take the thing whenever you want! I have my own, and if Turi's coach is gone, he'll have an excuse to not go when people ask him to visit. He loves that."

Shallan closed the other window shade as the coachman started the vehicle rolling, then got out her sketchbook. Pattern waited on the first blank white page. "We are going to find out," Shallan whispered, "just what we can do."

"Exciting!" Pattern said.

She got out her pouch of spheres and breathed in some of the Stormlight. Then, she puffed it out in front of her, trying to shape it, meld it.

Nothing.

Next, she tried holding a very specific image in her head—herself, with one small change: black hair instead of red. She puffed out the Stormlight, and this time it shifted around her and hung for a moment. Then it too vanished.

"This is silly," Shallan said softly, Stormlight trailing from her lips. She did a quick sketch of herself with dark hair. "What does it matter if I draw it first or not? The pencils don't even show color."

"It shouldn't matter," Pattern said. "But it matters to you. I do not know why."

She finished the sketch. It was very simple—it didn't show her features, only really her hair, everything else indistinct. Yet when she used Stormlight this time, the image took and her hair darkened to black.

Shallan sighed, Stormlight leaking from her lips. "So, how do I make the illusion vanish?"

"Stop feeding it."

"How?"

"I am supposed to know this?" Pattern asked. "You are the expert on feeding."

Shallan gathered all of her spheres—several were now dun—and set them on the seat across from her, out of reach. That wasn't far enough, for as her Stormlight ran out, she breathed in using instincts she hadn't realized she had. Light streamed from across the carriage and into her.

"I'm quite good at that," Shallan said sourly, "considering how short a time I've been doing it."

"Short time?" Pattern said. "But we first . . ."

She stopped listening until he was done.

"I really need to find another copy of *Words of Radiance*," Shallan said, starting another sketch. "Maybe it talks about how to dismiss the illusions."

She continued to work on her next sketch, a picture of Sebarial. She'd taken a Memory of him while dining the night before, just after returning from a session scouting Amaram's compound. She wanted to get the details of this sketch right for her collection, so it took some time. Fortunately, the level roadway meant no big bumps. It wasn't ideal, but she seemed to have less and less time these days, with her research, her work for Sebarial, infiltrating the Ghostbloods, and meetings with Adolin Kholin. She'd had so much more time when she was younger. She couldn't help thinking she'd wasted much of it.

She let the work consume her. The familiar sound of pencil on paper, the focus of creation. Beauty was out there, all around. To create art was not to capture it, but to *participate* in it.

When she finished, a glance out the window showed them approaching the Pinnacle. She held up the sketch, studying it, then nodded to herself. Satisfactory.

Next she tried using Stormlight to create an image. She breathed out a lot of it, and it formed immediately, snapping into an image of Sebarial sitting across from her in the carriage. He held the same position as he did in her sketch, hands out to slice food that was not included in her image.

Shallan smiled. The detail was *perfect*. Folds in skin, individual hairs. She hadn't drawn those—no sketch could capture all the hairs on a head, all the pores in skin. Her image had these things, so it didn't create exactly what she drew, but the drawing was a focus. A model that the image built from.

"Mmm," Pattern said, sounding satisfied. "One of your most truthful lies. Wonderful."

"He doesn't move," Shallan said. "Nobody would mistake this for something living, never mind the unnatural pose. The eyes are lifeless; the chest doesn't rise and fall with breath. The muscles don't shift. It's detailed—but like a statue can be detailed yet still dead."

"A statue of light."

"I didn't say it isn't impressive," Shallan said. "But the images will be much harder to use unless I can give them life." How strange that she should feel that her sketches were alive, but this thing—which was so much more realistic—was dead.

She reached out to wave her hand through the image. If she touched it slowly, the disturbance was minor. Waving her hand disturbed it like smoke. She noticed something else. While her hand was in the image . . .

Yes. She sucked in a breath and the image dissolved to glowing smoke, drawn into her skin. She could reclaim Stormlight from the illusion. *One question answered,* she thought, settling back and making notes about the experience in the back of the notebook.

She began packing up her satchel as the carriage arrived at the Outer

Market, where Adolin would be waiting for her. They'd gone on their promised walk the day before, and she felt things were going well. But she also knew she needed to impress him. Her efforts with Highlady Navani had not been fruitful so far, and she really *did* need an alliance with the Kholin house.

That made her consider. Her hair had dried, but she tended to keep it long and straight down her back, with only its natural curl to give it body. The Alethi women favored intricate braids instead.

Her skin was pale and dusted lightly with freckles, and her body was nowhere near curvaceous enough to inspire envy. She could change all of this with an illusion. An augmentation. Since Adolin had seen her without, she couldn't change anything dramatic—but she could enhance herself. It would be like wearing makeup.

She hesitated. If Adolin came to agree to the marriage, would it be because of her, or the lies?

Foolish girl, Shallan thought. *You were willing to change your appearance to get Vathah to follow you and to gain a place with Sebarial, but not now?*

But capturing Adolin's attention with illusions would lead her down a difficult path. She couldn't wear an illusion always, could she? In married life? Better to see what she could do without one, she thought as she climbed out of the carriage. She'd have to rely, instead, upon her feminine wiles.

She wished she knew if she had any.

48

NO MORE WEAKNESS

THREE YEARS AGO

These are really good, Shallan," Balat said, leafing through pages of her sketches. The two of them sat in the gardens, accompanied by Wikim, who sat on the ground tossing a cloth-wrapped ball for his axehound Sakisa to catch.

"My anatomy is off," Shallan said with a blush. "I can't get the proportions right." She needed models to pose for her so she could work on that.

"You're better than Mother ever was," Balat said, flipping to another page, where she had sketched Balat on the sparring grounds with his swordsmanship tutor. He tipped it toward Wikim, who raised an eyebrow.

Her middle brother was looking better and better these last four months. Less scrawny, more solid. He almost constantly had mathematical problems with him. Father had once railed at him for that, claiming it was feminine and unseemly—but, in a rare show of dissension, Father's ardents had approached him and told him to calm himself, and that the Almighty approved of Wikim's interest. They hoped Wikim might find his way into their ranks.

"I heard that you got another letter from Eylita," Shallan said, trying to distract Balat from the sketchbook. She couldn't keep herself from blushing as he turned page after page. Those weren't meant for others to look at. They weren't any good.

"Yeah," he said, grinning.

"You going to have Shallan read it to you?" Wikim asked, throwing the ball.

Balat coughed. "I had Malise do it. Shallan was busy."

"You're embarrassed!" Wikim said, pointing. "What is *in* those letters?"

"Things my fourteen-year-old sister doesn't need to know about!" Balat said.

"That racy, eh?" Wikim asked. "I wouldn't have figured that for the Tavinar girl. She seems too proper."

"No!" Balat blushed further. "They aren't racy; they are merely private."

"Private like your—"

"Wikim," Shallan cut in.

He looked up, and then noticed that angerspren were pooling underneath Balat's feet. "Storms, Balat. You are getting so touchy about that girl."

"Love makes us all fools," Shallan said, distracting the two.

"Love?" Balat asked, glancing at her. "Shallan, you're barely old enough to pin up your safehand. What do you know about love?"

She blushed. "I . . . never mind."

"Oh, look at that," Wikim said. "She's thought up something clever. You're going to have to say it now, Shallan."

"No use keeping something like that inside," Balat agreed.

"Ministara says I speak my mind too much. That it's not a feminine attribute."

Wikim laughed. "That hasn't seemed to stop any women *I've* known."

"Yeah, Shallan," Balat said. "If you can't say the things you think of to us, then who can you say them to?"

"Trees," she said, "rocks, shrubs. Basically anything that can't get me in trouble with my tutors."

"You don't have to worry about Balat, then," Wikim said. "He couldn't manage something clever even in repetition."

"Hey!" Balat said. Though, unfortunately, it wasn't far from the truth.

"Love," Shallan said, though partially just to distract them, "is like a pile of chull dung."

"Smelly?" Balat asked.

"No," Shallan said, "for even as we try to avoid both, we end up stepping in them anyway."

"Deep words for a girl who hit her teens precisely fifteen months ago," Wikim said with a chuckle.

"Love is like the sun," Balat said, sighing.

"Blinding?" Shallan asked. "White, warm, powerful—but also capable of burning you?"

"Perhaps," Balat said, nodding.

"Love is like a Herdazian surgeon," Wikim said, looking at her.

"And how is that?" Shallan asked.

"You tell me," Wikim said. "I'm seeing what you can make of it."

"Um . . . Both leave you uncomfortable?" Shallan said. "No. Ooh! The only reason you'd want one was if you'd taken a sharp blow to the head!"

"Ha! Love is like spoiled food."

"Necessary for life on one hand," Shallan said, "but also expressly nauseating."

"Father's snoring."

She shuddered. "You have to experience it to believe just how distracting it can be."

Wikim chuckled. Storms, but it was good to see him doing that.

"Stop it, you two," Balat said. "That kind of talk is disrespectful. Love . . . love is like a classical melody."

Shallan grinned. "If you end your performance too quickly, your audience is disappointed?"

"Shallan!" Balat said.

Wikim, however, was rolling on the ground. After a moment, Balat shook his head, and gave an agreeable chuckle. For her own part, Shallan was blushing. *Did I really just say that?* That last one had actually been somewhat witty, far better than the others. It had also been improper.

She got a guilty thrill from it. Balat looked embarrassed, and he blushed at the double meaning, collecting shamespren. Sturdy Balat. He wanted so much to lead them. So far as she knew, he'd given up his habit of killing cremlings for fun. Being in love strengthened him, changed him.

The sound of wheels on stone announced a carriage arriving at the house. No hoofbeats—father owned horses, but few other people in the area did. Their carriages were pulled by chulls or parshmen.

Balat rose to go see who had come, and Sakisa followed after, trumping in excitement. Shallan picked up her sketchpad. Father had recently forbidden her from drawing the manor's parshmen or darkeyes—he found it unseemly. That made it hard for her to find practice figures.

"Shallan?"

She started, realizing that Wikim hadn't followed Balat. "Yes."

"I was wrong," Wikim said, handing her something. A small pouch. "About what you're doing. I see through it. And . . . and still it's working. Damnation, but it's working. Thank you."

She moved to open the pouch he'd given her.

"Don't," he said.

"What is it?"

"Blackbane," Wikim said. "A plant, the leaves at least. If you eat them, they paralyze you. Your breathing stops too."

Disturbed, she pulled the top tight. She didn't even want to know how Wikim could recognize a deadly plant like this.

"I've carried those for the better part of a year," Wikim said softly. "The longer you have them, the more potent the leaves are supposed to become.

I don't feel like I need them any longer. You can burn them, or whatever. I just thought you should have them."

She smiled, though she felt unsettled. Wikim had been carrying this poison around? He felt he needed to give it to her?

He jogged after Balat, and Shallan stuffed the pouch in her satchel. She'd find a way to destroy it later. She picked up her pencils and went back to drawing.

Shouting from inside the manor distracted her a short time later. She looked up, uncertain even how much time had passed. She rose, satchel clutched to her chest, and crossed the yard. Vines shook and withdrew before her, though as her pace sped up, she stepped on more and more of them, feeling them writhe beneath her feet and try to yank back. Cultivated vines had poor instincts.

She reached the house to more shouting.

"Father!" Asha Jushu's voice. "Father, please!"

Shallan pushed open the slatted wood doors, silk dress rustling against the floor as she stepped in and found three men in old-style clothing—skirtlike ulatu to their knees, bright loose shirts, flimsy coats that draped to the ground—standing before Father.

Jushu knelt on the floor, hands bound behind his back. Over the years, Jushu had grown plump from his periods of excess.

"Bah," Father said. "I will not suffer this extortion."

"His credit is your credit, Brightlord," one of the men said in a calm, smooth voice. He was darkeyed, though he didn't sound it. "He promised us you would pay his debts."

"He lied," Father said, Ekel and Jix—house guards—at his sides, hands on weapons.

"Father," Jushu whispered through his tears. "They'll take me—"

"You were supposed to be riding our outer holdings!" Father bellowed. "You were supposed to be checking on our lands, not dining with thieves and gambling away our wealth and our good name!"

Jushu hung his head, sagging in his bonds.

"He's yours," Father said, turning and storming from the chamber.

Shallan gasped as one of the men sighed, then gestured toward Jushu. The other two grabbed him. They didn't seem pleased to be leaving without payment. Jushu trembled as they towed him away, past Balat and Wikim, who watched nearby. Outside, Jushu cried for mercy and begged the men to let him speak to Father again.

"Balat," Shallan said, walking to him, taking his arm. "Do something!"

"We all knew where the gambling would take him," Balat said. "We told him, Shallan. He wouldn't listen."

"He's still our brother!"

"What do you expect me to do? Where would I get spheres enough to pay his debt?"

Jushu's weeping grew softer as the men left the manor.

Shallan turned and dashed after her father, passing Jix scratching his head. Father had gone into his study two rooms over; she hesitated in the doorway, looking in at her father slumped in his chair beside the hearth. She stepped in, passing the desk where his ardents—and sometimes his wife—tallied his ledgers and read him reports.

Nobody stood there now, but the ledgers were open, displaying a brutal truth. She raised a hand to her mouth, noticing several letters of debt. She'd helped with minor accounts, but never seen so much of the full picture, and was stunned by what she saw. How could the family owe that much money?

"I'm not going to change my mind, Shallan," Father said. "Leave. Jushu prepared this pyre himself."

"But—"

"Leave me!" Father roared, standing.

Shallan cringed back, eyes widening, heart nearly stopping. Fearspren wriggled up around her. He never yelled at her. *Never.*

Father took a deep breath, then turned to the room's window. His back to her, he continued, "I can't afford the spheres."

"Why?" Shallan asked. "Father, is this because of the deal with Brightlord Revilar?" She looked at the ledgers. "No, it's bigger than that."

"I will finally make something of myself," Father said, "and of this house. I will stop them from whispering about us; I will end the questioning. House Davar will become a *force* in this princedom."

"By bribing favor from supposed allies?" Shallan asked. "Using money we don't have?"

He looked at her, face shadowed but eyes reflecting light, like twin embers in the dark of his skull. In that moment, Shallan felt a terrifying hatred from her father. He strode over, grabbing her by the arms. Her satchel dropped to the floor.

"I've done this for *you*," he growled, holding her arms in a tight, painful grip. "And you *will* obey. I've gone wrong, somewhere, in letting you learn to question me."

She whimpered at the pain.

"There will be changes in this house," Father said. "No more weakness. I've found a way . . ."

"Please, stop."

He looked down at her and seemed to see the tears in her eyes for the first time.

"Father . . ." she whispered.

He looked upward. Toward his rooms. She knew he was looking toward Mother's soul. He dropped her then, causing her to tumble to the floor, red hair covering her face.

"You are confined to your rooms," he snapped. "Go, and do not leave until I give you permission."

Shallan scrambled to her feet, snatching her satchel, then left the room. In the hallway, she pressed her back against the wall, panting raggedly, tears dripping from her chin. Things had been going better . . . her father had been better . . .

She squeezed her eyes shut. Emotion stormed inside of her, twisting about. She couldn't control it.

Jushu.

Father actually looked like he wanted to hurt me, Shallan thought, shivering. *He's changed so much.* She started to sink down toward the floor, arms wrapped around herself.

Jushu.

Keep cutting at those thorns, strong one . . . Make a path for the light . . .

Shallan forced herself to her feet. She ran, still crying, back into the feast hall. Balat and Wikim had taken seats, Minara quietly serving them drinks. The guards had left, perhaps to their post at the manor grounds.

When Balat saw Shallan, he stood, eyes widening. He rushed to her, knocking over his cup in his haste, spilling wine to the floor.

"Did he hurt you?" Balat asked. "Damnation! I'll kill him! I'll go to the highprince and—"

"He didn't hurt me," Shallan said. "Please. Balat, your knife. The one Father gave you."

He looked to his belt. "What of it?"

"It's worth good money. I'm going to try to trade it for Jushu."

Balat lowered his hand protectively to the knife. "Jushu built his pyre himself, Shallan."

"That's exactly what Father said to me," Shallan replied, wiping her eyes, then meeting those of her brother.

"I . . ." Balat looked over his shoulder in the direction Jushu had been taken. He sighed, then unhooked the sheath from his belt and handed it to her. "It won't be enough. They say he owes almost a hundred emerald broams."

"I have my necklace too," Shallan said.

Wikim, silently drinking his wine, reached to his belt and took off his knife. He set it at the edge of the table. Shallan scooped it up as she passed, then ran from the room. Could she catch the men in time?

Outside, she spotted the carriage only a short way down the road. She hurried as best she could on slippered feet down the cobbled drive and out the gates onto the road. She wasn't fast, but neither were chulls. As she drew closer, she saw that Jushu had been tied to walk behind the carriage. He didn't look up as Shallan passed him.

The carriage stopped, and Jushu dropped to the ground and curled up. The darkeyed man with the haughty air pushed open his door to look at Shallan. "He sent the child?"

"I came on my own," she said, holding up the daggers. "Please, they are very fine work."

The man raised an eyebrow, then gestured for one of his companions to step down and fetch them. Shallan unhooked her necklace and dropped it into the man's hands with the two knives. The man took out one of the knives, inspecting it as Shallan waited, apprehensive, shifting from foot to foot.

"You've been weeping," said the man in the carriage. "You care for him that much?"

"He is my brother."

"So?" the man asked. "I killed my brother when he tried to cheat me. You shouldn't let relations cloud your eyes."

"I love him," Shallan whispered.

The man looking over the daggers slid them both back in their sheaths. "They are masterworks," he admitted. "I'd value them at twenty emerald broams."

"The necklace?" Shallan asked.

"Simple, but of aluminum, which can only be made by Soulcasting," the man said to his boss. "Ten emerald."

"Together half what your brother owes," said the man in the carriage.

Shallan's heart sank. "But . . . what would you do with him? Selling him as a slave cannot redeem so great a debt."

"I'm often in the mood to remind myself that lighteyes bleed the same as darkeyes," the man said. "And sometimes it is useful to have a deterrent for others, a way to remind them not to take loans they cannot repay. He may save me more than he cost, if I display him prudently."

Shallan felt small. She clasped her hands, one covered, one not. Had she lost, then? The women from Father's books, the women she was coming to admire, would not have made pleas to win this man's heart. They would have tried logic.

She wasn't good at that. She didn't have the training for it, and she certainly didn't currently have the temperament. But as the tears began again, she forced out the first thing that came to mind.

"He may save you money that way," Shallan said. "But he may not. It is a gamble, and you do not strike me as the kind of man who gambles."

The man laughed. "What makes you say that? Gambling is what brought me here!"

"No," she said, blushing at her tears. "You are the type of man who profits from the gambling of others. You know that it usually leads to loss. I give you items of real value. Take them. Please?"

The man considered. He held out his hands for the daggers, and his man passed them over. He unsheathed one of the daggers and inspected it. "Name for me one reason I should show this man pity. In my house, he was an arrogant glutton, acting without thought for the difficulty he would cause you, his family."

"Our mother was murdered," Shallan said. "That night, as I cried, Jushu held me." It was all she had.

The man considered. Shallan felt her heart pounding. Finally, he tossed the necklace back to her. "Keep that." He nodded to his man. "Cut the little cremling free. Child, if you are wise, you will teach your brother to be more . . . conservative." He pulled the door closed.

Shallan stepped back as the servant cut Jushu free. The man then climbed onto the back of the vehicle and knocked. It pulled away.

Shallan knelt beside Jushu. He blinked one eye—the other was bruised and beginning to swell shut—as she untied his bloodied hands. It had not been a quarter hour since Father had declared that the men could have him, but they had obviously taken that time to show Jushu what they thought of not being paid.

"Shallan?" he asked, lips bloodied. "What happened?"

"You weren't listening?"

"My ears ring," he said. "Everything is spinning. I . . . am I free?"

"Balat and Wikim traded their knives for you."

"Mill took so little in trade?"

"Obviously, he did not know your true worth."

Jushu smiled a toothy smile. "Always quick with your tongue, aren't you?" He climbed to his feet with Shallan's help and began to limp back toward the house.

Halfway there, Balat joined them, taking Jushu under his arm. "Thank you," Jushu whispered. "She says you saved me. Thank you, Brother." He started weeping.

"I . . ." Balat looked to Shallan, then back to Jushu. "You're my brother. Let's get you back and cleaned up."

Content that Jushu would be cared for, Shallan left them and entered the manor house. She climbed the stairs, passed Father's glowing room, and entered her chambers. She sat down on the bed.

There, she waited for the highstorm.

Shouts rose from below. Shallan squeezed her eyes shut.

Finally, the door to her rooms opened.

She opened her eyes. Father stood outside. Shallan could make out a crumpled form beyond him, lying on the floor of the hallway. Minara, the serving maid. Her body didn't lie right, one arm bent at the wrong angle. Her figure stirred, whimpering, leaving blood on the wall as she tried to crawl away.

Father entered Shallan's room and shut the door behind him. "You know I would never hurt you, Shallan," he said softly.

She nodded, tears leaking from her eyes.

"I've found a way to control myself," her father said. "I just have to let the anger out. I can't blame myself for that anger. Others create it when they disobey me."

Her objection—that he hadn't told her to go *immediately* to her room, only that she shouldn't leave it once she was there—died on her lips. A foolish excuse. They both knew she'd intentionally disobeyed.

"I would not want to have to punish anyone else because of you, Shallan," Father said.

This cold monster, was this really her father?

"It is time." Father nodded. "No more indulgences. If we are to be important in Jah Keved, we cannot be seen as weak. Do you understand?"

She nodded, unable to stop the tears.

"Good," he said, resting his hand on her head, then running his fingers through her hair. "Thank you."

He left her, shutting the door.

This folio page shows contemporary
designs out of Azir, using local models.
Though these are specifically male civil
servant outfits, the styles have
deeply influenced all Azish fashion

49

WATCHING THE WORLD TRANSFORM

These Lightweavers, by no coincidence, included many who pursued the arts; namely: writers, artists, musicians, painters, sculptors. Considering the order's general temperament, the tales of their strange and varied mnemonic abilities may have been embellished.

—From *Words of Radiance*, chapter 21, page 10

After leaving her carriage at a stable in the Outer Market, Shallan was led to a stairwell carved into the stone of a hillside. She climbed this, then stepped hesitantly out onto a terrace that had been cut from the side of the hill here. Lighteyes wearing stylish clothing chatted over cups of wine at the patio's numerous ironwork tables.

They were high enough here to look out over the warcamps. The perspective was eastward, toward the Origin. What an unnatural arrangement; it made her feel exposed. Shallan was accustomed to balconies, gardens, and patios all facing away from the storms. True, nobody was likely to be out here when a highstorm was expected, but it just felt *off* to her.

A master-servant in black and white arrived and bowed, calling her Brightness Davar without need of an introduction. She'd have to get used to that; in Alethkar she was a novelty, and an easily recognizable one. She let the servant lead her among the tables, sending her guards for the day off toward a larger room cut farther into the stone to the right. This one had a proper roof and walls, so it could be completely closed off, and a group of other guards waited here upon the whims of their masters.

Shallan drew the eyes of the other patrons. Well, good. She had come here to upset their world. The more people spoke of her, the better her chances of persuading them, when the time came, to listen to her regarding the parshmen. Those were everywhere in camp, even here in this luxurious winehouse. She spotted three in the corner, moving wine bottles from wall-mounted racks to crates. They moved at a plodding yet implacable pace.

A few more steps brought her to the marble balustrade right at the edge of the terrace. Here Adolin had a table set off by itself with an unobstructed view directly east. Two members of Dalinar's house guard stood by the wall a short distance away; Adolin was important enough, apparently, that his guards didn't need to wait with the others.

Adolin browsed a folio, oversized by design so it wouldn't be mistaken for a woman's book. Shallan had seen some folios containing battle maps, others with designs for armor or pictures of architecture. She was amused as she caught sight of the glyphs for this one, with women's script underneath for further clarification. Fashions out of Liafor and Azir.

Adolin looked as handsome as he had before. Maybe more so, now that he was obviously more relaxed. She would *not* let him muddle her mind. She had a purpose to this meeting: an alliance with House Kholin to help her brothers and give her resources for exposing the Voidbringers and discovering Urithiru.

She couldn't afford to come off as weak. She had to control the situation, could not act like a sycophant, and she couldn't—

Adolin saw her and closed the portfolio. He stood up, grinning.

—oh, *storms*. That *smile*.

"Brightness Shallan," he said, holding out a hand toward her. "You are settling well in Sebarial's camp?"

"Yeah," she said, grinning at him. That mop of unruly hair just made her want to reach out and run her fingers through it. *Our children would have the strangest hair ever,* she thought. *His gold and black Alethi locks, my red ones, and . . .*

And was she really thinking about their *children*? Already? Foolish girl.

"Yes," she continued, trying to de-melt a little. "He has been quite kind to me."

"It's probably because you're family," Adolin said, letting her sit, then pushing in her chair. He did it himself, rather than allowing the master-servant to do so. She would not have expected that of someone so high-born. "Sebarial only does what he feels he's forced to."

"I think he may surprise you," Shallan said.

"Oh, he's already done *that* on several occasions."

"Really? When?"

"Well," Adolin said, sitting, "he once produced a very, um, loud and inappropriate noise at a meeting with the king. . . ." Adolin smiled, shrugging as if embarrassed, but he didn't blush as Shallan might have in a similar situation. "Does that count?"

"I'm not sure. Knowing what I do of Uncle Sebarial, I doubt that such a thing is particularly *surprising* from him. Expected is more like it."

Adolin laughed, tossing his head back. "Yes, I suppose you're right. That you are."

He seemed so *confident*. Not in a particularly conceited way, not like her father had been. In fact, it occurred to her that her father's attitude had been caused not by confidence, but the opposite.

Adolin seemed perfectly at ease both with his station and those around him. When he waved for the master-servant to bring him a list of wines, he smiled at the woman, though she was darkeyed. That smile was enough to produce a blush even in a master-servant.

Shallan was supposed to get this man to court her? Storms! She'd felt far more capable when trying to scam the leader of the Ghostbloods. *Act refined*, Shallan told herself. *Adolin has moved with the elite, and has been in relationships with the most sophisticated ladies of the world. He will expect that from you.*

"So," he said, flipping through the list of wines, described by glyphs, "we are supposed to get *married*."

"I would lighten that phrasing, Brightlord," Shallan said, choosing her words carefully. "We aren't *supposed* to get married. Your cousin Jasnah merely wanted us to consider a union, and your aunt seemed to agree."

"The Almighty save a man when his female relatives collude about his future," Adolin said with a sigh. "Sure, it's all right for *Jasnah* to run about into her middle years without a spouse, but if I reach my twenty-third birthday without a bride, it's like I'm some kind of menace. Sexist of her, don't you think?"

"Well, she wanted me to get married too," Shallan said. "So I wouldn't call her sexist. Merely . . . Jasnah-ist?" She paused. "Jasnagynistic? No, drat. It would have to be Misjasnahistic, and that doesn't work nearly as well, does it?"

"You're asking me?" Adolin asked, turning around the menu so she could see it. "What do you think we should order?"

"Storms," she breathed. "Those are *all* different kinds of wine?"

"Yeah," Adolin said. He leaned toward her, as if conspiratorial. "Honestly, I don't pay a lot of attention. Renarin knows the difference between them—he'll drone on if you let him. Me, I order something that sounds important, but I'm really just choosing based on color." He grimaced.

"We're technically at war. I won't be able to take anything too intoxicating, just in case. Kind of silly, as there won't be any plateau runs today."

"You're sure? I thought they were random."

"Yeah, but my warcamp isn't up. They almost never come too close before a highstorm, anyway." He leaned back, scanning the menu, before pointing at one of the wines and winking at the serving woman.

Shallan felt cold. "Wait. *Highstorm?*"

"Yeah," Adolin said, checking the clock in the corner. Sebarial had mentioned that those were growing more and more common around here. "Should come any time now. You didn't know?"

She sputtered, looking eastward, across the cracked landscape. *Act poised!* she thought. *Elegant!* Instead, a primal part of her wanted to scramble for a hole and hide. Suddenly she imagined she could sense the pressure dropping, as if the air itself were trying to escape. Could she see it out there, starting? No, that was nothing. She squinted anyway.

"I didn't look at the list of storms Sebarial keeps," Shallan forced herself to say. In all honesty, it was probably outdated, knowing him. "I've been busy."

"Huh," Adolin said. "I wondered why you didn't ask about this place. I just assumed you'd heard of it already."

This place. The open balcony, facing east. The lighteyes drinking wine now seemed anticipatory to her, with an air of nervousness. The second room—the large one for bodyguards she'd seen with the substantial doors—made far more sense now.

"We're here to watch?" Shallan whispered.

"It's the new fad," Adolin said. "Apparently we're supposed to sit here until the storm is almost upon us, then run into that other room and take shelter. I've wanted to come for weeks now, and only just managed to convince my minders that I'd be safe here." He said that last part somewhat bitterly. "We can go move into the safe room now, if you want."

"No," Shallan said, forcing herself to pry her fingers from the table edge. "I'm fine."

"You look pale."

"It's natural."

"Because you're Veden?"

"Because I'm always at the edge of panic these days. Oh, is that our wine?"

Poised, she reminded herself yet again. She pointedly did not look eastward.

The servant had brought them two cups of brilliant blue wine. Adolin picked his up and studied it. He smelled it, sipped it, then nodded in satisfaction and dismissed the servant with a parting smile. He watched the woman's backside as she retreated.

Shallan raised an eyebrow at him, but he didn't seem to notice that he'd done anything wrong. He looked back at Shallan and leaned in again. "I know you're supposed to swish the wine about and taste it and things," he whispered, "but nobody has ever explained to me what I'm looking for."

"Bugs floating in the liquid, perhaps?"

"Nah, my new food taster would have spotted one of those." He smiled, but Shallan realized he probably wasn't joking. A thin man who didn't wear a uniform had walked over to chat with the bodyguards. Probably the food taster.

Shallan sipped her wine. It was good—slightly sweet, a tad spicy. Not that she could spare much thought for its taste, with that storm—

Stop it, she told herself, smiling at Adolin. She needed to make sure this meeting went well for him. *Get him to talk about himself.* That was one piece of advice she remembered from books.

"Plateau runs," Shallan said. "How *do* you know when to begin one, anyway?"

"Hmm? Oh, we have spotters," Adolin said, lounging back in his chair. "Men who stand atop towers with these enormous spyglasses. They inspect every plateau we can reach in a reasonable time, watching for a chrysalis."

"I hear you've captured your share of those."

"Well, I probably shouldn't talk about it. Father doesn't want it to be a competition anymore." He looked at her, expectant.

"But surely you can talk about what happened before," Shallan said, feeling as if she were filling an expected role.

"I suppose," Adolin said. "There was one run a few months back where I seized the chrysalis basically by myself. You see, Father and I, we would usually jump the chasm first and clear the way for the bridges."

"Isn't that dangerous?" Shallan asked, dutifully looking at him with widened eyes.

"Yes, but we're Shardbearers. We have strength and power granted by the Almighty. It's a great responsibility, and it's our duty to use it for the protection of our men. We save hundreds of lives by going across first. Lets us lead the army, firsthand."

He paused.

"So brave," Shallan said, in what she hoped was a breathy, adoring voice.

"Well, it's the right thing to do. But it *is* dangerous. That day, I leaped across, but my father and I got pushed too far apart by the Parshendi. He was forced to jump back across, and a blow to his leg meant that when he landed, his greave—that's a piece of armor on the leg—cracked. That made it dangerous for him to jump back again. I was left alone while he waited for the bridge to lock down."

He paused again. She was probably supposed to ask what happened next.

"What if you need to poop?" she asked instead.

"Well, I put my back to the chasm and laid about me with my sword, intending to . . . Wait. What did you say?"

"Poop," Shallan said. "You're out there on the battlefield, encased in metal like a crab in its shell. What do you do if nature calls?"

"I . . . er . . ." Adolin frowned at her. "That is not something any woman has ever asked me before."

"Yay for originality!" Shallan said, though she blushed as she said it. Jasnah would have been displeased. Couldn't Shallan mind her tongue for a single conversation? She'd gotten him talking about something he liked; everything had been going well. Now this.

"Well," Adolin said slowly, "every battle has breaks in the flow, and men rotate in and out of the front lines. For every five minutes you're fighting, you often have almost as many resting. When a Shardbearer pulls back, men inspect his armor for cracks, give him something to drink or eat, and help him with . . . what you just mentioned. It's not something that makes a good topic of conversation, Brightness. We don't really talk about it."

"That's precisely *what* makes it a good topic of conversation," she said. "I can find out about wars and Shardbearers and glorious killing in the official accounts. The grimy details, though—nobody writes those down."

"Well, it *does* get grimy," Adolin said with a grimace, taking a drink. "You can't really . . . I can't believe I'm saying this . . . you can't really wipe yourself in Shardplate, so someone has to do it for you. Makes me feel like an infant. Then, sometimes, you just don't have time . . ."

"And?"

He inspected her, narrowing his eyes.

"What?" she asked.

"Just trying to determine if you're secretly Wit wearing a wig. This is something he would do to me."

"I'm not doing anything to you," she said. "I'm just curious." And honestly, she was. She'd thought about this. Perhaps more than it deserved consideration.

"Well," Adolin said, "if you must know, an old adage on the battlefield teaches that it's better to be embarrassed than dead. You can't let anything draw your attention from fighting."

"So . . ."

"So yes, I, Adolin Kholin—cousin to the king, heir to the Kholin princedom—have shat myself in my Shardplate. Three times, all on purpose." He downed the rest of his wine. "You are a very strange woman."

"If I must remind you," Shallan said, "you are the one who opened our conversation today with a joke about Sebarial's flatulence."

"I guess I did at that." He grinned. "This is not exactly going the way it's supposed to, is it?"

"Is that a bad thing?"

"No," Adolin said, then his grin widened. "Actually, it's kind of refreshing. Do you know how many times I've told that story about saving the plateau run?"

"I'm sure you were quite brave."

"Quite."

"Though probably not as brave as the poor men who have to clean your armor."

Adolin bellowed out a laugh. For the first time it seemed like something genuine—an emotion from him that wasn't scripted or expected. He pounded his fist on the table, then waved for more wine, wiping a tear from his eye. The grin he gave her threatened to bring out another blush.

Wait, Shallan thought, *did that just . . . work?* She was supposed to be acting feminine and delicate, not asking men what it's like to have to defecate in battle.

"All right," Adolin said, taking the cup of wine. He didn't even glance at the serving woman this time. "What other dirty secrets do you want to know? You've got me laid bare. There are tons of things the stories and official histories don't mention."

"The chrysalises," Shallan said, eager. "What do they look like?"

"That's what you want to know?" Adolin said, scratching his head. "I thought for sure you'd want to know about the chafing. . . ."

Shallan got out her satchel, setting a piece of paper on the table and starting a sketch. "From what I've been able to determine, nobody has done a solid study on the Chasmfiends. There are some sketches of dead ones, but that's it, and the anatomy on those is dreadful.

"They must have an interesting life cycle. They haunt these chasms, but I doubt they actually live here. There's not enough food to support creatures of their size. That means they come here as part of some migratory pattern. They come here to *pupate.* Have you ever seen a juvenile? Before they form the chrysalis?"

"No," Adolin said, scooting his chair around the table. "It often happens at night, and we don't spot them until morning. They're hard to see out there, colored like rock. Makes me think that the Parshendi must be watching us. We end up fighting over plateaus so often. It might mean they spot us mobilizing, then use the direction we're going to judge where to find the chrysalis. We get a head start, but they move faster over the Plains, so we arrive near the same time. . . ."

He trailed off, cocking his head to get a better look at her sketch. "Storms! That's really good, Shallan."

"Thanks."

"No, I mean *really* good."

She'd done a quick sketch of several types of chrysalises she had read about in her books, along with quick depictions of a man beside them for size reference. It wasn't very good—she'd done it for speed. Yet Adolin seemed genuinely impressed.

"The shape and texture of the chrysalis," Shallan said, "could help place the chasmfiends in a family of similar animals."

"It looks most like this one," Adolin said, scooting closer and pointing at one of the sketches. "When I've touched one, they've been hard as rock. It's hard to dig into one without a Shardblade. It can take men with hammers forever to break into one."

"Hmmm," Shallan said, making a note. "You're sure?"

"Yeah. That's how they look. Why?"

"That's the chrysalis of a yu-nerig," Shallan said. "A greatshell from the seas around Marabethia. The people there feed criminals to them, I'm told."

"Ouch."

"This might be a false positive, a coincidence. The yu-nerig are an aquatic species. The only time they come onto land is to pupate. Seems tenuous to assume a relationship to the chasmfiends . . ."

"Sure," Adolin said, taking a drink of wine. "If you say so."

"This is probably important," Shallan said.

"For research. Yeah, I know. Aunt Navani is always talking about things like that."

"This could be of more practical import than that," Shallan said. "About how many of these things total are killed by your armies and the Parshendi each month?"

Adolin shrugged. "One every three days or so, I'd guess. Sometimes more, sometimes less. So . . . fifteen or so a month?"

"You see the problem?"

"I . . ." Adolin shook his head. "No. Sorry. I'm kind of useless at anything that doesn't involve someone getting stabbed."

She smiled at him. "Nonsense. You proved skilled at choosing wine."

"I did that basically at random."

"And it tastes delicious," Shallan said. "Empirical proof of your methodology. Now, you probably don't see the problem because you don't have the proper facts. Greatshells, generally, are slow to breed and slow to grow.

This is because most ecosystems can only support a small population of apex predators of this size."

"I've heard some of those words before."

She looked to him, raising an eyebrow. He'd gotten a lot closer to her, in order to look at her drawing. He wore a faint cologne, a brisk woody scent. *Oh my . . .*

"All right, all right," he said, chuckling as he inspected her drawings. "I'm not as dense as I feign. I see what you're saying. You really think we could kill enough of them that it could be a problem? I mean, people have been doing greatshell hunts for generations, and the beasts are still around."

"You're not hunting them here, Adolin. You're *harvesting* them. You're systematically destroying their juvenile population. Have fewer of them been pupating lately?"

"Yeah," he said, though he sounded reluctant. "We think it might be the season."

"It might be. Or, it might be that, after over five years of harvesting, the population is starting to dwindle. Animals like the chasmfiends don't normally have predators. Suddenly losing a hundred and fifty or more of their numbers a year could be catastrophic to their population."

Adolin frowned. "The gemhearts we get feed the people of the war-camps. Without a constant flow of new stones of reasonable size, the Soulcasters will eventually crack the ones we have, and we won't be able to support the armies here."

"I'm not telling you to stop your hunts," Shallan said, blushing. This probably wasn't the point she should be making. Urithiru and the parshmen, that was the immediate problem. Still, she needed to gain Adolin's trust. If she could provide useful help regarding the chasmfiends, perhaps he'd listen when she approached him with something even more revolutionary.

"All I'm saying," Shallan continued, "is that it's worth thinking about and studying. What would it be like if you could start raising chasmfiends, growing them to juveniles in batches like men raise chulls? Instead of hunting three a week, what if you could breed and harvest hundreds?"

"That *would* be useful," Adolin said thoughtfully. "What would you need in order to make it happen?"

"Well, I wasn't saying . . . I mean . . ." She stopped herself. "I need to get out onto the Shattered Plains," she said more firmly. "If I'm going to try to figure out how to breed them, I'd need to see one of these chrysalises before it's been cut into. Preferably, I get to see an adult chasmfiend, and— ideally—I'd like a captured juvenile to study."

"Just a small list of impossibilities."

"Well, you *did* ask."

"I might be able to get you onto the Plains," Adolin said. "Father promised that he'd show Jasnah a dead chasmfiend, so I think he was planning to take her out after a hunt. Seeing a chrysalis, though . . . those rarely appear close to camp. I'd have to take you dangerously close to Parshendi territory."

"I'm sure you can protect me."

He looked at her, expectant.

"What?" Shallan asked.

"I'm waiting for a wisecrack."

"I was serious," Shallan said. "With you there, I'm certain the Parshendi wouldn't dare get close."

Adolin smiled.

"I mean," she said, "the stench alone—"

"I suspect I'm never going to live down telling you about that."

"Never," Shallan agreed. "You were honest, detailed, and engaging. Those aren't the sorts of things I let myself forget about a man."

His smile broadened. Storms, those eyes . . .

Careful, Shallan told herself. *Careful! Kabsal took you in easily. Don't repeat that.*

"I'll see what I can do," Adolin said. "The Parshendi might not be an issue in the near future."

"Really?"

He nodded. "It's not widely known, though we've told the highprinces. Father is going to be meeting with some of the Parshendi leaders tomorrow. It could end up starting a peace negotiation."

"That's *fantastic!*"

"Yeah," Adolin said. "I'm not hopeful. The assassin . . . anyway, we'll see what happens tomorrow, though I'll have to do this between the other work Father has for me."

"The duels," Shallan said, leaning in. "What is going on there, Adolin?"

He seemed hesitant.

"Whatever is going on in the camps now," she said, speaking more softly, "Jasnah didn't know about it. I feel woefully ignorant about politics here, Adolin. Your father and Highprince Sadeas had a falling-out, I've gathered. The king has changed the nature of these plateau runs, and everyone is talking about how you're dueling now. But from what I've been able to gather, you never *stopped* dueling."

"It's different," he said. "Now I'm dueling to win."

"And you didn't before?"

"No, then I dueled to punish." He glanced about, then met her eyes. "It began when my father started seeing visions . . ."

He continued. He poured out a surprising story, one with far greater detail than she'd anticipated. A story of betrayal, and of hope. Visions of the past. A unified Alethkar, prepared to weather a coming storm.

She didn't know what to make of it all, though she gathered that Adolin was telling her of it because he knew the rumors in camp. She'd heard of Dalinar's fits, of course, and had an inkling of what Sadeas had done. When Adolin mentioned that his father wanted the Knights Radiant to return, Shallan felt a chill. She glanced about for Pattern—he'd be close—but couldn't find him.

The meat of the story, at least in Adolin's estimation, was the betrayal by Sadeas. The young prince's eyes grew dark, face flushed, as he talked of being abandoned on the Plains, surrounded by enemies. He seemed embarrassed when he spoke of salvation by a lowly bridge crew.

He's actually confiding in me, Shallan thought, feeling a thrill. She rested her freehand on his arm as he spoke, an innocent gesture, but it seemed to spur him forward as he quietly explained Dalinar's plan. She wasn't certain he should be sharing all of this with her. They barely knew one another. But speaking of it seemed to lift a weight from Adolin's back, and he grew more relaxed.

"I guess," Adolin said, "that's the end of it. I'm supposed to win Shardblades off the others, taking away their bite, embarrassing them. But I don't know if it will work."

"Why not?" Shallan asked.

"The ones who agree to duel me aren't important enough," he said, forming a fist. "If I win too much from them, the real targets—the highprinces—will get scared of me and refuse duels. I need matches that are more high profile. No, what I *need* is to duel Sadeas. Pound that grinning face of his into the stones and take back my father's Blade. He's too oily, though. We'll never get him to agree."

She found herself wishing desperately to do something, anything, to help. She felt herself melting at the intense concern in those eyes, the passion.

Remember Kabsal . . . she reminded herself again.

Well, Adolin wasn't likely to try to assassinate her—but then, that didn't mean she should let her brain turn to curry paste around him. She cleared her throat, tearing her eyes away from his and looking down at her sketch.

"Bother," she said. "I've left you upset. I'm not very good at this wooing thing."

"Could have fooled me . . ." Adolin said, resting his hand on her arm.

Shallan covered another blush by ducking her head and digging into her satchel. "You," she said, "need to know what your cousin was working on before she died."

"Another volume in her father's biography?"

"No," Shallan said, getting out a sheet of paper. "Adolin, Jasnah thought that the Voidbringers were going to return."

"What?" he said, frowning. "She didn't even believe in the Almighty. Why would she believe in the Voidbringers?"

"She had evidence," Shallan said, tapping the paper with one finger. "A lot of that sank in the ocean, I'm afraid, but I do have some of her notes, and . . . Adolin, how hard do you think it would be to convince the high-princes to get rid of their parshmen?"

"Get rid of *what*?"

"How hard would it to be to make everyone stop using parshmen as slaves? Give them away, or . . ." Storms. She didn't want to start a genocide here, did she? But these were the *Voidbringers*. ". . . or set them free or something. Get them out of the warcamps."

"How difficult would it be?" Adolin said. "Off the cuff, I'd say impossible. That, or *really* impossible. Why would we even want to do something like that?"

"Jasnah thought they might be related to the Voidbringers and their return."

Adolin shook his head, looking bemused. "Shallan, we can barely get the highprinces to fight this war properly. If my father or the king were to require everyone to get rid of their parshmen . . . Storms! It would break the kingdom in a heartbeat."

So Jasnah was right on that count as well. Unsurprising. Shallan *was* interested to see how violently Adolin himself opposed the idea. He took a big gulp of wine, seeming utterly floored.

Time to pull back, then. This meeting had gone very well; she wouldn't want to end it on a sour note. "It was something Jasnah said," Shallan said, "but really, I'd rather that Brightlady Navani judge how important a suggestion it was. She would know her daughter, her notes, better than anyone."

Adolin nodded. "So go to her."

Shallan tapped the paper in her fingers. "I've tried. She's not been very accommodating."

"Aunt Navani can be overbearing sometimes."

"It's not that," Shallan said, scanning the words on the letter. It was a reply she'd gotten after requesting to meet the woman and discuss her daughter's work. "She doesn't want to meet with me. She barely seems to want to acknowledge I exist."

Adolin sighed. "She doesn't want to believe. About Jasnah, I mean. You represent something to her—the truth, in a way. Give her time. She just needs to grieve."

"I'm not certain if this is something that should wait, Adolin."

"I'll talk to her," he said. "How about that?"

"Wonderful," she said. "Much like you yourself."

He grinned. "It's nothing. I mean, if we're going to halfway-almost-kind-of-maybe-get-married, we should probably look out for one another's interests." He paused. "Don't mention that parshman thing to anyone else, though. That's not something that will go over well."

She nodded absently, then realized she'd been staring at him. She was going to kiss those lips of his someday. She let herself imagine it.

And, Ash's eyes . . . he had a very friendly way about him. She hadn't expected that in someone so highborn. She'd never actually met anyone of his rank before coming to the Shattered Plains, but all the men she knew near his level had been stiff and even angry.

Not Adolin. Storms, but being with him was something else she could get very, very used to.

People began to stir on the patio. She ignored them for a moment, but then many began to stand up from their seats, looking eastward.

Highstorm. Right.

Shallan felt a spike of alarm as she looked toward the Origin of Storms. The wind picked up, leaves and bits of refuse fluttering across the patio. Down below, the Outer Market had been packed up, tents folded away, awnings withdrawn, windows closed. The entirety of the warcamps braced itself.

Shallan stuffed her things into her satchel, then rose to her feet, stepping to the edge of the terrace, freehand fingers on the stone railing there. Adolin joined her. Behind them, people whispered and gathered. She heard iron grinding across stone; the parshmen had begun pulling away the tables and chairs, stowing them to both protect them and make a path for the lighteyes to retreat to safety.

The horizon had bled from light to dark, like a man flushing with anger. Shallan gripped the railing, watching the entire world transform. Vines withdrew, rockbuds closed. Grass hid in its holes. They knew, somehow. They all knew.

The air grew chill and wet, and prestorm winds gusted against her, blowing her hair back. Below and just to the north, the warcamps had piled refuse and waste to be blown away with the storm. It was a forbidden practice in most civilized areas, where that waste could blow into the next town. Out here, there was no next town.

The horizon grew even darker. A few people on the balcony fled to the back room's safety, their nerves getting the better of them. Most stayed, silent. Windspren zipped in tiny rivers of light overhead. Shallan took Adolin by the arm, staring eastward. Minutes passed until finally, she saw it.

The stormwall.

A huge sheet of water and debris blown before the storm. In places, it flashed with light from behind, revealing movement and shadows within. Like the skeleton of a hand when light illuminated the flesh, there was something *inside* this wall of destruction.

Most of the people fled the balcony, though the stormwall was still distant. In moments, only a handful remained, Shallan and Adolin among them. She watched, transfixed, as the storm approached. It took longer than she'd expected. It was moving at a terrible speed, but it was so large, they'd been able to spot it from quite a distance.

It consumed the Shattered Plains, one plateau at a time. Soon, it loomed over the warcamps, coming on with a roar.

"We should go," Adolin eventually said. She barely heard him.

Life. Something *lived* inside that storm, something that no artist had ever drawn, no scholar had ever described.

"Shallan!" Adolin began to tow her toward the protected room. She grabbed the railing with her freehand, remaining in place, clutching her satchel to her chest with her safehand. That humming, that was Pattern.

She'd never been so close to a highstorm. Even when she'd been only inches away from one, separated by a window shutter, she had not been as close as she was now. Watching that darkness descend upon the warcamps . . .

I need to draw.

"Shallan!" Adolin said, pulling her away from the railing. "They'll close the doors if we don't go now!"

With a start, she realized that everyone else had left the balcony. She allowed Adolin to get her moving, and she joined him in a dash across the empty patio. They reached the room at the side, packed with huddled lighteyes who watched in terror. Adolin's guards entered right after her, and several parshmen slammed the thick doors. The bar *thumped* in place, locking out the sky, leaving them to the light of spheres on the walls.

Shallan counted. The highstorm hit—she could *feel* it. Something beyond the thumping of the door and the distant sound of thunder.

"Six seconds," she said.

"What?" Adolin asked. His voice was hushed, and others in the room spoke in whispers.

"It took six seconds after the servants closed the doors until the storm hit. We could have spent that much longer out there."

Adolin regarded her with an incredulous expression. "When you first realized what we were doing on that balcony, you seemed *terrified*."

"I was."

"Now you wish you'd stayed out until the last moment before the storm hit?"

"I . . . yeah," she said, blushing.

"I have no idea what to make of you." Adolin regarded her. "You're not like anyone I've met."

"It's my air of feminine mystique."

He raised an eyebrow.

"It's a term we use," she said, "when we're feeling particularly erratic. It's considered polite not to point out that you know this. Now, do we just . . . wait in here?"

"In this box of a room?" Adolin asked, sounding amused. "We're light-eyes, not livestock." He gestured to the side, where several servants had opened doors leading to places burrowed deeper into the mountain. "Two sitting rooms. One for men, the other for women."

Shallan nodded. Sometimes during a highstorm, the genders would retire to separate rooms to chat. It looked like the winehouse followed this tradition. They'd probably have finger food. Shallan walked toward the indicated room, but Adolin rested a hand on her arm, making her pause.

"I'll see about getting you out onto the Shattered Plains," he said. "Amaram wants to go explore more, he's said, than he gets to during a plateau run. I think he and Father are having dinner to talk about it tomorrow night, and I can ask then if I can bring you. I'll also talk to Aunt Navani. Maybe we can discuss what I've come up with at the feast next week?"

"There's a feast next week?"

"There's always a feast next week," Adolin said. "We just have to figure out who's throwing it. I'll send to you."

She smiled, and then they separated. *Next week is not soon enough,* she thought. *I'll have to find a way to drop in on him when it's not too awkward.*

Had she really promised to help him breed chasmfiends? As if she needed something *else* to take her time. Still, she felt good about the day as she entered the women's sitting room, her guards taking their places in the appropriate waiting room.

Shallan strolled through the women's room, which was well lit with gemstones gathered in goblets—cut stones, but not in spheres. An expensive display.

She felt that, if her teachers had been watching, both would have been disappointed at her conversation with Adolin. Tyn would have wanted her to manipulate the prince more; Jasnah would have wanted Shallan to be more poised, more in control of her tongue.

It seemed that Adolin liked her anyway. That made her want to cheer.

The looks of the women about her washed away that emotion. Some turned backs toward Shallan, and others pressed their lips together and looked her up and down skeptically. Courting the kingdom's most eligible bachelor was not going to make her popular, not when she was an outsider.

That didn't bother Shallan. She didn't need acceptance from these women; she just needed to find Urithiru and the secrets it contained. Gaining Adolin's trust was a big step in that direction.

She decided to reward herself by stuffing her face with sweets and thinking further on her plan to sneak into Brightlord Amaram's house.

And now, if there was an uncut gem among the Radiants, it was the Willshapers; for though enterprising, they were erratic, and Invia wrote of them, "capricious, frustrating, unreliable," as taking it for granted that others would agree; this may have been an intolerant view, as often Invia expressed, for this order was said to be most varied, inconsistent in temperament save for a general love of adventure, novelty, or oddity.

—From *Words of Radiance,* chapter 7, page 1

Adolin sat in a high-backed chair, cup of wine in his hand, listening to the highstorm rumble outside. He should have felt safe in this bunker of rock, but there was something about storms that undercut any sense of security, no matter how rational. He'd be glad for the Weeping, and the end of the highstorms for a few weeks.

Adolin raised his cup toward Elit, who stomped past. He hadn't seen the man above, on the winehouse terrace, but this chamber also served as a highstorm bunker for several shops in the Outer Market.

"Are you ready for our duel?" Adolin asked. "You've made me wait an entire week so far, Elit."

The short, balding man took a drink of wine, then lowered his cup, not looking at Adolin. "My cousin is planning to kill you for challenging me," he said. "Right after he kills me for agreeing to the challenge." He finally turned toward Adolin. "But when I stomp you into the sands and claim all of your family's Shards, I'll be the rich one and he'll be forgotten. Am I ready for our duel? I *long* for it, Adolin Kholin."

"You're the one who wanted to wait," Adolin noted.

"The more time to savor what I'm going to do to you." Elit smiled with white lips, then moved on.

Creepy fellow. Well, Adolin would deal with him in two days, the date of their duel. Before that, though, was tomorrow's meeting with the Parshendi Shardbearer. It loomed over him like a thunderhead. What would it mean, if they finally found peace?

He mulled over that thought, regarding his wine and listening with half an ear to Elit chatting behind him with someone. Adolin recognized that voice, didn't he?

Adolin sat upright, then looked over his shoulder. How long had *Sadeas* been back there, and why hadn't Adolin spotted him when first entering?

Sadeas turned to him, a calm smile on his face.

Maybe he'll just . . .

Sadeas strolled up to Adolin, hands clasped behind his back, wearing a fashionable open-fronted short brown coat and an embroidered green stock. The buttons along the front of the coat were gemstones. Emeralds to match the stock.

Storms. He did *not* want to deal with Sadeas today.

The highprince took the seat beside Adolin, their backs to a hearth that a parshman had begun stoking. The room contained a low hum of nervous conversation. You could never quite be comfortable, no matter how pretty the decor, when a highstorm raged outside.

"Young Adolin," Sadeas said. "What do you think of my coat?"

Adolin took a gulp of wine, not trusting himself to reply. *I should just get up and walk away.* But he didn't. A small part of him wished for Sadeas to provoke him, push away his inhibitions, drive him to do something stupid. Killing the man right here, right now, would likely earn Adolin an execution—or at least an exile. It might be worth either punishment.

"You've always been so keen-eyed when it comes to style," Sadeas continued. "I'd know your opinion. I do think the coat is splendid, but I worry that the short cut might be trending out of fashion. What is the latest from Liafor?"

Sadeas pulled out the front of his jacket, moving his hand to display a ring that matched the buttons. The ring's emerald, like those on the jacket, was uncut. They glowed softly with Stormlight.

Uncut emeralds, Adolin thought, then looked up to meet Sadeas's eyes. The man smiled.

"The gemstones are recent acquisitions," Sadeas noted. "I am fond of them."

Gained from doing a plateau run with Ruthar that he wasn't supposed to have been on. Racing ahead of the other highprinces, like this was the old days, where each prince tried to be first and claim their winnings.

"I hate you," Adolin whispered.

"As well you should," Sadeas said, letting go of his coat. He nodded toward Adolin's bridgeman guards, watching with overt hostility nearby. "My former property is treating you well? I've seen their like patrolling the market here. I find that amusing for reasons I doubt I could ever properly express."

"They patrol," Adolin said, "to create a better Alethkar."

"Is that what Dalinar wants? I am surprised to hear it. He talks of justice, of course, but he doesn't allow justice to take its course. Not properly."

"And I know where you're going, Sadeas," Adolin snapped. "You're annoyed that we haven't been letting you put judges into our warcamp as Highprince of Information. Well, I'll have you know that Father has decided to let—"

"Highprince of . . . Information? You didn't hear? I recently renounced the title."

"*What?*"

"Yes," Sadeas said. "I fear I was never a good match for the position. My Shalashian temperament, perhaps. I wish Dalinar good fortune in finding a replacement—though from what I've heard, the other highprinces have come to an agreement that none of us are . . . suited to these kinds of appointments."

He renounces the king's authority, Adolin thought. Storms, this was bad. He gritted his teeth, and found himself reaching his hand to the side to summon his Blade. No. He pulled the hand back. He'd find a way to force this man into the dueling ring. Killing Sadeas now—no matter how much he deserved it—would undermine the very laws and codes Adolin's father was working so hard to uphold.

But storms . . . Adolin was tempted.

Sadeas smiled again. "Do you think me an evil man, Adolin?"

"That's too simple a term," Adolin snapped. "You're not just evil, you're a selfish, crem-crusted eel who is trying to strangle this kingdom with his bulbous, bastard hand."

"Eloquent," Sadeas said. "You realize I *created* this kingdom."

"You only helped my father and uncle."

"Men who are both gone," Sadeas said. "The Blackthorn is as dead as old Gavilar. Instead, two *idiots* rule this kingdom, and each one is—in a way—a shadow of a man I loved." He leaned forward, looking Adolin straight in the eyes. "I'm not strangling Alethkar, son. I'm trying with everything I have to keep a few chunks of it strong enough to weather the collapse your father is bringing."

"Don't call me son," Adolin hissed.

"Fine," Sadeas said, standing. "But I'll tell you one thing. I'm glad you survived the events on the Tower that day. You'll make a fine highprince in the coming months. I have a feeling that in ten years or so—following an extended civil war between the two of us—our alliance will be a strong one. By then, you'll understand why I did what I did."

"I doubt it. I'll have rammed my sword through your gut long before that, Sadeas."

Sadeas raised his cup of wine, then walked off, joining a different group of lighteyes. Adolin let out a long sigh of exhaustion, then leaned back against the chair. Nearby, his short bridgeman guard—the one with the silver at his temples—gave Adolin a nod of respect.

Adolin slumped there, feeling drained, until long after the highstorm ended and people started to depart. Adolin preferred to wait until the rain stopped completely before leaving, anyway. He never had liked how his uniform looked when it got wet.

Eventually, he rose, collected his two guards, and stepped out of the winehouse to a grey sky and a deserted Outer Market. He was mostly over the conversation with Sadeas, and kept reminding himself that up to that point the day had been going very well.

Shallan and her carriage had already gone, of course. He could have ordered a ride for himself, but after being locked away for so long, it felt good to be walking in the open air; chill, wet, and fresh from the storm.

Hands in the pockets of his uniform, he started along a pathway through the Outer Market, strolling around puddles. Gardeners had begun growing ornamental shalebark along the sides of the path, though it wasn't very high yet, just a few inches. A good shalebark ridge could take years to grow properly.

Those two insufferable bridgemen followed along behind him. Not that Adolin minded the men personally—they seemed like amiable enough fellows, particularly when away from their commander. Adolin just didn't like needing minders. Though the storm had passed into the west, the afternoon felt gloomy. Clouds obscured the sun, which had moved from its zenith and was drooping slowly toward the distant horizon. He didn't pass many people, so his only companions were the bridgemen—well, those and a legion of cremlings that had emerged to feast upon plants that lapped at water in pools.

Why did plants spend so much more time in their shells out here than they did back home? Shallan probably knew. He smiled, forcing thoughts of Sadeas into the back of his mind. This thing with Shallan, it was working. It always worked at first though, so he contained his enthusiasm.

She *was* marvelous. Exotic, witty, and not smothered in Alethi propriety. She was smarter than he was, but she didn't make him feel stupid. That was a large point in her favor.

He passed out of the market, then crossed the open ground beyond it, eventually reaching Dalinar's warcamp. The guards let him through with crisp salutes. He idled in the warcamp market, comparing the wares he saw here with those in the market near the Pinnacle.

What will happen to this place, Adolin thought, *when the war stops?* It would end someday. Perhaps tomorrow, with the negotiations with the Parshendi Shardbearer.

The Alethi presence wouldn't end here, not with the chasmfiends to hunt, but surely this large a population couldn't continue, could it? Could he really be witnessing a permanent shift of the king's seat?

Hours later—after spending some time at jewelry shops looking for something for Shallan—Adolin and his guards reached his father's complex. By then, Adolin's feet were starting to ache and the camp had grown dark. He yawned, making his way through the cavernous guts of his father's bunkerish dwelling. Wasn't it about time they built a proper mansion? Being an example for the men was all well and good, but there were certain standards a family like theirs should uphold. Particularly if the Shattered Plains were going to remain as important as they had been. It was . . .

He hesitated, stopping at an intersection and looking right. He'd been intending to visit the kitchens for a snack, but a group of men moved and threw shadows in the other direction. Hushed whispers.

"What is this?" Adolin demanded, marching toward the gathering, his two guards following. "Soldiers? What have you found?"

The men scrambled to turn and salute, spears to shoulders. They were more bridgemen from Kaladin's unit. Just beyond them were the doors to the wing where Dalinar, Adolin, and Renarin all made their quarters. Those doors lay open, and the men had set spheres on the ground.

What was going on? Normally, two or maybe four men would be on guard here. Not eight. And . . . why was there a *parshman* wearing a guardsman uniform, holding a spear with the others?

"Sir!" said a lanky, long-armed man at the front of the bridgemen. "We were just heading in to check on the highprince, when . . ."

Adolin didn't hear the rest. He pushed through the bridgemen, finally seeing what the spheres illuminated on the floor of the sitting room.

More scratched glyphs. Adolin knelt down, trying to read them. Unfortunately, they hadn't been drawn in any kind of picture to help. He thought they were numbers . . .

"Thirty-two days," said one of the bridgemen, a short Azish man. "Seek the center."

Damnation. "Have you told anyone of this?" Adolin asked.

"We just found it," the Azish man said.

"Post guards at either end of the hallway," Adolin said. "And send for my aunt."

⁌⁍

Adolin summoned his Blade, then dismissed it, then summoned it again. A nervous habit. The white fog appeared—manifesting as little vines sprouting in the air—before *snapping* into the form of a Shardblade, which suddenly weighed down his hand.

He stood in the sitting room, those foreboding markings staring up at him, as if in silent challenge. The closed door kept the bridgemen out so only he, Dalinar, and Navani would be privy to the discussion. Adolin wanted to use the Blade to cut those cursed glyphs away. Dalinar had *proven* that he was sane. Aunt Navani almost had an entire document of the Dawnchant translated, using the words of Father's visions as a guide!

The visions were from the Almighty. It all made sense.

Now this.

"They were made with a knife," Navani said, kneeling beside the glyphs. The sitting room was a large open area, used for receiving callers or holding meetings. Doors beyond led to the study and the bedrooms.

"This knife," Dalinar replied, holding up a side knife of the style most lighteyes wore. "My knife."

The edge was blunted and still bore flecks of stone from the gouges. The scratches matched the size of the blade. They'd found it just in front of the door to Dalinar's study, where he'd spent the highstorm. Alone. Navani's carriage had been delayed, and she'd been forced to return to the palace or risk being caught in the storm.

"Someone else could have taken it and done this," Adolin snapped. "They could have sneaked into your study, grabbed it while you were consumed by the visions, and come out here . . ."

The other two looked at him.

"Often," Navani said, "the simplest answer is the right one."

Adolin sighed, dismissing his Blade and slumping down in a chair beside the offending glyphs. His father stood tall. In fact, Dalinar Kholin never seemed to have stood as tall as he did now, hands clasped behind his back, eyes away from the glyphs, toward the wall—eastward.

Dalinar was a rock, a boulder too big for even storms to move. He seemed so *sure*. It was something to cling to.

"You don't remember anything?" Navani asked Dalinar, rising.

"No." He turned to Adolin. "I think it's obvious now that I was behind each of these. Why does that bother you so, son?"

"It's the idea of you scribbling on the ground," Adolin said, shivering. "Lost in one of those visions, not in control of yourself."

"The Almighty's path for me is a strange one," Dalinar said. "Why do I need to get the information this way? Scratches on the ground or the wall? Why not say it to me plainly in the visions?"

"It's foretelling, you realize," Adolin said softly. "Seeing the future. A thing of the Voidbringers."

"Yes." Dalinar narrowed his eyes. "Seek the center. What do you think, Navani? The center of the Shattered Plains? What truths hide there?"

"The Parshendi, obviously."

They talked about the center of the Shattered Plains as if they knew of the place. But no man had been there, only Parshendi. To the Alethi, the word "center" just referred to the vast open expanse of unexplored plateaus beyond the scouted rims.

"Yes," Adolin's father said. "But where? Maybe they move around? Maybe there is no Parshendi city in the center."

"They would only be able to move if they had Soulcasters," Navani said, "which I personally doubt. They'll have entrenched somewhere. They aren't a nomadic people, and there's no reason for them to move."

"If we can make peace," Dalinar mused, "reaching the center would be a lot easier. . . ." He looked to Adolin. "Have the bridgemen fill those scratches with crem, then have them pull the rug over that section of floor."

"I'll see it done."

"Good," Dalinar said, seeming distant. "After that, get some sleep, son. Tomorrow is a big day."

Adolin nodded. "Father. Were you aware that there is a *parshman* among the bridgemen?"

"Yes," Dalinar said. "There has been one among their numbers from the beginning, but they didn't arm him until I gave them permission."

"Why would you do such a thing?"

"Out of curiosity," Dalinar said. He turned and nodded toward the glyphs on the floor. "Tell me, Navani. Assuming these numbers are counting toward a date, is it a day when a highstorm will come?"

"Thirty-two days?" Navani asked. "That will be in the middle of the Weeping. Thirty-two days won't even be the exact end of the year, but two days ahead of it. I can't fathom the significance."

"Ah, it was too convenient an answer anyway. Very well. Let's allow the guards back in and swear them to secrecy. Wouldn't want to inspire a panic."

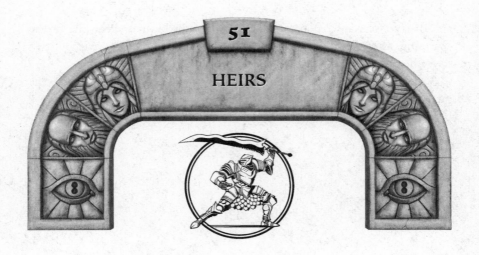

In short, if any presume Kazilah to be innocent, you must look at the facts and deny them in their entirety; to say that the Radiants were destitute of integrity for this execution of one their own, one who had obviously fraternized with the unwholesome elements, indicates the most slothful of reasoning; for the enemy's baleful influence demanded vigilance on all occasions, of war and of peace.

—From *Words of Radiance,* chapter 32, page 17

The next day, Adolin stomped his feet into his boots, hair still damp from a morning bath. It was amazing the difference a little hot water and some time to reflect could make. He'd come to two decisions.

He wasn't going to worry about his father's disconcerting behavior during the visions. The whole of it—the visions, the command to refound the Knights Radiant, the preparation for a disaster that might or might not come—was a package. Adolin had already decided to believe that his father wasn't mad. Further worry was pointless.

The other decision might get him into trouble. He left his quarters, entering the sitting room, where Dalinar was already planning with Navani, General Khal, Teshav, and Captain Kaladin. Renarin, frustratingly, guarded the door wearing a Bridge Four uniform. He'd refused to give up on that decision of his, despite Adolin's insistence.

"We'll need the bridgemen again," Dalinar said. "If something goes wrong, we may need a quick retreat."

"I'll prepare Bridges Five and Twelve for the day, sir," Kaladin said.

"Those two seem nostalgic for their bridges, and talk about the bridge runs with fondness."

"Weren't those *bloodbaths*?" Navani asked.

"They were," Kaladin said, "but soldiers are a strange lot, Brightness. A disaster unifies them. These men would never want to go back, but they still identify as bridgemen."

Nearby, General Khal nodded in understanding, though Navani still seemed baffled.

"I'll take my position here," Dalinar said, holding up a map of the Shattered Plains. "We can scout the meeting plateau first, while I wait. It apparently has some odd rock formations."

"That sounds good," Brightness Teshav said.

"It does," Adolin said, joining the group, "except for one thing. You won't be there, Father."

"Adolin," Dalinar said with a suffering tone. "I know you think this is too dangerous, but—"

"It *is* too dangerous," Adolin said. "The assassin is still out there—and he attacked us last on the very *day* the Parshendi messenger came to camp. Now, we have a meeting with the enemy out on the Shattered Plains? Father, you can't go."

"I have to," Dalinar said. "Adolin, this could mean an end to the war. It could mean answers—why they attacked in the first place. I will not give up this opportunity."

"We're not going to give it up," Adolin said. "We're just going to do things a little differently."

"How?" Dalinar asked, narrowing his eyes.

"Well for one thing," Adolin said, "I'm going to go in your place."

"Impossible," Dalinar said, "I won't risk my son on—"

"Father!" Adolin snapped. "This is *not* subject to discussion!"

The room fell silent. Dalinar lowered his hand from the map. Adolin stuck out his jaw, meeting his father's eyes. Storms, it was difficult to deny Dalinar Kholin. Did his father realize the presence he had, the way he moved people about by sheer force of expectation?

Nobody contradicted him. Dalinar did what he wanted. Fortunately, these days those motives had a noble purpose. But in many ways he was the same man he had been twenty years ago, when he'd conquered a kingdom. He was the Blackthorn, and he got what he wanted.

Except today.

"You are too important," Adolin said, pointing. "Deny that. Deny that your visions are vital. Deny that if you die, Alethkar would fall apart. Deny that every single person in this room is less important than you are."

Dalinar drew in a deep breath, then exhaled slowly. "It shouldn't be so. The kingdom needs to be strong enough to survive the loss of one man, no matter who."

"Well, it's not there yet," Adolin said. "To get it there, we're going to need you. And that means you need to let us watch out for you. I'm sorry, Father, but once in a while you just have to let someone else do their job. You can't fix every problem with your own hands."

"He's right, sir," Kaladin said. "You really shouldn't be risking yourself out on those Plains. Not if there's another option."

"I fail to see that there is one," Dalinar said, his tone cool.

"Oh, there is," Adolin said. "But I'm going to need to borrow Renarin's Shardplate."

⁂

The strangest thing about this experience, in Adolin's estimation, wasn't wearing his father's old armor. Despite the outward stylistic differences, suits of Shardplate all tended to fit similarly. The armor adapted, and within a short time after donning it, the Plate felt exactly like Adolin's own.

It also wasn't strange to ride at the front of the force, Dalinar's banner flapping over his head. Adolin had been leading them to battle on his own for six weeks now.

No, the strangest part was riding his father's horse.

Gallant was a large black animal, bulkier and squatter than Sureblood, Adolin's horse. Gallant looked like a warhorse even when compared to other Ryshadium. So far as Adolin knew, no man had ever ridden him but Dalinar. Ryshadium were finicky that way. It had taken a lengthy explanation from Dalinar to even get the horse to allow Adolin to hold the reins, let alone climb into the saddle.

It had eventually worked, but Adolin wouldn't dare ride Gallant into battle; he was pretty sure the beast would throw him off and run away, looking to protect Dalinar. It did feel odd climbing on a horse that wasn't Sureblood. He kept expecting Gallant to move differently than he did, turn his head at the wrong times. When Adolin patted his neck, the horse's mane felt off to him in ways he couldn't explain. He and his Ryshadium were more than simply rider and horse, and he found himself oddly melancholy to be out on a ride without Sureblood.

Foolishness. He had to stay focused. The procession approached the meeting plateau, which had a large, oddly shaped mound of rock near the center. This plateau was close to the Alethi side of the Plains, but much farther south than Adolin had ever gone. Early patrols had said chasmfiends were more common out in this region, but they never spotted a chrysalis here. Some kind of hunting ground, but not a place for pupating?

The Parshendi weren't there yet. When the scouts reported that the plateau was secure, Adolin urged Gallant across the mobile bridge. He felt warm in his Plate; the seasons, it seemed, had finally decided to inch through spring and maybe even toward summer.

He approached the rock mound at the center. It really *was* odd. Adolin circled it, noticing its shape, ridged in places, almost like . . .

"It's a chasmfiend," Adolin realized. He passed the face, a hollowed-out piece of stone that evoked the exact feeling of a chasmfiend's head. A statue? No, it was too natural. A chasmfiend had died here centuries ago, and instead of being blown away, had slowly crusted over with crem.

The result was eerie. The crem had duplicated the creature's form, clinging to the carapace, entombing it. The hulking rock seemed like a creature born of stone, like the ancient stories of Voidbringers.

Adolin shivered, nudging the horse away from the stone corpse and toward the other side of the plateau. Shortly, he heard alarms from the outrunners. Parshendi coming. He steeled himself, ready to summon his Shardblade. Behind him arrayed a group of bridgemen, ten in number, including that parshman. Captain Kaladin had remained with Dalinar back in the warcamp, just in case.

Adolin was the one more exposed. Part of him *wished* for the assassin to come today. So Adolin could try himself again. Of all the duels he hoped to fight in the future, this one—against the man who had killed his uncle—would be the most important, even more than taking down Sadeas.

The assassin did not make an appearance as a group of two hundred Parshendi crossed from the next plateau, jumping gracefully and landing on the meeting plateau. Adolin's soldiers stirred, armor clanking, spears lowering. It had been years since men and Parshendi had met without blood being spilled.

"All right," Adolin said in his helm. "Fetch my scribe."

Brightness Inadara was carried up through the ranks in a palanquin. Dalinar wanted Navani with him—ostensibly because he wanted her advice, but probably also to protect her.

"Let's go," Adolin said, nudging Gallant forward. They crossed the plateau, just him and Brightness Inadara, who rose from her palanquin to walk. She was a wizened matron, with grey hair she cut short for simplicity. He'd seen sticks with more flesh on them than she had, but she was keen-minded and as trustworthy a scribe as they had.

The Parshendi Shardbearer emerged from the ranks and strode forward on the rocks alone. Uncaring, unworried. This was a confident one.

Adolin dismounted and went the rest of the way on foot, Inadara at his side. They stopped a few feet from the Parshendi, the three of them alone on an expanse of rock, the fossilized chasmfiend staring at them from the left.

"I am Eshonai," the Parshendi said. "Do you remember me?"

"No," Adolin said. He pitched his voice down to try and match the voice of his father, and hoped that—with the helm in place—it would be enough to fool this woman, who couldn't know well what Dalinar sounded like.

"Not surprising," Eshonai said. "I was young and unimportant when we first met. Barely worth remembering."

Adolin had originally expected Parshendi conversation to be sing-songish, from what he'd heard said of them. That wasn't the case at all. Eshonai had a rhythm to her words, the way she emphasized them and where she paused. She changed tones, but the result was more of a chant than a song.

Inadara took out a writing board and spanreed, then started writing down what Eshonai said.

"What is this?" Eshonai demanded.

"I came alone, as you asked," Adolin said, trying to project his father's air of command. "But I *will* record what is said and send it back to my generals."

Eshonai did not raise her faceplate, so Adolin had a good excuse not to raise his. They stared at each other through eye slits. This was not going as well as his father had hoped, but it was about what Adolin had expected.

"We are here," Adolin said, using the words his father had suggested he begin with, "to discuss the terms of a Parshendi surrender."

Eshonai laughed. "That is not the point at all."

"Then what?" Adolin demanded. "You seemed eager to meet with me. Why?"

"Things have changed since I spoke with your son, Blackthorn. Important things."

"What things?"

"Things you cannot imagine," Eshonai said.

Adolin waited, as if pondering, but actually giving Inadara time to correspond with the warcamps. Inadara leaned up to him, whispering what Navani and Dalinar had written for him to say.

"We tire of this war, Parshendi," Adolin said. "Your numbers dwindle. We know this. Let us make a truce, one that would benefit us both."

"We are not as weak as you believe," Eshonai said.

Adolin found himself frowning. When she'd spoken to him before, she'd seemed passionate, inviting. Now she was cold and dismissive. Was that right? She was Parshendi. Perhaps human emotions didn't apply to her.

Inadara whispered more to him.

"What do you want?" Adolin asked, speaking the words his father sent. "How can there be peace?"

"There will be peace, Blackthorn, when one of us is dead. I came here because I wanted to see you with my own eyes, and I wanted to warn you. We have just changed the rules of this conflict. Squabbling over gemstones no longer matters."

No longer matters? Adolin started to sweat. *She makes it sound like they were playing their own game all this time. Not desperate at all.* Could the Alethi have misjudged everything so profoundly?

She turned to go.

No. All of this, just to have the meeting puff into smoke? Storm it!

"Wait!" Adolin cried, stepping forward. "Why? Why are you acting like this? What is wrong?"

She looked back at him. "You really want to end this?"

"Yes. Please. I want peace. Regardless of the cost."

"Then you will have to destroy us."

"Why?" Adolin repeated. "Why did you kill Gavilar, all those years ago? Why betray our treaty?"

"King Gavilar," Eshonai said, as if mulling over the name. "He should not have revealed his plans to us that night. Poor fool. He did not know. He bragged, thinking we would welcome the return of our gods." She shook her head, then turned again and jogged off, armor clinking.

Adolin stepped back, feeling useless. If his father had been there, would he have been able to do more? Inadara still wrote, sending the words to Dalinar.

A reply from him finally came. "Return to the warcamps. There is nothing you, or I myself, could have done. Clearly, her mind is already made up."

Adolin spent the return ride brooding. When he finally reached the warcamps a few hours later, he found his father in conference with Navani, Khal, Teshav, and the army's four battalionlords.

Together, they pored over the words that Inadara had sent. A group of parshman servants quietly brought wine and fruit. Teleb—wearing the Plate that Adolin had won from his duel with Eranniv—watched from the side of the room, Shardhammer on his back, faceplate up. His people had once ruled Alethkar. What did he think of all this? The man usually kept his opinions to himself.

Adolin stomped into the room, pulling off his father's—well, Renarin's—helm. "I should have let you go," Adolin said. "It wasn't a trap. Perhaps you could have talked sense to her."

"These are the people who murdered my brother on the very night they signed a treaty with him," Dalinar said, inspecting maps on the table. "It seems they have not changed at all from that day. You did perfectly, son; we know everything we need to."

"We do?" Adolin said, walking up to the table, helm under arm.

"Yes," Dalinar said, looking up. "We know that they will not agree to peace, no matter what. My conscience is clear."

Adolin looked over the outspread maps. "What is this?" he asked, noting troop movement symbols. They were all pointed across the Shattered Plains.

"A plan of assault," Dalinar said quietly. "The Parshendi will not deal with us, and they are planning something big. Something to change the war. The time has come to bring the fight directly to them and end this war, one way or another."

"Stormfather," Adolin said. "And if we're surrounded while we're out there?"

"We will take everyone," Dalinar said, "our whole army, and as many of the highprinces as will join me. Soulcasters for food. The Parshendi won't be able to surround that large a force, and even if they did, it wouldn't matter. We'd be able to stand against them."

"We can leave right after the final highstorm before the Weeping," Navani said, writing some numbers on the side of the map. "It is the Light Year, and so we'll have steady rains, but no highstorms for weeks. We won't be exposed to one while out on the Plains."

It would also put them out on the Shattered Plains, alone, within days of the date that had been scratched on the walls and floor. . . . Adolin's spine crawled.

"We have to beat them to it," Dalinar said softly, scanning the maps. "Interrupt whatever it is they are planning. Before the countdown ends." He looked up at Adolin. "I need you to duel more. High-profile matches, as high profile as you can manage. Win Shards for me, son."

"I'm dueling Elit tomorrow," Adolin said. "From there, I have a plan for my next target."

"Good. To succeed out on the Plains, we will need Shardbearers—and we will need the loyalty of as many highprinces as will follow me. Focus your dueling on the Shardbearers of the faction loyal to Sadeas, and beat them with as much fanfare as you can manage. I will go to the neutral highprinces, and will remind them of their oaths to fulfill the Vengeance Pact. If we can take Shards from those who follow Sadeas and use them to end the war, it will go a long way toward proving what I've been saying all along. That unity is the path to Alethi greatness."

Adolin nodded. "I'll see it done."

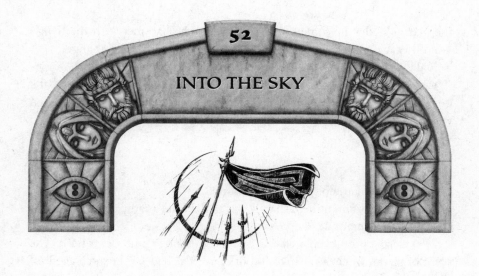

Now, as the Truthwatchers were esoteric in nature, their order being formed entirely of those who never spoke or wrote of what they did, in this lies frustration for those who would see their exceeding secrecy from the outside; they were not naturally inclined to explanation; and in the case of Corberon's disagreements, their silence was not a sign of an exceeding abundance of disdain, but rather an exceeding abundance of tact.

—From *Words of Radiance*, chapter 11, page 6

Kaladin strolled along the Shattered Plains at night, passing tufts of shalebark and vines, lifespren spinning about them as motes. Puddles still lingered in low spots from the previous day's highstorm, fat with crem for the plants to feast upon. To his left, Kaladin heard the sounds of the warcamps, busy with activity. To the right . . . silence. Just those endless plateaus.

When he'd been a bridgeman, Sadeas's troops hadn't stopped him from walking this path. What was there for men out here, on the Plains? Instead, Sadeas had posted guards at the edges of the camps and at bridges, so the slaves couldn't escape.

What was there for men out here? Nothing but salvation itself, discovered in the depths of those chasms.

Kaladin turned and strolled out along one of the chasms, passing soldiers on guard duty at bridges, torches shivering in the wind. They saluted him.

There, he thought, picking his way along a particular plateau. The warcamps to his left stained the air with light, enough to see where he was. At the plateau's edge he came to the place where he had met with the King's Wit on that night weeks ago. A night of decision, a night of change.

Kaladin stepped up to the edge of the chasm, looking eastward.

Change and decision. He checked over his shoulder. He'd passed the guard post, and now nobody was close enough to see him. So, belt laden with bags of spheres, Kaladin stepped off into the chasm.

∴

Shallan did not care for Sadeas's warcamp.

The air was different here than it was in Sebarial's camp. It stank, and it smelled of desperation.

Was desperation even a smell? She thought she could describe it. The scent of sweat, of cheap drink, and of crem that had not been cleaned off the streets. That all churned above roads that were poorly lit. In Sebarial's camp, people walked in groups. Here, they loped along in packs.

Sebarial's camp smelled of spice and industry—of new leather and, sometimes, livestock. Dalinar's camp smelled of polish and oil. Around every second corner in Dalinar's camp, someone was doing something practical. There were too few soldiers in Dalinar's camp these days, but each wore his uniform, as if it were a shield against the chaos of the times.

In Sadeas's camp, the men who wore their uniforms wore them with unbuttoned jackets and wrinkled trousers. She passed tavern after tavern, each spitting forth a racket. The women who idled in front of some indicated that not all were simply taverns. Whorehouses were common in every camp, of course, but they seemed more blatant here.

She passed fewer parshmen than she commonly saw in Sebarial's camp. Sadeas preferred traditional slaves: men and women with branded foreheads, scurrying about with backs bowed and shoulders slumped.

This was, honestly, what she'd expected from all of the warcamps. She'd read accounts of men at war—of camp followers and discipline problems. Of tempers flaring, of the attitudes of men who were trained to kill. Perhaps, instead of wondering at the awfulness of Sadeas's camp, she should be marveling that the others weren't the same.

Shallan hurried on her way. She wore the face of a young darkeyed man, her hair pushed up into her cap. She wore a pair of sturdy gloves. Even disguised as a boy, she wasn't about to go around with her safehand exposed.

Before leaving tonight, she had done a series of sketches to use as new faces, if need be. Testing had proven she could draw a sketch in the morning, then use it for an image in the afternoon. If she waited longer than about a day, though, the image she created was blurred and sometimes looked melted. That made perfect sense to Shallan. The process of creation left a picture in her mind that eventually wore thin.

Her current face had been based on the messenger youths who moved in Sadeas's camp. Though her heart thumped every time she passed a pack of soldiers, nobody gave her a second glance.

Amaram was a highlord—a man of third dahn, which made him a full rank higher than Shallan's father had been, two ranks higher than Shallan herself. That entitled him to his own little domain within his liege's warcamp. His manor flew his own banner, and he had his own personal military force occupying nearby buildings. Posts set into the stone and striped with his colors—burgundy and forest green—delineated his sphere of influence. She passed them without pausing.

"Hey, you!"

Shallan froze in place, feeling very small in the darkness. Not small enough. She turned slowly as a pair of patrolling guards walked up. Their uniforms were sharper than any she'd seen in this camp. Even the buttons were polished, though at the waists they wore skirtlike takama instead of trousers. Amaram was a traditionalist, and his uniforms reflected that.

The guards loomed over her, as most Alethi did. "Messenger?" one asked. "This time of night?" He was a solid fellow with a greying beard and a thick, wide nose.

"It's not even second moon yet, sir," Shallan said in what she hoped was a boyish voice.

He frowned at her. What had she said? *Sir,* she realized. *He's not an officer.*

"Report at the guard posts from now on when you visit," the man said, pointing toward a small, lit area in the distance behind them. "We're going to start keeping a secure perimeter."

"Yes, Sergeant."

"Oh, stop harassing the lad, Hav," the other soldier said. "You can't expect him to know rules that half the soldiers don't even know yet."

"On with you," Hav said, waving Shallan through. She hastened to obey. A secure perimeter? She didn't envy these men that task. Amaram didn't have a wall to keep people out, just some striped posts.

Amaram's manor was relatively small—two stories, with a handful of rooms on each floor. It might once have been a tavern, and was temporary, as he'd only just arrived at the warcamps. Stacked piles of crembrick and stone nearby indicated some far grander building was being planned. Near the piles stood other buildings that had been appropriated as barracks for Amaram's personal guard, which included only about fifty men. Most of the soldiers he'd brought, recruited from Sadeas's lands and sworn to him, would billet elsewhere.

Once she got close to Amaram's home, she ducked beside an outbuilding and squatted down. She'd spent three evenings scouting this area, wearing a different face each time. Perhaps that had been overly cautious. She wasn't certain. She'd never done anything like this before. Fingers trembling, she took off her cap—that part of the costume was real—and let her hair spill around her shoulders. Then she dug a folded picture out of her pocket and waited.

Minutes passed as she stared at the manor. *Come on . . .* she thought. *Come on . . .*

Finally, a young darkeyed woman stepped out of the manor, arm-in-arm with a tall man in trousers and a loose buttoned shirt. The woman tittered as her friend said something, then she scampered off into the night, the man calling after her and following. The maid—Shallan *still* hadn't been able to learn her name—left every night at this time. Twice with this man. Once with another.

Shallan took a deep breath, drawing in Stormlight, then held up the picture she'd drawn of the girl earlier. About Shallan's height, hair about the same length, similar enough build . . . It would have to do. She breathed out, and became someone else.

She giggles and laughs, Shallan thought, plucking off her masculine gloves and replacing the one on the safehand with a tan feminine one, *and often prances about, walking on her toes. Her voice is higher than mine, and she doesn't have an accent.*

Shallan had practiced sounding right, but hopefully she wouldn't need to find out how believable her voice was. All she had to do was go in the door, up the stairs, and slip into the appropriate room. Easy.

She stood up, holding her breath and living off the Stormlight, and strode toward the building.

⁘

Kaladin hit the bottom of the chasm in a glowing storm of Light. He took off at a jog, spear over his shoulder. It was difficult to stand still with Stormlight in his veins.

He dropped a few of the pouches of spheres to use later. The Stormlight rising from his exposed skin was enough to illuminate the chasm, and it cast shadows on the walls as he ran. Those seemed to become figures, crafted by the bones and branches stretching from the heaps on the ground. Bodies and souls. His movement made the shadows twist, as if turning to regard him.

He ran with a silent audience, then. Syl flew down as a ribbon of light and took up position beside his head, matching his speed. He leaped over obstacles and splashed through puddles, letting his muscles warm to the exercise.

Then he jumped up onto the wall.

He hit awkwardly, tripping and rolling through some frillblooms. He came to rest facedown, lying on the wall. He growled and pushed himself to his feet as Stormlight sealed a small cut on his arm.

Jumping onto the wall felt too unnatural; when he hit, it took time to orient himself.

He started running again, sucking in more Stormlight, accustoming himself to the change of perspective. When he reached the next gap between plateaus, to his eyes it looked as if he'd reached a deep pit. The walls of the chasm were his floor and ceiling.

He hopped off the wall, focused on the floor of the chasm, and blinked—willing that direction to become *down* to him again. He landed in another stumble, and this time tripped into a puddle.

He rolled over onto his back, sighing, lying in the cold water. Crem that had settled to the bottom squished between his fingers as he clenched fists.

Syl landed on his chest, taking the form of a young woman. She put hands on her hips.

"What?" he asked.

"That was pathetic."

"Agreed."

"Maybe you're taking it a little too quickly," she said. "Why not try to jump onto the wall without a running start?"

"The assassin could do it this way," Kaladin said. "I need to be able to fight like he does."

"I see. And I suppose he started doing all of this the moment he was born, without any practice at all."

Kaladin exhaled softly. "You sound like Tukks used to."

"Oh? Was he brilliant, beautiful, and always right?"

"He was loud, intolerant, and profoundly acerbic," Kaladin said, standing up. "But yes, he was basically always right." He faced the wall and leaned his spear against it. "Szeth called this 'Lashing.'"

"A good term," Syl said, nodding.

"Well, to get this down, I'm going to have to practice some fundamentals." Just like learning a spear.

That probably meant hopping onto and off the wall a couple hundred times.

Better than dying on that assassin's Shardblade, he thought, and got to it.

⁂

Shallan stepped into Amaram's kitchens, trying to move with the energetic grace of the girl whose face she wore. The large room smelled strongly of the curry simmering over the hearth—the remnants of the night's meal, waiting in case any lighteyes got peckish. The cook browsed a novel in the corner while her girls scrubbed pots. The room was well lit with spheres. Amaram apparently trusted his servants.

A long flight of steps led up to the second floor, providing quick access for servants to bring meals to Amaram. Shallan had drawn a layout of the building from guesses based on window locations. The room with the secrets had been easy to locate—Amaram had the windows shuttered, and never opened them. She'd guessed right about the stairwell in the kitchens, it seemed. She strode toward those steps, humming to herself, as the woman she imitated often did.

"Back already?" the cook said, not looking up from her novel. She was Herdazian, from the accent. "His gift tonight wasn't nice enough? Or did the other one spot you two together?"

Shallan said nothing, trying to cover her anxiety with the humming.

"Might as well put you to use," the cook said. "Stine wanted someone to polish mirrors for him. He's in the study, cleaning the master's flutes."

Flutes? A soldier like Amaram had flutes?

What would the cook do if Shallan bolted up the stairs and ignored the order? The woman was probably high ranked for a darkeyes. An important member of the household staff.

The cook didn't look up from her novel, but continued softly. "Don't think we haven't noticed you sneaking off during midday, child. Just because the master is fond of you doesn't mean you can take advantage. Go to work. Spending your free evening cleaning instead of playing might remind you that you have duties."

Gritting her teeth, Shallan looked up those steps toward her goal. The cook slowly lowered her novel. Her frown seemed the type that one didn't disobey.

Shallan nodded, moving away from the steps and into the corridor beyond. There would be another set of steps upward in the front hall. She'd just have to make her way in that direction and—

Shallan froze in place as a figure stepped into the hallway from a side room. Tall with a square face and angular nose, the man wore a lighteyed outfit of modern design: an open jacket over a buttoned shirt, stiff trousers, a stock tied in place at his neck.

Storms! Highlord Amaram—fashionable or otherwise—was *not* supposed to be in the building today. Adolin had said that Amaram was dining with Dalinar and the king tonight. Why was he here?

Amaram stood looking over a ledger in his hand, and didn't seem to have noticed her. He turned away from her and strolled down the corridor.

Run. It was her immediate reaction. Escape out the front doors, vanish into the night. The problem was, she'd spoken to the cook. When the woman Shallan was imitating came back later, she'd be in a storm of trouble—and she'd be able to prove, with witnesses, that she hadn't come back into the house earlier. Whatever Shallan did, there was a good chance that once she was gone, Amaram would find out that someone had been sneaking about, imitating one of his maids.

Stormfather! She'd only just stepped into the building, and already she'd messed everything up.

Stairs creaked up ahead. Amaram was going up to his room, the one Shallan was supposed to inspect.

The Ghostbloods will be mad at me for alerting Amaram, Shallan thought, *but they'll be even angrier if I do that and then return with no information.*

She had to get into that room, alone. That meant she couldn't let Amaram enter it.

Shallan scrambled after him, rushing into the entry hall and twisting around the newel post to propel herself up the stairs. Amaram reached the top landing and turned toward the hallway. Maybe he wouldn't go in that room.

She wasn't so lucky. As Shallan scurried up the steps, Amaram turned toward just that door and raised a key, slipping it into the lock and turning it.

"Brightlord Amaram," Shallan said, out of breath as she reached the top landing.

He turned toward her, frowning. "Telesh? Weren't you going out tonight?"

Well, at least she knew her name now. Did Amaram really take such an interest in his servants as to be aware of a lowly maid's evening plans?

"I did, Brightlord," Shallan said, "but I came back."

Need a distraction. But not something too suspicious. Think! Was he going to notice that the voice was different?

"Telesh," Amaram said, shaking his head. "You still can't choose between them? I promised your good father I'd see you cared for. How can I do that if you won't settle down?"

"It's not that, Brightlord," Shallan said quickly. "Hav stopped a messenger on the perimeter coming for you. He sent me back to tell you."

"Messenger?" Amaram said, slipping the key back out of the lock. "From whom?"

"Hav didn't say, Brightlord. He seemed to think it was important, though."

"That man . . ." Amaram said with a sigh. "He's too protective. He thinks he can keep a tight perimeter in this mess of a camp?" The highlord considered, then stuffed the key back in his pocket. "Better see what it's about."

Shallan gave him a bow as he passed her by and trotted down the stairs. She counted to ten once he was out of sight, then scrambled to the door. It was still locked.

"Pattern!" Shallan whispered. "Where are you?"

He came out from the folds of her skirts, moving across the floor and then up the door until he was just before her, like a raised carving on the wood.

"The lock?" Shallan asked.

"It is a pattern," he said, then grew very small and moved into the keyhole. She'd had him try a few more times on locks back in her rooms, and he'd been able to unlock those as he had Tyn's trunk.

The lock clicked, and she opened the door and slipped into the dark room. A sphere plucked from her dress pocket lit it for her.

The secret room. The room with shutters always closed, kept locked at all times. A room that the Ghostbloods wanted so desperately to see.

It was filled with maps.

⁘

The trick to jumping between surfaces wasn't the landing, Kaladin discovered. It wasn't about reflexes or timing. It wasn't even about changing perspective.

It was about fear.

It was about that moment when, hanging in the air, his body lurched from being pulled *down* to being pulled *sideways*. His instincts weren't equipped to deal with this shift. A primal part of him panicked every time down stopped being down.

He ran at the wall and jumped, throwing his feet to the side. He couldn't hesitate, couldn't be afraid, couldn't flinch. It was like teaching himself to dive face-first onto a stone surface without raising his hands for protection.

He shifted his perspective and used Stormlight to make the wall become downward. He positioned his feet. Even still, in that brief moment, his instincts rebelled. The body knew, it *knew*, that he was going to fall back to the chasm floor. He would break bones, hit his head.

He landed on the wall without stumbling.

Kaladin stood up straight, surprised, and exhaled a deep breath, puffing with Stormlight.

"Nice!" Syl said, zipping around him.

"It's unnatural," Kaladin said.

"No. I could never be involved in anything unnatural. It's just . . . *extra*-natural."

"You mean supernatural."

"No I don't." She laughed and zipped on ahead of him.

It *was* unnatural—as walking wasn't natural for a child who was just learning. It became natural over time. Kaladin was learning to crawl—and unfortunately, he'd soon be required to run. Like a child dropped in a whitespine's lair. Learn quickly or be lunch.

He ran along the wall, hopping over a shalebark outcropping, then jumped to the side and shifted to the floor of the chasm. He landed with only a slight stumble.

Better. He ran after Syl and kept at it.

⋅⋅

Maps.

Shallan crept forward, her solitary sphere revealing a room draped with maps and strewn with papers. They were covered in glyphs that had been scribbled quickly, not made to be beautiful. She could barely read most of them.

I've heard of this, she thought. *The stormwarden script. The way they get around the restrictions on writing.*

Amaram was a stormwarden? A chart of times on one wall, listing highstorms and calculations of their next arrival—written in the same hand as the notes on the maps—seemed proof of that. Perhaps this was what the Ghostbloods were seeking: blackmail material. Stormwardens, as male scholars, made most people uncomfortable. Their use of glyphs in a way that was basically the same as writing, their secretive nature . . . Amaram was one of the most accomplished generals in all of Alethkar. He was respected even by those he fought. Exposing him as a stormwarden could seriously damage his reputation.

Why would he bother with such strange hobbies? All of these maps faintly reminded her of the ones she'd discovered in her father's study, after his death—though those had been of Jah Keved. "Watch outside, Pattern," she said. "Bring me word quickly when Amaram returns to the building."

"Mmmm," he buzzed, withdrawing.

Aware that her time was short, Shallan hurried to the wall, holding up her sphere and taking Memories of the maps. The Shattered Plains? This map was far more extensive than any she'd seen before—and that included the Prime Map that she'd studied in the king's Gallery of Maps.

How had Amaram obtained something so extensive? She tried to work out the use of glyphs—there was no grammar to them that she could see. Glyphs weren't meant to be used that way. They conveyed a single idea, not a string of thoughts. She read a few in a row.

Origin . . . direction . . . uncertainty. . . . The place of the center is uncertain? That was probably what it meant.

Other notes were similar, and she translated in her head. *Perhaps pushing this direction will yield results. Warriors spotted watching from here.* Other groupings of glyphs made no sense to her. This script was bizarre. Perhaps Pattern could translate it, but she certainly couldn't.

Aside from the maps, the walls were covered in long sheets of paper filled with writing, figures, and diagrams. Amaram was working on something, something big—

Parshendi! she realized. *That's what those glyphs mean. Parap-shenesh-idi.* The three glyphs individually meant three separate things—but together, their sounds made the word "Parshendi." That was why some of the writings seemed like gibberish. Amaram was using some glyphs phonetically. He underlined them when he did this, and that allowed him to write in glyphs things that never should have worked. The stormwardens really *were* turning glyphs into a full script.

Parshendi, she translated, still distracted by the nature of the characters, *must know how to return the Voidbringers.*

What?

Remove secret from them.

Reach center before Alethi armies.

Some of the writings were lists of references. Though they'd been translated to glyphs, she recognized some of the quotes from Jasnah's work. They referred to the Voidbringers. Others were purported sketches of Voidbringers and other creatures of mythology.

This was it, full proof that the Ghostbloods were interested in the same things Jasnah was. As was Amaram, apparently. Heart beating with excitement, Shallan turned around, looking over the room. Was the secret to Urithiru here? Had he found it?

There was too much for Shallan to translate fully at the moment. The script was too difficult, and her thumping heart made her too nervous. Besides, Amaram would likely return very soon. She took Memories so she could sketch this all out later.

As she did, the writings she translated in passing caused a new species of dread to rise within her. It seemed . . . it seemed that Highlord Amaram— paragon of Alethi honor—was *actively* trying to bring about the return of the Voidbringers.

I have to stay a part of this, Shallan thought. *I can't afford to have the Ghostbloods cast me out for making a mess of this incursion. I need to discover what else they know. And I have to know why Amaram is doing what he does.*

She couldn't just run tonight. She couldn't risk leaving Amaram alerted that someone had infiltrated his secret room. She couldn't botch this assignment.

Shallan had to craft better lies.

She pulled a sheet of paper from her pocket and slapped it onto the desk, then began to frantically draw.

⬦

Kaladin jumped off the wall at a careful speed, twisting to the side and landing back on the ground without breaking step. He wasn't going very quickly, but at least he didn't stumble anymore.

With each jump, he shoved the visceral panic farther down. Up, back onto the wall. Down again. Again and again, sucking in Stormlight.

Yes, this was natural. Yes, this was *him*.

He continued running along the chasm bottom, feeling a surge of excitement. Shadows waved him on as he dodged between piles of bone and moss. He leaped over a large pool of water, but misjudged its size. He came down—about to splash into the shallow water.

But by reflex, he looked upward and Lashed himself toward the sky.

For a brief moment, Kaladin stopped falling down and fell up instead. His momentum continued forward, and he cleared the pool, then Lashed himself downward again. He landed in a trot, sweating.

I could Lash myself upward, he thought, *and fall into the sky forever.*

But no, that was how an ordinary person thought. A skyeel didn't fear falling, did it? A fish didn't fear drowning.

Until he began thinking in a new way, he wouldn't control this gift he had been given. And it *was* a gift. He would embrace this.

The sky was now his.

Kaladin shouted, dashing forward. He leaped and Lashed himself to the wall. No pausing, no hesitance, no *fear*. He hit at a dead run, and nearby, Syl laughed for joy.

But that, that was simple. Kaladin jumped off the wall and looked directly above him at the opposite wall. He Lashed himself in that direction, and flung his body into a flip. He landed, going down on one knee upon what had been the ceiling to him a moment before.

"You did it!" Syl said, flitting around him. "What changed?"

"I did."

"Well, yeah, but what about you?" Syl asked.

"Everything."

She frowned at him. He grinned back, then took off at a run along the side of the chasm.

Shallan strode down the mansion's back steps to the kitchen, thumping each foot down harder than it would normally fall, trying to imitate being heavier than she was. The cook looked up from her novel and dropped it in a wide-eyed panic, moving to stand. "Brightlord!"

"Remain seated," Shallan mouthed, scratching at her face to mask her lips. Pattern spoke the words she'd told him to say in a perfect imitation of Amaram's voice.

The cook remained seated, as ordered. Hopefully, from that position, she wouldn't notice that Amaram was shorter than he should be. Even walking on her tiptoes—which was masked by the illusion—she was much shorter than the highlord.

"You spoke to the maid Telesh earlier," Pattern said as Shallan mouthed the words.

"Yes, Brightlord," the cook said, speaking softly to match Pattern's tone of voice. "I sent her off to work with Stine for the evening. I thought the girl needed a little direction."

"No," Pattern said. "Her return was at my command. I have sent her out again, and told her not to speak of what happened tonight."

The cook frowned. "What . . . happened tonight?"

"You are not to speak of this event. You interfered with something that is not of your concern. Pretend you did not see Telesh. Never speak of this event to me. If you do, I will pretend none of this happened. Do you understand?"

The cook grew pale, and nodded her head, sinking down in her chair.

Shallan nodded to her curtly, then walked from the kitchens out into the night. There, she ducked to the side of the building, heart pounding. A grin formed on her face anyway.

Out of sight, she exhaled Stormlight in a cloud, then stepped forward. As she passed through it, the image of Amaram vanished, replaced by that of the messenger boy she'd been imitating before. She scrambled back to the front of the building and sat down on the steps, slumping and leaning with her head on her hand.

Amaram and Hav walked up through the night, speaking softly. ". . . I didn't notice that the girl had seen me talking to the messenger, Highlord," Hav was saying. "She must have realized . . ." He trailed off as they saw Shallan.

She hopped to her feet and bowed to Amaram.

"It's no matter now, Hav," Amaram said, waving the soldier back to his rounds.

"Highlord," Shallan said. "I bring you a message."

"Obviously, darkborn," the man said, stepping up to her. "What does he want?"

"He?" Shallan asked. "This is from Shallan Davar."

Amaram cocked his head. "Who?"

"Betrothed of Adolin Kholin," she said. "She is trying to update the accounting of all of the Shardblades in Alethkar with pictures. She would like to schedule a time to come and do a sketch of yours, if you are willing."

"Oh," Amaram said. He seemed to relax. "Yes, well, that would be fine. I am free most afternoons. Have her send someone to speak with my steward to arrange a meeting."

"Yes, Highlord. I'll see that it is done." Shallan moved to leave.

"You came this late?" Amaram asked. "To ask such a simple question."

Shallan shrugged. "I don't question the commands of lighteyes, Highlord. But my mistress, well, she can be distracted at times. I suppose she wanted me on her task while it was fresh in her mind. And she's really interested in Shardblades."

"Who isn't?" Amaram mused, turning away, speaking softly. "They're wondrous things, aren't they?"

Was he talking to her, or to himself? Shallan hesitated. A sword formed in his hand, mist coalescing, water beading on its surface. Amaram held it up, looking at himself in the reflection.

"Such beauty," he said. "Such art. Why must we kill with our grandest creations? Ah, but I'm babbling, delaying you. I apologize. The Blade is still new to me. I find excuses to summon it."

Shallan was barely listening. A Blade with the back edge ridged like flowing waves. Or perhaps tongues of fire. Etchings all along its surface. Curved, sinuous.

She knew this Blade.

It belonged to her brother Helaran.

⁖

Kaladin charged through the chasm, and the wind joined him, blowing at his back. Syl soared before him as a ribbon of light.

He reached a boulder in his way and jumped into the air, Lashing himself upward. He soared a good thirty feet upward before Lashing himself to the side and downward at the same time. The downward Lashing slowed his momentum upward; the sideways Lashing brought him to the wall.

He dismissed the downward Lashing and hit the wall with one hand, twisting and throwing himself to his feet. He kept running along the chasm wall. When he reached the end of the plateau, he leaped toward the next one and Lashed himself at its wall instead.

Faster! He held nearly all of the Stormlight he had left, fetched from the pouches he'd dropped earlier. He held so much that he glowed like a bonfire. It encouraged him as he jumped and Lashed himself forward, eastward. This made him fall *through* the chasm. The floor of the chasm whipped along beneath him, plants a blur to his sides.

He had to remember that he was falling. This was not flight, and every second he moved, his speed increased. That didn't stop the feeling of liberty, of ultimate freedom. It just meant this could be dangerous.

The winds picked up and he Lashed himself backward at the last moment, slowing his descent as he crashed against a chasm wall before him.

That direction was down to him now, so he stood and ran along it. He was using the Stormlight at a furious rate, but he didn't need to scrimp. He was paid like a lighteyed officer of the sixth dahn, and his spheres held not tiny chips of gemstone, but broams. A month's pay for him now was more than he had ever seen at a time, and the Stormlight it held was a vast fortune compared to what he'd once known.

He shouted as he jumped a group of frillblooms, their fronds pulling in beneath him. He Lashed himself to the other chasm wall and crossed the chasm, landing on his hands. He threw himself back upward, and somehow Lashed himself only *slightly* in that direction.

Now much lighter, he was able to twist in the air and come down on his feet. He stood on the wall, facing down the chasm, hands in fists and Light pouring off him.

Syl hesitated, flitting around him back and forth. "What?" she asked.

"More," he said, then Lashed himself forward again, down the corridor.

Fearless, he fell. This was his ocean to swim, his winds upon which to soar. He fell face-first toward the next plateau. Just before he arrived, he Lashed himself sideways and backward.

His stomach lurched. He felt like someone had tied a rope around him and pushed him off a cliff, then yanked on the rope right as he reached the end of it. The Stormlight inside, however, made the discomfort negligible. He pulled sideways, into another chasm.

Lashings sent him eastward again down another corridor, and he wove around plateaus, keeping to the chasms—like an eel swimming through the waves, swerving around boulders. Onward, faster, still falling . . .

Teeth clenched at both the wonder and the forces twisting him, he tossed caution aside and Lashed himself upward. Once, twice, three times. He let go of all else, and amid the streaming Light, he shot from the chasms out into the open air above.

He Lashed himself back to the east so that he could fall in that direction again, but now no plateau walls got in his way. He soared toward the horizon, distant, lost in the darkness. He gained speed, coat flapping, hair whipping behind him. Air buffeted his face, and he narrowed his eyes, but did not close them.

Beneath, dark chasms passed one after another. Plateau. Pit. Plateau. Pit. This sensation . . . flying over the land . . . he had felt this before, in dreams. What took bridgemen hours to cross, he passed in minutes. He felt as if something were boosting him from behind, the wind itself carrying him. Syl zipped along to his right.

And to his left? No, those were other windspren. He'd accumulated dozens of them, flying around him as ribbons of light. He could pick out Syl. He didn't know how; she didn't look different, but he could tell. Like you could pick a family member out of a crowd just by their walk.

Syl and her cousins twisted around him in a spiral of light, free and loose, but with a hint of coordination.

How long had it been since he felt this good, this triumphant, this *alive*? Not since before Tien's death. Even after saving Bridge Four, darkness had shadowed him.

That evaporated. He saw a spire of rock ahead on the plateaus, and nudged himself toward it with a careful Lashing to the right. Other Lashings to his rear slowed his fall enough that when he hit the tip of the spire of rock, he could clutch to it and spin around it, fingers on the smooth cremstone.

A hundred windspren broke around him, like the crash of a wave, spraying outward from Kaladin in a fan of light.

He grinned. Then he looked upward, toward the sky.

⁘

Highlord Amaram continued to stare at the Shardblade in the night. He held it up before him in the light spilling from the front of the manor house.

Shallan remembered her father's quiet terror as he looked upon that weapon, leveled toward him. Could it be a coincidence? Two weapons that looked the same? Perhaps her memory was flawed.

No. No, she would *never* forget the look of that Blade. It *was* the one Helaran had held. And no two Blades were the same.

"Brightlord," Shallan said, drawing Amaram's attention. He seemed startled, as if he'd forgotten she was there.

"Yes?"

"Brightness Shallan," she said, "wants to make certain the records are all correct and that the histories of the Blades and Plate in the Alethi army have been properly traced. Your Blade is not in them. She asked if you would mind sharing the origin of your Blade, in the name of scholarship."

"I've explained this to Dalinar already," Amaram said. "I don't know the history of my Shards. Both were in the possession of an assassin who tried to kill me. A younger man. Veden, with red hair. We don't know his name, and his face was ruined in my counterattack. I had to stab him through his faceplate, you see."

Young man. Red hair.

She stood before her brother's killer.

"I . . ." Shallan stammered, feeling sick. "Thank you. I will pass the information along."

She turned, trying not to stumble as she walked away. She finally knew what had happened to Helaran.

You were involved in all of this, weren't you, Helaran? she thought. *Just like Father was. But how, why?*

It seemed that Amaram was trying to bring back the Voidbringers. Helaran had tried to kill him.

But would anyone really *want* to bring back the Voidbringers? Perhaps she was mistaken. She needed to get to her rooms, draw those maps from the Memories she'd taken, and try to figure this all out.

The guards, blessedly, did not give her any further troubles as she slipped away from Amaram's camp and into the anonymity of the darkness. That was well, for if they'd looked closely, they'd have seen the messenger boy with tears in his eyes. Crying for a brother that now, once and for all, Shallan knew was dead.

⁙

Upward.

One Lashing, then another, then a third. Kaladin shot up into the sky. Nothing but open expanse, an infinite sea for his delight.

The air grew cold. Still upward he went, reaching for the clouds. Finally, worried about running out of Stormlight before returning to the ground—he had only one infused sphere left, carried in his pocket for an emergency—Kaladin reluctantly Lashed himself downward.

He didn't fall downward immediately; his momentum upward merely slowed. He was still Lashed to the sky; he hadn't dismissed the upward Lashings.

Curious, he Lashed himself downward to slow further, then dismissed all of his Lashings except one up and one down. He eventually came to a stop hanging in midair. The second moon had risen, bathing the Plains in light far below. From here, they looked like a broken plate. *No . . .* he thought, squinting. *It's a pattern.* He'd seen this before. In a dream.

Wind blew against him, causing him to drift like a kite. The windspren he'd attracted scampered away now that he wasn't riding upon the winds. Funny. He'd never realized one could attract windspren as one attracted the spren of emotions.

All you had to do was fall into the sky.

Syl remained, spinning around him in a swirl until finally coming to rest on his shoulder. She sat, then looked down.

"Not many men ever see this view," she noted. From up here, the warcamps—circles of fire to his right—seemed insignificant. It was cold enough to be uncomfortable. Rock claimed the air was thinner up high, though Kaladin couldn't tell any difference.

"I've been trying to get you to do this for a while now," Syl said.

"It's like when I first picked up a spear," Kaladin whispered. "I was just a child. Were you with me back then? All that time ago?"

"No," Syl said, "and yes."

"It can't be both."

"It can. I knew I needed to find you. And the winds knew you. They led me to you."

"So everything I've done," Kaladin said. "My skill with the spear, the way I fight. That's not me. It's you."

"It's *us.*"

"It's cheating. Unearned."

"Nonsense," Syl said. "You practice every day."

"I have an advantage."

"The advantage of talent," Syl said. "When the master musician first picks up an instrument and finds music in it that nobody else can, is that cheating? Is that art unearned, just because she is naturally more skilled? Or is it genius?"

Kaladin Lashed himself westward, back toward the warcamps. He didn't want to leave himself stranded in the middle of the Shattered Plains without Stormlight. The tempest within had calmed greatly since he started. He fell in that direction for a time—getting as close as he dared before slowing himself—then removed part of the upward Lashing and began to drift downward.

"I'll take it," Kaladin said. "Whatever it is that gives me that edge. I'll use it. I'll need it to beat *him.*"

Syl nodded, still sitting on his shoulder.

"You don't think he has a spren," Kaladin said. "But how does he do what he does?"

"The weapon," Syl said, more confidently than she had before. "It's something special. It was created to give abilities to men, much as our bond does."

Kaladin nodded, light wind ruffling his jacket as he fell through the night. "Syl . . ." How to broach this? "I can't fight him without a Shardblade."

She looked the other way, squeezing her arms together, hugging herself. Such human gestures.

"I've avoided the training with the Blades that Zahel offers," Kaladin continued. "It's hard to justify. I *need* to learn how to use one of those weapons."

"They're evil," she said in a small voice.

"Because they're symbols of the knights' broken oaths," Kaladin said. "But where did they come from in the first place? How were they forged?"

Syl didn't answer.

"Can a new one be forged? One that doesn't bear the stain of broken promises?"

"Yes."

"How?"

She didn't reply. They floated downward for a time in silence until gently coming to rest on a dark plateau. Kaladin got his bearings, then walked over and drifted off the edge, going down into the chasms. He wouldn't want to walk back using the bridges. The scouts would find it odd that he was coming back without having gone out.

Storms. They'd have seen him flying out here, wouldn't they? What would they think? Were any close enough to have seen him land?

Well, he couldn't do anything about that now. He reached the bottom of the chasm and started walking back toward the warcamps, his Stormlight slowly dying out, leaving him in darkness. He felt deflated without it, sluggish, tired.

He fished the last infused sphere from his pocket and used it to light his path.

"There's a question you're avoiding," Syl said, landing on his shoulder. "It's been two days. When are you going to tell Dalinar about those men that Moash took you to meet?"

"He didn't listen when I told him about Amaram."

"This is *obviously* different," Syl said.

It was, and she was right. So why hadn't he told Dalinar?

"Those men didn't seem the type who would wait long," Syl said.

"I'll do something about them," Kaladin said. "I just want to think about it some more. I don't want Moash to get caught in the storm when we bring them down."

She fell silent as he walked the rest of the way, retrieving his spear, then climbed the ladder up onto the plateaus. The sky overhead had grown cloudy, but the weather had been turning toward spring lately.

Enjoy it while you can, he thought. *The Weeping comes soon.* Weeks of ceaseless rain. No Tien to cheer him up. His brother had always been able to do that.

Amaram had taken that from him. Kaladin lowered his head and started walking. At the warcamps' edge, he turned right and walked northward.

"Kaladin?" Syl asked, flitting in beside him. "Why are you walking this way?"

He looked up. This was the way toward Sadeas's camp. Dalinar's camp was the other direction.

Kaladin kept walking.

"Kaladin? What are you doing?"

Finally, he stopped in place. Amaram would be there, just ahead, inside Sadeas's camp somewhere. It was late, Nomon inching toward its zenith.

"I *could* end him," Kaladin said. "Enter his window in a flash of Stormlight, kill him, and be off before anyone has time to react. So easy. Everyone would blame it on the Assassin in White."

"Kaladin . . ."

"It's *justice*, Syl," he said, suddenly angry, turning toward her. "You tell me that I need to protect. If I kill him, that's what I'm doing! Protecting people, keeping him from ruining them. Like he ruined me."

"I don't like how you get," she said, seeming small, "when you think about him. You stop being you. You stop thinking. Please."

"He killed Tien," Kaladin said. "I *will* end him, Syl."

"But tonight?" Syl asked. "After what you just discovered, after what you just did?"

He took a deep breath, remembering the thrill of the chasms and the freedom of flight. He'd felt true joy for the first time in what seemed like ages.

Did he want to taint that memory with Amaram? No. Not even with the man's demise, which would surely be a wonderful day.

"All right," he said, turning back toward Dalinar's camp. "Not tonight."

Evening stew was finished by the time Kaladin arrived back at the barracks. He passed the fire, where embers still glowed, and made his way to his room. Syl zipped up into the air. She'd ride the winds overnight, playing with her cousins. So far as he knew, she didn't need sleep.

He stepped into his private room, feeling tired and drained, but in a pleasing way. It—

Someone stirred in the room.

Kaladin spun, leveling his spear, and sucked in the last light of the sphere he'd been using to guide his way. The Light that streamed off him revealed a red and black face. Shen looked disturbingly eerie in those shadows, like an evil spren from the stories.

"Shen," Kaladin said, lowering his spear. "What in the—"

"Sir," Shen said. "I must leave."

Kaladin frowned.

"I am sorry," Shen added speaking in his slow, deliberate way. "I cannot tell you why." He seemed to be waiting for something, his hands tense on his spear. The spear Kaladin had given him.

"You're a free man, Shen," Kaladin said. "I won't keep you here if you feel you must go, but I don't know that there is another place you can go where you will be able to make good on your freedom."

Shen nodded, then moved to walk past Kaladin.

"You are leaving tonight?"

"Immediately."

"The guards at the edges of the Plains might try to stop you."

Shen shook his head. "Parshmen do not flee captivity. They will see only a slave doing some assigned task. I will leave your spear beside the fire." He walked to the door, but then hesitated beside Kaladin, and placed a hand on his shoulder. "You are a good man, Captain. I have learned much. My name is not Shen. It is Rlain."

"May the winds treat you well, Rlain."

"The winds are not what I fear," Rlain said. He patted Kaladin's shoulder, then took a deep breath as if anticipating something difficult, and stepped from the chamber.

As to the other orders that were inferior in this visiting of the far realm of spren, the Elsecallers were prodigiously benevolent, allowing others as auxiliary to their visits and interactions; though they did never relinquish their place as prime liaisons with the great ones of the spren; and the Lightweavers and Willshapers both also had an affinity to the same, though neither were the true masters of that realm.

—From *Words of Radiance*, chapter 6, page 2

A dolin slapped away Elit's Shardblade with his forearm. Shard-bearers didn't use shields—each section of Plate was stronger than stone.

He swept in, using Windstance as he moved across the sand of the arena.

Win Shards for me, son.

Adolin flowed through the stance's strikes, one direction then the other, forcing Elit away. The man scrambled, Plate leaking from a dozen places where Adolin had struck him.

Any hope for a peaceful end to the war on the Shattered Plains was gone. Done for. He knew how much his father had wanted that end, and the Parshendi arrogance made him angry. Frustrated.

He kept that down. He could not be consumed by it. He moved smoothly through the stance, careful, maintaining a calm serenity.

Elit had apparently expected Adolin to be reckless, as in his first duel for Shards. Elit kept backing up, waiting for that moment of recklessness. Adolin didn't give it to him.

Today, he fought with precision—exacting form and stance, nothing out of place. Downplaying his ability in his previous duel had not coaxed anyone powerful into agreeing to a bout. Adolin had barely persuaded Elit.

Time for a different tactic.

Adolin passed where Sadeas, Aladar, and Ruthar watched. The core of the coalition against Father. By now, each of them had gone on plateau runs illicitly, getting to the plateau and stealing the gemheart before those assigned could arrive. Each time, they paid the fines Dalinar levied for their disobedience. Dalinar couldn't do anything more to them without risking open war.

But Adolin could punish them in other ways.

Elit stumbled back, wary, as Adolin swept in. The man tested forward, and Adolin slapped the Blade away, then brought in a backhand and clipped Elit's forearm. It, too, started to leak Stormlight.

The crowd murmured, conversations rising over the arena. Elit came in again, and Adolin slapped away his strikes, but did not counterattack.

Ideal form. Each step in place. The Thrill rose within him, but he shoved it down. He was disgusted by the highprinces and their squabbling, but today he would not show them that fury. Instead, he'd show them *perfection*.

"He's trying to wear you down, Elit!" Ruthar's voice from the stands nearby. In his younger years, he'd been something of a duelist himself, though nowhere near as good as Dalinar or Aladar. "Don't let him!"

Adolin smiled inside his helm as Elit nodded and dashed forward in Smokestance, thrusting with his Blade. A gamble. Most contests against Plate were won by breaking sections, but at times you could drive the point of your Blade through a joint between plates, cracking them and scoring a hit.

It was also a way to try to wound your opponent, more than just defeat him.

Adolin calmly stepped back and used the proper Windstance sweeps for parrying a thrust. Elit's weapon clanged away, and the crowd grumbled further. First, Adolin had given them a brutal show, which had annoyed them. Then, he'd given them a close fight, with plenty of excitement.

This time, he did something opposite of both, refusing the exciting clashes that were often so much a part of a duel.

He stepped to the side and swung to score a slight hit on Elit's helm. It leaked from a small crack. Not as much as it should, however.

Excellent.

Elit growled audibly from within his helm, then came in with another thrust. Right at Adolin's faceplate.

Trying to kill me, are you? Adolin thought, taking one hand from his Blade and raising it just under Elit's oncoming Blade, letting it slide between his thumb and forefinger.

Elit's Blade ground along Adolin's hand as he lifted upward and to the right. It was a move that you could never perform without Plate—you'd end with your hand sliced in half if you tried that on a regular sword, worse if you tried it on a Shardblade.

With Plate, he easily guided the thrust up past his head, then swept in with his other hand, slamming his Blade against Elit's side.

Some in the crowd cheered at the straight-on blow. Others booed, however. The classical strike there would have been to hit Elit's head, trying to shatter the helm.

Elit stumbled forward, knocked off balance by the missed thrust and subsequent blow. Adolin heaved against him with a shoulder, throwing him to the ground. Then, instead of pouncing, he stepped backward.

More booing.

Elit stood up, then took a step. He lurched slightly, then took another step. Adolin backed up and set his Blade with the point toward the ground, waiting. Overhead, the sky rumbled. It would probably rain later today—not a highstorm, thankfully. Just a mundane rainshower.

"Fight me!" Elit shouted from within his helm.

"I have." Adolin replied quietly. "And I've won."

Elit lurched forward. Adolin backed up. To the boos of the crowd, he waited until Elit locked up completely—his Plate out of Stormlight. The dozens of small cracks Adolin had put in the man's armor had finally added up.

Then, Adolin strolled forward, placed a hand against Elit's chest, and shoved him over. He crashed to the ground.

Adolin looked up at Brightlady Istow, highjudge.

"Judgment," the highjudge said with a sigh, "again goes to Adolin Kholin. The victor. Elit Ruthar forfeits his Plate."

The crowd didn't much like it. Adolin turned to face them, sweeping his Blade a few times before dismissing it to mist. He removed his helm and bowed to their boos. Behind, his armorers—whom he'd prepared for this—rushed out and pushed away those of Elit. They pulled off the Plate, which now belonged to Adolin.

He smiled, and when they were done, followed them into the staging room beneath the seats. Renarin waited by the door, wearing his own Plate, and Aunt Navani sat by the room's brazier.

Renarin peeked out at the dissatisfied crowds. "Stormfather. The first duel like this you did, you were done in under a minute, and they hated you. Today you were at it for the better part of an hour, and they seem to hate you more."

Adolin sat down with a sigh on one of the benches. "I won."

"You did," Navani said, stepping up, inspecting him as if for wounds. She was always worried when he dueled. "But weren't you supposed to do it with great fanfare?"

Renarin nodded. "That's what Father asked for."

"This will be remembered," Adolin said, accepting a cup of water from Peet, one of the bridgeman guards for the day. He nodded thankfully. "Fanfare is about making everyone pay attention. This will work."

He hoped. The next part was as important.

"Aunt," Adolin said as she started writing a prayer of thanks. "Have you given any thought to what I asked?"

Navani kept drawing.

"Shallan's work really does sound important," Adolin said. "I mean—"

A knock came at the door to the chamber.

So quickly? Adolin thought, rising. One of the bridgemen opened the door.

Shallan Davar burst in, wearing a violet dress, red hair flaring as she crossed the room. "That was incredible!"

"Shallan!" She wasn't the person he'd been expecting—but he wasn't unhappy to see her. "I checked your seat before the fight and you weren't there."

"I forgot to burn a prayer," she said, "so I stopped to do so. I caught most of the fight, though." She hesitated right before him, seeming awkward for a moment. Adolin shared that awkwardness. They had only been officially courting for little more than a week, but with the causal in place . . . what *was* their relationship?

Navani cleared her throat. Shallan spun and raised her freehand to her lips, as if having only just noticed the former queen. "Brightness," she said, and bowed.

"Shallan," Navani said. "I hear only good things from my nephew regarding you."

"Thank you."

"I will leave you two, then," Navani said, walking toward the door, her glyphward unfinished.

"Brightness . . ." Shallan said, raising a hand toward her.

Navani left and pulled the door closed.

Shallan lowered her hand, and Adolin winced. "Sorry," Adolin said. "I've been trying to talk to her about it. I think she needs a few more days, Shallan. She'll come around—she knows that she shouldn't be ignoring you, I can sense it. You just remind her of what happened."

Shallan nodded, looking disappointed. Adolin's armorers came over to help him remove his Plate, but he waved them away. It was bad enough to show her his sloppy hair, plastered to his head from being in the helm. His clothing underneath—a padded uniform—would look awful.

"So, uh, you liked the duel?" he asked.

"You were *wonderful*," Shallan said, turning back to him. "Elit kept jumping at you, and you just brushed him off like an annoying cremling trying to crawl up your leg."

Adolin grinned. "The rest of the crowd didn't think it was wonderful."

"They came to see you get stomped," she said. "You were so inconsiderate for not giving that to them."

"I'm quite stingy in that regard," Adolin said.

"You almost never lose, from what I've discovered. Awfully boring of you. Maybe you should try for a tie now and then. For variety."

"I'll consider it," he said. "We can discuss it, perhaps over dinner this evening? At my father's warcamp?"

Shallan grimaced. "I'm busy this evening. Sorry."

"Oh."

"But," she said, stepping closer. "I might have a gift for you soon. I haven't had much time to study—I've been working hard to reconstruct Sebarial's house ledgers—but I might have stumbled upon something that can help you. With your duels."

"What?" he asked, frowning.

"I remembered something from King Gavilar's biography. It would require you to win a duel in a spectacular way, though. Something amazing, something that would awe the crowd."

"Fewer boos, then," Adolin said, scratching at his head.

"I think everyone would appreciate that," Renarin noted from beside the door.

"Spectacular . . ." Adolin said.

"I'll explain more tomorrow," Shallan said.

"What happens tomorrow?"

"You're feeding me dinner."

"I am?"

"And taking me on a walk," she said.

"I am?"

"Yes."

"I'm a lucky man." He smiled at her. "All right, then, we can—"

The door slammed open.

Adolin's bridgeman guards jumped, and Renarin cursed, standing up. Adolin just turned, gently moving Shallan to the side so he could see who was standing beyond. Relis, current dueling champion and Highprince Ruthar's eldest son.

As expected.

"What," Relis demanded, stalking into the room, "was *that*?" He was followed by a small gaggle of other lighteyes, including Brightlady Istow, the highjudge. "You insult me and my house, Kholin."

Adolin clasped his gauntleted hands behind his back as Relis stalked right up to him, shoving his face into Adolin's.

"You didn't like the duel?" Adolin asked casually.

"That was *not* a duel," Relis snapped. "You embarrassed my cousin by refusing to fight properly. I *demand* that this farce be invalidated."

"I've told you, Prince Relis," Istow said from behind. "Prince Adolin didn't break any—"

"You want your cousin's Plate back?" Adolin asked quietly, meeting Relis's eyes. "Fight me for it."

"I won't be goaded by you," Relis said, tapping the center of Adolin's breastplate. "I won't let you pull me into another of your dueling farces."

"Six Shards, Relis," Adolin said. "Mine, those of my brother, Eranniv's Plate, and your cousin's Plate. I wager them all on a single bout. You and me."

"You are a dunnard if you think I'll agree to that," Relis snapped.

"Too afraid?" Adolin asked.

"You're beneath me, Kholin. These last two fights prove it. You don't even know how to duel anymore—all you know are tricks."

"Then you should be able to beat me easily."

Relis wavered, shifting from one foot to the other. Finally, he pointed at Adolin again. "You're a bastard, Kholin. I know you fought my cousin to embarrass my father and myself. I refuse to be goaded." He turned to leave.

Something spectacular, Adolin thought, glancing at Shallan. *Father asked for fanfare. . . .*

"If you're afraid," Adolin said, looking back to Relis, "you don't have to duel me alone."

Relis stopped in place. He looked back. "Are you saying you'll take me on with anyone else at the *same time*?"

"I am," Adolin said. "I'll fight you and whomever you bring, together."

"You *are* a fool," Relis breathed.

"Yes or no?"

"Two days," Relis snapped. "Here in the arena." He looked to the highjudge. "You witness this?"

"I do," she said.

Relis stormed out. The others trailed after. The highjudge lingered, regarding Adolin. "You realize what you have done."

"I know the dueling conventions quite well. Yes. I'm aware."

She sighed, but nodded, walking out.

Peet closed the door, then looked at Adolin, raising an eyebrow. Great. Now he was getting attitude from the bridgemen. Adolin sank back down on the bench. "Will that do for spectacular?" he asked Shallan.

"You really think you can beat two at once?" she asked.

Adolin didn't reply. Fighting two men at once was hard, particularly if they were both Shardbearers. They could gang up on you, flank you, blindside you. It was far harder than fighting two in a row.

"I don't know," he said. "But you wanted spectacular. So I'll try for spectacular. Now, I hope you *actually* have a plan."

Shallan sat down next to him. "What do you know of Highprince Yenev . . . ?"

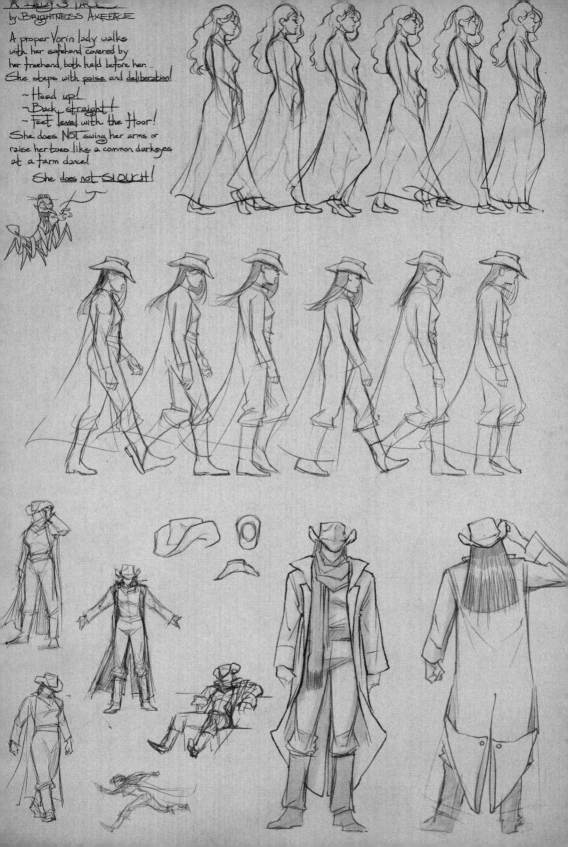

A LADY'S GAIT
by BRIGHTNESS AXEFACE

A proper Vorin lady walks
with her safehand covered by
her freehand, both held before her.
She steps with poise and deliberation!

~ Head up!
~ Back straight!
~ Feet level with the floor!
She does NOT swing her arms or
raise her toes like a common darkeyes
at a farm dance!

She does not SLOUCH!

54

VEIL'S LESSON

There came also sixteen of the order of Windrunners, and with them a considerable number of squires, and finding in that place the Skybreakers dividing the innocent from the guilty, there ensued a great debate.

—From *Words of Radiance,* chapter 28, page 3

Shallan stepped from the carriage into a light rainfall. She wore the white coat and trousers of the darkeyed version of herself that she'd named Veil. Rain sprinkled on the brim of her hat. She'd spent too long talking with Adolin after his duel, and had needed to rush to make it to this appointment, which was happening in the Unclaimed Hills a good hour's ride out of the warcamps.

But she was here, in costume, on time. Barely. She strode forward, listening to the rain patter on stone around her. She had always liked rainfalls like these. The younger sisters of highstorms, they brought life without the fury. Even the desolate stormlands here west of the warcamps bloomed with the advent of water. Rockbuds split, and though these didn't have blossoms like the ones back home, they did put out vibrant green vines. Grass rose thirstily from holes and refused to retreat until it was practically stepped on. Some reeds produced flowers to entice cremlings, which would feast upon the petals and in so doing rub themselves with spores that would give rise to the next generation, once mixed with the spores of other plants.

If she'd been at home, there would be far more vines—so many that it would be hard to walk without tripping. Going out in a wooded area would require a machete to move more than a couple of feet. Here, the vegetation became colorful, but not an impediment.

Shallan smiled at the wonderful surroundings, the light rainfall, the beautiful plant life. A little dampness was a small price to pay for the melodious sound of sprinkling rain, for fresh clean air and a beautiful sky full of clouds that varied in every shade of grey.

Shallan walked with a waterproof satchel under her arm, the hired carriage driver—she couldn't use Sebarial's coach for today's activity—awaiting her return as she'd instructed. This coach was pulled by parshmen instead of horses, but they were faster than chulls and had worked well enough.

She hiked toward a hillside ahead of her, the destination indicated on the map she'd received via spanreed. She wore a nice pair of sturdy boots. This clothing of Tyn's might be unusual, but Shallan was glad for it. The coat and hat kept off the rain, and the boots gave her sure footing on the slick rock.

She rounded the hill and found that it was broken on the other side, the rock having cracked and fallen in a small avalanche. The strata of hardened crem were clearly visible on the edges of the chunks of rock, which meant this was a newer fracture. If it had been old, new crem would have obscured that coloring.

The crack made a small valley in the hillside—full of clefts and ridges from the crumbled rock. These had caught spores and windborne stems, and that in turn had created an explosion of life. Wherever sheltered from the wind, plants would find purchase and start to grow.

The snarl of green grew haphazardly—this was not a true lait, where life would be safe over time, but instead a temporary shelter, good for a few years at most. For now, plants grew eagerly, sometimes atop one another, sprouting, blossoming, shaking, twisting, alive. It was an example of raw nature.

The pavilion, however, was not.

It covered four people who sat in chairs too fine for the surroundings. Snacking, they were warmed by a brazier at the center of the open-sided tent. Shallan approached, taking Memories of the people's faces. She'd draw those later, as she had done with the first group of the Ghostbloods she'd met. Two of them were the same as last time. Two were not. The discomforting woman with the mask did not seem to be present.

Mraize, standing tall and proud, inspected his long blowgun. He did not look up as Shallan stepped under the awning.

"I like to learn to use the local weapons," Mraize said. "It is a quirk, though I feel it is justified. If you want to understand a people, learn their weapons. The way men kill one another says far more about a culture than any scholar's ethnography."

He raised his weapon toward Shallan, and she froze in place. Then he turned toward the crack and puffed, blowing a dart into the foliage.

Shallan stepped up beside him. The dart pinned a cremling to one of the plant stems. The small, many-legged creature spasmed and thrashed, trying to get free, though surely having a dart sticking through it would prove lethal.

"This is a Parshendi blowgun," Mraize noted. "What does it say about them, do you suppose, little knife?"

"It's obviously not for killing big game," Shallan said. "Which makes sense. The only big game I know of in the area are the chasmfiends, which the Parshendi are said to have worshipped as gods."

She wasn't convinced that they actually did. Early reports—which she'd read in detail at Jasnah's insistence—made the *assumption* that the Parshendi gods were the chasmfiends. It wasn't actually clear.

"They probably used it for stalking small game," Shallan continued. "Which means they hunted for food, rather than pleasure."

"Why do you say this?" Mraize asked.

"Men who glory in the hunt seek grand captures," Shallan said. "Trophies. That blowgun is the weapon of a man who simply wants to feed his family."

"And if he used it against other men?"

"It wouldn't be useful in war," Shallan said. "Too short a range, I'd guess, and the Parshendi have bows anyway. Maybe this could be used in assassination, though I'd be very curious to discover if it was."

"And why is that?" Mraize asked.

A test of some sort. "Well," Shallan said, "most indigenous populations—the Silnasen natives, the Reshi peoples, the runners of the Iri plains—have no real concept of assassination. From what I know, they don't seem to have much use for battle at all. Hunters are too valuable, and so a 'war' in these cultures will involve a lot of shouting and posturing, but few deaths. That kind of boastful society doesn't seem the type to have assassins."

And yet the Parshendi had sent one. Against the Alethi.

Mraize was studying her—watching her with unreadable eyes, long blowgun held lightly in his fingertips. "I see," he finally said, "Tyn chose a *scholar* to be her apprentice this time around? I find that unusual."

Shallan blushed. It occurred to her that this person she became when she put on the hat and dark hair was not an imitation of someone else, not a different person. It was just a version of Shallan herself.

That could be dangerous.

"So," Mraize said, fishing another dart from his shirt pocket, "what excuse did Tyn give you today?"

"Excuse?" Shallan asked.

"For failing in her mission." Mraize loaded the dart.

Failing? Shallan began to sweat, cold prickles on her forehead. But she'd watched to see if anything out of the ordinary happened at Amaram's camp! This morning, she'd gone back—the real reason she'd been late to Adolin's duel—while wearing the face of a worker. She'd listened to see if anyone spoke of a break-in, or of Amaram being suspicious. She'd found nothing.

Well, obviously Amaram had not made his suspicions public. After all the work she'd done to cover up her incursion, she had failed. She probably shouldn't be surprised, but she was anyway.

"I—" Shallan began.

"I'm beginning to wonder if Tyn really is sick," Mraize said, raising the blowgun and shooting another dart into the foliage. "To not even try to carry out the assigned task."

"Not even try?" Shallan asked, baffled.

"Oh, is that the excuse?" Mraize asked. "That she made an attempt, and failed? I have people watching that house. If she had . . ."

He trailed off as Shallan shook the water from her satchel, then carefully undid it and lifted out a sheet of paper. It was a representation of Amaram's locked room with its maps on the walls. She'd had to guess at some of the details—it had been dark, and her single sphere hadn't illuminated much—but she figured it was close enough.

Mraize took the picture from her and raised it. He studied it, leaving Shallan to sweat nervously.

"It is rare," Mraize said, "that I am proven a fool. Congratulations."

Was that a good thing?

"Tyn doesn't have this skill," Mraize continued, still inspecting the sheet. "You saw this room yourself?"

"There is a reason that she chose a scholar as her assistant. My skills are meant to complement her own."

Mraize lowered the sheet. "Surprising. Your mistress might be a brilliant thief, but her choice of associates has always been unenlightened." He had such a refined way of speaking. It didn't seem to match his scarred face, misaligned lip, and weathered hands. He talked like a man who had spent his days sipping wine and listening to fine music, but he looked like someone who had repeatedly had his bones broken—and likely returned the favor many times over.

"Pity there is not more detail to these maps," Mraize noted, inspecting the picture again.

Shallan obligingly got out the other five pictures she'd drawn for him. Four were the maps on the walls in detail, the other a closer depiction of the wall scrolls with Amaram's script. In each one, the actual writing was indecipherable, just wiggled lines. Shallan had done this on purpose. Nobody would expect an artist to be able to capture such detail from memory, even though she could.

She would keep the details of the script from them. She intended to gain their trust, to learn what she could, but she would *not* help them more than she had to.

Mraize passed his blowgun to the side. The short, masked girl was there, holding the cremling that Mraize had speared along with a dead mink, a blowgun dart in its neck. No, its leg twitched. It was merely stunned. Some poison on the dart, then?

Shallan shivered. Where had this woman been hiding? Those dark eyes stared at Shallan, unblinking, the rest of the face hidden behind the mask of paint and shell. She took the blowgun.

"Amazing," Mraize said of Shallan's pictures. "How *did* you get in? We watched the windows."

Was that how Tyn would have done it, sneaking in during the dead of night through one of the windows? She hadn't trained Shallan in that sort of thing, only accents and imitation. Perhaps she had spotted that Shallan, who sometimes stumbled over her own feet, would not be best at acrobatic larceny.

"These are masterful," Mraize said, walking to a table and setting out the pictures. "A triumph, certainly. Such artistry."

What had happened to the dangerous, emotionless man who had confronted her at her first meeting with the Ghostbloods? Animated with emotion, he leaned down, studying the pictures one at a time. He even got out a magnifying glass in order to inspect the details.

She did not ask what she wondered. What is Amaram doing? Do you know how he got his Shardblade? How he . . . killed Helaran Davar? Her breath caught in her throat even still as she thought about it, but a part of her had admitted years ago that her brother wasn't coming back.

That didn't stop her from feeling a distinct, and surprising, hatred for the man Meridas Amaram.

"Well?" Mraize asked, glancing at her. "Come sit down, child. You did this yourself?"

"I did," Shallan said, shoving down her emotions. Had Mraize just called her "child"? She'd intentionally made this version of her look older, with a more angular face. What did she need to do? Start adding grey hairs to her head?

She settled into the seat beside the table. The woman with the mask appeared beside her, holding a cup and a kettle of something steaming. Shallan nodded hesitantly, and was rewarded with a cup of mulled orange wine. She sipped it—she probably didn't need to worry about poison, as these people could have killed her at any time. The others under the pavilion spoke with one another in hushed voices, but Shallan couldn't make out any of it. She felt like she was on display before an audience.

"I copied some of the text for you," Shallan said, fishing out one page of script. These were lines she had specifically chosen to show them—they didn't reveal too much, but might act as a primer to get Mraize talking about the topic. "We didn't have much time in the room, so I only got a few lines."

"You spent so long in there drawing the pictures, and so little recording the text?" Mraize asked.

"Oh," Shallan said. "No, I did those pictures from memory."

He looked up at her, jaw lowered a fraction, an expression of genuine surprise crossing his face before he quickly restored his usual confident equanimity.

That . . . probably wasn't wise to admit, Shallan realized. How many people could draw so well from memory? Had Shallan publicly demonstrated her skill in the warcamps?

So far as she knew, she hadn't. Now she would have to keep that aspect of her skill secret, lest the Ghostbloods make a connection between Shallan the lighteyed lady and Veil the darkeyed con artist. Storms.

Well, she was bound to make some mistakes. At least this one wasn't life threatening. Probably.

"Jin," Mraize snapped.

A golden-haired man with a bare chest beneath a flowing outer robe stood up from one of the chairs.

"Look at him," Mraize said to Shallan.

She took a Memory.

"Jin, leave us. You will draw him, Veil."

She had no choice but to oblige. As Jin walked off, grumbling to himself at the rain, Shallan started sketching. She did a full sketch—not just his face and shoulders, but an environment study, including the background of fallen boulders. Nervous, she didn't do as good a job as she could have, but Mraize still cooed over her picture like a proud father. She finished and got out her lacquer—this was in charcoal, and would want it—but Mraize plucked it from her fingers first.

"Incredible," he said, holding the sheet up. "You are wasted with Tyn. You can't do this with text, however?"

"No," Shallan lied.

"Pity. Still, this is marvelous. *Marvelous.* There should be ways to use this, yes indeed." He looked to her. "What is your goal, child? I might have a place for you in my organization, if you prove reliable."

Yes! "I wouldn't have agreed to come in Tyn's place if I hadn't wanted that opportunity."

Mraize narrowed his eyes at Shallan. "You killed her, didn't you?"

Oh, blast. Shallan blushed immediately, of course. "Uh . . ."

"Ha!" Mraize exclaimed. "She finally picked an assistant who was too capable. Delightful. After all of her arrogant posturing, she was brought down by someone she thought to make into a sycophant."

"Sir," Shallan said. "I didn't . . . I mean, I didn't want to. She turned on me."

"That must be quite the story," Mraize said, smiling. It was not a pleasant smile. "Know that what you have done is not forbidden, but it is hardly encouraged. We cannot run an organization properly if subordinates consider hunting their superiors to be a primary method of advancement."

"Yes, sir."

"*Your* superior, however, was not a member of our organization. Tyn thought herself to be the hunter, but she was game all along. If you are to join us, you should understand. We are not like others you may have known. We have a greater purpose, and we are . . . protective of one another."

"Yes, sir."

"So who are you?" he asked, waving for his servant to bring back the blowgun. "Who are you *really*, Veil?"

"Someone who wants to be part of things," Shallan said. "Things more important than stealing from the odd lighteyes or scamming for a weekend of luxury."

"So it is a hunt, then," Mraize said softly, grinning. He turned away from her, walking back to the edge of the pavilion. "More instructions will follow. Do the task assigned to you. Then we shall see."

It is a hunt, then. . . .

What kind of hunt? Shallan felt chilled by that statement.

Once again, her dismissal was uncertain, but she did up her satchel and started to leave. As she did so, she glanced at the remaining seated people. Their expressions were cold. Frighteningly so.

Shallan left the pavilion and found that the rain had stopped. She walked away, feeling eyes on her back. *They all know that I can identify them with exactness,* she realized, *and can present accurate pictures of them for any who request.*

They would not like that. Mraize had made it clear that Ghostbloods didn't often kill one another. But he'd *also* made it clear that she wasn't one of them, not yet. He'd said it pointedly, as if granting permission to those listening in.

Talat's hand, what had she gotten herself into?

You're only considering that now? she thought as she rounded the hillside. Her carriage was ahead, the coachman lounging on top, his back to her. Shallan looked anxiously over her shoulder. Nobody had followed yet, at least not that she could see.

"Is anyone watching, Pattern?" she asked.

"Mmm. Me. No people."

A rock. She'd drawn a boulder in the picture for Mraize. Not thinking—working by instinct and no small amount of panic—she breathed out Stormlight and shaped an image of that boulder before her.

Then, she promptly hid inside of it.

It was dark in there. She curled up in the boulder, sitting with her legs pulled against her. It felt undignified. The other people Mraize worked with probably didn't do silly things like this. They were practiced, smooth, capable. Storms, she probably didn't need to be hiding in the first place.

She sat there anyway. The looks in the eyes of the others . . . the way that Mraize had spoken . . .

Better to be overly cautious than naive. She was tired of people assuming she couldn't care for herself.

"Pattern," she whispered. "Go to the carriage driver. Tell him this, in my exact voice. 'I have entered the carriage when you weren't looking. Do not look. My exit must be stealthy. Carry me back to the city. Pull up to the warcamps and wait to a count of ten. I will leave. Do not look. You have your payment, and discretion was part of it.'"

Pattern hummed and moved off. A short time later, the carriage rattled away, pulled by its parshmen. It didn't take long for hoofbeats to follow. She hadn't seen horses.

Shallan waited, anxious. Would any of the Ghostbloods realize this boulder wasn't supposed to be here? Would they come back, looking for her once they didn't see her leave the carriage at the warcamps?

Perhaps they hadn't even gone after her. Perhaps she was being paranoid. She waited, pained. It started raining again. What would that do to her illusion? The stone she'd drawn had already been wet, so dryness wouldn't give it away—but from the way the rain fell on her, it obviously was passing through the image.

I need to find a way to see the outside while I'm hiding like this, she thought. Eyeholes? Could she make those inside her illusion? Perhaps she—

Voices.

"We will need to find how much he knows." Mraize's voice. "You will bring these pages to Master Thaidakar. We are close, but so—it appears—are Restares's cronies."

The response came in a rasping voice. Shallan couldn't make it out.

"No, I'm not worried about that one. The old fool sows chaos, but does not reach for the power offered by opportunity. He hides in his insignificant city, listening to its songs, thinking he plays in world events. He has no idea. His is not the position of the hunter. This creature in Tukar, however, is different. I'm not convinced he is human. If he is, he's certainly not of the local species. . . ."

Mraize continued speaking, but Shallan heard no more as they moved off. A short time later, she heard more hoofbeats.

She waited, water soaking though her coat and trousers. She shivered, satchel in her lap, and clenched her teeth to keep them from chattering. Weather lately had been warmer, but sitting in the rain belied that. She waited until her spine complained and her muscles screamed at her. She waited until finally, the boulder broke into luminescent smoke and faded away.

Shallan started. What had happened?

Stormlight, she realized, stretching her legs. She checked the pouch in her pocket. She'd drained every sphere, unconsciously, while holding up the illusion of the boulder.

Hours had passed, the sky darkening as evening approached. Maintaining something simple like the boulder didn't take much Light, and she didn't have to consciously think about it to keep it going. That was good to know.

She'd also proven herself a fool again for not even worrying about how much Light she had been using. Sighing, she climbed to her feet. She wobbled, her legs protesting the sudden motion. She took a deep breath, then walked over and peeked around the corner. The pavilion was gone and all signs of the Ghostbloods with it.

"I guess this means I'm walking," Shallan said, turning back toward the warcamps.

"Did you expect otherwise?" Pattern asked from his place on her coat, sounding genuinely curious.

"No," Shallan said. "I'm just talking to myself."

"Mmm. No, you talk to me."

She walked on into the evening, cold. However, it wasn't the deadly coldness she'd suffered in the south. This was uncomfortable, but nothing more. If she hadn't been wet, the air probably would have been pleasant, despite the shade. She passed the time practicing her accents with Pattern—she'd speak, then have him repeat back to her exactly what she'd said, in her voice and tone. Being able to hear it that way helped a great deal.

She had the Alethi accent down, she was certain. That was good, since Veil pretended to be Alethi. That one was easy, however, as Veden and

Alethi were so similar you could almost understand one by knowing the other.

Her Horneater accent was quite good too, in both Alethi and Veden. She was getting better and not overdoing it, as Tyn had suggested. Her Bav accent in both Veden and Alethi was passable, and through most of the time walking back, she practiced speaking both tongues with a Herdazian accent. Palona gave her a good example of this in Alethi, and Pattern could repeat to her things the woman had said, which was helpful for practice.

"What I need to do," Shallan said, "is train you to speak along with my images."

"You should have them speak themselves," Pattern said.

"Can I *do* that?"

"Why not?"

"Because . . . well, I use Light for the illusion, and so they create an imitation of light. Makes sense. I don't use sound to make them, though."

"This is a Surge," Pattern said. "Sound is a part of it. Mmm . . . Cousins of one another. Very similar. It can be done."

"How?"

"Mmmm. Somehow."

"You're very helpful."

"I am glad . . ." He trailed off. "Lie?"

"Yup." Shallan stuffed her safehand into her pocket, which was also wet, and continued walking through patches of grass that pulled away in front of her. Distant hills showed lavis grain growing in orderly fields of polyps, though she didn't see any farmers at this hour.

At least it had stopped raining. She *did* still like rain, though she hadn't considered how unpleasant it might be to have to walk a long distance in it. And—

What was that?

She pulled up short. A clump of something dark shadowed the ground ahead of her. She approached hesitantly, and found that she could smell smoke. The sodden, wet kind of smoke you smelled after a campfire was doused.

Her carriage. She could make it out now, partially burned in the night. The rains had put out the fire; it hadn't burned long. They'd probably started the blaze on the inside, where it would have been dry.

It was certainly the one she'd hired. She recognized the trim on the wheels. She approached hesitantly. Well, she'd been right in her worry. It was a good thing she'd stayed behind. Something nagged at her. . . .

The coachman!

She ran ahead, fearing the worst. His corpse was there, lying beside the broken carriage, staring up at the sky. His throat had been slit. Beside him, his parshman porters lay dead in a pile.

Shallan sat back on the wet stones, feeling sick, hand to her mouth. "Oh . . . Almighty above . . ."

"Mmm . . ." Pattern hummed, somehow conveying a morose tone.

"They're dead because of me," Shallan whispered.

"You did not kill them."

"I did," Shallan said. "As sure as if I'd held the knife. I knew the danger I was going into. The coachman didn't."

And the parshmen. How did she feel about that? Voidbringers, yes, but it was difficult not to feel sick at what had been done.

You'll cause something far worse than this if you prove what Jasnah claims, part of her said.

Briefly, while watching Mraize's excitement over her art, she'd wanted to like the man. Well, she'd best remember *this* moment. He'd allowed these murders. He might not have been the one to slit the coachman's throat, but he'd all but assured the others it was all right to remove her if they could.

They'd burned the carriage to make it look like bandits had been behind this, but no bandits would come this close to the Shattered Plains.

You poor man, she thought toward the coachman. But if she hadn't arranged a ride, she wouldn't have been able to hide as she did while the coach laid a false trail. Storms! How could she have handled this so nobody died? Would it have been possible?

She eventually forced herself to her feet and, with slumped shoulders, continued to walk back toward the warcamps.

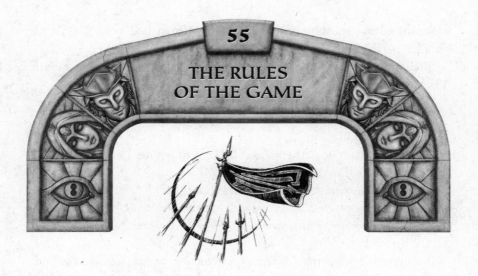

The considerable abilities of the Skybreakers for making such
amounted to an almost divine skill, for which no specific Surge or
spren grants capacity, but however the order came to such an apti-
tude, the fact of it was real and acknowledged even by their rivals.

—From *Words of Radiance*, chapter 28, page 3

"Great. You're the one guarding me today?"

Kaladin turned as Adolin came out of his room. The prince
wore a sharp uniform, as always. Monogrammed buttons, boots
that cost more than some houses, side sword. An odd choice for a Shardbearer, but Adolin probably wore it as an ornament. His hair was a mess of
blond sprinkled with black.

"I don't trust her, princeling," Kaladin said. "Foreign woman, secret betrothal, and the only person who could vouch for her is dead. She could be
an assassin, and that means putting you under the watch of the best I
have."

"Humble, aren't we?" Adolin said, striding down the stone hallway, Kaladin falling into step beside him.

"No."

"That was a joke, bridgeboy."

"My mistake. I was under the impression that jokes were supposed to be
funny."

"Only to people with a sense of humor."

"Ah, of course," Kaladin said. "I traded in my sense of humor long ago."

"And what did you get for it?"

"Scars," Kaladin said softly.

Adolin's eyes flicked toward the brands on Kaladin's forehead, though most would be obscured by hair. "This is great," Adolin said under his breath. "Just great. I'm so *happy* you're coming along."

At the end of the hallway, they stepped into daylight. Not much of it, though. The sky was still overcast from the rains of the last few days.

They emerged into the warcamp. "We collecting any other guards?" Adolin asked. "Usually there's two of you."

"Just me today." Kaladin was short-manned, with the king under his watch and with Teft taking the new recruits out patrolling again. He had two or three men on everyone else, but Adolin he figured he could watch on his own.

A carriage waited, pulled by two mean-looking horses. All horses looked mean, with those too-knowing eyes and sudden movements. Unfortunately, a prince couldn't arrive in a carriage pulled by chulls. A footman opened the door for Adolin, who settled into the confines. The footman closed the door, then climbed into a place at the back of the carriage. Kaladin prepared to swing up into the seat beside the carriage driver, then stopped.

"You!" he said, pointing at the driver.

"Me!" the King's Wit replied from where he sat holding the reins. Blue eyes, black hair, black uniform. What was he doing driving the carriage? He wasn't a servant, was he?

Kaladin clambered cautiously up into his seat, and Wit shook the reins, prodding the horses into motion.

"What are you doing here?" Kaladin asked him.

"Trying to find mischief," Wit replied cheerfully, as the horses' hooves rang against the stone. "Have you been practicing with my flute?"

"Uh . . ."

"Don't tell me you left it in Sadeas's camp when you moved out."

"Well—"

"I said *not* to tell me," Wit replied. "You don't need to, since I already know. A shame. If you knew the history of that flute, it would make your brain flip upside-down. And by that, I mean that I would shove you off the carriage for having spied on me."

"Uh . . ."

"Eloquent today, I see."

Kaladin *had* left the flute behind. When he had gathered the bridgemen left in Sadeas's camp—the wounded from Bridge Four, and the members of the other bridge crews—he'd been focused on people, not things. He hadn't bothered with his little bundle of possessions, forgetting that the flute was among them.

"I'm a soldier, not a musician," Kaladin said. "Besides, music is for women."

"All people are musicians," Wit countered. "The question is whether or not they share their songs. As for music being feminine, it's interesting that the woman who wrote that treatise—the one you all practically *worship* in Alethkar—decided that all of the feminine tasks involve sitting around having fun while all the masculine ones involve finding someone to stick a spear in you. Telling, eh?"

"I guess so."

"You know, I'm working very hard to come up with engaging, clever, meaningful points of interest to offer you. I can't help thinking you're not upholding your side of the conversation. It's a little like playing music for a deaf man. Which I might try doing, as it sounds fun, if only someone hadn't *lost my flute*."

"I'm sorry," Kaladin said. He'd rather be thinking about the new sword stances that Zahel had taught him, but Wit *had* shown him kindness before. The least Kaladin could do was chat with him. "So, uh, did you keep your job? As King's Wit, I mean. When we met before, you implied you were in danger of losing your title."

"I haven't checked yet," Wit said.

"You . . . you haven't . . . Does the king know you're back?"

"Nope! I'm trying to think of a properly dramatic way to inform him. Perhaps a hundred chasmfiends marching in unison, singing an ode to my magnificence."

"That sounds . . . hard."

"Yeah, the storming things have real trouble tuning their tonic chords and maintaining just intonation."

"I have no idea what you just said."

"Yeah, the storming things have real trouble tuning their tonic chords and maintaining just intonation."

"That didn't help, Wit."

"Ah! So you're going deaf, are you? Let me know when the process is complete. I have something I want to try. If I can just remember—"

"Yes, yes," Kaladin said, sighing. "You want to play the flute for one."

"No, that's not it . . . Ah! Yes. I've always wanted to sneak up and poke a deaf man in the back of the head. I think it will be *hilarious*."

Kaladin sighed. It would take an hour or so, even moving quickly, to reach Sebarial's warcamp. A very *long* hour.

"So you're just here," Kaladin said, "to mock me?"

"Well, it's kind of what I *do*. But I'll go easy on you. I wouldn't want you to go flying off on me."

Kaladin jolted with a start.

"You know," Wit said, nonchalant, "flying off in an angry tirade. That kind of thing."

Kaladin narrowed his eyes at the tall lighteyed man. "What do you know?"

"Almost everything. That *almost* part can be a real kick in the teeth sometimes."

"What do you want, then?"

"What I can't have." Wit turned to him, eyes solemn. "Same as everyone else, Kaladin Stormblessed."

Kaladin fidgeted. Wit knew about him and about Surgebinding. Kaladin was sure of it. So, should he expect some kind of demand?

"What do you want," Kaladin said, trying to speak more precisely, "from *me*?"

"Ah, so you're thinking. Good. From you, my friend, I want one thing. A story."

"What kind of story?"

"That is for you to decide." Wit smiled at him. "I hope it will be dynamic. If there is one thing I cannot stomach, it is boredom. Kindly avoid being dull. Otherwise I might have to sneak up and poke you in the back of the head."

"I'm *not* going deaf."

"It's also hilarious on people who aren't deaf, obviously. What, you think I'd torment someone just because they were deaf? That would be immoral. No, I torment all people equally, thank you very much."

"Great." Kaladin settled back, waiting for more. Amazingly, Wit seemed content to let the conversation die.

Kaladin watched the sky, so dull. He hated days like these, which reminded him of the Weeping. Stormfather. Grey skies and miserable weather made him wonder why he'd even bothered to get out of bed. Eventually, the carriage reached Sebarial's warcamp, a place that looked even more like a city than the other warcamps. Kaladin marveled at the fully constructed tenements, the markets, the—

"Farmers?" he asked as they rolled past a group of men hiking toward the gates, carrying worming reeds and buckets of crem.

"Sebarial has them setting up lavis fields on the southwestern hills," Wit explained.

"The highstorms out here are too powerful for farming."

"Tell that to the Natan people. They used to farm this entire area. Requires a strain of plant that doesn't grow as large as you're accustomed to."

"But why?" Kaladin asked. "Why wouldn't farmers go someplace where it's easier? Like Alethkar proper."

"You don't know a lot about human nature, do you, Stormblessed?"

"I . . . No, I don't."

Wit shook his head. "So frank, so blunt. You and Dalinar are alike, certainly. Someone needs to teach the pair of you how to have a good time now and then."

"I know full well how to have a good time."

"Is that so?"

"Yes. It involves being anywhere *you* aren't."

Wit stared at him, then chuckled, shaking the reins so the horses danced a little. "So you *do* have some spark of wit in you."

It came from Kaladin's mother. She'd often said things like that, though never so insulting. *Being around Wit must be corrupting me.*

Eventually, Wit pulled the carriage up to a nice manor home, the likes of which Kaladin would have expected in some fine lait, not here in a warcamp. With those pillars and beautiful glass windows, it was even finer than the citylord's manor back in Hearthstone.

In the carriageway, Wit asked the footman to fetch Adolin's causal betrothed. Adolin climbed out to await her, straightening his jacket, polishing the buttons on one sleeve. He glanced up toward the driver's seat, then started.

"You!" Adolin exclaimed.

"Me!" Wit replied. He swung down from the top of the carriage and performed a flowery bow. "Ever at your service, Brightlord Kholin."

"What did you do with my usual carriage driver?"

"Nothing."

"Wit—"

"What, you're implying that I *hurt* the poor fellow? Does that sound like me, Adolin?"

"Well, no," Adolin said.

"Exactly. Besides, I'm certain he's gotten the ropes undone by now. Ah, and here's your lovely almost-but-not-quite bride."

Shallan Davar had emerged from the house. She bobbed down the steps, not gliding down them as most lighteyed ladies would have. *She's certainly an enthusiastic one,* Kaladin thought idly, holding the reins, which he'd picked up after Wit had dropped them.

Something just felt *off* about this Shallan Davar. What was she hiding behind that eager attitude and ready smile? That buttoned sleeve on the safehand of a lighteyed woman's dress, that could hide any number of deadly implements. A simple poisoned needle, stuck through the fabric, would be enough to end Adolin's life.

Unfortunately, he couldn't watch her every moment she was with Adolin. He had to show more initiative than that; could he instead confirm that she was who she said she was? Decide from her past if she was a threat or not?

Kaladin stood up, planning to jump down onto the ground to keep an eye on her as she approached Adolin. She suddenly started, eyes widening. She pointed at Wit with her freehand.

"You!" Shallan exclaimed.

"Yes, yes. People certainly are good at identifying me today. Perhaps I need to wear—"

Wit cut off as Shallan lunged at him. Kaladin dropped to the ground, reaching for his side knife, then hesitated as Shallan grabbed Wit in an embrace, her head against his chest, her eyes squeezed shut.

Kaladin took his hand off his knife, raising an eyebrow at Wit, who looked completely flabbergasted. He stood with his arms at his sides, as if he didn't know what to do with them.

"I always wanted to say thank you," Shallan whispered. "I never had a chance."

Adolin cleared his throat. Finally, Shallan released Wit and looked at the prince.

"You hugged Wit," Adolin said.

"Is that his name?" Shallan asked.

"One of them," Wit said, apparently still unsettled. "There are too many to count, really. Granted, most of them are related to one form of curse or another. . . ."

"You hugged *Wit*," Adolin said.

Shallan blushed. "Was that improper?"

"It's not about propriety," Adolin said. "It's about common sense. Hugging him is like hugging a whitespine or, or a pile of nails or something. I mean it's Wit. You're not supposed to *like* him."

"We need to talk," Shallan said, looking up at Wit. "I don't remember everything we talked about, but some of it—"

"I'll try to squeeze it into my schedule," Wit said. "I'm fairly busy, though. I mean, insulting Adolin alone is going to take until sometime next week."

Adolin shook his head, waving away the footman and helping Shallan into the carriage himself. After he did so, he leaned in to Wit. "Hands off."

"She's *far* too young for me, child," Wit said.

"That's right," Adolin said with a nod. "Stick to women your own age."

Wit grinned. "Well, that might be a little harder. I think there's only one of those around these parts, and she and I never did get along."

"You are so bizarre," Adolin said, climbing into the carriage.

Kaladin sighed, then moved to follow them in.

"You intend to ride in there?" Wit asked, grin widening.

"Yeah," Kaladin said. He wanted to watch Shallan. She wasn't likely to try something in the open, while riding in the carriage with Adolin. But Kaladin might learn something by watching her, and he couldn't be *absolutely* certain she wouldn't try to harm him.

"Try not to flirt with the girl," Wit whispered. "Young Adolin seems to be growing possessive. Or . . . what am I saying? Flirt with the girl, Kaladin. It might make the prince's eyes bulge."

Kaladin snorted. "She's lighteyed."

"So?" Wit asked. "You people are too fixated on that."

"No offense," Kaladin whispered, "but I'd sooner flirt with a chasmfiend." He left Wit to drive the carriage, hauling himself into it.

Inside, Adolin looked toward the heavens. "You're kidding."

"It's my job," Kaladin said, seating himself next to Adolin.

"Surely I'm safe in here," Adolin said through gritted teeth, "with my betrothed."

"Well, maybe I just want a comfortable seat, then," Kaladin said, nodding to Shallan Davar.

She ignored him, smiling at Adolin as the carriage started rolling. "Where are we going today?"

"Well, you said something about a dinner," Adolin said. "I know of a new winehouse in the Outer Market, and it actually serves food."

"You always know the best places," Shallan said, her smile widening.

Could you be any more obvious with your flattery, woman? Kaladin thought.

Adolin smiled back. "I just listen."

"Now if you only paid more attention to what wines were good . . ."

"I don't because it's easy!" He grinned. "They're *all* good."

She giggled.

Storms, lighteyes were annoying. Particularly when they fawned over one another. Their conversation continued, and Kaladin found it blatantly obvious how badly this woman wanted a relationship with Adolin. Well, that wasn't surprising. Lighteyes were always looking for chances to get ahead—or to stab one another in the back, if they were in that mood instead. His job wasn't to figure out if this woman was an opportunist. Every lighteyes was an opportunist. He just had to find out if she was an opportunistic fortune hunter or an opportunistic assassin.

They continued talking, and Shallan circled the conversation back toward the day's activity.

"Now, I'm not saying I mind another winehouse," Shallan said. "But I *do* wonder if those are becoming a tad too obvious a choice."

"I know," Adolin replied. "But there's storming little to do out here otherwise. No concerts, no art shows, no sculpture contests."

Is that really what you people spend your time on? Kaladin wondered. *Almighty save you if you don't have* sculpture contests *to watch.*

"There's a menagerie," Shallan said, eager. "In the Outer Market."

"A menagerie," Adolin said. "Isn't that a little . . . low?"

"Oh, come on. We could look at all of the animals, and you could tell me which ones you've bravely slaughtered while hunting. It'll be very diverting." She hesitated, and Kaladin thought he saw something in her eyes. A flash of something deeper. Pain? Worry? "And I could use some distraction," Shallan added more softly.

"I actually despise hunting," Adolin said, as if he hadn't noticed. "No real contest to it." He looked to Shallan, who pasted on a smile and nodded eagerly. "Well, something different could be a pleasant change. All right, I'll tell Wit to take us there instead. Hopefully he'll do it, instead of driving us into a chasm to laugh at our screams of horror."

Adolin turned to open the small sliding shutter up to the driver's perch and gave the order. Kaladin watched Shallan, who sat back, a self-satisfied smile on her face. She had an ulterior motive for going to the menagerie. What was it?

Adolin turned back around and asked after her day. Kaladin listened with half an ear, studying Shallan, trying to pick out any knives hidden on her person. She blushed at something Adolin said, then laughed. Kaladin didn't really like Adolin, but at least the prince was honest. He had his father's earnest temperament, and had always been straight with Kaladin. Dismissive and spoiled, but straight.

This woman was different. Her movements were calculated. The way she laughed, the way she chose her words. She would giggle and blush, but her eyes were always discerning, always watching. She exemplified what made him sick about lighteyed culture.

You're just in an irritable mood, part of him acknowledged. It happened sometimes, more often when the sky was cloudy. But did they *have* to act nauseatingly cheery?

He kept an eye on Shallan as the ride continued, and eventually decided he was being too suspicious of her. She wasn't an immediate threat to Adolin. He found his mind drifting back toward the night in the chasms. Riding the winds, Light churning inside of him. Freedom.

No, not just freedom. Purpose.

You have a purpose, Kaladin thought, dragging his mind back to the present. *Guard Adolin.* This was an ideal job for a soldier, one others dreamed of. Great pay, his own squad to command, an important task. A dependable commander. It was perfect.

But those winds . . .

"Oh!" Shallan said, reaching for her satchel and digging into it.

"I brought that account for you, Adolin." She hesitated, glancing at Kaladin.

"You can trust him," Adolin said, somewhat grudgingly. "He's saved my life twice, and Father lets him guard us at even the most important meetings."

Shallan took out several sheets of paper with notes on them in the scribble-like women's script. "Eighteen years ago, Highprince Yenev was a force in Alethkar, one of the most powerful highprinces who opposed King Gavilar's unification campaign. Yenev wasn't defeated in battle. He was killed in a duel. By *Sadeas.*"

Adolin nodded, leaning forward, eager.

"Here is Brightness Ialai's own account of events," Shallan said. "'Bringing down Yenev was an act of inspired simplicity. My husband spoke with Gavilar regarding the Right of Challenge and the King's Boon, ancient traditions that many of the lighteyes knew, but ignored in modern circumstances.

"'As traditions that shared a relationship to the historical crown, invoking them echoed our right of rule. The occasion was a gala of might and renown, and my husband first entered into a duel with another man.'"

"A what of might and renown?" Kaladin asked.

Both looked at him, as if surprised to hear him speak. *Keep forgetting I'm here, do you?* Kaladin thought. *You prefer to ignore darkeyes.*

"A gala of might and renown," Adolin said. "It's fancy speak for a tournament. They were common back then. Ways for the highprinces who happened to be at peace with one another to show off."

"We need a way for Adolin to duel, or at least discredit, Sadeas," Shallan explained. "While thinking about it, I remembered a reference to the Yenev duel in Jasnah's biography of the old king."

"All right . . ." Kaladin said, frowning.

"'The purpose,'" Shallan continued, holding up her finger as she read further from the account, "'of this preliminary duel was to conspicuously awe and impress the highprinces. Though we had plotted this earlier, the first man to be defeated did not know of his role in our ploy. Sadeas defeated him with calculated spectacle. He paused the fighting at several points and raised the stakes, first with money, then with lands.

"'In the end, the victory was dramatic. With the crowd so engaged, King Gavilar stood and offered Sadeas a boon for having pleased him, after the ancient tradition. Sadeas's reply was simple: 'I will have no boon other than Yenev's cowardly heart on the end of my sword, Your Majesty!'"

"You're kidding," Adolin said. "Blowhard Sadeas said it like that?"

"The event, along with his words, is recorded in several major histories,"

Shallan said. "Sadeas then dueled Yenev, killed the man, and made an opening for an ally—Aladar—to take control of that princedom instead."

Adolin nodded thoughtfully. "It *could* work, Shallan. I can try the same thing—make a spectacle of my fight with Relis and the other person he brings, wow the crowd, earn a boon from the king and demand a Right of Challenge to Sadeas himself."

"It has a certain charm to it," Shallan agreed. "Taking a maneuver that Sadeas himself employed, then using it against him."

"He'd never agree," Kaladin said. "Sadeas won't let himself be trapped like that."

"Perhaps," Adolin said. "But I think you underestimate the position he'd be in, if we do this correctly. The Right of Challenge is an ancient tradition—some say the Heralds instituted it. A lighteyed warrior who has proven himself before the Almighty and the king, turning and demanding justice from one who wronged him . . ."

"He'll agree," Shallan said. "He'll *have* to. But can you be *spectacular*, Adolin?"

"The crowd expects me to cheat," Adolin said. "They won't come thinking much of my recent duels—that should work to my favor. If I can give them a *real* show, they'll be thrilled. Besides, defeating two men at once? That alone should give us the attention we need."

Kaladin looked from one to the other. They were taking this very seriously. "You really think this could work?" Kaladin said, growing thoughtful.

"Yes," Shallan said, "though, by this tradition, Sadeas could appoint a champion to fight on his behalf, so Adolin might not get to duel him personally. He'd still win Sadeas's Shards, though."

"It wouldn't be quite as satisfying," Adolin said. "But it would be acceptable. Beating his champion in a duel would cut Sadeas off at the knees. He'd lose immense credibility."

"But it wouldn't *really* mean anything," Kaladin said. "Right?"

The other two looked at him.

"It's just a duel," Kaladin said. "A game."

"This would be different," Adolin said.

"I don't see why. Sure, you might win his Shards, but his title and authority would be the same."

"It's about perception," Shallan said. "Sadeas has formed a coalition against the king. That implies he is stronger than the king. Losing to the king's champion would deflate that."

"But it's all just *games*," Kaladin said.

"Yes," Adolin said—Kaladin hadn't expected him to agree. "But it's a game that Sadeas is playing. They are rules he's accepted."

Kaladin sat back, letting it sink in. *This tradition might be an answer,* he thought. *The solution I've been looking for . . .*

"Sadeas used to be such a strong ally," Adolin said, sounding regretful. "I'd forgotten things like his defeat of Yenev."

"So what changed?" Kaladin asked.

"Gavilar died," Adolin said softly. "The old king was what kept Father and Sadeas pointed in the same direction." He leaned forward, looking at Shallan's sheets of notes, though he obviously couldn't read them. "We *have* to make this happen, Shallan. We have to yank this noose around that eel's throat. This is brilliant. Thank you."

She blushed, then packed away the notes in an envelope and handed it to him. "Give this to your aunt. It details what I've found. She and your father will know better if this is a good idea or not."

Adolin accepted the envelope, and took her hand in his as he did so. The two shared a moment, melting over one another. Yes, Kaladin was increasingly convinced that the woman wasn't going to be of immediate danger to Adolin. If she was some kind of con woman, she wasn't after Adolin's life. Just his dignity.

Too late, Kaladin thought, watching Adolin sit back with a stupid grin on his face. *That's dead and burned already.*

The carriage soon reached the Outer Market, where they passed several groups of men on patrol in Kholin blue. Bridgemen from the various bridges other than Bridge Four. Being guardsmen here was one of the ways Kaladin was training them.

Kaladin climbed out of the carriage first, noting the lines of stormwagons set up in rows nearby. Ropes on posts blocked off the area, ostensibly to keep people from sneaking in, though the men with cudgels lounging beside some of the posts probably did a better job of that.

"Thanks for the ride, Wit," Kaladin said, turning. "I'm sorry again about that flute you—"

Wit was gone from the top of the carriage. Another man sat there instead, a younger fellow in brown trousers and a white shirt, a cap on his head. He pulled that off, looking embarrassed.

"Oi'm sorry, sir," the man said. He had an accent Kaladin didn't recognize. "He paid me well, he did. Said exactly where Oi was to stand so we could swap places."

"What's this?" Adolin said, climbing from the carriage and looking up. "Oh. Wit does this, bridgeboy."

"This?"

"Likes to vanish mysteriously," Adolin said.

"It weren't so mysterious, sir," the lad said, turning and pointing. "It was joust back there a short ways, where the carriage stopped 'fore turning. Oi was to wait for him, then take over driving this here coach. Oi had to hop on without jostling things. He ran off giggling like a child, he did."

"He just likes to surprise people," Adolin said, helping Shallan from the carriage. "Ignore him."

The new carriage driver hunched down as if embarrassed. Kaladin didn't recognize him; he wasn't one of Adolin's regular servants. *I'll have to ride up there on the way back. Keep an eye on the man.*

Shallan and Adolin walked off toward the menagerie. Kaladin retrieved his spear from the back of the carriage, then jogged to catch up, eventually falling in a few steps behind them. He listened to them both laughing, and wanted to punch them in the face.

"Wow," Syl's voice said. "You're supposed to harness the storms, Kaladin. Not carry them about behind your eyes."

He glanced at her as she flew over and danced around him in the air, a ribbon of light. He set his spear on his shoulder and kept walking.

"What's wrong?" Syl asked, settling down in the air in front of him. Whichever way he turned his head, she automatically glided that way, as if seated on an invisible shelf, girlish dress fluttering to mist just below her knees.

"Nothing's wrong," Kaladin said softly. "I'm just tired of listening to those two."

Syl looked over her shoulder at the pair just ahead. Adolin paid their way in, thumbing back toward Kaladin, paying for him as well. A pompous-looking Azish man in an odd patterned hat and long coat with an intricate design waved them forward, pointing to the different rows of cages and indicating which animals were where.

"Shallan and Adolin seem happy," Syl said. "What's wrong with that?"

"Nothing," Kaladin said. "So long as I don't have to listen to it."

Syl wrinkled her nose. "It's not them, it's you. You're being sour. I can practically taste it."

"Taste?" Kaladin asked. "You don't eat, Syl. I doubt you have a sense of taste."

"It's a metaphor. And I can imagine it. And you taste sour. And stop arguing, because I'm *right*." She zipped off to dangle near Shallan and Adolin as they inspected the first cage.

Blasted spren, Kaladin thought, walking up beside Shallan and Adolin. *Arguing with her is like . . . well, arguing with the wind, I guess.*

This stormwagon looked a lot like the slaver cage he'd ridden in on his way to the Shattered Plains, though the animal within looked to have been treated far better than the slaves had. It sat on a rock, and the cage had been covered over with crem on the inside as if to imitate a cave. The creature itself was little more than a lump of flesh with two bulbous eyes and four long tentacles.

"Ooo . . ." Shallan said, eyes wide. She looked like she'd been given a pile of jewelry—only instead, it was a slimy lump of something that Kaladin would have expected to find stuck to the bottom of his boot.

"That," Adolin said, "is the ugliest thing I've ever seen. It's like the stuff in the middle of a hasper, only without the shell."

"It's one of the sarpenthyn," Shallan said.

"Poor thing," Adolin said. "Did its mother give it that name?"

Shallan swatted him on the shoulder. "It's a family."

"So the mother *was* behind it."

"A family of animals, idiot. They have more of them in the west, where the storms aren't as strong. I've only seen a few of them—we've got little ones in Jah Keved, but nothing like this. I don't even know what species this is." She hesitated, then stuck her fingers through the bars and grabbed one of the tentacle arms.

The thing pulled away immediately, inflating to look bigger, raising two of its arms behind its head in a threatening way. Adolin yelped and pulled Shallan back.

"He said not to touch any of them!" Adolin said. "What if it's poisonous?"

Shallan ignored him, digging a notebook from her satchel. "Warm to the touch," she mumbled to herself. "Truly warm-blooded. Fascinating. I need a sketch of it." She squinted at a little plaque on the cage. "Well, that's useless."

"What does it say?" Adolin asked.

"'Devil rock captured in Marabethia. The locals claim it is the reborn vengeful spirit of a child who was murdered.' Not even a mention of its species. What kind of scholarship is this?"

"It's a menagerie, Shallan," Adolin said, chuckling. "Brought all this distance to entertain soldiers and camp followers."

Indeed, the menagerie was popular. As Shallan sketched, Kaladin kept busy watching those who passed by, making certain they kept their distance. He saw everything from washmaids and tenners to officers, and even some higher lighteyes. Behind them, a lighteyed woman was paraded past in her palanquin, barely even glancing at the cages. It provided quite a contrast to Shallan's eager drawing and Adolin's good-natured gibes.

Kaladin wasn't giving those two enough credit. They might ignore him, but they weren't actively *mean* to him. They were happy and pleasant. Why did that annoy him so?

Eventually, Shallan and Adolin moved on to the next cage, which contained skyeels and a large tub of water for them to dip in. They didn't look as comfortable as the "devil rock." There wasn't much room to move in the cage, and they didn't often take to the air. Not very interesting.

Next was a cage with a creature that looked like a small chull, but with larger claws. Shallan wanted a sketch of this one too, so Kaladin found himself lounging beside the cage, watching people pass and listening to Adolin try to crack jokes to amuse his betrothed. He wasn't very good at it, but Shallan laughed anyway.

"Poor thing," Syl said, landing on the floor of the cage, looking at its crab occupant. "What kind of life is this?"

"A safe one." Kaladin shrugged. "At least it has no need to worry about predators. Always kept fed. I doubt a chull-thing could ask for more than that."

"Oh?" Syl asked. "And *you'd* be all right if that were you."

"Of course not. I'm not a chull-thing. I'm a soldier."

They moved on, passing cage after cage of animals. Some Shallan wanted to draw, others she concluded didn't need an immediate sketch. The one she found the most fascinating was also the strangest, a kind of colorful chicken with red, blue, and green feathers. She dug out colored pencils to do that sketch. Apparently, she'd missed a chance at sketching one of these a long time ago.

Kaladin had to admit the thing *was* pretty. How did it survive, though? It had shell on the very front of its face, but the rest of it wasn't squishy, so it couldn't hide in cracks like the devil rock. What did this chicken do when a storm came?

Syl landed on Kaladin's shoulder.

"I'm a soldier," Kaladin repeated, speaking very softly.

"That's what you *were*," Syl said.

"It's what I want to be again."

"Are you sure?"

"Mostly." He folded his arms, spear leaning against his shoulder. "The only thing is . . . It's crazy, Syl. Insane. My time as a bridgeman was the worst in my life. We suffered death, oppression, indignity. Yet I don't think I've ever felt so alive as I did in those final weeks."

Next to the work he'd done with Bridge Four, being a simple soldier— even a highly respected one, like captain of a highprince's guard—just felt mundane. Ordinary.

But soaring on the winds—*that* had been anything but ordinary.

"You're almost ready, aren't you?" Syl whispered.

He nodded slowly. "Yeah. Yeah, I think I am."

The next cage in line had a large crowd around it, and even a few fear-spren wiggling out of the ground. Kaladin pushed in, though he didn't have to clear a space—the people made room for Dalinar's heir as soon as they realized who he was. Adolin walked past them without a second glance, obviously accustomed to such deference.

This cage was different from the others. The bars were closer together, the wood reinforced. The animal inside didn't seem to deserve the special treatment. The sorry beast lay in front of some rocks, eyes closed. The square face showed sharpened mandibles—like teeth, only somehow more vicious—and a pair of long, toothlike tusks that pointed down from the upper jaw. The stark spikes running from the head along the sinuous back, along with powerful legs, were clues as to what this beast was.

"Whitespine," Shallan breathed, stepping closer to the cage.

Kaladin had never seen one. He remembered a young man, lying dead on the operating table, blood everywhere. He remembered fear, frustration. And then misery.

"I expected," Kaladin said, trying to sort through it all, "the thing to be . . . *more*."

"They don't do well in captivity," Shallan said. "This one probably would have gone dormant in crystal long ago, if it had been allowed. They must keep dousing it to wash away the shell."

"Don't feel sorry for the thing," Adolin said. "I've seen what they can do to a man."

"Yeah," Kaladin said softly.

Shallan got out her drawing things, though as she started, people began to move away from the cage. At first, Kaladin thought it was something about the beast itself—but the animal continued to just lie there, eyes closed, occasionally snorting out of its nose holes.

No, people were congregating at the other side of the menagerie. Kaladin caught Adolin's attention, then pointed. *I'm going to go check that out,* the gesture implied. Adolin nodded and rested his hand on his sword. *I'll be on the watch,* that said.

Kaladin jogged off, spear on his shoulder, to investigate. Unfortunately, he soon recognized a familiar face above the crowd. Amaram was a tall man. Dalinar stood at his side, guarded by several of Kaladin's men, who were keeping the gawking crowd back a safe distance.

". . . heard my son was here," Dalinar was saying to the well-dressed owner of the menagerie.

"You needn't pay, Highprince!" the menagerie owner said, speaking with a lofty accent similar to Sigzil's. "Your presence is a grand blessing from the Heralds upon my humble collection. And your distinguished guest."

Amaram. He wore a strange cloak. Bright yellow-gold, with a black glyph on the back. Oath? Kaladin didn't recognize the shape. It looked familiar, though.

The double eye, he realized. Symbol of . . .

"Is it true?" the menagerie owner asked, inspecting Amaram. "The rumors around camp are most intriguing. . . ."

Dalinar sighed audibly. "We were going to announce this at the feast tonight, but as Amaram insists on wearing the cloak, I suppose it needs to be stated. Under the king's direction, I have commanded the refounding of the Knights Radiant. Let it be spoken of in the camps. The ancient oaths are spoken again, and Brightlord Amaram was—at my request—the first to speak them. The Knights Radiant have been reestablished, and he stands at their head."

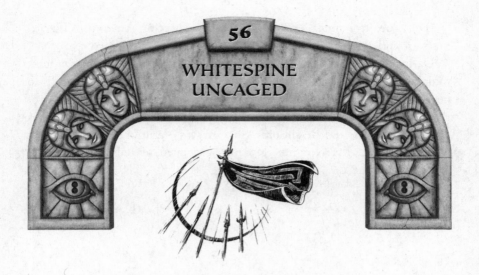

Twenty-three cohorts followed behind, that came from the contri-butions of the King of Makabakam, for though the bond between man and spren was at times inexplicable, the ability for bonded spren to manifest in our world rather than their own grew stronger through the course of the oaths given.

—From *Words of Radiance,* chapter 35, page 9

maram obviously doesn't have any Surgebinding abilities," Sigzil said softly, standing beside Kaladin.

Dalinar, Navani, the king, and Amaram climbed out of their carriage ahead. The dueling arena rose before them, another of the crater-like formations that rimmed the Shattered Plains. It was much smaller than the ones that held the warcamps, however, and had tiered seats in-side.

With both Elhokar and Dalinar in attendance—not to mention Navani and both of Dalinar's sons—Kaladin had brought every guard he could. That included some of the men from Bridge Seventeen and Bridge Two. Those stood proudly, with spears held high, obviously excited to finally be trusted with their first bodyguard assignment. In total, he had forty men on duty.

None of them would be worth a drop of rain if the Assassin in White attacked.

"Can we be certain?" Kaladin asked, nodding toward Amaram, who still wore his yellow-gold cloak with the symbol of the Knights Radiant on the back. "I haven't shown anyone my powers. There have to be others training as I am. Storms, Syl all but promised me there *were*."

"He'd have displayed the abilities if he had them," Sigzil said. "Gossip is moving through the ten warcamps like floodwater. Half the people think it's blasphemous and stupid, what Dalinar is doing. The other half are undecided. If Amaram displayed Surgebinding powers, Brightlord Dalinar's move would look a lot less precarious."

Sigzil was probably right. But . . . Amaram? The man walked with such pride, head held high. Kaladin felt his neck growing hot, and for a moment it seemed the only thing he could see was Amaram. Golden cloak. Haughty face.

Bloodstained. That man was *bloodstained*. Kaladin *told* Dalinar about it! Dalinar wouldn't do anything.

Someone else would have to.

"Kaladin?" Sigzil asked.

Kaladin realized he'd stepped toward Amaram, hands clenched on his spear. He took a deep breath, then pointed. "Put men up on the rim of the arena there. Skar and Eth are in the preparation room with Adolin, for all the good it will do him out on the field. Put another few down at the arena bottom, just in case. Three men at every door. I'll take six with me to the king's seats." Kaladin paused, then added, "Let's also put two men guarding Adolin's betrothed, just in case. She'll be sitting with Sebarial."

"Will do."

"Tell the men to keep focused, Sig. This is likely to be a dramatic fight. I want their minds on the possibility of assassins, not on the duel."

"Is he really going to fight two men at once?"

"Yeah."

"Can he possibly win that?"

"I don't know, and I don't really care. Our job is to watch for other threats."

Sigzil nodded, and moved to leave. He hesitated, however, taking Kaladin by the arm. "You could join them, Kal," he said softly. "If the king's refounding the Knights Radiant, you have an excuse to show what you are. Dalinar is trying, but so many think of the Radiants as an evil force, forgetting the good they did before they betrayed mankind. But if you showed your powers, it could change minds."

Join. Under Amaram. Not likely.

"Go pass my orders," Kaladin said, gesturing, then pulled his arm free of Sigzil's grip and jogged after the king and his retinue. At least the sun was out today, the spring air warm.

Syl bobbed along behind Kaladin. "Amaram is ruining you, Kaladin," she whispered. "Don't let him."

He gritted his teeth and didn't reply. Instead, he moved up beside Moash, who was in charge of a team who would watch Brightness

Navani—she preferred to watch the duels from down below, in the preparation rooms.

A part of him wondered if he should let Moash guard anyone other than Dalinar, but storm it, Moash had *sworn* to him that he'd take no more actions against the king. Kaladin trusted him on that count. They were Bridge Four.

I'll get you out of this, Moash, Kaladin thought, pulling the man aside. *We'll fix this.*

"Moash," Kaladin said, speaking softly. "Starting tomorrow, I'm putting you on patrol duty."

Moash frowned. "I thought you always wanted me guarding . . ." His expression grew hard. "This is about what happened. In the tavern."

"I want you to take a deep patrol," Kaladin said. "Head out toward New Natanan. I don't want you here when we move against Graves and his people." It had been too long already.

"I'm not leaving."

"You will, and it's not subject to—"

"What they're doing is *right*, Kal!"

Kaladin frowned. "Have you still been meeting with them?"

Moash looked away. "Only once. To assure them that you'd come around."

"You still disobeyed an order!" Kaladin said. "Storm it, Moash!"

The noise inside the arena was building.

"Almost time for the match," Moash said, pulling his arm free of Kaladin's grip. "We can talk about this later."

Kaladin ground his teeth, but unfortunately, Moash was right. This wasn't the time.

Should have grabbed him this morning, Kaladin thought. *No, what I should have done was make a decision on this days ago.*

It was his own fault. "You *will* go on that patrol, Moash," he said. "You don't get to be insubordinate just because you're my friend. Go on."

The man jogged ahead, collecting his squad.

⁕

Adolin knelt beside his sword in the preparation room and found he didn't know what to say.

He looked at his reflection in the Blade. Two Shardbearers at once. He'd never even tried that outside of the practice grounds.

Fighting multiple opponents was tough. In the histories, if you heard of a man fighting six men at once or whatnot, the truth was probably that he managed to take them one at a time somehow. Two at once was hard, if they were prepared and careful. Not impossible, but really hard.

"It comes down to this," Adolin said. He had to say *something* to the sword. It was tradition. "Let's go be spectacular. Then let's wipe that smile off Sadeas's face."

He stood up, dismissing his Blade. He left the small preparation room, walking down the tunnel with carved, painted duelists. In the room beyond, Renarin sat in his Kholin uniform—he wore that to official functions like this, instead of the blasted Bridge Four uniform—waiting anxiously. Aunt Navani was screwing the lid off a jar of paint to do a glyphward.

"No need," Adolin said, taking one from his pocket. Painted in Kholin blue, it read "excellence."

Navani cocked an eyebrow. "The girl?"

"Yeah," Adolin said.

"The calligraphy isn't bad," Navani said, grudgingly.

"She's quite wonderful, Aunt," Adolin said. "I wish you'd give her more of a chance. And she *does* want to share her scholarship with you."

"We'll see," Navani said. She sounded more thoughtful than she had before, regarding Shallan. A good sign.

Adolin placed the glyphward in the brazier, then bowed his head as it burned. A prayer to the Almighty for aid. His combatants for the day would probably be burning their own prayers. How did the Almighty decide whom to help?

I can't believe, Adolin thought, raising his head from the prayer, *that he'd want those who serve Sadeas, even indirectly, to succeed.*

"I'm worried," Navani said.

"Father thinks the plan could work, and Elhokar really likes it."

"Elhokar can be impulsive," Navani said, folding her arms and watching the remnants of the glyphward burn. "The terms change things."

The terms—agreed upon with Relis and spoken in front of the high-judge just earlier—indicated that this duel would go until surrender, not until a certain number of Plate sections were broken. That meant if Adolin did manage to beat one of his foes, making the man give in, the other could keep fighting.

It also meant that Adolin didn't have to stop fighting until he was convinced he was bested.

Or until he was incapacitated.

Renarin walked over, resting a hand on Adolin's shoulder. "I think the plan is a good one," he said. "You can do this."

"They're going to try to break you," Navani said. "That's why they insisted this be a match until the surrender. They'll leave you crippled if they can, Adolin."

"No different from the battlefield," he said. "Actually, in this case, they will want to leave me alive. I'll work better as an object lesson with Blade-dead legs than I would as ashes."

Navani closed her eyes, drawing in a breath. She looked pale. It was a little like having his mother back. A little.

"Make *sure* you don't give Sadeas any outs," Renarin said to him as the armorers entered with Adolin's Shardplate. "When you corner him with a challenge, he will look for a way to escape. Don't let him. Bring him down on those sands and beat him bloody, Brother."

"With pleasure."

"Now, you ate chicken?" Renarin asked.

"Two plates of the stuff, with curry."

"Mother's chain?"

Adolin felt in his pocket.

Then he felt in his other one.

"What?" Renarin asked, fingers tightening on Adolin's shoulder.

"I could have *sworn* I slipped it in."

Renarin cursed.

"Might be back in my rooms," Adolin said. "In the warcamps. On my end table." Assuming he hadn't grabbed it, then lost it on the way. *Storms.*

It was just a good luck charm. It didn't mean anything. He started sweating anyway as Renarin scrambled to send a runner off to search. They wouldn't get back in time. Already he could hear the crowd outside, the growing roar that came before a duel. Adolin reluctantly allowed his armorers to begin putting on his Plate.

By the time they gave him his helm, he had recovered most of his rhythm—the anticipation that was an odd blend of anxiety in his stomach and relaxation in his muscles. You couldn't fight while tense. You could fight while nervous, but not while tense.

He nodded to the servants, and they pushed open the doors, letting him stride out onto the sand. He could tell from their cheering where the darkeyes sat. In contrast, the lighteyes grew softer, instead of louder, when he emerged. It was good that Elhokar reserved space for the darkeyes. Adolin liked the noise. It reminded him of a battlefield.

There was a time, he thought, *when I didn't like the battlefield because it wasn't quiet, like a duel.* Despite his original reluctance, he had become a soldier.

He strode out into the center of the arena. The others hadn't left their preparation room yet. *Take Relis first,* Adolin told himself. *You know his dueling style.* The man preferred Vinestance, slow and steady, but with sudden, quick lunges. Adolin wasn't sure whom he'd bring along to fight with him, though he'd borrowed a full set of the King's Blade and Plate. Perhaps his cousin wanted to try again, for vengeance?

Shallan was there, on the opposite side of the arena, her red hair standing out like blood on stone. She had two bridgeman guards. Adolin found himself nodding in appreciation of that, and raised a fist to her. She waved back.

Adolin danced from one foot to the other, letting the power of the Plate flow through him. He could win, even without Mother's chain. The problem was, he intended to challenge Sadeas after this. So he had to retain enough strength for that duel.

He checked, anxious. Was Sadeas there? Yes; he sat only a little ways from Father and the king. Adolin narrowed his eyes, remembering the crushing moment of realization when he'd seen Sadeas's armies retreating from the Tower.

That steadied him. He'd stewed long about that betrayal. It was time, finally, to do something.

The doors across from him opened.

Four men in Shardplate strode out.

·_··

"Four?" Dalinar said, leaping to his feet.

Kaladin took a step downward toward the arena floor. Yes, those were all Shardbearers, entering the sands of the dueling arena below. One wore a set of the King's Plate; the other three wore their own, ornamented and painted.

Down below, the highjudge for the bout turned and cocked her head toward the king.

"What is this?" Dalinar bellowed toward Sadeas, who sat only a short distance away. The lighteyes on the benchlike rows of seats between them hunched down or fled, leaving a direct line of sight between the highprinces.

Sadeas and his wife turned about, lazily. "Why do you ask me?" Sadeas called back. "None of those men are mine. I'm just an observer today."

"Oh, don't be tiresome, Sadeas," Elhokar called. "You know full well what is happening. Why are there four? Is Adolin supposed to pick the two he wants to duel?"

"Two?" Sadeas asked. "When was it said that he would fight two?"

"That's what he said when he set up the duel!" Dalinar shouted. "Paired disadvantaged duel, two against one, as per the dueling conventions!"

"Actually," Sadeas replied, "that is *not* what young Adolin agreed to. Why, I have it on very good authority that he told Prince Relis: 'I'll fight you and whomever you bring.' I don't hear a specification of a number in there—which subjects Adolin to a *full* disadvantaged duel, not a paired duel. Relis may bring as many as he wishes. I know several scribes who recorded Adolin's precise words, and I hear the highjudge asked him *specifically* if he understood what he was doing, and he said that he did."

Dalinar growled softly. It was a sound Kaladin had never heard from him, the growl of a beast on a chain. It surprised him. The highprince contained himself, however, sitting down with a curt motion.

"He outthought us," Dalinar said softly to the king. "Again. We'll need to retreat and consider our next move. Someone tell Adolin to pull out of the contest."

"Are you certain?" the king said. "Pulling out would require that Adolin forfeit, Uncle. That's six Shards, I believe. Everything you own."

Kaladin could read the conflict in Dalinar's features—the scrunched-up brow, the red fury rising on his cheeks, the indecision in his eyes. Give up? Without a fight? It was probably the right thing to do.

Kaladin doubted he could have done it.

Below, after an extended pause—frozen on the sand—Adolin raised his hand in a sign of agreement. The judge began the duel.

·⁘·

I'm an idiot. I'm an idiot. I'm a storm-cursed idiot!

Adolin jogged backward across the sand-covered circle of the arena. He'd need to put his back to the wall to avoid being completely surrounded. That meant he'd start the duel with no place to retreat, locked in a box. Cornered.

Why hadn't he been more specific? He could see the holes in his challenge—he'd agreed to a full disadvantaged duel without realizing it. He should have stated, specifically, that Relis could bring *one* other. But no, doing so would have been smart. And Adolin was a storming idiot!

He recognized Relis from his Plate and Blade, colored completely a deep black, breakaway cloak bearing his father's glyphpair. The man in King's Plate—judging by his height and the way he walked—would indeed be Elit, Relis's cousin, returned for a rematch. He carried an enormous hammer, rather than a Blade. The two moved across the field carefully, and their two companions took the flanks. One in orange, the other in green.

Adolin recognized the Plate. That would be Abrobadar, a full Shardbearer from Aladar's camp and . . . and Jakamav, bearing the King's Blade that Relis had borrowed.

Jakamav. Adolin's friend.

Adolin cursed. Those two were among the best duelists in the camp. Jakamav would have won his own Blade years ago if he'd been allowed to risk his Plate. That had apparently changed. Had he, and his house, been bought with a promise of a share in the spoils?

Blade forming in his hand, Adolin backed into the cool shade of the wall around the arena grounds. Just above him, darkeyes roared on their benches. Whether they were thrilled or horrified by what he faced, Adolin could not tell. He'd come here intending to give a spectacular show. They'd get the opposite instead. A quick slaughter.

Well, he'd made this pyre himself. If he was going to burn on it, he'd at least put up a fight first.

Relis and Elit prowled closer—one in slate grey, the other in black—as their allies worked around the sides. Those would hang back to try to make Adolin focus on the two in front of him. Then the others could attack him from the sides.

"One at a time, lad!" One shout from the stands seemed to separate from the others. Was that Zahel's voice? "You're not cornered!"

Relis stepped forward in a quick motion, testing Adolin. Adolin danced away in Windstance—certainly the best against so many foes—with both hands holding the Blade in front of him, positioned sideways with one foot forward.

You're not cornered! What did Zahel mean? Of course he was cornered! It was the only way to face four. And how could he possibly face them one at a time? They'd never allow that.

Relis tested forward again, making Adolin shuffle sideways along the wall, focused on him. He had to turn somewhat to face Relis, however, and that put Abrobadar—moving up the other way, wearing orange—in his blind spot. Storms!

"They're scared of you." Zahel's voice, drifting again above the crowd. "Do you see it in them? Show them *why*."

Adolin hesitated. Relis stepped forward, making a Stonestance strike. Stonestance, to be immobile. Elit came in next, hammer held wardingly. They backed Adolin along the wall toward Abrobadar.

No. Adolin had demanded this duel. He had wanted it. He would not become a frightened rat.

Show them why.

Adolin attacked. He leaped forward, sweeping with a barrage of strikes at Relis. Elit jumped away with a curse as he did so. They were like men with spears prodding at a whitespine.

And this whitespine was not yet caged.

Adolin shouted, beating against Relis, scoring strikes on his helm and left vambrace, cracking the latter. Stormlight rose from Relis's forearm. As Elit recovered, Adolin spun on him and struck, leaving Relis dazed from the attack. His assault forced Elit to hold his hammer back and block with his forearm, lest Adolin slice the hammer in two and leave him unarmed.

This was what Zahel meant. Attack with fury. Don't allow them time to respond or assess. Four men. If he could intimidate them into hesitating . . . Maybe . . .

Adolin stopped thinking. He let the flow of the fight consume him, let the rhythm of his heart guide the beating of his sword. Elit cursed and pulled away, leaking Stormlight from his left shoulder and forearm.

Adolin turned and smashed his shoulder into Relis, who was stepping back into his stance. His shove threw the black-Plated man tumbling to the ground. Then, with a shout, Adolin turned and met Abrobadar head-on as the man came dashing up to help. Adolin fell into Stonestance himself, smashing his Blade down again and again against Abrobadar's raised sword until he heard grunts, curses. Until he could *feel* the fear coming off the man in orange like a stench, and could see fearspren on the ground.

Elit approached, wary, as Relis scrambled up to his feet. Adolin fell back into Windstance and swept about himself in a wide, fluid motion. Elit jumped away and Abrobadar stumbled back, gauntleted hand against the wall of the arena.

Adolin turned back toward Relis, who had recovered well, all things considered. Still, Adolin got in a second strike at the champion's breastplate. If this had been a battlefield and these common foes, Relis would be dead, Elit maimed. Adolin was yet untouched.

But they weren't common foes. They were Shardbearers, and a second strike against Relis's breastplate didn't break the armor. Adolin was forced to turn on Abrobadar before he wanted to, and the man was now braced for the fury of the assault, sword raised defensively. Adolin's barrage didn't stun him this time. The man weathered it while Elit and Relis got into position.

Just need to—

Something crashed into Adolin from behind.

Jakamav. Adolin had taken too long, and had allowed the fourth man—his supposed friend—to get into position. Adolin spun about, moving into a puff of Stormlight rising from his back plate. He raised his sword into Jakamav's next attack, but that opened his left flank. Elit swung, hammer crashing into Adolin's side. Plate cracked, and the blow shoved Adolin off balance.

He swept around himself, growing desperate. This time, his foes didn't back away. Instead, Jakamav charged in, head down, not even swinging. Smart man. His green armor was unscored. Even though the move let Adolin slam his sword down and hit the man on the back, it threw Adolin completely out of his stance.

Adolin stumbled backward, barely keeping from being thrown to the ground as Jakamav crashed into him. Adolin shoved the man aside, somehow keeping hold of his Shardblade, but the other three moved in. Blows rained on his shoulders, helm, breastplate. Storms. That hammer hit *hard*.

Adolin's head rang from a blow. He'd almost done it. He let himself grin as they beat on him. Four at once. And he'd almost *done it.*

"I yield," he said, voice muffled by his helm.

They continued attacking. He said it louder.

Nobody listened.

He raised his hand to signal to the judge to stop the proceedings, but someone slammed his arm downward.

No! Adolin thought, swinging about himself in a panic.

The judge could not end the fight. If he left this duel alive, he would do so as a cripple.

* * *

"That's it," Dalinar said, watching the four Shardbearers take turns coming in to swing at Adolin, who was obviously disoriented, barely able to fight them off. "The rules allow Adolin to have help, so long as his side is disadvantaged—one less than Relis's team. Elhokar, I'll need your Shardblade."

"No," Elhokar said. The king sat with folded arms beneath the shade. Those around them watched the duel . . . no, the beating . . . in silence.

"Elhokar!" Dalinar said, turning. "That is my *son.*"

"You're without Plate," Elhokar said. "If you take the time to put some on, you'll be too late. If you go down, you won't save Adolin. You'll simply lose *my* Blade as well as all the others."

Dalinar clenched his teeth. There was a drop of wisdom in that, and he knew it. Adolin was finished. They needed to end the match now and not put more on the line.

"You could help him, you know." Sadeas's voice.

Dalinar spun toward the man.

"The dueling conventions don't forbid it," Sadeas said, speaking loudly enough for Dalinar to hear. "I checked to make sure. Young Adolin can be helped by up to two people. The Blackthorn I once knew would have been down there already, fighting with a *rock* if he had to. I guess you're not that man anymore."

Dalinar sucked in a breath, then stood. "Elhokar, I'll pay the fee and borrow your Blade by right of the tradition of the King's Blade. You won't risk it that way. I'm going to fight."

Elhokar caught him by the arm, standing. "Don't be a fool, Uncle.

Listen to him! Do you see what he's doing? He obviously *wants* you to go down and fight."

Dalinar turned to meet the king's eyes. Pale green. Like his father's.

"Uncle," Elhokar said, grip tightening on his arm, "*listen* to me for once. Be a little paranoid. Why would Sadeas want you down there? It's so that an 'accident' can occur! He wants you *removed*, Dalinar. I guarantee that if you step onto those sands, all four will attack you straight out. Shardblade or none, you'll be dead before you get into stance."

Dalinar puffed in and out. Elhokar was right. Storm him, but he was right. Dalinar had to do *something* though.

A murmur rose from the watching crowd, whispers like scratches on paper. Dalinar spun to see that someone else had joined the battle, stepping from the preparation room, Shardblade held nervously in two hands but wearing no Plate.

Renarin.

Oh no . . .

⁙

One of the attackers moved away, Plated feet crunching on sand. Adolin threw himself in that direction, battering his way out from among the three others. He spun and backed away. His Plate was starting to feel heavy. How much Stormlight had he lost?

No broken sections, he thought, keeping his sword toward the three other men who fanned out to advance on him. He could maybe . . .

No. Time to end this. He felt a fool, but better a live fool than a dead one. He turned toward the highjudge to signal his surrender. Surely she could see him now.

"Adolin," Relis said, prowling forward, his Plate leaking from small cracks on his chest. "Now, we wouldn't want to end this prematurely, would we?"

"What glory do you think will come of such a fight?" Adolin spat back, sword held carefully, ready to give the signal. "You think people will cheer you? For beating a man four against one?"

"This isn't for honor," Relis said. "It's simple punishment."

Adolin snorted. Only then did he notice something on the other side of the arena. Renarin in Kholin blue, holding a wobbly Shardblade and facing down Abrobadar, who stood with sword on his shoulder as if completely unthreatened.

"Renarin!" Adolin shouted. "What in the storms are you doing! Go back—"

Abrobadar attacked, and Renarin parried awkwardly. Renarin had done all of his sparring in Shardplate so far, but hadn't had the time to fetch his Plate. Abrobadar's blow just about knocked the weapon from Renarin's hands.

"Now," Relis said, stepping closer to Adolin, "Abrobadar there is fond of young Renarin, and doesn't want to hurt him. So he'll just keep the young man engaged, make a good fight of it. So long as you're willing to keep up what you promised, and have a good duel with us. Surrender like a coward, or get the king to end the bout, and Abrobadar's sword might just slip."

Adolin felt a panic rising. He looked toward the highjudge. She could call this on her own, if she felt it had gone too far.

She sat imperiously in her seat, watching him. Adolin thought he saw something behind her calm expression. *They got to her*, he thought. *With a bribe, perhaps.*

Adolin tightened his grip on his Blade and looked back toward his three foes. "You bastards," he whispered. "Jakamav, how *dare* you be a part of this?"

Jakamav didn't reply, and Adolin could not see his face behind his green helm.

"So," Relis said. "Shall we?"

Adolin's response was a charge.

.·.

Dalinar reached the judge's seat, which sat on its own small, stone dais hanging out a few inches over the dueling grounds.

Brightness Istow was a tall, greying woman who sat with hands in her lap, watching the duel. She did not turn as Dalinar stepped up beside her.

"It is time to end this, Istow," Dalinar said. "Call the fight. Award the victory to Relis and his team."

The woman kept her eyes forward, watching the duel.

"Did you *hear* me?" Dalinar demanded.

She said nothing.

"Fine," he said. "I'll end it then."

"*I* am highprince here, Dalinar," the woman said. "In this arena, my word is the only law, granted me by the authority of the king." She turned to him. "Your son has not surrendered and he is not incapacitated. The terms of the duel have not been met, and I will not end it until they have been. Have you no respect for the law?"

Dalinar ground his teeth together, then looked back at the arena. Renarin fought one of the men. The lad had barely any training in the sword. In fact, as Dalinar watched, Renarin's shoulder began to twitch, pulling up toward his head violently. One of his fits.

Adolin fought the other three, having cast himself among them again. He fought marvelously, but could not fend off all of them. The three surrounded him and struck.

The pauldron on Adolin's left shoulder exploded into a burst of molten metal, bits trailing smoke through the air, the main chunk of it skidding to the sands a short distance away. That left Adolin's flesh exposed to the air, and to the Blades facing him.

Please . . . Almighty . . .

Dalinar turned upon the stands full of spectating lighteyes. "You can watch this?" he shouted at them. "My sons fight alone! There are Shardbearers among you. Is there not one of you who will fight with them?"

He scanned the crowd. The king was looking at his feet. Amaram. What of Amaram? Dalinar found him seated near the king. Dalinar met the man's eyes.

Amaram looked away.

No . . .

"What has happened to us?" Dalinar asked. "Where is our honor?"

"Honor is dead," a voice whispered from beside him.

Dalinar turned and looked at Captain Kaladin. He hadn't noticed the bridgeman walking down the steps behind him.

Kaladin took a deep breath, then looked at Dalinar. "But I'll see what I can do. If this goes poorly, take care of my men." Spear in hand, he grabbed the edge of the wall and flung himself over, dropping to the sands of the arena floor below.

*Malchin was stymied, for though he was inferior to none in the arts
of war, he was not suitable for the Lightweavers; he wished for his
oaths to be elementary and straightforward, and yet their spren
were liberal, as to our comprehension, in definitions pertaining to
this matter; the process included speaking truths as an approach
to a threshold of self-awareness that Malchin could never attain.*

—From *Words of Radiance*, chapter 12, page 12

Shallan stood up in her seat, watching Adolin's beating below. Why
didn't he surrender? Give up the bout?

Four men. She should have seen that loophole. As his wife,
watching for intrigue like this would be her duty. Now, barely betrothed,
she'd already failed him disastrously. Beyond that, this fiasco had been her
idea.

Adolin seemed about to give in, but then for some reason, he threw
himself back into the fight instead.

"Fool man," Sebarial said, lounging beside her, Palona on his other side.
"Too arrogant to see that he's beaten."

"No," Shallan said. "There's something more." Her eyes flicked down
toward poor Renarin, completely overwhelmed as he tried to fight a Shardbearer.

For the briefest instant, she considered going down to help. Sheer stupidity; she'd be even more useless than Renarin down there. Why didn't
anyone else help them? She glared across at the gathered Alethi lighteyes,
including Highlord Amaram, the supposed Knight Radiant.

Bastard.

Shocked at how quickly that sentiment rose inside of her, Shallan looked away from him. *Don't think about it.* Well, as nobody was going to help, both princes seemed to stand a good chance of dying.

"Pattern," she whispered. "Go see if you can distract that Shardbearer fighting Prince Renarin." She would not interfere with Adolin's fight, not as he'd obviously decided he needed to keep going for some reason. But she would try to keep Renarin from getting maimed, if she could.

Pattern hummed and slipped from her skirt, moving across the stone of the arena benches. He seemed painfully obvious to her, moving in the open, but everybody was focused on the fighting below.

Don't you get yourself killed on me, Adolin Kholin, she thought, glancing back up at him as he struggled against his three opponents. *Please . . .*

Someone else dropped to the sands.

⁘

Kaladin dashed across the arena floor.

Again, he thought, remembering coming to Amaram's rescue so long ago. "This had better end differently than it did that time."

"It will," Syl promised, zipping along beside his head, a line of light. "Trust me."

Trust. He'd trusted her and spoken to Dalinar about Amaram. That had gone wonderfully.

One of the Shardbearers—Relis, the one in black armor—trailed Stormlight from a crack in the vambrace on his left forearm. He glanced at Kaladin as he approached, then turned back away, indifferent. Relis obviously didn't think a simple spearman was a threat.

Kaladin smiled, then sucked in some Stormlight. On this bright day, with the sun blazing white overhead, he could risk more than he normally would. Nobody would see it. Hopefully.

He sped up, then lunged between two of the Shardbearers, ramming his spear into Relis's cracked vambrace. The man let out a shout of pain and Kaladin pulled his spear back, twisting between the attackers and getting close to Adolin. The young man in blue armor glanced at him, then quickly turned to put his back toward Kaladin.

Kaladin put his own back toward Adolin, preventing either of them from being attacked from behind.

"What are you doing here, bridgeboy?" Adolin hissed from within his helmet.

"Playing one of the ten fools."

Adolin grunted. "Welcome to the party."

"I won't be able to get through their armor," Kaladin said. "You'll need to crack it for me." Nearby, Relis shook his arm, cursing. The tip of Kaladin's spear had blood on it. Not much, unfortunately.

"Just keep one of them distracted from me," Adolin said. "I can handle two."

"I— All right." It was probably the best plan.

"Keep an eye on my brother, if you can," Adolin said. "If things go sour for these three, they might decide to use him as leverage against us."

"Done," Kaladin said, then pulled away and jumped to the side as the one with a hammer—Dalinar had named him Elit—tried to attack Adolin. Relis came in from the other side, swinging, as if to cut right through Kaladin and hit Adolin.

His heart thumped, but training with Zahel had done its job. He could stare down that Shardblade and feel only a *mild* panic. He twisted around Relis, dodging the Blade.

The black-Plated man glanced at Adolin and took a step in that direction, but Kaladin lunged as if to strike him in the arm again.

Relis turned back, then reluctantly let Kaladin draw him away from the fight with Adolin. The man attacked quickly, using what Kaladin could now identify as Vinestance—a style of fighting that focused on defensive footing and flexibility.

He went more offensive against Kaladin, but Kaladin twisted and spun, always getting *just* out of the way of the attacks. Relis started cursing, then turned back to the fight with Adolin.

Kaladin slapped him on the side of the head with the butt of his spear. It was a terrible weapon for fighting a Shardbearer, but the blow got the man's attention again. Relis turned and swept out with his Blade.

Kaladin pulled back a hair too slowly, and the Blade sheared the pointed end off his spear. A reminder. His own flesh would put up less resistance than that. Severing his spine would kill him, and no amount of Stormlight would undo that.

Careful, he tried to lead Relis farther away from the fight. However, when he pulled back too far, the man just turned and moved toward Adolin.

The prince fought desperately against his two opponents, swinging his Blade back and forth between the men on either side of him. And *storms* he was good. Kaladin had never seen this level of skill from Adolin on the practice grounds—nothing there had ever challenged him this much. Adolin moved between sweeps of his Blade, deflecting the Shardblade of the one in green, then warding away the one with the hammer.

He frequently came within inches of striking his opponents. Two-on-one against Adolin actually seemed an even match.

Three would obviously be too much for him. Kaladin needed to keep Relis distracted. But how? He couldn't get through that Plate with a spear. The only weak points were the eye slit and the small crack on the vambrace.

He had to do something. The man was striding back toward Adolin, weapon raised. Gritting his teeth, Kaladin charged.

He crossed the sands in a quick dash and then, right before reaching Relis, Kaladin jumped to put his feet toward the Shardbearer and Lashed himself that direction many times in quick succession. As many as he dared, so many that he burned through all of his Stormlight.

Though Kaladin fell only a short distance—enough that it wouldn't look too unusual to those watching—he hit with the force of having fallen much farther. His feet smashed against the Plate as he *kicked* with everything he had.

Pain shot up his legs like lightning striking, and he heard his bones crack. The kick flung the black-armored Shardbearer forward as if he'd been struck by a boulder. Relis went sprawling on his face, Blade flung from his hands. It vanished to mist.

Kaladin crashed to the sand, groaning, his Stormlight exhausted and the Lashings ended. By reflex, he sucked in more Light from the spheres in his pocket, letting it heal his legs. He'd broken them both, and his feet.

The healing process seemed to take forever, and he forced himself to roll over and look at Relis. Incredibly, Kaladin's attack had *cracked* the Shardplate. Not the center of the back plate where he'd hit, but at the shoulders and sides. Relis climbed to his knees, shaking his head. He looked back at Kaladin with what seemed like an attitude of awe.

Beyond the fallen man, Adolin spun and came in at one of his opponents—Elit, the one with the hammer—and slammed his Shardblade two-handed into the man's chest. The breastplate there exploded into molten light. Adolin took a hit on the side of the helm from the man in green to do it.

Adolin was in bad shape. Practically every piece of Plate the young man wore was leaking Stormlight. At this rate, he'd soon have none left, and the Plate would grow too heavy to move in.

For now, fortunately, he'd basically incapacitated one of his adversaries. A Shardbearer could fight with his breastplate broken, but it was supposed to be storming difficult. Indeed, as Elit backed away, his steps were awkward, as if his Plate suddenly weighed a lot more.

Adolin had to turn to fight the other Shardbearer near him. On the other side of the arena, the fourth man—the one who had been "fighting" Renarin—was waving his sword at the ground for some reason. He looked up and saw how poorly things were going for his allies, then left Renarin and dashed across the arena floor.

"Wait," Syl said. "What is *that*?" She zipped away toward Renarin, but Kaladin couldn't spare much thought for her behavior. When the man in orange reached Adolin, he'd again be surrounded.

Kaladin scrambled to his feet. Blessedly, they worked; the bones had reknit enough for him to walk. He charged Elit, kicking up sand as he ran, spear clutched in one hand.

Elit wobbled toward Adolin, intending to continue the fight despite his disabled Plate. Kaladin reached him first, however, ducking under the man's hasty hammer strike. Kaladin came in swinging from the shoulder, holding his broken spear in two hands, giving the attack all he had.

It smashed into Elit's exposed chest, making a satisfying *crunch*. The man let out an enormous gasp, doubling over. Kaladin raised his spear to swing again, but the man lifted a wobbling hand, trying to say something. "Yield . . ." his weak voice said.

"Louder!" Kaladin snapped at him.

The man tried, out of breath. The hand he raised, however, was enough. The watching judge spoke. "Brightlord Elit yields the combat," she said, sounding reluctant.

Kaladin backed away from the cowering man, light on his feet, Stormlight thundering inside of him. The crowd roared, even many of the lighteyes making noise.

Three Shardbearers remained. Relis had now returned to his companion in green, both harrying Adolin. They had the prince backed up against a wall. The final Shardbearer, wearing orange, arrived to join them, having left Renarin behind.

Renarin sat on the sand, head bowed, Shardblade stuck into the ground before him. Had he been defeated? Kaladin had heard no announcement from the judge.

No time to worry. Adolin once again had *three* people to fight. Relis scored a hit on his helm, and the thing exploded, exposing the prince's face. He would not last much longer.

Kaladin charged up to Elit, who was trying to hobble off the field in defeat. "Remove your helm," Kaladin shouted at him.

The man turned to him with a shocked posture.

"Your helm!" Kaladin screamed, raising his weapon to strike again.

In the stands, people shouted. Kaladin wasn't sure of the rules, but he had a suspicion that if he struck this man, he would forfeit the duel. Maybe even face criminal charges. Fortunately, he wasn't forced to make good on the threat, as Elit removed his helm. Kaladin snatched it from his hand, then left him and ran toward Adolin.

As he ran, Kaladin dropped his broken spear and shoved his hand into the helm from the bottom. He'd learned something about Shardplate—it attached itself automatically to its bearer. He'd hoped it might work for the helm now, and it did—the inside tightened around his wrist. When he let go, the helm remained on his hand like a very strange glove.

Taking a deep breath, Kaladin yanked out his side knife. He'd started carrying one meant for throwing again, as he had as a spearman before his captivity, though he was out of practice with that. Throwing wouldn't work against that armor anyway; this was a pitiful weapon against Shardbearers. Still, he could not use the spear one-handed. He charged Relis again.

This time, Relis backed away immediately. He watched Kaladin, sword held out. At least Kaladin had managed to worry him.

Kaladin advanced, backing him away. Relis went easily, keeping his distance. Kaladin made a show of it, darting in, backing the man away as if to give the two of them space to fight. The Shardbearer would be eager for this; with his Blade, he would want a good open area around them. Tight quarters would favor Kaladin's knife.

However, once a sufficient distance away, Kaladin turned and dashed back toward Adolin and the two men he was fighting. He left Relis standing there in an anxious pose, momentarily befuddled by Kaladin's retreat.

Adolin glanced at Kaladin, then nodded.

The man in green turned with surprise at Kaladin's advance. He swung, and Kaladin caught the blow on the Shardplate helm he carried, deflecting it. The man grunted as Adolin threw everything he had at the other Shardbearer, the one in orange, slamming his weapon down again and again.

For a short time, Adolin had only one foe to fight. Hopefully he could use that time well, though his steps were lethargic and his Plate's leaking Stormlight had slowed to a trickle. His legs were nearly immobile.

Green Plate attacked Kaladin again, who deflected the blow off the helm, which cracked and began leaking Stormlight. Relis came charging up on the other side, but didn't join the fight against Adolin—instead, he thrust at Kaladin.

Kaladin gritted his teeth, dodging to the side, feeling the Blade pass in the air. He had to buy Adolin time. Moments. He needed moments.

The wind began to blow around him. Syl returned to him, zipping through the air as a ribbon of light.

Kaladin ducked another blow, then slammed his improvised shield against the Blade of the other, throwing it back. Sand flew as Kaladin leaped back, a Shardblade biting the ground before him.

Wind. Motion. Kaladin fought two Shardbearers at once, knocking their Blades aside with the helm. He couldn't attack—didn't dare *try* to attack. He could only survive, and in this, the winds seemed to urge him.

Instinct . . . then something deeper . . . guided his steps. He danced between those Blades, cool air wrapping around him. And for a moment, he felt—impossibly—that he could have dodged just as well if his eyes had been closed.

The Shardbearers cursed, trying again and again. Kaladin heard the judge say something, but was too absorbed in the fight to pay attention. The crowd was growing louder. He leaped one attack, then stepped just to the side of another.

You could not kill the wind. You could not stop it. It was beyond the touch of men. It was infinite. . . .

His Stormlight ran out.

Kaladin stumbled to a halt. He tried to suck in more, but all of his spheres were drained.

The helm, he realized, noticing that it was *gushing* Stormlight from its numerous cracks, yet hadn't exploded. It had somehow fed upon his Stormlight.

Relis attacked and Kaladin barely scrambled out of the way. His back hit the wall of the arena.

Green Plate saw his opening and raised his Blade.

Someone hopped on him from behind.

Kaladin watched, dumbfounded, as Adolin grappled Green Plate, latching on to him. Adolin's armor hardly leaked at all anymore; his Stormlight was exhausted. It seemed that he could barely move—the sand nearby displayed a set of lurching tracks that led away from Orange Plate, who lay in the sand defeated.

That was what the judge had said just earlier: the man in orange had yielded. Adolin had beaten his foe, then walked slowly—one laborious step after another—over to where Kaladin fought. It looked like he'd used his final bit of energy to hop up on Green Plate's back and grab hold.

Green Plate cursed, swatting at Adolin. The prince held on, and his Plate had locked, as they called it—becoming heavy and almost impossible to move.

The two teetered, then toppled over.

Kaladin looked at Relis, who glanced from the fallen Green Plate to the man in orange, then to Kaladin.

Relis turned and dashed across the sands toward Renarin.

Kaladin cursed, scrambling after him and tossing the helm aside. His body felt sluggish without the Stormlight to help.

"Renarin!" Kaladin yelled. "Yield!"

The boy looked up. Storms, he'd been crying. Was he hurt? He didn't look it.

"Surrender!" Kaladin said, trying to run faster, summoning every drop of energy from muscles that felt drained, exhausted from being inflated by Stormlight.

The lad focused on Relis, who was bearing down on him, but said nothing. Instead, Renarin dismissed his Blade.

Relis skidded to a stop, raising his Blade high over his head toward the defenseless prince. Renarin closed his eyes, looking upward, as if exposing his throat.

Kaladin wasn't going to arrive in time. He was too slow compared to a man in Plate.

Relis hesitated, fortunately, as if unwilling to strike Renarin.

Kaladin arrived. Relis spun around and swung at him instead.

Kaladin skidded to his knees in the sand, momentum carrying him forward a short distance as the Blade fell. He raised his hands and snapped them together.

Catching the Blade.

Screaming.

Why could he hear *screaming*? Inside his head? Was that *Syl's* voice?

It reverberated through Kaladin. That horrible, awful screech shook him, made his muscles tremble. He released the Shardblade with a gasp, falling backward.

Relis dropped the Blade as if bitten. He backed away, raising his hands to his head. "What is it? What is it! No, I didn't kill you!" He shrieked as if in great pain, then ran across the sands and pulled open the door to the preparation room, fleeing inside. Kaladin heard his screams echoing inside the hallways there long after the man vanished.

The arena grew still.

"Highlord Relis Ruthar," the judge finally called, sounding disturbed, "forfeits by cause of leaving the dueling arena."

Kaladin climbed, trembling, to his feet. He glanced at Renarin—the lad was fine—then slowly crossed the arena. Even the watching darkeyes had grown silent. Kaladin was pretty sure they hadn't heard that strange scream, though. It had only been audible to him and Relis.

He stepped up to Adolin and Green Plate.

"Stand up and fight me!" Green Plate shouted. He lay faceup on the ground, Adolin buried beneath him and holding on in a wrestling grip.

Kaladin knelt down. Green Plate struggled more as Kaladin retrieved his side knife from the sand, then pressed the tip of it into the opening in Green Plate's armor.

The man grew perfectly still.

"You going to yield?" Kaladin growled. "Or do I get to kill my second Shardbearer?"

Silence.

"Storms curse you both!" Green Plate finally shouted inside his helm. "This wasn't a duel, this was a circus! Grappling is the way of the coward!"

Kaladin pressed the knife in farther.

"I yield!" the man yelled, holding up his hand. "Storm you, I yield!"

"Brightlord Jakamav yields," the judge said. "The day goes to Brightlord Adolin."

The darkeyes in their seats cheered. The lighteyes seemed stunned. Above, Syl spun with the winds, and Kaladin could feel her joy. Adolin released Green Plate, who rolled off him and stomped away. Underneath, the prince lay in a depression in the sand, head and shoulder exposed through broken pieces of Plate.

He was laughing.

Kaladin sat down beside the prince as Adolin laughed himself silly, tears streaming from his eyes.

"That was the most ridiculous thing I've ever done," Adolin said. "Oh, wow. . . . Ha! I think I just won three full suits of Plate and two Blades, bridgeboy. Here, help me get this armor off."

"Your armorer can do that," Kaladin said.

"No time," Adolin said, trying to sit up. "Storms. Completely drained. Hurry, help with this. There's something yet for me to do."

Challenge Sadeas, Kaladin realized. That was the point of all of this. He reached in under Adolin's gauntlet, helping him undo the strap there. The gauntlet didn't come off automatically, as it was supposed to. Adolin really had completely drained the suit.

They pulled the gauntlet off, then worked on the other one. A few minutes later, Renarin wandered over and helped. Kaladin didn't ask him about what had happened. The lad provided some spheres, and after Kaladin had tucked those in under Adolin's loosened breastplate, the armor started to function again.

They worked to the roar of the crowd as Adolin finally got free of the Plate and stood up. Ahead, the king had stepped up beside the judge, one foot on the railing around the arena. He looked down at Adolin, who nodded.

This is Adolin's chance, Kaladin realized, *but it can be my chance too.*

The king raised his hands, quieting the crowd.

"Warrior, duelmaster," the king shouted, "I am greatly pleased by what you have accomplished today. This was a fight the like of which hasn't been seen in Alethkar for generations. You have pleased your king greatly."

Cheering.

I could do this, Kaladin thought.

"I offer you a boon," the king proclaimed, pointing to Adolin as the cheering quieted. "Name what you wish of me or of this court. It shall be yours. No man, having seen this display, could deny you."

The Right of Challenge, Kaladin thought.

Adolin sought out Sadeas, who had stood and was making his way up the steps to flee. He understood.

Far to the right, Amaram sat in his golden cloak.

"For my boon," Adolin shouted to the quiet arena, "I demand the Right of Challenge. I demand the chance to duel Highprince Sadeas, right here and now, as redress for the crimes he committed against my house!"

Sadeas stopped upon the steps. A murmur ran through the crowd. Adolin looked as if he were going to say something more, but hesitated as Kaladin stepped up beside him.

"And for my boon!" Kaladin shouted, "I demand the Right of Challenge against the murderer Amaram! He stole from me and slaughtered my friends to cover it up. Amaram branded me a slave! I will duel him here, right now. That is the boon I demand!"

The king's jaw dropped.

The crowd grew very, very still.

Beside him, Adolin groaned.

Kaladin didn't spare either one a thought. Across the distance, he met the eyes of Brightlord Amaram, the murderer.

He saw horror therein.

Amaram stood up, then stumbled back. He hadn't known, hadn't recognized Kaladin, until just then.

You should have killed me, Kaladin thought. The crowd started to shout and yell.

"Arrest him!" the king bellowed over the din.

Perfect. Kaladin grinned.

Until he noticed the soldiers were coming for him and not Amaram.

So Melishi retired to his tent, and resolved to destroy the Void-bringers upon the next day, but that night did present a different stratagem, related to the unique abilities of the Bondsmiths; and being hurried, he could make no specific account of his process; it was related to the very nature of the Heralds and their divine duties, an attribute the Bondsmiths alone could address.

—From *Words of Radiance,* chapter 30, page 18

Captain Kaladin is a man of honor, Elhokar!" Dalinar shouted, gesturing toward Kaladin, who sat nearby. "He was the only one who went to help my sons."

"That's his job!" Elhokar snapped back.

Kaladin listened dully, chained to a seat inside Dalinar's rooms back in the warcamp. They hadn't gone to the palace. Kaladin didn't know why.

The three of them were alone.

"He insulted a highlord in front of the *entire court*," Elhokar said, pacing beside the wall. "He *dared* challenge a man so high above his station, the gap between them could hold a kingdom."

"He was caught up in the moment," Dalinar said. "Be reasonable, Elhokar. He'd just helped bring down four Shardbearers!"

"On a dueling ground, where his help was invited," Elhokar said, throwing his hands into the air. "I still don't agree with letting a darkeyes duel Shardbearers. If you hadn't held me back . . . Bah! I won't stand for this, Uncle. I *won't.* Common soldiers challenging our highest and most important generals? It is *madness.*"

"What I said was true," Kaladin whispered.

"Don't you speak!" Elhokar shouted, stopping and leveling a finger at Kaladin. "You've ruined everything! We lost our chance at Sadeas!"

"Adolin made his challenge," Kaladin said. "Surely Sadeas can't ignore it."

"Of course he can't," Elhokar shouted. "He's already responded!"

Kaladin frowned.

"Adolin didn't get a chance to pin down the duel," Dalinar said, looking at Kaladin. "As soon as he was free of the arena, Sadeas sent word agreeing to duel Adolin—in one year's time."

One *year*? Kaladin felt a hollowness in his stomach. By the time a year had passed, chances were the duel wouldn't matter anymore.

"He wiggled out of the noose," Elhokar said, throwing up his hands. "We *needed* that moment in the arena to pin him down, to shame him into a fight! You stole that moment, bridgeman."

Kaladin lowered his head. He'd have stood up to confront them, except for the chains. They were cold around his ankles, locking him to the chair.

He remembered chains like those.

"This is what you get, Uncle," Elhokar said, "for putting a slave in charge of our guard. Storms! What were you thinking? What was *I* thinking in allowing you?"

"You saw him fight, Elhokar," Dalinar said softly. "He is good."

"It's not his skill but his discipline that is the problem!" The king folded his arms. "Execution."

Kaladin looked up sharply.

"Don't be ridiculous," Dalinar said, stepping up beside Kaladin's chair.

"It is the punishment for slandering a highlord," Elhokar said. "It is the *law*."

"You can pardon any crime, as king," Dalinar said. "Don't tell me you honestly want to see this man hanged after what he did today."

"Would you stop me?" Elhokar said.

"I wouldn't stand for it, that's certain."

Elhokar crossed the room, stepping right up to Dalinar. For a moment, Kaladin seemed forgotten.

"Am I king?" Elhokar asked.

"Of course you are."

"You don't act like it. You're going to have to decide something, *Uncle*. I won't continue letting you rule, making a puppet of me."

"I'm not—"

"I say the boy is to be executed. What do you say of that?"

"I'd say that in attempting such a thing, you'd make an enemy of me,

Elhokar." Dalinar had grown tense.

Just try to execute me . . . Kaladin thought. *Just try.*

The two stared at each other for a long moment. Finally, Elhokar turned away. "Prison."

"How long?" Dalinar said.

"Until I say he's done!" the king said, waving a hand and stalking toward the exit. He stopped there, looking at Dalinar, a challenge in his eyes.

"Very well," Dalinar said.

The king left.

"Hypocrite," Kaladin hissed. "He's the one who insisted you put me in charge of his guard. Now he blames you?"

Dalinar sighed, kneeling down beside Kaladin. "What you did today was a wonder. In protecting my sons, you justified my faith in you before the entire court. Unfortunately, you then threw it away."

"He asked me for a boon!" Kaladin snapped, raising his manacled hands. "I got one, it seems."

"He asked *Adolin* for a boon. You knew what we were about, soldier. You heard the plan in conference with us this morning. You overshadowed it in the name of your own petty vengeance."

"Amaram—"

"I don't know where you got this idea about Amaram," Dalinar said, "but you have to *stop*. I checked into what you said, after you brought it to my attention the first time. Seventeen witnesses told me that Amaram won his Shardblade only four months ago, long after your ledger says you were made a slave."

"Lies."

"Seventeen men," Dalinar repeated. "Lighteyed and dark, along with the word of a man I've known for decades. You're wrong about him, soldier. You're just plain *wrong*."

"If he is so honorable," Kaladin whispered, "then why didn't *he* fight to save your sons?"

Dalinar hesitated.

"It doesn't matter," Kaladin said, looking away. "You're going to let the king put me in prison."

"Yes," Dalinar said, rising. "Elhokar has a temper. Once he cools down, I'll get you free. For now, it might be best if you had some time to think."

"They'll have a tough time forcing me to go to prison," Kaladin said softly.

"Have you even been listening?" Dalinar suddenly roared.

Kaladin sat back, eyes widening, as Dalinar leaned down, red-faced, taking Kaladin by the shoulders as if to shake him. "Have you not *felt* what is coming? Have you not seen how this kingdom squabbles? We don't have time for this! We don't have time for games! Stop being a child, and start being a *soldier*! You'll go to prison, and you'll go happily. That's an order. Do you *listen* to orders anymore?"

"I . . ." Kaladin found himself stammering.

Dalinar stood up, rubbing his hands on his temples. "I thought we had Sadeas cornered, there. I thought maybe we'd be able to cut his feet out from under him and save this kingdom. Now I don't know what to do." He turned and walked to the door. "Thank you for saving my sons."

He left Kaladin alone in the cold stone room.

⁘

Torol Sadeas slammed the door to his quarters. He walked to his table and leaned over it, hands flat on the surface, looking down at the slice through the center he'd made with Oathbringer.

A drop of sweat smacked the surface right beside that slot. He'd kept himself from trembling all the way back to the safety of his warcamp— he'd actually managed to paste on a smile. He'd shown no concern, even as he dictated to his wife a response to the challenge.

And all the while, in the back of his mind a voice had laughed at him.

Dalinar. Dalinar had almost *outmaneuvered* him. If that challenge had been sustained, Sadeas would quickly have found himself in the arena with a man who had just defeated not one, but *four* Shardbearers.

He sat down. He did not look for wine. Wine made a man forget, and he didn't want to forget this. He must never forget this.

How satisfying it would be to someday ram Dalinar's own sword into his chest. Storms. To think he'd almost felt pity for his former friend. Now the man pulled something like this. How had he grown so deft?

No, Sadeas told himself. *This was not deftness. It was luck. Pure and simple luck.*

Four Shardbearers. *How?* Even allowing for the help of that slave, it was now obvious that Adolin was at last growing into the man his father had once been. That terrified Sadeas, because the man Dalinar had once been—the Blackthorn—had been a large part of what had conquered this kingdom.

Isn't this what you wanted? Sadeas thought. *To reawaken him?*

No. The deeper truth was that Sadeas *didn't* want Dalinar back. He wanted his old friend out of the way, and it had been such for months now, no matter what he wanted to tell himself.

A while later, the door to his study opened and Ialai slipped in. Seeing him lost in thought, she stopped by the door.

"Organize all of your informants," Sadeas said, looking up at the ceiling. "Every spy you have, every source you know. Find me something, Ia-lai. Something to *hurt* him."

She nodded.

"And after that," Sadeas said, "it will be time to make use of those assassins you've planted."

He had to ensure that Dalinar was desperate and wounded—had to guarantee that the others viewed him as broken, ruined.

Then he'd end this.

.·.

Soldiers arrived for Kaladin a short time later. Men that Kaladin didn't know. They were respectful as they unchained him from the chair, though they left the chains binding his hands and feet. One gave him a lifted fist, a sign of respect. *Stay strong,* the fist said.

Kaladin bowed his head and shuffled with them, led through camp before the watching eyes of soldiers and scribes alike. He caught a glimpse of Bridge Four uniforms in the crowd.

He reached Dalinar's camp prison, where soldiers did time for fighting or other offenses. It was a small, nearly windowless building with thick walls.

Inside, in an isolated section, Kaladin was placed in a cell with stone walls and a door of steel bars. They left the chains on as they locked him in.

He sat down on a stone bench, waiting, until Syl finally drifted into the room.

"This," Kaladin said, looking at her, "is what comes of trusting lighteyes. Never again, Syl."

"Kaladin . . ."

He closed his eyes, turning and lying down on the cold stone bench.

He was in a cage once again.

THE END OF

Part Three

INTERLUDES

LIFT • SZETH • ESHONAI

Lift had never robbed a palace before. Seemed like a dangerous thing to try. Not because she might get caught, but because once you robbed a starvin' palace, where did you go next?

She climbed up onto the outer wall and looked in at the grounds. Everything inside—trees, rocks, buildings—reflected the starlight in an odd way. A bulbous-looking building stuck up in the middle of it all, like a bubble on a pond. In fact, most of the buildings were that same round shape, often with small protrusions sprouting out of the top. There wasn't a straight line in the whole starvin' place. Just lots and lots of curves.

Lift's companions climbed up to peek over the top of the wall. A scuffling, scrambling, rowdy mess they were. Six men, supposedly master thieves. They couldn't even climb a wall properly.

"The Bronze Palace itself," Huqin breathed.

"Bronze? Is that what everythin' is made of?" Lift asked, sitting on the wall with one leg over the side. "Looks like a bunch of breasts."

The men looked at her, aghast. They were all Azish, with dark skin and hair. She was Reshi, from the islands up north. Her mother had told her that, though Lift had never seen the place.

"What?" Huqin demanded.

"Breasts," Lift said, pointing. "See, like a lady layin' on her back. Those points on the tops are nipples. Bloke who built this place musta been single for a *looong* time."

Huqin turned to one of his companions. Using their ropes, they scuttled back down the outside of the wall to hold a whispered conference.

"Grounds at this end look empty, as my informant indicated would be the case," Huqin said. He was in charge of the lot of them. Had a nose like someone had taken hold of it when he was a kid and pulled real, *real* hard.

Lift was surprised he didn't smack people in the face with it when he turned.

"Everyone's focused on choosing the new Prime Aqasix," said Maxin. "We could really do this. Rob the Bronze Palace itself, and right under the nose of the vizierate."

"Is it . . . um . . . safe?" asked Huqin's nephew. He was in his teens, and puberty hadn't been kind to him. Not with that face, that voice, and those spindly legs.

"Hush," Huqin snapped.

"No," Tigzikk said, "the boy is right to express caution. This will be very dangerous."

Tigzikk was considered the learned one in the group on account of his being able to cuss in three languages. Downright scholarly, that was. He wore fancy clothing, while most of the others wore black. "There will be chaos," Tigzikk continued, "because so many people move through the palace tonight, but there will also be danger. Many, many bodyguards and a likelihood of suspicion on all sides."

Tigzikk was an aging fellow, and was the only one of the group Lift knew well. She couldn't say his name. That "quq" sound on the end of his name sounded like choking when someone pronounced it correctly. She just called him Tig instead.

"Tigzikk," Huqin said. Yup. Choking. "You were the one who suggested this. Don't tell me you're getting cold now."

"I'm not backing down. I'm pleading caution."

Lift leaned down over the wall toward them. "Less arguing," she said. "Let's move. I'm hungry."

Huqin looked up. "*Why* did we bring her along?"

"She'll be useful," Tigzikk said. "You'll see."

"She's just a child!"

"She's a youth. She's at least twelve."

"I *ain't* twelve," Lift snapped, looming over them.

They turned up toward her.

"I ain't," she said. "Twelve's an unlucky number." She held up her hands. "I'm only this many."

". . . Ten?" Tigzikk asked.

"Is that how many that is? Sure, then. Ten." She lowered her hands. "If I can't count it on my fingers, it's unlucky." And she'd been that many for three years now. So there.

"Seems like there are a lot of unlucky ages," Huqin said, sounding amused.

"Sure are," she agreed. She scanned the grounds again, then glanced back the way they had come, into the city.

A man walked down one of the streets leading to the palace. His dark clothing blended into the gloom, but his silver buttons glinted each time he passed a streetlight.

Storms, she thought, a chill running up her spine. *I didn't lose him after all.*

She looked down at the men. "Are you coming with me or not? 'Cuz I'm *leaving.*" She slipped over the top and dropped into the palace yards. Lift squatted there, feeling the cold ground. Yup, it was metal. Everything was bronze. Rich people, she decided, loved to stick with a theme.

As the boys finally stopped arguing and started climbing, a thin, twisting trail of vines grew out of the darkness and approached Lift. It looked like a little stream of spilled water picking its way across the floor. Here and there, bits of clear crystal peeked out of the vines, like sections of quartz in otherwise dark stone. Those weren't sharp, but smooth like polished glass, and didn't glow with Stormlight.

The vines grew super-fast, curling about one another in a tangle that formed a face.

"Mistress," the face said. "Is this *wise?*"

"'Ello, Voidbringer," Lift said, scanning the grounds.

"I am *not* a Voidbringer!" he said. "And you know it. Just . . . just stop saying that!"

Lift grinned. "You're my pet Voidbringer, and no lies are going to change that. I got you captured. No stealing souls, now. We ain't here for souls. Just a little thievery, the type what never hurt nobody."

The vine face—he called himself Wyndle—sighed. Lift scuttled across the bronze ground over to a tree that was, of course, also made of bronze. Huqin had chosen the darkest part of night, between moons, for them to slip in—but the starlight was enough to see by on a cloudless night like this.

Wyndle grew up to her, leaving a small trail of vines that people didn't seem to be able to see. The vines hardened after a few moments of sitting, as if briefly becoming solid crystal, then they crumbled to dust. People spotted that on occasion, though they certainly couldn't see Wyndle himself.

"I'm a spren," Wyndle said to her. "Part of a proud and noble—"

"Hush," Lift said, peeking out from behind the bronze tree. An open-topped carriage passed on the drive beyond, carrying some important Azish folk. You could tell by the coats. Big, drooping coats with really wide sleeves and patterns that argued with each other. They all looked like kids who had snuck into their parents' wardrobe. The hats were nifty, though.

The thieves followed behind her, moving with reasonable stealth. They really weren't *that* bad. Even if they didn't know how to climb a wall properly.

They gathered around her, and Tigzikk stood up, straightening his coat—which was an imitation of one of those worn by the rich scribe types who worked in the government. Here in Azir, working for the government was real important. Everyone else was said to be "discrete," whatever that meant.

"Ready?" Tigzikk said to Maxin, who was the other one of the thieves dressed in fine clothing.

Maxin nodded, and the two of them moved off to the right, heading toward the palace's sculpture garden. The important people would supposedly be shuffling around in there, speculating about who should be the next Prime.

Dangerous job, that. The last two had gotten their heads chopped off by some bloke in white with a Shardblade. The most recent Prime hadn't lasted two starvin' days!

With Tigzikk and Maxin gone, Lift only had four others to worry about. Huqin, his nephew, and two slender brothers who didn't talk much and kept reaching under their coats for knives. Lift didn't like their type. Thieving shouldn't leave bodies. Leaving bodies was easy. There was no *challenge* to it if you could just kill anyone who spotted you.

"You *can* get us in," Huqin said to Lift. "Right?"

Lift pointedly rolled her eyes. Then she scuttled across the bronze grounds toward the main palace structure.

Really does look like a breast . . .

Wyndle curled along the ground beside her, his vine trail sprouting tiny bits of clear crystal here and there. He was as sinuous and speedy as a moving eel, only he *grew* rather than actually moving. Voidbringers were a strange lot.

"You realize that *I* didn't choose you," he said, a face appearing in the vines as they moved. His speaking left a strange effect, the trail behind him clotted with a sequence of frozen faces. The mouth seemed to move because it was growing so quickly beside her. "*I* wanted to pick a distinguished Iriali matron. A grandmother, an accomplished gardener. But no, the Ring said we should choose you. 'She has visited the Old Magic,' they said. 'Our mother has blessed her,' they said. 'She will be young, and we can mold her,' they said. Well, *they* don't have to put up with—"

"Shut it, Voidbringer," Lift hissed, drawing up beside the wall of the palace. "Or I'll bathe in blessed water and go listen to the priests. Maybe get an exorcism."

Lift edged sideways until she could look around the curve of the wall to
spot the guard patrol: men in patterned vests and caps, with long halberds.

She looked up the side of the wall. It bulged out just above her, like a rock-bud, before tapering up further. It was of smooth bronze, with no hand-holds.

She waited until the guards had walked farther away. "All right," she whispered to Wyndle. "You gotta do what I say."

"I do *not*."

"Sure you do. I captured you, just like in the stories."

"I came to *you*," Wyndle said. "Your powers come from me! Do you even *listen* to—"

"Up the wall," Lift said, pointing.

Wyndle sighed, but obeyed, creeping up the wall in a wide, looping pattern. Lift hopped up, grabbing the small handholds made by the vine, which stuck to the surface by virtue of thousands of branching stems with sticky discs on them. Wyndle wove ahead of her, making a ladder of sorts.

It wasn't easy. It was starvin' difficult, with that bulge, and Wyndle's handholds weren't very big. But she did it, climbing all the way to the near-top of the building's dome, where windows peeked out at the grounds.

She glanced toward the city. No sign of the man in the black uniform. Maybe she'd lost him.

She turned back to examine the window. Its nice wooden frame held very thick glass, even though it pointed east. It was unfair how well Azi-mir was protected from highstorms. They should have to live with the wind, like normal folk.

"We need to Voidbring that," she said, pointing at the window.

"Have you realized," Wyndle said, "that while you *claim* to be a master thief, *I* do all of the work in this relationship?"

"You do all the complainin' too," she said. "How do we get through this?"

"You have the seeds?"

She nodded, fishing in her pocket. Then in the other one. Then in her back pocket. Ah, there they were. She pulled out a handful of seeds.

"I can't affect the Physical Realm except in minor ways," Wyndle said. "This means that you will need to use Investiture to—"

Lift yawned.

"Use Investiture to—"

She yawned *wider*. Starvin' Voidbringers never could catch a hint.

Wyndle sighed. "Spread the seeds on the frame."

She did so, throwing the handful of seeds at the window.

"Your bond to me grants two primary classes of ability," Wyndle said. "The first, manipulation of friction, you've already—don't yawn at me!—discovered. We have been using that well for many weeks now, and it is time for you to learn the second, the power of Growth. You aren't ready for what was once known as Regrowth, the healing of—"

Lift pressed her hand against the seeds, then summoned her awesomeness.

She wasn't sure how she did it. She just *did*. It had started right around when Wyndle had first appeared.

He hadn't talked then. She kind of missed those days.

Her hand glowed faintly with white light, like vapor coming off the skin. The seeds that saw the light started to grow. Fast. Vines burst from the seeds and wormed into the cracks between the window and its frame.

The vines grew at her will, making constricted, straining sounds. The glass cracked, then the window frame *popped* open.

Lift grinned.

"Well done," Wyndle said. "We'll make an Edgedancer out of you yet."

Her stomach grumbled. When had she last eaten? She'd used a lot of her awesomeness practicing earlier. She probably should have stolen something to eat. She wasn't quite so awesome when she was hungry.

She slipped inside the window. Having a Voidbringer was useful, though she wasn't *completely* sure her powers came from him. That seemed the sorta thing a Voidbringer would lie about. She *had* captured him, fair and square. She'd used words. A Voidbringer had no body, not really. To catch something like that, you had to use words. Everybody knew it. Just like curses made evil things come find you.

She had to get out a sphere—a diamond mark, her lucky one—to see properly in here. The small bedroom was decorated after the Azish way with lots of intricate patterns on the rugs and the fabric on the walls, mostly gold and red here. Those patterns were everything to the Azish. They were like words.

She looked out the window. Surely she'd escaped Darkness, the man in the black and silver with the pale crescent birthmark on his cheek. The man with the dead, lifeless stare. Surely he hadn't followed her all the way from Marabethia. That was half a continent away! Well, a quarter one, at the least.

Convinced, she uncoiled the rope that she wore wrapped around her waist and over her shoulders. She tied it to the door of a built-in closet, then fed it out the window. It tightened as the men started climbing. Nearby, Wyndle grew up around one of the bedposts, coiled like a skyeel.

She heard whispered voices below. "Did you *see* that? She climbed right up it. Not a handhold in sight. How . . . ?"

"Hush." That was Huqin.

Lift began poking through cabinets and drawers as the boys clambered in the window one at a time. Once inside, the thieves pulled up the rope and shut the window as best they could. Huqin studied the vines she'd grown from seeds on the frame.

Lift stuck her head in the bottom of a wardrobe, groping around. "Ain't nothing in this room but moldy shoes."

"You," Huqin said to her, "and my nephew will hold this room. The three of us will search the bedrooms nearby. We will be back shortly."

"You'll probably have a whole *sack* of moldy shoes . . ." Lift said, pulling out of the wardrobe.

"Ignorant child," Huqin said, pointing at the wardrobe. One of his men grabbed the shoes and outfits inside, stuffing them in a sack. "This clothing will sell for bundles. It's exactly what we're looking for."

"What about real riches?" Lift said. "Spheres, jewelry, art . . ." She had little interest in those things herself, but she'd figured it was what Huqin was after.

"That will all be *far* too well guarded," Huqin said as his two associates made quick work of the room's clothing. "The difference between a successful thief and a dead thief is knowing when to escape with your takings. This haul will let us live in luxury for a year or two. That is enough."

One of the brothers peeked out the door into the hallway. He nodded, and the three of them slipped out. "Listen for the warning," Huqin said to his nephew, then eased the door almost closed behind him.

Tigzikk and his accomplice below would listen for any kind of alarm. If anything seemed to be amiss, they'd slip off and blow their whistles. Huqin's nephew crouched by the window to listen, obviously taking his duty very seriously. He looked to be about sixteen. Unlucky age, that.

"How did you climb the wall like that?" the youth asked.

"Gumption," Lift said. "And spit."

He frowned at her.

"I gots magic spit."

He seemed to believe her. Idiot.

"Is it strange for you here?" he asked. "Away from your people?"

She stood out. Straight black hair—she wore it down to her waist—tan skin, rounded features. Everyone would immediately mark her as Reshi.

"Don't know," Lift said, strolling to the door. "Ain't never been around my people."

"You're not from the islands?"

"Nope. Grew up in Rall Elorim."

"The . . . City of Shadows?"

"Yup."

"Is it—"

"Yup. Just like they say."

She peeked through the door. Huqin and the others were well out of the way. The hallway was bronze—walls and everything—but a red and blue rug, with lots of little vine patterns, ran down the center. Paintings hung on the walls.

She pulled the door all the way open and stepped out.

"Lift!" The nephew scrambled to the door. "They told us to wait here!"

"And?"

"And we should *wait here*! We don't want to get Uncle Huqin in trouble!"

"What's the point of sneaking into a palace if not to get into trouble?" She shook her head. Odd men, these. "This should be an interesting place, what with all of the rich folk hanging around." There ought to be some *really* good food in here.

She padded out into the hallway, and Wyndle grew along the floor beside her. Interestingly, the nephew followed. She'd expected him to stay in the room.

"We shouldn't be doing this," he said as they passed a door that was open a crack, shuffles sounding from inside. Huqin and his men, robbing the place silly.

"Then stay," Lift whispered, reaching a large stairwell. Servants whisked back and forth below, even a few parshmen, but she didn't catch sight of anyone in one of those coats. "Where are the important folk?"

"Reading forms," the nephew said from beside her.

"Forms?"

"Sure," he said. "With the Prime dead, the viziers, scribes, and arbiters were all given a chance to fill out the proper paperwork to apply to take his place."

"You *apply* to be emperor?" Lift said.

"Sure," he said. "Lots of paperwork involved in that. And an essay. Your essay has to be *really* good to get this job."

"Storms. You people are crazy."

"Other nations do it better? With bloody succession wars? This way, everyone has a chance. Even the lowest of clerks can submit the paperwork. You can even be *discrete* and end up on the throne, if you are convincing enough. It happened once."

"Crazy."

"Says the girl who talks to herself."

Lift looked at him sharply.

"Don't pretend you don't," he said. "I've seen you doing it. Talking to the air, as if somebody were there."

"What's your name?" she asked.

"Gawx."

"Wow. Well then, Gaw. I don't talk to myself because I'm crazy."

"No?"

"I do it because I'm *awesome*." She started down the steps, waited for a gap between passing servants, then made for a closet across the way. Gawx cursed, then followed.

Lift was tempted to use her awesomeness to slide across the floor quickly, but she didn't need that yet. Besides, Wyndle kept complaining that she used the awesomeness too often. That she was at risk of malnutrition, whatever that meant.

She slipped up to the closet, using just her normal everyday sneakin' skills, and moved inside. Gawx scrambled into the closet with her just before she pulled it shut. Dinnerware on a serving cart clinked behind them, and they could barely crowd into the space. Gawx moved, causing more clinks, and she elbowed him. He stilled as two parshmen passed, bearing large wine barrels.

"You should go back upstairs," Lift whispered to him. "This could be dangerous."

"Oh, sneaking into the storming *royal palace* is dangerous? Thanks. I hadn't realized."

"I mean it," Lift said, peeking out of the closet. "Go back up, leave when Huqin returns. He'll abandon me in a heartbeat. Probably will you, too."

Besides, she didn't want to be awesome with Gawx around. That started questions. And rumors. She hated both. For once, she'd like to be able to stay someplace for a while without being forced to run off.

"No," Gawx said softly. "If you're going to steal something good, I want a piece of it. Then maybe Huqin will stop making me stay behind, giving me the easy jobs."

Huh. So he had some spunk to him.

A servant passed carrying a large, plate-filled tray. The food smells wafting from it made Lift's stomach growl. Rich-person food. So *delicious*.

Lift watched the woman go, then broke out of the closet, following after. This was going to get difficult with Gawx in tow. He'd been trained well enough by his uncle, but moving unseen through a populated building wasn't easy.

The serving woman pulled open a door that was hidden in the wall. Servants' hallways. Lift caught it as it closed, waited a few heartbeats, then eased it open and slipped through. The narrow hallway was poorly lit and smelled of the food that had just passed.

Gawx entered behind Lift, then silently pulled the door closed. The serving woman disappeared around a corner ahead—there were probably lots of hallways like this in the palace. Behind Lift, Wyndle grew around the doorframe, a dark green, funguslike creep of vines that covered the door, then the wall beside her.

He formed a face in the vines and spots of crystal, then shook his head.

"Too narrow?" Lift asked.

He nodded.

"It's dark in here. Hard to see us."

"Vibrations on the floor, mistress. Someone coming this direction."

She looked longingly after the servant with the food, then shoved past Gawx and pushed open the door, entering the main hallways again.

Gawx cursed. "Do you even know what you're doing?"

"No," she said, then scuttled around a corner into a large hallway lined with alternating green and yellow gemstone lamps. Unfortunately, a servant in a stiff, black and white uniform was coming right at her.

Gawx let out a "meep" of worry, ducking back around the corner. Lift stood up straight, clasped her hands behind her back, and strolled forward.

She passed the man. His uniform marked him as someone important, for a servant.

"You, there!" the man snapped. "What is this?"

"Mistress wants some cake," Lift said, jutting out her chin.

"Oh, for Yaezir's sake. Food is served in the gardens! There is cake *there*!"

"Wrong type," Lift said. "Mistress wants berry cake."

The man threw his hands into the air. "Kitchens are back the other way," he said. "Try and persuade the cook, though she'll probably chop your hands off before she takes another special request. Storming country scribes! Special dietary needs are supposed to be sent ahead of time, with the proper forms!" He stalked off, leaving Lift with hands behind her back, watching him.

Gawx slunk around the corner. "I thought we were dead for sure."

"Don't be stupid," Lift said, hurrying down the hallway. "This ain't the dangerous part yet."

At the other end, this hallway intersected another one—with the same wide rug down the center, bronze walls, and glowing metal lamps. Across the way was a door with no light shining under it. Lift checked in both directions, then dashed to the door, cracked it, peeked in, then waved for Gawx to join her inside.

"We should go right down that hallway outside," Gawx whispered as she shut the door all but a crack. "Down that way, we'll find the vizier quarters. They're probably empty, because everyone will be in the Prime's wing deliberating."

"You know the palace layout?" she asked, crouching in near darkness beside the door. They were in a small sitting room of some sort, with a couple of shadowed chairs and a small table.

"Yeah," Gawx said. "I memorized the palace maps before we came. You didn't?"

She shrugged.

"I've been in here once before," Gawx said. "I watched the Prime sleeping."

"You *what*?"

"He's public," Gawx said, "belongs to everyone. You can enter a lottery to come look at him sleeping. They rotate people through every hour."

"What? On a special day or something?"

"No, every day. You can watch him eat too, or watch him perform his daily rituals. If he loses a hair or cuts off a nail, you might be able to keep it as a relic."

"Sounds creepy."

"A little."

"Which way to his rooms?" Lift asked.

"That way," Gawx said, pointing left down the hallway outside—the opposite direction from the vizier chambers. "You don't want to go there, Lift. That's where the viziers and everyone important will be reviewing applications. In the Prime's presence."

"But he's dead."

"The new Prime."

"He ain't been chosen yet!"

"Well, it's kind of strange," Gawx said. By the dim light of the cracked door, she could see him blushing, as if he knew how starvin' odd this all was. "There's never *not* a Prime. We just don't know who he is yet. I mean, he's alive, and he's already Prime—right now. We're just catching up. So, those are his quarters, and the scions and viziers want to be in his presence while they decide who he is. Even if the person they decide upon isn't in the room."

"That makes no sense."

"Of course it makes sense," Gawx said. "It's government. This is all *very* well detailed in the codes and . . ." He trailed off as Lift yawned. Azish could be *real* boring. At least he could take a hint, though.

"Anyway," Gawx continued, "everyone outside in the gardens is hoping to be called in for a personal interview. It might not come to that, though. The scions can't be Prime, as they're too busy visiting and blessing villages around the kingdom—but a vizier can, and they tend to have the best applications. Usually, one of their number is chosen."

"The Prime's quarters," Lift said. "That's the direction the food went."

"What is it with you and food?"

"I'm going to eat their dinner," she said, soft but intense.

Gawx blinked, startled. "You're . . . *what*?"

"I'm gonna eat their food," she said. "Rich folk have the best food."

"But . . . there might be spheres in the vizier quarters. . . ."

"Eh," she said. "I'd just spend 'em on food."

Stealing regular stuff was no fun. She wanted a *real* challenge. Over the last two years, she'd picked the most difficult places to enter. Then she'd snuck in.

And eaten their dinners.

"Come on," she said, moving out of the doorway, then turned left toward the Prime's chambers.

"You really *are* crazy," Gawx whispered.

"Nah. Just bored."

He looked the other way. "I'm going for the vizier quarters."

"Suit yourself," she said. "I'd go back upstairs instead, if I were you. You aren't practiced enough for this kind of thing. You leave me, you're probably going to get into trouble."

He fidgeted, then slipped off in the direction of the vizier quarters. Lift rolled her eyes.

"Why did you even come with them?" Wyndle asked, creeping out of the room. "Why not just sneak in on your own?"

"Tigzikk found out about this whole election thing," she said. "He told me tonight was a good night for sneaking. I owed it to him. Besides, I wanted to be here in case he got into trouble. I might need to help."

"Why bother?"

Why indeed? "Someone has to care," she said, starting down the hallway. "Too few people care, these days."

"You say this while coming in to *rob* people."

"Sure. Ain't gonna hurt them."

"You have an odd sense of morality, mistress."

"Don't be stupid," she said. "Every sense of morality is odd."

"I suppose."

"Particularly to a Voidbringer."

"I'm not—"

She grinned and hurried her pace toward the Prime's quarters. She knew she'd found those when she glanced down a side hallway and spotted guards at the end. Yup. That door was so nice, it *had* to belong to an emperor. Only super-rich folk built fancy doors. You needed money coming out your ears before you spent it on a *door*.

Guards were a problem. Lift knelt down, peeking around the corner. The hallway leading to the emperor's rooms was narrow, like an alleyway. Smart. Hard to sneak down something like that. And those two guards, they weren't the bored type. They were the "we gotta stand here and look real angry" type. They stood so straight, you'd have thought someone had shoved brooms up their backsides.

She glanced upward. The hallway was tall; rich folk liked tall stuff. If they'd been poor, they'd have built another floor up there for their aunts and cousins to live in. Rich people wasted space instead. Proved they had so much money, they could waste it.

Seemed perfectly rational to steal from them.

"There," Lift whispered, pointing to a small ornamented ledge that ran along the wall up above. It wouldn't be wide enough to walk on, unless you were Lift. Which, fortunately, she was. It was dim up there too. The chandeliers were the dangly kind, and they hung low, with mirrors reflecting their spherelight downward.

"Up we go," she said.

Wyndle sighed.

"You gotta do what I say or I'll prune you."

"You'll . . . prune me."

"Sure." That sounded threatening, right?

Wyndle grew up the wall, giving her handholds. Already, the vines he'd trailed through the hallway behind them were vanishing, becoming crystal and disintegrating into dust.

"Why don't they notice you?" Lift whispered. She'd never asked him, despite their months together. "Is it 'cuz only the pure in heart can see you?"

"You're not serious."

"Sure. That'd fit into legends and stories and stuff."

"Oh, the theory itself isn't ridiculous," Wyndle said, speaking out of a bit of vine near her, the various cords of green moving like lips. "Merely the idea that *you* consider yourself to be pure in heart."

"I'm pure," Lift whispered, grunting as she climbed. "I'm a child and stuff. I'm so storming pure I practically belch rainbows."

Wyndle sighed again—he liked to do that—as they reached the ledge. Wyndle grew along the side of it, making it slightly wider, and Lift stepped onto it. She balanced carefully, then nodded to Wyndle. He grew further along the ledge, then doubled back and grew up the wall to a point above her head. From there, he grew horizontally to give her a handhold. With the extra inch of vine on the ledge and the handhold above, she managed to sidle along, stomach to the wall. She took a deep breath, then turned the corner into the hallway with the guards.

She moved along it slowly, Wyndle wrapping back and forth, enhancing both footing and handholds for her. The guards didn't cry out. She was *doing* it.

"They can't see me," Wyndle said, growing up beside her to create another line of handholds, "because I exist mostly in the Cognitive Realm, even though I've moved my consciousness to this Realm. I can make myself visible to anyone, should I desire, though it's not easy for me. Other spren are more skilled at it, while some have the opposite trouble. Of course, no matter *how* I manifest, nobody can touch me, as I barely have any substance in this Realm."

"Nobody but me," Lift whispered, inching down the hallway.

"You shouldn't be able to either," he said, sounding troubled. "What did you ask for, when you visited my mother?"

Lift didn't have to answer that, not to a storming Voidbringer. She eventually reached the end of the hallway. Beneath her was the door. Unfortunately, that was exactly where the guards stood.

"This does not seem very well thought out, mistress," Wyndle noted. "Had you considered *what* you were going to do once you got here?"

She nodded.

"Well?"

"Wait," she whispered.

They did, Lift with her front pressed to the wall, her heels hanging out above a fifteen-foot drop onto the guards. She didn't want to fall. She was pretty sure she was awesome enough to survive it, but if they saw her, that would end the game. She'd have to run, and she'd *never* get any dinner.

Fortunately, she'd guessed right, unfortunately. A guard appeared at the other end of the hallway, looking out of breath and not a little annoyed. The other two guards jogged over to him. He turned, pointing the other way.

That was her chance. Wyndle grew a vine downward, and Lift grabbed it. She could feel the crystals jutting out between the tendrils, but they were smooth and faceted—not angular and sharp. She dropped, vine smooth between her fingers, pulling herself to a stop just before the floor.

She only had a few seconds.

". . . caught a thief trying to ransack the vizier quarters," said the newer guard. "Might be more. Keep watch. By Yaezir himself! I can't believe they'd dare. Tonight of all nights!"

Lift cracked open the door to the emperor's rooms and peeked in. Big room. Men and women at a table. Nobody looking her direction. She slipped through the door.

Then became awesome.

She ducked down, kicked herself forward, and for a moment, the floor—the carpet, the wood beneath—had no purchase on her. She glided as if on ice, making no noise as she slid across the ten-foot gap. Nothing could hold her when she got Slick like this. Fingers would slip off her, and she could glide forever. She didn't think she'd ever stop unless she turned off the awesomeness. She'd slide all the way to the storming ocean itself.

Tonight, she stopped herself under the table, using her fingers—which weren't Slick—then removed the Slickness from her legs. Her stomach growled in complaint. She needed food. Real fast, or no more awesomeness for her.

"Somehow, you are partly in the Cognitive Realm," Wyndle said, coiling beside her and raising a twisting mesh of vines that could make a face. "It is the only answer I can find to why you can touch spren. And you can metabolize food *directly* into Stormlight."

She shrugged. He was always saying words like those. Trying to confuse her, starvin' Voidbringer. Well, she wouldn't talk back to him, not now. The men and women standing around the table might hear her, even if they couldn't hear Wyndle.

That food was in here somewhere. She could smell it.

"But *why*?" Wyndle said. "Why did She give you this incredible talent? Why a child? There are soldiers, grand kings, incredible scholars among humankind. Instead she chose you."

Food, food, food. Smelled *great*. Lift crawled along under the long table. The men and women up above were talking in very concerned voices.

"Your application was *clearly* the best, Dalksi."

"What! I misspelled three words in the first paragraph alone!"

"I didn't notice."

"You didn't . . . Of course you noticed! But this is pointless, because *Axikk's* essay was obviously superior to mine."

"Don't bring me into this again. We disqualified me. I'm not fit to be Prime. I have a bad back."

"Ashno of Sages had a bad back. He was one of the greatest Emuli Primes."

"Bah! My essay was utter rubbish, and you know it."

Wyndle moved along beside Lift. "Mother has given up on your kind. I can feel it. She doesn't care any longer. Now that He's gone . . ."

"This arguing does not befit us," said a commanding female voice. "We should take our vote. People are waiting."

"Let it go to one of those fools in the gardens."

"Their essays were *dreadful*. Just look at what Pandri wrote across the top of hers."

"My . . . I . . . I don't know what half of that even means, but it *does* seem insulting."

This finally caught Lift's attention. She looked up toward the table above. Good cusses? *Come on*, she thought. *Read a few of those.*

"We'll have to pick one of them," the other voice—she sounded very in charge—said. "Kadasixes and Stars, this is a puzzle. What do we do when *nobody* wants to be Prime?"

Nobody wanted to be Prime? Had the entire country suddenly grown some sense? Lift continued on. Being rich seemed fun and all, but being in charge of that many people? Pure misery, that would be.

"Perhaps we should pick the *worst* application," one of the voices said. "In this situation, that would indicate the cleverest applicant."

"Six different monarchs killed . . ." one of the voices said, a new one. "In a mere two months. Highprinces slaughtered throughout the East. Religious leaders. And then, two Primes murdered in a matter of a single week. Storms . . . I almost think it's another Desolation come upon us."

"A Desolation in the form of a single man. Yaezir help the one we choose. It is a death sentence."

"We have stalled too long as it is. These weeks of waiting with no Prime have been harmful to Azir. Let's just pick the worst application. From this stack."

"What if we pick someone who is legitimately terrible? Is it not our *duty* to care for the kingdom, regardless of the risk to the one we choose?"

"But in picking the best from among us, we doom our brightest, our best, to die by the sword . . . Yaezir help us. Scion Ethid, a prayer for guidance would be appreciated. We need Yaezir himself to show us his will. Perhaps if we choose the right person, he or she will be protected by his hand."

Lift reached the end of the table and looked out at a banquet that had been set onto a smaller table at the other side of the room. This place was *very* Azish. Curls of embroidery everywhere. Carpets so fine, they probably drove some poor woman blind weaving them. Dark colors and dim lights. Paintings on the walls.

Huh, Lift thought, *someone scratched a face off of that one.* Who'd ruin a painting like that, and such a fine one, the Heralds all in a row?

Well, nobody seemed to be touching that feast. Her stomach growled, but she waited for a distraction.

It came soon after. The door opened. Likely the guards coming to report about the thief they'd found. Poor Gawx. She'd have to go break him out later.

Right now, it was time for food. Lift shoved herself forward on her knees and used her awesomeness to Slick her legs. She slid across the floor and grabbed the corner leg of the food table. Her momentum smoothly pivoted her around and behind it. She crouched down, the tablecloth neatly hiding her from the people at the room's center, and unSlicked her legs.

Perfect. She reached up a hand and plucked a dinner roll off the table. She took a bite, then hesitated.

Why had everyone grown quiet? She risked a glance over the tabletop.

He had arrived.

The tall Azish man with the white mark on his cheek, like a crescent. Black uniform with a double row of silver buttons down the coat's front, a stiff silver collar poking up from a shirt underneath. His thick gloves had collars of their own that extended halfway back around his forearms.

Dead eyes. This was Darkness himself.

Oh no.

"What is the meaning of this!" demanded one of the viziers, a woman in one of their large coats with the too-big sleeves. Her cap was of a different pattern, and it clashed quite spectacularly with the coat.

"I am here," Darkness said, "for a thief."

"Do you realize where you are? How *dare* you interrupt—"

"I have," Darkness said, "the proper forms." He spoke completely without emotion. No annoyance at being challenged, no arrogance or pomposity. Nothing at all. One of his minions entered behind him, a man in a black and silver uniform, less ornamented. He proffered a neat stack of papers to his master.

"Forms are all well and good," the vizier said. "But this is *not* the time, constable, for—"

Lift bolted.

Her instincts finally battered down her surprise and she ran, leaping over a couch on her way to the room's back door. Wyndle moved beside her in a streak.

She tore a hunk off the roll with her teeth; she was going to need the food. Beyond that door would be a bedroom, and a bedroom would have a window. She slammed open the door, dashing through.

Something swung from the shadows on the other side.

A cudgel took her in the chest. Ribs cracked. Lift gasped, dropping face-first to the floor.

Another of Darkness's minions stepped from the shadows inside the bedroom.

"Even the chaotic," Darkness said, "can be predictable with proper study." His feet thumped across the floor behind her.

Lift gritted her teeth, curled up on the floor. *Didn't get enough to eat . . .* So hungry.

The few bites she'd taken earlier worked within her. She felt the familiar feeling, like a storm in her veins. Liquid awesomeness. The pain faded from her chest as she healed.

Wyndle ran around her in a circle, a little lasso of vines sprouting leaves on the floor, looping her again and again. Darkness stepped up close.

Go! She leaped to her hands and knees. He seized her by the shoulder, but she could escape that. She summoned her awesomeness.

Darkness thrust something toward her.

The little animal was like a cremling, but with *wings*. Bound wings, tied-up legs. It had a strange little face, not crabbish like a cremling. More like a tiny axehound, with a snout, mouth, and eyes.

It seemed sickly, and its shimmering eyes were pained. How could she tell that?

The creature sucked the awesomeness from Lift. She actually *saw* it go, a glistening whiteness that streamed from her to the little animal. It opened its mouth, drinking it in.

Suddenly, Lift felt very tired and very, *very* hungry.

Darkness handed the animal to one of his minions, who made it vanish into a black sack he then tucked in his pocket. Lift was certain that the viziers—standing in an outraged cluster at the table—hadn't seen any of this, not with Darkness's back to them and the two minions crowding around.

"Keep all spheres from her," Darkness said. "She must not be allowed to Invest."

Lift felt terror, panicked in a way she hadn't known for years, ever since her days in Rall Elorim. She struggled, thrashing, biting at the hand that held her. Darkness didn't even grunt. He hauled her to her feet, and another minion took her by the arms, wrenching them backward until she gasped at the pain.

No. She'd freed herself! She couldn't be taken like this. Wyndle continued to spin around her on the ground, distressed. He was a good type, for a Voidbringer.

Darkness turned to the viziers. "I will trouble you no further."

"Mistress!" Wyndle said. "Here!"

The half-eaten roll lay on the floor. She'd dropped it when the cudgel hit. Wyndle ran into it, but he couldn't do anything more than make it wobble. Lift thrashed, trying to pull free, but without that storm inside of her, she was just a child in the grip of a trained soldier.

"I am *highly* disturbed by the nature of this incursion, constable," the lead vizier said, shuffling through the stack of papers that Darkness had dropped. "Your paperwork is in order, and I see you even included a plea— granted by the arbiters—to search the palace itself for this urchin. Surely you did not need to disturb a holy conclave. For a common thief, no less."

"Justice waits upon no man or woman," Darkness said, completely calm. "And this thief is anything but common. With your leave, we will cease disturbing you."

He didn't seem to care if they gave him leave or not. He strode toward the door, and his minion pulled Lift along after. She got her foot out to the roll, but only managed to kick it forward, under the long table by the viziers.

"This is a leave of *execution*," the vizier said with surprise, holding up the last sheet in the stack. "You will kill the child? For mere thievery?"

Kill? *No. No!*

"That, in addition to trespassing in the Prime's palace," Darkness said, reaching the door. "And for interrupting a holy conclave in session."

The vizier met his gaze. She held it, then *wilted*. "I . . ." she said. "Ah, of course . . . er . . . constable."

Darkness turned from her and pulled open the door. The vizier set one hand on the table and raised her other hand to her head.

The minion dragged Lift up to the door.

"Mistress!" Wyndle said, twisting up nearby. "Oh . . . oh dear. There is something very wrong with that man! He is not right, not right at all. You must use your powers."

"Trying," Lift said, grunting.

"You've let yourself grow too thin," Wyndle said. "Not good. You always use up the excess. . . . Low body fat . . . That might be the problem. I don't know *how* this works!"

Darkness hesitated beside the door and looked at the low-hanging chandeliers in the hallway beyond, with their mirrors and sparkling gemstones. He raised his hand and gestured. The minion not holding Lift moved out into the hallway and found the chandelier ropes. He unwound those and pulled, raising the chandeliers.

Lift tried to summon her awesomeness. Just a little more. She just needed a *little*.

Her body felt exhausted. Drained. She really *had* been overdoing it. She struggled, increasingly panicked. Increasingly desperate.

In the hallway, the minion tied off the chandeliers high in the air. Nearby, the vizier leader glanced from Darkness to Lift.

"Please," Lift mouthed.

The vizier pointedly *shoved* the table. It clipped the elbow of the minion holding Lift. He cursed, letting go with that hand.

Lift dove for the floor, ripping out of his grip. She squirmed forward, getting underneath the table.

The minion seized her by the ankles.

"What was that?" Darkness asked, his voice cold, emotionless.

"I slipped," the vizier said.

"Watch yourself."

"Is that a threat, constable? I am beyond your reach."

"Nobody is beyond my reach." Still no emotion.

Lift thrashed underneath the table, kicking at the minion. He cursed softly and hauled Lift out by her legs, then pulled her to her feet. Darkness watched, face emotionless.

She met his gaze, eye to eye, a half-eaten roll in her mouth. She stared him down, chewing quickly and swallowing.

For once, he showed an emotion. Bafflement. "All that," he said, "for a roll?"

Lift said nothing.

Come on . . .

They walked her down the hallway, then around the corner. One of the minions ran ahead and purposefully removed the spheres from the lamps on the walls. Were they *robbing* the place? No, after she passed, the minion ran back and restored the spheres.

Come on . . .

They passed a palace guard in the larger hallway beyond. He noted something about Darkness—perhaps that rope tied around his upper arm, which was threaded with an Azish sequence of colors—and saluted. "Constable, sir? You found another one?"

Darkness stopped, looking as the guard opened the door beside him. Inside, Gawx sat on a chair, slumped between two other guards.

"So you did have accomplices!" shouted one of the guards in the room. He slapped Gawx across the face.

Wyndle gasped from just behind her. "That was *certainly* uncalled for!"

Come on . . .

"This one is not your concern," Darkness said to the guards, waiting as one of his minions did the strange gemstone-moving sequence. Why *did* they worry about that?

Something stirred inside of Lift. Like the little swirls of wind at the advent of a storm.

Darkness looked at her with a sharp motion. "Something is—"

Awesomeness returned.

Lift became Slick, every part of her but her feet and the palms of her hands. She yanked her arm—it slipped from the minion's fingers—then kicked herself forward and fell to her knees, sliding under Darkness's hand as he reached for her.

Wyndle let out a whoop, zipping along beside her as she began slapping the floor like she was swimming, using each swing of her arms to push herself forward. She skimmed the floor of the palace hallway, knees sliding across it as if it were greased.

The posture wasn't particularly dignified. Dignity was for rich folk who had time to make up games to play with one another.

She got going real fast real quick—so fast it was hard to control herself as she relaxed her awesomeness and tried to leap to her feet. She crashed into the wall at the end of the hallway instead, a sprawling heap of limbs.

She came out of it with a grin. That had gone *way* better than the last few times she'd tried this. Her first attempt had been super embarrassing. She'd been so Slick, she hadn't even been able to stay on her knees.

"Lift!" Wyndle said. "Behind."

She glanced down the hallway. She could *swear* he was glowing faintly, and he was certainly running too quickly.

Darkness was awesome too.

"That is *not* fair!" Lift shouted, scrambling to her feet and dashing down a side hallway—the way she'd come when sneaking with Gawx. Her body had already started to feel tired again. One roll didn't get it far.

She sprinted down the lavish hallway, causing a maid to jump back, shrieking as if she'd seen a rat. Lift skidded around a corner, dashed toward the nice scents, and burst into the kitchens.

She ran through the mess of people inside. The door slammed open behind her a second later. Darkness.

Ignoring startled cooks, Lift leaped up onto a long counter, Slicking her leg and riding on it sideways, knocking off bowls and pans, causing a clatter. She came down off the other end of the counter as Darkness shoved his way past cooks in a clump, his Shardblade held up high.

He didn't curse in annoyance. A fellow should curse. Made people feel real when they did that.

But of course, Darkness wasn't a real person. Of that, though little else, she was sure.

Lift snatched a sausage off a steaming plate, then pushed into the servant hallways. She chewed as she ran, Wyndle growing along the wall beside her, leaving a streak of dark green vines.

"Where are we going?" he asked.

"*Away.*"

The door into the servant hallways slammed open behind her. Lift turned a corner, surprising an equerry. She went awesome, and threw herself to the side, easily slipping past him in the narrow hallway.

"What has become of me?" Wyndle asked. "Thieving in the night, chased by abominations. I was a gardener. A wonderful gardener! Cryptics and honorspren alike came to see the crystals I grew from the minds of your world. Now this. What *have* I become?"

"A whiner," Lift said, puffing.

"Nonsense."

"So you were always one of those, then?" She looked over her shoulder. Darkness casually shoved down the equerry, barely breaking stride as he charged over the man.

Lift reached a doorway and slammed her shoulder against it, scrambling out into the rich hallways again.

She needed an exit. A window. Her flight had just looped her around back near the Prime's quarters. She picked a direction by instinct and started running, but one of Darkness's minions appeared around a corner that way. He *also* carried a Shardblade. Some starvin' luck, she had.

Lift turned the other way and passed by Darkness striding out of the servant hallways. She barely dodged a swing of his Blade by diving, Slicking herself, and sliding along the floor. She made it to her feet without stumbling this time. That was something, at least.

"Who *are* these men?" Wyndle asked from beside her.

Lift grunted.

"Why do they care so much about you? There's something about those weapons they carry . . ."

"Shardblades," Lift said. "Worth a whole kingdom. Built to kill Voidbringers." And they had *two* of the things. Crazy.

Built to kill Voidbringers . . .

"You!" she said, still running. "They're after you!"

"What? Of course they aren't!"

"They *are*. Don't worry. You're mine. I won't lettem have you."

"That's endearingly loyal," Wyndle said. "And not a little insulting. But they are not after—"

The second of Darkness's minions stepped out into the hallway ahead of her. He held Gawx.

He had a knife to the young man's throat.

Lift stumbled to a halt. Gawx, in far over his head, whimpered in the man's hands.

"Don't move," the minion said, "or I will kill him."

"Starvin' bastard," Lift said. She spat to the side. "That's dirty."

Darkness thumped up behind her, the other minion joining him. They penned her in. The entrance to the Prime's quarters was actually just ahead, and the viziers and scions had flooded out into the hallway, where they jabbered to one another in outraged tones.

Gawx was crying. Poor fool.

Well. This sorta thing never ended well. Lift went with her gut—which was basically what she always did—and called the minion's bluff by dashing forward. He was a lawman type. Wouldn't kill a captive in cold—

The minion slit Gawx's throat.

Crimson blood poured out and stained Gawx's clothing. The minion dropped him, then stumbled back, as if startled by what he'd done.

Lift froze. He couldn't— He didn't—

Darkness grabbed her from behind.

"That was poorly done," Darkness said to the minion, tone emotionless. Lift barely heard him. *So much blood.* "You will be punished."

"But . . ." the minion said. "I had to do as I threatened . . ."

"You have not done the proper paperwork in this kingdom to kill that child," Darkness said.

"Aren't we above their laws?"

Darkness actually let go of her, striding over to slap the minion across the face. "Without the law, there is nothing. You will subject yourself to their rules, and accept the dictates of justice. It is all we have, the only sure thing in this world."

Lift stared at the dying boy, who held his hands to his neck, as if to stop the blood flow. Those tears . . .

The other minion came up behind her.

"Run!" Wyndle said.

She started.

"Run!"

Lift ran.

She passed Darkness and pushed through the viziers, who gasped and yelled at the death. She barreled into the Prime's quarters, slid across the table, snatched another roll off the platter, and burst into the bedroom. She was out the window a second later.

"Up," she said to Wyndle, then stuffed the roll in her mouth. He streaked up the side of the wall, and Lift climbed, sweating. A second later, one of the minions leaped out the window beneath her.

He didn't look up. He charged out onto the grounds, twisting about, searching, his Shardblade flashing in the darkness as it reflected starlight.

Lift safely reached the upper reaches of the palace, hidden in the shadows there. She squatted down, hands around her knees, feeling cold.

"You barely knew him," Wyndle said. "Yet you mourn."

She nodded.

"You've seen much death," Wyndle said. "I know it. Aren't you accustomed to it?"

She shook her head.

Below, the minion moved off, hunting farther and farther for her. She was free. Climb across the roof, slip down on the other side, disappear.

Was that motion on the wall at the edge of the grounds? Yes, those moving shadows were men. The other thieves were climbing their wall and disappearing into the night. Huqin had left his nephew, as expected.

Who would cry for Gawx? Nobody. He'd be forgotten, abandoned.

Lift released her legs and crawled across the curved bulb of the roof toward the window she'd entered earlier. Her vines from the seeds, unlike the ones Wyndle grew, were still alive. They'd overgrown the window, leaves quivering in the wind.

Run, her instincts said. *Go.*

"You spoke of something earlier," she whispered. "Re . . ."

"Regrowth," he said. "Each bond grants power over two Surges. You can influence how things grow."

"Can I use this to help Gawx?"

"If you were better trained? Yes. As it stands, I doubt it. You aren't very strong, aren't very practiced. And he might be dead already."

She touched one of the vines.

"Why do you care?" Wyndle asked again. He sounded curious. Not a challenge. An attempt to understand.

"Because someone has to."

For once, Lift ignored what her gut was telling her and, instead, climbed through the window. She crossed the room in a dash.

Out into the upstairs hallway. Onto the steps. She soared down them, leaping most of the distance. Through a doorway. Turn left. Down the hallway. Left again.

A crowd in the rich corridor. Lift reached them, then wiggled through. She didn't need her awesomeness for that. She'd been slipping through cracks in crowds since she started walking.

Gawx lay in a pool of blood that had darkened the fine carpet. The viziers and guards surrounded him, speaking in hushed tones.

Lift crawled up to him. His body was still warm, but the blood seemed to have stopped flowing. His eyes were closed.

"Too late?" she whispered.

"I don't know," Wyndle said, curling up beside her.

"What do I do?"

"I . . . I'm not sure. Mistress, the transition to your side was difficult and left holes in my memory, even with the precautions my people took. I . . ."

She set Gawx on his back, face toward the sky. He *wasn't* really anything to her, that was true. They'd barely just met, and he'd been a fool. She'd told him to go back.

But this was who she was, who she had to be.

I will remember those who have been forgotten.

Lift leaned forward, touched her forehead to his, and breathed out. A shimmering something left her lips, a little cloud of glowing light. It hung in front of Gawx's lips.

Come on . . .

It stirred, then drew in through his mouth.

A hand took Lift by the shoulder, pulling her away from Gawx. She sagged, suddenly exhausted. *Real* exhausted, so much so that even standing was difficult.

Darkness pulled her by the shoulder away from the crowd. "Come," he said.

Gawx stirred. The viziers gasped, their attention turning toward the youth as he groaned, then sat up.

"It appears that you are an Edgedancer," Darkness said, steering her down the corridor as the crowd moved in around Gawx, chattering. She stumbled, but he held her upright. "I had wondered which of the two you would be."

"Miracle!" one vizier said.

"Yaezir has spoken!" said one of the scions.

"Edgedancer," Lift said. "I don't know what that is."

"They were once a glorious order," Darkness said, walking her down the hallway. Everyone ignored them, focused instead on Gawx. "Where you blunder, they were elegant things of beauty. They could ride the thinnest rope at speed, dance across rooftops, move through a battlefield like a ribbon on the wind."

"That sounds . . . amazing."

"Yes. It is unfortunate they were always so concerned with small-minded things, while ignoring those of greater import. It appears you share their temperament. You have become one of them."

"I didn't mean to," Lift said.

"I realize this."

"Why . . . why do you hunt me?"

"In the name of justice."

"There are *tons* of people who do wrong things," she said. She had to force out every word. Talking was hard. *Thinking* was hard. So tired. "You . . . you coulda hunted big crime bosses, murderers. You chose me instead. Why?"

"Others may be detestable, but they do not dabble in arts that could return Desolation to this world." His words were so cold. "What you are must be stopped."

Lift felt numb. She tried to summon her awesomeness, but she'd used it all up. And then some, probably.

Darkness turned her and pushed her against the wall. She couldn't stand, and slumped down, sitting. Wyndle moved up beside her, spreading out a starburst of creeping vines.

Darkness knelt next to her. He held out his hand.

"I *saved* him," Lift said. "I did something good, didn't I?"

"Goodness is irrelevant," Darkness said. His Shardblade dropped into his fingers.

"You don't even care, do you?"

"No," he said. "I don't."

"You should," she said, exhausted. "You should . . . should try it, I mean. I wanted to be like you, once. Didn't work out. Wasn't . . . even like being alive . . ."

Darkness raised his Blade.

Lift closed her eyes.

"She is pardoned!"

Darkness's grip on her shoulder tightened.

Feeling completely drained—like somebody had held her up by the toes and squeezed everything out of her—Lift forced her eyes to open. Gawx stumbled to a stop beside them, breathing heavily. Behind, the viziers and scions moved up as well.

Clothing bloodied, his eyes wide, Gawx clutched a piece of paper in his hand. He thrust this at Darkness. "I pardon this girl. Release her, constable!"

"Who are you," Darkness said, "to do such a thing?"

"I am the Prime Aqasix," Gawx declared. "Ruler of Azir!"

"Ridiculous."

"The Kadasixes have spoken," said one of the scions.

"The Heralds?" Darkness said. "They have done no such thing. You are mistaken."

"We have voted," said a vizier. "This young man's application was the best."

"What application?" Darkness said. "He is a thief!"

"He performed the miracle of Regrowth," said one of the older scions. "He was dead and he returned. What better application could we ask for?"

"A sign has been given," said the lead vizier. "We have a Prime who can survive the attacks of the One All White. Praise to Yaezir, Kadasix of Kings, may he lead in wisdom. This youth is Prime. He has *been* Prime always. We have only now realized it, and beg his forgiveness for not seeing the truth sooner."

"As it always has been done," the elderly scion said. "As it will be done again. Stand down, constable. You have been given an order."

Darkness studied Lift.

She smiled tiredly. Show the starvin' man some teeth. That was the right of it.

His Shardblade vanished to mist. He'd been bested, but he didn't seem to care. Not a curse, not even a tightening of the eyes. He stood up and pulled on his gloves by the cuffs, first one, then the other. "Praise Yaezir," he said. "Herald of Kings. May he lead in wisdom. If he ever stops drooling."

Darkness bowed to the new Prime, then left with a sure step.

"Does anyone know the name of that constable?" one of the viziers asked. "When did we start letting officers of the law requisition Shard-blades?"

Gawx knelt beside Lift.

"So you're an emperor or something now," she said, closing her eyes, settling back.

"Yeah. I'm still confused. It seems I performed a miracle or something."

"Good for you," Lift said. "Can I eat your dinner?"

SZETH

Szeth-son-son-Vallano, Truthless of Shinovar, sat atop the highest tower in the world and contemplated the End of All Things.

The souls of the people he had murdered lurked in the shadows. They whispered to him. If he drew close, they screamed.

They also screamed when he shut his eyes. He had taken to blinking as little as possible. His eyes felt dry in his skull. It was what any . . . sane man would do.

The highest tower in the world, hidden in the tops of the mountains, was perfect for his contemplation. If he had not been bound to an Oathstone, if he had been another man entirely, he would have stayed here. The only place in the East where the stones were not cursed, where walking on them was allowed. This place was holy.

Bright sunlight shone down to banish the shadows, which kept those screams to a minimum. The screamers deserved their deaths, of course. They should have killed Szeth. *I hate you. I hate . . . everyone.* Glories within, what a strange emotion.

He did not look up. He would not meet the gaze of the God of Gods. But it *was* good to be in the sunlight. There were no clouds here to bring the darkness. This place was above them all. Urithiru ruled even the clouds.

The massive tower was also empty; that was another reason he liked it. A hundred levels, built in ring shapes, each one beneath larger than the one above it to provide a sunlit balcony. The eastern side, however, was a sheer, flat edge that made the tower look from a distance as if that side had been sliced off by an enormous Shardblade. What a strange shape.

He sat on that edge, right at the top, feet swinging over a drop of a hundred massive stories and a plummet down the mountainside below. Glass sparkled on the smooth surface of the flat side there.

Glass windows. Facing *east*, toward the Origin. The first time he had visited this place—just after being exiled from his homeland—he hadn't understood just how odd those windows were. Back then, he'd still been accustomed to gentle highstorms. Rain, wind, and meditation.

Things were different in these cursed lands of the stonewalkers. These hateful lands. These lands flowing with blood, death, and screams. And . . . And . . .

Breathe. He forced the air in and out and stood up on the rim of the parapet atop the tower.

He had fought an impossibility. A man with Stormlight, a man who knew the storm within. That meant . . . problems. Years ago, Szeth had been banished for raising the alarm. The *false* alarm, it had been said.

The Voidbringers are no more, they had told him.

The spirits of the stones themselves promised it.

The powers of old are no more.

The Knights Radiant are fallen.

We are all that remains.

All that remains. . . . Truthless.

"Have I not been faithful?" Szeth shouted, finally looking up to face the sun. His voice echoed against the mountains and their spirit-souls. "Have I not obeyed, kept my oath? Have I not done as you *demanded* of me?"

The killing, the murder. He blinked tired eyes.

SCREAMS.

"What does it mean if the Shamanate are wrong? What does it mean if they banished me in error?"

It meant the End of All Things. The end of truth. It would mean that nothing made sense, and that his oath was meaningless.

It would mean he had killed for no reason.

He dropped off the side of the tower, white clothing—now a symbol to him of many things—flapping in the wind. He filled himself with Stormlight and Lashed himself southward. His body lurched in that direction, falling across the sky. He could only travel this way for a short time; his Stormlight did not last long.

Too imperfect a body. The Knights Radiant . . . they'd been said . . . they'd been said to be better at this . . . like the Voidbringers.

He had just enough Light to free himself from the mountains and land in a village in the foothills. They often set out spheres for him there as an offering, considering him some kind of god. He would feed upon that

Light, and it would let him go a farther distance until he found another city and more Stormlight.

It would take days to get where he was going, but he *would* find answers. Or, barring that, someone to kill.

Of his own choice, this time.

NEW RHYTHMS

E shonai waved her hand as she climbed the central spire of Narak, trying to shoo away the tiny spren. It danced around her head, shedding rings of light from its cometlike form. Horrid thing. Why would it not leave her alone?

Perhaps it could not stay away. She was experiencing something wonderfully new, after all. Something that had not been seen in centuries. Stormform. A form of true power.

A form given of the gods.

She continued up the steps, feet clinking in her Shardplate. It felt good on her.

She had held this form for fifteen days now, fifteen days of hearing new rhythms. At first, she had attuned those often, but this had made some people very nervous. She had backed off, and forced herself to attune the old, familiar ones when speaking.

It was difficult, for those old rhythms were so *dull*. Buried within those new rhythms, the names of which she intuited somehow, she could almost hear voices speaking to her. Advising her. If her people had received such guidance over the centuries, they surely would not have fallen so far.

Eshonai reached the top of the spire, where the other four awaited her. Again, her sister Venli was also there, and she wore the new form as well—with its spiking armor plates, its red eyes, its lithe danger. This meeting would proceed very differently from the previous one. Eshonai cycled through the new rhythms, careful not to hum them. The others weren't ready yet.

She sat down, then gasped.

That rhythm! It sounded like . . . like her own voice yelling at her. Screaming in pain. What was *that*? She shook her head, and found that she had reflexively pulled her hand to her chest in anxiety. When she opened it, the cometlike spren shot out.

She attuned Irritation. The others of the Five regarded her with heads cocked, a couple humming to Curiosity. Why did she act as she did?

Eshonai settled herself, Shardplate grinding against stone. This close to the lull—the time called the Weeping by the humans—highstorms were growing more rare. That had created a small impediment in her march to see every listener given stormform. There had only been one storm since Eshonai's own transformation, and during it, Venli and her scholars had taken stormform along with two hundred soldiers chosen by Eshonai. Not officers. Common soldiers. The type she was *sure* would obey.

The next highstorm was mere days away, and Venli had been gathering her spren. They had thousands ready. It was time.

Eshonai regarded the others of the Five. Today's clear sky rained down white sunlight, and a few windspren approached on a breeze. They stopped when they grew near, then zipped away in the opposite direction.

"Why have you called this meeting?" Eshonai asked the others.

"You've been speaking of a plan," Davim said, broad worker's hands clasped before him. "You've been telling everyone of it. Shouldn't you have brought it to the Five first?"

"I'm sorry," Eshonai said. "I am merely excited. I believe, however, we should now be the Six."

"That has not been decided," Abronai said, weak and plump. Mateform was disgusting. "This moves too quickly."

"We *must* move quickly," Eshonai replied to Resolve. "We have only two highstorms before the lull. You know what the spies report. The humans are planning a final push toward us, toward Narak."

"It is a pity," Abronai said to Consideration, "that your meeting with them went so poorly."

"They wanted to tell me of the destruction they planned to bring," Eshonai lied. "They wanted to gloat. That was the only reason they met with me."

"We need to be ready to fight them," Davim said to Anxiety.

Eshonai laughed. A blatant use of emotion, but she truly felt it. "Fight them? Haven't you been listening? I can summon a *highstorm*."

"With help," Chivi said to Curiosity. Nimbleform. Another weak form. They should expunge that one from their ranks. "You have said you cannot do it alone. How many others would you need? Certainly the two hundred you have now are enough."

"No, that is not *nearly* enough," Eshonai replied. "I feel that the more people we have in this form, the more likely we are to succeed. I would like, therefore, to move that we transform."

"Yes," Chivi said. "But how many of us?"

"All of us."

Davim hummed to Amusement, thinking it must be a joke. He trailed off as the rest sat in silence.

"We will have just one chance," Eshonai said to Resolve. "The humans will leave their warcamps together, in one large army that intends to reach Narak during the lull. They will be completely exposed on the plateaus, with no shelter. A highstorm at that time would *destroy* them."

"We don't even truly know if you can summon one," Abronai said to Skepticism.

"That is why we need as many of us in stormform as possible," Eshonai said. "If we miss this opportunity, our children will sing us the songs of Cursing, assuming they even live long enough to do so. This is our chance, our one chance. Imagine the ten armies of men, isolated on the plateaus, buffeted and overwhelmed by a tempest they could never have expected! With stormform, we would be immune to its effects. If any survive, we could destroy them easily."

"It *is* tempting," Davim said.

"I do not like the look of those who have taken this form," Chivi said. "I do not like how people clamor to be given it. Perhaps two hundred are enough."

"Eshonai," Davim said, "how does this form feel?"

He was asking more than he actually said. Each form changed a person in some ways. Warform made you more aggressive, mateform made you easy to distract, nimbleform encouraged focus, and workform made you obedient.

Eshonai attuned Peace.

No. *That* was the screaming voice. How had she spent weeks in this form and not noticed?

"I feel alive," Eshonai said to Joy. "I feel strong, and I feel powerful. I feel a connection to the world that I should have always known. Davim, this is like the change from dullform to one of the other forms—it is *that* much of an upgrade. Now that I hold this strength, I realize I wasn't fully alive before."

She lifted her hand and made a fist. She could feel the energy coursing down her arm as the muscles flexed, though it was hidden beneath the Shardplate.

"Red eyes," Abronai whispered. "Have we come to this?"

"If we decide to do this," Chivi said. "Perhaps we four should assess it first, then say if the others should join us." Venli opened her mouth to speak, but Chivi waved her hand, interrupting her. "You have had your say, Venli. We know what you wish."

"We cannot wait, unfortunately," Eshonai said. "If we want to trap the

Alethi armies, we will need time to transform everyone before the Alethi leave to search for Narak."

"I'm willing to try it," Abronai said. "Perhaps we should propose a mass transformation to our people."

"No." Zuln spoke to Peace.

The dullform member of the Five sat slouched, looking at the ground before her. She almost never said anything.

Eshonai attuned Annoyance. "What was that?"

"No," Zuln repeated. "It is not right."

"I would have us all be in agreement," Davim said. "Zuln, can you not listen to reason?"

"It is not right," the dullform said again.

"She is dull," Eshonai said. "We should ignore her."

Davim hummed to Anxiety. "Zuln represents the past, Eshonai. You shouldn't say such things of her."

"The past is dead."

Abronai joined Davim in humming to Anxiety. "Perhaps this is worth more thought. Eshonai, you . . . do not speak as you used to. I hadn't realized the changes were so stark."

Eshonai attuned one of the new rhythms, the Rhythm of Fury. She held the song inside, and found herself humming. These were so cautious, so weak! They would see her people destroyed.

"We will meet again later today," Davim said. "Let us spend time considering. Eshonai, I would speak with you alone during that period, if you are willing."

"Of course."

They rose from their places atop the pillar. Eshonai stepped to the edge and looked down as the others filed down. The spire was too high to jump from, even in Shardplate. She so wanted to try.

It seemed that every person in the city had gathered around the base to await the decision. In the weeks since Eshonai's transformation, talk of what had happened to her—then the others—had infused the city with a certain mixture of anxiety and hope. Many had come to her, begging to be given the form. They saw the chance it offered.

"They're not going to agree to it," Venli said from behind once the others were down. She spoke to Spite, one of the new rhythms. "You spoke too aggressively, Eshonai."

"Davim is with us," Eshonai said to Confidence. "Chivi will come too, with persuasion."

"That isn't enough. If the Five do not come to a consensus—"

"Don't worry."

"Our people *must* take that form, Eshonai," Venli said. "It is inevitable."

Eshonai found herself attuning the new version of Amusement . . . Ridicule, it was. She turned to her sister. "You knew, didn't you? You knew *exactly* what this form would do to me. You knew this before you took the form yourself."

"I . . . Yes."

Eshonai grabbed her sister by the front of her robe, then yanked her forward, holding her tightly. With Shardplate it was easy, though Venli resisted more than she should have been able to, and a small spark of red lightning ran across the woman's arms and face. Eshonai was not accustomed to such strength from her scholar of a sister.

"You could have destroyed us," Eshonai said. "What if this form had done something terrible?"

Screaming. In her head. Venli smiled.

"How did you discover this?" Eshonai asked. "It didn't come from the songs. There is more."

Venli did not speak. She met Eshonai's eyes and hummed to Confidence. "We must make certain the Five agree to this plan," she said. "If we are to survive, and if we are to defeat the humans, we must be in this form—all of us. We *must* summon that storm. It has been . . . waiting, Eshonai. Waiting and building."

"I will see to it," Eshonai said, dropping Venli. "You can gather enough spren for us to transform all of our people?"

"My staff have been working on it these three weeks. We will be ready to transform thousands upon thousands over the course of the final two highstorms before the lull."

"Good." Eshonai started down the steps.

"Sister?" Venli asked. "You are planning something. What is it? How will you persuade the Five?"

Eshonai continued down the steps. With the added balance and strength of Shardplate, she didn't need to bother with the chains to steady herself. As she neared the bottom, where the others of the Five were speaking to the people, she stopped a short distance above the crowd and drew in a deep breath.

Then, as loudly as she could, Eshonai shouted, "In two days, I will take any who wish to go into the storm and give them this new form."

The crowd stilled, their humming dropping off.

"The Five seek to deny you this right," Eshonai bellowed. "They don't want you to have this form of power. They are frightened, like cremlings hiding in cracks. They *cannot* deny you! It is the right of every person to choose their own form."

She raised her hands above her head, humming to Resolve, and summoned a storm.

A tiny one, a mere trickle compared to what waited. It grew between her hands, a wind coursing with lightning. A miniature tempest in her palms, light and power, wind spinning in a vortex. It had been centuries since this power had been used, and so—like a river that had been dammed—the energy waited impatiently to be freed.

The tempest grew so that it whipped at her clothing, spinning around her in a swirl of wind, crackling red lightning, and dark mist. Finally, it dissipated. She heard Awe being sung throughout the crowd—full songs, not humming. Their emotions were strong.

"With this power," Eshonai declared, "we can destroy the Alethi and protect our people. I have seen your despair. I have heard you sing to Mourning. It need not be so! Come with me into the storms. It is your right, your *duty*, to join with me."

Behind her on the steps, Venli hummed to Tension. "This will divide us, Eshonai. Too aggressive, too abrupt!"

"It will work," Eshonai said to Confidence. "You do not know them as I do."

Below, the other members of the Five were glaring up at her, looking betrayed, though she could not hear their songs.

Eshonai marched to the bottom of the spire, then pushed her way through the crowd, being joined by her soldiers in stormform. The people made way for her, many humming to Anxiety. Most who had come were workers or nimbleforms. That made sense. The warforms were too pragmatic for gawking.

Eshonai and her stormform warriors left the town's center ring. She allowed Venli to tag along behind, but paid the woman no heed. Eshonai eventually approached the barracks on the leeward side of the city, a large group of buildings built together to form a community for the soldiers. Though her troops were not required to sleep here, many did so.

The practice grounds one plateau over were busy with the sounds of warriors honing their skills, or—more likely—newly transformed soldiers being trained. The second division, a hundred and twenty-eight in number, were away watching for humans entering the middle plateaus. Scouts in warpairs roamed the Plains. She'd set them on this task soon after obtaining her form, as she had known even then that she would need to change the way this battle worked. She wanted every bit of information about the Alethi and their current tactics that she could get.

Her soldiers would ignore chrysalises for the time being. She would not lose soldiers to that petty game any longer, not when each man and woman under her command represented the potential of stormform.

The other divisions were all here, however. Seventeen thousand soldiers total. A mighty force in some ways, but also so few, compared to what they had once been. She raised her hand in a fist, and her stormform division raised the call for all soldiers in the listener army to gather. Those practicing set down their weapons and jogged over. Others left the barracks. In a short time, all had joined her.

"It is time to end the fight against the Alethi," Eshonai announced in a loud voice. "Which of you are willing to follow me in doing so?"

Humming to Resolve moved through the crowd. So far as she could hear, not a one hummed to Skepticism. Excellent.

"This will require each soldier to join me in this form," Eshonai shouted, her words being relayed through the ranks.

More humming to Resolve.

"I am proud of you," Eshonai said. "I am going to have the Storm Division go among you and take your word, each of you, on this transformation. If there are any here who do not wish to change, I would know of it personally. It is your decision, by right, and I will not force you—but I must know."

She looked to her stormforms, who saluted and broke apart, moving in warpairs. Eshonai stepped back, folding her arms, watching as these visited each other division in turn. The new rhythms thrummed in her skull, though she stayed away from the Rhythm of Peace, with its strange screams. There was no fighting against what she had become. The eyes of the gods were too strongly upon her.

Nearby, some soldiers gathered, familiar faces beneath hardened skullplates, the men bearing bits of gemstone tied to their beards. Her own division, once her friends.

She could not quite explain why she had not chosen them at first for the transformation, instead picking two hundred soldiers from across many divisions. She'd needed soldiers who were obedient, but not known for their brightness.

Thude and the soldiers of Eshonai's former division . . . they knew her too well. They would have questioned.

Soon, she had gotten word. Of her seventeen thousand troops, only a handful refused the required transformation. Those who had declined were gathered on the practice grounds.

As she contemplated her next move, Thude approached. Tall and thick-limbed, he had always worn warform save for two weeks as a mate to Bila. He hummed to Resolve—the way for a soldier to indicate a willingness to obey orders.

"I am worried about this, Eshonai," he said. "Do so many need to change?"

"If we do not transform," Eshonai said, "we are dead. The humans will ruin us."

He continued to hum to Resolve, to indicate he trusted her. His eyes seemed to tell another story.

Melu, of her stormforms, returned and saluted. "The counting is finished, sir."

"Excellent," Eshonai said. "Pass word to the troops. We're going to do the same thing for everyone in the city."

"*Everyone?*" Thude said to Anxiety.

"Our time is short," Eshonai said. "If we do not act, we will miss our opportunity to move against the humans. We have two storms left; I want every willing person in this city ready to take up stormform before those have passed us. Those who will not are given that right, but I want them gathered so we may know where we stand."

"Yes, General," Melu said.

"Use a tight scouting formation," Eshonai said, pointing toward parts of the city. "Move through the streets, counting every person. Use the non-stormform divisions too, for speed. Tell the common people that we're trying to determine how many soldiers we will have for the coming battle, and have our soldiers be calm and sing to Peace. Put those people who are willing to transform into the central ring. Send those who are unwilling out here. Give them an escort so that they do not get lost."

Venli stepped up to her as Melu passed the word, sending ranks out to obey. Thude rejoined his division.

Every half year, they did an accounting to determine their numbers and see if the forms were properly balanced. Once in a while, they would need more volunteers to become mates or workers. Most often, they needed more warforms.

That meant this exercise was familiar to the soldiers, and they took easily to the orders. After years of war, they were accustomed to doing as she said. Many had the same depression that the regular people expressed—only for the troops, it manifested as bloodlust. They just wanted to fight. They would probably have charged head-on against the human encampments, and ten times their own numbers, if Eshonai ordered.

The Five all but handed this to me, she thought as the first of the unwilling began to trickle out of the city, guarded by her soldiers. *For years I've been absolute leader of our armies, and every person among us with a hint of aggression has been given to me as a soldier.*

Workers would obey; it was their nature. Many of the nimbles who hadn't transformed yet were loyal to Venli, as the majority of them aspired to be scholars. The mates wouldn't care, and the few dulls would be too numb of brain to object.

The city was hers.

"We'll have to kill them, unfortunately," Venli said, watching the unwilling be gathered. They huddled together, afraid, despite the soft songs of the soldiers. "Will your troops be able to do it?"

"No," Eshonai said, shaking her head. "Many would resist us if we did this now. We will have to wait for all of my soldiers to be transformed. They will not object then."

"That's sloppy," Venli said to Spite. "I thought you commanded their loyalty."

"Do not question me," Eshonai said. "I control this city, not you."

Venli quieted, though her humming to Spite continued. She would attempt to seize control from Eshonai. It was an uncomfortable realization, as was the realization of how deeply Eshonai herself wanted to be in control. That didn't feel like her. Not at all.

None of this feels like me. I . . .

The new rhythms' beats surged in her mind. She turned from such thoughts as a group of soldiers approached, towing a shouting figure. Abronai, of the Five. She should have realized that he'd be trouble; he maintained mateform too easily, avoiding its distractions.

Transforming him would have been dangerous, she thought. *He has too much control over himself.*

As the stormform soldiers pulled him to Eshonai, his shouts beat against her. "This is outrageous! The dictates of the Five rule us, not the will of a single person! Can't you see that the form, the new form is overriding her! You've all lost your minds! Or . . . or *worse.*"

It was discomfortingly close to the truth.

"Put him with the others," Eshonai said, gesturing toward the group of dissidents. "What of the rest of the Five?"

"They agreed," Melu said. "Some were reluctant, but they agreed."

"Go and fetch Zuln. Put her with the dissenters. I don't trust her to do what is needed."

The soldier didn't question as she towed Abronai away. There were perhaps a thousand dissenters there on the large plateau that made up the practice grounds. An acceptably small number.

"Eshonai . . ." The song was sung to Anxiety. She turned as Thude approached. "I don't like this, what we're doing here."

Bother. She had worried that he would be difficult. She took him by the arm, leading him a ways off. The new rhythms cycled through her mind as her armored feet crunched on the stones. Once they were far enough away from Venli and the others for some privacy, she turned Thude to look him in the eyes.

"Out with it," she said to Irritation, picking one of the old, familiar rhythms for him.

"Eshonai," he said quietly. "This isn't right. You *know* it's not right. I agreed to change—every soldier did—but it's not right."

"Do you disagree that we needed new tactics in this war?" Eshonai said to Resolve. "We were dying slowly, Thude."

"We did need new tactics," Thude said. "But this . . . Something's wrong with you, Eshonai."

"No, I just needed an excuse for such extreme action. Thude, I've been considering something like this for months."

"A coup?"

"Not a coup. A refocusing. We are *doomed* if we don't change our methods! My only hope was Venli's research. The only thing she turned up was this form. Well, I've got to try and use it, make one last attempt to save our people. The Five tried to stop me. I've heard you yourself complain about how much they talk instead of acting."

He hummed to Consideration. She knew him well enough, however, to sense when he was forcing a rhythm. The beat was too obvious, too strong.

I almost convinced him, she thought. *It's the red eyes. I've instilled in him, and some of the others of my own division, too much of a fear of our gods.*

It was a shame, but she'd probably have to see him, and her other former friends, executed.

"I see you're not convinced," Eshonai said.

"I just . . . I don't know, Eshonai. This seems bad."

"I'll talk you through it later," Eshonai said. "I don't have time right now."

"And what are you going to do to those?" Thude asked, nodding toward the dissenters. "This looks an awful lot like a roundup of people who don't agree with you. Eshonai . . . did you realize your own mother was among them?"

She started, looking and seeing her aging mother being guided to the group by two stormforms. They hadn't even come to her with the question. Did that mean they were extra obedient, following her orders no matter what, or were they worried she would weaken because her mother refused to change?

She could hear her mother singing. One of the old songs, as she was guided.

"You can watch over that group," Eshonai said to Thude. "You and soldiers you trust. I'll put my own division in charge of the people there, you at their head. That way, nothing will happen to them without your agreement."

He hesitated, then nodded, humming to Consideration for real this time. She let him go and he jogged over to Bila and a few others of Eshonai's former division.

Poor, trusting Thude, she thought as he took command of guarding the dissenters. *Thank you for rounding yourself up so neatly.*

"This was handled well," Venli said as Eshonai walked back to her. "Can you control the city long enough for the transformation?"

"Easily," Eshonai said, nodding to the soldiers who came to give her a report. "Just make certain you can deliver the proper spren and in the proper quantities."

"I will," Venli said to Satisfaction.

Eshonai took the reports. Everyone who had agreed was gathered in the center of the city. It was time to speak to them and deliver the lies she'd prepared. That the Five would be reinstated once the humans were dealt with, that there was no reason to worry. That everything was just fine.

Eshonai strode into a city that was now hers, flanked by soldiers in the new form. She summoned her Blade for effect, the last one her people owned, resting it on her shoulder.

She made her way to the center of the city, passing melted buildings and shacks built from carapace. It was a wonder that those things survived the storms. Her people deserved better. With the return of the gods, they would *have* better.

Irritatingly, it took some time to get the people ready for her speech. Some twenty thousand non-warforms gathered together was quite a sight; looking upon them, the city's population did not seem nearly so small. Still, this was a fraction of their original numbers.

Her soldiers seated them all, prepared messengers to deliver her words to those not near enough to hear. As she waited for the preparations, she listened to reports regarding the population. Surprisingly, the majority of those who had dissented were workers. They were supposed to be obedient. Well, the greater number of them were elderly, the ones who had not fought in the war against the Alethi. Those who had not been forced to watch their friends be killed.

She waited by the base of the pillar until everything was ready. She climbed the steps to begin her speech, but stopped as she noticed Varanis, one of her lieutenants, running toward her. He was one she had chosen for stormform.

Suddenly alert, Eshonai attuned the Rhythm of Destruction.

"General," he said to Anxiety. "They've escaped!"

"Who?"

"The ones you had us set apart, the ones who did not want to transform. They've fled."

"Well, chase them down," Eshonai said to Spite. "They can't get far. The workers won't be able to jump chasms; they can only go as far as the bridges allow."

"General! They cut down one of the bridges, then used the ropes to climb down into the chasm itself. They've fled through those."

"Then they're dead anyway," Eshonai said. "There is a storm in two days. They'll be caught in the chasms and killed. Ignore them."

"What of their guards?" Venli demanded to Spite, shoving her way up beside Eshonai. "Why weren't they being watched?"

"The guards went with them," Varanis said. "Eshonai, Thude was leading those—"

"No matter," Eshonai said. "You are dismissed."

Varanis retreated.

"You aren't surprised," Venli said to Destruction. "Who are these guards that are willing to *help* their prisoners escape? What have you done, Eshonai?"

"Do not challenge me."

"I—"

"Do *not* challenge me," Eshonai said, grabbing her sister by the neck with a gauntleted hand.

"Kill me, and you'll ruin everything," Venli said, not a hint of fear in her voice. "They'll never follow a woman who murdered her own sister in public, and only I can provide the spren you need for this transformation."

Eshonai hummed to the Rhythm of Derision, but let go. "I'm going to make my speech." She turned her back on Venli and stepped up to address the people.

PART
FOUR

The Approach

KALADIN • SHALLAN • DALINAR

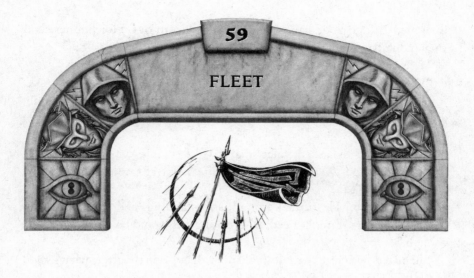

59

FLEET

I'll address this letter to my "old friend," as I have no idea what name you're using currently.

Kaladin had never been in prison before.

Cages, yes. Pits. Pens. Under guard in a room. Never a proper prison.

Perhaps that was because prisons were too nice. He had two blankets, a pillow, and a chamber pot that was changed regularly. They fed him far better than he'd ever been fed as a slave. The stone shelf wasn't the most comfortable bed, but with the blankets, it wasn't too bad. He didn't have any windows, but at least he wasn't out in the storms.

All in all, the room was very nice. And he hated it.

In the past, the only times he'd been stuck in a small space had been to weather a highstorm. Now, being enclosed here for hours on end, with nothing to do but lie on his back and think . . . Now he found himself restless, sweating, missing the open spaces. Missing the wind. The solitude didn't bother him. Those walls, though. They felt like they were crushing him.

On the third day of his imprisonment, he heard a disturbance from farther inside the prison, beyond his chamber. He stood up, ignoring Syl, who sat on an invisible bench on his wall. What *was* that shouting? It echoed in from the hallway.

His little cell was in its own room. The only people he'd seen since being locked up were the guards and the servants. Spheres glowed on the walls, keeping the place well lit. Spheres in a room meant for criminals. Were they there to taunt the men locked away? Riches just beyond reach.

He pressed against the cold bars, listening to the indistinct shouts. He imagined Bridge Four having come to break him out. Stormfather send they didn't try something so foolish.

He eyed one of the spheres in its setting on the wall.

"What?" Syl asked him.

"I might be able to get close enough to suck that Light out. It's only a little farther than the Parshendi were when I drew the Light from their gemstones."

"Then what?" Syl asked, voice small.

Good question. "Would you help me break out, if I wanted to?"

"Do you want to?"

"I'm not sure." He turned around, still standing, and rested his back against the bars. "I might need to. Breaking out would be against the law, though."

She lifted her chin. "I'm no highspren. Laws don't matter; what's *right* matters."

"On that point, we agree."

"But you came willingly," Syl said. "Why would you leave now?"

"I won't let them execute me."

"They're not going to," Syl said. "You heard Dalinar."

"Dalinar can go rot. He let this happen."

"He tried to—"

"He let it happen!" Kaladin snapped, turning and slamming his hands against the bars. Another *storming* cage. He was right back where he'd begun! "He's the same as the others," Kaladin growled.

Syl zipped over to him, coming to rest between the bars, hands on hips. "Say that again."

"He . . ." Kaladin turned away. Lying to her was hard. "All right, fine. He's not. But the king is. Admit it, Syl. Elhokar is a terrible king. At first he *lauded* me for trying to protect him. Now, at the snap of his fingers, he's willing to execute me. He's a child."

"Kaladin, you're scaring me."

"Am I? You told me to trust you, Syl. When I jumped down into the arena, you said this time things would be different. *How* is this different?"

She looked away, seeming suddenly very small.

"Even Dalinar admitted that the king had made a big mistake in letting Sadeas wiggle out of the challenge," Kaladin said. "Moash and his friends are right. This kingdom would be better off without Elhokar."

Syl dropped to the floor, head bowed.

Kaladin walked back to his bench, but was too stirred up to sit. He found himself pacing. How could a man be expected to live trapped in a little room, without fresh air to breathe? He wouldn't let them leave him

here.

You'd better keep your word, Dalinar. Get me out. Soon.

The disturbance, whatever it had been, quieted. Kaladin asked the servant about it when she came with his food, pushing it through the small opening at the bottom of the bars. She wouldn't speak to him, and scurried off like a cremling before a storm.

Kaladin sighed, retrieving the food—steamed vegetables, dribbled with a salty black sauce—and flopping back on his bench. They gave him food he could eat with his fingers. No forks or knives for him, just in case.

"Nice place you have here, bridgeboy," Wit said. "I considered moving in here myself on several occasions. The rent might be cheap, but the price of admission is quite steep."

Kaladin scrambled up to his feet. Wit sat on a bench by the far wall, outside the cell and under the spheres, tuning some kind of strange instrument on his lap made of taut strings and polished wood. He hadn't been there a moment ago. Storms . . . had the *bench* even been there before?

"How did you get in?" Kaladin asked.

"Well, there are these things called *doors* . . ."

"The guards let you?"

"Technically?" Wit asked, plucking at a string, then leaning down to listen as he plucked another. "Yes."

Kaladin sat back down on the bench in his cell. Wit wore his black-on-black, his thin silver sword undone from his waist and sitting on the bench beside him. A brown sack slumped there as well. Wit leaned down to tune his instrument, one leg crossed over the other. He hummed softly to himself and nodded. "Perfect pitch," Wit said, "makes this all so much easier than it once was. . . ."

Kaladin sat, waiting, as Wit settled back against the wall. Then did nothing.

"Well?" Kaladin asked.

"Yes. Thank you."

"Are you going to play music for me?"

"No. You wouldn't appreciate it."

"Then why are you here?"

"I like visiting people in prison. I can say whatever I want to them, and they can't do anything about it." He looked up at Kaladin, then rested his hands on his instrument, smiling. "I've come for a story."

"What story?"

"The one you're going to tell me."

"Bah," Kaladin said, lying back down on his bench. "I'm in no mood for your games today, Wit."

Wit plucked a note on his instrument. "Everyone always says that— which, first off, makes it a cliche. I am led to wonder. Is anyone *ever* in the mood for my games? And if they are, would that not defeat the point of my type of game in the first place?"

Kaladin sighed as Wit continued to pluck out notes. "If I play along today," Kaladin asked, "will that get rid of you?"

"I will leave as soon as the story is done."

"Fine. A man went to jail. He hated it there. The end."

"Ah . . ." Wit said. "So it's a story about a child, then."

"No, it's about—" Kaladin cut off.

Me.

"Perhaps a story *for* a child," Wit said. "I will tell you one, to get you in the mood. A bunny rabbit and a chick went frolicking in the grass together on a sunny day."

"A chick . . . baby chicken?" Kaladin said. "And a what?"

"Ah, forgot myself for a moment," Wit said. "Sorry. Let me make it more appropriate for you. A piece of wet slime and a disgusting crab thing with seventeen legs slunk across the rocks together on an insufferably rainy day. Is that better?"

"I suppose. Is the story over?"

"It hasn't started yet."

Wit abruptly slapped the strings, then began to play them with ferocious intent. A vibrant, energetic repetition. One punctuated note, then seven in a row, frenzied.

The rhythm got inside of Kaladin. It seemed to shake the entire room.

"What do you see?" Wit demanded.

"I . . ."

"Close your eyes, idiot!"

Kaladin closed his eyes. *This is stupid.*

"What do you see?" Wit repeated.

Wit was playing with him. The man was said to do that. He was supposedly Sigzil's old mentor. Shouldn't Kaladin have earned a reprieve by helping out his apprentice?

There was nothing of humor to those notes. Those powerful notes. Wit added a second melody, complementing the first. Was he playing that with his other hand? Both at the same time? How could one man, one instrument, produce so much music?

Kaladin saw . . . in his mind . . .

A race.

"That's the song of a man who is running," Kaladin said.

"In the driest part of the brightest day, the man set off from the eastern sea." Wit said it perfectly to the beat of his music, a chant that was almost a song. "And where he went or why he ran, the answer comes from you to me."

"He ran from the storm," Kaladin said softly.

"The man was Fleet, whose name you know; he's spoken of in song and lore. The fastest man e'er known to live. The surest feet e'er known to roam. In time long past, in times I've known, he raced the Herald Chan-a-rach. He won that race, as he did each one, but now the time for defeat had come.

"For Fleet so sure, and Fleet the quick, to all that heard he yelled his goal: to beat the wind, and race a storm. A claim so brash, a claim too bold. To race the wind? It can't be done. Undaunted, Fleet was set to run. So to the east, there went our Fleet. Upon the shore his mark was set.

"The storm grew strong, the storm grew wild. Who was this man all set to dash? No man should tempt the God of Storms. No fool had ever been so rash."

How did Wit play this music with only two hands? Surely another hand had joined him. Should Kaladin look?

In his mind's eye, he saw the race. Fleet, a barefooted man. Wit claimed all knew of him, but Kaladin had never heard of such a story. Lanky, tall, with tied-back long hair that went to his waist. Fleet took his mark on the shore, leaning forward in a running posture, waiting as the stormwall thundered and crashed across the sea toward him. Kaladin jumped as Wit hit a burst of notes, signaling the race's start.

Fleet tore off just in front of an angry, violent wall of water, lightning, and wind-blown rocks.

Wit did not speak again until Kaladin prompted him. "At first," Kaladin said, "Fleet did well."

"O'er rock and grass, our Fleet did run! He leaped the stones and dodged the trees, his feet a blur, his soul a sun! The storm so grand, it raged and spun, but away from it our Fleet did run! The lead was his, the wind behind, did man now prove that storms could *lose*?

"Through land he ran so quick and sure, and Alethkar he left behind. But now the test he saw ahead, for mountains he would have to climb. The storm surged on, released a howl; it saw its chance might now approach.

"To the highest mounts and the coldest peaks, our hero Fleet did make his way. The slopes were steep and paths unsure. Would he maintain his mighty lead?"

"Obviously not," Kaladin said. "You can never stay ahead. Not for long."

"No! The storm grew close, 'til it chewed his heels. Upon his neck, Fleet felt its chill. Its breath of ice was all around, a mouth of night and wings of frost. Its voice was of the breaking rocks; its song was of the crashing rain."

Kaladin could feel it. Icy water seeping through his clothing. Wind buffeting his skin. A roar so loud that soon, he could hear nothing at all.

He'd been there. He'd felt it.

"Then the tip he reached! The point he found! Fleet climbed no more; he crossed the peak. And down the side, his speed returned! Outside the storm, Fleet found the sun. Azir's plains were now his path. He sprinted west, more broad his stride."

"But he was growing weak," Kaladin said. "No man can run that far without getting tired. Even Fleet."

"Yet soon the race its toll did claim. His feet like bricks, his legs like cloth. In gasps our runner drew his breath. The end approached, the storm outdone, but slowly did our hero run."

"More mountains," Kaladin whispered. "Shinovar."

"A final challenge raised its head, a final shadow to his dread. The land did rise up once again, the Misted Mountains guarding Shin. To leave the storming winds behind, our Fleet again began to climb."

"The storm caught up."

"The storms again came to his back, the winds again did spin around! The time was short, the ending near, as through those mounts our Fleet did dash."

"It was right upon him. Even going down the other side of the mountains, he was unable to stay very far ahead."

"He crossed the peaks, but lost his lead. The last paths lay before his feet, but strength he'd spent and might he'd lost. Each step was toil, each breath in pain. A sunken land he crossed with grief, the grass so dead it did not move.

"But here the storm, it too did wilt, with thunder lost and lightning spent. The drops slipped down, now weak as wet. For Shin is not a place for them.

"Ahead the sea, the race's end. Fleet stayed ahead, his muscles raw. Eyes barely saw, legs barely walked, but on he went to destiny. The end you know, the end will live, a shock for men to me you'll give."

Music, but no words. Wit waited for Kaladin's reply. *Enough of this,* Kaladin thought. "He died. He didn't make it. The end."

The music stopped abruptly. Kaladin opened his eyes, looking toward Wit. Would he be mad that Kaladin had made such a poor conclusion to the story?

Wit stared at him, instrument still in his lap. The man didn't seem angry. "So you *do* know this story," Wit said.

"What? I thought you were making it up."

"No, you were."

"Then what is there to know?"

Wit smiled. "All stories told have been told before. We tell them to ourselves, as did all men who ever were. And all men who ever will be. The only things new are the names."

Kaladin sat up. He tapped one finger against his stone block of a bench.

"So . . . Fleet. Was he real?"

"As real as I am," Wit said.

"And he died?" Kaladin said. "Before he could finish the race?"

"He died." Wit smiled.

"What?"

Wit attacked the instrument. Music ripped through the small room. Kaladin rose to his feet as the notes reached new heights.

"Upon that land of dirt and soil," Wit shouted, "our hero fell and did not stir! His body spent, his strength undone, Fleet the hero was no more.

"The storm approached and found him there. It stilled and stopped upon its course! The rains they fell, the winds they blew, but forward they could not progress.

"For glory lit, and life alive, for goals unreached and aims to strive. All men must try, the wind did see. It is the test, it is the dream."

Kaladin stepped slowly up to the bars. Even with eyes open, he could see it. Imagine it.

"So in that land of dirt and soil, our hero stopped the storm itself. And while the rain came down like tears, our Fleet refused to end this race. His body dead, but not his will, within those winds his soul did *rise*.

"It flew upon the day's last song, to win the race and claim the dawn. Past the sea and past the waves, our Fleet no longer lost his breath. Forever strong, forever fast, forever free to race the wind."

Kaladin rested his hands against the bars of his cage. The music rang in the room, then slowly died.

Kaladin gave it a moment, Wit looking at his instrument, a proud smile on his lips. Finally, he tucked his instrument under his arm, took his bag and sword, and walked toward the doorway out.

"What does it mean?" Kaladin whispered.

"It's your story. You decide."

"But you already knew it."

"I know most stories, but I'd never sung this one before." Wit looked back at him, smiling. "What *does* it mean, Kaladin of Bridge Four? Kaladin Stormblessed?"

"The storm caught him," Kaladin said.

"The storm catches everyone, eventually. Does it matter?"

"I don't know."

"Good." Wit tipped his sword up toward his forehead, as if in respect. "Then you have something to think about."

He left.

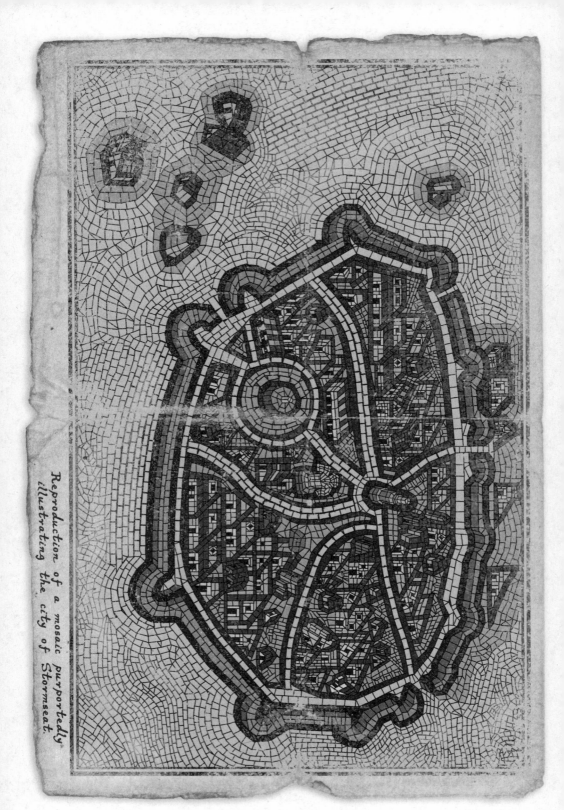

Reproduction of a mosaic purportedly illustrating the city of Stormseat.

60

VEIL WALKS

*Have you given up on the gemstone, now that it is dead? And do
you no longer hide behind the name of your old master? I am told
that in your current incarnation you've taken a name that references
what you presume to be one of your virtues.*

"Aha!" Shallan said. She scrambled across her fluffy bed—sinking
down practically to her neck with each motion—and leaned precariously over the side. She scrabbled among the stacks of papers
on the floor, tossing aside irrelevant sheets.

Finally, she retrieved the one she wanted, holding it up while pushing
hair out of her eyes and tucking it behind her ears. The page was a map, one
of those ancient ones that Jasnah had talked about. It had taken forever to
find a merchant at the Shattered Plains who had a copy.

"Look," Shallan said, holding the map beside a modern one of the same
area, copied by her own hand from Amaram's wall.

Bastard, she noted to herself.

She turned the maps around so that Pattern—who decorated the wall
above her headboard—could see them.

"Maps," he said.

"A pattern!" Shallan exclaimed.

"I see no pattern."

"Look right here," she said, edging over beside the wall. "On this old
map, the area is . . ."

"Natanatan," Pattern read, then hummed softly.

"One of the Epoch Kingdoms," Shallan said. "Organized by the Heralds
themselves for divine purposes and blah blah. But *look.*" She stabbed the

page with her finger. "The capital of Natanatan, Stormseat. If you were to judge where we'd find the ruins of it, comparing this old map to the one Amaram had . . ."

"It would be in those mountains somewhere," Pattern said, "between the words 'Dawn's Shadow' and the *U* in 'Unclaimed Hills.'"

"No, no," Shallan said. "Use a little imagination! The old map is wildly inaccurate. Stormseat was *right here*. On the Shattered Plains."

"That is not what the map says," Pattern said, humming.

"Close enough."

"That is *not* a pattern," he said, sounding offended. "Humans; you do not understand patterns. Like right now. It is second moon. Each night, you sleep during this time. But not tonight."

"I can't sleep tonight."

"More information, please," Pattern said. "Why *not* tonight? Is it the day of the week? Do you always not sleep on Jesel? Or is it the weather? Has it grown too warm? The position of the moons relative to—"

"It's none of that," Shallan said, shrugging. "I just can't sleep."

"Your body is capable of it, surely."

"Probably," Shallan said. "But not my head. It surges with too many ideas, like waves against the rocks. Rocks that . . . I guess . . . are also in my head." She cocked her head. "I don't think that metaphor makes me sound particularly bright."

"But—"

"No more complaints," Shallan said, raising a finger. "Tonight, I am doing *scholarship*."

She put the page down on her bed, then leaned over the side, fishing out several others.

"I *wasn't* complaining," Pattern complained. He moved down onto the bed beside her. "I do not remember well, but did Jasnah not use a *desk* when . . . 'doing scholarship'?"

"Desks are for boring people," Shallan said. "And for people who don't have a squishy bed." Would Dalinar's camp have had such a plush bed for her? Likely, the workload would have been smaller. Though, finally, she'd managed to finish sorting through Sebarial's personal finances and was almost ready to present him with a set of relatively neat books.

In a stroke of insight, she'd slipped a copy of one of her pages of quotes about Urithiru—its potential riches, and its connection to the Shattered Plains—in among the other reports she'd sent Palona. At the bottom, she wrote, "Among Jasnah Kholin's notes are these indications of something valuable hidden out on the Shattered Plains. Will keep you informed of my discoveries." If Sebarial thought there was opportunity beyond gemhearts out on the Plains, she might be able to get him to take her out there with his armies, in case Adolin's promises didn't come through.

Getting all of that ready had left her with little time for studying, unfortunately. Perhaps that was why she couldn't sleep. *This would be easier,* Shallan thought, *if Navani would agree to meet with me.* She'd written again, and gotten the reply that Navani was busy caring for Dalinar, who had come down with a sickness. Nothing life-threatening, apparently, but he had withdrawn for a few days to recuperate.

Did Adolin's aunt blame her for botching the dueling agreement? After what Adolin had decided to do last week . . . Well, at least his preoccupation left Shallan with some time to read and think about Urithiru. Anything other than worrying about her brothers, who still hadn't responded to her letters pleading for them to leave Jah Keved and come to her.

"I find sleeping very odd," Pattern said. "I know that all beings in the Physical Realm engage in it. Do you find it pleasant? You fear nonexistence, but is not unconsciousness the same thing?"

"With sleep, it's only temporary."

"Ah. It is all right, because in the morning, you each return to sentience."

"Well, that depends on the person," Shallan said absently. "For many of them, 'sentience' might be too generous a term. . . ."

Pattern hummed, trying to sort through to the meaning of what she said. Finally, he buzzed an approximation of a laugh.

Shallan cocked an eyebrow at him.

"I have guessed that what you said is humorous," Pattern said. "Though I do not know why. It was not a joke. I know of jokes. A soldier came running into camp after going to see the prostitutes. He was white in the face. His friends asked if he had found a good time. He said that he had not. They asked why. He said that when he'd asked how much the woman charged, she'd said one mark plus the tip. He told his friends that he hadn't realized they were charging body parts now."

Shallan grimaced. "You heard that from Vathah's men, didn't you?"

"Yes. It is funny because the word 'tip' means several different things. A payment made in addition to the sum initially charged, usually given voluntarily, and the top piece of something. In addition, I believe that 'the tip' means something in the slang of the soldiers, and so the man in the joke thought she was going to cut off his—"

"Yes, thank you," Shallan said.

"That is a joke," Pattern continued. "I understand why it is funny. Ha ha. Sarcasm is similar. You replace an expected result with one grossly unexpected, and the humor is in the juxtaposition. But why was your earlier comment funny?"

"It's debatable whether it was, at this point. . . ."

"But—"

"Pattern, nothing is *less* funny than explaining humor," Shallan said. "We have more important things to discuss."

"Mmm . . . Such as why you have forgotten how to make your images produce sound? You did it once, long ago."

. . .

Shallan blinked, then held up the modern map. "The capital of Natanatan *was* here, on the Shattered Plains. The old maps are misleading. Amaram notes that the Parshendi use weapons of masterly design, far beyond their skill in craftsmanship. Where would they have gotten those? From the ruins of the city that once was here."

Shallan dug in her stacks of papers, getting out a map of the city itself. It didn't show the surrounding area—it was just a city map, and a rather vague one, taken from a book she'd purchased. She thought it was the one that Jasnah referenced in her notes.

The merchant she'd bought it from claimed it was ancient—that it was a copy of a copy from a book in Azir that claimed to be a drawing of a tile mosaic depiction of the city of Stormseat. The mosaic no longer existed—so much of what they had of the shadowdays came from fragments like these.

"Scholars reject the idea that Stormseat was here on the Plains," Shallan said. "They say that the craters of the warcamps don't match the descriptions of the city. Instead, they propose that the ruins must be hidden up in the highlands, where you indicated. But Jasnah didn't agree with them. She points out that few of the scholars have actually been here, and that this area in general is poorly explored."

"Mmm," Pattern said. "Shallan . . ."

"I agree with Jasnah," Shallan said, turning from him. "Stormseat wasn't a large city. It could have been in the middle of the Plains, and these craters something else. . . . Amaram says here he thinks they might once have been domes. I wonder if that is even possible. . . . They'd be so large. . . . Anyway, this might have been a satellite city of some sort."

Shallan felt like she was getting close to something. Amaram's notes spoke mostly of trying to meet with the Parshendi, to ask them about the Voidbringers and how to return them. He did mention Urithiru, however, and seemed to have come to the same conclusion as Jasnah—that the ancient city of Stormseat would have contained a path to Urithiru. Ten of them had once connected the ten capitals of the Epoch Kingdoms to Urithiru, which had some kind of conference room for the ten monarchs of the Epoch Kingdoms—and a throne for each one.

That was why none of the maps placed the holy city in the same location. It was ridiculous to walk there; instead, you made for the nearest city with an Oathgate and used that.

He's searching for the information there, Shallan thought. *Same as I am. But he wants to return the Voidbringers, not fight them. Why?*

She held up the antique map of Stormseat, the copy from the mosaic. It had artistic stylings instead of specific indications of things like distance and location. While she appreciated the former, the latter was truly frustrating.

Are you on here? she thought. *The secret, the Oathgate? Are you here, on this dais, as Jasnah thought?*

"The Shattered Plains haven't always been shattered," Shallan whispered to herself. "That's what the scholars, all but Jasnah, are missing. Stormseat was destroyed during the Last Desolation, but it was so long ago, nobody talks about *how*. Fire? Earthquake? No. Something more terrible. The city was broken, like a piece of fine dinnerware hit with a hammer."

"Shallan," Pattern said, moving closer to her. "I know that you have forgotten much of what once was. Those lies attracted me. But you cannot continue like this; you must admit the truth about me. About what I can do, and what we have done. Mmm . . . More, you *must* know yourself. And remember."

She sat cross-legged on the too-nice bed. Memories tried to claw their way out of the boxes inside her head. Those memories all pointed one way, toward carpet bloodied. And carpet . . . not.

"You wish to help," Pattern said. "You wish to prepare for the Everstorm, the spren of the unnatural one. You must become something. I did not come to you merely to teach you tricks of light."

"You came to learn," Shallan said, staring at her map. "That's what you said."

"I came to learn. We became to do something greater."

"Would you have me unable to laugh?" she demanded, suddenly holding back tears. "Would you have me crippled? That is what those memories would do to me. I can *be* what I *am* because I cut them off."

An image formed in front of her, born of Stormlight, created by instinct. She hadn't needed to draw this image first, for she knew it too well.

The image was of herself. Shallan, as she *should* be. Curled in a huddle on the bed, unable to weep for she had long since run out of tears. This girl . . . not a woman, a girl . . . flinched whenever spoken to. She expected everyone to shout at her. She could not laugh, for laughter had been squeezed from her by a childhood of darkness and pain.

That was the real Shallan. She knew it as surely as she knew her own name. The person she had become instead was a lie, one she had fabricated in the name of survival. To remember herself as a child, discovering Light in the gardens, Patterns in the stonework, and dreams that became real . . .

. . .

"Mmmm . . . Such a deep lie," Pattern whispered. "A deep lie indeed. But still, you must obtain your abilities. Learn again, if you have to."

"Very well," Shallan said. "But if we did this before, can't you just tell me how it is done?"

"My memory is weak," Pattern said. "I was dumb so long, nearly dead. Mmm. I could not speak."

"Yeah," Shallan said, remembering him spinning on the ground and running into the wall. "You were kind of cute, though." She banished the image of the frightened, huddled, whimpering girl, then got out her drawing implements. She tapped a pencil against her lips, then did something simple, a drawing of Veil, the darkeyed con woman.

Veil was not Shallan. Her features were different enough that the two of them would be distinct individuals to anyone who happened to see them both. Still, Veil did bear echoes of Shallan. She was a darkeyed, tan-skinned, Alethi version of Shallan—a Shallan that was a few years older and had a pointier nose and chin.

Finished with the drawing, Shallan breathed out Stormlight and created the image. It stood beside the bed, arms folded, looking as confident as a master duelist facing a child with a stick.

Sound. How would she do sound? Pattern had called it a force, part of the Surge of Illumination—or at least similar to it. She situated herself on the bed, one leg folded beneath her, inspecting Veil. Over the next hour, Shallan tried everything she could think of, from straining herself and concentrating, to trying to *draw* sounds to make them appear. Nothing worked.

Finally, she climbed off the bed and walked to get herself a drink from the bottle chilling in the bucket in the next room. As she approached it, however, she felt a *tugging* inside of her. She looked over her shoulder into the bedroom, and saw that the image of Veil had started to blur, like smudged pencil lines.

Blast, but that was inconvenient. Sustaining the illusion required Shallan to provide a constant source of Stormlight. She walked back into the bedroom and set a sphere on the floor inside of Veil's foot. When she walked away, the illusion still grew indistinct, like a bubble preparing to pop. Shallan turned and put her hands on her hips, staring at the version of Veil that had gone all fuzzy.

"Annoying!" she snapped.

Pattern hummed. "I'm sorry that your mystical, godlike powers do not instantly work as you would like them to."

She raised an eyebrow at him. "I thought you didn't understand humor."

"I do. I just explained . . ." He paused for a moment. "Was I being funny? Sarcasm. I was *sarcastic*. By accident!" He seemed surprised, even gleeful.

"I guess you're learning."

"It is the bond," he explained. "In Shadesmar, I do not communicate this way, this . . . human way. My connection to you gives me the means by which I can manifest in the Physical Realm as more than a mindless glimmer. Mmmm. It links me to you, helps me communicate as you do. Fascinating. Mmmm."

He settled down like a trumping axehound, perfectly content. And then Shallan noticed something.

"I'm not glowing," Shallan said. "I'm holding a lot of Stormlight, but I'm not glowing."

"Mmm . . ." Pattern said. "Large illusion transforms the Surge into another. Feeds off your Stormlight."

She nodded. The Stormlight she held fed the illusion, drawing the excess from her that would normally float above her skin. That could be useful. As Pattern moved up onto the bed, Veil's elbow—which was closest to him—grew more distinct.

Shallan frowned. "Pattern, move closer to the image."

He obliged, crossing the cover of her bed toward where Veil stood. She unfuzzed. Not completely, but his presence made a noticeable difference.

Shallan walked over, her proximity making the illusion snap back to full clarity.

"Can you hold Stormlight?" Shallan asked Pattern.

"I don't . . . I mean . . . Investiture is the means by which I . . ."

"Here," Shallan said, pressing her hand down on him, muffling his words to an annoyed buzzing. It was an odd sensation, as if she'd trapped an angry cremling under the bedsheets. She pushed some Stormlight into him. When she lifted her hand, he was trailing wisps of it, like steam off a hotplate fabrial.

"We're bonded," she said. "My illusion is your illusion. I'm going to get a drink. See if you can keep the image from breaking apart." She backed to the sitting room and smiled. Pattern, still buzzing with annoyance, moved down off the bed. She couldn't see him—the bed was in the way—but she guessed he'd gone to Veil's feet.

It worked. The illusion stayed. "Ha!" Shallan said, getting herself a cup of wine. She walked back and eased onto the bed—flopping down with a cup of red wine did not seem prudent—and looked over the side at the floor, where Pattern sat beneath Veil. He was visible because of the Stormlight.

I'll need to take that into account, Shallan thought. *Build illusions so that he can hide in them.*

"It worked?" Pattern said. "How did you know it would work?"

"I didn't." Shallan took a sip of wine. "I guessed."

She drank another sip as Pattern hummed. Jasnah would not have approved. *Scholarship requires a sharp mind and alert senses. These do not mix with alcohol.* Shallan drank the rest of the wine in a gulp.

"Here," Shallan said, reaching down. She did the next bit by instinct. She had a connection to the illusion, and she had a connection to Pattern, so . . .

With a *push* of Stormlight, she attached the illusion to Pattern as she often attached them to herself. His glow subsided. "Walk around," she said.

"I don't walk . . ." Pattern said.

"You know what I mean," Shallan said.

Pattern moved, and the image moved with him. It didn't walk, unfortunately. The image just kind of glided. Like light reflected onto the wall from a spoon you idly turned in your hands. She cheered to herself anyway. After so long failing to get sounds from one of her creations, this different discovery seemed a major victory.

Could she get it to move more naturally? She settled down with her sketchpad and started drawing.

61

OBEDIENCE

ONE AND A HALF YEARS AGO

Shallan became the perfect daughter.

She kept quiet, particularly in Father's presence. She spent most days in her room, sitting by the window, reading the same books over and over or sketching the same objects again and again. He had proven several times by this point that he would not touch her if she angered him.

Instead, he would beat others in her name.

The only times she allowed herself to drop the mask was when she was with her brothers, times when her father couldn't hear. Her three brothers often cajoled her—with an edge of desperation—to tell them stories from her books. For their hearing only, she made jokes, poked fun at Father's visitors, and invented extravagant tales by the hearth.

Such an insignificant way to fight back. She felt a coward for not doing more. But surely . . . surely things would get better now. Indeed, as Shallan was involved more by the ardents in accounts, she noted a shrewdness to the way her father stopped being bullied by other lighteyes and started playing them against each other. He impressed her, but frightened her, in how he seized for power. Father's fortunes changed further when a new marble deposit was discovered on his lands—providing resources to keep up with his promises, bribes, and deals.

Surely that would make him start laughing again. Surely that would drive the darkness from his eyes.

It did not.

"She is too low for you to marry," Father said, setting down his mug. "I won't have it, Balat. You will break off contact with that woman."

"She belongs to a good family!" Balat said, standing, palms on the table. It was lunch, and so Shallan was expected to be here, rather than remaining shut up in her room. She sat to the side, at her private table. Balat stood facing Father across the high table.

"Father, they're your vassals!" Balat snapped. "You yourself have invited them to dine with us."

"My axehounds dine at my feet," Father said. "I do not allow my sons to court them. House Tavinar is not nearly ambitious enough for us. Now, Sudi Valam, that might be worth considering."

Balat frowned. "The highprince's daughter? You can't be serious. She's in her fifties!"

"She is single."

"Because her husband died in a duel! Anyway, the highprince would never approve it."

"His perception of us will change," Father said. "We are a wealthy family now, with much influence."

"Yet still headed by a murderer," Balat snapped.

Too far! Shallan thought. On Father's other side, Luesh laced his fingers in front of him. The new house steward had a face like a well-worn glove, leathery and wrinkled in the places most used—notably the frown lines.

Father stood up slowly. This new anger of his, the cold anger, terrified Shallan. "Your new axehound pups," he said to Balat. "Terrible that they caught a sickness during the latest highstorm. Tragic. It is unfortunate they need to be put down." He gestured, and one of his new guards—a man Shallan did not know well—stepped outside, pulling his sword from its sheath.

Shallan grew very cold. Even Luesh grew concerned, placing a hand on Father's arm.

"You bastard," Balat said, growing pale. "I'll—"

"You'll *what*, Balat?" Father asked, shaking off Luesh's touch, leaning toward Balat. "Come on. Say it. Will you challenge me? Don't think I wouldn't kill you if you did. Wikim may be a pathetic wreck, but he will serve just as well as you for what this house needs."

"Helaran is back," Balat said.

Father froze, hands on the table, unmoving.

"I saw him two days ago," Balat said. "He sent for me, and I rode out to meet him in the city. Helaran—"

"That name is *not* to be spoken in this house!" Father said. "I mean it, *Nan* Balat! Never."

Balat met his father's gaze, and Shallan counted ten beats of her thumping heart before Balat broke the stare and looked away.

Father sat down, looking exhausted as Balat stalked out of the room. The hall fell completely silent, Shallan too frightened to speak. Father eventually stood up, shoving his chair back and leaving. Luesh trailed soon after.

That left Shallan alone with the servants. Timidly she stood up, then went after Balat.

He was in the kennel. The guard had worked swiftly. Balat's new pod of pups lay dead in a pool of violet blood on the stone floor.

She'd encouraged Balat to breed these. He'd been making progress with his demons, over the years. He rarely hurt anything larger than a cremling. Now he sat on a box, looking down at the small corpses, horrified. Painspren cluttered the ground near him.

The metal gate into the kennel rattled as Shallan pushed it open. She raised her safehand to her mouth as she drew closer to the pitiful remains.

"Father's guards," Balat said. "It's like they were *waiting* for a chance to do something like this. I don't like the new group he has. That Levrin, with the angry eyes, and Rin . . . that one frightens me. What ever happened to Ten and Beal? Soldiers that you could joke with. Almost friends . . ."

She rested a hand on his shoulder. "Balat. Did you really see Helaran?"

"Yes. He said I wasn't to tell anyone. He warned me that this time when he left, he might not be coming back for a long time. He told me . . . told me to watch over the family." Balat buried his head in his hands. "I can't be him, Shallan."

"You don't need to be."

"He's brave. He's strong."

"He abandoned us."

Balat looked up, tears running down his cheeks. "Maybe he was right. Maybe that's the only way, Shallan."

"Leave our house?"

"What of it?" Balat asked. "You spend every day locked away, brought out only for Father to display. Jushu has gone back to his gambling—you know he has, even if he's smarter about it. Wikim talks about becoming an ardent, but I don't know if Father will ever let go of him. He's insurance."

It was, unfortunately, a good argument. "Where would we go?" Shallan asked. "We have nothing."

"I have nothing here either," Balat said. "I'm not going to give up on Eylita, Shallan. She's the only beautiful thing that has happened in my life. If she and I have to go live in Vedenar as tenth dahn, with me working as a house guard or something like that, we'll do it. Doesn't that seem a better life than this?" He gestured toward the dead pups.

"Perhaps."

"Would you go with me? If I took Eylita and left? You could be a scribe. Earn your own way, be free of Father."

"I . . . No. I need to stay."

"Why?"

"Something has hold of Father, something awful. If we all leave, we give him to it. Someone has to help him."

"Why do you defend him so? You know what he did."

"He didn't do it."

"You can't remember," Balat said. "You've told me over and over that your mind blanks. You saw him kill her, but you don't want to admit that you witnessed it. Storms, Shallan. You're as broken as Wikim and Jushu. As . . . as I am sometimes . . ."

She shook off her numbness.

"It doesn't matter," she said. "If you go, are you going to take Wikim and Jushu with you?"

"I couldn't afford to," Balat said. "Jushu in particular. We'd have to live lean, and I couldn't trust that he'd . . . you know. But if you came, it might be easier for one of us to find work. You're better at writing and art than Eylita."

"No, Balat," Shallan said, frightened of how eager a part of her was to say yes to him. "I *can't*. Particularly if Jushu and Wikim remain here."

"I see," he said. "Maybe . . . maybe there's another way out. I'll think."

She left him in the kennel, worried that Father would find her there and that it would upset him. She entered the manor, but couldn't help feeling that she was trying to hold together a carpet as dozens of people pulled out threads from the sides.

What would happen if Balat left? He backed down from fights with Father, but at least he resisted. Wikim merely did what he was told, and Jushu was still a mess. *We have to just weather this,* Shallan thought. *Stop provoking Father, let him relax. Then he'll come back. . . .*

She climbed the steps and passed Father's door. It was open a crack; she could hear him inside.

". . . find him in Valath," Father said. "Nan Balat claims to have met him in the city, and that is what he must have meant."

"It will be done, Brightlord." That voice. It was Rin, captain of Father's new guards. Shallan backed up, peeking into the room. Father's strongbox shone behind the picture on the back wall, bright light bursting through the canvas. To her it was almost blinding, though the men in the room didn't seem able to see it.

Rin bowed before Father, hand on sword.

"Bring me his head, Rin," Father said. "I want to see it with my own eyes. He is the one who could ruin all of this. Surprise him, kill him before he can summon his Shardblade. That weapon will be yours in payment so long as you serve House Davar."

Shallan stumbled back from the door before Father could look up and see her. Helaran. Father had just ordered *Helaran's assassination*.

I have to do something. I have to warn him. How? Could Balat contact him again? Shallan—

"How dare you," said a feminine voice within.

Stunned silence followed. Shallan edged back to look into the room. Malise, her stepmother, stood in the doorway between the bedroom and the sitting room. The small, plump woman had never seemed threatening to Shallan before. But the storm on her face today could have frightened a whitespine.

"Your own *son*," Malise said. "Have you no morals left? Have you no compassion?"

"He is no longer my son," Father growled.

"I believed your story about the woman before me," Malise said. "I've supported you. I've lived with this cloud over the house. Now I hear *this*? It is one thing to beat the servants, but to kill your *son*?"

Father whispered something to Rin. Shallan jumped, and barely got down the hallway to her room before the man slipped out of the room, then closed Father's door with a *click*.

Shallan shut herself in her room as the shouting started, a violent, angry back-and-forth between Malise and her father. Shallan huddled up beside the bed, tried to use a pillow to keep out the sounds. When she thought it was over, she removed the pillow.

Her father stormed out into the hallway. "Why will nobody in this house *obey*?" he shouted, thumping down the stairs. "This wouldn't happen if you all just obeyed."

62

THE ONE WHO KILLED PROMISES

This is, I suspect, a little like a skunk naming itself for its stench.

Life continued in Kaladin's cell. Though the accommodations were nice for a dungeon, he found himself wishing he were back in the slave wagon. At least then he'd been able to watch the scenery. Fresh air, wind, an occasional rinse in the highstorm's last rains. Life certainly hadn't been good, but it had been better than being locked away and forgotten.

They took the spheres away at night, abandoning him to blackness. In the dark, he found himself imagining that he was someplace deep, with miles of stone above him and no pathway out, no hope of rescue. He could not conceive a worse death. Better to be gutted on the battlefield, looking up at the open sky as your life leaked away.

⁘

Light awoke him. He sighed, watching the ceiling as the guards—lighteyed soldiers he didn't know—replaced the lamp spheres. Day after day, everything was the storming *same* in here. Waking to the frail light of spheres, which only made him wish for the sun. The servant arrived to give him his breakfast. He'd placed his chamber pot in reach of the opening at the bottom of the bars, and it scraped stone as she pulled it out and replaced it with a fresh one.

She scurried away. He frightened her. With a groan at stiff muscles, Kaladin sat up and regarded his meal. Flatbread stuffed with bean paste. He stood, waving away some strange spren like taut wires crossing before him, then forced himself to do a set of push-ups. Keeping his strength up would be difficult if the imprisonment continued too long. Perhaps he could ask for some stones to use for training.

Was this what happened to Moash's grandparents? Kaladin wondered, taking the food. *Waiting for a trial until they died in prison?*

Kaladin sat back on his bench, nibbling on the flatbread. There'd been a highstorm yesterday, but he'd barely been able to hear it, locked away in this room.

He heard Syl humming nearby, but couldn't find where she'd gone. "Syl?" he asked. She kept hiding from him.

"There was a Cryptic at the fight," her voice said softly.

"You mentioned those before, didn't you? A type of spren?"

"A revolting type." She paused. "But not evil, I don't think." She sounded begrudging. "I was going to follow it, as it fled, but you needed me. When I went back to look, it had hidden from me."

"What does it mean?" Kaladin asked, frowning.

"Cryptics like to plan," Syl said slowly, as if recalling something long lost. "Yes . . . I remember. They debate and watch and never *do* anything. But . . ."

"What?" Kaladin asked, rising.

"They're looking for someone," Syl said. "I've seen the signs. Soon, you might not be alone, Kaladin."

Looking for someone. To choose, like him, as a Surgebinder. What kind of Knight Radiant had been made by a group of spren Syl so obviously detested? It didn't seem like someone he'd want to get to know.

Oh, storms, Kaladin thought, sitting back down. *If they choose Adolin . . .*

The thought should have made him sick. Instead, he found Syl's revelation oddly comforting. Not being alone, even if it *did* turn out to be Adolin, made him feel better and drove away some small measure of his gloom.

As he was finishing his meal, a thump came from the hallway. The door opening? Only lighteyes could visit him, though so far none had. Unless you counted Wit.

The storm catches everyone, eventually. . . .

Dalinar Kholin stepped into the room.

Despite his sour thoughts, Kaladin's immediate reaction—drilled into him over the years—was to stand and salute, hand to breast. This was his commanding officer. He felt an idiot as soon as he did it. He stood behind bars and saluted the man who'd put him here?

"At ease," Dalinar said with a nod. The wide-shouldered man stood with hands clasped behind his back. Something about Dalinar was imposing, even when he was relaxed.

He looks like the generals from the stories, Kaladin thought. Thick of face and greying of hair, solid in the same way that a brick was. He didn't wear a uniform, the uniform wore *him*. Dalinar Kholin represented an ideal that Kaladin had long since decided was a mere fancy.

"How are your accommodations?" Dalinar asked.

"Sir? I'm in storming *prison*."

A smile cracked Dalinar's face. "So I see. Calm yourself, soldier. If I'd ordered you to guard a room for a week, would you have done it?"

"Yes."

"Then consider this your duty. Guard this room."

"I'll make sure nobody unauthorized runs off with the chamber pot, sir."

"Elhokar is coming around. He's finished cooling off, and now only worries that releasing you too quickly will make him look weak. I'll need you to stay here a few more days, then we'll draft a formal pardon for your crime and have you reinstated to your position."

"I don't see that I have any choice, sir."

Dalinar stepped closer to the bars. "This is hard for you."

Kaladin nodded.

"You are well cared for, as are your men. Two of your bridgemen guard the way into the building at all times. There is nothing to worry you, soldier. If it's your reputation with me—"

"Sir," Kaladin said. "I guess I'm just not convinced that the king will ever let me go. He has a history of letting inconvenient people rot in dungeons until they die."

As soon as he said the words, Kaladin couldn't believe they'd come from his lips. They sounded insubordinate, even treasonous. But they'd been sitting there, in his mouth, *demanding* to be spoken.

Dalinar remained in his posture with hands clasped behind his back. "You speak of the silversmiths back in Kholinar?"

So he did know. Stormfather . . . had Dalinar been involved? Kaladin nodded.

"How did you hear of that incident?"

"From one of my men," Kaladin said. "He knew the imprisoned people."

"I had hoped we could escape those rumors," Dalinar said. "But of course, rumor grows like lichen, crusted on and impossible to completely scrub free. What happened with those people was a mistake, soldier. I'll admit that freely. The same won't happen to you."

"Are the rumors about them true, then?"

"I would really rather not speak of the Roshone affair."

Roshone.

Kaladin remembered screams. Blood on the floor of his father's surgery room. A dying boy.

A day in the rain. A day when one man tried to steal away Kaladin's light. He eventually succeeded.

"Roshone?" Kaladin whispered.

"Yes, a minor lighteyes," Dalinar said, sighing.

"Sir, it's important that I know of this. For my own peace of mind."

Dalinar looked him up and down. Kaladin just stared straight ahead, mind . . . numb. Roshone. Everything had started to go wrong when Roshone had arrived in Hearthstone to be the new citylord. Before then, Kaladin's father had been respected.

When that horrid man had arrived, dragging petty jealousy behind him like a cloak, the world had twisted upon itself. Roshone had infected Hearthstone like rotspren on an unclean wound. He was the reason Tien had gone to war. He was the reason Kaladin had followed.

"I suppose I owe you this," Dalinar said. "But it is not to be spread around. Roshone was a petty man who gained Elhokar's ear. Elhokar was crown prince then, commanded to rule over Kholinar and watch the kingdom while his father organized our first camps here in the Shattered Plains. I was . . . away at the time.

"Anyway, do not blame Elhokar. He was taking the advice of someone he trusted. Roshone, however, sought his own interests instead of those of the Throne. He owned several silversmith shops . . . well, the details are not important. Suffice it to say that Roshone led the prince to make some errors. I cleared it up when I returned."

"You saw this Roshone punished?" Kaladin asked, voice soft, feeling numb.

"Exiled," Dalinar said, nodding. "Elhokar moved the man to a place where he couldn't do any more harm."

A place he couldn't do any more harm. Kaladin almost laughed.

"You have something to say?"

"You don't want to know what I think, sir."

"Perhaps I don't. I probably need to hear it anyway."

Dalinar *was* a good man. Blinded in some ways, but a good man. "Well, sir," Kaladin said, controlling his emotions with difficulty, "I find it . . . troubling that a man like this Roshone could be responsible for the deaths of innocent people, yet escape prison."

"It was complicated, soldier. Roshone was one of Highprince Sadeas's sworn liegemen, cousin to important men whose support we needed. I originally argued that Roshone should be stripped of station and made a tenner, forced to live his life in squalor. But this would have alienated allies, and could have undermined the kingdom. Elhokar argued for leniency toward Roshone, and his father agreed via spanreed. I relented, figuring that mercy was not an attribute I should discourage in Elhokar."

"Of course not," Kaladin said, clenching his teeth. "Though it seems that such mercy often ends up serving the cousins of powerful lighteyes, and rarely someone lowly." He stared through the bars between himself and Dalinar.

"Soldier," Dalinar asked, voice cool. "Do you think I've been unfair toward you or your men?"

"You. No, sir. But this isn't about you."

Dalinar exhaled softly, as if in frustration. "Captain, you and your men are in a unique position. You spend your daily lives around the king. You don't see the face that is presented to the world, you see the *man*. It has ever been so for close bodyguards.

"So your loyalty needs to be extra firm and generous. Yes, the man you guard has flaws. Every man does. He is still your king, and I *will* have your respect."

"I can and do respect the Throne, sir," Kaladin said. Not the man sitting in it, perhaps. But he did respect the office. Somebody needed to rule.

"Son," Dalinar said after a moment's thought, "do you know why I put you into the position that I did?"

"You said it was because you needed someone you could trust not to be a spy for Sadeas."

"That's the rationale," Dalinar said, stepping up closer to the bars, only inches from Kaladin. "But it's not the *reason*. I did it because it felt right."

Kaladin frowned.

"I trust my hunches," Dalinar said. "My gut said you were a man who could help change this kingdom. A man who could live through Damnation itself in Sadeas's camp and still somehow inspire others was a man I wanted under my command." His expression grew harder. "I gave you a position no darkeyes has ever held in this army. I let you into conferences with the king, and I listened when you spoke. Do *not* make me regret those decisions, soldier."

"You don't already?" Kaladin asked.

"I've come close," Dalinar said. "I understand, though. If you truly believe what you told me about Amaram . . . well, if I'd been in your place, I'd have been hard pressed not to do the same thing you did. But storm it, man, you're still a *darkeyes*."

"It shouldn't matter."

"Maybe it shouldn't, but it *does*. You want to change that? Well, you're not going to do it by screaming like a lunatic and challenging men like Amaram to duels. You'll do it by distinguishing yourself in the position I gave you. Be the kind of man that others admire, whether they be light-eyed or dark. Convince Elhokar that a darkeyes can lead. *That* will change the world."

Dalinar turned and walked away. Kaladin couldn't help thinking that the man's shoulders seemed more bowed than when he'd entered.

After Dalinar left, Kaladin sat back on his bench, letting out a long, annoyed breath. "Stay calm," he whispered. "Do as you're told, Kaladin. Stay in your cage."

"He's trying to help," Syl said.

Kaladin glanced to the side. Where *was* she hiding? "You heard about Roshone."

Silence.

"Yes," Syl finally said, voice sounding small.

"My family's poverty," Kaladin said, "the way the town ostracized us, Tien being forced into the army, these things were all Roshone's fault. Elhokar sent him to us."

Syl didn't respond. Kaladin fished a bit of flatbread from his bowl, chewing on it. Stormfather—Moash really *was* right. This kingdom would be better off without Elhokar. Dalinar tried his best, but he had an enormous blind spot regarding his nephew.

It was time someone stepped in and cut the ties binding Dalinar's hands. For the good of the kingdom, for the good of Dalinar Kholin himself, the king had to die.

Some people—like a festering finger or a leg shattered beyond repair— just needed to be removed.

*Now, look what you've made me say. You've always been able to
bring out the most extreme in me, old friend. And I do still name
you a friend, for all that you weary me.*

---

*W*hat are you doing? the spanreed wrote to Shallan.
        Nothing much, she wrote back by spherelight, *just working
        on Sebarial's income ledgers.* She peeked out through the hole
in her illusion, regarding the street far below. People flowed through the
city as if marching to some strange rhythm. A dribble, then a burst, then
back to a dribble. Rarely a constant flow. What caused that?

You want to come visit? the pen wrote. *This is getting really boring.*

Sorry, she wrote back to Adolin, *I really need to get this work done. It
might be nice to have a spanreed conversation to keep me company, though.*

Pattern hummed softly beside her at the lie. Shallan had used an illusion
to expand the size of the shed atop this tenement in Sebarial's warcamp,
providing a hidden place to sit and watch the street below. Five hours of
waiting—comfortable enough, with the stool and spheres for light—had
revealed nothing. Nobody had approached the lone stone-barked tree
growing beside the pathway.

She didn't know the species. It was too old to have been planted there
recently; it must predate Sebarial's arrival. The gnarled, sturdy bark made
her think it was some variety of dendrolith, but the tree also had long
fronds that rose into the air like streamers, twisting and fluttering in the
wind. Those were reminiscent of a dalewillow. She'd already done a sketch;
she would look it up in her books later.

The tree was used to people, and didn't pull in its fronds as they passed it. If someone had approached carefully enough to avoid brushing the fronds, Shallan would have spotted them. If, instead, they'd moved quickly, the fronds would have felt the vibrations and withdrawn—which she also would have spotted. She was reasonably certain that if anyone had tried to fetch the item in the tree, she'd have known it, even if she'd been looking away for a moment.

I suppose, the pen wrote, *I can continue to keep you company. Shoren isn't doing anything else.*

Shoren was the ardent who wrote for Adolin today, come to visit by Adolin's order. The prince had pointedly noted that he was using an ardent, rather than one of his father's scribes. Did he think she'd grow jealous if he used another woman for scribing duties?

He did seem surprised that she didn't get jealous. Were the women of the court so petty? Or was Shallan the odd one, too relaxed? His eyes *did* wander, and she had to admit that wasn't something that pleased her. And there was his reputation to consider. Adolin was said to have, in the past, changed relationships as frequently as other men changed coats.

Perhaps she should cling more firmly, but the thought of it nauseated her. Such behavior reminded her of Father, holding so tightly to everything that he eventually broke it all.

Yes, she wrote back to Adolin, using the board set on a box beside her, *I'm certain the good ardent has nothing at all better to do than transcribe notes between two courting lighteyes.*

He's an ardent, Adolin sent. *He likes to serve. It's what they do.*

I thought, she wrote, *that saving souls was what they did.*

He's tired of that, Adolin sent. *He told me that he already saved three this morning.*

She smiled, checking on the tree—still no change. *He did, did he?* she wrote. *Has them tucked away in his back pocket for safekeeping, I assume?*

No, Father's way was not right. If she wanted to keep Adolin, she had to try something far more difficult than just clinging to him. She'd have to be so irresistible that he didn't want to let go. Unfortunately, this was one area where neither Jasnah's training nor Tyn's would help. Jasnah had been indifferent toward men, while Tyn had not talked about keeping men, only distracting them for a quick con.

Is your father feeling better? she wrote.

Yes, actually. He's been up and about since yesterday, looking as strong as ever.

Good to hear, she wrote. The two continued exchanging idle comments, Shallan watching the tree. Mraize's note had instructed her to come at sunrise and search the hole in the tree trunk for her instructions. So she'd come four hours early, while the sky was still dark, and sneaked up to the top of this building to watch.

Apparently, she hadn't come early enough. She'd really wanted to get a view of them placing the instructions. "I don't like this," Shallan said, whispering to Pattern and ignoring the pen, which scribed Adolin's next line to her. "Why didn't Mraize just give me the instructions via spanreed? Why make me come here?"

"Mmm . . ." Pattern said from the floor beneath her.

The sun had long since risen. She needed to go get the instructions, but still she hesitated, tapping her finger against the paper-covered board beside her.

"They're watching," she realized.

"What?" Pattern said.

"They are doing exactly what I did. They are hiding somewhere, and want to watch me pick up the instructions."

"Why? What does it accomplish?"

"It gives them information," Shallan said. "And that is the sort of thing these people thrive upon." She leaned to the side, peering out of her hole, which would appear from the outside as a gap between two of the bricks.

She didn't think Mraize wanted her dead, despite the sickening incident with the poor carriage driver. He'd given leave for the others around him to kill her, if they feared her, but that—like so much about Mraize—had been a test. *If you really are strong and clever enough to join us,* that incident implied, *then you'll avoid being assassinated by these people.*

This was another test. How did she pass it in a way that didn't leave anyone dead this time?

They'd be watching for her to come get her instructions, but there weren't many good places to keep an eye on the tree. If she were Mraize and his people, where would she go to observe?

She felt silly thinking it. "Pattern," she whispered, "go look in the windows of this building that face the street. See if anyone is sitting in one of them, watching as we are."

"Very well," he said, sliding out of her illusion.

She was suddenly conscious of the fact that Mraize's people might be hiding somewhere very close, but shoved aside her nervousness, reading Adolin's reply.

Good news, by the way, the pen wrote. *Father visited last night, and we talked at length. He's preparing his expedition out onto the Plains to fight the Parshendi, once and for all. Part of getting ready involves some scouting missions in the coming days. I got him to agree to bring you out onto the plateaus during one of them.*

And we can find a chrysalis? Shallan asked.

Well, the pen wrote, *even if the Parshendi aren't fighting over those anymore, Father doesn't take risks. I can't bring you on a run when there is a chance they might come and contest us. But, I've been thinking we can probably arrange the scouting mission so it passes by a plateau with a chrysalis a day or so after it was harvested.*

Shallan frowned. *A dead, harvested chrysalis?* she wrote. *I don't know how much that will tell me.*

Well, Adolin replied, *it's better than not seeing one at all, right? And you did say you wanted the chance to cut one up. This is almost the same thing.*

He was right. Besides, getting out onto the Plains was the real goal. *Let's do it. When?*

In a few days.

"Shallan!"

She jumped, but it was only Pattern, buzzing with excitement. "You were right," he said. "Mmmm. She watches below. Only one level down, second room."

"She?"

"Mmm. The one with the mask."

Shallan shivered. Now what? Go back to her rooms, then write to Mraize and say that she didn't appreciate being spied upon?

It wouldn't accomplish anything useful. Looking down at her pad of paper, she realized that her relationship with Mraize was similar to her relationship with Adolin. In both cases, she couldn't just do as expected. She needed to excite, exceed.

I'll need to go, she wrote to Adolin. *Sebarial is asking for me. It might take me a while.*

She clicked off the spanreed and tucked it and the board away in her satchel. Not her usual one, but a rugged bag with a leather strap that went over her shoulder, like Veil would carry. Then, before she could lose her nerve, she ducked out of her illusory hiding place. She put her back to the wall of the shed, facing away from the street, then touched the side of the illusion and withdrew the Stormlight.

That made the illusory section of wall vanish, quickly breaking down and streaming into her hand. Hopefully, nobody had been looking at the shed at that moment. If they had been, though, they would probably just think the change a trick of the eyes.

Next, she knelt and used Stormlight to infuse Pattern and bind to him an image of Veil from a drawing she'd done earlier. Shallan nodded for him to move, and as he did, the image of Veil walked.

She looked good. A confident stride, a swishing coat, peaked hat shading her face against the sun. The illusion even blinked and turned her head on occasion, as prescribed by the drawing sequence Shallan had done earlier.

She watched, hesitating. Was that actually how she looked while wearing

Veil's face and clothing? She didn't feel nearly that poised, and the clothing always seemed exaggerated, even silly, to her. On this image, it looked appropriate.

"Go down," Shallan whispered to Pattern, "and walk to the tree. Try to approach carefully, slowly, and buzz loudly to get the tree's leaves to pull back. Stand at the trunk for a moment, as if retrieving the thing inside, then walk to the alleyway between this building and the next."

"Yes!" Pattern said. He zipped off toward the stairs, excited to be part of the lie.

"Slower!" Shallan said, wincing to see Veil's pace not matching her speed. "As we practiced!"

Pattern slowed and reached the steps. Veil's image moved down them. Awkwardly. The illusion could walk and stand still on flat ground, but other terrain—such as steps—wasn't accommodated. To anyone watching, it would seem like Veil was stepping on nothing and gliding down the stairs.

Well, it was the best they could do for the moment. Shallan took a deep breath and pulled on her hat, breathing out a second image, one that covered her over and transformed her into Veil. The one on Pattern would remain so long as he had Stormlight. That Stormlight drained from him a lot faster than it did from Shallan, though. She didn't know why.

She went down the steps, but only one level, walking as quietly as she could. She counted over two doors in the dim hallway. The masked woman was inside that one. Shallan left it alone, instead ducking into an alcove by the stairwell, where she would be hidden from anyone in the hallway.

She waited.

A door eventually clicked open, and clothing rustled in the hallway. The masked woman passed Shallan's hiding place, amazingly quiet as she moved down the steps.

"What is your name?" Shallan asked.

The woman froze on the steps. She spun—gloved safehand on the knife at her side—and saw Shallan standing in the alcove. The woman's masked eyes flicked back toward the room she'd left.

"I sent a double," Shallan said, "wearing my clothing. That's what you saw."

The woman did not move, still crouched on the steps.

"Why did he want you to follow me?" Shallan asked. "He's that interested in finding out where I'm staying?"

"No," the woman finally said. "The instructions in the tree call for you to set about a task immediately, with no time to waste."

Shallan frowned, considering. "So your job wasn't to follow me home, but to follow me on the mission. To watch how I accomplished it?"

The woman said nothing.

Shallan strolled forward and seated herself on the top step, crossing her arms on her legs. "So what is the job?"

"The instructions are in—"

"I'd rather hear it from you," Shallan said. "Call me lazy."

"How did you find me?" the woman asked.

"A sharp-eyed ally," Shallan said. "I told him to watch the windows, then send me word of where you were. I was waiting up above." She grimaced. "I was hoping to catch one of you placing the instructions."

"We placed them before even contacting you," the woman said. She hesitated, then took a few steps upward. "Iyatil."

Shallan cocked her head.

"My name," the woman said. "Iyatil."

"I've never heard one like it."

"Unsurprising. Your task today was to investigate a certain new arrival into Dalinar's camp. We wish to know about this person, and Dalinar's allegiances are uncertain."

"He's loyal to the king and the Throne."

"Outwardly," the woman said. "His brother knew things of an extraordinary nature. We are uncertain if Dalinar was told of these things or not, and his interactions with Amaram worry us. This newcomer is linked."

"Amaram is making maps of the Shattered Plains," Shallan said. "Why? What is out there that he wants?" *And why would he want to return the Voidbringers?*

Iyatil didn't answer.

"Well," Shallan said, rising, "let's get to it, then. Shall we?"

"Together?" Iyatil said.

Shallan shrugged. "You can sneak along behind, or you can just go with me." She extended her hand.

Iyatil inspected the hand, then clasped it with her own gloved freehand in acceptance. She kept her other hand on the dagger at her side the entire time, though.

⁘

Shallan flipped through the instructions Mraize had left, as the oversized palanquin lurched along toward Dalinar's warcamp. Iyatil sat across from Shallan, legs tucked beneath her, watching with beady, masked eyes. The woman wore simple trousers and a shirt, such that Shallan had originally mistaken her for a boy that first time.

Her presence was *thoroughly* unsettling.

"A madman," Shallan said, flipping to the next page of instructions. "Mraize is this interested in a simple madman?"

"Dalinar and the king are interested," Iyatil said. "So, then, are we."

There *did* seem to be some sort of cover-up involved. The madman had arrived in the custody of a man named Bordin, a servant whom Dalinar had stationed in Kholinar years ago. Mraize's information indicated that this Bordin was no simple messenger, but instead one of Dalinar's most trusted footmen. He had been left behind in Alethkar to spy on the queen, or so the Ghostbloods inferred. But why would someone need to keep an eye on the queen? The briefing didn't say.

This Bordin had come to the Shattered Plains in haste a few weeks ago, bearing the madman and other mysterious cargo. Shallan's charge was to find out who this madman was and why Dalinar had hidden him away in a monastery with strict instructions that nobody was to be allowed access save specific ardents.

"Your master knows more about this," Shallan said, "than he is telling me."

"My master?" Iyatil asked.

"Mraize."

The woman laughed. "You mistake. He is not my master. He is my student."

"In what?" Shallan asked.

Iyatil stared at her with a level gaze and gave no reply.

"Why the mask?" Shallan asked, leaning forward. "What does it mean? Why do you hide?"

"I have many times asked myself," Iyatil said, "why those of you here go about so brazenly with features exposed to all who would see them. My mask reserves my self. Besides, it gives me the ability to adapt."

Shallan sat back, thoughtful.

"You are willing to ponder," Iyatil said. "Rather than asking question after question. This is good. Your instincts, however, must be judged. Are you the hunter, or are you the quarry?"

"Neither," Shallan said immediately.

"All are one or the other."

The palanquin's porters slowed. Shallan peeked out the curtains and found that they had finally reached the edge of Dalinar's warcamp. Here, soldiers at the gates stopped each person in line waiting to enter.

"How will you get us in?" Iyatil asked as Shallan closed the curtains. "Highprince Kholin has grown cautious of late, with assassins appearing in the night. What lie will gain us access to his realm?"

Delightful, she thought, revising her list of tasks. Shallan not only had to infiltrate the monastery and discover information about this madman, she had to do it without revealing too much about herself—or what she could do—to Iyatil.

She had to think quickly. The soldiers at the front called for the palanquin to approach—lighteyes wouldn't be required to wait in the ordinary line, and the soldiers would assume this nice a vehicle had someone rich inside. Taking a deep breath, Shallan removed her hat, pulled her hair forward over her shoulder, then pushed her face out of the curtains so that her hair hung down before her outside the palanquin. At the same moment, she withdrew her illusion and pulled the curtains closed behind her head, tight against her neck, to prevent Iyatil from seeing the transformation.

The porters were parshmen, and she doubted the parshmen would say anything about what they saw her do. Their lighteyed master was turned away, fortunately. Her palanquin wobbled up to the front of the line, and the guards started when they saw her. They waved her through immediately. The face of Adolin's betrothed was well known by this point.

Now, how to get Veil's appearance back on? There were people on the street here; she wasn't about to breathe Stormlight while hanging out the window.

"Pattern," she whispered. "Go make a noise at the window on the other side of the palanquin."

Tyn had drilled into her the need to make a distracting motion with one hand while palming an object with the other. The same principle might work here.

A sharp yelp sounded from the other window. Shallan moved her head back into the palanquin with a quick motion, breathing out Stormlight. She flipped the curtains in a diverting way and obscured her face with the hat as she put it on.

Iyatil looked back toward her from the window where the yelp had sounded, but Shallan was Veil again. She settled back, meeting Iyatil's gaze. Had the smaller woman seen?

They rode in silence for a moment.

"You bribed the guards ahead of time," Iyatil finally guessed. "I would know how you did this. Kholin's men are difficult to bribe. You got to one of the supervisors, perhaps?"

Shallan smiled in what she hoped was a frustrating way.

The palanquin continued on toward the warcamp's temple, a part of Dalinar's camp that she'd never visited. Actually, she hadn't been to visit Sebarial's ardents very often either—though when she had gone, she'd found them surprisingly devout, considering who owned them.

She peeked out the window as they approached. Dalinar's temple grounds were as plain as she would have expected. Grey-robed ardents passed the palanquin in pairs or small groups, mixing among people of all stations. Those had come for prayers, instruction, or advice—a good temple, properly equipped, could provide each of these things and more. Darkeyes from almost any nahn could come to be taught a trade, exercising their divine Right to Learn, as mandated by the Heralds. Lesser lighteyes came to learn trades as well, and the higher dahns came to learn the arts or progress in their Callings to please the Almighty.

A large population of ardents like this one would have true masters in every art and trade. Perhaps she should come and seek Dalinar's artists for training.

She winced, wondering where she would find time for such a thing. What with courting Adolin, infiltrating the Ghostbloods, researching the Shattered Plains, and doing Sebarial's ledgers, it was a wonder she had time to sleep. Still, it felt impious of her to expect success in her duties while ignoring the Almighty. She did need to have more concern for such things.

And what is the Almighty to think of you? she wondered. *And the lies you're growing so proficient at producing.* Honesty was among the divine attributes of the Almighty, after all, which everyone was supposed to seek.

The temple complex here included more than one building, though most people would only visit the main structure. Mraize's instructions had included a map, so she knew the specific building she needed—one near the back, where the ardent healers saw to the sick and cared for people with long-term illnesses.

"It will not be easy to enter," Iyatil said. "The ardents are protective of their charges, and have them locked away in the back, kept from the eyes of other men. They will not welcome an attempt at intrusion."

"The instructions indicated that today was the perfect time to sneak in," Shallan said. "I was to make haste to not miss the opportunity."

"Once a month," Iyatil said, "all may come to the temple to ask questions or see a physician with no offering requested. Today will be a busy day, a day of confusion. That will make for an easier time infiltrating, but it does not mean they will simply let you saunter in."

Shallan nodded.

"If you would rather do this at night," Iyatil said, "perhaps I can persuade Mraize that the matter can wait until then."

Shallan shook her head. She had no experience sneaking about in the darkness. She'd just make a fool of herself.

But how to get in . . .

"Porter," she commanded, sticking her head out the window and pointing, "take us to that building there, then set us down. Send one of your number to seek the master healers. Tell them I need their aid."

The tenner who led the parshmen—hired with Shallan's spheres—nodded brusquely. Tenners were a strange lot. This one didn't own the parshmen; he just worked for the woman who rented them out. Veil, with dark eyes, would be beneath him socially, but was also the one paying his wage, and so he just treated her as he would any other master.

The palanquin settled down and one of the parshmen walked off to deliver her request.

"Going to feign sickness?" Iyatil asked.

"Something like that," Shallan said as footsteps arrived outside. She climbed out to meet a pair of square-bearded ardents, conferring as the parshmen led them in her direction. They looked her over, noting her dark eyes and her clothing—which was well-made but obviously intended for rugged use. Likely, they placed her in one of the upper-middle nahns, a citizen, but not a particularly important one.

"What is the problem, young woman?" asked the older of the two ardents.

"It is my sister," Shallan said. "She has put on this strange mask and refuses to remove it."

A soft groan rose from inside the palanquin.

"Child," said the lead ardent, his tone suffering, "a stubborn sister is not a matter for the ardents."

"I understand, good brother," Shallan said, raising her hands before her. "But this is no simple stubbornness. I think . . . I think one of the Voidbringers has inhabited her!"

She pushed aside the curtains of the palanquin, revealing Iyatil inside. Her strange mask made the ardents pull back and break off their objections. The younger of the two men peered in at Iyatil with wide eyes.

Iyatil turned to Shallan, and with an almost inaudible sigh, started rocking back and forth in place. "Should we kill them?" she muttered. "No. No, we shouldn't. But someone will see! No, do not say these things. No. I will not listen to you." She started humming.

The younger ardent turned to look back at the senior.

"This is dire," the ardent said, nodding. "Porter, come. Have your parshmen bring the palanquin."

⁘

A short time later, Shallan waited in the corner of a small monastery room, watching Iyatil sit and resist the ministration of several ardents. She kept warning them that if they removed her mask, she would have to kill them.

That did not seem to be part of the act.

Fortunately, she otherwise played her part well. Her ravings, mixed with her hidden face, gave even Shallan shivers. The ardents seemed alternately fascinated and horrified.

Concentrate on the drawing, Shallan thought to herself. It was a sketch of one of the ardents, a portly man about her own height. The drawing was rushed but capable. She idly found herself wondering what a beard would feel like. Would it itch? But no, hair on your head didn't itch, so why should hair on your face? How did they keep food out of the things?

She finished with a few quick marks, then rose quietly. Iyatil kept the ardents' attention with a new bout of raving. Shallan nodded to her in thanks, then slipped out of the door, entering the hallway. After glancing to the sides to see that she was alone, she used a cloud of Stormlight to transform into the ardent. That done, she reached up and tucked her straight red hair—the only part of her that threatened to pop out of the illusion—inside the back of her coat.

"Pattern," she whispered, turning and walking down the hallway with a relaxed demeanor.

"Mmm?"

"Find him," she said, removing from her satchel a sketch of the madman that Mraize had left in the tree. The sketch had been done at a distance, and wasn't terribly good. Hopefully . . .

"Second hallway on the left," Pattern said.

Shallan looked down at him, though her new costume—an ardent's robe—obscured him where he sat on her coat. "How do you know?"

"You were distracted by your drawing," he said. "I peeked about. There is a very interesting woman four doors down. She appears to be rubbing excrement on the wall."

"Ew." Shallan thought she could smell it.

"Patterns . . ." he said as they walked. "I did not get a good look at what she was writing, but it seemed very interesting. I think I shall go and—"

"No," Shallan whispered, "stay with me." She smiled, nodding to several ardents who strolled past. They didn't speak to her, fortunately, merely nodding back.

The monastery building, like most everything in Dalinar's warcamp, was sliced through with dull, unornamented hallways. Shallan followed Pattern's instructions to a thick door set into the stone. The lock clicked open with Pattern's help, and Shallan quietly slipped inside.

A single small window—more of a slit—proved insufficient to fully illuminate the large figure sitting on the bed. Dark-skinned, like a man from the Makabaki kingdoms, he had dark, ragged hair and hulking arms. Those were the arms of either a laborer or a soldier. The man sat slumped, back bowed, head down, frail light from the window cutting a slice across his back in white. It made for a grim, powerful silhouette.

The man was whispering. Shallan couldn't make out the words. She shivered, her back to the door, and held up the sketch Mraize had given her. This seemed to be the same person—at least, the skin color and stout build were the same, though this man was far more muscled than the picture indicated. Storms . . . those hands of his looked as if they could crush her like a cremling.

The man did not move. He did not look up, did not shift. He was like a boulder that had rolled to a stop here.

"Why is it kept so dark in this room?" Pattern asked, perfectly cheerful.

The madman didn't react to the comment, or even Shallan, as she stepped forward.

"Modern theory for helping the mad suggests dim confines," Shallan whispered. "Too much light stimulates them, and can reduce the effectiveness of treatment." That was what she remembered, at least. She hadn't read much on this subject. The room *was* dark. That window couldn't be more than a few fingers wide.

What was he whispering? Shallan cautiously continued forward. "Sir?" she asked. Then she hesitated, realizing that she was projecting a young woman's voice from an old, fat ardent's body. Would that startle the man? He wasn't looking, so she withdrew the illusion.

"He doesn't seem angry," Pattern said. "But you call him mad."

"'Mad' has two definitions," Shallan said. "One means to be angry. The other means broken in the head."

"Ah," Pattern said, "like a spren who has lost his bond."

"Not exactly, I'd guess," Shallan said, stepping up to the madman. "But similar." She knelt down by the man, trying to figure out what he was saying.

"The time of the Return, the Desolation, is at hand," he whispered. She would have expected an Azish accent from him, considering the skin color, but he spoke perfect Alethi. "We must prepare. You will have forgotten much, following the destruction of times past."

She looked over at Pattern, lost in the shadows at the side of the room, then back at the man. Light glinted off his dark brown eyes, two bright pinpricks on an otherwise shadowed visage. That slumped posture seemed so morose. He whispered on, about bronze and steel, about preparations and training.

"Who are you?" Shallan whispered.

"Talenel'Elin. The one you call Stonesinew."

She felt a chill. Then the madman continued, whispering the same things he had before, repeated exactly. She couldn't even be certain if his comment had been a reply to her question, or just a part of his recitation. He did not answer further questions.

Shallan stepped back, folding her arms, satchel over her shoulder.

"Talenel," Pattern said. "I know that name."

"Talenelat'Elin is the name of one of the Heralds," Shallan said. "This is almost the same."

"Ah." Pattern paused. "Lie?"

"Undoubtedly," Shallan said. "It defies reason that Dalinar Kholin would have one of the *Heralds of the Almighty* locked away in a temple's back rooms. Many madmen think themselves someone else."

Of course, many said that Dalinar himself was mad. And he *was* trying to refound the Knights Radiant. Scooping up a madman who thought he was one of the Heralds could be in line with that.

"Madman," Shallan said, "where do you come from?"

He continued ranting.

"Do you know what Dalinar Kholin wishes of you?"

More ranting.

Shallan sighed, but knelt and wrote his exact words to deliver to Mraize. She got the entire sequence down, and listened to it twice through to make sure he wasn't going to say anything new. He didn't say his supposed name this time, though. So that was one deviation.

He couldn't *actually* be one of the Heralds, could he?

Don't be silly, she thought, tucking away her writing implements. *The Heralds glow like the sun, wield the Honorblades, and speak with the voices of a thousand trumpets.* They could cast down buildings with a command, force the storms to obey, and heal with a touch.

Shallan walked to the door. By now, her absence in the other room would have been noticed. She should get back and give her lie, of seeking a drink for her parched throat. First, though, she'd want to put back on the ardent disguise. She sucked in some Stormlight, then breathed out, using the still-fresh memory of the ardent to create—

"Aaaaaaaah!"

The madman leaped to his feet, screaming. He lurched for her, moving with incredible speed. As Shallan yelped in surprise, he grabbed her and shoved her out of her cloud of Stormlight. The image fell apart, evaporating, and the madman smashed her up against the wall, his eyes wide, his breathing ragged. He searched her face with frantic eyes, pupils darting back and forth.

Shallan trembled, breath catching.

Ten heartbeats.

"One of Ishar's Knights," the madman whispered. His eyes narrowed. "I remember . . . He founded them? Yes. Several Desolations ago. No longer just talk. It hasn't been talk for thousands of years. But . . . When . . ."

He stumbled back from her, hand to his head. Her Shardblade dropped into her hands, but she no longer appeared to need it. The man turned his back to her, walked to his bed, then lay down and curled up.

Shallan inched forward, and found he was back to whispering the same things as before. She dismissed the Blade.

Mother's soul . . .

"Shallan?" Pattern asked. "Shallan, are you mad?"

She shook herself. How much time had passed? "Yes," she said, walking hurriedly for the door. She peeked outside. She couldn't risk using Storm-light again in this room. She'd just have to slip out—

Blast. Several people approached down the hallway. She would have to wait for them to pass. Except, they seemed to be heading right to this very door.

One of those men was Highlord Amaram.

Yes, I'm disappointed. Perpetually, as you put it.

K aladin lay on his bench, ignoring the afternoon bowl of steamed, spiced tallew on the floor.

He had begun to imagine himself as that whitespine in the menagerie. A predator in a cage. Storms send that he didn't end up like that poor beast. Wilted, hungry, confused. *They don't do well in captivity,* Shallan had said.

How many days had it been? Kaladin found himself not caring. That worried him. During his time as a slave, he'd also stopped caring about the date.

He wasn't so far removed from that wretch he'd once been. He felt himself slipping back toward that same mindset, like a man climbing a cliff covered in crem and slime. Each time he tried to pull himself higher, he slid back. Eventually he'd fall.

Old ways of thinking . . . a slave's ways of thinking . . . churned within him. Stop caring. Worry only about the next meal, and keeping it away from the others. Don't think too much. Thinking is dangerous. Thinking makes you hope, makes you want.

Kaladin shouted, throwing himself off his bench and pacing in the small room, hands to his head. He'd thought himself so strong. A fighter. But all they had to do to take that away was stuff him in a box for a few weeks, and the truth returned! He slammed himself against the bars and stretched a hand between them, toward one of the lamps on the wall. He sucked in a breath.

Nothing happened. No Stormlight. The sphere continued to glow, even and steady.

Kaladin cried out, reaching farther, pushing his fingertips toward that distant light. *Don't let the darkness take me,* he thought. He . . . prayed. How long had it been since he'd done that? He didn't have someone to properly write and burn the words, but the Almighty listened to hearts, didn't he? *Please. Not again. I can't go back to that.*

Please.

He strained for that sphere, breathing in. The Light seemed to *resist,* then gloriously streamed out into his fingertips. The storm pulsed in his veins.

Kaladin held his breath, eyes shut, savoring it. The power strained against him, trying to escape. He pushed off the bars and started pacing again, eyes closed, not so frantic as before.

"I'm worried about you." Syl's voice. "You're growing dark."

Kaladin opened his eyes and finally found her, sitting between two of the bars as if on a swing.

"I'll be all right," Kaladin said, letting Stormlight rise from his lips like smoke. "I just need to get out of this cage."

"It's worse than that. It's the darkness . . . the darkness . . ." She looked to the side, then giggled suddenly, streaking off to inspect something on the floor. A little cremling that was creeping along the edge of the room. She stood over it, eyes widening at the stark red and violet color of its shell.

Kaladin smiled. She was still a spren. Childlike. The world was a place of wonder to Syl. What would that be like?

He sat down and ate his meal, feeling as if he'd pushed aside the gloom for a time. Eventually, one of the guards checked on him and found the dun sphere. He pulled it out, frowning, shaking his head before replacing it and moving on.

⁘

Amaram was coming into this room.

Hide!

Shallan was proud of how quickly she spat out the rest of her Stormlight, wreathing herself in it. She didn't even give thought to how the madman had reacted to her Lightweaving before, though perhaps she should have. Regardless, this time he didn't seem to notice.

Should she become an ardent? No. Something much simpler, something faster.

Darkness.

Her clothing turned black. Her skin, her hat, her hair—everything pure black. She scrambled back away from the door into the corner of the room, farthest from the slot of a window, stilling herself. With her illusion in place, the Lightweaving consumed the trails of Stormlight that would normally rise from her skin, further masking her presence.

The door opened. Her heart thundered within her. She wished she'd had time to create a false wall. Amaram entered the room with a young darkeyed man, obviously Alethi, with short dark hair and prominent eyebrows. He wore Kholin livery. They shut the door quietly behind themselves, Amaram pocketing a key.

Shallan felt an immediate anger at seeing her brother's murderer here, but found that it had quieted somewhat. A smoldering loathing instead of an intense hatred. It had been a long time since she'd seen Helaran, now. And Balat had a point in that her older brother had abandoned them.

To try to kill this man, apparently—or so she'd been able to put together from what she'd read of Amaram and his Shardblade. Why had Helaran gone to kill this man? And could she really blame Amaram when, in truth, he'd probably just been defending himself?

She felt like she knew so little. Though Amaram was still a bastard, of course.

Together, Amaram and the Alethi darkeyes turned to the madman. Shallan couldn't make out much of their features in the mostly dark room. "I don't know why you need to hear it for yourself, Brightlord," the servant said. "I told you what he said."

"Hush, Bordin," Amaram said, crossing the room. "Listen at the door."

Shallan stood stiff, pressed back in the corner. They'd see her, wouldn't they?

Amaram knelt beside the bed. "Great Prince," he whispered, hand to the madman's shoulder. "Turn. Let me see you."

The madman looked up, still muttering.

"Ah . . ." Amaram said, breathing out. "Almighty above, ten names, all true. You are beautiful. Gavilar, we have done it. We have finally *done it.*"

"Brightlord?" Bordin said from the door. "I don't like being here. If we're discovered, people might ask questions. The treasure . . ."

"He truly spoke of Shardblades?"

"Yes," Bordin said. "A whole cache of them."

"The Honorblades," Amaram whispered. "Great Prince, please, give me the same words you spoke to this one."

The madman muttered on, the same as Shallan had heard. Amaram continued kneeling, but eventually he turned toward the nervous Bordin. "Well?"

"He repeated those words every day," Bordin said, "but he only spoke of the Blades once."

"I would hear of them for myself."

"Brightlord . . . We could wait here days and not hear those words. Please. We must go. The ardents will eventually come by on their rounds."

Amaram stood up with obvious reluctance. "Great Prince," he said to the huddled figure of the madman, "I go to recover your treasures. Speak not of them to the others. I will put the Blades to good use." He turned to Bordin. "Come. Let us search out this place."

"Today?"

"You said it was close."

"Yes, well, that was why I brought him all the way out here. But—"

"If he accidentally speaks of this to others, I would have them go to the place and find it empty of treasures. Come, quickly. You will be rewarded."

Amaram strode out. Bordin lingered at the door, looking at the madman, then trailed out and shut the door with a *click*.

Shallan breathed out a long, deep breath, slumping down to the floor. "It's like that sea of spheres."

"Shallan?" Pattern asked.

"I've fallen in," she said, "and it isn't that the water is over my head—it's that the stuff isn't even water, and I have no idea how to swim in it."

"I do not understand this lie," Pattern said.

She shook her head, the color bleeding back into her skin and clothing. She made herself look like Veil again, then walked to the door, accompanied by the sound of the madman's rambling. *Herald of War. The time of the Return is near at hand. . . .*

Outside, she found her way back to the room with Iyatil, then apologized profusely to the ardents there who were looking for her. She pled that she had gotten lost, but said she'd accept an escort to take her back to her palanquin.

Before going, however, she leaned down to hug Iyatil, as if to wish her sister farewell.

"You can escape?" Shallan whispered.

"Don't be stupid. Of course I can."

"Take this," Shallan said, pressing a sheet of paper into Iyatil's gloved freehand. "I wrote upon it the ramblings of the madman. They repeat without change. I saw Amaram sneak into the room; he seems to think these words are authentic, and he seeks a treasure the madman spoke of earlier. I will write a thorough report via spanreed to you and the others tonight."

Shallan moved to pull back, but Iyatil held on. "Who are you really, Veil?" the woman asked. "You caught me in stealth spying upon you, and you can lose me in the streets. This is not easily accomplished. Your clever drawings fascinate Mraize, another near-impossible task, considering all that he has seen. Now what you have done today."

Shallan felt a thrill. Why should she feel so excited to have the respect of these people? They were murderers.

But storms take her, she had *earned* that respect.

"I seek the truth," Shallan said. "Wherever it may be, whoever may hold it. That's who I am." She nodded to Iyatil, then pulled away and escaped the monastery.

Later on that night, after sending in a full report of the day's events—as well as promising drawings of the madman, Amaram, and Bordin for good measure—she received back a simple message from Mraize.

The truth destroys more people than it saves, Veil. But you have proven yourself. You no longer need fear our other members; they have been instructed not to touch you. You are required to get a specific tattoo, a symbol of your loyalty. I will send a drawing. You may add it to your person wherever you wish, but must prove it to me when we next meet.

Welcome to the Ghostbloods.

recollection of the metamorphosis, and training will have to resume as if with a new beast. There's no guarantee that a docile grub will pupate into

To encourage pupation of the mature larvae, feed them a consistent diet of rocklily leaves. To discourage pupation of your adult chulls, add drops of shalebark oil to the drinking water and feed chulls crushed shelltick before a storm. Sheltering your livestock during a highstorm remains the most-proven method to keep your chulls from pupating.

FIG. 38 -- METAMORPHOSIS OF THE CHULL: LARVA (THE CHULL CREMLING), FIRST PUPATION, ADULT CHULL, SECOND PUPATION, SENESCENCE.

ONE AND A HALF YEARS AGO

W hat is a woman's place in this modern world? Jasnah Kholin's
words read. *I rebel against this question, though so many of my
peers ask it. The inherent bias in the inquiry seems invisible to so
many of them. They consider themselves progressive because they are willing to
challenge many of the assumptions of the past.*

*They ignore the greater assumption—that a "place" for women must be defined
and set forth to begin with. Half of the population must somehow be reduced to the
role arrived at by a single conversation. No matter how broad that role is, it will
be—by nature—a reduction from the infinite variety that is womanhood.*

*I say that there is no role for women—there is, instead, a role for each woman,
and she must make it for herself. For some, it will be the role of scholar; for others,
it will be the role of wife. For others, it will be both. For yet others, it will be
neither.*

*Do not mistake me in assuming I value one woman's role above another. My
point is not to stratify our society—we have done that far too well already—my
point is to diversify our discourse.*

*A woman's strength should not be in her role, whatever she chooses it to be, but
in the power to choose that role. It is amazing to me that I even have to make this
point, as I see it as the very foundation of our conversation.*

Shallan closed the book. Not two hours had passed since Father had
ordered Helaran's assassination. After Shallan had retreated to her room, a
pair of Father's guards had appeared in the hallway outside. Probably not
to watch her—she doubted that Father knew that she'd overheard his order for Helaran to be killed. The guards were to see that Malise, Shallan's
stepmother, did not try to flee.

That could be a mistaken assumption. Shallan didn't even know if Malise was still alive, following her screaming and Father's cold, angry ranting.

Shallan wanted to hide, to hunker down in her closet with blankets wrapped around her, eyes squeezed shut. The words in Jasnah Kholin's book strengthened her, though in some ways it seemed laughable for Shallan to even be reading it. Highlady Kholin talked about the nobility of choice, as if every woman had such opportunity. The decision between being a mother or a scholar seemed a difficult decision in Jasnah's estimation. That wasn't a difficult choice at all! That seemed like a *grand* place to be! Either would be delightful when compared to a life of fear in a house seething with anger, depression, and hopelessness.

She imagined what Highlady Kholin must be, a capable woman who did not do as others insisted she must. A woman with power, authority. A woman who had the luxury of seeking her dreams.

What would that be like?

Shallan stood up. She walked to the door, then cracked it open. Though the evening had grown late, the two guards still stood at the other end of the hallway. Shallan's heart thumped, and she cursed her timidity. Why couldn't she be like women who acted, instead of being someone who hid in her room with a pillow around her head?

Shaking, she slipped from the room. She padded toward the soldiers, feeling their eyes on her. One raised his hand. She didn't know the man's name. Once, she'd known all of the guards' names. Those men, whom she'd grown up with, had been replaced now.

"My father will need me," she said, not stopping at the guard's gesture. Though he was lighteyed, she did not need to obey him. She might spend most of every day in her rooms, but she was still of a much higher rank than he.

She walked by the men, trembling hands clenched tight. They let her go. When she passed her father's door, she heard soft weeping inside. Malise still lived, thankfully.

She found Father in the feast hall, sitting alone with both firepits roaring, full of flames. He slumped at the high table, lit by harsh light, staring at the tabletop.

Shallan slipped into the kitchen before he noticed her, and mixed his favorite. Deep violet wine, spiced with cinnamon and warmed against the chill day. He looked up as she walked back into the feast hall. She set the cup before him, looking into his eyes. No darkness there today. Just him. That was very rare, these days.

"They won't *listen*, Shallan," he whispered. "Nobody will listen. I hate that I have to fight my own house. They should support me." He took the drink. "Wikim just stares at the wall half the time. Jushu is worthless, and Balat fights me every step. Now Malise too."

"I will speak to them," Shallan said.

He drank the wine, then nodded. "Yes. Yes, that would be good. Balat is still out with those cursed axehound corpses. I'm glad they're dead. That litter was full of runts. He didn't need them anyway. . . ."

Shallan stepped into the chill air. The sun had set, but lanterns hung on the eaves of the manor house. She had rarely seen the gardens at night, and they took on a mysterious cast in the darkness. Vines looked like fingers reaching from the void, seeking something to grab and pull away into the night.

Balat lay on one of the benches. Shallan's feet crunched on something as she stepped up to him. Claws from cremlings, pulled free of their bodies one after another, then tossed to the ground. She shivered.

"You should go," she said to Balat.

He sat up. "What?"

"Father can no longer control himself," Shallan said softly. "You need to leave, while you can. I want you to take Malise with you."

Balat ran his hand through his mess of curly dark hair. "Malise? Father will never let her go. He'd hunt us down."

"He'll hunt you anyway," Shallan said. "He hunts Helaran. Earlier today, he ordered one of his men to find our brother and assassinate him."

"What!" Balat stood. "That bastard! I'll . . . I . . ." He looked to Shallan in the darkness, face lit by starlight. Then he crumpled, sitting back down, holding his head in his hands. "I'm a coward, Shallan," he whispered. "Oh, Stormfather, I'm a coward. I won't face him. I can't."

"Go to Helaran," Shallan said. "Could you find him, if you needed to?"

"He . . . Yes, he left me the name of a contact in Valath who could put me in touch with him."

"Take Malise and Eylita. Go to Helaran."

"I won't have time to find Helaran before Father catches up."

"Then we will contact Helaran," Shallan said. "We will make plans for you to meet him, and you can schedule your flight for a time when Father is away. He is planning another trip to Vedenar a few months from now. Leave when he's gone, get a head start."

Balat nodded. "Yes . . . Yes, that is good."

"I will draft a letter to Helaran," Shallan said. "We need to warn him about Father's assassins, and we can ask him to take the three of you in."

"You shouldn't have to do this, small one," Balat said, head down. "I'm the eldest after Helaran. I should have been able to stop Father by now. Somehow."

"Take Malise away," Shallan said. "That will be doing enough."

He nodded.

Shallan returned to the house, passing Father mulling over his disobedient family, and fetched some things from the kitchen. Then she returned to the steps and looked upward. Taking a few deep breaths, she went over what she would say to the guards if they stopped her. Then she raced up them and opened the door into her father's sitting room.

"Wait," the hallway guard said. "He left orders. Nobody in or out."

Shallan's throat tightened, and even with her practice, she stammered as she spoke. "I just talked to him. He wants me to speak with her."

The guard inspected her, chewing on something. Shallan felt her confidence wilt, heart racing. Confrontation. She was as much a coward as Balat.

He gestured to the other guard, who went downstairs to check. He eventually returned, nodding, and the first man reluctantly waved for her to continue. Shallan entered.

Into the Place.

She had not entered this room in years. Not since . . .

Not since . . .

She raised a hand, shading her eyes against the light coming from behind the painting. How could Father sleep in here? How was it that nobody else looked, nobody else cared? That light was *blinding*.

Fortunately, Malise was curled in an easy chair facing that wall, so Shallan could put her back to the painting and obstruct the light. She rested a hand on her stepmother's arm.

She didn't feel that she knew Malise, despite years living together. Who was this woman who would marry a man everyone whispered had killed his previous wife? Malise oversaw Shallan's education—meaning she searched for new tutors each time the women fled—but Malise herself couldn't do much to teach Shallan. One could not teach what one did not know.

"Mother?" Shallan asked. She used the word.

Malise looked. Despite the blazing light of the room, Shallan saw the woman's lip was split and bleeding. She cradled her left arm. Yes, it was broken.

Shallan took out the gauze and cloth she had fetched from the kitchen, then began to wipe down the wounds. She would have to find something to use as a splint for that arm.

"Why doesn't he hate you?" Malise said harshly. "He hates everyone else but you."

Shallan dabbed at the woman's lip.

"Stormfather, why did I come to this cursed household?" Malise shuddered. "He'll kill us all. One by one, he'll break us and kill us. There's a darkness inside of him. I've seen it, behind his eyes. A beast . . ."

"You're going to leave," Shallan said softly.

Malise barked a laugh. "He'll never let me go. He never lets go of anything."

"You're not going to ask," Shallan whispered. "Balat is going to run and join Helaran, who has powerful friends. He's a Shardbearer. He'll protect the both of you."

"We'll never reach him," Malise said. "And if we do, why would Helaran take us in? We have nothing."

"Helaran is a good man."

Malise twisted in her seat, staring away from Shallan, who continued her ministrations. The woman whimpered when Shallan bound her arm, but wouldn't respond to questions. Finally, Shallan gathered up the bloodied cloths to throw away.

"If I go," Malise whispered, "and Balat with me, who will he hate? Who will he hit? Maybe you, finally? The one who actually deserves it?"

"Maybe," Shallan whispered, then left.

Is not the destruction we have wrought enough? The worlds you now tread bear the touch and design of Adonalsium. Our interference so far has brought nothing but pain.

Feet scraped on the stone outside of Kaladin's cage. One of the jailers checking on him again. Kaladin continued to lie motionless with closed eyes, and did not look.

In order to keep the darkness at bay, he had begun planning. What would he do when he got out? *When* he got out. He had to tell himself that forcibly. It wasn't that he didn't trust Dalinar. His mind, though . . . his mind betrayed him, and whispered things that were not true.

Distortions. In his state, he could believe that Dalinar lied. He could believe that the highprince secretly wanted Kaladin in prison. Kaladin was a terrible guard, after all. He'd failed to do anything about the mysterious countdowns scrawled on walls, and he'd failed to stop the Assassin in White.

With his mind whispering lies, Kaladin could believe that Bridge Four was happy to be rid of him—that they pretended they wanted to be guards, just to make him happy. They secretly wanted to go on with their lives, lives they'd enjoy, without Kaladin spoiling them.

These untruths *should* have seemed ridiculous to him. They didn't.

Clink.

Kaladin snapped his eyes open, growing tense. Had they come to take him, to execute him, as the king wished? He leaped to his feet, coming down in a battle stance, the empty bowl from his meal held to throw.

The jailer at the cell door stepped back, eyes widening. "Storms, man," he said. "I thought you were asleep. Well, your time is served. King signed a pardon today. They didn't even strip your rank or position." The man rubbed his chin, then pulled the cell door open. "Guess you're lucky."

Lucky. People always said that about Kaladin. Still, the prospect of freedom forced away the darkness inside of him, and Kaladin approached the door. Wary. He stepped out, the guard backing away.

"You are a distrustful one, aren't you?" the jailer said. A lighteyes of low rank. "Guess that makes you a good bodyguard." The man gestured for Kaladin to leave the room first.

Kaladin waited.

Finally, the guard sighed. "Right, then." He walked out the doorway into the hall beyond.

Kaladin followed, and with each step felt himself traveling back a few days in time. Shut the darkness away. He wasn't a slave. He was a soldier. Captain Kaladin. He'd survived this . . . what had it been? Two, three weeks? This short time back in a cage.

He was free now. He could return to his life as a bodyguard. But one thing . . . one thing had changed.

Nobody will ever, ever, do this to me again. Not king or general, not brightlord or brightlady.

He would die first.

They passed a leeward window, and Kaladin stopped to breathe in the cool, fresh scent of open air. The window gave an ordinary, mundane view of the camp outside, but it seemed glorious. A small breeze stirred his hair, and he let himself smile, reaching a hand to his chin. Several weeks' growth. He'd have to let Rock shave that.

"Here," the jailer said. "He's free. Can we finally be done with this farce, Your Highness?"

"Your Highness"? Kaladin turned down the hallway to where the guard had stopped at another cell—one of the larger ones set into the hallway itself. Kaladin had been put in the deepest cell, away from the windows.

The jailer twisted a key in the lock of the wooden door, then pulled it open. Adolin Kholin—wearing a simple tight uniform—stepped out. He also had several weeks of growth on his face, though the beard was blond, speckled black. The princeling took a deep breath, then turned toward Kaladin and nodded.

"He locked *you* away?" Kaladin said, baffled. "How . . . ? What . . . ?"

Adolin turned to the jailer. "Were my orders followed?"

"They wait in the room just beyond, Brightlord," the jailer said, sounding nervous.

Adolin nodded, moving in that direction.

Kaladin reached the jailer, taking him by the arm. "What is happening? The king put Dalinar's *heir* in here?"

"The king didn't have anything to do with it," the jailer said. "Brightlord Adolin insisted. So long as you were in here, he wouldn't leave. We tried to stop him, but the man's a prince. We can't storming make him do anything, not even leave. He locked himself away in the cell and we just had to live with it."

Impossible. Kaladin glanced at Adolin, who walked slowly down the hallway. The prince looked a lot better than Kaladin felt—Adolin had obviously seen a few baths, and his prison cell had been much larger, with more privacy.

It had still been a cell.

That was the disturbance I heard, Kaladin thought, *on that day, early after I was imprisoned. Adolin came and shut himself in.*

Kaladin jogged up to the man. "Why?"

"Didn't seem right, you in here," Adolin said, eyes forward.

"I ruined your chance to duel Sadeas."

"I'd be crippled or dead without you," Adolin said. "So I wouldn't have had the chance to fight Sadeas anyway." The prince stopped in the hallway, and looked at Kaladin. "Besides. You saved Renarin."

"It's my job," Kaladin said.

"Then we need to pay you more, bridgeboy," Adolin said. "Because I don't know if I've ever met another man who would jump, unarmored, into a fight among six Shardbearers."

Kaladin frowned. "Wait. Are you wearing cologne? In *prison*?"

"Well, there was no need to be barbaric, just because I was incarcerated."

"Storms, you're spoiled," Kaladin said, smiling.

"I'm refined, you insolent farmer," Adolin said. Then he grinned. "Besides, I'll have you know that I had to use *cold* water for my baths while here."

"Poor boy."

"I know." Adolin hesitated, then held out a hand.

Kaladin clasped it. "I'm sorry," he said. "For ruining the plan."

"Bah, you didn't ruin it," Adolin said. "Elhokar did that. You think he couldn't have simply ignored your request and proceeded, letting me expand on my challenge to Sadeas? He threw a tantrum instead of taking control of the crowd and pushing forward. Storming man."

Kaladin blinked at the audacious tone, then glanced toward the jailer, who stood a distance behind, obviously trying to look inconspicuous.

"The things you said about Amaram," Adolin said. "Were they true?"

"Every one."

Adolin nodded. "I've always wondered what that man was hiding." He continued walking.

"Wait," Kaladin said, jogging to catch up, "you *believe* me?"

"My father," Adolin said, "is the best man I know, perhaps the best man *alive*. Even he loses his temper, makes bad judgment calls, and has a troubled past. Amaram never seems to do anything wrong. If you listen to the stories about him, it's like everyone expects him to glow in the dark and piss nectar. That stinks, to me, of someone who works too hard to maintain his reputation."

"Your father says I shouldn't have tried to duel him."

"Yeah," Adolin said, reaching the door at the end of the hallway. "Dueling is formalized in a way I suspect you just don't get. A darkeyes can't challenge a man like Amaram, and you certainly shouldn't have done it like you did. It embarrassed the king, like spitting on a gift he'd given you." Adolin hesitated. "Of course, that shouldn't matter to you anymore. Not after today."

Adolin pushed open the door. Beyond, most of the men of Bridge Four crowded into a small room where the jailers obviously spent their days. A table and chairs had been shoved to the corner to make room for the twenty-something men who saluted Kaladin as the door opened. Their salutes dissolved immediately as they started to cheer.

That sound . . . that sound quashed the darkness until it vanished completely. Kaladin found himself smiling as he stepped out to meet them, taking hands, listening to Rock make a wisecrack about his beard. Renarin was there in his Bridge Four uniform, and he immediately joined his brother, speaking to him quietly in a jovial way, though he had out his little box that he liked to fidget with.

Kaladin glanced to the side. Who were those men beside the wall? Members of Adolin's retinue. Was that one of Adolin's armorers? They carried some items draped with sheets. Adolin stepped into the room and loudly clapped his hands, quieting Bridge Four.

"It turns out," Adolin said, "that I'm in possession of not one, but *two* new Shardblades and *three* sets of Plate. The Kholin princedom now owns a quarter of the Shards in all of Alethkar, and I've been named dueling champion. Not surprising, considering Relis was on a caravan back to Alethkar the night after our duel, sent by his father in an attempt to hide the shame of being beaten so soundly.

"One complete set of those Shards is going to General Khal, and I've ordered two of the sets of Plate given to appropriate lighteyes of rank in my father's army." Adolin nodded toward the sheets. "That leaves one full set. Personally, I'm curious to know if the stories are true. If a darkeyes bonds a Shardblade, will his eyes change color?"

Kaladin felt a moment of sheer panic. Again. It was happening again.

The armorers removed the sheets, revealing a shimmering silvery Blade. Edged on both sides, a pattern of twisting vines ran up its center. At their feet, the armorers uncovered a set of Plate, painted orange, taken from one of the men Kaladin had helped defeat.

Take these Shards, and everything changed. Kaladin immediately felt sick, almost cripplingly so. He turned back to Adolin. "I can do with these as I wish?"

"Take them," Adolin said, nodding. "They are yours."

"Not anymore," Kaladin said, pointing toward one of the members of Bridge Four. "Moash. Take these. You're now a Shardbearer."

All of the color drained from Moash's face. Kaladin prepared himself. Last time . . . He flinched as Adolin grabbed him by the shoulder, but the tragedy of Amaram's army did not repeat. Instead, Adolin yanked Kaladin back into the hallway, holding up a hand to stop the bridgemen from talking.

"Just a second," Adolin said. "Nobody move." Then, in a quieter voice, he hissed to Kaladin. "I'm *giving* you a *Shardblade* and *Shardplate*."

"Thank you," Kaladin said. "Moash will use them well. He's been training with Zahel."

"I didn't give them to him. I gave them to you."

"If they're really mine, then I can do with them as I wish. Or are they not really mine?"

"What's *wrong* with you?" Adolin said. "This is the dream of every soldier, darkeyed or light. Is this out of spite? Or . . . is it . . ." Adolin seemed completely baffled.

"It's not out of spite," Kaladin said, speaking softly. "Adolin, those Blades have killed too many people I love. I can't look at them, can't *touch* them, without seeing blood."

"You'd be lighteyed," Adolin whispered. "Even if it didn't change your eye color, you'd count as one. Shardbearers are immediately of the fourth dahn. You could challenge Amaram. Your whole life would change."

"I don't want my life to change because I've become a lighteyes," Kaladin said. "I want the lives of people like me . . . like I am now . . . to change. This gift is not for me, Adolin. I'm not trying to spite you or anyone else. I just don't want a Shardblade."

"That assassin is going to come back," Adolin said. "We both know it. I'd rather have you there with Shards to back me up."

"I'll be more useful without them."

Adolin frowned.

"Let me give the Shards to Moash," Kaladin said. "You saw, on that field, that I can handle myself fine without a Blade and Plate. If we Shard-up one of my best men, there will be three of us to fight him, not just two."

Adolin looked into the room, then skeptically back at Kaladin. "You *are* crazy, you realize."

"I'll accept that."

"Fine," Adolin said, striding back into the room. "You. Moash, was it? I guess those Shards are yours, now. Congratulations. You now outrank ninety percent of Alethkar. Pick yourself a family name and ask to join one of the houses under Dalinar's banner, or start your own if you are inclined."

Moash glanced at Kaladin for confirmation. Kaladin nodded.

The tall bridgeman walked to the side of the room, reaching out a hand to rest his fingers on the Shardblade. He ran those fingers all the way down to the hilt, then seized it, lifting the Blade in awe. Like most, it was enormous, but Moash held it easily in one hand. The heliodor set into the pommel flashed with a burst of light.

Moash looked to the others of Bridge Four, a sea of wide eyes and speechless mouths. Gloryspren rose around him, a spinning mass of at least two dozen spheres of light.

"His eyes," Lopen said. "Shouldn't they be changing?"

"If it happens," Adolin said, "it might not be until he's bonded the thing. That takes a week."

"Put the Plate on me," Moash said to the armorers. Urgent, as if he feared it would be taken from him.

"Enough of this!" Rock said as the armorers began to work, his voice filling the room like captive thunder. "We have party to give! Great Captain Kaladin, Stormblessed and dweller in prisons, you will come eat my stew now. Ha! I have been cooking it as long as you were locked away."

Kaladin let the bridgemen usher him out into the sunlight, where a crowd of soldiers waited—including many of the bridgemen from other crews. These cheered, and Kaladin caught sight of Dalinar waiting off to the side. Adolin moved to join his father, but Dalinar watched Kaladin. What did that look mean? So pensive. Kaladin looked away, accepting the greetings of bridgemen as they clasped his hand and clapped him on the back.

"What did you say, Rock?" Kaladin said. "You cooked a stew for each day I was locked in prison?"

"No," Teft said, scratching his beard. "The storming Horneater has been cooking a single pot, letting it simmer for weeks now. He won't let us try it, and insists on getting up at night and tending it."

"Is celebratory stew," Rock said, folding his arms. "Must simmer long time."

"Well, let's get to it, then," Kaladin said. "I could certainly use something better than prison food."

The men cheered, piling off toward their barrack. As they moved, Kaladin grabbed Teft by the arm. "How did the men take it?" he asked. "My imprisonment?"

"There was talk of breaking you out," Teft admitted softly. "I beat some sense into them. Ain't no good soldier who hasn't spent a day or two locked up. It's part of the job. They didn't demote you, so they just wanted to slap your wrist a little. The men saw the truth of it."

Kaladin nodded.

Teft glanced at the others. "There's quite a lot of anger among them about this Amaram fellow. And a lot of interest. Anything about your past gets them talking, you know."

"Lead them back to the barrack," Kaladin said. "I'll join you in a moment."

"Don't take too long," Teft said. "The lads have been guarding this doorway for three weeks now. You owe them their celebration."

"I'll be along," Kaladin said. "I just want to say a few things to Moash."

Teft nodded and jogged off to wrangle the others. The prison's front room felt empty when Kaladin walked back in. Only Moash and the armorers remained. Kaladin walked up to them, watching Moash make a fist with his gauntlet.

"I'm still having trouble believing this, Kal," Moash said as the armorers fit on his breastplate. "Storms . . . I'm now worth more than some *kingdoms*."

"I wouldn't suggest selling the Shards, at least not to a foreigner," Kaladin said. "That sort of thing can be considered treason."

"Sell?" Moash said, looking up sharply. He made another fist. "Never." He smiled, a grin of pure joy as the breastplate locked into place.

"I'll help him with the rest," Kaladin said to the armorers. They withdrew reluctantly, leaving Kaladin and Moash alone.

He helped Moash fit one of the pauldrons to his shoulder. "I had a lot of time to think, in there," Kaladin said.

"I can imagine."

"The time led me to a few decisions," Kaladin said as the section of Plate locked into place. "One is that your friends are right."

Moash turned to him sharply. "So . . ."

"So tell them I agree with their plan," Kaladin said. "I'll do what they want me to in order to help them . . . accomplish their task."

The room grew strangely still.

Moash took him by the arm. "I told them you'd see." He gestured to the Plate he wore. "This will help too, with what we must do. And once we've finished, I think a certain man you challenged might need the same treatment."

"I only agree," Kaladin said, "because it's for the best. For you, Moash, this is about revenge—and don't try to deny it. *I* really think it is what Alethkar needs. Maybe what the world needs."

"Oh, I know," Moash said, putting on the helmet, visor up. He took a deep breath, then took a step and stumbled, nearly crashing to the ground.

He steadied himself by grabbing a table, which he crunched beneath his fingers, the wood splitting.

He stared at what he'd done, then laughed. "This . . . this is going to change *everything*. Thank you, Kaladin. Thank you."

"Let's get those armorers and help you take it off," Kaladin said.

"*No.* You go to Rock's storming feast. I'm going to the sparring grounds to practice! I won't take this off until I can move in it naturally."

Having seen how much work Renarin was putting into learning his Plate, Kaladin suspected that might take longer than Moash wanted. He didn't say anything, instead stepping back out into the sunlight. He enjoyed that for a moment, eyes closed, head toward the sky.

Then, he jogged off to rejoin Bridge Four.

My path has been chosen very deliberately. Yes, I agree with everything you have said about Rayse, including the severe danger he presents.

D alinar stopped on the switchbacks down from the Pinnacle, Navani at his side. In the waning light, they watched a river of men flowing back into the warcamps from the Shattered Plains. The armies of Bethab and Thanadal were returning from their plateau run, following their highprinces, who had probably gotten back somewhat earlier.

Down below, a rider approached the Pinnacle, likely with news for the king on the runs. Dalinar looked to one of his guards—he had four tonight, two for him, two for Navani—and gestured.

"You want the details, Brightlord?" asked the bridgeman.

"Please."

The man jogged off down the switchbacks. Dalinar watched him go, thoughtful. These men were remarkably disciplined, considering their origin—but they were not career soldiers. They did not like what he had done in throwing their captain into prison.

He suspected they wouldn't let it become a problem. Captain Kaladin led them well—he was the exact type of officer Dalinar looked for. The kind that showed initiative not because of a desire for advancement, but because of the satisfaction of a job well done. Those kinds of soldiers often had rocky starts until they learned to keep their heads. Storms. Dalinar himself had needed similar lessons pounded into him at various points in his life.

He continued with Navani down the switchbacks, walking slowly. She looked radiant tonight, hair done with sapphires that glowed softly in the light. Navani liked these strolls together, and they were in no hurry to arrive at the feast.

"I keep thinking," Navani said, continuing their previous conversation, "that there should be a way to use fabrials as *pumps*. You have seen the gemstones built to attract certain substances, but not others—it is most useful with something like smoke above a fire. Could we make this work with water?"

Dalinar grunted, nodding.

"More and more buildings in the warcamps are plumbed," she continued, "after the Kharbranthian manner—but those use gravity itself as a way to conduct the liquid through their piping. I imagine true motion, with gemstones at the ends of piping segments to pull water through at a flow, against the pull of the earth. . . ."

He grunted again.

"We made a breakthrough in the design of new Shardblades the other day."

"What, really?" he asked. "What happened? How soon will you have one ready?"

She smiled, arm around his.

"What?"

"Just seeing if you are still you," she said. "Our breakthrough was realizing that the gemstones in the Blades—used to bond them—might not have originally been part of the weapons."

He frowned. "That's important?"

"Yes. If this is true, it means the Blades aren't powered by the stones. Credit goes to Rushu, who asked why a Shardblade can be summoned and dismissed even if its gemstone has gone dun. We had no answers, and she spent the last few weeks in contact with Kharbranth, using one of those new information stations. She came up with a scrap from several decades after the Recreance which talks about men learning to summon and dismiss Blades by adding gemstones to them, an accident of ornamentation it seems."

He frowned as they passed a shalebark outcropping where a gardener was working late, carefully filing away and humming to himself. The sun had set; Salas had just risen in the east.

"If this is true," Navani said, sounding happy, "we're back to knowing absolutely nothing about how Shardblades were crafted."

"I don't see why that's a breakthrough at all."

She smiled, patting him on the arm. "Imagine you had spent the last five years believing an enemy had been following Dialectur's *War* as a model for tactics, but then heard it reported they instead had never heard of the treatise."

"Ah . . ."

"We had been assuming that somehow, the strength and lightness of the Blades was a fabrial construct powered by the gemstone," Navani said. "This might not be the case. It seems the gemstone's purpose is *only* used in initially bonding the Blade—something that the Radiants didn't need to do."

"Wait. They didn't?"

"Not if this fragment is correct. The implication is that the Radiants could always dismiss and summon Blades—but for a time the ability was lost. It was only recovered when someone added a gemstone to his Blade. The fragment says the weapons actually shifted *shape* to adopt the stones, but I'm not certain if I trust that.

"Either way, after the Radiants fell but before men learned to put gemstones into their Blades and bond them, the weapons were apparently *still* supernaturally sharp and light, though bonding was impossible. This would explain several other fragments of records I've read and found confusing. . . ."

She continued, and he found her voice pleasant. The details of fabrial construction, however, were not pressing to him at the moment. He did care. He had to care. Both for her, and for the needs of the kingdom.

He just couldn't care *right now*. In his head, he went over preparations for the expedition out onto the Shattered Plains. How to protect the Soulcasters from sight, as they preferred. Sanitation shouldn't be an issue, and water would be plentiful. How many scribes would he need to bring? Horses? Only one week remained, and he had the majority of the preparations in place, such as mobile bridge construction and supply estimations. There was always more to plan, however.

Unfortunately, the biggest variable was one he couldn't plan for, not specifically. He didn't know how many troops he'd have. It depended on which of the highprinces, if any, agreed to go with him. Less than a week out, and he still wasn't certain if *any* of them would.

I could use Hatham most, Dalinar thought. *He runs a tight army. If only Aladar hadn't sided with Sadeas so vigorously; I can't figure that man out. Thanadal and Bethab . . . storms, will I bring their mercenaries if either of those two agree to come? Is that the kind of force I want? Dare I refuse any spear that comes to me?*

"I'm not going to get a good conversation out of you tonight, am I?" Navani asked.

"No," he admitted as they reached the base of the Pinnacle and turned south. "I'm sorry."

She nodded, and he could see the mask cracking. She talked about her work because it was something to talk about. He stopped beside her. "I know it hurts," he said softly. "But it will get better."

"She wouldn't let me be a mother to her, Dalinar," Navani said, staring into the distance. "Do you know that? It was almost like . . . like once Jasnah climbed into adolescence, she no longer *needed* a mother. I would try to get close to her, and there was this *coldness,* like even being near me reminded her that she had once been a child. What happened to my little girl, so full of questions?"

Dalinar pulled her close; propriety could seek Damnation. Nearby, the three guards shuffled, looking the other way.

"They'll take my son too," Navani whispered. "They're trying."

"I will protect him," Dalinar promised.

"And who will protect you?"

He had no answer to that. Answering that his guards would do it sounded trite. That wasn't the question she'd asked. *Who will protect you when that assassin returns?*

"I almost wish that you would fail," she said. "In holding this kingdom together, you make a target of yourself. If everything just collapsed, and we fractured back to princedoms, perhaps he'd leave us alone."

"And then the storm would come," Dalinar replied softly. Eleven days.

Navani eventually pulled back, nodding, composing herself. "You're right, of course. I just . . . this is the first time, for me. Dealing with this. How did you manage it, when *Shshshsh* died? I know you loved her, Dalinar. You don't have to deny it for my ego."

He hesitated. *The first time;* an implication that when Gavilar had died, she had not been broken up about it. She had never stated so outright an implication of the . . . difficulties the two had been having.

"I'm sorry," she said. "Was that too difficult a question, considering its source?" She tucked away her kerchief, which she'd used to dab her eyes dry. "I apologize; I know that you don't like to talk about her."

It wasn't that it was a difficult question. It was that Dalinar didn't remember his wife. How odd, that he could go weeks without even noticing this hole in his memories, this change that had ripped out a piece of him and left him patched over. Without even a prick of emotion when her name, which he could not hear, was mentioned.

Best to move to some other topic. "I cannot help but assume that the assassin is involved in all of this, Navani. The storm that comes, the secrets of the Shattered Plains, even Gavilar. My brother knew something, something he never shared with any of us." *You must find the most important words a man can say.* "I would give almost anything to know what it was."

"I suppose," Navani said. "I will go back to my journals of the time. Perhaps he said something that would give us clues—though I warn you, I've pored over those accounts dozens of times."

Dalinar nodded. "Regardless, that isn't a worry for today. Today, *they* are our goal."

They turned, looking as coaches clattered past, making their way to the nearby feasting basin, where lights glowed a soft violet in the night. He narrowed his eyes and found Ruthar's coach approaching. The highprince had been stripped of Shards, all but his own Blade. They had cut off Sadeas's right hand in this mess, but the head remained. And it was venomous.

The other highprinces were almost as big a problem as Sadeas. They resisted him because they wanted things to be easy, as they had been. They glutted themselves on their riches and their games. Feasts manifested that all too much, with their exotic food, their rich costumes.

The world itself seemed close to ending, and the Alethi threw a party.

"You must not despise them," Navani said.

Dalinar's frown deepened. She could read him too well.

"Listen to me, Dalinar," she said, turning him to meet her eyes. "Has any good ever come from a father hating his children?"

"I don't hate them."

"You loathe their excess," she said, "and you are close to applying that emotion to them as well. They live the lives they have known, the lives that society has taught them are proper. You won't change them with contempt. You aren't Wit; it isn't your job to scorn them. Your job is to enfold them, encourage them. Lead them, Dalinar."

He drew a deep breath, and nodded.

"I will go to the women's island," she said, noticing the bridgeman guard returning with news on the plateau assault. "They consider me an eccentric vestige of things better left in the past, but I think they still listen to me. Sometimes. I'll do what I can."

They parted, Navani hurrying to the feast, Dalinar idling as the bridgeman passed his news. The plateau run had been successful, a gemheart captured. It had taken quite a long time to reach the target plateau, which was deep into the Plains—almost to the edge of the scouted area. The Parshendi had not appeared to contest the gemheart, though their scouts had watched from a distance.

Again they decide not to fight, Dalinar thought, walking the last distance to the feast. *What does the change mean? What are they planning?*

The feast basin was made up of a series of Soulcast islands beside the Pinnacle complex. It had been flooded, as it often was, in a way that made the Soulcast mounds rise between small rivers. The water glowed. Spheres, and a lot of them, must have been dumped into the water to give it that ethereal cast. Purple, to match the moon that was just rising, violet and frail on the horizon.

Lanterns were placed intermittently, but with dim spheres, perhaps to not distract from the glowing water. Dalinar crossed the bridges to the farthest island—the king's island, where the genders mixed and only the most powerful were invited. This was where he knew he'd find the highprinces. Even Bethab, who had just returned from his plateau run, was already in attendance—though, as he preferred to use mercenary companies for the bulk of his army, it wasn't surprising he had returned so quickly from the run. Once they captured the gemheart, he'd often ride back quickly with the prize, letting them sort out how to return.

Dalinar passed Wit—who had arrived back at the warcamps with characteristic mystery—insulting everyone who passed. He had no wish to fence words with the man today. Instead, he sought out Vamah; the highprince seemed to have actually listened to Dalinar's pleas during their most recent dinner. Perhaps with more nudging, he would commit to joining Dalinar's assault on the Parshendi.

Eyes followed Dalinar as he crossed the island, and whispered conversations broke out like rashes as he passed. He expected those looks by now, though they still unnerved him. Were they more plentiful this night? More lingering? He couldn't move in Alethi society these days without catching a smile on the lips of too many people, as if they were all part of some grand joke that he had not been told.

He found Vamah speaking with a group of three older women. One was Sivi, a highlady from Ruthar's court who—contrary to custom—had left her husband at home to see to their lands, coming to the Shattered Plains herself. She eyed Dalinar with a smile and eyes like daggers. The plot to undermine Sadeas had to a large extent failed—but that was in part because the damage and shame had been deflected to Ruthar and Aladar, who had suffered the loss of Shardbearers in the men who had dueled Adolin.

Well, those two were never going to have been Dalinar's—they were Sadeas's strongest supporters.

The four people grew silent as Dalinar stepped up to them. Highprince Vamah squinted in the dim light, looking Dalinar up and down. The round-faced man had a cupbearer standing behind him with a bottle of some exotic liquor or another. Vamah often brought his own spirits to feasts, regardless of who hosted them; being engaging enough a conversationalist to earn a sip of what he'd managed to import was considered a political triumph by many attendees.

"Vamah," Dalinar said.

"Dalinar."

"There's a matter I've been wanting to discuss with you," Dalinar said. "I find it impressive what you've been able to do with light cavalry on your plateau runs. Tell me, how do you decide when to risk an all-out assault with your riders? The loss of horses could easily overwhelm your earnings

from gemhearts, but you have managed to balance this with clever strata-
gems."

"I . . ." Vamah sighed, looking to the side. A group of young men nearby
was snickering as they looked toward Dalinar. "It is a matter of . . ."

Another sound, louder, came from the opposite side of the island. Vamah
started again, but his eyes flicked in that direction, and a round of laughter
burst out more loudly. Dalinar forced himself to look, noting women with
hands to mouths, men covering their exclamations with coughs. A half-
hearted attempt at maintaining Alethi propriety.

Dalinar looked back at Vamah. "What is happening?"

"I'm sorry, Dalinar."

Beside him, Sivi tucked some sheets of paper under her arm. She met
Dalinar's gaze with a forced nonchalance.

"Excuse me," Dalinar said. Hands forming fists, he crossed the island
toward the source of the disturbance. As he neared, they quieted and people
broke up into smaller groups, moving off. It almost seemed *planned* how
quickly they dispersed, leaving him to face Sadeas and Aladar, standing
side by side.

"What are you doing?" Dalinar demanded of the two of them.

"Feasting," Sadeas said, then shoved a piece of fruit into his mouth.
"Obviously."

Dalinar drew in a deep breath. He glanced at Aladar, long-necked and
bald, with his mustache and tuft of hair on his bottom lip. "You should be
ashamed," Dalinar growled at him. "My brother once called you a friend."

"And not me?" Sadeas said.

"What have you done?" Dalinar demanded. "What is everyone talking
about, snickering about behind their hands?"

"You always assume it's me," Sadeas said.

"That's because any time I think it *isn't* you, I'm wrong."

Sadeas gave him a thin-lipped smile. He started to reply, but then
thought a moment, and finally just stuffed another chunk of fruit in his
mouth. He chewed and smiled.

"Tastes good," was all he said. He turned to walk away.

Aladar hesitated. Then he shook his head and followed.

"I never figured you for a pup to follow at a master's heels, Aladar,"
Dalinar called after him.

No reply.

Dalinar growled, moving back across the island, looking for someone
from his own warcamp who might have heard what was happening. Elhokar
was late to his own feast, it seemed, though Dalinar did see him approaching outside now. No sign of Teshav or Khal yet—they would undoubtedly
make an appearance, now that he was a Shardbearer.

Dalinar might have to move to one of the other islands, where lesser lighteyes would be mingling. He started that way, but stopped as he heard something.

"Why, Brightlord Amaram," Wit cried. "I was *hoping* I'd be able to see you tonight. I've spent my life learning to make others feel miserable, and so it's a true joy to meet someone so innately talented in that very skill as you are."

Dalinar turned, noticing Amaram, who had just arrived. He wore his cape of the Knights Radiant and carried a sheaf of papers stuck under his arm. He stopped beside Wit's chair, the nearby water casting a lavender tone across their skin.

"Do I know you?" Amaram asked.

"No," Wit said lightly, "but fortunately, you can add it to the list of many, many things of which you are ignorant."

"But now I've met you," Amaram said, holding out a hand. "So the list is one smaller."

"Please," Wit said, refusing the hand. "I wouldn't want it to rub off on me."

"It?"

"Whatever you've been using to make your hands look clean, Brightlord Amaram. It must be powerful stuff indeed."

Dalinar hurried over.

"Dalinar," Wit said, nodding.

"Wit. Amaram, what are those papers?"

"One of your clerks seized them and brought them to me," Amaram said. "Copies were being passed around the feast before your arrival. Your clerk thought Brightness Navani might want to see them if she hasn't already. Where is she?"

"Staying away from you, obviously," Wit noted. "Lucky woman."

"Wit," Dalinar said sternly, "do you mind?"

"Rarely."

Dalinar sighed, looking back to Amaram and taking the papers. "Brightness Navani is on another island. Do you know what these say?"

Amaram's expression grew grim. "I wish I didn't."

"I could hit you in the head with a hammer," Wit said happily. "A good bludgeoning would make you forget *and* do wonders for that face of yours."

"Wit," Dalinar said flatly.

"I'm only joking."

"Good."

"A hammer would hardly dent that thick skull of his."

Amaram turned to Wit, a look of bafflement on his face.

"You're *very* good at that expression," Wit noted. "A great deal of prac-

tice, I assume?"

"*This* is the new Wit?" Amaram asked.

"I mean," Wit said, "I wouldn't want to call Amaram an imbecile . . ." Dalinar nodded.

". . . because then I'd have to explain to him what the word means, and I'm not certain any of us have the requisite time."

Amaram sighed. "Why hasn't anyone killed him yet?"

"Dumb luck," Wit said. "In that I'm lucky you're all so dumb."

"Thank you, Wit," Dalinar said, taking Amaram by the arm and towing him to the side.

"One more, Dalinar!" Wit said. "Just one last insult, and I leave him alone."

They continued walking.

"Lord Amaram," Wit called, standing to bow, his voice growing solemn. "I salute you. You *are* what lesser cretins like Sadeas can only aspire to be."

"The papers?" Dalinar said to Amaram, pointedly ignoring Wit.

"They are accounts of your . . . experiences, Brightlord," Amaram said softly. "The ones you have during the storms. Written by Brightness Navani herself."

Dalinar took the papers. His visions. He looked up and saw groups of people collecting on the island, chatting and laughing, shooting glances at him.

"I see," he said softly. It made sense now, the hidden snickering. "Find Brightness Navani for me, if you would."

"As you request," Amaram said, but stopped short, pointing. Navani stalked across the next island over, heading toward them with a tempestuous air about her.

"What do you think, Amaram?" Dalinar said. "Of the things that are being said of me?"

Amaram met his eyes. "They are obviously visions from the Almighty himself, given to us in a time of great need. I wish I had known their contents earlier. They give me great confidence in my position, and in your appointment as prophet of the Almighty."

"A dead god can have no prophets."

"Dead . . . No, Dalinar! You obviously misinterpret that comment from your visions. He speaks of being dead in the minds of men, that they no longer listen to his commands. God cannot die."

Amaram seemed so earnest. *Why didn't he help your sons?* Kaladin's voice rang in Dalinar's mind. Amaram had come to him that day, of course, professing his apologies and explaining that—with his appointment as a Radiant—he couldn't possibly have helped one faction against another. He said he needed to be above the squabbles between highprinces, even when it pained him.

"And the supposed Herald?" Dalinar asked. "The thing I asked you about?"

"I am still investigating."

Dalinar nodded.

"I was surprised," Amaram noted, "that you left the slave as head of your guard." He glanced to the side, to where Dalinar's guards for the night stood, just off the island in their own area, waiting with the other bodyguards and attendants, including many of the wards of the highladies present.

There had been a time not too long ago when few had felt the need to bring their guards with them to a feast. Now, the place was crowded. Captain Kaladin wasn't there; he was resting, after his imprisonment.

"He's a good soldier," Dalinar said softly. "He just carries a few scars that are having trouble healing." *Vedeledev knows,* Dalinar thought, *I have a few of those myself.*

"I merely worry that he is incapable of properly protecting you," Amaram said. "Your life is important, Dalinar. We *need* your visions, your leadership. Still, if you trust the slave, then so be it—though I certainly wouldn't mind hearing an apology from him. Not for my own ego, but to know that he's put aside this misconception of his."

Dalinar gave no reply as Navani strode across the short bridge onto their island. Wit started to proclaim an insult, but she swatted him in the face with a stack of papers, giving him barely a glance as she continued on toward Dalinar. Wit watched after, rubbing his cheek, and grinned.

She noted the papers in his hand as she joined the two of them, who seemed to stand among a sea of amused eyes and hushed laughter.

"They added words," Navani hissed.

"What?" Dalinar demanded.

She shook the papers. "These! You've heard what they contain?"

He nodded.

"They aren't as I wrote them," Navani said. "They've changed the tone, some of my words, to imply a ridiculousness to the entire experience—and to make it sound as if I am merely indulging you. What's worse, they added a commentary in another handwriting that pokes fun at what you say and do." She took a deep breath, as if to calm herself. "Dalinar, they're trying to destroy any shred of credibility left to your name."

"I see."

"How did they get these?" Amaram asked.

"Through theft, I do not doubt," Dalinar said, realizing something. "Navani and my sons always have guards—but when they leave their rooms, those are relatively unprotected. We may have been too lax in that regard. I misunderstood. I thought his attacks would be physical."

Navani looked out at the sea of lighteyes, many congregating in groups around the various highprinces in the soft, violet light. She stepped closer to Dalinar, and though her eyes were fierce, he knew her well enough to guess what she was feeling. Betrayal. Invasion. That which was private to them, opened up, mocked and then displayed for the world.

"Dalinar, I'm sorry," Amaram said.

"They did not change the visions themselves?" Dalinar asked. "They copied them accurately."

"So far as I can tell, yes," Navani said. "But the tone is different, and that *mockery*. Storms. It's nauseating. When I find the woman who did this . . ."

"Peace, Navani," Dalinar said, resting his hand on her shoulder.

"How can you say that?"

"Because this is the act of childish men who assume that I can be embarrassed by the truth."

"But the commentary! The changes. They've done everything they can to discredit you. They even managed to undermine the part where you offer a translation of the Dawnchant. It—"

"'As I fear not a child with a weapon he cannot lift, I will never fear the mind of a man who does not think.'"

Navani frowned at him.

"It's from *The Way of Kings*," Dalinar said. "I am not a youth, nervous at his first feast. Sadeas makes a mistake in believing I will respond to this as he would. Unlike a sword, scorn has only the bite you give it."

"This *does* hurt you," Navani said, meeting his eyes. "I can see it, Dalinar."

Hopefully, the others would not know him well enough to see what she did. Yes, it did hurt. It hurt because these visions were *his*, entrusted to him—to be shared for the good of men, not to be held up for mockery. It was not the laughter itself that pained him, but the loss of what could have been.

He stepped away from her, passing through the crowd. Some of those eyes he now interpreted as being sorrowful, not just amused. Perhaps he was imagining it, but he thought some pitied him more than scorned him.

He wasn't certain which emotion was more damaging.

Dalinar reached the food table at the back of the island. There, he picked up a large pan and handed it to a bewildered serving woman, then hauled himself up onto the table. He set one hand on the lantern pole beside the table and looked out over the small crowd. They were the most important people in Alethkar.

Those who hadn't already been watching him turned with shock to see him up there. In the distance, he noticed Adolin and Brightness Shallan rushing onto the island. They'd likely only just arrived, and heard the talk.

Dalinar looked to the crowd. "What you have read," he bellowed, "is true."

Stunned silence. Making a spectacle of oneself in this way was not done in Alethkar. He, however, had *already been* this evening's spectacle.

"Commentary has been added to discredit me," Dalinar said, "and the tone of Navani's writing has been changed. But I will not hide what has been happening to me. I see visions from the Almighty. They come with almost every storm. This should not surprise you. There have been rumors circulating about my experiences for weeks now. Perhaps I should have released these visions already. In the future, each one I receive will be published, so that scholars around the world can investigate what I have seen."

He sought out Sadeas, who stood with Aladar and Ruthar. Dalinar gripped the lantern pole, looking back at the Alethi crowd. "I do not blame you for thinking I am mad. It is natural. But in the coming nights, when rain washes your walls and the wind howls, you will wonder. You will question. And soon, when I offer you proof, you will know. This attempt to destroy me will then vindicate me instead."

He looked over their faces, some aghast, some sympathetic, others amused.

"There are those among you who assume I will flee, or be broken, because of this attack," he said. "They do not know me as well as they presume. Let the feast continue, for I wish to speak with each and every one of you. The words you hold may mock, but if you must laugh, do it while looking me in the eyes."

He stepped down from the table.

Then he went to work.

◆◆

Hours later, Dalinar eventually let himself sit down in a seat beside a table at the feast, exhaustionspren swirling around him. He'd spent the rest of the evening moving through the crowd, forcing his way into conversations, drumming up support for his excursion onto the Plains.

He had pointedly ignored the pages with his visions on them, except when asked direct questions about what he'd seen. Instead, he had presented them with a forceful, confident man—the Blackthorn turned politician. Let them chew on that and compare him to the frail madman the falsified transcripts would make him out to be.

Outside, past the small rivers—they now glowed blue, the spheres having been changed to match the second moon—the king's carriage rolled away, bearing Elhokar and Navani the short distance to the Pinnacle, where porters would carry them in a palanquin up to the top. Adolin had already retired, escorting Shallan back to Sebarial's warcamp, which was a fair ride away.

Adolin seemed to be fonder of the young Veden woman than of any woman in the recent past. For that reason alone, Dalinar was increasingly inclined to encourage the relationship, assuming he could ever get some straight answers out of Jah Keved about her family. That kingdom was a mess.

Most of the other lighteyes had retired, leaving him on an island populated by servants and parshmen who cleared away food. A few master-servants, trusted for such duties, began to scoop the spheres out of the river with nets on long poles. Dalinar's bridgemen, at his suggestion, were attacking the feast's leftovers with the voracious appetite exclusive to soldiers who had been offered an unexpected meal.

A servant strolled by, then stopped, resting his hand on his side sword. Dalinar started, realizing he'd mistaken Wit's black military uniform for that of a master-servant in training.

Dalinar put on a firm face, though inwardly he groaned. Wit? Now? Dalinar felt as if he'd been fighting on the battlefield for ten hours straight. Odd, how a few hours of delicate conversation could feel so similar to that.

"What you did tonight was clever," Wit said. "You turned an attack into a promise. The wisest of men know that to render an insult powerless, you often need only to embrace it."

"Thank you," Dalinar said.

Wit nodded curtly, following the king's coach with his eyes as it vanished. "I found myself without much to do tonight. Elhokar was not in need of Wit, as few sought to speak to him. All came to you instead."

Dalinar sighed, his strength seeming to drain away. Wit hadn't said it, but he hadn't needed to. Dalinar read the implication.

They came to you, instead of the king. Because essentially, you are king.

"Wit," Dalinar found himself asking, "am I a tyrant?"

Wit cocked an eyebrow, and seemed to be looking for a clever quip. A moment later, he discarded the thought. "Yes, Dalinar Kholin," he said softly, consolingly, as one might speak to a tearful child. "You are."

"I do not wish to be."

"With all due respect, Brightlord, that is not *quite* the truth. You seek for power. You take hold, and let go only with great difficulty."

Dalinar bowed his head.

"Do not sorrow," Wit said. "It is an era for tyrants. I doubt this place is ready for anything more, and a benevolent tyrant is preferable to the disaster of weak rule. Perhaps in another place and time, I'd have denounced you with spit and bile. Here, today, I praise you as what this world needs."

Dalinar shook his head. "I should have allowed Elhokar his right of rule, and not interfered as I did."

"Why?"

"Because he is king."

"And that position is something sacrosanct? Divine?"

"No," Dalinar admitted. "The Almighty, or the one claiming to be him, is dead. Even if he hadn't been, the kingship didn't come to our family naturally. We claimed it, and forced it upon the other highprinces."

"So then why?"

"Because we were wrong," Dalinar said, narrowing his eyes. "Gavilar, Sadeas, and I were wrong to do as we did all those years ago."

Wit seemed genuinely surprised. "You unified the kingdom, Dalinar. You did a good work, something that was sorely needed."

"*This* is unity?" Dalinar asked, waving a hand back toward the scattered remnants of the feast, the departing lighteyes. "No, Wit. We failed. We crushed, we killed, and we have *failed miserably*." He looked up. "I receive, in Alethkar, only what I have demanded. In taking the throne by force, we implied—no we *screamed*—that strength is the right of rule. If Sadeas thinks he is stronger than I am, then it is his *duty* to try to take the throne from me. These are the fruits of my youth, Wit. It is why we need more than tyranny, even the benevolent kind, to transform this kingdom. That is what Nohadon was teaching. And *that* is what I've been missing all along."

Wit nodded, looking thoughtful. "I need to read that book of yours again, it seems. I wanted to warn you, however. I'll be leaving soon."

"Leave?" Dalinar said. "You only just arrived."

"I know. It's incredibly frustrating, I must admit. I have discovered a place that I must be, though to be honest I'm not *exactly* sure why I need to be there. This doesn't always work as well as I'd like it to."

Dalinar frowned at him. Wit smiled back affably.

"Are you one of them?" Dalinar asked.

"Excuse me?"

"A Herald."

Wit laughed. "No. Thank you, but no."

"Are you what I've been looking for, then?" Dalinar asked. "Radiant?"

Wit smiled. "I am but a man, Dalinar, so much as I wish it were not true at times. I am no Radiant. And while I *am* your friend, please understand that our goals do not completely align. You must not trust yourself with me. If I have to watch this world crumble and burn to get what I need, I will do so. With tears, yes, but I would let it happen."

Dalinar frowned.

"I will do what I can to help," Wit said, "and for that reason, I must go. I cannot risk too much, because if *he* finds me, then I become nothing—

a soul shredded and broken into pieces that cannot be reassembled. What I do here is more dangerous than you could ever know."

He turned to go.

"Wit," Dalinar called.

"Yes?"

"If who finds you?"

"The one you fight, Dalinar Kholin. The father of hatred." Wit saluted, then jogged off.

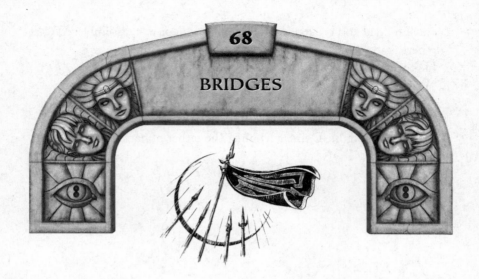

However, it seems to me that all things have been set up for a purpose, and if we—as infants—stumble through the workshop, we risk exacerbating, not preventing, a problem.

The Shattered Plains.

Kaladin did not claim these lands as he did the chasms, where his men had found safety. Kaladin remembered all too well the pain of bloodied feet on his first run, battered by this broken stone wasteland. Barely anything grew out here, only the occasional patch of rockbuds or set of enterprising vines draping down into a chasm on the leeward side of a plateau. The bottoms of the cracks were clogged with life, but up here it was barren.

The aching feet and burning shoulders from running a bridge had been nothing compared to the slaughter that had awaited his men at the end of a bridge run. Storms . . . even looking across the Plains made Kaladin flinch. He could hear the hiss of arrows in the air, the screams of terrified bridgemen, the song of the Parshendi.

I should have been able to save more of Bridge Four, Kaladin thought. *If I'd been faster to accept my powers, could I have done so?*

He breathed in Stormlight to reassure himself. Only it didn't come. He stood, dumbfounded, while soldiers marched across one of Dalinar's enormous mechanical bridges. He tried again. Nothing.

He fished a sphere from his pouch. The firemark glowed with its customary light, tinting his fingers red. Something was wrong. Kaladin couldn't *feel* the Stormlight inside as he once had.

Syl flitted across the chasm high in the air with a group of windspren.

Her giggling laughter rained down upon him, and he looked up. "Syl?" he asked quietly. Storms. He didn't want to look like an idiot, but something deep within him was panicking like a rat caught by its tail. "Syl!"

Several marching soldiers glanced at Kaladin, then up toward the air. Kaladin ignored them as Syl zipped down in the form of a ribbon of light. She swirled around him, still giggling.

The Stormlight returned to him. He could feel it again, and he greedily sucked it from the sphere—though he did have the presence of mind to clutch the sphere in a fist and hold it to his chest to make the process less obvious. The Light of one mark wasn't enough to expose him, but he felt far, far better with that Stormlight raging inside of him.

"What happened?" Kaladin whispered to Syl. "Is something wrong with our bond? Is it because I haven't found the Words soon enough?"

She landed on his wrist and took the form of a young woman. She peered at his hand, cocking her head. "What's inside?" she asked with a conspiratorial whisper.

"You know what this is, Syl," Kaladin said, feeling chilled, as if he'd been hit by a wave of stormwater. "A sphere. Didn't you see it just now?"

She looked at him, face innocent. "You are making bad choices. Naughty." Her features mimicked his for a moment and she jumped forward, as if to startle him. She laughed and zipped away.

Bad choices. Naughty. So, this was because of his promise to Moash that he'd help assassinate the king. Kaladin sighed, continuing forward.

Syl couldn't see why his decision was the right one. She was a spren, and had a stupid, simplistic morality. To be human was often to be forced to choose between distasteful options. Life wasn't clean and neat like she wanted it to be. It was messy, coated with crem. No man walked through life without getting covered in it, not even Dalinar.

"You want too much of me," he snapped at her as he reached the other side of the chasm. "I'm not some glorious knight of ancient days. I'm a broken man. Do you hear me, Syl? I'm *broken*."

She zipped up to him and whispered, "That's what they *all* were, silly." She streaked away.

Kaladin watched as the soldiers filed across the bridge. They weren't doing a plateau run, but Dalinar had brought plenty of soldiers anyway. Going out onto the Shattered Plains was entering a war zone, and the Parshendi were ever a threat.

Bridge Four tromped across the mechanical bridge, carrying their smaller one. Kaladin wasn't *about* to leave the camps without that. These mechanisms Dalinar employed—the massive, chull-pulled bridges that could be ratcheted down into place—were amazing, but Kaladin didn't trust them. Not nearly as much as he did a good bridge on his shoulders.

Syl flitted by again. Did she really expect him to live according to *her* perception of what was right and wrong? Was she going to yank his powers away every time he did something that risked offending her?

That would be like living with a noose around his neck.

Determined to not let his worries ruin the day, he went to check on Bridge Four. *Look at the open sky,* he told himself. *Breathe the wind. Enjoy the freedom.* After so much time in captivity, these things were wonders.

He found Bridge Four beside their bridge at parade rest. It was odd to see them with their old padded-shoulder leather vests on over their new uniforms. It transformed them into a weird mix of what they had been and what they were now. They saluted him together, and he saluted back.

"At ease," he told them, and they broke formation, laughing and joking with one another as Lopen and his assistants distributed waterskins.

"Ha!" Rock said, settling down on the side of the bridge to drink. "This thing, it is not so hard as I remember it being."

"It's because we're going slower," Kaladin said, pointing at Dalinar's mechanical bridge. "And because you're remembering the early days of bridge carries, not the later ones when we were well-fed and well-trained. It got easier then."

"No," Rock said. "The bridge is light because we have defeated Sadeas. Is the proper way of things."

"That makes no sense."

"Ha! Perfect sense." He took a drink. "Airsick lowlander."

Kaladin shook his head, but let himself find a smile at Rock's familiar voice. After slaking his own thirst, he jogged across the plateau toward where Dalinar had just finished crossing. Nearby, a tall rock formation surmounted the plateau, and atop it was a wooden structure like a small fort. Sunlight glinted off one of the spyglasses fitted there.

No permanent bridge led to this plateau, which was just outside the secure area closest to the warcamp. These scouts positioned here were vaulters, who leaped chasms at narrow points with the use of long poles. It seemed like a job that would require a special brand of craziness—and because of that, Kaladin had always felt respect for these men.

One of the vaulters was speaking with Dalinar. Kaladin would have expected the man to be tall and limber, but he was short and compact, with thick forearms. He wore a Kholin uniform with white stripes edging the coat.

"We *did* see something out here, Brightlord," the vaulter said to Dalinar. "I saw it with my own two eyes, and recorded the date and time in glyphs on my ledger. It was a man, a glowing one, who flew around in the sky back and forth over the Plains."

Dalinar grunted.

"I'm not crazy, sir," the vaulter said, shuffling from one foot to the other. "The other lads saw it too, once I—"

"I believe you, soldier," Dalinar said. "It was the Assassin in White. He looked like that when he came for the king."

The man relaxed. "Brightlord, sir, that's what I thought. Some of the men back at camp told me I was just seeing what I wanted."

"Nobody wants to see that one," Dalinar said. "But why would he spend his time out here? Why hasn't he come back to attack, if he's this close?"

Kaladin cleared his throat, uncomfortable, and pointed at the watchman's post. "That fort up there, is it wood?"

"Yes," the vaulter said, then noticed the knots on Kaladin's shoulders. "Uh, sir."

"That can't possibly withstand a highstorm," Kaladin said.

"We break it down, sir."

"And carry it back to camp?" Kaladin asked, frowning. "Or do you leave it out here for the storm?"

"Leave it, sir?" the short man said. "We stay here with it." He pointed toward a burrowed-out section of rock, cut with hammers or a Shardblade, at the base of the stone formation. It didn't look very large—just a cubby, really. It looked like they took the wooden floor of the platform up above, then locked it into place with clasps at the side of the cubby to form a kind of door.

A special kind of crazy indeed.

"Brightlord, sir," the vaulter said to Dalinar, "the one in white might be out here somewhere. Waiting."

"Thank you, soldier," Dalinar said, nodding his dismissal. "Keep an eye out for us while we travel. We've had reports of a chasmfiend moving in close to the camps."

"Yes, sir," the man said, saluting and then jogging back toward the rope ladder leading up to his post.

"What if the assassin does come for you?" Kaladin asked softly.

"I don't see how it would be any different out here," Dalinar said. "He'll be back eventually. On the Plains or in the palace, we'll have to fight him."

Kaladin grunted. "I wish you'd accept one of those Shardblades that Adolin has been winning, sir. I'd feel more comfortable if you could defend yourself."

"I think you'd be surprised," Dalinar said, shading his eyes, turning toward the warcamp. "I do feel wrong leaving Elhokar alone back there, though."

"The assassin said he wanted you, sir," Kaladin said. "If you're apart from the king, that will only serve to protect him."

"I suppose," Dalinar said. "Unless the assassin's comments were misdirection." He shook his head. "I might order you to stay with him next time. I can't help but feel I'm missing something important, something right in front of me."

Kaladin set his jaw, trying to ignore the chill he felt. *Order you to stay with him next time. . . .* It was almost like fate itself was pushing Kaladin to be in a position to betray the king.

"About your imprisonment," the highprince said.

"Already forgotten, sir," Kaladin said. Dalinar's part in it, at least. "I appreciate not being demoted."

"You're a good soldier," Dalinar said. "Most of the time." His eyes flicked toward Bridge Four, picking up their bridge. One of the men at the side drew his attention in particular: Renarin, wearing his Bridge Four uniform, hefting the bridge into place. Nearby, Leyten laughed and gave him pointers on how to hold the thing.

"He's actually starting to fit in, sir," Kaladin said. "The men like him. I never thought I'd see the day."

Dalinar nodded.

"How was he?" Kaladin asked softly. "After what happened in the arena?"

"He refused to go practice with Zahel," Dalinar said. "So far as I know, he hasn't summoned his Shardblade in weeks." He watched for a moment longer. "I can't decide if his time with your men is good for him—helping him think like a soldier—or if it's just encouraging him to avoid his greater responsibilities."

"Sir," Kaladin said. "If I may say so, your son seems like kind of a misfit. Out of place. Awkward, alone."

Dalinar nodded.

"Then, I can say with confidence that Bridge Four is probably the *best* place he could find himself." It felt odd to be saying it of a lighteyes, but it was true.

Dalinar grunted. "I'll trust your judgment. Go. Make sure those men of yours are on the watch for the assassin, in case he does come today."

Kaladin nodded, leaving the highprince behind. He'd heard about Dalinar's visions before—and had had an inkling of their contents. He didn't know what he thought, but he intended to get a copy of the vision records in their entirety so he could have Ka read it to him.

Perhaps these visions were why Syl was always so determined to trust Dalinar.

As the day passed, the army moved across the Plains like the flow of some viscous liquid—mud dribbling down a shallow incline. All of this so Shallan could see a chasmfiend chrysalis. Kaladin shook his head, crossing a plateau. Adolin was certainly smitten; he'd managed to roll out an entire strike force, his father included, just to sate the girl's whims.

"Walking, Kaladin?" Adolin said, trotting up. The prince rode that white beast of a horse, the thing with the hooves like hammers. Adolin wore his full suit of blue Shardplate, helm tied to a knob on the back of the saddle. "I thought you had full requisition right from my father's stables."

"I have full requisition right from the quartermasters too," Kaladin said, "but you don't see me hiking out here with a cauldron on my back just because I *can*."

Adolin chuckled. "You should try riding more. You have to admit that there are advantages. The speed of the gallop, the height of attack." He patted his horse on the neck.

"I guess I just trust my own feet too much."

Adolin nodded, as if that had been the wisest thing a man had ever said, before riding back to check on Shallan in her palanquin. Feeling a little fatigued, Kaladin fished in his pocket for another sphere, just a diamond chip this time, and held it to his chest. He breathed in.

Again, nothing happened. Storm it! He looked about for Syl, but couldn't find her. She'd been so playful lately, he was starting to wonder if this was all some kind of trick. He actually hoped it was that, and not something more. Despite his inward grousing and complaints, he desperately wanted this power. He had claimed the sky, the winds themselves. Giving them up would be like giving up his own hands.

He eventually reached the edge of their current plateau, where Dalinar's mechanical bridge was setting up. Here, blessedly, he found Syl inspecting a cremling crawling across the rocks toward the safety of a nearby crack.

Kaladin sat down on a rock beside her. "So you're punishing me," he said. "For agreeing to help Moash. That's why I'm having trouble with the Stormlight."

Syl followed along behind the cremling, which was a kind of beetle with a round, iridescent shell.

"Syl?" Kaladin asked. "Are you all right? You seem . . ."

Like you were before. When we first met. It made a feeling of dread rise within him to acknowledge it. If his powers were withdrawing, was it because the bond itself was weakening?

She looked up at him, and her eyes became more focused, her expression like that of her normal self. "You have to decide what you want, Kaladin," she said.

"You don't like Moash's plan," Kaladin said. "Are you trying to force me to change my mind regarding him?"

She scrunched up her face. "I don't want to *force* you to do anything. You have to do what you think is right."

"That's what I'm trying to do!"

"No. I don't think you are."

"Fine. I'll tell Moash and his friends that I'm out, that I'm not going to help them."

"But you gave Moash your word!"

"I gave my word to Dalinar too. . . ."

She drew her lips to a line, meeting his eyes.

"That's the problem, isn't it," Kaladin whispered. "I've made two promises, and I can't keep my word to both." Oh, storms. Was this the sort of thing that had destroyed the Knights Radiant?

What happened to your honorspren when you confronted them with a choice like this? A broken vow either way.

Idiot, Kaladin thought at himself. It seemed he couldn't make any right choices these days.

"What do I do, Syl?" he whispered.

She flitted up until she was standing in the air just before him, eyes meeting his. "You must speak the Words."

"I don't know them."

"Find them." She looked toward the sky. "Find them soon, Kaladin. And no, simply telling Moash you won't help isn't going to work. We've gone too far for that. You need to do what your heart needs to do." She rose upward toward the sky.

"Stay with me, Syl," he whispered after her, standing. "I'll figure this out. Just . . . don't lose yourself. Please. I need you."

Nearby, gears on Dalinar's bridge mechanism turned as soldiers twisted levers, and the entire thing started to unfold.

"Stop, stop, *stop!*" Shallan Davar jogged up, a flurry of red hair and blue silk, a large floppy hat on her head to keep off the sun. Two of her guards jogged after her, but neither was Gaz.

Kaladin spun about, alarmed at her tone, searching for signs of the Assassin in White.

Shallan, puffing, raised her safehand to her chest. "Storms, what is wrong with palanquin porters? They absolutely refuse to move quickly. 'It's not stately,' they say. Well, I don't really *do* stately. All right, give me a minute, then you can continue."

She settled down on a rock near the bridge. The baffled soldiers regarded her as she dug out her drawing pad, then started sketching. "All right," she said. "Continue. I've been trying all *day* to get a progressive sketch of that bridge as it unfolds. Storming porters."

What a bizarre woman.

The soldiers hesitantly continued positioning the bridge, unfolding it beneath the watchful eyes of three of Dalinar's engineers—widowed wives of his fallen officers. Several carpenters were also on hand to work at their orders if the bridge got stuck or a piece snapped.

Kaladin gripped his spear, trying to sort through his emotions regarding Syl, and the promises he'd made. Surely he could work this out somehow. Couldn't he?

Seeing this bridge intruded on his mind with thoughts of bridge runs, and he found that a welcome distraction. He could see why Sadeas had preferred the simple, if brutal, method of the bridge crews. Those bridges were faster, cheaper, and less prone to problems. These massive things were ponderous, like big ships trying to maneuver in a bay.

Armored bridge runners is the natural solution, Kaladin thought. *Men with shields, with full support from the army to get them into position. You could have fast, mobile bridges, but also not leave men to be slaughtered.*

Of course, Sadeas had wanted the bridgemen killed, as bait to keep arrows away from his soldiers.

One of the carpenters helping with the bridge—examining one of the wooden steadying pins and talking about carving a new one—was familiar to Kaladin. The stout man had a birthmark across his forehead, shaded by the carpenter's cap he wore.

Kaladin knew that face. Had the man been one of Dalinar's soldiers, one of those who had lost the will to fight following the slaughter on the Tower? Some of those had switched to other duties in camp.

He was distracted as Moash walked over, raising a hand toward Bridge Four, who cheered him. Moash's brilliant Shardplate—which he'd had repainted blue with red accents at the points—looked surprisingly natural on him. It hadn't even been a week yet, but Moash walked in the armor easily.

He stepped up to Kaladin, then knelt down on one knee, Plate clinking. He saluted, arm across chest.

His eyes . . . they *were* lighter in color; tan instead of deep brown as they'd once been. He wore his Shardblade strapped across his back in a guarded sheath. Only one more day until he had it bonded.

"You don't need to salute me, Moash," Kaladin said. "You're lighteyed now. You outrank me by a mile or two."

"I'll never outrank you, Kal," Moash said, faceplate of his helm up. "You're my captain. Forever." He grinned. "But I can't tell you how much storming *fun* it is to watch the lighteyes try to figure out how to deal with me."

"Your eyes are really changing."

"Yeah," Moash said. "But I'm not one of them, you hear me? I'm one of us. Bridge Four. I'm our . . . secret weapon."

"Secret?" Kaladin asked, raising an eyebrow. "They've probably heard about you all the way in *Iri* by now, Moash. You're the first darkeyed man to be given a Blade and Plate in over a lifetime."

Dalinar had even granted Moash lands and a stipend from them, a lavish sum, and not just by bridgeman standards. Moash still stopped by for stew some nights, but not all. He was too busy arranging his new quarters.

There was nothing wrong with that. It was natural. It was also part of why Kaladin had turned down the Blade himself—and perhaps why he'd always been worried about showing his powers to the lighteyes. Even if they didn't find a way to take the abilities from him—he knew that fear was irrational, though he felt it all the same—they might find a way to take Bridge Four from him. His men . . . his very self.

They might not be the ones who take it from you, Kaladin thought. *You might be doing it to yourself, better than any lighteyes could.*

The thought nauseated him.

"We're getting close," Moash said softly as Kaladin took out his water-skin.

"Close?" Kaladin asked. He lowered the waterskin and looked over his shoulder across the plateaus. "I thought we still had a few hours to go before we reached the dead chrysalis."

It was far out, almost as far out as the armies went on bridge runs. Bethab and Thanadal had claimed it yesterday.

"Not *that*," Moash said, looking to the side. "Other things."

"Oh. Moash, are you . . . I mean . . ."

"Kal," Moash said. "You're with us, right? You said it."

Two promises. Syl told him to follow his heart.

"Kaladin," Moash said, more solemnly. "You gave me these Shards, even after you were angry with me for disobeying you. There's a reason. You know, deep down, that what I'm doing is right. It's the only solution."

Kaladin nodded.

Moash glanced around, then stood up, Plate clinking. He leaned in to whisper. "Don't worry. Graves says you aren't going to have to do much. We just need an opening."

Kaladin felt sick. "We can't do it when Dalinar is in the warcamp," he whispered. "I won't risk him being hurt."

"No problem," Moash said. "We feel the same way. We'll wait for the right moment. The newest plan is to hit the king with an arrow, so there's no risk of implicating you or anyone else. You lead him to the right spot, and Graves will fell the king with his own bow. He's an excellent shot."

An arrow. It felt so cowardly.

It needed to be done. It *needed* to be.

Moash patted him on the shoulder, stepping off in his clinking Shard-plate. Storms. All Kaladin had to do was lead the king into a specific spot . . . that, and betray Dalinar's trust in him.

And if I don't help kill the king, won't I be betraying justice and honor? The king had murdered—or as good as murdered—many people, some through indifference, others through incompetence. And storms, Dalinar wasn't innocent either. If he'd been as noble as he pretended, wouldn't he have seen Roshone imprisoned, rather than shipped off somewhere where he "couldn't do any more harm"?

Kaladin walked over to the bridge, watching the men march across. Shallan Davar sat primly on a rock, continuing her sketches of the bridge mechanism. Adolin had climbed off his horse and handed it to some grooms for watering. He waved Kaladin over.

"Princeling?" Kaladin asked, stepping up.

"The assassin has been seen out here," Adolin said. "On the Plains at night."

"Yes. I heard the scout telling your father about it."

"We need a plan. What if he attacks out here?"

"I hope he does."

Adolin looked to him, frowning.

"From what I saw," Kaladin said, "and from what I've learned about the assassin's initial attack on the old king, he depends on confusion in his victims. He jumps off walls and onto ceilings; he sends men falling the wrong direction. Well, there aren't any walls or ceilings out here."

"So he can just full-on fly," Adolin said with a grimace.

"Yes," Kaladin said, pointing with a smile, "since we have, what is it, *three hundred* archers with us?"

Kaladin had used his abilities effectively against Parshendi arrows, and so perhaps archers wouldn't be able to kill the assassin. But he imagined it would be hard for the man to fight with wave after wave of arrows flying at him.

Adolin nodded slowly. "I'll talk to them, get them ready for the possibility." He started walking toward the bridge, so Kaladin joined him. They passed Shallan, who was still absorbed in her sketching. She didn't even notice Adolin waving at her. Lighteyed women and their diversions. Kaladin shook his head.

"Do you know anything about women, bridgeboy?" Adolin asked, looking over his shoulder and watching Shallan as the two of them crossed the bridge.

"Lighteyed women?" Kaladin asked. "Nothing. Thankfully."

"People think I know a lot about women," Adolin said. "The truth is, I know how to get them—how to make them laugh, how to make them interested. I don't know how to keep them." He hesitated. "I really want to keep this one."

"So . . . tell her that, maybe?" Kaladin said, thinking back to Tarah, and the mistakes he'd made.

"Do such things work on darkeyed women?"

"You're asking the wrong man," Kaladin said. "I haven't had much time for women lately. I was too busy trying to avoid being killed."

Adolin seemed to be barely listening. "Perhaps I could say something like that to her. . . . Seems too simple, and she's anything but simple. . . ." He turned back to Kaladin. "Anyway. Assassin in White. We need more of a plan than just telling the archers to be ready."

"Do you have any ideas?" Kaladin said.

"You won't have a Shardblade, but won't need one, because of . . . you know."

"I know?" Kaladin felt a spike of alarm.

"Yeah . . . you know." Adolin glanced away and shrugged, as if trying to act nonchalant. "That thing."

"What thing?"

"The thing . . . with the . . . um, stuff?"

He doesn't know, Kaladin realized. *He's just fishing, trying to figure out why I can fight so well.*

And he's doing a really, really bad job of it.

Kaladin relaxed, and even found himself smiling at Adolin's awkward attempt. It was nice to feel an emotion other than panic or worry. "I don't think you have any idea what you're talking about."

Adolin scowled. "There's something odd about you, bridgeboy," he said. "Admit it."

"I admit nothing."

"You survived that fall with the assassin," Adolin said. "And at first, I worried you were working with him. Now . . ."

"Now what?"

"Well, I've decided that whatever you are, you're on my side." Adolin sighed. "Anyway, the assassin. My instincts say the best plan is the one we used when fighting together in the arena. You distract him while I kill him."

"That could work, though I worry that he's not the type to let himself get distracted."

"Neither was Relis," Adolin said. "We'll do it, bridgeboy. You and I. We're going to bring that monster down."

"We'll need to be fast," Kaladin said. "He'll win a drawn-out fight. And Adolin, strike for the spine or the head. Don't try a weakening blow first. Go right for the kill."

Adolin frowned at him. "Why?"

"I saw something when the two of us fell together," Kaladin said. "I cut him, but he healed the wound somehow."

"I have a Blade. He won't be able to heal from *that* . . . right?"

"Best to not find out. Strike to kill. Trust me."

Adolin met his eyes. "Oddly, I do. Trust you, I mean. It's a very strange sensation."

"Yeah, well, I'll try to hold myself back from going skipping across the plateau in joy."

Adolin grinned. "I'd pay to see that."

"Me skipping?"

"You happy," Adolin said, laughing. "You've got a face like a storm! I half think you could *frighten off* a storm."

Kaladin grunted.

Adolin laughed again, slapping him on the shoulder, then turned as Shallan finally crossed the bridge, her sketching apparently done. She looked to Adolin fondly, and as he reached out to take her hand, she rose up on her toes and gave him a kiss on the cheek. Adolin drew back, startled. Alethi were more reserved than that in public.

Shallan grinned at him. Then she turned and gasped, raising a hand to her mouth. Kaladin jumped, *again,* looking for danger—but Shallan just went dashing off to a nearby clump of rocks.

Adolin raised his hand to his cheek, then looked to Kaladin with a grin. "She probably saw an interesting bug."

"No, it's moss!" Shallan called back.

"Ah, of course," Adolin said, strolling over, Kaladin following. "Moss. So *exciting.*"

"Hush, you," Shallan said, wagging her pencil at him as she bent down, inspecting the rocks. "The moss grows in a strange pattern here. What could cause that?"

"Alcohol," Adolin said.

She glanced at him.

He shrugged. "Makes *me* do crazy things." He looked at Kaladin, who shook his head. "That was *funny,*" Adolin said. "It was a joke! Well, kind of."

"Oh hush," Shallan said. "This looks almost like the same pattern as a flowering rockbud, the kind common here on the Plains. . . ." She started sketching.

Kaladin folded his arms. Then he sighed.

"What does that sigh mean?" Adolin asked him.

"Boredom," Kaladin said, glancing back at the army, still crossing the bridge. With a force of three thousand—that was about half of Dalinar's current army, following heavy recruitment—moving out here took time. On bridge runs, these crossings had felt so quick. Kaladin had always been exhausted, savoring the chance to rest. "I guess out here, it's so barren that there's not much to get excited about other than moss."

"You hush too," Shallan told him. "Go polish your bridge or something." She leaned in, then poked her pencil at a bug that was crawling across the moss. "Ah . . ." she said, then hurriedly scribbled some notes. "Anyway, you're wrong. There's a *lot* out here to get excited about, if you look in the right places. Some of the soldiers said a chasmfiend has been spotted. Do you think it might attack us?"

"You sound entirely too hopeful saying that, Shallan," Adolin said.

"Well, I *do* still need a good sketch of one."

"We'll get you to the chrysalis. That will have to be enough."

Shallan's scholarship was an excuse; the truth was obvious to Kaladin. Dalinar had brought an unusual number of scouts with him today, and Kaladin suspected once they reached the chrysalis—which was on the border of unexplored lands—they'd range ahead and gather information. This was all preparation for Dalinar's expedition.

"I don't understand why we need so many soldiers," Shallan said, noticing Kaladin's gaze as he studied the army. "Didn't you say the Parshendi haven't been showing up to fight over chrysalises lately?"

"No, they haven't," Adolin said. "That's precisely *what* makes us worried."

Kaladin nodded. "Whenever your enemy changes established tactics, you need to worry. It could mean they're getting desperate. Desperation is very, very dangerous."

"You're good at military thinking, for a bridgeboy," Adolin said.

"Coincidentally," Kaladin said, "you're good at not being unobnoxious, for a prince."

"Thanks," Adolin said.

"That was an insult, dear," Shallan said.

"What?" Adolin said. "It was?"

She nodded, still sketching, though she glanced up to eye Kaladin. He met the expression calmly.

"Adolin," Shallan said, turning back to the small rock formation in front of her, "would you slay this moss for me, please?"

"Slay . . . the moss." He looked at Kaladin, who just shrugged. How was he to know what a lighteyed woman meant? They were a strange breed.

"Yes," Shallan said, standing up. "Give that moss, and the rock behind it, a good chop. As a favor for your betrothed."

Adolin looked baffled, but he did as she asked, summoning his Shardblade and hacking at the moss and rock. The top of the small pile of stones slipped free, cut with ease, and clattered to the floor of the plateau.

Shallan stepped up eagerly, crouching down beside the perfectly flat top of the sliced stone. "Mmm," she said, nodding to herself. She started sketching.

Adolin dismissed his Blade. "Women!" he said, shrugging at Kaladin. Then he went jogging off to get a drink without asking her for an explana-

tion.

Kaladin took a step after him, but then hesitated. What *did* Shallan find so interesting here? This woman was a puzzle, and he knew he wouldn't be completely comfortable until he understood her. She had too much access to Adolin, and therefore Dalinar, to leave uninvestigated.

He stepped closer, looking over her shoulder as she drew. "Strata," he said. "You're counting the strata of crem to guess how old the rock is."

"Good guess," she said, "but this is a bad location for strata dating. The wind blows across the plateaus too strongly, and the crem doesn't collect in pools evenly. So the strata here are erratic and inaccurate."

Kaladin frowned, narrowing his eyes. The cross section of rock was normal cremstone on the outside, some strata visible as different shades of brown. The center of the stone, though, was white. You didn't see white rock like that often; it had to be quarried. Which meant this was either a very strange occurrence, or . . .

"There was a structure here once," Kaladin said. "A long time ago. It must have taken centuries for the crem to get that thick on something sticking out of the ground."

She glanced at him. "You're smarter than you look." Then, turning back to her drawing, she added, "Good thing . . ."

He grunted. "Why does everything you say have to include some quip? Are you that desperate to prove how clever you are?"

"Perhaps I'm merely annoyed at you for taking advantage of Adolin."

"Advantage?" Kaladin asked. "Because I called him obnoxious?"

"You deliberately said it in a way you expected he wouldn't understand. To make him look like a fool. He's trying very hard to be nice to you."

"Yes," Kaladin said. "He's always so munificent to all of the little dark-eyes who flock around to worship him."

Shallan snapped her pencil against the page. "You really are a hateful man, aren't you? Underneath the mock boredom, the dangerous glares, the growls—you just hate people, is that it?"

"What? No, I—"

"Adolin is *trying*. He feels bad for what happened to you, and he's doing what he can to make up for it. He is a *good man*. Is it too much for you to stop provoking him?"

"He calls me bridgeboy," Kaladin said, feeling stubborn. "He's been provoking *me*."

"Yes, because *he* is the one storming around with alternating scowls and insults," Shallan said. "Adolin Kholin, the most difficult man to get along with on the Shattered Plains. I mean *look* at him! He's so unlikable!"

She gestured with the pencil toward where Adolin was laughing with the darkeyed water boys. The groom walked up with Adolin's horse, and Adolin took his Shardplate helm off the carrying post, handing it over, letting one of the water boys try it on. It was ridiculously large on the lad.

Kaladin flushed as the boy took a Shardbearer's pose, and they all laughed again. Kaladin looked back to Shallan, who folded her arms, drawing pad resting on the flat-topped cut rock before her. She smirked at him.

Insufferable woman. *Bah!*

Kaladin left her and hiked across the rough ground to join Bridge Four, where he insisted on taking a turn hauling the bridge, despite Teft's protests that he was "above that sort of thing" now. He was no storming lighteyes. He'd never be above doing an honest day's work.

The familiar weight of the bridge settled onto his shoulders. Rock was right. It *did* feel lighter than it once had. He smiled as he heard cursing from Lopen's cousins, who—like Renarin—were being initiated on this run into their first bridge carry.

They hiked the bridge over a chasm—crossing on one of Dalinar's larger, less mobile ones—and started across the plateau. For a time, marching at the front of Bridge Four, Kaladin could imagine that his life was simple. No plateau assaults, no arrows, no assassins or bodyguarding. Just him, his team, and a bridge.

Unfortunately, as they neared the other side of the large plateau, he started to feel weary and—by reflex—tried to suck in some Stormlight to bolster him. It wouldn't come.

Life was not simple. It never *had* been, certainly not while running bridges. To pretend otherwise was to paint over the past.

He helped set the bridge down, then—noticing the vanguard moving out in front of the army—he and the bridgemen shoved their bridge into place across the chasm. The vanguard cheerfully welcomed the chance to get ahead, marching over the bridge and securing the next plateau.

Kaladin and the others followed, then—a half hour later—they let the vanguard onto the next plateau. They continued like that for a time, waiting for Dalinar's bridge to arrive before crossing, then leading the vanguard onto the next plateau. Hours passed—sweaty, muscle-straining hours. Good hours. Kaladin didn't come to any realizations about the king, or his place in the man's potential assassination. But for the moment, he carried his bridge and enjoyed the progress of an army moving toward their goal beneath an open sky.

As the day grew long, they approached the target plateau, where the hollowed-out chrysalis awaited Shallan's study. Kaladin and Bridge Four let the vanguard across as they'd been doing, then settled in to wait. Eventually, the bulk of the army approached, and Dalinar's lumbering bridges moved into position, ratcheting down to span the chasm.

Kaladin gulped deeply of warm water as he watched. He washed his face with the water, then wiped his brow. They were getting close. This plateau was far out onto the Plains, almost to the Tower itself. Getting back would take hours, assuming they moved at the same relaxed speed they had taken getting out here. It would be well after dark when they returned to the warcamps.

If Dalinar does want to assault the center of the Shattered Plains, Kaladin thought, *it will take days of marching, all the while exposed on the plateaus, with the potential of being surrounded and cut off from the warcamps.*

The Weeping *would* make a great chance for that. Four straight weeks of rain, but no highstorms. This was the off year, when there wouldn't even be a highstorm on Lightday in the middle—part of the thousand-day cycle of two years that made up a full storm rotation. Still, he knew that many Alethi patrols had tried exploring eastward before. They'd all been destroyed by highstorms, chasmfiends, or Parshendi assault teams.

Nothing short of an all-out, full-on movement of resources toward the center would work. An assault that would leave Dalinar, and whoever came with him, isolated.

Dalinar's bridge thumped down into place. Kaladin's men traversed their own bridge and prepared to pull it across to go move the vanguard. Kaladin crossed, then waved them on ahead of him. He walked over to where the larger bridge had settled down.

Dalinar was crossing it while walking with some of his scouts, all vaulters, with servants behind carrying long poles. "I want you to spread out," the highprince said to them. "We won't have much time before we need to head back. I want a survey of as many plateaus as you can see from here. The more of our route we can plan now, the less time we'll have to waste during the actual assault."

The scouts nodded, saluting as he dismissed them. He stepped off the bridge and nodded to Kaladin. Behind them, Dalinar's generals, scribes, and engineers crossed the bridge. They'd be followed by the bulk of the army, and finally the rearguard.

"I hear you've been building mobile bridges, sir," Kaladin said. "You realize those mechanical ones are too slow for your assault, I assume."

Dalinar nodded. "But I will have soldiers carry them. No need for your men to do so."

"Sir, that is thoughtful of you, but I don't think you have to worry. The bridge crews will carry for you, if ordered. Many of them will probably welcome the familiarity."

"I thought you and your men considered assignment to those bridge crews a death sentence, soldier," Dalinar said.

"The way Sadeas ran them, it was. You could do a better job. Armored men, trained in formations, running the bridges. Soldiers marching in front with shields. Archers with instructions to defend the bridge crews. Besides, the danger is only for an assault."

Dalinar nodded. "Prepare the crews, then. Having your men on the bridges will free the soldiers in case we get attacked." He started to walk across the plateau, but one of the carpenters on the other side of the chasm called to him. Dalinar turned and started to cross the bridge again.

He passed officers and scribes crossing the bridge, including Adolin and Shallan, who walked side by side. She'd given up on the palanquin and he had given up on his horse, and she seemed to be explaining to him about the hidden remnants of a structure she'd found inside that rock earlier.

Behind them, on the other side of the chasm, stood the worker who had called Dalinar back across.

It's that same carpenter, Kaladin thought. The stout man with the cap and the birthmark. *Where* have *I seen him . . . ?*

It clicked. Sadeas's lumberyards. The man had been one of the carpenters there, overseeing the construction of bridges.

Kaladin started running.

He was charging toward the bridge before the connection fully solidified in his mind. Ahead of him, Adolin spun immediately and started running, searching for whatever danger Kaladin had spotted. He left a bewildered Shallan standing in the bridge's center. Kaladin approached her in a rush.

The carpenter grabbed a lever on the side of the bridge contraption.

"The carpenter, Adolin!" Kaladin screamed. "Stop that man!"

Dalinar still stood on the bridge. The highprince had been distracted by something else. What? Kaladin realized he had heard something too. Horns, the call that the enemy had been spotted.

It happened all in an instant. Dalinar turning toward the horns. The carpenter pulling the lever, Adolin in his glimmering Shardplate reaching Dalinar.

The bridge lurched.

Then it collapsed.

*Rayse is captive. He cannot leave the system he now inhabits. His
destructive potential is, therefore, inhibited.*

As the bridge fell out from beneath him, Kaladin reached for Stormlight.

Nothing.

Panic surged through him. His stomach dropped and he tumbled into
the air.

The fall into the darkness of the chasm was a brief moment, but also an
eternity. He caught a glimpse of Shallan and several men in blue uniforms
falling and flailing in terror.

Like a drowning man struggling toward the surface, Kaladin thrashed
for the Stormlight. He would *not* die this way! The sky was his! The winds
were his. The chasms were his.

He would not!

Syl screamed, a terrified, painful sound that vibrated Kaladin's very
bones. In that moment, he got a breath of Stormlight, life itself.

He crashed into the ground at the bottom of the chasm and all went
black.

⁂

Swimming through pain.

The pain washed over him, a liquid, but did not get *inside*. His skin kept
it out.

WHAT HAVE YOU DONE? The distant voice sounded like rumbling thunder.

Kaladin gasped and opened his eyes, and the pain crawled inside. Suddenly, his entire body hurt.

He lay on his back, staring upward at a streak of light in the air. Syl? No . . . no, that was sunlight. The opening at the top of the chasm, high above him. This far out onto the Shattered Plains, the chasms here were hundreds of feet deep.

Kaladin groaned and sat up. That strip of light seemed impossibly distant. He'd been swallowed by the darkness, and the chasm nearby was shadowed, obscure. He put a hand to his head.

I got some Stormlight right at the end, he thought. *I survived. But that scream!* It haunted him, echoing in his mind. It had sounded too much like the scream he'd heard when touching the duelist's Shardblade in the arena.

Check for wounds, his father's teachings whispered from the back of his mind. The body could go into shock with a bad break or wound, and not notice the damage that had been done. He went through the motions of checking his limbs for breaks, and did not reach for any of the spheres in his pouch. He didn't want to light the gloom, and potentially face the dead around him.

Was Dalinar among them? Adolin had been running toward his father. Had the prince managed to get to Dalinar before the bridge collapsed? He'd been wearing Plate, and had jumped at the end.

Kaladin felt at his legs, then his ribs. He found aches and scrapes, but nothing broken or ripped. That Stormlight he'd held at the end . . . it had protected him, perhaps even healed him, before running out. He finally reached into his pouch and fished out spheres, but found those all drained. He tried his pocket, then froze as he heard something scraping nearby.

He leaped to his feet and spun, wishing he had a weapon. The chasm bottom grew *brighter.* A steady glow revealed fanlike frillblooms and draping vines on the walls, gathered twigs and moss on the floor in patches. Was that a voice? He felt a surreal moment of confusion as shadows moved on the wall ahead of him.

Then someone wandered around the corner, wearing a silk dress and carrying a pack over her shoulder. Shallan Davar.

She screamed when she saw him, throwing the pack to the ground and stumbling backward, hands to her sides. She even dropped her sphere.

Rolling his arm in its socket, Kaladin stepped closer into the light. "Calm down," he said. "It's me."

"Stormfather!" Shallan said, scrambling to grab the sphere off the ground again. She stepped forward, thrusting the light toward him. "It *is* you . . . the bridgeman. How . . . ?"

"I don't know," he lied, looking upward. "I've got a wicked crick in my neck and my elbow hurts like thunder. What happened?"

"Someone threw the emergency latch on the bridge."

"What emergency latch?"

"It topples the bridge into the chasm."

"Sounds like a storming *stupid* thing to have," Kaladin said, fishing in his pocket for his other spheres. He glanced at them covertly. Also drained. Storms. He'd used them all?

"Depends," Shallan said. "What if your men have retreated over the bridge and enemies are pouring across it after you? The emergency latch is supposed to have some kind of safety lock so it can't be thrown by accident, but you can release it in a hurry if you need to."

He grunted as Shallan shone her sphere past him toward where the two halves of the bridge had smashed into the ground of the chasm. There were the bodies he'd expected.

He looked. He *had* to. No sign of Dalinar, though several of the officers and lighteyed ladies who had been crossing the bridge lay in twisted, broken heaps on the ground. A drop of two hundred feet or more did not leave survivors.

Except Shallan. Kaladin didn't remember grabbing her as he fell, but he didn't remember much of that fall beyond Syl's scream. That *scream . . .*

Well, he must have managed to grab Shallan by reflex, infusing her with Stormlight to slow her fall. She looked disheveled, her blue dress scuffed and her hair a mess, but she was apparently otherwise unharmed.

"I woke up down here in the darkness," Shallan said. "It's been a while since we fell."

"How can you tell?"

"It's almost dark up there," Shallan said. "It will be night soon. When I woke I heard echoes of yelling. Fighting. I saw something glowing from around that corner. Turned out to be a soldier who had fallen, his sphere pouch ripped." She shivered visibly. "He'd been killed by something before the fall."

"Parshendi," Kaladin said. "Just before the bridge collapsed, I heard horns from the vanguard. We got attacked." Damnation. That probably meant that Dalinar had retreated, assuming he'd actually survived. There was nothing worth fighting for out here.

"Give me one of those spheres," Kaladin said.

She handed one over, and Kaladin went searching among the fallen. For pulses, ostensibly, but really for any equipment or spheres.

"You think any of these might be alive?" Shallan asked, voice sounding small in the otherwise silent chasm.

"Well, *we* survived somehow."

"How do you think that happened?" Shallan said, looking upward toward the gap far, far above.

"I saw some windspren just before we fell," Kaladin said. "I've heard folktales of them protecting a person as he falls. Perhaps that's what happened."

Shallan went silent as he searched the bodies. "Yes," she finally said. "That sounds logical."

She seemed convinced. Good. So long as she didn't start wondering about the stories told of "Kaladin Stormblessed."

Nobody else was alive, but he verified for certain that neither Dalinar nor Adolin were among the corpses.

I was a fool not to spot that an assassination attempt was coming, Kaladin thought. Sadeas had tried hard to undermine Dalinar at the feast a few days back, with the revelation of the visions. It was a classic ploy. Discredit your enemy, *then* kill him, to make certain he didn't become a martyr.

The corpses had little of value. A handful of spheres, some writing implements that Shallan greedily snatched up and stuffed into her satchel. No maps. Kaladin had no specific idea where they were. And with night imminent . . .

"What do we do?" Shallan asked softly, staring at the darkened realm, with its unexpected shadows, its gently moving frills, vines, polyplike staccatos, their tendrils out and wafting in the air.

Kaladin remembered his first times down in this place, which always felt too green, too muggy, too alien. Nearby, two skulls peeked out from beneath the moss, watching. Splashing sounded from a distant pool, which made Shallan spin wildly. Though the chasms were a home to Kaladin now, he did not deny that at times they were distinctly unnerving.

"It's safer down here than it seems," Kaladin said. "During my time in Sadeas's army, I spent days upon days in the chasms, gathering salvage from the fallen. Just watch for rotspren."

"And the chasmfiends?" Shallan asked, spinning to look in another direction as a cremling scuttled along the wall.

"I never saw one." Which was true, though he *had* seen a shadow of one once, scraping its way down a distant chasm. Even thinking of that day gave him chills. "They aren't as common as people claim. The real danger is highstorms. You see, if it rains, even far away from here—"

"Yes, flash flooding," Shallan said. "Very dangerous in a slot canyon. I've read about them."

"I'm sure that will be very helpful," Kaladin said. "You mentioned some dead soldiers nearby?"

She pointed, and he strode in that direction. She followed, sticking close to his light. He found a few dead spearmen who had been shoved off the plateau above. The wounds were fresh. Just beyond them was a dead Parshendi, also fresh.

The Parshendi man had uncut gems in his beard. Kaladin touched one, hesitated, then tried to draw the Stormlight out. Nothing happened. He sighed, then bowed his head for the fallen, before finally pulling a spear from underneath one of the bodies and standing up. The light above had faded to a deep blue. Night.

"So, we wait?" Shallan asked.

"For what?" Kaladin asked, raising the spear to his shoulder.

"For them to come back . . ." She trailed off. "They're not coming back for us, are they?"

"They'll assume we're dead. Storms, we *should* be dead. We're too far out for a corpse-recovery operation, I'd guess. That's doubly true since the Parshendi attacked." He rubbed his chin. "I suppose we could wait for Dalinar's major expedition. He was indicating he'd come this way, searching for the center. It's only a few days away, right?"

Shallan paled. Well, she paled *further*. That light skin of hers was so strange. It and the red hair made her look like a very small Horneater. "Dalinar is planning to march just after the final highstorm before the Weeping. That storm is close. And it will involve lots, and lots, and *lots* of rain."

"Bad idea, then."

"You could say so."

He'd tried to imagine what a highstorm would be like down here. He had seen the aftereffects when salvaging with Bridge Four. The twisted, broken corpses. The piles of refuse crushed against walls and into cracks. Boulders as tall as a man casually washed through chasms until they got wedged between two walls, sometimes fifty feet up in the air.

"When?" he asked. "*When* is that highstorm?"

She stared at him, then dug into her satchel, flipping through sheets of paper with her freehand while holding the satchel through the fabric of her safehand. She waved him over with his sphere, as she had to tuck hers away.

He held it up for her as she looked over a page with lines of script. "Tomorrow night," she said softly. "Just after first moonset."

Kaladin grunted, holding up his sphere and inspecting the chasm. *We're just to the north of the chasm we fell from,* he thought. *So the way back should be . . . that way?*

"All right then," Shallan said. She took a deep breath, then snapped her satchel closed. "We walk back, and we start immediately."

"You don't want to sit for a moment and catch your breath?"

"My breath is quite well caught," Shallan said. "If it's all the same to you, I'd rather be moving. Once back, we can sit sipping mulled wine and laugh about how silly it was of us to hurry all that way, since we had so much time to spare. I'd like very much to feel that foolish. You?"

"Yeah." He liked the chasms. It didn't mean he wanted to risk a highstorm in one of them. "You don't have a map in that satchel, do you?"

"No," Shallan said with a grimace. "I didn't bring my own. Brightness Velat has the maps. I was using hers. But I might be able to remember some of what I've seen."

"Then I think we should go this way," Kaladin said, pointing. He started walking.

⁘

The bridgeman started walking off in the direction he'd pointed, not even giving her a chance to state her opinion on the matter. Shallan kept a huff to herself, snatching up her pack—she'd found some waterskins on the soldiers—and satchel. She hurried after him, her dress catching on something she *hoped* was a very white stick.

The tall bridgeman deftly stepped over and around debris, eyes forward. Why did *he* have to be the one who survived? Though to be honest, she was pleased to find anyone. Walking down here alone would not have been pleasant. At least he was superstitious enough to believe that he'd been saved by some twist of fate and spren. She had no idea how she'd saved herself, let alone him. Pattern rode on her skirts, and before she'd found the bridgeman, he'd been speculating that the Stormlight had kept her alive.

Alive after a fall of at least two hundred feet? It only proved how little she knew about her abilities. Stormfather! She'd saved this man too. She was sure of it; he'd been falling right beside her as they plummeted.

But *how*? And could she figure out how to do it again?

She hurried to keep up with him. Blasted Alethi and their freakishly long legs. He marched like a soldier, giving no thought to how she had to pick her way more carefully than he did. She didn't want to get her skirt caught on *every* branch they passed.

They reached a pool of water on the chasm floor, and he hopped up onto a log that bridged the water, barely breaking stride as he crossed. She stopped at the edge.

He looked back at her, holding up a sphere. "You aren't going to demand I give you my boots again, are you?"

She raised a foot, revealing the military-style boots she wore underneath her dress. That got him to cock an eyebrow.

"I wasn't *about* to come out onto the Shattered Plains in slippers," she said, blushing. "Besides, nobody can see your shoes under a dress this long." She regarded the log.

"You want me to help you across?" he asked.

"Actually, I'm wondering how the trunk of a stumpweight tree got here," she confessed. "They can't possibly be native to this area of the Shattered Plains. Too cold out here. It might have grown along the coast, but a highstorm really carried it that far? Four hundred miles?"

"You're not going to demand we stop for you to sketch a picture, are you?"

"Oh please," Shallan said, stepping up onto the log and picking her way across. "Do you know how many sketches I have of stumpweights?"

The other things down here were a different matter entirely. As they continued on their way, Shallan used her sphere—which she had to juggle in her freehand, trying to manage it along with the satchel in her safehand and the pack over her shoulder—to illuminate her surroundings. They were stunning. Dozens of different varieties of vines, frillblooms of red, orange, and violet. Tiny rockbuds on the walls, and haspers in little clusters, opening and closing their shells as if breathing.

Motes of lifespren drifted around a patch of shalebark that grew in knobby patterns like fingers. You almost never saw that formation above. The tiny glowing specks of green light drifted through the chasm toward an entire wall of fist-size tube plants with little feelers wiggling out the top. As Shallan passed, the feelers retracted in a wave running up the wall. She gasped softly and took a Memory.

The bridgeman stopped ahead of her, turning. "Well?"

"Don't you even notice how beautiful it is?"

He looked up at the wall of tube plants. She was certain she'd read about those somewhere, but the name escaped her.

The bridgeman continued on his way.

Shallan jogged after him, pack thumping against her back. She almost tripped over a snarled pile of dead vines and sticks as she reached him. She cursed, hopping on one foot to stay upright before steadying herself.

He reached out and took the pack from her.

Finally, she thought. "Thank you."

He grunted, slipping it over his shoulder before continuing on without another word. They reached a crossroads in the chasms, a path going right and another going left. They'd have to weave around the next plateau before them to continue westward. Shallan looked up at the rift—getting a good picture in her mind of how this side of the plateau looked—as Kaladin chose one of the paths.

"This is going to take a while," he said. "Even longer than it took to get out here. We had to wait upon the whole army then, but we could also cut through the centers of the plateaus. Having to go around every one of them will add a lot to the trip."

"Well, at least the companionship is pleasant."

He eyed her.

"For you, I mean," she added.

"Am I going to have to listen to you prattle all the way back?"

"Of course not," she said. "I also intend to do some blathering, a little nattering, and the occasional gibber. But not too much, lest I overdo a good thing."

"Great."

"I've been practicing my burble," she added.

"I just can't wait to hear."

"Oh, well, that was it, actually."

He studied her, those severe eyes of his boring into her own. She turned away from him. He didn't trust her, obviously. He was a bodyguard; she doubted that he trusted many people.

They reached another intersection, and Kaladin took longer to make this decision. She could see why—down here, it was difficult to determine which way was which. The plateau formations were varied and erratic. Some were long and thin, others almost perfectly round. They had knobs and peninsulas off to their sides, and that made a maze of the twisted paths between them. It should have been easy—there were few dead ends, after all, and so they really just had to keep moving westward.

But which direction was westward? It would be very, very easy to get lost down here.

"You're not picking our course at random, are you?" she asked.

"No."

"You seem to know a lot about these chasms."

"I do."

"Because the gloomy atmosphere matches your disposition, I assume."

He kept his eyes forward, walking without comment.

"Storms," she said, hurrying to catch up. "That was supposed to be lighthearted. What would it take to make you relax, bridgeboy?"

"I guess I'm just a . . . what was it again? A 'hateful man'?"

"I haven't seen any proof to the contrary."

"That's because you don't care to look, lighteyes. Everyone beneath you is just a plaything."

"What?" she said, taking it like a slap to the face. "Where would you get that idea?"

"It's obvious."

"To *whom*? To you only? *When* have you seen me treat someone of a lesser station like a plaything? Give me one example."

"When I was imprisoned," he said immediately, "for doing what any lighteyes would have been applauded for doing."

"And that was *my* fault?" she demanded.

"It's the fault of your entire class. Each time one of us is defrauded, enslaved, beaten, or broken, the blame rests upon all of you who support it. Even indirectly."

"Oh please," she said. "The world isn't fair? What a huge revelation! Some people in power abuse those they have power over? Amazing! When did this start happening?"

He gave no reply. He'd tied his spheres to the top of his spear with a pouch formed from the white handkerchief he'd found on one of the scribes. Held high, it lit the chasm nicely for them.

"I think," she said, tucking away her own sphere for convenience, "that you're just looking for excuses. Yes, you've been mistreated. I admit it. But I think *you're* the one who cares about eye color, that it's just easier for you to pretend that every lighteyes is abusing you because of your status. Have you ever asked yourself if there's a simpler explanation? Could it be that people don't like you, not because you're darkeyed, but because you're just a *huge pain in the neck*?"

He snorted, then moved on more quickly.

"No," Shallan said, practically running to keep even with him and his long stride. "You're not wiggling out of this. You don't get to imply that I'm abusing my station, then walk off without a response. You did this earlier, with Adolin. Now with me. What is your *problem*?"

"You want a better example of you playing with people beneath you?" Kaladin asked, dodging her question. "Fine. You stole my boots. You pretended to be someone you weren't and bullied a darkeyed guard you'd barely met. Is that a good enough example of you playing with someone you saw as beneath you?"

She stopped in her tracks. He was right, there. She wanted to blame Tyn's influence, but his comment cut the bite out of her argument.

He stopped ahead of her, looking back. Finally, he sighed. "Look," he said. "I'm not holding a grudge about the boots. From what I've seen lately, you're not as bad as the others. So let's just leave it at that."

"Not as bad as the others?" Shallan said, walking forward. "What a delightful compliment. Well, let's say you're right. Perhaps I *am* an insensitive rich woman. That doesn't change the fact that you can be downright mean and offensive, Kaladin Stormblessed."

He shrugged.

"That's it?" she asked. "I apologize, and all I get in return is a shrug?"

"I am what the lighteyes have made me to be."

"So you're not culpable at all," she said flatly. "For the way you act."

"I'd say not."

"Stormfather. I can't say anything to change the way you treat me, can I? You're just going to continue to be an intolerant, odious man, full of spite. Incapable of being pleasant around others. Your life must be very lonely."

That seemed to get under his skin, as his face turned red in the sphere-light. "I'm starting to revise my opinion," he said, "of you not being as bad as the others."

"Don't lie," she said. "You've never liked me. Right from the start. And not just because of the boots. I see how you watch me."

"That's because," he said, "I know you're lying through your smile at everyone you meet. The only time you seem honest is when you're insulting someone!"

"The only honest things I can say to you *are* insults."

"Bah!" he said. "I just . . . Bah! Why is it that being around you makes me want to claw my face off, woman?"

"I have special training," she said, glancing to the side. "And I collect faces." What was that?

"You can't just—"

He cut off as the scraping noise, echoing from one of the chasms, grew louder.

Kaladin immediately put his hand over his improvised sphere lantern, plunging them into darkness. In Shallan's estimation, that did *not* help. She stumbled toward him in the darkness, grabbing his arm with her free-hand. He was annoying, but he was also *there*.

The scraping continued. A sound like rock on rock. Or . . . carapace on rock.

"I guess," she whispered nervously, "having a shouting match in an echoing network of chasms was not terribly wise."

"Yeah."

"It's getting closer, isn't it?" she whispered.

"Yeah."

"So . . . run?"

The scraping seemed just beyond the next turn.

"Yeah," Kaladin said, pulling his hand off his spheres and charging away from the noise.

A variety of vinebud that
is unknown to me.

It is difficult to study,
as it mostly clings to the stone
above the waterline.

It blooms a tremendous flower
of bright leaves, and the vines
grow to be dozens of feet long!

The vines appear to seek, not
just water, but others of their
own kind, creating the occasional
tangle in the chasms above.

The volume seems incredibly
elastic! When withdrawn, both
the length and diameter visibly
compress more than any
variety I've ever seen.

A standard, though
very large variety of
Frillbloom grows here.

Whether this was Tanavast's design or not, millennia have passed
without Rayse taking the life of another of the sixteen. While I
mourn for the great suffering Rayse has caused, I do not believe we
could hope for a better outcome than this.

Kaladin scrambled down the chasm, leaping branches and refuse, splashing through puddles. The girl kept up better than he'd expected, but—hampered by her dress—she was nowhere near as swift as he was.

He held himself back, matching her pace. Exasperating though she might be, he wasn't going to abandon Adolin's betrothed to be eaten by a chasmfiend.

They reached an intersection and chose a path at random. At the next intersection, he only paused long enough to check to see if they were being followed.

They were. Thumping from behind them, claws on stone. Scraping. He grabbed the girl's satchel—he was already carrying her pack—as they ran down another corridor. Either Shallan was in excellent shape, or the panic got to her, because she didn't even seem winded when they reached the next intersection.

No time for hesitation. He barreled down a pathway, ears full of the sound of grinding carapace. A sudden four-voiced trump echoed through the chasm, as loud as a thousand horns being blown. Shallan screamed, though Kaladin barely heard her over the horrible sound.

The chasm plants withdrew in large waves. In moments, the entire place went from fecund to barren, like the world preparing for a highstorm.

They hit another intersection, and Shallan hesitated, looking back toward the sounds. She held her hands out, as if preparing to embrace the thing. Storming woman! He grabbed her and pulled her after him. They ran down two chasms without stopping.

It was still chasing, though he could only hear it. He had no idea how close it was, but it had their scent. Or their sound? He had no idea how they hunted.

Need a plan! Can't just—

At the next intersection, Shallan turned the opposite way from the one he had picked. Kaladin cursed, pounding to a stop and running after her.

"This is no time," he said, puffing, "to argue about—"

"Shut it," she said. "Follow."

She led them to an intersection, then another. Kaladin was feeling winded, his lungs protesting. Shallan stopped, then pointed and ran down a chasm. He followed, looking over his shoulder.

He could see only blackness. Moonlight was too distant, too choked, to illuminate these depths. They wouldn't know if the beast was upon them until it entered the light of his spheres. But *Stormfather,* it sounded close.

Kaladin turned his attention back to his running. He nearly tripped over something on the ground. A corpse? He leaped it, catching up to Shallan. The hem of her dress was snarled and ripped from the running, her hair a mess, her face flushed. She led them down another corridor, then slowed to a stop, hand to the wall of the chasm, puffing.

Kaladin closed his eyes, breathing in and out. *Can't rest long. It will be coming.* He felt as if he were going to collapse.

"Cover that light," Shallan hissed.

He frowned at her, but did so. "We can't rest long," he hissed back.

"Quiet."

The darkness was complete save for the thin light escaping between his fingers. The scraping seemed almost on top of them. Storms! Could he fight one of these monsters? Without Stormlight? Desperate, he tried to suck in the Light he held in his palm.

No Stormlight came, and he hadn't seen Syl since the fall. The scraping continued. He prepared to run, but . . .

The sounds didn't seem to be getting closer anymore. Kaladin frowned. The body he'd stumbled over, it had been one of the fallen from the fight earlier. Shallan had led them back to where they'd started.

And . . . to food for the beast.

He waited, tense, listening to his heartbeat thumping in his chest. Scraping echoed in the chasm. Oddly, some light flashed in the chasm behind. What was that?

"Stay here," Shallan whispered.

Then, incredibly, she started to move *toward* the sounds. Still holding the spheres awkwardly with one hand, he reached out with the other and snatched her.

She turned back to him, then looked down. Inadvertently, he'd grabbed her by the safehand. He let go immediately.

"I have to see it," Shallan whispered to him. "We're so close."

"Are you *insane?*"

"Probably." She continued toward the beast.

Kaladin debated, cursing her in his mind. Finally, he put his spear down and dropped her pack and satchel over its spheres to muffle the light. Then he followed. What else could he do? Explain to Adolin? *Yes, princeling. I let your betrothed wander off alone in the darkness to get eaten by a chasmfiend. No, I didn't go with her. Yes, I'm a coward.*

There *was* light ahead. It showed Shallan—her outline, at least—crouching beside a turn in the chasm, peeking around. Kaladin stepped up to her, crouching down and taking a look.

There it was.

The beast filled the chasm. Long and narrow, it wasn't bulbous or bulky, like some small cremlings. It was sinuous, sleek, with that arrowlike face and sharp mandibles.

It was also *wrong*. Wrong in a way difficult to describe. Big creatures were supposed to be slow and docile, like chulls. Yet this enormous beast moved with ease, its legs up on the sides of the chasm, holding it so that its body barely touched the ground. It ate the corpse of a fallen soldier, grasping the body in smaller claws by its mouth, then ripping it in half with a gruesome bite.

That face was like something from a nightmare. Evil, powerful, almost *intelligent*.

"Those spren," Shallan whispered, so soft he could barely hear. "I've seen those . . ."

They danced around the chasmfiend, and were the source of the light. They looked like small glowing arrows, and they surrounded the beast in schools, though occasionally one would drift away from the others and then vanish like a small plume of smoke rising into the air.

"Skyeels," Shallan whispered. "They follow skyeels too. The chasmfiend likes corpses. Could its kind be carrion feeders by nature? No, those claws, they look like they're meant for breaking shells. I suspect we'd find herds of wild chulls near where these things live naturally. But they come to the Shattered Plains to pupate, and here there's very little food, which is why they attack men. Why has this one remained after pupating?"

The chasmfiend was almost done with its meal. Kaladin took her by the shoulder, and she allowed him—with obvious reluctance—to pull her away.

They returned to their things, gathered them up, and—as silently as possible—retreated farther into the darkness.

·•·

They walked for hours, going in a completely different direction from the one they'd taken before. Shallan allowed Kaladin to lead again, though she tried her best to keep track of the chasms. She'd need to draw it out to be certain of their location.

Images of the chasmfiend tumbled in her head. What a majestic animal! Her fingers practically *itched* to sketch it from the Memory she'd taken. The legs were larger than she'd imagined; not like a legger, with spindly little spinelike legs holding up a thick body. This creature had exuded power. Like the whitespine, only enormous and more alien.

They were far from it now. Hopefully that meant they were safe. The night was dragging on her, after she'd risen early to get moving on the expedition.

She covertly checked the spheres in her pouch. She'd drained them all dun in their flight. Bless the Almighty for the Stormlight—she would need to make a glyphward in thanks. Without the strength and endurance it lent, she'd never have been able to keep up with Kaladin longlegs.

Now, however, she was *storming* exhausted. As if the Light had inflated her capacity, but now left her deflated and worn out.

At the next intersection, Kaladin paused and looked her over.

She gave him a weak smile.

"We'll need to stop for the night," he said.

"Sorry."

"It's not just you," he said, looking up at the sky. "I honestly have no idea if we're going the right direction or not. I'm all turned around. If we can get an idea in the morning of where the sun is rising, it will tell us which direction to walk."

She nodded.

"We should still be able to get back in plenty of time," he added. "No need to worry."

The way he said it immediately made her start worrying. Still, she helped him find a relatively dry portion of ground, and they settled down, spheres in the center like a little mock fire. Kaladin dug in the pack she'd found— she'd taken it off a dead soldier—and came out with some rations of flatbread and dried chull jerky. Not the most appetizing of food by any stretch, but it was something.

She sat with her back to the wall and ate, looking upward. The flatbread was from Soulcast grain—that stale taste was obvious. Clouds above prevented her from seeing the stars, but some starspren moved in front of those, forming distant patterns.

"It's strange," she whispered as Kaladin ate. "I've only been down here half a night, but it feels like so much longer. The tops of the plateaus seem so distant, don't they?"

He grunted.

"Ah yes," she said. "The bridgeman grunt. A language unto itself. I'll need to go over the morphemes and tones with you; I'm not quite fluent yet."

"You'd make a terrible bridgeman."

"Too short?"

"Well, yes. And too female. I doubt you'd look good in the traditional short trousers and open vest. Or, rather, you'd probably look *too* good. It might be a little distracting for the other bridgemen."

She smiled at that, digging into her satchel and pulling out her sketchbook and pencils. At least she had fallen with those. She started sketching, humming softly to herself and stealing one of the spheres for light. Pattern still lay on her skirts, content to be silent in Kaladin's presence.

"Storms," Kaladin said. "You're not drawing a *picture* of you wearing one of those outfits . . ."

"Yes, of course," she said. "I'm drawing salacious pictures of myself for you after only a few hours together in the chasm." She scratched at a line. "You have quite the imagination, bridgeboy."

"Well it's what we were talking about," he grumbled, rising and walking over to look at what she was doing. "I thought you were tired."

"I'm exhausted," she said. "So I need to relax." Obviously. This first sketch wouldn't be the chasmfiend. She needed a warm-up.

So she drew their path through the chasms. A map, kind of, but more a picture of the chasms as if she could see them from above. It was imaginative enough to be interesting, though she was certain she got a few of the ridges and corners wrong.

"What *is* that?" Kaladin asked. "A picture of the Plains?"

"Something of a map," she said, though she grimaced. What did it say about her that she couldn't just draw a few lines giving their location, like a regular person? She had to do it like a picture. "I don't know the full shapes of the plateaus we walked around, just the chasm pathways we used."

"You remember it that well?"

Stormwinds. Hadn't she intended to keep her visual memory more secret than this? "Uh . . . No, not really. I'm guessing at a lot of this."

She felt foolish for revealing her skill. Veil would have had words with her. It was too bad Veil wasn't down here, actually. She would be better at this whole surviving-in-the-wilderness thing.

Kaladin took the picture from her fingers, standing up and using his sphere to light it. "Well, if your map is correct, we've been making our way southward instead of westward. I need light to navigate better."

"Perhaps," she said, taking out another sheet to begin her sketch of the chasmfiend.

"We'll wait for the sun tomorrow," he said. "That will tell me which way to go."

She nodded, beginning her sketch as he made a place for himself and settled down, coat folded into a pillow. She wanted to turn in herself, but this sketch would *not* wait. She at least had to get something down.

She only lasted about a half hour—finishing perhaps a quarter of the sketch—before she had to put it away, curl up on the hard ground with the pack as a pillow, and fall asleep.

.·.

It was still dark when Kaladin nudged her awake with the butt of his spear. Shallan groaned, rolling over on the chasm floor, and drowsily tried to put her pillow over her head.

Which, of course, spilled dried chull meat onto her. Kaladin chuckled.

Sure, *that* got a laugh out of him. Storming man. How long had she been able to sleep? She blinked bleary eyes and focused on the open crack of the chasm far above.

Nope, not a single glimmer of light. Two, perhaps three hours of sleep, then? Or, rather, "sleep." The definition of what she'd done was debatable. She'd probably have called it "tossing and turning on the rocky ground, occasionally waking with a start to find that she'd drooled a small puddle." That didn't really roll off the tongue, though. Unlike the aforementioned drool.

She sat up and stretched sore limbs, checking to make sure her sleeve hadn't come unbuttoned in the night or anything equally embarrassing. "I need a bath," she grumbled.

"A bath?" Kaladin asked. "You have only been away from civilization for *one day*."

She sniffed. "Just because you're accustomed to the stench of unwashed bridgeman does not mean I need to join in."

He smirked, taking a piece of dried chull meat from her shoulder and popping it in his mouth. "In my home town growing up, bath day was once a week. I think even the local lighteyes would have found it strange that everyone out here, even the common soldiers, finds a bath more frequently."

How *dare* he be this chipper in the morning? Or, rather, the "morning."

She threw another piece of chull meat at him when he wasn't looking. The storming man caught it.

I hate him.

"We didn't get eaten by that chasmfiend while we slept," he said, refilling the pack save for a single waterskin. "I'd say that was about as much a blessing as we could expect, under the circumstances. Come on, up on your toes. Your map gives me an idea of which way to go, and we can watch for sunlight to make certain we're on the right path. We want to beat that highstorm, right?"

"You're the one I want to beat," she grumbled. "With a stick."

"What was that?"

"Nothing," she said, standing up and trying to make something of her frazzled hair. Storms. She must look like the aftereffect of a lightning bolt hitting a jar of red ink. She sighed. She didn't have a brush, and he didn't look like he was going to give her time for a proper braid, so she put on her boots—wearing the same pair of socks two days in a row was the least of her indignities—and picked up her satchel. Kaladin carried the pack.

She trailed after him as he led the way through the chasm, her stomach complaining about how little she'd eaten the night before. Food didn't sound good, so she let it growl. *Serves it right,* she thought. Whatever that meant.

Eventually, the sky did start to brighten, and from a direction that indicated that they were going the right way. Kaladin fell into his customary quiet, and his chipper mien from earlier in the morning evaporated. Instead, he looked like he was consumed by difficult thoughts.

She yawned, pulling up beside him. "What are you thinking about?"

"I was considering how nice it was to have a little silence," he said. "With nobody bothering me."

"Liar. Why do you try so hard to put people off?"

"Maybe I just don't want to have another argument."

"You won't," she said, yawning again. "It's far too early for arguments. Try it. Give me an insult."

"I don't—"

"Insult! Now!"

"I'd rather walk these chasms with a compulsive murderer than you. At least then, when the conversation got tedious, I'd have an easy way out."

"And your feet stink," she said. "See? Too early. I can't possibly be witty at this hour. So no arguments." She hesitated, then continued more softly. "Besides, no murderer would agree to accompany you. Everyone needs to have *some* standards, after all."

Kaladin snorted, lips tugging up to the sides.

"Be careful," she said, hopping over a fallen log. "That was *almost* like a smile—and earlier this morning, I could swear that you were cheerful.

Well, mildly content. Anyway, if you start to be in a better mood, it will destroy the whole variety of this trip."

"Variety?" he asked.

"Yes. If we're both pleasant, there's no artistry to it. You see, great art is a matter of contrast. Some lights and some darks. The happy, smiling, radiant lady and the dark, brooding, malodorous bridgeman."

"That—" He stopped. "Malodorous?"

"A great figure painting," she said, "shows the hero with inherent contrast—strong, yet hinting at vulnerability, so that the viewer can relate to him. Your little problem would make for a dynamic contrast."

"How would you even convey that in a painting?" Kaladin said, frowning. "Besides, I'm *not* malodorous."

"Oh, so you're getting better? Yay!"

He looked at her, dumbfounded.

"Confusion," she said. "I will graciously take that as a sign that you're amazed that I can be so humorous at such an early hour." She leaned in conspiratorially, whispering. "I'm really not very witty. You just happen to be stupid, so it *seems* that way. Contrast, remember?"

She smiled at him, then continued on her way, humming to herself. Actually, the day was looking much better. Why had she been in a bad mood earlier?

Kaladin jogged to catch up with her. "Storms, woman," he said. "I don't know what to make of you."

"Preferably not a corpse."

"I'm surprised someone hasn't already done that." He shook his head. "Give me an honest answer. Why are you here?"

"Well, there was this bridge that collapsed, and I fell . . ."

He sighed.

"Sorry," Shallan said. "Something about you encourages me to crack wise, bridgeboy. Even in the *morning*. Anyway, why did I come here? You mean to the Shattered Plains in the first place?"

He nodded. There *was* a sort of rugged handsomeness to the fellow. Like the beauty of a natural rock formation, as opposed to a fine sculpture like Adolin.

But Kaladin's *intensity*, that frightened her. He seemed like a man who constantly had his teeth clenched, a man who couldn't let himself—or anyone else—just sit down and take a nice rest.

"I came here," Shallan said, "because of Jasnah Kholin's work. The scholarship she left behind must not be abandoned."

"And Adolin?"

"Adolin is a delightful surprise."

They passed an entire wall covered in draping vines that were rooted in a broken section of rock above. They wriggled and pulled up as Shallan passed. *Very alert,* she noted. *Faster than most vines.* These were the opposite of those in the gardens back home, where the plants had been sheltered for so long. She tried to snatch one for a cutting, but it moved too quickly.

Drat. She needed a bit of one so that when they got back, she could grow a plant for experimentation. Pretending she was here to explore and record new species helped push back the gloom. She heard Pattern humming softly from her skirt, as if he realized what she was doing, distracting herself from the predicament and the danger. She swatted at him. What would the bridgeman think if he heard her clothing buzz?

"Just a moment," she said, finally snatching one of the vines. Kaladin watched, leaning on his spear, as she cut the tip off the vine with the small knife from her satchel.

"Jasnah's research," he said. "It had something to do with structures hidden out here, beneath the crem?"

"What makes you say that?" She tucked the tip of the vine away in an empty ink jar she'd kept for specimens.

"You made too much of an effort to get out here," he said. "Ostensibly all to investigate a chasmfiend's chrysalis. A dead one, even. There has to be more."

"You don't understand the compulsive nature of scholarship, I see." She shook the jar.

He snorted. "If you'd really wanted to see a chrysalis, you could have just had them tow one back for you. They have those chull sleds for the wounded; one of those might have worked. There was no need for you to come all the way out here yourself."

Blast. A solid argument. It was a good thing Adolin hadn't thought of that. The prince *was* wonderful, and he certainly wasn't stupid, but he was also . . . mentally direct.

This bridgeman was proving himself different. The way he watched her, the way he thought. Even, she realized, the way he spoke. He talked like an educated lighteyes. But what of those *slave brands* on his forehead? The hair got in the way, but she thought that one of them was a *shash* brand.

Perhaps she should spend as much time wondering about this man's motives as he apparently fretted about hers.

"Riches," he said, as they continued on. He held back some dead branches sticking from a crack so she could pass. "There's a treasure of some sort out here, and that's what you seek? But . . . no. You could have wealth easily enough by marriage."

She didn't say anything, stepping through the gap he made for her.

"Nobody had heard of you before this," he continued. "The Davar house really does have a daughter your age, and you match the description. You could be an impostor, but you're actually lighteyed, and that Veden house isn't particularly significant. If you were going to bother to impersonate someone, wouldn't you pick someone more important?"

"You seem to have thought about this a great deal."

"It's my job."

"I'm being truthful with you—Jasnah's research *is* why I came to the Shattered Plains. I think the world itself could be in danger."

"That's why you talked to Adolin about the parshmen."

"Wait. How do you . . . Your guards were there on that terrace with us. They told you? I didn't realize they were close enough to listen."

"I made a point of telling them to stay close," Kaladin said. "At the time, I was half convinced you were here to assassinate Adolin."

Well, he was nothing if not honest. And blunt.

"My men said," Kaladin continued, "that you seemed to want to get the parshmen murdered."

"I said nothing of the sort," she said. "Though I am worried that they might betray us. It's a moot point, as I doubt I'll persuade the highprinces without more evidence."

"If you got your way, though," Kaladin said, sounding curious, "what would you do? About the parshmen?"

"Have them exiled," Shallan said.

"And who will replace them?" Kaladin said. "Darkeyes?"

"I'm not saying it would be easy," Shallan said.

"They'd need more slaves," Kaladin said, contemplative. "A lot of honest men might find themselves with brands."

"Still sore about what happened to you, I assume."

"Wouldn't you be?"

"Yes, I suppose I would. I *am* sorry that you were treated in such a way, but it could have been worse. You could have been hanged."

"I wouldn't have wanted to be the executioner who tried that." He said it with a quiet intensity.

"Me neither," Shallan said. "I think hanging people is a poor choice of professions for an executioner. Better to be the guy with an axe."

He frowned at her.

"You see," she said, "with the axe, it's easier to get ahead. . . ."

He stared. Then, after a moment, he winced. "Oh, storms. That was awful."

"No, it was *funny*. You seem to get those two mixed up a lot. Don't worry. I'm here to help."

He shook his head. "It's not that you aren't witty, Shallan. I just feel like you try too hard. The world is not a sunny place, and frantically trying to turn everything into a joke is not going to change that."

"Technically," she said, "it *is* a sunny place. Half the time."

"To people like you, perhaps," Kaladin said.

"What does that mean?"

He grimaced. "Look, I don't want to fight again, all right? I just . . . Please. Let's let the topic drop."

"What if I promise not to get angry?"

"Are you capable of that?"

"Of course. I spend most of my time not being angry. I'm terribly proficient at it. Most of those times aren't around you, granted, but I think I'll be all right."

"You're doing it again," he said.

"Sorry."

They walked in silence for a moment, passing plants in bloom with a shockingly well-preserved skeleton underneath them, somehow barely disturbed by the flowing of water in the chasm.

"All right," Kaladin said. "Here it is. I can imagine how the world must appear to someone like you. Growing up pampered, with everything you want. To someone like you, life is wonderful and sunny and worth laughing over. That's not your fault, and I shouldn't blame you. You haven't had to deal with pain or death like I have. Sorrow is not your companion."

Silence. Shallan didn't reply. How *could* she reply to that?

"What?" Kaladin finally asked.

"I'm trying to decide how to react," Shallan said. "You see, you just said something very, very funny."

"Then why aren't you laughing?"

"Well, it isn't that kind of funny." She handed him her satchel and stepped onto a small dry rise of rock running through the middle of a deep pond on the chasm floor. The ground was usually flat—all of that crem settling—but the water in this pool looked a good two or three feet deep.

She crossed with hands out to the sides, balancing. "So, let me see," she said as she stepped carefully. "You think I've lived a simple, happy life full of sunshine and joy. But you also imply that I've got dark, evil secrets, so you're suspicious of and even hostile to me. You tell me I'm arrogant and assume that I consider darkeyes to be playthings, but when I tell you what I'm trying to do to protect them—and everyone else—you imply I'm meddling and should just leave well enough alone."

She reached the other side and turned about. "Would you say that's an accurate summary of our conversations up to this point, Kaladin Stormblessed?"

He grimaced. "Yes. I suppose."

"Wow," she said, "you sure do seem to know me well. Particularly considering that you started this conversation by professing that you don't know what to make of me. An odd statement from someone who seems, from my perspective, to have figured it all out. Next time I'm trying to decide what to do, I'll just ask you, since you appear to understand me better than I understand myself."

He crossed the same ridge of rock in the path, and she watched anxiously, as he was carrying her satchel. She trusted him better with it over the water than she trusted herself, though. She reached for it when he arrived on the other side, but found herself taking his arm to draw his attention.

"How about this?" she said, holding his eyes. "I promise, solemnly and by the tenth name of the Almighty, that I mean no harm to Adolin or his family. I mean to prevent a disaster. I might be wrong, and I might be misguided, but I vow to you that I'm sincere."

He stared into her eyes. So *intense*. She felt a shiver meeting that expression. This was a man of passion.

"I believe you," he said. "And I guess that will do." He looked upward, then cursed.

"What?" she asked, looking toward the distant light above. The sun was peeking out over the lip of the ridge there.

The wrong ridge. They weren't going west any longer. They'd strayed again, pointing southward.

"Blast," Shallan said. "Give me that satchel. I need to draw this out."

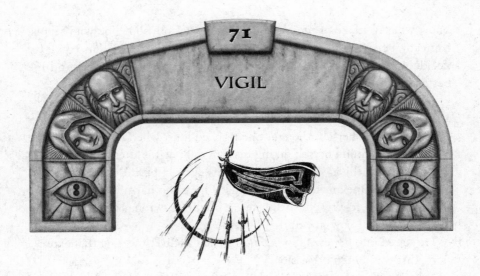

*He bears the weight of God's own divine hatred, separated from
the virtues that gave it context. He is what we made him to be, old
friend. And that is what he, unfortunately, wished to become.*

"I was young," Teft said, "so I didn't hear much. Kelek, I didn't *want* to
hear much. The things my family did, they weren't the sort of things
you want your parents doing, all right? I didn't want to know. So it's
not surprising I can't remember."

Sigzil nodded in that mild, yet infuriating way of his. The Azish man
just *knew* things. And he made you tell him things too. Unfair, that was.
Terribly. Why did Teft have to end up with him on watch duty?

The two sat on rocks near the chasms just east of Dalinar's warcamp.
A cold wind blew in. Highstorm tonight.

He'll be back before then. Surely by then.

A cremling scuttled past. Teft threw a rock at it, driving it toward a
nearby crack. "I don't know why you want to hear all of these things anyway. They aren't any use."

Sigzil nodded. Storming foreigner.

"All right, fine," Teft said. "It was some kind of cult, you see, called the
Envisagers. They . . . well, they thought if they could find a way to return
the Voidbringers, then the Knights Radiant would return as well. Stupid,
right? Only, they knew things. Things they shouldn't, things like what
Kaladin can do."

"I see this is hard for you," Sigzil said. "Want to play another hand of
michim to pass the time instead?"

"You just want my storming spheres," Teft snapped, wagging his finger at the Azish man. "And don't call it by that name."

"Michim is the game's actual name."

"That's a holy word, and ain't no *game* named a holy word."

"The word isn't holy where it came from," Sigzil said, obviously annoyed.

"We ain't there now, are we? Call it something else."

"I thought you'd like it," Sigzil said, picking up the colored rocks that were used in the game. You bet them, in a pile, while trying to guess the ones your opponent had hidden. "It's a game of skill, not chance, so it doesn't offend Vorin sensibilities."

Teft watched him pick up the rocks. Maybe it would be better if he just lost all of his spheres in that storming game. It wasn't good for him to have money again. He couldn't be trusted with money.

"They thought," Teft said, "that people were more likely to manifest powers if their lives were in danger. So . . . they'd put lives in danger. Members of their own group—never an innocent outsider, bless the winds. But that was bad enough. I watched people let themselves be pushed off cliffs, watched them tied in place with a candle slowly burning a rope until it snapped and dropped a rock to crush them. It was bad, Sigzil. Awful. The sort of thing nobody should have to watch, especially a boy of six."

"So what did you do?" Sigzil asked softly, pulling tight the string on his little bag of rocks.

"Ain't none of your business," Teft said. "Don't know why I'm even talking to you."

"It's all right," Sigzil said. "I can see—"

"I turned them in," Teft blurted out. "To the citylord. He held a trial for them, a big one. Had them all executed in the end. Never did understand that. They were only a danger to themselves. Their punishment for threatening suicide was to be killed. Nonsense, that is. Should have found a way to help them . . ."

"Your parents?"

"Mother died in that rock–string contraption," Teft said. "She really believed, Sig. That she had it in her, you know? The powers? That if she were about to die, they'd come out in her, and she'd save herself . . ."

"And you watched?"

"Storms, no! You think they'd let her son watch that? Are you mad?"

"But—"

"Did watch my father die, though," Teft said, looking out over the Plains. "Hanged." He shook his head, digging in his pocket. Where had he put that flask? As he turned, however, he caught sight of that other lad sitting back there, fiddling with his little box as he often did. Renarin.

Teft wasn't one for all that nonsense like Moash had talked about, wanting to overturn lighteyes. The Almighty had put them in their place, and who had business questioning him? Not spearmen, that's for certain. But in a way, Prince Renarin was as bad as Moash. Neither one knew their place. A lighteyes wanting to join Bridge Four was as bad as a darkeyes talking stupid and lofty to the king. It didn't fit, even if the other bridgemen seemed to like the lad.

And, of course, Moash was one of them now. Storms. Had he left his flask back at the barrack?

"Heads up, Teft," Sigzil said, rising.

Teft turned around and saw men in uniform approaching. He scrambled to his feet, grabbing his spear. It was Dalinar Kholin, accompanied by several of his lighteyed advisors, along with Drehy and Skar from Bridge Four, the day's guards. With Moash promoted away and Kaladin . . . well, not there . . . Teft had taken over daily assignments. Nobody else would storming do it. They said he was in command now. Idiots.

"Brightlord," Teft said, slapping his chest in salute.

"Adolin told me you men were coming here," the highprince said. He spared a glance for Prince Renarin, who had also stood and saluted, as if this weren't his own father. "A rotation, I understand?"

"Yes, sir," Teft said, looking toward Sigzil. It *was* a rotation.

Teft was just on nearly every shift.

"You really think he's alive out there, soldier?" Dalinar asked.

"He is, sir," Teft said. "It's not about what I or anyone thinks."

"He fell hundreds of feet," Dalinar said.

Teft continued to stand at attention. The highprince hadn't asked a question, so Teft didn't give a reply.

He did have to banish a few terrible images in his head. Kaladin having knocked his head while falling. Kaladin having been crushed by the falling bridge. Kaladin lying with a broken leg, unable to find spheres to heal himself. The fool boy thought he was immortal, sometimes.

Kelek. They all thought he was.

"He *is* going to come back, sir," Sigzil said to Dalinar. "He's going to come climbing right up out of that chasm right there. It will be well if we're here to meet him. Uniforms on, spears polished."

"We wait on our own time, sir," Teft said. "Neither of us three are supposed to be anywhere else." He blushed as soon as he said it. And here he'd been thinking about how *Moash* talked back to his betters.

"I didn't come to order you away from your chosen task, soldier," Dalinar said. "I came to make certain you were caring for yourselves. No men are to skip meals to wait here, and I don't want you getting any ideas about waiting during a highstorm."

"Er, yes, sir," Teft said. He had used his morning meal break to put in duty here. How had Dalinar known?

"Good luck, soldier," Dalinar said, then continued on his way, flanked by attendants, apparently off to inspect the battalion that was nearest to the eastern edge of camp. Soldiers there scurried like cremlings after a storm, carrying supply bags and piling them inside their barracks. The time for Dalinar's full expedition onto the Plains was quickly approaching.

"Sir," Teft called after the highprince.

Dalinar turned back toward him, his attendants pausing mid-sentence.

"You don't believe us," Teft said. "That he'll come back, I mean."

"He's dead, soldier. But I understand that you need to be here anyway." The highprince touched his hand to his shoulder, a salute to the dead, then continued on his way.

Well, Teft supposed that was all right, Dalinar not believing. He'd just be that much more surprised when Kaladin *did* return.

Highstorm tonight, Teft thought, settling back down on his rock. *Come on, lad. What are you doing out there?*

※

Kaladin felt like one of the ten fools.

Actually, he felt like all of them. Ten times an idiot. But most specifically Eshu, who spoke of things he did not understand in front of those who did.

Navigation this deep in the chasms was hard, but he could usually read directions by the way that the debris was deposited. Water blew in from the east to the west, but then it drained out the other way—so cracks on walls where debris was smashed in tight usually marked a western direction, but places where debris had been deposited more naturally—as water drained—marked where water had flowed east.

His instincts told him which way to go. They'd been wrong. He shouldn't have been so confident. This far from the warcamps, the waterflows must be different.

Annoyed at himself, he left Shallan drawing and walked out a ways. "Syl?" he asked.

No response.

"Sylphrena!" he said, louder.

He sighed and walked back to Shallan, who knelt on the mossy ground—she'd obviously given up on protecting the once-fine dress from stains and rips—drawing on her sketchpad. She was another reason he felt like a fool. He shouldn't let her provoke him so. He could hold in the retorts against other, far more annoying lighteyes. Why did he lose control when talking with her?

Should have learned my lesson, he thought as she sketched, her expression growing intense. *She's won every argument so far, hands down.*

He leaned against a section of the chasm wall, spear in the crook of his arm, light shining from the spheres tied tightly at its head. He *had* made invalid assumptions about her, as she had so poignantly noted. Again and again. It was like a part of him frantically *wanted* to dislike her.

If only he could find Syl. Everything would be better if he could see her again, if he could know that she was all right. That scream . . .

To distract himself, he moved over to Shallan, then leaned down to see her sketch. Her map was more of a picture, one that looked eerily like the view Kaladin had had, nights ago, when flying above the Shattered Plains.

"Is all that necessary?" he asked as she shaded in the sides of a plateau.

"Yes."

"But—"

"Yes."

It took longer than he'd have preferred. The sun passed through the crack overhead, vanishing from sight. Already past noon. They had seven hours until the highstorm, assuming the timing prediction was right—even the best stormwardens got the calculations wrong sometimes.

Seven hours. *The hike out here,* he thought, *took about that long.* But surely they'd made some progress toward the warcamps. They'd been walking all morning.

Well, no use rushing Shallan. He left her to it, walking back along the chasm, looking up at the shape of the rift up above and comparing it to her drawing. From what he could see, her map was dead on. She was drawing, from memory, their entire path as if seen from above—and she did it perfectly, every little knob and ledge accounted for.

"Stormfather," he whispered, jogging back. He'd known she had skill in drawing, but this was something entirely different.

Who was this woman?

She was still drawing when he arrived. "Your picture is amazingly accurate," he said.

"I may have . . . underplayed my skill a little last night," Shallan said. "I can remember things pretty well, though to be honest, I didn't realize how far off our path was until I drew it. A lot of these plateau shapes are unfamiliar to me; we might be into the areas that haven't been mapped yet."

He looked to her. "You remember the shapes of *all* of the plateaus on the maps?"

"Uh . . . yes?"

"That's incredible."

She sat back on her knees, holding up her sketch. She brushed aside an unruly lock of red hair. "Maybe not. Something's very odd here."

"What?"

"I think my sketch must be off." She stood up, looking troubled. "I need more information. I'm going to walk around one of the plateaus here."

"All right . . ."

She started walking, still focused on her sketch, barely paying attention to where she was going as she stumbled over rocks and sticks. He kept up with ease, but didn't bother her as she turned her eyes toward the rift ahead. She walked them all the way around the base of the plateau to their right.

It took a painfully long time, even walking quickly. They were losing minutes. Did she know where they were or not?

"Now that plateau," she said, pointing to the next wall. She began walking around the base of *that* plateau.

"Shallan," Kaladin said. "We don't have—"

"This is important."

"So is not getting crushed in a highstorm."

"If we don't find out where we are, we won't ever escape," she said, handing him the sheet of paper. "Wait here. I'll be right back." She jogged off, skirt swishing.

Kaladin stared at the paper, inspecting the path she'd drawn. Though they'd started the morning going the right way, it was as he'd feared—Kaladin had eventually wound them around until they were going directly south again. He'd even somehow turned them back going *east* for a while!

That put them even farther from Dalinar's camp than when they'd begun the night before.

Please let her be wrong, he thought, going around the plateau the other direction to meet her halfway.

But if she *was* wrong, they wouldn't know where they were at all. Which option was worse?

He got a short distance down the chasm before freezing. The walls here were scraped free of moss, the debris on the floor pushed around and scratched. Storms, this was fresh. Since the last highstorm at least. The chasmfiend had come this way.

Maybe . . . maybe it had gone past on its way farther out into the chasms.

Shallan, distracted and muttering to herself, appeared around the other side of the plateau. She walked, still staring at the sky, muttering to herself. ". . . I know I said that I saw these patterns, but this is too grand a scale for me to know instinctively. You should have said something. I—"

She cut off abruptly, jumping as she saw Kaladin. He found himself narrowing his eyes. That had sounded like . . .

Don't be silly. She's no warrior. The Knights Radiant had been soldiers, hadn't they? He didn't really know much about them.

Still, Syl *had* seen several strange spren about.

Shallan gave a glance to the wall of the chasm and the scrapes. "Is that what I think it is?"

"Yeah," he said.

"Delightful. Here, give me that paper."

He handed it back and she slipped a pencil out of her sleeve. He gave her the satchel, which she set on the floor, using the stiff side as a place to sketch. She filled in the two plateaus closest to them, the ones she'd walked around to get a full view.

"So is your drawing off or not?" Kaladin asked.

"It's accurate," Shallan said as she drew, "it's just strange. From my memory of the maps, this set of plateaus nearest to us should be farther to the north. There is another group of them up there that are *exactly* the same shape, only mirrored."

"You can remember the maps that well?"

"Yes."

He didn't press further. From what he'd seen, maybe she could do just that.

She shook her head. "What are the chances that a series of plateaus would take the exact same shape as those on another part of the Plains? Not just one, but an entire sequence . . ."

"The Plains are symmetrical," Kaladin said.

She froze. "How do you know that?"

"I . . . it was a dream. I saw the plateaus arrayed in a wide symmetrical formation."

She looked back at her map, then gasped. She began scribbling notes on the side. "Cymatics."

"What?"

"I know where the Parshendi are." Her eyes widened. "And the Oathgate. The center of the Shattered Plains. I can see it all—I can map almost the entire thing."

He shivered. "You . . . what?"

She looked up sharply, meeting his eyes. "We have to get back."

"Yes, I know. The highstorm."

"More than that," she said, standing. "I know too much now to die out here. The Shattered Plains *are* a pattern. This isn't a natural rock formation." Her eyes widened further. "At the center of these Plains was a city. Something broke it apart. A weapon . . . Vibrations? Like sand on a plate? An earthquake that could break rock . . . Stone became sand, and at the blowing of the highstorms, the cracks full of sand were hollowed out."

Her eyes seemed eerily distant, and Kaladin didn't understand half of what she'd said.

"We need to reach the center," Shallan said. "I can find it, the heart of these Plains, by following the pattern. And there will be . . . things there . . ."

"The secret you're searching for," Kaladin said. What had she said just earlier? "Oathgate?"

She blushed deeply. "Let's keep moving. Didn't you mention how little time we had? Honestly, if *one* of us weren't chatting away all the time and distracting everyone, I'm half certain we'd be back already."

He cocked an eyebrow at her, and she grinned, then pointed the direction for them to go. "I'm leading now, by the way."

"Probably for the best."

"Though," she said, "as I consider, it might be better to let you lead. That way, we might find our way to the center by accident. Assuming we don't end up in Azir."

He gave her a chuckle at that because it seemed the right thing to do. Inside, however, it ripped him apart. He'd failed.

The next few hours were excruciating. After walking the length of two plateaus, Shallan had to stop and update her map. It was correct to do so—they *couldn't* risk getting off track again.

It just took so much time. Even moving as quickly as they could between drawing sessions, practically running the entire way, their progress was too slow.

Kaladin shuffled from foot to foot, watching the sky as Shallan filled in her map again. She cursed and grumbled, and he noticed her brushing away a drop of sweat that had fallen from her brow onto the increasingly crumpled paper.

Maybe four hours left until the storm, Kaladin thought. *We aren't going to make it.*

"I'll try for scouts again," he said.

Shallan nodded. They had entered the territory where Dalinar's pole-wielding scouts watched for new chrysalises. Shouting to them was a slim hope—even if they were lucky enough to find one of those groups, he doubted they had enough rope handy to reach to the bottom of the chasm.

But it was a chance. So he moved away—so as to not disturb her drawing—cupped his mouth, and began shouting. "Hello! Please reply! We're trapped in the chasms! Please reply!"

He walked for a time, shouting, then stopped to listen. Nothing came back. No questioning shouts echoing down from above, no signs of life.

They've probably all withdrawn into their cubbies by now, Kaladin thought. *They've broken down their watchposts and are waiting for the highstorm.*

He stared up with frustration at that slot of attenuated sky. So distant.

He remembered this feeling, being down here with Teft and the others, longing to climb out and escape the horrible life of a bridgeman.

For the hundredth time, he tried drawing in the Stormlight of those spheres. He clutched the sphere until his hand and the glass were sweaty, but the Stormlight—the power within—did not flow to him. He couldn't feel the Light anymore.

"Syl!" he yelled, tucking away the sphere, cupping his hands around his mouth. "Syl! Please! Are you there, anywhere . . . ?" He trailed off. "I still don't know," he said more softly. "Is this a punishment? Or is it something more? What is wrong?"

No reply. Surely if she were watching him, she wouldn't let him die down here. Assuming she could think to notice. He had a horrible image of her riding the winds, mingling with the windspren, having forgotten herself and him—becoming terribly, blissfully ignorant of what she truly was.

She'd feared that. She'd been terrified of it.

Shallan's boots scratched the ground as she walked up. "No luck?"

He shook his head.

"Well, onward, then." She took a deep breath. "Through soreness and exhaustion we go. You wouldn't be willing to carry me a little ways . . ."

He glared at her.

She shrugged with a smile. "Think how grand it would be! I could even get a reed to whip you with. You'd be able to go back and tell all the other guards what an awful person I am. It'll be a wonderful opportunity for griping. No? Well, all right then. Off we go."

"You're a strange woman."

"Thank you."

He fell into step beside her.

"My," she noted, "you've brewed another storm over your head, I see."

"I've killed us," he whispered. "I took the lead, and I got us lost."

"Well, I didn't notice we were going the wrong way either. I wouldn't have done any better."

"I should have thought to have you map our progress from the start today. I was too confident."

"It's done," she said. "If I'd been more clear with you about how well I could draw these plateaus, then you'd probably have made better use of my maps. I didn't, and you didn't know, so here we are. You can't blame yourself for everything, right?"

He walked in silence.

"Uh, right?"

"It's my fault."

She rolled her eyes exaggeratedly. "You are really intent on beating yourself up, aren't you?"

His father had said the same thing time and time again. It was who Kaladin was. Did they expect him to change?

"We'll be fine," Shallan said. "You'll see."

That darkened his mood further.

"You still think I'm too optimistic, don't you?" Shallan said.

"It's not your fault," Kaladin said. "I'd rather be like you. I'd rather not have lived the life I have. I would that the world was only full of people like you, Shallan Davar."

"People who don't understand pain."

"Oh, all people understand pain," Kaladin said. "That's not what I'm talking about. It's . . ."

"The sorrow," Shallan said softly, "of watching a life crumble? Of struggling to grab it and hold on, but feeling hope become stringy sinew and blood beneath your fingers as everything collapses?"

"Yes."

"The sensation—it's not sorrow, but something deeper—of being broken. Of being crushed so often, and so hatefully, that emotion becomes something you can only *wish* for. If only you could cry, because then you'd feel *something*. Instead, you feel nothing. Just . . . haze and smoke inside. Like you're already dead."

He stopped in the chasm.

She turned and looked to him. "The crushing guilt," she said, "of being powerless. Of wishing they'd hurt *you* instead of those around you. Of screaming and scrambling and hating as those you love are ruined, popped like a boil. And you have to watch their joy seeping away while you *can't do anything*. They break the ones you love, and not you. And you plead. Can't you just beat me instead?"

"Yes," he whispered.

Shallan nodded, holding his eyes. "Yes. It would be nice if nobody in the world knew of those things, Kaladin Stormblessed. I agree. With everything I have."

He saw it in her eyes. The anguish, the frustration. The terrible nothing that clawed inside and sought to smother her. She knew. It was there, inside. She had been broken.

Then she smiled. Oh, storms. She smiled *anyway*.

It was the single most beautiful thing he'd seen in his entire life.

"How?" he asked.

She shrugged lightly. "Helps if you're crazy. Come on. I do believe we're under a slight time constraint . . ."

She started down the chasm. He stood behind, feeling drained. And oddly brightened.

He should feel like a fool. He'd done it again—he'd been telling her how easy her life was, while she'd had *that* hiding inside of her all along. This time, though, he didn't feel like an idiot. He felt like he understood. Something. He didn't know what. The chasm just seemed a little brighter.

Tien always did that to me . . . he thought. *Even on the darkest day.*

He stood still long enough that frillblooms opened around him, their wide, fanlike fronds displaying veined patterns of orange, red, and violet. He eventually jogged after Shallan, shocking the plants closed.

"I think," she said, "we need to focus on the *positive* side of being down here in this terrible chasm."

She eyed him. He didn't say anything.

"Come on," she said.

"I . . . have the sense that it would be better not to encourage you."

"What's the fun in that?"

"Well, we *are* about to get hit by a highstorm's flood."

"So our clothing will get washed," she said with a grin. "See! Positive."

He snorted.

"Ah, that bridgeman grunt dialect again," she noted.

"That grunt meant," he said, "that at least if the waters come, it will wash away some of your stench."

"Ha! Mildly amusing, but no points to you. I already established that you're the malodorous one. Reuse of jokes is strictly forbidden on pain of getting dunked in a highstorm."

"All right then," he said. "It's a good thing we're down here because I had guard duty tonight. Now I'm going to miss it. That is practically like getting the day off."

"To go swimming, no less!"

He smiled.

"I," she proclaimed, "am glad we are down here because the sun is far too bright up above, and it tends to give me a sunburn unless I wear a hat. It is much better to be down in the dank, dark, smelly, moldy, potentially life-threatening depths. No sunburns. Just monsters."

"I'm glad to be down here," he said, "because at least it was me, and not one of my men, who fell."

She hopped over a puddle, then eyed him. "You're not very good at this."

"Sorry. I meant that I'm glad to be down here because when we get out, everyone will cheer me for being a hero for rescuing you."

"Better," Shallan said. "Except for the fact that I *do* believe that I am the one rescuing *you.*"

He glanced at her map. "Point."

"I," she said, "am glad to be down here because I've always wondered what it's like to be a chunk of meat traveling through a digestive system, and these chasms remind me of the intestines."

"I hope you're not serious."

"What?" She looked shocked. "Of *course* I'm not. Ew."

"You really *do* try too hard."

"It's what keeps me insane."

He scrambled up a large pile of debris, then offered a hand to help her. "I," he said, "am happy to be here because it reminds me of how lucky I am to be free of Sadeas's army."

"Ah," she said, stepping up to the top with him.

"His lighteyes sent us down here to gather," Kaladin said, sliding down the other side. "And didn't pay us much at all for the effort."

"Tragic."

"You could say," he told her as she stepped down off the pile, "that we were given only a pittance."

He grinned at her.

She cocked her head.

"Pit-tance," he said, gesturing toward the depth of the hole they were in. "You know. We're in a pit . . ."

"Oh, *storms*," she said. "You don't actually expect that to count. That was terrible!"

"I know. I'm sorry. My mother would be disappointed."

"She didn't like wordplay?"

"No, she loved it. She'd just be mad I tried to do it when she wasn't around to laugh at me."

Shallan smiled, and they continued on, keeping a brisk pace. "I am glad we're down here," she said, "because by now, Adolin will be worried sick about me—so when we get back, he'll be *ecstatic*. He might even let me kiss him in public."

Adolin. Right. That dampened his mood.

"We probably need to stop so I can draw out our map," Shallan said, frowning at the sky. "And so that you can yell some more for our potential salvation."

"I suppose," he said as she settled down to get out her map. He cupped his hands. "Hey, up there? Anyone? We're down here, and we're making bad puns. Please save us from ourselves!"

Shallan chuckled.

Kaladin smiled, then started as he actually heard something echoing back. Was that a voice? Or . . . Wait . . .

A trumping sound—like a horn's call, but overlapping itself. It grew louder, washing over them.

Then an enormous, skittering mass of carapace and claws crashed around the corner.

Chasmfiend.

Kaladin's mind panicked, but his body simply *moved*. He snatched Shallan by the arm, hauling her to her feet and pulling her into a run. She shouted, dropping her satchel.

Kaladin pulled her after him and did not look back. He could *feel* the thing, too close, the walls of the chasm shaking from its pursuit. Bones, twigs, shell, and plants cracked and snapped.

The monster trumped again, a deafening sound.

It was almost upon them. Storms, but it could move. He'd never have imagined something so large being so quick. There was no distracting it this time. It was almost upon them; he could *feel* it right behind . . .

There.

He whipped Shallan in front of him and thrust her into a fissure in the wall. As a shadow loomed over him, he threw himself into the fissure, shoving Shallan backward. She grunted as he pressed her against some of the refuse of twigs and leaves that had been packed into this crack by flood-waters.

The chasm fell silent. Kaladin could hear only Shallan's panting and his own heartbeat. They'd left most of their spheres on the ground, where Shallan had been preparing to draw. He still had his spear, his improvised lantern.

Slowly, Kaladin twisted about, putting his back to Shallan. She held him from behind, and he could feel her tremble. Stormfather. He trembled himself. He twisted his spear to give light, peering out at the chasm. This fissure was shallow, and only a few feet stood between him and the opening.

The frail, washed-out light of his diamond spheres twinkled off the wet floor. It illuminated broken frillblooms on the walls and several writhing vines on the ground, severed from their plants. They twisted and flopped, like men arching their backs. The chasmfiend . . . Where was it?

Shallan gasped, arms tightening around his waist. He looked up. There, higher up the crack, a large, inhuman eye watched them. He couldn't see the bulk of the chasmfiend's head; just part of the face and jaw, with that terrible glassy green eye. A large claw slammed against the side of the hole, trying to force its way in, but the crack was too small.

The claw dug at the hole, and then the head withdrew. Scraping rock and chitin sounded in the chasm, but the thing didn't go far before stopping.

Silence. A steady drip somewhere fell into a pool. But otherwise, silence.

"It's *waiting*," Shallan whispered, head near his shoulder.

"You sound proud of it!" Kaladin snapped.

"A little." She paused. "How long, do you suppose, until . . ."

He looked upward, but couldn't see the sky. The crack didn't run all the way up the side of the chasm, and was barely ten or fifteen feet tall. He leaned forward to look at the slot high above, not extending all the way out of the crack, just getting a little closer to the lip so he could see the sky. It was getting dark. Not sunset yet, but getting close.

"Two hours, maybe," he said. "I—"

A crashing tempest of carapace charged down the chasm. Kaladin jumped back, pressing Shallan against the refuse again as the chasmfiend tried— without success—to get one of its legs into the fissure. The leg was still too large, and though the chasmfiend could shove the tip in toward them— getting close enough to brush Kaladin—it wasn't enough to hurt them.

That eye returned, reflecting the image of Kaladin and Shallan—tattered and dirtied from their time in the chasm. Kaladin looked less frightened than he felt, staring that thing in the eye, spear held up wardingly. Shallan, rather than looking terrified, seemed fascinated.

Crazy woman.

The chasmfiend withdrew again. It stopped just down the chasm. He could hear it settling down to watch.

"So . . ." Shallan said, "we wait?"

Sweat trickled down the sides of Kaladin's face. Wait. How long? He could imagine staying in here, like a frightened rockbud trapped in its shell, until the waters came crashing through the chasms.

He'd survived a storm once. Barely, and only then with the aid of Stormlight. In here, it would be far different. The waters would whip them in a surge through the chasms, smashing them into walls, boulders, churning them with the dead until they drowned or were ripped limb from limb . . .

It would be a very, very bad way to die.

His grip tightened on his spear. He waited, sweating, worrying. The chasmfiend didn't leave. Minutes passed.

Finally, Kaladin made his decision. He moved to step forward.

"What are you doing!" Shallan hissed, sounding terrified. She tried to hold him back.

"When I'm out," he said, "run the other way."

"Don't be stupid!"

"I'll distract it," he said. "Once you're free, I'll lead it away from you, then escape. We can meet back up."

"Liar," she whispered.

He twisted about, meeting her eyes. "You can get back to the warcamps on your own," he said. "I can't. You have information that needs to get to Dalinar. I don't. I have combat training. I might be able to get away from the thing after distracting it. You couldn't. If we wait here, we both die. Do you need more logic than that?"

"I hate logic," she whispered. "Always have."

"We don't have time to talk about it," Kaladin said, twisting around, his back to her.

"You can't do this."

"I can." He took a deep breath. "Who knows," he said more softly, "maybe I'll get in a lucky hit." He reached up and ripped the spheres off his spearhead, then tossed them out into the chasm. He'd need a steadier light. "Get ready."

"Please," she whispered, sounding more frantic. "Don't leave me down in these chasms alone."

He smiled wryly. "Is it really this hard for you to let me win one single argument?"

"Yes!" she said. "No, I mean . . . Storms! Kaladin, it *will* kill you."

He gripped his spear. The way things had been going with him lately, perhaps that was what he deserved. "Apologize to Adolin for me. I actually kind of like him. He's a good man. Not just for a lighteyes. Just . . . a good person. I've never given him the credit he deserves."

"Kaladin . . ."

"It has to happen, Shallan."

"At least," she said, reaching her hand over his shoulder and past his head, "take this."

"Take what?"

"*This*," Shallan said.

Then she summoned a Shardblade.

*I suspect that he is more a force than an individual now, despite
your insistence to the contrary. That force is contained, and an
equilibrium reached.*

Kaladin stared at the glistening length of metal, which dripped with
condensation from its summoning. It glowed softly the color of
garnet along several faint lines down its length.

Shallan had a Shardblade.

He twisted his head toward her, and in so doing, his cheek brushed the
flat of the blade. No screams. He froze, then cautiously raised a finger and
touched the cold metal.

Nothing happened. The screech he had heard in his mind when fighting alongside Adolin did not recur. It seemed a very bad sign to him.
Though he did not know the meaning of that terrible sound, it *was* related
to his bond with Syl.

"How?" he asked.

"It's not important."

"I rather think it *is*."

"Not at the moment! Look, are you going to take this thing? Holding it
this way is awkward. If I drop it by accident and cut off your foot, it's going
to be your fault."

He hesitated, regarding his face reflected in its metal. He saw corpses,
friends with burning eyes. He'd refused these weapons each time one was
offered to him.

But always before, it had been after the fight, or at least on the practice grounds. This was different. Besides, he wasn't choosing to become a Shardbearer; he would only use this weapon to protect someone's life.

Making a decision, he reached up and seized the Shardblade by the hilt. At least this told him one thing—Shallan wasn't likely to be a Surgebinder. Otherwise, he suspected she'd hate this Blade as much as he did.

"You're not supposed to let people use your Blade," Kaladin said. "By tradition, only the king and the highprinces do that."

"Great," she said. "You can report me to Brightness Navani for being wildly indecent and ignorant of protocol. For now, can we just survive, please?"

"Yeah," he said, hefting the Blade. "That sounds wonderful." He barely knew how to use one of these. Training with a practice sword did not make you an expert with the real thing. Unfortunately, a spear was going to be of little use against a creature so large and so well armored.

"Also . . ." Shallan said. "Could you not do that 'reporting me' thing I mentioned? That was a joke. I don't think I'm supposed to have that Blade."

"Nobody would believe me anyway," Kaladin said. "You *are* going to run, right? As I instructed?"

"Yes. But if you could, please lead the monster to the left."

"That's toward the warcamps," Kaladin said, frowning. "I was planning to lead it deeper into the chasms, so that you—"

"I need to get back to my satchel," Shallan said.

Crazy woman. "We're fighting for our *lives*, Shallan. The satchel is unimportant."

"No, it's *very* important," she said. "I need it to . . . Well, the sketches in there show the pattern of the Shattered Plains. I'll need that to help Dalinar. Please, just do it."

"Fine. If I can."

"Good. And, um, please don't die, all right?"

He was suddenly aware of her pressed against his back. Holding him, breath warm on his neck. She trembled, and he thought he could hear in her voice both terror and fascination at their situation.

"I'll do my best," he said. "Get ready."

She nodded, letting go of him.

One.

Two.

Three.

He leaped out into the chasm, then turned and dashed left, *toward* the chasmfiend. Storming woman. The beast lurked in the shadows in that direction. No, it *was* a shadow. An enormous, looming shadow, long and eel-like, lifted above the floor of the chasm and gripping the walls with its legs.

It trumped and surged forward, carapace scraping on rock. Holding tightly to the Shardblade, Kaladin threw himself to the ground and ducked underneath the monster. The ground *heaved* as the beast smashed claws toward him, but Kaladin came up unscathed. He swung wildly with the Shardblade, carving a line in the rock wall beside him but missing the chasmfiend.

It curled in the chasm, twisting underneath itself, then turning about. The maneuver went far more smoothly for the monster than Kaladin would have hoped.

How do I even kill something like this? Kaladin wondered, backing up as the chasmfiend settled on the floor of the chasm to inspect him. Hacking at that enormous body was unlikely to kill it quickly enough. Did it have a heart? Not the stone gemheart, but a real one? He'd have to try to get underneath it again.

Kaladin continued to back down the chasm, trying to lead the creature away from Shallan. It moved more carefully than Kaladin would have expected. He was relieved to catch sight of Shallan escaping the crack and scrambling away down the passage.

"Come on, you," Kaladin said, waving the Shardblade at the chasmfiend. It reared up in the chasm, but did not strike at him. It watched, eyes hidden in its darkened face. The only light came from the distant slit high above and the spheres he'd tossed out into the chasm, which now were behind the monster.

Shallan's Blade glowed softly too, from a strange pattern along its length. Kaladin had never seen one do that before, but then, he'd never seen a Shardblade in the dark before.

Looking up at the rearing, alien silhouette before him—with its too many legs, its twisted head, its segmented armor—Kaladin thought he must know what a Voidbringer looked like. Surely nothing more terrible than this could exist.

Stepping backward, Kaladin stumbled on an outcropping of shalebark sprouting from the floor.

The chasmfiend struck.

Kaladin regained his balance easily, but had to throw himself into a roll—which required dropping the Shardblade, lest he slice himself. Shadowy claws smashed around him as he came out of his roll and sprang one way, then the other. He ended up pressed against the slimy side of the chasm just in front of the monster, puffing. He was too close for the claws to get him, perhaps, and—

The head snapped down, mandibles gaping. Kaladin cursed, hurling himself to the side again. He grunted, rolling to his feet and scooping up the discarded Shardblade. It hadn't vanished—he knew enough about them to understand that once Shallan instructed it to remain, it would stay until she summoned it back.

Kaladin turned around as a claw came down where he had just been. He got a swipe at it, cutting through the claw's tip as it crashed into rock.

His cut didn't seem to do much. The Blade scored the carapace and killed the flesh inside—prompting a trump of anger—but the claw was enormous. He'd done the equivalent of cutting off the tip of an enemy soldier's big toe. Storms. He wasn't fighting the beast; he was just annoying it.

It came more aggressively, sweeping at him with a claw. Fortunately, the confines of the chasm made it difficult for the creature to swing; its arms brushed the walls, and it couldn't pull back for full leverage. That was probably why Kaladin was still alive. He got out of the way of the sweep, barely, but tripped in the darkness again. He could hardly see.

As another claw crashed toward him, Kaladin got to his feet and dashed away—running farther down the corridor, farther from the light, passing plants and flotsam. The chasmfiend trumped and charged after him, clacking and scraping.

Kaladin felt so *slow* without Stormlight. So clumsy and awkward.

The chasmfiend was close. He judged his next move by instinct. *Now!* He stopped with a lurch, then sprinted back toward the creature. It slowed with great difficulty, carapace grinding on the walls, and Kaladin ducked and ran beneath it. He slammed the Shardblade upward, sinking it deep into the creature's underside.

The beast trumped more frantically. He seemed to have actually hurt it, for it immediately lifted upward to pull itself off the sword. Then it twisted down upon itself in an eyeblink, and Kaladin found those frightful jaws coming at him. He threw himself forward, but the snapping jaws caught his leg.

Blinding pain ran up the limb, and he struck out with the Blade even as the beast flung him about. He thought he hit its face, though he couldn't be certain.

The world spun.

He hit the ground and rolled.

No time to be dizzy. With everything still spinning, he groaned and turned over. He'd lost the Shardblade—he didn't know where it was. His leg. He couldn't feel it.

He looked down, expecting to see nothing but a ragged stump. It wasn't quite so bad. Bloodied, the trousers ripped, but he couldn't see bone. The numbness was from shock.

His mind had gone analytical and focused on the wounds. That wasn't good. He needed the soldier at the moment, not the surgeon. The chasmfiend was righting itself in the chasm, and a chunk of its facial carapace was missing.

Get. Away.

Kaladin turned over and climbed to hands and knees, then lurched to his feet. The leg worked, kind of. His boot squished as he stepped.

Where was the Shardblade? There, ahead. It had flown far, embedding itself in the ground near the spheres he'd tossed from the rift. Kaladin hobbled toward it, but had trouble walking, let alone running. He was halfway there when his leg gave out. He hit hard, scraping his arm on shalebark.

The chasmfiend trumped and—

"Hey! Hey!"

Kaladin twisted about. Shallan? What was that fool woman doing, standing in the chasm, waving her hands like a maniac? How had she even gotten past him?

She yelled again, getting the chasmfiend's attention. Her voice echoed oddly.

The chasmfiend turned from Kaladin to Shallan, then began to smash at her.

"No!" Kaladin yelled. But what was the use in shouting? He needed his weapon. Gritting his teeth, he twisted about and scrambled—as best he could—to the Shardblade. Storms. Shallan . . .

He ripped the sword from the rock, but then he collapsed again. The leg just wouldn't hold him. He twisted back, holding out the Blade, searching the chasm. The monster continued to swipe about, trumping, the terrible sound echoing and reverberating in the narrow confines. Kaladin couldn't see a corpse. Had Shallan escaped?

Stabbing the blasted thing through the chest only seemed to have made it angrier. The head. His only chance was the head.

Kaladin struggled to his feet. The monster stopped smashing against the ground and with a trump surged toward him. Kaladin gripped the sword in two hands, then wavered. His leg buckled beneath him. He tried to go down on one knee, but the leg gave out completely, and he slumped to the side and narrowly avoided slicing himself with the Shardblade.

He splashed into a pool of water. In front of him, one of the spheres he'd tossed shone with a bright white light.

He reached into the water, snatching it, clutching the chilled glass. He needed that Light. Storms, his life depended on it.

Please.

The chasmfiend loomed above.

Kaladin sucked in a breath, straining, like a man gasping for air. He heard . . . as if distantly . . .

Weeping.

No power entered him.

The chasmfiend swung and Kaladin twisted, and strangely found *himself.*

The other version of him stood above him, sword raised, larger than life. It was bigger than him by half.

What in the Almighty's own eyes . . . ? Kaladin thought, dumbfounded, as the chasmfiend smashed an arm down onto the figure beside Kaladin. That not-him shattered into a puff of Stormlight.

What had he done? How had he done it?

No matter. He lived. With a cry of desperation, he threw himself back to his feet and lurched toward the chasmfiend. He needed to get close, as he had before, too close for the claws to swing in these confines.

So close that . . .

The chasmfiend reared, then snapped down for a bite, mandibles extending, terrible eyes bearing down.

Kaladin thrust upward.

◆⁙◆

The chasmfiend crashed down, chitin snapping, legs spasming. Shallan cried out, freehand to mouth, from where she hid behind a boulder, her skin and clothing turned deep black.

The chasmfiend had fallen on Kaladin.

Shallan dropped her paper—it bore a drawing of her and another of Kaladin—and scrambled across the rocks, dismissing the blackness around her. She'd needed to be close to the fighting for the illusions to work. Better if she'd been able to send them on Pattern, but that was problematic because—

She stopped in front of the still-twitching beast, a heap of flesh and carapace like a fallen avalanche of stone. She shifted from one foot to another, uncertain what to do. "Kaladin?" she called out. Her voice was frail in the darkness.

Stop it, she told herself. *No timidity. You're past that.* Taking a deep breath, she moved forward, picking her way over the huge armored legs. She tried to shove aside a claw, but it was far too heavy for her, so she climbed over it and skidded down the other side.

She froze as she heard something. The chasmfiend's head lay nearby, massive eyes cloudy. Spren started to rise from it, like trails of smoke. The same ones as before, only . . . leaving? She held her light closer.

The bottom half of Kaladin's body protruded from the chasmfiend's mouth. Almighty above! Shallan gasped, then scrambled forward. She tried, with difficulty, to pull Kaladin from the closed maw before summoning her Shardblade and cutting away at several mandibles.

"Kaladin?" she asked, nervously peering into the thing's mouth from the side, where she'd removed a mandible.

"Ow," a weak voice trailed back to her.

Alive! "Hang on!" she said, hacking at the thing's head, careful not to cut too close to Kaladin. Violet ichor spurted out, coating her arms, smelling like wet mold.

"This is kind of uncomfortable . . ." Kaladin said.

"You're alive," Shallan said. "Stop complaining."

He was alive. Oh, Stormfather. Alive. She would have a whole *heap* of prayers to burn when they got back.

"Smells awful in here," Kaladin said weakly. "Almost as bad as you do."

"Be glad," Shallan said as she worked. "Here, I have a reasonably perfect specimen of a chasmfiend—with only a minor case of being dead—and I'm chopping it apart for you instead of studying it."

"I'm eternally grateful."

"How did you get in its mouth, anyway?" Shallan asked, prying off a piece of carapace with a sickening sound. She tossed it aside.

"Stabbed it through the roof of its mouth," Kaladin said, "into the brain. Only way I could figure to kill the blasted thing."

She leaned down, reaching her hand through the large hole she'd opened. With some work—and with a little cutting at the front mandibles—she managed to help Kaladin wiggle out the side of the mouth. Covered in ichor and blood, face pale from apparent blood loss, he looked like death itself.

"Storms," she whispered, as he lay back on the rocks.

"Bind my leg," Kaladin said weakly. "The rest of me should be fine. Heal right up . . ."

She looked at the mess of his leg, and shivered. It looked like . . . Like . . . Balat . . .

Kaladin wouldn't be walking on that leg anytime soon. *Oh, Stormfather,* she thought, cutting off the skirt of her dress at the knees. She wrapped his leg tightly, as he instructed. He seemed to think he didn't need a tourniquet. She listened to him; he'd probably bound far more wounds than she had.

She cut the sleeve off her right arm and used that to bind a second wound on his side, where the chasmfiend had started to rip him in half as it bit. Then she settled down next to him, feeling drained and cold, legs and arm now exposed to the chill air of the chasm bottom.

Kaladin took a deep breath, resting on the rock ground, eyes closed. "Two hours until the highstorm," he whispered.

Shallan checked the sky. It was almost dark. "If that long," she whispered. "We beat it, but we're dead anyway, aren't we?"

"Seems unfair," he said. Then he groaned, sitting up.

"Shouldn't you—"

"Bah. I've had far worse wounds than this."

She raised an eyebrow at him as he opened his eyes. He looked dizzy.

"I have," he insisted. "That's not just soldier bravado."

"This bad?" she asked. "How often?"

"Twice," he admitted. He looked over the hulking form of the chasmfiend. "We actually killed the thing."

"Sad, I know," she said, feeling depressed. "It was beautiful."

"It would be more beautiful if it hadn't tried to eat me."

"From my perspective," Shallan noted, "it didn't try, it succeeded."

"Nonsense," Kaladin said. "It didn't manage to swallow me. Doesn't count." He held his hand out to her, as if for help getting to his feet.

"You want to try to keep going?"

"You expect me to just lie here in the chasm until the waters come?"

"No, but . . ." She looked up. The chasmfiend was big. Maybe twenty feet tall, as it lay on its side. "What if we climbed up that thing, then tried to scale up to the top of the plateau?" The farther westward they'd gone, the shallower the chasms had grown.

Kaladin looked up. "That's still a good eighty feet of climbing, Shallan. And what would we do on the top of the plateau? The storm would blow us off."

"We could at least try to find some kind of shelter . . ." she said. "Storms, it really is hopeless, isn't it?"

Oddly, he cocked his head. "Probably."

"Only 'probably'?"

"Shelter . . . You have a Shardblade."

"And?" she asked. "I can't cut away a wall of water."

"No, but you *can* cut stone." He looked up, toward the wall of the chasm.

Shallan's breath caught in her throat. "We can carve out a cubby! Like the scouts use."

"High up the wall," he said. "You can see the water line up there. If we can get above that . . ."

It still meant climbing. She wouldn't have to go all the way to where the chasm got narrow at the top, but it wouldn't be an easy climb, by any means. And she had very little time.

But it was a chance.

"You're going to have to do it," Kaladin said. "I might be able to stand, with help. But climbing while wielding a Shardblade . . ."

"Right," Shallan said, standing up. She took a deep breath. "Right."

She started by scaling the back of the chasmfiend. The smooth carapace made for slippery climbing, but she found footholds between plates. Once on its back, she looked up toward the water line. It seemed much higher than it had from below.

"Cut handholds," Kaladin called.

Right. She kept forgetting about the Shardblade. She didn't want to think about it . . .

No. No time for that now. She summoned the Blade and cut out a series of long strips of rock, sending chunks falling to bounce off the carapace. She tucked her hair behind her ear, working in the dim light to create a ladderlike series of handholds up the side of the wall.

She started climbing them. Standing on one and clinging to the highest one, she summoned the Blade again and tried to cut a step even higher, but the thing was just so blasted long.

Obligingly, it shrank in her hand to the size of a much shorter sword, really a big knife.

Thank you, she thought, then cut out the next line of rock.

Up she went, handhold after handhold. It was sweaty work, and she periodically had to climb back down and rest her hands from clinging. Eventually, she got about as high as she figured she could, just over the water line. She hung there awkwardly, then began hacking out sections of rock, trying to cut them so they wouldn't tumble backward onto her head.

Falling stone made a beating sound on the dead chasmfiend's armor. "You're doing great!" Kaladin called up to her. "Keep at it!"

"When did you get so peppy?" she shouted.

"Ever since I assumed I was dead, then I suddenly wasn't."

"Then remind me to try to kill you once in a while," she snapped. "If I succeed, it will make me feel better, and if I fail, it will make you feel better. Everyone wins!"

She heard him chuckling as she dug deeper into the stone. It was more difficult than she'd have imagined. Yes, the Blade cut the rock easily, but she kept cutting sections that just *wouldn't* fall out. She had to chop them to pieces, then dismiss the Blade and grab chunks to pull them out.

After over an hour of frantic work, however, she managed to craft a semblance of a refuge. She didn't get the cubby hollowed out as deeply as she wanted, but it would have to do. Drained, she crawled back down her improvised ladder one last time and flopped on the chasmfiend's back amid the rubble. Her arms felt like she'd been lifting something heavy— and technically she probably had, since climbing meant lifting herself.

"Done?" Kaladin called up from the chasm floor.

"No," Shallan said, "but close enough. I think we might fit."

Kaladin was silent.

"You *are* coming up into the hole I just cut, Kaladin bridgeboy, chasmfiend-slayer and gloombringer." She leaned over the side of the chasmfiend to look at him. "We are *not* having another stupid conversation about you dying in here while I bravely continue on. Understand?"

"I'm not sure if I can walk, Shallan," Kaladin said with a sigh. "Let alone climb."

"You're going," Shallan said, "if I have to *carry* you."

He looked up, then grinned, face covered in dried violet ichor that he'd wiped away as best he could. "I'd like to see that."

"Come on," Shallan said, rising with some difficulty herself. Storms, she was tired. She used the Blade to hack a vine off the wall. It took two hits to get it free, amusingly. The first severed its soul. Then, dead, it could actually be cut by the sword.

The upper part withdrew, curling like a corkscrew to get height. She tossed down one side of the length she'd cut free. Kaladin took it with one hand, and—favoring his bad leg—carefully made his way up to the top of the chasmfiend. Once up, he flopped down beside her, sweat making trails through the grime on his face. He looked up at the ladder cut into the rock. "You're really going to make me climb that."

"Yes," she said. "For perfectly selfish reasons."

He looked to her.

"I'm not going to have your last sight in life be a view of me standing in half a filthy dress, covered in purple blood, my hair an utter mess. It's undignified. On your feet, bridgeboy."

In the distance, she heard a rumbling. *Not good* . . .

"Climb up," he said.

"I'm not—"

"Climb up," he said more firmly, "and lie down in the cubby, then reach your hand over the edge. Once I near the top, you can help me the last few feet."

She fretted for a moment, then fetched her satchel and made the climb. Storms, those handholds were slick. Once up, she crawled into the shallow cubby and perched precariously, reaching down with one hand as she braced herself with the other. He looked up at her, then set his jaw and started climbing.

He mostly pulled himself with his hands, wounded leg dangling, the other one steadying him. Heavily muscled, his soldier's arms slowly pulled him up slot by slot.

Below, water trickled down the chasm. Then it started to gush.

"Come on!" she said.

Wind howled through the chasms, a haunting, eerie sound that called through the many rifts. Like the moaning of spirits long dead. The high sound was accompanied by a low, rumbling roar.

All around, plants withdrew, vines twisting and pulling tight, rockbuds closing, frillblooms folding away. The chasm hid.

Kaladin grunted, sweating, his face tense with pain and exertion, his fingers trembling. He pulled himself up another rung, then reached his hand up toward hers.

The stormwall hit.

73

A THOUSAND SCURRYING CREATURES

ONE YEAR AGO

Shallan slipped into Balat's room, holding a short note between her fingers.

Balat spun, standing. He relaxed. "Shallan! You nearly killed me with fright."

The small room, like many in the manor house, had open windows with simple reed shutters—those were closed and latched today, as a highstorm was approaching. The last one before the Weeping. Servants outside pounded on the walls as they affixed sturdy stormshutters over the reed ones.

Shallan wore one of her new dresses, the expensive kind that Father bought for her, after the Vorin style, straight and slim-waisted with a pocket on the sleeve. A woman's dress. She also wore the necklace he had given her. He liked it when she did that.

Jushu lounged on a chair nearby, rubbing some kind of plant between his fingers, his face distant. He had lost weight during the two years since his creditors had dragged him from the house, though with those sunken eyes and the scars on his wrists, he still didn't look much like his twin.

Shallan eyed the bundles Balat had been preparing. "Good thing Father never checks in on you, Balat. Those bundles look so fishy, we could make a stew out of them."

Jushu chuckled, rubbing the scar on one wrist with the other hand. "Doesn't help that he jumps every time a servant so much as sneezes out in the hallway."

"Quiet, both of you," Balat said, eyeing the window where workers locked a stormshutter in place. "This is not a time for levity. Damnation. If he discovers that I'm planning to leave . . ."

"He won't," Shallan said, unfolding the letter. "He's too busy getting ready to parade himself in front of the highprince."

"Does it feel odd to anyone else," Jushu said, "to be this rich? How many deposits of valuable stone are there on our lands?"

Balat turned back to packing his bundles. "So long as it keeps Father happy, I don't care."

The problem was, it hadn't made Father happy. Yes, House Davar was now wealthy—the new quarries provided a fantastic income. Yet, the better off they were, the darker Father grew. Walking the hallways grumbling. Lashing out at servants.

Shallan scanned the letter's contents.

"That's not a pleased face," Balat said. "They still haven't been able to find him?"

Shallan shook her head. Helaran had vanished. Really vanished. No more contact, no more letters; even the people he'd been in touch with earlier had no idea where he'd gone.

Balat sat down on one of his bundles. "So what do we do?"

"You will need to decide," Shallan said.

"I have to get out. I *have* to." He ran his hand through his hair. "Eylita is ready to go with me. Her parents are away for the month, visiting Alethkar. It's the perfect time."

"If you can't find Helaran, then what?"

"I'll go to the highprince. His bastard said that he'd listen to anyone willing to speak against Father."

"That was years ago," Jushu said, leaning back. "Father's in favor now. Besides, the highprince is nearly dead; everyone knows it."

"It's our only chance," Balat said. He stood up. "I'm going to leave. Tonight, after the storm."

"But Father—" Shallan began.

"Father wants me to ride out and check on some of the villages along the eastern valley. I'll tell him I'm doing that, but instead I'll pick up Eylita and we'll ride for Vedenar and go straight to the highprince. By the time Father arrives a week later, I'll have had my say. It might be enough."

"And Malise?" Shallan asked. The plan was still for him to take their stepmother to safety.

"I don't know," Balat said. "He's not going to let her go. Maybe once he leaves to visit the highprince, you can send her away someplace safe? I don't know. Either way, I *have* to go. Tonight."

Shallan stepped forward, laying a hand on his arm.

"I'm tired of the fear," Balat said to her. "I'm tired of being a coward. If Helaran has vanished, then I really am eldest. Time to show it. I won't just run, spending my life wondering if Father's minions are hunting us. This way . . . this way it will be over. Decided."

The door slammed open.

For all her complaints that Balat was acting suspicious, Shallan jumped just as high as he did, letting out a squeak of surprise. It was only Wikim.

"Storms, Wikim!" Balat said. "You could at least knock or—"

"Eylita is here," Wikim said.

"*What?*" Balat leaped forward, grabbing his brother. "She wasn't to come! I was going to pick her up."

"Father summoned her," Wikim said. "She arrived with her handmaid just now. He's speaking with her in the feast hall."

"Oh *no*," Balat said, shoving Wikim aside, barreling through the door.

Shallan followed, but stopped in the doorway. "Don't do anything foolish!" she called after him. "Balat, the plan!"

He didn't appear to have heard her.

"This could be bad," Wikim said.

"Or it could be wonderful," Jushu said from behind them, still lounging. "If Father pushes Balat too far, maybe he'll stop whining and do something."

Shallan felt cold as she stepped into the hallway. That coldness . . . was that panic? Overwhelming panic, so sharp and strong it washed away everything else.

This had been coming. She'd *known* this had been coming. They tried to hide, they tried to flee. Of course that wouldn't work.

It hadn't worked with Mother either.

Wikim passed her, running. She stepped slowly. Not because she was calm, but because she felt *pulled* forward. A slow pace resisted the inevitability.

She turned up the steps instead of going down to the feast hall. She needed to fetch something.

It took only a minute. She soon returned, the pouch given to her long ago tucked into the safepouch in her sleeve. She walked down the steps and to the doorway of the feast hall. Jushu and Wikim waited just outside of it, watching tensely.

They made way for her.

Inside the feast hall, there was shouting, of course.

"You shouldn't have done this without talking to me!" Balat said. He stood before the high table, Eylita at his side, holding to his arm.

Father stood on the other side of the table, half-eaten meal before him. "Talking to you is useless, Balat. You don't hear."

"I *love* her!"

"You're a child," Father said. "A foolish child without regard for your house."

Bad, bad, bad, Shallan thought. Father's voice was soft. He was most dangerous when his voice was soft.

"You think," Father continued, leaning forward, palms on the tabletop, "I don't know about your plan to leave?"

Balat stumbled back. *"How?"*

Shallan stepped into the room. *What is that on the floor?* she thought, walking along the wall toward the door into the kitchens. Something blocked the door from closing.

Rain began to pelt the rooftop outside. The storm had come. The guards were in their guardhouse, the servants in their quarters to wait the storm's passing. The family was alone.

With the windows closed, the only light in the room was the cool illumination of spheres. Father did not have a fire burning in the hearth.

"Helaran is dead," Father said. "Did you know that? You can't find him because he's been killed. I didn't even have to do it. He found his own death on a battlefield in Alethkar. Idiot."

The words threatened Shallan's cold calm.

"How did you find out I was leaving?" Balat demanded. He stepped forward, but Eylita held him back. "Who told you?"

Shallan knelt by the obstruction in the kitchen doorway. Thunder rumbled, making the building vibrate. The obstruction was a body.

Malise. Dead from several blows to the head. Fresh blood. Warm corpse. He had killed her recently. Storms. He'd found out about the plan, had sent for Eylita and waited for her to arrive, *then* killed his wife.

Not a crime of the moment. He'd murdered her as punishment.

So it has come to this, Shallan thought, feeling a strange, detached calm. *The lie becomes the truth.*

This was Shallan's fault. She stood up and rounded the room toward where servants had left a pitcher of wine, with cups, for Father.

"Malise," Balat said. He hadn't looked toward Shallan; he was just guessing. "She broke down and told you, didn't she? Damnation. We shouldn't have trusted her."

"Yes," Father said. "She talked. Eventually."

Balat's sword made a whispering rasp as he pulled it from its leather sheath. Father's sword followed.

"Finally," Father said. "You show hints of a backbone."

"Balat, no," Eylita said, clinging to him.

"I won't fear him any longer, Eylita! I *won't!*"

Shallan poured wine.

They clashed, Father leaping over the high table, swinging in a two-handed blow. Eylita screamed and scrambled back while Balat swung at his father.

Shallan did not know much of swordplay. She had watched Balat and the others spar, but the only real fights she'd seen were duels at the fair.

This was different. This was *brutal*. Father bashing his sword down again and again toward Balat, who blocked as best he could with his own sword. The *clang* of metal on metal, and above it all the storm. Each blow seemed to shake the room. Or was that the thunder?

Balat stumbled before the onslaught, falling on one knee. Father batted the sword out of Balat's fingers.

Could it really be over that quickly? Only seconds had passed. Not like the duels at all.

Father loomed over his son. "I've always despised you," Father said. "The coward. Helaran was noble. He resisted me, but he had *passion*. You . . . you crawl about, whining and complaining."

Shallan moved up to him. "Father?" She handed the wine toward him. "He's down. You've won."

"I always wanted sons," Father said. "And I got four. All worthless! A coward, a drunkard, and a weakling." He blinked. "Only Helaran . . . Only Helaran . . ."

"Father?" Shallan said. *"Here."*

He took the wine, gulping it down.

Balat grabbed his sword. Still on one knee, he struck with a lunge. Shallan screamed, and the sword made a strange *clang* as it barely missed Father, stabbing through his coat and out the back, connecting with something metallic.

Father dropped the cup. It smashed, empty, to the ground. He grunted, feeling at his side. Balat pulled the sword back and stared upward at his father in horror.

Father's hand came back with a touch of blood on it, but not much. "That's the best you have?" Father demanded. "Fifteen years of sword training, and that's your best attack? Strike at me! Hit me!" He held his sword out to the side, raising his other hand.

Balat started to blubber, sword slipping from his fingers.

"Bah!" Father said. "Useless." He tossed his sword onto the high table, then stepped over to the hearth. He grabbed an iron poker, then walked back. "Useless."

He slammed the poker down on Balat's thigh.

"Father!" Shallan screamed, trying to take his arm. He shoved her aside as he struck again, smashing his poker against Balat's leg.

Balat screamed.

Shallan hit the ground hard, knocking her head against the floor. She could only hear what happened next. Shouts. The poker connecting with a sound like a dull thump. The storm raging above.

"Why." *Smack.* "Can't." *Smack.* "You." *Smack.* "Do." *Smack.* "Anything." *Smack.* "Right?"

Shallan's vision cleared. Father drew deep breaths. Blood had splattered his face. Balat whimpered on the floor. Eylita held to him, face buried in his hair. Balat's leg was a bloody mess.

Wikim and Jushu still stood in the doorway to the hall, looking horrified.

Father looked to Eylita, murder in his eyes. He raised his poker to strike. But then the weapon slipped from his fingers and clanged to the ground. He looked at his hand as if surprised, then stumbled. He grabbed the table for support, but fell to his knees, then slumped to the side.

Rain pelted the roof. It sounded like a thousand scurrying creatures looking for a way into the building.

Shallan forced herself to her feet. Coldness. Yes, she recognized that coldness inside of her now. She'd felt it before, on the day when she'd lost her mother.

"Bind Balat's wounds," she said, approaching the weeping Eylita. "Use his shirt."

The woman nodded through her tears and began working with trembling fingers.

Shallan knelt beside her father. He lay motionless, eyes open and dead, staring at the ceiling.

"What . . . what happened?" Wikim asked. She hadn't noticed him and Jushu timidly entering the room, rounding the table and joining her. Wikim peered over her shoulder. "Did Balat's strike to the side . . ."

Father was bleeding there; Shallan could feel it through the clothing. It wasn't nearly bad enough to have caused this though. She shook her head.

"You gave me something a few years ago," she said. "A pouch. I kept it. You said it grows more potent over time."

"Oh, *Stormfather,*" Wikim said, raising his hand to his mouth. "The blackbane? You . . ."

"In his wine," Shallan said. "Malise is dead by the kitchen. He went too far."

"You've killed him," Wikim said, staring at their father's corpse. "You've *killed* him!"

"Yes," Shallan said, feeling exhausted. She stumbled over to Balat, then began helping Eylita with the bandages. Balat was conscious and grunting at the pain. Shallan nodded to Eylita, who fetched him some wine. Unpoisoned, of course.

Father was dead. She'd killed him.

"What is this?" Jushu asked.

"Don't do that!" Wikim said. "Storms! You're going through his pockets already?"

Shallan glanced over to see Jushu pulling something silvery from Father's coat pocket. It was shrouded in a small black bag, mildly wet with blood, only pieces of it showing from where Balat's sword had struck.

"Oh, *Stormfather*," Jushu said, pulling it out. The device consisted of several chains of silvery metal connecting three large gemstones, one of which was cracked, its glow lost. "Is this what I think it is?"

"A *Soulcaster*," Shallan said.

"Prop me up," Balat said as Eylita returned with the wine. "Please."

Reluctantly the girl helped him sit. His leg . . . his leg was not in good shape. They would need to get him a surgeon.

Shallan stood, wiping bloodied hands on her dress, and took the Soulcaster from Jushu. The delicate metal was broken where the sword had struck it.

"I don't understand," Jushu said. "Isn't that blasphemy? Don't those belong to the king, only to be used by ardents?"

Shallan rubbed her thumb across the metal. She couldn't think. Numbness . . . shock. That was it. Shock.

I killed Father.

Wikim yelped suddenly, jumping back. "His leg twitched."

Shallan spun on the body. Father's fingers spasmed.

"Voidbringers!" Jushu said. He looked up at the ceiling, and at the raging storm. "They're here. They're inside of him. It—"

Shallan knelt next to the body. The eyes trembled, then focused on her. "It wasn't enough," she whispered. "The poison wasn't strong enough."

"Oh, storms!" Wikim said, kneeling next to her. "He's still breathing. It didn't kill him, it just paralyzed him." His eyes widened. "And he's waking."

"We need to finish the job, then," Shallan said. She looked to her brothers.

Jushu and Wikim stumbled away, shaking their heads. Balat, dazed, was barely conscious.

She turned back to her father. He was looking at her, his eyes moving easily now. His leg twitched.

"I'm sorry," she whispered, unhooking her necklace. "Thank you for what you did for me." She wrapped the necklace around his neck.

Then she began to twist.

She used the handle of one of the forks that had fallen from the table as her father tried to steady himself. She looped one side of the closed necklace around it, and in twisting, pulled the chain very tight around Father's throat.

"Now go to sleep," she whispered, "in chasms deep, with darkness all around you . . ."

A lullaby. Shallan spoke the song through her tears—the song he'd sung for her as a child, when she was frightened. Red blood speckled his face and covered her hands.

"Though rock and dread may be your bed, so sleep my baby dear."

She felt his eyes on her. Her skin squirmed as she held the necklace tight.

"Now comes the storm," she whispered, "but you'll be warm, the wind will rock your basket . . ."

Shallan had to watch as his eyes bulged out, his face turning colors. His body trembling, straining, trying to move. The eyes looked to her, demanding, *betrayed*.

Almost, Shallan could imagine that the storm's howls were part of a nightmare. That soon she would awaken in terror, and Father would sing to her. As he'd done when she was a child . . .

"The crystals fine . . . will glow sublime . . ."

Father stopped moving.

"And with a song . . . you'll sleep . . . my baby dear."

*You, however, have never been a force for equilibrium. You tow
chaos behind you like a corpse dragged by one leg through the
snow. Please, hearken to my plea. Leave that place and join me in
my oath of nonintervention.*

Kaladin caught Shallan's hand.

Boulders crashed above, smashing against the plateaus, breaking
off chunks and tossing them down around him. Wind raged. Water swelled below, rising toward him. He clung to Shallan, but their wet
hands started to slip.

And then, in a sudden *surge*, her grip tightened. With a strength that
seemed to belie her smaller form, she heaved. Kaladin shoved with his
good leg as water washed over it, and forced himself up the remaining
distance to join her in the rocky alcove.

The hollow was barely three or four feet deep, shallower than the crack
they'd hid in. Fortunately, it faced westward. Though icy wind twisted
about and sprayed water on them, the brunt of the storm was broken by
the plateau.

Puffing, Kaladin pulled against the wall of the alcove, his injured leg
smarting like nothing else, Shallan clinging to him. She was a warmth
in his arms, and he held to her as much as she did him, both of them sitting hunched against the rock, his head brushing the top of the hollowed
hole.

The plateau shuddered, quivering like a frightened man. He couldn't see
much; the blackness was absolute except when lightning came. And the
sound. Thunder crashing, seemingly disconnected from the sprays of light-

ning. Water roared like an angry beast, and the flashes illuminated a frothing, churning, raging river in the chasm.

Damnation . . . it was almost up to their alcove. It had risen fifty or more feet in moments. The dirty water was filled with branches, broken plants, vines ripped from their mountings.

"The sphere?" Kaladin asked in the blackness. "You had a sphere with you for light."

"Gone," she shouted over the roar. "I must have dropped it when I grabbed you!"

"I didn't—"

A *crash* of thunder, accompanied by a blinding flash of light, sent him stuttering. Shallan pulled more tightly against him, fingers digging into his arm. The light left an afterimage in his eyes.

Storms. He could swear that afterimage was a face, horribly twisted, the mouth pulled open. The next lightning bolt lit the flood just outside with a sequence of crackling light, and it showed water bobbing with corpses. Dozens of them pulled past in the current, dead eyes toward the sky, many just empty sockets. Men and Parshendi.

The water surged upward, and a few inches of it flooded the chamber. The water of dead men. The storm went dark again, as black as a cavern beneath the ground. Just Kaladin, Shallan, and the bodies.

"That was," Shallan said, her head near his, "the most surreal thing I've ever seen."

"Storms are strange."

"You speak from experience?"

"Sadeas hung me out in one," he said. "I was supposed to die."

That tempest had tried to rip the skin, then muscles, from his skeleton. Rain like knives. Lightning like a cauterizing iron.

And a small figure, all white, standing before him with hands forward, as if to part the tempest for him. Tiny and frail, yet as strong as the winds themselves.

Syl . . . what have I done to you?

"I need to hear the story," Shallan said.

"I'll tell it to you sometime."

Water washed up over them again. For a moment, they became lighter, floating in the sudden burst of water. The current pulled with unexpected strength, as if eager to tow them out into the river. Shallan screamed and Kaladin gripped the rock on either side, holding on in a panic. The river retreated, though he could still hear it rushing. They settled back into the alcove.

Light came from above, too steady to be lightning. Something was *glowing* on the plateau. Something that moved. It was hard to see, since water streamed off the side of the plateau above, falling in a sheet before their refuge. He *swore* he saw an enormous figure walking up there, a glowing inhuman form, followed by another, alien and sleek. Striding the storm. Leg after leg, until the glow passed.

"Please," Shallan said. "I need to hear something other than *that*. Tell me."

He shivered, but nodded. Voices. Voices would help. "It started when Amaram betrayed me," he said, tone hushed, just loud enough for her—pressed close—to hear. "He made me a slave for knowing the truth, that he'd killed my men in his lust to get a Shardblade. That it mattered more to him than his own soldiers, more to him than honor . . ."

He continued on, talking of his days as a slave, of his attempts to escape. Of the men he'd gotten killed for trusting him. It gushed from him, a story he'd never told. Who would he have told it to? Bridge Four had lived most of it with him.

He told her of the wagon and of Tvlakv—that name earned a gasp. She apparently knew him. He spoke of the numbness, the . . . *nothing*. The thinking he should kill himself, but the trouble believing that it was worth the effort.

And then, Bridge Four. He didn't talk about Syl. Too much pain there right now. Instead, he talked of bridge runs, of terror, of death, and of decision.

Rain washed over them, blown in swirls, and he swore he could hear chanting out there somewhere. Some kind of strange spren zipped past their enclosure, red and violet and reminiscent of lightning. Was that what Syl had seen?

Shallan listened. He would have expected questions from her, but she didn't ask a single one. No pestering for details, no chattering. She apparently *did* know how to be quiet.

He got through it all, amazingly. The last bridge run. Rescuing Dalinar. He wanted to spill it all out. He talked about facing the Parshendi Shardbearer, about how he'd offended Adolin, about holding the bridgehead on his own . . .

When he finished, they both let the silence settle on them, and shared warmth. Together, they stared out at the rushing water just out of reach and lit by flashing.

"I killed my father," Shallan whispered.

Kaladin looked toward her. In a flash of light, he saw her eyes as she looked up from where her head had been resting against his chest, beads of water on her eyelashes. With his hands around her waist, hers around him, it was as close as he'd held a woman since Tarah.

"My father was a violent, angry man," Shallan said. "A murderer. I loved him. And I strangled him as he lay on the floor, watching me, unable to move. I killed my own father . . ."

He didn't prod her, though he wanted to know. *Needed* to know.

She went on, fortunately, speaking of her youth and the terrors she had known. Kaladin had thought his life terrible, but there was one thing he'd had, and perhaps not cherished enough: parents who loved him. Roshone had brought Damnation itself to Hearthstone, but at least Kaladin's mother and father had always been there to rely upon.

What would he have done, if his father had been like the abusive, hateful man Shallan described? If his mother had died before his own eyes? What would *he* have done if, instead of living off Tien's light, *he* had been required to bring light to the family?

He listened with wonder. Storms. Why wasn't this woman broken, truly broken? She described herself that way, but she was no more broken than a spear with a chipped blade—and a spear like that could still be as sharp a weapon as any. He preferred one with a score or two on the blade, a worn handle. A spearhead that had known fighting was just . . . better than a new one. You could know it had been used by a man fighting for his life, and that it had remained sure and not broken. Marks like those were signs of strength.

He did feel a chill as she mentioned her brother Helaran's death, anger in her voice.

Helaran had been killed in Alethkar. At Amaram's hands.

Storms . . . I killed him, didn't I? Kaladin thought. *The brother she loved.* Had he told her about that?

No. No, he hadn't mentioned that he'd killed the Shardbearer, only that Amaram had killed Kaladin's men to cover up his lust for the weapon. He'd gotten used to, over the years, referencing the event without mentioning that he'd killed a Shardbearer. His first few months as a slave had beaten into him the dangers of talking about an event like that. He hadn't even realized he'd fallen into that habit of speaking here.

Did she realize? Had she inferred that Kaladin, not Amaram, had been the one to actually kill the Shardbearer? She didn't seem to have made that connection. She continued talking, speaking of the night—also during a storm—when she'd poisoned, then murdered her father.

Almighty above. This woman was stronger than he'd ever been.

"And so," she continued, pressing her head back against his chest, "we decided that I would find Jasnah. She . . . had a Soulcaster, you see."

"You wanted to see if she could fix yours?"

"That would have been too rational." He couldn't see her scowl at herself, but he heard it, somehow. "My plan—being stupid and naive—was to *swap* mine for hers and bring back a working one to make money for the family."

"You had never left your family's lands before."

"Yes."

"And you went to *rob* one of the smartest women in the world?"

"Er . . . yes. Remember that bit about 'stupid and naive'? Anyway, Jasnah found out. Fortunately, I intrigued her and she agreed to take me on as a ward. The marriage to Adolin was her idea, a way to protect my family while I trained."

"Huh," he said. Lightning flashed outside. The winds seemed to be building even further, if that was possible, and he had to raise his voice even though Shallan was right there. "Generous, for a woman you intended to rob."

"I think she saw something in me that—"

Silence.

Kaladin blinked. Shallan was gone. He panicked for a moment, searching about himself, until he realized that his leg no longer hurt and the fuzziness in his head—from blood loss, shock, and possible hypothermia—was gone too.

Ah, he thought. *This again.*

He took a deep breath and stood up, stepping out of the blackness to the lip of the opening. The stream below had stopped, as if frozen solid, and the opening of the alcove—which Shallan had made far too low to stand up in—could now hold him standing at full height.

He looked out and met the gaze of a face as wide as eternity itself.

"Stormfather," Kaladin said. Some named him Jezerezeh, Herald. This didn't fit what Kaladin had heard of any Herald, however. Was the Stormfather a spren, perhaps? A god? It seemed to stretch forever, yet he could see it, make out the face in its infinite expanse.

The winds had stopped. Kaladin could hear his own heartbeat.

CHILD OF HONOR. It spoke to him this time. Last time, in the middle of the storm, it had not—though it had done so in dreams.

Kaladin looked to the side, again checking to see if Shallan was there, but he couldn't see her any longer. She wasn't part of this vision, whatever it was.

"She's one of them, isn't she?" he asked. "Of the Knights Radiant, or at least a Surgebinder. That's what happened when fighting the chasmfiend, that's how she survived the fall. It wasn't me either time. It was her."

The Stormfather rumbled.

"Syl," Kaladin said, looking back to the face. The plateaus in front of him had vanished. It was just him and the face. He had to ask. It hurt him, but he *had* to. "What have I done to her?"

YOU HAVE KILLED HER. The voice shook everything. It was as if . . . as if the shaking of the plateau and his own body *made* the sounds for the voice.

"No," Kaladin whispered. "No!"

IT HAPPENED AS IT ONCE DID, the Stormfather said, angry. A human emotion. Kaladin recognized it. MEN CANNOT BE TRUSTED, CHILD OF TANAVAST. YOU HAVE TAKEN HER FROM ME. MY BELOVED ONE.

The face seemed to withdraw, fading.

"Please!" Kaladin screamed. "How can I fix it? What can I do?"

IT CANNOT BE FIXED. SHE IS BROKEN. YOU ARE LIKE THE ONES WHO CAME BEFORE, THE ONES WHO KILLED SO MANY OF THOSE I LOVE. FARE-WELL, SON OF HONOR. YOU WILL NOT RIDE MY WINDS AGAIN.

"No, I—"

The storm returned. Kaladin collapsed back into the alcove, gasping at the sudden restoration of pain and cold.

"Kelek's breath!" Shallan said. "What was *that*?"

"You saw the face?" Kaladin asked.

"Yes. So vast . . . I could see stars in it, stars upon stars, infinity . . ."

"The Stormfather," Kaladin said, tired. He reached around beneath him for something that was suddenly glowing. A sphere, the one Shallan had dropped earlier. It had gone dun, but was now renewed.

"That was amazing," she whispered. "I need to draw it."

"Good luck," Kaladin said, "in this rain." As if to punctuate his point, another wave of it washed over them. It would swirl in between the chasms, twisting about and sometimes blowing back at them. They sat in water a few inches deep, but it didn't threaten to pull them away again.

"My poor drawings," Shallan said, pulling her satchel to her breast with her safehand as she held to him—the only thing *to* hold to—with her other. "The satchel is waterproof, but . . . I don't know that it's highstorm-proof."

Kaladin grunted, staring out at the rushing water. There was a mesmer-izing pattern to it, surging with broken plants and leaves. No corpses, not anymore. The flowing water rose in a large bump before them, as if rush-ing over something large beneath. The chasmfiend's carcass, he realized, was still wedged down there. It was too heavy for even the flood to budge.

They fell silent. With light, the need to speak had passed, and though he considered confronting her about what he was increasingly sure she was, he said nothing. Once they were free, there would be time.

For now, he wanted to think—though he was still glad for her presence. And aware of it in more ways than one, pushed against him and wearing the wet, increasingly tattered dress.

His conversation with the Stormfather, however, drew his attention away from that sort of thought.

Syl. Had he really . . . killed her? He had heard her weeping earlier, hadn't he?

He tried, just out of futile experimentation, to pull in some Stormlight. He kind of wanted Shallan to see, to gauge her reaction. It didn't work, of course.

The storm slowly passed, the floodwaters receding bit by bit. After the rains slackened to the level of an ordinary storm, the waters started flowing in the other direction. It was as he'd always assumed, though never seen. Now rain was falling more on the ground west of the Plains than on the Plains themselves, and the drainage was all to the east. The river churned—far more lethargically—back out the way it had come.

The chasmfiend's corpse emerged from the river. Then, finally, the flood was done—the river reduced to a trickle, the rain a drizzle. The drops that dripped from the plateaus above were far larger and heavier than the rain itself.

He shifted to move to climb down, but realized that Shallan, curled up against him, had fallen asleep. She snored softly.

"You must be the only person," he whispered, "to ever fall asleep while outside in a highstorm."

Uncomfortable though he was, he realized he *really* didn't fancy the idea of climbing down with this wounded leg. Strength sapped, feeling a crushing darkness at what the Stormfather had said about Syl, he let himself succumb to the numbness, and fell asleep.

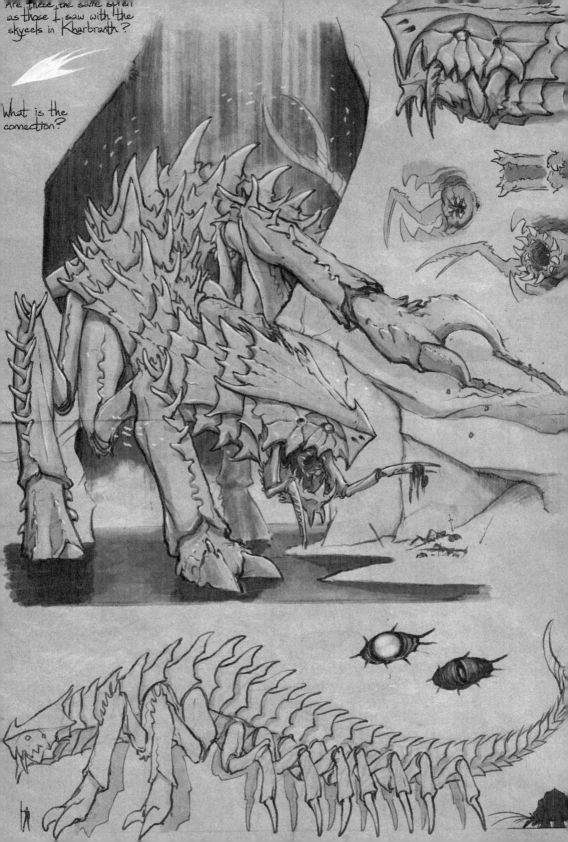

Are these the same spren
as those I saw with the
skyeels in Kharbranth?

What is the
connection?

The cosmere itself may depend upon our restraint.

A t least speak with him, Dalinar," Amaram said. The man walked quickly to match Dalinar's pace, his cloak of the Knights Radiant billowing behind him, as they inspected the lines of troops loading up wagons with supplies for the trip out onto the Shattered Plains. "Come to an accommodation with Sadeas before you leave. Please."

Dalinar, Navani, and Amaram passed a group of spearmen running to get into place with their battalion, which was counting ranks. Just beyond them, the men and women of the camp acted similarly excited. Cremlings scuttled this way and that, moving through pools of water left by the storm.

Last night's highstorm was the final one of the season. Sometime tomorrow, the Weeping would begin. Wet though it would be, it provided a window. Safety from storms, time to strike out. He planned to leave by midday.

"Dalinar?" Amaram asked. "Will you talk to him?"

Careful, Dalinar thought. *Don't make any judgments just yet.* This had to be done with precision. At his side, Navani eyed him. He'd shared his plans regarding Amaram with her.

"I—" Dalinar began.

A series of horns interrupted him, blaring above through the camp. They seemed more urgent than usual. A chrysalis had been spotted. Dalinar counted the rhythms, placing the plateau location.

"Too far," he said, pointing to one of his scribes, a tall, lanky woman that often helped Navani with her experiments. "Who is on the schedule for today's runs?"

"Highprinces Sebarial and Roion, sir," the scribe said, consulting her ledger.

Dalinar grimaced. Sebarial never sent troops, even when commanded. Roion was slow. "Send the signal flags to tell those two the gemheart is too far out to try for. We'll be marching for the Parshendi camp later today, and I can't have some of our troops splitting off and running for a gemheart."

He made the order as if either man would commit any troops to his march. He had hopes for Roion. Almighty send that the man didn't get frightened at the last minute and refuse to go on the expedition.

The attendant rushed away to call off the plateau run. Navani pointed to a group of scribes who were tabulating supply lists, and he nodded, stopping while she walked over to talk to the women and get an estimate on readiness.

"Sadeas won't like a gemheart being left unharvested," Amaram said as the two of them waited. "When he hears you called off the run, he'll send his own troops for it."

"Sadeas will do as he wishes, regardless of my intervention."

"Each time you allow him to disobey openly," Amaram said, "it drives a wedge between him and the Throne." Amaram took Dalinar by the arm. "We have bigger problems than you and Sadeas, my friend. Yes, he betrayed you. Yes, he likely will again. But we can't afford to let the two of you go to war. The Voidbringers *are* coming."

"How can you be certain of that, Amaram?" Dalinar asked.

"Instinct. You gave me this title, this position, Dalinar. I can feel something from the Stormfather himself. I know that a disaster is coming. Alethkar needs to be strong. That means you and Sadeas working together."

Dalinar shook his head slowly. "No. The opportunity for Sadeas to work with me has long since passed. The road to unity in Alethkar is not at the table of negotiation, it's out there."

Across the plateaus, to the Parshendi camp, wherever it was. An end to this war. Closure for both him and his brother.

Unite them.

"Sadeas *wants* you to try this expedition," Amaram said. "He's certain you will fail."

"And when I do not," Dalinar said, "he will lose all credibility."

"You don't even know where you'll find the Parshendi!" Amaram said, throwing his hands into the air. "What are you going to do, just wander out there until you run across them?"

"Yes."

"Madness. Dalinar, you appointed me to this position—an impossible position, mind you—with the charge to be a light to all nations. I'm finding it hard to even get *you* to listen to me. Why should anyone else?"

Dalinar shook his head, looking eastward, over those broken plains.

"I have to go, Amaram. The answers are out there, not here. It's like we walked all the way to the shore, then huddled there for years, peering out at the waters but afraid to get wet."

"But—"

"Enough."

"Eventually, you're going to have to give away authority and let it stay *given*, Dalinar," Amaram said softly. "You can't hold it all, pretending you aren't in charge, but then ignore orders and advice as if you were."

The words, problematically truthful, slapped him hard. He did not react, not outwardly.

"What of the matter I assigned you?" Dalinar asked him.

"Bordin?" Amaram said. "So far as I can tell, his story checks out. I really think that the madman is only raving about having had a Shardblade. It's patently ridiculous that he might have actually had one. I—"

"Brightlord!" A breathless young woman in a messenger uniform—narrow skirt slit up the sides, with silk leggings beneath—scrambled up to him. "The plateau!"

"Yes," Dalinar said, sighing. "Sadeas is sending out troops?"

"No, sir," the woman said, flush in the cheeks from her run. "Not . . . I mean . . . He came *out* of the chasms."

Dalinar frowned, looking sharply toward her. "Who?"

"Stormblessed."

⁘

Dalinar ran the entire way.

When he drew close to the triage pavilion at the edge of camp—normally reserved for tending to the wounded who came back from plateau runs—he had trouble seeing because of the crowd of men in cobalt blue uniforms blocking the path. A surgeon was yelling for them to back up and give him room.

Some of the men saw Dalinar and saluted, hastily pulling out of the way. The blue parted like waters blown in a storm.

And there he was. Ragged, hair matted in snarls, face scratched and leg wrapped in an improvised bandage. He sat on a triage table and had removed his uniform coat, which sat on the table beside him, tied into a round bundle with what looked like a vine wrapping it.

Kaladin looked up as Dalinar approached, and then moved to pull himself to his feet.

"Soldier, don't—" Dalinar began, but Kaladin didn't listen. He hauled himself up tall, using a spear to support his bad leg. Then he raised hand to breast, a slow motion, as if the arm were tied with weights. It was, Dalinar figured, the most tired salute he'd ever seen.

"Sir," Kaladin said. Exhaustionspren puffed around Kaladin like little jets of dust.

"How . . ." Dalinar said. "You fell *into* a chasm!"

"I fell face-first, sir," Kaladin said, "and fortunately, I'm particularly hard-headed."

"But . . ."

Kaladin sighed, leaning on his spear. "I'm sorry, sir. I don't really know how I survived. Some spren were involved, we think. Anyway, I hiked back through the chasms. I had a duty to see to." He nodded to the side.

Farther into the triage tent, Dalinar saw something he hadn't originally noticed. Shallan Davar—a tangle of red hair and ripped clothing—sat amid a pack of surgeons.

"One future daughter-in-law," Kaladin said, "delivered safe and sound. Sorry about the damage done to the packaging."

"But there was a highstorm!" Dalinar said.

"We really wanted to get back before that," Kaladin said. "Ran into some troubles along the way, I'm afraid." With lethargic movements, he took out his side knife and cut the vines off the package beside him. "You know how everyone kept saying there was a chasmfiend prowling about in the nearby chasms?"

"Yes . . ."

Kaladin lifted the remnants of his coat away from the table, revealing a massive green gemstone. Though bulbous and uncut, the gemheart shone with a powerful inner light.

"Yeah," Kaladin said, taking the gemheart in one hand and tossing it to the ground before Dalinar. "We took care of that for you, sir." In the blink of an eye, gloryspren replaced his exhaustionspren.

Dalinar stared mutely at the gemheart as it rolled and tapped against the front of his boot, its light almost blinding.

"Oh, don't be so melodramatic, bridgeman," Shallan called. "Brightlord Dalinar, we found the beast already dead and rotting in the chasm. We survived the highstorm by climbing up its back to a crack in the side of the plateau, where we waited out the rains. We could only get the gemheart out because the thing was half-rotted already."

Kaladin looked to her, frowning. He turned back to Dalinar almost immediately. "Yes," Kaladin said. "That's what happened."

He was a far worse liar than Shallan was.

Amaram and Navani finally arrived, the former having remained behind to escort the latter. Navani gasped when she saw Shallan, then ran to her, snapping angrily at the surgeons. She fussed and bustled around Shallan, who seemed far less the worse for wear than Kaladin, despite the terrible state of her dress and hair. In moments, Navani had Shallan wrapped in a blanket to cover her exposed skin, then she sent a runner back to prepare a warm bath and meal at Dalinar's complex, to be had in whichever order Shallan wished.

Dalinar found himself smiling. Navani pointedly ignored Shallan's protests that none of this was necessary. The mother axehound had finally emerged. Shallan was apparently no longer an outsider, but one of Navani's clutch—and Chana help the man or woman who stood between Navani and one of her own.

"Sir," Kaladin said, finally letting the surgeons settle him back on the table. "The soldiers are gathering supplies. The battalions forming up. Your expedition?"

"You needn't worry, soldier," Dalinar said. "I could hardly expect you to guard me in your state."

"Sir," Kaladin said, more softly, "Brightness Shallan found something out there. Something you need to know. Talk to her before you set out."

"I'll do so," Dalinar said. He waited for a moment, then waved the surgeons aside. Kaladin seemed to be in no immediate danger. Dalinar stepped closer, leaning in. "Your men waited for you, Stormblessed. They skipped meals, pulled triple shifts. I half think they'd have sat out here, at the head of the chasms, through the highstorm itself if I hadn't intervened."

"They are good men," Kaladin said.

"It's more than that. They *knew* you would return. What is it they understand about you that I don't?"

Kaladin met his eyes.

"I've been searching for you, haven't I?" Dalinar said. "All this time, without seeing it."

Kaladin looked away. "No, sir. Maybe once, but . . . I'm just what you see, and not what you think. I'm sorry."

Dalinar grunted, inspecting Kaladin's face. He had almost thought . . . But perhaps not.

"Give him anything he wants or needs," Dalinar said to the surgeons, letting them approach. "This man is a hero. Again."

He withdrew, letting the bridgemen crowd around—which, of course, started the surgeons cursing at them again. Where *had* Amaram gone? The man had been here just a few minutes ago. As the palanquin arrived for Shallan, Dalinar decided to follow and find out just what it was that Kaladin said the girl knew.

⁂

One hour later, Shallan snuggled into a nest of warm blankets, wet hair on her neck, smelling of flowered perfume. She wore one of Navani's dresses—which was too big for her. She felt like a child in her mother's clothing.

That was, perhaps, exactly what she was. Navani's sudden affection was unexpected, but Shallan would certainly accept it.

The bath had been glorious. Shallan wanted to curl up on this couch and sleep for ten days. For the moment, however, she let herself revel in the distinctive feeling of being clean, warm, and safe for the first time in what seemed like an eternity.

"You can't take her, Dalinar." Navani's voice came from Pattern on the table beside Shallan's couch. She didn't feel a moment's guilt for sending him to spy on the two of them while she bathed. After all, they had been talking about her.

"This map . . ." Dalinar's voice said.

"She can draw you a better map and you can take it."

"She can't draw what she hasn't seen, Navani. She'll need to be there, with us, to draw out the center of the pattern on the Plains once we penetrate in that direction."

"Someone else—"

"Nobody else has been able to do this," Dalinar said, sounding awed. "Four years, and none of our scouts or cartographers saw the pattern. If we're going to find the Parshendi, I'm going to need her. I'm sorry."

Shallan winced. She was *not* doing a very good job of keeping her drawing ability hidden.

"She just got *back* from that terrible place," Navani's voice said.

"I won't let a similar accident occur. She will be safe."

"Unless you all die," Navani snapped. "Unless this entire expedition is a disaster. Then everything will be taken from me. Again." Pattern stopped, then spoke further in his own voice. "He held her at this point, and whispered some things I did not hear. From there, they got *very* close and made some interesting noises. I can reproduce—"

"No," Shallan said, blushing. "Too private."

"Very well."

"I need to go with them," Shallan said. "I need to complete that map of the Shattered Plains and find some way to correlate it with the ancient ones of Stormseat."

It was the only way to find the Oathgate. *Assuming it wasn't destroyed in whatever shattered the Plains,* Shallan thought. *And, if I do find it, will I even be able to open it?* Only one of the Knights Radiant was said to be able to open the pathway.

"Pattern," she said softly, clutching a mug of warmed wine, "I'm not a Radiant, right?"

"I do not think so," he said. "Not yet. There is more to do, I believe, though I cannot be certain."

"How can you not know?"

"I was not me when the Knights Radiant existed. It is complex to explain. I have always existed. We are not 'born' as men are, and we cannot truly die as men do. Patterns are eternal, as is fire, as is the wind. As are all spren. Yet, I was not in this state. I was not . . . aware."

"You were a mindless spren?" Shallan said. "Like the ones that gather around me when I draw?"

"Less than that," Pattern said. "I was . . . everything. In everything. I cannot explain it. Language is insufficient. I would need numbers."

"Surely there are others among you, though," Shallan said. "Older Cryptics? Who *were* alive back then?"

"No," Pattern said softly. "None who experienced the bond."

"Not a single one?"

"All dead," Pattern said. "To us, this means they are mindless—as a force cannot truly be destroyed. These old ones are patterns in nature now, like Cryptics unborn. We have tried to restore them. It does not work. Mmmm. Perhaps if their knights still lived, something could be done . . ."

Stormfather. Shallan pulled the blanket around her closer. "An entire people, all killed?"

"Not just one people," Pattern said, solemn. "Many. Spren with minds were less plentiful then, and the majorities of several spren peoples were all bonded. There were very few survivors. The one you call Stormfather lived. Some others. The rest, thousands of us, were killed when the *event* happened. You call it the Recreance."

"No wonder you're certain I will kill you."

"It is inevitable," Pattern said. "You will eventually betray your oaths, breaking my mind, leaving me dead—but the opportunity is worth the cost. My kind is too static. We always change, yes, but we change in the same way. Over and over. It is difficult to explain. You, though, you are *vibrant.* Coming to this place, this world of yours, I had to give up many things. The transition was . . . traumatic. My memory returns slowly, but I am pleased at the chance. Yes. Mmm."

"Only a Radiant can open the pathway," Shallan said, then took a sip of her wine. She liked the warmth it built inside of her. "But we don't know why, or how. Maybe I'll count as enough of a Radiant to make it work."

"Perhaps," Pattern said. "Or you could progress. Become more. There *is* something more you must do."

"Words?" Shallan said.

"You have said the Words," Pattern said. "You said them long ago. No . . . it is not words that you lack. It is truth."

"You prefer lies."

"Mmm. Yes, and you are a lie. A powerful one. However, what you do is not *just* lie. It is truth and lie mixed. You must understand both."

Shallan sat in thought, finishing her wine, until the door to the sitting room burst open, letting in Adolin. He stopped, wild-eyed, regarding her.

Shallan stood up, smiling. "It appears that I have failed at properly—"

She cut off as he grabbed her in an embrace. Drat. She'd had a perfectly clever quip prepared too. She'd worked on it during the entire bath.

Still, it was nice to be held. This was the most physically forward he'd ever been. Surviving an impossible journey did have its benefits. She let herself wrap her arms around him, feel the muscles on his back through his uniform, breathe in his cologne. He held her for several heartbeats. Not enough. She twisted her head and forced a kiss, her mouth enclosing his, firm in his embrace.

Adolin melted into the kiss, and did not pull back. Eventually, though, the perfect moment ended. Adolin took her head in his hands, looking into her eyes, and smiled. Then he grabbed her in another hug and laughed that barking, exuberant laugh of his. A *real* laugh, the one of which she was so fond.

"Where were you?" she asked.

"Visiting the other highprinces," Adolin said, "one at a time and delivering Father's final ultimatum—to join us in this assault, or forever be known as those who refused to see the Vengeance Pact fulfilled. Father thought giving me something to do would help distract me from . . . well, you."

He leaned back, holding her by the arms, and gave her a silly grin.

"I have pictures to draw for you," Shallan said, grinning back. "I saw a chasmfiend."

"A dead one, right?"

"Poor thing."

"Poor thing?" Adolin said, laughing. "Shallan, if you'd seen a live one, you'd have surely been killed!"

"Almost surely."

"I still can't believe . . . I mean, you fell. I should have saved you. Shallan, I'm sorry. I ran for Father first—"

"You did what you should have," she said. "No person on that bridge would have had you rescue one of us instead of your father."

He embraced her once more. "Well, I won't let it happen again. Nothing like it. I'll protect you, Shallan."

She stiffened.

"I will make *sure* you aren't ever hurt," Adolin said fiercely. "I should have realized that you could be caught in an assassination attempt intended for Father. We'll have to make it so that you aren't ever in that kind of position again."

She pulled away from him.

"Shallan?" Adolin said. "Don't worry, they won't get to you. I'll protect you. I—"

"Don't say things like that," she hissed.

"What?" He ran his hand through his hair.

"Just *don't*," Shallan said, shivering.

"The man who did this, who threw that lever, is dead now," Adolin said. "Is that what you're worried about? He was poisoned before we could get answers—though we're sure he belonged to Sadeas—but you don't need to worry about him."

"I will worry about what I wish to worry about," Shallan said. "I don't need to be protected."

"But—"

"I don't!" Shallan said. She breathed in and out, calming herself. She reached out and took him by the hand. "I won't be locked away again, Adolin."

"Again?"

"It's not important." Shallan raised his hand and wove his fingers between her own. "I appreciate the concern. That's all that matters."

But I won't let you, or anyone else, treat me like a thing to be hidden away. Never, never again.

Dalinar opened the door into his study, letting Navani pass through first, then followed her into the room. Navani looked serene, her face a mask.

"Child," Dalinar said to Shallan, "I have a somewhat difficult request to make of you."

"Anything you wish, Brightlord," Shallan said, bowing. "But I do wish to make a request of you in turn."

"What is it?"

"I need to accompany you on your expedition."

Dalinar smiled, shooting a glance at Navani. The older woman did not react. *She can be so good with her emotions,* Shallan thought. *I can't even read what she's thinking.* That would be a useful skill to learn.

"I believe," Shallan said, looking back to Dalinar, "that the ruins of an ancient city are hidden on the Shattered Plains. Jasnah was searching for them. So, then, must I."

"This expedition will be dangerous," Navani said. "You understand the risks, child?"

"Yes."

"One would think," Navani continued, "that considering your recent ordeal, you would wish for a time of shelter."

"Uh, I wouldn't say things like that to her, Aunt," Adolin said, scratching at his head. "She's kind of funny about them."

"It is not a matter of humor," Shallan said, lifting her head high. "I have a duty."

"Then I shall allow it," Dalinar said. He liked anything having to do with duty.

"And your request of me?" Shallan asked him.

"This map," Dalinar said, crossing the room and holding up the crinkled map detailing her path back through the chasms. "Navani's scholars say this is as accurate as any map we have. You can truly expand this? Deliver a map of the entire Shattered Plains?"

"Yes." Particularly if she used what she remembered of Amaram's map to fill in some details. "But Brightlord, might I make a suggestion?"

"Speak."

"Leave your parshmen behind in the warcamp," she said.

He frowned.

"I cannot accurately explain why," Shallan said, "but Jasnah felt that they were dangerous. Particularly to bring out onto the Plains. If you wish my help, if you trust me to create this map for you, then trust me on this one single point. Leave the parshmen. Conduct this expedition without them."

Dalinar looked to Navani, who shrugged. "Once our things are packed, they won't be *needed* really. The only ones inconvenienced will be the officers, who will have to set up their own tents."

Dalinar considered, chewing on her request. "This comes from Jasnah's notes?" Dalinar asked.

Shallan nodded. To the side, blessedly, Adolin piped in. "She's told me some of it, Father. You should listen to her."

Shallan shot him a grateful smile.

"Then it shall be done," Dalinar said. "Gather your things and send word to your uncle Sebarial, Brightness. We're leaving within the hour. Without parshmen."

THE END OF

Part Four

INTERLUDES

LHAN • ESHONAI • TARAVANGIAN

LHAN

"ongratulations," Brother Lhan said. "You have found your way to the easiest job in the world."

The young ardent pursed her lips, looking him up and down. She had obviously not expected her new mentor to be rotund, slightly drunk, and yawning.

"You are the . . . *senior* ardent I've been assigned to?"

"'To whom I've been assigned,'" Brother Lhan corrected, putting an arm around the young woman's shoulders. "You're going to have to learn how to speak punctiliously. Queen Aesudan likes to feel that those around her are refined. It makes her feel refined by association. My job is to mentor you on these items."

"I have been an ardent here in Kholinar for over a year," the woman said. "I hardly think that I need mentoring at all—"

"Yes, yes," Brother Lhan said, guiding her out of the monastery's entryway. "It's just that, you see, your superiors say you might need a little extra direction. Being assigned to the queen's own retinue is a marvelous privilege! One, I understand, you have requested with some measure of . . . ah . . . persistence."

She walked with him, and each step revealed her reluctance. Or perhaps confusion. They passed into the Circle of Memories, a round room with ten lamps on the walls, one for each of the ancient Epoch Kingdoms. An eleventh lamp represented the Tranquiline Halls, and a large ceremonial keyhole set into the wall represented the need for ardents to ignore borders, and look only at the hearts of men . . . or something like that. He wasn't sure, honestly.

Outside the Circle of Memories, they entered one of the covered walkways between monastery buildings, a light rain sprinkling the rooftops.

The last leg of the walkways, the sunwalk, gave a wonderful view of Kholinar—at least on a clear day. Even today, Lhan could see much of the city, as both the temple and the high palace occupied a flat-topped hill.

Some said that the Almighty himself had drawn Kholinar in rock, scooping out sections of ground with a fluent finger. Lhan wondered how drunk he'd been at the time. Oh, the city was beautiful, but it was the beauty of an artist who wasn't quite right in the mind. The rock took the shape of rolling hills and steeply sloping valleys, and when the stone was cut into, it exposed thousands of brilliant strata of red, white, yellow, and orange.

The most majestic formations were the windblades—enormous, curving spines of rock that cut through the city. Beautifully lined with colorful strata on the sides, they curved, curled, rose, and fell unpredictably, like fish leaping from the ocean. Supposedly, this all had to do with how the winds blew through the area. He *did* mean to get around to studying why that was. One of these days.

Slippered feet fell softly on glossy marble, accompanying the sound of the rains, as Lhan escorted the girl—what was her name again? "Look at that city," he said. "Everyone out there has to work, even the lighteyes. Bread to bake, lands to oversee, cobblestones to . . . ah . . . cobble? No, that's shoes. Damnation. What do you call people who cobble, but don't *actually* cobble?"

"I don't know," the young woman said softly.

"Well, it's no matter to us. You see, we have only one job, and it's an easy one. To serve the queen."

"That is not easy work."

"But it is!" Lhan said. "So long as we're all serving the same way. In a very . . . ah . . . careful way."

"We are sycophants," the young woman said, staring out over the city. "The queen's ardents tell her only what she wants to hear."

"Ah, and here we are, at the point of the matter." Lhan patted her on the arm. What *was* her name again? They'd told it to him. . . .

Pai. Not a very Alethi name; she'd probably chosen it upon being made an ardent. It happened. A new life, a new name, often a simple one.

"You see, Pai," he said, watching to notice if she reacted. Yes, it did seem he'd gotten the name right. His memory must be improving. "This is what your superiors wanted me to talk to you about. They fear that if you're not properly instructed, you might cause a bit of a storm here in Kholinar. Nobody wants that."

He and Pai passed other ardents along the sunwalk, and Lhan nodded to them. The queen had a lot of ardents. A *lot* of ardents.

"Here's the thing," Lhan said. "The queen . . . she sometimes worries that maybe the Almighty isn't pleased with her."

"Rightly so," Pai said. "She—"

"Hush, now," Lhan said, wincing. "Just . . . hush. Listen. The queen figures that if she treats her ardents well, it will buy her favor with the One who makes the storms, so to speak. Nice food. Nice robes. Fantastic quarters. Lots of free time to do whatever we want. We get these things as long as she thinks she's on the right path."

"Our duty is to give her the truth."

"We do!" Lhan said. "She's the Almighty's chosen, isn't she? Wife of King Elhokar, ruler while he's off fighting a holy war of retribution against the regicides on the Shattered Plains. Her life is very hard."

"She throws feasts every night," Pai whispered. "She engages in debauchery and excess. She wastes money while Alethkar languishes. People in outer towns starve as they send food here, with the understanding that it will be passed on to soldiers who need it. It rots because the queen can't be bothered."

"They have plenty of food on the Shattered Plains," Lhan said. "They've got gemstones coming out of their ears there. And nobody is starving here either. You're exaggerating. Life is good."

"It is if you're the queen or one of her lackeys. She even canceled the Beggars' Feasts. It is reprehensible."

Lhan groaned inside. This one . . . this one was going to be hard. How to persuade her? He wouldn't want the child to do anything that endangered her. Or, well, him. Mostly him.

They entered the palace's grand eastern hall. The carved pillars here were considered one of the greatest artworks of all time, and one could trace their history back to before the shadowdays. The gilding on the floor was ingenious—a lustrous gold that had been placed beneath Soulcast ribbons of crystal. It ran like rivulets between floor mosaics. The ceiling had been decorated by Oolelen himself, the great ardent painter, and depicted a storm blowing in from the east.

All of this could have been crem in the gutter for the reverence Pai gave it. She seemed to see only the ardents strolling about, contemplating the beauty. And eating. And composing new poems for Her Majesty—though honestly, Lhan avoided that sort of thing. It seemed like work.

Perhaps Pai's attitude came from a residual jealousy. Some ardents were envious of the queen's personal chosen. He tried to explain some of the luxuries that were now hers: warm baths, horseback riding using the queen's personal stables, music and art . . .

Pai's expression grew darker with each item. Bother. This wasn't working. New plan.

"Here," Lhan said, steering her toward the steps. "There's something I want to show you."

The steps twisted down through the palace complex. He loved this place, every bit of it. White stone walls, golden sphere lamps, and an *age*. Kholinar had never been sacked. It was one of the few eastern cities that hadn't suffered that fate in the chaos after the Hierocracy's fall. The palace had burned once, but that fire had died out after consuming the eastern wing. Rener's miracle, it was called. The arrival of a highstorm to put out the fire. Lhan swore the place still smelled of smoke, three hundred years later. And . . .

Oh, right. The girl. They continued down the steps and eventually entered the palace kitchens. Lunch had ended, though that didn't stop Lhan from snatching a plate of fried bread, Herdazian style, from the counter as they passed. Plenty was laid out for the queen's favorites, who might find themselves peckish at any time. Being a proper sycophant could work up an appetite.

"Trying to lure me with exotic foods?" Pai asked. "For the past five years, I have eaten only a bowl of boiled tallew for each meal, with a piece of fruit on special occasions. This will not tempt me."

Lhan stopped in place. "You're not serious, are you?"

She nodded.

"What is *wrong* with you?"

She blushed. "I am of the Devotary of Denial. I wished to experience separation from the physical needs of my—"

"This is worse than I thought," Lhan said, taking her by the hand and pulling her through the kitchens. Near the back, they found the door leading out to the service yard, where supplies were delivered and refuse taken away. There, shaded from the rain by an awning, they found piles of uneaten food.

Pai gasped. "Such waste! You bring me here to convince me *not* to make a storm? You are doing quite the opposite!"

"There used to be an ardent who took all of this and distributed it to the poor," Lhan said. "She died a few years back. Since then, the others have made some effort to take care of it. Not much, but some. The food does get taken away eventually, usually dumped into the square to be picked through by beggars. It's mostly rotten by then."

Storms. He could almost *feel* the heat of her anger.

"Now," Lhan said, "if there were an ardent among us whose only hunger was to do good, think how much she could accomplish. Why, she could feed hundreds just from what is wasted."

Pai eyed the piles of rotting fruit, the sacks of open grain, now ruined in the rain.

"Now," Lhan said, "let us contemplate the opposite. If some ardent tried to take away that which we have . . . well, what might happen to her?"

"Is that a threat?" she asked softly. "I do not fear physical harm."

"Storms," Lhan said. "You think we'd— Girl, I have someone else put my *slippers* on for me in the morning. Don't be dense. We're not going to hurt you. Too much work." He shivered. "You'd get sent away, quickly and quietly."

"I do not fear that either."

"I doubt you fear anything," Lhan said, "except maybe having a little fun. But what good would it do anyone if you were sent away? Our lives wouldn't change, the queen would remain the same, and that food out there would still spoil. But if you *stay*, you can do good. Who knows, maybe your example will help all of us reform, eh?"

He patted her on the shoulder. "Think about it for a few minutes. I want to go finish my bread." He wandered off, checking over his shoulder a few times. Pai settled down beside the heaps of rotting food and stared at them. She didn't seem bothered by the ripe odor.

Lhan watched her from inside until he got bored. When he got back from his afternoon massage, she was still there. He ate dinner in the kitchen, which wasn't terribly luxurious. The girl was entirely too interested in those heaps of garbage.

Finally, as evening fell, he ambled back to her.

"Don't you even wonder?" she asked, staring at those piles of refuse, rain pattering just beyond. "Don't you stop to think about the cost of your gluttony?"

"Cost?" he asked. "I told you nobody starves because we—"

"I don't mean the monetary cost," she whispered. "I mean the spiritual cost. To you, to those around you. Everything's wrong."

"Oh, it's not that bad," he said, settling down.

"It *is*. Lhan, it's bigger than the queen, and her wasteful feasts. It wasn't much better before that, with King Gavilar's hunts and the wars, prince-dom against princedom. The people hear of the glory of the battle on the Shattered Plains, of the riches there, but none of it ever materializes here.

"Does anyone among the Alethi elite *care* about the Almighty anymore? Sure, they curse by his name. Sure, they talk about the Heralds, burn glyph-wards. But what do they *do*? Do they change their lives? Do they listen to the Arguments? Do they transform, recasting their souls into something greater, something better?"

"They have Callings," Lhan said, fidgeting with his fingers. Digiting, then? "The devotaries help."

She shook her head. "Why don't we hear from Him, Lhan? The Heralds said we defeated the Voidbringers, that Aharietiam was the great victory for mankind. But shouldn't He have sent them to speak with us, to counsel us? Why didn't they come during the Hierocracy and denounce us? If what the Church had been doing was so evil, where was the word of the Almighty against it?"

"I . . . Surely you're not suggesting we *return* to that?" He pulled out his handkerchief and dabbed at his neck and head. This conversation was getting worse and worse.

"I don't know what I'm suggesting," she whispered. "Only that something is wrong. All of this is just so very wrong." She looked to him, then climbed to her feet. "I have accepted your proposal."

"You have?"

"I will not leave Kholinar," she said. "I will stay here and do what good I can."

"You won't get the other ardents into trouble?"

"My problem is not with the ardents," she said, offering a hand to help him to his feet. "I will simply try to be a good example for all to follow."

"Well, then. That seems like a fine choice."

She walked off, and he dabbed his head. She hadn't promised, not exactly. He wasn't certain how worried he should be about that.

Turned out, he should have been *very* worried.

The next morning, he stumbled into the People's Hall—a large, open building in the shadow of the palace where the king or queen addressed the concerns of the masses. A murmuring crowd of horrified ardents stood just inside the perimeter.

Lhan had already heard, but he had to see for himself. He forced his way to the front. Pai knelt on the floor here, head bowed. She'd painted all night, apparently, writing glyphs on the floor by spherelight. Nobody had noticed. The place was usually locked up tight when not in use, and she'd started working well after everyone was either asleep or drunk.

Ten large glyphs, written directly on the stone of the floor running up to the dais with the king's Common Throne. The glyphs listed the ten foolish attributes, as represented by the ten fools. Beside each glyph was a written paragraph in women's script explaining how the queen exemplified each of the fools.

Lhan read with horror. This . . . this didn't just chastise. It was a condemnation of the entire government, of the lighteyes, and of the Throne itself!

Pai was executed the very next morning.

The riots started that evening.

A PART TO PLAY

That voice deep within Eshonai still screamed. Even when she didn't attune the old Rhythm of Peace. She kept herself busy to quiet it, walking the perfectly circular plateau just outside of Narak, the one where her soldiers often practiced.

Her people had become something old, yet something new. Something powerful. They stood in lines on this plateau, humming to Fury. She divided them by combat experience. A new form would not a soldier make; many of these had been workers all their lives.

They would have a part to play. They would bring about something grand.

"The Alethi will come," Venli said, strolling at Eshonai's side and absently bringing energy to her fingers and letting it play between two of them. Venli smiled often while wearing this new form. Otherwise, it didn't seem to have changed her at all.

Eshonai knew that she herself had changed. But Venli . . . Venli acted the same.

Something felt wrong about that.

"The agent who sent this report is certain of it," Venli continued. "Your visit to the Blackthorn seems to have encouraged them to action, and the humans intend to strike toward Narak in force. Of course, this could still turn into a disaster."

"No," Eshonai said. "No. It is perfect."

Venli looked to her, stopping on the rock field. "We need no more training. We should act, right now, to bring a highstorm."

"We will do it when the humans near," Eshonai said.

"Why? Let us do it tonight."

"Foolishness," Eshonai said. "This is a tool to use in battle. If we produce an unexpected storm now, the Alethi won't come, and we won't win this war. We *must* wait."

Venli seemed thoughtful. Finally, she smiled, then nodded.

"What do you know that you aren't telling me?" Eshonai demanded, taking her sister by the shoulder.

Venli smiled more broadly. "I'm simply persuaded. We must wait. The storm will blow the wrong way, after all. Or is it all other storms that have blown the wrong way, and this one will be the first to blow the right way?"

The wrong way? "How do you know? About the direction?"

"The songs."

The songs. But . . . they said nothing about . . .

Something deep within Eshonai nudged her to move on. "If that is true," she said, "we'll have to wait until the humans are practically on top of us to catch them in it."

"Then that is what we do," Venli said. "I will set to the teaching. Our weapon will be ready."

She spoke to the Rhythm of Craving, a rhythm like the old Rhythm of Anticipation, but more violent.

Venli walked away, joined by her once-mate and many of her scholars. They seemed comfortable in these forms. Too comfortable. They couldn't have held these forms before . . . could they?

Eshonai shoved down the screams and went to prepare another battalion of new soldiers. She had always hated being a general. How ironic, then, that she would be recorded in their songs as the warleader who had finally crushed the Alethi.

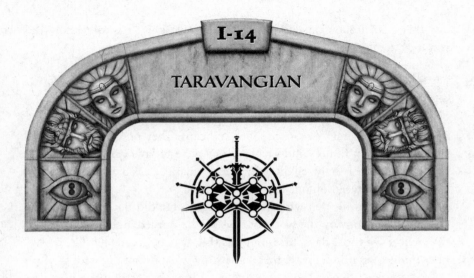

TARAVANGIAN

Taravangian, king of Kharbranth, awoke to stiff muscles and an ache in his back. He didn't feel stupid. That was a good sign.

He sat up with a groan. Those aches were perpetual now, and his best healers could only shake their heads and promise him that he was fit for his age. Fit. His joints cracked like logs on the fire and he couldn't stand quickly, lest he lose his balance and topple to the floor. To age truly was to suffer the ultimate treason, that of one's body against oneself.

He sat up in his cot. Water lapped quietly against the hull of his cabin, and the air smelled of salt. He heard shouts in the near distance, however. The ship had arrived on schedule. Excellent.

As he settled himself, one servant approached with a table and another with a warm, wet cloth for wiping his eyes and hands. Behind them waited the King's Testers. How long had it been since Taravangian had been alone, truly alone? Not since before the aches had come upon him.

Maben knocked on the open door, bearing his morning meal on a tray, stewed and spiced grain mush. It was supposed to be good for his constitution. Tasted like dishwater. Bland dishwater. Maben stepped forward to set out the meal, but Mrall—a Thaylen man in a black leather cuirass who wore both his head and eyebrows shaved—stopped her with a hand to the arm.

"Tests first," Mrall said.

Taravangian looked up, meeting the large man's gaze. Mrall could loom over a mountain and intimidate the wind itself. Everyone assumed he was Taravangian's head bodyguard. The truth was more disturbing.

Mrall was the one who got to decide whether Taravangian would spend the day as king or as a prisoner.

"Surely you can let him eat first!" Maben said.

"This is an important day," Mrall said, voice low. "I would know the result of the testing."

"But—"

"It is his right to demand this, Maben," Taravangian said. "Let us be on with it."

Mrall stepped back, and the testers approached, a group of three stormwardens in deliberately esoteric robes and caps. They presented a series of pages covered in figures and glyphs. They were today's variation on a sequence of increasingly challenging mathematical problems devised by Taravangian himself on one of his better days.

He picked up his pen with hesitant fingers. He did not *feel* stupid, but he rarely did. Only on the worst of days did he immediately recognize the difference. On those days, his mind was thick as tar, and he felt like a prisoner in his own mind, aware that something was profoundly wrong.

Today wasn't one of those, fortunately. He wasn't a complete idiot. At worst, he'd just be very stupid.

He set to his task, solving what mathematical problems he could. It took the better part of an hour, but during the process, he was able to gauge his capacity. As he had suspected, he was not terribly smart—but he was not stupid, either. Today . . . he was average.

That would do.

He turned over the problems to the stormwardens, who consulted in low voices. They turned to Mrall. "He is fit to serve," one proclaimed. "He may not offer binding commentary on the Diagram, but he may interact outside of supervision. He may change government policy so long as there is a three-day delay before the changes take effect, and he may also freely pass judgment in trials."

Mrall nodded, looking to Taravangian. "Do you accept this assessment and these restrictions, Your Majesty?"

"I do."

Mrall nodded, then stepped back, allowing Maben to set out Taravangian's morning meal.

The trio of stormwardens tucked away the papers he'd filled out, then they retreated to their own cabins. The testing was an extravagant procedure, and consumed valuable time each morning. Still, it was the best way he had found to deal with his condition.

Life could be tricky for a man who awoke each morning with a different level of intelligence. Particularly when the entire world might depend upon his genius, or might come crashing down upon his idiocy.

"How is it out there?" Taravangian asked softly, picking at his meal, which had gone cold during the testing.

"Horrible," Mrall said with a grin. "Just as we wanted it."

"Do not take pleasure in suffering," Taravangian replied. "Even when it is a work of our hands." He took a bite of the mush. "*Particularly* when it is a work of our hands."

"As you wish. I will do so no more."

"Can you really change that easily?" Taravangian asked. "Turn off your emotions on a whim?"

"Of course," Mrall said.

Something about that tickled at Taravangian, some thread of interest. If he had been in one of his more brilliant states, he might have seized upon it—but today, he sensed thought seeping away like water between fingers. Once, he had fretted about these missed opportunities, but he had eventually made his peace. Days of brilliance—he had come to learn—brought their own problems.

"Let me see the Diagram," he said. Anything to distract from this slop they insisted on feeding him.

Mrall stepped aside, allowing Adrotagia—head of Taravangian's scholars—to approach, bearing a thick, leatherbound volume. She set it onto the table before Taravangian, then bowed.

Taravangian rested his fingers upon the leatherbound cover, feeling a moment of . . . reverence? Was that right? Did he revere anything anymore? God was dead, after all, and Vorinism therefore a sham.

This book, though, *was* holy. He opened it to one of the pages marked with a reed. Inside were scribbles.

Frenetic, bombastic, majestic scribbles that had been painstakingly copied from the walls of his former bedroom. Sketches laid atop one another, lists of numbers that seemed to make no sense, lines upon lines upon lines of script written in a cramped hand.

Madness. And genius.

Here and there, Taravangian could find hints that this writing was his own. The way he wiggled a line, the way he wrote along the edge of a wall, much like how he would write along the side of a page when he was running out of room. He didn't remember any of this. It was the product of twenty hours of lucid insanity, the most brilliant he had ever been.

"Does it strike you as odd, Adro," Taravangian asked the scholar, "that genius and idiocy are so similar?"

"Similar?" Adrotagia asked. "Vargo, I do not see them as similar at all." He and Adrotagia had grown up together, and she still used Taravangian's boyhood nickname. He liked that. It reminded him of days before all of this.

"On both my most stupid days and my most incredible," Taravangian said, "I am unable to interact with those around me in a meaningful way. It is like . . . like I become a gear that cannot fit those turning beside it. Too small or too large, it does not matter. The clock will not work."

"I had not considered that," Adrotagia said.

When Taravangian was at his stupidest, he was not allowed from his room. Those were the days he spent drooling in a corner. When he was merely dull-minded, he was allowed out under supervision. He spent those nights crying for what he had done, knowing that the atrocities he committed were important, but not understanding why.

When he was dull, he could not change policy. Interestingly, he had decided that when he was too brilliant, he was *also* not allowed to change policy. He'd made this decision after a day of genius where he'd thought to fix all of Kharbranth's problems with a series of very rational edicts—such as requiring people to take an intelligence test of his own devising before being allowed to breed.

So brilliant on one hand. So stupid on another. *Is that your joke here, Nightwatcher?* he wondered. *Is that the lesson I'm to learn? Do you even care about lessons, or is what you do to us merely for your own amusement?*

He turned his attention back to the book, the Diagram. That grand plan he had devised on his singular day of unparalleled brilliance. Then, too, he'd spent the day staring at a wall. He'd *written* on it. Babbling the whole time, making connections no man had ever before made, he had scribbled all over his walls, floor, even parts of the ceiling he could reach. Most of it had been written in an alien script—a language he himself had devised, for the scripts he had known had been unable to convey ideas precisely enough. Fortunately, he'd thought to carve a key on the top of his bedside table, otherwise they wouldn't have been able to make sense of his masterpiece.

They could barely make sense of it anyway. He flipped through several pages, copied exactly from his room. Adrotagia and her scholars had made notations here and there, offering theories on what various drawings and lists might mean. They wrote those in the women's script, which Taravangian had learned years ago.

Adrotagia's notes on one page indicated that a picture there appeared to be a sketch of the mosaic on the floor of the Veden palace. He paused on that page. It might have relevance to this day's activities. Unfortunately, he wasn't smart enough today to make much sense of the book or its secrets. He had to trust that his smarter self was correct in his interpretations of his even *smarter* self's genius.

He shut the book and put down his spoon. "Let us be on with it." He stood up and left the cabin, Mrall on one side of him and Adrotagia on the other. He emerged into sunlight and to the sight of a smoldering coastal city, complete with enormous terraced formations—like plates, or sections of shalebark, the remnants of city covering them and practically spilling over the sides. Once, this sight had been wondrous. Now, it was black, the buildings—even the palace—destroyed.

Vedenar, one of the great cities of the world, was now little more than a heap of rubble and ash.

Taravangian idled by the rail. When his ship had sailed into the harbor the night before, the city had been dotted with the red glow of burning buildings. Those had seemed alive. More alive than this. The wind was blowing in off the ocean, pushing at him from behind. It swept the smoke inland, away from the ship, so that Taravangian could barely smell it. An entire city burned just beyond his fingertips, and yet the stench vanished into the wind.

The Weeping would come soon. Perhaps it would wash away some of this destruction.

"Come, Vargo," Adrotagia said. "They are waiting."

He nodded, joining her in climbing into the rowboat for tendering to shore. There had once been grand docks for this city. No more. One faction had destroyed them in an attempt to keep out the others.

"It's amazing," Mrall said, settling down into the tender beside him.

"I thought you said you weren't going to be pleased any longer," Taravangian said, stomach turning as he saw one of the heaps at the edge of the city. Bodies.

"I am not pleased," Mrall said, "but in awe. Do you realize that the Eighty's War between Emul and Tukar has lasted six years, and hasn't produced nearly this level of desolation? Jah Keved *ate* itself in a matter of months!"

"Soulcasters," Adrotagia whispered.

It was more than that. Even in his painfully normal state, Taravangian could see it was so. Yes, with Soulcasters to provide food and water, armies could march at speed—no carts or supply lines to slow them—and commence a slaughter in almost no time at all. But Emul and Tukar had their share of Soulcasters as well.

Sailors started rowing them toward shore.

"There was more," Mrall said. "Each highprince sought to seize the capital. That made them converge. It was almost like the wars of some Northern savages, with a time and place appointed for the shaking of spears and chanting of threats. Only here, it depopulated a kingdom."

"Let us hope, Mrall, that you make an overstatement," Taravangian said. "We will need this kingdom's people." He turned away, stifling a moment of emotion as he saw bodies upon the rocks of the shore, men who had died by being shoved over the side of a nearby cliff into the ocean. That ridge normally sheltered the dock from highstorms. In war, it had been used to kill, one army pressing the other back off the drop.

Adrotagia saw his tears, and though she said nothing, she pursed her lips in disapproval. She did not like how emotional he became when he was low of intellect. And yet, he knew for a fact that the old woman still burned a glyphward each morning as a prayer for her deceased husband. A strangely devout action for blasphemers such as they.

"What is the day's news from home?" Taravangian asked to draw attention from the tears he wiped away.

"Dova reports that the number of Death Rattles we're finding has dropped even further. She didn't find a single one yesterday, and only two the day before."

"Moelach moves, then," Taravangian said. "It is certain now. The creature must have been drawn by something westward." What now? Did Taravangian suspend the murders? His heart yearned to—but if they could discover even one more glimmer about the future, one fact that could save hundreds of thousands, would it not be worth the lives of the few now?

"Tell Dova to continue the work," he said. He had not anticipated that their covenant would attract the loyalty of an ardent, of all things. The Diagram, and its members, knew no boundaries. Dova had discovered their work on her own, and they'd needed to either induct her or assassinate her.

"It will be done," Adrotagia said.

The boatmen moved them up alongside some smoother rocks at the harbor's edge, then hopped out into the water. The men were servants of his, and were part of the Diagram. He trusted them, for he needed to trust some people.

"Have you researched that other matter I requested?" Taravangian asked.

"It is a difficult matter to answer," Adrotagia said. "The exact intelligence of a man is impossible to measure; even your tests only give us an approximation. The speed at which you answer questions and the *way* you answer them . . . well, it lets us make a judgment, but it is a crude one."

The boatmen hauled them up onto the stony beach with ropes. Wood scraped stone with an awful sound. At least it covered up the moans in the near distance.

Adrotagia took a sheet from her pocket and unfolded it. Upon it was a graph, with dots plotted in a kind of hump shape, a small trail to the left rising to a mountain in the center, then falling off in a similar curve to the right.

"I took your last five hundred days' test results and assigned each one a number between zero and ten," Adrotagia said. "A representation of how intelligent you were that day, though as I said, it is not exact."

"The hump near the middle?" Taravangian asked, pointing.

"When you were average intelligence," Adrotagia said. "You spend most of your time near there, as you can see. Days of pure intelligence and days of ultimate stupidity are both rare. I had to extrapolate from what we had, but I think this graph is somewhat accurate."

Taravangian nodded, then allowed one of the boatmen to help him debark. He had known that he spent more days average than he did otherwise. What he had asked her to figure out, however, was when he could expect another day like the one during which he'd created the Diagram. It had been years now since that day of transcendent mastery.

She climbed out of the boat and Mrall followed. She stepped up to him with her sheet.

"So this is where I was most intelligent," Taravangian said, pointing at the last point on the chart. It was far to the right, and very close to the bottom. A representation of high intelligence and a low frequency of occurrence. "This was that day, that day of perfection."

"No," Adrotagia said.

"What?"

"That was the time you were the most intelligent during the last five hundred days," Adrotagia explained. "This point represents the day you finished the most complex problems you'd left for yourself, and the day you devised new ones for use in future tests."

"I remember that day," he said. "It was when I solved Fabrisan's Conundrum."

"Yes," she said. "The world may thank you for that, someday, if it survives."

"I was smart on that day," he said. Smart enough that Mrall had declared he needed to be locked in the palace, lest he reveal his nature. He'd been convinced that if he could just explain his condition to the city, they would all listen to reason and let him control their lives perfectly. He'd drafted a law requiring that all people of less than average intellect be required to commit suicide for the good of the city. It had seemed reasonable. He had considered they might resist, but thought that the brilliance of the argument would sway them.

Yes, he had been smart on that day. But not nearly as smart as the day of the Diagram. He frowned, inspecting the paper.

"This is why I can't answer your question, Vargo," Adrotagia said. "That graph, it's what we call a logarithmic scale. Each step from that center point is not equal—they compound on one another the farther out you get. How smart *were* you on the day of the Diagram? Ten times smarter than your smartest otherwise?"

"A hundred," Taravangian said, looking at the graph. "Maybe more. Let me do the calculations. . . ."

"Aren't you stupid today?"

"Not stupid. Average. I can figure this much. Each step to the side is . . ."

"A measureable change in intelligence," she said. "You might say that each step sideways is a doubling of your intelligence, though that is hard to quantify. The steps upward are easier; they measure how frequently you have days of the given intelligence. So if you start at the center of the peak, you can see that for every five days you spend being average, you spend one day being mildly stupid and one day mildly smart. For every five of those, you spend one day moderately stupid and one day moderately genius. For every five days like that . . ."

Taravangian stood on the rocks, his soldiers waiting above, as he counted on the graph. He moved sideways off the graph until he reached the point where he guessed the day of the Diagram might have been. Even that seemed conservative to him.

"Almighty above . . ." he whispered. Thousands of days. Thousands upon thousands. "It should never have happened."

"Of course it should have," she said.

"But it's so unlikely as to be impossible!"

"It's perfectly possible," she said. "The likelihood of it having happened is one, as it *already occurred*. That is the oddity of outliers and probability, Taravangian. A day like that could happen again tomorrow. Nothing forbids it. It's all pure chance, so far as I can determine. But if you want to know the likelihood of it happening again . . ."

He nodded.

"If you were to live another *two thousand years,* Vargo," she said, "you'd maybe have one single day like this among them. Maybe. Even odds, I'd say."

Mrall snorted. "So it was luck."

"No, it was simple probability."

"Either way," Taravangian said, folding the paper. "This was not the answer I wanted."

"Since when has it mattered what we want?"

"Never," he said. "And it never will." He tucked the sheet into his pocket.

They picked their way up the rocks, passing corpses bloated from too long in the sun, and joined a small group of soldiers at the top of the beach. They wore the burnt-orange crest of Kharbranth. He had few soldiers to his name. The Diagram called for his nation to be unthreatening.

The Diagram was not perfect, however. They caught errors in it now and then. Or . . . not truly errors, just missed guesses. Taravangian had been supremely brilliant that day, but he had *not* been able to see the future. He had made educated guesses—very educated—and had been right an eerie amount of the time. But the farther they went from that day and the knowledge he'd had then, the more the Diagram needed tending and cultivation to stay on course.

That was why he'd hoped for another such day soon, a day to revamp the Diagram. That would not come, most likely. They would have to continue, trusting in that man that he had once been, trusting his vision and

understanding.

Better that than anything else in this world. Gods and religion had failed them. Kings and highlords were selfish, petty things. If he was going to trust one thing to believe in, it would be himself and the raw genius of a human mind unfettered.

It *was* difficult at times, though, to stay the course. Particularly when he faced the consequences of his actions.

They entered the battlefield.

Most of the fighting had apparently moved outside of the city, once the fire began. The men had continued warring even as their capital burned. Seven factions. The Diagram had guessed six. Would that matter?

A soldier handed him a scented handkerchief to hold over his face as they passed the dead and dying. Blood and smoke. Scents he would come to know all too well before this was through.

Men and women in the burnt-orange livery of Kharbranth picked through the dead and wounded. Throughout the East, the color had become synonymous with healing. Indeed, tents flying his banner—the banner of the surgeon—dotted the battlefield. Taravangian's healers had arrived just before the battle, and had started ministering to the wounded immediately.

As he left the fields of the dead, Veden soldiers began to stand up from where they sat in a dull-eyed stupor at the edges of the battlefield. Then they started to cheer him.

"Pali's mind," Adrotagia said, watching them rise. "I don't believe it."

The soldiers sat separated in groups by banner, being tended to by Taravangian's surgeons, water-bearers, and comforters. Wounded and unwounded alike, any who could stand rose for the king of Kharbranth and cheered him.

"The Diagram said it would happen," Taravangian said.

"I thought for certain that was an error," she replied, shaking her head.

"They know," Mrall said. "We are the only victors this day. Our healers, who earned the respect of all sides. Our comforters who helped the dying pass. Their highlords brought them only misery. You brought them life and hope."

"I brought them death," Taravangian whispered.

He had ordered the execution of their king, along with specific highprinces the Diagram indicated. In doing so, he had pushed the various factions into war with one another. He had brought this kingdom to its knees.

Now they cheered him for it. He forced himself to stop with one of the groups, asking after their health, seeing if there was anything he could do for them. It was important to be seen by the people as a compassionate man. The Diagram explained this in casual sterility, as if compassion were something one could measure in a cup next to a pint of blood.

He visited another group of soldiers, then a third. Many stepped up to him, touching his arms or his robe, weeping tears of thanks and joy. Many more of the Veden soldiers remained sitting in the tents, however, staring out over the fields of dead. Numb of mind.

"The Thrill?" he whispered to Adrotagia as they left the latest group of men. "They fought through the night as their capital burned. It must have been in force."

"I agree," she said. "It gives us a further reference point. The Thrill is at least as strong here as it is in Alethkar. Maybe stronger. I will speak to our scholars. Perhaps this will help pinpoint Nergaoul."

"Do not spend too much effort on that," Taravangian said, approaching another group of Veden soldiers. "I'm not sure what we would even do if we found the thing." An ancient, evil spren was not something he had the resources to tackle. Not yet at least. "I would rather know where Moelach is moving."

Hopefully, Moelach hadn't decided to slumber again. The Death Rattles had, so far, offered them the best way that they'd found to augment the Diagram.

There was one answer, however, he'd never been able to determine. One he'd give almost anything to know.

Would all of this be enough?

He met with the soldiers, and adopted the air of a kindly—if not bright—old man. Caring and helpful. He was almost that man in truth, today. He tried to do an imitation of himself when he was a little dumber. People accepted that man, and when he was of that intellect, he did not need to feign compassion nearly as much as he did when smarter.

Blessed with intelligence, cursed with compassion to feel pain for what he had done. They came inversely. Why couldn't he have both at once? He did not think that in other people, intelligence and compassion were tied in such a way. The Nightwatcher's motives behind her boons and curses were unfathomable.

Taravangian moved through the crowd of men, listening to them beg for more relief and for drugs to ease their pain. Listening to their thanks. These soldiers had suffered a fight that—even yet—seemed to have no victor. They wanted *something* to hold to, and Taravangian was neutral, supposedly. It was shocking how easily they bared their souls to him.

He came to the next soldier in line, a cloaked man clutching an apparently broken arm. Taravangian looked into the man's hooded eyes.

It was Szeth-son-son-Vallano.

Taravangian felt a moment of sheer panic.

"We need to speak," the Shin man said.

Taravangian grabbed the assassin by the arm, hauling him away from the crowd of Veden soldiers. With his other hand, Taravangian felt in his pocket for the Oathstone he carried on his person at all times. He pulled it out just to see. Yes, it was no fake. Damnation, seeing Szeth there had made him think that he'd been bested somehow, the stone stolen and Szeth sent to kill him.

Szeth let himself be pulled away. What had he said? *That he needed to talk, you fool,* Taravangian thought to himself. *If he'd come to kill you, you would be dead.*

Had Szeth been seen here? What would people say if they saw Taravangian interacting with a bald Shin man? Rumors had started from less. If anyone got even a *hint* that Taravangian had been involved with the infamous Assassin in White . . .

Mrall noticed immediately that something was wrong. He barked orders to the guards, separating Taravangian from the Veden soldiers. Adrotagia—who had been sitting with crossed arms nearby, watching and tapping her foot—leaped to stride over. She peeked at the person under the hood, then gasped, the color draining from her face.

"How *dare* you come here?" Taravangian said to Szeth, speaking under his breath while maintaining a cheerful pose and expression. He was of only average intelligence today, but he was still a king, raised and trained to the court. He could maintain his composure.

"A problem has arisen," Szeth said, face hooded, voice emotionless. Speaking to this creature was like speaking to one of the dead themselves.

"Why have you failed to kill Dalinar Kholin?" Adrotagia demanded with quiet urgency. "We know you fled. Return and do the job!"

Szeth glanced at her, but did not reply. She did not hold his Oathstone. He did seem to note her, however, with those too-blank eyes of his.

Damnation. Their plan had been to keep Szeth from meeting or knowing of Adrotagia, just in case he decided to turn against Taravangian and kill him. The Diagram hypothesized this possibility.

"Kholin has a Surgebinder," Szeth said.

So, Szeth knew about Jasnah. Had she faked her death, then, as he'd suspected? Damnation.

The battlefield seemed to grow still. To Taravangian, the moans of the wounded faded away. Everything narrowed to just him and Szeth. Those eyes. The tone of the man's voice. A dangerous tone. What—

He spoke with emotion, Taravangian realized. *That last sentence was said with passion.* It had sounded like a plea. As if Szeth's voice were being squeezed on the sides.

This man was not sane. Szeth-son-son-Vallano was the most dangerous weapon on all of Roshar, and he was broken.

Storms, why couldn't this have happened on a day when Taravangian had more than half a wit?

"What makes you say this?" Taravangian said, trying to buy time for his mind to lumber through the implications. He held Szeth's Oathstone before him, almost as if it could chase away problems like a superstitious woman's glyphward.

"I fought him," Szeth said. "He protected Kholin."

"Ah, yes," Taravangian said, thinking furiously. Szeth had been banished from Shinovar, made Truthless for something relating to a claim that the Voidbringers had returned. If he discovered that he wasn't wrong about that claim, then what—

Him?

"You fought a Surgebinder?" Adrotagia said, glancing at Taravangian.

"Yes," Szeth said. "An Alethi man who fed upon Stormlight. He healed a Blade-severed arm. He is . . . Radiant . . ." That strain in his voice did not sound safe. Taravangian glanced at Szeth's hands. They were clenching into fists time and time again, like hearts beating.

"No, no," Taravangian said. "I have learned this only recently. Yes, it makes sense now. One of the Honorblades has vanished."

Szeth blinked, and he focused on Taravangian, as if returning from a distant place. "One of the other seven?"

"Yes," Taravangian said. "I have heard only hints. Your people are secretive. But yes . . . I see, it is one of the two that allow Regrowth. Kholin must have it."

Szeth swayed back and forth, though he did not seem conscious of the motion. Even now, he moved with a fighter's grace. *Storms.*

"This man I fought," Szeth said, "he summoned no Blade."

"But he used Stormlight," Taravangian said.

"Yes."

"So he must have an Honorblade."

"I . . ."

"It is the *only* explanation."

"It . . ." Szeth's voice grew colder. "Yes, the only explanation. I will kill him and retrieve it."

"No," Taravangian said firmly. "You are to return to Dalinar Kholin and do the task assigned you. Do not fight this other man. Attack when he is not present."

"But—"

"Have I your Oathstone?" Taravangian demanded. "Is my word to be questioned?"

Szeth stopped swaying. His gaze locked with Taravangian's. "I am Truthless. I do as my master requires, and I do not ask for an explanation."

"Stay away from the man with the Honorblade," Taravangian repeated. "Kill Dalinar."

"It will be done." Szeth turned and strode away. Taravangian wanted to yell further instructions. *Don't be seen! Don't ever come to me in public again!*

Instead, he sat right there on the path, composure crumbling. He gasped, trembling, sweat streaming down his brow.

"Stormfather," Adrotagia said, settling on the ground beside him. "I thought we were dead."

Servants brought Taravangian a chair while Mrall made excuses for him. *The king is overcome with grief at the deaths of so many. He is old, you know. And so caring . . .*

Taravangian breathed in and out, struggling to regain control. He looked to Adrotagia, who sat in the middle of a circle of servants and soldiers, all sworn to the Diagram. "Who is it?" he asked softly. "Who is this Surgebinder?"

"Jasnah's ward?" Adrotagia said.

They had been startled when that one arrived on the Shattered Plains. Already they hypothesized that the girl had been trained. If not by Jasnah, then by the girl's brother, before his death.

"No," Taravangian said. "A male. One of Dalinar's family members?" He thought for a time. "We need the Diagram itself."

She went to fetch it from the ship. Nothing else—his visits to the soldiers, more important meetings with Veden leaders—mattered right now. The Diagram was off. They strayed into dangerous territory.

She returned with it, and with the stormwardens, who set up a tent around Taravangian right there on the path. Excuses continued. *The king is weak from the sun. He must rest and burn glyphwards to the Almighty for the preservation of your nation. Taravangian cares while your own lighteyes sent you to the slaughter . . .*

By the light of spheres, Taravangian picked through the tome, poring over translations of his own words written in a language he had invented and then forgotten. Answers. He *needed* answers.

"Did ever I tell you, Adro, what I asked for?" he whispered as he read.

"Yes."

He was barely listening. "Capacity," he whispered, turning a page. "Capacity to stop what was coming. The capacity to save humankind."

He searched. He was not brilliant today, but he had spent many days reading these pages, going over, and over, and over passages. He knew them.

The answers would be here. They *would*. Taravangian worshipped only one god now. It was the man he had been on that day.

There.

He found it on a reproduction of one corner of his room, where he'd written in tiny script sentences over the top of one another because he'd run out of space. In his clarity of genius, the sentences had looked easy to separate, but it had taken his scholars years to piece together what this said.

They will come. You cannot stop their oaths. Look for those who survive when they should not. That pattern will be your clue.

"The bridgemen," Taravangian whispered.

"What?" Adrotagia asked.

Taravangian looked up, blinking bleary eyes. "Dalinar's bridgemen, the ones he took from Sadeas. Did you read the account of their survival?"

"I didn't think it important. Just another game of power between Sadeas and Dalinar."

"No. It's more." They had survived. Taravangian stood up. "Wake every Alethi sleeper we have; send every agent in the area. There will be stories told of one of these bridgemen. Miraculous survival. Favored of the winds. One is among them. He might not know yet exactly what he's doing, but he has bonded a spren and sworn at least the First Ideal."

"If we find him?" Adrotagia asked.

"We keep him away from Szeth at all costs." Taravangian handed her the Diagram. "Our lives depend upon it. Szeth is a beast who gnaws at his leg to escape his bonds. If he gets free . . ."

She nodded, moving off to do as he commanded. She hesitated at the flaps to their temporary tent. "We might have to reassess our methods of determining your intelligence. What I have seen in the last hour makes me question whether 'average' can be applied to you today."

"The assessments are not inaccurate," he said. "You simply underestimate the average man."

Besides, in dealing with the Diagram, he might not remember what he had written or why—but there were *echoes* sometimes.

She left, making way as Mrall stepped in. "Your Majesty," he said. "Time runs short. The highprince is dying."

"He's been dying for years." Still, Taravangian did hasten his step—as much as he was capable of doing these days—as he resumed his hike. He didn't stop with any more of the soldiers, and gave only brief waves toward the cheers he received.

Eventually, Mrall led him over a hillside away from the immediate stench of the battle and the smoldering city. A series of stormwagons here flew an optimistic flag, that of the king of Jah Keved. The guards there let Taravangian enter their ring of wagons, and he approached the largest one, an enormous vehicle almost like a mobile building on wheels.

They found Highprince Valam . . . *King* Valam . . . in bed coughing. His hair had fallen out since Taravangian had last seen him, and his cheeks were so sunken that rainwater would have pooled in them. Redin, the king's bastard son, stood at the foot of the bed, head bowed. With the three guards who stood in the room, there wasn't room for Taravangian, so he stopped in the doorway.

"Taravangian," Valam said, then coughed into his handkerchief. The cloth came back bloodied. "You've come for my kingdom, have you?"

"I don't know what you mean, Your Majesty," Taravangian said.

"Don't play coy," Valam snapped. "I can't stand it in women or in rivals. Stormfather . . . I don't know what they're going to make of you. I half think they'll have you assassinated by the end of the week." He waved with a sickly hand, all draped in cloth, and the guards made way for Taravangian to enter the small bedchamber.

"Clever ploy," the king said. "Sending that food, those healers. The soldiers love you, I've heard. What would you have done if one side had won decisively?"

"I'd have had a new ally," Taravangian said. "Grateful for my aid."

"You helped all sides."

"But the winner the most, Your Majesty," Taravangian said. "We can minister to survivors, but not the dead."

Valam coughed again, a great hacking mess. His bastard stepped up, concerned, but the king waved him back. "Would have figured," the king said to him between wheezes, "you'd be the only one of my children to live, bastard." He turned to Taravangian. "Turns out, you have a legitimate claim on the throne, Taravangian. Through your mother's side, I think? A marriage to a Veden princess some three generations back?"

"I am not aware," Taravangian said.

"Didn't you hear me about being coy?"

"We both have a role to play in this production, Your Majesty," Taravangian said. "I am merely speaking the lines as they were written."

"You talk like a woman," Valam said. He spat blood to the side. "I know what you're up to. In a week or so, after caring for my people, your scribes will 'discover' your claim on the throne. You'll reluctantly step in to save the kingdom, as urged by my own storming people."

"I see you've had the script read to you," Taravangian said softly.

"That assassin will come for you."

"He very well might." That was the truth.

"Don't know why I even storming tried for this throne," Valam said. "At least I'll die as king." He heaved a deep breath, then raised his hand, gesturing impatiently at the scribes huddled outside the room. The women perked up, peeking around Taravangian.

"I'm making this idiot my heir," Valam said, waving at Taravangian. "Ha! Let the other highprinces chew on that."

"They're dead, Your Majesty," Taravangian said.

"What? All of them?"

"Yes."

"Even Boriar?"

"Yes."

"Huh," Valam said. "Bastard."

At first, Taravangian thought that was a reference to one of the deceased. Then, however, he noticed the king waving at his illegitimate son. Redin stepped up, going onto one knee beside the bed as Taravangian made room.

Valam struggled with something beneath his blankets; his side knife. Redin helped him get it out, then held the knife awkwardly.

Taravangian inspected this Redin, curious. This was the king's ruthless executioner that he had read about? This concerned, helpless-looking man?

"Through my heart," Valam said.

"Father, no . . ." Redin said.

"Through my storming heart!" Valam shouted, spraying bloody spittle across his sheet. "I won't lie here and let Taravangian coax my own servants into poisoning me. Do it, boy! Or can't you do a single thing that—"

Redin slammed the knife down into his father's chest with such force, it made Taravangian jump. Redin then stood, saluted, and shoved his way out of the room.

The king heaved a final gasp, eyes glazing over. "So the night will reign, for the choice of honor is life . . ."

Taravangian raised an eyebrow. A Death Rattle? Here, now? Blast, and he wasn't in a position where he could write down the exact phrasing. He'd have to remember it.

Valam's life faded away until he was simply meat. A Shardblade appeared from vapor beside the bed, then thumped to the wooden floor of the wagon. Nobody reached for it, and the soldiers in the room and scribes outside it looked to Taravangian, then knelt.

"Cruel, what Valam did to that one," Mrall said, nodding toward the bastard, who shoved his way out of the stormwagon and into the light.

"More than you know," Taravangian said, reaching out to touch the knife protruding through blanket and clothing from the old king's chest. He hesitated, fingers inches from the handle. "The bastard will be known as a patricide on the official records. If he had interest in the throne, this will make it . . . difficult for him, even more so than his parentage." Taravangian pulled his fingers away from the knife. "Might I have a moment with the fallen king? I would speak a prayer for him."

The others left him, even Mrall. They shut the small door, and Taravangian sat down on the stool beside the corpse. He had no intention of saying any sort of prayer, but he did want a moment. Alone. To think.

It had worked. Just as the Diagram instructed, Taravangian was king of

Jah Keved. He had taken the first major step toward unifying the world, as Gavilar had insisted would need to happen if they were to survive.

That was, at least, what the visions had proclaimed. Visions Gavilar had confided in him six years ago, the night of the Alethi king's death. Gavilar had seen visions of the Almighty, who was also now dead, and of a coming storm.

Unite them.

"I am doing my best, Gavilar," Taravangian whispered. "I *am* sorry that I need to kill your brother."

That would not be the only sin upon his head when this was done. Not by a faint breeze or a stormwind.

He wished, once again, that this day had been a day of brilliance. Then he wouldn't have felt so guilty.

PART FIVE

Winds Alight

KALADIN • SHALLAN • DALINAR • ADOLIN • WIT

THE HIDDEN BLADE

They will come you cannot stop their oaths look for those who
survive when they should not that pattern will be your clue.

—From the Diagram, Coda of the
Northwest Bottom Corner: paragraph 3

You have killed her. . . .

Kaladin couldn't sleep.

He knew he *should* sleep. He lay in his dark barrack room, surrounded by familiar stone, comfortable for the first time in days. A soft pillow, a mattress as good as the one he'd had back home in Hearthstone.

His body felt wrung out, like a rag after the washing was done. He'd survived the chasms and brought Shallan home safely. Now he needed to sleep and heal.

You have killed her. . . .

He sat up in his bed, and felt a wave of dizziness. He gritted his teeth and let it pass. His leg wound throbbed inside his bandage. The camp surgeons had done a good job with that; his father would have been pleased.

The camp outside felt too quiet. After showering him with praise and enthusiasm, the men of Bridge Four had gone to join the army for its expedition, along with all of the other bridge crews, who would be carrying bridges for the army. Only a small force from Bridge Four would remain behind to guard the king.

Kaladin reached out in the darkness, feeling beside the wall until he found his spear. He took hold, then propped himself up and stood. The leg flared with immediate pain, and he gritted his teeth, but it wasn't so bad.

He'd taken fathom bark for the pain, and it was working. He'd refused the firemoss the surgeons had tried to give him. His father had hated using the addictive stuff.

Kaladin forced his way to the door of his small room, then shoved it open and stepped into the sunlight. He shaded his eyes and scanned the sky. No clouds yet. The Weeping, the worst part of the year, would roll in sometime tomorrow. Four weeks of ceaseless rain and gloom. It was a Light Year, so not even a highstorm in the middle. Misery.

Kaladin longed for the storm within. That would have awakened his mind, made him feel like moving.

"Hey, gancho?" Lopen said, popping up from where he sat beside the firepit. "You need something?"

"Let's go watch the army leave."

"You're not supposed to be walking, I think. . . ."

"I'll be fine," Kaladin said, hobbling with difficulty.

Lopen rushed over to help him, getting up under Kaladin's arm, lifting weight off the bad leg. "Why don't you glow a bit, gon?" Lopen asked softly. "Heal that problem?"

He'd prepared a lie: something about not wanting to alert the surgeons by healing too quickly. He couldn't force it out. Not to a member of Bridge Four.

"I've lost the ability, Lopen," he said softly. "Syl has left me."

The lean Herdazian fell unusually silent. "Well," he finally said, "maybe you should buy her something nice."

"Buy something nice? For a *spren*?"

"Yeah. Like . . . I don't know. A nice plant, maybe, or a new hat. Yes, a hat. Might be cheap. She's small. If a tailor tries to charge you full price for a hat that small, you thump him real good."

"That's the most ridiculous piece of advice I've ever been given."

"You should rub yourself with curry and go prancing through the camp singing Horneater lullabies."

Kaladin looked at Lopen, incredulous. *"What?"*

"See? Now the bit about the hat is only the *second* most ridiculous piece of advice you've ever been given, so you should try it. Women like hats. I have this cousin who makes them. I can ask her. You might not even need the actual hat. Just the spren of the hat. That'll make it even cheaper."

"You're a very special kind of weird, Lopen."

"Of course I am, gon. There's only *one* of *me*."

They continued through the empty camp. Storms, the place seemed hollow. They passed empty barrack after empty barrack. Kaladin walked with care, glad for Lopen's help, but even this was draining. He shouldn't be moving on the leg. Father's words, the words of a surgeon, floated up from the depths of his mind.

Torn muscles. Bind the leg, ward against infection, and keep the subject from putting weight on it. Further tearing could lead to a permanent limp, or worse.

"You want to get a palanquin?" Lopen asked.

"Those are for women."

"Ain't nothing wrong with being a woman, gancho," Lopen said. "Some of my relatives are women."

"Of course they . . ." He trailed off at Lopen's grin. Storming Herdazian. How much of what he said was to deliberately sound obtuse? Well, Kaladin had heard men telling jokes about how stupid Herdazians were, but Lopen could talk rings around those men. Of course, half of Lopen's own jokes were about Herdazians. He seemed to find those extra funny.

As they approached the plateaus, the dead silence gave way to the low roar of thousands of people assembled in a limited area. Kaladin and Lopen finally broke free of the barrack rows, emerging onto the natural terrace just above the parade grounds that debouched onto the Shattered Plains. Thousands of soldiers were gathered there. Spearmen in huge blocks, lighteyed archers in thinner ranks, officers prancing on horseback in gleaming armor.

Kaladin gasped softly.

"What?" Lopen asked.

"It's what I always thought I'd find."

"What? Today?"

"As a young man in Alethkar," Kaladin said, unexpectedly emotional. "When I dreamed of the glory of war, this is what I imagined." He hadn't pictured the greenvines and barely capable soldiers that Amaram had trained in Alethkar. Neither had he pictured the crude, if effective, brutes of Sadeas's army—or even the quick strike teams of Dalinar's plateau runs.

He'd imagined *this*. A full army, arrayed for a grand march. Spears held high, banners fluttering, drummers and trumpeters, messengers in livery, scribes on horses, even the king's Soulcasters in their own sectioned-off square, hidden from sight by walls of cloth carried on poles.

Kaladin knew the truth of battle now. Fighting was not about glory, but about men lying on the ground screaming and thrashing, tangled in their own viscera. It was about bridgemen thrown against a wall of arrows, or of Parshendi cut down while they sang.

Yet in this moment, Kaladin let himself dream again. He gave his youthful self—still there deep inside him—the spectacle he'd always imagined. He pretended that these soldiers were about something wonderful, instead of just another pointless slaughter.

"Hey, someone else is actually coming," Lopen said, pointing. "Look at that."

By the banners, Dalinar had been joined by only a single highprince: Roion. However, as Lopen pointed out, another force—not quite as large or as well organized—was flowing northward up the wide, open pathway along the eastern rim of the warcamps. At least one other highprince had responded to Dalinar's call.

"Let's find Bridge Four," Kaladin said. "I want to see the men off."

"Sebarial?" Dalinar asked. "*Sebarial's* troops are joining us?"

Roion grunted, wringing his hands—as if wishing to wash them—as he sat in the saddle. "I guess we should be glad for any support at all."

"Sebarial," Dalinar said, dumbfounded. "He wouldn't even send troops on close plateau runs, where there was no risk of Parshendi. Why would he send men now?"

Roion shook his head and shrugged.

Dalinar turned Gallant and trotted the horse toward the oncoming group, as did Roion. They passed Adolin, who rode just behind with Shallan, side by side, her guards and his following. Renarin was over with the bridgemen, of course.

Shallan was riding one of Adolin's own horses, a petite gelding over which Sureblood towered. Shallan wore a traveling dress of the kind messenger women preferred, with the front and back slit all the way to the waist. She wore leggings—basically silk trousers, but women preferred other names—underneath.

Behind them rode a large group of Navani's scholars and cartographers, including Isasik, the ardent who was the royal cartographer. These passed around the map Shallan had drawn, Isasik riding to the side, chin raised, as if pointedly ignoring the praise the women were giving Shallan's map. Dalinar needed all these scholars, though he wished he didn't. Each scribe he brought was another life he risked. That was made worse by Navani herself coming. He couldn't dismiss her argument. *If you think it's safe enough for you to bring the girl, then it's safe enough for me.*

As Dalinar made his way toward Sebarial's oncoming procession, Amaram rode up, wearing his Shardplate, his golden cloak trailing behind. He had a fine warhorse, the hulking breed used in Shinovar to pull heavy carts. It still looked like a pony beside Gallant.

"Is that *Sebarial*?" Amaram asked, pointing at the oncoming force.

"Apparently."

"Should we send him away?"

"Why would we do that?"

"He's untrustworthy," Amaram said.

"He keeps his word, so far as I know," Dalinar said. "That is more than I can say for most."

"He keeps his word because he never promises anything."

Dalinar, Roion, and Amaram trotted up to Sebarial, who stepped out of a carriage at the front of the army. A carriage. For a war procession. Well, it wouldn't slow Dalinar any more than all of these scribes. In fact, he should probably have a few more carriages made ready. It would be nice for Navani to have a way to ride in comfort once the days wore long.

"Sebarial?" Dalinar asked.

"Dalinar!" the plump man said, shading his eyes. "You look surprised."

"I am."

"Ha! That's reason enough to have come. Wouldn't you say, Palona?"

Dalinar could barely make out the woman sitting in the carriage, wearing an enormous fashionable hat and a sleek gown.

"You brought your mistress?" Dalinar asked.

"Sure. Why not? If we fail out there, I'll be dead and she'll be out on her ear. She insisted, anyway. Storming woman." Sebarial walked up right beside Gallant. "I've got a feeling about you, Dalinar old man. I think it's wise to stay close to you. Something's going to happen out there on the Plains, and opportunity rises like the dawn."

Roion sniffed.

"Roion," Sebarial said, "shouldn't you be hiding under a table somewhere?"

"Perhaps I should, if only to get away from you."

Sebarial laughed. "Well said, you old turtle! Maybe this trip won't be a complete bore. Onward, then! To glory and some such nonsense. If we find riches, remember that I get my part! I got here before Aladar. That has to count for something."

"Before . . ." Dalinar said with a start. He twisted around, looking back toward the warcamp bordering his own to the north.

There, an army wearing Aladar's colors of white and dark green spilled out onto the Shattered Plains.

"Now *that*," Amaram said, "I *really* didn't expect."

⁂

"We could try a coup," Ialai said.

Sadeas turned in his saddle toward his wife. Their guards scattered the hills around them, distant enough to be out of earshot as the highprince and his wife enjoyed a gentle "ride through the hills." In reality, the two of them had wanted a closer look at Sebarial's expansions out here west of the warcamps, where he was setting up full-scale farming operations.

Ialai rode with eyes forward. "Dalinar will be gone from the camp, and with him Roion, his only supporter. We could seize the Pinnacle, execute the king, and take the throne."

Sadeas turned his horse, looking eastward over the warcamps. He could just barely make out Dalinar's army gathering distantly on the Shattered Plains.

A coup. One last step, a slap in the face of old Gavilar. He'd do it. Storm it, he would.

Except for the fact that he didn't need to.

"Dalinar has committed to this foolish expedition," Sadeas said. "He'll be dead soon, surrounded and destroyed on those Plains. We don't need a coup; if I'd known that he would actually *do* this, we wouldn't have even needed your assassin."

Ialai looked away. Her assassin had failed. She considered it a strong fault on her part, though the plan had been executed with exactness. These things were never certain. Unfortunately, now that they'd tried and failed, they'd need to be careful about . . .

Sadeas turned his horse, frowning as a messenger approached on horseback. The youth was allowed to pass the guards and proffered a letter to Ialai.

She read it, and her disposition darkened.

"You aren't going to like this," she said, looking up.

•፧•

Dalinar kicked Gallant into motion, tearing across the landscape, startling plants into their dens. He passed his army in a few minutes of hard riding and approached the new force.

Aladar sat on horseback here, surveying his army. He wore a fashionable uniform, black with maroon stripes on the sleeves and a matching stock at the neck. Soldiers swarmed around him. He had one of the largest forces on the Plains—storms, with Dalinar's numbers reduced, Aladar's army might be *the* largest.

He was also one of Sadeas's greatest supporters.

"How are we going to do this, Dalinar?" Aladar asked as Dalinar trotted up. "Do we all go out on our own, crossing different plateaus but meeting back up, or do we march in an enormous column?"

"Why?" Dalinar asked. "Why have you come?"

"You made such passionate arguments all along, and now you act surprised that someone listened?"

"Not someone. You."

Aladar pressed his lips to a line, finally turning to meet Dalinar's eyes. "Roion and Sebarial, the two biggest cowards in our midst, are marching to war. Am I to stay behind and let them seek the fulfillment of the Vengeance Pact without me?"

"The other highprinces seem content to do so."

"I suspect they are better at lying to themselves than I am."

Suddenly, all of Aladar's vehement arguments—at the forefront of the faction against Dalinar—took on a different cast. *He was arguing to convince himself,* Dalinar thought. *He was worried all along that I was right.*

"Sadeas will not be pleased," Dalinar said.

"Sadeas can storm off. He doesn't own me." Aladar fiddled with his reins for a moment. "He wants to, though. I can feel it in the deals he forces me to make, the knives he slowly places at everyone's throats. He'd have us all as his slaves by the end of this."

"Aladar," Dalinar said, moving his horse right up alongside the other man's so the two of them faced each other directly. He held Aladar's eyes. "Tell me Sadeas didn't put you up to this. Tell me this isn't part of another plot to abandon or betray me."

Aladar smiled. "You think I'd just tell you if it were?"

"I would hear a promise from your own lips."

"And you'll trust that promise? How well did that serve you, Dalinar, when Sadeas professed his friendship?"

"A promise, Aladar."

Aladar met his eyes. "I think the things you say about Alethkar are naive at best, and undoubtedly impossible. Those delusions of yours aren't a sign of madness, as Sadeas wants us to think—they're just the dreams of a man who wants desperately to believe in something, something foolish. 'Honor' is a word applied to the actions of men from the past who have had their lives scrubbed clean by historians." He hesitated. "But . . . storm me for a fool, Dalinar, I wish they *could* be true. I came for myself, not Sadeas. I won't betray you. Even if Alethkar can't ever be what you want, we *can* at least crush the Parshendi and avenge old Gavilar. It's just the right thing to do."

Dalinar nodded.

"I could be lying," Aladar said.

"But you aren't."

"How do you know?"

"Honestly? I don't. But if this is all going to work, I am going to have to trust some of you." To an extent. He would never put himself in another position like the Tower.

Either way, Aladar's presence meant this incursion was actually possible. Together, the four of them would likely outnumber the Parshendi—though he wasn't certain how trustworthy the scribes' counts of their numbers were.

It was not the grand coalition of all highprinces that Dalinar had wanted, but even with the chasms favoring the Parshendi, this could be enough.

"We march together," Dalinar said, pointing. "I don't want us spread out. We keep to plateaus next to one another, or the same plateau when possible. And you'll need to leave your parshmen behind."

"That's an unusual requirement," Aladar said with a frown.

"We're marching against their cousins," Dalinar said. "Best to not risk the possibility of them turning against us."

"But they'd never . . . Bah, whatever. It can be done."

Dalinar nodded, extending a hand to Aladar as, behind, Roion and Amaram finally trotted up; Dalinar had outstripped them on Gallant.

"Thank you," Dalinar said to Aladar.

"You really do believe in all of this, don't you?"

"Yes."

Aladar extended his hand, but hesitated. "You realize that I'm stained through and through. I've got blood on these hands, Dalinar. I'm not some perfect, honorable knight as you seem to want to pretend."

"I know you're not," Dalinar said, taking the hand. "I'm not either. We will have to do."

They shared a nod, then Dalinar turned Gallant and began to trot back toward his own army. Roion groaned, complaining about his thighs after having galloped all the way over. The ride today was not going to be pleasant for him.

Amaram fell in beside Dalinar. "First Sebarial, then Aladar? Your trust seems to come cheaply today, Dalinar."

"Would you have me turn them away?"

"Think how spectacular this victory would be if we did it on our own."

"I hope we're above such vainglory, old friend," Dalinar said. They rode for a time, passing Adolin and Shallan again. Dalinar scanned his force and noticed something. A tall man in blue sat on a stone in the midst of Bridge Four's bodyguards.

Speaking of fools . . .

"Come with me," Dalinar said to Amaram.

Amaram let his horse lag behind. "I think I should go see to—"

"Come," Dalinar said sharply. "I want you to speak to that young man so we can put a stop to the rumors and the things he's been saying about you. Those don't do anyone any good."

"Very well," Amaram said, catching up.

⋄⋄

Kaladin found himself standing up amid the bridgemen, despite the pain of his leg, as he noticed Adolin and Shallan riding past. He followed the pair with his eyes. Adolin, astride his thick-hooved Ryshadium, and Shallan on a more modestly sized brown animal.

She looked gorgeous. Kaladin was willing to admit it, if only to himself. Brilliant red hair, ready smile. She said something clever; Kaladin could almost hear the words. He waited, hoping that she'd look toward him, meet his eyes across the short distance.

She didn't. She rode on, and Kaladin felt like an utter fool. A part of him wanted to hate Adolin for holding her attention, but he found that he couldn't. The truth was, he *liked* Adolin. And those two were good for one another. They *fit*.

Perhaps Kaladin could hate that.

He settled back down on a rock, bowing his head. The bridgemen crowded in around him. Hopefully they hadn't seen Kaladin following Shallan with his eyes, straining to hear her voice. Renarin stood, like a shade, at the back of the group. The bridgemen were coming to accept him, but he still seemed very awkward around them. Of course, he seemed awkward around most people.

I need to talk to him more about his condition, Kaladin thought. Something seemed off to him about that man and his explanation of the epilepsy.

"Why are you here, sir?" Bisig asked, drawing Kaladin's attention back to the other bridgemen.

"I wanted to see you off," Kaladin said, sighing. "I assumed you'd be happy to see me."

"You are like child," Rock said, wagging a thick finger at Kaladin. "What would you do, great Captain Stormblessed, if you caught one of *these* men walking about with hurt leg? You would have that man beaten! Once he healed, of course."

"I thought," Kaladin noted, "that I was your *commander*."

"Nah, can't be," Teft said, "because our commander would be smart enough to stay in bed."

"And eat much stew," Rock said. "I left you stew to eat while I am gone."

"You're going on the expedition?" Kaladin asked, looking up at the large Horneater. "I thought you were just seeing the men off. You aren't willing to fight. What will you do out there?"

"Someone must fix food for them," Rock said. "This expedition, it will take days. I will not leave my friends to the mercy of camp chefs. Ha! The food they cook will all be from Soulcast grain and meat. Tastes like crem! Someone must come with proper spices."

Kaladin looked up at the group of frowning men. "Fine," he said. "I'll go back. Storms, I . . ."

Why were the bridgemen parting? Rock looked over his shoulder, then laughed, backing away. "Now we shall see real trouble."

Behind them, Dalinar Kholin was climbing from his saddle. Kaladin sighed, then waved for Lopen to help him to his feet so he could salute properly. He got upright—earning a glare from Teft—before noticing that Dalinar was not alone.

Amaram. Kaladin stiffened, straining to keep his face expressionless.

Dalinar and Amaram approached. The pain in Kaladin's leg seemed to fade, and for the moment he could only see that man. That *monster* of a man. Wearing Plate Kaladin had earned, a golden cloak billowing out behind, bearing the symbol of the Knights Radiant.

Control yourself, Kaladin thought. He managed to swallow his rage. Last time it had gotten the better of him, he'd earned himself weeks in prison.

"You should be resting, soldier," Dalinar said.

"Yes, sir," Kaladin replied. "My men have already made that abundantly clear."

"Then you trained them well. I'm proud to have them along with me on this expedition."

Teft saluted. "If there is danger to you, Brightlord, it will be out there on the Plains. We can't protect you if we wait back here."

Kaladin frowned, realizing something. "Skar is here . . . Teft . . . so who is watching the king?"

"We've seen to it, sir," Teft said. "Brightlord Dalinar asked me leave our best man behind with a team of his own selection. They'll watch the king."

Their best man . . .

Coldness. Moash. *Moash* had been left in charge of the king's safety, and had a team of his own choosing.

Storms.

"Amaram," Dalinar said, waving for the highlord to step up. "You told me that you'd never seen this man before arriving here on the Shattered Plains. Is that true?"

Kaladin met the eyes of a murderer.

"Yes," Amaram said.

"What of his claim that you took your Blade and Plate from him?" Dalinar asked.

"Brightlord," Amaram said, taking Dalinar by the arm, "I don't know if the lad is touched in the head or merely starved for attention. Perhaps he served in my army, as he claims—he certainly bears the correct slave brand. But his allegations regarding me are *obviously* preposterous."

Dalinar nodded to himself, as if this were all expected. "I believe an apology is due."

Kaladin struggled to remain upright, his leg feeling weak. So this would be his final punishment. Apologizing to Amaram in public. A humiliation above all others.

"I—" Kaladin began.

"Not you, son," Dalinar said softly.

Amaram turned, posture suddenly more alert—like that of a man preparing for a fight. "Surely you don't believe these allegations, Dalinar!"

"A few weeks ago," Dalinar said, "I received two special visitors in camp. One was a trusted servant who had come from Kholinar in secret, bringing a precious cargo. The other was that cargo: a madman who had arrived at the gates of Kholinar carrying a Shardblade."

Amaram paled and stepped back, hand going to his side.

"I told my servant," Dalinar said calmly, "to go drinking with your personal guard—he knew many of them—and talk of a treasure that the madman said had been hidden for years outside the warcamp. By my order, he then placed the madman's Shardblade in a nearby cavern. After that, we waited."

He's summoning his Blade, Kaladin thought, looking at Amaram's hand. Kaladin reached for his side knife, but Dalinar was already raising his own hand.

White mist coalesced in Dalinar's fingers, and a Shardblade appeared, tip to Amaram's throat. Wider than most, it was almost cleaverlike in appearance.

A Blade formed in Amaram's hand a second later—a second too late. His eyes went wide as he stared at the silvery Blade held to his throat.

Dalinar had a Shardblade.

"I thought," Dalinar said, "that if you *had* been willing to murder for one Blade, you would certainly be willing to lie for a second. And so, after I knew you'd sneaked in to see the madman on your own, I asked you to investigate his claims for me. I gave your conscience plenty of time to come clean, out of respect for our friendship. When you told me you'd found nothing—but in fact you had actually recovered the Shardblade—I knew the truth."

"How?" Amaram hissed, looking at the Blade Dalinar held. "How did you get it back? I removed it from the cave. My men had it safe!"

"I wasn't about to risk it just to prove a point," Dalinar said, cold. "I bonded this Blade before we hid it away."

"That week you spent ill," Amaram said.

"Yes."

"Damnation."

Dalinar exhaled, a hissing sound through his teeth. "Why, Amaram? Of all people, I thought that you . . . Bah!" Dalinar's grip on the weapon tightened, knuckles white. Amaram raised his chin, as if thrusting his neck toward the point of the Shardblade.

"I did it," Amaram said, "and I would do it again. The Voidbringers will soon return, and we must be strong enough to face them. That means practiced, accomplished Shardbearers. In sacrificing a few of my soldiers, I planned to save many more."

"Lies!" Kaladin said, stumbling forward. "You just wanted the Blade for yourself!"

Amaram looked Kaladin in the eyes. "I am sorry for what I did to you and yours. Sometimes, good men must die so that greater goals may be accomplished."

Kaladin felt a gathering chill, a numbness that spread from his heart outward.

He's telling the truth, he thought. *He . . . honestly believes that he did the right thing.*

Amaram dismissed his Blade, turning back to Dalinar. "What now?"

"You are guilty of murder—of killing men for personal wealth."

"And what is it," Amaram said, "when you send thousands of men to their deaths so that you may secure gemhearts, Dalinar? Is that different somehow? We all know that sometimes lives must be spent for the greater good."

"Take off that cloak," Dalinar growled. "You are no Radiant."

Amaram reached up and undid it, then dropped it to the rock. He turned and started to walk away.

"No!" Kaladin said, stumbling after him.

"Let him go, son," Dalinar said, sighing. "His reputation is broken."

"He is still a murderer."

"And we will try him fairly," Dalinar said, "once I return. I can't imprison him—Shardbearers are above that, and he'd cut his way out anyway. Either you execute a Shardbearer or you leave him free."

Kaladin sagged, and Lopen appeared on one side, holding him up while Teft got under his other arm. He felt drained.

Sometimes lives must be spent for the greater good. . . .

"Thank you," Kaladin said to Dalinar, "for believing me."

"I *do* listen sometimes, soldier," Dalinar said. "Now go back to camp and *get some rest*."

Kaladin nodded. "Sir? Stay safe out there."

Dalinar smiled grimly. "If possible. At least now I've got a way to fight that assassin, if he arrives. With all of these Shardblades flying around lately, I figured having one myself made too much sense to ignore." He narrowed his eyes, turning eastward. "Even if it feels . . . wrong somehow to hold one. Strange, that. Why should it feel wrong? Perhaps I just miss my old Blade."

Dalinar dismissed the Blade. "Go," he said, walking back toward his horse, where Highprince Roion—looking stunned—was watching Amaram stalk away, his personal guard of fifty joining him.

Yes, that *was* Aladar's banner, joining Dalinar's. Sadeas could make it out through the spyglass.

He lowered it, and sat quietly for a long, long time. So long that his guards, and even his wife, started to fidget and looked nervous. But there was no reason.

He quelled his annoyance.

"Let them die out there," he said. "All four. Ialai, make a report for me. I would like to know . . . Ialai?"

His wife started, looking toward him.

"Is all well?"

"I was merely thinking," she said, seeming distant. "About the future. And what it is going to bring. For us."

"It is going to bring Alethkar new highprinces," Sadeas said. "Make a report of which among our sworn highlords would be appropriate to take the place of those who will fall on Dalinar's trip." He tossed the spyglass back to the messenger. "We do nothing until they're dead. This will end, it appears, with Dalinar killed by the Parshendi after all. Aladar can go with him, and to Damnation with the lot of them."

He turned his horse and continued the day's ride, his back pointedly toward the Shattered Plains.

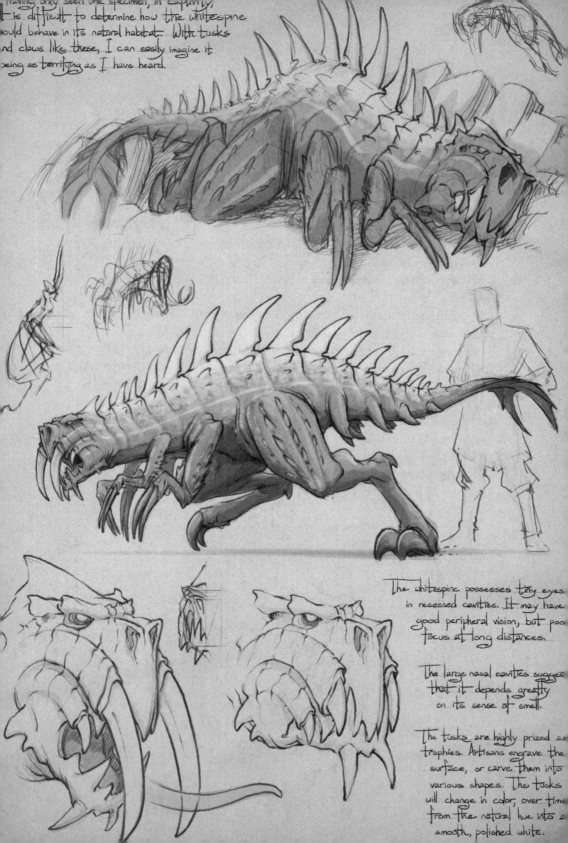

having only seen one specimen in captivity, is difficult to determine how the whitespine would behave in its natural habitat. With tusks and claws like these, I can easily imagine it being as terrifying as I have heard.

The whitespine possesses tiny eyes in recessed cavities. It may have good peripheral vision, but poor focus at long distances.

The large nasal cavities suggest that it depends greatly on its sense of smell.

The tusks are highly prized as trophies. Artisans engrave the surface, or carve them into various shapes. The tusks will change in color over time from the natural hue into a smooth, polished white.

One danger in deploying such a potent weapon will be the potential encouragement of those exploring the Nahel bond. Care must be taken to avoid placing these subjects in situations of powerful stress unless you accept the consequences of their potential Investiture.

—From the Diagram, Floorboard 27: paragraph 6

Like a river suddenly undammed, the four armies flooded out onto the plateaus. Shallan watched from horseback, excited, anxious. Her little part of the convoy included Vathah and her soldiers, along with Marri, her lady's maid. Gaz, notably, hadn't arrived yet, and Vathah claimed to not know where he was. Perhaps she should have looked more into the nature of his debts. She'd been so busy with other things . . . storms, if the man vanished, how would she feel about that?

She would have to deal with that later. Today, she was part of something extremely important—a story that had begun with Gavilar and Dalinar's first hunting expedition into the Unclaimed Hills years ago. Now came the final chapter, the mission that would unearth the truth and determine the future of the Shattered Plains, the Parshendi, and perhaps Alethkar itself.

Shallan kicked her horse forward, eager. The gelding started to walk, placid despite Shallan's prodding.

Storming animal.

Adolin trotted up beside her on Sureblood. The beautiful animal was pure white—not dusty grey, like some horses she'd seen, but actually white.

That Adolin should have the larger horse was patently unfair. She was shorter than he was, so she should be on the taller horse.

"You purposely gave me a slow one," Shallan complained, "didn't you?"

"Sure did."

"I'd smack you. If I could reach you up there."

He chuckled. "You said you don't have a lot of experience riding, so I picked a horse that had a lot of experience being ridden. Trust me, you'll be thankful."

"I want to ride in a majestic charge as we begin our expedition!"

"And you can do so."

"Slowly."

"Technically, slow speeds can be very majestic."

"Technically," she said, "a man doesn't need all of his toes. Shall we remove a few of yours and prove it?"

He laughed. "As long as you don't hurt my face, I suppose."

"Don't be ridiculous. I like your face."

He grinned, Shardplate helm hanging from his saddle so as to not mess up his hair. She waited for him to add a quip to hers, but he didn't.

That was all right. She liked Adolin as he was. He was kind, noble, and *genuine*. It didn't matter that he wasn't brilliant or . . . or whatever else Kaladin was. She couldn't even define it. So there.

Passionate, with an intense, smoldering resolve. A leashed anger that he used, because he had dominated *it. And a certain tempting arrogance. Not the haughty pride of a highlord. Instead, the secure, stable sense of determination that whispered that no matter who you were—or what you did—you could not hurt him. Could not change him.*

He was. Like the wind and rocks were.

Shallan completely missed what Adolin said next. She blushed. "What was that?"

"I said that Sebarial has a carriage. You might want to travel with him."

"Because I'm too delicate for riding?" Shallan said. "Did you miss that I *walked* back through the chasms in the middle of a *highstorm*?"

"Um, no. But walking and riding are different. I mean, the soreness . . ."

"Soreness?" Shallan asked. "Why would I be sore? Doesn't the horse do all of the work?"

Adolin looked at her, eyes widening.

"Um," she said. "Dumb question?"

"You said you'd ridden before."

"Ponies," she said, "on my father's estates. Around in circles . . . All right, from that expression, I'm led to believe I'm being an idiot. When I get sore, I'll go ride with Sebarial."

"*Before* you get sore," Adolin said. "We'll give it an hour."

As annoyed as she was at this turn, she couldn't deny his expertise. Jasnah had once defined a fool as a person who ignored information because it disagreed with desired results.

She determined to not be bothered, and instead enjoy the ride. The army as a whole moved slowly, considering that each piece seemed to be so efficient. Spearmen in blocks, scribes on horseback, scouts roving outward. Dalinar had six of the massive mechanical bridges, but he had also brought all of the former bridgemen and their simpler, man-carried bridges, designed as copies of the ones they'd left in Sadeas's camp. That was good, since Sebarial only had a couple of bridge crews.

She allowed herself a moment of personal satisfaction at the fact that he'd come on the expedition. As she was thinking on that, she noticed someone running up the line of troops behind her. A short man, with an eye patch, who drew glares from Adolin's bridgeman guards for the day.

"Gaz?" Shallan said with relief as he hustled up, carrying a package under his arm. Her fears that he'd been knifed in an alley somewhere were unfounded.

"Sorry, sorry," he said. "It came. You owe the merchant two sapphire broams, Brightness."

"It?" Shallan asked, accepting the package.

"Yeah. You asked me to find one for you. I storming did." He seemed proud of himself.

She unwrapped the cloth around the rectangular object, and found inside a book. *Words of Radiance,* the cover said. The sides were worn, and the pages faded—one patch across the top was even stained from spilled ink sometime in the past.

Rarely had she been as pleased to receive something so damaged. "Gaz!" she said. "You're wonderful!"

He grinned, shooting Vathah a triumphant smile. The taller man rolled his eyes, muttering something Shallan didn't hear.

"Thank you," Shallan said. "Thank you truly, Gaz."

⁂

As the time passed and one day led into another, Shallan found the distraction of the book extremely welcome. The armies moved about as fast as a herd of sleepy chulls, and the scenery was actually quite boring, though she'd never admit that to Kaladin or Adolin, considering what she'd told them last time she was out here.

The book, though. The book was wonderful. And frustrating.

But what was the "wicked thing of eminence" that led to the Recreance? she thought, writing the quote in her notebook. It was the second day of their travels on the Plains, and she had agreed to ride in the coach Adolin had provided—alone, though it baffled Adolin why she wouldn't want her lady's maid with her. Shallan did not want to explain Pattern to the girl.

The book had a chapter for each order of Knights Radiant, with talk of their traditions, their abilities, and their attitudes. The author admitted that a lot of it was hearsay—the book had been written two hundred years after the Recreance, and by then facts, lore, and superstition had mixed freely. Beyond that, it was in an old dialect of Alethi, using the protoscript, a precursor to the true women's script of modern day. She spent a lot of her time sorting out meanings, occasionally calling over some of Navani's scholars to provide definitions or interpretation.

Still, she had learned a great deal. For example, each order had different Ideals, or standards, to determine advancement. Some were specific, others left to the interpretation of the spren. Also, some orders were individualistic, while others—like the Windrunners—functioned in teams, with a specific hierarchy.

She settled back, thinking about the powers described. Would the others be appearing, then? As she and Jasnah had? Men who could glide elegantly across the ground as if they weighed nothing, women who could melt stone with a touch. Pattern had offered some few insights, but mostly he had been of use telling her what sounded likely to have been real, and what from the book was a mistake based on hearsay. His memory was spotty, but growing much better, and hearing what the book said often made him remember more.

Right now, he buzzed on the seat beside her in a contented way. The carriage hit a bump—it was rough out here—but at least in the coach, she could read and reference other books at the same time. That would have been practically impossible while riding.

The coach did make her feel shut away, though. *Not everyone who tries to take care of you is trying to do what your father did,* she told herself firmly.

Adolin's warned-of soreness had never manifested, of course. Originally, she'd felt a small amount of pain in her thighs from holding herself in place in the saddle, but Stormlight had made it vanish.

"Mmm," Pattern said, climbing onto the door of the carriage. "It comes."

Shallan looked out the window and felt a drop of water sprinkle against her face. Rock darkened as rain coated it. Soon, the air filled with a steady drizzle, light and pleasant. Though colder, it reminded her of some of the rainfalls back in Jah Keved. Here in the stormlands, it seemed that rain was rarely this soft.

She pulled down the shades and scooted to the center of the seat so she wouldn't get rained on. She soon found that the pleasing sound of water muffled the soldiers' voices and the monotonous sound of marching feet, making it a nice accompaniment to reading. A quote sparked her interest, and so she dug out her sketch of the Shattered Plains and her old maps of Stormseat.

I need to find out how these maps relate, she thought. *Multiple points of reference, preferably.* If she could identify two places on the Shattered Plains that matched points on her map of Stormseat, she could judge how large Stormseat had been—the old map had no scale—and then overlay it on the map of the Shattered Plains. That would give them some context.

What really drew her attention was the Oathgate. On the map of Stormseat, Jasnah thought it was represented by a round disc, like a dais, on the southwestern side of the city. Was there a doorway there on that dais somewhere? A magical portal to Urithiru? How did one of the knights operate it?

"Mmm," Pattern said.

Shallan's carriage started to slow. She frowned, scooting to the door, meaning to peek out the window. The door opened, however, to reveal Highlady Navani standing outside, Dalinar himself holding up an umbrella for her.

"Would you mind company?" Navani asked.

"Not at all, Brightness," Shallan said, scrambling to pick up her papers and books, which she'd spread about on all of the seats. Navani patted Dalinar fondly on the arm, then climbed into the coach, using a towel to dry her feet and legs. She sat once Dalinar shut the door.

They started rolling again, and Shallan fidgeted with her papers. What was her relationship with Navani? She was Adolin's aunt, but she was romantically involved with his father. So she was kind of Shallan's future mother-in-law, though by Vorin tradition Dalinar would never be allowed to marry her.

Shallan had tried for weeks to get this woman to listen to her, and had failed. Now, she seemed to have been forgiven for bearing the news of Jasnah's death. Did that mean Navani . . . liked her?

"So," Shallan said, feeling awkward, "did Dalinar exile you to the coach to protect you from getting sore, as Adolin did to me?"

"Sore? Heavens no. If anyone should be riding in the coach, it's Dalinar. When there is fighting to be done, we'll need him rested and ready. I came because it's rather difficult to read while riding in the rain."

"Oh." Shallan shifted in her seat.

Navani studied her, then finally sighed. "I have been ignoring things," the older woman said, "that I should not. Because they bring me pain."

"I am sorry."

"You have nothing to apologize for." Navani held out her hand toward Shallan. "May I?"

Shallan looked at her handful of notes, diagrams, and maps. She hesitated.

"You are engaged in work you obviously think very important," Navani said softly. "This city Jasnah was searching for, according to the notes you sent me? Perhaps I can help you interpret my daughter's intentions."

Was there anything in these pages that would incriminate Shallan and reveal her powers? Her activities as Veil?

She didn't think so. She'd been studying the Knights Radiant as part of it, but she was searching for their center of power, so that made sense. Hesitant, she handed over the papers.

Navani leafed through them, reading by spherelight. "The organization of these notes is . . . interesting."

Shallan blushed. The organization made sense to her. As Navani continued to look through the notes, Shallan found herself growing oddly anxious. She'd wanted Navani's help—she'd all but begged for it. Now, however, she found herself feeling like this woman was intruding. This had become Shallan's project, her duty and her quest. Now that Navani had apparently overcome her grief, would she insist on taking over completely?

"You think like an artist," Navani said. "I can see it in the way you put the notes together. Well, I suppose I can't expect everything you do to be annotated precisely as I'd wish. A magical portal to another city? Jasnah actually believed in this?"

"Yes."

"Hmm," Navani said. "Then it's probably true. That girl never did have the decency to be *wrong* an appropriate amount of the time."

Shallan nodded, glancing at the notes, feeling anxious.

"Oh, don't get so touchy," Navani said. "I'm not going to steal the project from you."

"I'm that transparent?" Shallan said.

"This research is obviously very important to you. I assume Jasnah persuaded you that the fate of the world itself rested upon the answers you find?"

"She did."

"Damnation," Navani said, flipping to the next page. "I shouldn't have ignored you. It was petty."

"It was the act of a grieving mother."

"Scholars don't have time for such nonsense." Navani blinked, and Shallan caught a tear in the woman's eye.

"You're still human," Shallan said, reaching across, putting her hand on Navani's knee. "We can't all be emotionless chunks of rock like Jasnah."

Navani smiled. "She sometimes had the empathy of a corpse, didn't she?"

"Comes from being too brilliant," Shallan said. "You grow accustomed to everyone else being something of an idiot, trying to keep up with you."

"Chana knows, I wondered sometimes how I raised that child without strangling her. By age six, she was pointing out my logical fallacies as I tried to get her to go to bed on time."

Shallan grinned. "I always just assumed she was born in her thirties."

"Oh, she was. It just took thirty-some years for her body to catch up." Navani smiled. "I won't take this from you, but neither should I allow you to attempt a project so important on your own. I would be part. Figuring out the puzzles that captivated her . . . it will be like having her again. My little Jasnah, insufferable and wonderful."

How surreal it was to imagine Jasnah as a child being held by a mother. "It would be an honor to have your aid, Brightness Navani."

Navani held up the page. "You're trying to overlay Stormseat with the Shattered Plains. It's not going to work unless you have a point of reference."

"Preferably two," Shallan said.

"It's been centuries since that city fell. It was destroyed during Aharietiam itself, I believe. We're going to have trouble finding clues out here, though your list of descriptions will help." She tapped her finger against the papers. "This isn't my area of expertise, but I have several archaeologists among Dalinar's scribes. I should show them these pages."

Shallan nodded.

"We'll want copies of everything here," Navani said. "I don't want to lose originals to all of this rain. I could have the scribes work on it tonight, after we camp."

"If you wish."

Navani looked up at her, then frowned. "It is your decision."

"You're serious?" Shallan asked.

"Absolutely. Think of me as an additional resource."

All right then. "Yes, have them make copies," Shallan said, digging in her satchel. "And copies of this too—it's my attempt at re-creating one of the murals described as being on the outer wall of the temple to Chanaranach in Stormseat. It faced leeward, and was supposedly shaded, so we might be able to find hints of it.

"Also, I need a surveyor to measure each new plateau we cross, once we get farther in. I can draw them out, but my spatial reasoning can be off. I want exact sizes to make the map more accurate. I'll need guards and scribes to ride out with me ahead of the army to visit plateaus parallel to our course. It would really help if you could convince Dalinar to allow this.

"I'd like a team to study the quotes on that page underneath the map. They talk about methods for opening the Oathgate, which was supposed to be the duty of the Knights Radiant. Hopefully we can discover another method. Also, alert Dalinar that we'll be trying to open the portal if we find it. I do not expect there to be anything dangerous on the other side, but he'll undoubtedly want to send soldiers through first."

Navani raised an eyebrow at her. "You've done a touch of thinking about this, I see."

Shallan nodded, blushing.

"I'll see it done," Navani said. "I myself will head the research team studying those quotes you mention." She hesitated. "Do you know *why* Jasnah thought this city, Urithiru, was so important?"

"Because it was the seat of the Knights Radiant, and she expected to find information on them—and the Voidbringers—there."

"So she was like Dalinar," Navani said, "trying to bring back powers that—perhaps—we should leave alone."

Shallan felt a sudden spike of anxiety. *I need to say it. Say something.* "She wasn't trying. She succeeded."

"Succeeded?"

Shallan took a deep breath. "I don't know what she said regarding the origin of her Soulcaster, but the truth was that it was a fake. Jasnah could Soulcast on her own, without any fabrial. I saw her do it. She knew secrets from the past, secrets I don't think anyone else knows. Brightness Navani . . . your daughter *was* one of the Knights Radiant." Or as close to one as the world was going to have again.

Navani raised an eyebrow, obviously skeptical.

"I swear this is true," Shallan said, "on the tenth name of the Almighty."

"That is disturbing. Radiants, Heralds, and Voidbringers alike are supposed to be gone. We won that war."

"I know."

"I will go get to work on this," Navani said, knocking for the carriage driver to halt the vehicle.

⁘

The Weeping began.

A steady stream of rain. Kaladin could hear it inside his room, like a whisper in the background. Weak, miserable rain, without the fury and passion of a true highstorm.

He lay in the darkness, listening to the patter, feeling his leg throb. Wet, cold air leaked into his room, and he dug for the extra blankets that the quartermaster had delivered. He curled up and tried to sleep, but after sleeping most of the day yesterday—the day that Dalinar's army had left—he found himself wide awake.

He hated being wounded. Bed rest wasn't supposed to happen to him. Not anymore.

Syl . . .

The Weeping was a bad time for him. Days spent trapped indoors. A perpetual gloom in the sky that seemed to affect him more than it did others, leaving him lethargic and uncaring.

A knock came at his door. Kaladin raised his head in the darkness, then sat up and settled himself on his bench of a bed. "Come," he said.

The door opened and let in the sound of rain, like a thousand little footsteps scrambling about. Very little light accompanied the sounds. The overcast sky of the Weeping left the land in perpetual twilight.

Moash stepped in. He wore his Shardplate, as always. "Storms, Kal. Were you asleep? I'm sorry!"

"No, I was awake."

"In the darkness?"

Kaladin shrugged. Moash clicked the door shut behind him, but took off his gauntlet and hung it from a clip at the waist of his Shardplate. He reached beneath a fold in the metal and pulled out a handful of spheres to light his way. Riches that would have seemed incredible to bridgemen were now pocket change to Moash.

"Aren't you supposed to be guarding the king?" Kaladin asked.

"On and off," Moash said, sounding eager. "They quartered the five of us guards up by his rooms. In the palace itself! Kaladin, it's *perfect*."

"When?" Kaladin asked softly.

"We don't want to ruin Dalinar's expedition," Moash said, "so we're going to wait until he's out there some distance, maybe until he's engaged the enemy. That way, he'll be committed and won't turn back when he gets news. Better for Alethkar if he succeeds at defeating the Parshendi. He will return a hero . . . and a king."

Kaladin nodded, feeling sick.

"We have everything planned out," Moash said. "We'll raise an alert in the palace that the Assassin in White has been seen. Then we'll do what was done last time—send all of the servants into hiding in their rooms. Nobody will be around to see what we do, nobody will get hurt, and they'll all believe that the Shin assassin was behind this. We couldn't have *asked* for this to play out better! And you won't have to do anything, Kal. Graves says that we won't need your help after all."

"So why are you here?" Kaladin asked.

"I just wanted to check on you," Moash said. He stepped in closer. "Is it true, what Lopen says? About your . . . abilities?"

Storming Herdazian. Lopen had stayed behind—with Dabbid and

Hobber—to take care of the barrack and watch over Kaladin. They'd been talking to Moash, it seemed.

"Yes," Kaladin said.

"What happened?"

"I'm not sure," he lied. "I offended Syl. I haven't seen her in days. Without her, I can't draw in Stormlight."

"We'll have to fix that somehow," Moash said. "Either that, or get you Plate and Blade of your own."

Kaladin looked up at his friend. "I think she left because of the plot to kill the king, Moash. I don't think a Radiant could be involved in something like this."

"Shouldn't a Radiant care about doing what is right? Even if it means a difficult decision?"

"Sometimes lives must be spent for the greater good," Kaladin said.

"Yes, exactly!"

"That's what Amaram said. In regards to my friends, whom he murdered to cover up his secrets."

"Well, that's different, obviously. He's a lighteyes."

Kaladin looked to Moash, whose eyes had turned as light a tan as those of any Brightlord. Same color as Amaram's, actually. "So are you."

"Kal," Moash said. "You're worrying me. Don't say things like that."

Kaladin looked away.

"The king wanted me to deliver a message," Moash said. "That's my excuse for being here. He wants you to come talk to him."

"What? Why?"

"I don't know. He's been dipping into the wine, now that Dalinar is gone. Not the orange stuff, either. I'll tell him you're too wounded to come."

Kaladin nodded.

"Kal," Moash said. "We can trust you, right? You're not having second thoughts?"

"You said it yourself," Kaladin said. "I don't have to do anything. I just have to stay away." *What could I do, anyway? Wounded, with no spren?*

Everything was in motion. It was too far along for him to stop.

"Great," Moash said. "You heal up, all right?"

Moash walked out, leaving Kaladin in the darkness again.

CONTRADICTIONS

Ahbuttheywereleftbehindltisobviousfromthenatureofthebond
ButwherewherewherewhereSetoffObviousRealizationlikeapricity
TheyarewiththeShinWemustfindoneCanwemaketouseaTruthless
Canwecraftaweapon

—From the Diagram, Floorboard 17: paragraph 2,
every second letter starting with the first

In the darkness, Shallan's violet spheres gave life to the rain. Without the spheres, she couldn't see the drops, only hear their deaths upon the stones and the cloth of her pavilion. With the light, each falling speck of water flashed briefly, like starspren.

She sat at the edge of the pavilion, as she liked to watch the rainfall between bouts of sketching, while the other scholars sat closer to the center. So did Vathah and a couple of his soldiers, watching over her like nesting skyeels with a single pup. It amused her that they'd grown so protective; they seemed actively *proud* to be her soldiers. She'd honestly expected them to run off after gaining their clemency.

Four days into the Weeping, and she still enjoyed the weather. Why did the soft sound of gentle rain make her feel more imaginative? Around her, creationspren slowly vanished, most having taken the shapes of things about the camp. Swords that sheathed and unsheathed repeatedly, tiny tents that untied and blew in unseen wind. Her picture was of Jasnah as she'd been on that night just over a month ago, when Shallan had last seen her. Leaning upon the desk of a darkened ship's cabin, hand pushing back hair freed from its customary twists and braids. Exhausted, overwhelmed, terrified.

The drawing didn't depict a single faithful Memory, not as Shallan usually did them. This was a re-creation of what she remembered, an interpretation that was not exact. Shallan was proud of it, as she'd captured Jasnah's contradictions.

Contradictions. Those were what made people real. Jasnah exhausted, yet somehow still strong—stronger, even, because of the vulnerability she revealed. Jasnah terrified, yet also brave, for one allowed the other to exist. Jasnah overwhelmed, yet powerful.

Shallan had recently been trying to do more drawings like this—ones synthesized from her own imaginings. Her illusions would suffer if she could only reproduce what she'd experienced. She needed to be able to create, not just copy.

The last creationspren faded away, this one imitating a puddle that was being splashed by a boot. Her sheet of paper dimpled as Pattern moved up onto it.

He sniffed. "Useless things."

"The creationspren?"

"They don't *do* anything. They flit around and watch, admire. Most spren have a purpose. These are merely attracted by someone *else's* purpose."

Shallan sat back, thinking on that, as Jasnah had taught her. Nearby, the scholars and ardents argued about how large Stormseat had been. Navani had done her part well—better than Shallan could have hoped. The army's scholars now worked at Shallan's command.

Around her in the night, an uncountable array of lights both near and far indicated the breadth of the army. The rain continued to sprinkle down, catching the purple spherelight. She had chosen all spheres of one color.

"The artist Eleseth," Shallan observed to Pattern, "once did an experiment. She set out only ruby spheres, in their strength, to light her studio. She wanted to see what effect the all-red light would have upon her art."

"Mmmm," Pattern said. "To what result?"

"At first, during a painting session, the color of light affected her strongly. She would use too little red, and fields of blossoms would look washed out."

"Not unexpected."

"The interesting thing, however, was what happened if she continued working," Shallan said. "If she painted for hours by that light, the effects diminished. The colors of her reproductions grew more balanced, the pictures of flowers more vivid. She eventually concluded that her mind *compensated* for the colors she saw. Indeed, if she switched the color of the light during a session, she'd continue for a time to paint as if the room were still red, reacting against the new color."

"Mmmmmm . . ." Pattern said, content. "Humans can see the world as it is not. It is why your lies can be so strong. You are able to *not* admit that they are lies."

"It frightens me."

"Why? It is wonderful."

To him, she was a subject of study. For a moment, she understood how Kaladin must have seen Shallan as she spoke of the chasmfiend. Admiring its beauty, the form of its creation, oblivious to the present reality of its danger.

"It frightens me," Shallan said, "because we all see the world by some kind of light personal to us, and that light changes our perception. I don't see clearly. I want to, but I don't know if I ever truly can."

Eventually, a pattern broke through the sound of rain, and Dalinar Kholin entered the tent. Straight-backed and greying, he looked more like a general than a king. She had no sketches of him. It seemed a gross omission on her part, so she took a Memory of him walking into the pavilion, an aide holding an umbrella for him.

He strode up to Shallan. "Ah, here you are. The one who has taken command of this expedition."

Shallan belatedly scrambled to her feet and bowed. "Highprince?"

"You have co-opted my scribes and cartographers," Dalinar said, sounding amused. "They hum of it like the rainfall. Urithiru. Stormseat. How did you do it?"

"I didn't. Brightness Navani did."

"She says you convinced her."

"I . . ." Shallan blushed. "I was really just there, and she changed her mind . . ."

Dalinar nodded curtly to the side, and his aide stepped over to the debating scholars. The aide spoke with them softly, and they rose—some quickly, others with reluctance—and departed into the rain, leaving their papers. The aide followed them, and Vathah looked to Shallan. She nodded, excusing him and the other guards.

Soon Shallan and Dalinar were alone in the pavilion.

"You told Navani that Jasnah had discovered the secrets of the Knights Radiant," Dalinar said.

"I did."

"You're certain that Jasnah didn't mislead you somehow," Dalinar said, "or allow you to mislead yourself—that would be far more like her."

"Brightlord, I . . . I don't think that is . . ." She took a breath. "No. She did not mislead me."

"How can you be sure?"

"I saw it," Shallan said. "I witnessed what she did, and we spoke of it. Jasnah Kholin did not *use* a Soulcaster. She was one."

Dalinar folded his arms, looking past Shallan into the night. "I think

I'm supposed to refound the Knights Radiant. The first man I thought I could trust for the job turned out to be a murderer and a liar. Now you tell me that Jasnah might have had actual power. If that is true, then I am a fool."

"I don't understand."

"In naming Amaram," Dalinar said. "I did what I thought was my task. I wonder now if I was mistaken all along, and that refounding them was never my duty. They might be refounding themselves, and I am an arrogant meddler. You have given me a great deal to think upon. Thank you."

He did not smile as he said it; in fact, he looked severely troubled. He turned to leave, clasping his hands behind his back.

"Brightlord Dalinar?" Shallan said. "What if your task *wasn't* to refound the Knights Radiant?"

"That is what I just said," Dalinar replied.

"What if instead, your task was to *gather* them?"

He looked back to her, waiting. Shallan felt a cold sweat. What was she doing?

I have to tell someone sometime, she thought. *I can't do as Jasnah did, holding it all. This is too important.* Was Dalinar Kholin the right person?

Well, she certainly couldn't think of anyone better.

Shallan held out her palm, then breathed in, draining one of her spheres. Then she breathed back out, sending a cloud of shimmering Stormlight into the air between herself and Dalinar. She formed it into a small image of Jasnah, the one she'd just drawn, on top of her palm.

"Almighty above," Dalinar whispered. A single awespren, like a ring of blue smoke, burst out above him, spreading like the ripple from a stone dropped in a pond. Shallan had seen such a spren only a handful of times in her life.

Dalinar stepped closer, reverent, leaning down to inspect Shallan's image. "Can I?" he asked, reaching out a hand.

"Yes."

He touched the image, causing it to fuzz back into shifting light. When he withdrew his finger, the image re-formed.

"It's just an illusion," Shallan said. "I can't create anything real."

"It's amazing," Dalinar said, his voice so soft she could barely hear it over the pattering rain. "It is wonderful." He looked up at her, and there were—shockingly—tears in his eyes. "You're one of them."

"Maybe, kind of?" Shallan said, feeling awkward. This man, so commanding, so much larger than life, should not be crying in front of her.

"I'm not mad," he said, more to himself, it seemed. "I had decided that I wasn't, but that's not the same as knowing. It's all true. They're returning." He tapped at the image again. "Jasnah taught you this?"

"I more stumbled into it on my own," Shallan said. "I think I was led to her so she could teach me. We didn't have much time for that, unfortunately." She grimaced, withdrawing the Stormlight, heart beating quickly because of what she'd done.

"I need to give *you* the golden cape," Dalinar said, standing up straight, wiping his eyes and growing firm of voice again. "Put you in charge of them. So we—"

"*Me?*" Shallan yelped, thinking of what that would mean to her alternate identity. "No, I can't! I mean, Brightlord, sir, what I can do is mostly useful if nobody knows it's possible. I mean, if everyone is *looking* for my illusions, I'll never fool them."

"Fool them?" Dalinar said.

Perhaps the not best choice of words for Dalinar.

"Brightlord Dalinar!"

Shallan spun, alert, suddenly worried that someone had seen what she did. A lithe messenger approached the tent, dripping wet, locks of hair undone from her braids and sticking to her face. "Brightlord Dalinar! Parshendi spotted, sir!"

"Where?"

"Eastern side of this plateau," the messenger said, panting. "Scouting party, we think."

Dalinar looked from the messenger to Shallan, then cursed and started out into the rain.

Shallan tossed her sketchpad onto her chair and followed.

"This could be dangerous," Dalinar said.

"I appreciate the concern, Brightlord," she said softly. "But I think I could actually take a spear through the stomach, and my abilities would heal me up without a scar. I'm probably the most difficult person to kill in this entire camp."

Dalinar strode in silence for a moment. "The fall into the chasm?" he asked softly.

"Yes. I think I must have rescued Captain Kaladin too, though I don't know how I managed that."

He grunted. They moved quickly through the rain, the water wetting Shallan's hair and clothing. She practically had to jog to keep pace with Dalinar. Storming Alethi and their long legs. Guards ran up, members of Bridge Four, and fell in around them.

She heard shouting in the distance. Dalinar sent the guards into a wider perimeter to give himself and Shallan a measure of privacy.

"Can you Soulcast?" Dalinar asked softly. "Like Jasnah did?"

"Yes," Shallan said. "But I haven't practiced it much."

"It could prove very useful."

"It's also very dangerous. Jasnah didn't want me practicing without her, though now that she's gone . . . Well, I will do more with it, eventually. Sir, please don't tell anyone about this. For now, at least."

"This was why Jasnah took you on as a ward," Dalinar said. "It's why she wanted you marrying Adolin, isn't it? To bind you to us?"

"Yes," Shallan said, blushing in the darkness.

"A great many things make more sense now. I will tell Navani about you, but nobody else, and I will swear her to secrecy. She *can* keep a secret, if she has to."

She opened her mouth to say yes, but stopped herself. Was that what Jasnah would have said?

"We'll send you back to the warcamps," Dalinar continued, eyes forward, speaking softly. "Immediately, with an escort. I don't care how hard you are to kill. You're too valuable to risk on this expedition."

"Brightlord," Shallan said, splashing through a pool of water, glad she was wearing boots and leggings under the skirt, "you are not my king, nor are you my highprince. You have no authority over me. My duty is to find Urithiru, so you will *not* be sending me back. And, by your honor, I will have your promise not to tell a soul what I can do unless I give leave. That includes Brightness Navani."

He stopped in place, and stared at her in surprise. Then he grunted, his face barely visible. "I see Jasnah in you."

Rarely had Shallan been given such a compliment.

Lights bobbed and approached in the rain, soldiers bearing sphere lanterns. Vathah and his men jogged up, having been left behind, and Bridge Four held them back for the moment.

"Very well, Brightness," Dalinar said to Shallan. "Your secret will remain one, for now. We *will* consult further, once this expedition is done. You have read of the things I have been seeing?"

She nodded.

"The world is about to change," Dalinar said. He took a deep breath. "You give me hope, true hope, that we can change it in the right way."

The approaching scouts saluted, and Bridge Four parted to allow their leader access to Dalinar. He was a portly man with a brown hat that reminded her of the one Veil wore, except it was wide-brimmed. The scout wore soldier's trousers, but a leather jacket over them, and certainly didn't seem in fighting shape.

"Bashin," Dalinar said.

"Parshendi on that plateau next to us, sir," Bashin said, pointing. "The Parshendi stumbled over one of my scouting teams. The lads raised the alarm quickly, but we lost all three men."

Dalinar cursed softly, then turned toward Highlord Teleb, who had approached from the other direction, wearing his Shardplate, which he'd painted silver. "Wake the army, Teleb. Everyone on alert."

"Yes, Brightlord," Teleb said.

"Brightlord Dalinar," Bashin said, "the lads took down one of those shell-heads before being killed themselves. Sir . . . you need to see this. Something has changed."

Shallan shivered, feeling sodden and cold. She'd brought clothing that would last well in the rain, of course, but that didn't mean standing out here was *comfortable*. Though they wore coats, nobody else seemed to pay much heed. Likely, they took it for granted that during the Weeping, you were going to get soaked. That was something else for which her sheltered childhood had not prepared her.

Dalinar did not object as Shallan joined him in walking toward a nearby bridge—one of the more mobile ones run by Kaladin's bridge teams, who wore raincoats and front-brimmed caps. A group of soldiers on the other side of the bridge dragged something across, pushing a little wave of water before it. A Parshendi corpse.

Shallan had only seen the one that she'd found with Kaladin in the chasm. She'd done a sketch of that earlier, and this one looked very different. It had hair—well, a kind of hair. Leaning down, she found that it was thicker than human hair, and felt too . . . slick. Was that the right word? The face was marbled, like that of a parshman, this one with prominent red streaks through the black. The body was lean and strong, and something seemed to grow *under* the skin of the exposed arms, peeking out. Shallan prodded at it, and found it hard and ridged, like a crab shell. In fact, the face was crusted with a kind of thin, bumpy carapace just above the cheeks and running back around the sides of the head.

"This isn't a type we've seen before, sir," Bashin said to Dalinar. "Look at those ridges. Sir . . . some of the lads that were killed, they had *burn marks* on them. In the rain. Shakiest thing I've ever seen . . ."

Shallan looked up at them. "What do you mean by a 'type,' Bashin?"

"Some Parshendi have hair," the man said—he was a darkeyes, but clearly well respected, though he didn't bear an obvious military rank. "Others have carapace. The ones we met with King Gavilar long ago, they were . . . *shaped* different from the ones we fight."

"They have specialized subspecies?" Shallan said. Some cremlings were like that, working in a hive, with different specializations and varied forms.

"We might be depleting their numbers," Dalinar said to Bashin. "Forcing them to send out their equivalent of lighteyes to fight."

"And the burns, Dalinar?" Bashin said, scratching his head under his hat.

Shallan reached out to check the Parshendi's eye color. Did they have lighteyes and dark, like humans? She lifted the eyelid.

The eye beneath was completely red.

She screamed, jumping back, pulling her hand up to her chest. The soldiers cursed, looking around, and Dalinar's Shardblade appeared in his hand a few seconds later.

"Red eyes," Shallan whispered. "It's happening."

"The red eyes are just a legend."

"Jasnah had an entire notebook of references to this, Brightlord," Shallan said, shivering. "The Voidbringers are here. Time is short."

"Throw the body into the chasm," Dalinar said to his men. "I doubt we'd be able to easily burn it. Keep everyone alert. Be prepared for an attack tonight. They—"

"Brightlord!"

Shallan spun as a hulking armored figure came up, rainwater trailing down his silvery Plate. "We've found another one, sir," Teleb said.

"Dead?" Dalinar said.

"No, sir," the Shardbearer said, pointing. "He walked right up to us, sir. He's sitting on a rock over there."

Dalinar looked to Shallan, who shrugged. Dalinar started off in the direction Teleb had pointed.

"Sir?" Teleb said, voice resonating inside his helm. "Should you . . ."

Dalinar ignored the warning, and Shallan hastened after him, collecting Vathah and his two guards.

"Should you head back?" Vathah said under his breath to her. Storms, but that face of his looked dangerous in the dim light, even if his voice was respectful. She couldn't help but still see him as the man who had almost killed her, back in the Unclaimed Hills.

"I will be safe," Shallan replied softly.

"You might have a Blade, Brightness, but you could still die to an arrow in the back."

"Unlikely, in this rain," she said.

He fell in behind her, offering no further objection. He was trying to do the job she had assigned him. Unfortunately, she was discovering that she didn't much like being guarded.

They found the Parshendi after a hike through the rain. The rock he sat on was about as high as a man was tall. He seemed to have no weapons, and about a hundred Alethi soldiers stood around the base of his seat, spears pointed upward. Shallan couldn't make out much more, as he sat across the chasm from them, a portable bridge in place to his plateau.

"Has he said anything?" Dalinar asked softly as Teleb stepped up.

"Not that I know of," the Shardbearer said. "He just sits there."

Shallan peered across the chasm toward the solitary Parshendi man. He stood up, and shaded his eyes against the rain. The soldiers below shuffled, spears rising into more threatening positions.

"Skar?" the Parshendi's voice called. "Skar, is that you? And Leyten?"

Nearby, one of Dalinar's bridgeman guards cursed. He ran across the bridge, and several other bridgemen followed.

They returned a moment later. Shallan crowded in closely to hear what their leader whispered to Dalinar.

"It's him, sir," Skar said. "He's changed, but storm me for a fool if I'm wrong—it's *him*. Shen. He ran bridges with us for months, then vanished. Now he's here. He says he wants to surrender to you."

Q: For what essential must we strive? A: The essential of preservation, to shelter a seed of humanity through the coming storm. Q: What cost must we bear? A: The cost is irrelevant. Mankind must survive. Our burden is that of the species, and all other considerations are but dust by comparison.

—From the Diagram, Catechism of the
Back of the Flowered Painting: paragraph 1

Dalinar stood with hands behind his back, waiting in his command tent and listening to the patter of rain on the cloth. The floor of the tent was wet. You couldn't avoid that, in the Weeping. He knew that from miserable experience—he'd been out on more than one military excursion during this time of year.

It was the day after they'd discovered the Parshendi on the Plains—both the dead one and the one the bridgemen called Shen, or Rlain, as he had said his name was. Dalinar himself had allowed the man to be armed.

Shallan claimed that all parshmen were Voidbringers in embryo. He had ample reason to believe her word, considering what she'd shown him. But what was he to *do*? The Radiants had returned, the Parshendi had manifested red eyes. Dalinar felt as if he were trying to stop a dam from breaking, all the while not knowing where the leaks were actually coming from.

The tent flaps parted and Adolin ducked in, escorting Navani. She hung her stormcoat on the rack beside the flap, and Adolin grabbed a towel and began drying his hair and face.

Adolin was betrothed to a member of the Knights Radiant. *She says she's not one yet*, Dalinar reminded himself. That made sense. One could be a trained spearman without being a soldier. One implied skill, the other a position.

"They are bringing the Parshendi man?" Dalinar asked.

"Yes," Navani said, sitting down in one of the room's chairs. Adolin didn't take his seat, but found a pitcher of filtered rainwater and poured himself a cup. He tapped the side of the tin cup as he drank.

They were restless, all of them, following the discovery of red-eyed Parshendi. After no attack had come that night, Dalinar had pushed the four armies into another day of marching.

Slowly, they approached the middle of the Plains, at least as Shallan's projections indicated. They were already well beyond the regions that scouts had explored. Now, they had to rely on the young woman's maps.

The flaps opened again, and Teleb marched in with the prisoner. Dalinar had put the highlord and his personal guard in charge of this "Rlain," as he didn't like how defensive the bridgemen were about him. He did invite their lieutenants—Skar and the Horneater cook they called Rock—to come to the interrogation, and those two entered after Teleb and his men. General Khal and Renarin were in another tent with Aladar and Roion, going over tactics for when they approached the Parshendi encampment.

Navani sat up, leaning forward, narrowing her eyes at the prisoner. Shallan had wanted to attend, but Dalinar had promised to have everything written down for her. The Stormfather had given her some sense, fortunately, and she hadn't insisted. Having too many of them near this spy felt dangerous to Dalinar.

He had a vague recollection of the parshman guard who had occasionally joined the men of Bridge Four. Parshmen were practically invisible, but once this one had started carrying a spear, he had become instantly noticeable. Not that there had been anything else distinctive about him—same squat parshman body, marbled skin, dull eyes.

This creature before him was nothing like that. He was a full Parshendi warrior, complete with orange-red skullplate and armored carapace at the chest, thighs, and outer arms. He was as tall as an Alethi, and more muscular.

Though he carried no weapon, the guards still treated him as if he were the most dangerous thing on this plateau—and perhaps he was just that. As he stepped up, he saluted Dalinar, hand to chest. Like the other bridgemen. He bore their tattoo on his forehead, reaching up and blending into his skullplate.

"Sit," Dalinar ordered, nodding toward a stool at the center of the room. Rlain obeyed.

"I'm told," Dalinar said, "that you refuse to tell us anything about the Parshendi plans."

"I don't know them," Rlain said. He had the rhythmic intonations common to the Parshendi, but he spoke Alethi very well. Better than any parshman Dalinar had heard.

"You were a spy," Dalinar said, hands clasped behind his back, trying to loom over the Parshendi—but staying far enough away that the man could not grab him without Adolin getting in the way first.

"Yes, sir."

"For how long?"

"About three years," Rlain said. "In various warcamps."

Nearby, Teleb—faceplate up—turned and raised an eyebrow at Dalinar.

"You answer me when I ask," Dalinar said. "But not the others. Why?"

"You're my commanding officer," Rlain said.

"You're Parshendi."

"I . . ." The man looked down at the ground, shoulders bowing. He raised a hand to his head, feeling at the ridge of skin just where his skull-plate ended. "Something is very wrong, sir. Eshonai's voice . . . on the plateau that day, when she came to meet with Prince Adolin . . ."

"Eshonai," Dalinar prompted. "The Parshendi Shardbearer?" Nearby, Navani scribbled on a pad of paper, writing down each word spoken.

"Yes. She was my commander. But now . . ." He looked up, and despite the alien skin and the strange way of speaking, Dalinar recognized grief in this man's face. Terrible grief. "Sir, I have reason to believe that everyone I know . . . everyone I loved . . . has been destroyed, monsters left in their place. The listeners, the Parshendi, may be no more. I have nothing left . . ."

"Yes you do," Skar said from outside the ring of guards. "You're Bridge Four."

Rlain looked at him. "I'm a traitor."

"Ha!" Rock said. "Is little problem. Can be fixed."

Dalinar gestured to quiet the bridgemen. He glanced at Navani, who nodded for him to continue.

"Tell me," Dalinar said, "how you hid among the parshmen."

"I . . ."

"Soldier," Dalinar barked. "That was an order."

Rlain sat up. Amazingly, he seemed to want to obey—as if he needed something to lend him strength. "Sir," Rlain said, "it's just something my people can do. We choose a form based on what we need, the job required of us. Dullform, one of those forms, looks a lot like a parshman. Hiding among them is easy."

"We account our parshmen with precision," Navani said.

"Yes," Rlain replied, "and we are noticed—but rarely questioned. Who questions when you find an extra sphere lying on the ground? It's not something suspicious. It's merely fortune."

Dangerous territory, Dalinar thought, noticing the change in Rlain's voice—the beat to which he was speaking. This man did not like how the parshmen were treated.

"You spoke of the Parshendi," Dalinar said. "This has to do with the red eyes?"

Rlain nodded.

"What does it mean, soldier?" Dalinar asked.

"It means our gods have returned," Rlain whispered.

"Who are your gods?"

"They are the souls of those ancient. Those who gave of themselves to destroy." A different rhythm to his words this time, slow and reverent. He looked up at Dalinar. "They hate you and your kind, sir. This new form they have given my people . . . it is something terrible. It will *bring* something terrible."

"Can you lead us to the Parshendi city?" Dalinar asked.

Rlain's voice changed again. A different rhythm. "My people . . ."

"You said they are gone," Dalinar said.

"They might be," Rlain said. "I got close enough to see an army, tens of thousands. But surely they left some in other forms. The elderly? The young? Who watches our children?"

Dalinar stepped up to Rlain, waving back Adolin, who raised an anxious hand. He stooped down, laying an arm on the Parshendi man's shoulder.

"Soldier," Dalinar said, "if what you're telling me is correct, then the most important thing you can do is lead us to your people. I will see that the noncombatants are protected, my word of honor on it. If something terrible is happening to your people, you need to help me stop it."

"I . . ." Rlain took a deep breath. "Yes, sir," he said to a different rhythm.

"Meet with Shallan Davar," Dalinar said. "Describe the route to her, and get us a map. Teleb, you may release the prisoner into the custody of Bridge Four."

The Oldblood Shardbearer nodded. As the group of them left, letting in a gust of rainy wind, Dalinar sighed and sat down beside Navani.

"You trust his word?"

"I don't know," Dalinar said. "But something *did* shake that man, Navani. Soundly."

"He's Parshendi," she said. "You may be misreading his body language."

Dalinar leaned forward, clasping his hands before him. "The countdown?" he asked.

"Three days away," Navani said. "Three days before Lightday."

So little time. "We hasten our pace," he said.

Inward. Toward the center.

And destiny.

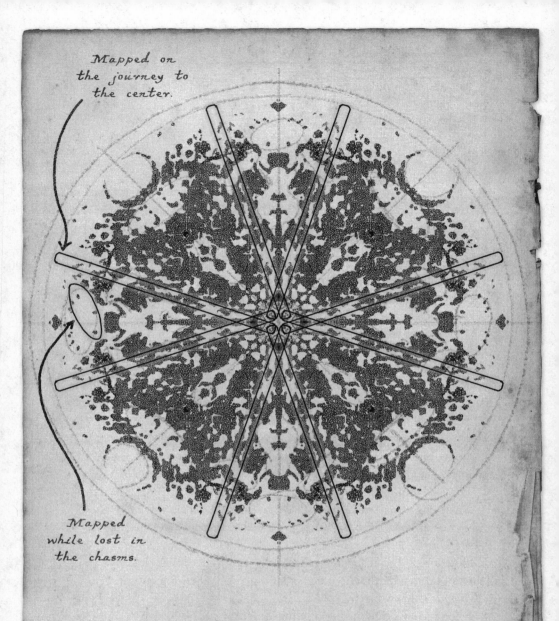

Mapped on
the journey to
the center.

Mapped
while lost in
the chasms.

Note: Eastern side of the Plains is much more eroded
than this. Light areas are plateaus packed closely together.
Dark areas represent plateaus less densely packed.

I know you wanted me to draw every plateau, but shadows,
woman! Even I'm not THAT crazy.

TO FIGHT THE RAIN

You must become king. Of Everything.

—From the Diagram, Tenets of Instruction,
Back of the Footboard: paragraph 1

Shallan fought against the wind, pulling her stormcoat—stolen from a soldier—close around her as she struggled up the slick incline.

"Brightness?" Gaz asked. He grabbed his cap to keep it from blowing free. "Are you certain you want to do this?"

"Of course I am," Shallan said. "Whether or not what I'm doing is wise . . . well, that's another story."

These winds were unusual for the Weeping, which was supposed to be a period of placid rainfall, a time for contemplating the Almighty, a respite from highstorms.

Maybe things were different out here in the stormlands. She pulled herself up the rocks. The Shattered Plains had grown increasingly rough as the armies traveled inward—now on their eighth day of the expedition—following Shallan's map, created with the help of Rlain, the former bridgeman.

Shallan crested the rock formation and found the view that the scouts had described. Vathah and Gaz stomped up behind her, muttering about the cold. The heart of the Shattered Plains extended before Shallan. The inner plateaus, never explored by men.

"It's here," she said.

Gaz scratched at the socket beneath his eye patch. "Rocks?"

"Yes, guardsman Gaz," Shallan said. "Rocks. Beautiful, wonderful rocks."

In the distance, she saw shadows draped in a veil of misty rain. Seen together in a group like this, it was unmistakable. This *was* a city. A city covered over with centuries' worth of crem, like children's blocks dribbled with many coats of melted wax. To the innocent eye, it undoubtedly looked much like the rest of the Shattered Plains. But it was oh so much more.

It was proof. Even this formation Shallan stood upon had probably once been a building. Weathered on the stormward side, dribbled with crem down the leeward side to create the bulbous, uneven slope they had climbed.

"Brightness!"

She ignored the voices from down below, instead waving impatiently for the spyglass. Gaz handed it to her, and she raised it to inspect the plateaus ahead. Unfortunately, the thing had fogged up on one end. She tried to rub it clean, rain washing over her, but the fog was on the inside. Blasted device.

"Brightness?" Gaz asked. "Shouldn't we, uh, listen to what they're saying down below?"

"More twisted Parshendi spotted," Shallan said, raising the spyglass again. Wouldn't the designer of the thing have built it to be sealed on the inside, to prevent moisture from getting in?

Gaz and Vathah stepped back as several members of Bridge Four reached the top of the incline.

"Brightness," one of the bridgemen said, "Highprince Dalinar has withdrawn the vanguard and ordered a secure perimeter on the plateau behind us." He was a tall, handsome man whose arms seemed entirely too long for his body. Shallan looked with dissatisfaction at the inner plateaus.

"Brightness," the bridgeman continued reluctantly, "he did say that if you wouldn't come, he would send Adolin to . . . um . . . cart you back over his shoulder."

"I would like to see him do that," Shallan said. It *did* sound kind of romantic, the sort of thing you'd read of in a novel. "He's that worried about the Parshendi?"

"Shen . . . er, Rlain . . . says we're practically to their home plateau, Brightness. Too many of their patrols have been spotted. Please."

"We need to get in there," Shallan said, pointing. "That's where the secrets are."

"Brightness . . ."

"Very well," she said, turning and hiking down the incline. She slipped, which did not help her dignity, but Vathah caught her arm before she tumbled onto her face.

Once down, they quickly crossed this smaller plateau, joining scouts who were jogging back toward the bulk of the army. Rlain claimed to know nothing himself of the Oathgate—or even really much about the city, which he called "Narak" instead of Stormseat. He said his people had only taken up permanent residence here following the Alethi invasion.

During the push inward, Dalinar's soldiers had spotted an increasing number of Parshendi and had clashed with them in brief skirmishes. General Khal thought that the forays had been intended to draw the army off course, though how they would figure that, Shallan didn't know—but she *did* know she was growing tired of feeling damp all the time. They had been out here nearly two weeks now, and some of the soldiers had begun to mutter that the army would need to return to the warcamps soon, or risk not getting back before the highstorms resumed.

Shallan stalked across the bridge and passed several lines of spearmen setting up behind short, wavelike ridges in the stone—likely the footings of old walls. She found Dalinar and the other highprinces in a tent set up at the center of camp. It was one of six identical tents, and it wasn't immediately obvious which one held the four highprinces. A safety precaution of some sort, she assumed. As Shallan stepped in out of the rain, she intruded upon their conversation.

"The current plateau does have very favorable defensible positions," Aladar said, gesturing toward a map set out on the travel table before them. "I prefer our chances against an assault here to moving deeper."

"And if we move deeper," Dalinar said with a grunt, "we'll be in danger of getting split during an attack, half on one plateau, half on the other."

"But do they even *need* to attack?" Roion said. "If I were them, I'd just form up out there as if to prepare for an attack—but then I wouldn't. I'd stall, forcing my enemy to get stuck out here waiting for an attack until the highstorms returned!"

"He makes a valid point," Aladar admitted.

"Trust a coward," Sebarial said, "to know the smartest way to stay out of fighting." He sat with Palona beside the table, eating fruit and smiling pleasantly.

"I am *not* a coward," Roion said, forming fists at his sides.

"I didn't mean it as an insult," Sebarial said. "My insults are far more pithy. *That* was a compliment. If I had my way, I'd hire you to run all wars, Roion. I suspect there would be far fewer casualties, and the price of undergarments would double once soldiers were told that you were in charge. I'd make a fortune."

Shallan handed her dripping coat to a servant, then took off her cap and began drying her hair with a towel. "We need to press closer to the center of the Plains," she said. "Roion is right. I refuse to let us bivouac. The Parshendi will just wait us out."

The others looked to her.

"I wasn't aware," Dalinar said, "that you decided our tactics, Brightness Shallan."

"It's our own fault, Dalinar," Sebarial said, "for giving her so much leeway. We probably should have tossed her off the Pinnacle weeks ago, the moment she arrived at that meeting."

Shallan was stirring up a retort as the tent flaps parted and Adolin trudged in, Shardplate streaming. He pushed up his faceplate. Storms . . . he looked so good, even when you could see only half his face. She smiled.

"They are *definitely* agitated," Adolin said. He saw her, and gave her a quick smile before clinking up to the table. "There are at least ten thousand of those twisted Parshendi out there, moving in groups around the plateaus."

"Ten thousand," Aladar said with a grunt. "We can take ten thousand. Even with them having the terrain advantage, even if we have to assault rather than defend, we should handle that many with ease. We have over thirty thousand."

"This *is* what we came to do," Dalinar said. He looked at Shallan, who blushed at her forwardness earlier. "Your portal, the one you think is out here. Where would it be?"

"Closer to the city," Shallan said.

"What of those red eyes?" Roion asked. He looked very uncomfortable. "And the flashes of light they cause when they fight? Storms, when I spoke earlier, I didn't mean that I wanted us to go farther. I was just worried at what the Parshendi would do. I . . . there's no easy way to do this, is there?"

"So far as Rlain has said," Navani said from her seated position at the side of the room, "only their soldiers can jump between plateaus, but we can assume the new form capable of it as well. They can flee us if we push forward."

Dalinar shook his head. "They set up on the Plains, rather than fleeing all those years ago, because they knew it was their best chance for survival. On the open, unbroken rock of the stormlands, they could be hunted and destroyed. Out here they have the advantage. They won't abandon it now. Not if they think they can fight us."

"If we want to make them fight, then," Aladar said, "we need to threaten their homes. I guess we really should press toward the city."

Shallan relaxed. Each step closer to the center—by Rlain's explanations, they were but half a day away—got her closer to the Oathgate.

Dalinar leaned forward, spreading his hands to the sides, his shadow falling on the battle maps. "Very well. I did not come all this way to timidly wait upon Parshendi whims. We'll march inward tomorrow, threaten their city, and force them to engage."

"The closer we get," Sebarial noted, "the more likely we are to become cut off without hope of retreat."

Dalinar didn't respond, but Shallan knew what he was thinking. *We gave up hope of retreat days ago.* A flight across days and days of plateaus would be a disaster if the Parshendi decided to harry. The Alethi fought here, and they won, seizing the shelter of Narak.

That was their only option.

Dalinar adjourned the meeting, and the highprinces left, surrounded by groups of aides holding umbrellas. Shallan waited as Dalinar caught her eyes. In moments only she, Dalinar, Adolin, and Navani remained.

Navani walked up to Dalinar, taking his arm with both of hers. An intimate posture.

"This portal of yours," Dalinar said.

"Yes?" Shallan asked.

Dalinar looked up and met her eyes. "How real is it?"

"Jasnah was convinced it was completely real. She was never wrong."

"This would be a storming *bad* time for her to break her record," he said softly. "I agreed to press forward, in part, because of your exploration."

"Thank you."

"I did not do it for scholarship," Dalinar said. "From what Navani tells me, this portal offers a unique opportunity for retreat. I had hoped to defeat the Parshendi before danger overtook us, whatever it was. Judging by what we've seen, danger has arrived early."

Shallan nodded.

"Tomorrow is the last day of the countdown," Dalinar said. "Scribbled on the walls during highstorms. Whatever it is, whatever it was, we meet it tomorrow—and you are my backup plan, Shallan Davar. You will find this portal, and you will make it work. If the evil overwhelms us, your pathway will be our escape. You may be the only chance that our armies—and indeed, Alethkar itself—have for survival."

⁘

Days passed, and Kaladin refused to let the rain overcome him.

He limped through the camp, using a crutch that Lopen had fetched for him despite objecting that it was too soon for Kaladin to be up and about.

The place was still empty, save for the occasional parshmen lugging wood from the forests outside or carrying sacks of grain. The camp didn't get any news about the expedition. The king was probably being sent word via spanreed, but he didn't share it with everyone else.

Storms, this place feels eerie, Kaladin thought, limping past deserted barracks, rain pattering against the umbrella that Lopen had tied to Kaladin's crutch. It worked. Kind of. He passed rainspren, like blue candles sprouting from the ground, each with a single eye in the center of its top. Creepy things. Kaladin had always disliked them.

He fought the rain. Did that make any sense? It seemed that the rain wanted him to stay inside, so he went out. The rain wanted him to give in to the despair, so he forced himself to think. Growing up, he'd had Tien to help lighten the gloom. Now, even thinking of Tien increased that gloom instead—though he couldn't avoid it. The Weeping reminded him of his brother. Of laughter when the darkness threatened, of cheerful joy and carefree optimism.

Those images warred with ones of Tien's death. Kaladin squeezed his eyes shut, trying to banish that memory. Of the frail young man, barely trained, being cut down. Tien's own company of soldiers had put him at the front as a distraction, a sacrifice to slow the enemy.

Kaladin set his jaw, opening his eyes. No more moping. He would not whine or wallow. Yes, he'd lost Syl. He'd lost many loved ones during his life. He would survive this agony as he had survived the others.

He continued his limping circuit of the barracks. He did this four times a day. Sometimes Lopen came with him, but today Kaladin was alone. He splashed through puddles of water, and found himself smiling because he wore the boots Shallan had stolen from him.

I never did believe she was a Horneater, he thought. *I need to make sure she knows that.*

He stopped, leaning on the crutch and looking out through the rain toward the Shattered Plains. He couldn't see far. The haze of rainfall prevented that.

You come back safely, he thought to those out there. *All of you. This time, I can't help you if something goes wrong.*

Rock, Teft, Dalinar, Adolin, Shallan, everyone in Bridge Four—all out on their own. How different a place would the world be if Kaladin had been a better man? If he'd used his powers and had returned to the warcamp with Shallan full of Stormlight? He had been so close to revealing what he could do . . .

You'd been thinking that for weeks, he thought to himself. *You'd never have done it. You were too scared.*

He hated admitting it, but it was true.

Well, if his suspicions about Shallan were true, perhaps Dalinar would have his Radiant anyway. May she make a better run of it than Kaladin had.

He continued on his limping way, rounding back to Bridge Four's barrack. He stopped when he saw a fine carriage, pulled by horses bearing the king's livery, waiting in front of it.

Kaladin cursed, hobbling forward. Lopen ran out to meet him, not carrying an umbrella. A lot of people gave up on trying to stay dry during the Weeping.

"Lopen!" Kaladin said. "What?"

"He's waiting for you, gancho," Lopen said, gesturing urgently. "The king himself."

Kaladin limped more quickly toward his room. The door was open, and Kaladin peeked in to find King Elhokar standing inside, looking about the small chamber. Moash guarded the door, and Taka—a former member of the King's Guard—stood nearer to the king.

"Your Majesty?" Kaladin asked.

"Ah," the king said, "bridgeman." Elhokar's cheeks were flushed. He'd been drinking, though he didn't appear drunk. Kaladin understood. With Dalinar and that disapproving glare of his gone for a time, it was probably nice to relax with a bottle.

When Kaladin had first met the king, he'd thought Elhokar lacked regality. Now, oddly, he thought Elhokar did look like a king. It wasn't that the king had changed—the man still had his imperious features, with that overly large nose and condescending manner. The change was in Kaladin. The things he'd once associated with kingship—honor, strength of arms, nobility—had been replaced with Elhokar's less inspiring attributes.

"This is really all that Dalinar assigns one of his officers?" Elhokar asked, gesturing around the room. "That man. He expects everyone to live with his own austerity. It is as if he's completely forgotten how to enjoy himself."

Kaladin looked to Moash, who shrugged, Shardplate clinking.

The king cleared his throat. "I was told you were too weak to make the trip to see me. I see that might not be the case."

"I'm sorry, Your Majesty," Kaladin said. "I'm not well, but I walk the camp each day to rebuild my strength. I feared that my weakness and appearance might be offensive to the Throne."

"You've learned to speak politically, I see," the king said, folding his arms. "The truth is that my command is meaningless, even to a darkeyes. I no longer have authority in the eyes of men."

Great. Here we go again.

The king waved curtly. "Out, you other two. I'd speak to this man alone."

Moash glanced at Kaladin, looking concerned, but Kaladin nodded. With reluctance, Moash and Taka walked out, shutting the door, leaving them to the light of a few dwindling spheres that the king set out. Soon, those wouldn't have any Stormlight to them at all—it had been too long without a highstorm. They'd need to break out candles and oil lamps.

"How did you know," the king asked him, "how to be a hero?"

"Your Majesty?" Kaladin asked, sagging against his crutch.

"A hero," the king said, waving flippantly. "Everyone loves you, bridge-man. You saved Dalinar, you fought Shardbearers, you came back after falling into the storming chasms! How do you do it? How do you know?"

"It's really just luck, Your Majesty."

"No, no," the king said. He began pacing. "It's a pattern, though I can't figure it out. When I try to be strong, I make a fool of myself. When I try to be merciful, people walk all over me. When I try to listen to counsel, it turns out I've picked the wrong men! When I try to do everything on my own, Dalinar has to take over lest I ruin the kingdom.

"How do people know what to do? Why don't *I* know what to do? I was born to this office, given the throne by the Almighty himself! Why would he give me the title, but not the capacity? It defies reason. And yet, every-one seems to know things that I do not. My father could rule even the likes of Sadeas—men loved Gavilar, feared him, and served him all at once. I can't even get a darkeyes to obey a command to come visit the palace! Why doesn't this work? What do I have to *do*?"

Kaladin stepped back, shocked at the frankness. "Why are you asking me this, Your Majesty?"

"Because you know the secret," the king said, still pacing. "I've seen how your men regard you; I've heard how people speak of you. You're a *hero,* bridgeman." He stopped, then walked up to Kaladin, taking him by the arms. "Can you teach me?"

Kaladin regarded him, baffled.

"I want to be a king like my father was," Elhokar said. "I want to lead men, and I want them to respect me."

"I don't . . ." Kaladin swallowed. "I don't know if that's possible, Your Majesty."

Elhokar narrowed his eyes at Kaladin. "So you do still speak your mind. Even after the trouble it brought you. Tell me. Do you think me a bad king, bridgeman?"

"Yes."

The king drew in a sharp breath, still holding Kaladin by the arms.

I could do it right here, Kaladin realized. *Strike the king down. Put Dalinar on the throne. No hiding, no secrets, no cowardly assassination. A fight, him and me.*

That seemed a more honest way to be about it. Sure, Kaladin would probably be executed, but he found that didn't bother him. Should he do it, for the good of the kingdom?

He could imagine Dalinar's anger. Dalinar's disappointment. Death didn't bother Kaladin, but failing Dalinar . . . *Storms.*

The king let go and stalked away. "Well, I did ask," he muttered to him-self. "I merely have to win you over as well. I *will* figure this out. I will be a king to be remembered."

"Or you could do what is best for Alethkar," Kaladin said, "and step down."

The king stopped in place. He turned on Kaladin, expression darkening. "Do *not* overstep yourself, bridgeman. Bah. I should never have come here."

"I agree," Kaladin said. He found this entire experience surreal.

Elhokar made to leave. He stopped at the door, not looking at Kaladin. "When you came, the shadows went away."

"The . . . shadows?"

"I saw them in mirrors, in the corners of my eyes. I could swear I even heard them whispering, but you frightened them. I haven't seen them since. There's something about you. Don't try to deny it." The king looked to him. "I am sorry for what I did to you. I watched you fight to help Adolin, and then I saw you defend Renarin . . . and I grew jealous. There you were, such a champion, so loved. And everyone hates me. I should have gone to fight myself.

"Instead, I overreacted to your challenge of Amaram. You weren't the one who ruined our chance against Sadeas. It was me. Dalinar was right. Again. I'm so tired of him being right, and me being wrong. In light of that, I am not at all surprised that you find me a bad king."

Elhokar pushed open the door and left.

The Unmade are a deviation, a flair, a conundrum that may not be
worth your time. You cannot help but think of them. They are fas-
cinating. Many are mindless. Like the spren of human emotions,
only much more nasty. I do believe a few can think, however.

—From the Diagram, Book of the 2nd Desk Drawer: paragraph 14

Dalinar strode from the tent into a subtle rain, joined by Navani
and Shallan. The rain sounded softer out here than it had inside
the tent, where the drops had drummed upon the fabric.

They had marched farther inward all that morning, bringing them to
the very heart of the ruined plateaus. They were close now. So close, they
had the Parshendi's full attention.

It was happening.

An attendant offered an umbrella to each person leaving the tent, but
Dalinar waved his away. If his men had to stand in this, he'd join them.
He'd be soaked by the end of this day anyway.

He strode through the ranks, following bridgemen in stormcoats who
led the way with sapphire lanterns. It was still day, but the thick cloud
cover rendered everything dim. He used blue light to identify himself.
Roion and Aladar, seeing that Dalinar had eschewed an umbrella, stepped
out into the rain with him. Sebarial, of course, stayed underneath his.

They reached the edge of the mass of troops who had formed up in a
large oval, facing outward. He knew his soldiers well enough to sense their
anxiety. They stood too stiffly, with no shuffling or stretching. They were

968

also silent, not chattering to distract themselves—not even griping. The only voices he heard were occasional barked orders as officers trimmed the lines. Dalinar soon saw what was causing the uneasiness.

Glowing red eyes amassed on the next plateau.

They hadn't glowed before. Red eyes yes, but not with those uncanny glows. In the dim light, the Parshendi bodies were indistinct, no more than shadows. The crimson eyes hovered like Taln's Scar—like spheres in the darkness, deeper in color than any ruby. Parshendi beards often bore bits of gemstone woven into them in patterns, but today those didn't glow.

Too long without a highstorm, Dalinar thought. Even the gems in Alethi spheres—cut with facets and so able to hold light longer—had almost all failed by this point of the Weeping, though larger gemstones might last another week or so.

They had entered the darkest part of the year. The time when Stormlight did not shine.

"Oh, Almighty!" Roion whispered, looking at those red eyes. "Oh, by the names of God himself. What have you brought us to, Dalinar?"

"Can you do anything to help?" Dalinar asked softly, looking to Shallan, who stood beneath her umbrella at his side, her guards just behind.

Face pale, she shook her head. "I'm sorry."

"The Knights Radiant were warriors," Dalinar said, very softly.

"If they were, then I've got a long way to go. . . ."

"Go, then," Dalinar told the girl. "When there is an opening in the fighting, find that pathway to Urithiru, if it exists. You're my only contingency plan, Brightness."

She nodded.

"Dalinar," Aladar said, sounding horrified as he watched the red eyes, which were forming into ordered ranks on the other side of the chasm, "tell me straight. When you brought us on this march, did you *expect* to find these horrors?"

"Yes." It was true enough. He didn't know what horrors he'd find, but he had known that something was coming.

"You came anyway?" Aladar demanded. "You hauled us all the way out onto these cursed plains, you let us be surrounded by monsters, to be slaughtered and—"

Dalinar grabbed Aladar by the front of the jacket and hauled him forward. The move caught the other man completely off guard, and he quieted, eyes widening.

"Those are *Voidbringers* out there," Dalinar hissed, rain dribbling down his face. "They've returned. Yes, it is true. And we, Aladar, *we* have a chance to stop them. I don't know if we can prevent another Desolation, but I'd do *anything*—including sacrificing myself and this entire army—to protect Alethkar from those things. Do you understand?"

Aladar nodded, wide-eyed.

"I hoped to get here before this happened," Dalinar said, "but I didn't. So now we're going to fight. And storm it, we're going to destroy those things. We're going to stop them, and we're going to hope that will stop this evil from spreading to the world's parshmen, as my niece feared. If you survive this day, you'll be known as one of the greatest men of our generation."

He released Aladar, letting the highprince stumble back. "Go to your men, Aladar. Go lead them. Be a champion."

Aladar stared at Dalinar, mouth gaping. Then, he straightened. He slapped his arm to his chest, giving a salute as crisp as any Dalinar had seen. "It will be done, Brightlord," Aladar said. "Highprince of War." Aladar barked to his attendants—including Mintez, the highlord that Aladar usually had use his Shardplate in battle—then put his hand to his side-sword and dashed away in the rain.

"Huh," Sebarial said from beneath his umbrella. "He's actually buying into it. He thinks he's going to be a storming hero."

"He now knows I was right about the need to unify Alethkar. He's a good soldier. Most of the highprinces are . . . or were, at some point."

"Pity you ended up with us two instead of them," Sebarial said, nodding toward Roion, who still stared out at the shifting red eyes. There were thousands now, still increasing as more Parshendi arrived. Scouts reported that they were gathering on all three plateaus bordering the large one that the Alethi occupied.

"I'm useless in a battle," Sebarial continued, "and Roion's archers will be wasted in this rain. Besides, he's a coward."

"Roion is not a coward," Dalinar said, laying a hand on the shorter highprince's arm. "He's careful. That did not serve him well in the squabbling over gemhearts, where men like Sadeas threw away lives in exchange for prestige. But out here, care is an attribute I'd choose over recklessness."

Roion turned to Dalinar, blinking away water. "Is this really happening?"

"Yes," Dalinar said. "I want you with your men, Roion. They need to see you. This is going to terrify them, but not you. You're careful, in control."

"Yeah," Roion said. "Yes. You . . . you're going to get us out of this, right?"

"No, I'm not," Dalinar said.

Roion frowned.

"We're all going to get ourselves out of it *together.*"

Roion nodded, and didn't object. He saluted as Aladar had, if less crisply, then headed toward his army on the northern flank, calling for his aides to give him the numbers of his reserves.

"Damnation," Sebarial said, watching Roion go. "Dam*nation*. What about me? Where's my impassioned speech?"

"You," Dalinar said, "are to go back to the command tent and not get in the way."

Sebarial laughed. "All right. That I can do."

"I want Teleb in command of your army," Dalinar said. "And I'm sending both Serugiadis and Rust to join him. Your men will fight better against these things with a few Shardbearers at their head." All three were men who had been given Shards following Adolin's dueling spree.

"I'll give the order that Teleb is to be obeyed."

"And Sebarial?" Dalinar asked.

"Yes?"

"If you have a mind for it, burn some prayers. I don't know if anyone up there is listening anymore, but it can't hurt." Dalinar turned toward the sea of red eyes. Why were they just standing there watching?

Sebarial hesitated. "Not as confident as you acted to the other two, eh?" He smiled, as if that comforted him, then sauntered off. What a strange man. Dalinar nodded to one of his aides, who went to give the orders to the three Kholin Shardbearers, first picking Serugiadis—a lanky young man whose sister Adolin had once courted—out of his command post along the ranks, then running off to fetch Teleb and explain Dalinar's orders.

That seen to, Dalinar stepped up to Navani. "I need to know you're safe in the command tent. As safe as anyone can be."

"Then pretend I'm there," she said.

"But—"

"You want my help with fabrials?" Navani said. "I can't set up that sort of thing remotely, Dalinar."

He ground his teeth, but what could he say? He was going to need every edge he could get. He looked out at the red eyes again.

"Campfire tales come alive," said Rock, the massive Horneater bridgeman. Dalinar had never seen that one guarding him or his sons; he was a quartermaster, Dalinar believed. "These things should not be. Why do they not move?"

"I don't know," Dalinar said. "Send a few of your men to fetch Rlain. I want to see if he can provide any explanations." As two bridgemen ran off, Dalinar turned to Navani. "Gather your scribes to write my words. I will speak to the soldiers."

Within moments, she had a pair of scribes—shivering as they stood under umbrellas with pencils out to write—ready to record his words. They'd send women down the lines and read his message to all the men.

Dalinar climbed into Gallant's saddle to get a little height. He turned toward the ranks of men nearby. "Yes," he shouted over the sound of the rain, "these are Voidbringers. Yes, we're going to fight them. I don't know what they can do. I don't know why they've returned. But we came here to *stop them*.

"I know you're scared, but you have heard of my visions in the high-storms. In the warcamps, the lighteyes mocked me and dismissed what I'd seen as delusions." He thrust his arm to the side, pointing at the sea of red eyes. "Well out there, you see proof that my visions were true! Out there, you see what I have been told would come!"

Dalinar licked wet lips. He had given many battlefield speeches in his life, but never had he said anything like what came to him now. "I," he shouted, "have been sent by the Almighty himself to save this land from another Desolation. I have *seen* what those things can do; I have lived lives broken by the Voidbringers. I've seen kingdoms shattered, peoples ruined, technology forgotten. I've seen civilization itself brought to the trembling edge of collapse.

"*We will prevent this!* Today you fight not for the wealth of a lighteyes, or even for the honor of your king. Today, you fight for the good of all men. You will not fight alone! Trust in what I have seen, trust in my words. If those *things* have returned, then so must the forces that once defeated them. We will see miracles before this day is out, men! We merely have to be strong enough to deserve them."

He looked across a sea of hopeful eyes. Storms. Were those gloryspren about his head, spinning like golden spheres in the rain? His scribes finished writing down the short speech, then hurriedly started making copies to send with runners. Dalinar watched them go, hoping to the Tranquiline Halls that he hadn't just lied to everyone.

His force seemed small in this darkness, surrounded by enemies. Soon, he heard his own words being spoken in the distance, read out to the troops. Dalinar remained seated, Shallan beside his horse, though Navani moved off to see to several of her contraptions.

The battle plan called for them to wait a little longer, and Dalinar was content to do so. With these chasms to cross, it was far better to be assaulted than to assault. Perhaps the separate armies forming up would encourage the Parshendi to start the battle by coming to him. Fortunately, the rain meant no arrows. The bowstrings wouldn't stand the dampness, nor would the animal glue in the Parshendi recurve bows.

The Parshendi started singing.

It came in a sudden roar over the rains, startling his men, making them shy backward in a wave. The song wasn't one Dalinar had ever heard during plateau runs. This was more staccato, more frenetic. It rose all around, coming from the three surrounding plateaus, shouted like thrown axes at the Alethi in the center.

Dalinar shivered. Wind blew against him, stronger than was normal during the Weeping. The gust drove raindrops against the side of his face. Cold bit his skin.

"Brightlord!"

Dalinar turned in his saddle, noting four bridgemen approaching along with Rlain—he still had the man under guard at all times. He waved for his guards to part, allowing the Parshendi bridgeman to scramble up to his horse.

"That song!" Rlain said. "That *song*."

"What is it, man?"

"It is death," Rlain whispered. "Brightlord, I have never heard it before, but the rhythm is one of destruction. Of power."

Across the chasm, the Parshendi started to glow. Tiny lines of red sparked around their arms, blinking and shaking, like lightning.

"What is *that*?" Shallan asked.

Dalinar narrowed his eyes, and another burst of wind washed over him.

"You have to stop it," Rlain said. "Please. Even if you have to kill them. *Do not let them finish that song.*"

It was the day of the countdown he had scribbled on the walls without knowing. The last day.

Dalinar made his decision based on instinct. He called for a messenger, and one jogged up—Teshav's ward, a girl in her fifteenth year. "Pass the word," he commanded her. "Send to General Khal at the command tent, the battalionlords, my son, Teleb, and the other highprinces. We're changing strategies."

"Brightlord?" the messenger asked. "What change?"

"We attack. *Now!*"

⁘

Kaladin stopped at the entrance to the lighteyed training grounds, rainwater streaming off his umbrella's waxed cloth, surprised at what he saw. In preparation for a storm, the ardents normally swept and shoveled the sand into covered trenches at the edges of the ground to keep it from being blown away.

He had expected to see something similar during the Weeping. Instead, they had left the sand out, but had then placed a short wooden barrier across the gateway in. It plugged the front of the sparring grounds, allowing them to fill up with water. A small cascade of rainwater poured over the lip of the barrier and into the roadway.

Kaladin regarded the small lake that now filled the courtyard, then sighed and reached down, undoing his laces, then pulling off both boots and socks. When he stepped in, the cold water came up to his calves.

Soft sand squished between his toes. What was the purpose of this? He crossed the courtyard, crutch under his arm, boots joined by the laces and slung over his shoulder. The chill water numbed his wounded foot, which actually felt nice, though his leg still hurt with each step. It seemed that the two weeks of healing hadn't done much for his wounds. His continued insistence that he walk so much probably wasn't helping.

He'd been spoiled by his abilities; a soldier with such a wound normally would take months to recover. Without Stormlight, he'd just have to be patient and heal like everyone else.

He had expected to find the training grounds as abandoned as most of the camp. Even the markets were relatively empty, people preferring to remain indoors during the Weeping. Here, however, he found the ardents laughing and chatting as they sat in chairs in the raised arcades framing the sparring grounds. They sewed leather practice jerkins, cups of auburn wine on tables at their sides. That area rose enough above the yard floor to stay dry.

Kaladin walked along, searching among them, but didn't find Zahel. He even peeked in the man's room, but it was empty.

"Up above, bridgeman!" one of the ardents called. The bald woman pointed toward the stairwell at the corner, where Kaladin had often sent guards to secure the roof when Adolin and Renarin practiced.

Kaladin waved in thanks, then hobbled over and awkwardly made his way up the steps. He had to close his umbrella to fit. Rain fell on his head as he poked it out of the opening in the roof, where the stairwell ended. The roof was made of tile set into hardened crem, and Zahel lay there in a hammock he'd strung between two poles. Kaladin thought they might be lightning rods, which didn't strike him as safe. A tarp hung above the hammock and kept Zahel almost dry.

The ardent swung gently, eyes closed, holding a square bottle of hard honu, a type of lavis grain liquor. Kaladin inspected the rooftop, judging his ability to cross those sloped tiles without toppling off and breaking his neck.

"Ever been to the Purelake, bridgeman?" Zahel asked.

"No," Kaladin said. "One of my men talks about it, though."

"What have you heard?"

"It's an ocean that's so shallow, you can wade across it."

"It's ridiculously shallow," Zahel said. "Like an endless bay, mere feet deep. Warm water. Calm breezes. Reminds me of home. Not like this cold, damp, godsforsaken place."

"So why aren't you there instead of here?"

"Because I can't stand being reminded of home, idiot."

Oh. "Why are we talking about it, then?"

"Because you were wondering why we made our own little Purelake down below."

"I was?"

"Of course you were. Damnation boy. I know you well enough by now to know that questions bother you. You don't think like a spearman."

"Spearmen can't be curious?"

"No. Because if they are, they either get killed or they end up showing someone in charge how smart they are. Then they get put somewhere more useful."

Kaladin raised an eyebrow, waiting for more explanation. Finally, he sighed, and asked, "Why have you blocked off the courtyard below?"

"Why do you think?"

"You are a really annoying person, Zahel. Do you realize that?"

"Sure do." He took a drink of his honu.

"I assume," Kaladin said, "that you blocked off the front of the practice grounds so that the rain wouldn't wash the sand away."

"Excellent deduction," Zahel said. "Like fresh blue paint on a wall."

"Whatever that means. The problem is, why is it necessary to keep the sand in the courtyard? Why not just put it away, like you do before highstorms?"

"Did you know," Zahel said, "that rains during the Weeping don't drop crem?"

"I . . ." Did he know that? Did it matter?

"Good thing too," Zahel said, "or our entire camp here would end up clogged with the stuff. Anyway, rain like this, it's great for washing."

"You're telling me that you've turned the floor of the dueling grounds into a *bath*?"

"Sure did."

"You wash in that?"

"Sure do. Not ourselves, of course."

"Then what?"

"Sand."

Kaladin frowned, then peered over the side, looking at the pool below.

"Every day," Zahel said, "we go in there and stir it up. The sand settles back down to the bottom, and all the yuck floats away, carried by the rain in little streams out of the camp. Did you ever consider that sand might need washing?"

"No, actually."

"Well it does. After a year's worth of being kicked by stinky bridgeman feet and equally stinky—but far more refined—lighteyes feet, after a year of having people like me spill food on it, or having animals find their way in here to do business, the sand needs cleaning."

"Why are we talking about this?"

"Because it's important," Zahel said, taking a drink. "Or something. I don't know. You came to me, kid, interrupting my vacation. That means you have to listen to me blab."

"You're supposed to say something profound."

"Did you miss the part about me being on vacation?"

Kaladin stood in the rain. "Do you know where the King's Wit is?"

"That fool, Dust? Not here, blessedly. Why?"

Kaladin needed someone to talk to, and had spent the better part of the day searching for Wit. He hadn't found the man, though he had broken down and bought some chouta from a lonely street vendor.

It had tasted good. That hadn't helped his mood.

So, he'd given up on finding Wit and had come to Zahel instead. That appeared to have been a mistake. Kaladin sighed, turning back down the stairs.

"What was it you wanted?" Zahel called to him. The man had cracked an eye, looking toward Kaladin.

"Have you ever had to choose between two equally distasteful choices?"

"Every day I choose to keep breathing."

"I worry something awful is going to happen," Kaladin said. "I can prevent it, but the awful thing . . . it might be best for everyone if it *does* happen."

"Huh," Zahel said.

"No advice?" Kaladin asked.

"Choose the option," Zahel said, rearranging his pillow, "that makes it easiest for you to sleep at night." The old ardent closed his eyes and settled back. "That's what I wish I'd done."

Kaladin continued down the steps. Below, he didn't get out his umbrella. He was already soaked anyway. Instead, he poked through the racks at the side of the practice grounds until he found a spear—real, not practice. Then he set down his crutch and hobbled out into the water.

There, he fell into a spearman's stance and closed his eyes. Rain fell around him. It splattered in the water of the pool, sprinkled the rooftop, pattered the streets outside. Kaladin felt drained, like his blood had been sucked from him. The gloom made him want to sit still.

Instead, he started dancing with the rain. He went through spear forms, doing his best to avoid putting weight on his wounded leg. He splashed in the waters. He sought peace and purpose in the comfortable forms.

He didn't find either.

His balance was off, and his leg screamed. The rain didn't accompany him; it just annoyed him. Worse, the wind didn't blow. The air felt *stale*.

Kaladin stumbled over his own feet. He twisted the spear about him, then dropped it clumsily. It spun away to splash into the pool. As he fetched it, he noticed the ardents watching him with looks ranging from befuddled to amused.

He tried again. Simple spear forms. No spinning the weapon, no showing off. Step step thrust.

The spear's shaft felt wrong in his fingers. Off balance. Storms. He'd come here seeking solace, but he only grew more and more frustrated as he tried to practice.

How much of his ability with the spear had come from his powers? Was he nothing without them?

He dropped the spear again after trying a simple twist and thrust. He reached for it, and found a rainspren sitting next to it in the water, looking upward, unblinking.

He snatched the spear with a growl, then looked up toward the sky. "He deserves it!" he bellowed at those clouds.

Rain pelted him.

"Give me a reason why he doesn't!" Kaladin yelled, uncaring if the ardents heard. "It might not be his fault, and he might be trying, but he's still *failing*."

Silence.

"It's right to remove the wounded limb," Kaladin whispered. "This is what we have to do. To . . . To . . ."

To stay alive.

Where had those words come from?

Gotta do what you can to stay alive, son. Turn a liability into an advantage whenever you can.

Tien's death.

That moment, that horrible moment, when he watched unable to do anything as his brother died. Tien's own squadleader had sacrificed the untrained to gain a moment's advantage.

That squadleader had spoken to Kaladin after it was all over. *Gotta do what you can to stay alive. . . .*

It made a twisted, horrible kind of sense.

It hadn't been Tien's fault. Tien had tried. He'd still failed. So they'd killed him.

Kaladin fell to his knees in the water. "Almighty, oh Almighty."

The king . . .

The king was Dalinar's Tien.

❖

"Attack?" Adolin asked. "Are you certain that is what my father said?"

The young woman who had run the message nodded a rain-slicked head, looking miserable in her slitted dress and runner's sash. "You're to stop that singing, if you can, Brightlord. Your father indicated it was important."

Adolin looked over his battalions, which held the southern flank. Just beyond them, on one of the three plateaus that surrounded their army, the Parshendi sang a horrible song. Sureblood danced, snorting.

"I don't like it either," Adolin said softly, patting the horse on the neck. That song put him on edge. And those threads of red light on their arms, in their hands. What were those?

"Perel," he said to one of his field commanders, "tell the men to get ready for the mark. We're going to charge across those bridges onto the southern plateau. Heavy infantry first, shortspears behind, longspears at the ready in case we're overrun. I want the men ready to form blocks on the other side until we're sure where the Parshendi lines will fall. Storms, I wish we had archers. Go!"

The word spread, and Adolin nudged Sureblood up beside one of the bridges, which had already been set. His bridgeman guards for the day followed, a pair named Skar and Drehy.

"You two going to sit out?" Adolin asked the bridgemen, his eyes forward. "Your captain doesn't like you going into battle against Parshendi."

"To Damnation with that!" Drehy said. "We'll fight, sir. Those aren't Parshendi anyway. Not anymore."

"Good answer. They'll advance once we start our assault. We need to hold the bridgehead for the rest of our army. Try to keep up with me, if you can." He glanced over his shoulder, waiting. Watching until . . .

A large blue gemstone rose into the air, hoisted high on a distant pole near the command tent.

"Go!" Adolin kicked Sureblood into motion, thundering across the bridge and splashing through a pool on the other side. Rainspren wavered. His two bridgemen followed at a run. Behind them, the heavy infantry in thick armor with hammers and axes—perfect for splitting Parshendi carapace—surged into motion.

The bulk of the Parshendi continued their chanting. A smaller group broke off, perhaps two thousand in number, and moved to intercept Adolin. He growled, leaning low, Shardblade appearing in his hand. If they—

A flash of light.

The world lurched, and Adolin found himself skidding on the ground, his Shardplate grinding against stones. The armor absorbed the blow of the fall, but could do nothing for Adolin's own shock. The world spun, and a spray of water spurted in through the slits in his helm, washing over his face.

As he came to rest, he heaved himself backward, up to his feet. He stumbled, clanking, thrashing about in case any Parshendi had gotten close. He blinked away water inside his helm, then oriented himself on a change in the landscape in front of him. White amid the brown and grey. What was that . . .

He finally blinked his eyes clear enough to get a good look. The whiteness was a horse, fallen to the ground.

Adolin screamed something raw, a sound that echoed in his helm. He ignored the shouts of soldiers, the sound of rain, the sudden and unnatural *crack* behind him. He ran to the body on the ground. Sureblood.

"No, no, no," Adolin said, skidding to his knees beside the horse. The animal bore a strange, branching burn all down the side of his white coat. Wide, jagged. Sureblood's dark eyes, open to the rain, did not blink.

Adolin raised his hands, suddenly hesitant to touch the animal.

A youth on an unfamiliar field.

Sureblood wasn't moving.

More nervous that day than during the duel that won his Blade.

Shouts. Another *crack* in the air, sharp, immediate.

They pick their rider, son. We fixate on Shards, but any man—courageous or coward—can bond a Blade. Not so here, on this ground. Only the worthy win here . . .

Move.

Grieve later.

Move!

Adolin roared, leaping to his feet and charging past the two bridgemen who nervously stood guard over him with spears. He started the process of summoning his Blade and ran toward the fighting up ahead. Only moments had passed, but already the Alethi lines were collapsing. Some infantry advanced in clusters while others had hunkered down, stunned and confused.

Another flash, accompanied by a *crack*ing of the air. Lightning. Red lightning. It appeared in flashes from groups of Parshendi, then was gone in the blink of an eye. It left a bright afterimage—glowing, forked—that briefly obscured Adolin's sight.

Ahead of him, men dropped, fried in their armor. Adolin shouted as he charged, bellowing for the men to hold their lines.

More *crack*s sounded, but the strikes didn't seem well aimed. They'd sometimes flash backward or would follow strange paths, rarely going straight toward the Alethi. As he ran, he saw a blast come from a pair of Parshendi, but it arced immediately down into the ground.

The Parshendi stared downward, befuddled. It was as if the lightning worked . . . well, like lightning from the sky, not following any sort of predictable path.

"Charge them, you cremlings!" Adolin shouted, running through the middle of the soldiers. "Back into your lines! It's just like advancing on archers! Keep your heads. Tighten up. If we break, we're dead!"

He wasn't certain how much of that they heard, but the image of him yelling, crashing into the line of Parshendi, did something. Shouts rose from officers, lines re-formed.

Lightning flashed right at Adolin.

The sound was incredible, and the *light*. He stood in place, blinded. When it faded, he found himself completely unharmed. He looked down at the armor, which was *vibrating* softly—a hum that rattled his skin in a strangely comforting way. Nearby, another crack of lightning left a small group of Parshendi, but it didn't blind him. His helm—which as always was partially translucent from the inside—darkened in a jagged streak, perfectly overlaying the lightning.

Adolin grinned with clenched teeth, feeling a savage satisfaction as he pushed into the Parshendi and swung his Shardblade through their necks. By the old stories, the suit he wore had been created to fight these very monsters.

Though these Parshendi soldiers were sleeker and more ferocious-looking than the ones he'd previously fought, their eyes burned just as easily. Then they dropped dead and something wiggled out of their chests—small red spren, like tiny lightning, that zipped into the air and vanished.

"They *can* be killed!" one of the soldiers yelled nearby. "They can die!"

Others raised the call, passing it down the lines. Obvious though the revelation seemed, it bolstered his troops, and they surged forward.

They can die.

⁘

Shallan drew. Frantic.

A map in ink. Each line precise. The large sheet, crafted at her order, covered a wide board on the floor. It was the largest drawing she'd ever done; she'd filled it in, section by section, as they traveled.

She listened with half an ear to the other scholars in the tent. They were a distraction, but an important one.

Another line, rippled on the sides, forming a thin plateau. It was a copy of the one she'd drawn in seven other places on the map. The Plains were a fourfold radial pattern mirrored down the center of each quadrant, and so anything she drew in one quadrant she could repeat in the others, mirrored as appropriate. The eastern side was worn down, yes, so her map wouldn't be accurate in that area—but for cohesion, she needed to finish those parts. So she could see the whole pattern.

"Scout reporting in," a messenger woman said, bursting into the tent, letting in a gust of the wet wind. This unexpected wind . . . it almost felt like the wind before a highstorm.

"What is the report?" Inadara asked. The severe woman was supposed to be a great scholar. She reminded Shallan of her father's ardents. In the corner of the room, Prince Renarin stood in his Shardplate, arms folded. He had orders to protect them all, should the Parshendi try to break onto the command plateau.

"The large center plateau is just as the parshman told us," the scout said, breathless. "It's only one plateau over, to the east." Lyn was a solid-looking woman with long black hair and keen eyes. "It's obviously inhabited, though there doesn't seem to be anyone there right now."

"And the plateaus surrounding it?" Inadara asked.

"Shim and Felt are scouting those," Lyn said. "Felt should be back soon. I can do a rough drawing of what I saw of the center plateau for you."

"Do it," Inadara said. "We need to find that Oathgate."

Shallan wiped a stray drop of water—fallen from Lyn's coat—off her map, then continued drawing. The army's path from the warcamps inward had allowed her to extrapolate and draw eight chains of plateaus, two each—mirrored—starting from the four "sides" of the Plains and working inward.

She had almost completed the last of the eight arms reaching toward the center. This close, earlier scout reports—and what Shallan had seen herself—allowed her to fill in everything around the center. Rlain's explanations had helped, but he hadn't been able to draw out the center plateaus for her. He'd never paid attention to their shapes, and Shallan needed precision.

Fortunately, earlier reports had almost been enough. She didn't need much more. She was almost done.

"What do you think?" Lyn asked.

"Show it to Brightness Shallan." Inadara sounded displeased, which seemed her normal state.

Shallan glanced over Lyn's hastily sketched map, then nodded, turning back to her drawing. It would be better if she could see the center plateau herself, but the corner this woman had drawn gave Shallan an idea.

"Not going to say anything?" Inadara asked.

"Not done yet," Shallan said, dipping her pen in the ink.

"We have been given an order by the highprince himself to find the Oathgate."

"I will."

Something crashed outside, like distant lightning.

"Mmm . . ." Pattern said. "Bad. Very bad."

Inadara looked at Pattern, who dimpled the floor near Shallan. "I do not like this thing. Spren should not speak. It may be of *them*, a Voidbringer."

"I am *not* a Voidspren," Pattern said.

"Brightness Shallan—"

"He's not a Voidspren," Shallan said absently.

"We should study it," Inadara said. "How long did you say it has been following you?"

A heavy footstep sounded on the floor, Renarin stepping forward. Shallan would have preferred to keep Pattern secret, but when the winds had started picking up, he'd started buzzing loudly. There was no avoiding it now that he'd drawn the scholars' attention. Renarin leaned down. He seemed fascinated by Pattern.

He wasn't the only one. "It is likely involved," Inadara said. "You should not dismiss one of my theories so quickly. I still think it might be related to the Voidbringers."

"Know you nothing of Patterns, old human?" Pattern said, huffing. When had he picked up how to huff? "Voidbringers have no pattern. Besides, I have read of them in your lore. They speak of spindly arms like bone, and horrific faces. I should think, if you wish to find one, the mirror might be a location where you can begin your search."

Inadara recoiled. Then she stomped away, moving to chat with Brightness Velat and the ardent Isasik about their interpretation of Shallan's map.

Shallan smiled as she drew. "That was clever."

"I am trying to learn," Pattern replied. "Insults in particular will be of great use to my people, as they are truths and lies combined in a quite interesting manner."

The pops continued outside. "What is that?" she asked softly, finishing another plateau.

"Stormspren," Pattern said. "They *are* a variety of Voidspren. It is not good. I feel something very dangerous brewing. Draw more quickly."

"The Oathgate must be in that center plateau somewhere," Inadara said to her group of scholars.

"We will never search the entire thing in time," said one of the ardents, a man who seemed to be constantly removing his spectacles and wiping them down. He put them back on. "That plateau is by far the largest we've found on the Plains."

It *was* a problem. How to find the Oathgate? It could be anywhere. *No,* Shallan thought, drawing with precise motions, *the old maps placed what Jasnah thought was the Oathgate southwest of the city center.* Unfortunately, she still didn't have a scale for reference. The city was too ancient, and all the maps were copies of copies of copies or re-creations from descriptions. She was certain by now that Stormseat hadn't made up the entire Shattered Plains—the city hadn't been nearly so huge. Structures like the warcamps had been outbuildings, or satellite cities.

But that was just a guess. She needed something concrete. Some sign.

The tent flaps opened again. It had grown cold outside. Was the rain harder than it had been?

"Damnation!" the newcomer swore, a thin man in a scout's uniform. "Have you *seen* what is happening out there? Why are we split across the plateaus? Wasn't the plan to fight a defensive battle?"

"Your report?" Inadara asked.

"Get me a towel and some paper," the scout said. "I rounded the southern side of the central plateau. I'll draw what I saw . . . but *Damnation*! They're throwing lightning, Brightness. Throwing it! It's insane. How do we fight such things?"

Shallan finished the last plateau on her drawing. She settled back on her heels, lowering her pen. The Shattered Plains, drawn almost in their entirety. But what was she doing? What was the point?

"We will make an expedition into the central plateau," Inadara said. "Brightlord Renarin, we will need your protection. Perhaps in the Parshendi city we will find the elderly or the workers, and we can protect them, as Brightlord Dalinar has instructed. They might know about the Oathgate. If not, we can begin breaking into buildings and searching for clues."

Too slow, Shallan thought.

The newly arrived scout stepped up to Shallan's large map. He leaned over, inspecting it as he dried himself off with a towel. Shallan gave him a glare. If he dripped water on this after all she'd done . . .

"That's wrong," he said.

Wrong? Her art? Of *course* it wasn't wrong. "Where?" she asked, exhausted.

"That plateau there," the man said, pointing. "It's not long and thin, as you drew it. It's a perfect circle, with big gaps between it and the plateaus on its east and west."

"That's unlikely," Shallan said. "If it were that way—" She blinked.

If it were that way, it wouldn't match the pattern.

⁂

"Well then, find Brightness Shallan a squad of soldiers and do as she says!" Dalinar said, turning and raising his arm against the wind.

Renarin nodded. Blessedly, he'd agreed to put on his Plate for the battle, rather than continuing on with Bridge Four. Dalinar barely understood the lad these days. . . . *Storms.* Dalinar had never known a man who could look awkward in Shardplate, but his son managed it. The sheet of wind-driven rain passed. Light from blue lanterns reflected from Renarin's wet armor.

"Go," Dalinar said. "Protect the scholars on their mission."

"I . . ." Renarin said. "Father, I don't know . . ."

"It wasn't a request, Renarin!" Dalinar shouted. "Do as you're told, or give that storming Plate to someone who will!"

The boy stumbled back, then saluted with a metallic slap. Dalinar pointed at Gaval, who barked orders, gathering a squad of soldiers. Renarin followed Gaval as the two of them moved off.

Stormfather. The sky had grown darker and darker. They'd need Navani's fabrials soon. That wind came in bursts, blowing rain that was entirely too strong for the Weeping. "We have to interrupt that singing!" Dalinar shouted against the rain, making his way to the edge of the plateau, joined by officers and messengers, including Rlain and several members of Bridge Four. "Parshman. Is this storm their doing?"

"I believe so, Brightlord Dalinar!"

On the other side of the chasm, Aladar's army fought a desperate battle against the Parshendi. Red lightning came in bursts, but according to field reports, the Parshendi didn't know how to control it. It could be very dangerous to those who stood close by, but was not the terrible weapon it had first seemed.

In direct combat, unfortunately, these new Parshendi were another thing entirely. A group of them prowled close to the chasm, where they ripped through a squad of spearmen like a whitespine through a patch of ferns. They fought with a ferocity beyond what the Parshendi had ever shown on the plateau runs, and their weapons connected with flashes of red.

It was difficult to watch, but Dalinar's place was not out there fighting. Not today.

"Aladar's eastern flank needs reinforcement," Dalinar said. "What do we have?"

"Light infantry reserves," General Khal said, wearing only his uniform. His son wore his Shards, fighting with Roion's army. "Fifteenth spear division from Sebarial's army. But those were supposed to support Brightlord Adolin. . . ."

"He'll survive without them. Get those men over here and see Aladar reinforced. Tell him to punch through to those Parshendi in the back, engage the ones singing at all costs. What's Navani's status?"

"She is ready with the devices, Brightlord," a messenger said. "She wants to know where she should begin."

"Roion's flank," Dalinar said immediately. He sensed a disaster brewing there. Speeches were all well and good, but even with Khal's son fighting on that front, Roion's troops were the worst he had. Teleb was supporting them with some of Sebarial's troops, who were surprisingly good. The man himself was practically useless in a battle, but he knew how to hire the right people—and that had always been his genius. Sebarial probably assumed that Dalinar didn't know that.

He'd kept many of Sebarial's troops as a reserve up until now. With them on the field, they'd committed almost every soldier they had.

Dalinar hiked back toward the command tent, passing Shallan, Inadara, some bridgemen, and a squad of soldiers—Renarin included—crossing the plateau at a trot, heading out on their mission. They'd have to skirt across the southern plateau, near the fighting, to get where they were going. Kelek speed their way.

Dalinar himself pushed through the rain, soaked to the very bones, reading the battle through what he could see of the flanks. His force had the size advantage, as anticipated. But now, this red lightning, this wind . . . The Parshendi moved through the darkness and the gusts of wind with ease while the humans slipped, squinted, and were battered.

Still, the Alethi were holding their own. The problem was that this was only half of the Parshendi. If the other half attacked, his people would be in serious trouble—but they didn't attack, so they must consider that singing to be important. They saw the wind they were creating as more damaging, more deadly to the humans, than simply joining the battle.

That terrified him. What was coming would be worse.

"I am sorry that you have to die this way."

Dalinar stood still. Rain streamed down. He looked to the flock of messengers, aides, bodyguards, and officers who attended him. "Who spoke?"

They looked at one another.

Wait . . . He recognized that voice, didn't he? It was familiar to him.

Yes. He'd heard it many times. In his visions.

It was the voice of the Almighty.

82

FOR GLORY LIT

There is one you will watch. Though all of them have some rele-
vance to precognition, Moelach is one of the most powerful in this
regard. His touch seeps into a soul as it breaks apart from the
body, creating manifestations powered by the spark of death itself.
But no, this is a distraction. Deviation. Kingship. We must discuss
the nature of kingship.

—From the Diagram, Book of the 2nd Desk Drawer: paragraph 15

Kaladin limped up the switchbacks to the palace, his leg a knotted
mass of pain. Almost falling as he reached the doors, he slumped
against them, gasping, his crutch under one arm, spear in the
other hand. As if he could do anything with that.

Have . . . to get . . . to the king. . . .

How would he get Elhokar away? Moash would be watching. Storms.
The assassination could happen any day . . . any *hour* now. Surely Dalinar
was already far enough from the warcamps.

Keep. Moving.

Kaladin stumbled into the entryway. No guards at the doors. Bad sign.
Should he have raised the alarm? There weren't any soldiers in camp to
help, and if he'd come in force, Graves and his men would know something was wrong. Alone, Kaladin might be able to see the king. His best
hope was to get Elhokar to safety quietly.

Fool, Kaladin thought to himself. *You change your mind now? After all of*
this? What are you doing?

But storm it . . . the king tried. He actually tried. The man was arrogant, perhaps incapable, but he *tried*. He was sincere.

Kaladin stopped, exhausted, leg screaming, and leaned against the wall. Shouldn't this be easier? Now that he'd made the decision, shouldn't he be focused, confident, energized? He felt none of that. He felt wrung out, confused, and uncertain.

He pushed himself forward. *Keep going.* Almighty send that he wasn't too late.

Was he back to praying now?

He picked through darkened corridors. Shouldn't there be more light? With some difficulty, he reached the king's upper rooms, with the conference chamber and its balcony to the side. Two men in Bridge Four uniforms guarded the door, but Kaladin didn't recognize either of them. They weren't Bridge Four—they weren't even members of the old King's Guard. Storms.

Kaladin hobbled up to them, knowing he must look a sight, soaked through and through, limping on a leg that—he noticed—was trailing blood. He'd split the sutures on his wounds.

"Stop," said one of the men. The fellow had a chin so cleft, it looked like he'd taken an axe to the face as a baby. He looked Kaladin up and down. "You're the one they call Stormblessed."

"You're Graves's men."

The two looked at each other.

"It's all right," Kaladin said. "I'm with you. Is Moash here?"

"He's off for the moment," the soldier said. "Getting some sleep. It's an important day."

I'm not too late, Kaladin thought. Luck was with him. "I want to be part of what you're doing."

"It's taken care of, bridgeman," the guard said. "Go back to your barrack and pretend nothing is happening."

Kaladin leaned in close, as if to whisper something. The guard leaned forward.

So Kaladin dropped his crutch and slammed his spear up between the man's legs. Kaladin immediately turned, spinning on his good leg and dragging the other one, whipping his spear toward the other man.

The man got his spear up to block, and tried to shout. "To arms! To—"

Kaladin slammed against him, knocking aside his spear. Kaladin dropped his own spear and grabbed the man by the neck with numb, wet fingers and cracked his head against the wall. Then he twisted and dropped, bringing his elbow down onto Cleft-chin's head, driving it down into the floor.

Both men fell still. Light-headed from the sudden exertion, Kaladin slammed himself back against the door. The world spun. At least he knew he could still fight without Stormlight.

He found himself laughing, though it turned into a cough. Had he really just attacked those men? He was committed now. Storms, he didn't even really know why he was doing this. The king's sincerity was part of it, but that wasn't the true reason, not deep down. He knew this was what he should do, but *why*? The thought of the king dying for no good reason made him sick. It reminded him of what had been done to Tien.

But that wasn't the full reason either. Storms, he wasn't making any sense, not even to himself.

Neither guard moved save for a few twitches. Kaladin coughed and coughed, gasping for breath. No time for weakness. He reached up a claw-like hand and twisted the door handle, forcing it open. He half fell into the room, then stumbled to his feet.

"Your Majesty?" he called, propping himself up on his spear and dragging his bad leg. He reached the back of a couch and used it to pull himself fully upright. Where was the—

The king lay on the couch, unmoving.

⁂

Adolin swept broadly with his Blade, maintaining perfect Windstance, the sword's point spraying water as he sheared through the neck of a Parshendi soldier. Red lightning crackled from the corpse in a bright flare, connecting the soldier to the ground as he died. Nearby Alethi were careful not to step in puddles beside the corpse. They had learned the hard way that this strange lightning could kill quickly via water.

Raising his sword and charging, Adolin led a rush against the nearest Parshendi group. Curse this storm and the winds that had brought it! Fortunately, the darkness had been pushed back somewhat, as Navani had sent fabrials to bathe the battlefield in an extraordinarily even white light.

Adolin and his team clashed again with the Parshendi. However, as soon as he got among the enemy, he felt something tug on his left arm. A loop of rope? He jerked back. No rope could hold Shardplate. He growled and yanked the rope free of the hands holding it. Then he jerked as another rope looped his neck and pulled him backward.

He shouted, spinning and sweeping his Blade through the rope, severing it. Three more loops leaped from the darkness for him; the Parshendi had sent an entire team. Adolin turned to defensive sweeps, as he'd been trained by Zahel to resist a dedicated rope strike. They'd have strung other ropes across the ground in front of him, expecting that he'd charge them . . . Yes, there they were.

Adolin backed away, slicing free the ropes that reached him. Unfortunately, his men had been depending on him to break the Parshendi line. As he backed away instead, the enemy pressed against the Alethi line in force. As always, they didn't use traditional battle formations, instead attacking in squads and pairs. That was frightfully effective on this chaotic, rain-soaked battlefield, with cracks of lightning and bursts of wind.

Perel, the field commander that he'd put in charge near the lights, called the retreat for Adolin's flank. Adolin let out a series of curses, cutting loose one final rope and stepping backward, sword out in case the Parshendi pursued.

They didn't. Two figures, however, shadowed him as he joined the retreat.

"Still alive, bridgemen?" Adolin asked.

"Still alive," Skar said.

"You've got some loops of rope stuck to you still, sir," Drehy said.

Adolin held out his arm and let Drehy cut them free with his side knife. Over his shoulder, Adolin watched the Parshendi re-form their lines. From farther back, the sound of that harsh chanting reached him between crashes of lightning and bursts of wind.

"They keep sending teams to engage and distract me," Adolin said. "They don't intend to defeat me; they just want to keep me out of the battle."

"They'll have to really fight you sooner or later," Drehy said, cutting off another of the ropes. Drehy reached up and ran his hand over his bald head, wiping the rain off. "They can't just leave a Shardbearer alone."

"Actually," Adolin said, narrowing his eyes, listening to that chanting. "That's exactly what they're doing."

Through sheets of windborne rain, Adolin jogged in a clanking run up to the command position, near the lights. Perel—wrapped in a large stormcoat—stood there bellowing orders. He gave Adolin a quick salute.

"Status?" Adolin asked.

"Treading water, Brightlord."

"I have no idea what that means," Adolin said.

"Swimming term, sir," Perel said. "We're fighting back and forth, but we're not making any headway. We're fairly evenly matched; each side is looking for an edge. I'm most worried about those Parshendi reserves. They should have committed those by now."

"The reserves?" Adolin asked, peering across the dim plateau. "You mean the singers." To both right and left, Alethi troops engaged other Parshendi units. Men shouted and screamed, weapons clashed, the familiar deadly sounds of a battlefield.

"Yes, sir," Perel said. "They're up against that rock formation at the middle of the plateau, singing their storming hearts out."

Adolin remembered that rock outcropping, looming in the dim light. It was easily large enough for a battalion on top. "Could we climb it from behind?"

"In this rain, Brightlord?" Perel asked. "Not likely. Maybe *you* could, but would you really want to go alone?"

Adolin waited for the familiar eagerness to urge him forward, the desire to rush into the fight without concern for the consequences. He'd trained himself to resist that urge, and was surprised to find it . . . gone. Nothing.

He frowned. He was tired. Was that the reason? He considered the situation, thinking to the sound of rain on his helmet.

We need to get to those Parshendi at the back, he thought. *Father wants the reserves engaged, the song broken off . . .*

What had Shallan said about these inner plateaus? And the rock formations on them?

"Gather me a battalion," Adolin said. "A thousand men, heavy infantry. Once I've been gone with them for a half hour, send the rest of the men in a full assault against the Parshendi. I'm going to try something, and I want you to provide a distraction."

·:·

"You're dead," Dalinar shouted toward the sky. He spun about, still on the central plateau between the three battlefields, startling the aides and attendants near him. "You told me you had been killed!"

Rain pelted his face. Were his ears playing tricks on him in this havoc of rain and shouting?

"I am not the Almighty," the voice said. Dalinar turned, searching among his startled companions. Four bridgemen in stormcoats stepped back, as if frightened. His captains watched the clouds unsteadily, holding hands on swords.

"Did any of you hear that voice?" Dalinar asked.

Women and men alike shook heads.

"Are you . . . hearing the Almighty?" asked one of the messenger women.

"Yes." It was the simplest answer, though he wasn't sure what was happening. He continued to cross the central plateau, intending to check on Adolin's battlefront.

"I am sorry," the voice repeated. Unlike in the visions, Dalinar could find no avatar speaking the words. They came out of nowhere. "You have striven hard. But I can do nothing for you."

"Who are you?" Dalinar hissed.

"I am the one left behind," the voice said. It wasn't exactly as he'd heard it in the visions; this voice had a depth to it. A density. "I am the sliver of Him that remains. I saw His corpse, saw Him die when Odium murdered Him. And I . . . I fled. To continue as I always have. The piece of God left in this world, the winds that men must feel."

Was he responding to Dalinar's question, or speaking a mere monologue? In the visions, Dalinar had originally assumed he was having conversations with this voice, only to find that its half of the seeming dialogue had been preset. He could not tell if this was the same or not.

Storms . . . was he in the middle of a vision now? He froze in place, suddenly imagining a horrible picture of himself, sprawled on the floor of the palace, having imagined everything leading up to this battle in the rain.

No, he thought forcefully. *I will not travel down that path.* He had always recognized when he was in a vision before; he had no reason to believe that had changed.

The reserves he'd ordered for Aladar trotted past, spearmen with points toward the sky. That would be storming dangerous if real lightning came, but they didn't have much choice.

Dalinar waited for the voice to say more, but nothing happened. He proceeded, and soon approached Adolin's plateau.

Was that thunder?

No. Dalinar turned and picked out a horse galloping across the plateau toward him, a messenger on its back. He held up a hand, interrupting a tactical report by Captain Javih.

"Brightlord!" the messenger shouted. She reared the horse. "Brightlord Teleb has fallen! Highprince Roion has been routed. His lines are broken, his remaining men surrounded by Parshendi! He's trapped on the northern plateau!"

"Damnation! Captain Khal?"

"Still up, fighting toward where Roion was last seen. He's nearly overwhelmed."

Dalinar spun to Javih. "Reserves?"

"I don't know what we have left," the man said, face pale in the dim light. "Depends on if any have rotated out."

"Find out and bring them here!" Dalinar said, running to the messenger. "Off," he told her.

"Sir?"

"Off!"

The woman scrambled from the saddle as Dalinar placed foot into stirrup and swung into position. He turned the horse—thankful, for once, he didn't have on any Shardplate. This light horse wouldn't have been able to carry him.

"Gather whatever you can and follow!" he shouted. "I need men, even if you have to pull that battalion of spearmen back from Aladar."

Captain Javih's reply was lost in the rain as Dalinar leaned low and cued the horse with his heels. The animal snorted, and Dalinar had to fight it before getting it to move. The pops of lightning in the distance had the creature skittish.

Once pointed the right direction, he gave the horse its head, and it galloped eagerly. Dalinar crossed the plateau in a rush, triage tents, command posts, and food stations passing in a blur. As he neared the northern plateau, he reined in the horse and scanned the area for Navani.

No sign of her, though he did see several large tarps laid on the ground here—expansive squares of black cloth. She'd been at work. He called a question to an engineer, and she pointed, so Dalinar rode along the chasm in that direction. He passed a succession of other tarps that had been arranged on the stone.

Across the chasm to his left, men died with shouts and screams. He saw firsthand how terribly Roion's battle was progressing. The danger was manifest in broken groups of men flying beleaguered banners, split into vulnerable small bunches by red-eyed enemies. The Alethi would fight on, but with their line fragmenting, their prospects were grim.

Dalinar remembered fighting like that himself two months ago, surrounded by a sea of enemies, without hope for salvation. Dalinar pushed his horse faster, and soon spotted Navani. She stood beneath an umbrella directing a group of workers with another large tarp.

"Navani!" Dalinar shouted, pulling his horse to a slippery stop across the tarp from her. "I need a miracle!"

"Working on it," she shouted back.

"No time for working. Execute your plan. *Now.*"

He was too distant to see her glare, but he felt it. Fortunately, she waved workers away from her current tarp and began shouting orders to her engineers. The women ran up to the chasm, where a line of rocks was arrayed. They were attached to ropes, Dalinar thought, though he wasn't sure how this process worked. Navani shouted instructions.

Too much time, Dalinar thought, anxious, watching across the chasm. Had they recovered Teleb's Plate and the King's Blade he was wielding? He couldn't spare grief for the man, not now. They *needed* those Shards.

Behind Dalinar, soldiers gathered. Roion's archers, finest in the warcamps, had been useless in this rain. The engineers backed up at a barked order from Navani, and the workers shoved the line of some forty rocks into the chasm.

As the rocks fell, tarps jumped fifty feet into the air, pulled at the front corners and centers. In an instant, a long line of improvised pavilions flanked the chasm.

"Move!" Dalinar said, urging his horse between two of the pavilions. "Archers forward!"

Men dashed into the protected areas under the tarps, some muttering at the lack of any visible poles holding them in the air. Navani had pulled up only the fronts, so the tarps slanted backward, away from the chasm. The rain streamed down in that direction. They also had sides, like tents, so only the open faces were toward Roion's battlefront.

Dalinar swung from the horse and handed the reins to a worker. He jogged under one of the pavilions to where archers were forming ranks. Navani entered, carrying a large sack over her shoulder. She opened it to reveal a large glowing garnet suspended within a delicate wire lacework fabrial.

She fiddled with it for a moment, then stepped back.

"We really should have had more time to test this," she warned to Dalinar, folding her arms. "Attractors are new inventions. I'm still half afraid this thing will suck the blood out of anyone who touches it."

It didn't. Instead, water quickly started to pool around the thing. Storms, it worked! The fabrial was pulling moisture from the air. Roion's archers removed bowstrings from protected pockets, bending bows and stringing them at the orders of their lieutenants. Many of the men here were lighteyes—archery was seen as an acceptable Calling for a lighteyed man of modest means. Not everyone could be an officer.

The archers began loosing waves of arrows across the chasm into the Parshendi who had surrounded Roion's forces. "Good," Dalinar said, watching the arrows fly. "Very good."

"The rain and wind are still going to make aiming the arrows difficult," Navani said. "And I don't know how well the fabrials will work; with the front of the pavilions open, humidity is going to flood in constantly. We might run out of Stormlight after just a short time."

"It's enough," Dalinar said. The arrows made an almost immediate difference, drawing Parshendi attention away from the beleaguered men. It wasn't a maneuver to try unless you were desperate—the risk of hitting allies was great—but Roion's archers proved deserving of their reputation.

He pulled Navani close with one arm. "You did well." Then he called for his horse—*his* horse, not that wild messenger beast—as he charged out of the pavilion. Those archers would give him an opening. Hopefully it wasn't too late for Roion.

⁘

No! Kaladin thought, rounding the couch to the king's side. Was he dead? There was no obvious wound.

The king shifted, then groaned in a lazy way and sat upright. Kaladin let out a deep breath. An empty wine bottle rested on the end table, and Kaladin could smell the spilled wine now that he was closer.

"Bridgeman?" Elhokar's speech was slurred. "Have you come to gloat over me?"

"Storms, Elhokar," Kaladin said. "How much have you had?"

"They all . . . they *all* talk about me," Elhokar said, flopping down on the couch. "My own guards . . . every one. Bad king, they say. Everyone hates him, they say."

Kaladin felt a chill. "They wanted you to drink, Elhokar. Makes their job easier."

"Huh?"

Storms. The man was barely conscious.

"Come on," Kaladin said. "Assassins are coming for you. We're getting out of here."

"Assassins?" Elhokar leapt to his feet, then wobbled. "He wears white. I knew he'd come . . . but then . . . he only cared about Dalinar . . . Not even the assassin thinks I'm worthy of the throne. . . ."

Kaladin managed to get under Elhokar's arm, holding his spear for support with one hand. The king slumped against him, and Kaladin's leg cried out. "Please, Your Majesty," Kaladin said, almost collapsing, "I need you to try to walk."

"Assassins probably want you, bridgeman," the king muttered. "You're more a leader than I am. I wish . . . wish you'd teach me . . ."

Thankfully, Elhokar then did support himself to an extent. It was a struggle to walk the two of them to the doorway, where the guard's body still lay—

Body? Where was the other one?

Kaladin twisted out of the king's grip as a blur with a knife lunged at him. By instinct, Kaladin snapped his spear haft back—bringing his hands up near to the head for a close-quarters fight—then thrust. The spearhead sank in deep into Cleft-chin's stomach. The man grunted.

But he *hadn't* been lunging for Kaladin.

He'd plunged his knife into the king's side.

Cleft-chin flopped to the floor, falling off Kaladin's spear and dropping his knife. Elhokar reached—a stunned expression on his face—to his side. The hand came away bloody. "I'm dead," Elhokar whispered, regarding the blood.

In that moment, Kaladin's pain and weakness seemed to fade. The moment of panic was a moment of strength, and he used it to rip at Elhokar's clothing while kneeling on his good leg. The knife had glanced off a rib. The king was bleeding heavily, but it was a very survivable wound, with medical attention.

"Keep pressure on that," Kaladin said, pushing a cut section of the king's shirt against the wound, then placing the king's hand over it. "We need to get out of the palace. Find safety somewhere." The dueling grounds, maybe? The ardents could be relied upon, and they could fight too. But would that be too obvious?

Well, first they had to actually get out of the palace. Kaladin grabbed his spear and turned to lead the way out, but his leg nearly betrayed him. He managed to catch himself, but it left him gasping in pain, clinging to his spear to keep from falling.

Storms. Was that pool of blood at his feet *his*? He'd ripped his sutures out, and then some.

"I was wrong," the king said. "We're both dead."

"Fleet kept running," Kaladin growled, getting back under Elhokar's arm.

"What?"

"He couldn't win, but he kept running. And when the storm caught him, it didn't matter that he'd died, because he'd run for all he had."

"Sure. All right." The king sounded groggy, though Kaladin couldn't tell if it was the alcohol or the blood loss.

"We all die in the end, you see," Kaladin said. The two of them walked down the corridor, Kaladin leaning on his spear to keep them upright. "So I guess what truly matters is just how well you've run. And Elhokar, you've kept running since your father was killed, even if you screw up all the *storming* time."

"Thank you?" the king said, drowsy.

They reached an intersection, and Kaladin decided on escaping through the bowels of the palace complex, rather than the front gates. It was equally fast, but might not be the first place the plotters would look.

The palace was empty. Moash had done as he'd said, sending the servants away into hiding, using the precedent of the Assassin in White's attack. It *was* a perfect plan.

"Why?" the king whispered. "Shouldn't you hate me?"

"I don't like you, Elhokar," Kaladin said. "But that doesn't mean it's right to let you die."

"You said I should step down. Why, bridgeman? Why help me?"

I don't know.

They turned down a hallway, but only made it about halfway before the king stopped walking and slumped to the ground. Kaladin cursed, kneeling beside Elhokar, checking his pulse and the wound.

This is the wine, Kaladin decided. That, plus the blood loss, left the king too light-headed.

Bad. Kaladin worked to rebind the wound as best he could, but then what? Try to pull the king out on a litter? Go for help, and risk leaving him alone?

"Kaladin?"

Kaladin froze, still kneeling over the king.

"Kaladin, what are you *doing*?" Moash's voice demanded from behind. "We found the men at the door to the king's room. Storms, did *you* kill them?"

Kaladin rose and turned, putting his weight on his good leg. Moash stood at the other end of the corridor, resplendent in his blue and red Shardplate. Another Shardbearer accompanied him, Blade up on the shoulder of his Plate, faceplate down. Graves.

The assassins had arrived.

Obviously they are fools The Desolation needs no usher It can and will sit where it wishes and the signs are obvious that the spren anticipate it doing so soon The Ancient of Stones must finally begin to crack It is a wonder that upon his will rested the prosperity and peace of a world for over four millennia

—From the Diagram, Book of the 2nd Ceiling Rotation: pattern 1

Shallan stepped off the bridge onto a deserted plateau.

The rain muffled the sounds of warfare, making the area feel even more isolated. Darkness like dusk. Rainfall like hushed whispers.

This plateau was higher than most, so she could see Stormseat's center arrayed around her. Pillars with crem accreting at their bases, transforming them to stalagmites. Buildings that had become mounds, overgrown with stone like snow covering a fallen log. In the darkness and rain, the ancient city presented a sketch of skyline for the imagination to fill in.

This city hid beneath time's own illusion.

The others followed her across the bridge. They'd skirted the fighting on Aladar's battlefront, slipping along the Alethi lines to attain this farther plateau. Getting up here had taken time, as the bridgemen had needed to locate a usable landing. They'd had to climb a slope on the adjoining plateau and place their bridge there to get across the chasm.

"How can you be sure this is the right place?" Renarin asked, clinking down onto the plateau beside her. Shallan had opted for an umbrella, but Renarin stood in the rain, helm under his arm, letting the water stream down his face. Didn't he wear spectacles? She hadn't seen them on him much lately.

"It is the right place," Shallan said, "because it's deviant."

"That's hardly a logical conclusion," Inadara said, joining the two of them as soldiers and bridgemen crossed to the empty plateau. "A portal of this nature would be kept hidden; it would not be deviant."

"The Oathgates were not hidden," Shallan said. "That is beside the point, however. This plateau is a circle."

"Many are circular."

"Not *this* circular," Shallan said, striding forward. Now that she was here, she could see just how irregularly . . . well, *regular* the plateau was. "I was looking for a dais on a plateau, but didn't realize the scale of what I was searching for. This entire *plateau* is the dais upon which the Oathgate sat.

"Don't you see? The other plateaus were created by some kind of disaster—they are jagged, broken. This place is not. That's because it was *already here* when the shattering happened. On the old maps it was a raised section, like a giant pedestal. When the Plains were broken, it remained this way."

"Yes . . ." Renarin said, nodding. "Imagine a plate with a circle etched into the center . . . if a force shattered the plate, it might break along the already weakened lines."

"Leaving you with a bunch of irregular pieces," Shallan agreed, "and one shaped like a circle."

"Perhaps," Inadara said. "But I find it odd that something so tactically important would be exposed."

"The Oathgates were a symbol," Shallan said, continuing to walk. "The Vorin Right of Travel, given to all citizens of sufficient rank, is based on the Heralds' declaration that all borders should be open. If you were going to create a symbol of that unity—a portal that connected all of the Silver Kingdoms together—where would you put it? Hidden in a locked room? Or on a stage that rose above the city? It was out here because they were proud of it."

They continued through the blowing rain. There was a hallowed quality to this place, and honestly, that was part of how she knew she was right.

"Mmmm," Pattern said softly. "They are raising a storm."

"The Voidspren?" Shallan whispered.

"The bonded ones. They craft a storm."

Right. Her task was urgent; she didn't have time to stand around thinking. She was about to order the search begun, but paused as she noticed Renarin staring westward, his eyes distant.

"Prince Renarin?" she asked.

"The wrong way," he whispered. "The wind is blowing from the *wrong direction*. West to east . . . Oh, Almighty above. It's terrible."

She followed his gaze, but could see nothing.

"It's actually real," Renarin said. "The Everstorm."

"What are you talking about?" Shallan asked, feeling a chill at the tone of his voice.

"I . . ." He looked to her and wiped the water from his eyes, gauntlet hanging from his waist. "I should be with my father. I should be able to fight. Only I'm useless."

Great. He was creepy *and* whiny. "Well, your father ordered you to help me, so deal with your issues. Everyone, let's search this place."

"What are we looking for, cousin?" asked Rock, one of the bridgemen.

Cousin, she thought. *Cute.* Because of the red hair. "I don't know," she said. "Anything strange, out of the ordinary."

They split up and spread out across the plateau. Along with Inadara, Shallan had a small group of ardents and scholars to help her, including one of Dalinar's stormwardens. She sent teams of several scholars, one bridgeman, and one soldier each in different directions.

Renarin and the majority of the bridgemen insisted on going with her. She couldn't complain about that—this *was* a war zone. Shallan passed a lump on the ground, part of a large ring. Perhaps once a low ornamental wall. How would this place have looked? She pictured it in her mind, and wished she could have drawn it. That would certainly have helped her visualize.

Where would the portal be? Most likely at the center, so that was the direction she went. There she found a large stone mound.

"This is all?" Rock asked. "He is just more rock."

"That is exactly what I was hoping to find," Shallan said. "Anything exposed to the air would have weathered away or become immured with crem. If we're to discover anything useful, it will have to be inside."

"Inside?" asked one of the bridgemen. "Inside what?"

"The buildings," Shallan said, feeling at the wall until she found a ripple in the back of the rock. She turned to Renarin. "Prince Renarin, would you kindly slay this rock for me?"

·⁙·

Adolin raised his sphere in the dark chamber, shining light on the wall. After so long outdoors in the Weeping, it felt strange *not* to have rain tapping against his helm. The musty air in this place was already growing humid, and even with the shuffling of soldiers and men coughing, Adolin felt like it was too silent. Within this rocky tomb, they may as well have been miles away from the battlefield just outside.

"How did you know, sir?" asked Skar, the bridgeman. "How'd you guess that this rock mound would be hollow?"

"Because a clever woman," Adolin said, "once asked me to attack a boulder for her."

Together, he and these men had circled to the other side of the large rock formation that the chanting Parshendi were using to guard their backs. With a few twists of the Shardblade, Adolin had cut an entrance into the mound, which had proven to be hollow as he'd hoped.

He picked his way through the dusty chambers, passing bones and dried debris that might once have been furniture. Presumably it had rotted away before the crem had finished sealing the building. Had it been a kind of communal dwelling, long ago? Or perhaps a market? It did have a lot of rooms; many doorways still bore rusted hinges that had once held doors.

A thousand men moved through the building with him, holding lanterns that carried large cut gems—five times bigger than broams, though even some of those were starting to fail, as it had been so long since a highstorm.

A thousand men was a large number to navigate through these eerie confines. But, unless he was completely off, they should now be approaching the opposite wall—the one just behind the Parshendi. Some of his men scouted nearby rooms, and came back with the confirmation. The building ended here. Adolin now saw the outlines of windows, sealed up with crem that had spilled in through gaps over the years, dribbling down the wall and piling on the floor.

"All right," he called out to the company commanders and their captains. "Let's gather everyone we can in this room here and the hall right outside. I'll cut an exit hole. As soon as it's open, we need to spill out and attack those singing Parshendi.

"First Company, you split to either side and secure this exit. Don't get pushed back! I'll charge and try to draw attention. Everyone else move through and join the assault as quickly as you can manage."

The men nodded. Adolin took a deep breath, then closed his faceplate and stepped up to the wall. They were on the second floor of the building, but he estimated the buildup of crem outside would place that at about ground level. Indeed, from outside he heard a faint sound. Humming, resonating through the wall.

Storms, the Parshendi were *right there*. He summoned his Blade, waited until the company commanders passed the word back that their men were ready, then hacked at the wall in several long ribbons. He sliced it the other way with sweeping blows, then slammed his Plate shoulder into it.

The wall broke down and fell out, stone blocks cascading away from him. The rain returned in force. He was only a few feet off the ground, and he eagerly pushed his way out onto the slick wet rocks. Just to his left, Parshendi reserves stood in rows facing away from him, absorbed in their chanting. The clamor of battle was nearly inaudible here, all but drowned out by the spine-tingling sound of that inhuman singing.

Perfect. The rain and chanting had covered the noise of the hole opening. He hacked open another hole as men spilled out from the first one, bearing lights. He began to open a third exit, but heard a shout. One of the Parshendi had finally noticed him. She was female—with this new form of theirs, that was more obvious than it had been before.

He charged the short distance to the Parshendi and launched himself into their ranks, sweeping lethally with his Blade. Bodies fell dead with burned eyes. Five, then ten. His soldiers joined him, thrusting spears into the Parshendi, cutting off their awful song.

It was shockingly easy. These Parshendi abandoned their song reluctantly, coming out of their trance disoriented and confused. Those who fought did so without coordination, and Adolin's swift attack didn't allow time for them to summon their strange sparking energy.

It was like killing sleeping men. Adolin had done dirty work with his Shards before. Damnation, any time you took the field with Plate and Blade against ordinary men, you did dirty work—slaughtering those who might as well have been children with sticks. This was worse though. Often they'd come to just before he killed them—blinking to consciousness, shaking themselves awake, only to find themselves face-to-face with a full Shardbearer in the rain, murdering their friends. Those looks of horror haunted Adolin as he sent corpse after corpse to the ground.

Where was the Thrill that usually propelled him through this kind of butchery? He needed it. Instead, he felt only nausea. Standing amid a field of the newly dead—the acrid smoke of burned-out eyes curling up through the rain—he trembled and dropped his Blade in disgust. It vanished to mist.

Something crashed into him from behind.

He lurched over a corpse—stumbling but keeping his feet—and spun about. A Shardblade smashed against his chest, spreading a glowing web of cracks across his breastplate. He deflected the next blow with his forearm and stepped back, taking a battle stance.

She stood before him, rain streaming from her armor. What had she named herself? Eshonai.

Inside his helm, Adolin grinned at the Shardbearer. *This* he could do.

An honest fight. He raised his hands, the Shardblade forming from mist as he swung upward and deflected her attack in a sweeping parry.

Thank you, he thought.

∴

Dalinar rode Gallant back across the bridge from Roion's plateau, nursing a bloody wound at his side. Stupid. He should have seen that spear. He'd been too focused on that red lightning and the quickly shifting Parshendi fighting pairs.

The truth, Dalinar thought, sliding from his horse so a surgeon could inspect the wound, *is that you're an old man now.* Perhaps not by the measuring of lifespans, as he was only in his fifties, but by the yardstick of soldiers he was *certainly* old. Without Shardplate to assist, he was getting slow, getting weak. Killing was a young man's game, if only because the old men fell first.

That cursed rain kept coming, so he escaped it under one of Navani's pavilions. The archers kept the Parshendi from following across the chasm to harry Roion's beleaguered retreat. With the help of the bowmen, Dalinar had successfully saved the highprince's army, half of it at least—but they'd lost the entire northern plateau. Roion rode across to safety, followed by an exhausted Captain Khal on foot—General Khal's son wore his own Plate and bore the King's Blade that he'd blessedly recovered from Teleb's corpse after the other man had fallen.

They'd been forced to leave the body, and the Plate. Just as bad, the Parshendi singing continued unabated. Despite the soldiers saved, this was a terrible defeat.

Dalinar undid his breastplate and sat down with a grunt as the surgeon ordered him a stool. He suffered the woman's ministration, though he knew the wound was not terrible. It was bad—any wound was bad on the battlefield, particularly if it impaired the sword arm—but it wouldn't kill him.

"Storms," the surgeon said. "Highprince, you're all scars under here. How many times have you been wounded in the shoulder?"

"Can't remember."

"How can you still use your arm?"

"Training and practice."

"That's not how it works . . ." she whispered, eyes wide. "I mean . . . storms . . ."

"Just sew the thing up," he said. "Yes, I'll stay off the battlefield today. No, I won't stress it. Yes, I've heard all the lectures before."

He shouldn't have been out there in the first place. He'd told himself he wouldn't ride into battle anymore. He was supposed to be a politician now, not a warlord.

But once in a while, the Blackthorn needed to come out. The men needed it. Storms, *he* needed it. The—

Navani thundered into the tent.

Too late. He sighed as she stalked up to him, passing this tent's fabrial—which glowed on a little pedestal, collecting water around it in a shimmering globe. That water streamed off along two metal rods at the sides of the fabrial, spilling onto the ground, then running out of the tent and over the plateau's edge.

He looked up at Navani grimly, expecting to be dressed down like a re-cruit who had forgotten his whetstone. Instead, she took him by his good side, then pulled him close.

"No reprimand?" Dalinar asked.

"We're at war," she whispered. "And we're losing, aren't we?"

Dalinar glanced at the archers, who were running low on arrows. He didn't speak too loudly, lest they hear. "Yes." The surgeon glanced at him, then lowered her head and kept sewing.

"You rode to battle when someone needed you," Navani said. "You saved the lives of a highprince and his soldiers. Why would you expect anger from me?"

"Because you're you." He reached up with his good hand and ran his fingers through her hair.

"Adolin has won his plateau," Navani said. "The Parshendi there are scattered and routed. Aladar holds. Roion has failed, but we're still evenly matched. So how are we losing? I can sense that we are, from your face, but I don't see it."

"An even match is a loss for us," Dalinar said. He could *feel* it building. Distant, to the west. "If they complete that song, then as Rlain warned, that is the end."

The surgeon finished as best she could, wrapping the wound and giving Dalinar leave to replace his shirt and coat, which would hold the bandage tight. Once dressed, he climbed to his feet, intending to go to the com-mand tent and get an update on the situation from General Khal. He was interrupted as Roion burst into the pavilion.

"Dalinar!" the tall, balding man rushed in, grabbing him by the arm. The bad one. Dalinar winced. "It's a storming bloodbath out there! We're dead. Storms, we're dead!"

Nearby archers shuffled, their arrows spent. A sea of red eyes gathered on the plateau across the chasm, smoldering coals in the darkness.

For all that Dalinar wanted to slap Roion, that wasn't the sort of thing you did to a highprince, even a hysterical one. Instead, he towed Roion out of the pavilion. The rain—now a full-blown storm—felt icy as it washed over his soaked uniform.

"Control yourself, Brightlord," Dalinar said sternly. "Adolin has won his plateau. Not all is as bad as it seems."

"It should not end this way," the Almighty said.

Storm it! Dalinar shoved Roion away and strode out into the center of the plateau, looking up toward the sky. "Answer me! Let me know if you can hear me!"

"I can."

Finally. Some progress. "Are you the Almighty?"

"I said I am not, child of Honor."

"Then what are you?"

I AM THAT WHICH BRINGS LIGHT AND DARKNESS. The voice took on more of a rumbling, distant quality.

"The Stormfather," Dalinar said. "Are you a Herald?"

No.

"Then are you a spren or a god?"

BOTH.

"What is the point of talking to me?" Dalinar shouted at the sky. "What is happening?"

THEY CALL FOR A STORM. MY OPPOSITE. DEADLY.

"How do we stop it?"

YOU DON'T.

"There has to be a way!"

I BRING YOU A STORM OF CLEANSING. IT WILL CARRY AWAY YOUR CORPSES. THIS IS ALL I CAN DO.

"No! Don't you *dare* abandon us!"

YOU MAKE DEMANDS OF ME, YOUR GOD?

"You aren't my god. You were *never* my god! You are a shadow, a lie!"

Distant thunder rumbled ominously. The rain beat harder against Dalinar's face.

I AM CALLED. I MUST GO. A DAUGHTER DISOBEYS. YOU WILL SEE NO FURTHER VISIONS, CHILD OF HONOR. THIS IS THE END.

FAREWELL.

"Stormfather!" Dalinar yelled. "There has to be a way! I will not die here!"

Silence. Not even thunder. People had gathered around Dalinar: soldiers, scribes, messengers, Roion and Navani. Frightened people.

"Don't abandon us," Dalinar said, voice trailing off. "Please . . ."

⁜

Moash stepped forward, his faceplate up, his face pained. "Kaladin?"

"I had to make the choice that would let me sleep at night, Moash," Kaladin said wearily, standing before the unconscious form of the king.

Blood pooled around Kaladin's boot from the wounds he'd reopened. Light-headed, he had to lean on his spear to keep on his feet.

"You said he was trustworthy," Graves said, turning toward Moash, his voice ringing inside his Shardplate helm. "You promised me, Moash!"

"Kaladin *is* trustworthy," Moash said. It was just the three of them— four, if you counted the king—standing in a lonely hallway of the palace.

This would be a sad place to die. A place away from the wind.

"He's just a little confused," Moash said, stepping forward. "This will still work. You didn't tell anyone, right, Kal?"

I recognize this hallway, Kaladin realized. *It's the very place we fought the Assassin in White.* To his left, windows lined the wall, though shutters kept out the light rainfall. Yes . . . there. He spotted where planks had been installed over the hole that the assassin had cut through the wall. The place where Kaladin had fallen into blackness.

Back here again. He took a deep breath and steadied himself as best he could on his good leg, then raised the spear, point toward Moash.

Storms, his leg hurt.

"Kal, the king is obviously wounded," Moash said. "We followed your trail of blood here. He's practically dead already."

Trail of blood. Kaladin blinked bleary eyes. Of course. His thoughts were coming slowly. He should have caught that.

Moash stopped a few feet from Kaladin, just out of easy striking range with the spear. "What are you going to do, Kal?" Moash demanded, look- ing at the spear pointed toward him. "Would you really attack a member of Bridge Four?"

"You left Bridge Four the moment you turned against our duty," Kala- din whispered.

"And you're different?"

"No, I'm not," Kaladin said, feeling a hollowness in his stomach. "But I'm trying to change that."

Moash took another step forward, but Kaladin pushed the spear point upward, toward Moash's face. His friend hesitated, raising his gauntleted hands in a warding gesture.

Graves moved forward, but Moash shooed him away, then turned to Kaladin. "What do you think this will accomplish, Kal? If you get in our way, you'll just get yourself killed, and the king will still be dead. You want me to know you don't agree with this? Fine. You tried. Now you're overmatched, and there is no point in fighting. Put down the spear."

Kaladin glanced over his shoulder. The king was still breathing.

Moash's armor clinked. Kaladin turned back, raising the spear again. Storms . . . his head was really throbbing now.

"I mean it, Kal," Moash said.

"You'd attack me?" Kaladin said. "Your captain? Your *friend*?"

"Don't turn this around on me."

"Why not? Which is more important to you? Me or petty vengeance?"

"He *murdered* them, Kaladin," Moash snapped. "That sorry excuse for a king killed the only family I ever had."

"I know."

"Then why are you protecting him?"

"It wasn't his fault."

"That's a load of—"

"It *wasn't his fault,*" Kaladin said. "But I'd be here even if it had been, Moash! We have to be better than this, you and I. It's . . . I can't explain it, not perfectly. You have to trust me. Back down. The king hasn't yet seen you or Graves. We'll go to Dalinar, and I'll see that you get justice against the *right* man, Roshone, the one truly behind your grandparents' deaths.

"But Moash, we're *not* going to be this kind of men. Murders in dark corridors, killing a drunk man because we find him distasteful, telling ourselves it's for the good of the kingdom. If I kill a man, I'm going to do it in the sunlight, and I'm going to do it only because there is no other way."

Moash hesitated. Graves clinked up beside him, but again Moash raised a hand, stopping him. Moash met Kaladin's eyes, then shook his head. "Sorry, Kal. It's too late."

"You won't have him. I won't back down."

"I guess I wouldn't want you to." Moash slammed his faceplate down, the sides misting as it sealed.

84

THE ONE
WHO SAVES

*1118251011127124915121010111410215117112101112171 3
448311107151425414341091614914934121225410101 25
127101519101112341255115251215755111234101112915 1
21061534*

—From the Diagram, Book of the 2nd Ceiling Rotation: pattern 15

The stone block slid inward, confirming Shallan's deduction. They had opened a building that hadn't been entered, or even seen, for centuries. Renarin stepped back from the hole he'd made, giving Shallan a chance to step forward. The air from inside smelled stale, musty.

Renarin dismissed his Blade, and oddly, as he did so, he let out a relieved sigh and relaxed against the outer wall of the building. Shallan moved to enter, but the bridgemen slipped in front of her to check the building's safety first, raising sapphire lanterns.

The light revealed majesty.

Shallan's breath caught in her throat. The large, circular room was a space worthy of a palace or temple. A mosaic mural covered the wall and floor with majestic images and dazzling color. Knights in armor stood before swirling skies of red and blue. People from all walks of life were depicted in all manner of settings, each crafted from vivid colors of every kind of stone—a masterwork that brought the whole world into one room.

Worried she'd damage the portal somehow, she'd placed Renarin's cuts near a ripple that she had hoped indicated a doorway, and it seemed that she'd been correct. She entered through the hole and walked a curving path through the circular chamber, silently counting the divisions in the floor mural. There were ten main ones, just as there had been ten orders of knights, ten kingdoms, ten peoples. And then—between the segments representing the first and tenth kingdoms—was a narrower eleventh section. It depicted a tall tower. Urithiru.

She'd found it, the portal. And this artwork! Such beauty. It was breathtaking.

No, there wasn't time to admire art right now. The large floor mosaic swirled around the center, but the swords of each knight pointed toward the same area of the wall, so Shallan walked in that direction. Everything in here seemed perfectly preserved, even the lamps on the walls, which appeared to still hold dun gemstones.

On the wall, she found a metal disc set into the stone. Was this steel? It hadn't rusted or even tarnished despite its long abandonment.

"It's coming," Renarin announced from the other side of the room, his quiet voice echoing across the domed chamber. Storms, that boy was disturbing, particularly when accompanied by a howling storm and the sound of rain pelting the plateau outside.

Brightness Inadara and several scholars arrived. Stepping into the chamber, they gasped and then began talking over one another as they rushed to examine the mural.

Shallan studied the strange disc set into the wall. It was shaped like a ten-pointed star and had a thin slot directly in the center. *The Radiants could operate this place,* she thought. *And what did the Radiants have that nobody else did?* Many things, but the shape of that slot in the metal gave her a pretty good guess why only they could make the Oathgate work.

"Renarin, get over here," Shallan said.

The boy clomped in her direction.

"Shallan," Pattern said warningly. "Time is very short. They have summoned the Everstorm. And . . . and there's something else, coming from the other direction. A highstorm?"

"It's the Weeping," Shallan said, looking to Pattern, who dimpled the wall just beside the steel disc. "No highstorms."

"One is coming anyway. Shallan, they're going to hit together. Two storms coming, one from each direction. They will crash into one another *right here.*"

"I don't suppose they'll just, you know, cancel each other out?"

"They will feed one another," Pattern said. "It will be like two waves hitting with their peaks coinciding . . . it will create a storm like none the world has ever seen. Stone will shatter, plateaus themselves might collapse. It's going to be bad. Very, *very* bad."

Shallan looked to Inadara, who had walked up beside her. "Thoughts?"

"I don't know what to think, Brightness," Inadara said. "You were right about this place. I . . . I no longer trust myself to judge what is correct and what is false."

"We need to move the armies to this plateau," Shallan said. "Even if they defeat the Parshendi, they're doomed unless we can make this portal work."

"It doesn't *look* like a portal at all," Inadara said. "What will it do? Open a doorway in the wall?"

"I don't know," Shallan said, looking to Renarin. "Summon your Shardblade."

He did so, wincing as it appeared. Shallan pointed at the slot like a keyhole in the wall—acting on a hunch. "See if you can scratch that metal with your Blade. Be *very* careful. We don't want to ruin the Oathgate, in case I'm wrong."

Renarin stepped up and carefully—using his hand to pinch the weapon from above—placed the tip of the blade on the metal around the keyhole. He grunted as the Blade wouldn't cut. He tried a little harder, and the metal resisted the Blade.

"Made of the same stuff!" Shallan said, growing excited. "And that slot is shaped like it might fit a Blade. Try sliding the weapon in, very slowly."

He did so, and as the point moved into the hole, the entire *shape* of the keyhole shifted, the metal flowing to match the shape of Renarin's Shardblade. It was working! He got the weapon placed, and they turned around, looking over the chamber. Nothing appeared to have changed.

"Did that do anything?" Renarin asked.

"It has to have," Shallan said. They'd unlocked a door, perhaps. But how to turn the equivalent of the doorknob?

"We need Highlady Navani to help," Shallan said. "More importantly, we need to bring everyone here. Go, soldiers, bridgemen! Run and tell Dalinar to gather his armies on this plateau. Tell him that if he doesn't, they are doomed. The rest of you scholars, we're going to put our heads together and figure out how this storming thing works."

⁘

Adolin danced through the storm, trading blows with Eshonai. She was good, though she didn't use stances he recognized. She dodged back and forth, feeling him out with her Blade, bursting through the storm like a crackling thunderbolt.

Adolin kept after her, sweeping with his Shardblade, forcing her away. A duel. He could win a duel. Even in the middle of a storm, even against a monster, this was something he could *do*. He backed her away across the battlefield, closer to where his armies had crossed the chasm to join this battle.

She was difficult to maneuver. He had only met this Eshonai twice, but he felt he knew her through the way she fought. He sensed her eagerness for blood. Her eagerness to kill. The Thrill. He did not feel it himself. He sensed it in her.

Around him, Parshendi fled or fought in pockets as his men harried them. He passed a Parshendi, forced to the ground by soldiers, being gutted in the rain as he tried to crawl away. Water and blood splashed on the plateau, frantic yells sounding amid the thunder.

Thunder. Distant thunder from the west. Adolin glanced in that direction, and nearly lost his concentration. He could *see* it building, wind and rain spinning in a gigantic pillar, flashing red.

Eshonai swung for him, and Adolin turned back, blocking the blow with his forearm. That section of his Plate was getting weak, the cracks leaking Stormlight. He stepped into the blow and swung his own Blade, one-handed, into Eshonai's side. He was rewarded by a grunt. She didn't fold, though. She didn't even step back. She raised her Blade and smashed it down against his forearm yet again.

The Plate there exploded in a flash of light and molten metal. Storms. Adolin was forced to pull the arm back and release the gauntlet—now too heavy, without the connecting Plate to help it—letting it drop off his hand. The wind that blew against his exposed skin was startlingly powerful.

A little more, Adolin thought, not backing away despite the lost section of Plate. He grabbed his Shardblade in two hands—one metal, the other flesh—and battered forward with a series of strikes. He transitioned out of Windstance. No sweeping majesty for him. He needed the frantic fury of Flamestance. Not just for the power, but because of what he needed to convey to Eshonai.

Eshonai growled, forced backward. "Your day has ended, destroyer," she said inside her helm. "Today, your brutality turns against you. Today, extinction turns from us to you."

A little more.

Adolin pressed her with a burst of swordplay, then he flagged, presenting her with an opening. She took it immediately, swinging for his helm, which leaked from an earlier blow. Yes, she was fully caught up in the Thrill. That lent her energy and strength, but it drove her to recklessness. To ignore her surroundings.

Adolin took the hit to the head and stumbled. Eshonai laughed with glee and moved to swing again.

Adolin lunged forward and slammed his shoulder and head into her chest. His helm exploded from the force of it, but his gambit succeeded.

Eshonai had not noticed how close they were to the chasm.

His shove threw her over the plateau's edge. He felt Eshonai's panic, heard her shout, as she was dropped into the open blackness.

Unfortunately, the exploding helm left Adolin momentarily blinded. He stumbled, and when he put a foot down, it landed only on empty air. He lurched, then fell toward the void of the chasm.

For a timeless moment, all he felt was panic and fright, a frozen eternity before he realized he wasn't falling. His vision cleared, and he looked down into the maw before him, rain falling in curtains all around. Then he looked back over his shoulder.

To where two bridgemen had grabbed hold of the steel link skirt of his Plate and were struggling to hold him back from the brink. Grunting, they clung to the slick metal, holding tight with feet thrust against stones to keep from being pulled off with him.

Other soldiers materialized, rushing to help. Hands grabbed Adolin around the waist and shoulders, and together they hauled him back from the brink of the void—to the point that he was able to get his balance again and stumble away from the chasm.

Soldiers cheered, and Adolin let out an exhausted laugh. He turned to the bridgemen, Skar and Drehy. "I guess," Adolin said, "I don't need to wonder if you two can keep up with me or not."

"This was nothing," Skar said.

"Yeah," Drehy added. "Lifting fat lighteyes is easy. You should try a bridge sometime."

Adolin grinned, then wiped water from his face with his exposed hand. "See if you can find a chunk of my helm or forearm piece. Regrowing the armor will go faster if we've got a seed. Collect my gauntlet too, if you would."

The two nodded. That red lightning in the sky was building, and that spinning column of dark rain was expanding, growing outward. That . . . that did *not* seem like a good sign.

He needed a better grasp on what was happening in the rest of the army. He jogged across the bridge to the central plateau. Where was his father? What was happening on Aladar's and Roion's fronts? Had Shallan returned from her expedition?

Everything seemed chaotic here on the central plateau. The rising winds tore at tents, and some of them had collapsed. People ran this way and that. Adolin spotted a figure in a thick cloak, striding purposefully through the rain. That person looked like he knew what he was doing. Adolin caught his arm as he passed.

"Where's my father?" he asked. "What orders are you delivering?"

The hood of the cloak fell down and the man turned to regard Adolin with eyes that were slightly too large, too rounded. A bald head. Filmy, loose clothing beneath the cloak.

The Assassin in White.

·⁖·

Moash stepped forward, but did not summon his Shardblade.

Kaladin struck with his spear, but it was futile. He'd used what strength he had to merely remain upright. His spear glanced off Moash's helm, and the former bridgeman slapped a fist down on the weapon, shattering the wood.

Kaladin lurched to a stop, but Moash wasn't done. He stepped forward and slammed an armored fist into Kaladin's gut.

Kaladin gasped, folding as things *broke* inside of him. Ribs snapped like twigs before that impossibly strong fist. Kaladin coughed, spraying blood across Moash's armor, then groaned as his friend stepped back, removing his fist.

Kaladin collapsed to the cold stone floor, everything shaking. His eyes felt like they'd pop from his face, and he curled around his broken chest, trembling.

"Storms." Moash's voice was distant. "That was a harder blow than I intended."

"You did what you had to." Graves.

Oh . . . Stormfather . . . the pain . . .

"Now what?" Moash.

"We end this. Kill the king with a Shardblade. It will still look like the assassin, hopefully. Those blood trails are frustrating. They might make people ask questions. Here, let me cut down these boards, so it looks like he came in through the wall, like last time."

Cold air. Rain.

Yelling? Very distant? He knew that voice. . . .

"Syl?" Kaladin whispered, blood on his lips. "Syl?"

Nothing.

"I ran until . . . until I couldn't any longer," Kaladin whispered. "End of . . . the race."

Life before death.

"I will do it." Graves. "I will bear this burden."

"It is my right!" Moash said.

He blinked, eyes resting on the king's unconscious body just beside him. Still breathing.

I will protect those who cannot protect themselves.

It made sense, now, why he'd had to make this choice. Kaladin rolled to his knees. Graves and Moash were arguing.

"I have to protect him," Kaladin whispered.

Why?

"If I protect . . ." He coughed. "If I protect . . . only the people I like, it means that I don't care about doing what is right." If he did that, he only cared about what was convenient for himself.

That wasn't protecting. That was selfishness.

Straining, agonized, Kaladin raised one foot. The good foot. Coughing blood, he shoved himself upward and stumbled to his feet between Elhokar and the assassins. Fingers trembling, he felt at his belt, and—after two tries—got his side knife out. He squeezed out tears of pain, and through blurry vision, saw the two Shardbearers looking at him.

Moash slowly raised his faceplate, revealing a stunned expression. "Stormfather . . . Kal, how are you standing?"

It made sense now.

That was why he'd come back. It was about Tien, it was about Dalinar, and it was what was right—but most of all, it was about protecting people.

This was the man he wanted to be.

Kaladin moved one foot back, touching his heel to the king, forming a battle stance. Then raised his hand before him, knife out. His hand shook like a roof rattling from thunder. He met Moash's eyes.

Strength before weakness.

"You. Will. Not. *Have. Him.*"

"Finish this, Moash," Graves said.

"Storms," Moash said. "There's no need. Look at him. He can't fight back."

Kaladin felt exhausted. At least he'd stood up.

It was the end. The journey had come and gone.

Shouting. Kaladin heard it now, as if it were closer.

He is mine! a feminine voice said. *I claim him.*

He betrayed his oath.

"He has seen too much," Graves said to Moash. "If he lives this day, he'll betray us. You know my words are true, Moash. Kill him."

The knife slipped from Kaladin's fingers, clanging to the ground. He was too weak to hold it. His arm flopped back to his side, and he stared down at the knife, dazed.

I don't care.

He will kill you.

"I'm sorry, Kal," Moash said, stepping forward. "I should have made it quick at the start."

The Words, Kaladin. That was Syl's voice. *You have to speak the Words!*

I forbid this.

Your will matters not! Syl shouted. You cannot hold me back if he speaks the Words! The Words, Kaladin! Say them!

"I will protect even those I hate," Kaladin whispered through bloody lips. "So long as it is right."

A Shardblade appeared in Moash's hands.

A distant rumbling. Thunder.

The Words are Accepted, the Stormfather said reluctantly.

"Kaladin!" Syl's voice. "Stretch forth thy hand!" She zipped around him, suddenly visible as a ribbon of light.

"I can't . . ." Kaladin said, drained.

"Stretch forth thy hand!"

He reached out a trembling hand. Moash hesitated.

Wind blew in the opening in the wall, and Syl's ribbon of light became mist, a form she often took. Silver mist, which grew larger, coalesced before Kaladin, extending into his hand.

Glowing, brilliant, a Shardblade emerged from the mist, vivid blue light shining from swirling patterns along its length.

Kaladin gasped a deep breath as if coming fully awake for the first time. The entire hallway went black as the Stormlight in every lamp down the length of the hall winked out.

For a moment, they stood in darkness.

Then Kaladin *exploded* with Light.

It erupted from his body, making him shine like a blazing white sun in the darkness. Moash backed away, face pale in the white brilliance, throwing up a hand to shade his eyes.

Pain evaporated like mist on a hot day. Kaladin's grip firmed upon the glowing Shardblade, a weapon beside which those of Graves and Moash looked dull. One after another, shutters burst open up and down the hallway, wind screaming into the corridor. Behind Kaladin, frost crystalized on the ground, growing backward away from him. A glyph formed in the frost, almost in the shape of wings.

Graves screamed, falling in his haste to get away. Moash backed up, staring at Kaladin.

"The Knights Radiant," Kaladin said softly, "have returned."

"Too late!" Graves shouted.

Kaladin frowned, then glanced at the king.

"The Diagram spoke of this," Graves said, scuttling back along the corridor. "We missed it. We missed it completely! We focused on making certain you were separated from Dalinar, and not on what our actions might push you to become!"

Moash looked from Graves back at Kaladin. Then he ran, Plate clinking as he turned and dashed down the corridor and disappeared.

Kaladin, Syl's voice spoke in his head. *Something is still very wrong. I feel it on the winds.*

Graves laughed like a madman.

"Separating me," Kaladin whispered. "From Dalinar? Why would they care?"

He turned, looking eastward.

Oh no . . .

*But who is the wanderer, the wild piece, the one who makes no
sense? I glimpse at his implications, and the world opens to me.
I shy back. Impossible. Is it?*

—From the Diagram, West Wall Psalm of Wonders: paragraph 8
(Note by Adrotagia: Could this refer to Mraize?)

S he didn't say if she could even open the pathway?" Dalinar asked as
he stalked toward the command tent. Rain pummeled the ground
around him, so dense that it was no longer possible to distinguish
separate windblown sheets in the glare of Navani's fabrial floodlights. It
was long past when he should have found cover.

"No, Brightlord," said Peet, the bridgeman. "But she was insistent that
we couldn't face what was coming at us. Two highstorms."

"How could there be *two*?" Navani asked. She wore a stout cloak but
was soaked clear through anyway, her umbrella having blown away long
ago. Roion walked on Dalinar's other side, his beard and mustache limp
with water.

"I don't know, Brightness," Peet said. "But that's what she said. A highstorm and something else. She called it an Everstorm. She expects they're
going to collide right here."

Dalinar considered, frowning. The command tent was just ahead. Inside, he'd talk to his field commanders, and—

The command tent shuddered, then ripped free in a burst of wind.
Trailing ropes and spikes, it blew right past Dalinar, almost close enough
to touch. Dalinar cursed as the light of a dozen lanterns—once contained

in the tent—spilled onto the plateau. Scribes and soldiers scrambled, trying to grab maps and sheets of paper as rain and wind claimed them.

"Storm it!" Dalinar said, turning his back to the powerful wind. "I need an update!"

"Sir!" Commander Cael, head of the field command, jogged over, his wife—Apara—following. Cael's clothing was mostly dry, though that was quickly changing. "Aladar has *won* his plateau! Apara was just composing you a message."

"Really?" Almighty bless that man. He'd done it.

"Yes, sir," Cael said. He had to shout against the wind and rain. "Highprince Aladar said the singing Parshendi went right down, letting him slaughter them. The rest broke and fled. Even with Roion's plateau fallen, we've won the day!"

"Doesn't feel like it," Dalinar shouted back. Just minutes ago, the rainfall had been light. The situation was degrading quickly. "Send orders immediately to Aladar, my son, and General Khal. There's a plateau just to the southeast, perfectly round. I want all of our forces to move there to brace for an oncoming storm."

"Yes, sir!" Cael said with a salute, fist to coat. With the other hand, however, he pointed over Dalinar's shoulder. "Sir, have you seen *that*?"

He turned, looking back toward the west. Red light flashed, lightning coursing down in repeated blasts. The sky itself seemed to spasm as something built there, swirling in an enormous storm cell that was rapidly expanding outward.

"Almighty above . . ." Navani whispered.

Nearby another tent shook, its stakes coming undone. "Leave the tents, Cael," Dalinar said. "Get everyone moving. *Now.* Navani, go to Brightness Shallan. Help her if you can."

The officer leaped away and began shouting orders. Navani went with him, vanishing into the night, and a squad of soldiers chased after her to provide protection.

"And me, Dalinar?" Roion asked.

"We'll need you to take command of your men and lead them to safety," Dalinar said. "If such a thing can be found."

That tent nearby shook again. Dalinar frowned. It didn't seem to be moving along with the wind. And was that . . . shouting?

Adolin crashed through the tent's fabric and skidded along the stones on his back, his armor leaking Light.

"Adolin!" Dalinar shouted, dashing to his son.

The young man was missing several segments of his armor. He looked up with gritted teeth, blood streaming from his nose. He said something, but it was lost to the wind. No helm, no left vambrace, the breastplate cracked just short of shattering, his right leg exposed. Who could have done such a thing to a Shardbearer?

Dalinar knew the answer immediately. He cradled Adolin, but looked up past the collapsed tent. It whipped in the storm and tore away as a man strode past it, glowing with spinning trails of Stormlight. Those foreign features, clothing all of white plastered to his body by the rain, a bowed, hairless head, shadows hiding eyes that glowed with Stormlight.

Gavilar's murderer. Szeth, the Assassin in White.

* *

Shallan worked through the inscriptions on the wall of the round chamber, frantically searching for some way to make the Oathgate function.

This had to work. It *had* to.

"This is all in the Dawnchant," Inadara said. "I can't make sense of any of it."

The Knights Radiant are the key.

Shouldn't Renarin's sword have been enough? "What's the pattern?" she whispered.

"Mmm . . ." Pattern said. "Perhaps you cannot see it because you are too close? Like the Shattered Plains?"

Shallan hesitated, then stood and walked to the center of the room, where the depictions of the Knights Radiant and their kingdoms met at a central point.

"Brightlord Renarin?" Inadara asked. "Is something wrong?" The young prince had fallen to his knees and was huddled next to the wall.

"I can see it," Renarin answered feverishly, his voice echoing in the chamber. Ardents who had been studying part of the murals looked up at him. "I can see the future itself. Why? Why, Almighty? Why have you cursed me so?" He screamed a pleading cry, then stood and cracked something against the wall. A rock? Where had he gotten it? He gripped the thing in a gauntleted hand and began to write.

Shocked, Shallan took a step toward him. A sequence of numbers?

All zeros.

"It's come," Renarin whispered. "It's come, it's come, it's come. We're dead. We're dead. We're dead. . . ."

* *

Dalinar knelt beneath a fracturing sky, holding his son. Rainwater washed the blood from Adolin's face, and the boy blinked, dazed from his thrashing.

"Father . . ." Adolin said.

The assassin stepped forward quietly, with no apparent urgency. The man seemed to glide through the rain.

"When you take the princedom, son," Dalinar said, "don't let them corrupt you. Don't play their games. Lead. Don't follow."

"Father!" Adolin said, his eyes focusing.

Dalinar stood up. Adolin lurched over onto all fours and tried to get to his feet, but the assassin had broken one of Adolin's greaves, which made it almost impossible to rise. The boy slipped back into the pooling water.

"You've been taught well, Adolin," Dalinar said, eyes on that assassin. "You're a better man than I am. I was always a tyrant who had to learn to be something else. But you, you've been a good man from the start. Lead them, Adolin. Unite them."

"Father!"

Dalinar walked away from Adolin. Nearby, scribes and attendants, captains and enlisted men all shouted and scrambled, trying to find order in the chaos of the storm. They followed Dalinar's order to evacuate, and most had yet to notice the figure in white.

The assassin stopped ten paces from Dalinar. Roion, pale-faced and stammering, backed away from the two of them and began shouting. "Assassin! Assassin!"

The rainfall was actually letting up a little. That didn't bring Dalinar much hope; not with that red lightning on the horizon. Was that . . . a stormwall building at the front of the new storm? His efforts to disrupt the Parshendi had fallen short.

The Shin man didn't strike. He stood opposite Dalinar, motionless, expressionless, water dripping down his face. Unnaturally calm.

Dalinar was far taller and broader. This small man in white, with his pale skin, seemed almost a youth, a stripling by comparison.

Behind him, Roion's cries were lost in the confusion. However, Bridge Four did run up to surround Dalinar, spears in hand. Dalinar waved them back. "There's nothing you can do here, lads," Dalinar said. "Let me face him."

Ten heartbeats.

"Why?" Dalinar asked the assassin, who still stood there in the rain. "Why kill my brother? Did they explain the reasoning behind your orders?"

"I am Szeth-son-son-Vallano," the man said. Harshly. "Truthless of Shinovar. I do as my masters demand, and I do not ask for explanations."

Dalinar revised his assessment. This man was not calm. He seemed that way, but when he spoke, he did it through clenched teeth, his eyes open too wide.

He's mad, Dalinar thought. *Storms.*

"You don't have to do this," Dalinar said. "If it's about pay . . ."

"What I am owed," the assassin shouted, rainwater spraying from his face and Stormlight rising from his lips, "will come to me eventually! Every bit of it. I will drown in it, stonewalker!"

Szeth put his hand to the side, Shardblade appearing. Then, with a curt, deprecatory motion—like he was merely trimming a bit of gristle from his meat—he strode forward and swung at Dalinar.

Dalinar caught the Blade with his own, which appeared in his hand as he raised it.

The assassin spared a glance for Dalinar's weapon, then smiled, lips drawn thin, showing only a hint of teeth. That eager smile matched with haunted eyes was one of the most evil things Dalinar had ever seen.

"Thank you," the assassin said, "for extending my agony by not dying easily." He stepped back and burst *afire* with white light.

He came at Dalinar again, inhumanly quick.

⁘

Adolin cursed, shaking out of his daze. Storms, his head hurt. He'd smacked it something good when the assassin tossed him to the ground.

Father was fighting Szeth. Bless the man for listening to reason and bonding that madman's Blade. Adolin gritted his teeth and struggled to get to his feet, something that was difficult with a broken greave. Though the rain was letting up, the sky remained dark. To the west, lightning plunged downward like red waterfalls, almost constant.

At the same time, wind gusted from the east. Something was building out there too, from the Origin. This was very bad.

Those things Father said to me . . .

Adolin stumbled, almost falling to the ground, but hands appeared to assist him. He glanced to the side to find those two bridgemen from before, Skar and Drehy, helping him to his feet.

"You two," Adolin said, "are getting a storming raise. Help me get this armor off." He frantically began removing sections of armor. The entire suit was so battered it was nearly useless.

Metal clanged nearby as Dalinar fought. If he could hold a little longer, Adolin would be able to help. He would *not* let that creature get the better of him again. Not again!

He spared a glance for what Dalinar was doing, and froze, hands on the straps for his breastplate.

His father . . . his father moved beautifully.

Dalinar did not fight for his life. His life hadn't been his own for years.

He fought for Gavilar. He fought as he wished he had all those years ago, for the chance he had missed. In that moment between storms—when the rain stilled and the winds drew in their breaths to blow—he danced with the slayer of kings, and somehow held his own.

The assassin moved like a shadow. His step seemed too quick to be human. When he jumped, he soared into the air. He swung his Shardblade like flashes of lightning, and would occasionally stretch forward with his other hand, as if to grab Dalinar.

Recalling their previous encounter, Dalinar recognized that as the more dangerous of Szeth's weapons. Each time, Dalinar managed to bring his Blade around and force the assassin away. The man attacked from different directions, but Dalinar didn't think. Thoughts could get jumbled, the mind disoriented.

His instincts knew what to do.

Duck when Szeth leaped over Dalinar's head. Step backward, avoiding a strike that should have severed his spine. Lash out, forcing the assassin away. Three quick steps backward, sword up wardingly, strike for the assassin's palm as it tried to touch him.

It worked. For this brief time, he fought this creature. Bridge Four remained back, as he'd commanded. They'd only have interfered.

He survived.

But he did not win.

Finally, Dalinar twisted away from a strike but was unable to move quickly enough. The assassin rounded on him and thrust a fist into his side.

Dalinar's ribs cracked. He grunted, stumbling, almost falling. He swung his Blade toward Szeth, warding the man back, but it didn't matter. The damage was done. He sank to his knees, barely able to remain upright for the pain.

In that instant he knew a truth he should always have known.

If I'd been there, on that night, awake instead of drunk and asleep . . . Gavilar would still have died.

I couldn't have beaten this creature. I can't do it now, and I couldn't have done it then.

I couldn't have saved him.

It brought peace, and Dalinar finally set down that boulder, the one he'd been carrying for over six years.

The assassin stalked toward him, glowing with terrible Stormlight, but a figure lunged for him from behind.

Dalinar expected it to be Adolin, perhaps one of the bridgemen.

Instead, it was Roion.

※

Adolin tossed aside the last bit of armor and went running for his father. He wasn't too late. Dalinar knelt before the assassin, defeated, but not dead.

Adolin shouted, drawing close, and an unexpected figure leapt out of the wreckage of a tent. Highprince Roion—incongruously holding a side sword and leading a small force of soldiers—rushed the assassin.

Rats had a better chance fighting a chasmfiend.

Adolin barely had time to shout as the assassin—moving at blinding speed—spun and cut the blade from the hilt of Roion's sword. Szeth's hand shot out and slammed against Roion's chest.

Roion shot into the air, trailing a wisp of Stormlight. He screamed as the sky swallowed him.

He lasted longer than his men. The assassin swept between them, deftly avoiding spears, moving with uncanny grace. A dozen soldiers fell in an instant, eyes burning.

Adolin jumped over one of the bodies as it collapsed. Storms. He could still hear Roion screaming up above somewhere.

Adolin thrust at the assassin, but the creature twisted and slapped the Shardblade away. The assassin was grinning. He didn't speak, though Stormlight leaked between his teeth.

Adolin tried Smokestance, attacking with a quick sequence of jabs. The assassin silently battered them away, unfazed. Adolin focused, dueling the best he could, but he was a *child* before this thing.

Roion, still screaming, plummeted from the sky and hit nearby with a sickening wet crunch. A quick glance at his corpse told Adolin that the highprince would never rise again.

Adolin cursed and lunged for the assassin, but a fluttering tarp—brushed by the assassin in passing—leaped toward Adolin. The monster could command inanimate objects! Adolin sliced through the tarp and then jumped forward to swing for the assassin.

He found nothing to fight.

Duck.

He threw himself to the ground as something passed over his head, the assassin flying through the air. Szeth's hissing Shardblade missed Adolin's head by inches.

Adolin rolled and came to his knees, puffing.

How . . . What could he do . . . ?

You can't beat it, Adolin thought. *Nothing can beat it.*

The assassin landed lightly. Adolin climbed back to his feet, and found himself in company. A dozen of the bridgemen formed up around him. Skar, at their head, looked to Adolin and nodded. Good men. They'd seen Roion's fall, and still they joined him. Adolin hefted his Shardblade and noticed that a short distance away, his father had managed to regain his feet. Another small group of bridgemen moved in around him, and he allowed it. He and Adolin had dueled and lost. Their only chance now was a mad rush.

Nearby, shouts arose. General Khal and a large strike force of soldiers, judging by the banner approaching. There wasn't time. The assassin stood on the wet plateau between Dalinar's small troop and Adolin's, head bowed. Fallen blue lanterns gave light. The sky had gone as black as night, except when broken by that red lightning.

Charge and mob a Shardbearer. Hope for a lucky blow. It was the only way. Adolin nodded to Dalinar. His father nodded back, grim. He knew. He *knew* there was no beating this thing.

Lead them, Adolin.

Unite them.

Adolin screamed, charging forward, sword out, men running with him. Dalinar advanced too, more slowly, one arm across his chest. Storms, the man could barely walk.

Szeth snapped his head up, face devoid of all emotion. As they arrived, he leaped, shooting into the air.

Adolin's eyes followed him up. Surely they hadn't chased him off . . .

The assassin twisted in the air, then crashed back down to the ground, glowing like a comet. Adolin barely parried a blow from the Blade; the *force* of it was incredible. It tossed him backward. The assassin spun, and a pair of bridgemen fell with burning eyes. Others lost spearheads as they tried to stab at him.

The assassin ripped free from the press of bodies, trailing blood from a couple of wounds. Those wounds *closed* as Adolin watched, the blood stopping. It was as Kaladin had said. With a horrible sinking feeling, Adolin realized just how *little* a chance they'd ever had.

The assassin dashed for Dalinar, who brought up the rear of the attack. The aging soldier raised his Blade, as if in respect, then thrust once.

An attack. That was the way to go.

"Father . . ." Adolin whispered.

The assassin parried the thrust, then placed his hand against Dalinar's

chest.

The highprince, suddenly glowing, lurched up into the dark sky. He didn't scream.

The plateau fell silent. Some bridgemen propped up wounded fellows. Others turned toward the assassin, pulling into a spear formation, looking frantic.

The assassin lowered his Blade, then started to walk away.

"Bastard!" Adolin spat, dashing after him. "Bastard!" He could barely see for the tears.

The assassin stopped, then leveled his weapon toward Adolin.

Adolin stumbled to a halt. Storms, his head hurt.

"It is finished," the assassin whispered. "I am done." He turned from Adolin and continued to walk away.

Like Damnation itself, you are! Adolin raised his Shardblade overhead.

The assassin spun and slapped the weapon so hard with his own Blade that Adolin distinctly heard something *snap* in his wrist. His Blade tumbled from his fingers, vanishing. The assassin's hand slapped out, knuckles striking Adolin in the chest, and he gasped, his breath suddenly gone from his throat.

Stunned, he sank to his knees.

"I suppose," the assassin snarled, "I can kill one more, on my own time." Then he grinned, a terrible smile with teeth clenched, eyes wide. As if he were in enormous pain.

Gasping, Adolin awaited the blow. He looked toward the sky. *Father, I'm sorry. I . . .*

I . . .

What was that?

He blinked as he made out something glowing in the air, drifting down, like a leaf. A figure. A man.

Dalinar.

The highprince fell slowly, as if he were no more weighty than a cloud. White Light streamed from his body in glowing wisps. Nearby bridgemen murmured, soldiers shouted, pointing.

Adolin blinked, certain he was delusional. But no, that *was* Dalinar. Like . . . one of the Heralds themselves, coming down from the Tranquiline Halls.

The assassin looked, then stumbled back, mouth open in horror. "No . . . *No!*"

And then, like a falling star, a blazing fireball of light and motion shot down in front of Dalinar. It crashed into the ground, sending out a ring of Stormlight like white smoke. At the center, a figure in blue crouched with one hand on the stones, the other clutching a glowing Shardblade.

His eyes afire with a light that somehow made the assassin's seem *dull* by comparison, he wore the uniform of a bridgeman, and bore the glyphs of slavery on his forehead.

The expanding ring of smoky light faded, save for a large glyph—a swordlike shape—which remained for a brief moment before puffing away.

"You sent him to the sky to die, assassin," Kaladin said, Stormlight puffing from his lips, "but the sky and the winds are mine. I claim them, as I now claim your life."

One is almost certainly a traitor to the others.

—From the Diagram, Book of the 2nd Desk Drawer: paragraph 27

K aladin let the Stormlight evaporate before him. He was running low—his frantic flight across the Plains had drained him. How shocked he had been when the flare of light rising into the darkening sky above a lit plateau had turned out to be Dalinar himself. Lashed to the sky by Szeth.

Kaladin had caught him quickly and sent him back to the ground with a careful Lashing of his own. Ahead, Szeth stumbled away from the princeling, holding out his sword wardingly toward Kaladin, eyes wide and lips trembling. Szeth looked horrified.

Good.

Dalinar finally landed on the plateau with a soft step, and Kaladin's Lashing ran out.

"Seek shelter," Kaladin said, the tempest in his veins dampening further. "I flew over a storm on my way here . . . a big one. Coming from the west."

"We're in the process of withdrawing."

"Hurry," Kaladin said. "I will deal with our friend."

"Kaladin?"

Kaladin turned, glancing at the highprince, who stood tall, despite cradling one arm against his chest. Dalinar met his eyes. "You *are* what I've been looking for."

"Yes. Finally."

Kaladin turned and strode toward the assassin. He passed Bridge Four in a tight formation, and the men—at a barked command from Teft—threw something down before Kaladin. Blue lanterns, lit by oversized gems that had lasted the Weeping.

Bless them. Stormlight streamed up as he passed, filling him. With a sinking feeling, however, he noticed two corpses with burned-out eyes at their feet. Pedin and Mart. Eth clutched his brother's body, weeping. Other bridgemen had lost limbs.

Kaladin snarled. No more. He would lose no further men to this monster.

"You ready?" he whispered.

Of course, Syl said in his head. *I'm not the one we've been waiting on.*

Burning with Stormlight, enraged and alight, Kaladin launched himself at the assassin and met him Blade against Blade.

⁘

"We're dead . . ." Renarin muttered.

"Someone shut him up," Shallan snapped. "Gag him if you have to." She pointedly turned around, ignoring the raving prince. She still stood in the center of the muraled chamber. The pattern. What was the pattern?

A circular room. A thing on one side that adapted to fit different Shardblades. Depictions of Knights on the floor, glowing with Stormlight, pointing at a tower city, just as the myths described. Ten lamps on the walls. The lock hung over what she thought was a depiction of Natanatan, the kingdom of the Shattered Plains. It—

Ten lamps. With gems in them. Latticework of metal enclosing each one.

Shallan blinked, a shock running through her.

"It's a fabrial."

⁘

The assassin hurtled into the air. Captain Kaladin flew upward, chasing him, trailing Light.

"Status of the retreat!" Dalinar bellowed, crossing the plateau, his ribs smarting like nothing else, his wound from before little better. Storms. That one had faded as he fought, but now it ached something fierce. "Someone get me information!"

Scribes and ardents appeared from the nearby wreckage of tents. Shouts rose from around the plateau. The wind started to pick up—their period of reprieve, the short calm, was over. They needed to escape these plateaus. *Now.*

Dalinar reached Adolin and helped the young man to his feet. He looked quite a bit worse for wear, bruised, battered, dizzy. He flexed his right hand and winced in pain, then gingerly let it relax.

"Damnation," Adolin said. "That bridgeboy is really one of them? The Knights Radiant?"

"Yes."

Oddly, Adolin smiled, seeming satisfied. "Ha! I *knew* there was something wrong with that man."

"Go," Dalinar said, pushing Adolin along. "We need to get the army to move two plateaus over, that direction, where Shallan waits. Get over there and organize what you can." He looked westward as the wind whipped up further, with bursts of rain. "Time is short."

Adolin shouted for the bridgemen to join him, which they did, helping their wounded—though they were unfortunately forced to leave their dead. Several of them carried Adolin's Shardplate as well, which was apparently spent.

Dalinar limped eastward across the plateau as fast as he could manage in his condition, searching for . . .

Yes. The place where he'd left Gallant. The horse snorted, shaking a wet mane. "Bless you, old friend," Dalinar said, reaching the Ryshadium. Through the thunder and the chaos, the horse had not fled.

Dalinar moved much more easily once in the saddle, and eventually found Roion's army pouring southward toward Shallan's plateau, in organized ranks. He allowed himself a sigh of relief at their orderly march; the majority of the army had already crossed to the southern plateau, only one away from Shallan's round one. That was wonderful. He couldn't remember where Captain Khal had been sent, but with Roion himself fallen, Dalinar had assumed he'd left this army in chaos.

"Dalinar!" a voice called.

He turned to find the utterly incongruous sight of Sebarial and his mistress sitting beneath a canopy, eating dried sellafruit off a plate held by an awkward-looking soldier.

Sebarial raised a cup of wine toward Dalinar. "Hope you don't mind," Sebarial said. "We liberated your stores. They were blowing past at the time, headed for certain doom."

Dalinar stared at them. Palona even had a *novel* out and was *reading*.

"You did this?" Dalinar asked, nodding toward Roion's army.

"They were making a racket," Sebarial said. "Wandering around, shouting at one another, weeping and wailing. Very poetic. Figured someone should get them moving. My army is already off on that other plateau. It's getting *rather* cramped there, you realize."

Palona flipped the page in her novel, barely paying attention.

"Have you seen Aladar?" Dalinar asked.

Sebarial gestured with his wine. "He should be about finished crossing as well. You'll find him that direction. Downwind, happily."

"Don't dally," Dalinar said. "You remain here, and you're a dead man."

"Like Roion?" Sebarial asked.

"Unfortunately."

"So it *is* true," Sebarial said, standing up, brushing off his trousers—which were somehow still dry. "Who am I going to make fun of now?" He shook his head sadly.

Dalinar rode off in the direction indicated. He noticed that, incredibly, a pair of bridgemen were still tailing him, only now catching up to where he'd found Sebarial. They saluted as Dalinar noticed them.

He told them where he was going, then sped up. Storms. In terms of pain, riding with broken ribs wasn't much better than walking with them. Worse, actually.

He did find Aladar on the next plateau over, supervising his army as it seeped onto the perfectly round plateau that Shallan had indicated. Rust Elthal was there as well, wearing his Plate—one of the suits Adolin had won—and guiding one of Dalinar's large, mechanical bridges. It settled down next to two others that spanned the chasm here, crossing in places the smaller bridges wouldn't have been able to.

The plateau everyone was crowding onto was relatively small, by the scale of the Shattered Plains—but it was still several hundred yards across. It would fit the armies, hopefully.

"Dalinar?" Aladar asked, trotting his horse over. Lit by a large diamond—stolen from one of Navani's fabrial lights, it seemed—hanging from his saddle, Aladar sported a soaked uniform and a bandage on his forehead, but appeared otherwise unharmed. "What in Kelek's tongue is going on out here? I can't get a straight answer from anyone."

"Roion is dead," Dalinar said wearily, reining in Gallant. "He fell with honor, attacking the assassin. The assassin, hopefully, has been distracted for a time."

"We won the day," Aladar said. "I scattered those Parshendi. We left well over half of them dead on that plateau, perhaps even three quarters. Adolin did even better on his plateau, and from reports, the ones on Roion's plateau have fled. The Vengeance Pact is fulfilled! Gavilar is avenged, and the war is over!"

So proud. Dalinar had difficulty finding the words to deflate him, so he just stared at the other man. Feeling numb.

Can't afford that, Dalinar thought, sagging in his saddle. *Have to lead.*

"It doesn't matter, does it?" Aladar asked more softly. "That we won?"

"Of course it matters."

"But . . . shouldn't it feel different?"

"Exhaustion," Dalinar said, "pain, suffering. This is what victory usually feels like, Aladar. We've won, yes, but now we have to survive with our victory. Your men are almost across?"

He nodded.

"Get everyone onto that plateau," Dalinar said. "Force them up against one another if you have to. We need to be ready to move through the portal as quickly as possible, once it is opened."

If it opened.

Dalinar urged Gallant forward, crossing one of the bridges to the packed ranks on the other side. From there, he forced his way—with difficulty—toward the center, where he hoped to find salvation.

* *

Kaladin shot into the air after the assassin.

The Shattered Plains fell away beneath him. Fallen gemstones twinkled across the plateau, abandoned where tents had blown down or soldiers had fallen. They illuminated not only the central plateau, but three others around it and one more beyond, one that looked oddly circular from above.

The armies gathered on that one. Small lumps dotted the others like freckles. Corpses. So many.

Kaladin looked toward the sky. He was free once again. Winds *surged* beneath him, seeming to lift him, propel him. Carry him. His Shardblade shattered into mist and Syl zipped out, becoming a ribbon of light that spun around him as he flew.

Syl lived. Syl *lived*. He still felt euphoric about that. Shouldn't she be dead? When he'd asked on their flight out, her response had been simple.

I was only as dead as your oaths, Kaladin.

Kaladin continued upward, out of the path of the oncoming storms. He could see those distinctly from this vantage. Two of them, one rolling from the west and bursting with red lightning, the other approaching more quickly from the east with a dark grey stormwall. They were going to *collide*.

"A highstorm," Kaladin said, shooting up through the sky after Szeth. "The red storm is from the Parshendi, but why is there a *highstorm* coming? This isn't the time for one."

"My father," Syl said, voice growing solemn. "He brought the storm, rushing its pace. He's . . . broken, Kaladin. He doesn't think any of this should be happening. He wants to end it all, wash everyone away, and try to hide from the future."

Her father . . . did that mean the *Stormfather* wanted them dead?

Great.

The assassin disappeared above, vanishing into the dark clouds. Kaladin gritted his teeth, Lashing himself upward again for more acceleration. He shot into the clouds, and all around him became featureless grey.

He kept watch for glimmers of light to announce the assassin coming for him. He might not have much warning.

The area around him lightened. Was that the assassin? Kaladin extended his hand to the side, and Syl formed into the Blade immediately.

"Not ten heartbeats?" he asked.

Not when I'm here with you, ready. The delay is primarily something of the dead. They need to be revived each time.

Kaladin burst out of the clouds and into sunlight.

He gasped. He'd forgotten that it was still daytime. Here, far above the earthy darkness of war, the sunlight beat upon the cover of clouds, making them glow with pale beauty. The thin air was frigid, but raging Stormlight inside him made that easy to ignore.

The assassin hovered nearby, toes pointed downward, head bowed, silvery Shardblade held to the side. Kaladin Lashed himself so that he stopped, then sank level with the assassin.

"I am Szeth-son-son-Vallano," the man said. "Truthless . . . Truthless." He looked up, eyes wide, teeth clenched. "You have stolen Honorblades. It is the only explanation."

Storms. Kaladin had always imagined the Assassin in White as a calm, cold killer. This was something different.

"I possess no such weapon," Kaladin said. "And I don't know why it would matter if I did."

"I hear your lies. I know them." Szeth shot forward, sword out.

Kaladin Lashed himself to the side, jerking out of the way. He swiped with his Blade, but didn't come close to connecting. "I should have practiced more with the sword," he muttered.

Oh. That's right. You probably want me to be a spear, don't you?

The weapon fuzzed to mist, then elongated and grew into the shape of a silvery spear, with glowing, swirling glyphs along the sharpened sides of the spearhead.

Szeth twisted in the air, Lashing himself back into a hovering position. He looked at the spear, then seemed to tremble. "No. Truthless. I am Truthless. No questions."

Stormlight streaming from his mouth, Szeth threw his head back and screamed; a futile, human sound that dissipated in the infinite expanse of sky.

Beneath them, thunder rumbled and the clouds shivered with color.

Shallan dashed from lamp to lamp in the circular chamber, infusing each one with Stormlight. She glowed brightly, having drawn the Light from the ardents' lanterns. There wasn't time for explanation.

So much for keeping her nature as a Surgebinder hidden.

This room was a giant fabrial, powered by the Stormlight of those lamps. She should have seen it. She passed Inadara, who stared at her. "How . . . how are you doing this, Brightness?"

Several of the scholars had settled onto the ground where they hurriedly sketched glyphward prayers onto cloths, using chalk because of the moisture. Shallan didn't know if those prayers were a request for safety from the storms or from Shallan herself. She did hear the words "Lost Radiant" murmured by one.

Two more lanterns. She infused a ruby with Stormlight, bringing it to life, but then ran out of Light.

"Gemstones!" she said, spinning on the room. "I need more Stormlight."

The people inside looked to one another, all but Renarin, who continued to scratch identical glyphs on the rocks as he wept. Stormfather. She'd bled them all dry. One of the scholars had dug an oil lantern from her pack, and it paled beside the lamps on the walls.

Shallan ducked out of the opening in the door, looking at the mass of soldiers who gathered there. Thousands upon thousands shuffled in the darkness. Fortunately, some of them carried lanterns.

"I need your Stormlight!" she said. "It—"

Was that *Adolin*? Shallan gasped, other thoughts fleeing for the moment as she spotted him in the front of the crowd, leaning on a bridgeman for support. Adolin was a mess, the left side of his face a patchwork of blood and bruises, his uniform ripped and bloodied. Shallan ran to him, pulling him close.

"Good to see you too," he said, burying his face in her hair. "I hear you're going to get us out of this mess."

"Mess?" she asked.

Thunder rumbled and cracked without pause as red lightning blasted down not in streaks but in sheets. Storms! She hadn't realized it was so close!

"Mmm . . ." Pattern said. She looked left. A stormwall was approaching. The storms were like two hands, closing in to crush the armies between them.

Shallan breathed in sharply, and Stormlight entered her, bringing her to life. Adolin had a gemstone or two on him, apparently. He pulled back, looking her over.

"You *too*?" he said.

"Um . . ." She bit her lip. "Yeah. Sorry."

"Sorry? Storms, woman! Can you fly like he does?"

"Fly?"

Thunder cracked. Impending doom. Right.

"Make sure everyone is ready to move!" she said, dashing back into the chamber.

⁘

Storms crashed together beneath Kaladin. The clouds broke apart, black, red, and grey mingling in enormous swirls, lightning arcing among them. It seemed to be Aharietiam again, the ending of all things.

Above all this, atop the world, Kaladin fought for his life.

Szeth flew by in a sweeping flash of silvery metal. Kaladin deflected the blow, the spear in his hand vibrating with a plangent *ding*. Szeth continued on, passing him, and Kaladin Lashed himself in that direction.

They fell westward, skimming the tops of the clouds—though to Kaladin's eyes, that direction was down. He fell with his spear aimed, point straight toward the murderous Shin.

Szeth jerked left, and Kaladin followed, quickly Lashing himself that way. Violent, churning, angry clouds mixed beneath him. The two storms seemed to be fighting; the lightning that lit them was like thrown punches. Crashes sounded, and not all of them thunder. Near Kaladin a large stone churned up through the clouds, spinning vapors across its length. It breached in the light like a leviathan, then sank back into the clouds.

Stormfather . . . He was hundreds, perhaps thousands of feet in the air. What kind of violence was happening below if boulders were thrown this high?

Kaladin Lashed himself toward Szeth, picking up speed, moving along the top surface of the storms. He drew close, then eased back, letting his acceleration match that of Szeth so they flew side by side.

Kaladin drove his spear toward the assassin. Szeth parried deftly, Shardblade held in one hand while supporting the Blade from behind with the other, diverting Kaladin's thrust to the side.

"The Knights Radiant," Szeth screamed, "cannot have returned."

"They have," Kaladin said, yanking his spear back. "And they're going to kill you." He Lashed himself slightly to the side as he swung, twisting in the air and sweeping toward Szeth.

Szeth jerked upward, however, passing over Kaladin's spear. As they continued to fall through the air, clouds just beside them, Szeth dove inward and struck. Kaladin cursed, barely Lashing himself away in time.

Szeth dove past him, disappearing into the clouds below, becoming just a shadow. Kaladin tried to trace that shadow, but failed.

Szeth burst up beside Kaladin a second later, striking with three quick blows. One took Kaladin in the arm, and he dropped Syl.

Damnation. He Lashed himself back away from Szeth, then forced Stormlight into his greying, lifeless hand. With an effort, he made the color return, but Szeth was already upon him with an airborne lunge.

Mist formed in Kaladin's left hand as he raised it to ward, and a silvery shield appeared, glowing with a soft light. Szeth's Blade deflected away, causing the man to grunt in surprise.

Strength returned to Kaladin's right hand, the severing healed, but forcing that much Stormlight through it left him feeling drained. He fell away from Szeth, trying to keep his distance, but the assassin kept on him, jerking each direction that Kaladin did as he tried to escape.

"You are new at this," Szeth called. "You cannot fight me. I will win."

Szeth zipped forward, and Syl formed into a spear in Kaladin's hands again. She seemed to be able to anticipate the weapon he wanted. Szeth slammed his weapon against Syl. It brought them face-to-face and they tumbled, eye to eye, their Lashings pulling them along the clouds.

"I *always* win," Szeth said. He said it in a strange way, as if *angry*.

"You're wrong," Kaladin said. "About me. I'm not new to this."

"You only just acquired your abilities."

"No. The wind is mine. The sky is mine. They have been mine since childhood. You are the trespasser here. Not me."

They broke apart, Kaladin throwing the assassin backward. He stopped thinking so much about his Lashings, about what he should be doing.

Instead, he let himself *be*.

He dove for Szeth, coat flapping, spear pointed for the man's heart. Szeth got out of the way, but Kaladin dropped the spear and swung his hand in a great arc. Syl formed an axehead halberd. It came within inches of Szeth's face.

The assassin cursed, but responded with his Blade. A shield was in Kaladin's hand a split second later, and he slammed away the attack. Syl shattered even as he did so, forming back into a sword as Kaladin thrust forward with empty hands. The sword appeared, and the weapon bit deeply into Szeth's shoulder.

The assassin's eyes widened. Kaladin twisted his Blade, pulling it out of the assassin's flesh, then tried a backhand to end the man permanently. Szeth was too fast. He Lashed himself backward, forcing Kaladin to follow, piling on Lashing after Lashing.

Szeth's hand still worked. Damnation. The strike to the shoulder hadn't fully severed the soul leading to the arm. And Kaladin's Stormlight was running out.

Szeth's looked even lower, fortunately. The assassin seemed to be using it up at a much faster rate than Kaladin, judging by the decreased glow around him. Indeed, he didn't try to heal his shoulder—which would have required a lot of Light—but continued to flee, jerking back and forth, trying to outrun Kaladin.

The shadowy battle continued below, a tangle of lightning, winds, and spinning clouds. As Kaladin chased Szeth, something gargantuan moved beneath the clouds, a shadow the size of a city. A second later, the top of an entire *plateau* broke through the dark clouds, twisting slowly, as if it had been thrown upward from below.

Szeth almost ran into it. Instead, he Lashed upward enough to crest it, then landed on the surface. He ran along it as it turned lethargically in the air, its momentum running out.

Kaladin landed behind him, though he retained most of a Lashing upward, keeping himself light. He ran up the side of the plateau, heading almost directly upward toward the sky, dodging to the side as Szeth suddenly twisted and cut through a rock formation, sending boulders tumbling downward.

Rocks clattered along the surface of the plateau, which itself began to tumble back down toward the ground. Szeth reached the peak and threw himself off, and Kaladin followed shortly thereafter, launching from the stone surface, which sank like a dying ship into the roiling clouds.

They continued their chase, but Szeth did it falling backward along the stormtop, his eyes on Kaladin. Wild eyes. "You're trying to convince me!" he shouted. "You can't be one of them!"

"You've seen that I am," Kaladin shouted back.

"The Voidbringers!"

"Are back," Kaladin shouted.

"THEY CAN'T BE. I AM TRUTHLESS!" The assassin panted. "I need not fight you. You are not my target. I have . . . I have work to do. I *obey*!"

He turned and Lashed himself downward.

Into the clouds, down toward the plateau where Dalinar had gone.

◆◆

Shallan rushed into the room as the storms crashed together outside.

What was she doing? There wasn't time. Even if she could open a portal, those storms were *here*. She wouldn't have time to get people through.

They were dead. All of them. Thousands had probably already been

swept to their deaths by the stormwall.

She ran to the last lamp anyway, infusing its spheres.

The floor started to glow.

Ardents jumped to their feet in surprise and Inadara yelped. Adolin stumbled in through the doorway, a crashing wind and a spray of angry rain trailing him.

Beneath them, the intricate design shone from within. It looked almost like stained glass. Gesturing frantically for Adolin to join her, Shallan ran across to the lock on the wall.

"Sword," she shouted at Adolin over the sounds of storms outside. "In there!" Renarin had long since dismissed his.

Adolin obeyed, scrambling forward, summoning his Shardblade. He rammed it into the slot, which again flowed to fit the weapon.

Nothing happened.

"It's not working," Adolin shouted.

Only one answer.

Shallan grabbed the hilt of his sword and whipped it out—ignoring the scream in her mind that came from touching it—then tossed it aside. Adolin's sword vanished to mist.

A deep truth.

"There is something wrong with your Blade, and with all Blades." She hesitated for just a second. "All but mine. Pattern!"

He formed in her hands, the Blade she'd used to kill. The hidden soul. Shallan rammed it into the slot, and the weapon vibrated in her hands and glowed. Something deep within the plateau *unlocked*.

Outside, lightning fell and men screamed.

Now the mechanism's operation became clear to her. Shallan threw her weight against the sword, pushing it before her like the spoke on a mill. The inner wall of the building was like a ring inside a tube—it could rotate, while the outer wall remained in place. The sword moved the inner wall as she pushed on it, though it stuck at first, the fallen blocks of the cut doorway getting in the way. Adolin threw his weight against the sword with her, and together they pushed it around the circle until they were above the picture of Urithiru, half the circumference from Natanatan where she'd begun. She pulled her Blade free.

The ten lamps faded like closing eyes.

※

Kaladin followed Szeth into the storm, diving into the blackness, falling amid the churning winds and the blasting lightning. Wind attacked him, tossing him about, and no Lashings could prevent this. He might be master of the winds, but storms were another thing.

Take care, Syl sent. *My father hates you. This is his domain. And it is mixed with something even more terrible, another storm. Their storm.*

Nevertheless, the highstorms were the source of Stormlight—and being in here *energized* Kaladin. His reserves of Stormlight burst alight, as they obviously did for Szeth. The assassin suddenly reappeared as a stark white explosion that zoomed through the maelstrom toward the plateaus.

Kaladin growled, Lashing himself after Szeth. Lightning of a dozen colors flashed around him, red, violet, white, yellow. Rain soaked him. Rocks spun past him, some colliding, but the Stormlight healed him as quickly as the debris did damage.

Szeth moved along the plateaus, coursing just above them, and Kaladin followed with difficulty. This churning wind was tough to navigate, and the darkness was near absolute. Flashes lit the Plains in fitful bursts. Fortunately, Szeth's glow could not be hidden, and Kaladin kept his attention on that blazing beacon.

Faster.

Just as Zahel had taught weeks ago, Szeth didn't need to defeat Kaladin to win. He just had to get to those Kaladin protected.

Faster.

A burst of lightning illuminated the battle plateaus. And beyond them, Kaladin caught a glimpse of the army. Thousands of men huddled on the large circular plateau. Many hunkered down. Others panicked.

The lightning was gone in a moment, and the land became dark again, though Kaladin had seen enough to know this was a disaster. A cataclysm. Men being blown off the edge, others crushed by falling rocks. In minutes, the army would be gone. Storms, Kaladin wasn't even certain if *he* could survive this nexus of destruction.

Szeth crashed down among them, a glowing light amid the blackness. As Kaladin Lashed himself down in that direction, lightning struck again.

Its light revealed Szeth standing on an empty plateau, baffled. The army was gone.

⁂

The sounds of the raging storm outside vanished. Shallan shivered, wet and cold.

"Almighty above . . ." Adolin breathed. "I'm almost scared of what we'll find."

Rotating the inside wall of the building had moved their doorway opposite hardened crem. Perhaps there had been a natural doorway here before; Adolin summoned his Blade to cut a hole.

Pattern . . . her Shardblade . . . vanished back to mist, and the room's mechanisms settled down. She didn't hear anything outside, no crashing of winds, no thunder.

Emotions fought inside of her. She'd saved herself and Adolin, it appeared. But the rest of the army . . . Adolin cut a doorway; sunlight spilled through it. Shallan walked to the opening, nervous, passing Inadara, who sat in the corner, looking overwhelmed.

At the doorway, Shallan looked out at the same plateau as before, only now it was sunlit and calm. Four armies' worth of men and women crouched, soggy and wet, many holding their heads and hunkering down against wind that no longer blew. Nearby, two figures stood beside a massive Ryshadium stallion. Dalinar and Navani, who had apparently been on their way to the central building.

Beyond them spread the peaks of an unfamiliar mountain range. It was the same plateau, and here was in a ring with nine others. To Shallan's left, an enormous ribbed tower—shaped like cups of increasingly smaller sizes stacked atop one another—broke the peaks. Urithiru.

The plateau hadn't contained the portal.

The plateau *was* the portal.

※

Szeth screamed words at Kaladin, but those were lost in the tempest. Rocks crashed down around them, ripped from somewhere distant. Kaladin was sure he heard terrible screams over the winds, as red spren he'd never seen before—like small meteors, trailing light behind them—zipped around him.

Szeth screamed again. Kaladin caught the word this time. "How!"

Kaladin's answer was to strike with his Blade. Szeth parried violently, and they clashed, two glowing figures in the blackness.

"I know this column!" Szeth screamed. "I have seen its like before! They went to the city, didn't they!"

The assassin launched himself into the air. Kaladin was all too eager to follow. He wanted out of this tempest.

Szeth screamed away, heading westward, away from the storm with the red lightning—following the path of the common highstorm. That alone was dangerous enough.

Kaladin gave chase, but that proved difficult in the buffeting winds. It wasn't that they served Szeth more than Kaladin; the tempest was simply unpredictable. They'd shove him one way and Szeth another.

What happened if Szeth lost him?

He knows where Dalinar went, Kaladin thought, gritting his teeth as a flash of sudden whiteness blinded him from one side. *I don't.*

He couldn't protect Dalinar if he couldn't find the man. Unfortunately, a chase through this darkness favored the person who was trying to escape. Slowly, Szeth pulled ahead.

Kaladin tried to follow, but a surge of wind drove him in the wrong direction. Lashings didn't really let him fly. He couldn't resist such unpredictable winds; they controlled him.

No! Szeth's glowing form dwindled. Kaladin shouted into the darkness, blinking eyes against the rain. He'd almost lost sight . . .

Syl spun into the air in front of him. But he was still carrying the spear. What?

Another one, then another. Ribbons of light, occasionally taking the shapes of young women or men, laughing. Windspren. A dozen or more spun around him, leaving trails of light, their laughter somehow strong over the sounds of the storm.

There! Kaladin thought.

Szeth was ahead. Kaladin Lashed himself through the tempest toward him, jerking one way, then the other. Dodging blitzes of lightning, ducking under hurled boulders, blinking away the sheets of driven rain.

A whirlwind of chaos. And ahead . . . light?

The stormwall.

Szeth burst free of the storm's very front. Through the mess of water and debris, Kaladin could just barely make out the assassin turning around to look backward, his posture confident.

He thinks he's lost me.

Kaladin exploded out of the stormwall, surrounded by windspren that spiraled away in a pattern of light. He shouted, driving his spear toward Szeth, who parried hastily, his eyes wide. "Impossible!"

Kaladin spun around and slashed his spear—which became a sword—through Szeth's foot.

The assassin lurched away along the length of the stormwall. Both Szeth and Kaladin continued to fall westward, just in front of the wall of water and debris.

Beneath them, the land passed in a blur. The two storms had finally separated, and the highstorm was moving along its normal path, east to west. The Shattered Plains were soon left behind, giving way to rolling hills.

As Kaladin chased, Szeth spun and fell backward, attacking, though Syl became a shield to block. Kaladin swung down and a hammer appeared in his hand, crashing against Szeth's shoulder, breaking bones. As Stormlight tried to heal the assassin, Kaladin pulled in close and slammed his hand against Szeth's stomach, a knife appearing there and digging deeply into the skin. He sought the spine.

Szeth gasped and frantically Lashed himself farther backward, pulling out of Kaladin's grip.

Kaladin followed. Boulders churned in the stormwall—which was now the ground from Kaladin's perspective. He had to repeatedly adjust his Lashing to stay in the right place, just ahead of the storm.

Kaladin leaped on churning boulders as they appeared, pursuing Szeth, who fell wildly, his clothing flapping. Windspren formed a halo around Kaladin, zipping in and out, spiraling, spinning around his arms and legs. The proximity of the storm kept his Stormlight stoked, never letting it grow dim.

Szeth slowed, his wounds healing. He hung in front of the crashing stormwall, holding his sword before him. He took a breath, meeting Kaladin's eyes.

An ending, then.

Kaladin drove forward, Syl forming a spear in his fingers, the most familiar weapon.

Szeth attacked in a sequence, a relentless blur of strikes.

Kaladin blocked each one. He ended with his spear against the hilt of Szeth's Blade, pressing the two together, mere inches from the assassin's face.

"It is actually true," Szeth whispered.

"Yes."

Szeth nodded, and the edge of tension seemed to fade from him, replaced by an emptiness in his eyes. "Then I was right all along. I was never Truthless. I could have stopped the murders at any time."

"I don't know what that means," Kaladin said. "But you never *had* to kill."

"My orders—"

"Excuses! If that was why you murdered, then you're not the evil man I assumed. You're a coward instead."

Szeth looked him in the eyes, then nodded. He pushed Kaladin back, then moved to swing.

Kaladin drove his hands forward, forming Syl into a sword. He expected a parry. The move was intended to draw Szeth out of his attack pattern.

Szeth did not parry. He just closed his eyes to accept the attack.

In that instant, for reasons he could not have articulated—pity, perhaps?—Kaladin diverted his blow, driving the Blade through Szeth's wrist. The skin greyed. Flashing with reflected lightning, the sword tumbled from the assassin's fingers, then *dulled* as it plummeted.

The glow fled the assassin's form. All his Stormlight vanished in a puff, all Lashings banished.

Szeth started to fall.

Get that sword! Syl sent to Kaladin, a mental shout. *Grab it.*

"The assassin!"

He has released the bond. He's nothing without that sword! It must not be lost!

Kaladin dove after the Blade, passing Szeth, who tumbled through the air like a rag doll, buffeted by winds toward the stormwall.

Kaladin furiously Lashed himself downward, snatching the Blade just before the storm consumed it. Nearby, the assassin dropped past him into the storm and was swallowed up, leaving Kaladin with the haunting image of Szeth's limp silhouette being driven into a plateau below with all the tempest's force.

Raising the assassin's Blade, Kaladin Lashed himself back upward, passing along the stormwall, the windspren he'd attracted spiraling about him and laughing with pure joy. As he crested the top of the storm, they burst around him and zipped away, moving off to dance in front of the still-advancing storm.

That left him with only one. Syl—in the form of a young woman in a fluttering dress, full-sized this time—hovered before him. She smiled as the storm moved beneath them.

"I didn't kill him," Kaladin said.

"Did you want to?"

"No," Kaladin said, surprised that it was the truth. "But I should have anyway."

"You have his Blade," she replied. "The Stormfather likely took him. And if not . . . well, he is no longer the weapon he once was. I must say, that was very nicely done. Perhaps I'll keep you around this time."

"Thank you."

"You almost killed me, you realize."

"I realize. I thought I had."

"And?"

"And . . . um . . . you are intelligent and articulate?"

"You forgot the compliment."

"But I just said—"

"Those were simple statements of fact."

"You're wonderful," he said. "Truly, Syl. You are."

"Also a fact," she said, grinning. "But I'll let it slide so long as you're willing to present me with a sufficiently sincere smile."

He did.

And it felt very, very good.

Chaos in Alethkar is, of course, inevitable. Watch carefully, and do not let power in the kingdom solidify. The Blackthorn could become an ally or our greatest foe, depending on whether he takes the path of the warlord or not. If he seems likely to sue for peace, assassinate him expeditiously. The risk of competition is too great.

—From the Diagram, Writings upon the Bedstand Lamp: paragraph 4
(Adrotagia's 3rd translation from the original hieroglyphics)

The Shattered Plains had been shattered again.

Kaladin strolled across them with Szeth's Shardblade on his shoulder. He passed heaps of rock and fresh cracks in the ground. Enormous puddles like small lakes shimmered amid huge chunks of broken stone. Just to his left, an entire plateau had crumbled into the chasms around it. The jagged, ripped-up base of the plateau had a black, charred cast to it.

He found no sign of Szeth's corpse. That could mean the man had survived somehow, or it could just mean the storm had buried the body in rubble or blown it away, leaving it in some forgotten chasm to rot until the bones were finally picked over by an unfortunate salvage crew.

For now, the fact that Szeth had not summoned his Blade back to him was enough. Either he was dead, or—as Syl had said—the strange weapon was no longer bound to him. Kaladin didn't know how to tell. This Shardblade had no gemstone at the pommel to indicate.

Kaladin stopped at a high point of the plateau and surveyed the wreckage.

Then he glanced toward Syl, who sat on his shoulder. "This is going to happen again?" he said. "That other storm is still out there?"

"Yes," Syl said. "A new storm. It's not of us, but of *him*."

"Will it be this bad every time it passes?" Of the plateaus he could see, only the one had been destroyed completely. But if the storm could do that to pure rock, what would it do to a city? Particularly since it blew the *wrong way*.

Stormfather . . . Laits would no longer be laits. Buildings that had been constructed to face away from the storms would suddenly be exposed.

"I don't know," Syl said softly. "This is a new thing, Kaladin. Not from before. I don't know how it happened or what it means. Hopefully, it won't be this bad except when a highstorm and an everstorm crash into each other."

Kaladin grunted, picking his way over to the edge of his current plateau. He breathed in a little Stormlight, then Lashed himself upward to offset the natural pull of the ground. He became weightless. He pushed off lightly with his foot and drifted across the chasm to the next plateau.

"So how did the army vanish like that?" he asked, removing his Lashing and settling down on the rock.

"Uh . . . how should I know?" Syl said. "I was *kind of* distracted."

He grunted. Well, this was the plateau where everyone had been. Perfectly round. Odd, that. On a nearby plateau, what had once been a large hill had been cracked wide open, exposing the remnants of a building inside. This perfectly circular one was far more flat, though it looked like there was a hill or something at the center. He strode in that direction.

"So they're all spren," he said. "Shardblades."

Syl grew solemn.

"Dead spren," Kaladin added.

"Dead," Syl agreed. "Then they live again a little when someone summons them, syncing a heartbeat to their essence."

"How can something be 'a little' alive?"

"We're spren," Syl said. "We're *forces*. You can't kill us completely. Just . . . sort of."

"That's perfectly clear."

"It's perfectly clear to us," Syl said. "You're the strange ones. Break a rock, and it's still there. Break a spren, and she's still there. Sort of. Break a person, and something leaves. Something changes. What's left is just meat. You're weird."

"I'm glad we established that," he said, stopping. He couldn't see any evidence of the Alethi. Had they really escaped? Or had a sudden surge of the storm swept them all into the chasms? It seemed unlikely such a disaster would have left *nothing* behind.

Please let it not be so. He lifted Szeth's sword off his shoulder and set it down, point first, in front of him. It sank a few inches into the rock.

"What about this?" he asked, looking over the thin, silvery weapon. An unornamented Blade. That was supposed to be odd. "It doesn't scream when I hold it."

"That's because it's not a spren," Syl said softly.

"What is it, then?"

"Dangerous."

She stood up from his shoulder, then walked as if down a flight of steps toward the sword. She rarely flew when she had a human form. She flew as a ribbon of light, or as a group of leaves, or as a small cloud. He'd never noticed before how odd, yet normal, it was that she stuck to the nature of the form she used.

She stopped just before the sword. "I think this is one of the Honor-blades, the swords of the Heralds."

Kaladin grunted. He'd heard of those.

"Any man who holds this weapon will become a Windrunner," Syl explained, looking back at Kaladin. "The Honorblades are what we are based on, Kaladin. Honor gave these to men, and those men gained powers from them. Spren figured out what He'd done, and we imitated it. We're bits of His power, after all, like this sword. Be careful with it. It is a treasure."

"So the assassin wasn't a Radiant."

"No. But Kaladin, you have to understand. With this sword, someone can do what you can, but without the . . . checks a spren requires." She touched it, then shivered visibly, her form blurring for a second. "This sword gave the assassin power to use Lashings, but it also fed upon his Storm-light. A person who uses this will need far, far more Light than you will. Dangerous levels of it."

Kaladin reached out and took the sword by the hilt, and Syl flitted away, becoming a ribbon of light. He hefted the weapon and set it back on his shoulder before continuing on his way. Yes, there was a hill up ahead, probably a crem-covered building. As he drew closer, blessedly, he saw motion around it.

"Hello?" he called.

The figures near it stopped and turned. "Kaladin?" a familiar voice called. "Storms, is that you?"

He grinned, the figures resolving into men in blue uniforms. Teft scrambled across the rock like a madman to meet him. Others came after, shouting and laughing. Drehy, Peet, Bisig, and Sigzil, Rock towering over them all.

"Another one?" Rock asked, eyeing Kaladin's Shardblade. "Or is he yours?"

"No," Kaladin said. "I took this from the assassin."

"He is dead, then?" Teft asked.

"Near enough."

"You *defeated* the Assassin in White," Bisig breathed. "It's truly over then."

"I suspect that it is just beginning," Kaladin said, nodding toward the building. "What is this place?"

"Oh!" Bisig said. "Come on! We need to show you the tower—that Radiant girl taught us how to summon the plateau back, so long as we have you."

"Radiant girl?" Kaladin asked. "Shallan?"

"You don't sound surprised," Teft said with a grunt.

"She has a Shardblade," Kaladin said. One that didn't scream in his mind. Either she was a Radiant or she had another of these Honorblades. As he stepped up to the building, he noticed a bridge in the shadows nearby.

"It's not ours," Kaladin said.

"No," Leyten said. "That belongs to Bridge Seventeen. We had to leave ours behind in the storm."

Rock nodded. "We were too busy stopping lighteyed heads from becoming too friendly with swords of enemies. Ha! But we needed bridge here. Way platform works, we had to get off him for Shallan Davar to transport herself back."

Kaladin poked his head into the chamber inside the hill, then paused at the beauty he found inside. Other members of Bridge Four waited here, including a tall man Kaladin didn't immediately recognize. Was that one of Lopen's cousins? The man turned around, and Kaladin realized what he'd mistaken for a cap was a reddish skullplate.

Parshendi. Kaladin tensed as the Parshendi man *saluted*. He was wearing a Bridge Four uniform.

And he had the tattoo.

"Rlain?" Kaladin said.

"Sir," Rlain said. His features were no longer rounded and plump, but instead sharp, muscular, with a thick neck and a stronger jaw, now lined by a red and black beard.

"It appears you are more than you seemed," Kaladin said.

"Pardon, sir," he said. "But I would suggest that applies to both of us." When he spoke now, his voice had a certain musicality to it—an odd rhythm to his words.

"Brightlord Dalinar has pardoned Rlain," Sigzil explained, walking around Kaladin and entering the chamber.

"For being Parshendi?" Kaladin asked.

"For being a spy," Rlain said. "A spy for a people who, it appears, no longer exist." He said this to a different beat, and Kaladin thought he could sense pain in that voice. Rock walked over and put a hand on Rlain's shoulder.

"We can give you the story once we get back to the city," Teft said.

"We figured you'd come back here," Sigzil added. "To this plateau, and so we needed to be here to greet you, for all Brightness Davar grumbled.

Anyway, there's a lot to tell—a lot is happening. I think that you're kind of going to be at the center of it."

Kaladin took a deep breath, but nodded. What else did he expect? No more hiding. He had made his decision.

What do I tell them about Moash? he wondered as the members of Bridge Four piled into the room around him, chattering about how he needed to infuse the spheres in the lanterns. A couple of the men bore wounds from the fighting, including Bisig, who kept his right hand in his coat pocket. Grey skin peeked out from the cuff. He'd lost the hand to the Assassin in White.

Kaladin pulled Teft aside. "Did we lose anyone else?" Kaladin asked. "I saw Mart and Pedin."

"Rod," Teft said with a grunt. "Dead to the Parshendi."

Kaladin closed his eyes, breathing out in a hiss. Rod had been one of Lopen's cousins, a jovial Herdazian who hardly spoke Alethi. Kaladin had barely known him, but the man had still been Bridge Four. Kaladin's responsibility.

"You can't protect us all, son," Teft said. "You can't stop people from feeling pain, can't stop men from dying."

Kaladin opened his eyes, but did not challenge those statements. Not vocally, at least.

"Kal," Teft said, voice getting even softer. "At the end there, right before you arrived . . . Storms, son, I swear I saw a couple of the lads glowing. Faintly, with Stormlight."

"What?"

"I've been listening to readings of those visions Brightlord Dalinar sees," Teft continued. "I think you should do the same. From what I can guess, it seems that the orders of the Knights Radiant were made up of more than just the knights themselves."

Kaladin looked over the men of Bridge Four, and found himself smiling. He shoved down the pain at his losses, at least for the time being. "I wonder," he said softly, "what it will do to Alethi social structure when an entire *group* of former slaves starts going about with glowing skin."

"Not to mention those eyes of yours," Teft said with a grunt.

"Eyes?" Kaladin said.

"Haven't you seen?" Teft said. "What am I saying? Ain't no mirrors out on the Plains. Your eyes, son. Pale blue, like glassy water. Lighter than that of any king."

Kaladin turned away. He'd hoped his eyes wouldn't change. The truth, that they had, made him uncomfortable. It said worrisome things. He didn't want to believe that lighteyes had any grounds upon which to build the oppression.

They still don't, he thought, infusing the gemstones in the lanterns as Sigzil instructed him. *Perhaps the lighteyes rule because of the memory, buried deeply, of the Radiants. But just because they* look *a little like Radiants doesn't mean they should have been able to oppress everyone.*

Storming lighteyes. He . . .

He was one of them now.

Storm it!

He summoned Syl as a Blade, following Sigzil's instructions, and used her as a key to work the fabrial.

⁂

Shallan stood at the front gates of Urithiru, looking up, trying to comprehend.

Inside, voices echoed in the grand hall and lights bobbed as people explored. Adolin had taken command of that endeavor, while Navani set up a camp to see to the wounded and to measure supplies. Unfortunately, they'd left most of their food and gear behind on the Shattered Plains. In addition, the travel through the Oathgate had not been as cheap as Shallan had first assumed. Somehow, the trip had drained the majority of the gemstones held by the men and women on the plateau—including Navani's fabrials, clutched in the hands of engineers and scholars.

They had run a few tests. The more people you moved, the more Light was required. It seemed that Stormlight, and not just the gemstones that contained it, would become a valuable resource. Already, they had to ration their gemstones and lanterns to explore the building.

Several scribes passed by, bringing paper to draw out maps of Adolin's exploration. They bobbed quick, uncomfortable bows to Shallan and called her "Brightness Radiant." She still hadn't talked at length with Adolin about what had happened to her.

"Is it true?" Shallan asked, tilting her head all the way back, looking up the side of the enormous tower toward the blue sky high above. "Am I one of them?"

"Mmm . . ." Pattern said from her skirt. "Almost you are. Still a few Words to say."

"What kind of words? An oath?"

"Lightweavers make no oaths beyond the first," Pattern said. "You must speak truths."

Shallan stared up at the heights for a time longer, then turned and walked back down toward their improvised camp. It was not the Weeping here. She wasn't certain if that was because they were actually *above* the rainclouds, or if the weather patterns had simply been thrown off by the arrival of the strange highstorms.

In camp, men sat on the stone, divided by ranks, shivering in their wet coats. Shallan's breath puffed before her, though she had taken in Stormlight—just a dash—to keep herself from noticing the cold. Unfortunately, there wasn't much to use for fires. The large stone field in front of the tower city bore very few rockbuds, and the ones that did grow were tiny, smaller than a fist. They would provide little wood for fires.

The field was ringed by ten columnar plateaus, with steps winding around their bases. The Oathgates. Beyond that extended the mountain range.

Crem did cover some of the steps here, and dripped over the sides of the open field. There wasn't nearly as much as there had been on the Shattered Plains. Less rain must fall up here.

Shallan stepped up to one edge of the stone field. A sheer drop. If Nohadon really *had* walked to this city, as *The Way of Kings* claimed, then his path would have included scaling cliff faces. So far, they had found no way down other than through the Oathgates—and even if there were such a way, one would still be stranded in the middle of the mountains, weeks from civilization. Judging from the sun height, the scholars placed them near the center of Roshar, somewhere in the mountains near Tu Bayla or maybe Emul.

The remote location made the city incredibly defensible, or so Dalinar said. It also left them isolated, potentially cut off. And that, in turn, explained why everyone looked at Shallan as they did. They'd tried other Shardblades; none were effective at making the ancient fabrial work. Shallan was literally their only way out of these mountains.

One of the soldiers nearby cleared his throat. "You certain you should be that close to the edge, Brightness Radiant?"

She gave the man a droll look. "I could survive that drop and stroll away, soldier."

"Um, yes, Brightness," he said, blushing.

She left the edge and continued on to find Dalinar. Eyes followed her as she walked: soldiers, scribes, lighteyes, and highlords alike. Well, let them see Shallan the Radiant. She could always find freedom later, wearing another face.

Dalinar and Navani supervised a group of women near the center of the army. "Any luck?" Shallan asked, approaching.

Dalinar glanced at her. The scribes wrote letters using every spanreed they had, delivering messages of warning to the warcamps and to the relay room in Tashikk. *A new storm might come, blowing in from the west, not the east. Prepare.*

New Natanan, on the very eastern coast of Roshar, would be struck today after the everstorm left the Shattered Plains. Then it would enter the eastern ocean and move toward the Origin.

None of them knew what would happen next. Would it round the world and come crashing into the western coast? Were the highstorms all one storm that rounded the planet, or did a new one start at the Origin each time, as mythology claimed?

Scholars and stormwardens thought the former, these days. Their calculations said that, assuming the everstorm moved at the same speed as a highstorm this time of year, they'd have a few days before it returned and hit Shinovar and Iri, then blew across the continent, laying waste to cities thought protected.

"No news," Dalinar said, voice tense. "The king seems to have vanished. What's more, Kholinar appears to be in a state of riot. I haven't been able to get straight answers on either question."

"I'm sure the king is somewhere safe," Shallan said, glancing at Navani. The woman maintained a composed face, but as she gave instructions to a scribe, her voice was terse and clipped.

One of the pillarlike plateaus nearby flashed. It happened with a wall of light revolving around its perimeter, leaving streaks of blurred afterimage to fade. Someone had activated the Oathgate.

Dalinar stepped up beside her and they waited tensely, until a group of figures in blue appeared at the plateau edge and started down the steps. Bridge Four.

"Oh, thank the *Almighty*," Shallan whispered. It was him, not the assassin.

One of the figures pointed down toward where Dalinar and the rest of them stood. Kaladin separated from his men, dropping *off* the steps and floating over the army. He landed on the stones in stride, carrying a Shardblade on his shoulder, his long officer's coat unbuttoned and coming down to his knees.

He still has the slave brands, she thought, though his long hair obscured them. His eyes had become a pale blue. They glowed softly.

"Stormblessed," Dalinar called.

"Highprince," Kaladin said.

"The assassin?"

"Dead," Kaladin said, hefting the Blade and sticking it down into the rock before Dalinar. "We need to talk. This—"

"My son, bridgeman," Navani asked from behind. She stepped up and took Kaladin by the arm, as if completely unconcerned by the Stormlight that drifted from his skin like smoke. "What happened to my son?"

"There was an assassination attempt," Kaladin said. "I stopped it, but the king was wounded. I put him someplace safe before coming to help Dalinar."

"Where?" Navani demanded. "We've had our people in the warcamps search monasteries, mansions, the barracks . . ."

"Those places were too obvious," Kaladin said. "If you could think to look there, so might the assassins. I needed someplace nobody would think of."

"Where, then?" Dalinar asked.

Kaladin smiled.

．．．

The Lopen made a fist with his hand, clutching the sphere inside. In the next room over, his mother scolded a king.

"No, no, Your Majesty," she said, words thickly accented, using the same stern tone she used with the axehounds. "You roll the whole thing up and eat it. You can't pick it apart like that."

"I don't feel so hungry, nanha," Elhokar said. His voice was weak, but he'd awoken from his drunken stupor, which was a good sign.

"You'll eat anyway!" Mother said. "I know what to do when I see a man that pale in the face, and pardon, Your Majesty, but you are pale as a sheet hung out for the sun to bleach! And that's the truth of it. You're going to eat. No complaints."

"I'm the king. I don't take orders from—"

"You're in my home now!" she said, and Lopen mouthed along with the words. "In a Herdazian woman's home, nobody's station means nothing beside her own. I'm not going to have them come and get you and find you not properly fed! I'll not have people saying that, Your Brightship, no I won't! Eat up. I've got soup cooking."

The Lopen smiled, and though he heard the king grumble, he *also* heard the sound of spoon against plate. Two of Lopen's strongest cousins sat out front of the hovel in Little Herdaz—which was technically in Highprince Sebarial's warcamp, though the Herdazians didn't pay much attention to that. Four more cousins sat at the end of the street, idly sewing some boots, watching for anything suspicious.

"All right," Lopen whispered, "you really need to work this time." He focused on that sphere in his hand. Just like he did every day, and had done every day since Captain Kaladin had started glowing. He'd figure it out sooner or later. He was as sure of it as he was sure of his name.

"Lopen." A wide face ducked in one of the windows, distracting him. Chilinko, his uncle. "Get the king man dressed up like a Herdazian again. We might need to move."

"Move?" Lopen said, standing.

"Word has come in to all the warcamps from Highprince Sebarial," Chilinko said in Herdazian. "They found something out there, on the Plains. Be ready. Just in case. Everyone's talking. I can't make sense of it." He shook his head. "First that highstorm nobody knew about, then the rains stop early, then the storming *king man of Alethkar* on my doorstep. Now this. I think we might be abandoning camp, even though nightfall's around the corner. Makes no sense to me, but get the king man taken care of."

The Lopen nodded. "I'll get to it. Just a sec."

Chilinko ducked away. Lopen opened his palm and stared at the sphere. He didn't want to miss a day practicing with his sphere, just in case. After all, sooner or later, he was going to look at one of these and—

The Lopen sucked in Light.

It happened in an eyeblink, and then there he sat, Stormlight streaming from his skin.

"Ha!" he shouted, leaping to his feet. "*Ha!* Hey, Chilinko, come back here. I need to stick you to the wall!"

The Light winked out. The Lopen stopped, frowning, and held his hand up in front of him. Gone so fast? What had happened? He hesitated. That tingling . . .

He felt at his shoulder, the one where he'd lost his arm so long ago. There, his fingers prodded a new nub of flesh that had begun sprouting from his scar.

"Oh, *storms* yes! Everybody, give the Lopen your spheres! I have glowing that needs to be done."

⁙

Moash sat on the back of the cart as it rattled and wound its way out of the warcamps. He could have ridden in front, but he didn't want to be far from his armor, which they'd wrapped up in packages and stacked back here. Hidden. The Blade and Plate might be his in name, but he had no illusions as to what would happen if the Alethi elite noticed him trying to flee with it.

His wagon crested the rise just outside of the warcamps. Behind them, enormous lines of people snaked out onto the Shattered Plains. Highprince Dalinar's orders had been clear, though baffling. The warcamps were being abandoned. All parshmen were to be left behind, and everyone was to make their way toward the center of the Shattered Plains.

Some of the highprinces obeyed. Others did not. Curiously, Sadeas was one of those who obeyed, his warcamp emptying almost as quickly as those of Sebarial, Roion, and Aladar. It seemed like everyone was going, even the children.

Moash's cart rolled to a stop. Graves stepped up beside the back a few moments later. "We needn't have worried about hiding," he mumbled, looking over the exodus. "They're too busy to pay attention to us. Look there."

Some groups of merchants gathered outside of Dalinar's warcamps. They pretended to be packing to leave, but weren't making any obvious progress.

"Scavengers," Graves said. "They'll head into the abandoned warcamps to loot. Storming fools. They deserve what is coming."

"What *is* coming?" Moash said. He felt as if he had been tossed into a roiling river, one that had burst its banks following a highstorm. He swam with the current, but could barely keep his head above water.

He'd tried to kill Kaladin. *Kaladin*. It had all fallen apart. The king survived, Kaladin's powers were back, and Moash . . . Moash was a traitor. Twice over.

"Everstorm," Graves said. He didn't look nearly so refined, now that he wore the patchwork overalls and shirt of a poor darkeyes. He'd used some strange eyedrops to change his eyes dark, then had instructed Moash to do the same.

"And that is?"

"The Diagram is vague," Graves said. "We only knew the term because of old Gavilar's visions. The Diagram says this will probably return the Void-bringers, though. Those have turned out to be the parshmen, it seems." He shook his head. "Damnation. That woman was right."

"Woman?"

"Jasnah Kholin."

Moash shook his head. He didn't understand *any* of what was happening. Graves's sentences felt like strings of words that shouldn't go together. Parshmen, Voidbringers? Jasnah Kholin? That was the king's sister. Hadn't she died at sea? What did Graves know of her?

"Who are you really?" Moash asked.

"A patriot," Graves said. "Just like I told you. We're allowed to pursue our own interests and goals until we're called up." He shook his head. "I thought for sure my interpretation was correct, that if we removed Elho-kar, Dalinar would become our ally in what is to come. . . . Well, it appears I was wrong. Either that, or I was too slow."

Moash felt sick.

Graves gripped him on the arm. "Head up, Moash. Bringing a Shard-bearer back with me will mean that my mission wasn't a *complete* loss. Besides, you can tell us about this new Radiant. I'll introduce you to the Diagram. We have an important work."

"Which is?"

"The salvation of the entire world, my friend." Graves patted him, then walked toward the front of the cart, where the others rode.

The salvation of the entire world.

I've been played for one of the ten fools, Moash thought, chin to his chest. *And I don't even know how.*

The wagon started rolling again.

88

THE MAN WHO OWNED THE WINDS

1173090605   1173090801   1173090901   1173091001
1173091004   1173100105   1173100205   1173100401
1173100603   1173100804

—From the Diagram, North Wall Coda,
Windowsill region: paragraph 2
(This appears to be a sequence of dates,
but their relevance is as yet unknown.)

They soon began to move into the tower.

There was nothing else they could do, though Adolin's explorations were far from finished. Night was approaching, and the temperature was dropping outside. Beyond that, the highstorm that had hit the Shattered Plains would be raging across the land currently, and would eventually hit these mountains. It took over a day for one to cross the entire continent, and they were probably somewhere near the center, so it would be growing close.

An unscheduled highstorm, Shallan thought, walking through the dark hallways with her guards. *And something* else *coming from the other direction.*

She could tell that this tower—its contents, every hallway—was a majestic wonder. It spoke worlds about how tired she was that she didn't want to draw any of it. She just wanted to sleep.

Their spherelight revealed something odd on the wall ahead. Shallan frowned, shaking off her fatigue and stepping up to it. A small folded piece of paper, like a card. She glanced back at her guards, who looked equally confused.

She pulled the card off the wall; it had been stuck in place with some weevilwax on the back. Inside was the triangle symbol of the Ghostbloods. Beneath it, Shallan's name. Not Veil's name.

Shallan's.

Panic. Alertness. In a moment, she had sucked in the Light of their lantern, plunging the corridor into darkness. Light shone from a doorway nearby, however.

She stared at it. Gaz moved to investigate, but Shallan stopped him with a gesture.

Run or fight?

Run where? she thought. Hesitant, she stepped up to the doorway, again motioning her guards back.

Mraize stood inside, gazing out a large, glassless window that overlooked another section of the innards of this tower. He turned toward her, twisted and scarred, yet somehow refined in his gentleman's clothing.

So. She had been found out.

I am no longer a child who hides in her room when the shouting comes, she thought firmly to herself, walking into the room. *If I run from this man, he will see me as something to be hunted.*

She stepped right up to him, ready to summon Pattern. He wasn't like other Shardblades; she acknowledged that now. He could come more quickly than the ten requisite heartbeats.

He'd done that before. She hadn't been willing to admit that he was capable of it. Admitting that would have meant too much.

How many more of my lies, she thought, *hold me back from things I could accomplish?*

But she needed those lies. *Needed* them.

"You led me on a grand hunt, Veil," Mraize said. "If your abilities had not been manifest during the course of saving the army, I perhaps never would have located your false identity."

"Veil is the false identity, Mraize," Shallan said. "I am me."

He inspected her. "I think not."

She met that gaze, but shivered inside.

"A curious position you are in," Mraize said. "Will you hide the true nature of your powers? I was able to guess what they are, but others will not be so knowledgeable. They might see only the Blade, and not ask what else you can do."

"I don't see how it's a concern of yours."

"You are one of us," Mraize said. "We look after our own."

Shallan frowned. "But you've seen through the lie."

"Are you saying you don't want to be one of the Ghostbloods?" His tone was not threatening, but those eyes . . . storms, those eyes could have drilled through stone. "We do not offer the invitation to just any-one."

"You killed Jasnah," Shallan hissed.

"Yes. After she, in turn, had assassinated a number of our members. You didn't think her hands were clean of blood, did you, Veil?"

She looked away, breaking his gaze.

"I should have guessed that you would turn out to be Shallan Davar," Mraize continued. "I feel a fool for not seeing it earlier. Your family has a long history of involvement in these events."

"I will not help you," Shallan said.

"Curious. You should know that I have your brothers."

She looked to him sharply.

"Your house is no more," Mraize said. "Your family's grounds seized by a passing army. I rescued your brothers from the chaos of the succession war, and am bringing them here. Your family, however, does owe me a debt. One Soulcaster. Broken."

He met her eyes. "How convenient that you, by my estimations, *are* one, little knife."

She summoned Pattern. "I will kill you before I let you use them as blackmail—"

"No blackmail," Mraize said. "They will arrive safe. A gift to you. You may wait upon my words and see. I mention your debt only so that it has a chance to find . . . purchase in your mind."

She frowned, holding her Shardblade, wavering. "Why?" she finally asked.

"Because, you are ignorant." Mraize stepped closer to her, towering over her. "You don't know who we are. You don't know what we're trying to accomplish. You don't know much of anything at all, Veil. Why did your father join us? Why did your brother seek out the Skybreakers? I have done some research, you see. I have answers for you." Surprisingly, he turned from her and walked toward the doorway. "I will give you time to consider. You seem to think that your newfound place among the Radiants makes you unfit for our numbers, but I see it differently, as does my *babsk*. Let Shallan Davar be a Radiant, conformist and noble. Let Veil come to us." He stopped by the doorway. "And let her find truth."

He disappeared into the hallway. Shallan found herself feeling even more drained than before. She dismissed Pattern and leaned back against the wall. Of *course* Mraize would have found his way here—he'd likely been among the armies, somewhere. Getting to Urithiru had been one of the Ghost-bloods' primary goals. Despite her determination not to help them, she'd transported them—along with the army—right where they wanted to go.

Her brothers? Would they actually be safe? What of her family servants, her brother's betrothed?

She sighed, walking to the doorway and collecting her guards. *Let her find truth.* What if she didn't want to find the truth? Pattern hummed softly.

After walking through the tower's ground floor—using her own glow for light—she found Adolin in the hallway beside a room, where he'd said he'd be. He had his wrist wrapped, and the bruises on his face were starting to purple. They made him look *slightly* less intoxicatingly handsome, though there was a rugged "I punched a lot of people today" quality to that, which was fetching in its own right.

"You look exhausted," he said, giving her a peck of a kiss.

"And you look like you let someone play sticks with your face," she said, but smiled at him. "You should get some sleep too."

"I will," he said. "Soon." He touched her face. "You're amazing, you realize. You saved everything. Everyone."

"No need to treat me like I'm glass, Adolin."

"You're a Radiant," he said. "I mean . . ." He ran his hand through his persistently messy hair. "Shallan. You're something greater than even a lighteyes."

"Was that a wisecrack about my girth?"

"What? No. I mean . . ." He blushed.

"I will *not* let this be awkward, Adolin."

"But—"

She grabbed him in an embrace and forced him into a kiss, a deep and passionate one. He tried to mumble something, but she kept on kissing, pressing her lips against his, letting him feel her desire. He melted into the kiss, then grabbed her by the torso and pulled her close.

After a moment, he pulled back. "Storms, that smarts!"

"Oh!" Shallan raised a hand to her mouth, remembering the bruises on his face. "Sorry."

He grinned, then winced again, as apparently that hurt too. "Worth it. Anyway, I'll promise to avoid being awkward if you avoid being too irresistible. At least until I'm healed up. Deal?"

"Deal."

He looked to her guards. "Nobody disturbs the Lady Radiant, understand?"

They nodded.

"Sleep well," he said, pushing open a door into the room. Many of the rooms still had wooden doors, despite their long abandonment. "Hopefully, the room is suitable. Your spren chose it."

Her spren? Shallan frowned, then stepped into the room. Adolin closed the door.

Shallan studied the windowless stone chamber. Why had Pattern chosen this particular place for her? The room didn't seem distinctive. Adolin had left a Stormlight lantern for her—that was extravagant, considering how few lit gemstones they had—and it showed a small square chamber with a stone bench in the corner. There were a few blankets on it. Where had Adolin found blankets?

She frowned at the wall. The rock here was faded in a square, as if someone had once hung a picture there. Actually, that looked oddly familiar. Not that she'd been here before, but the place that square hung on the wall . . .

It was exactly in the same place where the picture had hung on her father's wall back in Jah Keved.

Her mind started to fuzz.

"Mmm . . ." Pattern said from the floor beside her. "It is time."

"No."

"It is time," he repeated. "The Ghostbloods circle you. The people need a Radiant."

"They have one. The bridgeboy."

"Not enough. They need you."

Shallan blinked out tears. Against her will, the room started to change. White carpet appeared. A picture on the wall. Furniture. Walls painted light blue.

Two corpses.

Shallan stepped over one, though it was just an illusion, and walked to the wall. A painting had appeared, part of the illusion, and it was outlined with a white glow. Something was hidden behind it. She pulled aside the picture, or tried to. Her fingers only made the illusion blur.

This was nothing. Just a re-creation of a memory she wished she didn't have.

"Mmm . . . A better lie, Shallan."

She blinked away tears. Her fingers lifted, and she pressed them against the wall again. This time, she could *feel* the painting's frame. It wasn't real. For the moment, she pretended that it was, and let the image capture her.

"Can't I just keep pretending?"

"No."

She was there, in her father's room. Trembling, she pulled aside the picture, revealing the strongbox in the wall beyond. She raised the key, and hesitated. "Mother's soul is inside."

"Mmm . . . No. Not her soul. That which took her soul."

Shallan unlocked the safe, then tugged it open, revealing the contents. A small Shardblade. Thrust into the strongbox hastily, tip piercing through the back, hilt toward her.

"This was you," she whispered.

"Mmm . . . Yes."

"Father took you from me," Shallan said, "and tried to hide you in here.

Of course, that was useless. You vanished as soon as he closed the strongbox. Faded to mist. He wasn't thinking clearly. Neither of us were."

She turned.

Red carpet. Once white. Her mother's friend lay on the floor, bleeding from the arm, though that wound hadn't killed him. Shallan walked to the other corpse, the one facedown in the beautiful dress of blue and gold. Red hair spilled out in a pattern around the head.

Shallan knelt and rolled over her mother's corpse, confronting a skull with burned-out eyes.

"Why did she try to kill me, Pattern?" Shallan whispered.

"Mmm . . ."

"It started when she found out what I could do."

She remembered it now. Her mother's arrival, with a friend Shallan didn't recognize, to confront her father. Her mother's shouts, arguing with her father.

Mother calling Shallan one of *them*.

Her father barging in. Mother's friend with a knife, the two struggling, the friend getting cut in the arm. Blood spilled on the carpet. The friend had won that fight, eventually holding Father down, pinned on the ground. Mother took the knife and came for Shallan.

And then . . .

And then a sword in Shallan's hands.

"He let everyone believe that *he'd* killed her," Shallan whispered. "That he'd murdered his wife and her lover in a rage, when I was the one who had actually killed them. He lied to protect me."

"I know."

"That secret destroyed him. It destroyed our entire family."

"I know."

"I hate you," she whispered, staring into her mother's dead eyes.

"I know." Pattern buzzed softly. "Eventually, you will kill me, and you will have your revenge."

"I don't want revenge. I want my family."

Shallan wrapped her arms around herself and buried her head in them, weeping as the illusion bled white smoke, then vanished, leaving her in an empty room.

⁘

I can only conclude, Amaram wrote hurriedly, the glyphs a mess of sloppy ink, *that we have been successful, Restares. The reports from Dalinar's army indicate that Voidbringers were not only spotted, but fought. Red eyes, ancient powers. They have apparently unleashed a new storm upon this world.*

He looked up from his pad and peeked out the window. His carriage rattled down the roadway in Dalinar's warcamp. All of his soldiers were away, and his remaining guards had gone to oversee the exodus. Even with Amaram's reputation, he'd been able to pass into the camp with ease.

He turned back to his paper. *I do not exult in this success,* he wrote. *Lives will be lost. It has ever been our burden as the Sons of Honor. To return the Heralds, to return the dominance of the Church, we had to put the world into a crisis.*

That crisis we now have, a terrible one. The Heralds will return. How can they not, with the problems we now face? But many will die. So very many. Nalan send that it is worth the loss. Regardless, I will have more information soon. When I next write you, I hope to do so from Urithiru.

The coach pulled to a stop and Amaram pushed open the door. He handed the letter to the carriage driver, Pama. She took it and began digging in her satchel for the spanreed to send the communication to Restares. He would have done it himself, but you could not use a spanreed while moving.

She would destroy the papers when done. Amaram spared a glance for the trunks on the back of the coach; they contained a precious cargo, including all of his maps, notes, and theories. Should he have left those with his soldiers? Bringing the force of fifty into Dalinar's warcamp would have drawn attention for certain, even with the chaos here, so he'd ordered them to meet him on the Plains.

He needed to keep moving. He strode away from the coach, pulling up the hood on his cloak. The grounds of Dalinar's temple complex were even more frenzied than most of the warcamps, as many people had come to the ardents in this time of stress. He passed a mother begging for one of them to burn a prayer for her husband, who fought with Dalinar's army. The ardent kept repeating that she should gather her things and join the caravans heading out across the Plains.

It was happening. It was *really* happening. The Sons of Honor had, at long last, achieved their goal. Gavilar would be proud. Amaram hastened his pace, turning as another ardent bustled up to him, to ask if he needed anything. Before she could look in his hood and recognize him, however, her attention was drawn by a pair of frightened youths who complained that their father was too old to make the trip, and begged for the ardents to help them carry him somehow.

He made it to the corner of the monastery building where they kept the insane and rounded to the back wall, out of sight, near the rim of the warcamp itself. He looked about, then summoned his Blade. A few swift slices would—

What was that?

He spun, certain he'd seen someone approach. But it was nothing. Shadows playing tricks on him. He made his slices in the wall and then carefully pushed open the hole he'd made. The Great One—Talenelat'Elin, Herald of War himself—sat in the dark room, in much the same posture he'd borne before. Perched on the end of his bed, slumped forward, head bowed.

"Why must they keep you in such darkness?" Amaram said, dismissing his Blade. "This is not fit for the lowliest of men, let alone one such as yourself. I will have words with Dalinar about the way the insane are—"

No, he would not. Dalinar thought him a murderer. Amaram drew in a long, deep breath. Prices would need to be paid to see the Heralds return, but by Jezerezeh himself, the loss of Dalinar's friendship would be a stiff one indeed. Would that mercy had not stayed his hand, all those months ago, when he could have executed that spearman.

He hastened to the Herald's side. "Great Prince," Amaram whispered. "We must go."

Talenelat did not move. He was whispering again, though. The same things as before. Amaram could not help being reminded of the last time he had visited this place, in the company of someone who had been playing him for one of the ten fools all along. Who knew that Dalinar had grown so crafty in his old age? Time had changed both of them.

"Please, Great Prince," Amaram said, getting the Herald to his feet with some difficulty. The man was enormous, as tall as Amaram but built like a wall. The dark brown skin had surprised him the first time he'd seen the man—Amaram had, somewhat foolishly, expected that all of the Heralds would look Alethi.

The Herald's dark eyes were, of course, some kind of disguise.

"The Desolation . . ." Talenelat whispered.

"Yes. It comes. And with it, your return to glory." Amaram began to walk the Herald toward his opening. "We must get you to—"

The Herald's hand snapped up in front of him.

Amaram started, freezing in place, as he saw something in the Herald's fingers. A small dart, the tip dripping with some clear liquid.

Amaram glanced at the opening, which spilled sunlight into the room. A small figure there made a puffing sound, a blowgun held to lips beneath a half mask that covered the upper face.

The Herald's other hand shot out, quick as an eyeblink, and snatched the dart from the air mere inches from Amaram's face. The Ghostbloods. They weren't trying to kill the Herald.

They were trying to kill Amaram.

He cried out, reaching his hand to the side, summoning his Blade. Too slow. The figure looked from him to the Herald, then scuttled away with a soft curse. Amaram chased after, leaping the rubble of the wall and breaking out into light, but the figure was moving too quickly.

Heart thumping in his chest, he looked back toward Talenelat, worried for the Herald's safety. Amaram started as he found the Herald standing tall, straight-backed, head up. Dark brown eyes, startlingly lucid, reflected the light of the opening. Talenelat raised one dart before himself and inspected it.

Then he dropped both darts and sat back down on his bed. His strange, unchanging mantra started over again, muttered. Amaram felt a chill run down his spine, but when he returned to the Herald, he could not get the man to respond.

With effort, he made the Herald rise again and ushered him to the coach.

⋄

Szeth opened his eyes.

He immediately squeezed them closed again. "No. I died. I died!"

He felt rock beneath him. Blasphemy. He heard water dripping and felt the sun on his face. "Why am I not dead?" he whispered. "I released my bond to the Shardblade. I fell into the storm without Lashings. Why didn't I die?"

"You *did* die."

Szeth opened his eyes again. He lay on an empty rock expanse, his clothing a wet mess. The Frostlands? He felt cold, despite the heat of the sun.

A man stood before him, wearing a crisp black and silver uniform. He had dark brown skin like a man from the Makabaki region, but had a pale mark on his right cheek in the shape of a small hooked crescent. He held one hand behind his back, while his other hand tucked something away into his coat pocket. A fabrial of some sort? Glowing brightly?

"I recognize you," Szeth realized. "I've seen you somewhere before."

"You have."

Szeth struggled to rise. He managed to make it to his knees, then knelt back on them. "How?" he asked.

"I waited until you crashed to the ground," the man said, "until you were broken and mangled, your soul cut through, dead for certain. Then, I restored you."

"Impossible."

"Not if it is done before the brain dies. Like a drowned man restored with the proper ministrations, you could be restored with the right Surgebinding. If I had waited seconds longer, of course, it would have been too late. But surely you know this. Two of the Blades held by your people allow Regrowth. I suspect you have already seen the newly dead restored to life."

He spoke the words calmly, without emotion.

"Who are you?" Szeth asked.

"You spend this long obeying the precepts of your people and religion, yet you fail to recognize one of your gods?"

"My gods are the spirits of the stones," Szeth whispered. "The sun and the stars. Not men."

"Nonsense. Your people revere the spren of stone, but *you* do not worship them."

That crescent . . . He recognized it, didn't he?

"You, Szeth," the man said, "worship order, do you not? You follow the laws of your society to perfection. This attracted me, though I worry that emotion has clouded your ability to discern. Your ability to . . . judge."

Judgment.

"Nin," he whispered. "The one they call Nalan, or Nale, here. Herald of Justice."

Nin nodded.

"Why save me?" Szeth said. "Is my torment not enough?"

"Those words are foolishness," Nin said. "Unbecoming of one who would study beneath me."

"I don't want to study," Szeth said, curling up on the stone. "I want to be dead."

"Is that it? Truly, that is what you wish most? I will give it to you, if it is your honest desire."

Szeth squeezed his eyes shut. The screams awaited him in that darkness. The screams of those he'd killed.

I was not wrong, he thought. *I was never Truthless.*

"No," Szeth whispered. "The Voidbringers *have* returned. I was right, and my people . . . *they* were wrong."

"You were banished by petty men with no vision. I will teach you the path of one uncorrupted by sentiment. You will bring this back to your people, and will carry with you justice for the leaders of the Shin."

Szeth opened his eyes and looked up. "I am not worthy."

Nin cocked his head. "You? Not worthy? I watched you destroy yourself in the name of order, watched you obey your personal code when others would have fled or crumbled. Szeth-son-Neturo, I watched you keep your word with perfection. This is a thing lost to most people—it is the only genuine beauty in the world. I doubt I have ever found a man more worthy of the Skybreakers than you."

The Skybreakers? But that was an order of the Knights Radiant.

"I have destroyed myself," Szeth whispered.

"You did, and you died. Your bond to your Blade severed, all ties—both spiritual and physical—undone. You are reborn. Come along. It is time to visit your people. Your training begins immediately." Nin began to walk away, revealing that the thing he held behind his back was a sheathed sword.

You are reborn. Could he . . . could Szeth be reborn? Could he make the screams in the shadows go away?

You are a coward, the Radiant had said, the man who owned the winds. A small piece of Szeth thought it true. But Nin offered more. Something different.

Still kneeling, Szeth looked up after the man. "You are right. My people have the other Honorblades, and have kept them safe for millennia. If I am to bring judgment to them, I will face enemies with Shards and with power."

"This is not a problem," Nin said, looking back. "I have brought a replacement Shardblade for you. One that is a perfect match for your task and temperament." He tossed his large sword to the ground. It skidded on stone and came to a rest before Szeth.

He had not seen a sword with a metal sheath before. And who sheathed a Shardblade? And the Blade itself . . . was it black? An inch or so of it had emerged from the sheath as it slid on the rocks.

Szeth swore he could see a small trail of black smoke coming off the metal. Like Stormlight, only dark.

Hello, a cheerful voice said in his mind. *Would you like to destroy some evil today?*

*TherehastobeananswerWhatistheanswerStopTheParshendi
OneofthemYestheyarethemissingpiecePushfortheAlethitodestroy
themoutrightbeforethisoneobtainstheirpowerItwillformabridge*

—From the Diagram, Floorboard 17: paragraph 2,
every second letter starting with the second

Dalinar stood in darkness.

He turned about, trying to remember how he'd come to this place. In the shadows, he saw furniture. Tables, a rug, drapes from Azir with wild colors. His mother had always been proud of those drapes.

My home, he thought. *As it was when I was a child.* Back before conquest, back before Gavilar . . .

Gavilar . . . hadn't Gavilar died? No, Dalinar could hear his brother laughing in the next room. He was a child. They both were.

Dalinar crossed the shadowed room, feeling the fuzzy joy of familiarity. Of things being as they *should* be. He'd left his wooden swords out. He had a collection, each carved like a Shardblade. He was too old for those now, of course, but he still liked having them. As a collection.

He stepped to the balcony doors and pushed them open.

Warm light bathed him. A deep, enveloping, *piercing* warmth. A warmth that soaked down deep through his skin, into his very self. He stared at that light, and was not blinded. The source was distant, but he knew it. Knew it well.

He smiled.

Then he awoke. Alone in his new rooms in Urithiru, a temporary location for him to stay while they scouted the entire tower. A week had passed since they had arrived at this place, and the people of the warcamps had finally started to arrive, bearing spheres recharged during the unexpected highstorm. They needed those badly to make the Oathgate function.

Those from the warcamps arrived none too soon. The Everstorm had not yet returned, but if it moved like a regular highstorm, it should be striking any day now.

Dalinar sat in the darkness for a short time, contemplating that *warmth* he had felt. What had that been? It had been an odd time to get one of the visions. They always came during highstorms. Before, when he'd felt one coming on while sleeping, it had awakened him.

He checked with his guards. No highstorm was blowing. Contemplative, he started to dress. He wanted to see if he could get out onto the roof of the tower today.

※

As Adolin walked the dark halls of Urithiru, he tried not to show how overwhelmed he felt. The world had just *shifted,* like a door on its hinges. A few days ago, his causal betrothal had been that of a powerful man to a relatively minor scion of a distant house. Now, Shallan might be the most important person in the world, and he was . . .

What was he?

He raised his lantern, then made a few marks in chalk on the wall to indicate he'd been here. This tower was *huge.* How did the entire thing stay up? They could probably explore in here for months without opening every door. He had thrown himself into the duty of exploration because it seemed like something he could do. It also, unfortunately, gave him time to think. He didn't like how few answers he came up with.

He turned around, realizing he'd gotten far from the rest of his scouting party. He was doing that more and more often. The first groups from the Shattered Plains had started arriving, and they needed to decide where to house everyone.

Were those voices ahead? Adolin frowned, then continued down the corridor, leaving his lantern behind so it wouldn't give him away. He was surprised when he recognized one of the speakers down the hallway. Was that *Sadeas?*

It was. The highprince stood with a scouting party of his own. Silently, Adolin cursed the wind that had persuaded Sadeas—of all people— to heed the call to come to Urithiru. Everything would have been so much easier if he'd just stayed behind.

Sadeas gestured for a few of his soldiers to go down one branch of the tunnel-like corridor. His wife and a few of her scribes went the other way, two soldiers trailing. Adolin watched for a moment as the highprince himself raised a lantern, inspecting a faded painting on the wall. A fanciful picture, with animals from mythology. He recognized a few from children's stories, like the enormous, minklike creature with the mane of hair that burst out around and behind its head. What was it called again?

Adolin turned to go, but his boot scraped stone.

Sadeas spun, raising his lantern. "Ah, Prince Adolin." He wore white, which really didn't help his complexion—the pale color made his ruddy features seem downright bloody by comparison.

"Sadeas," Adolin said, turning back. "I wasn't aware that you had arrived." Storming man. He'd ignored Father all those months, and *now* he decided to obey?

The highprince strolled up the hallway, passing Adolin. "This place is remarkable. Remarkable indeed."

"So you acknowledge that my father was right," Adolin said. "That his visions are true. The Voidbringers have returned, and you are made a fool."

"I will admit," Sadeas said, "there is more fight left to your father than I'd once feared. A remarkable plan. Contacting the Parshendi, working out this deal with them. They put on quite a show, I hear. It certainly convinced Aladar."

"You can't possibly believe it was all a show."

"Oh please. You deny that he had a Parshendi among his *own guard*? Isn't it convenient that these new 'Radiants' include the head of Dalinar's guard and your own betrothed?"

Sadeas smiled, and Adolin saw the truth. No, he didn't believe this, but it was the lie he would tell. He would start the whisperings again, trying to undermine Dalinar.

"Why?" Adolin asked, stepping up to him. "*Why* are you like this, Sadeas?"

"Because," Sadeas said with a sigh, "it has to happen. You can't have an army with two generals, son. Your father and I, we're two old whitespines who both want a kingdom. It's him or me. We've been pointed that way since Gavilar died."

"It doesn't have to be that way."

"It does. Your father will never trust me again, Adolin, and you know it." Sadeas's face darkened. "I will take this from him. This city, these discoveries. It's just a setback."

Adolin stood for a moment, staring Sadeas in the eyes, and then something finally snapped.

That's it.

Adolin grabbed Sadeas by the throat with his unwounded hand, slamming the highprince back against the wall. The look of utter shock on Sadeas's face amused a part of Adolin, the very small part that wasn't completely, totally, and *irrevocably* enraged.

He squeezed, choking off a cry for help as he moved to pin Sadeas back against the wall, grabbing the man's arm with his own. But Sadeas was a trained soldier. He tried to break the hold, taking Adolin by the arm and twisting.

Adolin kept hold, but lost his balance. The two of them fell in a jumble, twisting, rolling. This wasn't the calculated intensity of the dueling grounds, or even the methodical butchery of the battlefield.

This was two sweating, straining men, both on the edge of panic. Adolin was younger, but he was still bruised from the fight with the Assassin in White.

He managed to come up on top, and as Sadeas struggled to yell, Adolin slammed the man's head down against the stone floor to daze him. Breathing in gasps, Adolin grabbed his side knife. He plunged the knife toward Sadeas's face, though the man managed to get his hands up to grab Adolin by the wrist.

Adolin grunted, forcing the knife closer, clutched in his off hand. He brought the right in anyway, the wrist flaring with pain, as he leaned it against the crossguard. Sweat prickled on Sadeas's brow, the knife's tip touching the end of his left nostril.

"My father," Adolin said with a grunt, sweat from his nose dripping down onto the blade of the knife, "thinks I'm a better man than he is." He strained, and felt Sadeas's grip weaken. "Unfortunately for you, he's wrong."

Sadeas whimpered.

With a surge, Adolin forced the blade up past Sadeas's nose and into the eye socket—piercing the eye like a ripe berry—then rammed it home into the brain.

Sadeas shook for a moment, blood pooling around the blade as Adolin worked it to be certain.

A second later, a Shardblade appeared beside Sadeas—his father's Shardblade. Sadeas was dead.

Adolin stumbled back to not get blood on his clothing, though his cuffs were already stained. Storms. Had he just done that? Had he just *murdered* a *highprince*?

Dazed, he stared at that weapon. Neither man had summoned his Blade for the fight. The weapons might be worth a fortune, but they'd do less good than a rock in such a close-quarters fight.

Thoughts coming more clearly, Adolin picked up the weapon and stumbled away. He ditched the Blade out a window, dropping it down into one of the planterlike outcroppings of the terrace below. It might be safe there.

After that, he had the presence of mind to cut off his cuffs, remove his chalk mark on the wall by scraping it free with his own Blade, and walk as far away as he could before finding one of his scouting parties and pretending he'd been in that area all along.

∴

Dalinar finally figured out the locking mechanism, then pushed on the metal door at the end of the stairwell. The door was set into the ceiling here, the steps running straight up to it.

The trapdoor refused to open, despite being unlocked. He'd oiled the parts. Why wasn't it moving?

Crem, of course, he thought. He summoned his Shardblade and made a series of quick cuts around the trapdoor. Then, with an effort, he was able to force it to open. The ancient trapdoor swung upward and let him out onto the very top of the tower city.

He smiled, stepping onto the roof. Five days of exploration had sent Adolin and Navani into the depths of the city-tower. Dalinar, however, had been driven to seek the top.

For such an enormous tower, the roof was actually relatively small, and not that encrusted with crem. This high, less rain likely dropped during highstorms—and everyone knew crem was thicker in the east than it was in the west.

Storms, this place was high. His ears had popped several times while riding to the top, using the fabrial lift that Navani had discovered. She spoke of counterweights and conjoined gemstones, sounding awed by the technology of the ancients. All he knew was that her discovery had let him avoid climbing up some hundred flights of steps.

He stepped up to the edge and looked down. Below, each ring of the tower expanded out a little farther than the one above it. *Shallan is right,* he thought. *They're gardens. Each outer ring is dedicated to planting food.* He did not know why the eastern face of the tower was straight and sheer, facing the Origin. No balconies along that side.

He leaned out. Distant, so far down it made him queasy, he picked out the ten pillars that held the Oathgates. The one to the Shattered Plains flashed, and a large group of people appeared on it. They flew Hatham's flag. With the maps Dalinar's scholars had sent, it had only taken Hatham and the others about a week of quick marching to reach the Oathgate. When Dalinar's army had crossed that same distance, they'd done so very cautiously, wary of Parshendi attacks.

Now that he saw those pillars from this perspective, he recognized that there was one of them in Kholinar. It made up the dais upon which the palace and royal temple had been built. Shallan suspected that Jasnah had tried to open the Oathgate there; the woman's notes said that Oathgates to each of the cities were locked tight. Only the one in the Shattered Plains had been left open.

Shallan hoped to figure out how to use the others, though their tests right now showed them to be locked somehow. If she managed to make them work, the world would become a much, much smaller place. Assuming there was anything left of it.

Dalinar turned and looked upward, regarding the sky. He took a deep breath. This was why he had come to the top.

"You sent that storm to destroy us!" he shouted toward the clouds. "You sent it to cover up what Shallan, and then Kaladin, were becoming! You tried to end this before it could begin!"

Silence.

"Why send me visions and tell me to prepare!" Dalinar shouted. "Then try to destroy us when we listen to them?"

I WAS REQUIRED TO SEND THOSE VISIONS ONCE THE TIME ARRIVED. THE ALMIGHTY DEMANDED IT OF ME. I COULD NO MORE DISOBEY THAN I COULD REFUSE TO BLOW THE WINDS.

Dalinar breathed in deeply. The Stormfather had replied. Blessedly, he had replied.

"The visions were his, then," Dalinar said, "and you the vehicle for choosing who received them?"

YES.

"Why did you pick me?" Dalinar demanded.

IT DOES NOT MATTER. YOU WERE TOO SLOW. YOU FAILED. THE EVERSTORM IS HERE, AND THE SPREN OF THE ENEMY COME TO INHABIT THE ANCIENT ONES. IT IS OVER. YOU HAVE LOST.

"You said that you were a fragment of the Almighty."

I AM HIS . . . SPREN, YOU MIGHT SAY. NOT HIS SOUL. I AM THE MEMORY MEN CREATE FOR HIM, NOW THAT HE IS GONE. THE PERSONIFICATION OF STORMS AND OF THE DIVINE. I AM NO GOD. I AM BUT A SHADOW OF ONE.

"I'll take what I can get."

HE WISHED FOR ME TO FIND YOU, BUT YOUR KIND HAVE BROUGHT ONLY DEATH TO MINE.

"What do you know of this storm that the Parshendi unleashed?"

THE EVERSTORM. IT IS A NEW THING, BUT OLD OF DESIGN. IT ROUNDS THE WORLD NOW, AND CARRIES WITH IT HIS SPREN. ANY OF THE OLD PEOPLE IT TOUCHES WILL TAKE ON THEIR NEW FORMS.

"Voidbringers."

THAT IS ONE TERM FOR THEM.

"This Everstorm *will* come again, for certain?"

Regularly, like highstorms, though less frequent. You are doomed.

"And it will transform the parshmen. Is there no way to stop it?"

No.

Dalinar closed his eyes. It was as he had feared. His army had defeated the Parshendi, yes, but they were only a fraction of what was coming. Soon he would face hundreds of thousands of them.

The other lands weren't listening. He'd managed to speak, via spanreed, with the emperor of Azir himself—a new emperor, as Szeth had visited the last one. There had been no succession war in Azir, of course. Those required too much paperwork.

The new emperor had invited Dalinar to visit, but obviously considered his words to be ravings. Dalinar hadn't realized that rumors of his madness had traveled so far. Even without that, however, he suspected his warnings would be ignored, as the things he spoke of were insane. A storm that blew the wrong way? Parshmen turning into Voidbringers?

Only Taravangian of Kharbranth—and now, apparently, Jah Keved—had seemed willing to listen. Heralds bless that man; hopefully he could bring some peace to that tortured land. Dalinar had asked for more information about how he'd obtained that throne; initial reports indicated he'd stumbled into the position unexpectedly. But he was too new, and Jah Keved too broken, for him to be able to do much.

Beyond that, there were sudden and unexpected reports, coming via spanreed, of Kholinar rioting. No straight answers there yet, either. And what was this he heard of a plague in the Purelake? Storms, what a mess this all had become.

He would need to do something about it. All of it.

Dalinar looked to the sky again. "I have been commanded to refound the Knights Radiant. I will need to join their number if I am to lead them."

Distant thunder rumbled in the sky, though there were no clouds.

"Life before death!" Dalinar shouted. "Strength before weakness! Journey before destination!"

I AM THE SLIVER OF THE ALMIGHTY HIMSELF! the voice said, sounding angry. I AM THE STORMFATHER. I WILL NOT LET MYSELF BE BOUND IN SUCH A WAY AS TO KILL ME!

"I need you," Dalinar said. "Despite what you did. The bridgeman spoke of oaths given, and of each order of knights being different. The First Ideal is the same. After that, each order is unique, requiring different Words."

The thunder rumbled. It sounded . . . like a challenge. Could Dalinar interpret thunder now?

This was a dangerous gambit. He confronted something primal, something unknowable. Something that had actively tried to murder him and his entire army.

"Fortunately," Dalinar said, "I know the second oath I am to make. I don't need to be told it. I *will* unite instead of divide, Stormfather. I will bring men together."

The thunder silenced. Dalinar stood alone, staring at the sky, waiting.

VERY WELL, the Stormfather finally said. THESE WORDS ARE ACCEPTED.

Dalinar smiled.

I WILL NOT BE A SIMPLE SWORD TO YOU, the Stormfather warned. I WILL NOT COME AS YOU CALL, AND YOU WILL HAVE TO DIVEST YOURSELF OF THAT . . . MONSTROSITY THAT YOU CARRY. YOU WILL BE A RADIANT WITH NO SHARDS.

"It will be what it must," Dalinar said, summoning his Shardblade. As soon as it appeared, screams sounded in his head. He dropped the weapon as if it were an eel that had snapped at him. The screams vanished immediately.

The Blade clanged to the ground. Unbonding a Shardblade was supposed to be a difficult process, requiring concentration and touching its stone. Yet this one was severed from him in an instant. He could feel it.

"What was the meaning of the last vision I received?" Dalinar said. "The one this morning, that came with no highstorm."

NO VISION WAS SENT THIS MORNING.

"Yes it was. I saw light and warmth."

A SIMPLE DREAM. NOT OF ME, NOR OF GODS.

Curious. Dalinar could have sworn it felt the same way as the visions, if not stronger.

GO, BONDSMITH, the Stormfather said. LEAD YOUR DYING PEOPLE TO FAILURE. ODIUM DESTROYED THE ALMIGHTY HIMSELF. YOU ARE NOTHING TO HIM.

"The Almighty could die," Dalinar said. "If that is true, then this Odium can be killed. I will find a way to do it. The visions mentioned a challenge, a champion. Do you know anything of this?"

The sky gave no reply beyond a simple rumble. Well, there would be time for more questions later.

Dalinar walked down off the top of Urithiru and entered the stairwell again. The flight of steps opened into a room that encompassed nearly the entire top floor of the tower city, and it shone with light through glass windows. Glass with no shutters or support, some of it facing east. How it survived highstorms Dalinar did not know, though lines of crem did streak it in places.

Ten short pillars ringed this room, with another at the center. "Well?" Kaladin asked, turning away from an inspection of one of them. Shallan rounded another; she looked far less ragged than she had when they'd first come to the city. Though their days here in Urithiru had been frantic, some good nights' sleep had served them all quite well.

In response to the question, Dalinar took a sphere from his pocket and held it up. Then he sucked in the Stormlight.

He knew to expect the feeling of a storm raging inside, as both Kaladin and Shallan had described it to him. It urged him to act, to move, to not stand still. It did not, however, feel like the Thrill of battle—which was what he had anticipated.

He felt his wounds healing in a familiar way. He'd done this before, he sensed. On the battlefield earlier? His arm felt fine now, and the cut on his side barely ached anymore.

"It's horribly unfair you managed that on your first try," Kaladin noted. "It took me forever."

"I had instruction," Dalinar said, walking into the room and tucking the sphere away. "The Stormfather called me Bondsmith."

"It was the name of one of the orders," Shallan said, resting her fingers on one of the pillars. "That makes three of us. Windrunner, Bondsmith, Lightweaver."

"Four," a voice said from the shadows of the stairwell. Renarin stepped up into the lit room. He looked at them, then shrank back.

"Son?" Dalinar asked.

Renarin remained in the darkness, looking down.

"No spectacles . . ." Dalinar whispered. "You stopped wearing them. I thought you were trying to look like a warrior, but no. Stormlight healed your eyes."

Renarin nodded.

"And the Shardblade," Dalinar said, stepping over and taking his son by the shoulder. "You hear screams. *That's* what happened to you in the arena. You couldn't fight because of those shouts in your head from summoning the Blade. Why? Why didn't you say anything?"

"I thought it was me," Renarin whispered. "My mind. But Glys, he says . . ." Renarin blinked. "Truthwatcher."

"Truthwatcher?" Kaladin said, glancing at Shallan. She shook her head. "I walk the winds. She weaves light. Brightlord Dalinar forges bonds. What do you do?"

Renarin met Kaladin's eyes across the room. "I *see*."

"Four orders," Dalinar said, squeezing Renarin's shoulder with pride. Storms, the lad was trembling. What made him so worried? Dalinar turned to the others. "The other orders must be returning as well. We need to find those whom the spren have chosen. Quickly, for the Everstorm is upon us, and it is worse than we feared."

"How?" Shallan asked.

"It will change the parshmen," Dalinar said. "The Stormfather confirmed it to me. When that storm hits it will bring back the Voidbringers."

"Damnation," Kaladin said. "I need to get to Alethkar, to Hearthstone." He strode toward the exit.

"Soldier?" Dalinar called. "I've done what I can to warn our people."

"My *parents* are back there," Kaladin said. "And the citylord of my town has parshmen. I'm going."

"How?" Shallan asked. "You'll fly the entire distance?"

"Fall," Kaladin said. "But yes." He paused at the doorway out.

"How much Light will that take, son?" Dalinar asked.

"I don't know," Kaladin admitted. "A lot, probably."

Shallan looked to Dalinar. They didn't have Stormlight to spare. Though those from the warcamps brought recharged spheres, activating the Oathgate took a great deal of Stormlight, depending on how many people were brought. Lighting the lamps in the room at the center of the Oathgate was merely the minimum amount needed to start the device—bringing many people partially drained the infused gemstones they carried as well.

"I will get you what I can, lad," Dalinar said. "Go with my blessing. Perhaps you will have enough left over to get to the capital afterward and help the people there."

Kaladin nodded. "I'll put together a pack. I need to leave within the hour." He ducked from the room into the stairwell down.

Dalinar sucked in more Stormlight, and felt the last of his wounds retreat. This seemed a thing a man could easily grow accustomed to having.

He sent Renarin with orders to speak with the king and requisition some emerald broams that Kaladin could borrow for his trip. Elhokar had finally arrived, in the company of a group of Herdazians, of all things. One claiming his name needed to be added to the lists of Alethi kings . . .

Renarin went eagerly to obey the order. He seemed to want something he could do.

He's one of the Knights Radiant, Dalinar thought, watching him go. *I'll probably need to stop sending him on errands.*

Storms. It was really happening.

Shallan had walked to the windows. Dalinar stepped up beside her. This was the eastern face of the tower, the flat edge that looked directly toward the Origin.

"Kaladin will only have time to save a few," Shallan said. "If that many. There are four of us, Brightlord. Only four against a storm full of destruction . . ."

"It is what it is."

"So many will die."

"And we will save the ones we can," Dalinar said. He turned to her. "Life before death, Radiant. It is the task to which we are now sworn."

She pursed her lips, still looking eastward, but nodded. "Life before death, Radiant."

EPILOGUE

ART AND EXPECTATION

"A blind man awaited the era of endings," Wit said, "contemplating the beauty of nature."

Silence.

"That man is me," Wit noted. "I'm not physically blind, just spiritually. And that other statement was actually *very* clever, if you think about it."

Silence.

"This is a lot more satisfying," he said, "when I have intelligent life whom I can render awed, rapt with attention for my clever verbosity."

The ugly lizard-crab-thing on the next rock over clicked its claw, an almost hesitant sound.

"You're right, of course," Wit said. "My usual audience isn't *particularly* intelligent. That was also the obvious joke, however, so shame on you."

The ugly lizard-crab-thing scuttled across its rock, moving onto the other side. Wit sighed. It was night, which was normally a good time for dramatic arrivals and meaningful philosophy. Unfortunately for him, there was nobody here upon which to philosophize or visit, dramatically or otherwise. A small river gurgled nearby, one of the few permanent waterways in this strange land. Extending in all directions were rolling hills, furrowed by passing water and grown over in the valleys with an odd kind of briar. Very few trees here, though farther west a true forest sprouted on the slopes down from the heights.

A couple of songlings made rattling sounds nearby, and he took out his pipes and tried to imitate them. He couldn't, not exactly. The singing sounds were too like percussion, a zipping rattle—musical, but not flute-like.

Still, the creatures seemed to alternate with him, responding to his music. Who knew? Maybe the things had a rudimentary intelligence. Those horses, the Ryshadium . . . those had surprised him. He was glad that there were still some things that could do that.

He finally set down his pipes and contemplated. An audience of ugly lizard-crab-things and songlings was *some* audience, at least.

"Art," he said, "is fundamentally unfair."

One songling continued to creak.

"You see, we pretend that art is eternal, that there is some kind of *persistence* to it. A Truth, you might say. Art is art because it is *art* and not because we say that it is art. I'm not going too quickly for you, am I?"

Creak.

"Good. But if art is eternal and meaningful and independent, why does it depend so damn much upon the audience? You've heard the story about the farmer visiting court during the Festival of Depiction, right?"

Creak?

"Oh, it's not that great a story. Utterly disposable. Standard beginning, the farmer who visits the big city, does something embarrassing, stumbles into the princess and—completely by accident—saves her from getting trampled. Princesses in these stories never do seem to be able to look where they are going. I think perhaps more of them should inquire with a reputable lensmaker and procure a suitable set of spectacles before attempting any further traversal of thoroughfares.

"Anyway, as this story is a comedy, the man is invited to the palace for a reward. Various nonsense follows, ending with the poor farmer wiping himself in the privy with one of the finest paintings ever painted, then strolling out to find all of the lighteyes staring at an empty frame and commenting on how beautiful the work is. Mirth and guffaws. Flourish and bow. Exit before anyone thinks too much about the tale."

He waited.

Creak?

"Well, don't you see?" Wit said. "The farmer found the painting near the privy, so assumed it was to be used for such a purpose. The lighteyes found the empty frame in the hall of art, and assumed it to be a masterwork. You may call this a silly story. It is. That does not depreciate its truthfulness. After all, I am frequently quite silly—but I am almost always truthful. Force of habit.

"Expectation. *That* is the true soul of art. If you can give a man more than he expects, then he will laud you his entire life. If you can create an air of anticipation and feed it properly, you will succeed.

"Conversely, if you gain a reputation for being *too* good, *too* skilled . . . beware. The better art will be in their heads, and if you give them an ounce less than they imagined, suddenly you have failed. Suddenly you are use-less. A man will find a single coin in the mud and talk about it for days, but when his inheritance comes and is accounted one percent less than he expected, then he will declare himself cheated."

Wit shook his head, standing up and dusting off his coat. "Give me an audience who have come to be entertained, but who expect nothing special. To them, I will be a god. That is the best truth I know."

Silence.

"I could use a little music," he said. "For dramatic effect, you see. Someone is coming, and I want to be prepared to welcome them."

The songling, obligingly, started its music again. Wit took a deep breath, then struck the appropriate pose—lazy expectation, calculated knowingness, insufferable conceit. After all, he did have a reputation, so he might as well *try* to live up to it.

The air in front of him blurred, as if heated in a ring near the ground. A streak of light spun about the ring, forming a wall five or six feet high. It faded immediately—really, it was just an afterimage, as if something glowing had spun in the circle very quickly.

In the center of it appeared Jasnah Kholin, standing tall.

Her clothing was ragged, her hair formed into a single utilitarian braid, her face lashed with burns. She'd once worn a fine dress, but that was tattered. She'd hemmed it at the knees and had sewn herself a glove out of something improvised. Curiously, she wore a kind of leather bandolier and a backpack. He doubted she'd had either one when her journey had begun.

She groaned a long groan, then looked to the side, where Wit stood.

He grinned at her.

She stabbed her hand out in the blink of an eye, mist twisting around her arm and snapping into the form of a long, thin sword pointed at Wit's neck.

He cocked an eyebrow.

"How did you find me?" she asked.

"You've been making quite a disturbance on the other side," Wit said. "It's been a long time since the spren had to deal with someone alive, particularly someone so demanding as yourself."

She hissed out a breath, then pushed the Shardblade closer. "Tell me what you know, Wit."

"I once spent the better part of a year inside of a large stomach, being digested."

She frowned at him.

"That *is* a thing that I know. You really should be more specific in your threats." He looked down as she twisted her Shardblade, rotating the tip, still pointed at him. "I'd be surprised if that little knife of yours poses me any real threat, Kholin. You can keep waving it about if you want, though. Perhaps it makes you feel more important."

She studied him. Then the sword burst to mist, vaporizing. She lowered her arm. "I don't have time for you. A storm is coming, a terrible storm. It will bring the Voidbringers to—"

"Already here."

"Damnation. We need to find Urithiru and—"

"Already found."

She hesitated. "The Knights—"

"Refounded," Wit said. "In part by your apprentice who, I might add, is exactly seventy-seven percent more agreeable than you are. I took a poll."

"You're lying."

"Okay, so it was a rather *informal* poll. But the ugly lizard-crab-thing gave you really poor marks for—"

"About the *other* things."

"I don't tell those kinds of lies, Jasnah. You know that. It's what you find so annoying about me."

She inspected him, then sighed. "It is *part* of what I find so annoying about you, Wit. Only a very small part of a vast, vast river."

"You only say that because you don't know me very well."

"Doubtful."

"No, really. If you *did* know me, that river of annoyance would be an ocean, obviously. Regardless. I know things that you do not, and I think you might *actually* know some that I do not. That gives us what is called synergy. If you can contain your annoyance, we might both learn something."

She looked him up and down, then drew her lips to a line and nodded. She started walking directly toward the nearest town. She had a good sense of direction, this woman.

Wit strolled up beside her. "You realize we're at *least* a week away from civilization. Did you need to Elsecall this far out in the middle of nowhere?"

"I was somewhat pressed at the time of my escape. I'm lucky to be here at all."

"Lucky? I don't know if I'd say that."

"Why?"

"You'd likely be better off on the other side, Jasnah Kholin. The Desolation has come, and with it, the end of this land." He looked at her. "I'm sorry."

"Don't be sorry," she said, "until we see how much I can salvage. The storm has come already? The parshmen have transformed?"

"Yes and no," Wit said. "The storm should hit Shinovar tonight, then work its way across the land. I believe that the storm will *bring* the transformation."

Jasnah stopped in place. "That's not how it happened in the past. I have learned things on the other side."

"You are correct. It is different this time."

She licked her lips, but otherwise did a good job containing her anxiety. "If it's not happening as it did before, then everything I know could be false. The words of the highspren could be inaccurate. The records I seek could be meaningless."

He nodded.

"We can't depend upon the ancient writings," she said. "And the supposed god of men is a fabrication. So we can't look to the heavens for salvation, but apparently we can't look toward the past either. So where *can* we look?"

"You're so convinced that there is no God."

"The Almighty is—"

"Oh," Wit said, "I don't mean the Almighty. Tanavast was a fine enough fellow—bought me drinks once—but he was *not* God. I'll admit, Jasnah, that I empathize with your skepticism, but I don't agree with it. I just think you've been looking for God in the wrong places."

"I suppose that you're going to tell me where you think I *should* look."

"You'll find God in the same place you're going to find salvation from this mess," Wit said. "Inside the hearts of men."

"Curiously," Jasnah said, "I believe I can actually agree with that, though I suspect for different reasons than you imply. Perhaps this walk won't be as bad as I had feared."

"Perhaps," he said, looking up toward the stars. "Whatever else might be said, at least the world chose a nice night upon which to end. . . ."

THE END OF

Book Two of

THE STORMLIGHT ARCHIVE

ENDNOTE

Alight, winds approach deadly approaching winds alight.

This ketek, written on Lightday, Jeseses 1174, adorns the cover of Navani Kholin's personal journal. Inside, she describes first-hand the events leading to the arrival of the Everstorm.

The glyphs of the ketek were drawn in the shape of two storms crashing into one another.

—Nazh

ARS ARCANUM

THE TEN ESSENCES AND THEIR HISTORICAL ASSOCIATIONS

NUMBER	GEMSTONE	ESSENCE	BODY FOCUS	SOULCASTING PROPERTIES	PRIMARY / SECONDARY DIVINE ATTRIBUTES
1 Jes	Sapphire	Zephyr	Inhalation	Translucent gas, air	Protecting / Leading
2 Nan	Smokestone	Vapor	Exhalation	Opaque gas, smoke, fog	Just / Confident
3 Chach	Ruby	Spark	The Soul	Fire	Brave / Obedient
4 Vev	Diamond	Lucentia	The Eyes	Quartz, glass, crystal	Loving / Healing
5 Palah	Emerald	Pulp	The Hair	Wood, plants, moss	Learned / Giving
6 Shash	Garnet	Blood	The Blood	Blood, all non-oil liquid	Creative / Honest
7 Betab	Zircon	Tallow	Oil	All kinds of oil	Wise / Careful
8 Kak	Amethyst	Foil	The Nails	Metal	Resolute / Builder
9 Tanat	Topaz	Talus	The Bone	Rock and stone	Dependable / Resourceful
10 Ishi	Heliodor	Sinew	Flesh	Meats, flesh	Pious / Guiding

The preceding list is an imperfect gathering of traditional Vorin symbolism associated with the Ten Essences. Bound together, these form the Double Eye of the Almighty, an eye with two pupils representing the creation of plants and creatures. This is also the basis for the hourglass shape that was often associated with the Knights Radiant.

Ancient scholars also placed the ten orders of Knights Radiant on this list, alongside the Heralds themselves, who each had a classical association with one of the numbers and Essences.

I'm not certain yet how the ten levels of Voidbinding or its cousin the Old Magic fit into this paradigm, if indeed they can. My research suggests that, indeed, there should be another series of abilities that is even more esoteric than the Voidbindings. Perhaps the Old Magic fits into those, though I am beginning to suspect that it is something entirely different.

Note that I currently believe the concept of the "Body Focus" to be more a matter of philosophical interpretation than an actual attribute of this Investiture and its manifestations.

THE TEN SURGES

As a complement to the Essences, the classical elements celebrated on Roshar, are found the Ten Surges. These—thought to be the fundamental forces by which the world operates—are more accurately a representation of the ten basic abilities offered to the Heralds, and then the Knights Radiant, by their bonds.

Adhesion: The Surge of Pressure and Vacuum
Gravitation: The Surge of Gravity
Division: The Surge of Destruction and Decay
Abrasion: The Surge of Friction
Progression: The Surge of Growth and Healing, or Regrowth
Illumination: The Surge of Light, Sound, and Various Waveforms
Transformation: The Surge of Soulcasting
Transportation: The Surge of Motion and Realmatic Transition
Cohesion: The Surge of Strong Axial Interconnection
Tension: The Surge of Soft Axial Interconnection

ON THE CREATION OF FABRIALS

Five groupings of fabrial have been discovered so far. The methods of their creation are carefully guarded by the artifabrian community, but they appear to be the work of dedicated scientists, as opposed to the more mystical Surgebindings once performed by the Knights Radiant. I am more and more convinced that the creation of these devices requires forced enslavement of transformative cognitive entities, known as "spren" to the local communities.

ALTERING FABRIALS

Augmenters: These fabrials are crafted to enhance something. They can create heat, pain, or even a calm wind, for instance. They are powered—like all fabrials—by Stormlight. They seem to work best with forces, emotions, or sensations.

The so-called half-shards of Jah Keved are created with this type of fabrial attached to a sheet of metal, enhancing its durability. I have seen fabrials of this type crafted using many different kinds of gemstone; I am guessing that any one of the ten Polestones will work.

Diminishers: These fabrials do the opposite of what augmenters do, and generally seem to fall under the same restrictions as their cousins. Those artifabrians who have taken me into confidence seem to believe that even greater fabrials are possible than what have been created so far, particularly in regard to augmenters and diminishers.

PAIRING FABRIALS

Conjoiners: By infusing a ruby and using methodology that has not been revealed to me (though I have my suspicions), you can create a conjoined pair of gemstones. The process requires splitting the original ruby. The two halves will then create parallel reactions across a distance. Spanreeds are one of the most common forms of this type of fabrial.

Conservation of force is maintained; for instance, if one is attached to a heavy stone, you will need the same strength to lift the conjoined fabrial that you would need to lift the stone itself. There appears to be some sort of process used during the creation of the fabrial that influences how far apart the two halves can go and still produce an effect.

Reversers: Using an amethyst instead of a ruby also creates conjoined halves of a gemstone, but these two work in creating *opposite* reactions. Raise one, and the other will be pressed downward, for instance.

These fabrials have only just been discovered, and already the possibilities for exploitation are being conjectured. There appear to be some unexpected limitations to this form of fabrial, though I have not been able to discover what they are.

WARNING FABRIALS

There is only one type of fabrial in this set, informally known as the Alerter. An Alerter can warn one of a nearby object, feeling, sensation, or phenomenon. These fabrials use a heliodor stone as their focus. I do not know whether this is the only type of gemstone that will work, or if there is another reason heliodor is used.

In the case of this kind of fabrial, the amount of Stormlight you can infuse into it affects its range. Hence the size of gemstone used is very important.

WINDRUNNING AND LASHINGS

Reports of the Assassin in White's odd abilities have led me to some sources of information that, I believe, are generally unknown. The Windrunners were an order of the Knights Radiant, and they made use of two primary types of Surgebinding. The effects of these Surgebindings were known—colloquially among the members of the order—as the Three Lashings.

BASIC LASHING: GRAVITATIONAL CHANGE

This type of Lashing was one of the most commonly used Lashings among the order, though it was not the easiest to use. (That distinction belongs to the Full Lashing below.) A Basic Lashing involved revoking a being's or object's spiritual gravitational bond to the planet below, instead temporarily linking that being or object to a different object or direction.

Effectively, this creates a change in gravitational pull, twisting the energies of the planet itself. A Basic Lashing allowed a Windrunner to run up walls, to send objects or people flying off into the air, or to create similar effects. Advanced uses of this type of Lashing would allow a Windrunner to make himself or herself lighter by binding part of his or her mass upward. (Mathematically, binding a quarter of one's mass upward would halve a person's effective weight. Binding half of one's mass upward would create weightlessness.)

Multiple Basic Lashings could also pull an object or a person's body downward at double, triple, or other multiples of its weight.

FULL LASHING: BINDING OBJECTS TOGETHER

A Full Lashing might seem very similar to a Basic Lashing, but they worked on very different principles. While one had to do with gravitation, the other had to do with the force (or Surge, as the Radiants called them) of Adhesion—binding objects together as if they were one. I believe this Surge may have had something to do with atmospheric pressure.

To create a Full Lashing, a Windrunner would infuse an object with Stormlight, then press another object to it. The two objects would become bound together with an extremely powerful bond, nearly impossible to break. In fact, most materials would themselves break before the bond holding them together would.

REVERSE LASHING: GIVING AN OBJECT
A GRAVITATIONAL PULL

I believe this may actually be a specialized version of the Basic Lashing. This type of Lashing required the least amount of Stormlight of any of the three Lashings. The Windrunner would infuse something, give a mental command, and create a *pull* to the object that yanked other objects toward it.

At its heart, this Lashing created a bubble around the object that imitated its spiritual link to the ground beneath it. As such, it was much harder for the Lashing to affect objects touching the ground, where their link to the planet was strongest. Objects falling or in flight were the easiest to influence. Other objects could be affected, but the Stormlight and skill required were much more substantial.

LIGHTWEAVING

A second form of Surgebinding involves the manipulation of light and sound in illusory tactics common throughout the cosmere. Unlike the variations present on Sel, however, this method has a powerful Spiritual element, requiring not just a full mental picture of the intended creation, but some level of connection to it as well. The illusion is based not simply upon what the Lightweaver imagines, but upon what they *desire* to create.

In many ways, this is the most similar ability to the original Yolish variant, which excites me. I wish to delve more into this ability, with the hope to gain a full understanding of how it relates to Cognitive and Spiritual attributes.

Turn the page for a sneak peek at
the next novel of the Stormlight Archive

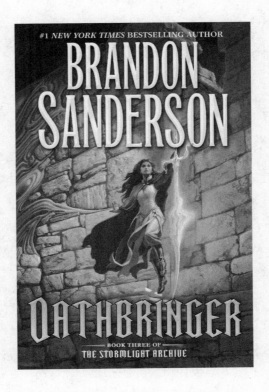

Available November 2017

1

Broken and Divided

I'm certain some will feel threatened by this record. Some few may feel liberated. Most will simply feel that it should not exist.

—From *Oathbringer,* preface

Dalinar Kholin appeared in the vision standing beside the memory of a dead god.

It had been six days since his forces had arrived at Urithiru, ancient holy tower city of the Knights Radiant. They had escaped the arrival of a new devastating storm, seeking refuge through an ancient portal. They were settling into their new home hidden in the mountains.

And yet, Dalinar felt as if he knew nothing. He didn't understand the force he fought, let alone how to defeat it. He barely understood the storm, and what it meant in returning the Voidbringers, ancient enemies of men.

So he came here, into his visions. Seeking to pull secrets from the god—named Honor, or the Almighty—who had left them. This particular vision was the first that Dalinar had ever experienced. It began with him standing next to an image of the god in human form, both perched atop a cliff overlooking Kholinar: Dalinar's home, seat of the government. In the vision, the city had been destroyed by some unknown force.

The Almighty started speaking, but Dalinar ignored him. Dalinar had become a Knight Radiant by bonding the Stormfather himself—soul of the highstorm, most powerful spren on Roshar—and Dalinar had discovered he could now have these visions replayed for him at will. He'd already heard this monologue three times, and had repeated it word for word to Navani for transcription.

This time, Dalinar instead walked to the edge of the cliff and knelt to look out upon the ruins of Kholinar. The air smelled dry here, dusty and warm. He squinted, trying to extract some meaningful detail from the chaos of broken buildings. Even the windblades—once magnificent, sleek rock formations exposing countless strata and variations—had been shattered.

The Almighty continued his speech. These visions were like a diary, a set of immersive messages the god had left behind. Dalinar appreciated the help, but right now he wanted details.

He searched the sky and discovered a ripple in the air, like heat rising from distant stone. A shimmer the size of a building.

"Stormfather," he said. "Can you take me down below, into the rubble?"

You are not supposed to go there. That is not part of the vision.

"Ignore what I'm supposed to do, for the moment," Dalinar said. "Can you do it? Can you transport me to those ruins?"

The Stormfather rumbled. He was a strange being, somehow connected to the dead god, but not exactly the same thing as the Almighty. At least today he wasn't using a voice that rattled Dalinar's bones.

In an eyeblink, Dalinar was transported. He no longer stood atop the cliff, but was on the plains down before the ruins of the city.

"Thank you," Dalinar said, striding the short remaining distance to the ruins.

Only six days had passed since their discovery of Urithiru. Six days since the awakening of the Parshendi, who gained strange powers and glowing red eyes. Six days since the arrival of the new storm—the Everstorm, a tempest of dark thunderheads and red lightning.

Some in his armies thought that it was finished, the storm over as one cataclysmic event. Dalinar knew otherwise. The Everstorm would return, and soon hit Shinovar in the far west. Following that, it would course across the land.

Nobody believed his warnings. Monarchs in places like Azir and Thaylenah admitted that a strange storm had appeared in the east, but they didn't believe it would return.

They couldn't guess how destructive this storm's return would be. When it had first appeared, it had clashed with the highstorm, creating a unique cataclysm. Hopefully it would not be as bad on its own—but it would still be a storm blowing the wrong way. And it would awaken the world's parshmen servants and make them into Voidbringers.

What do you expect to learn? the Stormfather said as Dalinar reached the rubble of the city. *This vision was constructed to draw you to the ridge to speak with Honor. The rest is backdrop, a painting.*

"Honor put this rubble here," Dalinar said, waving toward the broken walls heaped before him. "Backdrop or not, his knowledge of the world and our enemy couldn't help but affect the way he made this vision."

Dalinar hiked up the rubble of the outer walls. Kholinar had been . . . storm it, Kholinar *was* . . . a grand city, like few in the world. Instead of hiding in the shadow of a cliff or inside a sheltered chasm, Kholinar trusted in its enormous walls to buffer it from highstorm winds. It *defied* the winds, and did not bow to the storms.

In this vision, something had destroyed it anyway. Dalinar crested the detritus and surveyed the area, trying to imagine how it had felt to settle here so many millennia ago. Back when there had been no walls. It had been a hardy, stubborn lot who had grown this place.

He saw scrapes and gouges on the stones of the fallen walls, like those made by a predator in the flesh of its prey. The windblades had been smashed, and from up close he could see claw marks on one of those as well.

"I've seen creatures that could do this," he said, kneeling beside one of the stones, feeling the rough gash in the granite surface. "In my visions, I witnessed a stone monster that ripped itself free of the underlying rock.

"There are no corpses, but that's probably because the Almighty didn't populate the city in this vision. He just wanted a symbol of the coming destruction. He didn't think Kholinar would fall to the Everstorm, but to the Voidbringers."

Yes, the Stormfather said. *The storm will be a catastrophe, but not nearly on the scale of what follows. You can find refuge from storms, son of Honor. Not so with our enemies.*

Now that the monarchs of Roshar refused to listen to Dalinar's warning that the Everstorm would soon strike them, what else could Dalinar do? The real Kholinar was reportedly consumed by riots—and the queen had gone silent. Dalinar's armies had limped away from their first confrontation with the Voidbringers, and even many of his own highprinces hadn't joined him in that battle.

A war was coming. In awakening the Desolation, the enemy had rekindled a millennia-old conflict of ancient creatures with inscrutable motivations and unknown powers. Heralds were supposed to appear and lead the charge against the Voidbringers. The Knights Radiant should have already been in place, prepared and trained, ready to face the enemy. They were supposed to be able to trust in the guidance of the Almighty.

Instead, Dalinar had only a handful of new Radiants, and there was no sign of help from the Heralds. And beyond that, the Almighty—God himself—was dead.

Somehow, Dalinar was supposed to save the world anyway.

The ground started to tremble; the vision was ending with the land falling away. Atop the cliff, the Almighty would have just concluded his speech.

A final wave of destruction rolled across the land like a highstorm. A metaphor designed by the Almighty to represent the darkness and destruction that was coming upon humankind.

Our legends say that you won, he had said. *But the truth is that we lost. And we are losing. . . .*

The Stormfather rumbled. *It is time to go.*

"No," Dalinar said, standing atop the rubble. "Leave me."

But—

"Let me feel it!"

The wave of destruction struck, crashing against Dalinar, and he shouted defiance. He had not bowed before the highstorm; he would not bow before this! He faced it head-on, and in the blast of power that ripped apart the ground, he saw something.

A golden light, brilliant yet terrible. Standing before it, a dark figure in black Shardplate. The figure had nine shadows, each spreading out in a different direction, and its eyes glowed a brilliant red.

Dalinar stared deep into those eyes, and felt a chill wash through him. Though the destruction raged around him, vaporizing rocks, those *eyes* frightened him more. He saw something terribly familiar in them.

This was a danger far beyond even the storms.

This was the enemy's champion. And he was coming.

Unite them. Quickly.

Dalinar gasped as the vision shattered. He found himself sitting beside Navani in a quiet stone room in the tower city of Urithiru. Dalinar didn't need to be bound for visions any longer; he had enough control over them that he had ceased acting them out while living them.

He breathed deeply, sweat trickling down his face, his heart racing. Navani said something, but for the moment he couldn't hear her. She seemed distant compared to the rushing in his ears.

"What was that light I saw?" he whispered.

I saw no light, the Stormfather said.

"It was brilliant and golden, yet terrible," Dalinar whispered. "It bathed everything in its heat."

Odium, the Stormfather rumbled. *The enemy.*

The god who had killed the Almighty. The force behind the Desolations.

"Nine shadows," Dalinar whispered, trembling.

Nine shadows? The Unmade. His minions, ancient spren.

Storms. Dalinar knew of them from legend only. Terrible spren who twisted the minds of men.

Still, those eyes haunted him. As frightening as it was to contemplate the Unmade, he feared that figure with the red eyes the most. Odium's champion.

Dalinar blinked, looking to Navani, the woman he loved, her face painfully concerned as she held his arm. In this strange place and stranger time, she was something real. Something to hold on to. A mature beauty—in some ways the picture of a perfect Vorin woman: lush lips, light violet eyes, silvering black hair in perfect braids, curves accentuated by the tight silk havah. No man would ever accuse Navani of being scrawny.

"Dalinar?" she asked. "Dalinar, what happened? Are you well?"

"I'm . . ." He drew in a deep breath. "I'm well, Navani. And I know what we must do."

Her frown deepened. "What?"

"I have to unite the world against the enemy faster than he can destroy it."

He had to find a way to make the other monarchs of the world listen to him. He had to prepare them for the new storm, and the Voidbringers. And, barring that, he had to help them survive the effects.

And if he succeeded, he wouldn't have to face the Desolation alone. This was not a matter of one nation against the Voidbringers. He needed the kingdoms of the world to join him, and he needed to find the Knights Radiant who were being created among their populations.

Unite them.

"Dalinar," she said, "I think that's a worthy goal . . . but storms, what of ourselves? This mountainside is a wasteland—what are we going to feed our armies?"

"The Soulcasters—"

"Will run out of gemstones eventually," Navani said. "And they can create only the basic necessities. Dalinar, we're half frozen up here, broken and divided. Our command structure is in disarray, and it—"

"Peace, Navani," Dalinar said, rising. He pulled her to her feet. "I know. We have to fight anyway."

She embraced him. He held to her, feeling her warmth, smelling her perfume. She preferred a less floral scent than other women—a fragrance with spice to it, like the aroma of newly cut wood.

"We can do this," he told her. "My tenacity. Your brilliance. Together, we *will* convince the other kingdoms to join with us. They'll see when the storm returns that our warnings were right, and they'll unite against the enemy. We can use the Oathgates to move troops and to support each other."

The Oathgates. Ten portals, ancient fabrials, were gateways to Urithiru. When a Knight Radiant activated one of the devices, those people standing upon its surrounding platform were brought to Urithiru, appearing on a similar device here at the tower.

They only had one pair of Oathgates active now—the ones that moved people back and forth between Urithiru and the Shattered Plains. Nine more could theoretically be made to work—but unfortunately, their research determined that a mechanism inside each of them had to be unlocked from *both* sides before they'd work.

If he wanted to travel to Vedenar, Thaylen City, Azimir, or any of the other locations, they'd first need to get one of their Radiants to the city and unlock the device.

"All right," she said. "We'll do it. Somehow we'll make them listen—even if they've got their fingers planted firmly in their ears. Makes one wonder how they manage it, with their heads rammed up their own backsides."

He smiled, and suddenly thought himself foolish for idealizing her just earlier. Navani Kholin was not some timid, perfect ideal—she was a sour storm of a woman, set in her ways, stubborn as a boulder rolling down a mountain and increasingly impatient with things she considered foolish.

He loved her the most for that. For being open and genuine in a society that prided itself on secrets. She'd been breaking taboos, and hearts, since their youth. At times, the idea that she loved him back seemed as surreal as one of his visions.

A knock came at the door to his room, and Navani called for the person to enter. One of Dalinar's scouts poked her head in through the door. Dalinar turned, frowning, noting the woman's nervous posture and quick breathing.

"What?" he demanded.

"Sir," the woman said, saluting, face pale. "There's . . . been an incident. A corpse discovered in the corridors."

Dalinar felt something building, an energy in the air like the sensation of lightning about to strike. "Who?"

"Highprince Torol Sadeas, sir," the woman said. "He's been murdered."

ABOUT THE AUTHOR

BRANDON SANDERSON grew up in Lincoln, Nebraska. He lives in Utah with his wife and children and teaches creative writing at Brigham Young University. He is the author of such bestsellers as the Mistborn® trilogy and its sequels, *The Alloy of Law, Shadows of Self,* and *The Bands of Mourning;* the Stormlight Archive novels *The Way of Kings* and *Words of Radiance;* and other novels, including *The Rithmatist, Steelheart,* and the Alcatraz vs. the Evil Librarians series for young adults. In 2013, he won a Hugo Award for Best Novella for *The Emperor's Soul,* set in the world of his acclaimed first novel, *Elantris.* Additionally, he was chosen to complete Robert Jordan's Wheel of Time® sequence. For behind-the-scenes information on all of Brandon Sanderson's books, visit brandonsanderson.com.